THE COMPLETE MAHABHARATA

OF KRISHNA-DWAIPAYANA VYASA

VOLUME 4 of 4

BOOKS 13 to 18

TRANSLATED BY KISARI MOHAN GANGULI

A Digireads.com Book
Digireads.com Publishing

The Complete Mahabharata (Volume 4 of 4, Books 13 to 18)
By Krishna-Dwaipayana Vyasa
Translated by Kisari Mohan Ganguli
ISBN 10: 1-4209-4946-2
ISBN 13: 978-1-4209-4946-9

Please visit *www.digireads.com*

CONTENTS

4

6

8

BOOK 13. ANUSASANA PARVA

PART I.

SECTION I. (*Anusasanika Parva*)

OM! HAVING BOWED down unto Narayana, and Nara the foremost of male beings, and unto the goddess Saraswati, must the word Jaya be uttered.

"'Yudhishthira said, "O grandsire, tranquillity of mind has been said to be subtile and of diverse forms. I have heard all thy discourses, but still tranquillity of mind has not been mine. In this matter, various means of quieting the mind have been related (by thee), O sire, but how can peace of mind be secured from only a knowledge of the different kinds of tranquillity, when I myself have been the instrument of bringing about all this? Beholding thy body covered with arrows and festering with bad sores, I fail to find, O hero, any peace of mind, at the thought of the evils I have wrought. Beholding thy body, O most valiant of men, bathed in blood, like a hill overrun with water from its springs, I am languishing with grief even as the lotus in the rainy season. What can be more painful than this, that thou, O grandsire, hast been brought to this plight on my account by my people fighting against their foes on the battle-field? Other princes also, with their sons and kinsmen, having met with destruction on my account, alas, what can be more painful than this. Tell us, O prince, what destiny awaits us and the sons of Dhritarashtra, who, driven by fate and anger, have done this abhorrent act. O lord of men, I think the son of Dhritarashtra is fortunate in that he doth not behold thee in this state. But I, who am the cause of thy death as well as of that of our friends, am denied all peace of mind by beholding thee on the bare earth in this sorry condition. The wicked Duryodhana, the most infamous of his race, has, with all his troops and his brothers, perished in battle, in the observance of Kshatriya duties. That wicked-souled wight does not see thee lying on the ground. Verily, for this reason, I would deem death to be preferable to life. O hero that never swervest from virtue, had I with my brothers met with destruction ere this at the hands of our enemies on the battle-field, I would not have found thee in this pitiful plight, thus pierced with arrows. Surely, O prince, the Maker had created is to become perpetrators of evil deeds. O king, if thou wishest to do me good, do thou then instruct me in such a way that I may be cleansed of this sin in even another world."

"'Bhishma replied, "Why, O fortunate one, dost thou consider thy soul, which is dependent (on God and Destiny and Time) to be the cause of thy actions? The manifestation of its inaction is subtle and imperceptible to the senses. In this connection is cited the ancient story of the conversation between Mrityu and Gautami with Kala and the Fowler and the serpent. There was, O son of Kunti, an old lady of the name of Gautami, who was possessed of great patience and tranquillity of mind. One day she found her son dead in consequence of having been bitten by a serpent. An angry fowler, by name Arjunaka, bound the serpent with a string and brought it before Gautami. He then said to her,—'This wretched serpent has been the cause of thy son's death, O blessed lady. Tell me quickly how this wretch is to be destroyed. Shall I throw it into the fire or shall I hack it into pieces? This infamous destroyer of a child does not deserve to live longer.'

"'"Gautami replied, 'Do thou, O Arjunaka of little understanding, release this serpent. It doth not deserve death at thy hands. Who is so foolish as to disregard the inevitable lot that awaits him and burdening himself with such folly sink into sin? Those that have made themselves light by the practice of virtuous deeds, manage to cross the sea of the world even as a ship crosses the ocean. But those that have made themselves heavy with sin sink into the bottom, even as an arrow thrown into the water. By killing the serpent, this my boy will not be restored to life, and by letting it live, no harm will be caused to thee. Who would go to the interminable regions of Death by slaying this living creature?'

""The fowler said, 'I know, O lady that knowest the difference between right and wrong, that the great are afflicted at the afflictions of all creatures. But these words which thou hast spoken are fraught with instruction for only a self-contained person (and not for one plunged in sorrow). Therefore, I must kill this serpent. Those who value peace of mind, assign everything to the course of Time as the cause, but practical men soon assuage their grief (by revenge). People through constant delusion, fear loss of beatitude (in the next world for acts like these). Therefore, O lady, assuage thy grief by having this serpent destroyed (by me).'

""Gautami replied, 'People like us are never afflicted by (such misfortune). Good men have their souls always intent on virtue. The death of the boy was predestined: therefore, I am unable to approve of the destruction of this serpent. Brahmanas do not harbour resentment, because resentment leads to pain. Do thou, O good man, forgive and release this serpent out of compassion.'

""The fowler replied, 'Let us earn great and inexhaustible merit hereafter by killing (this creature), even as a man acquires great merit, and confers it on his victim sacrificed as well, by sacrifice upon the altar. Merit is acquired by killing an enemy: by killing this despicable creature, thou shalt acquire great and true merit hereafter.'

""Gautami replied, 'What good is there in tormenting and killing an enemy, and what good is won by not releasing an enemy in our power? Therefore, O thou of benign countenance, why should we not forgive this serpent and try to earn merit by releasing it?'

""The fowler replied, 'A great number (of creatures) ought to be protected from (the wickedness of) this one, instead of this single creature being protected (in preference to many). Virtuous men abandon the vicious (to their doom): do thou, therefore, kill this wicked creature.'

""Gautami replied, 'By killing this serpent, O fowler, my son will not be restored to life, nor do I see that any other end will be attained by its death: therefore, do thou, O fowler, release this living creature of a serpent.'

""The fowler said, 'By killing Vritra, Indra secured the best portion (of sacrificial offerings), and by destroying a sacrifice Mahadeva secured his share of sacrificial offerings: do thou, therefore, destroy this serpent immediately without any misgivings in thy mind!'"

"Bhishma continued, "The high-souled Gautami, although repeatedly incited by the fowler for the destruction of the serpent did not bend her mind to that sinful act. The serpent, painfully bound with the cord, sighing a little and maintaining its composure with great difficulty, then uttered these words slowly, in a human voice.

""The serpent said, 'O foolish Arjunaka, what fault is there of mine? I have no will of my own, and am not independent. Mrityu sent me on this errand. By his direction have I bitten this child, and not out of any anger or choice on my part. Therefore, if there be any sin in this, O fowler, the sin is his.'

""The fowler said, 'If thou hast done this evil, led thereto by another, the sin is thine also as thou art an instrument in the act. As in the making of an earthen vessel the potter's wheel and rod and other things are all regarded as causes, so art thou, O serpent, (cause in the production of this effect). He that is guilty deserves death at my hands. Thou, O serpent, art guilty. Indeed, thou confessest thyself so in this matter!'

""""The serpent said, 'As all these, viz., the potter's wheel, rod, and other things, are not independent causes, even so I am not an independent cause. Therefore, this is no fault of mine, as thou shouldst grant. Shouldst thou think otherwise, then these are to be considered as causes working in unison with one another. For thus working with one other, a doubt arises regarding their relation as cause and effect. Such being the case, it is no fault of mine, nor do I deserve death on this account, nor am I guilty of any sin. Or, if thou thinkest that there is sin (in even such causation), the sin lies in the aggregate of causes.'

""""The fowler said, 'If thou art neither the prime cause nor the agent in this matter, thou art still the cause of the death (of this child). Therefore, thou dost deserve death in my opinion. If, O serpent, thou thinkest that when an evil act is done, the doer is not implicated therein, then there can be no cause in this matter; but having done this, verily thou deservest death. What more dost thou think?'

""""The serpent said, 'Whether any cause exists or not,[1] no effect is produced without an (intermediate) act. Therefore, causation being of no moment in either case, my agency only as the cause (in this matter) ought to be considered in its proper bearings. If, O fowler, thou thinkest me to be the cause in truth, then the guilt of this act of killing a living being rests on the shoulders of another who incited me to this end.'[2]

""""The fowler said, 'Not deserving of life, O foolish one, why dost thou bandy so many words, O wretch of a serpent? Thou deservest death at my hands. Thou hast done an atrocious act by killing this infant.'

""""The serpent said, 'O fowler, as the officiating priests at a sacrifice do not acquire the merit of the act by offering oblations of clarified butter to the fire, even so should I be regarded with respect as to the result in this connection.'"

"'Bhishma continued, "The serpent directed by Mrityu having said this, Mrityu himself appeared there and addressing the serpent spoke thus.

""""Mrityu said, 'Guided by Kala, I, O serpent, sent thee on this errand, and neither art thou nor am I the cause of this child's death. Even as the clouds are tossed hither and thither by the wind, I am like the clouds, O serpent, influenced by Kala. All attitudes appertaining to Sattwa or Rajas, or Tamas, are provoked by Kala, and operate in all creatures. All creatures, mobile and immobile, in heaven, or earth, are influenced by Kala. The whole universe, O serpent, is imbued with this same influence of Kala. All acts in this world and all abstentions, as also all their modifications, are said to be influenced by Kala. Surya, Soma, Vishnu, Water, Wind, the deity of a hundred sacrifices, Fire, Sky, Earth, Mitra and Parjanya, Aditi, and the Vasus, Rivers and Oceans, all existent and non-existent objects, are created and destroyed by Kala. Knowing this, why dost thou, O serpent, consider me to be guilty? If any fault attaches to me in this, thou also wouldst be to blame.'

""""The serpent said, 'I do not, O Mrityu, blame thee, nor do I absolve thee from all blame. I only aver that I am directed and influenced (in my actions) by thee. If any blame

---

[1] The commentator explains this passage by the illustration that in the act of felling a tree the effect is produced by the intermediate act of raising the axe by some sentient agent, but that in the case of the burning of a forest, the fire is produced by the friction of the dry branches of trees without the intervention of any sentient agent.

[2] Even as the wind indicates the dry twigs to ignite, adds the commentator.

attaches to Kala, or, if it be not desirable to attach any blame to him, it is not for me to scan the fault. We have no right to do so. As it is incumbent on me to absolve myself from this blame, so it is my duty to see that no blame attaches to Mrityu.'"

"'Bhishma continued, "Then the serpent, addressing Arjunaka, said—'Thou hast listened to what Mrityu has said. Therefore, it is not proper for thee to torment me, who am guiltless, by tying me with this cord.'

"'"The fowler said, 'I have listened to thee, O serpent, as well as to the words of Mrityu, but these, O serpent, do not absolve thee from all blame. Mrityu and thyself are the causes of the child's death. I consider both of you to be the cause and I do not call that to be the cause which is not truly so. Accursed be the wicked and vengeful Mrityu that causes affliction to the good. Thee too I shall kill that art sinful and engaged in sinful acts!'

"'"Mrityu said, 'We both are not free agents, but are dependent on Kala, and ordained to do our appointed work. Thou shouldst not find fault with us if thou dost consider this matter thoroughly.'

"'"The fowler said, 'If ye both, O serpent and Mrityu, be dependent on Kala, I am curious to know how pleasure (arising from doing good) and anger (arising from doing evil) are caused.'

"'"Mrityu said, 'Whatever is done is done under the influence of Kala. I have said it before, O fowler, that Kala is the cause of all and that for this reason we both, acting under the inspiration of Kala, do our appointed work and therefore, O fowler, we two do not deserve censure from thee in any way!"'

"'Bhishma continued, "Then Kala arrived at that scene of disputation on this point of morality, and spoke thus to the serpent and Mrityu and the fowler Arjunaka assembled together.

"'"Kala said, 'Neither Mrityu, nor this serpent, nor I, O fowler, am guilty of the death of any creature. We are merely the immediate exciting causes of the event. O Arjunaka, the Karma of this child formed the exciting cause of our action in this matter. There was no other cause by which this child came by its death. It was killed as a result of its own Karma. It has met with death as the result of its Karma in the past. Its Karma has been the cause of its destruction. We all are subject to the influence of our respective Karma. Karma is an aid to salvation even as sons are, and Karma also is an indicator of virtue and vice in man. We urge one another even as acts urge one another. As men make from a lump of clay whatever they wish to make, even so do men attain to various results determined by Karma. As light and shadow are related to each other, so are men related to Karma through their own actions. Therefore, neither art thou, nor am I, nor Mrityu, nor the serpent, nor this old Brahmana lady, is the cause of this child's death. He himself is the cause here.' Upon Kala, O king, expounding the matter in this way, Gautami, convinced in her mind that men suffer according to their actions, spoke thus to Arjunaka.

"'"Gautami said, 'Neither Kala, nor Mrityu, nor the serpent, is the cause in this matter. This child has met with death as the result of its own Karma. I too so acted (in the past) that my son has died (as its consequence). Let now Kala and Mrityu retire from this place, and do thou too, O Arjunaka, release this serpent.'"

"'Bhishma continued, "Then Kala and Mrityu and the serpent went back to their respective destinations, and Gautami became consoled in mind as also the fowler. Having heard all this, O king, do thou forego all grief, and attain to peace of mind. Men attain to heaven or hell as the result of their own Karma. This evil has neither been of thy own creation, nor of Duryodhana's. Know this that these lords of Earth have all been slain (in this war) as a result of acts of Kala.'"

"Vaisampayana said, 'Having heard all this, the powerful and virtuous Yudhishthira became consoled in mind, and again enquired as follows.'"

SECTION II.

"'Yudhishthira said, "O grandsire, O wisest of men, O thou that art learned in all the scriptures, I have listened to this great story, O foremost of intelligent men. I am desirous of again hearing the recital of some history full of religious instruction, and it behoves thee to gratify me. O lord of Earth, tell me if any householder has ever succeeded in conquering Mrityu by the practice of virtue. Do thou recite this to me with all details!"

"'Bhishma said, "This ancient history is recited as an illustration of the subject of the conquest by a householder, over Mrityu, through the practice of virtue. The Prajapati Manu had a son, O king, of the name of the Ikshwaku. Of that king, illustrious as Surya, were born a hundred sons. His tenth son, O Bharata, was named Dasaswa, and this virtuous prince of infallible prowess became the king of Mahismati. Dasaswa's son, O king, was a righteous prince whose mind was constantly devoted to the practice of truth and charity and devotion. He was known by the name of Madiraswa and ruled over the Earth as her lord. He was constantly devoted to the study of the Vedas as also of the science of arms. Madiraswa's son was the king named Dyutimat who possessed great good fortune and power and strength and energy. Dyutimat's son was the highly devout and pious king who was famous in all the worlds under the name of Suvira. His soul was intent on religion and he possessed wealth like another Indra, the lord of the deities. Suvira too had a son who was invincible in battle, and who was the best of all warriors and known by the name of Sudurjaya. And Durjya too, possessed of a body like that of Indra, had a son who beamed with splendour like that of fire. He was the great monarch named Duryodhana who was one of the foremost of royal sages. Indra used to pour rain profusely in the kingdom of this monarch, who never fled from the battlefield and was possessed of valour like unto Indra himself. The cities and the kingdom of this king were filled with riches and gems and cattle and grain of various kinds. There was no miser in his kingdom nor any person afflicted with distress or poverty. Nor was there in his kingdom any person that was weak in body or afflicted with disease. That king was very clever, smooth in speech, without envy, a master of his passions, of a righteous soul, full of compassion, endued with prowess, and not given to boasting. He performed sacrifices, and was self-restrained and intelligent, devoted to Brahmanas and Truth. He never humiliated others, and was charitable, and learned in the Vedas and the Vedanta. The celestial river Narmada, auspicious and sacred and of cool waters, in her own nature, O Bharata, courted him. He begot upon that river, a lotus-eyed daughter, by name Sudarsana, who was, O king, endued with great beauty. No creature, O Yudhisthira, had ever been born before among womankind, that was possessed of such beauty as that excellent damsel who was the daughter of Duryodhana. The god Agni himself courted the beautiful princess Sudarsana, and taking the shape of a Brahmana, O monarch, sought her hand from the king. The king was unwilling to give his daughter in marriage to the Brahmana who was poor and not of the same rank with himself. Thereupon Agni vanished from his great sacrifice. The king, grieved at heart, then addressed the Brahmanas, saying,—'Of what sin have I, ye excellent Brahmanas, or you, been guilty, that Agni should disappear from this sacrifice, even as good done unto wicked men disappears from their estimation. Great, indeed, must that sin of ours be for which Agni has thus disappeared. Either must the sin be yours, or, it must be mine. Do you fully investigate the matter.'—Then hearing the king's words, O foremost prince of Bharata's race, the Brahmanas, restraining speech, sought with concentrated faculties the protection of the god of fire. The divine carrier of oblations, resplendent as the autumnal Sun, appeared before them, enveloping his self in glorious refulgence. The high-souled Agni then addressed those excellent Brahmanas, saying,—'I seek the daughter of Duryodhana for my own self.' At this all those Brahmanas were struck with wonder, and rising on the morrow, they related to the king what had been said by the fire-god. The wise monarch, hearing the words of those utterers of Brahma, was delighted at heart, and said,—'Be it so.'—The king craved a boon of the illustrious fire-god as the marriage dower,—'Do thou, O Agni, deign to remain always with us here.'—'Be it so'—said the divine Agni to that lord of Earth. For this reason Agni has always been present in the kingdom of Mahismati to this day, and was seen by Sahadeva in course of his conquering expedition to the south. Then the king gave his daughter, dressed in new garments and decked with jewels, to the high-souled deity, and Agni too accepted, according to Vedic rites, the princess Sudarsana as his bride, even as he accepts libations of clarified butter at sacrifices. Agni was well pleased with her appearance, her beauty, grace, character, and nobility of birth, and was minded to beget offspring upon her. And a son by Agni, of the name of Sudarsana, was soon born of her. Sudarsana also was, in appearance, as beautiful as the full moon, and even in his childhood he attained to a knowledge of the supreme and everlasting Brahma. There was also a king of the name of Oghavat, who was the grandfather of Nriga. He had a daughter of the name of Oghavati, and a son too of the name of Ogharatha born unto him. King Oghavat gave his daughter Oghavati, beautiful as a goddess, to the learned Sudarsana for wife. Sudarsana, O king, leading the life of a householder with Oghavati, used to dwell in Kurukshetra with her. This intelligent prince of blazing energy took the vow, O lord, of conquering Death by leading the life of even a householder. The son of Agni, O king, said to Oghavati,—'Do thou never act contrary to (the wishes of) those that seek our hospitality. Thou shouldst make no scruple about the means by which guests are to be welcomed, even if thou have to offer thy own person. O beautiful one, this vow is always present in the mind, since for householders, there is no higher virtue than hospitality accorded to guests. Do thou always bear this in mind without ever doubting it, if my words be any authority with thee. O sinless and blessed one, if thou hast any faith in me, do thou never disregard a guest whether I be at thy side or at a distance from thee!' Unto him, with hands clasped and placed on her head, Oghavati replied, saying,—'I shall leave nothing undone of what thou commandest me.'—Then Mrityu, O king, desiring to over-reach Sudarsana, began to watch him for finding out his laches. On a certain occasion, when the son of Agni went out to fetch firewood from the forest, a graceful Brahmana sought the hospitality of Oghavati with these words:—'O beautiful lady, if thou hast any faith in the virtue of hospitality as prescribed for householders, then I would request thee to extend the rites of hospitality to me to-day.'—The princess of great fame, thus addressed by that Brahmana, O king, welcomed him according to the rites prescribed in the Vedas. Having offered him a seat, and water to wash his feet, she enquired, saying,—'What is thy business? What can I offer thee?' The Brahmana said unto her,—'My business is with thy person, O blessed one. Do thou act accordingly without any hesitation in thy mind. If the duties prescribed for householders be acceptable to thee, do thou, O princess, gratify me by offering up thy person to me.'—Though tempted by the princess with offers of diverse other things, the Brahmana, however, did not ask for any other gift than the offer of her own person.

Seeing him resolved, that lady, remembering the directions which had before been given to her by her husband, but overcome with shame, said to that excellent Brahmana,—'Be it so.'—Remembering the words of her husband who was desirous of acquiring the virtue of householders, she cheerfully approached the regenerate Rishi. Meanwhile, the son of Agni, having collected his firewood, returned to his home. Mrityu, with his fierce and inexorable nature, was constantly by his side, even as one attends upon one's devoted friend. When the son of Pavaka returned to his own hermitage, he called Oghavati by name, and (receiving no answer) repeatedly, exclaimed,—'Whether art thou gone?'—But the chaste lady, devoted to her husband, being then locked in the arms of that Brahmana, gave no reply to her husband. Indeed, that chaste woman, considering herself contaminated became speechless, overcome with shame. Sudarsana, addressing her again, exclaimed,—'Where can my chaste wife be? Whither has she gone? Nothing can be of greater moment to me than this (her disappearance). Why does not that simple and truthful lady, devoted to her husband, alas, answer to my call today as she used to do before with sweet smiles?' Then that Brahmana, who was within the hut, thus replied to Sudarsana,—'Do thou learn, O son of Pavaka, that a Brahmana guest has arrived, and though tempted by this thy wife with diverse other offers of welcome, I have, O best of Brahmanas, desired only her person, and this fair-faced lady is engaged in welcoming me with due rites. Thou art at liberty to do whatever thou thinkest to be suitable to this occasion.' Mrityu, armed with the iron club, pursued the Rishi at that moment, desirous of compassing the destruction of one that would, he thought, deviate from his promise. Sudarsana was struck with wonder, but casting off all jealousy and anger by look, word, deed, or thought, said,—'Do thou enjoy thyself, O Brahmana. It is a great pleasure to me. A householder obtain the highest merit by honouring a guest. It is said by the learned that, as regards the householder, there is no higher merit than what results unto him from a guest departing from his house after having been duly honoured by him. My life, my wife, and whatever other worldly possessions I have, are all dedicated to the use of my guests. Even this is the vow that I have taken. As I have truly made this statement, by that truth, O Brahmana, I shall attain to the knowledge of Self. O foremost of virtuous men, the five elements, viz., fire, air, earth, water, and sky, and the mind, the intellect and the Soul, and time and space and the ten organs of sense, are all present in the bodies of men, and always witness the good and evil deeds that men do. This truth has today been uttered by me, and let the gods bless me for it or destroy me if I have spoken falsely.' At this, O Bharata, there arose in all directions, in repeated echoes, a voice, crying,—'This is true, this is not false.' Then that Brahmana came out of the hovel, and like the wind rising and encompassing both Earth and sky, and making the three worlds echo with Vedic sounds, and calling that virtuous man by name, and congratulating him said,—'O sinless one, I am Dharma. All glory to thee. I came here, O truth-loving one, to try thee, and I am well pleased with thee by knowing thee to be virtuous. Thou hast subdued and conquered Mrityu who always has pursued thee, seeking thy laches. O best of men, no one in the three worlds has the ability to insult, even with looks, this chaste lady devoted to her husband, far less to touch her person. She has been protected from defilement by thy virtue and by her own chastity. There can be nothing contrary to what this proud lady will say. This utterer of Brahma, endued with austere penances, shall, for the salvation of the world, be metamorphosed into a mighty river. And thou shalt attain to all the worlds in this thy body, and as truly as the science of Yoga is within her control, this highly blessed lady will follow thee with only half of her corporeal self, and with the other half will she be celebrated as the river Oghavati! And thou shalt attain with her to all the worlds that acquired through penances. Those eternal and everlasting worlds from which none cometh back will be attained by thee even in this gross body of thine. Thou hast conquered Death, and attained to the highest of all felicities, and by thy own power (of mind), attaining to the speed of thought, thou hast risen above the power of the five elements! By thus adhering to the duties of a householder, thou hast conquered thy passions, desires, and anger, and this princess, O prince of virtuous men has, by serving thee, conquered affliction, desire, illusion, enmity and lassitude of mind!'"

"'Bhishma continued, "Then the glorious Vasava (the lord of the gods), riding in a fine chariot drawn by a thousand white horses, approached that Brahmana. Death and Soul, all the worlds, all the elements, intellect, mind, time, and space as also desire and wrath, were all conquered. Therefore, O best of men, do thou bear this in mind, that to a householder there is no higher divinity than the guest. It is said by the learned that the blessings of an honoured guest are more efficacious than the merit of a hundred sacrifices. Whenever a deserving guest seeks the hospitality of a householder and is not honoured by him, he takes away (with him) all the virtues of the latter giving him his sins (in return). I have now recited to thee, my son, this excellent story as to how Death was conquered of old by a householder. The recital of this excellent story confers glory, fame, and longevity (upon those that listen to it). The man that seeks worldly prosperity should consider it as efficacious in removing all evil. And, O Bharata, the learned man that daily recites this story of the life of Sudarsana attains to the regions of the blessed.""''

SECTION III.

"'Yudhishthira said, "If, O prince, Brahmanahood be so difficult of attainment by the three classes (Kshatriyas, Vaisyas and Sudras), how then did the high souled Viswamitra, O king, though a Kshatriya (by birth), attain to the status of a Brahmana? I desire to know this, O sire. Therefore, do thou truly relate this matter to me. That powerful man, O sire, by virtue of his austerities, destroyed in a moment the hundred sons of the high-souled Vasishtha. While under the influence of anger, he created numerous evil spirits and Rakshasas of mighty vigour and resembling the great destroyer Kala himself. The great and learned race of Kusika, numbering hundreds of regenerate sages and belauded by the Brahmanas, was founded in this world of men by him. Sunasepha of austere penances, the son of Richika, having been sought to be slain as an animal in the great sacrifice of Amvarisha, obtained his deliverance through Viswamitra. Harischandra, having pleased the gods at a sacrifice, became a son of the wise Viswamitra. For not having honoured their eldest brother Devarat, whom Viswamitra got as a son from the gods, the other fifty brothers of his were cursed, and all of them became Chandalas. Trisanku, the son of Ikshwaku, through the curse of Vasishtha became a Chandala, and when abandoned by his friends, and remaining suspended with his head downwards in the lower regions, was translated to heaven at the pleasure of Viswamitra. Viswamitra had a large river, by name Kausika, that was frequented by celestial Rishis. This sacred and auspicious stream was frequented by the gods and regenerate Rishis. For disturbing his devotions, the famous celestial nymph Rambha of fine bracelets, was cursed and metamorphosed into a rock. Through fear of Viswamitra the glorious Vasishtha, in olden times, binding himself with creepers, threw himself down into a river and again rose released from his bonds. In consequence of this, that large and sacred river become thenceforth celebrated by the name of Vipasa.[3] He prayed to the glorious and puissant Indra who was pleased with him and absolved him from a curse.[4] Remaining on the northern side of the firmament, he sheds his lustre from a position in the midst of the seven regenerate Rishis,[5] and Dhruva the son of Uttanpada.[6] These are his achievements as well as many others. O descendant of Kuru, as they were performed by a Kshatriya, my curiosity has been roused in this matter. Therefore, O foremost one of Bharata's race, do thou relate this matter to me truly. How without casting off his corporeal frame and taking another tenement of flesh could he become a Brahmana? Do thou, O sire, truly relate this matter to me as thou hast related to me the story of Matanga. Matanga was born as a Chandala,[7] and could not attain to Brahmanahood, (with all his austerities) but how could this man attain to the status of a Brahmana?"'"

<h2 style="text-align:center">SECTION IV.</h2>

'"Bhishma said, "Listen truly in detail, O son of Pritha, how in olden times Viswamitra attained to the status of a Brahmana Rishi. There was, O foremost of Bharata's descendants, in the race of Bharata, a king of the name of Ajamida, who performed many sacrifices and was the best of all virtuous men. His son was the great king named Jahnu. Ganga was the daughter of this high-minded prince. The farfamed and equally virtuous Sindhudwipa was the son of this prince. From Sindhudwipa sprung the great royal sage Valakaswa. His son was named Vallabha who was like a second Dharma in embodied form. His son again was Kusika who was refulgent with glory like unto the thousand-eyed Indra. Kusika's son was the illustrious King Gadhi who, being childless and desiring to have a son born unto him, repaired to the forest. Whilst living there, a daughter was born unto him. She was called Satyavati by name, and in beauty of appearance she had no equal on Earth. The illustrious son of Chyavana, celebrated by the name of Richika, of the race of Bhrigu, endued with austere penances, sought the hand of this lady. Gadhi, the destroyer of his enemies, thinking him to be poor, did not bestow her in marriage upon the high-souled Richika. But when the latter, thus dismissed, was going away, the excellent king, addressing him said,—'If thou givest me a marriage dower thou shalt have my daughter for thy wife.'

'"Richika said, 'What dower, O king, shall I offer thee for the hand of thy daughter? Tell me truly, without feeling any hesitation in the matter.' Gadhi said,—'O descendant of Bhrigu, do thou give me a thousand horses fleet as the wind, and possessing the hue of moon-beams, and each having one ear black.'"

'"Bhishma said, "Then that mighty son of Chyavana who was the foremost of Bhrigu's race, besought the deity Varuna, the son of Aditi, who was the lord of all the waters.—'O best of gods, I pray to thee to give me a thousand horses, all endued with the speed of the wind and with complexion as effulgent as the moon's, but each having one ear black.' The god Varuna, the son of Aditi, said to that excellent scion of Bhrigu's

---

[3] Literally, the releaser from bonds.
[4] Refers to the curse pronounced on Viswamitra by the son of Vasishtha, when the former acted as the priest of Trisanku. The curse was that Viswamitra would partake of canine flesh by officiating as the priest of one who himself was the partaker of such flesh. It is said that at a time of great scarcity, Viswamitra was obliged to resort to dog's flesh for food, and that as he was about to cook it, Indra pounced upon it and took it away.
[5] The constellation of the Great Bear.
[6] The Pole Star.
[7] Matanga was begotten upon a Brahmana woman by a Sudra father.

race,—'Be it so. Wheresoever thou shalt seek, the horses shalt arise (in thy presence).'—As soon as Richika thought of them, there arose from the waters of Ganga thousand high-mettled horses, as lustrous in complexion as the moon. Not far from Kanyakubja, the sacred bank of Ganga is still famous among men as Aswatirtha in consequence of the appearance of those horses at that place. Then Richika, that best of ascetics, pleased in mind, gave those thousand excellent horses unto Gadhi as the marriage-dower. King Gadhi, filled with wonder and fearing to be cursed, gave his daughter, bedecked with jewels, unto that son of Bhrigu. That foremost of regenerate Rishis accepted her hand in marriage according to the prescribed rites. The princess too was well-pleased at finding herself the wife of that Brahmana. That foremost of regenerate Rishis, O Bharata, was well pleased with her conduct and expressed a wish to grant her boon. The princess, O excellent king, related this to her mother. The mother addressed the daughter that stood before her with down-cast eyes, saying,—'It behoves thee, O my daughter, to secure a favour for me also from thy husband. That sage of austere penances is capable of granting a boon to me, the boon, viz. of the birth of a son to me.'—Then, O king, returning quickly to her husband Richika, the princess related to him all that had been desired by her mother. Richika said,—'By my favour, O blessed one, she will soon give birth to a son possessed of every virtue. May thy request be fulfilled. Of thee too shall be born a mighty and glorious son who, endued with virtue, shall perpetuate my race. Truly do I say this unto thee! When you two shall bathe in your season, she shall embrace a peepul tree, and thou, O excellent lady, shalt likewise embrace a fig tree, and by so doing shall ye attain the object of your desire. O sweetly-smiling lady, both she and you shall have to partake of these two sacrificial offerings (charu)[8] consecrated with hymns, and then shall ye obtain sons (as desired).'—At this, Satyavati, delighted at heart, told her mother all that had been said by Richika as also of the two balls of charu. Then the mother, addressing her daughter Satyavati, said:—'O daughter, as I am deserving of greater consideration from thee than thy husband, do thou obey my words. The charu, duly consecrated with hymns, which thy husband has given to thee, do thou give unto me and thyself take the one that has been prescribed for me. O sweetly-smiling one of blameless character, if thou hast any respect for my word, let us change the trees respectively designed for us. Every one desires to possess an excellent and stainless being for his own son. The glorious Richika too must have acted from a similar motive in this matter, as will appear in the end. For this reason, O beautiful girl, my heart inclines towards thy charu, and thy tree, and thou too shouldst consider how to secure an excellent brother for thyself.'—The mother and the daughter Satyavati having acted in this way, they both, O Yudhishthira, became big with child. And that great Rishi, the excellent descendant of Bhrigu, finding his wife quick with child, was pleased at heart, and addressing her, said,—'O excellent lady, thou hast not done well in exchanging the charu as will soon become apparent. It is also clear that thou hast changed the trees. I had placed the entire accumulated energy of Brahma in thy charu and Kshatriya energy in the charu of thy mother. I had so ordered that thou wouldst give birth to a Brahmana whose virtues would be famous throughout the three worlds, and that she (thy mother) would give birth to an excellent Kshatriya. But now, O excellent lady, that thou hast reversed the order (of the charu) so, thy mother will give birth to an excellent Brahmana and thou too, O excellent lady, will give birth to a Kshatriya terrible in action. Thou hast not done will, O lady, by acting thus out of

---

[8] Charu is properly an oblation of rice, barley, and pulse, boiled with butter and milk, for presentation to the gods in a sacrifice or ordinary worship.

affection for thy mother.'—Hearing this, O king the excellent lady Satyavati, struck with sorrow, fell upon the ground like a beautiful creeper cut in twain. Regaining her senses and bowing unto her lord with head (bent), the daughter of Gadhi said to her husband, that foremost one of Bhrigu's race,—'O regenerate Rishi, O thou that art foremost amongst those versed in Brahma, do thou take pity on me, thy wife, who is thus appeasing thee and so order that a Kshatriya son may not be born unto me. Let my grandson be such a one as will be famous for his terrible achievements, if it be thy desire, but not my son, O Brahmana. Do thou confer this favour on me.'—'Be it so,'—said that man of austere penances to his wife and then, O king, she gave birth to a blessed son named Jamadagni. The celebrated wife of Gadhi too gave birth to the regenerate Rishi Viswamitra versed in the knowledge of Brahma, by favour of that Rishi. The highly devout Viswamitra, though a Kshatriya, attained to the state of a Brahmana and became the founder of a race of Brahmanas. His sons became high-souled progenitors of many races of Brahmanas who were devoted to austere penances, learned in the Vedas, and founders of many clans. The adorable Madhuchcchanda and the mighty Devrat, Akshina, Sakunta, Vabhru, Kalapatha, the celebrated Yajnavalkya, Sthula of high vows, Uluka, Mudgala, and the sage Saindhavayana, the illustrious Valgujangha and the great Rishi Galeva, Ruchi, the celebrated Vajra, as also Salankayana, Liladhya and Narada, the one known as Kurchamuka, and Vahuli, Mushala, as also Vakshogriva, Anghrika, Naikadrik, Silayupa, Sita, Suchi, Chakraka, Marrutantavya, Vataghna, Aswalayana, and Syamayana, Gargya, and Javali, as also Susruta, Karishi, Sangsrutya, and Para Paurava, and Tantu, the great sage Kapila, Tarakayana, Upagahana, Asurayani, Margama, Hiranyksha, Janghari, Bhavravayani, and Suti, Bibhuti, Suta, Surakrit, Arani, Nachika, Champeya, Ujjayana, Navatantu, Vakanakha, Sayanya, Yati, Ambhoruha, Amatsyasin, Srishin, Gardhavi Urjjayoni, Rudapekahin, and the great Rishi Naradin,—these Munis were all sons of Viswamitra and were versed in the knowledge of Brahma. O king Yudhishthira, the highly austere and devout Viswamitra, although a Kshatriya (by descent), became a Brahmana for Richika having placed the energy of supreme Brahma (in the charu). O foremost prince of Bharata's race, I have now related to you, with all details, the story of the birth of Viswamitra who was possessed of energy of the sun, the moon, and the fire-god. O best of kings, if thou hast any doubt with regard to any other matter, do thou let me know it, so that I may remove it.'"

SECTION V.

"'Yudhishthira said, "O thou that knowest the truths of religion, I wish to hear of the merits of compassion, and of the characteristics of devout men. Do thou, O sire, describe them to me."

"'Bhishma said, "In this connection, this ancient legend, the story of Vasava and the high-minded Suka, is cited as an illustration. In the territories of the king of Kasi, a fowler, having poisoned arrows with him went out of his village on a hunting excursion in search of antelopes. Desirous of obtaining meat, when in a big forest in pursuit of the chase, he discovered a drove of antelopes not far from him, and discharged his arrow at one of them. The arrows of that fowler of irresistible arms, discharged for the destruction of the antelope, missed its aim and pierced a mighty forest-tree. The tree, violently pierced with that arrow tipped with virulent poison, withered away, shedding its leaves and fruits. The tree having thus withered a parrot that had lived in a hollow of its trunk all his life, did not leave his nest out of affection for the lord of the forest. Motionless and without food silent and sorrowful, that grateful and virtuous parrot also withered away with the tree. The conqueror of Paka (Indra) was struck with wonder upon finding that high-souled, and generous-hearted bird thus uninfluenced by misery or happiness and possessing extraordinary resolution. Then the thought arose in Sakra's mind,—'How could this bird come to possess humane and generous feelings which are impossible in one belonging to the world of lower animals? Perchance, there is nothing wonderful in the matter, for all creatures are seen to evince kindly and generous feelings towards others.'—Assuming then the shape of a Brahmana, Sakra descended on the Earth and addressing the bird, said,—'O Suka, O best of birds, the grand-daughter (Suki) of Daksha has become blessed (by having thee as her offspring). I ask thee, for what reason dost thou not leave this withered tree?'—Thus questioned, the Suka bowed unto him and thus replied:—'Welcome to thee O chief of the gods, I have recognised thee by the merit of my austere penances'—'Well-done, well-done!'—exclaimed the thousand-eyed deity. Then the latter praised him in his mind, saying,—'O, how wonderful is the knowledge which he possesses.'—Although the destroyer of Vala knew that parrot to be of a highly virtuous character and meritorious in action, he still enquired of him about the reason of his affection for the tree. 'This tree is withered and it is without leaves and fruits and is unfit to be the refuge of birds. Why dost thou then cling to it? This forest, too, is vast and in this wilderness there are numerous other fine trees whose hollows are covered with leaves and which thou canst choose freely and to thy heart's content. O patient one exercising due discrimination in thy wisdom, do thou forsake this old tree that is dead and useless and shorn of all its leaves and no longer capable of any good."'

"'Bhishma said, "The virtuous Suka, hearing these words of Sakra, heaved a deep sigh and sorrowfully replied unto him, saying—'O consort of Sachi, and chief of the gods, the ordinances of the deities are always to be obeyed. Do thou listen to the reason of the matter in regard to which thou hast questioned me. Here, within this tree, was I born, and here in this tree have I acquired all the good traits of my character, and here in this tree was I protected in my infancy from the assaults of my enemies. O sinless one, why art thou, in thy kindness, tampering with the principle of my conduct in life? I am compassionate, and devoutly intent on virtue, and steadfast in conduct. Kindliness of feeling is the great test of virtue amongst the good, and this same compassionate and humane feeling is the source of perennial felicity to the virtuous. All the gods question thee to remove their doubts in religion, and for this reason, O lord, thou hast been placed in sovereignty over them all. It behoves thee not, O thousand-eyed one, to advise me now to abandon this tree for ever. When it was capable of good, it supported my life. How can I forsake it now?'—The virtuous destroyer of Paka, pleased with these well-meant words of the parrot, thus said to him:—'I am gratified with thy humane and compassionate disposition. Do thou ask a boon of me.'—At this, the compassionate parrot craved this boon of him, saying,—'Let this tree revive.'—Knowing the great attachment of the parrot to that tree and his high character, Indra, well-pleased, caused the tree to be quickly sprinkled over with nectar. Then that tree became replenished and attained to exquisite grandeur through the penances of the parrot, and the latter too, O great king, at the close of his life, obtained the companionship of Sakra by virtue of that act of compassion. Thus, O lord of men, by communion and companionship with the pious, people attain all the objects of their desire even as the tree die through its companionship with the parrot."'

23

SECTION VI.

"'Yudhishthira said, "Tell me, O learned sire that art versed in all the scriptures, of Exertion and Destiny which is the most powerful?"

"'Bhishma said, "This ancient story of the conversation of Vasishtha and Brahma, O Yudhishthira, is an illustration in point. In olden times the adorable Vasishtha enquired of Brahma as to which among these two, viz., the Karma of a creature acquired in this life, or that acquired in previous lives (and called Destiny), is the more potent in shaping his life. Then, O king, the great god Brahma, who had sprung from the primeval lotus, answered him in these exquisite and well-reasoned words, full of meaning.

"''Brahma said, 'Nothing comes into existence without seed. Without seed, fruits do not grow. From seeds spring other seeds. Hence are fruits known to be generated from seeds. Good or bad as the seed is that the husbandman soweth in his field, good or bad are the fruits that he reaps. As, unsown with seed, the soil, though tilled, becomes fruitless, so, without individual Exertion, Destiny is of no avail. One's own acts are like the soil, and Destiny (or the sum of one's acts in previous births) is compared to the seed. From the union of the soil and the seed doth the harvest grow. It is observed every day in the world that the doer reaps the fruit of his good and evil deeds; that happiness results from good deeds, and pain from evil ones; that acts, when done, always fructify; and that, if not done, no fruit arises. A man of (good) acts acquires merits with good fortune, while an idler falls away from his estate, and reaps evil like the infusion of alkaline matter injected into a wound. By devoted application, one acquires beauty, fortune, and riches of various kinds. Everything can be secured by Exertion: but nothing can be gained through Destiny alone, by a man that is wanting in personal Exertion. Even so does one attain to heaven, and all the objects of enjoyment, as also the fulfilment of one's heart's desires by well-directed individual Exertion. All the luminous bodies in the firmament, all the deities, the Nagas, and the Rakshasas, as also the Sun and the Moon and the Winds, have attained to their high status by evolution from man's status, through dint of their own action. Riches, friends, prosperity descending from generation to generation, as also the graces of life, are difficult of attainment by those that are wanting in Exertion. The Brahmana attains to prosperity by holy living, the Kshatriya by prowess, the Vaisya by manly exertion, and the Sudra by service. Riches and other objects of enjoyment do not follow the stingy, nor the impotent, nor the idler. Nor are these ever attained by the man that is not active or manly or devoted to the exercise of religious austerities. Even he, the adorable Vishnu, who created the three worlds with the Daityas and all the gods, even He is engaged in austere penances in the bosom of the deep. If one's Karma bore no fruit, then all actions would become fruitless, and relying on Destiny men would become idlers. He who, without pursuing the human modes of action, follows Destiny only, acts in vain, like unto the woman that has an impotent husband. In this world the apprehension that accrues from performance of good or evil actions is not so great if Destiny be unfavourable as one's apprehension of the same in the other world if Exertion be wanting while here.[9] Man's powers, if properly exerted, only follow his Destiny, but Destiny alone is incapable of conferring any good where Exertion is wanting. When it is seen that even in the celestial regions, the position of the deities themselves is unstable,

[9] The meaning seems to be that if Destiny be unfavourable, there need not be much fear with respect to this world. But if one be wanting in Exertion, great must his fear be with respect to the next world, for happiness can never be obtained in the next world unless one acts righteously while here.

how would the deities maintain their own position or that of others without proper Karma? The deities do not always approve of the good deeds of others in this world, for, apprehending their own overthrow, they try to thwart the acts of others. There is a constant rivalry between the deities and the Rishis, and if they all have to go through their Karma, still it can never be averted that there is no such thing as Destiny, for it is the latter that initiates all Karma. How does Karma originate, if Destiny form the prime spring of human action? (The answer is) that by this means, an accretion of many virtues is made even in the celestial regions. One's own self is one's friend and one's enemy too, as also the witness of one's good and evil deeds. Good and evil manifest themselves through Karma. Good and evil acts do not give adequate results. Righteousness is the refuge of the gods, and by righteousness is everything attained. Destiny thwarts not the man that has attained to virtue and righteousness.

"""In olden times, Yayati, falling from his high estate in heaven descended on the Earth but was again restored to the celestial regions by the good deeds of his virtuous grandsons. The royal sage Pururavas, celebrated as the descendant of Ila, attained to heaven through the intercession of the Brahmanas. Saudasa, the king of Kosala, though dignified by the performance of Aswamedha and other sacrifices, obtained the status of a man-eating Rakshasa, through the curse of a great Rishi. Aswatthaman and Rama, though both warriors and sons of Munis, failed to attain to heaven by reason of their own actions in this world. Vasu, though he performed a hundred sacrifices like a second Vasava, was sent to the nethermost regions, for making a single false statement. Vali, the son of Virochana, righteously bound by his promise, was consigned to the regions under the Earth, by the prowess of Vishnu. Was not Janamejaya, who followed the foot-prints of Sakra, checked and put down by the gods for killing a Brahmana woman? Was not the regenerate Rishi Vaisampayana too, who slew a Brahmana in ignorance, and was polluted by the slaughter of a child, put down by the gods? In olden times the royal sage Nriga became transmuted into a lizard. He had made gifts of kine unto the Brahmanas at his great sacrifice, but this availed him not. The royal sage Dhundhumara was overwhelmed with decrepitude even while engaged in performing his sacrifices, and foregoing all the merits thereof, he fell asleep at Girivraja. The Pandavas too regained their lost kingdom, of which they had been deprived by the powerful sons of Dhritarashtra, not through the intercession of the fates, but by recourse to their own valour. Do the Munis of rigid vows, and devoted to the practice of austere penances, denounce their curses with the aid of any supernatural power or by the exercise of their own puissance attained by individual acts? All the good which is attained with difficulty in this world is possessed by the wicked, is soon lost to them. Destiny does not help the man that is steeped in spiritual ignorance and avarice. Even as a fire of small proportions, when fanned by the wind, becomes of mighty power, so does Destiny, when joined with individual Exertion, increase greatly (in potentiality). As with the diminution of oil in the lamp its light is extinguished so does the influence of Destiny is lost if one's acts stop. Having obtained vast wealth, and women and all the enjoyments of this world, the man without action is unable to enjoy them long, but the high-souled man, who is even diligent, is able to find riches buried deep in the Earth and watched over by the fates. The good man who is prodigal (in religious charities and sacrifices) is sought by the gods for his good conduct, the celestial world being better than the world of men, but the house of the miser though abounding in wealth is looked upon by the gods as the house of dead. The man that does not exert himself is never contented in this world nor can Destiny alter the course of a man that has gone wrong. So there is no authority inherent in Destiny. As the pupil follows one's own individual perception, so the Destiny follows Exertion. The affairs in which one's own Exertion is put forth, there only Destiny shows its hand. O best of Munis, I have thus described all the merits of individual Exertion, after having always known them in their true significance with the aid of my yogic insight. By the influence of Destiny, and by putting forth individual Exertion, do men attain to heaven. The combined aid of Destiny and Exertion, becomes efficacious."'"

SECTION VII.

"'Yudhishthira said, "O the best of Bharata's race and the foremost of great men, I wish to know what the fruits are of good deed. Do thou enlighten me on this point."

"'Bhishma said, "I shall tell thee what thou hast asked. Do thou, O Yudhishthira, listen to this which constitutes the secret knowledge of the Rishis. Listen to me as I explain what the ends, long coveted, are which are attained by men after death. Whatever actions are performed by particular corporeal beings, the fruits thereof are reaped by the doers while endued with similar corporeal bodies; for example, the fruits of actions done with mind are enjoyed at the time of dreams, and those of actions performed physically are enjoyed in the working state physically. In whatever states creatures perform good or evil deeds, they reap the fruits thereof in similar states of succeeding lives. No act done with the aid of the five organs of sensual perception, is ever lost. The five sensual organs and the immortal soul which is the sixth, remain its witnesses. One should devote one's eye to the service of the guest and should devote one's heart on the same; one should utter words that are agreeable; one should also follow and worship (one's guest). This is called Panchadakshin Sacrifice, (the sacrifice with five gifts). He who offers good food to the unknown and weary travellers fatigued by a long journey, attains to great merit. Those that use the sacrificial platform as their only bed obtain commodious mansions and beds (in subsequent births). Those that wear only rags and barks of trees for dress, obtain good apparel and ornaments in next birth. One possessed of penances and having his soul on Yoga, get vehicles and riding animals (as the fruit of their renunciation in this life). The monarch that lies down by the side of the sacrificial fire, attains to vigour and valour. The man who renounces the enjoyment of all delicacies, attains to prosperity, and he that abstains from animal food, obtains children and cattle. He who lies down with his head downwards, or who lives in water, or who lives secluded and alone in the practice of Brahmacharya, attains to all the desired ends. He who offers shelter to a guest and welcomes him with water to wash his feet as also with food, light and bed, attains to the merits of the sacrifice with the five gifts. He who lays himself down on a warrior's bed on the battle-field in the posture of a warrior, goes to those eternal regions where all the objects of desire are fulfilled. A man, O king, attains to riches that makes charitable gifts. One secures obedience to one's command by the vow of silence, all the enjoyments of life by practice of austerities, long life by Brahmacharya, and beauty, prosperity and freedom from disease by abstaining from injury to others. Sovereignty falls to the lot of those that subsist on fruits and roots only. Residence in heaven is attained by those that live on only leaves of trees. A man, O king, is said to obtain happiness, by abstention from food. By confining one's diet to herbs alone, one becomes possessed of cows. By living on grass one attains to the celestial regions. By foregoing all intercourse with one's wife and making ablutions three times during the day and by inhaling the air only for purposes of subsistence, one obtains the merit of a sacrifice. Heaven is attained by the practice of truth, nobility of birth by sacrifices. The Brahmana of pure practices that subsists on water only, and performs the Agnihotra ceaselessly, and recites the Gayatri, obtains a kingdom. By abstaining food or by regulating it, one attains to residence in heaven. O king, by abstaining from all but the prescribed diet while engaged in sacrifices, and by making pilgrimage for twelve years, one attains to a place better than the abodes reserved for heroes. By reading all the Vedas, one is instantly liberated from misery, and by practising virtue in thought, one attains to the heavenly regions. That man who is able to renounce that intense yearning of the heart for happiness and material enjoyments,—a yearning that is difficult of conquest by the foolish and that doth not abate with the abatement of bodily vigour and that clings like a fatal disease unto him,—is able to secure happiness. As the young calf is able to recognise its dam from among a thousand cows, so does the previous acts of a man pursue him (in all his different transformations). As the flowers and fruits of a tree, unurged by visible influences, never miss their proper season, so does Karma done in a previous existence bring about its fruits in proper time. With age, man's hair grows grey, his teeth become loose; his eyes and ears too become dim in action; but the only thing that does not abate is his desire for enjoyments. Prajapati is pleased with those acts that please one's father, and the Earth is pleased with those acts that please one's mother, and Brahma is adored with those acts that please one's preceptor. Virtue is honoured by him who honours these three. The acts of those that despise these three do not avail them.'"

"Vaisampayana said, 'The princes of Kuru's race became filled with wonder upon listening to this speech of Bhishma. All of them became pleased in mind and overpowered with joy. As Mantras applied with a desire to win victory, or the performance of the Shoma sacrifice made without proper gifts, or oblations poured on the fire without proper hymns, become useless and lead to evil consequences, even so sin and evil results flow from falsehood in speech. O prince, I have thus related to thee this doctrine of the fruition of good and evil acts, as narrated by the Rishis of old. What else dost thou wish to hear?'"

SECTION VIII.

"'Yudhishthira said, "Who are deserving of worship? Who are they unto whom one may bow? Who are they, O Bharata, unto whom thou wouldst bend thy head? Who, again, are they whom thou likest? Tell me all this, O prince. What is that upon which thy mind dwells when affliction overwhelms thee? Do thou discourse to me on what is beneficial here, that is, in this region of human beings, as also hereafter."[10]

"'Bhishma said, "I like those regenerate persons whose highest wealth is Brahman, whose heaven consists in the knowledge of the soul, and whose penances are constituted by their diligent study of the Vedas. My heart yearns after those in whose race persons, young and old diligently bear the ancestral burthens without languishing under them. Brahmanas well-trained in several branches of knowledge, self-controlled, mild-speeched, conversant with the scriptures, well-behaved, possessed of the knowledge of Brahman and righteous in conduct, discourse in respectable assemblies like flights of swans.[11] Auspicious, agreeable, excellent, and well-pronounced are the words, O

---

[10] The commentator explains that hitam tad vada are understood in the last line.

[11] The commentator explains that the allusion here is to the adage that swans in drinking milk mixed with water always drink the milk leaving out the water. Learned Brahmanas are like swans for in discoursing upon even the topics of the world they select what is good and instructive but reject what is evil and sinful, or, as the Commentator puts it, they know the difference between what is soul and what is not soul.

Yudhishthira, which they utter with a voice as deep as that of the clouds. Fraught with happiness both temporal and spiritual, such words are uttered by them in the courts of monarchs, themselves being received with honour and attention and served with reverence by those rulers of men. Indeed, my heart yearns after them who listen to the words uttered in assemblies or the courts of kings by persons endued with knowledge and all desirable attributes, and are respected by others. My heart, O monarch, always yearns after them who, for the gratification of Brahmanas, O Yudhishthira, give unto them, with devotion, food that is well-cooked and clean and wholesome. It is easy to fight in battle, but not so to make a gift without pride or vanity. In this world, O Yudhishthira, there are brave men and heroes by hundreds. While counting them, he that is a hero in gifts should be regarded as superior. O amiable one, if I had been even a vulgar Brahmana, I would have regarded myself as very great, not to speak of one born in a good Brahmana family endued with righteousness of conduct, and devoted to penances and learning. There is no one, O son of Pandu, in this world that is dearer to me than thou, O chief of Bharata's race but dearer to me than thou are the Brahmanas. And since, O best of the Kurus, the Brahmanas are very much dearer to me than thou, it is by that truth that I hope to go to all those regions of felicity which have been acquired by my sire Santanu. Neither my sire, nor my sire's sire, nor any one else connected with me by blood, is dearer to me than the Brahmanas. I do not expect any fruit, small or great, from my worship of the Brahmanas (for I worship them as deities because they are deserving of such worship).[12] In consequence of what I have done to the Brahmanas in thought, word, and deed, I do not feel any pain now (even though I am lying on a bed of arrows). People used to call me as one devoted to the Brahmanas. This style of address always pleased me highly. To do good to the Brahmanas is the most sacred of all sacred acts. I behold many regions of beatitude waiting for me that have reverentially walked behind the Brahmanas. Very soon shall I repair to those regions for everlasting time, O son. In this world, O Yudhishthira, the duties of women have reference to and depend upon their husbands. To a woman, verily, the husband is the deity and he is the highest end after which she should strive. As the husband is to the wife, even so are the Brahmanas unto Kshatriyas. If there be a Kshatriya of full hundred years of age and a good Brahmana child of only ten years, the latter should be regarded as a father and the former as a son, for among the two, verily, the Brahmana is superior. A woman in the absence of her husband, takes his younger brother for her lord; even so the Earth, not having obtained the Brahmana, made the Kshatriya her lord. The Brahmanas should be protected like sons and worshipped like sires or preceptors. Indeed, O best of the Kurus, they should be waited upon with reverence even as people wait with reverence upon their sacrificial or Homa fires. The Brahmanas are endued with simplicity and righteousness. They are devoted to truth. They are always engaged in the good of every creature. Yet when angry they are like snakes of virulent poison. They should, for these reasons, be always waited upon and served with reverence and humility. One should, O Yudhishthira, always fear these two, viz., Energy and Penances. Both these should be avoided or kept at a distance. The effects of both are speedy. There is the superiority, however, of Penances, viz., that Brahmanas endued with Penances, O monarch, can, if angry, slay the object of their wrath (regardless of the measure of Energy with which that object may be endued). Energy and Penances, each of the largest measure, become neutralised if applied against a Brahmana that has conquered wrath. If the two,—that is, Energy and Penances,—be set against each other, then

---

[12] Vrijinam is explained by the commentator as 'Sankatam, phalasa iti yavat' etc.

destruction would overtake both but not destruction without a remnant, for while Energy, applied against Penances, is sure to be destroyed without leaving a remnant. Penances applied against Energy cannot be destroyed completely.[13] As the herdsman, stick in hand, protects the herd, even so should the Kshatriya always protect the Vedas and the Brahmanas. Indeed, the Kshatriya should protect all righteous Brahmanas even as a sire protects his sons. He should always have his eye upon the house of the Brahmanas for seeing that their means of subsistence may not be wanting.""'

SECTION IX.

"'Yudhisthira said, "O grandsire, O thou of great splendour, what do those men become who, through stupefaction of intellect, do not make gifts unto Brahmanas after having promised to make those gifts? O thou that art the foremost of all righteous persons, do tell me what the duties are in this respect. Indeed, what becomes the end of those wicked wights that do not give after having promised to give."

"'Bhishma said, "The person that, after having promised, does not give, be it little or much, has the mortification to see his hopes (in every direction) become fruitless like the hopes of a eunuch in respect of progeny. Whatever good acts such a person does between the day of his birth and that of his death, O Bharata, whatever libations he pours on the sacrificial fire, whatever gifts he makes, O chief of Bharata's race, and whatever penances he performs all become fruitless. They that are conversant with the scriptures declare this as their opinion, arriving at it, O chief of the Bharatas, with the aid of a well-ordered understanding. Persons conversant with the scriptures are also of opinion that such a man may be cleansed by giving away a thousand horses with ears of a dark hue. In this connection is cited the old narrative of the discourse between a jackal and an ape. While both were human beings, O scorcher of foes, they were intimate friends. After death one of them became a jackal and the other an ape. Beholding the jackal one day eating an animal carcase in the midst of a crematorium, the ape, remembering his own and his friend's former birth as human beings, addressed him, saying,—'Verily, what terrible sin didst thou perpetrate in thy former birth in consequence of which thou art obliged in this birth to feed in a crematorium upon such repulsive fare as the putrid carcase of an animal?'—Thus addressed, the jackal replied unto the ape, saying,—Having promised to give unto a Brahmana I did not make him the gift. It is for that sin, O ape, that I have fallen into this wretched order of existence. It is for that reason that, when hungry, I am obliged to eat such food.'"

"'Bhishma continued, "The jackal then, O best of men, addressed the ape and said,—'What sin didst thou commit for which thou hast become an ape?'

"'"The ape said, 'In my former life I used to appropriate the fruits belonging to Brahmanas. Hence have I become an ape. Hence it is clear that one possessed of intelligence and learning should never appropriate what belongs to Brahmanas. Verily, as one should abstain from this, one should avoid also all disputes with Brahmanas. Having promised, one should certainly make the promised gift unto them.'"

"'Bhishma continued, "I heard this, O king, from my preceptor while he was engaged in discoursing upon the subject of Brahmanas. I heard this from that righteous person when he recited the old and sacred declaration on this topic. I heard this from Krishna

---

[13] i.e., one should keep oneself aloof from both Energy and Penances, for both these can consume, if troubled or interfered with. By 'Energy' is meant both physical and mental force. It belongs to the Kshatriya as Penances belong to the Brahmana.

also, O king, while he was engaged in discoursing, O son of Pandu, upon Brahmanas.[14] The property of a Brahmana should never be appropriated. They should always be let alone. Poor, or miserly, or young in years, they should never be disregarded. The Brahmanas have always taught me this. Having promised to make them a gift, the gift should be made. A superior Brahmana should never be disappointed in the matter of his expectations. A Brahmana, O king, in whom an expectation has been raised, has, O king, been said to be like a blazing fire.[15] That man upon whom a Brahmana with raised expectations casts his eye, is sure, O monarch, to be consumed even as a heap of straw is capable of being consumed by a blazing fire.[16] When the Brahmana, gratified (with honours and gifts) by the king addresses the king in delightful and affectionate words, he becomes, O Bharata, a source of great benefit to the king, for he continues to live in the kingdom like a physician combating against diverse ills of the body.[17] Such a Brahmana is sure to maintain by his puissance and good wishes, the sons and grandsons and animals and relatives and ministers and other officers and the city and the provinces of the king.[18] Even such is the energy, so great, of the Brahmana like unto that of the thousand-rayed Surya himself, on the Earth. Therefore, O Yudhishthira, if one wishes to attain to a respectable or happy order of being in one's next birth, one should, having passed the promise to a Brahmana, certainly keep it by actually making the gift to him. By making gifts to a Brahmana one is sure to attain to the highest heaven. Verily, the making of gifts is the highest of acts that one can achieve. By the gifts one makes to a Brahmana, the deities and the pitris are supported. Hence one possessed of knowledge should ever make gifts unto the Brahmanas. O chief of the Bharatas, the Brahmana is regarded as the highest object unto whom gifts should be made. At no time should a Brahmana be received without being properly worshipped.""

SECTION X.

"'Yudhisthira said, "I wish to know, O royal sage, whether any fault is incurred by one who from interested or disinterested friendship imparts instructions unto a person belonging to a low order of birth! O grandsire, I desire to hear this, expounded to me in detail. The course of duty is exceedingly subtile. Men are often seen to be stupefied in respect of that course."

"'Bhishma said, "In this connection, O king, I shall recite to thee, in due order, what I heard certain Rishis say in days of yore. Instruction should not be imparted unto one that belongs to a low or mean caste. It is said that the preceptor who imparts instruction to such a person incurs great fault. Listen to me, O chief of Bharata's race, as I recite to thee, O Yudhishthira, this instance that occurred in days of old, O monarch, of the evil consequences of the imparting of instruction unto a low-born person fallen into distress. The incident which I shall relate occurred in the asylum of certain regenerate sages that stood on the auspicious breast of Himavat. There, on the breast of that prince of mountains, was a sacred asylum adorned with trees of diverse kinds. Overgrown also

---

[14] The commentator thinks that by Krishna, the Island-born Krishna or Vyasa is meant.

[15] The sense is that such a Brahmana, if his expectation be not gratified, is competent to consume the person that has falsely raised that expectation.

[16] Akshyayyam is fire, because it is fire that eats the food offered to the Pitris and makes it inexhaustible.

[17] The sense is that as a physician cures diverse ailments of the body, after the same manner, a gratified Brahmana cures diverse faults of the kingdom in which he continues to live honoured and gratified by the king.

[18] Santirishta is the rishti or benefits caused by santi. The commentator cites Medini for explaining that 'rishti' is 'kshema'.

with diverse species of creepers and plants, it was the resort of many animals and birds. Inhabited by Siddhas and Charanas also, it was exceedingly delightful in consequence of the woods that flowered these at every season. Many were the Brahmacharins that dwelt there, and many belonging to the forest mode of life. Many also were the Brahmanas that took up their residence there, that were highly blessed and that resembled the sun or the fire in energy and effulgence. Ascetics of diverse kinds, observant of various restraints and vows, as also others, O chief of the Bharatas, that had undergone Diksha and were frugal in fare and possessed of cleansed souls, took up their residence there. Large numbers of Valakhilyas and many that were observant of the vow of Sanyasa also, used to dwell there. The asylum, in consequence of all this, resounded with the chanting of the Vedas and the sacred Mantras uttered by its inhabitants. Once upon a time a Sudra endued with compassion for all creatures, ventured to come into that asylum. Arrived at that retreat, he was duly honoured by all the ascetics. Beholding those ascetics of diverse classes that were endued with great energy, that resembled the deities (in purity and power), and that were observing diverse kinds of Diksha, O Bharata, the Sudra became highly pleased at heart. Beholding everything, O chief of Bharata's race, the Sudra felt inclined to devote himself to the practice of penances. Touching the feet of the Kulapati (the head man of the group), O Bharata, he addressed him saying,[19] 'Through thy grace, O foremost of regenerate persons, I desire, to learn (and practise) the duties of religion. It behoveth thee, O illustrious one, to discourse to me on those duties and introduce me (by performing the rites of initiation) into a life of Renunciation. I am certainly inferior in colour, O illustrious one, for I am by caste a Sudra, O best of men. I desire to wait upon and serve you here. Be gratified with me that humbly seek thy shelter.'

""The Kulapati said, 'It is impossible that a Sudra should live here adopting the marks specially intended for those practising lives of Renunciation. If it pleases thee, thou mayest stay here, engaged in waiting upon and serving us. Without doubt, by such service thou shalt attain to many regions of high felicity.'"

"Bhishma continued, "Thus addressed by the ascetic, the Sudra began to reflect in his mind, O king, saying, 'How should I now act? Great is my reverence for those religious duties that lead to merit. Let this, however, be settled, that I shall do what would be for my benefit.'[20] Proceeding to a spot that was distant from that asylum, he made a hut of the twigs and leaves of trees. Erecting also a sacrificial platform, and making a little space for his sleep, and some platforms for the use of the deities, he began, O chief of the Bharatas, to lead a life regulated by rigid observances and vows and to practise penances, abstaining entirely from speech all the while. He began to perform ablutions thrice a day, observe other vows (in respect of food and sleep), make sacrifices to the deities, pour libations on the sacrificial fire, and adore the worship and deities in this way. Restraining all carnal desires, living abstemiously upon fruits and roots, controlling all his senses, he daily welcomed and entertained all that came to his retreat as guests, offering them herbs and fruits that grew plentifully around. In this way he passed a very long time in that hermitage of his.[21] One day an ascetic came to that Sudra's retreat for the purpose of making his acquaintance. The Sudra welcomed and worshipped the Rishi with

---

[19] Tapasye is Tapah karishye. There being no indirect narration in Sanskrit, such forms cannot be helped. A Kulapati is an ascetic that owns ten thousand ascetics for his disciples. Kanwa, the foster-father of Sakuntala, was a Kulapati.

[20] i.e. renouncing service which is the duty ordained for person of his order, he desired to betake himself to universal Renunciation or Sanyasa, without, however, the lingam or marks of that vow.

[21] Sankalpa-niyamopetah means Sankalpasya nigraha, of chittavritti nirodha; tena upetah.

due rites, and gratified him highly. Endued with great energy, and possessed of a righteous soul, that Rishi of rigid vows conversed with his host on many agreeable subjects and informed him of the place whence he had come. In this way, O chief of the Bharatas, that Rishi, O best of men, came into the asylum of the Sudra times out of a number for the object of seeing him. On one of these occasions, the Sudra, O king, addressing the Rishi said,—'I desire to perform the rites that are ordained for the Pitris. Do thou instruct me kindly in this matter.'—'Very well,'—the Brahmana said in reply unto him, O monarch. The Sudra then, purifying himself by a bath, brought water for the Rishi to wash his feet, and he also brought some Kusa grass, and wild herbs and fruits, and a sacred seat, and the seat called Vrishi. The Vrishi, however, was placed by the Sudra towards the south, with his head turned to the west. Beholding this and knowing that it was against the ordinance, the Rishi addressed the Sudra, saying,—'Place the Vrishi with its head turned towards the East, and having purified thyself, do thou sit with thy face turned towards the north'—The Sudra did everything as the Rishi directed. Possessed of great intelligence, and observant of righteousness, the Sudra received every direction, about the Sraddha, as laid down in the ordinance, from that Rishi endued with penances regarding the manner of spreading the Kusa grass, and placing the Arghyas, and as regards the rites to be observed in the matter of the libations to be poured and the food to be offered. After the rites in honour of the Pitris had been accomplished, the Rishi, was dismissed by the Sudra, whereupon he returned to his own abode.[22] After a long time, the whole of which he passed in the practice of such penances and vows, the Sudra ascetic met with his death in those woods. In consequence of the merit he acquired by those practices, the Sudra in the next life, took birth in the family of a great king, and in course of time became possessed of great splendour. The regenerate Rishi also, when the time came, paid his debt in Nature. In his next life, O chief of Bharata's race, he took birth in the family of a priest. It was in this way that those two, viz., that Sudra who had passed a life of penances and that regenerate Rishi who had in kindness given the former some instructions in the matter of the rites performed in honour of the Pitris, became reborn, the one as scion of a royal race and the other as the member of a priestly family. Both of them began to grow and both acquired great knowledge in the usual branches of study. The Brahmana became well versed in the Vedas as also in the Atharvans.[23] In the matter, again of all sacrifices ordained in the Sutras, of that Vedanga which deals with religious rites and observances, astrology and astronomy the reborn Rishi attained great excellence. In the Sankhya philosophy too he began to take great delight. Meanwhile, the reborn Sudra who had become a prince, when his father, the king died, performed his last rites; and after he had purified himself by accomplishing all the obsequial ceremonies, he was installed by the subjects of his father as their king on his paternal throne. But soon after his own installation as king, he installed the reborn Rishi as his priest. Indeed, having made the Brahmana his priest, the king began to pass his days in great happiness. He ruled his kingdom righteously and protected and cherished all his subjects. Everyday, however, the king on the occasion of receiving benedictions from his priest as also of the

---

[22] No Brahmana, the scriptures declare, should ever assist a Sudra in the performance of his religious or Pitri rites. Those Brahmanas that violate this injunction fall away from their superior position. They are condemned as Sudra-yajins. Here the Rishi, by only giving directions to the Sudra as to how the Pitri rites were to be performed, became a Sudra-yajin. There are many families to this day whose status has been lowered in consequence of such or similar acts of indiscretion on the part of their ancestors.

[23] Atharva Veda Veda cha implies that the Atharvans were not generally included under the term Veda by which the first three Vedas only were meant.

performance of religious and other sacred rites, smiled or laughed at him loudly. In this way, O monarch, the reborn Sudra who had become a king, laughed at sight of his priest on numberless occasions.[24] The priest, marking that the king always smiled or laughed whenever he happened to cast his eyes on him, became angry. On one occasion he met the king in a place where there was nobody else. He pleased the king by agreeable discourse. Taking advantage of that moment, O chief of Bharata's race, the priest addressed the king, saying,—'O thou of great splendour, I pray thee to grant me a single boon.'

""The king said, 'O best of regenerate persons, I am ready to grant thee a hundred of boons, what dost thou say then of one only? From the affection I bear thee and the reverence in which I hold thee, there is nothing that I cannot give thee.'

""The priest said, 'I desire to have only one boon, O king, thou hast been pleased with me. Swear that thou wouldst tell me the truth instead of any untruth.'"

"Bhishma continued, "Thus addressed by the priest, O Yudhishthira, the king said unto him—'So be it. If what thou wouldst ask me be known to me, I shall certainly tell thee truly. If on the other hand, the matter be unknown to me, I shall not say anything.'

""The priest said, 'Every day, on occasions of obtaining my benedictions, when, again, I am engaged in the performance of religious rites on thy behalf, on occasions also of the Homa and other rites of propitiation, why is it that thou laughest upon beholding me? Seeing thee laugh at me on all occasions, my mind shrinks with shame. I have caused thee to swear, O king, that thou wouldst answer me truly. It does not behove thee to say what is untrue. There must be some grave reason for thy behaviour. Thy laughter cannot be causeless. Great is my curiosity to know the reason. Do thou speak truly unto me.'

""The king said, 'When thou hast addressed me in this strain, O regenerate one, I am bound to enlighten thee, even if the matter be one that should not be divulged in thy hearing. I must tell thee the truth. Do thou listen to me with close attention, O regenerate one. Listen to me, O foremost of twice-born persons, as I disclose to thee what happened (to us) in our former births. I remember that birth. Do thou listen to me with concentrated mind. In my former life I was a Sudra employed in the practice of severe penances. Thou, O best of regenerate persons, wert a Rishi of austere penances. O sinless one, gratified with me, and impelled by the desire of doing me good, thou, O Brahmana, wert pleased to give me certain instructions in the rites I performed (on one occasion) in honour of my Pitris. The instructions thou gayest me were in respect of the manner of spreading the Vrishi and the Kusa blades and of offering libations and meat and other food to the manes, O foremost of ascetics. In consequence of this transgression of thine thou hast taken birth as a priest, and I have taken birth as a king, O foremost of Brahmanas. Behold the vicissitudes that Time brings about. Thou hast reaped this fruit in consequence of thy having instructed me (in my former birth). It is for this reason, O Brahmana, that I smile at sight of thee, O foremost of regenerate persons. I do not certainly laugh at thee from desire of disregarding thee. Thou art my preceptor.[25] At this change of condition I am really very sorry. My heart burns at the thought. I remember our former births, hence do I laugh at sight of thee. Thy austere penances were all destroyed by the instructions thou gayest me. Relinquishing thy present office of priest, do thou endeavour to regain a

---

[24] Punyaha-vachana is a peculiar rite. The priest or some other Brahmana is invited. Gifts are then made to him, and he utters benedictions in return upon the giver. Yudhishthira used to invite every day a large number of Brahmanas and make them very valuable presents for obtaining their benedictions.

[25] Or rather, superior. Guru is used to denote any senior as well as preceptor.

superior birth. Do thou exert so that thou mayst not obtain in thy next life a birth meaner than thy present one. Take as much wealth as thou wishest, O learned Brahmana, and cleanse thy soul, O best of men.'"

"'Bhishma continued, "Dismissed by the king (from the office of priest), the Brahmana made many gifts, unto persons of his own order, of wealth and land and villages. He observed many rigid and severe vows as laid down by the foremost of Brahmanas. He sojourned to many sacred waters and made many gifts unto Brahmanas in those places. Making gifts of kine unto persons of the regenerate order, his soul became cleansed and he succeeded in acquiring a knowledge of it. Repairing to that very asylum whither he had lived in his former birth, he practised very severe penances. As the consequence of all this, O foremost of kings, that Brahmana succeeded in attaining to the highest success. He became an object of veneration with all the ascetics that dwelt in that asylum. In this way, O best of monarchs, that regenerate Rishi fell into great distress. Unto Sudras, therefore, the Brahmanas should never give instructions. Hence, O king, the Brahmana should avoid imparting instructions (to such as are low-born), for it was by imparting instruction to a low-born person a Brahmana came to grief. O best of kings, the Brahmana should never desire to obtain instruction from, or impart instruction to, a person that belongs to the lowest order. Brahmanas and Kshatriyas and Vaisyas, the three orders, are regarded as twice-born. By imparting instruction unto these, a Brahmana does not incur any fault. They, therefore, that are good, should never discourse on any subject, for imparting any instruction, before persons of the inferior order. The course of morality is exceedingly subtle and incapable of being comprehended by persons of uncleansed souls. It is for this reason that ascetics adopt the vow of silence, and being respected by all, pass through Diksha (initiation) without indulging in speech.[26] For fear of saying what is incorrect or what may offend, ascetics often forego speech itself. Even men that are righteous and possessed of every accomplishment, and endued with truth and simplicity of behaviour, have been known to incur great fault in consequence of words spoken improperly. Instruction should never be imparted on anything unto any person. If in consequence of the instructions imparted, the instructed commit any sin, that sin, attaches to the Brahmana who imparted the instruction. The man of wisdom, therefore, that desires to earn merit, should always act with wisdom. That instruction which is imparted in barter for money always pollutes the instructor.[27] Solicited by others, one should say only what is correct after settling it with the aid of reflection. One should impart instruction in such a way that one may, by imparting it, earn merit. I have thus told thee everything respecting the subject of instructions. Very often persons become plunged into great afflictions in consequence of imparting instructions. Hence it is meet that one should abstain from giving instruction unto others."'"

SECTION XI.

"'Yudhishthira said, "Tell me, O grandsire, in what kind of man or woman, O chief of the Bharatas, does the goddess of prosperity always reside?"

"'Bhishma said, "I shall, in this connection, narrate to thee what occurred and what I have heard. Once on a time, beholding the goddess of prosperity blazing with beauty and endued with the complexion of the lotus, the princess Rukmini the mother of Pradyumna

---

[26] The Diksha is that rite which one passes through by way of preparation for those sacrifices and vows that one seeks to perform.

[27] Satyanrite is equivalent to trade or barter.

that bore the device of the Makara on his banner, filled with curiosity, asked this question in the presence of Devaki's son. 'Who are those beings by whose side thou stayest and whom thou favours? Who again, are those whom thou dost not bless with favour. O thou that art dear unto Him that is the lord of all creatures, tell me this truly, O thou that art equal to a great Rishi in penances and puissance.' Thus addressed by the princess, the goddess of prosperity, with a face as beautiful as the moon, and moved by grace, in the presence of him who has Garuda on his banner, said these words in reply that were sweet and charming.

""Sree said, 'O blessed lady, I always reside with him that is eloquent, active, attentive to business, free from wrath, given to the worship of the deities, endued with gratitude, has his passions under complete control, and is high-minded in everything. I never reside with one that is inattentive to business, that is an unbeliever, that causes an intermixture of races in consequence of his lustfulness, that is ungrateful, that is of impure practices, that uses harsh and cruel words, that is a thief, that cherishes malice towards his preceptors and other seniors, those persons that are endued with little energy, strength, life, and honour, that are distressed at every trifle, and that always indulge in wrath. I never reside with these that think in one strain and act in a different one.[28] I never reside also with him who never desires any acquisition for himself, of him who is so blinded as to rest content with the lot in which he finds himself without any exertion or with those that are contented with small acquisitions. I reside with those that are observant of the duties of their own order, or those that are conversant with the duties of righteousness, or those that are devoted to the service of the aged or those that have their passions under control, or those that are endued with cleansed souls or those that observe the virtue of forgiveness, or those that are able and prompt in action, or with such women as are forgiving and self-restrained. I reside with those women also that are devoted to truth and sincerity and that worship the deities. I do not reside with those women also that do not attend to household furniture and provisions scattered all around the house, and that always utter words contrary to the wishes of their husbands. I always avoid those women that are fond of the houses of other people and that have no modesty. On the other hand, I reside with those women that are devoted to their husbands, that are blessed in behaviour, and that are always decked in ornaments and attired in good robes. I always reside with those women that are truthful in speech, that are of handsome and agreeable features, that are blessed and that are endued with all accomplishments. I always avoid such women as are sinful and unclean or impure, as always lick the corners of their mouths, as have no patience or fortitude, and as are fond of dispute and quarrelling, as are given to much sleep, and as always lie down. I always reside in conveyances and the animals that drag them, in maidens, in ornaments and good vestments, in sacrifices, in clouds charged with rain, in full-blown lotuses, and in those stars that bespangle the autumnal firmament. I reside in elephants, in the cow pen, in good seats, and in lakes adorned with full-blown lotuses. I live also in such rivers as babble sweetly in their course, melodious with the music of cranes, having banks adorned with rows of diverse trees, and restored to by Brahmanas and ascetics and others crowned with success. I always reside in those rivers also that have deep and large volumes of rolling waters rendered turbid by lions and elephants plunging into them for bathing or slaking their thirst. I reside also in infuriate elephants, in bovine bulls, in kings, on the throne and good

---

[28] Sanguptamanoratheshu is explained by the commentator as persons who conceal their real sentiments by acting differently. The reference is to hypocrites.

men. I always reside in that house in which the inmate pours libation on the sacrificial fire and worships kine, Brahmanas and the deities. I reside in that house where at the proper time offerings are made unto the deities, in course of worship.[29] I always reside in such Brahmanas as are devoted to the study of the Vedas, in Kshatriyas devoted to the observance of righteousness, in Vaisyas devoted to cultivation, and the Sudras devoted to the (menial) service of the three upper classes. I reside, with a heart firm and unchangeable, in Narayana, in my embodied self. In Him is righteousness in its perfection and full measure, devotion to the Brahmanas, and the quality of agreeableness. Can I not say, O lady that I do not reside in my embodied form, (in any of these places that I have mentioned, except Narayana)? That person in whom I reside in spirit increases in righteousness and fame and wealth and objects of desire.'"""

SECTION XII.

"'Yudhishthira said, "It behoveth, O king to tell me truly which of the two viz., man or woman derives the greater pleasure from an act of union with each other. Kindly resolve my doubt in this respect."

"'Bhishma said, "In this connection is cited this old narrative of the discourse between Bhangaswana and Sakra as a precedent illustrating the question. In days of yore there lived a king of the name of Bhangaswana. He was exceedingly righteous and was known as a royal sage. He was, however, childless, O chief of men, and therefore performed a sacrifice from desire of obtaining an issue. The sacrifice which that mighty monarch performed was the Agnishtuta. In consequence of the fact that the deity of fire is alone adored in that sacrifice, this is always disliked by Indra. Yet it is the sacrifice that is desired by men when for the purpose of obtaining an issue they seek to cleanse themselves of their sins.[30] The highly blessed chief of the celestials, viz. Indra, learning that the monarch was desirous of performing the Agnishtuta, began from that moment to look for the laches of that royal sage of well-restrained soul (for if he could succeed in finding some laches, he could then punish his disregarder). Notwithstanding all his vigilance, however, O king, Indra failed to detect any laches, on the part of the high-souled monarch. Some time after, one day, the king went on a hunting expedition. Saying unto himself—This, indeed, is an opportunity,—Indra stupefied the monarch. The king proceeded alone on his horse, confounded because of the chief of the celestials having stupefied his senses. Afflicted with hunger and thirst, the king's confusion was so great that he could not ascertain the points of the compass. Indeed, afflicted with thirst, he began to wander hither and thither. He then beheld a lake that was exceedingly beautiful and was full of transparent water. Alighting from his steed, and plunging into the lake, he caused his animal to drink. Tying his horse then, whose thirst had been slaked, to a tree, the king plunged into the lake again for performing his ablutions. To his amazement he found that he was changed, by virtue of the waters, into a woman. Beholding himself thus transformed in respect of sex itself, the king became overpowered with shame. With his senses and mind completely agitated, he began to reflect with his whole heart in this strain:—'Alas, how shall I ride my steed? How shall I return to my capital? In

---

[29] Vali (sing. of valayah) means anything offered or dedicated to the deities. The sense of the second line is that the goddess of prosperity resides in that house in which flowers are offered to the deities instead of animal life.

[30] The belief is that a man remains childless in consequence of his sins. If these sins can be washed away, he may be sure to obtain children.

consequence of the Agnishtuta sacrifice I have got a hundred sons all endued with great might, and all children of my own loins. Alas, thus transformed, what shall I say unto them? What shall I say unto my spouses, my relatives and well-wishers, and my subjects of the city and the provinces? Rishis conversant with the truths of duty and religion and other matters say that mildness and softness and liability to extreme agitation are the attributes of women, and that activity, hardness, and energy are the attributes of men. Alas, my manliness has disappeared. For what reason has femininity come over me? In consequence of this transformation of sex, how shall I succeed in mounting my horse again?'—Having indulged in these sad thoughts, the monarch, with great exertion, mounted his steed and came back to his capital, transformed though he had been into a woman. His sons and spouses and servants, and his subjects of the city and the provinces, beholding that extraordinary transformation, became exceedingly amazed. Then that royal sage, that foremost of eloquent men, addressing them all, said,—'I had gone out on a hunting expedition, accompanied by a large force. Losing all knowledge of the points of the compass, I entered a thick and terrible forest, impelled by the fates. In that terrible forest, I became afflicted with thirst and lost my senses. I then beheld a beautiful lake abounding with fowl of every description. Plunging into that stream for performing my ablutions, I was transformed into a woman!'—Summoning then his spouses and counsellors, and all his sons by their names, that best of monarchs transformed into a woman said unto them these words:—'Do ye enjoy this kingdom in happiness. As regards myself, I shall repair to the woods, ye sons.'—Having said so unto his children, the monarch proceeded to the forest. Arrived there, she came upon an asylum inhabited by an ascetic. By that ascetic the transformed monarch gave birth to a century of sons. Taking all those children of hers, she repaired to where her former children were, and addressing the latter, said,—'Ye are the children of my loins while I was a man. These are my children brought forth by me in this state of transformation. Ye sons, do ye all enjoy my kingdom together, like brothers born of the same parents.'—At this command of their parent, all the brothers, uniting together, began to enjoy the kingdom as their joint property. Beholding those children of the king all jointly enjoying the kingdom as brothers born of the same parents, the chief of the celestials, filled with wrath, began to reflect—'By transforming this royal sage into a woman I have, it seems, done him good instead of an injury.' Saying this, the chief of the celestials viz., Indra of a hundred sacrifices, assuming the form of a Brahmana, repaired to the capital of the king and meeting all the children succeeded in disuniting the princes. He said unto them— 'Brothers never remain at peace even when they happen to be the children of the same father. The sons of the sage Kasyapa, viz., the deities and the Asuras, quarrelled with each other on account of the sovereignty of the three worlds. As regards ye princes, ye are the children of the royal sage Bhangaswana. These others are the children of an ascetic. The deities and the Asuras are children of even one common sire, and yet the latter quarrelled with each other. How much more, therefore, should you quarrel with each other? This kingdom that is your paternal property is being enjoyed by these children of an ascetic.' With these words, Indra succeeded in causing a breach between them, so that they were very soon engaged in battle and slew each other. Hearing this, king Bhangaswana, who was living as an ascetic woman, burnt with grief and poured forth her lamentations. The lord of the celestials viz. Indra, assuming the guise of a Brahmana, came to that spot where the ascetic lady was living and meeting her, said,—'O thou that art possessed of a beautiful face, with what grief dost thou burn so that thou art pouring forth thy lamentations?'—Beholding the Brahmana the lady told him in a piteous voice,—'Two hundred sons of mine O regenerate one, have been slain by Time. I was formerly a king, O learned Brahmana and in that state had a hundred sons. These were begotten by me after my own form, O best of regenerate persons. On one occasion I went on a hunting expedition. Stupefied, I wandered amidst a thick forest. Beholding at last a lake, I plunged into it. Rising, O foremost of Brahmanas, I found that I had become a woman. Returning to my capital I installed my sons in the sovereignty of my dominions and then departed for the forest. Transformed into a woman, I bore a hundred sons to my husband who is a high souled ascetic. All of them were born in the ascetic's retreat. I took them to the capital. My children, through the influence of Time, quarrelled with each other, O twice-born one. Thus afflicted by Destiny, I am indulging in grief.' Indra addressed him in these harsh words.—'In former days, O lady, thou gayest me great pain, for thou didst perform a sacrifice that is disliked by Indra. Indeed, though I was present, thou didst not invoke me with honours. I am that Indra, O thou of wicked understanding. It is I with whom thou hast purposely sought hostilities.' Beholding Indra, the royal sage fell at his feet, touching them with his head, and said,—'Be gratified with me, O foremost of deities. The sacrifice of which thou speakest was performed from desire of offspring (and not from any wish to hurt thee). It behoveth thee therefore, to grant me thy pardon.'—Indra, seeing the transformed monarch prostrate himself thus unto him, became gratified with him and desired to give him a boon. 'Which of your sons, O king, dost thou wish, should revive, those that were brought forth by thee transformed into a woman, or those that were begotten by thee in thy condition as a person of the male sex?' The ascetic lady, joining her hands, answered Indra, saying, 'O Vasava, let those sons of mine come to life that were borne by me as a woman.' Filled with wonder at this reply, Indra once more asked the lady, 'Why dost thou entertain less affection for those children of thine that were begotten by thee in thy form of a person of the male sex? Why is it that thou bearest greater affection for those children that were borne by thee in thy transformed state? I wish to hear the reason of this difference in respect of thy affection. It behoveth thee to tell me everything.'

""""The lady said, 'The affection that is entertained by a woman is much greater than that which is entertained by a man. Hence, it is, O Sakra, that I wish those children to come back to life that were borne by me as a woman.'"

"'Bhishma continued, "Thus addressed, Indra became highly pleased and said unto her, 'O lady that art so truthful, let all thy children come back into life. Do thou take another boon, O foremost of kings, in fact, whatever boon thou likest. O thou of excellent vows, do thou take from me whatever status thou choosest, that of woman or of man.'

""""The lady said, 'I desire to remain a woman, O Sakra. In fact, I do not wish to be restored to the status of manhood, O Vasava.'—Hearing this answer, Indra once more asked her, saying,—'Why is it, O puissant one, that abandoning the status of manhood thou wishest that of womanhood?' Questioned thus, that foremost of monarchs transformed into a woman answered, 'In acts of congress, the pleasure that women enjoy is always much greater than what is enjoyed by men. It is for this reason, O Sakra, that I desire to continue a woman; O foremost of the deities, truly do I say unto thee that I derive greater pleasure in my present status of womanhood. I am quite content with this status of womanhood that I now have. Do thou leave me now, O lord of heaven.'— Hearing these words of hers, the lord of the celestials answered,—'So be it,'—and bidding her farewell, proceeded to heaven. Thus, O monarch, it is known that woman derives much greater pleasure than man under the circumstances thou hast asked.""""

SECTION XIII.

"'Yudhishthira said, "What should a man do in order to pass pleasantly through this and the other world. How, indeed, should one conduct oneself? What practices should one adopt with this end in view?"

"'Bhishma said, "One should avoid the three acts that are done with the body, the four that are done with speech, the three that are done with the mind, and the ten paths of action. The three acts that are done with the body and should be wholly avoided are the destruction of the lives of other creatures, theft or appropriation of what belongs to other persons, and the enjoyment of other people's wives. The four acts that are done with speech, O king, and that should never be indulged in or even thought of, are evil conversation, harsh words, publishing other people's faults, and falsehood. Coveting the possessions of others, doing injury to others, and disbelief in the ordinances of the Vedas, are the three acts done with the mind which should always be avoided.[31] Hence, one should never do any evil act in word, body, or mind. By doing good and evil acts, one is sure to enjoy or endure the just consequences thereof. Nothing can be more certain than this."'"

SECTION XIV.

"'Yudhishthira said, "O son of the River Ganga, thou hast heard all the names of Maheshwara, the Lord of the universe. Do thou tell us, O grandsire, all the names that are applied, O puissant one, unto Him who is called Isa and Sambhu. Do thou tell us all those names that are applied unto Him who is called Vabhru or vast, Him that has the universe for his form, Him that is the illustrious preceptor of all the deities and the Asuras, that is called Swayambhu (self-creating) and that is the cause of the origin and dissolution of the universe. Do thou tell us also of the puissance of Mahadeva."

"'Bhishma said, "I am quite incompetent to recite the virtues of Mahadeva of highest intelligence. He pervades all things in the universe and yet is not seen anywhere. He is the creator of universal self and the Pragna (knowing) self and he is their master. All the deities, from Brahman to the Pisachas, adore and worship him. He transcends both Prakriti and Purusha. It is of Him that Rishis, conversant with Yoga and possessing a knowledge of the tattwas, think and reflect. He is indestructible and Supreme Brahman. He is both existent and non-existent. Agitating both Prakriti and Purusha by means of His energy, He created therefrom the universal lord of creatures, viz., Brahma. Who is there that is competent to tell the virtues of that god of gods, that is endued with supreme Intelligence? Man is subject to conception (in the mother's womb), birth, decrepitude, and death. Being such, what man like me is competent to understand Bhava? Only Narayana, O son, that bearer of the discus and the mace, can comprehend Mahadeva. He is without deterioration. He is the foremost of all beings in attributes. He is Vishnu, because of his pervading the universe. He is irresistible. Endued with spiritual vision, He is possessed of supreme Energy. He sees all things with the eye of Yoga. It is in consequence of the

---

[31] I give, in the affirmative form of speech, the three mental acts that are directed to be avoided. In the original, these are given in the negative form. Absence of coveting the possessions of others is the act that is directed to be followed. So compassion for all creatures is prescribed; and, lastly, the belief is directed to be entertained that acts have fruits, for the Vedas declare as such. He that does not believe that acts have fruits disbelieve the very Vedas which of course, is a sinful act.

devotion of the high-souled Krishna to the illustrious Rudra whom he gratified, O
Bharata, in the retreat of Vadari, by penances, that he has succeeded in pervading the
entire universe. O king of kings, it is through Maheswara of celestial vision that
Vasudeva has obtained the attribute of universal agreeableness,—an agreeableness that is
much greater than what is possessed by all articles included under the name of wealth.[32]
For a full thousand years this Madhava underwent the austerest penances and at last
succeeded in gratifying the illustrious and boon giving Siva, that Master of all the mobile
and the immobile universe. In every new Yuga has Krishna (by such penances) gratified
Mahadeva. In every Yuga has Mahadeva been gratified with the great devotion of the
high-souled Krishna. How great is the puissance of the high-souled Mahadeva,—that
original cause of the universe,—has been seen with his own eyes by Hari who himself
transcends all deterioration, on the occasion of his penances in the retreat of Vadari
undergone for obtaining a son.[33] I do not, O Bharata, behold any one that is superior to
Mahadeva. To expound the names of that god of gods fully and without creating the
desire of hearing more only Krishna is competent. This mighty-armed one of Yadu's race
is alone competent to tell the attributes of the illustrious Siva. Verily, O king, only he is
able to discourse on the puissance, in its entirety of the Supreme deity."'

"Vaisampayana continued, 'Having said these words, the illustrious Bhishma, the
grandsire of the Kurus, addressing Vasudeva, said the following words, dealing with the
subject of the greatness of Bhava, O monarch.

"'Bhishma said, "Thou art the Master of all the deities and the Asuras. Thou art
illustrious. Thou art Vishnu in consequence of thy pervading the whole universe. It
behoveth thee to discourse on those subjects connected with Siva of universal form about
which Yudhishthira has asked me. In days of yore, the Rishi Tandi, sprung from Brahma,
recited in Brahma's region and before Brahma himself the thousand names of Mahadeva.
Do thou recite those names before this conclave so that these Rishis endued with wealth
of asceticism, observant of high vows, possessed of self-restraint, and numbering the
Island-born Krishna among them, may hear thee. Do thou discourse on the high
blessedness of Him who is immutable, who is always cheerful and happy, who is Hotri,
who is the universal Protector, who is Creator, of the universe, and who is called Mundin
and Kaparddin."[34]

"'Vasudeva said, "The very deities with Indra, and the Grandsire Brahma numbering
among them, and the great Rishis also, are incompetent to understand the course of
Mahadeva's acts truly and in all their details. Even He is the end which all righteous
people attain. The very Adityas who are endued with subtile sight, are unable to behold
his abode. How then can one that is merely a man succeed in comprehending Him?[35] I

[32] The sense is this: wealth is always agreeable to all persons but Vasudeva is more agreeable than wealth.
This attribute of being more agreeable than wealth itself, that is being agreeable to all the universe,—is due to
the favour of Mahadeva. The commentator explains it in an esoteric sense, coming to the conclusion that arthat
priyataratwancha means the attribute of becoming the Soul of all things in the universe.

[33] The allusion is to Krishna's penances for gratifying Mahadeva in order to obtain a son. The son so
obtained,—that is, as a boon from Mahadeva, was Pradyumna begotten by Krishna upon Rukmini, his favourite
spouse.

[34] It is not necessary to explain these names here. They have been fully explained in previous portions and
will be explained later on in this very chapter.

[35] Such verses are explained by the esoteric school in a different way. Bhavanam is taken as standing for
Hardakasam, i.e., the firmament of the heart; adityas stand for the senses. The meaning then becomes,—'How
can one that is merely a man comprehend Sambhu whom the senses cannot comprehend, for Sambhu dwells in
the firmament of the heart and cannot be seen but by the internal vision that Yoga supplies.' Some texts read
'nidhanamadim meaning end and beginning.'

shall, therefore, truly recite to you some of the attributes of that illustrious slayer of Asuras, who is regarded as the Lord of all sacrifices and vows."'

"Vaisampayana continued, 'Having said these words, the illustrious Vasudeva began his discourse on the attributes of the high-souled Mahadeva endued with the highest intelligence, after having purified himself by touching water.'

"'Vasudeva said, "Hear, ye foremost of Brahmanas and thou Yudhishthira also, O sire, and hear thou too, O Ganga's son, the names that are applied unto Kaparddin. Hear ye, how in former days, I obtained a sight, so difficult to obtain, (of that great god), for the sake of Samva. Verily, in those days was the illustrious deity seen by me in consequence of Yoga-abstraction.[36] After twelve years had expired from the time when Pradyumna, the son of Rukmini, who is endued with great intelligence, slew the Asura Samvara in days of yore, my spouse Jamvavati addressed me. Indeed, beholding Pradyumna and Charudeshna and other sons born of Rukmini, Jamvavati, desirous of a son, said these words unto me, O Yudhishthira,—'Grant me, O thou of unfading glory, a son endued with heroism, the foremost of mighty men, possessed of the most agreeable features, sinless in conduct, and like unto thyself. And O, let there be no delay on thy part in granting this prayer of mine. There is nothing in the three worlds that is unattainable by thee, O perpetuator of Yadu's race, thou canst create other worlds if only thou wishest it. Observing a vow for twelve years and purifying thyself, thou hadst adored the Lord of all creatures (viz., Mahadeva) and then begot upon Rukmini the sons that she has obtained from thee, viz., Charudeshna and Sucharu and Charuvesa and Yasodhana and Charusravas and Charuyasas and Pradyumna and Sambhu. O slayer of Madhu, do thou grant to me a son like unto those of great powers whom thou hast begotten upon Rukmini?'—Thus addressed by the princess, I replied unto her of slender waist,—'Let me have thy permission (to leave thee for some time), O queen. I shall certainly obey thy behest.' She answered me, saying,—'Go, and may success and prosperity always attend thee. Let Brahma and Siva and Kasyapa, the Rivers, those deities that preside over the wind, the soil, all deciduous herbs, those Chhandas (Rhymes) that are regarded as bearers of the libations poured in sacrifices, the Rishis, Earth, the Oceans, the sacrificial presents, those syllables that are uttered for completing the cadences of Samans, the Rikshas, the Pitris, the Planets, the spouses of the deities, the celestial maidens, the celestial mothers, the great cycles, kine, Chandramas, Savitri, Agni, Savitri, the knowledge of the Vedas, the seasons, the year, small and big divisions of time, e.g., the Kshanas, the Labas, the Muhurtas, the Nimeshas, and the Yugas in succession, protect thee, O Yadava, and keep thee in happiness, wherever thou mayst stay. Let no danger overtake thee on thy way, and let no heedlessness be thine, O sinless one.'—Thus blessed by her, I took her leave, bidding farewell unto the daughter of the prince of apes. Repairing then into the presence of that foremost of men, viz., my father, of my mother, of the king, and of Ahuka, I informed them of what the daughter of the prince of the Vidyadharas, in great affliction, had said unto me. Bidding them farewell with a sorrowful heart, I then repaired to Gada and to Rama of great might. These two cheerfully addressed me saying,—Let thy penances increase without any obstruction.—Having obtained the permission of all of them, I thought of Garuda. He immediately came to me and bore me to Himavat (at my

---

[36] It is said that for obtaining a worthy son, Krishna underwent the austerest of penances on the breast of Himavat, with a view to gratifying the god Mahadeva. The son obtained as a boon from Mahadeva was Samva, as would appear from this and the succeeding verses. Elsewhere, however, it is stated that the son so obtained was Pradyumna begotten upon Rukmini. The inconsistency would disappear if we suppose that Krishna adored Mahadeva twice for obtaining sons.

bidding). Arrived at Himavat, I dismissed him. There on that foremost of mountains, I beheld many wonderful sights. I saw an excellent, wonderful, and agreeable retreat for the practice of penances. That delightful retreat was owned by the high-souled Upamanyu who was a descendant of Vyaghrapada. That retreat is applauded and reverenced by the deities and the Gandharvas, and seemed to be covered with Vedic beauty. It was adorned with Dhavas and Kakubhas and Kadamvas and Cocas, with Kuruvakas and Ketakas and Jamvus and Patalas, with banians and Varunakas and Vatsanabhas and Vilwas, with Saralas and Kapitthas and Piyalas and Salas and palmyras with Vadaris and Kundas and Punnagas and Asokas and Amras and Kovidaras and Champakas and Panasas, and with diverse other trees endued with fruits and flowers. And that retreat was also decked with the straight stems of the Musa Supienta.[37] Truly, that asylum was adorned with diverse other kinds of trees and with diverse kinds of fruits forming the food of diverse kinds of birds. Heaps of ashes (of sacrificial fires) were thrown in proper places all around, which added to the beauty of the scene. It abounded with Rurus and apes and tigers and lions and leopards, with deer of diverse species and peacocks, and with cats and snakes. Indeed, large numbers of other animals also were seen there, as also buffaloes and bears. Delicious breezes constantly blew bearing the melodious strains of celestial nymphs. The babblings of mountain rivulets and springs, the sweet notes of winged choristers, the gruntings of elephants, the delicious stains of Kinnaras, and the auspicious voice of ascetics singing the Samans, O hero, and diverse other kinds of music, rendered that retreat extremely charming. The very imagination cannot conceive another retreat as delightful as the one I beheld. There were also large houses in that asylum, intended for keeping the sacred fire, and covered all over with flowering creepers. It was adorned with the river Ganga of clear and sacred water. Indeed, the daughter of Jahnu always remained there. It was decked also with many ascetics who were the foremost of all righteous persons, who were endued with high souls, and who resembled fire itself in energy.[38] Some of those ascetics subsisted upon air and some upon water, some were devoted to Japa or the silent recitation of sacred Mantras, and some were engaged in cleansing their souls by practising the virtues of compassion while some amongst them were Yogins devoted to the abstraction of Yoga-meditation. Some amongst them subsisted upon smoke only, and some subsisted upon fire, and some upon milk. Thus was that retreat adorned with many foremost of regenerate persons. And some there were amongst them that had taken the vow of eating and drinking like kine,—that is, by giving up the use of the hands at once. And some used only two pieces of stone for husking their grain, and some used their teeth only for that purpose. And some subsisted by drinking only the rays of the moon, and some by drinking only froth. And some had betaken themselves to vow of living like deer.[39] And some there were that lived upon the fruits of the Ficus religiosa,

---

[37] Dhava is Anogeissus latifolia. Wall is Conocarpus latifolia Roxb. Kakubha is otherwise called Arjuna which is identified with Terminalia Arjuna, syn. Pentaptera Arjuna. Kadamva is Nauclea cadamba, Roxb. Kuruveka is Barleria cristata, Linn. Ketaka is Pandanus odoratissimus, Linn. Jamvu is Eugenia Jambolana. Patala is Stereospermum suaveolens syn. Bignonia suaveolens, Roxb. Varunaka is Crataea, religiosa, syn. Capparis trifoliata, Roxb. Vatsanabha is Aconitum ferox, Wall. Vilwa is Aegle Marmelos. Sarala is Pinus longifolia, Roxb. Kapittha is Feronia Elephantum. Piyala is Buchanania latifolia. Sala is Shorea robusta. Vadari is Zisyphus jujuba. Kunda is Balanites Roxburghii, Punnaga is Callophyllum inophyllum. Asoka is Saraca. Indica, Linn, syn Jonesia Asoka, Roxb. Amra is Mangifera Indica. Kovidara is Bauhinia, accuminata Linn. Champaka is Michelia Champaka, Linn. Panasa is Artocarpus integrifolia, Linn.

[38] Ganga is represented as the daughter of Rishi Jahnu, and hence is she known by the name of Jahnavi. What is meant by Jahnavi having been always represent there is that the goddess always stayed there in spirit, desirous of conferring merit upon those that would reverence her.

[39] i.e., never searching for food but taking what they saw, and never using their hands also.

and some that used to live upon water. And some dressed themselves in rags and some in animal skins and some in barks of trees. Indeed, I beheld diverse ascetics of the foremost order observing these and other painful vows. I desired then to enter that asylum. Verily, that asylum was honoured and adored by the deities and all high-souled beings, by Siva and others, O Bharata, and by all creatures of righteous acts. Thus addressed, it stood in all its beauty on the breast of Himavat, like the lunar disc in the firmament. The mongoose sported there with the snake, and the tiger with the deer, like friends, forgetting their natural enmity, in consequence of the energy of those ascetics of blazing penances and for their proximity to these high-souled ones. In that foremost of asylums, which was delightful to all creatures, inhabited by many foremost of Brahmanas fully conversant with the Vedas and their branches, and by many high-souled Rishis celebrated for the difficult vows they observed, I saw, as soon as I entered, a puissant Rishi with matted locks on head and dressed in rags, who seemed to blaze forth like fire with his penances and energy. Waited upon by his disciples and possessed of tranquil soul, that foremost of Brahmanas was young in aspect. His name was Upamanyu. Unto me who bowed unto him with a nod of the head, he said,—'Welcome art thou, O thou of eyes like lotus petals. Today, by this visit of thine, we see that our penances have borne fruit. Thou art worthy of our adoration, but thou adorest us still. Thou art worthy of being seen, but thou desirest to see me.'—Joining my hands I addressed him the usual enquiries respecting the well-being of the animals and birds that resided in his asylum, of the progress of his righteousness, and of his disciples. The illustrious Upamanyu then addressed me in words that were exceedingly sweet and delightful,—'Thou shalt, O Krishna, obtain without doubt a son like unto thyself. Betaking thyself to severe penances, do thou gratify Isana, the Lord of all creatures. That divine Master, O Adhokshaja, sporteth here with his spouse by his side. O Janarddana, it was here that the deities with all the Rishis, in days of yore, gratified that foremost of deities by their penances and Brahmacharyya and truth and self-restraint, and succeeded in obtaining the fruition of many high desires. That illustrious god is verily the vast receptacle of all energies and penances. Projecting into existence and withdrawing once more unto himself all things fraught with good and evil, that inconceivable Deity whom thou seekest, O destroyer of foes, lives here with his spouse. He who took his birth as the Danava named Hiranyakashipu, whose strength was so great that he could shake the very mountains of Meru, succeeded in obtaining from Mahadeva the puissance belonging to all the deities and enjoyed it for ten millions of years. He who was the foremost of all his sons and who was celebrated by the name of Mandara, succeeded, through the boon he had obtained from Mahadeva, in fighting Sakra for a million of years. The terrible discus of Vishnu and the thunderbolt of Indra were both unable to make the slightest impression, O Kesava, in days of yore, upon the body of that great cause of universal affliction.[40] The discus which thou bearest, O sinless one, was given unto thee by Mahadeva after he had slain a Daitya that was proud of his strength and used to live within the waters. That discus, blazing with energy and like unto fire, was created by the great god having for his device the bull. Wonderful and irresistible in energy it was given unto thee by that illustrious god. In consequence of its blazing energy it was incapable of being gazed at by any person save Siva the wielder of Pinaka. It was for this reason that Bhava (Siva) bestowed upon it the name of Sudarsana. From that time the name Sudarsana came to be

---

[40] Graha is literally a planet; here, Mandara who is likened to an evil planet in consequence of the mischief he did unto all.

current in all the worlds. Even the weapon, O Kesava, failed to make the slightest impression on the body of Hiranyakashipu's son Mandara, that appeared like an evil planet in the three worlds. Hundreds of Chakras like thine and thunderbolts like that of Sakra, could not inflict a scratch on the body of that evil planet endued with great might, who had obtained a boon from Mahadeva. Afflicted by the mighty Mandara, the deities fought hard against him and his associates, all of whom had obtained boons from Mahadeva. Gratified with another Danava named Vidyutprabha, Mahadeva granted to him the sovereignty of the three worlds. That Danava remained the sovereign of the three worlds for a hundred thousand years. And Mahadeva said unto him,—"Thou shalt become one of my attendants."—Indeed, the puissant Lord further bestowed upon him the boon of a hundred millions of children. The Master without birth, of all creatures further gave the Danava the region known by the name of Kusadwipa for his kingdom. Another great Asura, of the name of Satamukha, was created by Brahma. For a hundred years he poured on the sacrificial fire (as offerings unto Mahadeva) the flesh of his own body. Gratified with such penances, Sankara said unto him,—"What can I do for thee?"—Satamukha replied unto him, saying,—"O thou that art most wonderful, let me have the power of creating new creatures and animals. Give also unto me, O foremost of all deities, eternal power."—The puissant lord, thus addressed by him, said unto him,— "So be it."—The Self-born Brahma, concentrating his mind in Yoga,[41] in days of yore, made a sacrifice for three hundred years, with the object of obtaining children. Mahadeva granted him a thousand sons possessed of qualifications commensurate with the merits of the sacrifice. Without doubt, thou knowest, O Krishna, the lord of Yoga, him that is, who is sung by the deities. The Rishi known by the name of Yajnavalkya is exceedingly virtuous. By adoring Mahadeva he has acquired great fame. The great ascetic who is Parasara's son, viz., Vyasa, of soul set on Yoga, has obtained great celebrity by adoring Sankara. The Valikhilyas were on a former occasion disregarded by Maghavat. Filled with wrath at this, they gratified the illustrious Rudra. That lord of the universe, that foremost one of all the deities, thus gratified by the Valikhilyas, said unto them,—"Ye shall succeed by your penances in creating a bird that will rob Indra of the Amrita." Through the wrath of Mahadeva on a former occasion, all the waters disappeared. The deities gratified him by performing a sacrifice called Saptakapala, and caused, through his grace, other waters to flow into the worlds. Verily, when the three-eyed deity became gratified, water once more appeared in the world. The wife of Atri, who was conversant with the Vedas, abandoned her husband in a huff and said,—"I shall no longer live in subjection to that ascetic."—Having said these words, she sought the protection of Mahadeva. Through fear of her lord, Atri passed three hundred years, abstaining from all food. And all this time she slept on wooden clubs for the purpose of gratifying Bhava. The great deity then appeared unto her and then smilingly addressed her, saying—"Thou shalt obtain a son. And thou shalt get that son without the need of a husband, simply through the grace of Rudra. Without doubt that son, born in the race of his father, shall become celebrated for his worth, and assume a name after thee." The illustrious Vikarna also, O slayer of Madhu, full of devotion to Mahadeva, gratified him with severe penances and obtained high and happy success. Sakalya, too, of restrained soul, adored Bhava in a mental sacrifice that he performed for nine hundred years, O Kesava. Gratified with him the illustrious deity said unto him,—"Thou shalt become a great

---

[41] Yoga in verse 84 is explained by the commentator as meaning the power of creation. Chandra-Surya-parjanya-prithivyadi-sristi-samarthyam. Similarly, by Saswatam Valam is meant that power which arises from Brahmavidya.

author. O son, inexhaustible shall thy fame be in the three worlds. Thy race also shall never come to an end and shall be adorned by many great Rishis that shall take birth in it. Thy son will become the foremost of Brahmanas and will make the Sutras of thy work." There was a celebrated Rishi of the name of Savarni in the Krita age. Here, in this asylum, he underwent severe penances for six thousand years. The illustrious Rudra said,—"I am gratified with thee, O sinless one! Without being subject to decrepitude or death, thou shalt become an author celebrated through all the worlds!"—In days of yore, Sakra, also, in Baranasi, filled with devotion, O Janarddana, adored Mahadeva who has empty space alone for his garments and who is smeared with ashes as an agreeable unguent. Having adored Mahadeva thus, he obtained the sovereignty of the celestials. Narada also, in days of yore, adored the great Bhava with devotion of heart. Gratified with him, Mahadeva, that preceptor of the celestial preceptor, said these words.—"No one shall be thy equal in energy and penances. Thou shalt always attend upon me with thy songs and instrumental music." Hear also, O Madhava, how in former times I succeeded in obtaining a sight of that god of gods, that Master of all creatures, O Lord. Hear also in detail for what object, O thou of great puissance. I invoked with restrained senses and mind that illustrious deity endued with supreme energy. I shall, O sinless one, tell thee with full details all that I succeeded in obtaining from that god of gods, viz., Maheswara. In ancient times, viz., Krita age, O son, there was a Rishi of great fame, named Vyaghrapada. He was celebrated for his knowledge and mastery over the Vedas and their branches. I was born as the son of that Rishi and Dhaumya took birth as my younger brother. On a certain occasion, Madhava, accompanied by Dhaumya, I came upon the asylum of certain Rishis of cleansed souls. There I beheld a cow that was being milked. I saw the milk and it appeared to me to resemble Amrita itself in taste. I then came home, and impelled by childishness, I addressed my mother and said,—"Give me some food prepared with milk."—There was no milk in the house, and accordingly my mother was much grieved at my asking for it. My mother took a piece of (rice) cake and boiled it in water, Madhava. The water became whitened and my mother placed it before us saying that it was milk and bade us drink it. I had before that drunk milk on one occasion, for my father had, at the time of a sacrifice, taken me to the residence of some of our great kinsmen. A celestial cow, who delights the deities, was being milked on that occasion. Drinking her milk that resembled Amrita in taste, I knew what the virtues are of milk. I therefore, at once understood the origin of the substance that my mother offered me, telling me that it was milk. Verily, the taste of that cake, O son, did not afford me any pleasure whatever. Impelled by childishness I then addressed mother, saying,—"This O mother, that thou hast given me is not any preparation of milk."—Filled with grief and sorrow at this, and embracing me from parental affection and smelling my head, O Madhava, she said unto me,—"Whence, O child, can ascetics of cleansed souls obtain food prepared with milk? Such men always reside in the forest and subsist upon bulbs and roots and fruits. Whence shall we who live by the banks of rivers that are the resort of the Valikhilyas, we who have mountains and forest, for our home,—whence, indeed, O child, shall we obtain milk? We, dear child, live (sometimes) on air and sometimes on water. We dwell in asylums in the midst of forests and woods. We habitually abstain from all kinds of food that are taken by persons living in villages and towns. We are accustomed to only such food as is supplied by the produce of the wilderness. There cannot be any milk, O child, in the wilderness where there are no offspring of Surabhi.[42]

---

[42] Surabhi is the celestial cow, the original progenetrix of all kine in Heaven and on Earth.

Dwelling on the banks of rivers or in caves or on mountain-breasts, or in tirthas and other places of the kind, we pass our time in the practice of penances and the recitation of sacred Mantras, Siva being our highest refuge. Without gratifying the boon-giving Sthanu of unfading glory,—him, that is, who has three eyes,—whence, O child, can one obtain food prepared with milk and good robes and other objects of enjoyment in the world? Do thou devote thyself, O dear son, to Sankara with thy whole soul. Through his grace, O child, thou art sure to obtain all such objects as administer to the indulgence of all thy wishes,"—Hearing these words of my mother, O slayer of foes, that day, I joined my hands in reverence and bowing unto her, said,—"O mother, who this Mahadeva? In what manner can one gratify him? Where does that god reside? How may he be seen? With what does he become pleased? What also is the form of Sarva? How may one succeed in obtaining a knowledge of him? If gratified, will he, O mother, show himself unto me?"— After I had said these words, O Krishna, to my mother, she, filled with parental affection, smelt my head, O Govinda, her eyes covered with tears the while. Gently patting my body, O slayer of Madhu, my mother, adopting a tone of great humility, addressed me in the following words, O best of the deities.

"""My mother said, "Mahadeva is exceedingly difficult to be known by persons of uncleansed souls. These men are incapable of bearing him in their hearts or comprehending him at all. They can retain him in their minds. They cannot seize him, nor can they obtain a sight of him. Men of wisdom aver that his forms are many. Many, again, are the places in which he resides. Many are the forms of his Grace. Who is there that can understand in their details the acts, which are all excellent, of Isa, or of all the forms that he has assumed in days of yore? Who can relate how Sarva sports and how he becomes gratified? Maheswara of universal form resides in the hearts of all creatures. While Munis discoursed on the auspicious and excellent acts of Isana, I have heard from them how, impelled by compassion towards his worshippers, he grants them a sight of his person. For the purpose of showing a favour unto the Brahmanas, the denizens of heaven have recited for their information the diverse forms that were assumed by Mahadeva in days of yore. Thou hast asked me about these. I shall recite them to thee, O son."

"""My mother continued, "Bhava assumes the forms of Brahma and Vishnu and the chief of the celestials of the Rudras, the Adityas, and the Aswins; and of those deities that are called Viswadevas. He assumes the forms also of men and women, of Pretas and Pisachas, of Kiratas and Savaras, and of all aquatic animals. That illustrious deity assumes the forms of also those Savaras that dwell in the woods and forests. He assumes the forms of tortoises and fishes and conches. He it is that assumes the forms of those coral sprouts that are used as ornaments by men. He assumes also the forms of Yakshas, Rakshasas and Snakes, of Daityas and Danavas. Indeed, the illustrious god assumes the forms of all creatures too that live in holes. He assumes the forms of tigers and lions and deer, of wolves and bears and birds, of owls and of jackals as well. He it is that assumes the forms of swans and crows and peacocks, of chameleons and lizards and storks. He it is that assumes the forms of cranes and vultures and Chakravakas. Verily, he it is that assumes the forms of Chasas and of mountains also. O son, it is Mahadeva that assumes the forms of kine and elephants and horses and camels and asses. He assumes also the forms of goats and leopards and diverse other varieties of animals. It is Bhava who assumes the forms of diverse kinds of birds of beautiful plumage. It is Mahadeva who bears the forms of persons with sticks and those with umbrellas and those with calabashes among Brahmanas.[43] He sometimes becomes six-faced and sometimes becomes multifaced. He sometimes assumes forms having three eyes and forms having many heads. And he sometimes assumes forms having many millions of legs and forms having innumerable stomachs and faces and forms endued with innumerable arms and innumerable sides. He sometimes appears surrounded by innumerable spirits and ghosts. He it is that assumes the forms of Rishis and Gandharvas, and of Siddhas and Charanas. He sometimes assumes a form that is rendered white with the ashes he smears on it and is adorned with a half-moon on the forehead. Adored with diverse hymns uttered with diverse kinds of voice and worshipped with diverse Mantras fraught with encomiums, he, that is sometimes called Sarva, is the Destroyer of all creatures in the universe, and it is upon him, again, that all creatures rest as their common foundation. Mahadeva is the soul of all creatures. He pervades all things. He is the speaker of all discourses (on duties and rituals). He resides everywhere and should be known as dwelling in the hearts of all creatures in the universe. He knows the desire cherished by every one of his worshippers. He becomes acquainted with the object in which one pays him adorations. Do thou then, if it pleases thee, seek the protection of the chief of the deities. He sometimes rejoices, and sometimes yields to wrath, and sometimes utters the syllable Hum with a very loud noise. He sometimes arms himself with the discus, sometimes with the trident, sometimes with the mace, sometimes with the heavy mullets, sometimes with the scimitar, and sometimes with the battle axe. He it is that assumes the form of Sesha who sustains the world on his head. He has snakes for his belt, and his ears are adorned with ear-rings made of snakes. Snakes form also the sacred thread he wears. An elephant skin forms his upper garment.[44] He sometimes laughs and sometimes sings and sometimes dances most beautifully. Surrounded by innumerable spirits and ghosts, he sometimes plays on musical instruments. Diverse, again are the instruments upon which he plays, and sweet the sounds they yield. He sometimes wanders (over crematoria), sometimes yawns, sometimes cries, and sometimes causes others to cry. He sometimes assumes the guise of one that is mad, and sometimes of one that is intoxicated, and he sometimes utters words that are exceedingly sweet. Endued with appalling fierceness, he sometimes laughs loudly, frightening all creatures with his eyes. He sometimes sleeps and sometimes remains awake and sometimes yawns as he pleases. He sometimes recites sacred Mantras and sometimes becomes the deity of those Mantras which are recited. He sometimes performs penances and sometimes becomes the deity for whose adoration those penances are undergone. He sometimes makes gifts and sometimes receives those gifts; sometimes disposes himself in Yoga and sometimes becomes the object of the Yoga contemplation of others. He may be seen on the sacrificial platform or in the sacrificial stake; in the midst of the cow-pen or in the fire. He may not again be seen there. He may be seen as a boy or as an old man. He sports with the daughters and the spouses of the Rishis. His hair is long and stands erect. He is perfectly naked, for he has the horizon for his garments. He is endued with terrible eyes. He is fair, he is darkish, he is dark, he is pale, he is of the colour of smoke, and he is red. He is possessed of eyes that are large and terrible. He has empty space for his covering and he it is that covers all things. Who is there that can truly understand the limits of Mahadeva who is formless, who is one and indivisible, who

---

[43] A Sanyasin is one that bears the stick as the badge of the mode of life he has adopted. Chatrin is the king. Kundin is one with the calabash. The meaning is that it is Mahadeva who becomes the Sanyasin or the mendicant on the one hand and the monarch on the other.

[44] Every person belonging to the three superior orders bears the Upavita or sacred-thread as his badge. The deities also, including Mahadeva, bear the Upavita. Mahadeva's Upavita is made of living snakes.

conjures of illusions, who is of the cause of all actions and destructive operations in the universe, who assumes the form of Hiranyagarbha, and who is without beginning and without end, and who is without birth.[45] He lives in the heart (of every creature). He is the prana, he is the mind, and he is Jiva (that is invested in the material case). He is the soul of Yoga, and it is that is called Yoga. He is the Yoga-contemplation into which Yogins enter.[46] He is the Supreme Soul. Indeed Maheswara, the purity in essence, is capable of being comprehended not by the senses but through only the Soul seizing his existence. He plays on diverse musical instruments. He is a vocalist. He has a hundred thousand eyes, he has one mouth, he has two mouths, he has three mouths, and he has many mouths. Devoting thyself to him, setting thy heart upon him, depending upon him, and accepting him as thy one refuse, do thou, O son, adore Mahadeva and then mayst thou obtain the fruition of all thy wishes." Hearing those words of my mother, O slayer of foes, from that day my devotion was directed to Mahadeva, having nothing else for its object. I then applied myself to the practice of the austerest penances for gratifying Sankara. For one thousand years I stood on my left toe. After that I passed one thousand years, subsisting only upon fruits. The next one thousand years I passed, subsisting upon the fallen leaves of trees. The next thousand years I passed, subsisting upon water only. After that I passed seven hundred years, subsisting on air alone. In this way, I adored Mahadeva for a full thousand years of the celestials. After this, the puissant Mahadeva, the Master of all the universe, became gratified with me. Desirous of ascertaining whether I was solely devoted to him and him alone, he appeared before me in the form of Sakra surrounded by all the deities. As the celebrated Sakra, he had a thousand eyes on his person and was armed with the thunderbolt. And he rode on an elephant whose complexion was of the purest white, with eyes red, ears folded, the temporal juice trickling down his cheeks, with trunk contracted, terrible to look at, and endued with four tusks. Indeed, riding on such an elephant, the illustrious chief of the deities seemed to blaze forth with his energy. With a beautiful crown on his head and adorned with garlands round his neck and bracelets round his arms, he approached the spot where I was. A white umbrella was held over his head. And he was waited upon by many Apsaras, and many Gandharvas sang his praise. Addressing me, he said,—"O foremost of regenerate persons, I have been gratified with thee. Beg of me whatever boon thou desirest,"—Hearing these words of Sakra I did not become glad. Verily, O Krishna, I answered the chief of the celestials in these words.—"I do not desire any boon at thy hands, or from the hands of any other deity. O amiable deity, I tell thee truly, that it is Mahadeva only from whom I have boons to ask. True, true it is, O Sakra, true are these words that I say unto thee. No other words are at all agreeable to me save those which relate to Maheswara. At the command of Pashupati, that Lord of all creatures, I am ready to become a worm or a tree with many branches. If not obtained through the grace represented by Mahadeva's boons, the very sovereignty of the three worlds would not be acceptable to me. Let me be born among the very Chandalas but let me still be devoted to the feet of Hara. Without, again, being devoted to that Lord of all creatures, I would not

---

[45] Arupa is formless, or as the commentator explains, nishkala, i.e., without parts, being indivisible. Arupa is of the form of multifarious acts or operations or effects in the universe. Adyarupa is Hiranyagarbha.

[46] The commentator explains that by saying that Maheswara is in the heart, etc., what is stated is that he is the several cases of which Jiva is made up while in his unemancipate state, viz., the Annamaya kosha, the pranamaya kosha, the Manomaya kosha, and the Vijnanmaya kosha. What is meant by Yogatman is that he is the Soul or essence of Yoga of the Chidachidgranthi, i.e., the Anandamaya kosha. By Yogasanjnita is meant that he is Yoga or the Twam padarthah.

like to have birth in the palace of Indra himself. If a person be wanting in devotion to that Lord of the universe,—that Master of the deities and the Asuras,—his misery will not end even if from want of food he has to subsist upon only air and water.[47] What is the need of other discourses that are even fraught with other kinds of morality and righteousness, unto those persons who do not like to live even a moment without thinking of feet of Mahadeva? When the unrighteous or sinful Kali Yuga comes, one should never pass a moment without devoting his heart upon Mahadeva. One that has drunk the Amrita constituted by the devotion to Hara, one becomes freed from the fear of the world. One that has not obtained the grace of Mahadeva can never succeed to devote oneself to Mahadeva for a single day or for half a day or for a Muhurta or for a Kshana or for a Lava (very small unit of time). At the command of Mahadeva I shall cheerfully become a worm or an insect, but I have no relish for even the sovereignty of the three worlds, if bestowed by thee, O Sakra. At the word of Hara I would become even a dog. In fact, that would accord with my highest wish. If not given by Maheswara, I would not have the sovereignty of the very deities. I do not wish to have this dominion of the Heavens. I do not wish to have the sovereignty of the celestials. I do not wish to have the region of Brahma. Indeed, I do not wish to have that cessation of individual existence which is called Emancipation and which involves a complete identification with Brahma. But I want to become the slave of Hara. As long as that Lord of all creatures, the illustrious Mahesa, with crown on his head and body possessed of the pure white complexion of the lunar disc, does not become gratified with me, so long shall I cheerfully bear all those afflictions, due to a hundred repetitions of decrepitude, death and birth, that befall to the lot of embodied beings. What person in the universe can obtain tranquillity, without gratifying Rudra that is freed from decrepitude and death, that is endued with the effulgence of the Sun, the Moon, or the fire, that is the root or original cause of everything real and unreal in the three worlds, and that exists as one and indivisible entity? If in consequence of my faults, rebirths be mine, I shall, in those new births, devote myself solely to Bhava."

"'"Indra said, "What reason canst thou assign for the existence of a Supreme Being or for His being the cause of all causes?"'

"'"Upamanyu said, "'I solicit boons from that great Deity named Siva whom utterers of Brahma have described as existent and non-existent, manifest and unmanifest, eternal or immutable, one and many. I solicit boons from Him who is without beginning and middle and end, who is Knowledge and Puissance, who is inconceivable and who is the Supreme Soul. I solicit boons from Him whence comes all Puissance, who has not been produced by any one, who is immutable, and who, though himself unsprung from any seed, is the seed of all things in the universe. I solicit boons from Him who is blazing Effulgence, (beyond Darkness) who is the essence of all penances, who transcends all faculties of which we are possessed and which we may devote for the purpose of comprehending him, and by knowing whom every one becomes freed from grief or sorrow. I worship him, O Purandara, who is conversant with the creation of all elements and the thought of all living creatures, and who is the original cause of the existence or creation of all creatures, who is omnipresent, and who has the puissance to give

---

[47] The meaning seems to be this: the man that is not devoted to Mahadeva is sure to be subjected to misery. His distress will know no bounds. To think that such a man has reached the lowest depth of misery only when from want of food he has to live upon water or air would not be correct.

everything.[48] I solicit boons from Him who cannot be comprehended by argument, who represents the object of the Sankhya and the Yoga systems of philosophy, and who transcends all things, and whom all persons conversant with the topics of enquiry worship and adore.[49] I solicit boons from Him, O Maghavat, who is the soul of Maghavat himself, who is said to be the God of the gods, and who is the Master of all creatures. I solicit boons from Him who it is that first created Brahma, that creator of all the worlds, having filled Space (with His energy) and evoked into existence the primeval egg.[50] Who else than that Supreme Lord could be creator of Fire, Water, Wind, Earth, Space, Mind, and that which is called Mahat? Tell me, O Sakra, who else than Siva could create Mind, Understanding, Consciousness or Ego, the Tanmatras, and the senses? Who is there higher than Siva?[51] The wise say that the Grandsire Brahma is the creator of this universe. Brahma, however, acquired his high puissance and prosperity by adoring and gratifying Mahadeva, that God of gods. That high puissance (consisting of all the three attributes of creation, protection, and destruction), which dwells in that illustrious Being who is endowed with the quality of being one, who created Brahma, Vishnu, and Rudra, was derived from Mahadeva. Tell me who is there that is superior to the Supreme Lord?[52] Who else than that God of gods is competent to unite the sons of Diti with lordship and puissance, judging by the sovereignty and the power of oppressing conferred upon the foremost of the Daityas and Danavas?[53] The different points of the horizon, Time, the Sun, all fiery entities, planets, wind, water, and the stars and constellations,—these, know thou, are from Mahadeva. Tell us who is higher than the Supreme Lord? Who else is there, except Mahadeva, in the matter of the creation of Sacrifice and the destruction of Tripura? Who else except Mahadeva, the grinder of the foes, has offered lordship to the principal?[54] What need, O Purandara, of many well-sounding statements fraught with spacious sophisms, when I behold thee of a thousand eyes, O best of the deities,—thee that art worshipped by Siddhas and Gandharvas and the deities and the Rishis? O best of the Kusikas, all this is due to the grace of that God of gods viz., Mahadeva. Know, O Kesava, that this all, consisting of animate and inanimate existences with heaven and other unseen entities, which occur in this world, and which has the all-pervading Lord for their soul, has flowed from Maheswara and has been created (by him) for enjoyment by Jiva.[55] In the worlds that are known by the names of Bhu, Bhuva, Swah, and Maha, in the midst of the mountains of Lokaloka, in the islands, in the mountains of Meru, in all things

---

[48] Bhuta-bhavana-Bhavajnam is one acquainted with both the bhavana and the bhava of all bhutas, i.e., all the living creatures.

[49] Without the Srutis, He cannot be comprehended, for he is above all dialectics or arguments. The object which the Sankhya system has in view, flows from Him, and the object also which the Yogins have in view has its origin in Him.

[50] Mahadeva, as spoken of as Brahma, first filled Space with his energy. Space forming, as it were, the material with which everything else was created. Having filled Space as it were with creative energy, he created the primeval egg and placed Brahma or the Grandsire of the universe within it.

[51] Tanmatras are the subtile elements, those which we perceive being gross ones.

[52] Here Mahadeva is represented as Supreme Brahman. Hence, the Being that created Brahma, Vishnu, and Rudra, derived his power to create from Mahadeva. Thus Mahadeva is Unmanifest Brahma.

[53] Sampadayitum is aisaryyena samyojayitum. The difficulty lies in the first line; the ablative is to be taken as yabartha or lyablope.

[54] This is an instance of crux; adhipati is a verb of incomplete predication, implying etya or encountering.

[55] Here the compassion of Mahadeva is shown. The commentator explains that eshu refers to these words; chatanachetanani would include all animate and inanimate existences. The word adi following implies heaven and all unseen entities. Avyaktamuktakesa is a periphrasis for jiva; avyaktam aspashtam yathasyattatha muktah bhanti tirohitam nitya-muktatwama sya is the explanation offered. This is, no doubt correct. The sense then is that all this has flowed from Maheswara and exists for being enjoyed by Jiva.

that yield happiness, and in the hearts of all creatures, O illustrious Maghavat, resides Mahadeva, as persons conversant with all the topics of enquiry say. If, O Sakra, the Devas (deities) and the Asuras could see any other puissant form than Bhava's, would not both of them, especially the former, when opposed and afflicted by the latter, have sought the protection of that form? In all hostile encounters of the deities, the Yakshas, the Uragas and the Rakshasas, that terminating in mutual destruction, it is Bhava that gives unto those that meet with destruction, puissance commensurate with their respective locations as dependent upon their acts. Tell me, who else than Maheswara is there for bestowing boons upon, and once more chastising the Andhaka and Sukra and Dundubhi and Maharshi and many foremost of Yakshas, Indra and Vala and Rakshasas and the Nivatakavachas? Was not the vital seed of Mahadeva, that Master of both the deities and the Asuras, poured as a libation upon the fire? From that seed sprung a mountain of gold. Who else is there whose seed can be said to be possessed of such virtue?[56] Who else in this world is praised as having the horizon only for his garments? Who else can be said to be a Brahmacharin with his vital seed drawn up? Who else is there that has half his body occupied by his dear spouse?[57] Who else is there that has been able to subjugate Kama, the god of desire? Tell me, O Indra, what other Being possesses that high region of supreme felicity that is applauded by all the deities? Who else has the crematorium as his sporting ground? Who else is there that is so praised for his dancing? Whose puissance and worship remain immutable? Who else is there that sports with spirits and ghosts? Tell me, O deity, who else has associate that are possessed of strength like his own and that are, therefore, proud of that strength or puissance?[58] Who else is there whose status is applauded as unchangeable and worshipped with reverence by the three worlds? Who else is there that pours rain, gives heat, and blazes forth in Energy? From whom else do we derive our wealth of herbs? Who else upholds all kinds of wealth? Who else sports as much as he pleases in the three worlds of mobile and immobile things? O Indra, know Maheswara to be the original cause (of everything). He is adored by Yogins, by Rishis, by the Gandharvas, and by the Siddhas, with the aid of knowledge, (of ascetic) success, and of the rites laid down in the scriptural ordinances.[59] He is adored by both the deities and the Asuras with the aid of sacrifices by acts and the affliction of the ritual laid down in the scriptures. The fruits of action can never touch him for he transcends them all. Being such, I call him the original cause of everything.[60] He is both gross and subtile. He is without compare. He cannot be conceived by the senses. He is endued with attributes and he is divested of them. He is the lord of attributes, for they are under his control.

---

[56] The allusion is thus explained by the commentator; once upon a time the seed of Mahadeva fell upon a blazing fire. The deity of fire removed it, unable to consume it. The seed, however, thus removed became converted into a mountain of gold. Haimagiri is not Himavat or the mountains of Himalayas as the Burdwan translation wrongly renders it.

[57] Ardhe sthita kanta refers to the transformation of Mahadeva into a form half of which was male and half female, the male half being the half of his own usual form, and the female half the form of his dear spouse Uma or Parvati. This transformation is known by the name of Haragauri.

[58] The associates of Mahadeva are called Gana. Deva is in the vocative case. The Burdwan translator wrongly takes deva-ganah as a compound word and makes a mess of the meaning.

[59] The Bombay reading is Vihitam karanam param. The commentator adopts it, and explains it as vihitam, ajnatam sat jnapitam; param karanam avyaktasyapi karanam. The Bengal reading, however, is not faulty.

[60] The Bengal reading karmayoga is vicious. The Bombay text reads karmayajna which, of course, is correct. By karmayajna is meant that sacrifice which is performed with the aid of actual offerings of flowers and herbs and animals and libations of ghee, meat, etc. These are opposed to mental sacrifices or manasa yajna. It is curious to see that the Burdwan translator adheres to the vicious reading and misunderstands the meaning. Mahadeva transcends the fruits of action, i.e., he has no body unto which happiness and misery may attach.

Even such is the place that is Maheswara's. He is the cause of the maintenance and the creation (of the universe). He is the cause of the universe and the cause also of its destruction. He is the Past, the Present, and the Future. He is the parent of all things. Verily, He is the cause of every thing. He is that which is mutable, He is the unmanifest, He is Knowledge; He is ignorance; He is every act, He is every omission; He is righteousness; and He is unrighteousness. Him, O Sakra, do I call the cause of every thing. Behold, O Indra, in the image of Mahadeva the indications of both the sexes. That god of gods, viz., Rudra, that cause of both creation and destruction, displays in his form the indications of both the sexes as the one cause of the creation of the universe. My mother formerly told me that he is the cause of the universe and the one cause of everything. There is no one that is higher than Isa, O Sakra. If it pleases thee, do thou throw thyself on his kindness and protection. Thou hast visible evidence, O chief of the celestials, of the fact that the universe has sprung from the union of the sexes (as represented by Mahadeva). The universe, thou knowest, is the sum of what is vested with attributes and what else is divested of attributes and has for its immediate cause the seeds of Brahma and others. Brahma and Indra and Hutasana and Vishnu and all the other deities, along with the Daityas and the Asuras, crowned with the fruition of a thousand desires, always say that there is none that is higher than Mahadeva.[61] Impelled by desire, I solicit, with restrained mind, that god known to all the mobile and immobile universe,— him, that is, who has been spoken of as the best and highest of all the gods, and who is auspiciousness itself, for obtaining without delay that highest of all acquisitions, viz., Emancipation. What necessity is there of other reasons (for establishing) what I believe? The supreme Mahadeva is the cause of all causes. We have never heard that the deities have, at any time, adored the sign of any other god than Mahadeva. If Maheswara be not accepted, tell me, if thou hast ever heard of it, who else is there whose sign has been worshipped or is being worshipped by all the deities? He whose sign is always worshipped by Brahma, by Vishnu, by thee, O Indra, with all the other deities, is verily the foremost of all adorable deities. Brahma has for his sign the lotus, Vishnu has for his the discus, Indra has for his sign the thunder-bolt. But the creatures of the world do not bear any of the signs that distinguish these deities. On the other hand, all creatures bear the signs that mark Mahadeva and his spouse. Hence, all creatures must be regarded as belonging to Maheswara. All creatures of the feminine sex, have sprung from Uma's nature as their cause, and hence it is they bear the mark of femininity that distinguishes Uma; while all creatures that are masculine, having sprung from Siva, bear the masculine mark that distinguishes Siva. That person who says that there is, in the three worlds with their mobile and immobile creatures, any other cause than the Supreme Lord, and that which is not marked with the mark of either Mahadeva or his spouse should be regarded as very wretched and should not be counted among the creatures of the universe. Every being with the mark of the masculine sex should be known to be of Isana, while every being with the mark of the feminine sex should be known to be of Uma. This universe of mobile and immobile creatures is provided by two kinds of forms (viz., male and female). It is from Mahadeva that I wish to obtain boons. Failing in this, O Kausika, I would rather prefer dissolution itself. Go or remain, O Sakra, as thou, O slayer of Vala, desirest. I wish to have boons or curses from Mahadeva. No other deity shall I ever acknowledge, nor

---

[61] The Bombay reading savikara-nirguna-ganam is correct. The Bengal reading having gunam (and not ganam) as the last word of this compound, is vicious. The Burdwan translator adheres to the vicious reading and wrongly renders the compound. K. P. Singha skips over it. Of course, ganam means sum or total. Rectodbhavam is arsha for Retasodbhavam.

would I have from any other deity the fruition of all my wishes.—Having said these words unto the chief of the celestials, I became overwhelmed with grief at the thought of Mahadeva not having been gratified with me not withstanding my severe austerities. Within the twinkling of an eye, however, I saw the celestial elephant I had beheld before me transformed into a bull as white as a swan, or the Jasminum pubescens, or a stalk of the lotus or silver, or the ocean of milk. Of huge body, the hair of its tail was black and the hue of its eyes was tawny like that of honey. Its horns were hard as adamant and had the colour of gold. With their very sharp ends, whose hue was a mild red, the bull seemed to tear the Earth. The animal was adorned all over with ornaments made of the purest gold. Its face and hoofs and nose and ears were exceedingly beautiful and its waist too exceedingly well-formed. Its flanks were possessed of great beauty and its neck was very thick. Its whole form was exceedingly agreeable and beautiful to look at. Its hump shone with great beauty and seemed to occupy the whole of its shoulder-joint. And it looked like the summit of a mountain of snow or like a cliff of white clouds in the sky. Upon the back of that animal I beheld seated the illustrious Mahadeva with his spouse Uma. Verily, Mahadeva shone like the lord of stars while he is at his full. The fire born of his energy resembled in effulgence the lightening that flashes amid clouds. Verily, it seemed as if a thousand suns rose there, filling every side with a dazzling splendour. The energy of the Supreme Lord looked like the Samvartaka fire which destroys all creatures at the end of the Yuga. Overspread with that energy, the horizon became such that I could see nothing on any side. Filled with anxiety I once more thought what it could mean. That energy, however, did not pervade every side for any length of time, for soon, through the illusion of that god of gods, the horizon became clear. I then beheld the illustrious Sthanu or Maheswara seated on the back of his bull, of blessed and agreeable appearance and looking like a smokeless fire. And the great god was accompanied by Parvati of faultless features. Indeed, I beheld the blue-throated and high-souled Sthanu, unattached to everything, that receptacle of all kinds of force, endued with eight and ten arms and adorned with all kinds of ornaments. Clad in white vestments, he wore white garlands, and had white unguents smeared upon his limbs. The colour of his banner, irresistible in the universe, was white. The sacred thread round his person was also white. He was surrounded with associates, all possessed with prowess equal to his own, who were singing or dancing or playing on diverse kinds of musical instruments. A crescent moon, of pale hue, formed his crown, and placed on his forehead it looked like the moon that rises in the autumnal firmament. He seemed to dazzle with splendour, in consequence of his three eyes that looked like three suns. The garland of the purest white, that was on his body, shone like a wreath of lotuses, of the purest white, adorned with jewels and gems. I also beheld, O Govinda, the weapons in their embodied forms and fraught with every kind of energy, that belong to Bhava of immeasurable prowess. The high-souled deity held a bow whose hues resembled those of the rainbow. That bow is celebrated under the name of the Pinaka and is in reality a mighty snake. Indeed, that snake of seven heads and vast body, of sharp fangs and virulent poison, of large neck and the masculine sex, was twined round with the cord that served as its bowstring. And there was a shaft whose splendour looked like that of the sun or of the fire that appears at the end of the Yuga. Verily, that shaft was the excellent Pasupata that mighty and terrible weapon, which is without a second, indescribable for its power, and capable of striking every creature with fear. Of vast proportions, it seemed to constantly vomit sparks of fire. Possessed of one foot, of large teeth, and a thousand heads and thousand stomachs, it has a thousand arms, a thousand tongues, and a thousand eyes. Indeed, it seemed to continually vomit fire. O thou of mighty arms, that weapon is superior to the Brahma, the Narayana, the Aindra, the Agneya, and the Varuna weapons. Verily, it is capable of neutralising every other weapon in the universe. It was with that weapon that the illustrious Mahadeva had in days of yore, burnt and consumed in a moment the triple city of the Asuras. With the greatest ease, O Govinda, Mahadeva, using that single arrow, achieved that feat. That weapon, shot by Mahadeva's arms, can, without doubt consume in half the time taken up by a twinkling of the eyes the entire universe with all its mobile and immobile creatures. In the universe there is no being including even Brahma and Vishnu and the deities, that are incapable of being slain by that weapon. O sire, I saw that excellent, wonderful and incomparable weapon in the hand of Mahadeva. There is another mysterious and very powerful weapon which is equal or perhaps superior to the Pasupata weapon. I beheld that also. It is celebrated in all the worlds as the Sum of the Sula-armed Mahadeva. Hurled by the illustrious deity, that weapon is competent to rive the entire Earth or dry up the waters of the ocean or annihilate the entire universe. In days of yore, Yuvanaswa's son, king Mandhatri, that conqueror of the three worlds, possessed of imperial sway and endued with abundant energy, was, with all his troops, destroyed by means of that weapon. Endued with great might and great energy and resembling Sakra himself in prowess, the king, O Govinda, was slain by the Rakshasa Lavana with the aid of this Sula which he had got from Siva. The Sula has a very keen point. Exceedingly terrible, it is capable of causing everybody's hair stand on its end. I saw it in the hand of Mahadeva, as if roaring with rage, having contracted its forehead into three wrinkles. It resembled, O Krishna, a smokeless fire or the sun that rises at the end of the Yuga. The handle of that Sula, was made of a mighty snake. It is really indescribable. It looked like the universal Destroyer himself armed with his noose. I saw this weapon, O Govinda, in the hand of Mahadeva. I beheld also another weapon, viz., that sharp-edged battle-axe which, in days of yore, was given unto Rama by the gratified Mahadeva for enabling him to exterminate the Kshatriyas. It was with this weapon that Rama (of Bhrigu's race) slew in dreadful battle the great Kartaviryya who was the ruler of all the world. It was with that weapon that Jamadagni's son, O Govinda, was able to exterminate the Kshatriyas for one and twenty times. Of blazing edge and exceedingly terrible, that axe was hanging on the shoulder, adorned with a snake, of Mahadeva. Indeed, it shone on Mahadeva's person like the flame of a blazing fire. I beheld innumerable other celestial weapons with Mahadeva of great intelligence. I have, however named only a few, O sinless one, in consequence of their principal character. On the left side of the great god stood the Grandsire Brahma seated on an excellent car unto which were attached swans endued with the speed of the mind. On the same side could be seen Narayana also, seated on the son of Vinata, and bearing the conch, the discus, and the mace. Close to the goddess Uma was Skanda seated on his peacock, bearing his fatal dart and bells, and looking like another Agni. In the front of Mahadeva I beheld Nandi standing armed with his Sula and looking like a second Sankara (for prowess and energy). The Munis headed by the Self-born Manu and Rishis having Bhrigu for their first, and the deities with Sakra at their head, all came there. All the tribes of spirits and ghosts, and the celestial Mothers, stood surrounding Mahadeva and saluting him with reverence. The deities were engaged in singing the praises of Mahadeva by uttering diverse hymns. The Grandsire Brahma uttering a Rathantara, praised Mahadeva. Narayana also, uttering the Jyestha Saman, sang the praises of Bhava. Sakra also did the same with the aid of those foremost of Vedic Mantras, viz., the Sata-Rudriam. Verily, Brahma and Narayana and Sakra,—those three high-souled deities,—shone there like three sacrificial fires. In their midst shone the illustrious God like the sun in the midst of his corona, emerged from autumnal clouds. I beheld myriads of suns and moons, also in the sky, O Kesava. I then praised the illustrious Lord of everything, the supreme Master of the universe."'

"""Upamanyu continued, 'I said, "Salutations to thee, O illustrious one, O thou that constitutest the refuge of all things, O thou that art called Mahadeva! Salutations to thee that assumest the form of Sakra, that art Sakra, and that disguisest thyself in the form and vestments of Sakra. Salutations to thee that art armed with the thunder, to thee that art tawny, and thee that art always armed with the Pinaka. Salutations to thee that always bearest the conch and the Sula. Salutations to thee that art clad in black, to thee that art of dark and curly hair, to thee that hast a dark deer-skin for thy upper garment, to thee that presidest over the eighth lunation of the dark fortnight. Salutations to thee that art of white complexion, to thee that art called white, to thee that art clad in white robes, to thee that hast limbs smeared with white ashes, to thee that art ever engaged in white deeds. Salutations to thee that art red of colour, to thee that art clad in red vestments, to thee that ownest a red banner with red flags, to thee that wearest red garlands and usest red unguents. Salutations to thee that art brown in complexion, to thee that art clad in brown vestments, to thee that hast a brown banner with brown flags, to thee that wearest brown garlands and usest brown unguents. Salutations to thee that hast the umbrella of royalty held over thy head, to thee that wearest the foremost of crowns. Salutations unto thee that art adorned with half a garland and half an armlet, to thee that art decked with one ring for one year, to thee that art endued with the speed of the mind, to thee that art endued with great effulgence. Salutations to thee that art the foremost of deities, to thee that art the foremost of ascetics, to thee that art the foremost of celestials. Salutations to thee that wearest half a wreath of lotuses, to thee that hast many lotuses on thy body. Salutations to thee that hast half thy body smeared with sandal paste, to thee that hast half thy body decked with garlands of flowers and smeared with fragrant unguents.[62] Salutations to thee that art of the complexion of the Sun, to thee that art like the Sun, to thee whose face is like the Sun, to thee that hast eyes each of which is like the Sun. Salutations to thee that art Soma, to thee that art as mild as Soma, to thee that bearest the lunar disc, to thee that art of lunar aspect, to thee that art the foremost of all creatures, to thee that art adorned with a set of the most beautiful teeth. Salutations to thee that art of a dark complexion, to thee that art of a fair complexion, to thee that hast a form half of which is yellow and half white, to thee that hast a body half of which is male and half female, to thee that art both male and female. Salutations to thee that ownest a bull for thy vehicle, to thee that proceedest riding on the foremost of elephants, to thee that art obtained with difficulty, to thee that art capable of going to places unapproachable by others. Salutations to thee whose praises are sung by the Ganas, to thee that art devoted to the diverse Ganas, to thee that followest the track that is trod by the Ganas, to thee that art always devoted to the Ganas as to a vow. Salutations to thee that art of the complexion of white clouds, to thee that hast the splendour of the evening clouds, to thee that art incapable of being described by names, to thee that art of thy own form (having nothing else in the universe with which it can be compared). Salutations to thee that wearest a beautiful garland of red colour, to thee that art clad in robes of red colour. Salutations to thee that hast the crown of the head decked with gems, to thee that art adorned with a half-moon, to thee that wearest many beautiful gems in thy diadem, to thee that hast eight flowers on thy head.

---

[62] Mahadeva's body is half male and half female. The male half has garlands of bones, the female half garlands of flowers. The male half has everything that is rejected by others; the female half has all things that are coveted by others. This particular form of Mahadeva is called Hara-Gauri.

Salutations to thee that hast a fiery mouth and fiery eyes, to thee that hast eyes possessing the effulgence of a thousand moons, to thee that art of the form of fire, to thee that art beautiful and agreeable, to thee that art inconceivable and mysterious. Salutations to thee that rangest through the firmament, to thee that lovest and residest in lands affording pasture to kine, to thee that walkest on the Earth, to thee that art the Earth, to thee that art infinite, to thee that art exceedingly auspicious. Salutations to thee that art unclad (or has the horizon alone for thy vestments), to thee that makest a happy home of every place where thou mayst happen to be for the moment. Salutations to thee that hast the universe for thy home, to thee that hast both Knowledge and Felicity for thy Soul. Salutations to thee that always wearest a diadem, to thee that wearest a large armlet, to thee that hast a snake for the garland round thy neck, to thee that wearest many beautiful ornaments on thy person. Salutations to thee that hast the Sun, the Moon, and Agni for thy three eyes, to thee that art possessed of a thousand eyes, to thee that art both male and female, to thee that art divested of sex, to thee that art a Sankhya, to thee that art a Yogin. Salutations to thee that art of the grace of those deities who are worshipped in sacrifices, to thee that art the Atharvans, to thee that art the alleviator of all kinds of disease and pain, to thee that art the dispeller of every sorrow. Salutations to thee that roarest as deep as the clouds, to thee that puttest forth diverse kinds of illusions, to thee that presidest over the soil and over the seed that is sown in it, to thee that art the Creator of everything. Salutations to thee that art the Lord of all the celestials, to thee that art the Master of the universe, to thee that art endued with the speed of the wind, to thee that art of the form of the wind. Salutations to thee that wearest a garland of gold, to thee that sportest on hills and mountains,[63] to thee that art adorned by all who are enemies of the gods, to thee that art possessed of fierce speed and energy. Salutations to thee that torest away one of the heads of the Grandsire Brahma, to thee that hast slain the Asura named Mahisha, to thee that assumest three forms, to thee that bearest every form. Salutations to thee that art the destroyer of the triple city of the Asuras, to thee that art the destroyer of (Daksha's) sacrifice, to thee that art the destroyer of the body of Kama (the deity of Desire), to thee that wieldest the rod of destruction. Salutations to thee that art Skanda, to thee that art Visakha, to thee that art the rod of the Brahmana, to thee that art Bhava, to thee that art Sarva, to thee that art of universal form. Salutations to thee that art Isana, to thee that art the destroyer of Bhaga, to thee that art the slayer of Andhaka, to thee that art the universe, to thee that art possessed of illusion, to thee that art both conceivable and inconceivable.[64] Thou art the one end of all creatures, thou art the foremost, thou art the heart of everything. Thou art the Brahma of all the deities, thou art the Nilardhita Red and Blue of the Rudras. Thou art the Soul of the creatures, thou art He who is called Purusha in the Sankhya philosophy, thou art the Rishabha among all things sacred, thou art that which is called auspicious by Yogins and which, according to them, is without parts (being indivisible). Amongst those that are observant of the different modes of life, thou art the House-holder, thou art the great Lord amongst the lords of the universe. Thou art Kuvera among all the Yakshas, and thou art Vishnu amongst all the sacrifices.[65] Thou art Meru amongst mountains, thou art the Moon among all luminaries of the firmament, thou art Vasishtha amongst Rishis, thou art Surya among the planets. Thou art the lion among all wild animals, and among all domestic animals, thou art the bull that is worshipped by all

---

[63] Girimala is explained by the commentator as one that sports on hills and mountains.

[64] All the texts have Bhavaghnaya. The correct reading, however, seems to be Bhagaghnaya, especially as the reference to Andhaka occurs immediately after.

[65] Vishnu means here the foremost of sacrifices.

people. Among the Adityas thou art Vishnu (Upendra), among the Vasu thou art Pavaka, among birds thou art the son of Vinata (Garuda), and among snakes thou art Ananta (Sesha). Among the Vedas thou art the Samans, among the Yajushes thou art the Sata-Rudriyam, among Yogins thou art Sanatkumara, and among Sankhyas thou art Kapila. Among the Maruts thou art Sakra, among the Pitris thou art Devarat, among all the regions (for the residence of created beings) thou art the region of Brahman, and amongst all the ends that creatures attain to, thou art Moksha or Emancipation. Thou art the Ocean of milk among all oceans, among all rocky eminences thou art Himavat, among all the orders thou art the Brahmana, and among all learned Brahmanas thou art he that has undergone and is observant of the Diksha. Thou art the Sun among all things in the world, thou art the destroyer called Kala. Thou art whatever else possessed of superior energy of eminence that exists in the universe. Thou art possessed of supreme puissance. Even this is what represents my certain conclusion. Salutations to thee, O puissant and illustrious one, O thou that art kind to all thy worshippers. Salutations to thee, O lord of Yogins. I bow to thee, O original cause of the universe. Be thou gratified with me that am thy worshipper, that am very miserable and helpless. O Eternal Lord, do thou become the refuge of this adorer of thine that is very weak and miserable. O Supreme Lord, it behoveth thee to pardon all those transgressions of which I have been guilty, taking compassion upon me on the ground of my being thy devoted worshipper. I was stupefied by thee, O Lord of all the deities, in consequence of the disguise in which thou showest thyself to me. O Maheswara, I did not give thee the Arghya or water to wash thy feet."[66] Having hymned the praises of Isana in this way, I offered him, with great devotion, water to wash his feet and the ingredients of the Arghya, and then, with joined hands, I resigned myself to him, being prepared to do whatever he would bid. Then, O sire, an auspicious shower of flowers fell upon my head, possessed of celestial fragrance and bedewed with cold water. The celestial musicians began to play on their kettle-drums. A delicious breeze, fragrant and agreeable, began to blow and fill me with pleasure. Then Mahadeva accompanied by his spouse, and having the bull for his sign, having been gratified with me, addressed the celestials assembled there in these words, filling me with great joy,— "Behold, ye deities, the devotion of the high-souled Upamanyu. Verily, steady and great is that devotion, and entirely immutable, for it exists unalterably."—Thus addressed by the great God armed with the Sula, the deities, O Krishna, having bowed down unto him and joined their hands in reverence, said these words,—"O illustrious one, O God of the gods, O master of the universe, O Lord of all, let this best of regenerate persons obtain from thee the fruition of all his desires."—Thus addressed by all the deities, with the Grandsire Brahma among them. Sarva, otherwise called Isa and Sankara, said these words as if smiling unto me.'

"'"The illustrious Sankara said, "O dear Upamanyu, I am gratified with thee. Behold me, O foremost of Munis, O learned Rishi, thou art firmly devoted to me and well hast thou been tested by me. I have been very highly pleased with thee in consequence of this thy devotion to Siva. I shall, therefore, give thee today the fruition of whatever desires thou mayst have in thy heart." Thus addressed by Mahadeva of great wisdom, tears of joy came into my eyes and my hair stood on its end (through emotion). Kneeling down unto him and bowing unto him repeatedly, I then, with a voice that was choked with delight, said unto him,—"O illustrious god, it seems to me that I was hitherto dead and that it is only today that I have taken my birth, and that my birth hath today borne fruit, since I am

---

[66] These articles must be offered to a visitor, whether he stands in need of them or not.

staying now in the presence of Him who is the Master of both the deities and the Asuras! Who else is more praiseworthy than I, since I am beholding with these eyes of mine, Him of immeasurable prowess whom the very deities are unable to behold without first paying hearty worship? That which they that are possessed of learning and wisdom say is the highest of all topics, which is Eternal, which is distinguished from all else, which is unborn, which is Knowledge, which is indestructible, is identical with thee, O puissant and illustrious one, thee that art the beginning of all the topics, thee that art indestructible and changeless, thee that art conversant with the ordinances which govern all the topics, thee that art the foremost of Purushas, thee that art the highest of the high. Thou art he that hadst created from thy right side the Grandsire Brahma, the Creator of all things. Thou art he that hadst created from thy left side Vishnu for protecting the Creation. Thou art that puissant Lord who didst create Rudra when the end of the Yuga came and when the Creation was once more to be dissolved. That Rudra, who sprang from thee destroyed the Creation with all its mobile and immobile beings, assuming the form of Kala of great energy, of the cloud Samvartaka (charged with water which myriads of oceans are not capacious enough to bear), and of the all consuming fire. Verily, when the period comes for the dissolution of the universe, that Rudra stands, ready to swallow up the universe. Thou art that Mahadeva, who is the original Creator of the universe with all its mobile and immobile entities. Thou art he, who, at the end of the Kalpa, stands, withdrawing all things into thyself. Thou art he that pervadest all things, that art the Soul of all things, thou art the Creator of the Creator of all entities. Incapable of being seen by even any of the deities, thou art he that exists, pervading all entities. If, O lord, thou hast been gratified with me and if thou wouldst grant me boons, let this be the boon, O Lord of all the deities, that my devotion to thee may remain unchanged. O best of the deities, let me, through thy grace, have knowledge of the Present, the Past, and the Future. I shall also, with all my kinsmen and friends, always eat food mixed with milk. And let thy illustrious self be for ever present at our retreat."—Thus addressed by me, the illustrious Maheswara endued with supreme energy, that Master of all mobile and immobile, viz., Siva, worshipped of all the universe, then said unto me these words.'

""""The illustrious Deity said, "Be thou free from every misery and pain, and be thou above decrepitude and death. Be thou possessed of fame, be thou endued with great energy, and let spiritual knowledge be thine. Thou shalt, through my grace, be always sought for by the Rishis. Be thy behaviour good and righteous, be every desirable attribute thine, be thou possessed of universal knowledge, and be thou of agreeable appearance. Let undecaying youth be thine, and let thy energy be like that of fire. Wherever, again, thou mayst desire the presence of the ocean of milk that is so agreeable to thee, there shall that ocean appear before thee (ready for being utilised by thee and thy friends for purposes of thy food). Do thou, with thy friends, always obtain food prepared with milk, with the celestial nectar besides being mixed with it.[67] After the expiration of a Kalpa thou shalt then obtain my companionship. Thy family and race and kinsmen shall be exhaustless. O foremost of regenerate ones, thy devotion to me shalt be eternal. And, O best of Brahmanas, I shall always accord my presence to thy asylum. Live, O son, whithersoever thou likest, and let no anxiety be thine. Thought of by thee, I shall, O learned Brahmana, grant thee a sight of myself again."—Having said these words, and granted me these boons, the illustrious Isana, endued with the effulgence of millions of

---

[67] All the texts read Kshirodasagaraschaiva. The correct reading is Kshirodasagarasyaiva. The nominative may be construed with the previous line, but the genitive would be better.

Suns, disappeared there and then. It was even thus, O Krishna, that I beheld, with the aid of austere penances, that God of gods. I also obtained all that was said by the great Deity endued with supreme intelligence. Behold, O Krishna, before thy eyes, these Siddhas residing here and these Rishis and Vidyadharas and Yakshas and Gandharvas and Apsaras. Behold these trees and creepers and plants yielding all sorts of flowers and fruits. Behold them bearing the flowers of every season, with beautiful leaves, and shedding a sweet fragrance all around. O thou of mighty arms, all these are endued with a celestial nature through the grace of that god of gods, that Supreme Lord, that high-souled Deity.'

"'Vasudeva continued, "Hearing these words of his and beholding, as it were, with my own eyes all that he had related to me, I became filled with wonder. I then addressed the great ascetic Upamanyu and said unto him,—'Deserving of great praise art thou, O foremost of learned Brahmanas, for what righteous man is there other than thou whose retreat enjoys the distinction of being honoured with the presence of that God of gods? Will the puissant Siva, will the great Sankara, O chief of ascetics, grant me also a sight of his person and show me favour.'

"'"Upamanyu said, 'Without doubt, O thou of eyes like lotus-petals, thou wilt obtain a sight of Mahadeva very soon, even as, O sinless one, I succeeded in obtaining a sight of him. O thou of immeasurable prowess, I see with my spiritual eyes that thou wilt, in the sixth month from this, succeed in obtaining a sight of Mahadeva, O best of all persons. Thou, O foremost of the Yadus, wilt obtain from Maheswara and his spouse, four and twenty boons. I tell thee what is true. Through the grace of that Deity endued with supreme wisdom, the Past, the Future and the Present are known to me. The great Hara has favoured these Rishis numbering by thousands and others as numerous. Why will not the puissant Deity show favour to thee, O Mahadeva? The meeting of the gods is always commendable with one like thee, with one that is devoted to the Brahmanas, with one that is full of compassion and that is full of faith. I shall give thee certain Mantras. Recite them continuously. By this thou art certain to behold Sankara.'"

"'The blessed Vishnu continued, "I then said unto him, 'O regenerate one, through thy grace, O great ascetic, I shall behold the lord of the deities, that grinder of multitudes of Diti's sons.' Eight days, O Bharata, passed there like an hour, all of us being thus occupied with talk on Mahadeva. On the eighth day, I underwent the Diksha (initiation) according to due rites, at the hands of that Brahmana and received the staff from his hands. I underwent the prescribed shave. I took up a quantity of Kusa blades in my hand. I wore rags for my vestments. I rubbed my person with ghee. I encircled a cord of Munja grass round my loins. For one month I lived on fruits. The second month I subsisted upon water. The third, the fourth and the fifth months I passed, living upon air alone. I stood all the while, supporting myself upon one foot and with my arms also raised upwards, and foregoing sleep all the while. I then beheld, O Bharata, in the firmament an effulgence that seemed to be as dazzling as that of a thousand Suns combined together. Towards the centre of that effulgence, O son of Pandu, I saw a cloud looking like a mass of blue hills, adorned with rows of cranes, embellished with many a grand rainbow, with flashes of lightning and the thunder-fire looking like eyes set on it.[68] Within that cloud was the puissant Mahadeva. himself of dazzling splendour, accompanied by his spouse Uma. Verily, the great Deity seemed to shine with his penances, energy, beauty, effulgence,

---

[68] The commentator does not explain what is meant by Vidyunmalagavakshakam. The word go means the Thunder-fire. Very probably, what is implied is that flashes of lightning and the Thunder-fire looked like eyes set upon that cloud. Go may also mean jyoti or effulgence.

and his dear spouse by his side. The puissant Maheswara, with his spouse by his side, shone in the midst of that cloud. The appearance seemed to be like that of the Sun in the midst of racking clouds with the Moon by his side. The hair on my body, O son of Kunti, stood on its end, and my eyes expanded with wonder upon beholding Hara, the refuge of all the deities and the dispeller of all their griefs. Mahadeva was adorned with a diadem on his head. He was armed with his Sula. He was clad in a tiger-skin, had matted locks on his head, and bore the staff (of the Sanyasin) in one of his hands. He was armed, besides with his Pinaka and the thunderbolt. His teeth was sharp-pointed. He was decked with an excellent bracelet for the upper arm. His sacred thread was constituted by a snake. He wore an excellent garland of diversified colours on his bosom, that hung down to his toes. Verily, I beheld him like the exceedingly bright moon of an autumnal evening. Surrounded by diverse clans of spirits and ghosts, he looked like the autumnal Sun difficult of being gazed at for its dazzling brightness. Eleven hundred Rudras stood around that Deity of restrained soul and white deeds, then seated upon his bull. All of them were employed in hymning his praises. The Adityas, the Vasus, the Sadhyas, the Viswedevas, and the twin Aswins praised that Lord of the universe by uttering the hymns occurring in the scriptures. The puissant Indra and his brother Upendra, the two sons of Aditi, and the Grandsire Brahma, all uttered, in the presence of Bhava, the Rathantara Saman. Innumerable masters of Yoga, all the regenerate Rishis with their children, all the celestial Rishis, the goddess Earth, the Sky (between Earth and Heaven), the Constellations, the Planets, the Months, the Fortnights, the Seasons, Night, the Years, the Kshanas, the Muhurtas, the Nimeshas, the Yugas one after another, all the celestial Sciences and branches of knowledge, and all beings conversant with Truth, were seen bowing down unto that Supreme Preceptor, that great Father, that giver (or origin) of Yoga. Sanatkumara, the Vedas, the Histories, Marichi, Angiras, Atri, Pulastya, Pulaha, Kratu, the seven Manus, Soma, the Atharvans, and Vrihaspati, Bhrigu, Daksha, Kasyapa, Vasishtha, Kasya, the Schandas, Diksha, the Sacrifices, Dakshina, the Sacrificial Fires, the Havis (clarified butter) poured in sacrifices, and all the requisites of the sacrifices, were beheld by me, O Yudhishthira, standing there in their embodied forms. All the guardians of the worlds, all the Rivers, all the snakes, the mountains, the celestial Mothers, all the spouses and daughters of the celestials, thousands upon thousands and millions of ascetics, were seen to bow down to that puissant Lord who is the soul of tranquillity. The Mountains, the Oceans, and the Points of the compass also did the same, the Gandharvas and the Apsaras highly skilled in music, in celestial strains, sang and hymned the praises of Bhava who is full of wonder. The Vidyadharas, the Danavas, the Guhyakas, the Rakshasas, and all created beings, mobile and immobile, adorned, in thought, word and deed, that puissant Lord. Before me, that Lord of all the gods viz., Sarva, appeared seated in all his glory. Seeing that Isana had showed himself to me by being seated in glory before my eyes, the whole universe, with the Grandsire and Sakra, looked at me. I, however, had not the power to look at Mahadeva. The great Deity then addressed me saying, 'Behold, O Krishna, and speak to me. Thou hast adorned me hundreds and thousands of times. There is no one in the three worlds that is dearer to me than thou.' After I had bowed unto him, his spouse, viz., the goddess Uma, became gratified with me. I then addressed in these words the great God whose praises are hymned by all the deities with the Grandsire Brahma at their head.'"

"'The blessed Vishnu said, "I saluted Mahadeva, saying,—'Salutations to thee, O thou that art the eternal origin of all things. The Rishis say that thou art the Lord of the Vedas. The righteous say that thou art Penance, thou art Sattwa, thou art Rajas, thou art

Tamas, and thou art Truth. Thou art Brahman, thou art Rudra, thou art Varuna, thou art Agni, thou art Manu, thou art Bhava, thou art Dhatri, thou art Tashtri, thou art Vidhatri, thou art the puissant Master of all things, and thou art everywhere. All beings, mobile and immobile, have sprung from thee. This triple world with all its mobile and immobile entities, has been created by thee. The Rishis say that thou art superior to the senses, the mind, the vital breaths, the seven sacrificial fires, all others that have their refuge in the all-pervading Soul, and all the deities that are adored and worthy of adoration. Thou, O illustrious one, art the Vedas, the Sacrifices, Soma, Dakshina, Pavaka, Havi, and all other requisites of sacrifice. The merit obtained by sacrifices, gifts made to others, the study of the Vedas, vows, regulations in respect of restraint, Modesty, Fame, Prosperity, Splendour, Contentment, and Success, all exist for leading to thee.[69] Desire, Wrath, Fear, Cupidity, Pride, Stupefaction, and Malice, Pains and Diseases, are, O illustrious one, thy children. Thou art all acts that creatures do, thou art the joy and sorrow that flow from those acts, thou art the absence of joy and sorrow, thou art that Ignorance which is the indestructible seed of Desire, thou art the high origin of Mind, thou art Puissance, and thou art Eternity.[70] Thou art the Unmanifest, thou art Pavana, thou art inconceivable, thou art the thousand-rayed Sun, thou art the effulgent Chit, thou art the first of all the topics, and thou art the refuge of life.[71] The use of words like Mahat, Soul, Understanding, Brahman, Universe, Sambhu, and Self-born and other words occurring in succession (in the Vedas), show that thy nature has been judged (by persons conversant with the Vedas) as identical with Mahat and Soul. Verily, regarding thee as all this, the learned Brahmanas win over that ignorance which lies at the root of the world. Thou residest in the heart of all creatures, and thou art adored by the Rishis as Kshetrajna. Thy arms and feet extend to every place, and thy eyes, head, and face are everywhere. Thou hearest everywhere in the universe, and thou stayest, pervading all things. Of all acts that are performed in the Nimeshas and other divisions of time that spring in consequence of the puissance of the Sun, thou art the fruit.[72] Thou art the original effulgence (of the supreme Chit). Thou art Purusha, and thou residest in the hearts of all things. Thou art the various Yogic attributes of success, viz., Subtility and Grossness and Fruition and Supremacy and Effulgence and Immutability.[73] Understanding and intelligence and all the worlds rest upon thee. They that are devoted to meditation, that are always engaged in Yoga, that are devoted to or firm in Truth and that have subjugated their passions, seek thee and rest on thee.[74] They that know thee for one that is Immutable, or one that resides in all hearts, or one that is endued with supreme puissance, or one that is the ancient Purusha, or one that

---

[69] Tadarpani is explained by the commentator as Twatsarupasyaprapika.

[70] Kriti is Kriya, i.e., all acts that creatures do. Vikara is the fruits of kriya, i.e., joy or sorrow that creatures enjoy or endure. The Bengal texts read pralaya. The Bombay reading is pranaya. The latter is also the reading that the commentator notices, but when he explains it to mean tadabhavah, i.e., the absence of joy and sorrow, I think, through the scribe's mistake, the l has been changed into the palatal n. Prabhavah is explained as aiswaryya. Saswata is eternal, i.e., transcending the influence of acts.

[71] Thou art the adi of the ganas. By ganas is meant ganayante sankhyayante iti ganah, i.e., tattwah.

[72] The commentator explains this by saying that thou art the heavenly felicity which creatures earn by means of their righteous acts. Acts, again, are performed in course of Time whose divisions are caused by the Sun.

[73] It has been explained in previous Sections that by success in Yoga one may make oneself as subtile as possible or as gross as possible. One may also attain to the fruition of all desires, extending to the very creation of worlds upon worlds peopled with all kinds of creatures. That Yogins do not create is due to their respect for the Grandsire and their wish not to disturb the ordinary course of things.

[74] Satyasandhah is the Bengal reading. The Bombay reading is satrasatwah, meaning, as the commentator explains, satya-sankalpah.

is pure Knowledge, or one that is the effulgent Chit, or one that is the highest refuge of all persons endued with intelligence, are certainly persons of great intelligence. Verily, such persons stay, transcending intelligence.[75] By understanding the seven subtle entities (viz., Mahat, Ego, and five subtle primal elements called Tanmatras), by comprehending thy six attributes (of Omniscience, Contentment of Fullness, Knowledge without beginning, Independence, Puissance that is not at fault at any time and that is infinite), and being conversant with Yoga that is freed from every false notion, the man of knowledge succeeds in entering into thy great self.'—After I had said these words, O Partha, unto Bhava, that dispeller of grief and pain, the universe, both mobile and immobile, sent up a leonine shout (expressive of their approval of the correctness of my words). The innumerable Brahmanas there present, the deities and the Asuras, the Nagas, the Pisachas, the Pitris, the birds, diverse Rakshasas, diverse classes of ghosts and spirits, and all the great Rishis, then bowed down unto that great Deity. There then fell upon my head showers of celestial flowers possessed of great fragrance, and delicious winds blew on the spot. The puissant Sankara then, devoted to the good of the universe, looked at the goddess Uma and the lord of the celestials and myself also, and thus spoke unto me,— 'We know, O Krishna, that thou, O slayer of foes, art filled with the greatest devotion towards us. Do what is for thy good. My love and affection for thee is very great. Do thou ask for eight boons. I shall verily give them unto thee, O Krishna. O best of all persons, tell me what they are, O chief of the Yadavas. Name what thou wishest. However difficult of attainment they be, thou shalt have them still.'"'"[76]

SECTION XV.

"'The blessed Krishna said, "Bowing my head with great joy unto that mass of energy and effulgence, I said these words unto the great Deity, with a heart filled with gladness,—'Firmness in virtue, the slaughter of foes in battle, the highest fame, the greatest might, devotion to Yoga, thy adjacence, and hundreds upon hundreds of children, these are the boons I solicit of thee,'—'So be it,'—said Sankara repeating the words I had uttered. After this, the mother of the universe, the upholders of all things, who cleanses all things, viz., the spouse of Sarva, that vast receptacle of penances said with a restrained soul these words unto me,—'The puissant Mahadeva has granted thee, O sinless one, a son who shall be named Samva. Do thou take from me also eight boons which thou choosest. I shall certainly grant them to thee.'—Bowing unto her with a bend of my head, I said unto her, O son of Pandu,—'I solicit from thee non-anger against the Brahmanas, grace of my father, a hundred sons, the highest enjoyments, love for my family, the grace of my mother, the attainment of tranquillity and peace, and cleverness in every act!'
"'"Uma said, 'It shall be even so, O thou that art possessed of prowess and puissance equal to that of a celestial. I never say what is untrue. Thou shalt have sixteen thousand wives. Thy love for them and theirs also for thee shall be unlimited. From all thy kinsmen also, thou shalt receive the highest affection. Thy body too shall be most beautiful. Seven thousand guests will daily feed at thy palace.'"
"'Vasudeva continued, "Having thus granted me boons both the god and the goddess,

---

[75] Vigraham is explained by the commentator as visishthanubhanbhava-rupam or nishkalam jnaptimatram.
[76] In verse 369 ante Upamanyu says that Krishna is to receive from Mahadeva sixteen and eight boons. The commentator, stretching the words has tried to explain them as signifying a total of eight, and eight i.e., eight are to be obtained from Mahadeva, and eight from his divine spouse Uma. The language, however, is such that this meaning cannot be put upon it without doing violence to it.

O Bharata, disappeared there and then with their Ganas, O elder brother of Bhima. All those wonderful facts I related fully, O best of kings, to that Brahmana of great energy, viz., Upamanyu (from whom I had obtained the Diksha before adoring Mahadeva). Bowing down unto the great God, Upamanyu said these words to me.'

""'Upamanyu said, 'There is no deity like Sarva. There is no end or refuge like Sarva. There is none that can give so many or such high boons. There is none that equal him in battle.'""'

SECTION XVI.

""'Upamanyu said, 'There was in the Krita age, O sire, a Rishi celebrated under the name of Tandi. With great devotion of heart he adored, with the aid of Yoga-meditation, the great God for ten thousand years. Listen to me as I tell the fruit or reward he reaped of such extraordinary devotion. He succeeded in beholding Mahadeva and praised him by uttering some hymns. Thinking, with the aid of his penances, of Him who is the supreme Soul and who is immutable and undeteriorating, Tandi became filled with wonder, and said these words,—"I seek the protection of Him whom the Sankhyas describe and the Yogins think of as the Supreme, the Foremost, the Purusha, the pervader of all things, and the Master of all existent objects, of him who, the learned say, is the cause of both the creation and the destruction of the universe; of him who is superior to all the celestials, the Asuras, and the Munis, of him who has nothing higher, who is unborn, who is the Lord of all things, who has neither beginning nor end, and who is endued with supreme puissance, who is possessed of the highest felicity, and who is effulgent and sinless."—After he had said these words, Tandi beheld before him that ocean of penances, that great Deity who is immutable and undeteriorating, who is without compare, who is inconceivable, who is eternal, and who is without any change, who is indivisible, who is whole, who is Brahma, who transcends all attributes, and who is endued with attributes, who is the highest delight of Yogins, who is without deterioration, who is called Emancipation, who is the refuge of the Mind, of Indra, of Agni, of the god of wind, of the entire universe, and of the Grandsire Brahma; who is incapable of being conceived by the Mind, who is without mutation of any kind, who is pure, who is capable of being apprehended by understanding only and who is immaterial as the Mind; who is difficult of comprehension, who is incapable of being measured, who is difficult of being attained by persons of uncleansed souls, who is the origin of the universe, and who transcends both the universe and the attribute of darkness; who is ancient, who is Purusha, who is possessed of effulgence, and who is higher than the highest. The Rishi Tandi, desirous of beholding Him who making himself endued with life-breaths, resides in what results from it viz., Jiva, in the form of that effulgence which is called the Mind, passed many years in the practice of the severest austerities, and having succeeded in beholding Him as the reward of those penances, he praised the great God in the following terms.

""'Tandi said, "Thou art the holiest of holies[77] and the refuge of all, O foremost of all beings endued with intelligence. Thou art the fiercest energy of all kinds of energy. Thou art the austerest penance of all penances. Thou, O puissant one, art the liberal giver of blessings. Thou art the supreme Truth. Salutations to thee, O thou of a thousand rays,

[77] The commentator explains this as 'thou art the cleanser of all cleansing entities,' i.e., it is in consequence of thee, Ganga and the others have received the power of cleansing other things and creatures.

and, O refuge of all felicity. Thou art the giver of that Nirvana which, O puissant one, Yatis, standing in fear of birth and death, strive for so hard. The Grandsire Brahma, he of a hundred sacrifices, (viz., Indra) Vishnu, the Viswadevas, the great Rishis, are incapable of comprehending thee and thy real nature. How then can persons like ourselves hope to comprehend thee? From thee flows everything. Upon thee rests everything. Thou art called Kala, thou art called Purusha, thou art called Brahma. Celestial Rishis conversant with the Puranas, say that thou hast three bodies viz., those pertaining to Kalas, those pertaining to Purusha and those pertaining to Brahma or the three forms namely Brahma, Vishnu and Rudra. Thou art Adhi-Purusha, (occupying the physical frame from head to foot) thou art Adhyatma, thou art Adhibhuta, and Adhi-Daivata, thou art Adhi-loka, Adhi-Vijnanam and Adhi-Yajna.[78] Men of wisdom, when they succeed in knowing thee that residest in themselves and that art incapable of being known by the very gods, become freed from all bonds and pass into a state of existence that transcends all sorrow.[79] They that do not wish to know thee, O thou of great puissance, have to undergo innumerable births and deaths. Thou art the door of heaven and of Emancipation. Thou art he that projectest all beings into existence and withdrawest them again into thyself. Thou art the great giver. Thou art heaven, thou art Emancipation, thou art desire (the seed of action). Thou art wrath that inspires creatures. Thou art Sattwa, thou art Rajas, thou art Tamas, thou art the nether regions, and thou art the upper regions. Thou art the Grandsire Brahma, thou art Bhava, thou art Vishnu, thou art Skanda, thou art Indra, thou art Savitri, thou art Yama, thou art Varuna, Soma, thou art Dhatri, thou art Manu, thou art Vidhatri and thou art Kuvera, the Lord of treasures. Thou art Earth, thou art Wind, thou art Water, thou art Agni, thou art Space, thou art Speech, thou art the Understanding, thou art Steadiness, thou art Intelligence, thou art the acts that creatures do, thou art Truth, thou art Falsehood, thou art existent and thou art non-existent. Thou art the senses, thou art that which transcends Prakriti, thou art immutable. Thou art superior to the universe of existent objects, thou art superior to the universe of non-existent objects, thou art capable of being conceived, thou art incapable of being conceived. That which is supreme Brahman, that which is the highest entity, that which is the end of both the Sankhyas and the Yogins, is, without doubt, identical with thee. Verily, rewarded have I been today by thee in consequence of thy granting me a sight of thy form. I have attained the end which the righteous alone attain to. I have been rewarded with that end which is solicited by persons whose understandings have been cleansed by Knowledge. Alas, so long I was steeped in Ignorance; for this long period I was a senseless fool, since I had no knowledge of thee that art the Supreme Deity, thee that art the only eternal Entity as can be only known by all persons endued with wisdom. In course of innumerable lives have I at last succeeded in acquiring that Devotion towards thee in consequence of which thou hast shown thyself to me. O thou that art ever inclined to extend thy grace to those that are devoted to thee, he that succeeds in knowing thee is enable to enjoy immortality. Thou art that which is ever a mystery with the gods, the Asuras, and the ascetics. Brahman is concealed in the cave of the heart. The very ascetics are unable to behold or know Him.[80] Thou art that puissant deity who is the doer of everything and whose face is

[78] Adhyatma: that occupies the inner body. Adhibhuta: elements, prima, eyes, ears, etc.; Adhidaivata: sun, moon, etc. that control over the bhutas. Adhiloka—one occupying the lokas; Adhivijnana—one occupying the plane of consciousness; Adhiyajna—one conducting the sacrifices residing in the heart of the jivas.
[79] i.e., they attain to Emancipation when they behold thee in the firmament of their own hearts, or succeed in identifying their own souls with thee.
[80] The guha or cave in which Brahman is concealed is the heart of every living creature.

turned towards every direction. Thou art the Soul of all things, thou seest all things, thou pervadest all things, and thou knowest all things. Thou makest a body for thyself, and bearest that body. Thou art an embodied Being. Thou enjoyest a body, and thou art the refuge of all embodied creatures. Thou art the creator of the life-breaths, thou possessest the life-breaths, thou art one that is endued with life-breaths, thou art the giver of the life-breaths, and thou art the refuge of all beings endued with life-breaths. Thou art that Adhyatma which is the refuge of all righteous persons that are devoted to Yoga-meditation and conversant with the Soul and that are solicitous of avoiding rebirth. Verily, thou art that Supreme Lord who is identical with that refuge. Thou art the giver unto all creatures of whatever ends become theirs, fraught with happiness or misery. Thou art he that ordains all created beings to birth and death. Thou art the puissant Lord who grants success to Rishis crowned with success in respect of the fruition of their wishes. Having created all the worlds beginning with Bhu, together with all the denizens of heaven, that upholdest and cherishest them all, distributing thyself into thy well-known forms numbering Eight.[81] From thee flows everything. Upon thee rests all things. All things, again, disappear in thee. Thou art the sole object that is Eternal. Thou art that region of Truth which is sought by the righteous and regarded by them as the highest. Thou art that cessation of individual existence which Yogins seek. Thou art that Oneness which is sought by persons conversant with the soul. Brahma and the Siddhas expounding the mantras have concealed thee in a cave for preventing the deities and Asuras and human beings from beholding thee.[82] Although thou residest in the heart, yet thou are concealed. Hence, stupefied by thee, deities and Asuras and human beings are all unable to understand thee, O Bhava, truly and in all thy details. Unto those persons that succeed in attaining to thee after having cleansed themselves by devotion, thou showest thyself of thy own accord, O thou that residest in all hearts.[83] By knowing thee one can avoid both death and rebirth. Thou art the highest object of knowledge. By knowing thee no higher object remains for one to know. Thou art the greatest object of acquisition. The person that is truly wise, by acquiring thee, thinks that there is no higher object to acquire. By attaining to thee that art exceedingly subtile and that art the highest object of acquisition, the man of wisdom becomes immortal and immutable. The followers of the Sankhya system, well conversant with their own philosophy and possessing a knowledge of the attributes (of Sattwa, Rajas and Tamas) and of those called the topics of enquiry,— those learned men who transcend the destructible by attaining to a knowledge of the subtile or indestructible—succeed, by knowing thee, in freeing themselves from all bonds. Persons conversant with the Vedas regard thee as the one object of knowledge, which has been expounded in the Vedantas. These men, devoted to the regulation of the breaths, always meditate on thee and at last enter into thee as their highest end. Riding on the car made of Om, those men enter into Maheswara. Of that which is called the Devayana (the path of the deities) thou art the door called Aditya. Thou art again, the

---

[81] The worlds or regions commonly enumerated are Bhu, Bhuva, Swa, Maha, Jana, Tapa, and Satya. The eight well-known forms of Mahadeva are Water, Fire, Hotri, Sun, Moon, Space, Earth and Wind. In his form of water he is called Bhava; in that of fire, he is called Rudra; in that of Hotri he is called Pasupati; in that of the Sun, he is called Isana; in that of the Moon, he is called Mahadeva; in that of Space, he is called Bhima; in that of Earth, he is called Sarva; and in that of wind, he is called Ugra. Compare the benediction in Kalidasa's Shakuntalam.

[82] The cave in which Mahadeva has been concealed is the cave of the Scriptures: probably, difficult texts.

[83] The sense is that these persons have not to make any extraordinary efforts for beholding thee. Their devotion is sufficient to induce thee to show thyself unto them.

door, called Chandramas, of that which is called the Pitriyana (the path of the Pitris).[84]
Thou art Kashtha, thou art the points of the horizon, thou art the year, and thou art the
Yugas. Thine is the sovereignty of the heavens, thine is the sovereignty of the Earth, thou
art the Northern and the Southern declensions. The Grandsire Brahma in days of yore
uttered thy praises, O thou that art called Nilarohita (blue and red), by reciting diverse
hymns and urged thee to create living creatures. Brahmanas conversant with Richs praise
thee by uttering Richs, regarding thee as unattached to all things and as divested of all
forms. Adhyaryus, in sacrifices, pour libations, uttering Yajushes the while, in honour of
thee that art the sole object of knowledge, according to the three well-known ways.[85]
Persons of cleansed understandings, that are conversant with Samans, sing thee with the
aid of Samans. Those regenerate persons, again, that are conversant with the Atharvans,
hymn thee as Rita, as Truth, as the Highest, and as Brahma. Thou art the highest cause,
whence Sacrifice has flowed. Thou art the Lord, and thou art Supreme. The night and day
are thy sense of hearing and sense of sight. The fortnights and months are thy head and
arms. The seasons are thy energy, penances are thy patience, and the year is thy anus,
thighs and feet. Thou art Mrityu, thou art Yama, thou art Hutasana, thou art Kala, thou art
endued with speed in respect of destruction, thou art the original cause of Time, and thou
art eternal Time. Thou art Chandramas and Aditya, with all the stars and planets and the
atmosphere that fills space. Thou art the pole-star, thou art constellation called the seven
Rishis, thou art the seven regions beginning with Bhu. Thou art Pradhana and Mahat,
thou art Unmanifest, and thou art this world. Thou art the universe beginning with
Brahman and ending with the lowest forms of vegetation. Thou art the beginning or
original cause of all creatures. Thou art the eight Prakritis.[86] Thou art, again, above the
eight Prakritis. Everything that exists, represents a portion of thy divine Self. Thou art
that supreme Felicity which is also Eternal. Thou art the end which is attained to by all
things. Thou art that highest existence which is sought for by the Righteous. Thou art that
state which is freed from every anxiety. Thou art eternal Brahman! Thou art that highest
state which constitutes the meditation of persons learned in the scriptures and the
Vedantas. Thou art the highest Kashtha, thou art the highest Kala. Thou art the highest
Success, and thou art the highest Refuge. Thou art the highest Tranquillity. Thou art the
highest cessation of Existence. By attaining to thee, Yogins think that they attain to the
highest success that is open to them. Thou art Contentment, thou art Success, thou art the
Sruti, and thou art the Smriti. Thou art that Refuge of the Soul after which Yogins strive,
and thou art that indestructible Prapti which men of Knowledge pursue. Thou art, without
doubt, that End which those persons have in view that are habituated to sacrifices and that
pour sacrificial libations, impelled by specific desires, and that make large presents on
such occasions. Thou art that high End which is sought for by persons that waste and
scorch their bodies with severe penances, with ceaseless recitations, with those rigid
vows and fasts that appertain to their tranquil lives, and with other means of self-
affliction. O Eternal one, thou art that End which is theirs that are unattached to all things
and that have relinquished all acts. Thou, O Eternal one, art that End which is theirs that
are desirous of achieving Emancipation from rebirth, that live in dissociation from all

[84] Devayana and Pitriyana are the two courses or paths by which the departed have to attain to their ends.
Those going by the former reach the Sun; while those that go by the latter reach the Moon.
[85] The first is that which is according to the rites inculcated in the Srutis; second is according to the
procedure laid down in the Smritis, and the third is the way or manner constituted by Dhyana or meditation.
[86] Vide Sankhya karika. With original Prakriti, the seven beginning with Mahat and Ahankara and
numbering the five Tanmatras.

enjoyments, and that desire the annihilation of the Prakriti elements. Thou art that high End, O illustrious one, which is indescribable, which is stainless, which is the immutable one, and which is theirs that are devoted to knowledge and science. These are the five Ends that have been declared in the Vedas and the Scriptures and the Puranas. It is through thy grace that persons attain to those Ends, or, if they fail to attain to them, it is through thy grace being denied to them."—It was thus Tandi, who was a vast heap of penances, praised Isana. And he sang also that high Brahman which in ancient days was sung by the Creator himself (in honour of Mahadeva).'

""Upamanyu continued, 'Thus praised by that utterer of Brahma, viz., Tandi, Mahadeva that illustrious and puissant Deity, who was accompanied by his spouse Uma, said these words. Tandi had further said,—"Neither Brahma, nor Indra, nor Vishnu, nor the Viswedevas, nor the great Rishis, know thee." Gratified at this, Siva said the following words.'

"""The holy one said, "Thou shalt be indestructible and eternal. Thou shalt be freed from all sorrow. Great fame shall be thine. Thou shalt be endued with energy. Spiritual knowledge shall be thine. All the Rishis shall seek thee, and thy son, through my grace, shall become the author of Sutras, O foremost of regenerate persons. What wishes of thine shall I grant today? Tell me, O son, what those objects are which thou desirest."— At this, Tandi joined his hands and said—"O Lord, let my devotion to thee be steady."'

""Upamanyu continued, 'Having given unto Tandi these boons and having received the adorations of both the deities and the Rishis, the great Deity disappeared there and then. When the illustrious deity, O lord of the Yadavas, thus disappeared with all his followers, the Rishi came to my asylum and said unto me all that had happened to him. Do thou hear, O foremost of men, all those celebrated names (of Mahadeva) that Tandi said unto me for thy spiritual success. The Grandsire had at one time recited ten thousand names that apply to Mahadeva. In the scriptures, a thousand names occur of that illustrious deity. These names are not known to all. O thou that transcendest destruction, in days of yore, the Grandsire Brahma uttered these names for adoring the high-souled Deity. Having acquired them through the grace of the Grandsire, Tandi communicated them to me!"""[87]

SECTION XVII.

"'Vasudeva said, "Concentrating his mind, O Yudhishthira, the regenerate Rishi Upamanyu, with hands joined together in reverence uttered this abstract of names (applying to Mahadeva), commencing from the beginning.

""Upamanyu said, 'I shall adore that great Deity who deserves the adorations of all creatures, by uttering those names that are celebrated over all the worlds,—names some of which were uttered by the Grandsire Brahma, some by the Rishis, and some of which occur in the Vedas and the Vedantas. Those names have been applied (unto the great Deity) by persons that are eminent. Those names of him that are, again, true and fraught with success and are capable of accomplishing all the purposes which the utterer may have in view, have been applied unto Mahadeva by Tandi after calling them from the

---

[87] Both the vernacular translators render the last verse most erroneously. K.P. Singha skips over every difficulty. In the Anusasana, this characteristic of his is more marked than in the Santi. The Burdwan translators very rarely skip over a verse, but they are very generally in the wrong. Nilakantha explains that Devesah is Brahma. The meaning, therefore, is that Tandi said unto me those secret names which Brahma had applied unto the high-souled one or Mahadeva. The Bengal reading Devesa, in the vocative, is incorrect.

Vedic lore with the aid of his devotion. Indeed, with those names that have been uttered by many well-known persons of righteousness and by ascetics conversant with all the spiritual principles, I shall adore him who is the foremost, who is the first, who leads to heaven, who is ready to confer benefits upon all creatures, and who is auspicious. Those names have been heard everywhere in the universe, having spread from the region of Brahma (where they were originally invented). All of them are fraught with the element of Truth. With those names I shall adore him who is Supreme Brahman, who has been declared (unto the universe) by the Vedas, and who is Eternal. I shall now tell thee, O chief of Bharata's race those names. Do thou hear them with rapt attention. Thou art a devoted worshipper of the Supreme Deity. Do thou worship the illustrious Bhava, distinguishing him above all the deities. And because thou art devoted to him, I shall therefore, recite those names in thy hearing. Mahadeva is Eternal Brahman. Persons endued with Yoga and Yoga's achievements are unable to know in even a hundred years, the glory and puissance of the great Deity in their entirety. Verily, the beginning, middle or end of Mahadeva cannot be apprehended by the very deities. Indeed, when the case is such, who is there O Madhava, that can recite the attributes of Mahadeva in their entirety? For all that, I shall through the grace of that illustrious and supreme Deity of perfect wisdom, extended to me for my devotion to him, recite his attributes as embodied in an abstract of few words and letters. The Supreme Lord is incapable of being adored by any one if he does not grant his permission to the adorer. As regards myself, it is only when I become fortunate enough to receive his permission that I succeed in adoring him. I shall indicate only a few names of that great Deity who is without birth and without destruction, who is the original cause of the universe, who is endued with the highest Soul, and whose origin is unmanifest. Hear, O Krishna, a few names, that were uttered by Brahma himself, of that giver of boons, that adorable deity, that puissant one who has the universe for his form, and who is possessed of supreme wisdom. These names that I shall recite are extracted from the ten thousand names that the great Grandsire had uttered in days of yore, as ghee is extracted from curds. As gold represents the essence of rocky mountains, as honey represents the essence of flowers, as Manda represents the extract from ghee, even so have these names been extracted from and represent the essence of those ten thousand names that were uttered by Grandsire Brahma. This abstract of names is capable of cleansing every sin, however heinous. It possesses the same merit that is attached to the four Vedas. It should be comprehended with attention by spiritual aspirants and engraved on the memory. These names fraught with auspiciousness, leading to advancement, destructive of Rakshasas,[88] and great cleansers should be imparted to only him that is devoted to the great Lord, to him that has faith, to him that believes. Unto him that has no faith, him that is an unbeliever, him that has not subjugated his soul, it should never be communicated. That creature, O Krishna, who cherishes malice towards the illustrious Mahadeva who is the original cause of everything, who is the Supreme Soul, and who is the great Lord, has certainly to go to hell with all his ancestors before and all his children after him. This abstract of names that I shall recite to thee is looked upon as Yoga.[89] This is looked upon as the highest object of meditation. This is that which one should constantly recite as Japya. This is equivalent to Knowledge. This is the highest Mystery. If one, even during his last moments, recites it or hears it recited unto him, one succeeds in attaining to the highest end. This is holy. This is auspicious, this is

---

[88] i.e., if recited, it destroys all fear or Rakshasas, for these either fly away at its sound or are even killed.
[89] i.e., it has the merit that is attached to either Meditation or Yoga.

68

fraught with every kind of benefit. This is the best of all things. Brahma, the Grandsire of all the universe, having in days of old composed it, assigned to it the foremost place among all excellent hymns. From that time, this hymn to the greatness and glory of the high-souled Mahadeva, which is held in the highest esteem by all the deities, has come to be regarded as the king of all hymns. This king of all hymns was first conveyed from the region of Brahman to heaven, the region of the celestials. Tandi then obtained it from heaven. Hence is it known as the hymn composed by Tandi. From heaven Tandi brought it down on Earth. It is the most auspicious of all auspicious things, and is capable of cleansing the heart from all sins however heinous. O thou of mighty arms, I shall recite to thee that best of all hymns. "This hymn relates to him who is the Veda of the Vedas, and the most ancient of all ancient objects, to him who is the energy of all energies, and the penance of all penances; to him who is the most tranquil of all creatures endued with tranquillity, and who is the splendour of all splendours; to him who is looked upon as the most restrained of all creatures that are restrained, and him who is the intelligence of all creatures endued with intelligence; to him who is looked upon as the deity of all deities, and the Rishi of all Rishis; to him who is regarded as the sacrifice of all sacrifices and the most auspicious of all things fraught with auspiciousness; to him who is the Rudra of all Rudras and the effulgence of all things endued with effulgence; to him who is the Yogin of all Yogins, and the cause of all causes; to him from whom all the worlds start into existence, and unto whom all the worlds return when they cease to exist; to him who is the Soul of all existent creatures, and who is called Hara of immeasurable energy. Hear me recite those thousand and eight names of the great Sarva. Hearing those names, O foremost of all men, thou shalt be crowned with fruition in respect of all thy wishes,— Om! thou art Immobile, thou art Fixed, thou art Puissant, thou art Terrible, thou art Foremost, thou art boon-giving, and thou art Superior.[90] Thou art the Soul of all creatures, thou art celebrated over all creatures, thou art all things, thou art the Creator of all, and thou art Bhava.[91] Thou art the bearer of matted locks on thy head. Thou wearest animal skins for thy vestments. Thou wearest a crest of matted hair on thy head like the peacock. Thou art he who has the whole universe for thy limbs.[92] Thou art the Creator of all things. Thou art Hara in consequence of thy being the destroyer of all things. Thou art he that has eyes resembling those of the gazelle. Thou art the destroyer of all creatures. Thou art the supreme enjoyer of all things. Thou art that Pravritti whence all actions flow. Thou art that Nivritti or abstention from acts. Thou art observant of fasts and vows, thou art Eternal, thou art Unchangeable. Thou art he that residest in crematoria, thou art the possessor of the six well-known attributes of Lordship and the rest, thou residest in the heart of every creature, thou art he that enjoys all things with the senses, thou art the grinder of all sinful creatures.[93] Thou art he that deserves the salutations of all, thou art of

[90] Both Sthira and Sthanu imply immutability or freedom from change.
[91] The commentator explains that Bhava is here used in the sense of that from which all things now and into which all things merge when the universal dissolution comes. Or, it may imply, mere existence, without reference, that is, to any attribute by which it is capable of being described or comprehended.
[92] i.e., Virat or vast or Infinite.
[93] The task of rendering these names is exceedingly difficult. In the original, many of these names are such that they are capable of more than one interpretation. The commentator often suggests more than one meaning. Each name would require a separate note for explaining all its bearings. Niyata is literally one who is observant of fasts and vows and who has restrained his senses. Hence it means an ascetic. Mahadeva is an ascetic. Smasanu is either a crematorium, the place where dead creatures lie down, or, it may mean Varanasi, the sacred city of Siva, where creatures dying have not to take rebirth. Siva is both a resident of crematoria and of Varanasi.

great feats, thou art he that has penances for his wealth, thou createst all the elements at thy will, thou concealest thy real nature by putting on the guise of a lunatic. Thou art the Master of all the worlds and of all living creatures. Thou art of immeasurable form, thou art of vast body, thou art of the form of Righteousness, thou art of great fame, thou art of high Soul, thou art the Soul of all creatures, thou hast the universe for thy form.[94] Thou art of vast jaws (for thou swallowest the universe when the time comes for the dissolution of all things). Thou art the protector of all the lokas (the worlds). Thou art the soul residing in the inner heart and as such devoid of ahamkara originating from ignorance[95] and is one and undivided; Thou art anandam (gladness). Thou art he whose car is borne by mules. Thou art he that protects Jiva from the thunderbolt of rebirth. Thou art adorable. Thou art obtained by purity and self-restraint and vows. Thou art again the refuge of all kinds of vows and observances including purity and self-restraint.[96] Thou art the celestial artificer that is conversant with every art. Thou art Self-create (for no one has created thee). Thou art the beginning of all creatures and things. Thou art Hiranyagarbha, the Creator of all things. Thou art inexhaustible puissance and felicity.[97] Thou hast a hundred eyes, thou hast eyes of vast power. Thou art Soma.[98] Thou art he that causest all righteous creatures assume shapes of glory for shining in the firmament. Thou art Chandramas, thou art Surya, thou art the planet Saturn, thou art the descending node (of the moon), thou art the ascending node, thou art Mangala (Mars), and thou art Vrihaspati (Jupiter) and Sukra (Venus), thou art Vudha (Mercury) thou art the worshipper of Atri's wife, thou art he who shot his shaft in wrath at Sacrifice when Sacrifice fled away from him in the form of a deer. Thou art sinless.[99] Thou art possessed of penances that have conferred upon thee the power of creating the universe. Thou art possessed of penances that have rendered thee capable of destroying the universe. Thou art high minded (in consequence of thy great liberality towards thy devotees). Thou fulfillest the wishes of all who resign themselves to thee. Thou art the maker of the year (for it is thou who settest the wheel of Time revolving, by assuming the form of the sun and the planets). Thou art Mantra (in the form of Pranava and other sacred words and syllables). Thou art the authority for all acts (in the form of the Vedas and the scriptures). Thou art the highest Penance. Thou art devoted to Yoga. Thou art he who merges himself in Brahman (by Yoga-abstraction). Thou art the great seed (being the cause of causes). Thou art the displayer of what is unmanifest in the manifest form in which the universe exists. Thou

---

[94] Or, the universe is displayed in thee.

[95] Probably, what is said here is that Mahadeva is the Pratyag Soul free from ignorance.

[96] By Niyama is meant purity both internal and external, contentedness, with whatever is got, penances, Vedic studies, meditation on the Deity, etc.

[97] Nidhi implies the largest number that can be named in Arithmetical notation. Hence, it implies, as the commentator correctly explains, the possessor of inexhaustible felicity and gladness.

[98] Sahasraksha is either Indra or possessor of innumerable eyes in consequence of Mahadeva's being identical with the universe. Visalaksha is one whose eyes are of vast power, because the Past and the Future are seen by them even as the Present. Soma implies either the Moon or the juice of the Soma i.e. the libations poured in the sacrificial fire. All righteous persons, again, become luminaries in the firmament. It is Mahadeva that makes them so i.e., he is the giver of glorious forms to those that deserve them.

[99] Many of these names require comments to be intelligible. Ketu is no plant but Hindu astronomers name the descending node of the Moon by that name. Hence Rahu is the ascending node of the Moon. Graha, is that which seizes; Grahapati is Mangala, so called for its malevolence, Varah is Vrihaspati or Jupiter, who is the counterself of Sukra or Venus. In Hindu mythology, Sukra is a male person, the preceptor of the Daityas and Asuras. Atri is Vudha or Mercury, represented as the sons of Atri. Atryahnamaskarta is Durvasas who was the son of Atri's wife, got by the lady through a boon of Mahadeva. Daksha's Sacrifice sought to fly away from Siva, but the latter pursued it and shot his arrow at it for destroying it downright.

art possessed of infinite might. Thou art he whose seed is gold.[100] Thou art omniscient, (being as thou art all things and the great knower). Thou art the cause of all things. Thou art he that has the seed of action (viz., ignorance and desire) for the means of sojourning from this world to the other and the other to this.[101] Thou hast ten arms. Thou hast winkless eyes (for thou seest at all times). Thou hast a blue throat (in consequence of thy bearing in thy throat the poison that arose upon churning the ocean and which, if not so borne, was capable of destroying the universe). Thou art the Lord of Uma. Thou art the origin of all the infinite forms that occur in the universe. Thou art he whose superiority is due to thyself. Thou art a hero in might (in consequence of thy having achieved such grand feats as the quick destruction of the triple city of the Asuras). Thou art inert matter (which cannot move unless co-existing with the Soul). Thou art all the tattwas (subjects of enquiry as counted by the Sankhyas). Thou art the ordainer and ruler of the tattwas. Thou art the chief of those beings that wait upon thee and are called Ganas.[102] Thou coverest infinite space.[103] Thou art Kama, the God of Desire. Thou art conversant with Mantras (in the sense of knowledge being thy penance).[104] Thou art the highest Mantra for thou art that philosophy which consists in the ascertainment of the nature and attributes of the soul (and its differences from the Non-soul). Thou art the cause of the universe (since all that exists has sprung from thy Soul). Thou art universal destroyer (for all that ceases to exist becomes merged unto thee who art as the unmanifest Brahman). Thou bearest in one of thy hands the calabash, and in another thou holdest the bow; in another hand thou bearest shafts and in another thou bearest a skull. Thou bearest the thunder-bolt. Thou art armed with the hundred-killer.[105] Thou art armed with the sword. Thou wieldest the battle-axe. Thou art armed with the Sula (trident). Thou art adorable. Thou host the sacrificial ladle in one of thy hands. Thou art of beautiful form. Thou art endued with abundant energy. Thou givest in the most liberal measure all that tends to adorn those that are devoted to thee. Thou wearest a turban on thy head. Thou art of beautiful face. Thou art he who swells with splendour and puissance. Thou art he that is humble and modest. Thou art exceedingly tall. Thou art he who has the senses for thy rays.[106] Thou art the greatest of preceptors. Thou art Supreme Brahman (being a state of pure felicitous existence).[107] Thou art he that took the shape of a jackal (for consoling the

---

[100] Suvarna-retas is explained by the commentator as follows: At first he created water and then cast his seed into it. That seed became a golden egg. It may also mean that Mahadeva is Agni or the deity of fire, for gold represents the seed of Agni.

[101] The sense is this: Jiva carries that seed of acts, i.e., Ignorance and Desire, with him. In consequence of this seed, Jiva travels from one world into another ceaselessly. This seed, therefore, is the conveyance or the means of locomotion of Jiva. Mahadeva is Jiva. The soul is called the rider, and the body is the car that bears the Soul on it.

[102] Ganapati is Ganesa, the eldest son of Mahadeva. The Ganas are mighty beings that wait upon Mahadeva. This make up the first hundred names. The commentator takes Avala and Gana together.

[103] Digvasas means nude. The Puranas say that for stupefying the wives of certain ascetics, Mahadeva became nude on one occasion. The real meaning, however, is that he is capable of covering and does actually cover even infinite space. In the sense of nude, the word means one that has empty space for his cover or vestments.

[104] The meaning is that with thee Knowledge is penance instead of actual physical austerities being so. This is only another way of saying that thou hast Jnanamayam Tapah.

[105] Sataghni a killer of hundred; Wilson thinks it was a kind of rocket.

[106] Harikesa means one having the senses for one's rays, i.e., one who displays all objects before the soul through the doors of the senses. The meaning is that Mahadeva is he through whose puissance the mind succeeds in acquiring knowledge through the senses.

[107] Krishna is explained by the commentator thus. Krish is a word signifying Bhu or Existence. The letter n (the palatal one) signifies nivritti. Hence Krishna is anandatanmatra.

Brahmana who, when insulted by a wealthy Vaisya, had resolved to commit suicide). Thou art he whose objects are all crowned with fruition, of themselves and without waiting for the puissance (derivable from penances). Thou art one who bears a bald head (as the sign of the mendicant order). Thou art one who does good to all creatures. Thou art unborn. Thou hast innumerable forms. Thou bearest all kinds of fragrance on thy person. The matted locks on thy head had sucked up the river Ganga when it first fell from heaven (although they again gave out the waters at the earnest solicitations of king Bhagiratha). Thou art the giver of sovereignty and lordship.[108] Thou art a Brahmacharin without having ever fallen away from the rigid vow of continence. Thou art distinguished for thy sexual continence. Thou always liest on thy back. Thou hast thy abode in Puissance.[109] Thou hast three matted locks on thy head. Thou art he that is clad in rags. Thou art Rudra (in consequence of thy fierceness). Thou art the celestial generalissimo, and thou art all pervading. Thou art he that moves about during the day. Thou art he that moves about in the night.[110] Thou art of fierce wrath. Thou art possessed of dazzling effulgence (born of Vedic study and penances). Thou art the slayer of the mighty Asura who had come in the form of an infuriate elephant for destroying thy sacred city of Varanasi. Thou art the slayer of such Daityas as become the oppressors of the universe. Thou art Kala or Time which is the universal destroyer. Thou art the supreme ordainer of the universe. Thou art a mine of excellent accomplishments. Thou art of the form of the lion and the tiger. Thou art he that is clad in the skin of an elephant. Thou art the Yogin who deceives Time by transcending its irresistible influence. Thou art the original sound.[111] Thou art the fruition of all desires. Thou art he that is adored in four ways.[112] Thou art a night-wanderer (like Vetala and others). Thou art he that wanders in the company of spirits. Thou art he that wanders in the company of ghostly beings. Thou art the Supreme Lord of even Indra and the other celestials. Thou art he that hast multiplied himself infinitely in the form of all existent and non-existent things. Thou art the upholder of both Mahat and all the innumerable combinations of the five primal elements. Thou art the primeval Ignorance or Tamas that is known by the name of Rahu. Thou art without measure and hence infinite. Thou art the supreme End that is attained by the Emancipate. Thou art fond of dancing. Thou art he that is always engaged in dancing. Thou art he that causes others to dance. Thou art the friend of the universe. Thou art he whose aspect is calm and mild. Thou art endued with penances puissant enough to create and destroy the universe. Thou art he who binds all creatures with the bonds of thy illusion. Thou art he that transcends destruction. Thou art he who dwells on the mount Kailasa. Thou transcendest all bonds and art unattached in respect of all things, like Space. Thou art possessed of a thousand arms. Thou art victory. Thou art that perseverance which is the cause of success or victory. Thou art without idleness or

---

[108] Kaparddin is thus explained by the commentator Kam Jalam pivati iti kapah. So called because of the incident noted in the text, for the matted locks of Mahadeva had sucked up the river Ganga when it first fell from heaven. Then Rit means sovereignty or lordship. Riddah is one that gives sovereignty. Combining the two, the compound Kaparddin is formed.

[109] Nabhah means space which implies puissance. That Nabhah is the sthala or abode of Mahadeva. The Bengal texts which read Nabhastala are vicious.

[110] The deities are said to move about during the day, while the Asuras and Rakshasas during the night. What is said, therefore, here is that thou art the deities and thou art their foes of the Daityas and others.

[111] Sound, only when manifested, becomes perceptible. When unmanifest and lying in the womb of eternal space, it is believed to have an existence. Unmanifest Brahman is frequently represented as anahatah savdah or unstruck sound.

[112] These four ways are as enumerated by commentator, Visva, Taijasa, Prajna, Sivadhyana.

procrastination that interferes with persevering activity. Thou art dauntless. Thou art fear. Thou art he who put a stop to Vali's sacrifice.[113] Thou fulfillest the desires of all thy devotees. Thou art the destroyer of Daksha's sacrifice. Thou art amiable. Thou art slightly amiable. Thou art exceedingly fierce and robbest all creatures of their energy. Thou art the slayer of the Asura Vala. Thou art always cheerful. Thou art of the form of wealth which is coveted by all. Thou hast never been vanquished.[114] There is none more adorable than thou. Thou art he who utters deep roars (in the form of Ocean). Thou art that which is so deep that no one can measure it (because thou art of the form of space). Thou art he whose puissance and the might of whose companions and of the bull have never been measured by anybody. Thou art the tree of the world (whose roots extend upwards and branches hang downwards). Thou art the banian.[115] Thou art he that sleeps on a human leaf when the universe, after dissolution, becomes one infinite expanse of water. Thou art he that shows compassion to all worshippers assuming as thou listest, the form of Hari or Hara or Ganesa or Arka or Agni or Wind, etc. Thou art possessed of teeth that are exceedingly sharp (since thou art competent to chew innumerable worlds even as one munches nuts and swallows them speedily). Thou art of vast dimensions in respect of thy forms. Thou art possessed of a mouth that is vast enough to swallow the universe at once. Thou art he whose troops are adored everywhere.[116] Thou art he who dispelled all the fears of the deities when the prince of elephants had to be captured. Thou art the seed of the universe. Thou art he who has for his vehicle the same bull that forms again the device on his banner in battle. Thou hast Agni for thy soul. Thou art Surya who has green steeds yoked unto his car. Thou art the friend of Jiva. Thou art he that is conversant with the proper time for the accomplishment of all religious acts. Thou art he unto whom Vishnu paid his adorations (for obtaining his celebrated discus). Thou art the sacrifice being in the form of Vishnu. Thou art the ocean. Thou art the Barabanala Mare's head that ranges within the ocean, ceaselessly vomitting fire and drinking the saline waters as if they were sacrificial butter. Thou art Wind, the friend of Agni. Thou art of tranquil soul like the ocean when at rest and unstirred by the mildest breeze. Thou art Agni that drinks the libations of clarified butter poured in sacrifices with the aid of Mantras. Thou art he whom it is difficult to approach. Thou art he whose effulgence spreads over the infinite universe. Thou art ever skilful in battle. Thou art well conversant with the time when one should engage in battle so that victory may be achieved. Thou art that science which treats of the motions of heavenly bodies.[117] Thou art of the form of success or victory. Thou art he whose body is Time (for thy body is never subject to destruction). Thou art a householder for thou wearest a tuft of hair on thy head. Thou art a Sanyasin for thy head is bald. Thou wearest matted locks on thy head (being, as thou art, a Vanaprastha).[118] Thou art distinguished for thy fiery rays (for the effulgent path by which the righteous

---

[113] It may also mean that thou art he called Buddha who preached against all sacrifices.

[114] The commentator explains that Mahadeva's defeat at the hands of Krishna in the city of Vana was due to Mahadeva's kindness for Krishna, even as Krishna broke his own vow of never taking up arms in the battle of Kurukshetra, for honouring his worshipper Bhishma who had vowed that he would compel Krishna to take up arms.

[115] The sense is this: when the universal destruction comes and all becomes a mighty expanse of water, there appears a banian tree under whose shade the immortal Rishi Markandeya sees a boy who is Mahavishnu.

[116] It may also mean that thou art he at whose approach all the Daitya troops fled in all directions.

[117] i.e., thou art Time itself. This is the implication.

[118] By these three names what is indicated is that Mahadeva is a householder, a Sanyasin and a forest-recluse. House-holders bear a tuft of hair on their heads, Sanyasins have bald heads, while forest recluses or Vanaprasthis have matted locks.

proceed is identical with thee). Thou art he that appears in the firmament in the heart encased in the body of every creature.[119] Thou art he who enters into the cranium (brain) of every creature. Thou bearest the wrinkles of age. Thou bearest the bamboo flute. Thou hast also the tabour. Thou bearest the musical instrument called Tali. Thou hast the wooden vessel used for husking grain. Thou art he who covers that illusion which covers Yama.[120] Thou art an astrologer inasmuch as thy understanding is always directed towards the motion of the wheel of time which is made up of the luminaries in the firmament. Thou art Jiva whose understanding is directed to things that are the result of the attributes of Sattwa, Rajas, and Tamas. Thou art that in which all things merge when dissolution overtakes them. Thou art stable and fixed, there being nothing in thee that is subject to change or mutation of any kind. Thou art the Lord of all creatures. Thy arms extend all over the vast universe. Thou art displayed in innumerable forms that are but fractions of thyself. Thou pervadest all things.[121] Thou art he that has no mouth (for thou enjoyest not the objects of thy own creation). Thou art he who frees thy creatures from the bonds of the world. Thou art easily attainable.[122] Thou art he that manifested himself with a golden mail.[123] Thou art he that appears in the phallic emblem. Thou art he that wanders in the forests in quest of fowls and animals. Thou art he that wanders over the Earth. Thou art he that is omnipresent. Thou art the blare that is produced by all the trumpets blown in the three worlds. Thou art he that has all creatures for his relatives.[124] Thou art of the form of a snake (for thou art identical with the mighty Naga named Sesha). Thou art he that lives in mountain caves (like Jaigishavya), or any other Yogin. Thou art identical with Guha (the celestial generalissimo). Thou wearest garlands of flowers. Thou art he who enjoys the happiness that springs from the possession of worldly objects.[125] Thou art he from whom all creatures have derived their three states of birth, existence, and destruction. Thou art he that upholds all things that exist or occur in the three stages of time viz., the Past, the Present, and the Future. Thou art he that frees creatures from the effects of all acts belonging to previous lives as well as those accomplished in the present life and from all the bonds due to Ignorance and Desire. Thou art he who is the binder of Asura chiefs. Thou art he who is the slayer of foes in battle.[126] Thou art that which is attainable by knowledge alone. Thou art Durvasas. Thou art he who is waited upon and adored by all the righteous. Thou art he who causes the fall of even Brahma and the others. Thou art he that gives unto all creatures the just share of joy and grief that each deserves according to his own acts. Thou art he that is

---

[119] The sense is that Brahman is felt by every one in the firmament of his own heart. Mahadeva, as identical with Brahman is displayed in the heart that is within the physical case. Hence, he may be said to take birth or appear in his effulgence within every one's body.

[120] Kalakatankatah is explained by the commentator as follows:—Kala is Yama. He is covered over with the illusion of the Supreme Deity. This all covering illusion, again, has the Supreme Deity for its cover. Thou art that Supreme Deity.

[121] Vibhaga and Sarvaga, the commentator explains, are used for indicating that thou art the universe as Vyashti and Samashti.

[122] Some editions read susaranab, meaning thou art he who well protects the universe.

[123] The golden mail being the illusion of the Supreme Deity in consequence of which the universe has become displayed.

[124] Thou art Pasupati; atodyah pratodanarhah pasavah yasya iti.

[125] The commentator explains that Tarangavit, which is literally conversant with waves means one that is acquainted with the joys or pleasures that arise from the possession or enjoyment of worldly things, for such joys may truly be likened to waves which appear and disappear on the bosom of the sea or ocean of Eternity.

[126] The commentator explains that the binder of Asura chiefs refers to the Supreme Deity's form of Vishnu in which he had bound Vali, the chief of the Asuras. The plural form has reference to successive Kalpas.

74

incomparable. Thou art well conversant with the shares that are given and appropriated in sacrifices.[127] Thou residest in every place. Thou wanderest everywhere. Thou art he that has mean vestments.[128] Thou art Vasava. Thou art immortal. Thou art identical with the Himavat mountains. Thou art the maker of pure gold. Thou art without acts. Thou upholdest in thyself the fruits of all acts. Thou art the foremost of all creatures that are regarded as upholders.[129] Thou art he that has bloody eyes. Thou art he that has eyes whose vision extends over the infinite universe. Thou art he that has a car whose wheels are ever victorious. Thou art he that is possessed of vast learning. Thou art he that accepts thy devotees for thy servants. Thou art he that restrains and subjugates thy senses. Thou art he that acts. Thou wearest clothes whose warp and woof are made of snakes. Thou art Supreme. Thou art he who is the lowest of the celestials.[130] Thou art he that is well-grown. Thou ownest the musical instrument called Kahala. Thou art the giver of every wish. Thou art the embodiment of grace in all the three stages of Time, viz., the Past, the Present, and the Future. Thou art possessed of might that is always well spent. Thou art he who had assumed the form of Valarama (the elder brother of Krishna). Thou art the foremost of all collected things, being Emancipation or the highest of all ends to which creatures attain. Thou art the giver of all things. Thy face is turned towards all directions. Thou art he from whom diverse creatures have sprung even as all forms have sprung from space or are modifications of that primal element. Thou art he who falls into the pit called body.[131] Thou art he that is helpless (for, falling into the pit constituted by the body, thou canst not transcend the sorrow that is thy portion). Thou residest in the firmament of the heart. Thou art exceedingly fierce in form. Thou art the Deity called Ansu. Thou art the companion of Ansu and art called Aditya. Thou art possessed of innumerable rays. Thou art endued with dazzling effulgence. Thou hast the speed of the Wind.[132] Thou art possessed of speed that is greater than that of the Wind. Thou art possessed of the speed of the mind. Thou art Nishachara as thou enjoyest all things, being invested with Ignorance.[133] Thou dwellest in every body. Thou dwellest with Prosperity as thy companion. Thou art he that imparts knowledge and instruction. Thou art he who imparts instruction in utter silence. Thou art he that observes the vow of taciturnity (for thou instructest in silence). Thou art he who passes out of the body, looking at the soul.[134] Thou art he that is well adored. Thou art the giver of thousands (since the lord of all the treasures derived those treasures of his from thee). Thou art the prince of birds, (being Garuda the son of Vinata and Kasyapa). Thou art the friend that renders aid. Thou art possessed of exceeding effulgence (for thy splendour is like that of a million suns risen together). Thou art the Master of all created beings. Thou art he who provokes the appetites. Thou art the deity of Desire. Thou art of the form of lovely women that are coveted by all. Thou art the tree of the world. Thou art the Lord of Treasures. Thou art

[127] The sense is that thou art he that is well conversant with the ritual of sacrifices.
[128] Or, it may mean that thou art he that has no vestments, for no vestments can cover thy vast limbs.
[129] Those that uphold others are, for example, the elephants that stand at the different points of the compass, the snake Sesha, etc. What is said here is that thou art the best of all these or all such beings.
[130] The sense is that thou art Vishnu who is the foremost of the celestials and thou art Agni who is the lowest of the celestials; i.e., thou art all the celestials.
[131] The body is as it were a pit into which the soul falls, determined by Desire and Ignorance.
[132] Vasu, the commentator explains, indicates the Wind, for it means that which establishes all things into itself.
[133] Nisachara is one acting through nisa, or Avidya, i.e., one who enjoys all objects, implying Jiva invested with Ignorance.
[134] The Soul can view the Soul or itself, if it can transcend the body with the aid of Yoga.

the giver of fame. Thou art the Deity that distributes unto all creatures the fruits (in the form of joys and griefs) of their acts. Thou art thyself those fruits which thou distributest. Thou art the most ancient (having existed from a time when there was no other existent thing). Thou art competent to cover with a single footstep of thine all the three worlds. Thou art Vamana (the dwarf) who deceived the Asura chief Vali (and depriving him of his sovereignty restored it unto Indra). Thou art the Yogin crowned with success (like Sanatkumara and others). Thou art a great Rishi (like Vasishtha and others). Thou art one whose objects are always crowned with success (like Rishava or Dattatreya). Thou art a Sanyasin (like Yajnavalkya and others). Thou art he that is adorned with the marks of the mendicant order. Thou art he that is without such marks.[135] Thou art he that transcends the usages of the mendicant order. Thou art he that assures all creatures from every sort of fear. Thou art without any passions thyself (so that glory and humiliation are alike to thee). Thou art he that is called the celestial generalissimo. Thou art that Visakha who took his rise from the body of the celestial generalissimo when Indra hurled his thunder-bolt at him. Thou art conversant with the sixty tattwas or heads of enquiry in the universe. Thou art the Lord of the senses (for these achieve their respective functions guided by thee). Thou art he that is armed with the thunder-bolt (and that rives the mountains). Thou art infinite. Thou art the stupefier of Daitya ranks in the field of battle. Thou art he that moves his car in circles among his own ranks and that makes similar circles among the ranks of his foes and who comes back safe and sound after devastating them. Thou art he that is conversant with the lowest depth of the world's ocean (in consequence of thy knowledge of Brahman). Thou art he called Madhu (who has founded the race in which Krishna has taken his birth). Thou hast eyes whose colour resembles that of honey. Thou art he that has taken birth after Vrihaspati.[136] Thou art he that does the acts which Adhyaryus have to do in sacrifices. Thou art he who is always adored by persons whatever their modes of life. Thou art devoted to Brahman. Thou wanderest amongst the habitations of men in the world (in consequence of thy being a mendicant). Thou art he that pervadest all beings. Thou art he that is conversant with truth. Thou knowest and guidest every heart. Thou art he that overspreads the whole universe. Thou art he that collects or stores the good and bad acts of all creatures in order to award them the fruits thereof. Thou art he that lives during even the night that follows the universal dissolution. Thou art the protector wielding the bow called Pinaka. Thou residest in even the Daityas that are the marks at which shootest thy arrows. Thou art the author of prosperity. Thou art the mighty ape Hanuman that aided Vishnu in the incarnation of Rama in his expedition against Ravana. Thou art the lord of those Ganas that are thy associates. Thou art each member of those diverse Ganas. Thou art he that gladdens all creatures. Thou art the enhancer of the joys of all.[137] Thou takest away the sovereignty and prosperity of even such high beings as Indra and others. Thou art the universal slayer in the form of Death. Thou art he that resides in the four and sixty Kalas. Thou art very great. Thou art the Grandsire (being the sire of the great sire of all). Thou art the supreme phallic emblem that is adored by both deities and Asuras. Thou art of agreeable and beautiful features. Thou art he who presides over the variety of evidences and tendencies for action

---

[135] The commentator explains that the first word means that thou art Hansa and that the second word means thou art Paramahansa.

[136] Varhaspatya is a word that is applied to a priest. The deities first got their priest for assisting them at their sacrifices. Human beings then got theirs. Those born after Vrihaspati are Vrihaspatyas.

[137] This word Nandivardhanah may also mean he that withdraws or takes away the joys previously conferred.

and non-action. Thou art the lord of vision. Thou art the Lord of Yoga (in consequence of thy withdrawing all the senses into the heart and combining them together in that place). Thou art he that upholds the Krita and the other ages (by causing them to run ceaselessly). Thou art the Lord of seeds (in consequence of thy being the giver of the fruits of all acts good and bad). Thou art the original cause of such seeds. Thou actest in the ways that have been pointed out in the scriptures beginning with those that treat of the Soul. Thou art he in whom reside might and the other attributes. Thou art the Mahabharata and other histories of the kind. Thou art the treatises called Mimansa. Thou art Gautama (the founder of the science of dialectics). Thou art the author of the great treatise on Grammar that has been named after the Moon. Thou art he who chastises his foes. Thou art he whom none can chastise. Thou art he who is sincere in respect of all his religious acts and observances. Thou art he that becomes obedient to those that are devoted to thee. Thou art he that is capable of reducing others to subjection. Thou art he who foments quarrels among the deities and the Asuras. Thou art he who has created the four and ten worlds (beginning with Bhu). Thou art the protector and cherisher of all Beings commencing from Brahma and ending with the lowest forms of vegetable life (like grass and straw). Thou art the Creator of even the five original elements. Thou art he that never enjoys anything (for thou art always unattached). Thou art free from deterioration. Thou art the highest form of felicity. Thou art a deity proud of his might. Thou art Sakra. Thou art the chastisement that is spoken of in treatises on morality and is inflicted on offenders. Thou art of the form of that tyranny which prevails over the world. Thou art of pure Soul. Thou art stainless (being above faults of every kind). Thou art worthy of adoration. Thou art the world that appears and disappears ceaselessly. Thou art he whose grace is of the largest measure. Thou art he that has good dreams. Thou art a mirror in which the universe is reflected. Thou art he that has subjugated all internal and external foes. Thou art the maker of the Vedas. Thou art the maker of those declarations that are contained in the Tantras and the Puranas and that are embodied in language that is human.[138] Thou art possessed of great learning. Thou art the grinder of foes in battle. Thou art he that resides in the awful clouds that appear at the time of the universal dissolution. Thou art most terrible (in consequence of the dissolution of the universe that thou bringest about). Thou art he who succeeds in bringing all persons and all things into thy subjection. Thou art the great Destroyer. Thou art he that has fire for his energy. Thou art he whose energy is mightier than fire. Thou art the Yuga-fire that consumes all things. Thou art he that is capable of being gratified by means of sacrificial libations. Thou art water and other liquids that are poured in sacrifices with the aid of Mantras. Thou art in the form of the Deity of Righteousness, the distributor of the fruits that attach to acts good and bad. Thou art the giver of felicity. Thou art always endued with effulgence. Thou art of the form of fire. Thou art of the complexion of the emerald. Thou art always present in the phallic emblem. Thou art the source of blessedness. Thou art incapable of being baffled by anything in the prosecution of your objects. Thou art the giver of blessings. Thou art of the form of blessedness. Thou art he unto whom is given a share of sacrificial offerings. Thou art he who distributes unto each his share of that is offered in sacrifices. Thou art endued with great speed. Thou art he that is dissociated from all things. Thou art he that is possessed of the mightiest limb. Thou art he that is employed in the act of generation. Thou art of a dark complexion, (being of the form of Vishnu). Thou art of a white complexion (being of the form of Samva, the son of Krishna). Thou

---

[138] The language of the Veda is divine. That of the scriptures is human.

art the senses of all embodied creatures. Thou art possessed of vast feet. Thou hast vast hands. Thou art of vast body. Thou art endued with wide extending fame. Thou hast a vast head.[139] Thou art of vast measurements. Thou art of vast vision. Thou art the home of the darkness of ignorance. Thou art the Destroyer of the Destroyer. Thou art possessed of vast years. Thou hast vast lips. Thou art he that has vast cheeks. Thou hast a vast nose. Thou art of a vast throat. Thou hast a vast neck. Thou art he that tears the bond of body.[140] Thou hast a vast chest. Thou hast a vast bosom. Thou art the inner soul which resides in all creatures. Thou hast a deer on thy lap. Thou art he from whom innumerable worlds hang down like fruits hanging down from a tree. Thou art he who stretches his lips at the time of the universal dissolution for swallowing the universe. Thou art the ocean of milk. Thou hast vast teeth. Thou hast vast jaws. Thou hast a vast bristle.[141] Thou hast hair of infinite length. Thou hast a vast stomach. Thou hast matted locks of vast length. Thou art ever cheerful. Thou art of the form of grace. Thou art of the form of belief. Thou art he that has mountains for his bow (or weapons in battle). Thou art he that is full of affection to all creatures like a parent towards his offspring. Thou art he that has no affection. Thou art unvanquished. Thou art exceedingly devoted to (Yoga) contemplation.[142] Thou art of the form of the tree of the world.[143] Thou art he that is indicated by the tree of the world.[144] Thou art never satiated when eating (because of thy being of the form of fire, for of all elements, fire is never satiated with the quantity offered it for consumption). Thou art he that has the Wind for thy vehicle for going from place to place (in consequence of thy identity with fire). Thou art he that rangest over hills and little eminences. Thou art he that has his residence on the mountains of Meru. Thou art the chief of the celestials. Thou hast the Atharvans for thy head. Thou hast the Samans for thy mouth. Thou hast the thousand Richs for thy immeasurable eyes. Thou hast the Yajushes for thy feet and hands.[145] Thou art the Upanishads. Thou art the entire body of rituals (occurring in the scriptures). Thou art all that is mobile. Thou art he whose solicitations are never unfulfilled. Thou art he who is always inclined to grace. Thou art he that is of beautiful form. Thou art of the form of the good that one does to another. Thou art that which is dear. Thou art he that always advances towards thy devotees (in proportion as these advance for meeting thee). Thou art gold and other precious metals that are held dear by all. Thy effulgence is like that of burnished gold. Thou art the navel (of the universe). Thou art he that makes the fruits of sacrifices grow (for the benefit of those that perform sacrifices to thy glory). Thou art of the form of that faith and devotion which the righteous have in respect of sacrifices. Thou art the artificer of the universe. Thou art all that is immobile (in the form of mountains and other inert objects). Thou art

---

[139] Literally, crown of the head.

[140] i.e., that succeeds in effecting his Emancipation.

[141] Mahanakha refers to the incarnation of Narasingha or the Man-lion assumed for slaying the Daitya Hiranyakasipu, the father of Prahlada. Maharoman has reference to the form of the mighty or vast Boar that the Supreme Deity assumed for raising the submerged Earth on his tusks.

[142] Mahamuni may mean either one that is very mananasilah or one that is exceedingly taciturn.

[143] How the world has been likened to a tree has been explained in the Moksha sections of the Santi Parvan.

[144] This is explained in the sense of no one being able to enquire after Brahman unless he has a body, however subtle, with the necessary senses and understanding. It may also mean that the tree of the world furnishes evidence of the existence of the Supreme Deity.

[145] Both the vernacular translators have rendered many of these names most carelessly. The Burdwan translator takes Yaju as one name and Padabhuja as another. This is very absurd.

78

the two and ten stages of life through which a person passes.[146] Thou art he that causes fright (by assuming the intermediate states between the ten enumerated). Thou art the beginning of all things. Thou art he that unites Jiva with Supreme Brahman through Yoga. Thou art identifiable with that Yoga which causes such a union between Jiva and Supreme Brahman. Thou art unmanifest (being the deepest stupefaction). Thou art the presiding deity of the fourth age (in consequence of thy identity with lust and wrath and cupidity and other evil passions that flow from that deity).[147] Thou art eternal Time (because of thy being of the form of that ceaseless succession of birth and death that goes on in the universe). Thou art of the form of the Tortoise.[148] Thou art worshipped by the Destroyer himself. Thou livest in the midst of associates. Thou admittest thy devotees as members of thy Gana. Thou hast Brahma himself for the driver of thy car. Thou sleepest on ashes.[149] Thou protectest the universe with ashes.[150] Thou art he whose body is made of ashes.[151] Thou art the tree that grants the fruition of all wishes. Thou art of the form of those that constitute thy Gana. Thou art the protector of the four and ten regions. Thou transcendent all the regions. Thou art full, (there being no deficiency). Thou art adored by all creatures. Thou art white (being pure and stainless). Thou art he that has his body, speech and mind perfectly stainless. Thou art he who has attained to that purity of existence which is called Emancipation. Thou art he who is incapable of being stained by impurity of any kind. Thou art he who has been attained to by the great preceptors of old. Thou residest in the form of Righteousness or duly in the four modes of life. Thou art that Righteousness which is of the form of rites and sacrifices. Thou art of the form of that skill which is possessed by the celestial artificer of the universe. Thou art he who is adored as the primeval form of the universe. Thou art of vast arms. Thy lips are of a coppery hue. Thou art of the form of the vast waters that are contained in the Ocean. Thou art exceedingly stable and fixed (being of the form of mountains and hills). Thou art Kapila. Thou art brown. Thou art all the hues whose mixture produces white. Thou art the period of life. Thou art ancient. Thou art recent. Thou art a Gandharva. Thou art the mother of the celestials in the form of Aditi (or the mother of all things, in the form of Earth). Thou art Garuda, the prince of birds, born of Vinata by Kasyapa, otherwise called Tarkshya. Thou art capable of being comprehended with ease. Thou art of excellent and agreeable speech. Thou art he that is armed with the battle-axe. Thou art he that is desirous of victory. Thou art he that assists others in the accomplishment of their

---

[146] These are the ten previously enumerated, beginning with residence in the mother's womb and ending with death as the tenth, with heaven the eleventh and Emancipation the twelfth.

[147] It should be remembered that Kali which is either the age of sinfulness or the presiding deity of that age and, therefore, a malevolent one, is highly propitious to Emancipation. The world being generally sinful, those who succeed in living righteously in this age or under the sway of this malevolent deity, very quickly attain to heaven if heaven be their object, or Emancipation if they strive for Emancipation.

[148] Implying that thou assumest the form of the constellation called the Great Bear, and moving onward in space causest the lapse of Time. This constellation, in Hindu astronomy, is known by the name of Sisumara because of its resemblance with the form of a tortoise.

[149] The word bhashma, meaning ashes, literally signifies anything that dispels, tears off all bonds, and cures every disease. Ashes are used by Sanyasins for rubbing their bodies as a mark of their having consumed every sin and cut off every bond and freed themselves from all diseases.

[150] Mahadeva gave a quantity of ashes to his devotees for protecting them from sin.

[151] Vide the story of Mankanaka. The Rishi of that name, beholding vegetable juice issuing from his body, began to dance in joy. The whole universe, overpowered by a sympathetic influence, began to dance with him. At this, for protecting the universe, Mahadeva showed himself to Mankanaka and, pressing his fingers, brought out a quantity of ashes, thus showing that his body was made of ashes.

designs.[152] Thou art an excellent friend.[153] Thou art he that bears a Vina made of two hollow gourds. Thou art of terrible wrath (which thou displayest at the time of the universal dissolution). Thou ownest for thy offspring, beings higher than men and deities (viz., Brahma and Vishnu). Thou art of the form of that Vishnu who floats on the waters after the universal dissolution. Thou devourest all things with great ferocity. Thou art he that procreates offspring. Thou art family and race, continuing from generation to generation. Thou art the blare that a bamboo flute gives out. Thou art faultless. Thou art he every limb of whose body is beautiful. Thou art full of illusion. Thou dost good to others without expecting any return. Thou art Wind. Thou art Fire. Thou art the bonds of the worlds which bind Jiva. Thou art the creator of those bonds. Thou art the tearer of such bonds. Thou art he that dwells with even the Daityas (who are the foes of all sacrifices). Thou dwellest with those that are the foes of all acts (and that have abandoned all acts). Thou art of large teeth, and thou art of mighty weapons. Thou art he that has been greatly censured. Thou art he that stupefied the Rishis dwelling in the Daruka forest. Thou art he that did good unto even thy detractors, viz., those Rishis residing in the Daruka forest. Thou art he who dispels all fears and who dispelling all the fears of those Rishis gave them Emancipation. Thou art he that has no wealth (in consequence of his inability to procure even his necessary wearing apparel). Thou art the lord of the celestials. Thou art the greatest of the gods (in consequence of thy being adored by even Indra and others that are regarded as the highest of the celestials). Thou art an object of adoration with even Vishnu. Thou art the slayer of those that are the foes of the deities. Thou art he that resides (in the form of the snake Sesha) in the nethermost region.[154] Thou art invisible but capable of being comprehended, even as the wind which though invisible is perceived by every body. Thou art he whose knowledge extends to the roots of everything and unto whom all things, even in their inner nature, are known. Thou art the object that is enjoyed by him that enjoys it. Thou art he among the eleven Rudras who is called Ajaikapat. Thou art the sovereign of the entire universe. Thou art of the form of all Jivas in the universe (in consequence of thy being covered by the three well-known attributes of Sattwa, Rajas, and Tamas). Thou art he that is not subject to those three attributes. Thou art he that transcends all attributes and is a state of pure existence which is incapable of being described with the aid of any adjective that language can yield. Thou art the prince of physicians called Dhanwantari. Thou art a comet (in consequence of the calamities that flow from thee unto the sinful). Thou art the celestial generalissimo called Skanda. Thou art the king of the Yakshas, called Kuvera, who is thy inseparable associate and who is the Lord of all treasures in the world. Thou art Dhatri. Thou art Sakra. Thou art Vishnu. Thou art Mitra. Thou art Tashtri (the celestial artificer). Thou art the Pole Star. Thou art he that upholds all things. Thou art he called Prabhava amongst the Vasus. Thou art the wind which is capable of going everywhere (being the Sutra-atma that connects all things in the universe with a thread). Thou art Aryaman. Thou art Savitri. Thou art Ravi. Thou art that ancient king of great celebrity known by the name of Ushangu. Thou art he who protects all creatures in diverse ways. Thou art Mandhatri (because of thy competence to gratify all creatures). Thou art he from whom all creatures start into life. Thou art he who exists in diverse form. Thou art he who causes the diverse

---

[152] Anukari literally means an accessory. In the form of Vishnu or Krishna, the Supreme Deity addrest himself to aid Arjuna in slaying Bhishma.

[153] As Krishna the friend of Arjuna.

[154] In the Pauranik myth, the Earth is described as being supported in empty space by a mighty snake called Sesha. Mahadeva is that Sesha, otherwise called Ananta.

hues to exist in the universe. Thou art he who upholds all desires and all attributes (because of these flowing from thee). Thou art he who has the lotus on thy navel.[155] Thou art he within whose womb are innumerable mighty creatures. Thou art of face as beautiful as the moon. Thou art wind. Thou art fire. Thou art possessed of exceeding might. Thou art endued with tranquillity of soul. Thou art old. Thou art he that is known with the aid of Righteousness.[156] Thou art Lakshmi. Thou art the maker of the field of those actions (by which persons adore the supreme Deity). Thou art he who lives in the field of action. Thou art the soul of the field of action. Thou art the medicine or provoker of the attributes of sovereignty and the others.[157] All things lie in thee (for, as the Srutis declare, all things becomes one in thee, thyself being of the nature of that unconsciousness which exhibits itself in dreamless slumber). Thou art the lord of all creatures endued with life-breaths. Thou art the god of the gods. Thou art he who is attached to felicity. Thou art Sat (in the form of cause). Thou art Asat (in the form of effect). Thou art he who possesses the best of all things. Thou art he who resides on the mountains of Kailasa. Thou art he who repairs to the mountains of Himavat. Thou washest away all things besides thee like a mighty current washing away trees and other objects standing on its banks. Thou art the maker of Pushkara and other large lakes and pieces of natural water. Thou art possessed of knowledge of infinite kinds. Thou art the giver of infinite blessings. Thou art a merchant (who conveys the goods of this country to that country and brings the goods of that country to this for the convenience of human beings). Thou art a carpenter. Thou art the tree (of the world that supplies the timber for thy axe). Thou art the tree called Vakula (Mimusops Elengi, Linn.) Thou art the sandal-wood tree (Santalum album, Linn.). Thou art the tree called Chcchada (Alstonia Scholaris, syn Echitis, Scholaris, Roxb.). Thou art he whose neck is very strong. Thou art he whose shoulder joint is vast. Thou art not restless (but endued with steadiness in all thy acts and in respect of all thy faculties). Thou art the principal herbs and plants with their produce (in the form of rice and wheat and the other varieties of grain). Thou art he that grants success upon others in respect of the objects upon which they bestow their heart. Thou art all the correct conclusions in respect of both the Vedas and Grammar.[158] Thou art he who utters leonine roars. Thou art endued with leonine fangs. Thou ridest on the back of a lion for performing thy journeys. Thou ownest a car that is drawn by a lion. Thou art he called the truth of truth.[159] Thou art he whose dish or plate is constituted by the Destroyer of the universe.[160] Thou art always engaged in seeking the good of the worlds. Thou art he who rescues all creatures from distress (and leads them to the felicity of Emancipation). Thou art the bird called Saranga. Thou art a new (Young) swan. Thou art he who is displayed in beauty in consequence of the crest thou bearest on thy head (like the cock or the peacock). Thou art he who protects the place where assemblies of

---

[155] i.e., Mahavishnu, from whose navel arose the primeval lotus within which was born Brahma.

[156] The Bombay text has a misprint. It reads Punya-chanchu for Punya-chunchu. In printing the commentary also, the well-known grammatical Sutra vrittanschanchu etc. The Burdwan translator repeats the misprint in his rendering. K. P. Singha avoids it.

[157] The word Kurukshetra or its abbreviation Kuru means the field or department of action. It means also the actual field, so called, on which king Kuru performed his penances, and which is so sacred that its very dust cleanses a person of all sins.

[158] The commentator explains that Siddharthah means Siddhantah, and that the following compound is its adjective.

[159] Literally, the Soul of real existence.

[160] People eat off plates of silver or gold or of other metals. Mahadeva has for his plate Kala or destroyer of the universe. Both the vernacular translators have erred in rendering this word. K. P. Singha takes the compound as really consisting of two names, etc.

the wise sit for dispensing justice. Thou art the abode of all creatures. Thou art the cherisher of all creatures. Thou art Day and Night (which are the constituent elements of Eternity). Thou art he that is without fault and therefore, never censured. Thou art the upholder of all creatures. Thou art the refuge of all creatures. Thou art without birth. Thou art existent. Thou art ever fruitful. Thou art endued with Dharana and Dhyana and Samadhi. Thou art the steed Uchchaisravas. Thou art the giver of food. Thou art he who upholds the life-breaths of living creatures. Thou art endued with patience. Thou art possessed of intelligence. Thou art endued with exertion and cleverness. Thou art honoured by all. Thou art the giver of the fruits of Righteousness and sin. Thou art the cherisher of the senses (for the senses succeed in performing their respective functions in consequence of thee that presidest over them). Thou art the lord of all the luminaries. Thou art all collections of objects. Thou art he whose vestments are made of cowhides. Thou art he who dispels the grief of his devotees. Thou hast a golden arm. Thou art he who protects the bodies of Yogins who seek to enter their own selves. Thou art he who has reduced to nothingness all his foes.[161] Thou art he the measure of whose gladness is very great. Thou art he who achieved victory over the deity of desire that is irresistible. Thou art he who has subjugated his senses. Thou art the note called Gandhara in the musical octave. Thou art he who has an excellent and beautiful home (in consequence of its being placed upon the delightful mountains of Kailasa). Thou art he who is ever attached to penances. Thou art of the form of cheerfulness and contentment. Thou art he called vast or infinite.[162] Thou art he in whose honour the foremost of hymns has been composed. Thou art he whose dancing is characterised by vast strides and large leaps. Thou art he who is adored with reverence by the diverse tribes of Apsaras. Thou art he who owns a vast standard (bearing the device of the bull). Thou art the mountains of Meru. Thou art he who roves among all the summits of that great mountain. Thou art so mobile that it is very difficult to seize thee. Thou art capable of being explained by preceptors to disciples, although thou art incapable of being described in words. Thou art of the form of that instruction which preceptors impart to disciples. Thou art he that can perceive all agreeable scents simultaneously or at the same instant of time. Thou art of the form of the porched gates of cities and palaces. Thou art of the form of the moats and ditches that surround fortified towns and give the victory to the besieged garrison. Thou art the Wind. Thou art of the form of fortified cities and towns encompassed by walls and moats. Thou art the prince of all winged creatures, (being, as thou art, of the form of Garuda). Thou art he who multiplies the creation by union with the opposite sexes. Thou art the first of all in respect of virtues and knowledge. Thou art superior to even him who is the first of all in virtues and knowledge. Thou transcendest all the virtue and knowledge. Thou art eternal and immutable as also dependent on thyself. Thou art the master and protector of the deities and Asuras. Thou art the master and protector of all creatures. Thou art he who wears a coat of mail. Thou art he whose arms are competent to grind all foes. Thou art an object of adoration with even him who is called Suparvan in heaven.[163] Thou art he who grants the power of bearing or upholding all things.[164] Thou

---

[161] The sense is that Mahadeva is the foremost of Sadhakas or worshippers engaged in acquiring a particular object, for he has emaciated or reduced to nothingness all his foes in the form of all passions good and evil. Prakarshena tanukritah arayah kamadayo yena sah.

[162] Narah is thus explained by the commentator.

[163] The commentator explains that he who is called Suparvan in heaven is otherwise called Mahan.

[164] Sarva-sahana-samarthya pradah as the commentator explains. Hence, it means that Mahadeva is he who makes creatures competent to bear all things, i.e. all griefs and all joys, as also the influence all physical objects that is quietly borne without life being destroyed.

art thyself capable of bearing all things. Thou art fixed and steady (without being at all unstable). Thou art white or pure (being, as thou art, without any stain or blot). Thou bearest the trident that is competent to destroy (all things).[165] Thou art the grantor of bodies or physical forms unto those that constantly revolve in the universe of birth and death. Thou art more valuable than wealth. Thou art the conduct or way of the righteous (in the form of goodness and courtesy). Thou art he who had torn the head of Brahma after due deliberation (and not impelled by mere wrath). Thou art he who is marked with all those auspicious marks that are spoken of in the sciences of palmistry and phrenology and other branches of knowledge treating of the physical frame as the indicator of mental peculiarities. Thou art that wooden bar which is called the Aksha of a car and, therefore, art thou he who is attached to the car represented by the body. Thou art attached to all things (in consequence of thy pervading all things as their soul). Thou art endued with very great might, being as thou art a hero of heroes. Thou art the Veda. Thou art the Smritis, the Itihasas, the Puranas, and other scriptures. Thou art the illustrious deity of every sacred shrine. Thou art he who has the Earth for his car. Thou art the inert elements that enter into the composition of every creature. Thou art he who imparts life into every combination of those inert element. Thou art the Pranava and other sacred Mantras that instil life into dead matter. Thou art he that casts tranquil glances. Thou art exceedingly harsh (in consequence of thy being the destroyer of all things). Thou art he in whom are innumerable precious attributes and possessions. Thou hast a body that is red. Thou art he who has all the vast oceans as so many ponds filled for thy drinking.[166] Thou art the root of the tree of the world. Thou art exceedingly beautiful and shinest with surpassing grandeur. Thou art of the form of ambrosia or nectar. Thou art both cause and effect. Thou art an ocean of penances (being as thou art a great Yogin). Thou art he that is desirous of ascending to the highest state of existence. Thou art he that has already attained to that state. Thou art he who is distinguished for the purity of his conduct and acts and observances. Thou art he who art possessed of great fame (in consequence of the Righteousness of his behaviour). Thou art the ornament of armies (being as thou art of the form of prowess and courage). Thou art he who is adorned with celestial ornaments. Thou art Yoga. Thou art he from whom flow eternal time measured by Yugas and Kalpas. Thou art he who conveys all creatures from place.[167] Thou art of the form of Righteousness and sin and their intermixture (such as are displayed in the successive Yugas). Thou art great and formless. Thou art he who slew the mighty Asura that had approached against the sacred city of Varanasi in the form of an infuriate elephant of vast proportions. Thou art of the form of death. Thou givest to all creatures such fruition of their wishes as accords with their merits. Thou art approachable. Thou art conversant with all things that are beyond the ken of the senses. Thou art conversant with the Tattwas (and therefore, thoroughly fixed). Thou art he who incessantly shines in beauty. Thou wearest garlands that stretch down from thy neck to the feet. Thou art that Hara who has the Moon for his beautiful eye. Thou art the salt ocean of vast expanse. Thou art the first three Yugas (viz., Krita, Treta, and Dwapara). Thou art he whose appearance is always fraught with advantage to others. Thou art he who has three eyes (in the form of

---

[165] The etymology of Hara is thus explained by the commentator; Hanti iti ha sulah; tam rati or adatte. This is very fanciful.

[166] The sense is this: a nipana is a shallow pond or ditch where cattle drink. The very oceans are the nipanas or Mahadeva.

[167] The commentator thinks that this has reference to the incarnation of Trivikrama i.e., the dwarf suddenly expanding his form till with two steps he covered Heaven and Earth and demanded space for his third step.

the scriptures, the preceptor, and meditation). Thou art he whose forms are exceedingly subtile (being as thou art the subtile forms of the primal elements). Thou art he whose ears are bored for wearing jewelled Kundalas. Thou art the bearer of matted locks. Thou art the point (in the alphabet) which indicates the nasal sound. Thou art the two dots i.e., Visarga (in the Sanskrit alphabet which indicate the sound of the aspirated H). Thou art possessed of an excellent face. Thou art the shaft that is shot by the warrior for encompassing the destruction of his foe. Thou art all the weapons that are used by warriors. Thou art endued with patience capable of bearing all things. Thou art he whose knowledge has arisen from the cessation of all physical and mental functions.[168] Thou art he who has become displayed as Truth in consequence of the cessation of all other faculties. Thou art that note which, arising from the region called Gandhara, is exceedingly sweet to the ear. Thou art he who is armed with the mighty bow (called Pinaka). Thou art he who is the understanding and the desires that exist in all creatures, besides being the supreme upholder of all beings. Thou art he from whom all acts flow. Thou art that wind which rises at the time of the universal dissolution and which is capable of churning the entire universe even as the staff in the hands of the dairy-maid churns the milk in the milkpot. Thou art he that is full. Thou art he that sees all things. Thou art the sound that arises from slapping one palm against another. Thou art he the palm of whose hand serves as the dish or plate whence to take his food. Thou art he who is possessed of an adamantine body. Thou art exceedingly great. Thou art of the form of an umbrella. Thou art he who has an excellent umbrella. Thou art well-known to be identical with all creatures. Thou art he who having put forth three feet covered all the universe with two and wanted space for the remaining one. Thou art he whose head is bald. Thou art he whose form is exceedingly ugly and fierce. Thou art he who has undergone infinite modifications and become all things in the universe. Thou art he who bears the well-known badge of Sanyasa, viz., the stick. Thou art he who has a Kunda. Thou art he who is incapable of being attained to by means of acts. Thou art he who is identical with the green-eyed king of beasts (viz., the lion). Thou art of the form of all the points of the compass. Thou art he who is armed with the thunder. Thou art he who has a hundred tongues. Thou art he who has a thousand feet and thousand heads.[169] Thou art the lord and chief of the celestials. Thou art he that is made up of all the gods. Thou art the great Master or preceptor. Thou art he who has a thousand arms. Thou art he who is competent to obtain the fruition of every wish. Thou art he whose protection is sought by every one. Thou art he who is the creator of all the worlds. Thou art he who is the great cleanser of all from every kind of sin, in the form of shrines and sacred waters. Thou art he who has three high Mantras.[170] Thou art the youngest son of Aditi and Kasyapa, (being in the form of the dwarf who is otherwise known by the name of Upendra and who beguiled the Asura Vali of his lordship of the three worlds and restored it to the chief of the celestials). Thou art both black and tawny (being of the form which is known as Hari-Hara). Thou art the maker of the Brahmana's rod.[171] Thou art armed with the hundred-killer, the noose, and the dart. Thou art he that took his birth within the primeval lotus.

""""Thou art he who is endued with a vast womb. Thou art he who has the Vedas in

---

[168] i.e., thou art possessed of Yoga knowledge.

[169] The two together form one name.

[170] These are Vija, Sakti, and Kilakani. A kakud is a hump or elevated place in the body.

[171] The thin bamboo rod in the hand of the Brahmana is mightier than the thunderbolt of Indra. The thunder scorches all existing objects upon which it falls. The Brahmana's rod (which symbolizes the Brahmana's might in the form of his curse) blasts even unborn generations. The might of the rod is derived from Mahadeva.

his womb. Thou art he who takes his rise from that infinite waste of waters which succeeds the dissolution of the universe. Thou art he who is endued with rays of effulgent light. Thou art the creator of the Vedas. Thou art he who studies the Vedas. Thou art he who is conversant with the meaning of the Vedas. Thou art devoted to Brahman. Thou art the refuge of all persons devoted to Brahman. Thou art of infinite forms. Thou art the bearer of innumerable bodies. Thou art endued with irresistible prowess.[172] Thou art the soul or nature that transcends the three universal attributes (of Sattwa, Rajas, and Tamas). Thou art the lord of all Jivas. Thou art endued with the speed of the wind. Thou art possessed of the fleetness of the mind. Thou art always smeared with sandal-paste. Thou art the end of the stalk of the primeval lotus.[173] Thou art he who brought the celestial cow Surabhi down from a superior station to an inferior one by denouncing a curse upon her.[174] Thou art that Brahma who was unable to see thy end. Thou art adorned with a large wreath of Karnikara flowers. Thou art adorned with a diadem of blue gems. Thou art the wielder of the bow called Pinaka. Thou art the master of that knowledge which treats of Brahman.[175] Thou art he who has subjugated his senses by the aid of thy knowledge of Brahman. Thou art he who bearest Ganga on thy head.[176] Thou art the husband of Uma, the daughter of Himavat. Thou art mighty (in consequence of thy having assumed the form of the vast Boar for raising the submerged Earth). Thou art he who protects the universe by assuming diverse incarnations. Thou art worthy of adoration. Thou art that primeval Being with the equine head who recited the Vedas with a thundering voice. Thou art he whose grace is very great. Thou art the great subjugator. Thou art he who has slain all his foes (in the form of passions). Thou art both white and tawny (being as thou art half male and half female).[177] Thou art possessed of a body whose complexion is like that of gold.[178] Thou art he that is of the form of pure joy, (being, as thou art, above the five sheaths which the Jiva consists of, viz., the Anna-maya, the Prana-maya, the Mano-maya, the Vijnana-maya, and the Ananda-maya ones). Thou art of a restrained soul. Thou art the foundation upon which rests that Ignorance which is called Pradhana and which, consisting of the three attributes of Sattwa, Rajas, and Tamas is the cause whence the universe has sprung. Thou art he whose faces are turned to every direction.[179] Thou art he who has three eyes (in the forms of the Sun, the Moon, and Fire). Thou art he who is superior to all creatures (in consequence of thy righteousness whose measure is the greatest). Thou art the soul of all mobile beings. Thou art of the form of the subtile soul (which is incapable of being perceived). Thou art

---

[172] Sayambhuvah Tigmatejah is one name. The commentator explains that Brahman could not look at Mahadeva; hence this reference to his prowess.

[173] Brahma, after his birth within the primeval lotus, became desirous of seeing the end of the stalk of that lotus. He went on and on, without succeeding to find what he sought. The meaning of the word, therefore, by implication is that Mahadeva is infinite.

[174] Once Brahma asked Surabhi to bear evidence before Vishnu to the statement that Brahma has seen the foremost part of Siva. Surabhi having given false evidence out of fear for Brahma was cursed by Siva that her offspring will eat unholy substances.

[175] Uma is another name for Brahmavidya.

[176] Falling from the celestial regions, the river Ganga was held by Mahadeva on his head, among his matted locks. At the earnest solicitations of King Bhagiratha he gave her out so that flowing along the surface of the Earth she met the ocean, first passing over the spot where the ashes of Bhagiratha's ancestors, the sixty thousand sons of king Sagara of the solar race, lay.

[177] This form is called Hara-Gauri, as explained before.

[178] Some texts read Pritatma, implying one of contented soul. The reading noticed by the commentator is Pitatma, meaning gold-complexioned. The Burdwan translator takes Pritatma as one name. This is not correct.

[179] Mahadeva is represented as possessed of five heads, four on four sides and one above.

the giver of immortality in the form of Emancipation as the fruit of all acts of righteousness achieved by creatures without the desire of fruits.[180] Thou art the preceptor of even those that are the gods of the gods. Thou art Vasu, the son of Aditi. Thou art he who is endued with innumerable rays of light, who brings forth the universe, and who is of the form of that Soma which is drunk in sacrifices. Thou art Vyasa, the author of the Puranas and other sacred histories. Thou art the creations of Vyasa's brain (because of thy being identical with the Puranas and other sacred histories) both abridged and unabridged. Thou art the sum total of Jivas. Thou art the Season. Thou art the Year. Thou art the Month. Thou art the Fortnight. Thou art those sacred Days that end or conclude these periods. Thou art the Kalas. Thou art the Kashthas. Thou art the Lavas. Thou art the Matras. Thou art the Muhurtas and Days and Nights. Thou art the Kshanas.[181] Thou art the soil upon which the tree of the universe stands. Thou art the seed of all creatures [being of the form of that Unmanifest Chaitanya (consciousness) endued with Maya or illusion whence all creatures spring]. Thou art Mahattatwa. Thou art the sprout of Jiva, (being of the form of Consciousness which springs up after Mahattatwa). Thou art Sat or Effect. Thou art Asat or Cause. Thou art Manifest (being seizable by the senses). Thou art the Father. Thou art the Mother. Thou art the Grandfather. Thou art the door to Heaven (because of thy identity with Penances). Thou art the door of the generation of all creatures (because of thy identity with desire). Thou art the door of Emancipation (because of thy identity with the absence of Desire which alone can lead to the merging into Brahman). Thou art those acts of righteousness which lead to the felicity of heaven. Thou art Nirvana (or that cessation of individual or separate existence which is Emancipation). Thou art the gladdener (who gives all kinds of joy to every creature). Thou art that region of Truth (to which they that are foremost in righteousness attain). Thou art superior to even that region of Truth which is attainable by the righteous. Thou art he who is the creator of both the deities and the Asuras. Thou art he who is the refuge of both the deities and the Asuras. Thou art the preceptor of both the deities and the Asuras (being as thou art of the form of both Vrihaspati and Sukra). Thou art he who is ever victorious. Thou art he who is ever worshipped by the deities and the Asuras. Thou art he who guides the deities and the Asuras even as the Mahamatra guides the elephant. Thou art the refuge of all the deities and the Asuras. Thou art he who is the chief of both the deities and the Asuras (being as thou art of the form of both Indra and Virochana). Thou art he who is the leader in battle of both the deities and the Asuras (being as thou art of the form of Karttikeya and Kesi, the leaders of the celestial and the Daitya armies). Thou art he who transcends the senses and shines by himself. Thou art of the form of the celestial Rishis like Narada and others. Thou art the grantor of boons unto the deities and Asuras (in the form of Brahman and Rudra). Thou art he who rules the hearts of the deities and the Asuras. Thou art he into whom the universe enters (when it is dissolved). Thou art the refuge of even him who is the ruler of the hearts of both the deities and the Asuras. Thou art he whose body is made up of all the deities.[182] Thou art he who has no Being superior to thee of whom to think. Thou art he who is the inner soul of the deities. Thou art he who has sprung from his own self. Thou art of the form of immobile things. Thou art he who covers the three worlds with three steps of his. Thou art possessed of great learning. Thou art stainless. Thou art he who is freed from the quality of Rajas. Thou art he who transcends destruction. Thou art he in whose honour hymns should be

[180] Amritogovrisherwarah is one name.
[181] These are names for different portions of time.
[182] The Srutis declare that Fire is his head, the Sun and the Moon are his eyes, etc.

sung. Thou art the master of the irresistible elephant represented by Time. Thou art of the form of that lord of Tigers who is worshipped in the country of the Kalingas.[183] Thou art he who is called the lion among the deities (in consequence of the pre-eminence of thy prowess). Thou art he who is the foremost of men. Thou art endued with great wisdom. Thou art he who first takes a share of the offerings in sacrifice. Thou art imperceptible. Thou art the sum-total of all the deities. Thou art he in whom penances predominate. Thou art always in excellent Yoga. Thou art auspicious. Thou art armed with the thunder-bolt. Thou art the source whence the weapons called Prasas have taken their origin. Thou art he whom thy devotees attain to in diverse ways. Thou art Guha (the celestial generalissimo). Thou art the supreme limit of felicity.[184] Thou art identical with thy creation. Thou art he who rescues thy creatures from death (by granting them Emancipation). Thou art the cleanser of all including Brahma himself. Thou art of the form of bulls and other horned animals. Thou art he who is fond of mountain summits. Thou art the planet Saturn. Thou art Kuvera, the chief of the Yakshas. Thou art complete faultlessness. Thou art he who inspires gladness. Thou art all the celestials united together. Thou art the cessation of all things. Thou art all the duties that appertain to all the modes of life. Thou art he who has an eye on his forehead. Thou art he who sports with the universe as his marble ball. Thou art of the form of deer. Thou art endued with the energy that is of the form of knowledge and penance. Thou art the lord of all immobile things (in the form of Himavat and Meru). Thou art he who has subjugated his senses by various regulations and vows. Thou art he whose objects have all been fulfilled. Thou art identical with Emancipation. Thou art different from him whom we worship. Thou hast truth for thy penances. Thou art of a pure heart. Thou art he who presides over all vows and fasts (in consequence of thy being the giver of their fruits). Thou art the highest (being of the form of Turiya). Thou art Brahman. Thou art the highest refuge of the devotees. Thou art he who transcends all bonds (being Emancipate). Thou art freed from the linga body. Thou art endued with every kind of prosperity. Thou art he who enhances the prosperity of thy devotees. Thou art that which is incessantly undergoing changes.

"""'I have thus, O Krishna, hymned the praises of the illustrious Deity by reciting his names in the order of their importance. Who is there that can hymn the praises of the lord of the universe, that great Lord of all who deserves our adorations and worship and reverence, whom the very gods with Brahma at their head are unable to praise and whom the Rishis also fail to sing? Aided, however, by my devotion to him, and having received his permission, I have praised that Lord of sacrifices, that Deity of supreme puissance, that foremost of all creatures endued with intelligence. By praising with these names that enhance one's auspiciousness of the great lord of blessedness, a worshipper of devoted soul and pure heart succeeds in attaining to his own self. These names constitute a hymn that furnishes the best means of attaining to Brahman. With the aid of this hymn one is sure to succeed in attaining to Emancipation. Rishis and the deities all praise the highest deity by uttering this hymn. Hymned by persons of restrained soul Mahadeva becomes gratified with those that hymn his praises so. The illustrious deity is always full of compassion towards his devotees. Endued with omnipotence, he it is that gives Emancipation to those that worship him. So also, they among men that are foremost, that are possessed of faith and devotion hear and recite for others and utter with reverence the

---

[183] Mahadeva has an image in the country of the Kalingas that is called Vyaghreswara.
[184] Kantah is thus explained. Kasya Sukhasya antah sima.

praises of that highest and eternal Lord viz. Isana, in all their successive lives and adore him in thought, word, and deed, and adoring him thus at all times, viz. when they are lying or seated or walking or awake or opening the eyelids or shutting them, and thinking of him repeatedly, become objects of reverence with all their fellowmen and derive great gratification and exceeding joy. When a creature becomes cleansed of all his sins in course of millions of births in diverse orders of being, it is then that devotion springs up in his heart for Mahadeva. It is through good luck alone that undivided devotion to Bhava who is the original cause (of the universe) fully springs up in the heart of one that is conversant with every mode of worshipping that great Deity.[185] Such stainless and pure devotion to Rudra, that has singleness of purpose and that is simply irresistible in its course, is seldom to be found among even the deities, and never among men. It is through the grace of Rudra that such devotion arises in the hearts of human beings. In consequence of such devotion, men, identifying themselves wholly with Mahadeva, succeed in attaining to the highest success. The illustrious Deity who is always inclined to extend his grace towards them that seek him with humility, and throw themselves with their whole soul upon him rescues them from the world. Except the great Deity who frees creatures from rebirth, all other gods constantly nullify the penances of men, for men have no other source of puissance that is as great as these."[186] It was even thus Tandi of tranquil soul, resembling Indra himself in splendour, praised the illustrious Lord of all existent and non-existent things,—that great Deity clad in animal skins. Indeed, Brahma had sung this hymn in the presence of Sankara. Thou art a Brahmana (being conversant with Brahman and devoted to those that are conversant with Brahman). Thou shalt, therefore, comprehend it well. This is cleansing, and washes away all sins. This confers Yoga and Emancipation and heaven and contentment. He who recites this hymn with undivided devotion to Sankara succeeds in attaining to that high end which is theirs that are devoted to the doctrines of the Sankhya philosophy. That worshipper who recites this hymn daily for one year with singleness of devotion succeeds in obtaining the end that he desires. This hymn is a great mystery. It formerly resided in the breast of Brahma the Creator. Brahma imparted it unto Sakra. Sakra imparted unto Mrityu. Mrityu imparted it unto the Rudras. From the Rudras Tandi got it. Indeed Tandi acquired it in the region of Brahman as the reward of his severe austerities. Tandi communicated it to Sukra, and Sukra of Bhrigu's race communicated it to Gautama. Gautama in his turn, O descendant of Madhu, communicated it to Vaivaswata-Manu. Manu communicated it unto Narayana of great intelligence, numbered among the Sadhyas and held exceedingly dear by him. The illustrious Narayana, numbered among the Sadhyas and possessed of glory that knows no diminution, communicated it to Yama. Vaivaswat Yama communicated it to Nachiketa. Nachiketa, O thou of Vrishni's race, communicated to Markandeya. From Markandeya, O Janarddana, I obtained it as the reward of my vows and fasts. To thee, O slayer of foes, I communicate that hymn unheard by others. This hymn leads to heaven. It dispels disease and bestows long life. This is worthy of the highest praise, and is consistent with the Vedas."

"'Krishna continued, "That person, O Partha, who recites this hymn with a pure heart observing the vow of Brahmacharyya, and with his senses under control, regularly for

---

[185] Undivided, i.e., having nothing else for its object, Sarva-bhavatah is bhagvat. The sense is that unless one becomes conversant with all the modes of worshipping Bhava, i.e., in thought, word and deed, and unless one has special good luck, one cannot have such devotion to Bhava.

[186] There are numerous instances of the gods having become alarmed at the penances of men and done their best to nullify those penances by despatching celestial nymphs for attracting them of carnal pleasures.

one whole year, succeeds in obtaining the fruits of a horse-sacrifice. Danavas and Yakshas and Rakshasas and Pisachas and Yatudhanas and Guhyakas and snakes can do no injury to him."'''

SECTION XVIII.

"Vaisampayana said, 'After Vasudeva had ceased to speak, the great Yogin, viz. the Island-born Krishna, addressed Yudhisthira, saying,—"O son, do thou recite this hymn consisting of the thousand and eight names of Mahadeva, and let Maheswara be gratified with thee. In former days, O son, I was engaged in the practice of severe austerities on the breast of the mountains of Meru from desire of obtaining a son. It is this very hymn that was recited by me. As the reward of this, I obtained the fruition of all my wishes, O son of Pandu. Thou wilt also, by reciting this same hymn, obtain from Sarva the fruition of all thy wishes."—After this, Kapila, the Rishi who promulgated the doctrines that go by the name of Sankhya, and who is honoured by the gods themselves, said,—"I adore Bhava with great devotion for many lives together. The illustrious Deity at last became gratified with me and gave me knowledge that is capable of aiding the acquirer in getting over rebirth."—After this, the Rishi named Charusirsha, that dear friend of Sakra and known otherwise under the name of Alamvana's son and who is filled with compassion, said,— "I, in former days, repaired to the mountains of Gokarna and sat myself to practise severe penances for a hundred years. As the reward of those penances, I obtained from Sarva, O son of king Pandu, a hundred sons, all of whom were born without the intervention of woman, of well-restrained soul, conversant with righteousness, possessed of great splendour, free from disease and sorrow, and endued with lives extending over a hundred thousand years."—Then the illustrious Valmiki, addressing Yudhishthira, said,—"Once upon a time, in course of a dialectical disputation, certain ascetics that were possessors of the homa fire denounced me as one guilty of Brahmanicide. As soon as they had denounced me as such, the sin of Brahmanicide, O Bharata, possessed me. I then, for cleansing myself, sought the protection of the sinless Isana who is irresistible in energy. I become cleansed of all my sins. That dispeller of all sorrows, viz., the destroyer of the triple city of the Asuras, said unto me,—'Thy fame shall be great in the world.'"—Then Jamadagni's son, that foremost of all righteous persons, shining like the Sun with blazing splendour in the midst of that conclave of Rishis, said unto the son of Kunti these words:—"I was afflicted with the sin, O eldest son of Pandu, of Brahmanicide for having slain my brothers who were all learned Brahmanas. For purifying myself, I sought the protection, O king, of Mahadeva. I hymned the praises of the great Deity by reciting his names. At this, Bhava became gratified with me and gave me a battle-axe and many other celestial weapons. And he said unto me,—'Thou shalt be freed from sin and thou shalt be invincible in battle; Death himself shall not succeed in overcoming thee for thou shalt be freed from disease.'—Even thus did the illustrious and crested Deity of auspicious form said unto me. Through the grace of that Deity of supreme intelligence I obtained all that He had said." Then Viswamitra said,—"I was formerly a Kshatriya. I paid my adorations to Bhava with the desire of becoming a Brahmana. Through the grace of that great Deity I succeeded in obtaining the high status of a Brahmana that is so difficult to obtain."— Then the Rishi Asita-Devala, addressing the royal son of Pandu, said,—"In former days, O son of Kunti, through the curse of Sakra, all my merit due to the acts of righteousness I had performed, was destroyed. The puissant Mahadeva it was who kindly gave me back that merit together with great fame and a long life."—The illustrious Rishi Gritsamada, the dear friend of Sakra, who resembled the celestial preceptor Vrihaspati himself in splendour, addressing Yudhishthira of Ajamida's race said,—"The inconceivable Sakra had, in days of yore, performed a sacrifice extending over a thousand years. While that sacrifice was going on, I was engaged by Sakra in reciting the Samans. Vasishtha, the son of that Manu who sprung from the eyes of Brahma, came to that sacrifice and addressing me, said,—'O foremost of regenerate persons, the Rathantara is not being recited properly by thee. O best of Brahmanas, cease to earn demerit by reading so faultily, and with the aid of thy understanding do thou read the Samans correctly. O thou of wicked understanding, why dost thou perpetrate such sin that is destructive of sacrifice.'—Having said these words, the Rishi Vasishtha, who was very wrathful, gave way to that passion and addressing me once more, said,—'Be thou an animal divested of intelligence, subject to grief, ever filled with fear, and a denizen of trackless forests destitute of both wind and water and abandoned by other animals. Do thou thus pass ten thousand years with ten and eight hundred years in addition. That forest in which thou shalt have to pass this period will be destitute of all holy trees and will, besides, be the haunt of Rurus and lions. Verily, thou shalt have to become a cruel deer plunged in excess of grief.'—As soon as he had said these words, O son of Pritha, I immediately became transformed into a deer. I then sought the protection of Maheswara. The great Deity said unto me,—'Thou shalt be freed from disease of every kind, and besides immortality shall be thine. Grief shall never afflict thee. Thy friendship with Indra shall remain unchanged, and let the sacrifices of both Indra and thyself increase.' The illustrious and puissant Mahadeva favours all creatures in this way. He is always the great dispenser and ordainer in the matter of the happiness and sorrow of all living creatures. That illustrious Deity is incapable of being comprehended in thought, word, or deed. O son, O thou that are the best of warriors (through the grace of Mahadeva), there is none that is equal to me in learning."—After this, Vasudeva, that foremost of all intelligent men, once more said,—"Mahadeva of golden eyes was gratified by me with my penances. Gratified with me, O Yudhishthira, the illustrious Deity said unto me,—'Thou shalt, O Krishna, through my grace, become dearer to all persons than wealth which is coveted by all. Thou shalt be invincible in battle. Thy energy shall be equal to that of Fire.' Thousands of other boons Mahadeva gave unto me on that occasion. In a former incarnation I adored Mahadeva on the Manimantha mountain for millions of years. Gratified with me, the illustrious Deity said unto me these words:—'Blessed be thou, do thou solicit boons as thou wishest. Bowing unto him with a bend of my head, I said these words,—'If the puissant Mahadeva has been gratified with me, then let my devotion to him be unchanged, O Isana! Even this is the boon that I solicit.'—The great God said unto me,—'Be it so'—and disappeared there and then."

"'Jaigishavya said, "O Yudhishthira, formerly in the city of Varanasi, the puissant Mahadeva searching me out, conferred upon me the eight attributes of sovereignty."

"'Garga said,—"O son of Pandu, gratified with me in consequence of mental sacrifice which I had performed, the great God bestowed upon me, on the banks of the sacred stream Saraswati, that wonderful science, viz., the knowledge of Time with its four and sixty branches. He also bestowed upon me, a thousand sons, all possessed of equal merit and fully conversant with the Vedas. Through his grace, their periods of life as also that of mine have become extended to ten millions of years."

"'Parasara said,—"In former times I gratified Sarva, O king. I then cherished the desire of obtaining a son that would be possessed of great ascetic merit, endued with superior energy, and addressed to high Yoga, that would earn world-wide fame, arrange the Vedas, and become the home of prosperity, that would be devoted to the Vedas and the Brahmanas and be distinguished for compassion. Even such a son was desired by me from Maheswara. Knowing that this was the wish of my heart, that foremost of Deities said unto me,—'Through the fruition of that object of thine which thou wishest to obtain from me, thou shalt have a son of the name of Krishna. In that creation which shall be known after the name of Savarni-Manu, that son of thine shall be reckoned among the seven Rishis. He shall arrange the Vedas, and be the propagator of Kuru's race. He shall, besides, be the author of the ancient histories and do good to the universe. Endued with severe penances, he shall, again, be the dear friend of Sakra. Freed from diseases of every kind, that son of thine, O Parasara, shall besides, be immortal.'—Having said these words, the great Deity disappeared there and then. Even such is the good, O Yudhishthira, that I have obtained from that indestructible and immutable God, endued with the highest penances and supreme energy."

"'Mandavya said,—"In former times though not a thief and yet wrongly suspected of theft, I was impaled (under the orders of a king). I then adored the illustrious Mahadeva who said unto me,—'Thou shalt soon be freed from impalement and live for millions of years. The pangs due to impalement shall not be thine. Thou shalt also be freed from every kind of affliction and disease. And since, O ascetic, this body of thine hath sprung from the fourth foot of Dharma (viz., Truth), thou shalt be unrivalled on Earth. Do thou make thy life fruitful. Thou shalt, without any obstruction, be able to bathe in all the sacred waters of the Earth. And after the dissolution of thy body, I shall, O learned Brahmana, ordain that thou shall enjoy the pure felicity of heaven for unending Time.'— Having said these words unto me, the adorable Deity having the bull for his vehicle, viz., Maheswara of unrivalled splendour and clad in animal skin, O king, disappeared there and then with all his associates."

"'Galava said, "Formerly I studied at the feet of my preceptor Viswamitra. Obtaining his permission I set out for home with the object of seeing my father. My mother (having become a widow), was filled with sorrow and weeping bitterly, said unto me,—'Alas, thy father will never see his son who, adorned with Vedic knowledge, has been permitted by his preceptor to come home and who, possessed of all the graces of youth, is endued with self-restraint.'—Hearing these words of my mother, I became filled with despair in respect of again beholding my sire. I then paid my adoration with a rapt soul to Maheswara who, gratified with me, showed himself to me and said,—'Thy sire, thy mother, and thyself, O son, shall all be freed from death. Go quickly and enter thy abode; thou shall behold thy sire there.'—Having obtained the permission of the illustrious Deity, I then repaired to my home, O Yudhishthira, and beheld my father, O son, coming out after having finished his daily sacrifice. And he came out, bearing in his hands a quantity of Homa-fuel and Kusa grass and some fallen fruits. And he seemed to have already taken his daily food, for he had washed himself properly. Throwing down those things from his hand, my father, with eyes bathed in tears (of joy), raised me, for I had prostrated myself at his feet. Embracing me he smelt my head, O son of Pandu, and said.—'By good luck, O son, art thou seen by me. Thou hast come back, having acquired knowledge from the preceptor.'"

"Vaisampayana continued, 'Hearing these marvellous and most wonderful feats of the illustrious Mahadeva recited by the ascetics, the son of Pandu became amazed. Then Krishna, that foremost of all intelligent persons, spoke once more unto Yudhishthira, that ocean of righteousness, like Vishnu speaking unto Puruhuta.

"'Vasudeva said, "Upamanyu, who seemed to blaze with effulgence like the Sun, said unto me,—'Those sinful men that are stained with unrighteous deeds, do not succeed in attaining to Isana. Their dispositions being stained by the attributes of Rajas and Tamas, they can never approach the Supreme Deity. It is only those regenerate persons who are of cleansed souls that succeed in attaining to the Supreme Deity. Even if a person lives in the enjoyment of every pleasure and luxury, yet if he be devoted to the Supreme Deity, he comes to be regarded as the equal of forest recluses of cleansed souls. If Rudra be gratified with a person, he can confer upon him the states of either Brahma or of Kesava or of Sakra with all the deities under him, or the sovereignty of the three worlds. Those men, O sire, who worship Bhava even mentally, succeed in freeing themselves from all sins and attain to a residence in heaven with all the gods. A person who razes houses to the ground and destroys tanks and lakes indeed, who devastates the whole universe, does not become stained with sin, if he adores and worships the illustrious Deity of three eyes. A person that is destitute of every auspicious indication and that is stained by every sin, has all his sins destroyed by meditating upon Siva. Even worms and insects and birds, O Kesava, that devote themselves to Mahadeva, are enabled to rove in perfect fearlessness. Even this is my settled conviction that those men who devote themselves to Mahadeva become certainly emancipated from rebirth.' After this, Krishna again addressed Yudhishthira the son of Dharma in the following words.

"'Vishnu said, "O Great King, Aditya, Chandra, Wind, Fire, Heaven, Earth, the Vasus, the Viswedevas, Dhatri, Aryyaman, Sukra, Vrihaspati, the Rudras, the Saddhyas, Varuna, Brahma, Sakra, Maruts, the Upanishads that deal with knowledge of Brahman, Truth, the Vedas, the Sacrifices, Sacrificial Presents, Brahmanas reciting the Vedas, Soma, Sacrificer, the shares of the deities in sacrificial offerings or clarified butter poured in sacrifices, Raksha, Diksha, all kinds of restraints in the form of vows and fasts and rigid observances, Swaha, Vashat, the Brahmanas, the celestial cow, the foremost acts of righteousness, the wheel of Time, Strength, Fame, Self-restraint, the Steadiness of all persons endued with intelligence, all acts of goodness and the reverse, the seven Rishis, Understanding of the foremost order, all kinds of excellent touch, the success of all (religious) acts, the diverse tribes of the deities, those beings that drink heat, those that are drinkers of Soma, Clouds, Suyamas, Rishitas, all creatures having Mantras for their bodies, Abhasuras, those beings that live upon scents only, those that live upon vision only, those that restrain their speech, those that restrain their minds, those that are pure, those that are capable of assuming diverse forms through Yoga-puissance, those deities that live on touch (as their food), those deities that subsist on vision and those that subsist upon the butter poured in sacrifices, those beings that are competent to create by fiats of their will the objects they require, they that are regarded as the foremost ones among the deities, and all the other deities, O descendant of Ajamida, the Suparnas, the Gandharvas, the Pisachas, the Danavas, Yakshas, the Charanas, the snakes, all that is gross and all that is exceedingly subtle, all that is soft and all that is not subtle, all sorrows and all joys, all sorrows that come after joy and all joy that comes after sorrow, the Sankhya philosophy, Yoga, and that which transcends objects which are regarded as foremost and very superior,—all adorable things, all the deities, and all the protectors of the universe who entering into the physical forces sustain and uphold this ancient creation of that illustrious Deity,—have sprung from that Creator of all creatures. All this that I have mentioned is grosser than that which the wise think of with the aid of Penances. Indeed, that subtle Brahma is the cause of life. I bow my head in reverence to it. Let that immutable and indestructible Master, always adored by us, grant us desirable boons. That person who, subjugating his senses and purifying himself, recites this hymn, without interruption in respect of his vow, for one month, succeeds in obtaining the merit that is attached to a Horse-sacrifice. By reciting this hymn the Brahmana succeeds in acquiring all the Vedas; the Kshatriya becomes crowned with victory, O son of Pritha; the Vaisya becomes successful in obtaining wealth and cleverness; and the Sudra, in winning happiness here and a good end hereafter. Persons of great fame, by reciting this prince of hymns that is competent to cleanse every sin and that is highly sacred and purifying, set their hearts on Rudra. A man by reciting this prince of hymns succeeds in living in heaven for as many years as there are pores in his body.""'

SECTION XIX.

"'Yudhishthira said, "I ask, O chief of Bharata's race, what is the origin of the saying, about discharging all duties jointly at the time of a person's taking the hand of his spouse in marriage? Is that saying in respect of discharging all duties together, due only to what is laid down by the great Rishis in days of yore, or does it refer to the duty of begetting offspring from religious motives, or has it reference to only the carnal pleasure that is expected from such union? The doubt that fills my mind in this respect is very great. What is spoken of as joint duties by the sages is in my consideration incorrect. That which is called in this world the union for practising all duties together ceases with death and is not to be seen to subsist hereafter. This union for practising all duties together leads to heaven. But heaven, O grandsire, is attained to by persons that are dead. Of a married couple it is seen that only one dies at a time. Where does the other then remain? Do tell me this. Men attain to diverse kinds of fruits by practising diverse kinds of duties. The occupations again, to which men betake themselves are of diverse kinds. Diverse, again, are the hells to which they go in consequence of such diversity of duties and acts. Women, in particular, the Rishis have said, are false in behaviour. When human beings are such, and when women in particular have been declared in the ordinances to be false, how, O sire, can there be a union between the sexes for purposes of practising all duties together? In the very Vedas one may read that women are false. The word 'Duty', as used in the Vedas, seems to have been coined in the first instance for general application (so that it is applied to practices that have no merit in them). Hence the application of that word to the rites of marriage is, instead of being correct, only a form of speech forcibly applied where application it has none.[187] The subject seems to me to be inexplicable although I reflect upon it incessantly. O grandsire, O thou of great wisdom, it behoveth thee to expound this to me in detail, clearly and according to what has been laid down in the Sruti. In fact, do thou explain to me what its characteristics are, and the way in which it has come to pass!"[188]

"'Bhishma said, "In this connection is cited the old narrative of the discourse between Ashtavakra and the lady known by the name of Disa. In days of yore Ashtavakra of severe penances, desirous of marriage, begged the high-souled Rishi Vadanya of his daughter. The name by which the damsel was known was Suprabha. In beauty she was

---

[187] I expand this verse a little for bringing out the sense clearly.

[188] The subject propounded by Yudhishthira is this: marriage is always spoken of as a union of the sexes for practising all religious duties together. The king asks, how can this be. Marriage, as seems to him, is a union sought for pleasure. If it be said that the two individuals married together are married for practising religious duties jointly, such practice is suspended by death. Persons act differently and attain to different ends. There is, therefore, no prospect of a reunion after death. When, again, one of them dies, the joint practice of duties can no longer take place. The other objections, urged by Yudhishthira, to the theory of marriage being a union of the sexes for only practising religious duties jointly, are plain.

unrivalled on Earth. In virtues, dignity, conduct, and manners, she was superior to all the girls. By a glance alone that girl of beautiful eyes had robbed him of his heart even as a delightful grove in spring, adorned with flowers, robs the spectator of his heart. The Rishi addressed Ashtavakra and said,—'Yes, I shall bestow my daughter on thee. Listen, however, to me. Make a journey to the sacred North. Thou wilt see many things there!'[189]

""Ashtavakra said, 'It behoveth thee to tell me what I shall see in that region. Indeed, I am ready to execute whatever command may be laid upon me by thee.'

""Vadanya said, 'Passing over the dominions of the lord of Treasures thou will cross the Himavat mountains. Thou wilt then behold the plateau on which Rudra resides. It is inhabited by Siddhas and Charanas. It abounds with the associates of Mahadeva, frolicsome and fond of dance and possessed of diverse forms. It is peopled with also many Pisachas, O master, of diverse forms and all daubed with fragrant powders of diverse hues, and dancing with joyous hearts in accompaniment with instruments of different kinds made of brass. Surrounded by these who move with electric rapidity in the mazes of the dance or refrain at times altogether from forward or backward or transverse motion of every kind, Mahadeva dwells there. That delightful spot on the mountains, we have heard, is the favourite abode of the great Deity. It is said that that great god as also his associates are always present there. It was there that the goddess Uma practised the severest austerities for the sake of (obtaining for her lord) the three-eyed Deity. Hence, it is said, that spot is much liked by both Mahadeva and Uma. In days of yore there, on the heights of the Mahaparswa, which are situate to the north of the mountains sacred to Mahadeva, the sessions, and the last Night, and many deities, and many human beings also (of the foremost order), in their embodied forms, had adored Mahadeva.[190] Thou shalt cross that region also in thy northward journey. Thou will then see a beautiful and charming forest blue of hue and resembling a mass of clouds. There, in that forest, thou wilt behold a beautiful female ascetic looking like Sree herself. Venerable in age and highly blessed, she is in the observance of the Diksha. Beholding her there thou shouldst duly worship her with reverence. Returning to this place after having beheld her, thou wilt take the hand of my daughter in marriage. If thou wanteth to make this agreement, proceed then on thy journey and do what I command thee.'

""Ashtavakra said, 'So be it. I shall do thy bidding. Verily, I shall proceed to that region which thou speakest of, O thou of righteous soul. On thy side, let thy words, accord with truth.'"

"'Bhishma continued, "The illustrious Ashtavakra set out on his journey. He proceeded more and more towards the north and at last reached the Himavat mountains peopled by Siddhas and Charanas.[191] Arrived at the Himavat mountains, that foremost of Brahmanas then came upon the sacred river Vahuda whose waters produce great merit. He bathed in one of the delightful Tirthas of that river, which was free from mud, and gratified the deities with oblations of water. His ablutions being over, he spread a quantity of Kusa grass and laid himself down upon it for resting awhile at his ease.[192] Passing the night in this way, the Brahmana rose with the day. He once more performed his ablutions in the sacred waters of the Vahuda and then ignited his homa fire and

---

[189] The sense is that if after returning from thy journey to that region thou claimest thy bride, thou mayst obtain her from me. Thy journey will be a sort of trial or test to which I mean to put thee.

[190] Kala-ratri is the Night that precedes the universal dissolution.

[191] The commentator thinks that uttaram means the sacred north.

[192] Tirtha means here a Ghat, i.e., an easy descent from the bank for access to the water.

worshipped it with the aid of many foremost of Vedic mantras.[193] He then worshipped with due rites both Rudra and his spouse Uma, and rested for some more time by the side of that lake in the course of the Vahuda whose shores he had reached. Refreshed by such rest, he set out from that region and then proceeded towards Kailasa. He then beheld a gate of gold that seemed to blaze with beauty. He saw also the Mandakini and the Nalini of the high-souled Kuvera, the Lord of Treasures.[194] Beholding the Rishi arrived there, all the Rakshasas having Manibhadra for their head, who were engaged in protecting that lake abounding with beautiful lotuses, came out in a body for welcoming and honouring the illustrious traveller. The Rishi worshipped in return those Rakshasas of terrible prowess and asked them to report, without delay, his arrival unto the Lord of Treasures. Requested by him to do this, those Rakshasas, O king, said unto him,—'King Vaisravana, without waiting for the news from us, is coming of his own accord to thy presence. The illustrious Lord of Treasures is well acquainted with the object of this thy journey. Behold him,—that blessed Master,—who blazes with his own energy.' Then king Vaisravana, approaching the faultless Ashtavakra, duly enquired about his welfare. The usual enquiries of politeness being over, the Lord of Treasures then addressed the regenerate Rishi, saying,—'Welcome art thou here. Do tell me what it is thou seekest at my hands. Inform me of it. I shall, O regenerate one, accomplish whatever thou mayst bid me to accomplish. Do thou enter my abode as pleases thee, O foremost of Brahmanas. Duly entertained by me, and after thy business is accomplished, thou mayst go without any obstacles being placed in thy way.'—Having said these words, Kuvera took the hand of that foremost of Brahmanas and led him into his palace. He offered him his own seat as also water to wash his feet and the Arghya made of the usual ingredients. After the two had taken their seats, the Yakshas of Kuvera headed by Manibhadra, and many Gandharvas and Kinnaras, also sat down before them. After all of them had taken their seats, the Lord of Treasures said these words,—'Understanding what thy pleasure is, the diverse tribes of Apsaras will commence their dance. It is meet that I should entertain thee with hospitality and that thou shouldst be served with proper ministrations.' Thus addressed, the ascetic Ashtavakra said, in a sweet voice, 'Let the dance proceed.' Then Urvara and Misrakesi, and Rambha and Urvasi, and Alumvusha and Ghritachi, and Chitra and Chitrangada and Ruchi, and Manohara and Sukesi and Sumukhi and Hasini and Prabha, and Vidyuta, and Prasami and Danta and Vidyota and Rati,—these and many other beautiful Apsaras began to dance. The Gandharvas played on diverse kinds of musical instruments. After such excellent music and dance had commenced, the Rishi Ashtavakra of severe penances unconsciously passed a full celestial year there in the abode of king Vaisravana.[195] Then king Vaisravana said unto the Rishi,—'O learned Brahmana, behold, a little more than a year has passed away since thy arrival here. This music and dance, especially known by the name of Gandharva, is a stealer of the heart (and of time). Do thou act as thou wishes or let this go on if that be thy pleasure. Thou art my guest and, therefore, worthy of adoration. This is my house. Givest thou thy commands. We are all bound to thee.' The illustrious Ashtavakra, thus addressed by king Vaisravana, replied unto him, with a pleased heart, saying,—'I have been duly honoured by thee. I desire now, O Lord of Treasures, to go hence. Indeed, I am highly pleased. All this befits thee, O Lord of Treasures. Through thy grace, O illustrious one, and agreeably

---

[193] Pradhanatah is explained by the commentator to mean with foremost of Vedic mantras.

[194] Mandakini is that part of the river Ganga which flows through Kailasa, while Nalini is a celebrated lake owned by the king of the Yakshas, so called because of the lotuses which occur there in plenty.

[195] Divya is excellent Gandharva, meaning music and dance.

to the command of the high-souled Rishi Vadanya, I shall now proceed to my journey's end. Let growth and prosperity be thine.'—Having said these words, the illustrious Rishi set out of Kuvera's abode and proceeded northwards. He crossed the Kailasa and the Mandara as also the golden mountains. Beyond those high and great mountains is situated that excellent region where Mahadeva, dressed as an humble ascetic, has taken up his residence. He circumambulated the spot, with concentrated mind, bending his head in reverence the while. Descending then on the Earth, he considered himself sanctified for having obtained a sight of that holy spot which is the abode of Mahadeva. Having circumambulated that mountain thrice, the Rishi, with face turned towards the north, proceeded with a joyous heart. He then beheld another forest that was very delightful in aspect. It was adorned with the fruits and roots of every season, and it resounded with the music of winged warblers numbering by thousands. There were many delightful groves throughout the forest. The illustrious Rishi then beheld a charming hermitage. The Rishi saw also many golden hills decked with gems and possessed of diverse forms. In the begemmed soil he saw many lakes and tanks also. And he saw diverse other objects that were exceedingly delightful. Beholding these things, the mind of that Rishi of cleansed soul became filled with joy. He then saw a beautiful mansion made of gold and adorned with gems of many kinds. Of wonderful structure, that mansion surpassed the palace of Kuvera himself in every respect. Around it there were many hills and mounts of jewels and gems. Many beautiful cars and many heaps of diverse kinds of jewels also were visible in that place. The Rishi beheld there the river Mandakini whose waters were strewn with many Mandara flowers. Many gems also were seen there that were self-luminous, and the soil all around was decked with diamonds of diverse species. The palatial mansion which the Rishi saw contained many chambers whose arches were embellished with various kinds of stones. Those chambers were adorned also with nets of pearls interspersed with jewels and gems of different species. Diverse kinds of beautiful objects capable of stealing the heart and the eye, surrounded that palace. That delightful retreat was inhabited by numerous Rishis. Beholding these beautiful sights all around, the Rishi began to think where he would take shelter. Proceeding then to the gate of the mansion, he uttered these words:—'Let those that live here know that a guest has come (desirous of shelter).' Hearing the voice of the Rishi, a number of maidens came out together from that palace. They were seven in number, O King, of different styles of beauty, all of them were exceedingly charming. Every one of those maidens upon whom the Rishi cast his eyes, stole his heart. The sage could not, with even his best efforts, control his mind. Indeed, at the sight of those maidens of very superior beauty, his heart lost all its tranquillity. Seeing himself yielding to such influences, the Rishi made a vigorous effort and possessed as he was of great wisdom he at last succeeded in controlling himself. Those damsels then addressed the Rishi, saying,—'Let the illustrious one enter.' Filled with curiosity in respect of those exceedingly beautiful damsels as also of that palatial mansion, the regenerate Rishi entered as he was bidden. Entering the mansion he beheld an old lady, with indications of decrepitude, attired in white robes and adorned with every kind of ornament. The Rishi blessed her, saying,—'Good be to you.'—The old lady returned his good wishes in proper form. Rising up, she offered a seat to the Rishi. Having taken his seat, Ashtavakra said,—'Let all the damsels go to their respective quarters. Only let one stay here. Let that one remain here who is possessed of wisdom and who has tranquillity of heart. Indeed, let all the others go away at their will.'—Thus addressed, all those damsels circumambulated the Rishi and then left the chamber. Only that aged lady remained there. The day quickly passed and night came.

The Rishi seated on a splendid bed, addressed the old lady, saying,—'O blessed lady, the night is deepening. Do thou address thyself to sleep.' Their conversation being thus put a stop to by the Rishi, the old lady laid herself down on an excellent bed of great splendour. Soon after, she rose from her bed and pretending to tremble with cold, she left it for going to the bed of the Rishi. The illustrious Ashtavakra welcomed her with courtesy. The lady however, stretching her arms, tenderly embraced the Rishi, O foremost of men. Beholding the Rishi quite unmoved and as inanimate as a piece of wood, she became very sorry and began to converse with him. 'There is no pleasure, save that which waits upon Kama (desire), which women can derive from a person of the other sex. I am now under the influence of desire. I seek thee for that reason. Do thou seek me in return. Be cheerful, O learned Rishi, and unite thyself with me. Do thou embrace me, O learned one, for I desire thee greatly. O thou of righteous soul, even this union with me is the excellent and desirable reward of those severe penances which thou hast undergone. At the first sight I have become disposed to seek thee. Do thou also seek me. All this wealth, and everything else of value that thou seest here are mine. Do thou verily become the lord of all this along with my person and heart. I shall gratify every wish of thine. Do thou sport with me, therefore, in these delightful forests, O Brahmana, that are capable of granting every wish. I shall yield thee complete obedience in everything, and thou shall sport with me according to thy pleasure. All objects of desire that are human or that appertain to heaven shall be enjoyed by us. There is no pleasure more agreeable to women (than that which is derivable from the companionship of a person of the other sex). Verily, congress with a person of the opposite sex is the most delicious fruit of joy that we can reap. When urged by the god of desire, women become very capricious. At such times they do not feel any pain, even if they walk over a desert of burning sand.'

""Ashtavakra said, 'O blessed lady, I never approach one that is another's spouse. One's congress with another man's wife is condemned by persons conversant with the scriptures on morality. I am an utter stranger to enjoyments of every kind. O blessed lady, know that I have become desirous of wedlock for obtaining offspring. I swear by truth itself. Through the aid of offspring righteously obtained, I shall proceed to those regions of felicity which cannot be attained without such aid. O good lady, know what is consistent with morality, and knowing it, desist from thy efforts.'

""The lady said, 'The very deities of wind and fire and water, or the other celestials, O regenerate one, are not so agreeable to women as the deity of desire. Verily, women are exceedingly fond of sexual congress. Among a thousand women, or, perhaps, among hundreds of thousands, sometimes only one may be found that is devoted to her husband. When under the influence of desire, they care not for family or father or mother or brother or husband or sons or husband's brother (but pursue the way that desire points out). Verily, in pursuit of what they consider happiness, they destroy the family (to which they belong by birth or marriage) even as many queenly rivers eat away the banks that contain them. The Creator himself had said this, quickly marking the faults of women.'"[196]

"Bhishma continued, "The Rishi, bent upon finding out the faults of women, then addressed that lady, saying,—'Cease to speak to me in this strain. Yearning springs from liking. Tell me what (else) I am to do.'[197]—That lady then said in return,—'O illustrious

---

[196] A woman is said to destroy a family by staining it with her unchastity.
[197] Both the vernacular translators have totally misunderstood the second line. Asyatam is explained by the commentator as tushnim sthiyatam. Ruchitahchchandah means chchandah or yearning arises from ruchi or

one, thou shalt see according to time and place (as do whether I have anything agreeable in me). Do thou only live here (for some time), O highly blessed one, and I shall regard myself amply rewarded.'—Thus addressed by her, the regenerate Rishi, O Yudhishthira, expressed his resolution to comply with her request, saying,—'Verily, I shall dwell with thee in this place as long as I can venture to do so.'—The Rishi then, beholding that lady afflicted with decrepitude, began to reflect earnestly on the matter. He seemed to be even tortured by his thoughts. The eyes of that foremost of Brahmanas failed to derive any delight from those parts of that lady's person whereupon they were cast. On the other hand, his glances seemed to be dispelled by the ugliness of those particular limbs.—'This lady is certainly the goddess of this palace. Has she been made ugly through some curse? It is not proper that I should hastily ascertain the cause of this.'—Reflecting upon this in the secrecy of his heart, and curious to know the reason, the Rishi passed the rest of that day in an anxious state. The lady then addressed him, saying,—'O illustrious one, behold the aspect of the Sun reddened by the evening clouds. What service shall I do unto thee?'—The Rishi addressed her, saying,—.'Fetch water for my ablutions. Having bathed, I shall say my evening prayers, restraining my tongue and the senses.'"'"

SECTION XX.

"'Bhishma said, "Thus commanded, the lady said,—'Be it so.' She then brought oil (for rubbing the Rishi's body therewith) and a piece of cloth for his wear during the ablutions. Permitted by the ascetic, she rubbed every part of his body with the fragrant oil she had brought for him. Gently was the Rishi rubbed, and when the process of rubbing was over, he proceeded to the room set apart for the performance of ablutions. There he sat upon a new and excellent seat of great splendour.[198] After the Rishi had taken his seat upon it, the old lady began to wash his person with her own soft hands whose touch was exceedingly agreeable. One after another in due order, the lady rendered the most agreeable services to the Rishi in the matter of his ablutions. Between the lukewarm water with which he was washed, and the soft hands that were employed in washing him, the Rishi of rigid vows failed to understand that the whole night had passed away in the process. Rising from the bath the Rishi became highly surprised. He saw the Sun risen above the horizon on the East. He was amazed at this and asked himself,—'Was it really so or was it an error of the understanding?'—The Rishi then duly worshipped the god of a thousand rays. This done, he asked the lady as to what he should do. The old lady prepared some food for the Rishi that was as delicious to the taste as Amrita itself. In consequence of the delicious character of that food the Rishi could not take much. In taking that little, however, the day passed away and evening came. The old lady then asked the Rishi to go to bed and sleep. An excellent bed was assigned to the Rishi and another was occupied by herself. The Rishi and the old lady occupied different beds at first but when it was midnight, the lady left her own bed for coming to that of the Rishi.

"'"Ashtavakra said, 'O blessed lady, my mind turns away from sexual congress with one who is the spouse of another. Leave my bed, O good lady. Blessed be thou, do thou desist from this of thy own accord.'"[199]

---

like. What the Rishi says is, 'As yet I do not yearn after thy company, for I do not like thee. Of course, if, after staying with thee for some time, I begin to like thee, I may then feel a yearning for thee!'

[198] Utsaditah is explained by the commentator to mean chalitah. Here, however, I think it does not mean so.

[199] The last words may also mean—'Go to thy own bed and rest by thyself!'

"'Bhishma continued, "Thus dissuaded by that Brahmana with the aid of his self-restraint, the lady answered him, saying,—'I am my own mistress. In accepting me thou wilt incur no sin.'

""'Ashtavakra said, 'Women can never be their own mistresses. This is the opinion of the Creator himself, viz., that a woman never deserves to be independent.'

""'The lady said, 'O learned Brahmana, I am tortured by desire. Mark my devotion to thee. Thou incurrest sin by refusing to accost me lovingly.'

""'Ashtavakra said, 'Diverse faults, drag away the man that acts as he likes. As regards myself, I am able to control my inclinations by self-restraint. O good lady, do thou return to thy own bed.'

""'The lady said, 'I bow to thee, bending my head. It behoves thee to show me thy grace. O sinless one, I prostrate myself before thee, do thou become my refuge. If indeed, thou seest such sin in congress with one that is not thy spouse, I yield myself unto thee. Do thou, O regenerate one, accept my hand in marriage. Thou wilt incur no sin. I tell thee truly. Know that I am my own mistress. If there by any sin in this, let it be mine alone. My heart is devoted to thee. I am my own mistress. Do thou accept me.'

""'Ashtavakra said, 'How is it, O good lady, that thou art thy own mistress? Tell me the reason of this. There is not a single woman in the three worlds that deserves to be regarded as the mistress of her own self. The father protects her while she is a maiden. The husband protects her while she is in youth. Sons protect her when she is aged. Women can never be independent as long as they live!'

""'The lady said, 'I have since my maidenhood, adopted the vow of Brahmacharyya. Do not doubt it. I am still a maid. Do thou make me thy wife. O Brahmana, do not kill this devotion of mine to thee.'

""'Ashtavakra said, 'As thou art inclined to me, so I am inclined to thee. There is this question, however, that should be settled. Is it true that by yielding to my inclinations I shall not be regarded as acting in opposition to what the Rishi (Vadanya) wishes? This is very wonderful. Will this lead to what is beneficial? Here is a maiden adorned with excellent ornaments and robes. She is exceedingly beautiful. Why did decrepitude cover her beauty so long? At present she looks like a beautiful maiden. There is no knowing what form she may take hereafter.[200] I shall never swerve from that restraint which I have over desire and the other passions or from contentment with what I have already got. Such swerving does not seem to be good. I shall keep myself united with truth!'"[201]

SECTION XXI.

"'Yudhishthira said, "Tell me why had that lady no fear of Ashtavakra's curse although Ashtavakra was endued with great energy? How also did Ashtavakra succeed in coming back from that place?"

"'Bhishma said, "Ashtavakra asked her, saying,—'How dost thou succeed in altering thy form so? Thou shouldst not say anything that is untrue. I wish to know this. Speakest thou truly before a Brahmana.'

---

[200] The commentator takes the words kimivottaram bhavet to imply what will be better for me? Shall I adhere to Vadanya's daughter or shall I take this girl? I think this is rather far-fetched.

[201] By Sakti is implied kamadidamanasamarthyam and by dhriti purvapraptasya atyagah. The last half of the last line of verse 25 is rendered erroneously by both the vernacular translators. Adhering to the commentator's explanation, they add their own interpretation which is different. This sort of jumble is very peculiar.

""The lady said, 'O best of Brahmanas, wherever thou mayst reside in heaven or on Earth, this desire of union between the sexes is to be observed. O thou of infallible prowess, listen, with concentrated attention, to this all. This trial was devised by me, O sinless one, for testing thee aright. O thou of infallible prowess, thou hast subjugated all the worlds for not foregoing your previous resolution. Know that I am the embodiment of the Northern point of the compass. Thou hast seen the lightness of the female character. Even women that are aged are tortured by the desire of sexual union. The Grandsire himself and all the deities with Indra have been pleased with thee. The object for which thy illustrious self has come here (is known to me). O foremost of regenerate persons, thou hast been despatched higher by the Rishi Vadanya—the father of thy bride—in order that I may instruct thee. Agreeably to the wishes of that Rishi I have already instructed thee. Thou wilt return home in safety. Thy journey back will not be toilsome. Thou wilt obtain for wife any girl thou hast chosen. She will bear thee a son. Through desire I had solicited thee, thou madest me the very best answer. The desire for sexual union is incapable of being transcended in the three worlds. Go back to thy quarters, having achieved such merit. What else is there that thou wishest to hear from me? I shall discourse on it, O Ashtavakra, in accordance with the truth. I was gratified by the Rishi Vadanya in the first instance for thy sake, O regenerate ascetic. For the sake of honouring him, I have said all this to thee.'"

"'Bhishma continued, "Hearing these words of hers, the regenerate Ashtavakra joined his hands in a reverential attitude. He then solicited the lady for her permission to go back. Obtaining the permission he came back to his own asylum. Resting himself for some time at home and obtaining the permission of his kinsmen and friends, he then in a proper way, proceeded, O delighter of the Kurus, to the Brahmana Vadanya. Welcomed with the usual enquiries by Vadanya, the Rishi Ashtavakra, with a well-pleased heart, narrated all that he had seen (in course of his sojourn to the North). He said,— 'Commanded by thee I proceeded to the mountains of Gandhamadana. In the regions lying to the north of these mountains I beheld a very superior goddess. I was received by her with courtesy. She named you in my hearing and also instructed me in various matters. Having listened to her I have come back, O lord.' Unto him that said so, the learned Vadanya said,—'Take my daughter's hand according to due rites and under the proper constellations. Thou art the fittest bridegroom I can select for the girl.'"

"'Bhishma continued, "Ashtavakra said,—'So be it' and took the hand of the girl. Indeed, the highly righteous Rishi, having espoused the girl, became filled with joy. Having taken as his wife that beautiful damsel, the Rishi continued to dwell in his own asylum, freed from (mental) fever of every kind."'"

SECTION XXII.

"'Yudhishthira said, "Whom do the eternal Brahmanas strictly observing religious rites call a proper object of gifts? Is a Brahmana that bears the symbols of the order of life he follows to be regarded as such or one who does not bear such indications is to be so regarded?"[202]

"Bhishma said, "O monarch, it has been said that gifts should be made unto a

---

[202] Linga means signs or indications. A Lingin is one that bears signs and indications. Brahmanam (in both places) means one conversant with Brahman. The first, that is, Lingin implies either a Brahmacharin or a Sanyasin that always bears the marks of his order. An Alingin is one that is divested of such marks. Yudhishthira's question is, who, amongst these, should be considered worthy of gifts?

Brahmana that adheres to the duties of his own order, whether, he bears the indications of a Brahmachari or not, for both are faultless, viz., he that bears such indications and he that is divested of them."

"'Yudhishthira said, "What fault does an uncleansed person incur, if he makes gifts of sacrificial butter or food with great devotion unto persons of the regenerate order?"

"'Bhishma said, "Even one that is most destitute of self-restraint becomes, without doubt, cleansed by devotion. Such a man, O thou of great splendour, becomes cleansed in respect of every act (and not with reference to gift alone)."

"'Yudhishthira said, "It has been said that a Brahmana that is sought to be employed in an act having reference to the deities, should never be examined. The learned, however, say that with respect to such acts as have reference to the Pitris, the Brahmana that is sought to be employed, should be examined (in the matter of both his conduct and competence)."

"'Bhishma said, "As regards acts that have reference to the deities, these fructify not in consequence of the Brahmana that is employed in doing the rites but through the grace of the deities themselves. Without doubt, those persons that perform sacrifice obtain the merit attached to those acts, through the grace of the deities.[203] The Brahmanas, O chief of the Bharatas, are always devoted of Brahman. The Rishi Markandeya, one of the greatest Rishis endued with intelligence in all the worlds, said this in days of yore."

"'Yudhishthira said, "Why, O grandsire, are there five viz., he that is a stranger, he that is endued with learning (connected with the duties of his order), he that is connected by marriage, he that is endued with penances, and he that adheres to the performance of sacrifices, regarded as proper persons?"[204]

"'Bhishma said, "The first three, viz., strangers, relatives, and ascetics, when possessed of these attributes, viz., purity of birth, devotion to religious acts, learning, compassion, modesty, sincerity, and truthfulness, are regarded as proper persons. The other two, viz., men of learning and those devoted to sacrifices, when endued with five of these attributes, viz., purity of birth, compassion, modesty, sincerity, truthfulness, are also regarded as proper persons. Listen now to me, O son of Pritha, as I recite to thee the opinions of these four persons of mighty energy, viz., the goddess Earth, the Rishi Kasyapa, Agni (the deity of fire) and the ascetic Markandeya.

"'"The Earth said, 'As a clod of mud, when thrown into the great ocean quickly dissolves away, even so every kind of sin disappears in the three high attributes viz., officiation at sacrifices, teaching and receiving of gifts.'[205]

"'"Kasyapa said, 'The Vedas with their six branches, the Sankhya philosophy, the Puranas, and high birth, these fail to rescue a regenerate person if he falls away from good conduct.'[206]

"'"Agni said, 'That Brahmana who, engaged in study and regarding himself learned, seeks with the aid of his learning to destroy the reputation of others, falls away from

[203] The sense is that with respect to acts having reference to only the Pitris the conduct and competence of Brahmanas should be examined.
[204] The commentator explains that five persons are mentioned in the question of Yudhishthira. K. P. Singha omits one. The Burdwan translator repeats the words of the original without any explanation. I take sambandhi to mean relatives by marriage. To this day, in all India, people make gifts or presents unto sons-in-law, etc.
[205] The sense is that no sin can touch a Brahmana who observes these three acts. These three acts are efficacious in washing away all sins. The commentator points out that by this the attributes of birth and knowledge are referred to.
[206] By good conduct is implied modesty and candour.

righteousness, and comes to be regarded as dissociated from truth. Verily regions of felicity herein-after are never attained to by such a person of destructive genius.'

"'"Markandeya said, 'If a thousand Horse-sacrifices and Truth were weighed in the balance, I do not know whether the former would weigh even half as heavy as the latter.'"

"'Bhishma continued, "Having spoken these words, those four persons, each of whom is endued with immeasurable energy, viz., the goddess Earth, Kasyapa, Agni, and Bhrigu's son armed with weapons, quickly went away."

"'Yudhishthira said, "If Brahmanas observant of the vow of Brahmacharyya in this world solicit the offerings one makes (unto one's deceased ancestors in Sraddhas) I ask, can the Sraddha be regarded well-performed, if the performer actually makes over those offerings unto such Brahmanas?"

"'Bhishma said, "If, having practised the vow of Brahmacharyya for the prescribed period (of twelve years) and acquired proficiency in the Vedas and their branches, a Brahmana himself solicits the offering made in Sraddhas and eats the same, he is regarded to fall away from his vow. The Sraddha, however, is not regarded as stained in any way."

"'Yudhishthira said, "The wise have said that duty of righteousness has many ends and numerous doors. Tell me, O grandsire, what however are the settled conclusions in this matter."[207]

"'Bhishma said, "Abstention from injury to others, truthfulness, the absence of wrath (forgiveness), compassion, self-restraint, and sincerity or candour, O monarch, are the indications of Righteousness. There are persons who wander over the earth, praising righteousness but without practising what they preach and engaged all the while in sin, O king. He who gives unto such persons gold or gems or steeds, has to sink in hell and to subsist there for ten years, eating the while the faeces of such persons as live upon the flesh of dead kine and buffalos, of men called Pukkasas, of others that live in the outskirts of cities and villages, and of men that publish, under the influence of wrath and folly, the acts and the omissions of others.[208] Those foolish men who do give unto a Brahmana observant of the vow of Brahmacharyya the offerings made in Sraddhas (unto one's deceased ancestors), have to go, O monarch into regions of great misery."

"'Yudhishthira said, "Tell me, O grandsire, what is superior to Brahmacharyya? What is the highest indication of virtue? What is the highest kind of purity?"

"'Bhishma said,—"I tell thee, O son, that abstention from honey and meat is even superior to Brahmacharyya. Righteousness consists in keeping within boundaries or in self-restraint, the best indication of Righteousness is Renunciation (which is also the highest kind of purity)."[209]

"'Yudhishthira said, "In what time should one practise Righteousness? In what time

---

[207] Anekantam is explained by the commentator as Anekaphalakaram, i.e., of diverse kinds of fruits. The fruits attainable by a correct discharge of duties are of diverse kinds, because the objects of those duties, called Palms are of various kinds.

[208] Verse 22 contains 4 substantives in the genitive plural. All those are connected with vishtham in the previous verse. The commentator points out this clearly. Those living in the outskirts of towns and villages are tanners and other low castes. They who publish the acts and omissions of others are regarded as very vile persons, equivalent to such low caste men mentioned above. It is difficult to differ from the commentator, but it seems that genitives in the verse as are used for datives, in which case the meaning would be that they who give unto such persons shall also sink into hell. The Burdwan translator gives a ridiculous version of verse 22.

[209] The Bengal reading Brahmacharyya is better than the Bombay reading of that word in the accusative. Bhishma apparently gives two answers. These however involve three. By maryyada is meant boundaries or limits. The duties of men have known bounds. To transgress those bounds would be to transgress duty. The highest indication of Righteousness is samah or absence of desire for all worldly objects; hence Renunciation.

should wealth be sought? In what time should pleasure be enjoyed? O grandsire, do tell me this."

"'Bhishma said,—"One should earn wealth in the first part of one's life. Then should one earn Righteousness, and then enjoy pleasure. One should not, however, attach oneself to any of these. One should regard the Brahmanas, worship one's preceptor and seniors, show compassion for all creatures, be of mild disposition and agreeable speech. To utter falsehood in a court of justice, to behave deceitfully towards the king, to act falsely towards preceptors and seniors, are regarded as equivalent (in heinousness) to Brahmanicide. One should never do an act of violence to the king's person. Nor should one ever strike a cow. Both these offences are equivalent to the sin of foeticide. One should never abandon one's (homa) fire. One should also never cast off one's study of the Vedas. One should never assail a Brahmana by words or acts. All these offences are equivalent to Brahmanicide."

"'Yudhishthira said,—"What kind of Brahmanas should be regarded as good? By making presents unto (what kind of) Brahmanas one may acquire great merit? What kind of Brahmanas are they whom one should feed? Tell me all this, O grandsire!"

"'Bhishma said, "Those Brahmanas that are freed from wrath, that are devoted to acts of righteousness, that are firm in Truth, and that practise self-restraint are regarded as good. By making gifts unto them one acquires great merit. One wins great merit by making presents unto such Brahmanas as are free from pride, capable of bearing everything, firm in the pursuit of their objects, endued with mastery over their senses, devoted to the good of all creatures, and disposed to be friendly towards all. One earns great merit by making gifts unto such Brahmanas as are free from cupidity, as are pure of heart and conduct, possessed of learning and modesty, truthful in speech and observant of their own duties as laid down in the scriptures. The Rishis have declared that Brahmana to be a deserving object of gifts who studies the four Vedas with all their branches and is devoted to the six well-known duties (laid down in the scriptures). One acquires great merit by making gifts unto Brahmanas possessed of such qualifications. The man who makes gifts unto a deserving Brahmana multiplies his merit a thousand-fold. A single righteous Brahmana possessed of wisdom and Vedic lore, observant of the duties laid down in the scriptures, distinguished by purity of behaviour, is competent to rescue a whole race.[210] One should make gifts of kine and horses and wealth and food and other kinds of articles unto a Brahmana that is possessed of such qualifications. By making such gifts unto such persons one earns great happiness in the next world. As I have already told thee even one such Brahmana is fully competent to rescue the entire race to which the giver belongs. What need I say, therefore, O dear son, of the merit of making gifts unto many Brahmanas of such qualifications? In making gifts, therefore one should always select the object to whom the gifts are to be made. Hearing of a Brahmana possessed of proper qualifications and regarded with respect by all good people, one should invite him even if he resides at a distance and welcome him when he arrives and one should worship him by all means in his power."'"

---

[210] i.e., by making gifts unto even a single such Brahmana, one rescues all the ancestors and descendants of one's race.

SECTION XXIII.

"'Yudhishthira said, "I desire thee, O grandsire, to tell me what the ordinances are that have been laid down by the acts touching the deities and the (deceased) ancestors on occasions of Sraddhas."

"'Bhishma said, "Having purified oneself (by baths and other purificatory acts) and then going through the well-known auspicious rites, one should carefully do all acts relating to the deities in the forenoon, and all acts relating to the Pitris in the afternoon. What is given to men should be given in the midday with affection and regard. That gift which is made untimely is appropriated by Rakshasas.[211] Gifts of articles that have been leapt over by any one, or been licked or sucked, that are not given peacefully, that have been seen by women that are impure in consequence of their season having come, do not produce any merit. Such gifts are regarded as the portion belonging to the Rakshasas. Gifts of articles that have been proclaimed before many people or from which a portion has been eaten by a Sudra, or that have been seen or licked by a dog, form portions of Rakshasas. Food which is mixed with hair or in which there are worms, or which has been stained with spittle or saliva or which has been gazed at by a dog or into which tear-drops have fallen or which has been trodden upon should be known as forming the portion of Rakshasas. Food that has been eaten by a person incompetent to utter the syllable Om, or that has been eaten by a person bearing arms, O Bharata, or that has been eaten by a wicked person should be known to form the portion of Rakshasas.[212] The food that is eaten by a person from which a portion has already been eaten by another, or which is eaten without a part thereof having been offered to deities and guests and children, is appropriated by Rakshasas. Such stained food, if offered to the deities and Pitris is never accepted by them but is appropriated by Rakshasas. The food offered by the three regenerate classes in Sraddhas, in which Mantras are either not uttered or uttered incorrectly and in which the ordinances laid down in the scriptures are not complied with, if distributed to guests and other people, is appropriated by Rakshasas. The food that is distributed to guests without having been previously dedicated to the deities or the Pitris with the aid of libation on the sacred fire, which has been stained in consequence of a portion thereof having been eaten by a person that is wicked or of irreligious behaviour, should be known to form the portion of Rakshasas.

""I have told thee what the portions are of the Rakshasas. Listen now to me as I lay down the rules for ascertaining who the Brahmana is that is deserving of gift.[213] All Brahmanas that have been outcasted (on account of the commission of heinous sins), as also Brahmanas that are idiots and out of mind, do not deserve to be invited to Sraddhas in which offerings are made to either the deities or the Pitris. That Brahmana who is afflicted with leucoderma, or he that is destitute of virility, or he that has got leprosy, or he that has got phthisis or he that is labouring under epilepsy (with delusions of the

---

[211] One makes gifts unto the deities, the Pitris, and unto human beings. There is a time for each kind of gift. If made untimely, the gift, instead of producing any merit, becomes entirely futile, if not sinful. Untimely gifts are appropriated by Rakshasas. Even food that is taken untimely, does not strengthen the body but goes to nourish the Rakshasas and other evil beings.

[212] i.e., any food, a portion of which has been eaten by any of these persons, is unworthy of being given away. If given, it is appropriated by Rakshasas. One incompetent to utter Om is, of course, a Sudra.

[213] The speaker, by first mentioning who are unworthy, means to point out those that are worthy.

sensorium), or he that is blind, should not, O king, be invited.[214] Those Brahmanas that practise the calling of physicians, those that receive regular pay for worshipping the images of deities established by the rich, or live upon the service of the deities, those that are observant of vows from pride or other false motives, and those that sell Soma, do not deserve to be invited. Those Brahmanas that are, by profession, vocalists, or dancers or players or instrumental musicians, or reciters of sacred books, or warriors and athletes, do not, O king, deserve to be invited. Those Brahmanas who pour libations on the sacred fire for Sudras, or who are preceptors of Sudras, or who are servants of Sudra masters, do not deserve to be invited. That Brahmana who is paid for his services as preceptor, or who attends as pupil upon the lectures of some preceptor because of some allowance that is granted to him, does not deserve to be invited, for both of them are regarded as sellers of Vedic lore. That Brahmana who has been once induced to accept the gift of food in a Sraddha at the very outset, as also he who has married a Sudra wife, even if possessed of every kind of knowledge do not deserve to be invited.[215] Those Brahmanas that are destitute of their domestic fire, and they that attend upon corpses, they that are thieves, and they that have otherwise fallen away do not, O king, deserve to be invited.[216] Those Brahmanas whose antecedents are not known or are vile, and they that are Putrika-putras, do not, O king, deserve to be invited on occasions of Sraddhas.[217] That Brahmana who gives loans of money, or he who subsists upon the interest of the loans given by him, or he who lives by sale of living creatures, does not deserve, O king, to be invited. Persons who have been subjugated by their wives, or they who live by becoming the paramours of unchaste women, or they who abstain from their morning and evening prayers do not deserve, O king, to be invited to Sraddhas.

""Listen now to me as I mention who the Brahmana is that has been ordained for acts done in honour of the deities and the Pitris. Indeed, I shall tell thee what those merits are in consequence of which one may become a giver or a recipient of gifts in Sraddhas (notwithstanding the faults mentioned above).[218] Those Brahmanas that are observant of the rites and ceremonies laid down in the scriptures, or they that are possessed of merit, or they that are conversant with the Gayatri, or they that are observant of the ordinary duties of Brahmanas, even if they happen to betake themselves to agriculture for a living, are capable, O king, of being invited to Sraddhas. If a Brahmana happens to be wellborn, he deserves to be invited to Sraddhas notwithstanding his profession of arms for fighting the battle of others.[219] That Brahmana, however, O son, who happens to betake himself to trade for a living should be discarded (even if possessed of merit). The Brahmana who pours libations every day on the sacred fire, or who resides in a fixed habitation, who is not a thief and who does the duties of hospitality to guests arrived at his house, deserves, O king, to be invited to Sraddhas. The Brahmana, O chief of Bharata's race, who recites

---

[214] Apasmara is a peculiar kind of epilepsy in which the victim always thinks that he is pursued by some monster who is before his eyes. When epilepsy is accompanied by some delusion of the sensorium, it comes to be called by Hindu physicians as Apasmara.

[215] An Agrani or Agradani is that Brahmana unto whom the food and other offerings to the Preta in the first Sraddha are given away. Such a person is regarded as fallen.

[216] When corpses are taken to crematoria, certain rites have to be performed upon them before they can be consumed. Those Brahmanas that assist at the performance of those rites are regarded as fallen.

[217] Sometimes the father of a daughter bestows her upon a bridegroom under the contract that the son born of that daughter by her husband should be the son of the daughter's father. Such a son, who is dissociated from the race of his own father, is called a Putrika-putra.

[218] Anugraham is that merit in consequence of which faults become neutralised and the stained person may come to be regarded as deserving.

[219] As Drona, Aswatthaman, Kripa, Rama and others.

the Savitri morning, noon, and night, or who subsists upon eleemosynary charity, who is observant of the rites and ceremonies laid down in the scriptures for persons of his order, deserves, O king, to be invited to Sraddhas.[220] That Brahmana who having earned wealth in the morning becomes poor in the afternoon, or who poor in the morning becomes wealthy in the evening or who is destitute of malice, or is stained by a minor fault, deserves, O king, to be invited to Sraddhas. That Brahmana who is destitute of pride or sin, who is not given to dry disputation, or who subsists upon alms obtained in his rounds of mendicancy from house to house deserves, O king, to be invited to sacrifices. One who is not observant of vows, or who is addicted to falsehood (in both speech and conduct), who is a thief, or who subsists by the sale of living creatures or by trade in general, becomes worthy of invitation to Sraddhas, O king, if he happens to offer all to the deities first and subsequently drink Soma. That man who having acquired wealth by foul or cruel means subsequently spends it in adoring the deities and discharging the duties of hospitality, becomes worthy, O king, of being invited to Sraddhas. The wealth that one has acquired by the sale of Vedic lore, or which has been earned by a woman, or which has been gained by meanness (such as giving false evidence in a court of law), should never be given to Brahmanas or spent in making offerings to the Pitris. That Brahmana, O chief of Bharata's race, who upon the completion of a Sraddha that is performed with his aid, refuses to utter the words 'astu swadha,' incurs the sin of swearing falsely in a suit for land.[221] The time for performing Sraddha, O Yudhishthira, is that when one obtains a good Brahmana and curds and ghee and the sacred day of the new moon, and the meat of wild animals such as deer and others.[222] Upon the completion of a Sraddha performed by a Brahmana the word Swadha should be uttered. If performed by a Kshatriya the words that should be uttered are—Let thy Pitris be gratified.—Upon the completion of a Sraddha performed by a Vaisya, O Bharata, the words that should be uttered are—Let everything become inexhaustible.—Similarly, upon the conclusion of a Sraddha performed by a Sudra, the word that should be uttered is Swasti,—In respect of a Brahmana, the declaration regarding Punyaham should be accompanied with the utterance of the syllable Om. In the case of a Kshatriya, such declaration should be without the utterance of syllable Om. In the rites performed by a Vaisya, the words that should be uttered, instead of being the syllable Om, are,—Let the deities be gratified.[223]—Listen now to me as I tell thee the rites that should be performed, one after another, conformably to the ordinances, (in respect of all the orders). All the rites that go by the name of Jatakarma, O Bharata, are indispensable in the case of all the three orders (that are regenerate). All these rites, O Yudhishthira, in the case of both Brahmanas and Kshatriyas as also in that of Vaisyas are to be performed with the aid of mantras. The girdle of a Brahmana should be made of Munja grass. That for one belonging to the royal

---

[220] Uditastamita means one who having earned wealth spends it all in gifts. Astamitodita is one who though poor at first succeed in earning wealth afterwards; i.e., one who having become rich, keeps that wealth for spending it on good purposes.

[221] Upon the completion of a Sraddha, the Brahmana who is officiating at it should utter the words yukta which means well-applied. Certain other words such as Swadha, etc., have to be uttered. The meaning is that the Brahmana who assists the performer of the Sraddha by reciting the Mantras should, upon completion, say unto the performer that the Sraddha is well-performed. As the custom is, these words are still uttered by every Brahmana officiating at Sraddhas.

[222] K. P. Singha wrongly renders the word somakshayah as equivalent to somarasah.

[223] Upon the conclusion of a Sraddha or other rites, the Brahmana who officiates at it, addresses certain other Brahmanas that are invited on the occasion and says,—Do you say Punyaham—The Brahmana addressed say,—Om, let it be Punyaham!—By Punyaham is meant sacred day.

order should be a bowstring. The Vaisya's girdle should be made of the Valwaji grass. Even this is what has been laid down in the scriptures. Listen now to me as I expound to thee what constitutes the merits and faults of both givers and recipients of gifts. A Brahmana becomes guilty of a dereliction of duty by uttering a falsehood. Such an act on his part is sinful. A Kshatriya incurs four times and a Vaisya eight times the sin that a Brahmana incurs by uttering a falsehood. A Brahmana should not eat elsewhere, having been previously invited by a Brahmana. By eating at the house of the person whose invitation has been posterior in point of time, he becomes inferior and even incurs the sin that attaches to the slaughter of an animal on occasions other than those of sacrifices.[224] So also, if he eats elsewhere after having been invited by a person of the royal order or a Vaisya, he falls away from his position and incurs half the sin that attaches to the slaughter of an animal on occasions other than those of sacrifices. That Brahmana, O king, who eats on occasions of such rites as are performed in honour of the deities or the Pitris by Brahmanas and Kshatriyas and Vaisyas, without having performed his ablutions, incurs the sin of uttering an untruth for a cow. That Brahmana, O king, who eats on occasions of similar rites performed by persons belonging to the three higher orders, at a time when he is impure in consequence either of a birth or a death among his cognates, through temptation, knowing well that he is impure incurs the same sin.[225] He who lives upon wealth obtained under false pretences like that of sojourns to sacred places or who solicits the giver for wealth pretending that he would spend it in religious acts, incurs, O monarch, the sin of uttering a falsehood.[226] That person, belonging to any of the three higher orders, O Yudhishthira, who at Sraddhas and on other occasions distributes food with the aid of Mantras, unto such Brahmanas as do not study the Vedas and as are not observant of vows, or as have not purified their conduct, certainly incurs sin."

"'Yudhishthira said,—"I desire, O grandsire, to know by giving unto whom the things dedicated to the deities and the Pitris, one may earn the amplest rewards."

"'Bhishma said,—"Do thou, Yudhishthira, feed those Brahmanas whose spouses reverently wait for the remnants of the dishes of their husbands like tillers of the soil waiting in reverence for timely showers of rain. One earns great merit by making gifts unto those Brahmanas that are always observant of pure conduct, O king, that are emaciated through abstention from all luxuries and even full meals, that are devoted to the observances of such vows as lead to the emaciation of the body, and that approach givers with the desire of obtaining gifts. By making gifts unto such Brahmanas as regard conduct in this light of food, as regard conduct in the light of spouses and children, as regard conduct in the light of strength, as regard conduct in the light of their refuge for crossing this world and attaining to felicity in the next, and as solicit wealth only when wealth is absolutely needed, one earns great merit. By making gifts unto those persons, O Yudhishthira, that having lost everything through thieves or oppressors, approach the giver, one acquires great merit.[227] By making gifts unto such Brahmanas as solicit food

---

[224] The fact is, the slaughter of animals in a sacrifice leads to no sin but if slaughtered for nothing (i.e., for purposes of food only), such slaughter leads to sin.

[225] One is said to become impure when a birth or a death occurs among one's cognates of near degree. The period of impurity varies from one day to ten days in case of Brahmanas. Other periods have been prescribed for the other orders. During the period of impurity one cannot perform one's daily acts of worship, etc.

[226] In this country, to this day, there are many persons that go about begging, stating that they desire to go to Banaras or other places of the kind. Sometimes alms are sought on the ground of enabling the seeker to invest his son with the sacred thread or perform his father's Sraddha, etc. The Rishi declares such practices to be sinful.

[227] Literally that are afraid of thieves and others. The sense, of course, is that have suffered at the hands of thieves and others and are still trembling with fear.

from the hands of even a poor person of their order who has just got something from others, one earns great merit. By making gifts unto such Brahmanas as have lost their all in times of universal distress and as have been deprived of their spouses on such occasions, and as come to givers with solicitations for alms, one acquires great merit. By making gifts unto such Brahmanas as are observant of vows, and as place themselves voluntarily under painful rules and regulations, as are respectful in their conduct to the declaration laid down in the Vedas, and as come to solicit wealth for spending it upon the rites necessary to complete their vows and other observances, one earns great merit. By making gifts unto such Brahmanas as live at a great distance from the practices that are observed by the sinful and the wicked, as are destitute of strength for want of adequate support, and as are very poor in earthly possessions, one earns great merit. By making gifts unto such Brahmanas as have been robbed of all their possessions by powerful men but as are perfectly innocent, and as desire to fill their stomachs any how without, that is, any scruples respecting the quality of the food they take, one earns great merit. By making gifts unto such Brahmanas as beg on behalf of others that are observant of penances and devoted to them and as are satisfied with even small gifts, one earns great merit. Thou hast now, O bull of Bharata's race, heard what the declarations are of the scriptures in respect of the acquisition of great merit by the making of gifts. Listen now to me as I expound what those acts are that lead to hell or heaven. They, O Yudhishthira, that speak an untruth on occasions other than those when such untruth is needed for serving the purpose of the preceptor or for giving the assurance of safety to a person in fear of his life, sink into hell.[228] They who ravish other people's spouses, or have sexual congress with them, or assist at such acts of delinquency, sink in hell. They who rob others of their wealth or destroy the wealth and possessions of other people, or proclaim the faults of other people, sink in hell. They who destroy the containers of such pieces of water as are used by cattle for quenching thirst, as injure such buildings as are used for purposes of public meetings, as break down bridges and causeways, and as pull down houses used for purposes of habitation, have to sink to hell. They who beguile and cheat helpless women, or girls, or aged dames, or such women as have been frightened, have to sink to hell. They who destroy the means of other people's living, they who exterminate the habitations of other people, they who rob others of their spouses, they who sow dissensions among friends, and they who destroy the hopes of other people, sink into hell. They who proclaim the faults of others, they who break down bridges or causeways, they who live by following vocations laid down for other people, and they who are ungrateful to friends for services received, have to sink in hell. They who have no faith in the Vedas and show no reverence for them, they who break the vows made by themselves or oblige others to break them, and they who fall away from their status through sin, sink in hell. They who betake themselves to improper conduct, they who take exorbitant rates of interest, and they who make unduly large profits on sales, have to sink in hell. They who are given to gambling, they who indulge in wicked acts without any scruple, and they who are given to slaughter of living creatures, have to sink in hell. They who cause the

[228] The two exceptions have been much animadverted upon by unthinking persons. I have shown that according to the code of morality, that is in vogue among people whose Christianity and civilisation are unquestionable, a lie may sometimes be honourable. However casuists may argue, the world is agreed that a lie for saving life and even property under certain circumstances, and for screening the honour of a confiding woman, is not inexcusable. The goldsmith's son who died with a lie on his lips for saving the Prince Chevalier did a meritorious act. The owner also who hides his property from robbers, cannot be regarded as acting dishonourably.

dismissal by masters of servants that are hoping for rewards or are expectant of definite need or are in the enjoyment of wages or salaries or are waiting for returns in respect of valuable services already rendered, have to sink in hell. They who themselves eat without offering portions thereof unto their spouse or their sacred fires or their servants or their guests, and they who abstain from performing the rites laid down in the scriptures for honouring the Pitris and deities, have to sink in hell. They who sell the Vedas, they who find fault with the Vedas, and they who reduce the Vedas into writing, have all to sink in hell.[229] They who are out of the pale of the four well-known modes of life, they who betake themselves to practices interdicted by the Srutis and the scriptures, and they who live by betaking themselves to acts that are wicked or sinful or that do not belong to their order of birth, have to sink in hell. They who live by selling hair, they who subsist by selling poisons, and they who live by selling milk, have to sink in hell. They who put obstacles in the path of Brahmanas and kine and maidens, O Yudhishthira, have to sink in hell. They who sell weapons, they who forge weapons, they who make shafts, and they who make bows, have to sink in hell. They who obstruct paths and roads with stones and thorns and holes have to sink in hell. They who abandon and cast off preceptors and servants and loyal followers without any offence, O chief of Bharata's race, have to sink in hell. They who set bullocks to work before the animals attain to sufficient age, they who bore the noses of bullocks and other animals for controlling them the better while employed in work, and they who keep animals always tethered, have to sink in hell. Those kings that do not protect their subjects while forcibly taking from them a sixth share of the produce of their fields, and they who, though able and possessed of resources, abstain from making gifts, have to sink in hell. They who abandon and cast off persons that are endued with forgiveness and self-restraint and wisdom, or those with whom they have associated for many years, when these are no longer of services to them, have to sink in hell. Those men who themselves eat without giving portions of the food to children and aged men and servants, have to sink in hell.

""'All these men enumerated above have to go to hell. Listen now to me, O bull of Bharata's race, as I tell thee who those men are that ascend to heaven. The man who transgresses against a Brahmana by impeding the performances of all such acts in which the deities are adored, becomes afflicted with the loss of all his children and animals. (They who do not transgress against Brahmanas by obstructing their religious acts ascend to heaven). Those men, O Yudhishthira, who follow the duties as laid down in the scriptures for them and practise the virtues of charity and self-restraint and truthfulness, ascend to heaven. Those men who having acquired knowledge by rendering obedient services to their preceptors and observing austere penances, become reluctant to accept gifts, succeed in ascending to heaven. Those men through whom other people are relieved and rescued from fear and sin and the impediments that lie in the way of what they wish to accomplish and poverty and the afflictions of disease, succeed in ascending to heaven. Those men who are endued with a forgiving disposition, who are possessed of patience, who are prompt in performing all righteous acts, and who are of auspicious conduct, succeed in ascending to heaven. Those men who abstain from honey and meat, who abstain from sexual congress with the spouses of other people, and who abstain from wines and spirituous liquors, succeed in ascending to heaven. Those men that help in the establishment of retreats for ascetics, who become founders of families, O Bharata, who

---

[229] By selling the Vedas is meant the charging of fees for teaching them. As regards the Vedas, the injunction in the scriptures is to commit them to memory and impart them from mouth to mouth. Hence to reduce them into writing was regarded as a transgression.

open up new countries for purposes of habitation, and lay out towns and cities succeed in ascending to heaven. Those men who give away cloths and ornaments, as also food and drink, and who help in marrying others, succeed in ascending to heaven.[230] Those men that have abstained from all kinds of injury or harm to all creatures, who are capable of enduring everything, and who have made themselves the refuge of all creatures, succeed in ascending to heaven. Those men who wait with humility upon their fathers and mothers, who have subjugated their senses, and who are affectionate towards their brothers, succeed in ascending to heaven. Those men that subjugate their senses notwithstanding the fact of their being rich in worldly goods and strong in might and in the enjoyment of youth, succeed in ascending to heaven. Those men that are kind towards even those that offend against them, that are mild of disposition, that have an affection for all who are of mild behaviour, and that contribute to the happiness of others by rendering them every kind of service in humility, succeed in ascending to heaven. Those men that protect thousands of people, that make gifts unto thousands of people, and that rescue thousands of people from distress, succeed in ascending to heaven. Those men who make gifts of gold and of kine, O chief of Bharata's race, as also those of conveyances and animals, succeed in ascending to heaven. Those men who make gifts of such articles as are needed in marriages, as also those of serving men and maids, and cloths and robes, succeed in ascending to heaven.[231] Those men who make public pleasure-houses and gardens and wells, resting houses and buildings for public meetings and tanks for enabling cattle and men to quench their thirst, and fields for cultivation, O Bharata, succeed in ascending to heaven.[232] Those men who make gifts of houses and fields and populated villages unto persons that solicit them, succeed in ascending to heaven. Those men who having themselves manufactured juicy drinks of sweet taste and seeds and paddy or rice, make gifts of them unto others succeed in ascending to heaven. Those men who being born in families high or low beget hundreds of children and live long lives practising compassion and keeping wrath under complete subjection, succeed in ascending to heaven. I have thus expounded to thee, O Bharata, what the rites are in honour of the deities and the Pitris which are performed by people for the sake of the other world, what the ordinances are in respect of making gifts, and what the views are of the Rishis of former times in respect of both the articles of gift and the manner of giving them.""""

SECTION XXIV.

"'Yudhishthira said, "O royal son of Bharata's race, it behoveth thee to answer this question of mine truly and in detail. What are those circumstances under which a person may become guilty of Brahmanicide without actually slaying a Brahmana!"

"'Bhishma said, "Formerly, O monarch, I had one day requested Vyasa to explain to me this very subject. I shall now narrate to thee what Vyasa told me on that occasion. Do thou listen to it with undivided attention. Repairing to the presence of Vyasa, I addressed him, saying,—'Thou, O great ascetic, art the fourth in descent from Vasishtha. Do thou

---

[230] In this country to this day, the act of marrying a helpless person with a good girl by paying all the expenses of the marriage, is regarded as an act of righteousness. Of course, the man that is so married is also given sufficient property for enabling him to maintain himself and his wife.

[231] Articles needed in marriages are, of course, girls and ornaments.

[232] Vapra has various meanings. I think, it means here a field. Large waste lands often require to be enclosed with ditches and causeways. Unless so reclaimed, they cannot be fit for cultivation.

110

explain to me this. What are those circumstances under which one becomes guilty of Brahmanicide without actually slaying a Brahmana.'—Thus addressed by me, the son of Parasara's loins, O king, well-skilled in the science of morality, made me the following answer, at once excellent and fraught with certainty. 'Thou shouldst know that man as guilty of Brahmanicide who having of his own will invited a Brahmana of righteous conduct to his house for giving him alms subsequently refuses to give anything to him on the pretence of there being nothing in the house. Thou shouldst, O Bharata, know that man as guilty of Brahmanicide who destroys the means of living of a Brahmana learned in the Vedas and all their branches, and who is freed from attachments to worldly creatures and goods. Thou shouldst, O king, know that man to be guilty of Brahmanicide, who causes obstructions in the way of thirsty kine while employed in quenching that thirst. Thou shouldst take that man as guilty of Brahmanicide who, without studying the Srutis that have flowed from preceptor to pupil for ages and ages together, finds fault with the Srutis or with those scriptures that have been composed by the Rishis. Thou shouldst know that man as guilty of Brahmanicide who does not bestow upon a suitable bride-groom his daughter possessed of beauty and other excellent accomplishments. Thou shouldst know that foolish and sinful person to be guilty of Brahmanicide who inflicts such grief upon Brahmanas as afflict the very core of their hearts. Thou shouldst know that man to be guilty of Brahmanicide who robs the blind, the lame, and idiots of their all. Thou shouldst know that man to be guilty of Brahmanicide who sets fire to the retreats of ascetics or to woods or to a village or a town.'"""

SECTION XXV.

"'Yudhishthira said, "It has been said that sojourns to sacred waters as fraught with merit; that ablutions in such waters is meritorious; and that listening to the excellence of such waters is also meritorious. I desire to hear thee expatiate on this subject, O grandsire. It behoveth thee, O chief of Bharata's race, to mention to me the sacred waters that exist on this earth. I desire, O thou of great puissance, to hear thee discourse on this topic."

"'Bhishma said, "O thou of great splendour, the following enumeration of the sacred waters on the Earth was made by Angiras. Blessed be thou, it behoveth thee to listen to it for thou shalt then earn great merit. Once on a time, Gautama of rigid vows, approaching the great and learned Rishi Angiras endued with tranquillity of soul, while he was dwelling in a forest, questioned him, saying,—'O illustrious one, I have some doubts regarding the merits attaching to sacred waters and shrines. So I desire to hear thee discourse on that topic. Do thou, therefore, O ascetic, discourse to me. What merits are earned by a person in respect of the next world, by bathing in the sacred waters on the Earth, O thou of great wisdom? Do thou expound to me this truly and according to the ordinance.'

"""Angiras said, 'A person by bathing for seven days in succession in the Chandrabhaga or the Vitasta whose waters are always seen to dance in waves, observing a fast the while, is sure to become cleansed of all his sins and endued with the merit of an ascetic.[233] The very many rivers that flowing through Kasmira, fall into the great river called Sindhu (Indus). By bathing in these rivers one is sure to become endued with good

---

[233] The river Chenab in the Punjab was known in former times by the name of Chandrabhaga. So the river Jhelum was known by the name of Vitasta.

character and to ascend to heaven after departing from this world. By bathing in Pushkara, and Prabhasa, and Naimisha, and the ocean, and Devika, and Indramarga, and Swarnavindu, one is sure to ascend to heaven being seated on a celestial car, and filled with transports of joy at the adorations of Apsara. By plunging in the waters of Hiranyavindu with a concentrated mind and reverencing that sacred stream, and bathing next at Kusesaya and Devendra, one becomes cleansed of all one's sins. Repairing to Indratoya in the vicinity of the mountains of Gandhamadana and next to Karatoya in the country called Kuranga, one should observe a fast for three days and then bathe in those sacred waters with a concentrated heart and pure body. By doing this, one is sure to acquire the merit of a Horse-sacrifice. Bathing in Gangadwara and Kusavarta and Vilwaka in the Nita mountains, as also in Kankhala, one is sure to become cleansed of all one's sins and then ascend to heaven. If one becomes a Brahmacharin and subdues one's wrath, devotes oneself to truth and practises compassion towards all creatures, and then bathes in the Jala parda (Lake of Waters), one is sure to acquire the merit of a Horse-sacrifice. That part where Bhagirathi-Ganga flows in a northward direction is known as the union of heaven, earth, and the nether regions. Observing a fast for one month and bathing in that sacred Tirtha which is known to be acceptable to Maheswara, one becomes competent to behold the deities. One who gives oblations of water unto one's Pitris at Saptaganga and Triganga and Indramarga, obtains ambrosia for food, if one has still to undergo rebirth. The man who in a pure state of body and mind attends to his daily Agnihotra and observes a fast for one month and then bathes in Mahasrama, is sure to attain success in one month. By bathing, after a fast of three days and purifying the mind of all evil passions, in the large lake of Bhrigu Kunda, one becomes cleansed of even the sin of Brahmanicide. By bathing in Kanyakupa and performing one's ablutions in Valaka, one acquires great fame among even the deities and shines in glory. Bathing in Devika and the lake known by the name of Sundarika as also in the Tirtha called Aswini, one acquires, in one's next life, great beauty of form. By fasting for a fortnight and bathing in Mahaganga and Krittikangaraka, one becomes cleansed of all one's sins and ascends to heaven. Bathing in Vaimanika and Kinkinika, one acquires the power of repairing everywhere at will and becomes an object of great respect in the celestial region of the Apsaras.[234] If a person, subduing his wrath and observing the vow of Brahmacharyya for three days, bathes in the river Vipasa at the retreat called Kalika, he is sure to succeed in transcending the obligation of rebirth. Bathing in the asylum that is sacred to the Krittakas and offering oblations of water to the Pitris, and then gratifying Mahadeva, one becomes pure in body and mind and ascends to heaven. If one, observing a fast for three days with a purified body and mind, bathes in Mahapura, one becomes freed from the fear of all mobile and immobile animals as also of all animals having two feet. By bathing in the Devadaru forest and offering oblations of water to the Pitris and dwelling there for seven nights with a pure body and mind, one attains to the region of the deities on departing from this world. Bathing in the waterfalls at Sarastamva and Kusastambha and Dronasarmapada, one is sure to attain to the region of the Apsaras where one is waited upon with dutiful services by those superhuman beings. If one, observing a fast, bathes at Chitrakuta and Janasthana and the waters of Mandakini, one is sure to be united with prosperity that is royal.[235] By repairing to the retreat that is known by the name of Samya and residing there for a fortnight and bathing in the sacred water that exists there,

---

[234] The sense is that one proceeds to the region of the Apsaras and becomes an object of respect there.
[235] i.e., one acquires sovereignty.

one acquires the power of disappearing at will (and enjoy the happiness that has been ordained for the Gandharvas). Repairing to the tirtha known by the name of Kausiki and residing there with a pure heart and abstaining from all food and drink for three days, one acquires the power of dwelling (in one's next life) in the happy region of the Gandharvas. Bathing in the delightful tirtha that goes by the name of Gandhataraka and residing there for one month, abstaining all the while from food and drink, one acquires the power of disappearing at pleasure and, then one and twenty days, of ascending to heaven. He that bathes in the lake known by the name of Matanga is sure to attain to success in one night. He that bathes in Analamva or in eternal Andhaka, or in Naimisha, or the tirtha called Swarga, and offers oblations of water to the Pitris, subduing his senses the while, acquires the merit of a human sacrifice.[236] Bathing in Ganga hrada and the tirtha known by the name of Utpalavana and daily offering oblations of water there for a full month to the Pitris, one acquires the merit of a Horse-sacrifice. Bathing in the confluence of the Ganga and the Yamuna as also at the tirtha in the Kalanjara mountains and offering every day oblations of water to the Pitris for a full month, one acquires the merit that attaches to ten Horse-sacrifices. Bathing in the Shashthi lake one acquires merit much greater than what is attached to the gift of food. Ten thousand tirthas and thirty millions of other tirthas come to Prayaga (the confluence of Ganga and Yamuna), O chief of Bharata's race in the month of Magha. He who bathes in Prayaga, with a restrained soul and observing rigid vows the while, in the month of Magha, becomes cleansed of all his sins, O chief of Bharata's race, and attains to heaven. Bathing in the tirtha that is sacred to the Maruts, as also in that which is situate in the retreat of the Pitris, and also in that which is known by the name of Vaivaswata, one becomes cleansed of all one's sins and becomes as pure and sanctified as a tirtha. Repairing to Brahmasaras as also to the Bhagirathi and bathing there and offering oblations to the Pitris every day for a full month, abstaining from food all the while, one is sure to attain to the region of Soma. Bathing in Utpataka and then in Ashtavakra and offering oblations of water to the Pitris every day for twelve days in succession, abstaining the while from food, one acquires the merits of a Horse-sacrifice. Bathing in Asmaprishtha and Niravinda mountains and Kraunchapadi,—all three in Gaya—one becomes cleansed of the sin of Brahmanicide. A bath in the first place cleanses one of a single Brahmanicide; a bath in the second cleanses one of two offences of that character; and a bath in the third cleanses one of three such offences. Bathing in Kalavinga, one acquires a large quantity of water (for use in the next world). A man, by bathing in the city of Agni, acquires such merit as entitles him to live during his next birth in the city of Agni's daughter. Bathing in Visala in Karavirapura and offering oblations of water unto one's Pitris, and performing one's ablutions in Devahrada too, one becomes identified with Brahma and shines in glory as such. Bathing in Punaravarta-nanda as also Mahananda, a man of restrained senses and universal compassion repairs to the celestial gardens called Nandana of Indra and is waited upon there by Apsaras of diverse tribes. Bathing with concentrated soul in the tirtha that is called after the name of Urvasi and that is situate in the river Lohitya, on the day of full moon of the month of Kartika, one attains to the merits that attach to the sacrifice called Pundarika. Bathing in Ramahrada and offering oblations of water to the Pitris in the river Vipasa (Beas), and observing a fast for twelve days, one becomes cleansed of all sins. Bathing in the tirtha called Maha-hrada with a purified heart and after observing a fast for one month, one is sure to attain to the end which was the sage Jamadagni's. By exposing oneself to heat in the tirtha called Vindhya, a person devoted to truth and endued with compassion for all creatures should then betake himself to austere penances, actuated by humility. By so doing, he is sure to attain to ascetic success in course of a single month. Bathing in the Narmada as also in the tirtha known by the name of Surparaka, observing a fast for a full fortnight, one is sure to become in one's next birth a prince of the royal line. If one proceeds with restrained senses and a concentrated soul to the tirtha known under the name of Jamvumarga, one is sure to attain to success in course of a single day and night. By repairing to Chandalikasrama and bathing in the tirtha called Kokamukha, having subsisted for some time on potherbs alone and worn rags for vestments, one is sure to obtain ten maidens of great beauty for one's spouses. One who lives by the side of the tirtha known by the name of Kanya-hrada has never to go to the regions of Yama. Such a person is sure to ascend to the regions of felicity that belong to the celestials. One who bathes with restrained senses on the day of the new moon in the tirtha known by the name of Prabhasa, is sure, O thou of mighty arms, of at once attaining to success and immortality. Bathing in the tirtha known by the name of Ujjanaka which occurs in the retreat of Arshtisena's son, and next in the tirtha that is situate in the retreat of Pinga, one is sure to be cleansed of all one's sins. Observing a fast for three days and bathing in the tirtha known as Kulya and reciting the sacred mantras that go by the name of Aghamarshana, one attains the merit of a horse-sacrifice. Observing a fast for one night and bathing in Pindaraka, one becomes purified on the dawn of the next day and attains to the merit of an Agnishtoma sacrifice. One who repairs to Brahmasara which is adorned by the woods called Dharmaranya, becomes cleansed of all one's sins and attains to the merit of the Pundarika sacrifice. Bathing in the waters of the Mainaka mountain and saying one's morning and evening prayers there and living at the spot for a month, restraining desire, one attains to the merit of all the sacrifices. Setting out for Kalolaka and Nandikunda and Uttara-manasa, and reaching a spot that is hundred yojanas remote from any of them, one becomes cleansed of the sin of foeticide. One who succeeds in obtaining a sight of image of Nandiswara, becomes cleansed of all sins. Bathing in the tirtha called Swargamarga one is sure to proceed to the regions of Brahman. The celebrated Himavat is sacred. That prince of mountains is the father-in-law of Sankara. He is a mine of all jewels and gems and is the resort of the Siddhas and Charanas. That regenerate person who is fully conversant with the Vedas and who, regarding this life to be exceedingly unstable, casts off his body on those mountains, abstaining from all food and drink in accordance with the rites laid down in the scriptures, after having adored the deities and bent his head in worship of the ascetics, is sure to attain to success and proceed to the eternal regions of Brahman. There is nothing unattainable to him who resides in a tirtha, restraining lust and subjugating wrath, in consequence of such residence. For the purpose of repairing to all the tirthas in the world, one should mentally think of those amongst them that are almost inaccessible or sojourns to which are attended with insurmountable difficulties. Sojourns to tirthas is productive of the merits of sacrifices. They are competent to cleanse everybody of sin. Fraught with great excellence, they are capable of leading to heaven. The subject is truly a great mystery. The very deities should bathe in tirthas. To them also they are sin-cleansing. This discourse on tirthas should be imparted to Brahmanas, and to such honest or righteous persons as are bent upon achieving what is for their own good. It should also be recited in the hearing of one's well-wishers and friends and of one's obedient and devoted disciples. Angiras possessed of great ascetic merit, had imparted this discourse to Gautama.

Angiras himself had obtained it from Kasyapa of great intelligence. The great Rishi regard this discourse as worthy of constant repetition. It is the foremost of all cleansing things. If one recites it regularly every day, one is sure to become cleansed of every sin and to proceed to heaven after the termination of this life. One who listens to this discourse recited in his hearing,—this discourse, viz., of Angiras, that is regarded as a mystery,—is sure to attain in one's next life to be born in a good family and, what is more, one would become endued with the memory of one's previous existence."'"

SECTION XXVI.

"Vaisampayana said,—'Equal unto Vrihaspati in intelligence and Brahma himself in forgiveness, resembling Sakra in prowess and Surya in energy, Bhishma the son of Ganga, of infinite might, had been overthrown in battle by Arjuna. Accompanied by his brothers and many other people, king Yudhisthira asked him these questions. The old hero was lying on a bed that is coveted by heroes, in expectation of that auspicious time when he could take leave of the physical frame. Many great Rishis had come there for seeing that foremost one of Bharata's race. Amongst them were Atri and Vasishtha and Bhrigu and Pulastya and Pulaha and Kratu. There were also Angiras and Gotama and Agastya and Sumati of well-restrained soul, and Viswamitra and Sthulasiras and Samvarta and Pramati and Dama. There were also Vrihaspati and Usanas, and Vyasa and Chyavana and Kasyapa and Dhruva, and Durvasas and Jamadagni and Markandeya and Galava, and Bharadwaja and Raibhya and Yavakrita and Trita. There were Sthulaksha and Savalaksha and Kanwa and Medhatithi and Krisa and Narada and Parvata and Sudhanwa and Ekata and Dwita. There were also Nitambhu and Bhuvana and Dhaumya and Satananda and Akritavrana and Rama, the son of Jamadagni and Kacha. All these high-souled and great Rishis came there for seeing Bhishma lying on his bed of arrows. Yudhishthira with his brothers duly worshipped those high-souled Rishis who had come there, one after another in proper order. Receiving that worship, those foremost of Rishis sat themselves down and began to converse with one another. Their conversation related to Bhishma, and was highly sweet and agreeable to all the senses. Hearing that talk of theirs having reference to himself, Bhishma became filled with delight and regarded himself to be already in heaven. Those Rishis then, having obtained the leave of Bhishma and of the Pandava princes, made themselves invisible, vanishing in the very sight of all the beholders. The Pandavas repeatedly bowed and offered their adorations to those highly blessed Rishis, even after they had made themselves invisible. They then with cheerful souls waited upon the son of Ganga, even as Brahmanas versed in Mantras wait with reverence upon the rising Sun. The Pandavas beheld that the points of the compass blazed forth with splendour in consequence of the energy of their penances, and became filled with wonder at the sight. Thinking of the high blessedness and puissance of those Rishis, the Pandava princes began to converse on the subject with their grandsire Bhishma.'

"Vaisampayana continued, 'The conversation being over, the righteous Yudhishthira, the son of Pandu, touched Bhishma's feet with his head and then resumed his questions relating to morality and righteousness.'

"'Yudhishthira said, "Which countries, which provinces, which retreats, which mountains, and which rivers, O grandsire, are the foremost in point of sanctity?"

"'Bhishma said, "In this connection is cited the old narrative of a conversation between a Brahmana in the observance of the Sila and the Unccha vows, O Yudhishthira, and a Rishi crowned with ascetic success. Once on a time, a foremost person, having roamed over this entire earth adorned with mountains, arrived at last in the house of a foremost person leading the domestic mode of life in accordance with the Sila vow. The latter welcomed his guest with due rites. Received with such hospitality, the happy Rishi passed the night happily in the house of his host. The next morning the Brahmana in the observance of the Sila vow, having finished all his morning acts and rites and purified himself duly, very cheerfully approached his guest crowned with ascetic success. Meeting with each other and seated at their ease, the two began to converse on agreeable subjects connected with the Vedas and the Upanishads. Towards the conclusion of the discourse, the Brahmana in the observance of the Sila vow respectfully addressed the Rishi crowned with success. Endued with intelligence, he put this very question which thou, O Yudhisthira, hast put to me.

""The poor Brahmana said, 'What countries, what provinces, what retreats, what mountains, and what rivers should be regarded as the foremost in point of sanctity? Do thou discourse to me on this.'

""The Rishi crowned with success said, 'Those countries, those provinces, those retreats, and those mountains, should be regarded as the foremost in point of sanctity through which or by the side of which that foremost of all rivers, viz., Bhagirathi flows. That end which a creature is capable of attaining by penances, by Brahmacharyya, by sacrifices, or by practising renunciation, one is sure to attain by only living by the side of the Bhagirathi and bathing in its sacred waters. Those creatures whose bodies have been sprinkled with the sacred waters of Bhagirathi or whose bones have been laid in the channel of that sacred stream, have not to fall away from heaven at any time.[237] Those men, O learned Brahmana, who use the waters of Bhagirathi in all their acts, surely ascend to heaven after departing from this world. Even those men who, having committed diverse kinds of sinful deeds in the first part of their lives, betake themselves in after years to a residing by the side of Ganga, succeed in attaining to a very superior end. Hundreds of sacrifices cannot produce that merit which men of restrained souls are capable of acquiring by bathing in the sacred waters of Ganga. A person is treated with respect and worshipped in heaven for as long a period as his bones lie in the channel of the Ganga. Even as the Sun, when he rises at the dawn of day, blazes forth in splendour, having dispelled the gloom of night, after the same manner the person that has bathed in the waters of Ganga is seen to shine in splendour, cleansed of all his sins. Those countries and those points of the compass that are destitute of the sacred waters of Ganga are like nights without the moon or like trees without flowers. Verily, a world without Ganga is like the different orders and modes of life when they are destitute of righteousness or like sacrifices without Soma. Without doubt, countries and points of the compass that are without Ganga are like the firmament without the Sun, or the Earth without mountains, or the welkin without air. The entire body of creatures in the three worlds, if served with the auspicious waters of Ganga, derive a pleasure, the like of which they are incapable of deriving from any other source. He who drinks Ganga water that has been heated by the Sun's rays derives merit much greater than that which attaches to the vow of subsisting upon the wheat or grains of other corn picked up from cowdung. It cannot be said whether the two are equal or not, viz., he who performs a thousand Chandrayana rites for purifying his body and he who drinks the water of Ganga. It cannot be said whether the two are equal or not, viz., one who stands for a thousand years on one foot and one who

---

[237] Nyastani has Gangayam understood after it.

lives for only a month by the side of Ganga. One who lives permanently by the side of Ganga is superior in merit to one who stays for ten thousand Yugas with head hanging downwards. As cotton, when it comes into contact with fire, is burnt off without a remnant, even so the sins of the person that has bathed in Ganga become consumed without a remnant. There is no end superior to Ganga for those creatures who with hearts afflicted by sorrow, seek to attain to ends that may dispel that sorrow of theirs. As snakes become deprived of their poison at the very sight of Garuda, even so one becomes cleansed of all one's sins at the very sight of the sacred stream of Ganga. They that are without good name and that are addicted to deeds of sinfulness, have Ganga for their fame, their protection, their means of rescue, their refuge or cover. Many wretches among men who become afflicted with diverse sins of a heinous nature, when they are about to sink into hell, are rescued by Ganga in the next world (if, notwithstanding their sins, they seek the aid of Ganga in their after-years). They, O foremost of intelligent men, who plunge every day in the sacred waters of Ganga, become the equals of great Munis and the very deities with Vasava at their head. Those wretches among men that are destitute of humility or modesty of behaviour and that are exceedingly sinful, become righteous and good, O Brahmana, by betaking themselves to the side of Ganga. As Amrita is to the deities, as Swadha is to the Pitris, as Sudha is to the Nagas, even so is Ganga water to human beings. As children afflicted with hunger solicit their mothers for food, after the same manner do people desirous of their highest good pay court to Ganga. As the region of the self-born Brahma is said to be the foremost of all places, even so is Ganga said to be foremost of all rivers for those that desire to bathe. As the Earth and the cow are said to be the chief sustenance of the deities and other celestials, even so is Ganga the chief sustenance of all living creatures.[238] As the deities support themselves upon the Amrita that occurs in the Sun and the Moon and that is offered in diverse sacrifices, even so do human beings support themselves upon Ganga water. One besmeared with the sand taken from the shores of Ganga regards oneself as a denizen of heaven, adorned with celestial unguents. He who bears on his head the mud taken from the banks of Ganga presents an effulgent aspect equal to that of Sun himself bent on dispelling the surrounding darkness. When that wind which is moistened with the particles of Ganga-water touches one's person, it cleanses him immediately of every sin. A person afflicted by calamities and about to sink under their weight, finds all his calamities dispelled by the joy which springs up in his heart at sight of that sacred stream. By the melody of the swans and Kokas and other aquatic fowls that play on her breast, Ganga challenges the very Gandharvas and by her high banks the very mountains on the Earth. Beholding her surface teeming with swans and diverse other aquatic fowls, and having banks adorned with pasture lands with kine grazing on them. Heaven herself loses her pride. The high happiness which one enjoys by a residence on the banks of Ganga, can never be his who is residing even in heaven. I have no doubt in this that the person who is afflicted with sins perpetrated in speech and thought and overt act, becomes cleansed at the very sight of Ganga. By holding that sacred stream, touching it, and bathing in its waters, one rescues one's ancestors to the seventh generation, one's descendants to the seventh generation, as also other ancestors and descendants. By hearing of Ganga, by wishing to repair to that river, by drinking its waters, by touching its waters, and by bathing in them a person rescues both his paternal and maternal races. By seeing, touching, and drinking

---

[238] The deities are supported by the offerings made in sacrifices. These offerings consist of the productions of the Earth and the butter produced by the cow. The deities, therefore, are said to be chiefly supported by the Earth and the Cow. The Asuras, by afflicting the Earth and killing kine, used to weaken the deities.

the waters of Ganga, or even by applauding Ganga, hundreds and thousands of sinful men become cleansed of all their sins. They who wish to make their birth, life and learning fruitful, should repair to Ganga and gratify the Pitris and the deities by offering them oblations of water. The merit that one earns by bathing in Ganga is such that the like of it is incapable of being earned through the acquisition of sons or wealth or the performance of meritorious acts. Those who, although possessed of the physical ability, do not seek to have a sight of the auspicious Ganga of sacred current, are, without doubt, to be likened to persons afflicted with congenital blindness or those that are dead or those that are destitute of the power of locomotion through palsy or lameness. What man is there that would not reverence this sacred stream that is adored by great Rishis conversant with the Present, the Past, and the Future, as also by the very deities with Indra at their head. What man is there that would not seek the protection of Ganga whose protection is sought for by forest recluses and householders, and by Yatis and Brahmacharins alike? The man of righteous conduct who, with rapt soul, thinks of Ganga at the time when his life-breaths are about to leave his body, succeeds in attaining to the highest end. That man who dwells by the side of Ganga up to the time of his death, adoring her with reverence, becomes freed from the fear of every kind of calamity, of sin, and of kings. When that highly sacred stream fell from the firmament, Maheswara held it on his head. It is that very stream which is adored in heaven.[239] The three regions, viz., (Earth, Heaven, and the nether place called Patala) are adorned by the three courses of this sacred stream. The man who uses the waters of that stream becomes certainly crowned with success. As the solar ray is to the deities in heaven, as Chandramas is to the Pitris, as the king is to human beings, even such is Ganga unto all streams.[240] One who becomes bereaved of mother or father or sons or spouses or wealth does not feel that grief which becomes one's, when one becomes bereaved of Ganga. One does not obtain that joy through acts that lead to the region of Brahma, or through such sacrifices and rites that lead to heaven, or through children or wealth, which one obtain from a sight of Ganga.[241] The pleasures that men derive from a sight of Ganga is equal to what they derive from a sight of the full moon. That man becomes dear to Ganga who adores her with deep devotion, with mind wholly fixed upon her, with a reverence that refuses to take any other object within its sphere, with a feeling that there is nothing else to the universe worthy of similar adoration, and with a steadiness that knows no failing away. Creatures that live on Earth, in the welkin, or in Heaven, indeed, even beings that are very superior,—should always bathe in Ganga. Verily, this is the foremost of all duties with those that are righteous. The fame of Ganga for sanctity has spread over the entire universe, since she bore all the sons of Sagara, who had been reduced to ashes, from here to Heaven.[242] Men who are washed by the bright, beautiful, high, and rapidly moving waves, raised by the wind, of Ganga, become cleansed of all their sins and resemble in splendour the Sun with his thousand rays. Those men of tranquil souls that have cast off their bodies in the waters of Ganga whose sanctity is as great as that of the butter and other liquids poured in sacrifices and which are capable of conferring merits equal to those of the greatest of sacrifices, have certainly

---

[239] The river Ganga has three courses. On Earth it is called Bhagirathi or Ganga; in heaven it is called Mandakini; and in the nether regions it is known by the name of Bhogabati.

[240] Devesh is lit. the lord of the deities; but here it means the King or Emperor.

[241] Aranyaih is explained by the commentator as implying courses of conduct leading to Brahmaloka.

[242] The story referred to is this: King Sagara of the solar (?) race had sixty thousand sons, all of whom were reduced to ashes by the curse of Kapila. Afterwards Bhagiratha, a prince of the same race, brought down Ganga from heaven for their redemption.

attained to a station equal to that of the very deities. Verily, Ganga, possessed of fame and vast extent and identical with the entire universe and reverenced by the deities with Indra at their head, the Munis and human beings, is competent to bestow the fruition of all their wishes upon them that are blind, them that are idiots, and them that are destitute of all things.[243] They that sought the refuge of Ganga, that protectress of all the universe, that flows in three streams, that is filled with water at once highly sacred and sweet as honey and productive of every kind of good, have succeeded in attaining to the beatitude of Heaven.[244] That mortal who dwells by the side of Ganga and beholds her every day, becomes cleansed by her sight and touch. Unto him the deities give every kind of happiness here and a high end hereafter. Ganga is regarded as competent to rescue every creature from sin and lead him to the felicity of Heaven. She is held to be identical with Prisni, the mother of Vishnu. She is identical with the Word or Speech. She is very remote, being incapable of easy attainment. She is the embodiment of auspiciousness and prosperity. She is capable of bestowing the six well-known attributes beginning with lordship or puissance. She is always inclined to extend her grace. She is the displayer of all things in the universe, and she is the high refuge of all creatures. Those who have sought her protection in this life have surely attained heaven. The fame of Ganga has spread all over the welkin, and Heaven, and Earth, and all the points, cardinal and subsidiary, of the compass. Mortal creatures, by using the waters of that foremost of streams, always become crowned with high success. That person who himself beholding Ganga, points her out to others, finds that Ganga rescues him from rebirth and confers Emancipation on him. Ganga held Guha, the generalissimo of the celestial forces, in her womb. She bears the most precious of all metals, viz., gold, also in that womb of hers. They who bathe in her waters every day in the morning, succeed in obtaining the aggregate of three, viz., Righteousness, Wealth and Pleasure. Those waters are, again, equal in point of sanctity to the butter that is poured with Mantras on the sacrificial fire. Capable of cleansing one from every sin, she has descended from the celestial region, and her current is held in high esteem by every one. Ganga is the daughter of Himavat, the spouse of Hara, and the ornament of both Heaven and Earth. She is the bestower of everything auspicious, and is competent to confer the six well-known attributes beginning with lordship or puissance. Verily O king, Ganga is the one object of great sanctity in the three worlds and confers merit upon all. Truly, O monarch, Ganga is Righteousness in liquefied form. She is energy also running in a liquid form over the Earth. She is endued with the splendour or puissance that belongs to the butter that is poured with Mantras on the sacrificial fire. She is always adorned with large waves as also with Brahmanas who may at all times be seen performing their ablutions in her waters. Falling from Heaven, she was held by Siva on his head. The very mother of the heavens, she has sprung from the highest mountain for running over the plains and conferring the most precious benefits on all creatures of the Earth. She is the highest cause of all things; she is perfectly stainless. She is as subtile as Brahma. She affords the best bed for the dying. She leads creatures very quickly to heaven. She bears away a large volume of water. She bestows great fame on all. She is the protectress of the universe.[245] She is identical with every form. She is very much coveted by persons crowned with success. Verily, Ganga is

---

[243] Identical with the universe because capable of conferring the fruition of every wish. Vrihati—literally, large or vast, is explained by the commentator as implying foremost or superior.

[244] Madhumatim is explained as conferring the fruits of all good actions.

[245] Viswam avanti iti. Here the absence of num is arsha.

the path to Heaven of those that have bathed in her current.[246] The Brahmanas hold Ganga as equalling the Earth in forgiveness, and in the protection and upholding of those that live by her; further, as equalling Fire and Surya in energy and splendour; and, lastly, as always equalling Guha himself in the matter of showing favours unto the regenerate class.[247] Those men who, in this life, even mentally seek with their whole souls that sacred stream which is praised by the Rishis, which has issued out of the feet of Vishnu, which is very ancient, and which is exceedingly sacred, succeed in repairing to the regions of Brahman. Fully convinced that children and other possessions, as also regions possessed by every kind of felicity, are transitory or liable to destruction, men of subdued souls, who are desirous of attaining to that everlasting station which is identical with Brahma, always pay their adorations to Ganga with that reverence and love which are due from a son to mother. The men of cleansed soul who is desirous of achieving success should seek the protection of Ganga who is like a cow that yields Amrita instead of ordinary milk, who is prosperity's self, who is possessed of omniscience, who exists for the entire universe of creatures, who is the source of all kinds of food, who is the mother of all mountains, who is the refuge of all righteous persons, who is immeasurable in puissance and energy, and who charms the heart of Brahma himself. Having, with austere penances, gratified all the deities with the Supreme Lord (Vishnu), Bhagiratha brought Ganga down on the Earth. Repairing unto her, men always succeed in freeing themselves from every kind of fear both here and hereafter. Observing with the aid of intelligence, I have mentioned to thee only a small part of the merits of Ganga. My power, however, is inadequate to speak of all the merits of the sacred river, or, indeed, to measure her puissance and sanctity. One may, by putting forth one's best powers, count the stones that occur in the mountains of Meru or measure the waters that occur in the ocean, but one cannot count all the merits which belong to the waters of Ganga. Hence, having listened to these particular merits of Ganga which I have uttered with great devotion, one should, in thought, word and deed, reverence them with faith and devotion. In consequence of thy having listened to those merits which I have recited, thou art sure to fill all the three regions with fame and attain to a measure of success that is very large and that is difficult of being attained to by any other person. Verily, thou shalt, soon after that, sport in joy many a region of great felicity created by Ganga herself for those that reverence her. Ganga always extends her grace unto those that are devoted to her with humbleness of heart. She unites those that are so devoted to her with every kind of happiness. I pray that the highly-blessed Ganga may always inspire thy heart and mine with such attributes as are fraught with righteousness'.

"'Bhishma continued, "The learned ascetic endued with high intelligence and great illumination, and crowned with success, having in this manner discoursed unto that poor Brahmana in the observance of the Sila vow, on the subjects of the infinite merits of Ganga, then ascended the firmament. The Brahmana in the observance of Sila vow, awakened by the words of that ascetic crowned with success, duly worshipped Ganga and attained to high success. Do thou also, O son of Kunti, seek Ganga with great devotion, for thou shalt then, as the reward thereof, attain to high and excellent success.'"

"Vaisampayana continued, 'Hearing this discourse from Bhishma that was fraught with the praise of Ganga, Yudhishthira with his brothers became filled with great delight. That person who recites or hears recited this sacred discourse fraught with the praise of

---

[246] Bhuvanasya is swargasya.
[247] The construction of this verse is not difficult though the order of the words is a little involved. Both the vernacular translators have misunderstood it completely.

Ganga, becomes cleansed of every sin.'"

SECTION XXVII.

"'Yudhishthira said, "Thou O grandsire, art endued with wisdom and knowledge of the scriptures, with conduct and behaviour, with diverse kinds of excellent attributes, and also with years. Thou art distinguished above others by intelligence and wisdom and penances. I shall, therefore, O thou that art the foremost of all righteous men, desire to address enquiries to thee respecting Righteousness. There is not another man, O king, in all the worlds, who is worthier of being questioned on such subjects. O best of kings, how may one, if he happens to be a Kshatriya or a Vaisya or a Sudra, succeed in acquiring the status of a Brahmana? It behoveth thee to tell me the means. Is it by penances the most austere, or by religious acts, or by knowledge of the scriptures, that a person belonging to any of the three inferior orders succeeds in acquiring the status of a Brahmana? Do tell me this, O grandsire!"

"'Bhishma said, "The status of a Brahmana, O Yudhishthira, is incapable of acquisition by a person belonging to any of the three other orders. That status is the highest with respect to all creatures. Travelling through innumerable orders of existence, by undergoing repeated births, one at last, in some birth, becomes born as a Brahmana. In this connection is cited an old history, O Yudhishthira, of a conversation between Matanga and a she-ass. Once on a time a Brahmana obtained a son who, though procreated by a person belonging to a different order, had, however, the rites of infancy and youth performed in pursuance of the ordinances laid down for Brahmanas. The child was called by the name of Matanga and was possessed of every accomplishment. His father, desiring to perform a sacrifice, ordered him, O scorcher of foes, to collect the articles required for the act. Having received the command of his father, he set out for the purpose, riding on a car of great speed, drawn by an ass. It so happened that the ass yoked unto that car was of tender years. Instead therefore, of obeying the reins, the animal bore away the car to the vicinity of its dam, viz., the she-ass that had brought it forth. Matanga, dissatisfied with this, began to strike repeatedly the animal with his goad on its nose. Beholding those marks of violence on her child's nose, the she-ass, full of affection for him, said—'Do not grieve, O child, for his treatment. A Chandala it is that is driving thee. There is no severity in a Brahmana. The Brahmana is said to be the friend of all creatures. He is the teacher also of all creatures and their ruler. Can he chastise any creature so cruelly? This fellow, however, is of sinful deeds. He hath no compassion to show unto even a creature of such tender years as thou. He is simply proving the order of his birth by conducting himself in this way. The nature which he hath derived from his sire forbids the rise of those sentiments of pity and kindness that are natural to the Brahmana.' Hearing these harsh words of the she-ass, Matanga quickly came down from the car and addressing the she-ass, said,—'Tell me, O blessed dame, by what fault is my mother stained? How dost thou know that I am a Chandala? Do thou answer me without delay. How, indeed, dost thou know that I am a Chandala? How has my status as a Brahmana been lost? O thou of great wisdom, tell me all this in detail, from beginning to end.'

"''The she-ass said, 'Begotten thou wert, upon a Brahmana woman excited with desire, by a Sudra following the profession of a barber. Thou art, therefore, a Chandala by birth. The status of Brahmana thou hast not at all.'"

"'Brahmana continued, 'Thus addressed by the she-ass, Matanga retraced his way homewards. Seeing him return, his father said,—'I had employed thee in the difficult task of gathering the requisites of my intended sacrifice. Why hast thou come back without having accomplished thy charge? Is it the case that all is not right with thee?'

""'Matanga said, 'How can he who belongs to no definite order of birth, or to an order that is very low be regarded as all right and happy? How, O father, can that person be happy whose mother is stained? O father, this she-ass, who seems to be more than a human being, tells me that I have been begotten upon a Brahmani woman by a Sudra. I shall, for this reason, undergo the severest penances.'—Having said these words to his father, and firmly resolved upon what he had said he proceeded to the great forest and began to undergo the austerest of penances. Setting himself to the performance of those penances for the purpose of happily acquiring the status of a Brahmana, Matanga began to scorch the very deities by the severity of his asceticism. Unto him thus engaged in penances, the chief of the celestials, viz., Indra, appeared and said,—'Why, O Matanga, dost thou pass thy time in such grief, abstaining from all kinds of human enjoyments? I shall give thee boons. Do thou name the boons thou desirest. Do not delay, but tell me what is in thy breast. Even if that be unattainable, I shall yet bestow it on thee.'

""'Matanga said, 'Desirous of attaining to the status of Brahmana I have begun to practise these penances. After having obtained it, I shall go home. Even this is the boon solicited by me.'"

"'Bhishma continued, "Hearing these words of his, Purandara said unto him, 'The status of a Brahmana, O Matanga, which thou desirest to acquire is really unattainable by thee. It is true, thou desirest to acquire it, but then it is incapable of acquisition by persons begotten on uncleansed souls. O thou of foolish understanding, thou art sure to meet with destruction if thou persistest in this pursuit. Desist, therefore, from this vain endeavour without any delay. This object of thy desire, viz., the status of a Brahmana, which is the foremost of everything, is incapable of being won by penances. Therefore, by coveting that foremost status, thou wilt incur sure destruction. One born as a Chandala can never attain to that status which is regarded as the most sacred among the deities and Asuras and human beings!"""

SECTION XXVIII.

"'Bhishma said, "Thus addressed by Indra, Matanga of restrained vows and well regulated soul, (without hearkening to the counsels of the chief of the celestials), stood for a hundred years on one foot, O thou of unfading glory. Sakra of great fame once more appeared before him and addressing him, said,—'The status of a Brahmana, O child, is unattainable. Although thou covetest it, it is impossible for thee to obtain it. O Matanga, by coveting that very high status thou art sure to be destroyed. Do not, O son, betray such rashness. This cannot be a righteous path for thee to follow. O thou of foolish understanding, it is impossible for thee to obtain it in this world. Verily, by coveting that which is unattainable, thou art sure to meet with destruction in no time. I am repeatedly forbidding thee. By striving, however, to attain that high status by the aid of thy penances, notwithstanding my repeated admonition, thou art sure to meet with destruction. From the order of brute life one attains to the status of humanity. If born as human being, he is sure to take birth as a Pukkasa or a Chandala. Verily, one having taken birth in that sinful order of existence, viz., Pukkasa, one, O Matanga, has to wander in it for a very long time. Passing a period of one thousand years in that order, one attains next to the status of a Sudra. In the Sudra order, again, one has to wander for a long time. After thirty thousand years one acquire the status of a Vaisya. There, in that order, one has to pass a very long period. After a time that is sixty times longer than what has been stated as the period of Sudra existence, one becomes a person of the fighting order. In the Kshatriya order one has to pass a very long time. After a time that is measured by multiplying the period last referred to by sixty, one becomes born as a fallen Brahmana. In this order one has to wander for a long period. After a time measured by multiplying the period last named by two hundred, one becomes born in the race of such a Brahmana as lives by the profession of arms. There, in that order, one has to wander for a long period. After a time measured by multiplying the period last named by three hundred, one takes birth in the race of a Brahmana that is given to the recitation of the Gayatri and other sacred Mantras. There, in that order, one has to wander for a long period. After a time measured by multiplying the period last named by four hundred, one takes birth in the race of such a Brahmana as is conversant with the entire Vedas and the scriptures. There, in that order, one has to wander for a very long period. While wandering in that status of existence, joy and grief, desire and aversion, vanity and evil speech, seek to enter into him and make a wretch of him. If he succeeds in subjugating those foes, he then attains a high end. If, on the other hand, those enemies succeed in subjugating him, he falls down from that high status like a person falling down on the ground from the high top of a palmyra tree. Knowing this for certain, O Matanga, I say unto thee, do thou name some other boon, for the status of a Brahmana is incapable of being attained by thee (that hast been born as a Chandala)!'"'"

SECTION XXIX.

'"Bhishma said, "Thus advised by Indra, Matanga, observant of vows, refused to hear what he was bid. On the other hand, with regulated vows and cleansed soul, he practised austere penances by standing on one foot for a thousand years, and was deeply engaged in Yoga-meditation. After a thousand years had passed away, Sakra once more came to see him. Indeed, the slayer of Vala and Vritra said unto him the same words.

'"'Matanga said, 'I have passed these thousand years, standing on one foot, in deep meditation, observing of the vow of Brahmacharyya. Why is it that I have not yet succeeded in acquiring the status of a Brahmana?'

'"'Sakra said, 'One born on a Chandala cannot, by any means acquire the status of a Brahmana. Do thou, therefore name some boon so that all this labour of thine may not prove fruitless.'—Thus addressed by the chief of the celestials, Matanga became filled with grief. He repaired to Prayaga, and passed there a hundred years, standing all the while on his toes. In consequence of the observance of such Yoga which was extremely difficult to bear, he became very much emaciated and his arteries and veins became swollen and visible. He was reduced to only skin and bones. Indeed, it has been heard by us that the righteous-souled Matanga, while practising those austerities at Gaya, dropped down on the ground from sheer exhaustion. The lord and giver of boons, engaged in the good of all creatures, viz., Vasava beholding him falling down, quickly came to that spot and held him fast.

'"'Sakra said, 'It seems, O Matanga, that the status of a Brahmana which thou seekest is ill-suited to thee. That status is incapable of being attained by thee. Verily, in thy case, it is surrounded by many dangers. A person by worshipping a Brahmana obtains happiness; while by abstaining from such worship, he obtains grief and misery. The Brahmana is, with respect to all creatures, the giver of what they prize or covet and the protector of what they already have. It is through the Brahmanas that the Pitris and the deities become gratified. The Brahmana, O Matanga, is said to be foremost of all created Beings. The Brahmana grants all objects that are desired and in the way they are desired.[248] Wandering through innumerable orders of Being and undergoing repeated rebirths, one succeeds in some subsequent birth in acquiring the status of a Brahmana. That status is really incapable of being obtained by persons of uncleansed souls. Do thou, therefore, give up the idea. Do thou name some other boon. The particular boon which thou seekest is incapable of being granted to thee.'

""Matanga said, 'Afflicted as I am with grief, why, O Sakra, dost thou afflict me further (with such speeches as these)? Thou art striking one that is already dead, by this behaviour. I do not pity thee for having acquired the status of a Brahmana thou now failest to retain it (for thou hast no compassion to show for one like me). O thou of a hundred sacrifices, the status of a Brahmana as thou sayest be really unattainable by any of the three other orders, yet, men that have succeeded in acquiring (through natural means) that high status do not adhere to it (for what sins do not even Brahmanas commit). Those who having acquired the status of a Brahmana that, like affluence, is so difficult to acquire, do not seek to keep it up (by practising the necessary duties), must be regarded to be the lowest of wretches in this world. Indeed, they are the most sinful of all creatures. Without doubt, the status of a Brahmana is exceedingly difficult to attain, and once being attained, it is difficult to maintain it. It is capable of dispelling every kind of grief. Alas, having attained to it, men do not always seek to keep it up (by practising righteousness and the other duties that attach to it). When even such persons are regarded as Brahmanas why is it that I, who am contented with my own self, who am above all couples of opposites, who am dissociated from all worldly objects, who am observant of the duty of compassion towards all creatures and of self-restraint of conduct, should not be regarded as deserving of that status.[249] How unfortunate I am, O Purandara, that through the fault of my mother I have been reduced to this condition, although I am not unrighteous in my behaviour? Without doubt, Destiny is incapable of being warded off or conquered by individual exertion, since, O lord, I am unable to acquire, notwithstanding these persistent efforts of mine, the object, upon the acquisition of which I have set my heart. When such is the case, O righteous one, it behoves thee to grant me some other boon if, indeed, I have become worthy of thy grace or if I have a little of merit.'"

"'Bhishma continued, "The slayer of Vala and Vritra then said unto him,—'Do thou name the boon.'—Thus urged by the great Indra, Matanga said the following words:

""Matanga said, 'Let me be possessed of the power of assuming any form at will, and journeying through the skies and let me enjoy whatever pleasures I may set my heart upon. And let me also have the willing adorations of both Brahmanas and Kshatriyas. I bow to thee by bending my head, O god. It behoveth thee to do that also by which my fame, O Purandara, may live for ever in the world.'

""Sakra said, 'Thou shalt be celebrated as the deity of a particular measure of verse and thou shalt obtain the worship of all women. Thy fame, O son, shall become unrivalled in the three worlds.'—Having granted him these boons, Vasava disappeared there and then. Matanga also, casting off his life-breaths, attained to a high place. Thou mayst thus see, O Bharata, that the status of a Brahmana is very high. That status is

---

[248] Kurute may mean also makes. The sense is that the Brahmana grants to others whatever objects are desired by them. In his own case also, he creates those objects that he himself desires. His puissance is great and it is through his kindness that others get what they wish or seek.

[249] Ekaramah is one who sports with one's own self, i.e., who is not dependant on others for his joy or happiness; one who has understood the soul.

incapable of being acquired here (except in the natural way of birth) as said by the great Indra himself.""'

SECTION XXX.

"'Yudhishthira said, "I have heard this great narrative, O perpetuator of Kuru's race. Thou, O foremost of eloquent men, hast said that the status of a Brahmana is exceedingly difficult of acquisition. It is heard, however, that in former times the status of a Brahmana had been acquired by Viswamitra. Thou, however, O best of men, tellest us that status is incapable of being acquired. I have also heard that king Vitahavya in ancient times succeeded in obtaining the status of a Brahmana. I desire to hear, O puissant son of Ganga, the story of Vitahavya's promotion. By what acts did that best of kings succeed in acquiring the status of a Brahmana? Was it through some boon (obtained from some one of great puissance) or was it through the virtue of penances? It behoveth thee to tell me everything."

"'Bhishma said, "Hear, O monarch, how the royal sage Vitahavya of great celebrity succeeded in ancient times in acquiring the status of a Brahmana that is so difficult to attain and that is held in such high reverence by all the world. While the high-souled Manu in days of yore was employed in righteously ruling his subjects, he obtained a son of righteous soul who became celebrated under the name of Saryati. In Saryati's race, O monarch, two kings took their birth, viz., Haihaya and Talajangha. Both of them were sons of Vatsa, O foremost of victorious kings. Haihaya, O monarch, had ten wives. Upon them he begot, O Bharata, a century of sons all of whom were highly inclined to fighting. All of them resembled one another in features and prowess. All of them were endued with great strength and all of them were possessed of great skill in battle. They all studied the Vedas and the science of weapons thoroughly. In Kasi also, O monarch, there was a king who was the grandfather of Divodasa. The foremost of victorious men, he was known by the name of Haryyaswa. The sons of king Haihaya, O chief of men (who was otherwise known by the name of Vitahavya), invaded the kingdom of Kasi and advancing to the country that lies between the rivers Ganga and Yamuna, fought a battle with king Haryyaswa and also slew him in it. Having slain king Haryyaswa in this way, the sons of Haihaya, those great car-warriors, fearlessly went back to their own delightful city in the country of the Vatsas. Meanwhile Haryyaswa's son Sudeva, who looked like a deity in splendour and who was a second god of righteousness, was installed on the throne of Kasi as its ruler. The delighter of Kasi, that righteous-souled prince ruled his kingdom for some time, when the hundred sons of Vitahavya once more invaded his dominions and defeated him in battle. Having vanquished king Sudeva thus, the victors returned to their own city. After that Divodasa, the son of Sudeva, became installed on the throne of Kasi as its ruler. Realising the prowess of those high-souled princes, viz., the sons of Vitahavya, king Divodasa, endued with great energy, rebuilt and fortified the city of Baranasi at the command of Indra. The territories of Divodasa were full of Brahmanas and Kshatriyas, and abounded with Vaisyas and Sudras. And they teemed with articles and provisions of every kind, and were adorned with shops and marts swelling with prosperity. Those territories, O best of kings, stretched northwards from the banks of Ganga to the southern banks of Gomati, and resembled a second Amravati (the city of Indra). The Haihayas once again, O Bharata, attacked that tiger among kings, as he ruled his kingdom. The mighty king Divodasa endued with great splendour, issuing out of his capital, gave them battle. The engagement between the two parties proved so fierce as to resemble the encounter in days of old between the deities and the Asuras. King Divodasa fought the enemy for a thousand days at the end of which, having lost a number of followers and animals, he became exceedingly distressed.[250] King Divodasa, O monarch, having lost his army and seeing his treasury exhausted, left his capital and fled away. Repairing to the delightful retreat of Bhardwaja endued with great wisdom the king, O chastiser of foes joining his hands in reverence, sought the Rishi's protection. Beholding King Divodasa before him, the eldest son of Vrihaspati, viz., Bharadwaja of excellent conduct, who was the monarch's priest, said unto him, 'What is the reason of thy coming here? Tell me everything, O king. I shall do that which is agreeable to thee, without any scruple.'

""The king said, 'O holy one, the sons of Vitahavya have slain all the children and men of my house. I only have escaped with life, totally discomfited by the foe. I seek thy protection. It behoveth thee, O holy one, to protect me with such affection as thou hast for a disciple. Those princes of sinful deeds have slaughtered my whole race, leaving myself only alive.'"

"Bhishma continued, "Unto him who pleaded so piteously, Bharadwaja of great energy said, 'Do not fear! Do not fear! O son of Sudeva, let thy fears be dispelled. I shall perform a sacrifice, O monarch, in order that thou mayst have a son through whom thou shalt be able to smite thousands upon thousands of Vitahavya's party.' After this, the Rishi performed a sacrifice with the object of bestowing a son on Divodasa. As the result thereof, unto Divodasa was born a son named Pratarddana. Immediately on his birth he grew up like a boy of full three and ten years and quickly mastered the entire Vedas and the whole of arms. Aided by his Yoga powers, Bharadwaja of great intelligence had entered into the prince. Indeed, collecting all the energy that occurs in the object of the universe, Bharadwaja put them together in the body of prince Pratarddana. Put on shining mail on his person and armed with the bow, Pratarddana, his praises sung by bards and the celestial Rishis, shone resplendent like the risen star of day. Mounted on his car and with the scimitar tied to his belt, he shone like a blazing fire. With scimitar and shield and whirling his shield as he went, he proceeded to the presence of his sire. Beholding the prince, the son of Sudeva, viz., king Divodasa, became filled with joy. Indeed, the old king thought the sons of his enemy Vitahavya as already slain. Divodasa then installed his son Pratarddana as Yuvaraja, and regarding himself crowned with success became exceedingly happy. After this, the old king commanded that chastiser of foes, viz., prince Pratarddana to march against the sons of Vitahavya and slay them in battle. Endued with great powers, Pratarddana, that subjugator of hostile cities speedily crossed Ganga on his car and proceeded against the city of the Vitahavyas. Hearing the clatter produced by the wheels of his car, the sons of Vitahavya, riding on their own cars that looked like fortified citadels and that were capable of destroying hostile vehicles, issued out of their city. Issuing out of their capital, those tigers among men, viz., the sons of Vitahavya, who were all skilful warriors cased in mail, rushed with uplifted weapons towards Pratarddana, covering him with showers of arrows. Encompassing him with innumerable cars, O Yudhisthira, the Vitahavyas poured upon Pratarddana showers of weapons of various kinds like clouds pouring torrents of rain on the breast of Himavat. Baffling their weapons with his own, prince Pratarddana endued with mighty energy slew them all with his shafts that resembled the lighting fire of Indra. Their heads struck off, O king, with

---

[250] Dasatirdasa is ten times hundred or one thousand Dasati, like Saptati, Navati, etc., means ten times ten. Both the Vernacular translators have erred in rendering the word.

hundreds and thousands of broad-headed arrows, the warriors of Vitahavya fell down with blood-dyed bodies like Kinsuka trees felled by woodmen with their axes on every side. After all his warriors and sons had fallen in battle, king Vitahavya fled away from his capital to the retreat of Bhrigu. Indeed, arrived there, the royal fugitive sought the protection of Bhrigu. The Rishi Bhrigu, O monarch, assured the defeated king of his protection. Pratarddana followed in the footsteps of Vitahavya. Arrived at the Rishi's retreat, the son of Divodasa said in a loud voice.—'Ho, listen ye disciples of the high souled Bhrigu that may happen to be present, I wish to see the sage. Go and inform him of this. Recognising that it was Pratarddana who had come, the Rishi Bhrigu himself came out of his retreat and worshipped that best of kings according to due rites. Addressing him then, the Rishi said,—Tell me, O king, what is thy business.' The king, at this, informed the Rishi of the reason of his presence.'

"""The king said, 'King Vitahavya has come here, O Brahmana. Do thou give him up. His sons, O Brahmana, had destroyed my race. They had laid waste the territories and the wealth of the kingdom of Kasi. Hundred sons, however, of this king proud of his might, have all been slain by me. By slaying that king himself I shall today pay off the debt I owe to my father.' Unto him that foremost of righteous men, viz., the Rishi Bhrigu, penetrated with compassion, replied by saying,—'There is no Kshatriya in this retreat. They that are here are all Brahmanas.' Hearing these words of Bhrigu that must accord he thought with truth, Pratarddana touched the Rishi's feet slowly and, filled with delight, said,—'By this, O holy one, I am without doubt, crowned with success, since this king becomes abandoned by the very order of his birth in consequence of my prowess. Give me thy permission, O Brahmana, to leave thee, and let me solicit thee to pray for my welfare. This king, O founder of the race that goes by the name, has been compelled to leave of the very community of his birth, in consequence of my might. Dismissed by the Rishi Bhrigu, king Pratarddana then departed from that retreat, having even as a snake vomits forth its real poison and repaired to the place he had come from. Meanwhile, king Vitahavya attained to the status of a Brahmana sage by virtue of the words only of Bhrigu. And he acquired also a complete mastery over all the Vedas through the same cause. Vitahavya had a son named Gritsamada who in beauty of person was a second Indra. Once on a time the Daityas afflicted him much, believing him to be none else than Indra. With regard to that high-souled Rishi, one foremost of Srutis in the Richs goes like this viz., He with whom Gritsamada stays, O Brahmana, is held in high respect by all Brahmanas. Endued with great intelligence, Gritsamada become a regenerate Rishi in the observance of Brahmacharyya. Gritsamada had a regenerate son of the name of Sutejas. Sutejas had a son of the name of Varchas, and the son of Varchas was known by the name of Vihavya. Vihavya had a son of his loins who was named Vitatya and Vitatya had a son of name Satya. Satya had a son of name Santa. Santa had a son, viz., the Rishi Sravas. Sravas begot a son named Tama. Tama begot a son named Prakasa, who was a very superior Brahmana. Prakasa had a son named Vagindra who was the foremost of all silent reciters of sacred Mantras. Vagindra begot a son named Pramati who was a complete master of all the Vedas and their branches. Pramati begot upon the Apsara Ghritachi a son who was named Ruru. Ruru begot a son upon his spouse Pramadvara. That son was the regenerate Rishi Sunaka. Sunaka begot a son who is named Saunaka. It was even thus, O foremost of monarchs, that king Vitahavya, though a Kshatriya by the order of his birth, obtained the status of a Brahmana, O chief of Kshatriyas, through the grace of Bhrigu. I have also told thee the genealogy of the race that sprung from Gritsamada. What else wouldst thou ask?"""

SECTION XXXI.

"'Yudhishthira said, "What men, O chief of Bharata's race, are worthy of reverent homage in the three worlds? Tell me this in detail verily. I am never satiated with hearing thee discourse on these topics."

"'Bhishma said, "In this connection is cited the old narrative of the discourse between Narada and Vasudeva. Beholding Narada on one occasion worshipping many foremost of Brahmanas with joined hands, Kesava addressed him saying, 'Whom dost thou worship? Whom amongst these Brahmanas, O holy one dost thou worship with so great reverence? If it is a matter that I can hear of, I then wish to hear it. Do, O foremost of righteous men, tell me this!'[251]

"'"Narada said, 'Hear, O Govinda, as to who those are whom I am worshipping, O grinder of foes. Who else is there in this world that so much deserves to hear this? I worship the Brahmanas, O puissant one, who constantly worship Varuna and Vayu and Aditya and Parjanya and the deity of Fire, and Sthanu and Skanda and Lakshmi and Vishnu and the Brahmanas, and the lord of speech, and Chandramas, and the Waters and Earth and the goddess Saraswati. O tiger of Vrishni's race, I always worship those Brahmanas that are endued with penances, that are conversant with the Vedas, that are always devoted to Vedic study, and that are possessed of high worth. O puissant one, I bow down my head unto those persons who are freed from boastfulness, who discharge, with an empty stomach, the rites in honour of the deities, who are always contented with what they have and who are endued with forgiveness. I worship them, O Yadava, that are performers of sacrifices, that are of a forgiving disposition, and self restrained, that are masters of their own senses, that worship truth and righteousness, and that give away land and kine unto good Brahmanas.[252] I bow unto them, O Yadava, that are devoted to the observance of penances, that dwell in forests, that subsist upon fruits and roots, that never store anything for the morrow, and that are observant of all the acts and rites laid down in the scriptures. I bow unto them, O Yadava, that feed and cherish their servants, that are always hospitable to guests, and that eat only the remnants of what is offered to the deities. I worship them that have become irresistible by studying the Vedas, that are eloquent in discoursing on the scriptures, that are observant of the vow of Brahmacharyya, and that are always devoted to the duties of officiating at the sacrifices of others and of teaching disciples. I worship them that are endued with compassion towards all creatures, and that study the Vedas till noon (i.e. till their backs are heated by the sun). I bow unto them, O Yadava, that strive to obtain the grace of their preceptors, that labour in the acquisition of their Vedas, that are firm in the observance of vows, that wait, with dutiful obedience, upon their preceptors and seniors, and that are free from malice and envy. I bow unto them, O Yadava, that are observant of excellent vows, that practice taciturnity, that have knowledge of Brahman, that are firm in truth, that are givers of libations of clarified butter and oblations of meat. I bow to them, O Yadava, that subsist upon eleemosynary alms, that are emaciated for want of adequate food and drink, that have lived in the abodes of their preceptors, that are averse to and destitute of all enjoyments, and that are poor in the goods of this Earth. I bow unto them, O Yadava, that

---

[251] Teshu (Brahmaneshu) Vahumanaprah (san) kan namsvasi—this is the Grammar, as explained by the commentator.
[252] Yajanti with reference to truth and righteousness means worship, and with reference to land kine means give away.

have no affection for things of this Earth, that have no quarrels to wage with others, that do not clothe themselves, that have no wants, that have become irresistible through the acquisition of the Vedas, that are eloquent in the exposition of righteousness, and that are utterers of Brahma. I bow unto them that are devoted to the practice of the duty of compassion towards all creatures, that are firm in the observance of truth, that are self-restrained, and that are peaceful in their behaviour. I bow unto them, O Yadava, that are devoted to the worship of deities and guests, that are observant of the domestic mode of life, and that follow the practice of pigeons in the matter of their subsistence.[253] I always bow unto those persons whose aggregate of three exists, without being weakened, in all their acts, and who are observant of truth and righteous behaviour.[254] I bow unto them, O Kesava, that are conversant with Brahma, that are endued with knowledge of the Vedas, that are attentive to the aggregate of three, that are free from cupidity, and that are righteous in their behaviour. I bow unto them, O Madhava, that subsist upon water only, or upon air alone, or upon the remnants of the food that is offered to deities and guests, and that are observant of diverse kinds of excellent vows. I always worship them that have no spouses (in consequence of the vow of celibacy they observe), that have spouses and the domestic fire (in consequence of the domestic mode of life they lead), that are the refuge of the Vedas, and that are the refuge of all creatures in the universe (in consequence of the compassion they feel towards them). I always bow unto those Rishis, O Krishna, that are the creators of the universe, that are the elders of the universe, that are the eldest members of the race or the family, that are dispellers of the darkness of ignorance, and that are the best of all persons in the universe (for righteousness of behaviour and knowledge of the scriptures). For these reasons, do thou also, O scion of Vrishni's race, worship every day those regenerate persons of whom I speak. Deserving as they are of reverent worship, they will when worshipped, confer happiness on thee, O sinless one. Those persons of whom I speak are always givers of happiness in this world as well as in the next. Reverenced by all, they move about in this world, and if worshipped by thee are sure to grant thee happiness. They who are hospitable to all persons that come unto them as guests, and who are always devoted to Brahmanas and kine, as also to truth (in speech and behaviour), succeed in crossing all calamities and obstacles. They who are always devoted to peacefulness of behaviour, as also they who are freed from malice and envy, and they who are always attentive to the study of the Vedas, succeed in crossing all calamities and obstacles. They who bow unto all the deities (without showing a preference for any and thereby proving their tolerance), they who betake themselves to one Veda as their refuge, they who are possessed of faith and are self-restrained, succeed in crossing all calamities and obstacles. They who worship the foremost of Brahmanas with reverence and are firm in the observance of excellent vows and practise the virtue of charity, succeed in crossing all calamities and obstacles. They who are engaged in the practice of penances, they who are always observant of the vow of celibacy, and they whose souls have been cleansed by penances, succeed in crossing all calamities and obstacles. They who are devoted to the worship of the deities and guests and dependants, as also of the Pitris, and they who eat the remnant of the food that is offered to deities, Pitris, guests and dependants, succeed in crossing all calamities

---

[253] Pigeons pick up scattered grains and never store for the morrow. In the Sila and other vows, the picking up of scattered and cast off grains from the field after the crops have been taken away by the owners, is recommended as the means of filling the stomach.

[254] The aggregate of three is Righteousness, Wealth, and Pleasure. Persons who, in all the acts they do, keep an eye upon these three, are said to have their aggregate of three existing in all their acts.

and obstacles. They who, having ignited the domestic fire, duly keep it burning and worship it with reverence and they who have duly poured libations (to the deities) in Soma-sacrifices, succeed in crossing all calamities and obstacles. They who behave as they should towards their mothers and fathers and preceptors and other seniors even as thou, O tiger among the Vrishnis, dost behave, succeed in crossing all calamities and obstacles.'—Having said these words, the celestial Rishi ceased speaking."'

"'Bhishma continued, "For these reasons, do thou also, O son of Kunti, always worship with reverence the deities, the Pitris, the Brahmanas, and guests arrived at thy mansion and as the consequence of such conduct thou art sure to attain to a desirable end!"'"

SECTION XXXII.

"'Yudhishthira said,—"O grandsire, O thou of great wisdom, O thou that art conversant with all branches of knowledge, I desire to hear thee discourse on topics connected with duty and righteousness. Tell me truly, O chief of Bharata's race, what the merits are of those persons that grant protection to living creatures of the four orders when these pray for protection."

"'Bhishma said, "O Dharma's son of great wisdom and widespread fame, listen to this old history touching the great merit of granting protection to others when protection is humbly sought. Once on a time, a beautiful pigeon, pursued by a hawk, dropped down from the skies and sought the protection of the highly-blessed king Vrishadarbha. The pure-souled monarch, beholding the pigeon take refuge in his lap from fear, comforted him, saying, 'Be comforted, O bird; do not fear. Whence hast thou taken such great fright? What hast thou done and where hast thou done it in consequence of which thou hast lost thy senses in fear and art more dead than alive? Thy colour, beautiful bird, is such as to resemble that which adorns a fresh-blown lotus of the blue variety. Thy eyes are of the hue of the pomegranate or the Asoka flower. Do not fear. I bid thee, be comforted. When thou hast sought refuge with me, know that no one will have the courage to even think of seizing thee,—thee that hast such a protector to take care of thy person. I shall for thy sake, give up today the very kingdom of the Kasi and, if need be, my life too. Be comforted, therefore, and let no fear be thine, O pigeon.'

"'The hawk said, 'This bird has been ordained to be my food. It behoves thee not, O king, to protect him from me. I have outcoursed this bird and have got him. Verily, with great effort have I got at him at last. His flesh and blood and marrow and fat will be of great good to me. This bird will be the means of gratifying me greatly. Do not, O king, place thyself between him and me in this way. Fierce is the thirst that is afflicting me, and hunger is gnawing my bowels. Release the bird and cast him off. I am unable to bear the pains of hunger any longer. I pursued him as my prey. Behold, his body is bruised and torn by me with my wings and talons. Look, his breath has become very weak. It behoves thee not, O king, to protect him from me. In the exercise of that power which properly belongs to thee, thou art, indeed competent to interfere in protecting human beings when they are sought to be destroyed by human beings. Thou canst not, however, be admitted to have any power over a sky-ranging bird afflicted with thirst. Thy power may extend over thy enemies, thy servants, thy relatives, the disputes that take place between thy subjects. Indeed, it may extend over every part of thy dominions and over also thy own senses. Thy power, however, does not extend over the welkin. Displaying thy prowess over such foes as act against thy wishes, thou mayst establish thy rule over them. Thy rule, however, does not extend over the birds that range the sky. Indeed, if thou hast been desirous of earning merit (by protecting this pigeon), it is thy duty to look at me also (and do what is proper for enabling me to appease my hunger and save my life)!'"

"'Bhishma continued, "Hearing these words of the hawk, the royal sage became filled with wonder. Without disregarding these words of his, the king, desirous of attending to his comforts, replied unto him saying the following words.

"""The king said, 'Let a bovine bull or boar or deer or buffalo be dressed today for thy sake. Do thou appease thy hunger on such food today. Never to desert one that has sought my protection in my firm vow. Behold, O bird, this bird does not leave my lap!'

"""The hawk said, 'I do not, O monarch, eat the flesh of the boar or the ox or of any of the diverse kinds of fowl. What need have I of food of this or that kind? My concern is with that food which has been eternally ordained for beings of my order. Hawks feed on pigeons,—this is the eternal ordinance. O sinless Usinara, if thou feelest such affection for this pigeon, do thou then give me flesh from thy own body, of weight equal to that of this pigeon.'

"""The king said, 'Great is the favour thou showiest me today by speaking to me in this strain. Yes, I shall do what thou biddest.' Having said this, that best of monarchs began to cut off his own flesh and weigh it in a balance against the pigeon. Meanwhile, in the inner apartments of the palace, the spouses of king, adorned with jewels and gems, hearing what was taking place, uttered exclamations of woe and came out, stricken with grief. In consequence of those cries of the ladies, as also of the ministers and servants, a noise deep as the roar of the clouds arose in the palace. The sky that had been very clear became enveloped with thick clouds on every side. The Earth began to tremble, as the consequence of that act of truth which the monarch did. The king began to cut off the flesh from his flanks from the arms, and from his thighs, and quickly filled one of the scales for weighing it against the pigeon. In spite of all that, the pigeon continued to weigh heavier. When at last the king became a skeleton of bones, without any flesh, and covered with blood, he desired to give up his whole body and, therefore, ascended the scale in which he had placed the flesh that he had previously cut off. At that time, the three worlds, with Indra at their head, came to that spot for beholding him. Celestial kettle-drums and diverse drums were struck and played upon by invisible beings belonging to the firmament. King Vrishadarbha was bathed in a shower of nectar that was poured upon him. Garlands of celestial flowers, of delicious fragrance and touch, were also showered upon him copiously and repeatedly. The deities and Gandharvas and Apsaras in large bands began to sing and dance around him even as they sing and dance around the Grandsire Brahma. The king then ascended a celestial car that surpassed (in grandeur and beauty) a mansion made entirely of gold, that had arches made of gold and gems, and that was adorned with columns made of lapis lazuli. Through the merit of his act, the royal sage Sivi proceeded to eternal Heaven. Do thou also, O Yudhishthira, act in the same way towards those that seek thy protection. He who protects those that are devoted to him, those that are attached to him from love and affection, and those that depend upon him, and who has compassion for all creatures, succeeds in attaining great felicity hereafter. That king who is of righteous behaviour and who is observant of honesty and integrity, succeeds by his acts of sincerity in acquiring every valuable reward. The royal sage Sivi of pure soul and endued with great wisdom and unbaffled prowess, that ruler of the kingdom of Kasi, became celebrated over the three worlds for his deeds of righteousness. Anybody who would protect in the same way a seeker for protection, would certainly attain (like Sivi himself) to the same happy end, O best of the

Bharatas. He who recites this history of the royal sage Vrishadarbha is sure to become cleansed of every sin, and the person who hears this history recited by another is sure to attain to the same result."'"

SECTION XXXIII.

"'Yudhishthira said, "Which act, O grandsire, is the foremost of all those that have been laid down for a king? What is that act by doing which a king succeeds in enjoying both this world and the next?"

"'Bhishma said, "Even this viz., the worship of the Brahmanas, is the foremost of all those acts, O Bharata, which have been laid down for a king duly installed on the throne, if, indeed, he is desirous of obtaining great happiness. Even this is what the foremost of all kings should do. Know this well, O chief of Bharata's race. The king should always worship with reverence all righteous Brahmanas possessed of Vedic lore.[255] The king should, with bows and comforting speeches and gifts of all articles of enjoyment, worship all Brahmanas possessed of great learning who may dwell in his city or provinces. This is the foremost of all acts laid down for the king. Indeed, the king should always keep his eyes fixed on this. He should protect and cherish these, even as he protects his own self or his own children. The king should worship with greater reverence those amongst the Brahmanas that may be worthy of it (for their superior sanctity and learning). When such men are freed from all anxiety, the whole kingdom blazes forth in beauty. Such individuals are worthy of adoration. Unto such the king should bow his head. Verily, they should be honoured, even as one honours one's sires and grandsires. Upon them depends the course of conduct followed by men, even as the existence of all creatures depends upon Vasava. Of prowess incapable of being baffled and endued with great energy, such men, if enraged, are capable of consuming the entire kingdom to ashes by only fiat of their will, or by acts of incantation, or by other means (derived from the power of penance). I do not see anything that can destroy them. Their power seems to be uncontrolled, being capable of reaching to the farthest end of the universe. When angry, their glances fall upon men and things like a blazing flame of fire upon a forest. The most courageous men are struck with fear at their mein. Their virtues and powers are extraordinary and immeasurable. Some amongst them are like wells and pits with mouths covered by grass and creepers, while others resemble the firmament cleared of clouds and darkness. Some amongst them are of fierce dispositions (like Durvasas and others of that stamp). Some are as mild and soft in disposition as cotton (like Gautama and others). Some amongst them are very cunning (like Agastya who devoured the Asura Vatapi, and Rishis of that class). Some amongst them are devoted to the practice of penances. Some amongst them are employed in agricultural pursuits (like the preceptor of Uddalaka). Some amongst them are engaged in the keep of kine (as Upamanyu while attending his preceptor). Some amongst them live upon eleemosynary alms. Some amongst them are even thieves (like Valmiki in his early years and Viswamitra during a famine). Some amongst them are fond of fomenting quarrels and disputes (like Narada). Some, again, amongst them are actors and dancers (like Bharata). Some amongst them are competent to achieve all feats, ordinary and extraordinary (like Agastya drinking up the entire ocean, as if it were a palmful of water). The Brahmanas, O chief of Bharata's race are of

---

[255] Some texts read vriddhan for Ishtan. If the former reading be adopted, the meaning would be that kings should worship all aged Brahmanas possessed of Vedic lore.

diverse aspects and behaviour. One should always utter the praises of the Brahmanas who are conversant with all duties, who are righteous of behaviour, who are devoted to diverse kinds of act, and who are seen to derive their sustenance from diverse kinds of occupations.[256] The Brahmanas, O ruler of men, who are highly blessed, are elder in respect of their origin than the Pitris, the deities, human beings (belonging to the three other orders), the Snakes and the Rakshasas. These regenerate persons are incapable of being vanquished by the deities or the Pitris, or the Gandharvas or the Rakshasas, or the Asuras or the Pisachas. The Brahmanas are competent to make him a deity that is not a deity. They can, again, divest one that is a deity of his status as such. He becomes a king whom they wish to make a king. He, on the other hand, goes to the wall whom they do not love or like. I tell thee truly, O king, that those foolish persons, without doubt, meet with destruction who calumniate the Brahmanas and utter their dispraise. Skilled in praise and dispraise, and themselves the origin or cause of other people's fame and ignominy the Brahmanas, O king, always become angry with those that seek to injure others. That man whom the Brahmanas praise succeeds in growing in prosperity. That man who is censured and is cast off by the Brahmanas soon meets with discomfiture. It is in consequence of the absence of Brahmanas from among them that the Sakas, the Yavanas, the Kamvojas and other Kshatriya tribes have become fallen and degraded into the status of Sudras. The Dravidas, the Kalingas, the Pulandas, the Usinaras, the Kolisarpas, the Mahishakas and other Kshatriyas, have, in consequence of the absence of Brahmanas from among their midst, become degraded into Sudras. Defeat at their hands is preferable to victory over them, O foremost of victorious persons. One slaying all other living creatures in the world does not incur a sin so heinous as that of slaying a single Brahmana. The great Rishis have said that Brahmanicide is a heinous sin. One should never utter the dispraise or calumny of the Brahmanas. Where the dispraise of Brahmanas is uttered, one should sit with face hanging down or leave that spot (for avoiding both the utterer and his words). That man has not as yet been born in this world or will not take birth here, who has been or will be able to pass his life in happiness after quarrelling with the Brahmanas. One cannot seize the wind with one's hands. One cannot touch the moon with one's hand. One cannot support the Earth on one's arms. After the same manner, O king, one is not able to vanquish the Brahmanas in this world."'"

SECTION XXXIV.

"'Bhishma said, "One should always offer the most reverent worship unto the Brahmanas. They have Soma for their king, and they it is who confer happiness and misery upon others. They, O king, should always be cherished and protected as one cherishes and protects one's own sires and grandsires, and should be adored with bows and gifts of food and ornaments and other articles of enjoyment, as also with such things as they may desire. The peace and happiness of the kingdom flow from such respect shown to the Brahmanas even as the peace and happiness of all living creatures flow from Vasava, the chief of the celestials. Let Brahmanas of pure behaviour and Brahma-effulgence be born in a kingdom. Kshatriyas also that are splendid car-warriors and that are capable of scorching all foes, should be desired (amongst those that settle in a kingdom). This was said unto me by Narada. There is nothing higher, O king, than this,

---

[256] Though really conversant with all duties, and of righteous behaviour, the Brahmanas, nevertheless, for concealing their real natures or for protecting the world, are seen to be employed in diverse kinds of occupations.

viz., the act of causing a Brahmana possessed of good birth, having a knowledge of morality and righteousness, and steadfast in the observance of excellent vows, to take up his residence in one's mansion. Such an act is productive of every kind of blessing. The sacrificial offerings given unto Brahmanas reach the very deities who accept them. Brahmanas are the sires of all creatures. There is nothing higher than a Brahmana. Aditya, Chandramas, Wind, Water, Earth, Sky and the points of the compass, all enter the body of the Brahmana and take what the Brahmana eats.[257] In that house where Brahmanas do not eat, the Pitris refuse to eat. The deities also never eat in the house of the wretch who hates the Brahmanas. When the Brahmanas are gratified, the Pitris also are gratified. There is no doubt in this. They that give away the sacrificial butter unto the Brahmanas become themselves gratified (in this and the other world). Such men never meet with destruction. Verily, they succeed in attaining to high ends. Those particular offerings in sacrifices with which one gratifies the Brahmanas go to gratify both the Pitris and the deities. The Brahmana is the cause of that sacrifice whence all created things have sprung. The Brahmana is acquainted with that from which this universe has sprung and unto which, when apparently destroyed, it returns. Indeed the Brahmana knows the path that leads to Heaven and the other path that leads to the opposite place. The Brahmana is conversant with what has happened and what will happen. The Brahmana is the foremost of all two-legged beings. The Brahmana, O chief of the Bharatas, is fully conversant with the duties that have been laid down for his order. Those persons that follow the Brahmanas are never vanquished. Departing from this world, they never meet with destruction. Indeed victory is always theirs. Those high-souled persons,—indeed, those persons that have subdued their souls,—who accept the words that fall from the lips of the Brahmanas, are never vanquished. Victory always becomes theirs.[258] The energy and might of those Kshatriyas who scorch everything with their energy and might become neutralised when they encounter the Brahmanas. The Bhrigus conquered the Talajanghas. The son of Angiras conquered the Nipas. Bharadwaja conquered the Vitahavyas as also the Ailas, O chief of Bharata's race. Although all these Kshatriyas were capable of using diverse kinds of arms, yet the Brahmanas named, owning only black deer skins for their emblems, succeeded in conquering them effectually. Bestowing the Earth upon the Brahmanas and illuminating both the worlds by the splendour of such a deed, one should accomplish acts through which one may succeed in attaining to the end of all things.[259] Like fire concealed within wood, everything that is said or heard or read in this world, lies ensconced in the Brahmana. In this connection is cited the old history of the conversation between Vasudeva and the Earth, O chief of Bharata's race!

""'Vasudeva said, 'O mother of all creatures, O auspicious goddess, I desire to ask thee for a solution of this doubt of mine. By what act does a man leading the domestic mode of life succeed in cleansing all his sins?'

""'The Earth said, 'One should serve the Brahmanas. This conduct is cleansing and excellent. All the impurities are destroyed of that man who serves the Brahmanas with reverence. From this (conduct) arises prosperity. From this arises fame. From this springs forth intelligence or knowledge of the soul. A Kshatriya by this conduct, becomes a

---

[257] The argument, therefore, is that anything given to the Brahmana to eat and that is eaten by him apparently, is really eaten by these deities.

[258] Bhutatmanah is explained by the commentator as Bhuta praptahvasikritahatma yaih.

[259] The second line of verse 18 is a crux. The commentator explains that prakshipya means dattwa; Kun is the Earth. Van is diptim ukrvan, ubhaya-loke iti seshah. Para- [This footnote appears to have been truncated, as the last line begins with a hyphenated word.—JBH.]

mighty car-warrior and a scorcher of foes and succeeds in acquiring great fame. Even this is what Narada said unto me, viz., that one should always revere a Brahmana that is well-born, of rigid vows and conversant with the scriptures, if one desires every kind of prosperity. That man really grows in prosperity who is applauded by the Brahmanas, who are higher than those that are regarded superior to all men high or low. That man who speaks ill of the Brahmanas soon meets with discomfiture, even as a clod of unbaked earth meets with destruction when cast into the sea. After the same manner, all acts that are hurtful to the Brahmanas are sure to bring about discomfiture and ruin. Behold the dark spots on the Moon and the salt waters of the ocean. The great Indra had at one time been marked all over with a thousand sex-marks. It was through the power of the Brahmanas that those marks became altered into as so many eyes. Behold, O Mahadeva how all those things took place. Desiring fame and prosperity and diverse regions of beatitude in the next world, a person of pure behaviour and soul should, O slayer of Madhu, live in obedience to the dictates of the Brahmanas.'"[260]

"'Bhishma continued, "Hearing these words of the goddess Earth, the slayer of Madhu, O thou of Kuru's race, exclaimed,—Excellent, Excellent—and honoured the goddess in due form. Having heard this discourse between the goddess Earth and Madhava, do thou, O son of Pritha, always, with rapt soul, worship all superior Brahmanas. Doing this, thou shalt verily obtain what is highly beneficial for thee!"'"

SECTION XXXV.

"'Bhishma said, "O blessed king, Brahmana, by birth alone, becomes an object of adoration with all creatures and are entitled, as guests, to eat the first portion of all cooked food.[261] From them flow all the great objects of life (viz., Righteousness and Wealth and Pleasure and Emancipation). They are the friends of all creatures in the universe. They are again the mouths of the deities (for food poured into their mouths is eaten by the deities). Worshipped with reverence, they wish us prosperity by uttering words fraught with auspiciousness. Disregarded by our foes, let them be enraged with these, and let them wish evil unto those detractors of theirs, uttering words fraught with severe curses. In this connection, persons conversant with ancient history repeat the following verses sung of old respecting how in ancient times the Creator, after having created the Brahmanas, ordained their duties.—'A Brahmana should never do anything else than what has been ordained for him. Protected, they should protect others. By conducting themselves in this way, they are sure to attain to what is mightily advantageous for them. By doing those acts that are ordained for them, they are sure to obtain Brahma-prosperity. Ye shall become the exemplars of all creatures, and reins for restraining them. A Brahmana possessed of learning should never do that which is laid down for the Sudras. By doing such acts, a Brahmana loses merit.[262] By Vedic study he is sure to obtain prosperity and intelligence and energy and puissance competent to scorch all things, as also glory of the most exalted kind. By offering oblations of clarified butter

---

[260] The dark spots on the Moon were due to the curse of Daksha. The waters of the Ocean became saltish owing to the curse of a Rishi.

[261] The sense is that one becomes a Brahmana by birth alone, without the aid of those purificatory rites that have been laid down in the scriptures. When food is cooked, none else than a Brahmana is entitled in the first portion thereof.

[262] The commentator thinks that saudram karma has especial reference to the service of others. Hence what is interdicted for the Brahmanas is the service of others.

unto the deities, the Brahmanas attain to high blessedness and become worthy of taking the precedence of even children in the matter of all kinds of cooked food, and endued with Brahma-prosperity.[263] Endued with faith that is fraught with compassion towards all creatures, and devoted to self-restraint and the study of the Vedas, ye shall attain to the fruition of all your wishes. Whatever things exist in the world of men, whatever things occur in the region of the deities, can all be achieved and acquired with the aid of penances and knowledge and the observance of vows and restraints.' I have thus recited to thee, O sinless one, the verses that were sung by Brahma himself. Endued with supreme intelligence and wisdom, the Creator himself ordained this, through compassion for the Brahmanas. The puissance of those among them that are devoted to penances is equal to the might of kings. They are verily irresistible, fierce, possessed of the speed of lightning, and exceedingly quick in what they do. There are amongst them those that are possessed of the might of lions and those that are possessed of the might of tigers. Some of them are endued with the might of boars, some with that of the deer, and some with that of crocodiles. Some there are amongst them whose touch resembles that of snakes of virulent poison, and some whose bite resembles that of sharks. Some amongst them are capable of compassing by speech alone the destruction of those that are opposed to them; and some are competent to destroy by a glance only of their eyes. Some amongst them, as already said, are like snakes of virulent poison, and some of them are possessed of very mild dispositions. The dispositions, O Yudhisthira, of the Brahmanas, are of diverse kinds. The Mekalas, the Dravidas, the Lathas, the Paundras, the Konwasiras, the Saundikas, the Daradas, the Darvas, the Chauras, the Savaras, the Varvaras, the Kiratas, the Yavanas, and numerous other tribes of Kshatriyas, have become degraded into the status of Sudras through the wrath of Brahmanas. In consequence of having disregarded the Brahmanas, the Asuras have been obliged to take refuge in the depths of the ocean. Through the grace of the Brahmanas, the deities have become denizens of the happy regions of Heaven. The element of space or ether is incapable of being touched. The Himavat mountains are incapable of being moved from their site. The current of Ganga is incapable of being resisted by a dam. The Brahmanas are incapable of being subjugated. Kshatriyas are incapable of ruling the Earth without cultivating the good will of the Brahmanas. The Brahmanas are high-souled beings. They are the deities of the very deities. Do thou always worship them with gifts and obedient services: if, indeed, thou wishest to enjoy the sovereignty of the whole Earth with her belt of seas. The energy and might of Brahmanas, O sinless one, become abated in consequence of the acceptance of gift. Thou shouldst protect thy race. O king, from those Brahmanas that do not desire to accept gifts!""[264] (Anusasana Parva Continued in Volume XI)

---

[263] In this country to this day, when food is prepared in view of guests invited to a house, no portion of such food can be offered to any one before it is dedicated to the deities and placed before those for whom it is intended. An exception, however, is made for children. What is stated here is that a good Brahmana can take the precedence of even children in the matter of such food.

[264] What is stated here is that those Brahmanas that do not accept gifts are very superior. Their energy and might are great. Bhishma directs Yudhishthira to be always careful of how he would treat such superior Brahmanas. After rakshyam, the words swakulam are understood. The Burdwan translator misunderstands the second line of the verse.

SECTION XXXVI.

"'Bhishma said, "In this connection is cited the old history of the discourse between Sakra and Samvara. Do thou listen to it, O Yudhishthira. Once upon a time Sakra, assuming the guise of an ascetic with matted locks on his head and body smeared with ashes all over, rode on an ugly car and repaired to the presence of the Asura Samvara.

"'"Sakra said, 'Through what conduct, O Samvara, hast thou been able to get at the head of all individuals of thy race? For what reason do all people regard thee as superior? Do thou tell me this truly and in detail.'

"'"Samvara said, 'I never cherish any ill-feelings towards the Brahmanas. Whatever instructions they impart I accept with unquestioning reverence. When the Brahmanas are engaged in interpreting the scriptures, I listen to them with great happiness. Having heard their interpretations I never disregard them. Nor do I ever offend against the Brahmanas in any way. I always worship those Brahmanas that are endued with intelligence. I always seek information from them. I always worship their feet. Approaching me with confidence, they always address me with affection and enquire after my welfare. If they ever happen to be heedless, I am always heedful. If they happen to sleep, I always remain wakeful. Like bees drenching the cells of the comb with honey, the Brahmanas, who are my instructors and rulers, always drench me with the nectar of knowledge—me that am always devoted to the path pointed out by the scriptures, that am devoted to the Brahmanas, and that am perfectly free from malice or evil passion. Whatever they say with cheerful hearts, I always accept aided by memory and understanding. I am always careful of my own faith in them and I always think of my own inferiority to them. I always lick the nectar that dwells at the end of their tongue, and it is for this reason that I occupy a position far above that of all others of my race like the Moon transcending all the stars. The scriptural interpretations which fall from the lips of the Brahmanas and listening to which every wise man acts in the world, constitute nectar on earth and may also be likened to eyes of remarkable excellence.[265] Witnessing the encounter between the deities and the Asuras in days of old, and understanding the puissance of the instructions that fell from the Brahmanas, my father became filled with delight and wonder.[266] Beholding the puissance of high-souled Brahmanas, my sire asked Chandramas the question, "How do the Brahmanas attain to success?"

"'"Soma said, "The Brahmanas become crowned with success through their penances. Their strength consists in speech. The prowess of persons belonging to the kingly order resides in their arms. The Brahmanas, however, have speech for their weapons. Undergoing the discomforts of a residence in the abode of his preceptor, the Brahmana should study the Vedas or at least the Pranava. Divesting himself of wrath and renouncing earthly attachments, he should become a Yati, viewing all things and all creatures with equal eyes. If remaining in the abode of his sire he masters all the Vedas and acquiring great knowledge attains to a position that should command respect, people still condemn him as untravelled or homekeeping. Like a snake swallowing mice, the earth swallows up these two, viz., a king that is unwilling to fight and a Brahmana that is

---

[265] The construction is Etat Brahmana-mukhat sastram, yat srutwaiha pravartate, prithivyam etc, etc. Both the vernacular translators have misunderstood the verse.

[266] Etat karanam seems to refer to Brahmana-mukhat sastram. The sense seems to be that in the encounter between the deities and the Asuras the power of the Brahmanas was abundantly proved, for Sukra aided the Asuras with his Mantras and incantations, while Vrihaspati and others aided the deities by the same means.

unwilling to leave home for acquiring knowledge.[267] Pride destroys the prosperity of persons of little intelligence. A maiden, if she conceives, becomes stained. A Brahmana incurs reproach by keeping at home. Even this is what my father heard from Soma of wonderful aspect. My father, in consequence of this, began to worship and reverence the Brahmanas. Like him, I also worship and adore all Brahmanas of high vows."'"'

"'Bhishma continued, "Hearing these words that fell from the mouth of that prince of Danavas, Sakra began to worship the Brahmanas, and as a consequence thereof he succeeded in obtaining the chiefdom of the deities."'"

SECTION XXXVII.

"'Yudhishthira said, "Which amongst these three persons, O grandsire, should be regarded as the best for making gifts unto, viz., one who is a thorough stranger, or one who is living with and who has been known to the giver for a long time, or one who presents himself before the giver, coming from a long distance?"

"'Bhishma said, "All these are equal. The eligibility of some consists in their soliciting alms for performing sacrifices or for paying the preceptor's fee or for maintaining their spouses and children. The eligibility of some for receiving gifts, consists in their following the vow of wandering over the earth, never soliciting anything but receiving when given. We should also give unto one what one seeks.[268] We should, however, make gifts without afflicting those that depend upon us. Even this is what we have heard. By afflicting one's dependants, one afflicts one's own self. The stranger,— one, that is, who has come for the first time,—should be regarded as a proper object of gifts. He who is familiar and well-known and has been living with the giver, should be regarded in the same light. The learned know that he too who comes from a distant place should be regarded in an equal light."

"'Yudhishthira said, "It is true that we should make gifts unto others without afflicting anyone and without doing violence to the ordinances of the scriptures. One should, however, correctly ascertain who the person is that should be regarded as a proper object for making gifts. He should be such that the gift itself, by being made over to him, may not grieve."[269]

"'Bhishma said, "If the Ritwik, the Purohita, the preceptor, the Acharya, the disciple, the relative (by marriage), and kinsmen, happen to be possessed of learning and free from malice, then should they be deemed worthy of respect and worship. Those persons that do not possess such qualifications cannot be regarded as worthy of gifts or hospitality. Hence, one should with deliberation examine persons with whom one comes into contact. Absence of wrath, truthfulness of speech, abstention from injury, sincerity, peacefulness of conduct, the absence of pride, modesty, renunciation, self-restraint, and tranquillity or contentment of soul, he in whom these occur by nature, and in whom there are no wicked acts, should be regarded as a proper object. Such a person deserves honours. Whether the person be one who is well-known and familiar, or one who has come newly, whether he

---

[267] In some of the Bengal texts for Bhumiretau the reading Bhumireto occurs. The fact is, the latter is a misprint or a mere clerical error. The etau has reference to the two mentioned in the second line. The Burdwan translator actually takes Bhumireto as a correct reading and makes nonsense of the verse.

[268] I expand this verse. After kriya bhavati patratwam is understood. Kriya includes the diverse objects for which persons solicit alms or gifts. Upansuvratam is maunam parivrajyam.

[269] It is said that food or other things, when given to an undeserving person, feels grief. What Yudhishthira asks is who the proper person is unto whom gifts may be made.

has not been seen before, if he happens to possess these qualifications, he should be regarded as worthy of honours and hospitality. He who denies the authority of the Vedas, or strives to show that the scriptures should be disregarded, or approves of all breaches of restraint in society,—simply brings about his own ruin (and should not be regarded as worthy of gifts). That Brahmana who is vain of his learning, who speaks ill of the Vedas or who is devoted to the science of useless disputation, or who is desirous of gaining victory (in disputations) in assemblies of good men by disproving the reasons that exist for morality and religion and ascribing everything to chance, or who indulges in censuring and reproaching others or who reproves Brahmanas, or who is suspicious of all persons, or who is foolish and bereft of judgment, or who is bitter of speech, should be known to be as hateful as a dog. As a dog encounters others, barking the while and seeking to bite, such a person is even so, for he spends his breath in vain and seeks to destroy the authority of all the scriptures. Those practices that support society, the duties of righteousness, and all those acts which are productive of benefit to one's own self, should be attended to. A person that lives, attending to these, grows in prosperity for everlasting time. By paying off the debt one owes to the deities by performing sacrifices, that to the Rishis by studying the Vedas, that to the Pitris by procreating children, that to the Brahmanas by making presents unto them and that to guests by feeding them, in due order, and with purity of intention, and properly attending to the ordinances of the scriptures, a householder does not fall away from righteousness."""[270]

SECTION XXXVIII.

"'Yudhishthira said, "O best of the Bharatas, I wish to hear thee discourse on the disposition of women. Women are said to be the root of all evil. They are all regarded as exceedingly frail."

"'Bhishma said, "In this connection is cited the old history of the discourse between the celestial Rishi Narada and the (celestial) courtezan Panchachuda. Once in ancient times, the celestial Rishi Narada, having roamed over all the world, met the Apsara Panchachuda of faultless beauty, having her abode in the region of Brahman. Beholding the Apsara every limb of whose body was endued with great beauty, the ascetic addressed her, saying, 'O thou of slender waist, I have a doubt in my mind. Do thou explain it.'"

"'Bhishma continued, "Thus addressed by the Rishi, the Apsara said unto him, 'If the subject is one which is known to me and if thou thinkest me competent to speak on it, I shall certainly say what is in my mind.'

""""Narada said, 'O amiable one, I shall not certainly appoint thee to any task that is beyond thy competence. O thou of beautiful face, I wish to hear from thee of the disposition of women.'"

"'Bhishma continued, "Hearing these words of the celestial Rishi, that foremost of Apsaras replied unto him, saying, 'I am unable, being myself a woman, to speak ill of women. Thou knowest what women are and with what nature they are endued. It behoveth thee not, O celestial Rishi, to set me to such a task.' Unto her the celestial Rishi said, 'It is very true, O thou of slender waist! One incurs fault by speaking what is untrue. In saying, however, what is true, there can be no fault.' Thus addressed by him, the

---

[270] All these acts should be performed with purity of intention and according to the ordinances of the scriptures. For example, sacrifices should not be performed with vanity or pride. The Vedas should not be studied without faith. Children should not be procreated from lust, etc.

Apsara Panchachuda of sweet smiles consented to answer Narada's question. She then addressed herself to mention what the true and eternal faults of women are.

""Panchachuda said, 'Even if high-born and endued with beauty and possessed of protectors, women wish to transgress the restraints assigned to them. This fault truly stains them, O Narada! There is nothing else that is more sinful than women. Verily, women are the root of all faults. That is certainly known to thee, O Narada! Women, even when possessed of husbands having fame and wealth, of handsome features and completely obedient to them, are prepared to disregard them if they get the opportunity. This, O puissant one, is a sinful disposition with us women that, casting off modesty, we cultivate the companionship of men of sinful habits and intentions. Women betray a liking for those men who court them, who approach their presence, and who respectfully serve them to even a slight extent. Through want of solicitation by persons of the other sex, or fear of relatives, women, who are naturally impatient of all restraints, do not transgress those that have been ordained for them, and remain by the side of their husbands. There is none whom they are incapable of admitting to their favours. They never take into consideration the age of the person they are prepared to favour. Ugly or handsome, if only the person happens to belong to the opposite sex, women are ready to enjoy his companionship. That women remain faithful to their lords is due not to their fear of sin, nor to compassion, nor to wealth, nor to the affection that springs up in their hearts for kinsmen and children. Women living in the bosom of respectable families envy the condition of those members of their sex that are young and well-adorned with jewels and gems and that lead a free life. Even those women that are loved by their husbands and treated with great respect, are seen to bestow their favours upon men that are hump-backed, that are blind, that are idiots, or that are dwarfs. Women may be seen to like the companionship of even those men that are destitute of the power of locomotion or those men that are endued with great ugliness of features. O great Rishi, there is no man in this world whom women may regard as unfit for companionship. Through inability to obtain persons of the opposite sex, or fear of relatives, or fear of death and imprisonment, women remain, of themselves, within the restraints prescribed for them. They are exceedingly restless, for they always hanker after new companions. In consequence of their nature being unintelligible, they are incapable of being kept in obedience by affectionate treatment. Their disposition is such that they are incapable of being restrained when bent upon transgression. Verily, women are like the words uttered by the wise.[271] Fire is never satiated with fuel. Ocean can never be filled with the waters that rivers bring unto him. The Destroyer is never satiated with slaying even all living creatures. Similarly, women are never satiated with men. This, O celestial Rishi, is another mystery connected with women. As soon as they see a man of handsome and charming features, unfailing signs of desire appear on their persons. They never show sufficient regard for even such husbands as accomplish all their wishes, as always do what is agreeable to them and as protect them from want and danger. Women never regard so highly even articles of enjoyment in abundance or ornaments or other possessions of an agreeable kind as they do the companionship of persons of the opposite sex. The destroyer, the deity of wind, death, the nether legions, the equine mouth that roves through the ocean, vomiting ceaseless flames of fire, the sharpness of the razor, virulent poison, the snake, and Fire—all these exist in a state of union in women. That

---

[271] Such words are unseizable and unintelligible for their depth of meaning. Women are equally unseizable and unintelligible.

eternal Brahman whence the five great elements have sprung into existence, whence the Creator Brahma hath ordained the universe, and whence, indeed, men have sprung, verily from the same eternal source have women sprung into existence. At that time, again, O Narada, when women were created, these faults that I have enumerated were planted in them!"'"

SECTION XXXIX.

"'Yudhishthira said, "All men, O king, in this world, are seen to attach themselves to women, overcome by the illusion that is created by the divine Being. Similarly, women too are seen to attach themselves to men. All this is seen taking place everywhere in the world. On this subject a doubt exists in my mind. Why, O delighter of the Kurus, do men (when women are stained with so many faults) still attach themselves to women? Who, again, are those men with whom women are highly pleased and who are they with whom they are displeased? It behoveth thee, O chief of men, to explain to me how men are capable of protecting women? While men take pleasure in women and sport with them, women, it seems, are engaged in deceiving men. Then, again, if a man once falls into their hands, it is difficult for him to escape from them. Like kine ever seeking pastures new women seek new men one after another. That illusion which the Asura Samvara possessed, that illusion which the Asura Namuchi possessed, that illusion which Vali or Kumbbinasi had, the sum total thereof is possessed by women. If man laughs, women laugh. If man weeps, they weep. If the opportunity requires, they receive the man that is disagreeable to them with agreeable words. That science of policy which the preceptor of the Asuras knew, that science of policy which the preceptor of the celestials, Vrihaspati, knew, cannot be regarded to be deeper or more distinguished for subtility than what woman's intelligence naturally brings forth. Verily how can women, therefore, be restrained by men? They make a lie appear as truth, and a truth appear as a lie. They who can do this,—I ask, O hero,—how can they be ruled by persons of the opposite sex? It seems to me that Vrihaspati and other great thinkers, O slayer of foes, evolved the science of policy from observation of the understandings of women. Whether treated by men with respect or with disdain, women are seen to turn the heads and agitate the hearts of men.[272] Living creatures, O thou of mighty arms, are virtuous. Even this is what has been heard by us. (How then, can this be consistent with fact)? For treated with affection and respect or otherwise, women (forming a fair portion of living creatures) are seen to deserve censure for their conduct towards men.[273] This great doubt fills my mind, viz., when their behaviour is such, what man is there that can restrain them within the bounds of righteousness? Do thou explain this to me, O highly blessed scion of Kuru's race! It behoves thee to tell me, O chief of Kuru's race, whether women are truly capable of being restrained within the bonds prescribed by the scriptures or whether any one before our time did really succeed in so restraining them."'"

---

[272] The sense is this: women agitate the hearts of those that treat them with respect as of those that treat them with disdain. The commentator explains that Pujitah dhikkritahva tulyavat vikaram janayati.

[273] All living creatures are virtuous, for they are capable of progressing towards godship by their own acts.

SECTION XL.

"'Bhishma said, "It is even so as thou sayest, O thou of mighty arms. There is nothing untrue in all this that thou sayest, O thou of Kuru's race, on the subject of women. In this connection I shall recite to thee the old history of how in days of yore the high-souled Vipula had succeeded in restraining women within the bounds laid down for them. I shall also tell thee, O king, how women were created by the Grandsire Brahman and the object for which they were created by Him. There is no creature more sinful, O son, than women. Woman is a blazing fire. She is the illusion, O king, that the Daitya Maya created. She is the sharp edge of the razor. She is poison. She is a snake. She is fire. She is, verily, all these united together. It has been heard by us that all persons of the human race are characterised by righteousness, and that they, in course of natural progress and improvement, attain to the status of deities. This circumstance alarmed the deities. They, therefore, O chastiser of foes, assembled together and repaired to the presence of the Grandsire. Informing him of what was in their minds, they stood silent in his presence, with downcast eyes. The puissant Grandsire having ascertained what was in the hearts of the deities, created women, with the aid of an Atharvan rite. In a former creation, O son of Kunti, women were all virtuous. Those, however, that sprang from this creation by Brahman with the aid of an illusion became sinful. The grandsire bestowed upon them the desire of enjoyment, all kinds of carnal pleasure. Tempted by the desire of enjoyment, they began to pursue persons of the other sex. The puissant lord of the deities created Wrath as the companion of Lust. Persons of the male sex, yielding to the power of Lust and Wrath, sought the companionship of women. Women have no especial acts prescribed for them. Even this is the ordinance that was laid down. The Sruti declares that women are endued with senses the most powerful, that they have no scriptures to follow, and that they are living lies. Beds and seats and ornaments and food and drink and the absence of all that is respectable and righteous, indulgence in disagreeable words, and love of sexual companionship,—these were bestowed by Brahman upon women. Men are quite unable to restrain them within bounds. The Creator himself is incapable of restraining them within the limits that are proper: what need then be said of men? This, O chief of men, I heard in former days, viz., how Vipula had succeeded in protecting his preceptor's spouse in ancient times. There was in days of yore a highly blessed Rishi of the name of Devasarman of great celebrity. He had a wife, Ruchi by name, who was unequalled on earth for beauty. Her loveliness intoxicated every beholder among the deities and Gandharvas and Danavas. The chastiser of Paka, viz., Indra, the slayer of Vritra, O monarch, was in particular enamoured of her and coveted her person. The great ascetic Devasarman was fully cognisant of the disposition of women. He, therefore, to the best of his power and energy, protected her (from every kind of evil influence). The Rishi knew that Indra was restrained by no scruples in the matter of seeking the companionship of other people's wives. It was for this reason that he used to protect his spouse, putting forth all his power. Once on a time, O son, the Rishi became desirous of performing a sacrifice. He began to think of how (during his own absence from home) his wife could be protected. Endued with high ascetic merit, he at last hit upon the course he should adopt. Summoning his favourite disciple whose name was Vipula and who was of Bhrigu's race, he said as follows:

"""Devasarman said, 'I shall leave home (for a while) in order to perform a sacrifice. The chief of the celestials always covets this Ruchi of mine. Do thou, during my absence, protect her, putting forth all thy might! Thou shalt pass thy time heedfully in view of Purandara. O foremost one of Bhrigu's race, that Indra assumes various disguises.'"

"Bhishma continued, "Thus addressed by his preceptor, the ascetic Vipula with senses under control, always engaged in severe penances, possessed of the splendour, O king, of fire or the sun conversant with all the duties of righteousness, and ever truthful in speech, answered him, saying, 'So be it.' Once more, however, as his preceptor was about to set out Vipula asked him in these words.

"'"Vipula said, 'Tell me, O Muni, what forms does Sakra assume when he presents himself? Of what kind is his body and what is his energy? It behoveth thee to say all this to me."'

"'Bhishma continued, "The illustrious Rishi then truly described unto the high-souled Vipula all the illusions of Sakra, O Bharata.

"'"Devasarman said, 'The puissant chastiser of Paka, O regenerate Rishi, is full of illusion. Every moment he assumes those forms that he chooses. Sometimes he wears a diadem and holds the thunderbolt. Sometimes armed with the thunderbolt and wearing a crown on his head, he adorns himself with ear-rings, in a moment he transforms himself into the shape and aspect of Chandala. Sometimes, he appears with coronal locks on his head: soon again, O son, he shows himself with matted locks, his person clad the while in rags. Sometimes, he assumes a goodly and gigantic frame. The next moment he transforms himself into one of emaciated limbs, and dressed in rags. Sometimes he becomes fair, sometimes darkish, sometimes dark of complexion. Sometimes he becomes ugly and sometimes as possessed of great comeliness of person. Sometimes he shows himself as young and sometimes as old. Sometimes he appears as a Brahmana, sometimes as a Kshatriya, sometimes as a Vaisya, and sometimes as a Sudra. Verily, he of a hundred sacrifices appears at times as a person born of impure order, that is as the son of a superior father by an inferior mother or of an inferior father by a superior mother. Sometimes he appears as a parrot, sometimes as a crow, sometimes as a swan, and sometimes as a cuckoo. He assumes the forms also of a lion, a tiger, or an elephant. Sometimes he shows himself as a god, sometimes as a Daitya, and sometimes he assumes the guise of a king. Sometimes he appears as fat and plump. Sometimes as one whose limbs have been broken by the action of disordered wind in the system, sometimes as a bird, and sometimes as one of exceedingly ugly features. Sometimes he appears as a quadruped. Capable of assuming any form, he sometimes appears as an idiot destitute of all intelligence. He assumes also the forms of flies and gnats. O Vipula, no one can make him out in consequence of these innumerable disguises that he is capable of assuming. The very Creator of the universe is not equal to that feat. He makes himself invisible when he chooses. He is incapable of being seen except with the eye of knowledge. The chief of the celestials sometimes transforms himself into the wind. The chastiser of Paka always assumes these disguises. Do thou, therefore, O Vipula, protect this slender-waisted spouse of mine with great care. O foremost one of Bhrigu's race, do thou take every care for seeing that the chief of the celestials may not defile this spouse of mine like a wretched dog licking the Havi kept in view of a sacrifice.' Having said these words, the highly-blessed Muni, viz., Devasarman, intent upon performing a sacrifice, set out from his abode, O chief of the Bharatas. Hearing these words of his preceptor, Vipula began to think, 'I shall certainly protect this lady in every respect from the puissant chief of the celestials. But what should be the means? What can I do in this matter of protecting the wife of my preceptor? The chief of the celestials is endued with large powers of illusion. Possessed of great energy, he is difficult of being resisted. Indra cannot be kept out by enclosing this retreat of ours or fencing this yard, since he is capable of assuming innumerable forms. Assuming the form of the wind, the chief of the celestials may assault the spouse of my preceptor. The best course, therefore, for me, would be to enter (by Yoga-power) the body of this lady and remain there. By putting forth my prowess I shall not be able to protect the lady, for the puissant chastiser of Paka, it has been heard by me, is capable of assuming any form he likes. I shall, therefore, protect this one from Indra by my Yoga-power. For carrying out my object I shall with my body enter the body of this lady. If my preceptor, coming back, beholds his spouse defiled, he will, without doubt, curse me through wrath, for endued with great ascetic merit, he is possessed of spiritual vision. This lady is incapable of being protected in the way in which other women are protected by men, since the chief of the celestials is endued with large powers of illusion. Alas, the situation in which I find myself is very critical. The behest of my preceptor should certainly be obeyed by me. If, therefore, I protect her by my Yoga-power, the feat will be regarded by all as a wonderful one. By my Yoga-power, therefore, I shall enter the body of my preceptor's lady. I shall stay within her and yet not touch her person, like a drop of water on a lotus-leaf which lies on it and yet does not drench it at all. If I be free from the taint of passion, I cannot incur any fault by doing what I wish to do. As a traveller, in course of his sojourn, takes up his residence (for a while) in any empty mansion he finds, I shall, after the same manner, reside this day within the body of my preceptor's lady. Verily, with mind rapt up in Yoga, I shall dwell today in this lady's body!' Giving his best consideration to these points of righteousness, thinking of all the Vedas and their branches, and with eye directed to the large measure of penances which his preceptor had and which he himself also was possessed of, and having settled in his mind, with a view only to protect the lady, to enter her person by Yoga-power. Vipula of Bhrigu's race took great care (for accomplishing his purpose). Listen now to me, O monarch, as I recite to thee what he did. Endued with great penances, Vipula sat himself down by the side of his preceptor's spouse as she of faultless features was sitting in her cottage. Vipula then began to discourse to her bringing her over to the cause of righteousness and truth. Directing his eyes then to hers and uniting the rays of light that emanated from her organs of vision with those that issued from his, Vipula (in his subtle form) entered the lady's body even as the element of wind enters that of ether of space. Penetrating her eyes with his eyes and her face with his face, Vipula stayed, without moving, within her invisibly, like her shadow. Restraining every part of the lady's body, Vipula continued to dwell within her, intent on protecting her from Indra. The lady herself knew nothing of this. It was in this way, O monarch, that Vipula continued to protect the lady till the time of his high-souled preceptor's coming back after accomplishing the sacrifice which he had gone out to perform."'"

SECTION XLI.

"'Bhishma said, "One day the chief of the celestials assuming a form of celestial beauty, came to the retreat of the Rishi, thinking that the opportunity he had been expecting had at last come. Verily, O king, having assumed a form unrivalled for comeliness and exceedingly tempting to women and highly agreeable to look at, Indra entered the ascetic's asylum. He saw the body of Vipula staying in a sitting posture, immovable as a stake, and with eyes destitute of vision, like a picture drawn on the canvas. And he saw also that Ruchi was seated there, adorned with eyes whose ends were extremely beautiful, possessed of full and rotund hips, and having a deep and swelling bosom. Her eyes were large and expansive like the petals of the lotus, and her face was as beautiful and sweet as the moon at full. Seeing Indra come in that guise, the lady wished to rise up and offer him a welcome. Her wonder having been excited at the unrivalled beauty of form which the person possessed, she very much wished to ask him as to who he was. Although, however, she wished to rise up and offer him a welcome, yet her limbs having been restrained by Vipula who was dwelling within her, she failed, O king, to do what she wished. In fact, she was unable to move from the place where she sat. The chief of the celestials then addressed her in agreeable words uttered with a sweet voice. Indeed, he said, 'O thou of sweet smiles, know that I am Indra, arrived here for thy sake! Know, O sweet lady, that I am afflicted by the deity of desire provoked by thoughts of thee! O thou of beautiful brows, I have come to thy presence. Time wears off.'[274] These words that Indra spoke were heard by the ascetic Vipula. Remaining within the body of his preceptor's wife, he saw everything that occurred. The lady of faultless beauty, though she heard what Indra said, was, however, unable to rise up for welcoming or honouring the chief of the celestials. Her senses restrained by Vipula, she was unable to utter a word in reply. That scion of Bhrigu's race, of mighty energy, judging from the indications afforded by the body of his preceptor's wife that she was not unwilling to receive Indra with kindness, restrained her limbs and senses all the more effectually, O king, by his Yoga-powers. With Yoga-bonds he bound up all her senses. Beholding her seated without any indication of agitation on her person, the lord of Sachi, abashed a little, once more addressed that lady who was stupefied by the Yoga-powers of her husband's disciple, in these words, 'Come, come, O sweet lady!' Then the lady endeavoured to answer him. Vipula, however restrained the words that she intended to utter. The words, therefore, that actually escaped her lips (under the influence of Vipula) were. 'What is the reason of thy coming hither?' These words adorned with grammatical refinements, issued out of her mouth that was as beautiful as the moon.[275] Subject to the influence of another, she uttered these words, but became rather ashamed for uttering them. Hearing her, Purandara became exceedingly cheerless. Observing that awkward result, the chief of the celestials, O monarch, adorned with a thousand eyes saw every thing with his spiritual eye. He then beheld the ascetic staying within the body of the lady. Indeed, the ascetic remained within the body of his preceptor's wife like an image or reflection on a mirror. Beholding the ascetic endued with the terrible might of penances, Purandara, O monarch, fearing the Rishi's curse, trembled in fright. Vipula then, possessed of high ascetic might, left the body of his preceptor's wife and returned to his own body that was lying near. He then addressed the terrified Indra in the following words:

""'Vipula said, 'O wicked-souled Purandara, O thou of sinful mind, O wretch that hast no control over thy senses, neither the deities nor human beings will worship thee for any length of time! Hast thou forgotten it, O Sakra,—does it not still dwell in thy remembrance,—that Gautama had cursed thee in consequence of which thy body became disfigured with a thousand sex-marks, which, owing to the Rishi's compassion, were afterwards changed into organs of vision? I know that thou art of an exceedingly foolish understanding, that thy soul is uncleansed, and that thou art of an exceedingly unstable mind! O fool, know that this lady is being protected by me. O sinful wretch, go back to that place whence thou camest. O thou of foolish soul, I do not consume thee today into ashes with my energy. Verily, I am filled with compassion for thee. It is for this that I do

---

[274] Pura has little force here, implying 'first'. In the first place, know that I have come to thee.

[275] Ladies spoke in Prakrita and not in Sanskrit. The latter is refined, the former is unrefined. Hence Indra's surprise at hearing Sanskrit words from the lady's lips.

not, O Vasava, wish to burn thee. My preceptor, endued with great intelligence, is possessed of terrible might. With eyes blazing with wrath, he would, if he saw thee, have burnt thy sinful self today. Thou shouldst not, O Sakra, do like this again. The Brahmanas should be regarded by thee. See that thou dost not, with thy sons and counsellors, meet with destruction, afflicted by the might of the Brahmanas. Thou thinkest that thou art an immortal and that, therefore, art at liberty to proceed in this way. Do not, however, disregard the Brahmanas. Know that there is nothing unattainable by penance.'"

"'Bhishma continued, "Hearing these words of the high-souled Vipula, Sakra without saying anything, and overwhelmed with shame, made himself invisible. A moment after he had gone away, Devasarman of high ascetic merit, having accomplished the sacrifice he had intended to perform, came back to his own asylum. When his preceptor came back, Vipula, who had done an agreeable deed, gave unto him his wife of faultless beauty whom he had successfully protected against the machinations of Indra. Of tranquil soul and full of reverence for his preceptor, Vipula respectfully saluted him and stood in his presence with a fearless heart. After his preceptor had rested a while and when he was seated with his wife on the same seat, Vipula represented unto him everything that Sakra had done. Hearing these words of Vipula, that foremost of Munis, endued with great prowess, became highly gratified with him for his conduct and disposition, his penances, and his observances. Observing Vipula's conduct towards himself—his preceptor—and his devotion also, and noting his steadiness in virtue, the puissant Devasarman exclaimed, 'Excellent, excellent!' The righteous-souled Devasarman, receiving his virtuous disciple with a sincere welcome, honoured him with a boon. Indeed, Vipula, steady in virtue obtained from his preceptor the boon that he would never swerve or fall away from righteousness. Dismissed by his preceptor he left his abode and practised the most severe austerities. Devasarman also, of severe penances, with his spouse, began from that day to live in those solitary woods, perfectly fearless of him who had slain Vala and Vritra.'""

SECTION XLII.

"'Bhishma said, "Having accomplished his preceptor's behest, Vipula practised the most severe penances. Possessed of great energy, he at last regarded himself as endued with sufficient ascetic merit, Priding himself upon the feat he had achieved, he wandered fearlessly and contentedly over the earth, O monarch, regarded by all as one possessed of great fame for what he had done. The puissant Bhargava regarded that he had conquered both the worlds by that feat of his as also by his severe penances. After some time had passed away, O delighter of the Kurus, the occasion came for a ceremony of gifts to take place with respect to the sister of Ruchi. Abundant wealth and corn were to be given away in it.[276] Meanwhile, a certain celestial damsel endued with great beauty, was journeying through the skies. From her body as she coursed through the welkin, some flowers dropped down on the earth. Those flowers possessed of celestial fragrance fell on a spot not far from the retreat of Ruchi's husband. As the flowers lay scattered on the ground, they were picked up by Ruchi of beautiful eyes. Soon after an invitation came to Ruchi from the country of the Angas. The sister, referred to above, of Ruchi, named Prabhavati, was the spouse of Chitraratha, the ruler of the Angas. Ruchi, of very superior complexion, having attached those flowers to her hair, went to the palace of the king of

---

[276] The adana ceremony was a rite in course of which friends and kinsmen had to make presents unto the person performing the ceremony. The investiture with the sacred-thread, marriage, the rite performed in the sixth and the ninth month of pregnancy, are all ceremonies of this kind.

the Angas in answer to the invitation she had received. Beholding those flowers on her hair the queen of the Angas, possessed of beautiful eyes, urged her sister to obtain some for her. Ruchi, of beautiful face, speedily informed her husband of that request of her sister. The Rishi accepted the prayer of his sister-in-law. Summoning Vipula into his presence Devasarman of severe penances commanded his disciple to bring him some flowers of the same kind, saying, 'Go, go!' Accepting without hesitation the behest of his preceptor, the great ascetic Vipula, O king, answered, 'So be it!' and then proceeded to that spot whence the lady Ruchi had picked up the flowers that were coveted by her sister. Arrived at that spot where the flowers (picked up by Ruchi) had fallen from the welkin, Vipula saw some others still lying scattered. They were all as fresh as if they had been newly plucked from the plants whereon they had grown. None of them had drooped in the least. He took up those celestial flowers of great beauty. Possessed of celestial fragrance, O Bharata, Vipula got them there as the result of his severe penances. The accomplisher of his preceptor's behest, having obtained them, he felt great delight and set out speedily for the city of Champa adorned with festoons of Champaka flowers. As he proceeded, he saw on his way a human couple moving in a circle hand in hand. One of them made a rapid step and thereby destroyed the cadence of the movement. For this reason, O king, a dispute arose between them. Indeed, one of them charged the other, saying, 'Thou hast made a quicker step!' The other answered, 'No, verily', as each maintained his own opinion obstinately, each, O king, asserted what the other denied, and denied what the other asserted. While thus disputing with each other with great assurance, an oath was then heard among them. Indeed, each of them suddenly named Vipula in what they uttered. The oath each of them took was even this, 'That one amongst us two who speaketh falsely, shall in the next world, meet with the end which will be the regenerate Vipula's!' Hearing these words of theirs, Vipula's face became very cheerless. He began to reflect, saying unto himself, 'I have undergone severe penances. The dispute between this couple is hot. To me, again, it is painful. What is the sin of which I have been guilty that both these persons should refer to my end in the next world as the most painful one among those reserved for all creatures?' Thinking in this strain, Vipula, O best of monarchs, hung down his head, and with a cheerless mind began to recollect what sin he had done. Proceeding a little way he beheld six other men playing with dice made of gold and silver. Engaged in play, those individuals seemed to him to be so excited that the hair on their bodies stood on end. They also (upon a dispute having arisen among them) were heard by Vipula to take the same oath that he had already heard the first couple to take. Indeed, their words had reference in the same way to Vipula, 'He amongst us who, led by cupidity, will act in an improper way, shall meet with that end which is reserved for Vipula in the next world!' Hearing these words, however, Vipula, although he strove earnestly to recollect failed to remember any transgression of his from even his earliest years, O thou of Kuru's race. Verily he began to burn like a fire placed in the midst of another fire. Hearing that curse, his mind burnt with grief. In this state of anxiety a long time elapsed. At last he recollected the manner in which he had acted in protecting his preceptor's wife from the machinations of Indra. 'I had penetrated the body of that lady, placing limb within limb, face within face, Although I had acted in this way, I did not yet tell my preceptor the truth!' Even this was the transgression, O thou of Kuru's race which Vipula recollected in himself. Indeed, O blessed monarch, without doubt that was the transgression which he had actually committed. Coming to the city of Champa, he gave the flowers to his preceptor. Devoted to superiors and seniors, he worshipped his preceptor in due form.'"

SECTION XLIII.

"'Bhishma said, "Beholding his disciple returned from his mission, Devasarman of great energy addressed him in words which I shall recite to thee O king!

""Davasarman said, 'What hast thou seen, O Vipula, in course of thy progress, O disciple, through the great forest? They whom thou hast seen knew thee, O Vipula. I, as also my spouse Ruchi, know how thou hadst acted in the matter of protecting Ruchi.'

""Vipula said, 'O regenerate Rishi, who are those two whom I first saw? Who also are those other six whom I saw subsequently? All of them know me: who, indeed, are they to whom thou alludest in thy speech to me?'

""Devasarman said, 'The first couple, O regenerate one, whom thou sawest, are Day and Night. They are ceaselessly moving like a circle. Both of them know the transgression of which thou hast been guilty, those other men (six in number) whom, O learned Brahmana, thou sawest playing cheerfully at dice, are the six Seasons. They also are acquainted with thy transgressions. Having committed a sin in secrecy, no sinful man should cherish the assuring thought that his transgression is known only to himself and not to any one else. When a man perpetrates a sinful deed in secret, the Seasons as also Day and Night behold it always. Those regions that are reserved for the sinful shall be thine (for what thou hast done). What thou hadst done thou didst not tell me. That thy sin was not known to any one, was thy belief, and this conviction had filled thee with joy. Thou didst not inform the preceptor of the whole truth, choosing to hide from him a material portion. The Seasons, and Day and Night, whom thou hast heard speak in that strain, thought it proper to remind thee of thy transgression. Day and Night and the Seasons are ever conversant of all the good and the bad deeds that are in a man. They spoke to thee in that way, O regenerate one, because they have full knowledge of what thou hadst done but which thou hadst not the courage to inform me of, fearing thou hadst done wrong. For this reason those regions that are reserved for the sinful will be thine as much. Thou didst not tell me what thou hadst done. Thou wert fully capable, O regenerate one, of protecting my spouse whose disposition by nature is sinful. In doing what thou didst, thou didst not commit any sin. I was, for this, gratified with thee! O best of Brahmanas, if I had known thee to have acted wickedly, I would without hesitation, have cursed thee. Women become united with men. Such union is very desirable with men. Thou hadst, however, protected my wife in a different spirit. If thou hadst acted otherwise, a curse would have been uttered upon thee. Even this is what I think. Thou hadst O son, protected my spouse. The manner in which thou didst it hath now become known to me as if thou hadst thyself informed me of it. I have, O son, become gratified with thee. Relieved of all anxiety, thou shalt go to heaven!' Having said these words unto Vipula, the great Rishi Devasarman, ascended to heaven with his wife and his disciple and began to pass his time there in great happiness. In course of conversation, O king, on a former occasion, the great ascetic Markandeya had narrated to me this history on the banks of the Ganga. I, therefore, recite to thee. Women should always be protected by thee (from temptations and opportunities of every kind). Amongst them both kinds are to be seen, that is, those that are virtuous and those that are not so. Those women that are virtuous are highly blessed. They are the mothers of the universe (for they it is that cherish all creatures on every side). They it is, O king, that uphold the earth with all her waters and forests. Those women that are sinful, that are of wicked behaviour, that are the destroyers of their races, and that are wedded to sinful resolves, are capable of being ascertained by indications, expressive of the evil that is in them, which appear, O king, on their bodies. It is even thus that high-souled persons are capable of protecting women. They cannot, O tiger among kings, be protected in any other way. Women, O chief of men, are fierce. They are endued with fierce prowess. They have none whom they love or like so much as they that have sexual congress with them. Women are like those (Atharvan) incantations that are destructive of life. Even after they have consented to live with one, they are prepared to abandon him for entering into engagements with others. They are never satisfied with one person of the opposite sex, O son of Pandu! Men should feel no affection for them. Nor should they entertain any jealousy on account of them. O king, having a regard only for the considerations of virtue, men should enjoy their society, not with enthusiasm and attachment but with reluctance and absence of attachment. By acting otherwise, a man is sure to meet with destruction, O delighter of the Kurus. Reason is respected at all times and under all circumstances. Only one man, viz., Vipula, had succeeded in protecting woman. There is none else, O king, in the three worlds who is capable of protecting women."'"

SECTION XLIV.

"'Yudhishthira said, "Tell me of that, O grandsire, which is the root of all duties, which is the root of kinsmen, of home, of the Pitris and of guests. I think this should be regarded as the foremost of all duties, (viz., the marriage of one's daughter). Tell me, however, O king, upon what sort of a person should one bestow one's daughter?"

"'Bhishma said, "Having enquired into the conduct and disposition of the person, his learning and acquirements, his birth, and his acts, good people should then bestow their daughter upon accomplished bridegrooms. All righteous Brahmanas, O Yudhishthira, act in this way (in the matter of the bestowal of their daughters). This is known as the Brahma marriage, O Yudhishthira! Selecting an eligible bridegroom, the father of the girl should cause him to marry his daughter, having, by presents of diverse kinds, induced the bridegroom to that act. This form of marriage constitutes the eternal practice of all good Kshatriyas. When the father of the girl, disregarding his own wishes, bestows his daughter upon a person whom the daughter likes and who reciprocates the girl's sentiments, the form of marriage, O Yudhishthira, is called Gandharva by those that are conversant with the Vedas. The wise have said this, O king, to be the practice of the Asuras, viz., wedding a girl after purchasing her at a high cost and after gratifying the cupidity of her kinsmen. Slaying and cutting off the heads of weeping kinsmen, the bridegroom sometimes forcibly takes away the girl he would wed. Such wedding, O son, is called by the name of Rakshasa. Of these five (the Brahma, the Kshatra, the Gandharva, the Asura, and the Rakshasa), three are righteous, O Yudhishthira, and two are unrighteous. The Paisacha and the Asura forms should never be resorted to.[277] The Brahma, Kshatra, and Gandharva forms are righteous, O prince of men! Pure or mixed, these forms should be resorted to, without doubt. A Brahmana can take three wives. A

[277] It would be curious to see how the commentator Nilakantha seeks to include within these five the eight forms of marriage mentioned by Manu. The fact is, such parts of the Mahabharata are unquestionably more ancient than Manu. The mention of Manu is either an instance of interpolation or there must have been an older Manu upon whose work the Manu we know has been based. The Asura and the Rakshasa forms are unequivocally condemned. Yet the commentator seeks to make out that the Rakshasa form is open to the Kshatriyas. The fact is, the Rakshasa was sometimes called the Paisacha. The distinction between those two forms was certainly of later origin.

Kshatriya can take two wives. As regards the Vaisya, he should take a wife from only his own order. The children born of these wives should all be regarded as equal.[278] Of the three wives of a Brahmana, she taken from his own order should be regarded as the foremost. Similarly, of the two wives permitted to the Kshatriya, she taken from his own order should be regarded as superior. Some say that persons belonging to the three higher orders may take, only for purposes of enjoyment (and not for those of virtue), wives from the lowest or the Sudra order. Others, however, forbid the practice.

"'"The righteous condemn the practice of begetting issue upon Sudra women. A Brahmana, by begetting children upon a Sudra woman, incurs the liability of performing an expiation. A person of thirty years of age should wed a girl of ten years of age called a Nagnika.[279] Or, a person of one and twenty years of age should wed a girl of seven years of age. That girl who has no brother nor father should not be wed, O chief of Bharata's race, for she may be intended as Putrika of her sire.[280] After the appearance of puberty, the girl (if not married) should wait for three years. On the fourth year, she should look for a husband herself (without waiting any longer for her kinsmen to select one for her). The offspring of such a girl do not lose their respectability, nor does union with such a girl become disgraceful. If, instead of selecting a husband for herself, she acts otherwise, she incurs the reproach of Prajapati herself. One should wed that girl who is not a Sapinda of one's mother or of the same Gotra with one's father. Even this is the usage (consistent with the sacred law) which Manu has declared."[281]

"'Yudhishthira said, "Desirous of marriage someone actually gives a dower to the girl's kinsmen; someone says, the girl's kinsmen consenting promises to give a dower; someone says, 'I shall abduct the girl by force;' someone simply displays his wealth (to the girl's kinsmen, intending to offer a portion thereof as dower for her); someone, again, actually takes the hand of the girl with rites of wedding. I ask thee, O grandsire, whose wife does the girl actually become? Unto its that are desirous of knowing the truth, thou art the eye with which to behold."

"'Bhishma said, "Whatever acts of men have been approved or settled in consultation by the wise, are seen to be productive of good. False speech, however, is always sinful.[282]

---

[278] Thus, there was no difference, in status, in ancient times, between children born of a Brahmana, a Kshatriya or a Vaisya mother. The difference of status was of later origin.

[279] Nagnika is said to be one who wears a single piece of cloth. A girl in whom the signs of puberty have not appeared does not require more than a single piece of cloth to cover her. The mention of Nagnika, the commentator thinks, is due to an interdiction about wedding a girl of even ten years in whom signs of puberty have appeared.

[280] When a father happens to have an only daughter, he frequently bestows her in marriage upon some eligible youth on the understanding that the son born of her shall be the son, for purposes of both Sraddha rites and inheritance, not of the husband begetting him but of the girl's father. Such a contract would be valid whether expressed or not at the time of marriage. The mere wish of the girl's father, unexpressed at the time of marriage, would convert the son into a son not of the father who begets him but of the father of the girl herself. A daughter reserved for such a purpose is said to be a putrikadharmini or 'invested with the character of a son.' To wed such a girl was not honourable. It was in effect an abandonment of the fruits of marriage. Even if dead at the time of marriage, still if the father had, while living, cherished such a wish, that would convert the girl into a putrikadharmini. The repugnance to wedding girls without father and brothers exists to this day.

[281] For understanding the meanings of Sapinda and Sagotra see any work on Hindu law civil or canonical.

[282] These verses are exceedingly terse. The commentator explains that what is intended is that under the third and fourth circumstances the giver of the girl incurs no sin; under the second, the bestower of the girl (upon a person other than he unto whom a promise had been made) incurs fault. The status of wife, however, cannot attach simply in consequence of the promise to bestow upon the promiser of the dower. The relationship of husband and wife arises from actual wedding. For all that, when the kinsmen meet and say, with due rites, 'This girl is this one's wife,' the marriage becomes complete. Only the giver incurs sin by not giving her to the promised person.

The girl herself that becomes wife, the sons born of her, the Ritwiks and preceptors and disciples and Upadhyayas present at the marriage all become liable to expiation if the girl bestow her hand upon a person other than he whom she had promised to wed. Some are of opinion that no expiation is necessary for such conduct. Manu does not applaud the practice of a girl living with a person whom she does not like.[283] Living as wife with a person whom she does not like, leads to disgrace and sin. No one incurs much sin in any of these cases that follow. In forcibly abducting for marriage a girl that is bestowed upon the abductor by the girl's kinsmen, with due rites, as also a girl for whom dower has been paid and accepted, there is no great sin. Upon the girl's kinsmen having expressed their consent, Mantras and Homa should be resorted to. Such Mantras truly accomplish their purpose. Mantras and Homa recited and performed in the case of a girl that has not been bestowed by her kinsmen, do not accomplish their purpose. The engagement made by the kinsmen of a girl is, no doubt, binding and sacred. But the engagement that is entered into by the wedder and wedded, with the aid of Mantras, is very much more so (for it is this engagement that really creates the relationship of husband and wife). According to the dictates of the scriptures, the husband should regard his wife as an acquisition due to his own acts of a previous life or to what has been ordained by God. One, therefore, incurs no reproach by accepting for wife a girl that had been promised to another by her kinsmen or for whom dower had been accepted by them from another."

"'Yudhishthira said, "When after the receipt of dower for a girl, the girl's sire sees a more eligible person present himself for her hand,—one, that is who is endued with the aggregate of Three in judicious proportions, does the girl's sire incur reproach by rejecting the person from whom dower had been received in favour of him that is more eligible? In such a case either alternative seems to be fraught with fault, for to discard the person to whom the girl has been promised can never be honourable, while to reject the person that is more eligible can never be good (considering the solemn obligation there is of bestowing one's daughter on the most eligible person). I ask, how should the sire conduct himself so that he might be said to do that which is beneficial? To us, of all duties this seems to demand the utmost measure of deliberation. We are desirous of ascertaining the truth. Thou, indeed, art our eyes! Do thou explain this to us. I am never satiated with listening to thee!"

"'Bhishma said, "The gift of the dower does not cause the status of wife to attach to the girl. This is well-known to the person paying it. He pays it simply as the price of the girl. Then again they that are good never bestow their daughters, led by the dowers that others may offer. When the person desirous of wedding happens to be endued with such qualities as do not go down with the girl's kinsmen, it is then that kinsmen demand dower from him. That person, however, who won over by another's accomplishments, addresses him, saying, 'Do thou wed my girl, adorning her with proper ornaments of gold and gems,'—and that person who complies with this request, cannot be said to demand dower or give it, for such a transaction is not really a sale. The bestowal of a daughter upon acceptance of what may strictly be regarded as gifts (of affection or love) is the eternal practice. In matters of marriage some fathers say, 'I shall not bestow my daughter upon such and such a person;' some say, 'I shall bestow my daughter upon such a one.'—Some again say with vehemence, 'I must bestow my daughter upon such an individual.' These declarations do not amount to actual marriage. People are seen to solicit one another for

---

[283] Hence, having promised to wed such a one, she is at liberty to give him over and wed another whom she likes.

the hands of maidens (and promise and retreat). Till the hand is actually taken with due rites, marriage cannot be said to take place. It has been heard by us that even this was the boon granted to men in days of old by the Maruts in respect of maidens.[284] The Rishis have laid the command upon all men that maidens should never be bestowed upon persons unless the latter happen to be most fit or eligible. The daughter is the root of desire and of descendants of the collateral line. Even this is what I think.[285] The practice has been known to human beings from a long time,—the practice, of sale and purchase of the daughter. In consequence of such familiarity with the practice, thou mayst be able, upon careful examination, to find innumerable faults in it. The gift or acceptance of dower alone could not be regarded as creating the status of husband and wife. Listen to what I say on this head.

"'Formerly, having defeated all the Magadhas, the Kasis, and the Kosalas, I brought away by force two maidens for Vichitravirya. One of those two maidens was wedded with due rites. The other maiden was not formally wedded on the ground that she was one for whom dowry had been paid in the form of valour. My uncle of Kuru's race, viz., king Valhika, said that the maiden so brought away and not wedded with due rites should be set free. That maiden, therefore, was recommended to Vichitravirya for being married by him according to due rites. Doubting my father's words I repaired to others for asking their opinion. I thought that my sire was exceedingly punctilious in matters of morality. I then went to my sire himself, O king, and addressed him these words from desire of knowing something about the practices of righteous people in respect of marriage, 'I desire, O sire, to know what in truth the practices are of righteous people.' I repeated the expression of my wish several times, so great was my eagerness and curiosity. After I had uttered those words, that foremost of righteous men, viz., my sire, Valhika answered me, saying, 'If in your opinion the status of husband and wife be taken to attach on account of the gift and acceptance of dowry and not from the actual taking of the maiden's hand with due rites, the father of the maiden (by permitting his daughter to go away with the giver of the dowry) would so himself to be the follower of a creed other than that which is derivable from the ordinary scriptures. Even this is what the accepted scriptures declare. Persons conversant with morality and duty do not allow that their words are at all authoritative who say that the status of husband and wife arises from the gift and acceptance of dowry, and not from the actual taking of the hand with due rites. The saying is well-known that the status of husband and wife is created by actual bestowal of the daughter by the sire (and her acceptance by the husband with due rites). The status of wife cannot attach to maidens through sale and purchase. They who regard such status to be due to sale and the gift of dowry are persons that are certainly unacquainted with the scriptures. No one should bestow his daughter upon such persons. In fact, they are not men to whom one may marry his daughter. A wife should never be purchased. Nor should a father sell his daughter. Only those persons of sinful soul who are possessed, besides, by cupidity, and who sell and purchase female slaves for making serving women, regard the status of wife as capable of arising from the gift and acceptance of a dowry. On this subject some people on one occasion had asked prince Satyavat the following question, "If the giver of a dowry unto the kinsmen of a maiden happens to die before marriage, can another person take the hand of that maiden in marriage? We have doubts

---

[284] In consequence of that boon no one incurs sin by retracting promises of bestowing daughters upon others in view of more eligible husbands.

[285] Hence, no one should bestow his daughter upon a person that is not eligible, for the offspring of such marriage can never be good and such a marriage can never make the daughter's sire or kinsmen happy.

on this matter. Do thou remove these doubts of ours, for thou art endued with great wisdom and art honoured by the wise. Be thou the organ of vision unto ourselves that are desirous of learning the truth." Prince Satyavat answered saying, "The kinsmen of the maiden should bestow her upon him whom they consider eligible. There need be no scruples in this. The righteous act in this way without taking note of the giver of the dower even if he be alive; while, as regards the giver that is dead, there is not the slightest doubt. Some say that the virgin wife or widow,—one, that is, whose marriage has not been consummated with her husband by actual sexual congress in consequence of his absence or death,—may be allowed to unite herself with her husband's younger brother or such other relation. The husband dying before such consummation, the virgin-widow may either surrender herself to her husband's younger brother or betake herself to the practice of penances. In the opinion of some, the younger brother of the husband or such other relation may thus use the unused wife or widow, though others maintain that such practice, notwithstanding its prevalence, springs from desire instead of being a scriptural ordinance. They that say so are clearly of opinion that the father of a maiden has the right to bestow her upon any eligible person, disregarding the dowry previously given by another and accepted by himself. If after the hand of a maiden has been promised all the initial rites before marriage be performed, the maiden may still be bestowed upon a person other than the one unto whom she had been promised. Only the giver incurs the sin of falsehood: so far, however, as the status of wife is concerned, no injury can occur thereto. The Mantras in respect of marriage accomplish their object of bringing about the indissoluble union of marriage at the seventh step. The maiden becomes the wife of him unto whom the gift is actually made with water.[286] The gift of maidens should be made in the following way. The wise know it for certain. A superior Brahmana should wed a maiden that is not unwilling, that belongs to a family equal to his own in purity or status, and that is given away by her brother. Such a girl should be wed in the presence of fire, with due rites, causing her, amongst other things, to circumambulate for the usual number of times."'"

SECTION XLV.

"'Yudhishthira said, "If a person, after having given dowry for a maiden, goes away, how should the maiden's father or other kinsmen who are competent to bestow her, act? Do tell me this, O grandsire!"

"'Bhishma said, "Such a maiden, if she happens to be the daughter of a sonless and rich father, should be maintained by the father (in view of the return of him who has given the dowry). Indeed, if the father does not return the dowry unto the kinsmen of the giver, the maiden should be regarded as belonging to the giver of the dowry. She may even raise offspring for the giver (during his absence) by any of those means that are laid down in the scriptures. No person, however, can be competent to wed her according to due rites. Commanded by her sire, the princess Savitri had in days of old chosen a husband and united herself with him. This act of hers is applauded by some; but others conversant with the scriptures, condemn it. Others that are righteous have not acted in this way. Others hold that the conduct of the righteous should ever be regarded as the

---

[286] One of the most important rites of marriage is the ceremony of circumambulation. The girl is now borne around the bride-groom by her kinsmen. Formerly, she used to walk herself. All gifts, again, are made with water. The fact is, when a thing is given away, the giver, uttering the formula, sprinkles a drop of water upon it with a blade of Kusa grass.

foremost evidence of duty or morality.[287] Upon this subject Sukratu, the grandson of the high-souled Janaka, the ruler of the Videhas, has declared the following opinion. There is the well-known declaration of the scriptures that women are incompetent to enjoy freedom at any period of their life. If this were not the path trodden by the righteous, how could this scriptural declaration exist? As regards the righteous, therefore, how can there be any question or doubt in respect of this matter? How can people condemn that declaration by choosing to conduct themselves otherwise? The unrighteous dereliction of eternal usage is regarded as the practice of the Asuras. Such practice we never hear of in the conduct of the ancients.[288] The relationship of husband and wife is very subtle (having reference to the acquisition of destiny, and, therefore, capable of being understood with the aid of only the inspired declarations in scriptures). It is different from the natural relationship of male and female which consists only in the desire for sexual pleasure. This also was said by the king alluded to of Janaka's race."[289]

"'Yudhishthira said, "Upon what authority is the wealth of men inherited (by others when they happen to have daughters)? In respect of her sire the daughter should be regarded the same as the son."

"'Bhishma said, "The son is even as one's own self, and the daughter is like unto the son. How, therefore, can another take the wealth when one lives in one's own self in the form of one's daughter? Whatever wealth is termed the Yautuka property of the mother, forms the portion of the maiden daughter. If the maternal grandfather happens to die without leaving sons, the daughter's son should inherit it. The daughter's son offers pindas to his own father and the father of his mother. Hence, in accordance with considerations of justice, there is no difference between the son and the daughter's son. When a person has got only a daughter and she has been invested by him with the status of a son, if he then happens to have a son, such a son (instead of taking all the wealth of his sire) shares the inheritance with the daughter.[290] When, again, a person has got a daughter and she has been invested by him with the status of a son, if he then happens to take a son by adoption or purchase then the daughter is held to be superior to such a son (for she takes three shares of her father's wealth, the son's share being limited to only the remaining two). In the following case I do not see any reason why the status of a daughter's son should attach to the sons of one's daughter. The case is that of the daughter who has been sold by her sire. The sons born of a daughter that has been sold by her sire for actual price, belong exclusively to their father (even if he do not beget them himself but obtain them according to the rules laid down in the scriptures for the raising of issue through the agency of others). Such sons can never belong, even as daughter's sons, to their maternal grandfather in consequence of his having sold their mother for a price and lost all his rights in or to her by that act.[291] Such sons, again, become full of malice, unrighteous in conduct, the misappropriators of other people's wealth, and endued with deceit and

---

[287] Hence, what Savitri did at the bidding of her sire could not be against the course of duty or morality. The Burdwan translator has misunderstood the second line of this verse, while K.P. Singha has quietly dropped it.

[288] Dharmasya refers to the true or correct or eternal Aryan usage, Pradanam is khandanam, from da, to cut. The sense is that the grant of liberty to women is an Asura practice.

[289] Hence, no one should wed, led by desire alone. Nor should the maiden be permitted to choose for herself. She may be guided in her choice by improper considerations connected with only carnal pleasure.

[290] The property is divided into five parts, two of which are taken by the daughter under such circumstances and three by the son.

[291] I expand the verse for making it intelligible, by setting forth the reasons urged by Hindu lawyers and noticed by the commentator.

cunning. Having sprung from that sinful form of marriage called Asura, the issue becomes wicked in conduct. Persons acquainted with the histories of olden times, conversant with duties, devoted to the scriptures and firm in maintaining the restraints therein laid down, recite in this connection some metrical lines sung in days of yore by Yama. Even this is what Yama had sung. That man who acquires wealth by selling his own son, or who bestows his daughter after accepting a dower for his own livelihood, has to sink in seven terrible hells one after another, known by the name of Kalasutra. There that wretch has to feed upon sweat and urine and stools during the whole time. In that form of marriage which is called Arsha, the person who weds has to give a bull and a cow and the father of the maiden accepts the gift. Some characterise this gift as a dowry (or price), while some are of opinion that it should not be regarded in that light. The true opinion, however, is that a gift for such a purpose, be it of small value or large, should, O king, be regarded as dowry or price, and the bestowal of the daughter under such circumstances should be viewed as a sale. Notwithstanding the fact of its having been practised by a few persons it can never be taken as the eternal usage. Other forms of marriage are seen, practised by men, such as marrying girls after abducting them by force from amidst their kinsmen. Those persons who have sexual intercourse with a maiden, after reducing her to subjection by force, are regarded as perpetrators of sin. They have to sink in darkest hell.[292] Even a human being with whom one has no relationship of blood should not form the subject of sale. What need then be said of one's own issue? With the wealth that is acquired by doing sinful deeds, no action leading to merit can be performed.""'

SECTION XLVI.

"'Bhishma said, "They that are conversant with ancient history recite the following verse of Daksha, the son of Prachetas: That maiden, in respect of whom nothing is taken by her kinsmen in the form of dowry cannot be said to be sold.[293] Respect, kind treatment, and everything else that is agreeable, should all be given unto the maiden whose hand is taken in marriage. Her sire and brothers and father-in-law and husband's brothers should show her every respect and adorn her with ornaments, if they be desirous of reaping benefits, for such conduct on their part always leads to considerable happiness and advantage. If the wife does not like her husband or fails to gladden him, from such dislike and absence of joy, the husband can never have issue for increasing his race. Women, O king, should always be worshipped and treated with affection. There where women are treated with respect, the very deities are said to be filled with joy. There where women are not worshipped, all acts become fruitless. If the women of a family, in consequence of the treatment they receive, grieve and shed tears, that family soon becomes extinct. Those houses that are cursed by women meet with destruction and ruin as if scorched by some Atharvan rite. Such houses lose their splendour. Their growth and prosperity cease. O king, Manu, on the eve of his departure for Heaven, made over women to the care and protection of men, saying that they are weak, that they fall an easy prey to the seductive wiles of men,[294] disposed to accept the love that is offered them, and

---

[292] Valatah vasyam implies only those whose consent is obtained by force. Hence, such cases as those of Krishna abducting Rukmini and Arjuna abducting Subhadra, are excluded from this denunciation.

[293] The maiden may herself accept ornaments. That would not convert the transaction into a sale.

[294] Swalpa-kaupinah literally is covered with a small piece of cloth, hence, capable of being easily seduced.

devoted to truth. There are others among them that are full of malice, covetous of honours, fierce in disposition, unlovable, and impervious to reason. Women, however, deserve to be honoured. Do ye men show them honour. The righteousness of men depends upon women. All pleasures and enjoyments also completely depend upon them. Do ye serve them and worship them. Do ye bend your wills before them. The begetting of offspring, the nursing of children already born, and the accomplishment of all acts necessary for the needs of society, behold, all these have women for their cause. By honouring women, ye are sure to attain to the fruition of all objects. In this connection a princess of the house of Janaka the ruler of the Videhas, sang a verse. It is this: Women have no sacrifices ordained for them. There are no Sraddhas which they are called upon to perform. They are not required to observe any fasts. To serve their husbands with reverence and willing obedience is their only duty. Through the discharge of that duty they succeed in conquering heaven. In childhood, the sire protects her. The husband protects her in youth. When she becomes old, her sons protect her. At no period of her life does woman deserve to be free. Deities of prosperity are women. The person that desire affluence and prosperity should honour them. By cherishing women, O Bharata, one cherishes the goddess of prosperity herself, and by afflicting her, one is said to afflict the goddess of prosperity.""'

SECTION XLVII.

"'Yudhishthira said, "Thou art fully conversant with the ordinances of all the scriptures. Thou art the foremost of those that are acquainted with the duties of kings. Thou art celebrated over the whole world as a great dispeller of doubts. I have a doubt, do thou explain it to me, O grandsire! As regards this doubt that has arisen in my mind, I shall not ask any other person for its solution. It behoveth thee, O thou of mighty arms, to expound as to how a man should conduct himself who is desirous of treading along the path of duty and righteousness. It has been laid down, O grandsire, that a Brahmana can take four wives, viz., one that belongs to his own order, one that is a Kshatriya, one that is a Vaisya, and one that is a Sudra, if the Brahmana wishes to indulge in the desire of sexual intercourse. Tell me, O best of the Kurus, which amongst those sons deserves to inherit the father's wealth one after another? Who amongst them, O grandsire, shall take what share of the paternal wealth? I desire to hear this, viz., how the distribution has been ordained amongst them of the paternal property."

"'Bhishma said, "The Brahmana, the Kshatriya, and the Vaisya are regarded as the three regenerate orders. To wed in these three orders has been ordained to be the duty of the Brahmana, O Yudhishthira. Through erroneous judgment or cupidity or lust, O scorcher of foes, a Brahmana takes a Sudra wife. Such a wife, however, he is not competent to take according to the scriptures. A Brahmana, by taking a Sudra woman to his bed, attains to a low end in the next world. He should, having done such an act, undergo expiation according to the rites laid down in the scriptures. That expiation must be twice heavier or severer if in consequence of such an act, O Yudhishthira, the Brahmana gets offspring. I shall now tell thee, O Bharata, how the (paternal) wealth is to be distributed (among the children of the different spouses.) The son born of the Brahmana wife shall, in the first place, appropriate from his father's wealth a bull of good marks, and the best car or vehicle. What remains of the Brahmana's property, O Yudhishthira, after this should be divided into ten equal portions. The son by the Brahmana wife shall take four of such portions of the paternal wealth. The son that is born of the Kshatriya wife is, without doubt, possessed of the status of a Brahmana. In consequence, however, of the distinction attaching to his mother, he shall take three of the ten shares into which the property has been divided. The son that has been born of the wife belonging to the third order, viz., the woman of the Vaisya caste, by the Brahmana sire, shall take, O Yudhishthira, two of the three remaining shares of the father's property. It has been said that the son that has been begotten by the Brahmana sire upon the Sudra wife should not take any portion of the father's wealth, for he is not to be considered an heir. A little, however, of the paternal wealth should be given to the son of the Sudra wife, hence the one remaining share should be given to him out of compassion. Even this should be the order of the ten shares into which the Brahmana's wealth is to be divided. All the sons that are born of the same mother or of mothers of the same order, shall share equally the portion that is theirs. The son born of the Sudra wife should not be regarded as invested with the status of a Brahmana in consequence of his being unskilled (in the scriptures and the duties ordained for the Brahmana). Only those children that are born of wives belonging to the three higher orders should be regarded as invested with the status of Brahmanas. It has been said that there are only four orders, there is no fifth that has been enumerated. The son by the Sudra wife shall take the tenth part of his sire's wealth (that remains after the allotment has been made to the others in the way spoken of). That share, however, he is to take only when his sire has given it to him. He shall not take it if his sire does not give it unto him. Some portion of the sire's wealth should without doubt, be given, O Bharata, to the son of the Sudra wife. Compassion is one of the highest virtues. It is through compassion that something is given to the son of the Sudra wife. Whatever be the object in respect of which compassion arises, as a cardinal virtue it is always productive of merit. Whether the sire happens to have children (by his spouses belonging to the other orders) or to have no children (by such spouses), unto the son by the Sudra wife, O Bharata, nothing more than a tenth part of the sire's wealth should be given. If a Brahmana happens to have more wealth than what is necessary for maintaining himself and his family for three years, he should with that wealth perform sacrifices. A Brahmana should never acquire wealth for nothing.[295] The highest sum that the husband should give unto the wife is three thousand coins (of the prevailing currency). The wealth that the husband gives unto the wife, the latter may spend or dispose of as she likes. Upon the death of the childless husband, the wife shall enjoy all his wealth. (She shall not, however, sell or otherwise dispose of any portion of it). The wife should never take (without her husband's knowledge) any portion of her husband's wealth. Whatever wealth, O Yudhishthira, the Brahmana wife may acquire by gift from her father, should be taken (after her death) by her daughter, for the daughter is like the son. The daughter, O king, has been ordained in the scriptures, to be equal to the son, O delighter of the Kurus. Even thus hath the law of inheritance been ordained, O bull of Bharata's race. Remembering these ordinances about the distribution and disposal of wealth, one should never acquire wealth uselessly."

"'Yudhishthira said, "If the son born of a Sudra woman by a Brahmana father has been declared in the scriptures to be disentitled to any wealth, by what exceptional rule then is a tenth part of the paternal property to be given to him? A son born of a Brahmana wife by a Brahmana is unquestionably a Brahmana. One born of a Kshatriya wife or of a Vaisya wife, by a Brahmana husband, is similarly invested with the status of a Brahmana.

---

[295] i.e., he should not acquire for storing. He may acquire to spend in sacrifices and gifts or for maintaining himself and his family.

Why then, O best of kings, are such sons to share the paternal wealth unequally? All of them, thou hast said, are Brahmanas, having been born of mothers that belong to the three higher orders equally entitled to the name of regenerate."

"'Bhishma said, "O scorcher of foes, all spouses in this world are called by the name of Data. Although that name is applied to all, yet there is this great distinction to be observed. If, having married three wives belonging to the three other orders, a Brahmana takes a Brahmana wife the very last of all yet shall she be regarded as the first in rank among all the wives, and as deserving of the greatest respect. Indeed, among all the co-wives, she shall be the foremost in consideration. In her apartments should be kept all those articles that are necessary in view of the husband's baths, personal decorations, washing of teeth, and application of collyrium to the eyes. In her apartments should be kept the Havya and the Kavya and all else that the husband may require for the performance of his religious acts. If the Brahmana wife is in the house, no other wife is entitled to attend to these needs of the husband. Only the Brahmana wife, O Yudhishthira, should assist in these acts of the husband. The husband's food and drink and garlands and robes and ornaments, all these should be given by the Brahmana wife to the husband, for she is the foremost in rank and consideration among all the spouses of the husband. These are the ordinances of the scriptures as laid down by Manu, O delighter of the Kurus! Even this, O monarch, is seen to be the course of eternal usage. If a Brahmana, O Yudhishthira, led by lust, acts in a different way, he shall come to be regarded as a Chandala among Brahmanas.[296] The son born of the Kshatriya wife has been said to be equal in status to the son born of the Brahmana wife. For all that, a distinction attaches to the son of the Brahmana wife in consequence of the superiority of the Brahmana to the Kshatriya in respect of the order of birth. The Kshatriya cannot be regarded as equal to the Brahmana woman in point of birth. Hence, O best of kings, the son born of the Brahmana wife must be regarded as the first in rank and superior to the son born of the Kshatriya wife. Because, again the Kshatriya is not equal in point of birth to the Brahmana wife, hence the son of the Brahmana wife takes one after another, all the best things, O Yudhishthira, among his father's possessions. Similarly, the Vaisya cannot be regarded as the equal of the Kshatriya in point of birth. Prosperity, kingdom, and treasury, O Yudhishthira, belong to the Kshatriya. All these have been ordained for the Kshatriya. The whole earth, O king, with her belt of seas, is seen to belong to him. By following the duties of his own order, the Kshatriya acquires an extensive affluence. The sceptre of royalty is held by him. Without the Kshatriya, O king, there can be no protection. The Brahmanas are highly blessed, for they are the deities of the very deities. Following the ordinances laid down by the Rishis, the Kshatriyas should worship the Brahmanas according to due rites. Even this is the eternal usage. Coveted by thieves and others, the possessions of all men are protected by Kshatriyas in the observance of the duties assigned to their order. Indeed, wealth and spouses and every other possession owned by people would have been forcibly taken away but for this protection that the Kshatriyas afford. The Kshatriya, as the king, becomes the protector or rescuer of all the others. Hence, the son of the Kshatriya wife shall, without doubt, be held to be superior to him that is born of the Vaisya wife. The son of the Kshatriya wife, for this, takes a larger share of the paternal property than the son of the Vaisya mother."

"'Yudhishthira said, "Thou hast duly said what the rules are that apply to Brahmanas.

---

[296] i.e., if the Brahmana, led by affection for any other wife, disregards the wife belonging to his own order and shows preference for those of the other orders, he then incurs the liability of being regarded as a Chandala that has come to be numbered among Brahmanas.

What, however, are the rules that apply to the others?"

"'Bhishma said, "For the Kshatriya, O delighter of the Kurus, two wives have been ordained. The Kshatriya may take a third wife from the Sudra order. Such practice prevails, it is true, but it is not sanctioned by the scriptures. Even this should be the order, O Yudhisthira, of the spouses of a Kshatriya. The property of a Kshatriya should, O king, be divided into eight shares. The son of the Kshatriya wife shall take four of such shares of the paternal property. The son of the Vaisya wife shall take three of such shares. The remaining one or the eighth share shall be taken by the son of the Sudra wife. The son of the Sudra wife, however, shall take only when the father gives but not otherwise. For the Vaisya only one wife has been ordained. A second wife is taken from the Sudra order. The practice prevails, it is true, but it is not sanctioned by the scriptures. If a Vaisya has two wives, one of whom is a Vaisya and the other a Sudra, there is a difference between them in respect of status. The wealth of a Vaisya, O chief of Bharata's race, should be divided into five portions. I shall now speak of the sons of a Vaisya by a wife of his own order and by one belonging to the inferior order, as also of the manner in which, O king his wealth is to be distributed among those children. The son born of the Vaisya wife shall take four of such shares of his father's wealth. The fifth share, O Bharata, has been said to belong to the son born of the Sudra wife. Such a son, however, shall take when the father gives. He should not take anything unless the father gives it to him. The son that is begotten on a Sudra wife by persons of the three higher orders should always be regarded as disentitled to any share of the sire's wealth. The Sudra should have only one wife taken from his own order. He can under no circumstances, take any other spouse. Even if he happens to have a century of sons by such a spouse, all of them share equally the wealth that he may leave behind. As regards all the orders, the children born of the spouse taken from the husband's own order shall, it has been laid down, share equally the father's wealth. The eldest son's share shall be greater than that of every other son, for he shall take one share more than each of his brothers, consisting of the best things of his father. Even this is the law of inheritance, O son of Pritha, as declared by the Self-born himself. Amongst children all born of the spouse taken from the husband's own order, there is another distinction, O king! In marrying, the elder ones should always precede the younger ones. The spouses being all equal in respect of their order of birth, and the children also being all equal in respect of the status of their mothers, the son that is first-born shall take one share more than each of his other brothers. The son that comes next in point of age shall take a share that is next in value, while the son that is youngest shall take the share that belongs to the youngest.[297] Thus among spouses of all orders, they that belong to the same order with the husband are regarded as the first. Even this is what was declared by the great Rishi Kasyapa the son of Marichi.""

---

[297] The sense of this verse seems to be this: If a Brahmana takes in succession three spouses all belonging to his own order, the son born of his first wife shall take the share that is allotted to the eldest; that born of the second wife shall take a share next in value; and that born of the youngest wife shall take the share allotted to the youngest. After such especial shares are taken, the residue of the property is to be distributed unto equal shares each of which shall be taken by each of the children. If this interpretation be correct, it would appear that the contention waged some years ago in Bengal, that the scriptures do not allow a person the liberty of taking more than one spouse from his own order, falls to the ground. Upon other grounds also, that contention was absurd, for Kshatriya kings often took more than one Kshatriya spouse.

SECTION XLVIII.

"'Yudhishthira said, "Through inducements offered by wealth, or through mere lust, or through ignorance of the true order of birth (of both males and females), or through folly, intermixture happens of the several orders. What, O grandsire, are the duties of persons that are born in the mixed classes and what are the acts laid down for them? Do thou discourse to me on this!"

"'Bhishma said, "In the beginning, the Lord of all creatures created the four orders and laid down their respective acts or duties, for the sake of sacrifice.[298] The Brahmana may take four wives, one from each of the four orders. In two of them (viz., the wife taken from his own order and that taken from the one next below), he takes birth himself (the children begotten upon them being regarded as invested with the same status as his own). Those sons, however, that are begotten by him on the two spouses that belong to the next two orders (viz., Vaisya and Sudra), are inferior, their status being determined not by that of their father but by that of their mothers. The son that is begotten by a Brahmana upon a Sudra wife is called Parasara, implying one born of a corpse, for the Sudra woman's body is as inauspicious as a corpse. He should serve the persons of his (father's) race. Indeed, it is not proper for him to give up the duty of service that has been laid down for him. Adopting all means in his power, he should uphold the burden of his family. Even if he happens to be elder in age, he should still dutifully serve the other children of his father who may be younger to him in years, and bestow upon them whatever he may succeed in earning. A Kshatriya may take three wives. In two of them (viz., the one taken from his own order and the other that is taken from the order immediately below), he takes birth himself (so that those children are invested with the status of his own order). His third wife being of the Sudra order is regarded as very inferior. The son that he begets upon her comes to be called as an Ugra. The Vaisya may take two spouses. In both of them (viz., the one taken from his own order, and the other from the lowest of the four pure orders), he takes birth himself (so that those children become invested with the status of his own order). The Sudra can take only one wife, viz., she that is taken from his own order. The son begotten by him upon her becomes a Sudra. A son that takes birth under circumstances other than those mentioned above, comes to be looked upon as a very inferior one. If a person of a lower order begets a son upon a woman of a superior order, such a son is regarded as outside the pale of the four pure orders. Indeed, such a son becomes on object of censure with the four principal orders. If a Kshatriya begets a son upon a Brahmana woman, such a son, without being included in any of the four pure orders, comes to be regarded as a Suta. The duties of a Suta are all connected with the reciting of eulogies and encomiums of kings and other great men. The son begotten by a Vaisya upon a woman of the Brahmana order comes to be regarded as a Vaidehaka. The duties assigned to him are the charge of bars and bolts for protecting the privacy of women of respectable households. Such sons have no cleansing rites laid down for them.[299] If a Sudra unites with a woman belonging to the foremost of the four orders, the son that is begotten is called a Chandala. Endued with a fierce disposition, he must live in the outskirts of cities and towns and the duty assigned to him is that of the public executioner. Such sons are always regarded as wretches of

---

[298] i.e., each order was created for performing sacrifices. The Sudra is competent to perform sacrifice. Only his sacrifice should be by serving the three other orders.

[299] For them there is no investiture with the sacred-thread.

their race. These, O foremost of intelligent persons, are the offspring of intermixed orders. The son begotten by a Vaisya upon a Kshatriya woman becomes a Vandi or Magadha. The duties assigned to him are eloquent recitations of praise. The son begotten through transgression, by a Sudra upon a Kshatriya woman, becomes a Nishada and the duties assigned to him have reference to the catching of fish. If a Sudra happens to have intercourse with a Vaisya woman, the son begotten upon her comes to be called Ayogava. The duty assigned to such a person are those of a Takshan (carpenter). They that are Brahmanas should never accept gifts from such a person. They are not entitled to possess any kind of wealth. Persons belonging to the mixed castes beget upon spouses taken from their own castes children invested with the status that is their own. When they beget children in women taken from castes that are inferior to theirs, such children become inferior to their fathers, for they become invested with the status that belongs to their mothers. Thus as regards the four pure orders, persons beget children invested with their own status upon spouses taken from their own orders as also upon them that are taken from the orders immediately below their own. When, however, offspring are begotten upon other spouses, they come to be regarded as invested with a status that is, principally, outside the pale of the four pure orders. When such children beget sons in women taken from their own classes, those sons take the status of their sires. It is only when they take spouse from castes other than their own, that the children they beget become invested with inferior status. As an example of this it may be said that a Sudra begets upon a woman belonging to the most superior order a son that is outside the pale of the four orders (for such a son comes to be regarded as a Chandala who is much inferior). The son that is outside the pale of the four orders by uniting with women belonging to the four principal orders, begets offspring that are further degraded in point of status. From those outside the pale of the four orders and those again that are further outside that pale, children multiply in consequence of the union of persons with women of classes superior to their own. In this way, from persons of inferior status classes spring up, altogether fifteen in number, that are equally low or still lower in status. It is only from sexual union of women with persons who should not have such union with them that mixed classes spring up. Among the classes that are thus outside the pale of the four principal or pure orders, children are begotten upon women belonging to the class called Sairindhri by men of the class called Magadha. The occupation of such offspring is the adornment of the bodies of kinds and others. They are well-acquainted with the preparation of unguents, the making of wreaths, and the manufacture of articles used for the decoration of the person. Though free by the status that attaches to them by birth, they should yet lead a life of service. From the union of Magadhas of a certain class with women of the caste called Sairindhri, there springs up another caste called Ayogava. Their occupation consists in the making of nets (for catching fish and fowl and animals of the chase). Vaidehas, by uniting themselves with women of the Sairindhri caste, beget children called Maireyakas whose occupation consists in the manufacture of wines and spirits. From the Nishadas spring a caste called Madgura and another known by the name of Dasas whose occupation consists in plying boats. From the Chandala springs a race called Swapaka whose occupation consists in keeping guard over the dead. The women of the Magadhi caste, by union with these four castes of wicked dispositions produce four others who live by practising deceit. These are Mansa, Swadukara, Kshaudra, and Saugandha. From the Vaideha springs up a cruel and sinful caste that lives by practising deception. From the Nishadas again springs up the Madranabha caste whose members are seen to ride on cars drawn by asses. From the Chandalas springs up the caste called

Pukkasa whose members are seen to eat the flesh of asses, horses and elephants. These cover themselves with the garments obtained by stripping human corpses. They are again seen to eat from broken earthenware.[300] These three castes of very low status are born of women of the Ayogava caste (by fathers taken from different castes). The caste called Kshudra springs from the Vaidehaka. The caste called Andhra which takes up its residence in the outskirts of towns and cities, also springs up (from the Vaidehakas). Then again the Charmakara, uniting himself with a woman of Nishada caste, begets the class called Karavara. From the Chandala again springs up the caste known by the name of Pandusaupaka whose occupation consists in making baskets and other things with cleft bamboos. From the union of the Nishada with a woman of the Vaidehi caste springs one who is called by the name of Ahindaka. The Chandala begets upon a Saupaka woman, a son that does not differ from the Chandala in status or occupation. A Nishada woman, by union with a Chandala, brings forth a son who lives in the outskirts of villages and towns. Indeed, the members of such a caste live in crematoria and are regarded by the very lowest orders as incapable of being numbered among them. Thus to these mixed castes spring up from improper and sinful union of fathers and mothers belonging to different castes. Whether they live in concealment or openly, they should be known by their occupations. The duties have been laid down in the scriptures for only the four principal orders. As regards the others the scriptures are entirely silent. Among all the orders, the members of those castes that have no duties assigned to them by the scriptures, need have no fears as to what they do (to earn their livelihood). Persons unaccustomed to the performance or for whom sacrifices have not been laid down, and who are deprived of the company and the instructions of the righteous whether numbered among the four principal orders or out of their pale, by uniting themselves with women of other castes, led not by considerations of righteousness but by uncontrolled lust, cause numerous mixed castes to come into existence whose occupations and abodes depend on the circumstances connected with the irregular unions to which they owe their origin. Having recourse to spots where four roads meet, or crematoria, or hills and mountains, or forests and trees, they build their habitations there. The ornaments they wear are made of iron. Living in such places openly, they betake themselves to their own occupations to earn their livelihood. They may be seen to live in this way, adorning their persons with ornaments and employed in the task of manufacturing diverse kinds of domestic and other utensils. Without doubt, by assisting kine and Brahmanas, and practising the virtues of abstention from cruelty, compassion, truthfulness of speech, and forgiveness, and, if need be, by preserving others by laying down their very lives, persons of the mixed castes may achieve success. I have no doubt, O chief of men, that these virtues become the causes of their success. He that is possessed of intelligence, should, taking everything into consideration, beget offspring according to the ordinances of the scriptures, upon women that have been declared proper or fit for him. A son begotten upon a woman belonging to a degraded caste, instead of rescuing the sire, brings him to grief even as a heavy weight brings to grief a swimmer desirous of crossing water. Whether a man happens to be possessed of learning or not, lust and wrath are natural attributes of humanity in this world. Women, therefore, may always be seen to drag men into the wrong path. This natural disposition of women is such that man's contact with her is productive of misery to him. Hence, men possessed of wisdom do not suffer themselves to be excessively attached to women."

---

[300] Broken earthenpots are always cast off. They are some times utilised by persons of the lower orders.

"'Yudhishthira said, "There are men who belong to the mixed castes, and who are of very impure birth. Though presenting the features of respectability, they are in reality disrespectable. In consequence of these external aspects we may not be able to know the truth about their birth. Are there any signs, O grandsire, by which the truth may be known about the origin of such men?"'"

SECTION XLIX.

"'Bhishma said, "A person that is born of an irregular union presents diverse features of disposition. One's purity of birth, again, is to be ascertained from one's acts which must resemble the acts of those who are admittedly good and righteous. A disrespectable behaviour, acts opposed to those laid down in the scriptures, crookedness and cruelty, and abstention from sacrifices and other spiritual acts that lead to merit, proclaim one's impurity of origin. A son receives the disposition of either the sire or the mother. Sometimes he catches the dispositions of both. A person of impure birth can never succeed in concealing his true disposition. As the cub of a tiger or a leopard resembles its sire and dam in form and in (the matter of) its stripes of spots, even so a person cannot but betray the circumstance of his origin. However covered may the course of one's descent be, if that descent happens to be impure, its character or disposition is sure to manifest itself slightly or largely. A person may, for purposes of his own, choose to tread on an insincere path, displaying such conduct as seems to be righteous. His own disposition, however, in the matter of those acts that he does, always proclaims whether he belongs to a good order or to a different one. Creatures in the world are endued with diverse kinds of disposition. They are, again, seen to be employed in diverse kinds of acts. Amongst creatures thus employed, there is nothing that is so good or precious as pure birth and righteous conduct. If a person be born in a low order, that good understanding which arises from a study of the scriptures fails to rescue his body from low acts. Absolute goodness of understanding may be of different degrees. It may be high, middling, or low. Even if it appears in a person of low extraction, it disappears like autumnal clouds without producing any consequences. On the other hand, that other goodness of understanding which, according to its measure, has ordained the status in which the person has been born, shows itself in his acts.[301] If a person happens to belong to a superior order but still if he happens to be divested of good behaviour, he should receive no respect or worship. One may worship even a Sudra if he happens to be conversant with duties and be of good conduct. A person proclaims himself by his own good and acts and by his good or bad disposition and birth. If one's race of birth happens to be degraded for any reason, one soon raises it and makes it resplendent and famous by one's acts. For these reasons they that are endued with wisdom should avoid those women, among these diverse castes mixed or pure, upon whom they should not beget offspring."

"'Yudhishthira said, "Do thou discourse to us, O sire, upon the orders and classes separately, upon different kinds of sons begotten upon different types of women, upon the person entitled to have them as sons, and upon their status in life. It is known that

---

[301] The second line is exceedingly terse. The sense seems to be this: one who is of low birth must remain low in disposition. Absolute goodness may arise in his heart, but it disappears immediately without producing any effect whatsoever. The study of the scriptures, therefore, cannot raise such a person. On the other hand, the goodness which according to its measure has ordained for one (1) the status of humanity and (2) the rank in that status, is seen to manifest itself in his act.

disputes frequently arise with respect to sons. It behoveth thee, O king, to solve the doubts that have taken possession of our minds. Indeed, we are stupefied with respect to this subject."

"'Bhishma said, "The son of one's loins is regarded as one's own self. The son that is begotten upon one's wife by a person whom one has invited for the task, is called Niruktaja. The son that is begotten upon one's wife by somebody without one's permission, is Prasritaja. The son begotten upon his own wife by a person fallen away from his status is called Patitaja. There are two other sons, viz., the son given, and the son made. There is another called Adhyudha.[302] The son born of a maiden in her father's house is called Kanina. Besides these, there are six kinds of sons called Apadhwansaja and six others that are Apasadas. These are the several kinds of sons mentioned in the scriptures, learn, O Bharata!"

"'Yudhishthira said, "Who are the six that are called Apadhwansajas? Who also are the Apasadas? It behoveth thee to explain all these to me in detail."

"'Bhishma said, "The sons that a Brahmana begets upon spouses taken from the three inferior orders, those begotten by a Kshatriya upon spouses taken from the two orders inferior to his own, O Bharata, and the sons that a Vaisya begets upon a spouse taken from the one order that is inferior to his,—are all called Apadhwansajas. They are, as thus explained, of six kinds. Listen now to me as I tell thee who the Apasadas are. The son that a Sudra begets upon a Brahmana woman is called a Chandala. Begotten upon a Kshatriya woman by a person of the Sudra order, the son is called a Vratya. He who is born of a Vaisya woman by a Sudra father is called a Vaidya. These three kinds of sons are called Apasadas. The Vaisya, by uniting himself with a woman of the Brahmana order, begets a son that is called a Magadha, while the son that he gets upon a Kshatriya woman is called a Vamaka. The Kshatriya can beget but one kind of son upon a woman of a superior order. Indeed, the son begotten by a Kshatriya upon a Brahmana woman, is called a Suta. These three also are called Apasadas. It cannot be said, O king, that these six kinds of sons are no sons."

"'Yudhishthira said, "Some say that one's son is he that is born in one's soil. Some, on the other hand, say that one's son is he who has been begotten from one's seed. Are both these kinds of sons equal? Where, again, is the son to be? Do thou tell me this, O grandsire!"

"'Bhishma said, "His is the son from whose seed he has sprung. If, however, the owner of the seed abandons the son born of it, such a son then becomes his upon whose spouse he has been begotten. The same rule applies to the son called Adhyudha. He belongs to the person from whose seed he has taken his birth. If, however, the owner of the seed abandons him, he becomes the son of the husband of his mother.[303] Know that even this is what the law declares."

"'Yudhishthira said, "We know that the son becomes his from whose seed he has taken birth. Whence does the husband of the woman that brings forth the son derive his right to the latter? Similarly, the son called Adhyudha should be known to be the son of him from whose seed he has sprung. How can they be sons of others by reasons of the

[302] The son begotten upon a maiden by one who does not become her husband, and born after her marriage, is regarded as belonging not to the begetter but to the husband.

[303] Such a son becomes the property of the mother's husband and not of his begetter. If however, the begetter expresses a wish to have him and rear him, he should be regarded as the begetter's. The principle upon which he becomes the child of the mother's husband is that the begetter conceals himself and never wishes to have him.

engagement about owning and rearing them having been broken?"

"'Bhishma said, "He who having begotten a son of his own loins, abandons him for some reason or other, cannot be regarded as the sire of such a son, for vital seed only cannot create sonship. Such a son must be held to belong to the person who owns the soil. When a man, desiring to have a son, weds a girl quick with child, the son born of his spouse must belong to him, for it is the fruit of his own soil. The person from whose vital seed the son has sprung can have no right to such a son. The son that is born in one's soil but not begotten by the owner, O chief of Bharata's race, bears all the marks of the sire that has actually begotten him (and not the marks of one that is only the husband of his mother). The son thus born is incapable of concealing the evidences that physiognomy offers. He is at once known by eyesight (to belong to another).[304] As regards the son made, he is sometimes regarded as the child of the person who has made him a son and so brings him up. In his case, neither the vital seed of which he is born nor the soil in which he is born, becomes the cause of sonship."

"'Yudhishthira said, "What kind of a son is that who is said to be a made son and whose sonship arises from the fact of his being taken and brought up and in whose case neither the vital seed nor the soil of birth, O Bharata, is regarded as the cause of sonship?"

"'Bhishma said, "When a person takes up and rears a son that has been cast off on the road by his father and mother, and when the person thus taking and rearing him fails to find out his parents after search, he becomes the father of such a son and the latter becomes what is called his made son. Not having anybody to own him, he becomes owned by him who brings him up. Such a son, again, comes to be regarded as belonging to that order to which his owner or rearer belongs."

"'Yudhishthira said, "How should the purificatory rites of such a person be performed? In whose case what sort of rites are to be performed? With what girl should he be wedded? Do thou tell me all this, O grandsire!"

"'Bhishma said, "The rites of purification touching such a son should be performed conformably to the usage of the person himself that raises him, for, cast off by his parents, such a son obtains the order of the person that takes him and brings him up. Indeed, O thou of unfading glory, the rearer should perform all the purificatory rites with respect to such a son according to the practices of the rearer's own race and kinsmen. As regards the girl also, O Yudhishthira, that should be bestowed in marriage upon such a son, who belongs to the order of the rearer himself, all this is to be done only when the order of son's true mother cannot be ascertained. Among sons, he that is born of a maiden and he that is born of a mother that had conceived before her marriage but had brought him forth subsequent to that are regarded as very disgraceful and degraded. Even those two, however, should receive the same rites of purification that are laid down for the sons begotten by the father in lawful wedlock. With respect to the son that becomes his sire's in consequence of his birth in the sire's soil and of those sons that are called Apasadas and those conceived by the spouse in her maidenhood but brought forth after marriage, Brahmanas and others should apply the same rites of purification that hold good for their own orders. These are the conclusions that are to be found in the scriptures with respect to the different orders. I have thus told thee everything appertaining to thy questions. What else dost thou wish to hear?"'"

---

[304] The objects of Yudhishthira's question will appear clearly from the answer given to it by Bhishma.

SECTION L.

"'Yudhishthira said, "What is the nature of the compassion or pity that is felt at the sight of another's woe? What is the nature of that compassion or sympathy that one feels for another in consequence of one's living in the companionship of that other? What is the nature (and degree) of the high blessedness that attaches to kine? It behoveth thee, O grandsire, to expound all this to me."

"'Bhishma said, "I shall, in this connection, O thou of great effulgence, recite to thee an ancient narrative of a conversation between Nahusha and the Rishi Chyavana. In days of yore O Chief of Bharata's race, the great Rishi Chyavana of Bhrigu's race, always observant of high vows, became desirous of leading for some time the mode of life called Udavasa and set himself to commence it. Casting off pride and wrath and joy and grief, the ascetic, pledging himself to observe that vow, set himself to live for twelve years according to the rules of Udavasa. The Rishi inspired all creatures with a happy trust. And he inspired similar confidence in all creatures living in water. The puissant ascetic resembled the Moon himself in his behaviour to all. Bowing unto all the deities and having cleansed himself of all sins, he entered the water at the confluence of the Ganga and the Yamuna, and stood there like an inanimate post of wood. Placing his head against it, he bore the fierce and roaring current of the two streams united together,—the current whose speed resembled that of the wind itself. The Ganga and the Yamuna, however, and the other streams and lakes, whose waters unite together at the confluence at Prayaga, instead of afflicting the Rishi, went past him (to show him respect). Assuming the attitude of a wooden post, the great Muni sometimes laid himself down in the water and slept at ease. And sometimes, O chief of Bharata's race, the intelligent sage stood in an erect posture. He became quite agreeable unto all creatures living in water. Without the least fear, all these used to smell the Rishi's lips. In this way, the Rishi passed a long time at that grand confluence of waters. One day some fishermen came there. With nets in their hands, O thou of great effulgence, those men came to that spot where the Rishi was. They were many in number and all of them were bent upon catching fish. Well-formed and broad-chested, endued with great strength and courage and never returning in fear from water, those men who lived upon the earnings by their nets, came to that spot, resolved to catch fish. Arrived at the water which contained many fish, those fishermen, O chief of the Bharatas, tied all their nets together. Desirous of fish, those Kaivartas, many in number united together and surrounded a portion of the waters of the Ganga and the Yamuna with their nets. Indeed, they then cast into water their net which was made of new strings, capable of covering a large space, and endued with sufficient length and breadth. All of them, getting into the water, then began to drag with great force that net of theirs which was very large and had been well-spread over a large space. All of them were free from fear, cheerful, and fully resolved to do one another's bidding. They had succeeded in enmeshing a large number of fish and other aquatic animals. And as they dragged their net, O king, they easily dragged up Chyavana the son of Bhrigu along with a large number of fish. His body was overgrown with the river moss. His beard and matted locks had become green. And all over his person could be seen conchs and other molluscs attached with their heads. Beholding that Rishi who was well-conversant with the Vedas dragged up by them from water, all the fishermen stood with joined palms and then prostrated themselves on the ground and repeatedly bent their heads. Through fear and pain caused by the dragging of the net, and in consequence of their being brought upon land, the fish enmeshed in the net yielded up their lives. The ascetic, beholding that great slaughter of fishes, became filled with compassion and sighed repeatedly.

""""The fishermen said, 'We have committed this sin (of dragging thy sacred self from water) through ignorance. Be gratified with us! What wish of thine shall we accomplish? Command us, O great ascetic!'"

"Bhishma continued, "This addressed by them, Chyavana, from among that heap of fishes around him, said, 'Do ye with concentrated attention hear what my most cherished wish is. I shall either die with these fishes or do ye sell me with them. I have lived with them for a long time within the water. I do not wish to abandon them at such a time.' When he said these words unto them, the fishermen became exceedingly terrified. With pale faces they repaired to king Nahusha and informed him of all that had taken place.""""

SECTION LI.

"'Bhishma said, "King Nahusha hearing the pass to which Chyavana was reduced, quickly proceeded to that spot accompanied by his ministers and priest. Having cleansed himself duly, the king, with joined palms and concentrated attention, introduced himself unto the high-souled Chyavana. The king's priest then worshipped with due ceremonies that Rishi, O monarch, who was observant of the vow of truth and endued with a high soul, and who resembled a god himself (in splendour and energy).

""""Nahusha said, 'Tell me, O best of regenerate persons, what act shall we do that may be agreeable to thee? However difficult that act may be, there is nothing, O holy one, that I shall not be able to accomplish at thy bidding.'

""""Chyavana said, 'These men that live by catching fish have all been tired with labour. Do thou pay them the price that may be set upon me along with the value of these fish.'

""""Nahusha said, 'Let my priest give unto these Nishadas a thousand coins as a price for purchasing these sacred one as he himself has commanded.'

""""Chyavana said, 'A thousand coins cannot represent my price. The question depends upon your discretion. Give them a fair value, settling with thy own intelligence what it should be.'

""""Nahusha said, 'Let, O learned Brahmana, a hundred thousand coins be given unto these Nishadas. Shall this be thy price, O holy one, or dost think otherwise?'

""""Chyavana said, 'I should not be purchased for a hundred thousand coins, O best of monarchs! Let a proper price be given unto them. Do thou consult with thy ministers.'

""""Nahusha said, 'Let my priest give unto these Nishadas a crore of coins. If even this does not represent thy price, let more be paid unto them.'

""""Chyavana said, 'O king, I do not deserve to be purchased for a crore of coins or even more. Let that price be given unto those men which would be fair or proper. Do thou consult with the Brahmanas.'

""""Nahusha said, 'Let half of my kingdom or even the whole be given away unto these Nishadas. I think that would represent thy price. What, however, dost thou think, O regenerate one?'

""""Chyavana said, 'I do not deserve to be purchased with half thy kingdom or even the whole of it, O king! Let thy price which is proper be given unto these men. Do thou consult with the Rishis.'"

"Bhishma continued, "Hearing these words of the great Rishi, Nahusha became afflicted with great grief. With his ministers and priest he began to deliberate on the matter. There then came unto king Nahusha an ascetic living in the woods and subsisting upon fruit and roots and born of a cow. That best of regenerate persons, addressing the monarch, O king, said these words, 'I shall soon gratify thee. The Rishi also will be gratified. I shall never speak an untruth.—no, not even in jest, what then need I say of other occasions? Thou shouldst, without any scruple, do what I bid thee.'

"'"Nahusha said, 'Do thou, O illustrious one, say what the price is of that great Rishi of Bhrigu's race. O, save me from this terrible pass, save my kingdom, and save my race! If the holy Chyavana became angry, he would destroy the three worlds: what need I say them of my poor self who is destitute of penances and who depends only upon the might of his arm? O great Rishi, do thou become the raft unto us that have all fallen into a fathomless ocean with all our counsellors and our priest! Do thou settle what the price should be of the Rishi.'"

"'Bhishma said, "Hearing these words of Nahusha, the ascetic born of a cow and endued with great energy spoke in this strain, gladdening the monarch and all his counsellors, 'Brahmanas, O king, belong to the foremost of the four orders. No value, however great, can be set upon them. Cows also are invaluable. Therefore, O chief of men, do thou regard a cow as the value of the Rishi.' Hearing these words of the great Rishi, Nahusha became, O king, filled with joy along with all his counsellors and priest. Proceeding then to the presence of Bhrigu's son, Chyavana, of rigid vows, he addressed him thus, O monarch, for gratifying him to the best of his ability.

"'"Nahusha said, 'Rise, rise, O regenerate Rishi, thou hast been purchased, O son of Bhirgu, with a cow as thy price. O foremost of righteous persons, even this, I think, is thy price.'

"'"Chyavana said. 'Yes, O king of kings, I do rise up. I have been properly purchased by thee, O sinless one! I do not, O thou of unfading glory, see any wealth that is equal to kine. To speak of kine, to hear others speak of them, to make gifts of kine, and to see kine, O king, are acts that are all applauded, O hero, and that are highly auspicious and sin-cleansing. Kine are always the root of prosperity. There is no fault in kine. Kine always afford the best food, in the form of Havi, unto the deities. The sacred Mantras, Swaha and Vashat, are always established upon kine. Kine are the chief conductresses of sacrifices. They constitute the mouth of sacrifice. They bear and yield excellent and strength-giving nectar. They receive the worship of all the worlds and are regarded as the source of nectar. On earth, kine resemble fire in energy and form. Verily, kine represent high energy, and are bestowers of great happiness upon all creatures. That country where kine, established by their owners, breathe fearlessly, shines in beauty. The sins also of that country are all washed off. Kine constitute the stairs that lead to heaven. Kine are adored in heaven itself. Kine are goddesses that are competent to give everything and grant every wish. There is nothing else in the world that is so high or so superior!'"[305]

"'Bhishma continued, "Even this is what I say unto thee on the subject of the glory and superiority of kine, O chief of Bharata's race. I am competent to proclaim a part only of the merits that attach to kine. I have not the ability to exhaust the subject!

"'"Then Nishadas said, 'O ascetic, thou hast seen us and hast also spoken with us. It

---

[305] There is no fault in kine, etc., and kine are like fire etc. The Hindu idea is that kine are cleansing or sanctifying. The Rishis discovered that the magnetism of the cow is something that is possessed of extraordinary virtues. Give the same kind of food to a cow and a horse. The horse-dung emits an unhealthy stench, while the cowdung is an efficacious disinfectant. Western science has not yet turned its attention to the subject, but there can be little doubt that the urine and dung of the cow possess untold virtues.

has been said that friendship with those that are good, depends upon only seven words.[306] Do thou then, O lord, show us thy grace. The blazing sacrificial fire eats all the oblations of clarified butter poured upon it. Of righteous soul, and possessed of great energy thou art among men, a blazing fire in energy. We propitiate thee, O thou of great learning! We surrender ourselves to thee. Do thou, for showing us favour, take back from us this cow.'

""""Chyavana said, 'The eye of a person that is poor or that has fallen into distress, the eye of an ascetic, or the eye of a snake of virulent poison, consumes a man with his very roots, even as a fire that, blazing up with the assistance of the wind, consumes a stack of dry grass or straw. I shall accept the cow that ye desire to present me. Ye fishermen, freed from every sin, go ye to heaven without any delay, with these fishes also that ye have caught with your nets.'"

"'Bhishma continued, "After this, in consequence of the energy of the great Rishi of cleansed soul, those fishermen along with all those fish through virtue of those words that he had uttered, proceeded to heaven. King Nahusha, beholding the fishermen ascending to heaven with those fishes in their company, became filled with wonder, O chief of Bharata's race. After this, the two Rishis, viz., the one born of a cow and the other who was Chyavana of Bhrigu's race, gladdened king Nahusha by granting him many boons. Then king Nahusha of great energy, that lord of all the earth, filled with joy, O best of the Bharatas, said, 'Sufficient!' Like unto a second Indra, the chief of the celestials, he accepted the boon about his own steadiness in virtue. The Rishis having granted him the boon, the delighted king worshipped them both with great reverence. As regards Chyavana, his vow having been completed, he returned to his own asylum. The Rishi that had taken his birth from the cow, and who was endued with great energy, also proceeded to his own retreat. The Nishadas all ascended to heaven as also the fishes they had caught, O monarch. King Nahusha, too, having obtained those valuable boons, entered his own city. I have thus, O son, told thee everything respecting what thou hadst asked me. The affection that is generated by the sight alone of others as also by the fact of living with them, O Yudhishthira, and the high-blessedness of kine too, and the ascertainment of true righteousness, are the topics upon which I have discoursed. Tell me, O hero what else is in thy breast."""

SECTION LII.

"'Yudhishthira said, "O thou of great wisdom, a doubt I have that is very great and that is as vast as the ocean itself. Listen to it, O mighty-armed one and having learnt what it is, it behoves thee to explain it unto me. I have a great curiosity with respect to Jamadagni's son, O lord, viz., Rama, that foremost of all righteous persons. It behoveth thee to gratify that curiosity. How was Rama born who was endued with prowess incapable of being baffled? He belonged by birth to a race of regenerate Rishis. How did he become a follower of Kshatriya practices? Do thou, then, O king, recite to me in detail the circumstances of Rama's birth. How also did a son of the race of Kusika who was Kshatriya become a Brahmana? Great, without doubt, was the puissance of the high-souled Rama, O chief of men, as also of Viswamitra. Why did the grandson of Richika instead of his son become a Kshatriya in conduct? Why also did the grandson of Kusika and not his son become a Brahmana? Why did such untoward incidents overtake the

---

[306] Saptopadam mitram means that by speaking only seven words or walking only seven steps together, two persons, if they be good, become friends.

grandsons of both, instead of their sons? It behoveth thee to explain the truth in respect of these circumstances."

"'Bhishma said, "In this connection is cited an old history of the discourse between Chyavana and Kusika, O Bharata! Endued with great intelligence, Chyavana of Bhrigu's race, that best of ascetics beheld (with his spiritual eye) the stain that would affect his own race (in consequence of some descendant of his becoming wedded to Kshatriya practice). Reflecting upon the merits and faults of that incident, as also its strength and weakness, Chyavana endued with wealth of asceticism became desirous of consuming the race of the Kusikas (for it was from that race that the stain of Kshatriya practices would, he knew, affect his own race). Repairing then to the presence of king Kusika, Chyavana said unto him, 'O sinless one, the desire has arisen in my heart of dwelling with thee for some time.'

"''Kusika said, 'O holy one, residence together is an act which the learned ordain for girls when these are given away. They that are endued with wisdom always speak of the practice in such connection only. O Rishi endued with wealth of asceticism, the residence which thou seekest with me is not sanctioned by the ordinance. Yet, however opposed to the dictates of duty and righteousness, I shall do what thou mayst be pleased to command.'"

"'Bhishma continued, "Ordering a seat to be placed for the great ascetic Chyavana, king Kusika, accompanied by his wife, stood in the presence of the ascetic. Bringing a little jar of water, the king offered him water for washing his feet. He then, through his servants, caused all the rites to be duly performed in honour of his high-souled guest. The high-souled Kusika, who was observant of restraints and vows, then cheerfully presented, according to due forms, the ingredients consisting of honey and the other things, to the great Rishi and induced him to accept the same. Having welcomed and honoured the learned Brahmana in this way, the king once more addressed him and said, 'We two await thy orders! Command us what we are to do for thee, O holy one! If it is our kingdom or wealth or kine, O thou of rigid vows, or all articles that are given away in sacrifices, which thou wantest, tell us the word, and we shall bestow all upon thee! This palace, the kingdom, this seat of justice, await thy pleasure. Thou art the lord of all these! Do thou rule the earth! As regards myself, I am completely dependent upon thee.' Addressed in these words by the king, Chyavana of Bhrigu's race, filled with great delight, said unto Kusika these words in reply.

"''Chyavana said, 'I do not, O king, covet thy kingdom, nor thy wealth, nor the damsels thou hast, nor thy kine, nor thy provinces, nor articles needed for sacrifice. Do thou listen to me. If it pleases thee and thy wife, I shall commence to observe a certain vow. I desire thee and thy wife to serve me during that period without any scruples.' Thus addressed by the Rishi, the king and the queen became filled with joy, O Bharata, and answered him, saving, 'Be it so, O Rishi!' Delighted with the Rishi's words, the king led him into an apartment of the palace. It was an excellent one, agreeable to see. The king showed him everything in that room. And the king said. 'This, O holy one, is thy bed. Do thou live here as thou pleasest! O thou that art endued with wealth of asceticism, myself and my queen shall strive our best to give thee every comfort and every pleasure.' While they were thus conversing with each other, the sun passed the meridian. The Rishi commanded the king to bring him food and drink. King Kusika, bowing unto the Rishi, asked him, saying, 'What kind of food is agreeable to thee? What food, indeed, shall be brought for thee?' Filled with delight, the Rishi answered that ruler of men, O Bharata, saying, 'Let food that is proper be given to me.' Receiving these words with respect, the king said, 'So be it!' and then offered unto the Rishi food of the proper kind. Having finished his meals, the holy Chyavana, conversant with every duty, addressed the king and the queen, saying, 'I desire to slumber. O puissant one, sleep hinders me now.' Proceeding thence to a chamber that had been prepared for him, that best of Rishis then laid himself down upon a bed. The king and the queen sat themselves down. The Rishi said to them, 'Do not, while I sleep, awake me. Do ye keep yourselves awake and continually press my feet as long as I sleep.' Without the least scruple, Kusika, conversant with every duty, said, 'So be it!' Indeed, the king and the queen kept themselves awake all night, duly engaged in tending and serving the Rishi in the manner directed. The royal couple, O monarch accomplished the Rishi's bidding with earnestness and attention. Meanwhile the holy Brahmana, having thus laid his commands upon the king, slept soundly, without changing his posture or turning even once, for a space of one and twenty days. The king, O delighter of the Kurus, foregoing all food, along with his wife, sat joyfully the whole time engaged in tending and serving the Rishi. On the expiration of one and twenty days, the son of Bhrigu rose of his own accord. The great ascetic then went out of the room, without accosting them at all. Famished and toil-worn the king and the queen followed him, but that foremost of Rishis did not deign to cast a single glance upon any of them. Proceeding a little way, the son of Bhrigu disappeared in the very sight of the royal couple (making himself invisible by his Yoga-power). At this, the king, struck with grief, fell down on the earth. Comforted, he rose up soon, and accompanied by his queen, the monarch, possessed of great splendour, began to search everywhere for the Rishi."'"

SECTION LIII.

"'Yudhishthira said, "After the Rishi had disappeared, what did the king do and what also did highly-blessed spouse do? Tell me this, O grandsire!"

"'Bhishma said, "Having lost sight of the Rishi, the king, overwhelmed with shame, toil-worn and losing his senses, returned to his palace, accompanied by his queen. Entering his mansion in a cheerless mood, he spoke not a word with any one. He thought only of that conduct of Chyavana. With a despairing heart he then proceeded to his chamber. There he saw the son of Bhrigu stretched as before on his bed. Beholding the Rishi there, they wondered much. Indeed, they began to reflect upon that very strange incident. The sight of the Rishi dispelled their fatigue. Taking their seats once more by his side, they again set themselves to gently press his feet as before. Meanwhile, the great ascetic continued to sleep soundly as before. Only, he now lay on another side. Endued with great energy, he thus passed another period measured by one and twenty day. Agitated by their fears, the royal couple showed no change in their attitude or sentiment towards the Rishi. Awaking then from his slumber, the ascetic addressed the king and the queen, saying, 'Do ye rub my body with oil. I wish to have a bath.' Famishing and toil-worn though they were they readily assented, and soon approached the Rishi with a costly oil that had been prepared by boiling it a hundred times. While the Rishi was seated at his ease, the king and the queen, restraining speech, continued to rub him. Endued with high ascetic merit the son of Bhrigu did not once utter the word 'Sufficient.' Bhrigu's son, however, saw that the royal couple were totally unmoved. Rising up suddenly, he entered the bathing chamber. The diverse article necessary for a bath and such as were fit for a king's use, were ready there. Without honouring, however, any of those articles by appropriating them to his use, the Rishi once more disappeared there and then by his Yoga-power, in the very sight of king Kusika (and his spouse). This, however, O chief of the Bharatas, failed to disturb the equanimity of the royal couple. The next time the puissant Rishi was seen seated, after a bath on the throne. Indeed, it was from that place that he then showed himself to the king and the queen, O delighter of the Kurus. With a cheerful face, king Kusika, together with his wife, then offered the Rishi cooked food with great reverence. Endued with wisdom, and with heart totally unmoved, Kusika made this offer. 'Let the food be brought' were the words that were then uttered by the ascetic. Assisted by his spouse, the king soon brought thither the food. There were diverse kinds of meat and different preparations also thereof. There was a great variety of vegetables also and pot-herbs. There were juicy cakes too among those viands, and several agreeable kinds of confectionery, and solid preparations of milk. Indeed, the viands offered presented different kinds of taste. Among them there was also some food—the produce of the wilderness—such as ascetics liked and took. Diverse agreeable kinds of fruit, fit to be eaten by kings, were also there. There were Vadaras and Ingudas and Kasmaryas and Bhallatakas. Indeed, the food that was offered contained such things as are taken by persons leading a domestic mode of life as also such things as are taken by denizens of the wilderness. Through fear of the Rishi's curse, the king had caused all kinds of food to be collected and dressed for his guest. All this food, brought from the kitchen, was placed before Chyavana. A seat was also placed for him and a bed too was spread. The viands were then caused to be covered with white cloths. Soon, however, Chyavana of Bhrigu's race set fire to all the things and reduced them to ashes. Possessed of great intelligence, the royal couple showed no wrath at this conduct of the Rishi, who once more, after this made himself invisible before the very eyes of the king and the queen. The Royal sage Kusika thereupon stood there in the same posture for the whole night, with his spouse by his side, and without speaking a word. Endued with great prosperity, he did not give way to wrath. Every day, good and pure food of diverse kinds, excellent beds, abundant articles needed for bath, and cloths of various kinds, were collected and kept in readiness in the palace for the Rishi. Indeed, Chyavana failed to notice any fault in the conduct of the king. Then the regenerate Rishi, addressing king Kusika, said unto him, 'Do thou with thy spouse, yoke thyself unto a car and bear me on it to whichever place I shall direct.' Without the least scruple, the king answered Chyavana endued with wealth of asceticism, saying, 'So be it!' and he further enquired of the Rishi, asking, 'Which car shall I bring? Shall it be my pleasure-car for making progress of pleasure, or, shall it be my battle-car?' Thus addressed by the delighted and contented monarch, the ascetic said unto him, 'Do thou promptly equip that car of thine with which thou penetratest into hostile cities. Indeed that battle-car of thine, with every weapon, with its standard and flags, its darts and javelins and golden columns and poles, should be made ready. Its rattle resembles the tinkling of bells. It is adorned with numerous arches made of pure gold. It is always furnished with high and excellent weapons numbering by hundreds!' The king said, 'So be it!' and soon caused his great battle-car to be equipped. And he yoked his wife thereto on the left and his own self on the right. And the king placed on the car, among its other equipments, the goad which had three handles and which had a point at once hard as the thunderbolt and sharp as the needle.[307] Having placed every requisite upon the car, the king said unto the Rishi, 'O holy one, whither shall the car proceed? O, let the son of Bhrigu issue his command! This

---

[307] Vajrasuchyagram may also mean furnished with an end like that of the needle with which diamonds and other hard gems are bored through.

thy car shall proceed to the place which thou mayst be pleased to indicate.' Thus addressed the holy man replied unto the king, saying, 'Let the car go hence, dragged slowly, step by step. Obedient to my will, do ye two proceed in such a way that I may not feel any fatigue, I should be borne away pleasantly, and let all thy people see this progress that I make through their midst. Let no person that comes to me, as I proceed along the road, be driven away. I shall make gifts of wealth unto all. Unto them amongst the Brahmanas that may approach me on the way, I shall grant their wishes and bestow upon all of them gems and wealth without stint. Let all this be accomplished, O king, and do not entertain any scruples.' Hearing these words of the Rishi, the king summoned his servants and said, 'Ye should, without any fear, give away whatever the ascetic will order.' Then jewels and gems in abundance, and beautiful women, and pairs of sheep, and coined and uncoined gold, and huge elephants resembling hills or mountain summits, and all the ministers of the king, began to follow the Rishi as he was borne away on that car. Cries of 'Oh' and 'Alas' arose from every part of the city which was plunged in grief at that extraordinary sight. And the king and the queen were suddenly struck by the Rishi with that goad equipped with sharp point. Though thus struck on the back and the cheeks, the royal couple still showed no sign of agitation. On the other hand, they continued to bear the Rishi on as before. Trembling from head to foot, for no food had passed their lips for fifty nights, and exceedingly weak, the heroic couple somehow succeeded in dragging that excellent car. Repeatedly and deeply cut by the goad, the royal couple became covered with blood. Indeed, O monarch, they then looked like a couple of Kinsuka trees in the flowering season. The citizens, beholding the plight to which their king and queen had been reduced, became afflicted with great grief. Filled with fear at the prospect of the curse of the Rishi, they kept silent under their misery. Gathering in knots they said unto each other, 'Behold the might of penances! Although all of us are angry, we are still unable to look at the Rishi! Great is the energy of the holy Rishi of cleaned soul! Behold also the endurance of the king and his royal spouse! Though worn out with toil and hunger, they are still bearing the car!' The son of Bhrigu notwithstanding the misery he caused to Kusika and his queen, failed to mark any sign of dissatisfaction or agitation in them."

"'Bhishma continued, "The perpetuator of Bhrigu's race beholding the king and the queen totally unmoved, began to give away very largely (wealth obtained from the king's treasury) as if he were a second Lord of Treasures. At this act also, king Kusika showed no mark of dissatisfaction. He did as the Rishi commanded (in the matter of those gifts). Seeing all this, that illustrious and best of ascetics became delighted. Coming down from that excellent car, he unharnessed the royal couple. Having freed them, he addressed them duly. Indeed, the son of Bhrigu, in a soft, deep, and delighted voice, said, 'I am ready to give an excellent boon unto you both!' Delicate as they were, their bodies had been pierced with the goad. That best of ascetics, moved by affection, softly touched them with his hands whose healing virtues resembled those of nectar itself, O chief of the Bharatas. Then the king answered, 'My wife and I have felt no toil!' Indeed, all their fatigue had been dispelled by the puissance of the Rishi, and hence it was that the king could say so unto the Rishi. Delighted with their conduct, the illustrious Chyavana said unto them, 'I have never before spoken an untruth. It must, therefore, be as I have said. This spot on the banks of the Ganga is very delightful and auspicious. I shall, observant of a vow, dwell for a little while here, O king! Do thou return to thy city. Thou are fatigued! Thou shalt come again. Tomorrow, O king, thou shalt, returning with thy spouse, behold me even here. Thou shouldst not give way to wrath or grief. The time is come when thou shalt reap a great reward! That which is coveted by thee and which is in thy heart shall verily be accomplished.' Thus addressed by the Rishi, king Kusika, with a delighted heart, replied unto the Rishi in these words of grave import, 'I have cherished no wrath or grief, O highly-blessed one! We have been cleansed and sanctified by thee, O holy one! We have once more become endued with youth. Behold our bodies have become exceedingly beautiful and possessed of great strength. I do not any longer see those wounds and cicatrices that were caused by thee on our persons with thy goad. Verily, with my spouse, I am in good health. I see my goddess become as beautiful in body as an Apsara. Verily, she is endued with as much comeliness and splendour as she had ever been before. All this, O great ascetic, is due to thy grace. Verily, there is nothing astonishing in all this, O holy Rishi of puissance ever unbaffled.' Thus addressed by the king, Chyavana said unto him, 'Thou shalt, with thy spouse, return hither tomorrow, O monarch!' With these words, the royal sage Kusika was dismissed. Saluting the Rishi, the monarch, endued with a handsome body, returned to his capital like unto a second chief of the celestials. The counsellors then, with the priest, came out to receive him. His troops and the dancing women and all his subjects, also did the same. Surrounded by them all, king Kusika, blazing with beauty and splendour, entered his city, with a delighted heart, and his praises were hymned by bards and encomiasts. Having entered his city and performed all his morning rites, he ate with his wife. Endued with great splendour, the monarch then passed the night happily. Each beheld the other to be possessed anew of youth. All their afflictions and pains having ceased, they beheld each other to resemble a celestial. Endued with the spendour they had obtained as a boon from that foremost of Brahmanas, and possessed as they were of forms that were exceedingly comely and beautiful, both of them passed a happy night in their bed. Meanwhile, the spreader of the feats of Bhrigu's race, viz., the Rishi possessed of the wealth of penances, converted, by his Yoga-power, that delightful wood on the bank of the Ganga into a retreat full of wealth of every kind and adorned with every variety of jewels and gems in consequence of which it surpassed in beauty and splendour the very abode of the chief of the celestials."'"

SECTION LIV.

"'Bhishma said, "When that night passed away, the high-souled king Kusika awoke and went through his morning rites. Accompanied by his wife he then proceeded towards that wood which the Rishi had selected for his residence. Arrived there, the monarch saw a palatial mansion made entirely of gold. Possessed of a thousand columns each of which was made of gems and precious stones, it looked like an edifice belonging to the Gandharvas.[308] Kusika beheld in every part of that structure evidences of celestial design. And he beheld hills with delightful valleys, and lakes with lotuses on their bosom, and mansions full of costly and curious articles, and gateways and arches, O Bharata. And the king saw many open glades and open spots carpeted with grassy verdure, and resembling level fields of gold. And he saw many Sahakaras adorned with blossoms, and Ketakas and Uddalakas, and Dhavas and Asokas, and blossoming Kundas, and Atimuktas. And he saw there many Champakas and Tilakas and Bhavyas and Panasas and Vanjulas and Karnikaras adorned with flowers. And the king beheld many Varanapushpas and the

---

[308] The ever-changing beautiful masses of afternoon or evening clouds, presenting diverse kinds of forms almost every minute, are regarded as the abodes or mansions of the Gandharvas.

174

creepers called Ashtapadika all clipped properly and beautifully.[309] And the king beheld trees on which lotuses of all varieties bloomed in all their beauty, and some of which bore flowers of every season. And he noticed also many mansions that looked like celestial cars or like beautiful mountains. And at some places, O Bharata, there were tanks and lakes full of cool water and at others were those that were full of warm or hot water. And there were diverse kinds of excellent seats and costly beds, and bedsteads made of gold and gems and overlaid with cloths and carpets of great beauty and value. Of comestible there were enormous quantities, well-dressed and ready for use. And there were talking parrots and she-parrots and Bhringarajas and Kokilas and Catapatras with Koyashtikas and Kukkubhas, and peacocks and cocks and Datyuhas and Jivajivakas and Chakoras and monkeys and swans and Sarasas and Chakravakas.[310] Here and there he beheld bevies of rejoicing Apsaras and conclaves of happy Gandharvas, O monarch. And he beheld other Gandharvas at other places rejoicing with their dear spouses. The king sometimes beheld these sights and sometimes could not see them (for they seemed to disappear from before his eyes). The monarch heard also melodious strains of vocal music and the agreeable voices of preceptors engaged in lecturing to their disciples on the Vedas and the scriptures. And the monarch also heard the harmonious cackle of the geese sporting in the lakes. Beholding such exceedingly wonderful sights, the king began to reflect inwardly, saying, 'Is this a dream? Or is all this due to an aberration of my mind? Or, is it all real? O, I have, without casting off my earthly tenement, attained to the beatitude of heaven! This land is either the sacred country of the Uttara-Kurus, or the abode, called Amaravati, of the chief of the celestials! O, what are these wonderful sights that I behold!' Reflecting in this strain, the monarch at last saw that foremost of Rishis. In that palace of gold (endued) with columns (made) of jewels and gems, lay the son of Bhrigu stretched on a costly and excellent bed. With his wife by his side the king approached with a delighted heart the Rishi as he lay on that bed. Chyavana, however, quickly disappeared at this, with the bed itself upon which he lay. The king then beheld the Rishi at another part of those woods seated on a mat made of Kusa grass, and engaged in mentally reciting some high Mantras. By his Yoga-power, even thus did that Brahmana stupefy the king. In a moment that delightful wood, those bevies of Apsaras, those bands of Gandharvas, those beautiful trees,—all disappeared. The bank of the Ganga became as silent as usual, and presented the old aspect of its being covered with Kusa grass and ant-hills. King Kusika with his wife having beheld that highly wonderful sight and its quick disappearance also,

[309] Some of these trees and creepers are identifiable. Sahakara is Mangifera Indica, Linn. Ketaka is a variety of Pandanus Odoratissimus, Linn. Uddalaka is otherwise called Vahuvara and sometimes Selu. It is the Cordia Myxa, Linn. It may be a misreading for Uddanaka, which is the well-known Cirisha or the Mimosa Sirisca of Roxburgh. Dhava is Conocarpus latifolia, Roxb. Asoka is Saraca Indica, Linn., syn, Jonesia Asoka, Roxb. Kunda is Jasminum pubescens, Linn. Atimukta is otherwise called Madhavi. It is Gaertinera racemosa, Roxb. Champaka is Michelia Champaca, Linn. Tilaka sometimes stands for Lodhra, i.e., Symplocos racemosa, Roxb. The word is sometimes used for the Aswattha or Ficus religiosa, Linn. Bhavya is Dillenia Indica, Linn. Panasa is Artocarpus integrifolia, Linn. The Indian Jack-tree. Vyanjula stands for the Asoka, also Vetasa (Indian cane), and also for Vakula, i.e., Mimusops Elengi, Linn. Karnikara is Pterospermum accrifolium, Linn. Cyama is sometimes used for the Pilu, i.e., Salvadora Persica, Linn. Varanapushpa or Nagapushpa or Punnaga is Colophyllum inophyllum, Linn. Astapadika or padika is otherwise called Bhardravalli. It is the Vallaris dichotoma, Wall., Syn., Echites dichotoma, Roxb.

[310] Bhringaraja is the Lanius Malabaricus. Kokila is the well-known Indian Koel or cuckoo. Catapatra is the wood-pecker. Koyashtika is the Lapwing. Kukkubhas are wild-cocks (Phasinus gallus). Datyuhas are a variety of Chatakas or Gallinules. Their cry resembles the words (phatikjal). Jivajivaka is a species of partridges. Chakora is the Greek partridge. Sarasa is the Indian crane. Chakravaka is the Brahmini duck or goose.

became filled with amazement. With a delighted heart, the monarch addressed his wife and said unto her, 'Behold, O amiable one, the various agreeable scenes and sights, occurring nowhere else, which we two have just witnessed! All this is due to the grace of Bhrigu's son and the puissance of his penances. By penances all that becomes attainable which one cherishes in one's imagination. Penances are superior to even the sovereignty over the three worlds. By penances well-performed, emancipation itself may be achieved. Behold, the puissance of the high-souled and celestial Rishi Chyavana derived from his penances. He can, at his pleasure, create even other worlds (than those which exist). Only Brahmanas are born in this world to attain to speech and understanding and acts that are sacred. Who else than Chyavana could do all this? Sovereignty may be acquired with ease. But the status of a Brahmana is not so attainable. It was through the puissance of a Brahmana that we were harnessed to a car like well-broken animals!' These reflections that passed through the king's brain became known to Chyavana. Ascertaining the king's thoughts, the Rishi addressed him and said, 'Come hither quickly!' Thus addressed, the king and the queen approached the great ascetic, and, bending their heads, they worshipped him who deserved worship. Uttering a benediction upon the monarch, the Rishi, possessed of great intelligence, O chief of men, comforted the king and said, 'Sit down on that seat!' After this, O monarch, the son of Bhrigu, without guile or insincerity of any kind, gratified the king with many soft words, and then said, 'O king, thou hast completely subjugated the five organs of action and the five organs of knowledge with the mind as their sixth. Thou hast for this come out unscathed from the fiery ordeal I had prepared for thee. I have been properly honoured and adored, O son, by thee, O foremost of all persons possessed of speech. Thou hast no sin, not even a minute one, in thee! Give me leave, O king, for I shall now proceed to the place I came from. I have been exceedingly pleased with thee, O monarch! Do thou accept the boon I am ready to give.'

""Kusika said, 'In thy presence, O holy one, I have stayed like one staying in the midst of a fire. That I have not yet, O chief of Bhrigu's race been consumed, is sufficient! Even this is the highest boon that has been obtained, O delighter of Bhrigu! That thou hast been gratified by me, O Brahmana, and that I have succeeded in rescuing my race from destruction, O sinless one, constitute in my case the best boons. This I regard, O learned Brahmana, as a distinct evidence of thy grace. The end of my life has been accomplished. Even this is what I regard the very end of my sovereignty. Even this is the highest fruit of my penances![311] If, O learned Brahmana, thou hast been pleased with me, O delighter of Bhrigu, then do thou expound some doubts which are in my mind!""

SECTION LV.

""Chyavana said, 'Do thou accept a boon from me. Do thou also, O chief of men, tell me what the doubt is that is in thy mind. I shall certainly accomplish all thy purposes.'

""Kusika said, 'If thou hast been gratified by me, O holy one, do thou then, O son of Bhrigu, tell me thy object in residing in my palace for some time, for I desire to hear it. What was thy object in sleeping on the bed I assigned thee for one and twenty days continuously, without changing sides? O foremost of ascetics, what also was thy object, again, in going out of the room without speaking a single word? Why didst thou, again, without any ostensible reason, make thyself invisible, and once more become visible? Why, O learned Brahmana, didst thou again, lay thyself down on the bed and sleep as

---

[311] In verse 39 and 40 for asmi and tapacchaitat read asi and tapasaccha.

before for one and twenty days? For what reason didst thou go out after thou wert rubbed by us with oil in view of thy bath? Why also, after having caused diverse kinds of food in my palace to be collected, didst thou consume them with the aid of fire? What was the cause of thy sudden journey through my city on the car? What object hadst thou in view in giving away so much wealth? What was thy motive in showing us the wonders of the forest created by the Yoga-puissance? What indeed was thy motive for showing, O great ascetic, so many palatial mansions made of gold and so many bedsteads supported on posts of jewels, and gems? Why also did all these wonders vanish from our sight? I wish to hear the cause of all this. In thinking of all these acts of thine, O perpetuator of Bhrigu's race, I became stupefied repeatedly. I fail to find what the certain motive was which influenced thee! O thou, that art endued with wealth of penances, I wish to hear the truth about all those acts of thine in detail.'

""Chyavana said, 'Listen to me as I tell thee in detail the reasons which had impelled me in all these acts of mine. Asked by thee, O monarch, I cannot refuse to enlighten thee. In days past, on one occasion, when the deities had assembled together, the Grandsire Brahman said some words. I heard them, O king, and shall presently repeat them to thee. "In consequence of a contention between Brahmana and Kshatriya energy, there will occur an intermixture in my race.[312] Thy grandson, O king, will become endued with great energy and puissance." Hearing this, I came hither, resolved to exterminate thy race. Indeed, I came, O Kusika, seeking the utter extermination of thy race,—in fact, for consuming into ashes all thy descendants. Impelled by this motive I came to thy palace, O monarch, and said unto thee, "I shall observe some vow. Do thou attend upon me and serve me dutifully." While residing, however, in thy house I failed to find any laches in thee. It is for that reason, O royal sage, that thou art still alive, for otherwise thou wouldst have by this time been numbered with the dead. It was with this resolution that I slept for one and twenty days in the hope that somebody would awake me before I arose of my own accord. Thou, however, with thy wife, didst not awaken me. Even then, O best of kings, I became pleased with thee. Rising from my bed I went out of the chamber without accosting any of you. I did this, O monarch, in the hope that thou wouldst ask me and thus I would have an opportunity of cursing thee. I then made myself invisible, and again showed myself in the room of thy palace, and, once more betaking myself to Yoga, slept for one and twenty days. The motive that impelled me was this. Worn out with toil and hunger you two would be angry with me and do what would be unpleasant to me. It was from this intention that I caused thyself and thy spouse to be afflicted with hunger. In thy heart however, O king, the slightest feeling of wrath or vexation did not rise. For this, O monarch, I became highly delighted with thee. When I caused diverse kinds of food to be brought and then set fire to them, I hoped that thyself with thy wife wouldst give way to wrath at the sight. Even that act however, of mine was tolerated by thee. I then ascended the car, O monarch, and addressed thee, saying, "Do thou with thy wife bear me." Thou didst what I bade, without the least scruple, O king! I became filled with delight at this. The gifts of wealth I made could not provoke thy anger. Pleased with thee, O king, I created with the aid of my Yoga puissance that forest which thyself with thy wife didst behold here. Listen, O monarch, to the object I had. For gratifying thee and thy queen I caused thee to have a glimpse of heaven. All those things which thou hast seen in these woods, O monarch, are a foretaste of heaven. O best of kings, for a little while I caused

---

[312] The Grandsire spoke of somebody becoming a Kshatriya in Bhrigu's race, and referred to the incident as the result of a stain that would be communicated to that race from Kusika's. This is the full allusion.

thee and thy spouse to behold, in even your earthly bodies, some sights of heaven. All this was done for showing the puissance of penances and the reward that is in store for righteousness. The desire that arose in thy heart, O monarch, at the sight of those delightful objects, is known to me. Thou becamest desirous of obtaining the status of a Brahmana and the merit of penances, O lord of Earth, disregarding the sovereignty of the earth, nay, the sovereignty of very heaven! That which thou thoughtest, O king, was even this. The status of a Brahmana is exceedingly difficult to obtain; after becoming a Brahmana, it is exceedingly difficult to obtain the status of a Rishi; for even a Rishi it is difficult to become an ascetic! I tell thee that thy desire will be gratified. From thee, O Kusika, will spring a Brahmana, who shall be called after thy name. The person that will be the third in descent from thee shall attain to the status of a Brahmana. Through the energy of the Bhrigus, thy grandson, O monarch, will be an ascetic endued with the splendour of fire. He shall always strike all men, indeed, the inhabitants of the three worlds, with fear. I tell thee the truth. O royal sage, do thou accept the boon that is now in thy mind. I shall soon set out on a tour to all the sacred waters. Time is expiring.'

""""Kusika said, 'Even this, O great ascetic, is a high boon, in my case, for thou hast been gratified by me. Let that take place which thou hast said. Let my grandson become a Brahmana, O sinless one! Indeed, let the status of Brahmanahood attach to my race, O holy one. This is the boon I ask for. I desire to once more ask thee in detail, O holy one! In what way, O delighter of Bhrigu, will the status of Brahmanahood attach to my race? Who will be my friend? Who will have my affection and respect?'"""[313]

SECTION LVI.

""""Chyavana said, 'I should certainly, O chief of men, tell you everything about the circumstance for which, O monarch, I came hither for exterminating thy race. This is well-known, O king, that the Kshatriyas should always have the assistance of the sons of Bhrigu in the matter of sacrifices. Through an irresistible decree of Destiny, the Kshatriyas and the Bhargavas will fall out. The Kshatriyas, O king, will slay the descendants of Bhrigu. Afflicted by an ordinance of fate, they will exterminate the race of Bhrigu, not sparing even infants in their mothers' wombs. There will then spring in Bhrigu's race a Rishi of the name of Urva. Endued with great energy, he will in splendour certainly resemble fire or the sun. He will cherish such wrath (upon hearing of the extermination of his race) as will be sufficient to consume the three worlds. He will be competent to reduce the whole earth with all her mountains and forests into ashes. For a little while he will quell the flames of that fiery rage, throwing it into the Mare's mouth that wanders through the ocean. He will have a son of the name of Richika. The whole science of arms, O sinless one, in its embodied form will come to him, for the extermination of the entire Kshatriya race, through a decree of Destiny. Receiving that science by inward light, he will, by Yoga-puissance, communicate it to his son, the highly-blessed Jamadagni of cleansed soul. That tiger of Bhrigu's race will bear that science in his mind. O thou of righteous soul, Jamadagni will wed a girl, taking her from thy race, for spreading its glory, O chief of the Bharatas. Having obtained for wife the daughter of Gadhi and thy grand-daughter, O king that great ascetic will beget a regenerate son endued with Kshatriya accomplishments. In thy race will be born a son, a

---

[313] The sense seems to be that Kusika wishes to know what person of Bhrigu's race will confer this high benefit upon his race.

Kshatriya endued with the virtues of a Brahmana. Possessed of great righteousness, he will be the son of Gadhi. Known by the name of Viswamitra, he will in energy come to be regarded as the equal of Vrihaspati himself, the preceptor of the celestials. The illustrious Richika will grant this son to thy race, this Kshatriya that will be endued with high penances. In the matter of this exchange of sons, (viz., a Kshatriya son in the race of Bhrigu and a Brahmana son in thy race) the cause will be two women. All this will happen at the command of the grandsire. It will never be otherwise. Unto one that is third in descent from thee, the status of Brahmanahood will attach. Thou shalt become a relative (by marriage) of the Bhargavas.'"

"'Bhishma continued, "Hearing these words of the high-souled ascetic Chyavana, king Kusika became filled with joy, and made answer in the following words, 'Indeed, O best of the Bharatas', he said, 'So be it!' Endued with high energy, Chyavana once more addressed the king, and urged him to accept a boon from himself. The king replied, 'Very well. From thee, O great ascetic, I shall obtain the fruition of my wish. Let my race become invested with the status of Brahmanahood, and let it always set its heart upon righteousness.' The ascetic Chyavana, thus solicited, granted the king's prayer, and bidding farewell to the monarch, set out on his intended tour to the sacred waters. I have now told thee everything, O Bharata, relating to thy questions, viz., how the Bhrigus and the Kusikas became connected with each other by marriage. Indeed, O king, everything fell out as the Rishi Chyavana had said. The birth of Rama (of Bhrigu's race) and of Viswamitra (of Kusika's race) happened in the way that Chyavana had indicated."'"

SECTION LVII.

"'Yudhishthira said, "Hearing thy words I become stupefied, O grandsire! Reflecting that the earth is now destitute of a very large number of kings all of whom were possessed of great prosperity, my heart becomes filled with grief. Having conquered the earth and acquired kingdoms numbered by hundreds, O Bharata, I turn with grief, O Grandsire, at the thought of the millions of men I have slaughtered. Alas, what will be the plight of those foremost ladies who have been deprived by us of husbands and sons and maternal uncles and brothers? Having slain those Kurus—our kinsmen, that is, our friends and well-wishers,—we shall have to sink in hell, heads (hanging) downwards. There is no doubt of this. I desire, O Bharata, to address my body to severe penances. With that end in view, O king, I wish to receive instructions from thee.'"

"Vaisampayana continued, 'The high-souled Bhishma, hearing these words of Yudhishthira, reflected upon them acutely with the aid of his understanding, and addressed Yudhishthira in reply.'

"'Bhishma said, "Hear what I say unto thee. It is exceedingly wonderful, and constitutes a great mystery. The topic is the object that creatures obtain after death as the rewards of particular acts or courses of conduct they follow. One attains to Heaven by penances. By penances one attains to fame. By penances, O puissant king, one attains to length of life and all articles of enjoyment. By penances one attains to knowledge, to science, to health and freedom from disease, beauty of person, prosperity, and blessedness, O chief of Bharata's race. By penances one attains to wealth. By observing the vow of taciturnity one succeeds in bringing the whole world under one's sway. By making gifts one acquires all kinds of enjoyable articles. By observing the right of Diksha one acquires birth in a good and high family. Those that spend their lives subsisting only upon fruits and roots (and avoiding cooked food) succeed in obtaining kingdom and sovereignty. Those that live upon the leaves of plants and trees as their food succeed in attaining to heaven. One that subsists upon water only attains to heaven. By making gifts one simply increases one's wealth. By serving with reverence one's preceptor one acquires learning. By performing Sraddhas every day in honour of one's Pitris (manes), one acquires a large number of children. By observing Diksha upon potherbs and vegetables, one acquires a large number of kine. Those that subsist upon grass and straw succeed in attaining to heaven. By bathing thrice every day with the necessary rites one acquires a large number of spouses. By drinking water alone one acquires residence in the regions of Prajapati. The Brahmana, who bathes every day and recites sacred Mantras in the twilights, becomes possessed of the status of Daksha himself. By worshipping the deities in a wilderness or desert, one acquires a kingdom or sovereignty, and by observing the vow of casting off the body by a long fast, one ascends to Heaven. One possessed of the wealth of penances and always passing his days in Yoga obtains good beds and seats and vehicles. Casting off the body by entering a blazing fire, one becomes an object of reverence in the region of Brahman. Those that lie on the hard and bare ground acquire houses and beds. Those that clothe themselves in rags and barks obtain good robes and ornaments. By avoiding the several agreeable tastes one succeeds in acquiring great prosperity. By abstaining from meat and fish, one gets long-lived children. One who passes some time in that mode of life which is called Udavasa, becomes the very lord of Heaven. The man who speaks the truth, O best of men, succeeds in sporting happily with the deities themselves. By making gifts one acquires great fame in consequence of one's high achievements. By abstention from cruelty one acquires health and freedom from disease. By serving Brahmanas with reverence one attains to kingdom and sovereignty, and the high status of a Brahmana. By making gifts of water and other drinks, one acquires eternal fame in consequence of high achievements. By making gifts of food one acquires diverse articles of enjoyment. One who gives peace unto all creatures (by refraining from doing them any injury), becomes freed from every region. By serving the deities one obtains a kingdom and celestial beauty. By presenting lights at places which are dark and frequented by men, one acquires a good vision. By giving away good and beautiful objects one acquires a good memory and understanding. By giving away scents and garlands, one acquires fame that spreads over a large area. Those who abstain from shaving off their hair and beards succeed in obtaining excellent children. By observing fasts and Diksha and baths, O Bharata, for twelve years (according to the ordinance), one acquires a region that is superior to that attainable by unreturning heroes. By bestowing one's daughter on an eligible bridegroom according to the Brahma form, one obtains, O best of men, male and female slaves and ornaments and fields and houses. By performing sacrifices and observing fasts, one ascends to Heaven, O Bharata. The man who gives away fruits and flowers succeeds in acquiring auspicious knowledge. The man who gives a thousand kine with horns adorned with gold, succeeds in acquiring heaven. Even this has been said by the very deities in a conclave in heaven. One who gives away a Kapila cow with her calf, with a brazen pot of milking with horns adorned with gold, and possessed of diverse other accomplishments, obtains the fruition of all his wishes from that cow. Such a person, in consequence of that act of gift, resides in heaven for as many years as there are hairs on the body of the cow and rescues in the next world (from the misery of hell) his sons and grandsons and all his race to the seventh degree.[314] The regions of the Vasus become attainable to that man who gives away a cow with horns

---

[314] By ancestors to the seventh degree also descendants to the same degree are meant.

beautifully decorated with gold, accompanied with a brazen jar for milking, along with a piece of cloth embroidered with gold, a measure of sesame and a sum of money as Dakshina. A gift of kine rescues the giver in the next world when he finds himself falling into the deep darkness of hell and restrained by his own acts in this world, like a boat with sails that have caught the air rescuing a person from being drowned in the sea. He who bestows a daughter according to the Brahma form upon an eligible person, or who makes a gift of land unto a Brahmana, or who gives food (to a Brahmana) according to due rites, succeeds in attaining to the region of Purandara. That man who makes a gift of a house, equipped with every kind of furniture, unto a Brahmana given to Vedic studies and possessed of every accomplishment and good behaviour, acquires residence in the country of the Uttara-Kurus. By making gifts of draft bullocks, a person acquires the region of the Vasus. Gifts of gold lead to heaven. Gifts of pure gold lead to greater merit still. By making a gift of an umbrella one acquires a palatial mansion. By making a gift of a pair of sandals or shoes one acquires good vehicles. The reward attached to a gift of cloths is personal beauty, and by making gifts of scents one becomes a fragrant person in one's next life. One who gives flowers and fruits and plants and trees unto a Brahmana, acquires, without any labour, palatial mansion equipped with beautiful women and full of plenty of wealth. The giver of food and drink of different tastes and of other articles of enjoyment succeeds in acquiring a copious supply of such articles. The giver, again, of houses and cloths gets articles of a similar kind. There is no doubt about it. That person who makes gifts of garlands and incense and scents and unguents and the articles needed by men after a bath, and floral wreaths, unto Brahmanas, becomes freed from every disease and possessed of personal beauty, sports in joy in the region reserved for great kings. The man, O king, who makes unto a Brahmana the gift of a house that is stored with grain, furnished with beds full of much wealth, auspicious, and delightful, acquires a palatial residence. He who gives unto a Brahmana a good bed perfumed with fragrant scents, overlaid with an excellent sheet, and equipped with pillows, wins without any effort on his part a beautiful wife, belonging to a high family and of agreeable manners. The man who takes to a hero's bed on the field of battle becomes the equal of the Grandsire Brahman himself. There is no end higher than this. Even this is what the great Rishis have declared."'

"Vaisampayana continued, 'Hearing these words of his grandfather, Yudhishthira, the delighter of the Kurus, became desirous of the end that is reserved for heroes and no longer expressed any disgust at leading a householder's mode of life. Then, O foremost of men, Yudhishthira, addressing all the other sons of Pandu, said unto them, "Let the words which our grandfather has said command your faith." At this, all the Pandavas with the famous Draupadi amongst them, applauded the words of Yudhishthira and said, "Yes."'"

SECTION LVIII.

"'Yudhishthira said, "I desire, O chief of the Bharatas, to hear from thee what the rewards are which are attached, O best of the Kurus, to the planting of trees and the digging of tanks."

"'Bhishma said, "A piece of land that is agreeable to the sight, fertile, situate in the midst of delightful scenes adorned with diverse kinds of metals, and inhabited by all sorts of creatures, is regarded as the foremost of sports. A particular portion of such land should be selected for digging a tank. I shall tell thee, in due order, about the different kinds of tanks. I shall also tell thee what the merits also are that attach to the digging of tanks (with the view of drawing water for the benefit of all creatures). The man who causes a tank to be dug becomes entitled to the respect and worship of the three worlds. A tank full of water is as agreeable and beneficial as the house of a friend. It is gratifying to Surya himself. It also contributes to growth to the deities. It is the foremost of all things that lead to fame (with respect to the person who causes it to be excavated). The wise have said that the excavation of a tank contributes to the aggregate of three, Righteousness, Wealth and Pleasure. A tank is said to be properly excavated, if it is made on a piece of land that is inhabited by respectable persons. A tank is said to be subservient to all the four purposes of living creatures. Tanks, again, are regarded as constituting the excellent beauty of a country. The deities and human beings and Gandharvas and Pitris and Uragas and Rakshasas and even immobile beings—all resort to a tank full of water as their refuge. I shall, therefore, tell thee what the merits are that have been said by great Rishis to be attached to tanks, and what the rewards are that are attainable by persons that cause them to be excavated. The wise have said that that man reaps the merit of an Agnihotra sacrifice in whose tank water is held in the season of the rains. The high reward in the world that is reaped by the person who makes a gift of a thousand kine is won by that man in whose tank water is held in the season of autumn. The person in whose tank water occurs in the cold season acquires the merit of one who performs a sacrifice with plentiful gifts of gold. That person in whose tanks water occurs in the season of dew, wins, the wise have said, the merits of an Agnishtoma sacrifice. That man in whose well-made tank water occurs in the season of spring acquires the merit of the Atiratra sacrifice. That man in whose tank water occurs in the season of summer acquires, the Rishis say, the merits that attach to a horse-sacrifice. That man rescues all his race in whose tank kine are seen to allay their thirst and from which righteous men draw their water. That man in whose tank kine slake their thirst as also other animals and birds, and human beings, acquires the merits of a horse-sacrifice. Whatever measure of water is drunk from one's tank and whatever measure is taken therefrom by others for purposes of bathing, all become stored for the benefit of the excavator of the tank and he enjoys the same for unending days in the next world. Water, especially in the other world, is difficult to obtain, O son. A gift of drink produces eternal happiness. Make gifts of sesame here. Make gifts of water. Do thou also give lamps (for lighting dark places.) While alive and awake, do thou sport in happiness with kinsmen. These are acts which thou shalt not be able to achieve in the other world.[315] The gift of drink, O chief of men, is superior to every other gift. In point of merit it is distinguished above all other gifts. Therefore, do thou make gifts of water. Even thus have the Rishis declared what the high merits of the excavation of tanks are I shall now discourse to thee on the planting of trees. Of immobile objects six classes have been spoken of. They are Vrikshas, Gulmas, Latas, Vallis, Twaksaras, and Trinas of diverse kinds.[316] These are the several kinds of vegetables. Listen now to the merit that attaches to their planting. By planting trees one acquires fame in the world of men and auspicious rewards in the world hereafter. Such a man is applauded and reverenced in the world of the Pitris. Such a man's name does not perish even when he becomes a citizen of the world of deities. The man who plants trees rescues the ancestors and descendants of both his paternal and

---

[315] Heaven and Hell are places of only enjoyment and endurance. There can be no acts there leading to merit or demerit. This world is the only place which is called the field of acts.

[316] Vrikshas are large or small trees generally. Gulma is a shrub, or bushy plant. Lata is a creeper, which cannot grow without a support. Talli is of the same variety, with this difference, perhaps, that its stems are more tree-like than those of creepers. Twaksara is the bamboo. Trina includes all kinds of grass.

maternal lines. Do thou, therefore, plant trees, O Yudhishthira! The trees that a man plants become the planter's children. There is no doubt about this. Departing from this world, such a man ascends to Heaven. Verily many eternal regions of bliss become his. Trees gratify the deities by their flowers; the Pitris by their fruits; and all guests and strangers by the shadow they give. Kinnaras and Uragas and Rakshasas and deities and Gandharvas and human beings, as also Rishis, all have recourse to trees as their refuge. Trees that bear flowers and fruits gratify all men. The planter of trees is rescued in the next world by the trees he plants like children rescuing their own father. Therefore, the man that is desirous of achieving his own good, should plant trees by the side of tanks and cherish them like his own children. The trees that a man plants are, according to both reason and the scriptures, the children of the planter. That Brahmana who excavates a tank, and he that plants trees, and he that performs sacrifices, are all worshipped in heaven even as men that are devoted to truthfulness of speech. Hence one should cause tanks to be excavated and trees to be planted, worship the deities in diverse sacrifices, and speak the truth.""'

SECTION LIX.

"'Yudhishthira said, "Amongst all those gifts that are mentioned in the treatises other than the Vedas, which gift, O chief of Kuru's race, is the most distinguished in thy opinion? O puissant one, great is the curiosity I feel with respect to this matter. Do thou discourse to me also of that gift which follows the giver into the next world."[317]

"'Bhishma said, "An assurance unto all creatures of love and affection and abstention from every kind of injury, acts of kindness and favour done to a person in distress, gifts of articles made unto one that solicits with thirst and agreeable to the solicitor's wishes, and whatever gifts are made without the giver's ever thinking of them as gifts made by him, constitute, O chief of Bharata's race, the highest and best of gifts. Gift of gold, gift of kine, and gift of earth,—these are regarded as sin-cleansing. They rescue the giver from his evil acts. O chief of men, do thou always make such gifts unto those that are righteous. Without doubt, gifts rescue the giver from all his sins. That person who wishes to make his gifts eternal should always give unto persons possessed of the requisite qualifications whatever articles are desired by all and whatever things are the best in his house. The man who makes gifts of agreeable things and who does to others what is agreeable to others, always succeeds in obtaining things that are agreeable to himself. Such a person certainly becomes agreeable unto all, both here and hereafter. That man, O Yudhishthira, is a cruel wretch, who, through vanity, does not, to the extent of his means, attend to the wishes of one who is poor and helpless, and who solicits assistance.[318] He is verily the foremost of men who shows favour unto even an helpless enemy fallen into distress when such enemy presents himself and prays for help. No man is equal to him (in merit) who satisfies the hunger of a person that is emaciated, possessed of learning, destitute of the means of support, and weakened by misery. One should always, O son of Kunti, dispel by every means in one's power, the distress of righteous persons observant of vows and acts, who, though destitute of sons and spouses and plunged into misery, do not yet solicit others for any kind of assistance. Those persons who do not utter blessings

---

[317] The commentator explains that the drift of Yudhishthira's query is this: the giver and the receiver do not meet in the next world. How then can an object given away return or find its way back to the giver in the next world or next life?

[318] Abhimanat is differently understood by the commentator.

upon the deities and men (in expectation of gifts), who are deserving of reverence and always contented, and who subsist upon such alms as they get without solicitation of any kind, are regarded as veritable snakes of virulent poison. Do thou, O Bharata, always protect thyself from them by making gifts unto them. They are competent to make the foremost of Ritwikas. Thou art to find them out by means of thy spies and agents.[319] Thou shouldst honour those men by gifts of good houses equipped with every necessary article, with slaves and serving men, with good robes and vestments, O son of Kuru, and with all articles competent to contribute to one's pleasure and happiness. Righteous men of righteous deeds should make such gifts, impelled by the motive that it is their duty to act in that way and not from desire of reaping any rewards therefrom. Verily good men should act in this way so that the virtuous men described above might not, O Yudhishthira, feel any disinclination to accept those gifts sanctified by devotion and faith. There are persons bathed in learning and bathed in vows. Without depending upon anybody they obtain their means of subsistence. These Brahmanas of rigid vows are devoted to Vedic study and penances without proclaiming their practices to any one. Whatever gifts thou mayst make unto those persons of pure behaviour, of thorough mastery over their senses, and always contented with their own wedded spouses in the matter of desire, are sure to win for thee a merit that will accompany thee into all the worlds into which thou mayst go. One reaps the same merit by making gifts unto regenerate persons of restrained souls which one wins by properly pouring libations unto the sacred fire morning and evening. Even this is the sacrifice spread out for thee,—a sacrifice that is sanctified by devotion and faith and that is endued with Dakshina. It is distinguished above all other sacrifices. Let that sacrifice ceaselessly flow from thee as thou givest away.[320] Performed in view of such men, O Yudhishthira, a sacrifice in which the water that is sprinkled for dedicating gifts constitutes the oblations in honour of the Pitris, and devotion and worship rendered unto such superior men, serves to free one of the debts one owes to the deities.[321] Those persons that do not yield to wrath and that never desire to take even a blade of grass belonging to others, as also they that are of agreeable speech, deserve to receive from us the most reverent worship. Such persons and others (because free from desire) never pay their regards to the giver. Nor do they strive for obtaining gifts. They should, however, be cherished by givers as they cherish their own sons. I bend my head unto them. From them also both Heaven and Hell may become one's.[322] Ritwiks and Purohitas and preceptors, when conversant with the Vedas and when behaving mildly towards disciples, become such. Without doubt, Kshatriya energy loses its force upon a Brahmana when it encounters him. Thinking that thou art a king, that thou art possessed of great power, and that thou hast affluence, do not, O Yudhishthira, enjoy thy affluence without giving anything unto the Brahmanas.

---

[319] Yuktaih is the better reading, although muktaih may not be erroneous. Yuktain is charaih; while muktath is 'men charged with a commission to do a thing'.

[320] This sacrifice is the sacrifices of gifts. 'Spreading out a sacrifice' means 'spreading out the articles and placing them in proper order in view of the sacrifice.' 'Dadatah vartotam' means datustaya saryanastu.

[321] The sense is this: gifts made to such superior Brahmanas serve to free a person from the debts which he owes to the deities. The 'water of gifts' means the water that the giver sprinkles, with a blade of Kusa grass, over the article given away, saying, 'I give this away'. In the sacrifice constituted by gifts, such water is like the dedication of offerings to the Pitris. A knowledge of the ritual of sacrifice is needed to understand and appreciate the figures employed in such verses.

[322] Some texts read tathabham, meaning abhayam or fearlessness is from them—Tathobhayam (which I adopt) is that both, Heaven and Hell become one's through them; if gratified, they bestow Heaven; if angry, they hurl into Hell.

Observing the duties of thy own order, do thou worship the Brahmanas with whatever wealth thou hast, O sinless one, for purposes of adornment or sustaining thy power. Let the Brahmanas live in whatever way they like. Thou shouldst always bend thy head unto them with reverence. Let them always rejoice in thee as thy children, living happily and according to their wishes. Who else than thou, O best of the Kurus, is competent to provide the means of subsistence for such Brahmanas as are endued with eternal contentment as are thy well-wishers, and as are gratified by only a little? As women have one eternal duty, in this world, viz., dependence upon and obedient service to their husbands, and as such duty constitutes their only end, even so is the service to Brahmanas our eternal duty and end. If, at sight of cruelties and other sinful acts in Kshatriyas, the Brahmanas, O son, unhonoured by us, forsake us all, I say, of what use would life be to us, in the absence of all contact with the Brahmanas, especially as we shall then have to drag on our existence without being able to study the Vedas to perform sacrifices, to hope for worlds of bliss hereafter, and to achieve great feats? I shall, in this connection, tell thee what the eternal usage is. In days of yore, O king, the Kshatriyas used to serve the Brahmanas. The Vaisya in a similar manner used in those days to worship the royal order, and the Sudra to worship the Vaisya. Even this is what is heard. The Brahmana was like a blazing fire. Without being able to touch him or approach his presence, the Sudra used to serve the Brahmana from a distance. It was only the Kshatriya and the Vaisya who could serve the Brahmana by touching his person or approaching his presence. The Brahmanas are endued with a mild disposition. They are truthful in behaviour. They are followers of the true religion. When angry, they are like snakes of virulent poison. Such being their nature, do thou, O Yudhishthira, serve and attend upon them with obedience and reverence. The Brahmanas are superior to even those that are higher than the high and the low. The energy and penances of even those Kshatriyas who blaze forth with energy and might, become powerless and neutralised when they come in contact with the Brahmanas. My sire himself is not dearer to me than the Brahmanas. My mother is not dearer to me than they. My grandsire, O king, is not dearer, my own self is not dearer, my life itself is not dearer, O king, to me than the Brahmanas! On earth there is nothing, O Yudhishthira, that is dearer to me than thou. But, O chief of Bharata's race, the Brahmanas are dearer to me than even thou. I tell thee truly, O son of Pandu! I swear by this truth, by which I hope to acquire all those regions of bliss that have been Santanu's. I behold those sacred regions with Brahma shining conspicuously before them. I shall repair thither, O son, and reside in them for unending days. Beholding these regions, O best of the Bharatas (with my spiritual eyes), I am filled with delight at the thought of all these acts which I have done in aid and honour of the Brahmanas, O monarch!"'"

SECTION LX.

"'Yudhishthira said, "Unto which of two Brahmanas, when both happen to be equally pure in behaviour, equally possessed of learning and purity, of birth and blood, but differing from each other in only this, viz., the one solicits and the other does not,—I ask, O grandsire, unto which of these two would a gift be more meritorious?"

"'Bhishma said, "It has been said. O son of Pritha, that a gift made unto an unsoliciting person is productive of greater merit than one made to a person who solicits. One possessed of contentment is certainly more deserving than that person who is destitute of that virtue and is, therefore, helpless amidst the storms and buffets of the world. The firmness of a Kshatriya consists in the protection he gives to others. The firmness of a Brahmana consists in his refusal to solicit. The Brahmana possessed of steadiness and learning and contentment gladdens the deities. The wise have said that an act of solicitation on the part of a poor man is a great reproach. Those persons that solicit others are said to annoy the world like thieves and robbers.[323] The person who solicits is said to meet with death. The giver, however, is said not to meet with death. The giver is said to grant life unto him who solicits. By an act of gift, O Yudhishthira, the giver is said to rescue his own self also. Compassion is a very high virtue. Let people make gift from compassion unto those that solicit. Those, however, that do not beg, but are plunged into poverty and distress should be respectfully invited to receive assistance. If such Brahmanas, who must be regarded as the foremost of their order, live in thy kingdom, thou shouldst regard them as fire covered with ashes. Blazing with penances, they are capable of consuming the whole earth. Such persons, O son of Kuru's race, though not generally worshipped, should still be regarded as deserving of worship in every way. Endued with knowledge and spiritual vision and penances and Yoga, such persons always deserve our worship. O scorcher of foes, do thou always offer worship unto such Brahmanas. One should repair of one's own accord unto those foremost of Brahmanas that do not solicit anybody and make unto them gifts of diverse kinds of wealth in abundance. The merit that flows from properly pouring libations into the sacred fire every morning and evening is won by the person who makes gifts unto a Brahmana endued with learning, with the Vedas and with high and excellent vows. Thou shouldst, O son of Kunti, invite those foremost of Brahmanas who are cleansed by learning and the Vedas and vows, who live in independence, whose Vedic studies and penances are hidden without being proclaimed from the house-top, and who are observant of excellent vows, and honour them with gifts of well-constructed and delightful houses equipped with servitors and robes and furniture, and with all other articles of pleasure and enjoyment. Conversant with all duties and possessed of minute vision, those foremost of Brahmanas, O Yudhishthira, may accept the gifts offered to them with devotion and respect, thinking that they should not refuse and disappoint the giver. Thou shouldst invite those Brahmanas whose wives wait for their return like tillers in expectation of rain. Having fed them well thou shouldst make gifts of additional food unto them so that upon their return home their expectant wives might be able to distribute that food among their children that had clamoured for food but that had been pacified with promises Brahmacharins of restrained senses, O son, by eating at one's house in the forenoon, cause the three sacrificial fires to be gratified with the householder at whose house they eat. Let the sacrifice of gift proceed in thy house at midday, O son, and do thou also give away kine and gold and robes (unto thy guests after feeding them well). By conducting thyself, in this way, thou art sure to gratify the chief of the celestials himself. That would constitute thy third sacrifice, O Yudhishthira, in which offerings are made unto the deities, the Pitris, and the Brahmanas. By such sacrifice thou art sure to gratify the Viswedevas. Let compassion unto all creatures, giving unto all creatures what is due unto them, restraining the senses, renunciation, steadiness, and truth, constitute the final bath of that sacrifice which is constituted by gift. Even this is the sacrifice that is spread out for thee,—a sacrifice that is sanctified by devotion and faith, and that has a large

---

[323] Yachyam is yachanarupamkarma, Anisasya is daridrasya. Abhiharam is tirashkaram. Yachanti bhutani means those who beg or solicit. In the Santi Parva, Bhishma in one place directs beggars to be driven away from towns and cities as annoyers of respectable people. This, however, applies to professional beggars, and not persons in real distress.

Dakshina attached to it. This sacrifice which is constituted by gift is distinguished above all other sacrifices. O son, let this sacrifice be always performed by thee."'"

SECTION LXI.

"'Yudhishthira said, "I wish to know in detail, O Bharata, where one meets with the high rewards of gifts and sacrifices. Are those rewards earned here or are they to come hereafter? Which amongst these two (viz., Gift and Sacrifice) is said to be productive of superior merit? Unto whom should gifts be made? In what manner are gifts and sacrifices to be made? When also are they to be made? I ask thee all these, O learned sire! Do thou discourse to me on the duty of gifts! Do tell me, O grandsire, what leads to the highest reward, viz., gifts made from the sacrificial platform or those made out of that place?"[324]

"'Bhishma said, "O son, a Kshatriya is generally employed in deeds of fierceness. In his case, sacrifices and gifts are regarded as cleansing or sanctifying him. They, that are good and righteous, do not accept the gifts of persons of the royal order, who are given to sinful acts. For this reason, the king should perform sacrifices with abundant gifts in the form of Dakshina.[325] If the good and righteous would accept the gifts made unto them, the Kshatriya, O monarch, should incessantly make gifts with devotion and faith unto them. Gifts are productive of great merit, and are highly cleansing. Observant of vows, one should perform sacrifices and gratify with wealth such Brahmanas as are friends of all creatures, possessed of righteousness, conversant with the Vedas, and preeminent for acts, conduct, and penances. If such Brahmanas do not accept thy gifts, no merit becomes thine. Do thou perform sacrifices with copious Dakshina, and make gifts of good and agreeable food unto those that are righteous. By making an act of gift thou shouldst regard thyself as performing a sacrifice. Thou shouldst with gifts adore those Brahmanas who perform sacrifices. By doing this thou will acquire a share in the merits of those sacrifices of theirs. Thou shouldst support such Brahmanas as are possessed of children and as are capable of sending people to Heaven. By conducting thyself in this way thou art sure to get a large progeny—in fact as large a progeny as the Prajapati himself. They that are righteous support and advance the cause of all righteous acts. One should, by giving up one's all, support such men, as also those that do good unto all creatures. Thyself being in the enjoyment of affluence, do thou, O Yudhishthira, make unto Brahmanas gifts of kine and bullocks and food and umbrellas, and robes and sandals or shoes. Do thou give unto sacrificing Brahmanas clarified butter, as also food and cars and vehicles with horses harnessed thereto, and dwelling houses and mansions and beds. Such gifts are fraught with prosperity and affluence to the giver, and are regarded as pure, O Bharata. Those Brahmanas that are not censurable for anything they do, and that have no means of support assigned to them, should be searched out. Covertly or publicly do thou cherish such Brahmanas by assigning them the means of support. Such conduct always confers higher benefit upon Kshatriyas than the Rajasuya and the Horse-sacrifices. Cleansing thyself of sin, thou art sure of attaining to Heaven. Filling thy treasury thou shouldst do good to thy kingdom. By such conduct thou art sure to win much wealth and become a Brahmana (in thy next life). Do thou, O Bharata, protect thy own means (of support and of doing acts of righteousness), as also the means of other people's subsistence. Do thou support thy servants as thy own children. Do thou, O Bharata,

---

[324] Antarvedyan is within the platform; and Anrisamsyatah is vahirvedyan or outside the platform.
[325] Sacrifices are a means of giving away unto the Brahmanas.

protect the Brahmanas in the enjoyment of what they have and make gifts unto them of such articles as they have not. Let thy life be devoted to the purpose of the Brahmanas. Let it never be said that thou dost not grant protection to the Brahmanas. Much wealth or affluence, when possessed by a Brahmana, becomes a source of evil to him. Constant association with affluence and prosperity is certain to fill him with pride and cause him to be stupefied (in respect of his true duties). If the Brahmanas become stupefied and steeped in folly, righteousness and duties are sure to suffer destruction. Without doubt, if righteousness and duty come to an end, it will lead to the destruction of all creatures. That king who having amassed wealth makes it over (for safe keep) to his treasury officers and guards, and then commences again to plunder his kingdom, saying unto his officers, 'Do ye bring me as much wealth as you can extort from the kingdom,' and who spends the wealth that is thus collected at his command under circumstances of fear and cruelty, in the performance of sacrifices, should know that those sacrifices of his are never applauded by the righteous. The king should perform sacrifices with such wealth as is willingly paid into his treasury by prosperous and unpersecuted subjects. Sacrifices should never be performed with wealth acquired by severity and extortion. The king should then perform great sacrifices with large presents in the shape of Dakshina, when in consequence of his being devoted to the good of his subjects, the latter bathe him with copious showers of wealth brought willingly by them for the purpose. The king should protect the wealth of those that are old, of those that are minors, of those that are blind, and of those that are otherwise disqualified. The king should never take any wealth from his people, if they, in a season of drought, succeed in growing any corn with the aid of water obtained from wells. Nor should he take any wealth from weeping women.[326] The wealth taken from the poor and the helpless is sure to destroy the kingdom and the prosperity of the king. The king should always make unto the righteous gifts of all enjoyable articles in abundance. He should certainly dispel the fear of famishing which those men may have.[327] There are no men more sinful than those upon whose food children look with wistfulness without being able to eat them duly. If within thy kingdom any learned Brahmana languishes with hunger like any of those children, thou shalt then incur the sin of foeticide for having allowed such an act. King Sivi himself had said this, viz., 'Fie on that king in whose kingdom a Brahmana or even any other man languishes from hunger.' That kingdom in which a Brahmana of the Snataka class languishes with hunger becomes overwhelmed with adversity. Such a kingdom with its king also incurs reproach. That king is more dead than alive in whose kingdom women are easily abducted from the midst of husbands and sons, uttering cries and groans of indignation and grief The subjects should arm themselves to slay that King who does not protect them, who simply plunders their wealth, who confounds all distinctions, who is ever incapable of taking their lead, who is without compassion, and who is regarded as the most sinful of kings. That king who tells his people that he is their protector but who does not or is unable to protect them, should be slain by his combined subjects, like a dog that is affected with the rabies and has become mad. A fourth part of whatever sins are committed by the subjects clings to that king who does not protect, O Bharata. Some authorities say that the whole of those sins is taken by such a king. Others are of opinion that a half thereof becomes his. Bearing in mind, however, the declaration of Manu, it is our opinion that a fourth part of such sins becomes the unprotecting king's. That king, O

---

[326] Weeping women means women of destitute condition and, therefore, unable to pay.
[327] The first word in the first line is not kshatam but kritam.

Bharata, who grants protection to his subjects obtains a fourth part of whatever merits his subjects acquire living under his protection. Do thou, O Yudhishthira, act in such a way that all thy subjects may seek thee as their refuge as long as thou art alive, even as all creatures seek the refuge of the deity of rain or even as the winged denizens of the air seek the refuge of a large tree. Let all thy kinsmen and all thy friends and well-wishers, O scorcher of foes, seek thee as their refuge even as the Rakshasas seek Kuvera or the deities seek Indra as theirs."'"

SECTION LXII.

"'Yudhishthira said, "People accept with affection the declarations of the Srutis which say, 'This is to be given.' 'This other thing is to be given!' As regards kings, again, they make gifts of various things unto various men. What, however, O grandsire, is the best or foremost of all gifts."

"'Bhishma said, "Of all kinds of gifts, the gift of earth has been said to be the first (in point of merit). Earth is immovable and indestructible. It is capable of yielding unto him who owns it all the best things upon which his heart may be set. It yields robes and vestments, jewels and gems, animals, paddy and barley. Amongst all creatures, the giver of earth grows in prosperity for ever and ever. As long as the earth lasts, so long does the giver thereof grow in prosperity. There is no gift that is higher, O Yudhishthira, than the gift of earth. It hath been heard by us that all men have given a little quantity of earth. All men have made gifts of earth, hence all men enjoy a little of earth. Whether in this or in the next world all creatures live under conditions dependent upon their own acts. Earth is Prosperity's self. She is a mighty goddess. She makes him her lord (in next life) who makes gifts of her in this life to other people. That person, O best of kings, who gives away earth, which is indestructible, as Dakshina, becomes born in next life as a man and becomes also a lord of earth. The measure of one's enjoyment in this life is commensurate with the measure of one's gifts in a previous life. Even this is the conclusion to which the scriptures point. For a Kshatriya should either give away the earth in gift or cast off his life in battle. Even this constitutes the highest source of prosperity with regard to Kshatriyas. It has been heard by us that earth, when given away, cleanses and sanctifies the giver. The man that is of sinful behaviour, that is guilty of even the slaughter of a Brahmana and of falsehood, is cleansed by a gift of earth. Indeed, such a gift rescues even such a sinner from all his sins. The righteous accept gifts of earth only and no other thing from kings that are sinful. Like one's mother, earth, when given away, cleanses the giver and the taker. This is an eternal and secret name of earth, viz., Priyadatta.[328] Given away or accepted in gift, the name that is dear to her is Priyadatta. The gift of earth is desirable. That king who makes a gift of earth unto a learned Brahmana, obtains from that gift a kingdom. Upon re-birth in this world, such a man without doubt attains to a position that is equal to that of a king. Hence a king as soon as he gets earth, should make gifts of earth unto the Brahmanas. None but a lord of earth is competent to make gifts of earth. Nor should one that is not a deserving person accept a gift of earth. They who desire earth should, without doubt, conduct themselves in this way (i.e., make gifts of earth). That person who takes away earth belonging to a righteous person never gets any earth. By making gifts of earth unto the righteous, one gets good

---

[328] The Commentator explains that because giver by one that is dear or given to one that is dear, therefore is she called Priyadatta.

earth. Of virtuous soul, such a giver acquires great fame both here and hereafter. That righteous king respecting whom the Brahmanas say, 'We live on earth given to us by him,' is such that his very enemies cannot utter the least reproach respecting his kingdom.[329] Whatever sins a man commits from want of the means of support, are all washed off by gift of only so much earth as is covered by a cow-hide. Those kings that are mean in their acts or are of fierce deeds, should be taught that gift of earth is exceedingly cleansing and is at the same time the highest gift (in respect of merit). The ancients thought that there was always very little difference between the man who performs a Horse-sacrifice and him that makes a gift of earth unto one that is righteous. The learned doubt the acquisition of merit by doing all other acts of righteousness. The only act with respect to which they do not entertain doubt is the gift of earth which, indeed, is the foremost of all gifts. The man of wisdom who makes gifts of earth, gives away all these, viz., gold, silver, cloth, gems and pearls and precious stones. Penances, sacrifice, Vedic lore, good behaviour, absence of cupidity, firmness in truth, worship of seniors, preceptors, and the deities—all these dwell in him who makes a gift of earth. They who ascend to the region of Brahman by leaving off their lives in battle, after having fought without any regard for themselves to secure the benefit to their masters— even they are unable to transcend the merit of those that make gifts of earth. As the mother always nourishes her own child with milk from her breast, even so doth the earth gratify with all the tastes the person that makes a gift of earth. Mrityu, Vaikinkara, Danda, Yama, Fire who is possessed of great fierceness, and all heinous and terrible sins are incapable of touching the person that makes a gift of earth. That man of tranquil soul who makes a gift of earth gratifies (by that act) the Pitris dwelling in their own region and the deities also hailing from the region that is theirs. The man who makes a gift of earth unto one that is emaciated and cheerless and destitute of the means of life and languishing with weakness, and who thereby supplies one with the means of subsistence, becomes entitled to the honour and merit of performing a sacrifice. Even as an affectionate cow runs towards her calf, with full udders dropping milk, the highly-blessed earth after the same manner, runs towards the person who makes a gift of earth. That man who makes unto a Brahmana a gift of earth which has been tilled, or sown with seeds or which contains standing crops, or a mansion well-equipped with every necessary, succeeds in becoming (in next life) the accomplisher of the wishes of everybody. The man who causes a Brahmana possessed of the means of life, owning a domestic fire and of pure vows and practices, to accept a gift of earth, never falls into any danger or distress. As the moon waxes day by day, even so the merit of a gift of earth becomes enhanced every time such earth produces crops. Those conversant with ancient history sing this verse in connection with the gift of earth. Hearing that verse Jamadagni's son (Rama) gave away the whole earth unto Kasyapa. The verse to which I refer is this, 'Receive me in gift. Give me away. By giving me away, thou (O giver) shall obtain me again!' That which is given away in this life is re-acquired in the next.[330] That Brahmana who recites this high declaration of the Vedas at the time of a Sraddha attains to the highest reward. A gift of earth is a high expiation for the sin of those puissant men who betake themselves to Atharvan rites for doing injuries to others. Indeed, by making a gift of earth one rescues ten generations of one's paternal and maternal race. That person who is even conversant with this Vedic declaration respecting the merits of a gift of earth,

---

[329] This is evidently a crux. Prasamsanti means generally praise. Here it means reproach or censure. The second line may also mean, his enemies dare not attack his kingdom.

[330] This is the utterance or declaration of the earth herself.

succeeds in rescuing ten generations of both his paternal and maternal families. The earth is the original source of all creatures (for it is from earth that all creatures derive their sustenance). It has been said that the deity of fire is the presiding genius of the earth. After the coronation ceremony has been performed of a king, this Vedic declaration should be re-cited to him, so that he may make gifts of earth and may never take away earth from a righteous person. Without doubt, the entire wealth owned by the king belongs to the Brahmanas. A king well-conversant with the science of duty and morality is the first requisite of the kingdom's prosperity. Those people whose king is unrighteous and atheistic in conduct and belief can never be happy. Such people can never sleep or wake in peace. In consequence of his acts of wickedness his subjects become always filled with anxiety. Protection of what the subjects already have and new acquisitions according to lawful means are incidents that are not noticeable in the kingdom of such a ruler. Those people, again, who have a wise and righteous king, sleep happily and wake up in happiness. Through the blessed and righteous acts of such a king, his subjects become freed from anxiety. The subjects, restrained from wicked acts, grow in prosperity through their own conduct. Capable of retaining what they have, they go on making new acquisitions. That king who makes gifts of earth is regarded as well-born. He is regarded as a man. He is a friend. He is righteous in his acts. He is a giver. He is regarded as possessing prowess. Those men who make gifts of ample and fertile earth unto Brahmanas conversant with the Vedas, always shine in the world, in consequence of their energy, like so many suns. As seeds scattered on the soil grow and return a goodly crop, even so all one's wishes become crowned with fruition in consequence of one's making gifts of earth. Aditya and Varuna and Vishnu and Brahman and Soma and Hutasana, and the illustrious and trident-bearing Mahadeva, all applaud the man that makes a gift of earth. Living creatures spring into life from the earth and it is into the earth that they become merged when they disappear. Living creatures which are distributed into four classes (i.e., viviparous, oviparous, filthborn, and vegetables) have earth for their constituent essence. The earth is both the mother and father of the universe of creatures, O monarch. There is no element, O ruler of men, that can compare with earth. In this connection is cited the old narrative of a discourse between the celestial preceptor Vrihaspati and Indra the ruler of Heaven, O Yudhishthira. Having adored Vishnu in a hundred sacrifices each of which was distinguished by plentiful gifts as Dakshina, Maghavat put this question to Vrihaspati, that foremost of all eloquent persons.

""Maghavat said, 'O illustrious one, by what gift does one succeed in coming to Heaven and attaining to beatitude? O foremost of speakers, do thou tell me of that gift which is productive of high and inexhaustible merit.'"

"Bhishma continued, "Thus addressed by the chief of the celestials the preceptor of the deities, viz., Vrihaspati of great energy, said these words in reply unto him of a hundred sacrifices. 'Endued as he is with the merits that attach to the gift of earth, the region of felicity reserved for the person who makes gift of such earth as is auspicious and rich with every taste, never become exhausted.[331] That king, O Sakra, who desires to have prosperity and who wishes to win happiness for himself, should always make gifts of earth, with due rites, unto deserving persons. If after committing numerous sins a person makes gifts of earth unto members of the regenerate class, he casts off all those sins like a snake casting off its slough. The person that makes a gift of earth is said to

---

[331] Rich with every taste; the idea is that things have six tastes, viz., sweet, sour, etc. The quality of taste is drawn by things from the soil or earth. The tastes inhere in earth, for it is the same earth that produces the sugarcane and the tamarind.

make gifts of everything, that is, of seas and rivers and mountains and forests. By making a gift of earth, the person is said to give away lakes and tanks and wells and streams. In consequence of the moisture of earth, one is said to give away articles of diverse tastes by making a gift of earth. The man who makes a gift of earth is regarded as giving away herbs and plants possessed of high and efficacious virtues, trees adorned with flowers and fruit, delightful woods, and hillocks. The merit that a person acquires by making a gift of earth is incapable of being acquired by the performance of even such great sacrifices as the Agnishtoma and others with plentiful gifts in the shape of Dakshina. The giver of earth, it has been already said, rescues ten generations of both his paternal and maternal races. Similarly, by taking away earth that was given away, one hurls oneself into hell and casts ten generations of both one's paternal and maternal lines into the same place of misery. That man who having promised to make a gift of earth does not actually make it, or who having made a gift takes it back, has to pass a long time, in great misery in consequence of being tied with the noose of Varuna at the command of Death. Those men have never to go to Yama who honour and worship those foremost of Brahmanas that pour libations every day on their domestic fire, that are always engaged in the performance of sacrifices, that have scanty means of livelihood, and that receive with hospitality every guest seeking shelter in their abodes. The king, O Purandara, should free himself from the debt he owes to the Brahmanas and protect the helpless and the weak belonging to the other orders. The king should never resume, O chief of the deities, earth that has been given away by another unto a Brahmana, O ruler of the celestials, that is destitute of the means of life.[332] The tears that would fall from the eyes of such cheerless and destitute Brahmanas in consequence of their lands being taken back are capable of destroying the ancestors and descendants to the third generation of the resumer. That man who succeeds by his endeavours in re-establishing a king driven away from his kingdom, obtains residence in heaven and is much honoured by the denizens thereof. That king who succeeds in making gifts of earth with such crops standing thereon as sugar-cane or barley or wheat, or with kine and horses and other draft cattle,—earth that has been won with the might of the giver's arms,—that has mineral wealth in its bowels and that is covered with every kind of wealth of the surface, wins inexhaustible regions of felicity in the next world, and such a king it is that is said to perform the earth-sacrifice. That king who makes a gift of earth becomes washed of every sin and is, therefore, pure and approved of the righteous. In this world he is highly honoured and applauded by all righteous men. The merit that attaches to a gift of earth increases every time the earth given away bears crops for the benefit of the owner, even as a drop of oil, falling upon water, is seen to extend on every side, and cover the watery surface. Those heroic kings and ornaments of assemblies who cast off their lives in battle with faces towards the foe, attain, O Sakra, to the region of Brahman. Beautiful damsels skilled in music and dancing and adorned with garlands of celestial flowers, approach, O chief of the deities, the giver of earth as he comes to heaven departing from the earth. That king who makes gifts of earth with due rites unto persons of the regenerate order, sports in bliss in the celestial regions, adorned all the while by the deities and Gandharvas. A century of Apsaras, adorned with celestial garlands, approach, O chief of the deities, the giver of earth as he ascends to the region of Brahman. Flowers of excellent perfumes, an excellent conch and excellent seat, an umbrella and excellent steeds with excellent vehicles, are always ready for the person how makes gifts of earth. By making gifts of earth a king can always

---

[332] Sparsitam is dattam.

command flowers of excellent perfumes and heaps of gold. Possessed of all kinds of wealth the commands of such a king can never be disobeyed anywhere, and cries of victory hail him wheresoever he may approach. The rewards that attach to gifts of earth consist of residence in heaven, O Purandara, and gold, and flowers, and plants and herbs of medicinal virtue, and Kusa and mineral wealth and verdant grass. A person by making a gift of earth acquires in his next life nectar yielding earth. There is no gift that is equal to a gift of earth. There is no senior worthy of greater respect than the mother. There is no duty higher than truth. There is no wealth more precious than that which is given away.'"

"'Bhishma continued, "Hearing these words from the son of Angiras, Vasava made a gift unto him of the whole earth with all her jewels and gems and all her wealth of diverse kinds. If these verses declaring the merit attaching to gifts of earth be recited on the occasion of a Sraddha, neither Rakshasas nor Asuras can succeed in appropriating any share of the offerings made in it. Without doubt, the offerings one makes unto the Pitris at such a Sraddha become inexhaustible. Hence, on occasions of Sraddhas, the man of learning should recite these verses on the subject of the merits that attach to gifts of earth, in the presence and hearing of the invited Brahmanas when engaged in eating. I have thus, O chief of the Bharatas, discoursed unto thee of that gift which is the foremost of all gifts. What else dost thou wish to hear?"'"

SECTION LXIII.

"'Yudhishthira said, "When a king becomes desirous of making gifts in this world, what, indeed, are those gifts which he should make, O best of the Bharatas, unto such Brahmanas as are possessed of superior accomplishments? What gift is that by which the Brahmanas become immediately gratified? What fruits do they bestow in return? O thou of mighty arms, tell me what is the high reward attainable through the merit arising from gifts. What gifts, O king, are productive of rewards both here and hereafter? I desire to hear all this from thee. Do thou discourse to me on all this in detail."

"'Bhishma said, "These very questions were on a former occasion put by me to Narada of celestial appearance. Hear me as I recite to thee what that celestial sage told me in reply.

"'"Narada said, 'The deities and all the Rishis applaud food. The course of the world and the intellectual faculties have all been established on food. There has never been, nor will be any gift that is equal to the gifts of food. Hence, men always desire particularly to make gifts of food. In this world, food is the cause of energy and strength. The life-breaths are established on food. It is food that upholds the wide universe, O puissant one. All classes of men, householders and mendicants and ascetics, exist, depending upon food. The life-breaths depend upon food. There is no doubt in this. Afflicting (if need be) one's relatives, one that is desirous of one's own prosperity, should make gifts of food unto a high-souled Brahmana or a person of the mendicant order. That man who makes a gift of food unto an accomplished Brahmana who solicits the same, secures for himself in the world to come wealth of great value. The householder who is desirous of his own prosperity should receive with reverence a deserving old man that is spent with toil while proceeding on his way far from home, when such a man honours the householder's abode with his presence. That man who, casting off wrath that overleaps every bound and becoming righteous in disposition and freed from malice, makes gifts of food, is sure to attain to happiness, O king, both here and hereafter. The householder should never disregard the man that comes to his abode, nor should he insult him by sending him away. A gift of food made unto even a Chandala or a dog is never lost. That man who makes a gift of clean food unto a person on the way who is toil-worn and unknown to the giver, is sure to acquire great merit. The man who gratifies with gifts of food the Pitris, the deities, the Rishis, the Brahmanas, and guests arrived at his abode, acquires merit whose measure is very large. That person who having committed even a heinous sin makes a gift of food unto one that solicits, or unto a Brahmana, is never stupefied by that heinous sin. A gift of food made unto a Brahmana becomes inexhaustible. One made to a Sudra becomes productive of great merit. Even this is the difference between the merits that attach to gifts of food made unto Brahmanas and Sudras. Solicited by a Brahmana, one should not enquire about his race or conduct or Vedic lore. Asked for food, one should give food to him that asks. There is no doubt in this, O king, that he who makes gifts of food obtains both here and hereafter many trees yielding food and every other object of desire. Like tillers expecting auspicious showers of rain, the Pitris always expect that their sons and grandsons would make offerings unto them of food (in Sraddhas). The Brahmana is a great being. When he comes into one's abode and solicits, saying, "Give me," the owner of the abode, whether influenced or not by the desire of acquiring merit, is sure to win great merit by listening to that solicitation. The Brahmana is the guest of all creatures in the universe. He is entitled to the first portion of every food. That house increases in prosperity to which the Brahmanas repair from desire of soliciting alms and from which they return honoured in consequence of their desires being fulfilled. The owner of such a house takes birth in his next life in a family, O Bharata, that can command all the comforts and luxuries of life. A man, by making gifts of food in this world, is sure to attain to an excellent place hereafter. He who makes gifts of sweetmeat and all food that is sweet, attains to a residence in heaven where he is honoured by all the deities and other denizens. Food constitutes the life-breath of men. Everything is established upon food. He who makes gifts of food obtains many animals (as his wealth), many children, considerable wealth (in other shape), and a command in abundance of all articles of comfort and luxurious enjoyment. The giver of food is said to be the giver of life. Indeed, he is said to be the giver of everything. Hence, O king, such a man acquires both strength and beauty of form in this world. If food be given duly unto a Brahmana arrived at the giver's house as a guest, the giver attains to great happiness, and is adored by the very deities. The Brahmana, O Yudhishthira, is a great being. He is also a fertile field. Whatever seed is sown on that field produces an abundant crop of merit. A gift of food is visibly and immediately productive of the happiness of both the giver and the receiver. All other gifts produce fruits that are unseen. Food is the origin of all creatures. From food, comes happiness and delight. O Bharata, know that religion and wealth both flow from food. The cure of disease or health also flows from food. In a former Kalpa, the Lord of all creatures said that food is Amrita or the source of immortality. Food is Earth, food is Heaven, food is the Firmament. Everything is established on food. In the absence of food, the five elements that constitute the physical organism cease to exist in a state of union. From absence of food the strength of even the strongest man is seen to fail. Invitations and marriages and sacrifices all cease in the absence of food. The very Vedas disappear when food there is none. Whatever mobile and immobile creatures exist in the universe are dependent on food. Religion and wealth, in the three worlds, are all dependent on food. Hence the wise should make gifts of food. The strength, energy, fame and achievements of the man who makes gifts of food, constantly increase in the three worlds, O king. The lord of the life-breaths, viz., the deity of wind, places above the clouds (the water sucked up by the Sun). The water thus borne to the clouds is caused by Sakra to be poured upon the earth, O Bharata. The Sun, by means of his rays, sucks up the moisture of the earth. The deity of wind causes the moisture to fall down from the Sun.[333] When the water falls down from the clouds upon the Earth, the goddess Earth becomes moist, O Bharata. Then do people sow diverse kinds of crops upon whose outturn the universe of creatures depends. It is in the food thus produced that the flesh, fat, bones and vital seed of all beings have their origin. From the vital seed thus originated, O king, spring diverse kinds of living creatures. Agni and Soma, the two agents living within the body, create and maintain the vital seed. Thus from food, the Sun and the deity of wind and the vital seed spring and act. All these are said to constitute one element or quantity, and it is from these that all creatures spring. That man who gives food unto one who comes into his house and solicits it, is said, O chief of the Bharatas, to contribute both life and energy unto living creatures.'"

"'Bhishma continued, "Thus addressed by Narada, O king, I have always made gifts of food. Do thou also, therefore, freed from malice and with a cheerful heart, make gifts of food. By making gifts of food, O king, unto deserving Brahmanas with due rites, thou mayst be sure, O puissant one, of attaining to Heaven. Hear me, O monarch, as I tell thee what the regions are that are reserved for those that make gifts of food. The mansions of those high-souled persons shine with resplendence in the regions of Heaven. Bright as the stars in the firmament, and supported upon many columns, white as the disc of the moon, and adorned with many tinkling bells, and rosy like the newly-risen sun, those palatial abodes are either fixed or movable. Those mansions are filled with hundreds upon hundreds of things and animals that live on land and as many things and animals living in water. Some of them are endued with the effulgence of lapis lazuli and some are possessed of the resplendence of the sun. Some of them are made of silver and some of gold. Within those mansions are many trees capable of crowning with fruition every desire of the inmates. Many tanks and roads and halls and wells and lakes occur all around. Thousands of conveyances with horses and other animals harnessed thereto and with wheels whose clatter is always loud, may be seen there. Mountains of food and all enjoyable articles and heaps of cloths and ornaments are also to be seen there. Numerous rivers that run milk, and hills of rice and other edibles, may also be seen there. Indeed, many palatial residences looking like white clouds, with many beds of golden splendour, occur in those regions, All these are obtained by those men that make gifts of food in this world. Do thou, therefore, become a giver of food. Verily, these are the regions that are reserved for those high-souled and righteous persons that make gifts of food in this world. For these reasons, men should always make gifts of food in this world."'"

SECTION LXIV.

"'Yudhishthira said, "I have heard the discourse regarding the ordinance about the gift of food. Do thou discourse to me now about the conjunction of the planets and the stars in relation to the subject of making gifts."[334]

"'Bhishma said, "In this connection is recited this ancient narrative of the discourse between Devaki and Narada, that foremost of Rishis. Once on a time when Narada of godlike feature and conversant with every duty arrived at Dwaraka, Devaki asked him this question. Unto her that had asked him, the celestial Rishi Narada duly answered in

---

[333] The Bombay reading adityatastansha is better than the Bengal reading adityataptansha.
[334] What Yudhishthira wishes to know is what conjunctions should be utilized for making what particular gifts.

the following words. Do thou hear as I recite them.

""''Narada said, 'By gratifying, O blessed lady, deserving Brahmanas with Payasa mixed with ghee, under the constellation Krittika one attains to regions of great happiness.[335] Under the constellation Rohini, one should for freeing oneself from the debt one owes to the Brahmanas make gift unto them of many handfuls of venison along with rice and ghee and milk, and other kinds of edibles and drinks. One giving away a cow with a calf under the constellation called Somadaivata (or Mrigasiras), proceeds from this region of human beings to a region in heaven of great felicity. One undergoing a fast and giving away Krisara mixed with sesame, transcends all difficulties in the next world, including those mountains with rocks sharp as razors. By making gifts, O beautiful lady, of cakes and other food under the constellation Punarvasu one becomes possessed of personal beauty and great fame and takes birth in one's next life in a family in which there is abundance of food. Making a gift of wrought or unwrought gold, under the constellation Pushya, one shines in effulgence like Soma himself in regions of surrounding gloom. He who makes a gift, under the constellation Aslesha, of silver or a bull, becomes freed from every fear and attains to great affluence and prosperity. By making a gift, under the constellation Magha, of earthen dishes filled with sesame, one becomes possessed of children and animals in this world and attains to felicity in the next.[336] For making gifts unto Brahmanas, under the constellation called Purva-Phalguni of food mixed with Phanita the giver observing a fast the while, reward is great prosperity both here and hereafter.[337] By making a gift, under the constellation called Uttara-Phalguni, of ghee and milk with rice called Shashthika, one attains to great honours in heaven. Whatever gifts are made by men under the constellation of Uttara-Phalguni produce great merit, which, again, becomes inexhaustible. This is very certain. Observing a fast the while, the person that makes, under the constellation Hasta, a gift of a car with four elephants, attains to regions of great felicity that are capable of granting the fruition of every wish. By making a gift, under the constellation Chitra, of a bull and of good perfumes, one sports in bliss in regions of Apsaras like the deities sporting in the woods of Nandana. By making gifts of wealth under the constellation Swati, one attains to such excellent regions as one desires and wins besides great fame. By making gifts, under constellation Visakha, of a bull, and a cow that yields a copious measure of milk, a cart full of paddy, with a Prasanga for covering the same, and also cloths for wear,[338] a person never meets with any calamity and certainly reaches heaven. By making gifts unto the Brahmanas of whatever articles they solicit, one attains to such means of subsistence as one desires, and becomes rescued from hell and every calamity that visits a sinner after death. This is the certain conclusion of the scriptures. By making gifts, under the constellation Anuradha of embroidered cloth and other vestments and of food, observing a fast the while, one becomes honoured in heaven for a hundred Yugas. By making a gift under the constellation Jyeshtha, of the potherb called Kalasaka with the roots, one attains to great prosperity as also to such an end as is desirable. By making unto Brahmanas a gift under the constellation Mula, of fruits and roots, with a restrained soul, one gratifies the Pitris and attains to a desirable end. By making under the constellation Purvashadha, a gift, unto a Brahmana conversant with the Vedas and of good family and conduct, of cups filled with curds, while one is in the observance of a fast, one takes birth

---

[335] Payasa is rice boiled in sugared milk. It is a sort of liquid food that is regarded as very agreeable.
[336] Vardhamana, Sarava or Saravika. It is a flat certain cup or dish.
[337] Phanita is the inspissated juice of the sugarcane.
[338] A prasanga is a basket of bamboo or other material for covering paddy.

in one's next life in a family possessed of abundant kine. One obtains the fruition of every wish, by making gifts, under the constellation Uttarashadha, of jugs full of barley-water, with ghee and inspissated juice of sugarcane in abundance. By making a gift under the conjunction called Abhijit, of milk with honey and ghee unto men of wisdom, a righteous person attains to heaven and becomes an object of attention and honour there. By making under the conjunction Sravana, a gift of blankets or other cloth of thick texture, one roves freely through every region of felicity, riding on a white car of pure resplendence. By making with a restrained soul, under the constellation Dhanishtha, a gift of a vehicle with bulls yoked thereto, or heaps of cloths and wealth, one at once attains to heaven in one's next life. By making gifts, under the constellation Satabhisha, of perfumes with Aquilaria Agallocha and sandalwood, one attains in the next world to the companionship of Apsaras as also eternal perfumes of diverse kinds. By making gifts, under the constellation Purva-Bhadrapada, or Rajamasha, one attains to great happiness in the next life and becomes possessed of an abundant stock of every kind of edibles and fruits.[339] One who makes, under the constellation Uttara, a gift of mutton, gratifies the Pitris by such an act attains to inexhaustible merit in the next world. Unto one who makes a gift, under the constellation Revati, of a cow with a vessel of white copper for milking her, the cow so given away approaches in the next world, ready to grant the fruition of every wish. By making a gift, under the constellation Aswini, of a car with steeds yoked thereto, one is born in one's next life in a family possessed of numerous elephants and steeds and cars, and becomes endued with great energy. By making, under the constellation Bharani, a gift unto the Brahmanas of kine and sesame, one acquires in one's next life great fame and an abundance of kine.'"

"'Bhishma continued, "Even thus did Narada discourse unto Devaki upon the subject of what gifts should be made under what constellations. Devaki herself, having listened to this discourse, recited it in her turn unto her daughters-in-law (viz., the spouses of Krishna).'"'"

SECTION LXV.

"'Bhishma said, "The illustrious Atri, the son of the Grandsire Brahman, said, 'They who make gifts of gold are said to make gifts of everything in the world.' King Harischandra said that the gift of gold is sin-cleansing, leads to long life, and becomes productive of inexhaustible merit unto the Pitris. Manu has said that a gift of drink is the best of all gifts: therefore should a man cause wells and tanks and lakes to be excavated. A well full of water and from which diverse creatures draw water, is said to take off half the sinful acts of the person who has excavated it. The whole race of a person is rescued from hell and sin in whose well or tank or lake kine and Brahmanas and righteous people constantly quench their thirst. That man transcends every kind of calamity from whose well or tank every one draws water without restraint during the summer season. Ghee is said to gratify the illustrious Vrihaspati, Pushan, Bhaga, the twin Aswins, and the deity of fire. Ghee is possessed of high medicinal virtues. It is a high requisite for sacrifice. It is the best of all liquids. The merit a gift of ghee produces is very superior. That man who is desirous of the reward of happiness in the next world, who wishes for fame and prosperity, should with a cleansed soul and having purified himself make gifts of ghee unto the Brahmanas. Upon that man who makes gifts of ghee unto the Brahmanas in the

---

[339] Rajamasha is a kind of bean. It is the Vinga sinensis, syn. Dilicheos sinensis Linn.

month of Aswin, the twin Aswins, gratified, confer personal beauty. Rakshasas never invade the abode of that man who makes gifts unto the Brahmanas of Payasa mixed with ghee. That man never dies of thirst who makes gifts unto the Brahmanas of jars filled with water. Such a person obtains every necessary of life in abundance, and has never to undergo any calamity or distress. That man, who with great devotion and restrained senses makes gifts unto the foremost of Brahmanas, is said to take a sixth part of the merits won by the Brahmanas by their penances. That man who makes presents unto Brahmanas having the means of life, of firewood for purposes of cooking as also of enabling them to drive away cold, finds all his purposes and all his acts crowned with success. Such a one is seen to shine with great splendour over all his enemies. The illustrious deity of fire becomes pleased with such a man. As another reward, he never becomes divested of cattle, and he is sure to achieve victory in battles. The man who makes a gift of an umbrella obtains children and great prosperity. Such a person is never affected by any eye-disease. The merits also that spring from the performance of a sacrifice become his. That man who makes a gift of an umbrella in the season of summer or rains, has never to meet with any heart-burning on any account. Such a man quickly succeeds in freeing himself from every difficulty and impediment. The highly blessed and illustrious Rishi Sandilya has said that, of all gifts, the gift of a car, O king, is the best.'"'

SECTION LXVI.

"'Yudhishthira said, "I desire to hear, O grandsire, what the merits are of that person who makes the gift of a pair of sandals unto a Brahmana whose feet are burning or being scorched by hot sand, while he is walking."

"'Bhishma said, "The man, that gives unto the Brahmanas sandals for the protection of their feet, succeeds in crushing all thorns and gets over every kind of difficulty. Such a man, O Yudhishthira, stays over the heads of all his foes. Vehicles of pure splendour, with mules harnessed thereto, and made of gold and silver, O monarch, approach him. He who makes a gift of sandals is said to earn the merit of making the gift of a vehicle with well-broken steeds yoked thereto."

"'Yudhishthira said, "Do thou tell me in detail once more, O grandsire, of the merits that attach to gifts of sesame and land and kine and food."

"'Bhishma said, "Do thou hear, O son of Kunti, what the merits are that attach to the gift of sesame. Hearing me, do thou, then, O best of the Kurus, make gifts of sesame according to the ordinance. Sesame seeds were created by the Self-born Brahman as the best food for the Pitris. Hence, gifts of sesame seeds always gladden the Pitris greatly. The man who makes gifts of sesame seeds, in the month of Magha, unto the Brahmanas, has never to visit hell which abounds with all frightful creatures. He who adores the Pitris with offerings of sesame seeds is regarded as worshipping the deities at all the sacrifices. One should never perform a Sraddha with offerings of sesame seeds without cherishing some purpose.[340] Sesame seeds sprang from the limbs of the great Rishi Kasyapa. Hence, in the matter of gifts, they have come to be regarded as possessed of high efficacy. Sesame seeds bestow both prosperity and personal beauty and cleans the giver of all his sins. It is for this reason that the gift of sesame seeds is distinguished above the gift of

---

[340] There may be akama and sakama acts, i.e., acts without desires of fruit and acts with desires of fruit. A Sraddha with Tila or sesame should never be done without desire for fruit.

every other article. Apastamva of great intelligence, and Kankha and Likhita, and the great Rishi Gautama have all ascended to heaven by having made gifts of sesame seeds. Those Brahmanas that make Homa with offerings of sesame, abstain from sexual intercourse, and are observant of the religion of Pravritti or acts, are regarded as equal (in purity and efficacy) to bovine Havi. The gift of sesame seeds is distinguished above all gifts. Amongst all gifts, the gifts of sesame is regarded as productive of inexhaustible merit. In ancient times when Havi (clarified butter) on one occasion had become unobtainable the Rishi Kusika, O scorcher of foes, made offerings of sesame seeds to his three sacrificial fires and succeeded in attaining to an excellent end. I have thus said unto thee, O chief of the Kurus, what the regulations are respecting the excellent gift of sesame seeds. It is in consequence of these regulations that the gift of sesame seeds has come to be regarded as endued with very superior merit. After this, listen to what I would say. Once on a time the deities, desirous of making a sacrifice, repaired, O monarch, to the presence of the Self-born Brahman. Having met Brahman, being desirous of performing a sacrifice on earth, they begged him for a piece of auspicious earth, saying, 'We want it for our sacrifice.'

""The deities said, 'O illustrious one, thou art the lord of all the earth as also of all the deities. With thy permission, O highly blessed one, we desire to perform a sacrifice. The person who has not obtained by lawful means the earth whereon to make the sacrificial altar, earns not the merit of the sacrifice he performs. Thou art the Lord of all the universe consisting of its mobile and immobile objects. Hence, it behoveth thee to grant us a piece of earth for the sacrifice we wish to make.'

""Brahman said, 'Ye foremost of deities, I shall give you a piece of earth whereon, ye sons of Kasyapa, you shall perform your intended sacrifice.'

""The deities said, 'Our wishes, O holy one, have been crowned with fruition. We shall perform our sacrifice even here with large Dakshina. Let, however, the Munis always adore the piece of earth.' Then there came to that place Agastya and Kanwa and Bhrigu and Atri and Vrishakapi, and Asita and Devala. The high-souled deities then, O thou of unfading glory, performed their sacrifice. Those foremost of gods concluded it in due time. Having completed that sacrifice of theirs on the breast of that foremost of mountains, Himavat, the deities attached to the gift of earth a sixth part of the merit arising from their sacrifice. The man who makes a gift of even a span of earth (unto a Brahmana) with reverence and faith, has never to languish under any difficulty and has never to meet with any calamity. By making a gift of a house that keeps out cold, wind, and sun, and that stand upon a piece of clean land, the giver attains to the region of the deities and does not fall down even when his merit becomes exhausted. By making a gift of a residential house, the giver, possessed of wisdom, lives, O king, in happiness in the company of Sakra. Such a person receives great honours in heaven. That person in whose house a Brahmana of restrained sense, well-versed in the Vedas, and belonging by birth to a family of preceptors, resides in contentment, succeeds in attaining to and enjoying a region of high felicity.[341] After the same manner, O best of the Bharatas, by giving away a shed for the shelter of kine that can keep out cold and rain and that is substantial in structure, the giver rescues seven generations of his race (from hell). By giving away a piece of arable earth the giver attains to excellent prosperity. By giving a piece of earth containing mineral wealth, the giver aggrandises his family and race. One should never

---

[341] When a residential house is given away unto such a Brahmana and the receiver resides in it, the giver reaps the reward indicated. It does not refer to the hospitable shelter to such a Brahmana given by one in one's own house.

give away any earth that is barren or that is burnt (arid); nor should one give away any earth that is in close vicinity to a crematorium, or that has been owned and enjoyed by a sinful person before such gift. When a man performs a Sraddha in honour of the Pitris on earth belonging to another person, the Pitris render both the gift of that earth and the Sraddha itself futile.[342] Hence, one possessed of wisdom should buy even a small piece of earth and make a gift of it. The Pinda that is offered to one's ancestors on earth that has been duly purchased becomes inexhaustible.[343] Forests, and mountains, and rivers, and Tirthas are regarded as having no owners. No earth need be purchased here for performing Sraddhas. Even this has been said, O king, on the subject of the merits of making gifts of earth. After this, O sinless one, I shall discourse to thee on the subject of the gift of kine. Kine are regarded as superior to all the ascetics. And since it is so, the divine Mahadeva for that reason performed penance in their company. Kine, O Bharata, dwell in the region of Brahman, in the company of Soma. Constituting as it does the highest end, regenerate Rishis crowned with success strive to attain to that very region. Kine benefit human beings with milk, ghee, curds, dung, skin, bones, horns, and hair, O Bharata. Kine do not feel cold or heat. They always work. The season of rains also cannot afflict them at all. And since kine attain to the highest end (viz., residence in the region of Brahman), in the company of Brahmanas, therefore do the wise say that king and Brahmanas are equal. In days of yore, king Rantideva performed a grand sacrifice in which an immense number of kine were offered up and slaughtered. From the juice that was secreted by the skins of the slaughtered animals, a river was formed that came to be called by the name of Charmanwati. Kine no longer form animals fit for sacrifice. They now constitute animals that are fit for gift. That king who makes gifts of kine unto the foremost of Brahmanas, O monarch, is sure to get over every calamity even if he falls into it. The man who makes a gift of a thousand kine has not to go to hell. Such a person, O ruler of men, obtains victory everywhere. The very chief of the deities had said that the milk of kine is nectar. For this reason, one who makes a gift of a cow is regarded as making a gift of nectar. Persons conversant with the Vedas have declared that the Ghee manufactured from cows' milk is the very best of all libations poured into the sacrificial fire. For this reason, the man who makes a gift of a cow is regarded as making a gift of a libation for sacrifice. A bovine bull is the embodiment of heaven. He who makes the gift of a bovine bull unto an accomplished Brahmana, receives great honours in heaven. Kine, O chief of Bharata's race, are said to be the life-breath of living creatures. Hence, the man who makes the gift of a cow is said to make the gift of life-breath. Persons conversant with the Vedas have said that kine constitute the great refuge of living creatures. Hence, the man who makes the gift of a cow is regarded as making the gift of what is the high refuge for all creatures. The cow should never be given away for slaughter (i.e., unto one who will kill her); nor should the cow be given unto a tiller of the soil; nor should the cow be given unto an atheist. The cow should not also, O chief of the Bharatas, be given unto one whose occupation is the keeping of kine.[344] The wise have said that a person who gives away the cow unto any of such sinful persons has to sink into everlasting hell.

---

[342] To this day, in Bengal at least, a tenant never performs the first Sraddha or a Puja (worship of the deities) without obtaining in the first instance the permission of the landlord. There is in Sraddhas a Rajavarana or royal fee payable to the owner of the earth on which the Sraddha is performed.

[343] Tasyam is explained by the commentator as kritayam.

[344] Kinasa is either one who tills the soil with the aid of bulls or one who slays cattle. Having first mentioned vadhartham, kinasa should here be taken for a tiller. Kasai, meaning butcher, seems to be a corruption of the word kinasa.

One should never give unto a Brahmana a cow that is lean, or that produces calves that do not live, or that is barren, or that is diseased, or that is defective of limb, or that is worn out with toil. The man that gives away ten thousand kine attains to heaven and sports in bliss in the companionship of Indra. The man who makes gifts of kine by hundred thousand acquires many regions of inexhaustible felicity. Thus have I recited to thee the merits attaching to the gift of kine and of sesame, as also to the gift of earth. Listen now to me as I discourse to thee upon the gift of food, O Bharata. The gift of food, O son of Kunti, is regarded as a very superior gift. King Rantideva in days of yore ascended to heaven by having made gifts of food. That king, who make a gift of food unto one that is toil-worn and hungry, attains to that region of supreme felicity which is the Self-born's own. Men fail to attain by gifts of gold and robes and of other thing, to that felicity to which givers of food succeed in attaining, O thou of great puissance! Food is, indeed, the first article. Food is regarded as the highest prosperity. It is from food that life springs, as also energy and prowess and strength. He who always makes gifts of food, with attention, unto the righteous, never falls into any distress. Even this has been said by Parasara. Having worshipped the deities duly, food should be first dedicated to them. It has been said, O king, that the kind of food that is taken by particular men is taken also by the deities those men worship.[345] That man who makes a gift of food in the bright fortnight of the month of Kartika, succeeds in crossing every difficulty here and attains to inexhaustible felicity hereafter. That man who makes a gift of food unto a hungry guest arrived at his abode, attains to all those regions, O chief of Bharata's race, that are reserved for persons acquainted with Brahma. The man who makes gifts of food is sure to cross every difficulty and distress. Such a person comes over every sin and cleanses himself of every evil act. I have thus discoursed to thee upon the merits of making gifts of food, of sesame, of earth, and of kine.""

SECTION LXVII.

"'Yudhishthira said, "I have heard, O sire, of the merits of the different kinds of gift upon which thou hast discoursed to me. I understand, O Bharata, that the gift of food is especially laudable and superior. What however, are the great merits of making gifts of drink. I desire to hear of this in detail, O grandsire!"

"'Bhishma said, "I shall, O chief of Bharata's race, discourse to thee upon this subject. Listen to me, O thou of unbaffled prowess, as I speak to thee. I shall, O sinless one, discourse unto thee of gifts beginning with that of drink. The merit that a man acquires by making gifts of food and drink is such that the like of it, I think, is incapable of being acquired through any other gift. There is no gift, therefore, that is superior to that of either food or drink. It is by food that all living creatures are able to exist. For this reason, food is regarded as a very superior object in all the worlds. From food the strength and energy of living creatures constantly increases. Hence, the lord of all creatures has himself said that the gift of food is a very superior gift. Thou hast heard, O son of Kunti, what the auspicious words are of Savitri herself (on the subject of the gift of food). Thou knowest for what reason those words were said, what those words were, and how they were said in course of the sacred Mantras, O thou of great intelligence. A man, by making a gift of food, really makes a gift of life itself. There is no gift in this world

---

[345] One need not dedicate unto one's deities any other food than what one takes oneself. In the Ramayana it has been said that Rama offered unto the Pitris astringent fruits while he was in exile. The Pisachas dedicate carrion unto their deities for they themselves subsist upon carrion.

that is superior to the gift of life. Thou art not unacquainted with this saying of Lomasa, O thou of mighty arms! The end that was attained in former days by king Sivi in consequence of his having granted life to the pigeon is acquired by him, O monarch, who makes a gift of food unto a Brahmana. Hence, it has been heard by us that they that give life attain to very superior regions of felicity in after life. Food, O best of the Kurus, may or may not be superior to drink. Nothing can exist without the aid of what springs from water. The very lord of all the planets, viz., the illustrious Soma, has sprung from water. Amrita and Sudha and Swadha and milk as also every kind of food, the deciduous herbs, O monarch, and creepers (medicinal and of other virtues), spring from water. From these, O king, the life-breath of all living creatures flows. The deities have nectar for their food. The Nagas have Sudha. The Pitris have Swadha for theirs. The animals have herbs and plants for their food. The wise have said that rice, etc., constitute the food of human beings. All these, O chief of men, spring from water. Hence, there is nothing superior to the gift of water or drink. If a person wishes to secure prosperity for himself, he should always make gifts of drink. The gift of water is regarded as very praiseworthy. It leads to great fame and bestows long life on the giver. The giver of water, O son of Kunti, always stays over the heads of his enemies. Such a person obtains the fruition of all his wishes and earns everlasting fame. The giver, O chief of men, becomes cleansed of every sin and obtains unending felicity hereafter as he proceeds to heaven, O thou of great splendour. Manu himself has said that such a person earns regions of inexhaustible bliss in the other world."'"

SECTION LXVIII.

"'Yudhishthira said, "Do thou discourse to me once again, O grandsire, upon the merits attaching to gifts of sesame and of lamps for lighting darkness, as also of food and robes."

"'Bhishma said, "In this connection, O Yudhishthira, is recited the narrative of the discourse that took place in ancient times between a Brahmana and Yama. In the country lying between the rivers Ganga and Yamuna, at the foot of the hills called Yamuna, there was a large town inhabited by Brahmanas. The town was celebrated under the name of Parnasala and was very delightful in appearance, O king. A large number of learned Brahmanas lived in it. One day, Yama, the ruler of the dead, commanded a messenger of his, who was clad in black, endued with blood-red eyes and hair standing erect, and possessed of feet, eyes, and nose all of which resembled those of a crow, saying, 'Go thou to the town inhabited by Brahmanas and bring hither the person known by the name of Sarmin and belonging by birth to the race of Agastya. He is intent on mental tranquillity and possessed of learning. He is a preceptor engaged in teaching the Vedas and his practices are well-known. Do not bring me another person belonging to the same race and living in the same neighbourhood. This other man is equal unto him I want, in virtues, study, and birth. With respect to children and conduct, this other resembles the intelligent Sarmin. Do thou bring the individual I have in view. He should be worshipped with respect (instead of being dragged hither with irreverence).' The messenger having come to the place, did the very reverse of what he had been bidden to do. Attacking that person, he brought him who had been forbidden by Yama to be brought. Possessed of great energy, Yama rose up at the sight of the Brahmana and worshipped him duly. The king of the dead then commanded his messenger, saying, 'Let this one be taken back, and let the other one be brought to me.' When the great judge of the dead said these words, that

Brahmana addressed him and said, 'I have completed my study of the Vedas and am no longer attached to the world. Whatever period may yet remain of my mortal existence, I wish to pass, dwelling even here, O thou of unfading glory!'[346]

""Yama said, 'I cannot ascertain the exact period, ordained by Time, of one's life, and hence, unurged by Time, I cannot allow one to take up one's residence here. I take note of the acts of righteousness (or otherwise) that one does in the world. Do thou, O learned Brahmana of great splendour return immediately to thy abode. Tell me what also is in thy mind and what I can do for thee, O thou of unfading glory!'

""The Brahmana said, 'Do thou tell me what those acts are by accomplishing which one may earn great merit. O best of all beings, thou art the foremost of authorities (on the subject) even in the three worlds.'

""Yama said, 'Do thou hear, O regenerate Rishi, the excellent ordinances regarding gifts. The gift of sesame seeds is a very superior one. It produces everlasting merit. O foremost of regenerate ones, one should make gifts of as much sesame as one can. By making gifts of sesame every day, one is sure to attain the fruition of one's every wish. The gift of sesame at Sraddhas is applauded. Verily the gift of sesame is a very superior one. Do thou make gifts of sesame unto the Brahmanas according to the rites ordained in the scriptures. One should on the day of the full moon of the month of Vaisakha, make gifts of sesame unto the Brahmanas. They should also be made to eat and to touch sesame on every occasion that one can afford. They that are desirous of achieving what is beneficial to them should, with their whole souls, do this in their houses.[347] Without doubt, men should similarly make gifts of water and establish resting places for the distribution of drinking water.[348] One should cause tanks and lakes and wells to be excavated. Such acts are rare in the world, O best of regenerate persons! Do thou always make gifts of water. This act is fraught with great merit. O best of regenerate persons, thou shouldst establish resting places along the roads for the distribution of water. After one has eaten, the gift unto one should especially be made of water for drink.'"

"Bhishma continued, "After Yama had said these words unto him, the messenger who had borne him from his abode conveyed him back to it. The Brahmana, on his return, obeyed the instructions he had received. Having thus conveyed him back to his abode the messenger of Yama fetched Sarmin who had really been sought by Yama. Taking Sarmin unto him, he informed his master. Possessed of great energy, the judge of the dead worshipped that righteous Brahmana, and having conversed with him a while dismissed him for being taken back to his abode. Unto him also Yama gave the same instructions. Sarmin, too, coming back into the world of men, did all that Yama had said. Like the gift of water, Yama, from a desire of doing good to the Pitris, applauds the gift of lamps to light dark places. Hence, the giver of a lamp for lighting a dark place is regarded as benefiting the Pitris. Hence, O best of the Bharatas, one should always give lamps for lighting dark spots. The giving of lamps enhances the visual power of the

---

[346] The first line of 13 and the last line of 14 are very terse: Kalasya vihitam, as explained by the Commentator, is ayuh pramanam, na prapnami is na janami. The sense is that 'unurged by time, I cannot allow these to take up my residence here.'

[347] i.e., invite Brahmanas to feasts in which sesame should predominate.

[348] In Bengal, to this day, those who can afford, particularly pious ladies, establish shady resting places in the month of Vaisakha (the hottest month of the year), by the side of the public roads, for travellers, where good cool drinking water, a handfull of well-drenched oats, and a little of raw sugar, are freely distributed. Such institutions, on the old Benares Road and the Grand Trunk Road, considerably refresh travellers. There are miles upon miles along these roads where good water is not at all procurable.

deities, the Pitris, and one's own self.[349] It has been said, O king, that the gift of gems is a very superior gift. The Brahmana, who, having accepted a gift of gems, sells the same for performing a sacrifice, incurs no fault. The Brahmana, who, having accepted a gift of gems makes a gift of them unto Brahmanas, acquires inexhaustible merit himself and confers inexhaustible merit upon him from whom he had originally received them. Conversant with every duty Manu himself has said that he, who, observant of proper restraints, earns makes a gift of gems unto a Brahmana observant of proper restraints earns inexhaustible merit himself and confers inexhaustible merit upon the recipient. The man who is content with his own wedded wife and who makes a gift of robes, earns an excellent complexion and excellent vestments for himself. I have told thee, O foremost of men, what the merits are that attach to gifts of kine, of gold, and the sesame agreeably to deserve precepts of the Vedas and the scriptures. One should marry and raise offspring upon one's wedded wives. Of all acquisitions, O son of Kuru's race, that of male issue is regarded as the foremost.""

SECTION LXIX.

"'Yudhishthira said, "Do thou, O foremost one of Kuru's race, discourse unto me once again of the excellent ordinance regarding gifts, with especial reference, O thou of great wisdom, to the gift of earth. A Kshatriya should make gifts of earth unto a Brahmana of righteous deeds. Such a Brahmana should accept the gift with due rites. None else, however, than a Kshatriya is competent to make gifts of earth. It behoves thee now to tell me what these objects are that persons of all classes are free to bestow if moved by the desire of earning merit. Thou shouldst also tell me what has been said in the Vedas on this subject."

"'Bhishma said, "There are three gifts that go by the same name and that are productive of equal merits. Indeed, these three confer the fruition of every wish. The three objects whose gifts are of such a character are kine, earth, and knowledge.[350] That person who tells his disciple words of righteous import drawn from the Vedas acquires merit equal to that which is won by making gifts of earth and kine. Similarly are kine praised (as objects of gifts). There is no object of gift higher than they. Kine are supposed to confer merit immediately. They are also, O Yudhishthira, such that a gift of them cannot but lead to great merit. Kine are the mothers of all creatures. They bestow every kind of happiness. The person that desires his own prosperity should always make gifts of kine. No one should kick at kine or proceed through the midst of kine. Kine are goddesses and homes of auspiciousness. For this reason, they always deserve worship. Formerly, the deities, while tilling the earth whereon they performed a sacrifice, used the goad for striking the bullocks yoked to the plough. Hence, in tilling earth for such a purpose, one may, without incurring censure or sin, apply the goad to bullocks. In other acts, however, bullocks should never be struck with the goad or the whip. When kine are grazing or lying down no one should annoy them in any way. When the cows are thirsty and they do not get water (in consequence of any one obstructing their access to the pool or tank or river), they, by merely looking at such a person, can destroy him with all his relatives and friends. What creatures can be more sacred than kine when with the very dung of kine altars whereon Sraddhas are performed in honour of the Pitris, or those

---

[349] What is meant by the giving of lamps is the placing of lighted lamps in dark places which are the resorts of men, such as roads and ghats, etc.

[350] Of equal name, because the word go means cow, earth, and speech.

whereon the deities are worshipped, are cleansed and sanctified? That man, who, before eating himself gives every day, for a year, only a handful of grass unto a cow belonging to another, is regarded as undergoing a vow or observance which bestows the fruition of every wish. Such a person acquires children and fame and wealth and prosperity, and dispels all evils and dreams."

"'Yudhishthira said, "What should be the indications of those kine that deserve to be given away? What are those kine that should be passed over in the matter of gifts? What should be the character of those persons unto whom kine should be given? Who, again, are those unto whom kine should not be given?"

"'Bhishma said, "A cow should never be given unto one that is not righteous in behaviour, or one that is sinful, or one that is covetous or one that is untruthful in speech, or one that does not make offerings unto the Pitris and deities. A person, by making a gift of ten kine unto a Brahmana learned in the Vedas, poor in earthly wealth, possessed of many children, and owning a domestic fire, attains to numerous regions of great felicity. When a man performs any act that is fraught with merit assisted by what he has got in gift from another, a portion of the merit attaching to that act becomes always his with whose wealth the act has been accomplished. He that procreates a person, he that rescues a person, and he that assigns the means of sustenance to a person are regarded as the three sires. Services dutifully rendered to the preceptor destroys sin. Pride destroys even great fame. The possession of three children destroys the reproach of childlessness, and the possession of ten kine dispels the reproach of poverty. Unto one that is devoted to the Vedanta, that is endued with great learning, that has been filled with wisdom, that has a complete control over his senses, that is observant of the restraints laid down in the scriptures, that has withdrawn himself from all worldly attachments, unto him that says agreeable words unto all creatures, unto him that would never do an evil act even when impelled by hunger, unto one that is mild or possessed of a peaceful disposition, unto one that is hospitable to all guests,—verily unto such a Brahmana should a man, possessed of similar conduct and owning children and wives, assign the means of sustenance. The measure of merit that attaches to the gift of kine unto a deserving person is exactly the measure of the sin that attaches to the act of robbing a Brahmana of what belongs to him. Under all circumstances should the spoliation of what belongs to a Brahmana be avoided, and his spouses kept at a distance."'"

SECTION LXX.

"'Bhishma said, "In this connection, O perpetuator of Kuru's race, is recited by the righteous the narrative of the great calamity that overtook king Nriga in consequence of his spoliation of what had belonged to a Brahmana. Some time before, certain young men of Yadu's race, while searching for water, had come upon a large well covered with grass and creepers. Desirous of drawing water from it, they laboured very much for removing the creepers that covered its mouth. After the mouth had been cleaned, they beheld within the well a very large lizard residing within it. The young men made strong and repeated efforts for rescuing the lizard from that situation. Resembling a very hill in size, the lizard was sought to be freed by means of cords and leathern tongs. Not succeeding in their intention the young men then went to Janardana. Addressing him they said, 'Covering the entire space of a well, there is a very large lizard to be seen. Notwithstanding our best efforts we have not succeeded in rescuing it from that situation.' Even this was what they represented unto Krishna. Vasudeva then proceeded to the spot and took out the lizard and questioned it as to who it was. The lizard said that it was identical with the soul of king Nriga who had flourished in days of old and who had performed many sacrifices. Unto the lizard that said those words, Madhava spoke, 'Thou didst perform many righteous acts. No sin didst thou commit. Why, then, O king, hast thou come to such a distressful end? Do thou explain what this is and why it has been brought about. We have heard that thou didst repeatedly make gifts unto the Brahmanas of hundreds upon hundreds of thousands and once again eight times hundreds upon hundreds of ten thousands of kine.[351] Why, therefore, has this end overtaken thee?' Nriga then replied unto Krishna, saying, 'On one occasion a cow belonging to a Brahmana who regularly worshipped his domestic fire, escaping from the owner's abode while he was absent from home entered my flock. The keepers of my cattle included that cow in their tale of a thousand. In time that cow was given away by me unto a Brahmana, acting as I did from desire of happiness in heaven. The true owner, returning home, sought for his lost cow and at last saw it in the house of another. Finding her, the owner said, "This cow is mine!" The other person contested his claim, till both, disputing and excited with wrath, came to me. Addressing me one of them said, "Thou hast been the giver of this cow!" The other one said, "Thou hast robbed me of this cow—she is mine!" I then solicited the Brahmana unto whom I had given that cow, to return the gift in exchange for hundreds upon hundreds of other kine. Without acceding to my earnest solicitations, he addressed me, saying. "The cow I have got is well-suited to time and place. She yields a copious measure of milk, besides being very quiet and very fond of us. The milk she yields is very sweet. She is regarded as worthy of every praise in my house. She is nourishing, besides, a weak child of mine that has just been weaned. She is incapable of being given up by me." Having said these words, the Brahmana went away. I then solicited the other Brahmana offering him an exchange, and saying, "Do thou take a hundred thousand kine for this one cow." The Brahmana, however, replied unto me, saying, "I do not accept gifts from persons of the kingly order. I am able to get on without help. Do thou then, without loss of time, give me that very cow which was mine." Even thus, O slayer of Madhu, did that Brahmana speak unto me. I offered to make gifts unto him of gold and silver and horses and cars. That foremost of Brahmanas refused to accept any of these as gift and went away. Meanwhile, urged by time's irresistible influence, I had to depart from this world. Wending to the region of the Pitris I was taken to the presence of the king of the dead. Worshipping me duly Yama addressed me, saying, "The end cannot be ascertained, O king, of thy deed. There is, however, a little sin which was unconsciously perpetrated by thee. Do thou suffer the punishment for that sin now or afterwards as it pleases thee. Thou hadst (upon thy accession to the throne) sworn that thou wouldst protect (all persons in the enjoyment of their own). That oath of thine was not rigidly kept by thee. Thou tookest also what belonged to a Brahmana. Even this has been the two-fold sin thou hast committed." I answered, saying, "I shall first undergo the distress of punishment, and when that is over, I shall enjoy the happiness that is in store for me, O lord!" After I had said those words unto the king of the dead, I fell down on the Earth. Though fallen down I still could hear the words that Yama said unto me very loudly. Those words were, "Janardana the son of Vasudeva, will rescue thee! Upon the completion of a full thousand years, when the demerit will be exhausted of thy sinful act, thou shalt then attain to many regions of inexhaustible felicity that have been acquired by thee through thy own acts of righteousness." Falling down I found myself, with head downwards, within this well,

---

[351] No particular number is intended. What is meant is—innumerable.

transformed into a creature of the intermediate order. Memory, however, did not leave me. By thee I have been rescued today. What else can it testify to than the puissance of thy penances? Let me have thy permission, O Krishna! I desire to ascend to heaven.' Permitted then by Krishna, king Nriga bowed his head unto him and then mounted a celestial car and proceeded to heaven. After Nriga had thus proceeded to heaven, O best of the Bharatas, Vasudeva recited this verse, O delighter of the Kurus. No one should consciously appropriate anything belonging to a Brahmana. The property of a Brahmana, if taken, destroys the taker even as the Brahmana's cow destroyed king Nriga! I tell thee, again, O Partha, that a meeting with the good never proves fruitless. Behold, king Nriga was rescued from hell through meeting with one that is good. As a gift is productive of merit even so an act of spoliation leads to demerit. Hence also, O Yudhishthira, one should avoid doing any injury to kine.""'[352]

SECTION LXXI.

"'Yudhishthira said, "O sinless one, do thou discourse to me more in detail upon the merits that are attainable by making gifts of kine. O thou of mighty arms, I am never satiated with thy words!"

"'Bhishma said, "In this connection is recited the old history of the discourse between the Rishi Uddalaki and his son called Nachiketa. Once on a time the Rishi Uddalaki endued with great intelligence, approaching his son Nachiketa, said unto him, 'Do thou wait upon and serve me.' Upon the completion of the vow he had observed the great Rishi once more said unto his son, 'Engaged in performing my ablutions and deeply taken up with my Vedic study, I have forgotten to bring with me the firewood, the Kusa blades, the flowers, the water jar, and the potherbs I had gathered. Do thou bring me those things from the riverside.' The son proceeded to the spot indicated, but saw that all the articles had been washed away by the current. Coming back to his father, he said, 'I do not see the things!' Afflicted as he then was with hunger, thirst, and fatigue, the Rishi Uddalaki of high ascetic merit, in a sudden wrath, cursed his son, saying, 'Do thou meet with Yama today!' Thus struck by his sire with the thunder of his speech, the son, with joined palms, said, 'Be appeased with me!' Soon, however, he fell down on the earth, deprived of life. Beholding Nachiketa prostrated upon the earth, his sire became deprived of his senses through grief. He, too, exclaiming, 'Alas, what have I done,' fell down on the earth. Filled with grief, as he indulged in lamentations for his son, the rest of that day passed away and night came. Then Nachiketa, O son of Kuru's race, drenched by the tears of his father, gave signs of returning life as he lay on a mat of Kusa grass. His restoration to life under the tears of his sire resembled the sprouting forth of seeds when drenched with auspicious showers. The son just restored to consciousness was still weak. His body was smeared with fragrant unguents and he looked like one just awaking from a deep slumber. The Rishi asked him, saying, 'Hast thou, O son, acquired auspicious regions by thy own acts? By good luck, thou hast been restored to me! Thy body does not seem to be human!' Thus asked by high-souled father, Nachiketa who had seen every thing with his own eyes, made the following answer unto him in the midst of the Rishis, 'In obedience to thy command I proceeded to the extensive region of Yama which is possessed of a delightful effulgence. There I beheld a palatial mansion which extended for thousands of Yojanas

---

[352] The 'hence' in the last line has reference to what has been said before on the subject of kine, and not to the first line of the verse.

and emitted a golden splendour from every part. As soon as Yama beheld me approaching with face towards him, he commanded his attendants saying, "Give him a good seat, verily, the king of the dead, for thy sake worshipped we with the Arghya and the other ingredients." Thus worshipped by Yama and seated in the midst of his counsellors, I then said mildly, "I have come to thy abode, O judge of the dead! Do thou assign me those regions which I deserve for my acts!" Yama then answered me, saying, "Thou art not dead, O amiable one! Endued with penances, thy father said unto thee, 'Do thou meet with Yama!' The energy of thy sire is like that of a blazing fire. I could not possibly falsify that speech of his. Thou hast seen me. Do thou go hence, O child! The author of thy body is indulging in lamentations for thee. Thou art my dear guest. What wish of thine cherished by thee in thy heart shall I grant thee? Solicit the fruition of whatever desire thou mayst cherish." Thus addressed by him, I replied unto the king of the dead, saying, "I have arrived within thy dominions from which no traveller ever returns. If I really be an object deserving of thy attentions, I desire, O king of the dead, to have a sight of those regions of high prosperity and happiness that have been reserved for doers of righteous deeds." Thus addressed by me, Yama caused me to be mounted upon a vehicle of splendour as effulgent as that of the sun and unto which were harnessed many excellent steeds. Bearing me on that vehicle, he showed me, O foremost of regenerate persons, all those delightful regions that are reserved for the righteous. I beheld in those regions many mansions of great resplendence intended for high-souled persons. Those mansions are of diverse forms and are adorned with every kind of gem. Bright as the disc of the moon, they are ornamented with rows of tinkling bells. Hundreds among them are of many storeys. Within them are pleasant groves and woods and transparent bodies of water. Possessed of the effulgence of lapis lazuli and the sun, and made of silver and gold, their complexion resembles the colour of the morning sun. Some of them are immovable and some movable. Within them are many hills of viands and enjoyable articles and robes and beds in abundance. Within them are many trees capable of granting the fruition of every wish. There are also many rivers and roads and spacious halls and lakes and large tanks. Thousands of cars with rattling wheels may be seen there, having excellent steeds harnessed unto them. Many rivers that run milk, many hills of ghee, and large bodies of transparent water occur there. Verily, I beheld many such regions, never seen by me before of happiness and joy, approved by the king of the dead. Beholding all those objects, I addressed the ancient and puissant judge of the dead, saying, "For whose use and enjoyment have these rivers with eternal currents of milk and ghee been ordained?" Yama answered me saying, "These streams of milk and ghee, know thou, are for the enjoyment of those righteous persons, that make gifts in the world of men. Other eternal worlds there are which are filled with such mansions free from sorrow of every kind. These are reserved for those persons that are engaged in making gifts of kine.[353] The mere gift of kine is not worthy of praise. There are considerations of propriety or otherwise about the person unto whom kine should be given, the time for making those gifts, the kind of kine that should form the object of gifts, and the rites that should be observed in making the gifts. Gifts of kine should be made after ascertaining the distinctive qualifications of both Brahmanas (who are to receive them) and the kine themselves (which are to be given away). Kine should not be given unto one in whose abode they are likely to suffer from fire or the sun. That Brahmana who is possessed of

---

[353] Vitasokaih in the instrumental plural refers to Bhavanaih or some such substantive understood. It may also be read as a nominative plural, referring to Lokah.

Vedic lore, who is of austere penances, and who performs sacrifices, is regarded as worthy of receiving kine in gift. Those kine that have been rescued from distress situation, or that have been given by poor householders from want of sufficient means to feed and cherish them, are, for these reasons, reckoned as of high value.[354] Abstaining from all food and living upon water alone for three nights and sleeping the while on the bare earth, one should, having properly fed the kine one intends to give away, give them unto Brahmanas after having gratified them also (with other gifts). The kine given away should be accompanied by their calves. They should, again, be such as to bring forth good calves, at the proper seasons. They should be accompanied with other articles so given away. Having completed the gift, the giver should live for three days on only milk and forbearing from food of every other kind. He, who gives a cow that is not vicious, that brings forth good calves at proper intervals, and that does not fly away from the owners' house, and accompanies such gift with a vessel of white brass for milking her, enjoys the felicity of heaven for as many years as are measured by the number of hairs on the animal's body. He, who gives unto a Brahmana a bull well-broken and capable of bearing burdens, possessed of strength and young in years, disinclined to do any mischief, large-sized and endued with energy, enjoys those regions, that are reserved for givers of kine. He is regarded as a proper person for receiving a cow in gift who is known to be mild towards kine, who takes kine for his refuge, who is grateful, and who has no means of subsistence assigned unto him. When an old man becomes ill, or when a Brahmana intends to perform a sacrifice, or when one wishes to till for agriculture, or when one gets a son through the efficacy of a Homa performed for the purpose, or for the use of one's preceptor, or for the sustenance of a child (born in the usual way), one should give away a beloved cow. Even these are the considerations that are applauded (in the matter of making gifts of kine) in respect of place and time. The kine that deserve to be given away are those that yield copious measures of milk, or those that are well-known (for their docility and other virtues), or those that have been purchased for a price, or those that have been acquired as honoraria for learning, or those that have been obtained in exchange by offering other living creatures (such as sheep and goats, etc.), or those that have been won by prowess of arms, or those that have been gained as marriage-dower (from fathers-in-law and other relations of the wife)."

""""Nachiketa continued, 'Hearing these words of Vaivaswata, I once more addressed him, saying, "What are those objects by giving which, when kine are not procurable, givers may yet go to regions reserved for men making gifts of kine?" Questioned by me, the wise Yama answered, explaining further what the end is that is attainable by making gifts of kine. He said, "In the absence of kine, a person by making gifts of what has been regarded as the substitute of kine, wins the merit of making gifts of kine. If, in the absence of kine, one makes a gift of a cow made of ghee, observant of a vow the while, one gets for one's use these rivers of ghee all of which approach one like an affectionate mother approaching her beloved child. If, in the absence of even a cow made of ghee, one makes a gift of a cow made of sesame seeds, observing a cow the while, one succeeds with the assistance of that cow to get over all calamities in this world and to enjoy great happiness hereafter from these rivers of milk that thou beholdest! If in the absence of a cow made of sesame seeds, one makes a gift of a cow made of water one succeeds in coming to these happy regions and enjoying this river of cool and transparent water, that

---

[354] Very probably what is said here is that only such kine are worthy of being given away unto Brahmanas, and not lean animals.

is, besides capable of granting the fruition of every wish." The king of the dead explained to me all this while I was his guest, and, O thou of unfading glory, great was the joy that I felt at sight of all the wonders he showed me. I shall now tell thee what would certainly be agreeable to thee. I have now got a great sacrifice whose performance does not require much wealth. That sacrifice (constituted by gifts of kine) may be said to flow from me, O sire! Others will obtain it also. It is not inconsistent with the ordinances of the Vedas. The curse that thou hadst pronounced upon me was no curse but was in reality a blessing, since it enabled me to have a sight of the great king of the dead. There I have beheld what the rewards are that attach to gifts. I shall, henceforth, O thou of great soul, practise the duty of gift without any doubt lurking in my mind respecting its rewards. And, O great Rishi, the righteous Yama, filled with joy, repeatedly told me, "One, who, by making frequent gifts, has succeeded in acquiring purity of mind should then make gifts of kine specially. This topic (about gifts) is fraught with sanctity. Do thou never disregard the duties in respect of gifts. Gifts, again, should be made unto deserving persons, when time and place are suitable. Do thou, therefore, always make gifts of kine. Never entertain any doubts in this respect. Devoted to the path of gifts, many high-souled persons in days of yore used to make gifts of kine. Fearing to practise austere penances, they made gifts according to the extent of their power. In time they cast off all sentiments of pride and vanity, and purified their souls. Engaged in performing Sraddhas in honour of the Pitris and in all acts of righteousness, they used to make, according to the extent of their power, gifts of kine, and as the reward of those acts they have attained to heaven and are shining in effulgence for such righteousness. One should, on the eighth day of the moon that is known by the name of Kamyashtami, make gifts of kine, properly won, unto the Brahmanas after ascertaining the eligibility of the recipients (by the ordinances already laid down). After making the gift, one should then subsist for ten days together upon only the milk of kine, their dung and their urine (abstaining from all other food the while). The merit that one acquires by making a gift of a bull is equal to that which attaches to the divine vow. By making a gift of a couple of kine one acquires, as the reward thereof, a mastery of the Vedas. By making a gift of cars and vehicles with kine yoked thereto, one acquires the merit of baths in sacred waters. By making a gift of a cow of the Kapila species, one becomes cleansed of all one's sins. Verily, by giving away even a single cow of the Kapila species that has been acquired by legitimate means, one becomes cleansed of all the sins one may have committed. There is nothing higher (in point of tastes) than the milk which is yielded by kine. The gift of a cow is truly regarded as a very superior gift. Kine by yielding milk, rescue all the worlds from calamity. It is kine, again, that produce the food upon which creatures subsist. One, who, knowing the extent of the service that kine do, does not entertain in one's heart affection for kine, is a sinner that is certain to sink in hell.[355] If one gives a thousand or a hundred or ten or five kine, verily, if one gives unto a righteous Brahmana even a single cow which brings forth good calves at proper intervals, one is sure to see that cow approach one in heaven in the form of a river of sacred water capable of granting the fruition of every wish. In respect of the prosperity and the growth that kine confer, in the matter also of the protection that kine grant unto all creatures of the earth, kine are equal to the very rays of the sun that fall on the earth.[356] The word that signifies the cow stands also for the rays of the sun. The giver of a cow

---

[355] Kine produce food not only by assisting at tillage of the soil, but also by aiding in the performance of sacrifices. The ghee burnt in the sacrificial fire sustains the under-deities, who pour rain and cause crops to grow.

[356] That heat is the originating principle of the growth of many things was well understood by the Rishis.

becomes the progenitor of a very large race that extends over a large part of the earth. Hence, he that gives a cow shines like a second sun in resplendence. The disciple should, in the matter of making gifts of kine, select his preceptor. Such a disciple is sure to go to heaven. The selection of a preceptor (in the matter of the performance of pious deeds) is regarded as a high duty by persons conversant with the ordinances. This is, indeed, the initial ordinance. All other ordinances (respecting the gift of kine) depend upon it.[357] Selecting, after examination, an eligible person among the Brahmanas, one should make unto him the gift of a cow that has been acquired by legitimate means, and having made the gift cause him to accept it. The deities and men and ourselves also, in wishing good to other, say, 'Let the merits attaching to gifts be thine in consequence of thy righteousness!'" Even thus did the judge of the dead speak unto me, O regenerate Rishi. I then bowed my head unto the righteous Yama. Obtaining his permission I left his dominions and have now come to the sole of thy feet.'"''

SECTION LXXII.

"'Yudhishthira said, "Thou hast, O grandsire, discoursed to me the topic of gifts of kine in speaking of the Rishi Nachiketa. Thou hast also impliedly discoursed, O puissant one, on the efficacy and pre-eminence of that act. Thou hast also told me, O grandsire of great intelligence, of the exceedingly afflicting character of the calamity that overtook the high-souled king Nriga in consequence of a single fault of his. He had to dwell for a long time at Dwaravati (in the form of a mighty lizard) and how Krishna became the cause of his rescue from that miserable plight. I have, however, one doubt. It is on the subject of the regions of kine. I desire to hear, in detail, about those regions which are reserved for the residence of persons that make gifts of kine."

"'Bhishma said, "In this connection is recited the old narrative of the discourse between Him who sprang from the primeval lotus and him who performed a hundred sacrifices.

"'"Sakra said, 'I see, O Grandsire, that those who are residents of the region of kine transcend by their resplendence the prosperity of the denizens of heaven and pass them by (as beings of an inferior station). This has raised a doubt in my mind. Of what kind, O holy one, are the regions of kine? Tell me all about them, O sinless one! Verily, what is the nature of those regions that are inhabited by givers of kine? I wish to know this of what kind are those regions? What fruits do they bring? What is the highest object there which the denizens thereof succeeds in winning? What are its virtues? How also do men, freed from every kind of anxiety, succeed in going to those regions? For what period does the giver of a cow enjoy the fruits that are borne by his gift? How may persons make gifts of many kine and how may they make gifts of a few kine? What are the merits attaching to gifts of many kine and what those that attach to gifts of a few only? How also do persons become givers of kine without giving any kine in reality? Do thou tell me all this. How does one making gifts of even many kine, O puissant lord, become the equal of one that has made gift of only a few kine? How also does one who make gifts of only a few kine succeed in becoming the equal of one who has made gifts of many kine? What kind of Dakshina is regarded as distinguished for pre-eminence in the matter of gifts of kine?

---

[357] The sense seems to be this: in doing all pious acts, one should first take the aid of a preceptor, even if one be well-conversant with the ordinances one has to follow. Without the selection of a preceptor in the first place, there can be no pious act. In the matter, therefore, of making gifts of kine according to the ordinances laid down, one should seek the help of a preceptor as well as in the matter of every other act of piety.

It behoveth thee, O holy one, to discourse unto me on all this agreeably to truth.""""

SECTION LXXIII.

""""The Grandsire said, 'The questions thou hast asked me in respect of kine, beginning with their gift, are such that there is none else in the three worlds, O thou of a hundred sacrifices, who could put them! There are many kinds of regions, O Sakra, which are invisible to even thee. Those regions are seen by me, O Indra, as also by those women that are chaste and that have been attached to only one husband. Rishis observant of excellent vows, by means of their deeds of righteousness and piety, and Brahmanas of righteous souls, succeed in repairing to them in even their fleshy forms. Men that are observant of excellent vows behold those regions which resemble the bright creations of dreams, aided by their cleansed minds and by that (temporary) emancipation which succeeds the loss of one's consciousness of body.[358] Listen, O thou of a thousand eyes, to me as I tell thee what the attributes are with which those regions are endued. There the very course of Time is suspended. Decrepitude is not there, nor Fire which is omnipresent in the universe. There the slightest evil does not occur, nor disease, nor weakness of any kind. The kine that live there, O Vasava, obtain the fruition of every desire which they cherish in their hearts. I have direct experience of what I say unto thee. Capable of going everywhere at will and actually repairing from place to place with ease, they enjoy the fruition of wish after wish as it arises in their minds. Lakes and tanks and rivers and forests of diverse kinds, and mansions and hills and all kinds of delightful objects,— delightful, that is, to all creatures,—are to be seen there. There is no region of felicity that is superior to any of these of which I speak. All those foremost of men, O Sakra, who are forgiving unto all creatures, who endure everything, who are full of affection for all things, who render dutiful obedience unto their preceptors, and who are free from pride and vanity, repair to those regions of supreme felicity. He, who abstains from every kind of flesh, who is possessed of a cleansed heart, who is endued with righteousness, who worships his parents with reverence, who is endued with truthfulness of speech and conduct, who attends with obedience upon the Brahmanas, who is faultless in conduct, who never behaves with anger towards kine and towards the Brahmanas, who is devoted to the accomplishment of every duty, who serves his preceptors with reverence, who is devoted for his whole life to truth and to gifts, and who is always forgiving towards all transgression against himself, who is mild and self-restrained, who is full of reverence for the deities, who is hospitable to all guests, who is endued with compassion,—verily, he, who is adorned with these attributes,—succeeds in attaining to the eternal and immutable region of kine. He, who is stained with adultery, sees not such a region; nor he, who is a slayer of his preceptor; nor he, who speaks falsely or indulges in idle boasts; nor he, who always disputes with others; nor he who behaves with hostility towards the Brahmanas. Indeed, that wicked wight, who is stained with such faults fails to attain even a sight of these regions of felicity; also he that injures his friends; also he that is full of guile; also he that is ungrateful; also he that is a cheat; also he that is crooked in conduct; also he that is a disregarder of religion; also he that is a slayer of Brahmanas. Such men are incapable of beholding in even imagination the region of kine that is the abode of only those who are righteous of deeds. I have told thee everything about the region of kine in

---

[358] When consciousness of body is lost in Yoga or Samadhi, a temporary Moksha or Emancipation succeeds. Men with cleansed minds behold at such times those regions of supreme felicity to which the speaker refers. Such felicity, of course, is the felicity of Brahma itself.

minute detail, O chief of the deities! Hear now, O thou of a hundred sacrifices, the merit that is theirs who are engaged in making gifts of kine. He, who make gifts of kine, after purchasing them with wealth obtained by inheritance or acquired lawfully by him, attains, as the fruit of such an act to many regions of inexhaustible felicity. He, who makes a gift of a cow, having acquired it with wealth won at dice, enjoys felicity, O Sakra, for ten thousand years of celestial measure. He, who acquires a cow as his share of ancestral wealth is said to acquire her legitimately. Such a cow may be given away. They that make gifts of kine so acquired obtain many eternal regions of felicity that is inexhaustible. That person, who, having acquired a cow in gift makes a gift of her with a pure heart, succeeds without doubt, O lord of Sachi, in obtaining eternal regions of beatitude. That person, who, with restrained senses speaks the truth from his birth (to the time of his death) and who endures everything at the hands of his preceptor and of the Brahmanas, and who practises forgiveness, succeeds in attaining to an end that is equal to that of kine. That speech which is improper, O lord of Sachi, should never be addressed to a Brahmana. One, again, should not, in even one's mind, do an injury to a cow. One should, in one's conduct, imitate the cow, and show compassion towards the cow.[359] Hear, O Sakra, what the fruits are that become his, who is devoted to the duty of truth. If such a person gives away a single cow, that one cow becomes equal to a thousand kine. If a Kshatriya, possessed of such qualifications, makes a gift of a single cow, his merit becomes equal to that of a Brahmana's. That single cow, listen, O Sakra which such a Kshatriya gives away becomes the source of as much merit as the single cow that a Brahmana gives away under similar circumstances. Even this is the certain conclusion of the scriptures. If a Vaisya, possessed of similar accomplishments, were to make a gift of a single cow, that cow would be equal to five hundred kine (in respect of the merit she would produce). If a Sudra endued with humility were to make a gift of a cow, such a cow would be equal to a hundred and twenty-five kine (in respect of the merit it would produce). Devoted to penances and truth, proficient (in the scriptures and all acts) through dutiful services rendered to his preceptor, endued with forgiveness of disposition, engaged in the worship of the deities, possessed of a tranquil soul, pure (in body and mind), enlightened, observant of all duties, and freed from every kind of egotism, that man who makes a gift of a cow unto a Brahmana, certainly attains to great merit through that act of his, viz., the gift, according to proper rites, of a cow yielding copious milk. Hence, one, with singleness of devotion, observant of truth and engaged in humbly serving one's preceptor, should always make gifts of kine.[360] Hear, O Sakra, what the merit is of that person, who, duly studying the Vedas, shows reverence for kine, who always becomes glad at sight of kine, and who, since his birth has always bowed his head unto kine. The merit that becomes one's by performing the Rajasuya sacrifice, the merit that becomes one's by making gifts of heaps of gold, that high merit is acquired by a person who shows such reverence for kine. Righteous Rishis and high-souled persons crowned with success have said so. Devoted to truth, possessed of a tranquil soul, free from cupidity, always truthful in speech, and behaving with reverence towards kine with the steadiness of a vow, the man, who, for a whole year before himself taking any food, regularly presents some food to kine, wins the merit, by such an act, of the gift of a thousand kine. That man, who takes only one meal a day and who gives away the entire

---

[359] Govritti is imitating the cow in the matter of providing for the morrow. Hence, one, who never thinks of the morrow and never stores anything for future use, is meant.

[360] Etachcha in 25 implies gift of a cow, and enam refers to a Brahmana. Dwijaya dattwa, etc, in the first line of 26 seems to be an elaboration of Etachcha.

quantity of his other meal unto kine.—verily, that man, who thus reverences kine with the steadiness of a vow and shows such compassion towards them,—enjoys for ten years' unlimited felicity. That man, who confines himself to only one meal a day and with the other meal saved for some time purchases a cow and makes a gift of it (unto a Brahmana), earns, through that gift, O thou of a hundred sacrifices, the eternal merit that attaches to the gift of as many kine as there are hairs on the body of that single cow so given away. These are declarations in respect of the merit that Brahmanas acquire by making gifts of kine. Listen now to the merits that Kshatriyas may win. It has been said that a Kshatriya, by purchasing a cow in this manner and making a gift of it unto a Brahmana, acquires great felicity for five years. A Vaisya, by such conduct, acquires only half the merit of a Kshatriya, and a Sudra, by such conduct, earns half the merit that a Vaisya does. That man, who sells himself and with the proceeds thereof purchases kine and gives them away unto Brahmanas, enjoy felicity in heaven for as long a period as kine are seen on earth. It has been said, O highly blessed one, that in every hair of such kine as are purchased with the proceeds obtained by selling oneself, there is a region of inexhaustible felicity. That man, who having acquired kine by battle makes gifts of them (unto Brahmanas), acquires as much merit as he, who makes gifts of kine after having purchased the same with the proceeds of selling oneself. That man, who, in the absence of kine, makes a gift of a cow made of sesame seeds, restraining his senses the while, is rescued by such a cow from every kind of calamity or distress. Such a man sports in great felicity. The mere gift of kine is not fraught with merit. The considerations of deserving recipients, of time, of the kind of kine, and of the ritual to be observed, should be attended to. One should ascertain the proper time for making a gift of kine. One should also ascertain the distinctive qualifications of both Brahmanas (who are to receive them) and of kine themselves (which are to be given away). Kine should not be given unto one in whose abode they are likely to suffer from fire or the sun. One, who is rich in Vedic lore, who is of pure lineage, who is endued with a tranquil soul, who is devoted to the performance of sacrifices, who fears the commission of sin, who is possessed of varied knowledge, who is compassionate towards kine, who is mild in behaviour, who accords protection unto all that seek it of him, and who has no means of sustenance assigned unto him, is regarded as a proper person for receiving a gift of kine. Unto a Brahmana who has no means of sustenance, unto him while he is exceedingly afflicted for want of food (in a time, of famine, for example) for purposes of agriculture, for a child born in consequence of Homa, for the purposes of his preceptor, for the sustenance of a child born (in the ordinary course), should a cow be given. Verily, the gift should be made at a proper time and in a proper place.[361] Those kine, O Sakra, whose dispositions are well-known, which have been acquired as honoraria for knowledge, or which have been purchased in exchange for other animals (such as goats, sheep, etc.), or which have been won by prowess of arms, or obtained as marriage-dower; or which have been acquired by being rescued from situations of danger, or which incapable of being maintained by their poor owner have been made over for careful keep to another's house are, for such reasons, regarded as proper objects of gift. Those kine which are strong of body, which have good dispositions, and which emit an agreeable fragrance, are applauded in the matter of gifts. As Ganga is the foremost of all streams, even so is a Kapila cow the foremost of all

---

[361] Homyaheth prasute implies for a child born in consequence of a Homa. The fact is, ascetics sometimes created children without the intervention of women and by efficacy of the Homa alone. At such times should people make gifts of kine unto such sires. The mention of Vala-samvriddhaye afterwards implies the birth of children in the usual course.

animals of the bovine breed. Abstaining from all food and living only upon water for three nights, and sleeping for the same period upon the bare earth, one should make gifts of kine unto Brahmanas after having gratified them with other presents. Such kine, freed from every vice should, at the same time, be accompanied by healthy calves that have not been weaned. Having made the gift, the giver should live for the next three days in succession on food consisting only of the products of the cow.[362] By giving away a cow that is of good disposition, that quietly suffers herself to be milked, that always brings forth living and hale calves, and that does not fly away from the owner's abode, the giver enjoys felicity in the next world for as many years as there are hairs on her body. Similarly, by giving unto a Brahmana a bull that is capable of bearing heavy burden, that is young and strong and docile, that quietly bears the yoke of the plough, and that is possessed of such energy as is sufficient to undergo even great labour one attains to such regions as are his who gives away ten kine. That person, who rescues kine and Brahmanas (from danger) in the wilderness, O Kausika, becomes himself rescued from every kind of calamity. Hear what his merit is.[363] The merit such a man acquires is equal to the eternal merit of a Horse-sacrifice. Such a person attains to whatever end he desires at the hour of death. Many a region of felicity,—in fact, whatever happiness he covets in his heart,—becomes attainable to him in consequence of such an act of his. Verily, such man, permitted by kine, lives honoured in every region of felicity. That man, who follows kine every day in the woods himself subsisting the while on grass and cowdung and leaves of trees, his heart freed from desire of fruit, his senses restrained from every improper object and his mind purified of all dross,—that man,—O thou of a hundred sacrifices, lives in joy and freed from the dominion of desire in my region or in any other region of happiness that he wishes, in the company of the deities!"'"

SECTION LXXIV.

"'"Indra said, 'I wish to know, O Grandsire, what the end is that is attained by him who consciously steals a cow or who sells one from motives of cupidity.'

"'"The Grandsire said, 'Hear what the consequences are that overtake those persons that steal a cow for killing her for food or selling her for wealth, or making a gift of her unto a Brahmana. He, who, without being checked by the restraints of the scriptures, sells a cow, or kills one, or eats the flesh of a cow, or they, who, for the sake of wealth, suffer a person to kill kine,—all these, viz., he that kills, he that eats, and he that permits the slaughter,—rot in hell for as many years as there are hairs on the body of the cow so slain.[364] O thou of great puissance, those faults and those kinds of faults that have been said to attach to one that obstructs a Brahmana's sacrifice, are said to attach to the sale and the theft of kine. That man, who, having stolen a cow makes a gift of her unto a Brahmana, enjoys felicity in heaven as the reward of the gift but suffers misery in hell for

[362] Kshirapaih implies calves that are yet unweaned; that is, the cow should be given at such a time when she is still yielding milk; when, in fact, her calf has not learnt to eat or drink anything besides the milk or its dam.
[363] The correct reading of the second line is kshanene vipramuchya as in the Bombay text, and not kshemena vipramuchyeran. The latter reading yields almost no sense. The Burdwan translator, who has committed grave blunders throughout the Anusasana, adheres to the incorrect reading, and makes nonsense of the verse.
[364] In verse 3, vikrayartham is followed, as the Commentator rightly explains, by niyunkta or some such word. Vikrayartham hinsyat may mean 'killing for sale.' This, however should be pleonastic with reference to what follows.

the sin of theft for as long a period. Gold has been said to constitute the Dakshina, O thou of great splendour, in gifts of kine. Indeed, gold has been said to be the best Dakshina in all sacrifices. By making a gift of kine one is said to rescue one's ancestors to the seventh degree as also one's descendants to the seventh degree. By giving away kine with Dakshina of gold one rescues one's ancestors and descendants of double the number. The gift of gold is the best of gifts. Gold is, again, the best Dakshina. Gold is a great cleanser, O Sakra, and is, indeed, the best of all cleansing objects. O thou of a hundred sacrifices, gold has been said to be the sanctifier of the entire race of him who gives it away. I have thus, O thou of great splendour, told thee in brief of Dakshina.'"

"'Bhishma said, "Even this was said by the Grandsire unto Indra, O chief of Bharata's race! Indra imparted it unto Dasaratha, and Dasaratha in his turn unto his son Rama. Rama of Raghu's race imparted it unto his dear brother Lakshmana of great fame. While dwelling in the woods, Lakshmana imparted it unto the Rishis. It has then come down from generation to generation, for the Rishis of rigid vows held it amongst themselves as also the righteous kings of the earth. My preceptor, O Yudhishthira, communicated it to me. That Brahmana, who recites it every day in the assemblies of Brahmanas, in sacrifices or at gifts of kine, or when two persons meet together, obtains hereafter many regions of inexhaustible felicity where he always resides with the deities as his companions. The holy Brahman, the Supreme Lord, had said so (unto Indra on the subject of kine).""""

SECTION LXXV.

"'Yudhishthira said, "I have been greatly assured, O thou of puissance, by thee thus discoursing unto me of duties. I shall, however, give expression to the doubts I have. Do thou explain them to me, O grandsire! What are the fruits, declared in the scriptures, of the vows that men observe. Of what nature are the fruits, O thou of great splendour, of observances of other kinds? What, again, are the fruits, of one's studying the Vedas properly?[365] What are the fruits of gifts, and what those of holding the Vedas in memory? What are the fruits that attach to the teaching of the Vedas? I desire to know all this. What, O grandsire, are the merits attaching to the non-acceptance of gifts in this world? What fruits are seen to attach to him who makes gifts of knowledge? What are the merits acquired by persons that are observant of the duties of their order, as also by heroes that do not flee from battle? What are the fruits that have been declared to attach to the observance of purity and to the practice of Brahmacharya? What are the merits that attach to the service of the father and of the mother? What also are the merits of serving preceptors and teachers, and what are the merits of compassion and kindness? I desire to know all these, O grandsire, truly and in detail, O thou that art conversant with all the scriptures! Great is the curiosity I feel."

"'Bhishma said, "Eternal regions of felicity become his, who, having properly commenced a Vrata (vow) completes its observance according to the scriptures, without a break. The fruits of Niyamas, O king, are visible even in this world. These rewards that thou hast won are those of Niyamas and sacrifices. The fruits that attach to the study of the Vedas are seen both here and hereafter. The person, who is devoted to the study of the Vedas is seen to sport in felicity both in this world and in the region of Brahma. Listen

---

[365] Vratas (rendered as 'vows') and Niyamas (rendered as observances) differs in this respect that the former involves positive acts of worship along with the observance of, or abstention from, particular practices, while the latter involves only such observance or abstention.

now to me, O king, as I tell thee in detail what the fruits are of self-restraint. They that are self-restrained are happy everywhere. They that are self-restrained are always in the enjoyment of that felicity which attaches to the absence or subjugation of desire. They that are self-restrained are competent to go everywhere at will. They that are self-restrained are capable of destroying every foe. Without doubt, they that are self-restrained succeed in obtaining everything they seek. They that are self-restrained, O son of Pandu, obtain the fruition of every wish. The happiness that men enjoy in heaven through penances and prowess (in arms), through gift, and through diverse sacrifices, becomes theirs that are self-restrained and forgiving. Self-restraint is more meritorious than gift. A giver, after making a gift unto the Brahmanas, may yield to the influence of wrath. A self-restrained man, however, never yields to wrath. Hence, self-restraint is superior (in point of merit) to gift. That man, who makes gifts without yielding to wrath, succeeds in attaining to eternal regions of felicity. Wrath destroys the merit of a gift. Hence, self-restraint is superior to gift. There are various invisible places, O monarch, numbering by ten thousands, in heaven. Existing in all the regions of heaven, these places belong to the Rishis. Persons, leaving this world, attain to them and become transformed into deities. O king, the great Rishis repair thither, aided only by their self-restraint, and as the end of their efforts to attain to a region of superior happiness. Hence, self-restraint is superior (in efficacy) to gift. The person, who becomes a preceptor (for teaching the Vedas), and who duly worships the fire, taking leave of all his afflictions in this world, enjoys inexhaustible felicity, O king, in the region of Brahma. That man, who, having himself studied the Vedas, imparts a knowledge thereof unto righteous disciples, and who praises the acts of his own preceptor, attains to great honours in heaven. That Kshatriya, who takes to the study of the Vedas, to the performance of sacrifices, to the making of gifts, and who rescues the lives of others in battle, similarly attains to great honours in heaven. The Vaisya, who, observant of the duties of his order, makes gifts, reaps as the fruit of those gifts, a crowning reward. The Sudra, who duly observes the duties of his order (which consist of services rendered to the three other orders) wins heaven as the reward of such services. Diverse kinds of heroes have been spoken of (in the scriptures). Listen to me as I expound to thee what the rewards are that they attain to. The rewards are fixed of a hero belonging to a heroic race. There are heroes of sacrifice, heroes of self-restraint, heroes of truth, and others equally entitled to the name of hero. There are heroes of battle, and heroes of gift of liberality among men. There are many persons, who may be called the heroes of the Sankhya faith as, indeed, there are many others that are called heroes of Yoga. There are others that are regarded as heroes in the matter of forest-life, of householding or domesticity, and of renunciation (or Sannyasa). Similarly, there are others that are called heroes of the intellect, and also heroes of forgiveness. There are other men, who live in tranquillity and who are regarded as heroes of righteousness. There are diverse other kinds of heroes that practise diverse other kinds of vows and observances. There are heroes devoted to the study of the Vedas and heroes devoted to the teaching of the same. There are, again, men that come to be regarded as heroes for the devotion with which they wait upon and serve their preceptors, as indeed, heroes in respect of the reverence they show to their sires. There are heroes in respect of obedience to mothers, and heroes in the matter of the life of mendicancy they lead. There are heroes in the matter of hospitality to guests, whether living as householders. All these heroes attain to very superior regions of felicity which are, of course, acquired by them as the rewards of their own acts. Holding all the Vedas in memory, or ablutions performed in all the sacred waters, may or may not be equal to telling the Truth every day in one's life. A thousand horse sacrifices and Truth were once weighed in the balance. It was seen that Truth weighed heavier than a thousand horse-sacrifices. It is by Truth that the sun is imparting heat, it is by Truth that fire blazes up, it is by Truth that the winds blow; verily, everything rests upon Truth. It is Truth that gratifies the deities, the Pitris and the Brahmanas. Truth has been said to be the highest duty. Therefore, no one should ever transgress Truth. The Munis are all devoted to Truth. Their prowess depends upon Truth. They also swear by Truth. Hence, Truth is pre-eminent. All truthful men, O chief of Bharata's race, succeed by their truthfulness in attaining to heaven and sporting there in felicity. Self-restraint is the attainment of the reward that attaches to Truth. I have discoursed on it with my whole heart. The man of humble heart who is possessed of self-restraint, without doubt, attains to great honours in heaven. Listen now to me, O lord of Earth, as I expound to thee the merits of Brahmacharya. That man, who practises the vow of Brahmacharya from his birth to the time of his death, know, O king, has nothing unattainable! Many millions of Rishis are residing in the region of Brahma. All of them, while here, were devoted to Truth, and self-restrained and had their vital seed drawn up. The vow of Brahmacharya, O king, duly observed by a Brahmana, is sure to burn all his sins. The Brahmana is said to be a blazing fire. In those Brahmanas that are devoted to penances, the deity of fire becomes visible. If a Brahmacharin yields to wrath in consequence of any slight the chief of the deities himself trembles in fear. Even this is the visible fruit of the vow of Brahmacharya that is observed by the Rishis. Listen to me, O Yudhishthira, what the merit is that attaches to the worship of the father and the mother. He, who dutifully serves his father without ever crossing him in anything, or similarly serves his mother or (elder) brother or other senior or preceptor, it should be known, O king, earns a residence in heaven. The man of cleansed soul, in consequence of such service rendered to his seniors, has never even to behold hell."''

SECTION LXXVI.

"'Yudhishthira said, "I desire, O king, to hear thee discourse in detail upon those high ordinances which regulate gifts of kine, for it is by making gifts (of kine) according to those ordinances that one attains to innumerable regions of eternal felicity."

"'Bhishma said, "There is no gift, O lord of Earth, that is higher in point of merit than the gift of kine. A cow, lawfully acquired, if given away, immediately rescues the whole race of the giver. That ritual which sprang for the benefit of the righteous, was subsequently declared for the sake of all creatures. That ritual has come down from primeval time. It existed even before it was declared. Verily, O king, listen to me as I recite to thee that ritual which affects the gift of kine.[366] In days of yore when a number of kine (intended to be given away) was brought (before him), king Mandhatri, filled with doubt in respect of the ritual he should observe (in actually giving them away), properly questioned Vrihaspati (the preceptor of the celestials) for an explanation of that doubt. Vrihaspati said, 'Duly observing restraints the while, the giver of kine should, on the previous day, properly honour the Brahmanas and appoint the (actual) time of gift. As regards the kine to be given away, they should be of the class called Rohini. The kine also should be addressed with the words—Samange and Vahule—Entering the fold where the kine are kept, the following Srutis should be uttered,—The cow is my mother.

---

[366] The orthodox belief is that all rituals are literally eternal. As eternal, they existed before anybody declared them or set them down in holy writ. The ritual in respect of gifts of kine sprang in this way, i.e., in primeval time. It was only subsequently declared or set down in holy writ.

The bull is my sire. (Give me) heaven and earthly prosperity! The cow is my refuge!—
Entering the fold and acting in this way, the giver should pass the night there. He should
again utter the formula when actually giving away the kine.[367] The giver, thus residing
with the kine in the fold without doing anything to restrain their freedom, and lying down
on the bare earth (without driving away the gnats and other insects that would annoy him
as they annoy the kine), becomes immediately cleansed of all his sins in consequence of
his reducing himself to a state of perfect similitude with the kine. When the sun rises in
the morning, thou shouldst give away the cow, accompanied by her calf and a bull. As
the reward of such an act, heaven will certainly become attainable to thee. The blessings
also that are indicated by the Mantras will also be thine. The Mantras contain these
references to kine: Kine are endued with the elements of strength and energetic exertion.
Kine have in them the elements of wisdom. They are the source of that immortality which
sacrifice achieves. They are the refuge of all energy. They are the steps by which earthly
prosperity is won. They constitute the eternal course of the universe. They lead to the
extension of one's race. Let the kine (I give away) destroy my sins. They have that in
them which partakes in the nature of both Surya, and Soma. Let them be aids to my
attainment of heaven. Let them betake themselves to me as a mother takes to her
offspring. Let all other blessings also be mine that have not been named in the Mantras I
have uttered! In the alleviation or cure of phthisis and other wasting diseases, and in the
matter of achieving freedom from the body, if a person takes the help of the five products
of the cow, kine become inclined to confer blessings upon the person like the river
Saraswati—Ye kine, ye are always conveyers of all kinds of merit! Gratified with me, do
ye appoint a desirable end for me! I have today become what ye are! By giving you away,
I really give myself away. (After these words have been uttered by giver, the receiver
should say),—Ye are no longer owned by him who gives you away! Ye have now
become mine. Possessed of the nature of both Sutya and Soma, do ye cause both the giver
and the receiver to blaze forth with all kinds of prosperity!—(As already indicated), the
giver should duly utter the words occurring in the first part of the above verse. The
regenerate recipient, conversant with the ritual that regulates the gift of kine, should,
when receiving the kine in gift, utter (as already) said the words occurring in the latter
half of the above verse. The man who, instead of a cow, gives away the usual value
thereof or cloths or gold, comes to be regarded as the giver of a cow. The giver, when
giving away the usual value of a cow (as the substitute of a cow) should utter the
words,—This cow with face upturned is being given away. Do thou accept her!—The
man who gives away cloths (as the substitute of a cow) should utter the words,—
Bhavitavya—(meaning that the gift should be regarded as representing a cow). The man
who gives away gold (as the substitute of a cow) should utter the word,—Vaishnavi
(meaning, this gold that I give away is of the form and nature of a cow).—Even these are
the words that should be uttered in the order of the kind of gift mentioned above. The
reward that is reaped by making such vicarious gifts of kine is residence in Heaven for
six and thirty thousand years, eight thousand years, and twenty thousand years
respectively. Even these are the merits, respectively, of gifts of things as substitute of
kine. While as regards him who gives an actual cow all the merits that attach to vicarious

[367] In verse 5, if instead of the reading swah, swa be adopted, the meaning would be knowing that he
would have to die. A Rohini is a red cow. The words Samanga and Vahula are Vedic terms applied to the cow.
The Sandh in vahuleti is arsha. The formula or Mantras that should be uttered in actually giving away the kine
occur in the scriptures.

gifts of kine become his at only the eight step (homewards) of the recipient.[368] He that gives an actual cow becomes endued with righteous behaviour in this world. He that gives the value of a cow becomes freed from every kind of fear. He that gives a cow (as a substitute in way for a real cow) never meet with sorrow. All the three, as also they that regularly go through their ablutions and other acts at early dawn, and he that is well-conversant with the Mahabharata, it is well-known, attain to the regions of Vishnu and Soma. Having given away a cow, the giver should, for three nights, adopt the vaccine vow, and pass one night with kine. Commencing again from that lunation, numbering the eight, which is known by the name of Kamya, he should pass three nights, supporting himself entirely on milk and urine and dung of the cow.[369] By giving away a bull, one attains to the merit that attaches to the divine vow (Brahmacharya). By giving away a couple of kine, one acquires the mastery of the Vedas. That man who performs a sacrifice and makes gifts of kine agreeably to the ritual laid down, attains to many regions of a superior character. These, however, are not attainable by the person who is unacquainted with that ritual (and who, therefore, gives away kine without observing the scriptural declarations). That man who gives away even a single cow that yields a copious measure of milk, acquires the merit of giving away all desirable things on Earth collected together. What need, therefore, be said of the gift of many such kine as yield Havya and Kavya in consequence of their full udders? The merit that attaches to the gift of superior oxen is greater than that which attaches to the gift of kine. One should not, by imparting a knowledge of this ritual, benefit a person that is not one's disciple or that is not observant of vows or that is bereft of faith or that is possessed of a crooked understanding. Verily, this religion is a mystery, unknown to most people. One that knows it should not speak of it at every place. There are, in the world, many men that are bereft of faith. There are among men many persons that are mean and that resemble Rakshasas. This religion, if imparted unto them, would lead to evil. It would be productive of equal evil if imparted to such sinful men as have taken shelter in atheism.'—Listen to me, O king, as I recite to thee the names of those righteous monarchs that have attained to regions of great felicity as the reward of those gifts of kine which they made agreeable to the instructions of Vrihaspati, Usinara, Viswagaswa, Nriga, Bhagiratha, the celebrated Mandhatri the son of Yuvanaswa, king Muchukunda, Bhagiratha, Naishadha, Somaka, Pururavas, Bharata of imperial sway to whose race belongs all the Bharatas, the heroic Rama the son of Dasaratha, and many other celebrated kings of great achievement, and also king Dilipa of widely known deeds, all, in consequence of their gifts of kine agreeable to the ritual, attained to Heaven. King Mandhatri was always observant of sacrifices, gifts, penances, kingly duties, and gifts of kine. Therefore, O son of Pritha, do thou also bear in mind those instructions of Vrihaspati which I have recited unto thee (in respect of gifts of kine). Having obtained the kingdom of the Kurus, do thou, with a cheerful heart, make gifts of good kine unto foremost of Brahmanas!'"

"Vaisampayana continued, 'Thus addressed by Bhishma on the subject of properly making gifts of kine, king Yudhishthira did all that Bhishma wished. Verily, king

---

[368] The Commentator explains that gavadinam in the first line refers to gopratindhinam. The second line is very terse. The sense is that at only the eight step in the homeward journey of the recipient, all the merits attaching to vicarious gift become his who gives an actual cow: what need, therefore, be said of that merit when the recipient reaches home and draws from the cow the means of worshipping his domestic fire, entertaining his guests, etc?

[369] Ashtami is the eighth day of the lunar fortnight. There must be two Ashtamis in every lunar month. A particular Ashtami is known as the Kamya or the Goshtha. On that day, kine are worshipped with sandalpaste, vermilion, floral wreaths, etc.

Yudhishthira bore in mind the whole of that religion which the preceptor of the deities imparted unto the royal Mandhatri. Yudhishthira from that time began to make always gifts of kine and to support himself on grains of barley and on cowdung as both his food and drink. The king also began to sleep from that day on the bare earth, and possessed of restrained soul and resembling a bull in conduct, he became the foremost of monarchs.[370] The Kuru king from that day became very attentive to kine and always worshipped them, hymning their praises. From that day, the king gave up the practice of yoking kine unto his vehicles. Wheresoever he had occasion to go, he proceeded on cars drawn by horses of good mettle.'"

SECTION LXXVII.

"Vaisampayana said, 'King Yudhishthira endued with humility, once again questioned the royal son of Santanu on the subject of gifts of kine in detail.'

"'The king said, "Do thou, O Bharata, once more discourse to me in detail on the merits of giving away kine. Verily, O hero, I have not been satiated with hearing thy nectar-like words!"'

"Vaisampayana continued, 'Thus addressed by king Yudhishthira the just, Santanu's son began to discourse to him once again, in detail on the merits attaching to the gift of kine.'

"'Bhishma said, "By giving unto a Brahmana a cow possessed of a calf, endued with docility and other virtues, young in years, and wrapped round with a piece of cloth, one becomes cleansed of all one's sins. There are many regions (in Hell) which are sunless. One who makes the gift of a cow has not to go thither. That man, however, who gives unto a Brahmana a cow that is incapable of drinking or eating, that has her milk dried up, that is endued with senses all of which have been weakened, and that is diseased and overcome with decrepitude, and that may, therefore, be likened to a tank whose water has been dried up,—indeed, the man who gives such a cow unto a Brahmana and thereby inflicts only pain and disappointment upon him, has certainly to enter into dark Hell. That cow which is wrathful and vicious, or diseased, or weak or which has been purchased without the price agreed upon having been paid,—or which would only afflict the regenerate recipient with distress and disappointment, should never be given. The regions such a man may acquire (as the rewards of other acts of righteousness performed by him) would fail to give him any happiness or impart to him any energy. Only such kine as are strong, endued with good behaviour, young in years, and possessed of fragrance, are applauded by all (in the matter of gift). Verily, as Ganga is the foremost of all rivers, even so is a Kapila cow the foremost of all kine."

"'Yudhishthira said, "Why, O grandsire, do the righteous applaud the gift of a Kapila cow (as more meritorious) when all good kine that are given away should be regarded as equal? O thou of great puissance, I wish to hear what the distinction is that attaches to a Kapila cow. Thou art, verily, competent to discourse to me on this topic!"[371]

"'Bhishma said, "I have, O son, heard old men recite this history respecting the circumstances under which the Kapila cow was created. I shall recite that old history to thee! In days of yore, the Self-born Brahman commanded the Rishi Daksha, saying,—'Do thou create living creatures!' From desire of doing good to creatures, Daksha, in the first

---

[370] Sikhi means a bull, so called from the hump it carries. The construction is sikhi Vrishaiva etc.

[371] A Kapila cow is one that gives a copious measure of milk whenever she is milked, and is possessed of various other accomplishments and virtues.

instance, created food. Even as the deities exist, depending upon nectar, all living creatures, O puissant one, live depending upon the sustenance assigned by Daksha. Among all objects mobile and immobile, the mobile are superior. Among mobile creatures Brahmanas are superior. The sacrifices are all established upon them. It is by sacrifice that Soma (nectar) is got. Sacrifice has been established upon kine.[372] The gods become gratified through sacrifices. As regards the Creation then, the means of support came first, creatures came next. As soon as creatures were born, they began to cry aloud for food. All of them then approached their creator who was to give them food like children approaching their father or mother. Knowing the intention which moved all his creatures, the holy lord of all creatures, viz., Daksha, for the sake of the beings he had created, himself drank a quantity of nectar. He became gratified with the nectar he quaffed and thereupon an eructation came out, diffusing an excellent perfume all around. As the result of that eructation, Daksha saw that it gave birth to a cow which he named Surabhi. This Surabhi was thus a daughter of his, that had sprung from his mouth. The cow called Surabhi brought forth a number of daughters who came to be regarded as the mothers of the world. Their complexion was like that of gold, and they were all Kapilas. They were the means of sustenance for all creatures. As those kine, whose complexion resembled that of Amrita, began to pour milk, the froth of that milk arose and began to spread on every side, even as when the waves of a running stream dashing against one another, copious froth is produced that spreads on every side. Some of that froth fell, from the mouths of the calves that were sucking, upon the head of Mahadeva who was then sitting on the Earth. The puissant Mahadeva thereupon, filled with wrath, cast his eyes upon those kine. With that third eye of his which adorns his forehead, he seemed to burn those kine as he looked at them. Like the Sun tingeing masses of clouds with diverse colours the energy that issued from the third eye of Mahadeva produced, O monarch, diverse complexion in those kine. Those amongst them, however, which succeeded in escaping from the glance of Mahadeva by entering the region of Soma, remained of the same colour with which they were born, for no change was produced in their complexion. Seeing that Mahadeva had become exceedingly angry, Daksha, the lord of all creatures, addressed him, saying—'Thou hast, O great deity, been drenched with nectar. The milk or the froth that escapes from the mouths of calves sucking their dams is never regarded as impure remnant.[373] Chandramas, after drinking the nectar, pours it once more. It is not, however, on that account, looked upon as impure. After the same manner, the milk that these kine yield, being born of nectar, should not be regarded as impure (even though the udders have been touched by the calves with their mouths). The wind can never become impure. Fire can never become impure. Gold can never become impure. The Ocean can never become impure. The Nectar, even when drunk by the deities, can never become impure. Similarly, the milk of a cow, even when her udders are sucked by her calf, can never become impure. These kine will support all these worlds with the milk they will yield and the ghee that will be manufactured therefrom. All creatures wish to enjoy the auspicious wealth, identifiable with nectar, that kine possess!'—Having said these words, the lord of creatures, Daksha, made a present unto Mahadeva of a bull with certain kine.

---

[372] For without ghee, which is produced from milk, there can be no sacrifice. The sa may refer to Soma, but sacrifice is evidently meant.

[373] The idea of uchchishta, is peculiarly Hindu and cannot be rendered into any other language. Everything that forms the remnant of meal after one has left of eating, is uchchishta. The calf sucks its dam. The udders, however, are not washed before milking the dam, for the milk coming out of them is not held to be impure remnant.

Daksha gratified the heart of Rudra, O Bharata, with that present. Mahadeva, thus gratified, made that bull his vehicle. And it was after the form of that bull that Mahadeva adopted the device on the standard floating on his battle-car. For this reason it is that Rudra came to be known as the bull-bannered deity. It was on that occasion also that the celestials, uniting together, made Mahadeva the lord of animals. Indeed, the great Rudra became the Master of kine and is named as the bull-signed deity. Hence, O king, in the matter of giving away kine, the gift is regarded as primarily desirable of Kapila kine which are endued with great energy and possessed of colour unchanged (from white). Thus are kine, the foremost of all creatures in the world. It is from them that the means have flowed of the sustenance of all the worlds. They have Rudra for their master. They yield Soma (nectar) in the form of milk. They are auspicious and sacred, and grantors of every wish and givers of life. A person by making a gift of a cow come to be regarded as making a gift of every article that is desired to be enjoyed by men. That man who, desiring to attain to prosperity, reads with a pure heart and body these verses on the origin of kine, becomes cleansed of all his sins and attains to prosperity and children and wealth and animals. He who makes a gift of a cow, O king, always succeeds in acquiring the merits that attach to gifts of Havya and Kavya, to the offer of oblations of water unto the Pitris, to other religious acts whose performance brings peace and happiness, to the gift of vehicles and cloths, and to the cherishing of children and the old.'"

"Vaisampayana continued, 'Hearing these words of his grandsire, Pritha's son, viz., the royal Yudhishthira of Ajamida's race, uniting with his brothers, began to make gifts of both bulls and kine of different colours unto foremost of Brahmanas. Verily, for the purpose of subduing regions of felicity in the next, and winning great fame, king Yudhishthira performed many sacrifices and, as sacrificial presents, gave away hundreds of thousands of kine unto such Brahmanas.'"

SECTION LXXVIII.

"'Bhishma said, "In days of yore, king Saudasa born of Ikshvaku's race, that foremost of eloquent men, on one occasion approached his family priest, viz., Vasishtha, that foremost of Rishis, crowned with ascetic success, capable of wandering through every region, the receptacle of Brahma, and endued with eternal life and put him the following question.

""Saudasa said, 'O holy one, O sinless one, what is that in the three worlds which is sacred and by reciting which at all times a man may acquire high merit?'"

"'Bhishma said, "Unto king Saudasa who stood before him with head bent in reverence, the learned Vasishtha having first bowed unto kine and purified himself (in body and mind), discoursed upon the mystery relating to kine, a topic that is fraught with result highly beneficial to all persons.

""Vasishtha said, 'Kine are always fragrant. The perfume emanated by the exudation of the Amytis agallochum issues out of the bodies. Kine are the great refuge of all creatures. Kine constitute the great source of blessing unto all.[374] Kine are the Past and the Future. Kine are the source of eternal growth. Kine are the root of Prosperity. Anything given to kine is never lost. Kine constitute the highest food. They are the best Havi for the deities. The Mantras called Swaha and Vashat are forever established in

---

[374] Swastayana is a ceremony of propitiation, productive of blessing and destructive of misery of every kind.

kine. Kine constitute the fruit of sacrifices. Sacrifices are established in kine. Kine are the Future and the Past, and Sacrifice rest on them. Morning and evening kine yield unto the Rishis, O foremost of men, Havi for use in Homa, O thou of great effulgence. They who make gift of kine succeed in transcending all sins which they may have committed and all kinds of calamities into which they may fall, O thou of great puissance. The man possessing ten kine and making a gift of one cow, he possessing a hundred kine and making a gift of ten kine, and he possessing a thousand kine and making a gift of a hundred kine, all earn the same measure of merit. The man who, though possessed of hundred kine, does not establish a domestic fire for daily worship, that man who though possessed of a thousand kine does not perform sacrifices, and that man who though possessed of wealth acts as a miser (by not making gift and discharging the duties of hospitality), are all three regarded as not worthy of any respect. Those men who make gift of Kapila kine with their calves and with vessel of white brass for milking them,— kine, that is, which are not vicious and which while given away, are wrapped round with cloths,—succeed in conquering both this and the other world. Such persons as succeed in making gift of a bull that is still in the prime of youth, that has all its senses strong, and that may be regarded as the foremost one among hundreds of herds, that has large horns adorned with ornaments (of gold or silver), unto a Brahmana possessed of Vedic learning, succeed, O scorcher of foes, in attaining to great prosperity and affluence each time they take birth in the world. One should never go to bed without reciting the names of kine. Nor should one rise from bed in the morning without a similar recitation of the names of kine. Morning and evening one should bend one's head in reverence to kine. As the consequence of such acts, one is sure to attain to great prosperity. One should never feel any repugnance for the urine and the dung of the cow. One should never eat the flesh of kine. As the consequence of this, one is sure to attain to great prosperity. One should always take the names of kine. One should never show any disregard for kine in any way. If evil dreams are seen, men should take the names of kine. One should always bathe, using cow-dung at the time. One should sit on dried cowdung. One should never cast one's urine and excreta and other secretions on cowdung. One should never obstruct kine in any way. One should eat, sitting on a cowhide purified by dipping it in water, and then cast one's eyes towards the west. Sitting with restrained speech, one should eat ghee, using the bare earth as one's dish. One reaps, in consequence of such acts, that prosperity of which kine are the source.[375] One should pour libations on the fire, using ghee for the purpose. One should cause Brahmanas to utter blessings upon one, by presents of ghee. One should make gift of ghee. One should also eat ghee. As the reward of such acts one is sure to attain to that prosperity which kine confer. That man who inspires a vaccine form made of sesame seeds by uttering the Vedic Mantras called by the name of Gomati, and then adorns that form with every kind of gems and makes a gift of it, has never to suffer any grief on account of all his acts of omission and commission,—"Let kine that yield copious measures of milk and that have horns adorned with gold,—kine viz., that are Surabhis or the daughters of Surabhis.—approach me even as rivers approach the ocean! I always look at kine. Let kine always look at me. Kine are ours. We are theirs. Ourselves are there where kine are!"—Even thus, at night or day, in happiness or woe, verily, at times of even great fear,—should a man exclaim. By uttering such words he is

---

[375] The commentator explains that by a wet cowhide is meant a piece of cowhide that has been dipped in water and thus purified. Upavisya is understood after Charmani. The mention of bhumau implies the avoidance of dishes or plates or cups of white brass or other allowable metals. Gavam pushtim, I understand, means 'the prosperity in respect of kine.' i.e., the prosperity which kine confer.

certain to become freed from every fear.'"""

SECTION LXXIX.

"""Vasishtha said, 'The kine that had been created in a former age practised the austerest penances for a hundred thousand years with the desire of attaining to a position of great pre-eminence. Verily, O scorcher of foes, they said unto themselves,—"We shall, in this world, become the best of all kinds of Dakshina in sacrifices, and we shall not be liable to be stained with any fault! By bathing in water mixed with our dung people shall become sanctified. The deities and men shall use our dung for the purpose of purifying all creatures mobile and immobile. They also that will give us away shall attain to those regions of happiness which will be ours."[376]—The puissant Brahman, appearing unto them at the conclusion of their austerities, gave them the boons they sought, saying,—"it shall be as ye wish! Do ye (thus) rescue all the worlds!"—Crowned with fruition in respect of their wishes, they all rose up,—those mothers of both the Past and the Future. Every morning, people should bow with reverence unto kine. As the consequence of this, they are certain to win prosperity. At the conclusion of their penances O monarch, kine became the refuge of the world. It is for this that kine are said to be highly blessed, sacred, and the foremost of all things. It is for this that kine are said to stay at the very head of all creatures. By giving away a Kapila cow with a calf resembling herself, yielding a copious measure of milk, free from every vicious habit, and covered with a piece of cloth, the giver attains to great honours in the region of Brahma. By giving away a cow of red complexion, with a calf that resembles herself, yielding milk, free from every vice, and covered with a piece of cloth, one attains to great honours in the region of Surya. By giving away a cow of variegated hue, with a calf similar to herself, yielding milk, free from every vice, and covered with a piece of cloth, one attains to great honours in the region of Soma. By giving away a cow of white complexion, with a calf similar to herself, yielding milk, free from every vice, and covered with a piece of cloth, one attains to great honours in the region of Indra. By giving away a cow of dark complexion, with a calf similar to herself, yielding milk, free from every vice, and covered with a piece of cloth, one attains to great honours in the region of Agni. By giving away a cow of the complexion of smoke, with a calf similar to herself, yielding milk, free from every vice, and covered with a piece of cloth, one attains to great honours in the region of Yama. By giving away a cow of the complexion of the foam of water, with a calf and a vessel of white brass for milking her, and covered with a piece of cloth, one attains to the region of Varuna. By giving away a cow whose complexion is like that of the dust blown by the wind, with a calf, and a vessel of white brass for milking her, and covered with a piece of cloth, one attains to great honours in the region of the Wind-god. By giving a cow of the complexion of gold, having eyes of a tawny hue with a calf and a vessel of white brass for milking her and covered with a piece of cloth, one enjoys the felicity of the region of Kuvera. By giving away a cow of the complexion of the smoke of straw, with a calf and a vessel of white brass for milking her, and covered with a piece of cloth, one attains to great honours in the region of the Pitris. By giving away a fat cow with the flesh of its throat hanging down and accompanied by her calf, one attains with ease to the high region of the Viswedevas. By giving away a Gouri cow, with calf similar to her, yielding

---

[376] The first line of verse 4 seems to be connected with verse 3. The second line of 4 seems to stand by itself. By connecting the first line of 4 with the second, the meaning will be—All mobile and immobile creatures that will give us away etc. Immobile creatures making gifts of kine would be utter nonsense.

milk, free from every vice, and covered with a piece of cloth, one attains to the region of the Vasus. By giving away a cow of the complexion of a white blanket, with a calf and a vessel of white brass, and covered with a piece of cloth, one attains to the region of the Sadhyas. By giving away a bull with a high hump and adorned with every jewel, the giver, O king, attains to the region of the Maruts. By giving away a bull of blue complexion, that is full-grown in respect of years and adorned with every ornament, the giver attains to the regions of the Gandharvas and the Apsaras. By giving away a cow with the flesh of her throat hanging down, and adorned with every ornament, the giver, freed from every grief, attains to those regions that belong to Prajapati himself. That man, O king, who habitually makes gifts of kine, proceeds, piercing through the clouds, on a car of solar effulgence to Heaven and shines there in splendour. That man who habitually makes gifts of kine comes to be regarded as the foremost of his species. When thus proceeding to Heaven, he is received by a thousand celestial damsels of beautiful hips and adorned with handsome robes and ornaments. These girls wait upon him there and minister to his delight. He sleeps there in peace and is awakened by the musical laughter of those gazelle-eyed damsels, the sweet notes of their Vinas, the soft strains of their Vallakis, and the melodious tinkle of their Nupuras.[377] The men who makes gifts of kine resides in Heaven and is honoured there for as many years as there are hairs on the bodies of the kine he gives away. Falling off from Heaven (upon the exhaustion of his merit), such a man takes birth in the order of humanity and, in fact, in a superior family among men.""""

SECTION LXXX.

""""Vasishtha said, "'Kine are yielders of ghee and milk. They are the sources of ghee and they have sprung from ghee. They are rivers of ghee, and eddies of ghee. Let kine ever be in my house! Ghee is always my heart. Ghee is even established in my navel. Ghee is in every limb of mine. Ghee resides in my mind. Kine are always at my front. Kine are always at my rear. Kine are on every side of my person. I live in the midst of kine!'—Having purified oneself by touching water, one should, morning and evening, recite these Mantras every day. By this, one is sure to be cleansed of all the sins one may commit in course of the day. They who make gifts of a thousand kine, departing from this world, proceed to the regions of the Gandharvas and the Apsaras where there are many palatial mansions made of gold and where the celestial Ganga, called the current of Vasu, runs. Givers of a thousand kine repair thither where run many rivers having milk for their water, cheese for their mire, and curds for their floating moss. That man who makes gifts of hundreds of thousands of kine agreeably to the ritual laid down in the scriptures, attains to high prosperity (here) and great honours in Heaven. Such a man causes both his paternal and maternal ancestors to the tenth degree to attain to regions of great felicity, and sanctifies his whole race. Kine are sacred. They are the foremost of all things in the world. They are verily the refuge of the universe. They are the mothers of the very deities. They are verily incomparable. They should be dedicated in sacrifices. When making journeys, one should proceed by their right (i.e., keeping them to one's left). Ascertaining the proper time, they should be given away unto eligible persons. By giving away a Kapila cow having large horns, accompanied by a calf and a vessel of white brass for milking her, and covered with a piece of cloth, one succeeds in entering, freed from

---

[377] Vallaki is the Indian lute. The Nupura is an ornament for the ankles.

fear, the palace of Yama that is so difficult to enter. One should always recite this sacred Mantra, viz.,—"Kine are of beautiful form. Kine are of diverse forms. They are of universal form. They are the mothers of the universe. O, let kine approach me!"—There is no gift more sacred than the gift of kine. There is no gift that produces more blessed merit. There has been nothing equal to the cow, nor will there be anything that will equal her. With her skin, her hair, her horns, the hair of her tail, her milk, and her fat,—with all these together,—the cow upholds sacrifice. What thing is there that is more useful than the cow? Bending my head unto her with reverence, I adore the cow who is the mother of both the Past and the Future, and by whom the entire universe of mobile and immobile creatures is covered. O best of men, I have thus recited to thee only a portion of the high merits of kine. There is no gift in this world that is superior to the gift of kine. There is also no refuge in this world that is higher than kine.'"

"'Bhishma continued, "That high-souled giver of land (viz., king Saudasa), thinking these words of the Rishi Vasishtha to be foremost in point of importance, then made gifts of a very large number of kine unto the Brahmanas, restraining his senses the while, and as the consequence of those gifts, the monarch succeeded in attaining to many regions of felicity in the next world."'"[378]

SECTION LXXXI.

"'Yudhishthira said, "Tell me, O grandsire, what is that which is the most sacred of all sacred things in the world, other than that which has been already mentioned, and which is the highest of all sanctifying objects."

"'Bhishma said, "Kine are the foremost of all objects. They are highly sacred and they rescue men (from all kinds of sin and distress). With their milk and with the Havi manufactured therefrom, kine uphold all creatures in the universe. O best of the Bharatas, there is nothing that is more sacred than kine. The foremost of all things in the three worlds, kine are themselves sacred and capable of cleansing others. Kine reside in a region that is even higher than the region of the deities. When given away, they rescue their givers. Men of wisdom succeed in attaining to Heaven by making gifts of kine. Yuvanaswa's son Mandhatri, Yayati, and (his sire) Nahusha, used always to give away kine in thousands. As the reward of those gifts, they have attained to such regions as are unattainable by the very deities. There is, in this connection, O sinless one, a discourse delivered of old. I shall recite it to thee. Once on a time, the intelligent Suka, having finished his morning rites, approached with a restrained mind his sire, that foremost of Rishis, viz., the Island-born Krishna, who is acquainted with the distinction between that which is superior and that which is inferior, and saluting him, said, 'What is that sacrifice which appears to thee as the foremost of all sacrifices? What is that act by doing which men of wisdom succeed in attaining to the highest region? What is that sacred act by which the deities enjoy the felicity of Heaven? What constitutes the character of sacrifice as sacrifice? What is that upon which sacrifice rests? What is that which is regarded as the best by the deities? What is that sacrifice which transcends the sacrifices of this world? Do thou also tell me, O sire, what is that which is the most sacred of all things.' Having heard these words of his son, O chief of Bharata's race, Vyasa, the foremost of all persons conversant with duties, discoursed as follows unto him.

[378] Bhumidah is literally, a giver of land. King Saudasa, the commentator explains, was known by the name of Bhumidah in consequence of his liberality in the matter of giving away land unto the Brahmanas.

""""Vyasa said, 'Kine constitute the stay of all creatures. Kine are the refuge of all creatures. Kine are the embodiment of merit. Kine are sacred, and kine are sanctifiers of all. Formerly kine were hornless as it has been heard by us. For obtaining horns they adored the eternal and puissant Brahman. The puissant Brahman, seeing the kine paying their adorations to him and sitting in praya, granted unto each of them what each desired. Thereafter their horns grew and each got what each desired. Of diverse colours, and endued with horns, they began to shine in beauty, O son! Favoured by Brahman himself with boons, kine are auspicious and yielders of Havya and Kavya. They are the embodiments of merit. They are sacred and blessed. They are possessed of excellent form and attributes. Kine constitute high and highly excellent energy. The gift of kine is very much applauded. Those good men who, freed from pride, make gifts of kine, are regarded as doers of righteous deeds and as givers of all articles. Such men, O sinless one, attain to the highly sacred region of kine. The trees there produce sweet fruits. Indeed, those trees are always adorned with excellent flowers and fruits. Those flowers, O best of regenerate persons, are endued with celestial fragrance. The entire soil of that region is made of gems. The sands there are all gold. The climate there is such that the excellencies of every season are felt. There is no more mire, no dust. It is, indeed, highly auspicious. The streams that run there shine in resplendence for the red lotuses blooming upon their bosoms, and for the jewels and gems and gold that occur in their banks and that display the effulgence of the morning Sun. There are many lakes also in that region on whose breasts are many lotuses, mixed here and there with Nymphoea stellata, and having their petals made of costly gems, and their filaments adorned with a complexion like that of gold. They are also adorned with flowering forests of the Nerium odorum with thousands of beautiful creepers twining round them, as also with forests of Santanakas bearing their flowery burdens. There are rivers whose banks are variegated with many bright pearls and resplendent gems and shining gold. Portions of those regions are covered with excellent trees that are decked with jewels and gems of every kind. Some of them are made of gold and some display the splendour of fire. There stand many mountains made of gold, and many hills and eminences made of jewels and gems. These shine in beauty in consequence of their tall summits which are composed of all kinds of gems. The trees that adorn those regions always put forth flowers and fruits, and are always covered with dense foliage. The flowers always emit a celestial fragrance and the fruits are exceedingly sweet, O chief of Bharata's race. Those persons that are of righteous deeds, O Yudhishthira, always sport there in joy. Freed from grief and wrath, they pass their time there, crowned with the fruition of every wish. Persons of righteous deeds, possessed of fame, sport there in happiness, moving from place to place, O Bharata, on delightful vehicles of great beauty. Auspicious bands of Apsaras always amuse them there, with music and dance. Indeed O Yudhishthira, a person goes to such regions as the reward of his making gifts of kine. Those regions which have for their lords Pushan, and the Maruts of great puissance, are attained to by givers of kine. In affluence the royal Varuna is regarded as pre-eminent. The giver of kine attains to affluence like that of Varuna himself. One should, with the steadiness of a vow, daily recite these Mantras declared by Prajapati himself (in respect of kine). Viswarupa and viz.,—Yugandharah, Surupah, Vahurupah, and Matara.[379]—He who serves kine with reverence and who follows them

---

[379] These are the several names by which kine are known. The first is probably derived from kine bearing the plough and thus assisting the tillage of the soil. The second implies beauty of form. The third is derived from the cow being regarded as the origin of all things in the universe: all things, therefore, are only so many

with humility, succeeds in obtaining many invaluable boons from kine who become gratified with him. One should never, in even one's heart, do an injury to kine. One should, indeed, always confer happiness on them. One should always reverence kine and worship them, with bends of one's head. He who does this, restraining his senses the while and filled with cheerfulness, succeeds in attaining to that felicity which is enjoyed by kine (and which kine alone can confer). One should for three days drink the hot urine of the cow. For the next three days one should drink the hot milk of the cow. Having thus drunk for three days hot milk, one should next drink hot ghee for three days. Having in this way drunk hot ghee for three days, one should subsist for the next three days on air only. That sacred thing by whose aid the deities enjoy regions of felicity, that which is the most sacred of all sacred things, viz., ghee should then be borne on the head.[380] With the aid of ghee one should pour libations on the sacred fire. By making gifts of ghee, one should cause the Brahmana to utter benedictions on oneself. One should eat ghee and make gifts of ghee. As the reward of this conduct, one may then attain to that prosperity which belongs to kine. That man who, for a month, subsists upon the gruel of barley picked up every day from cow dung becomes cleansed of sins as grave as the slaughter of a Brahmana. After their defeat at the hands of the Daityas, the deities practised this expiation. It was in consequence of this expiation that they succeeded in regaining their position as deities. Verily, it was through this that they regained their strength and became crowned with success. Kine are sacred. They are embodiments of merit. They are high and most efficacious cleansers of all. By making gifts of kine unto the Brahmanas one attains to Heaven. Living in a pure state, in the midst of kine, one should mentally recite those sacred Mantras that are known by the name of Gomati, after touching pure water. By doing this, one becomes purified and cleansed (of all sins). Brahmanas of righteous deeds, who have been cleansed by knowledge, study of the Vedas, and observance of vows, should, only in the midst of sacred fires or kine or assemblies of Brahmanas, impart unto their disciples a knowledge of the Gomati Mantras which are every way like unto a sacrifice (for the merit they produce). One should observe a fast for three nights for receiving the boon constituted by a knowledge of the import of the Gomati Mantras. The man who is desirous of obtaining a son may obtain one by adoring these Mantras. He who desires the possession of wealth may have his desire gratified by adoring these Mantras. The girl desirous of having a good husband may have her wish fulfilled by the same means. In fact, one may acquire the fruition of every wish one may cherish, by adoring these sacred Mantras. When kine are gratified with the service one renders them, they are, without doubt, capable of granting the fruition of every wish. Even so, kine are highly blessed. They are the essential requisites of sacrifices. They are grantors of every wish. Know that there is nothing superior to kine.'"

"'Bhishma continued, "Thus addressed by his high-souled sire, Suka, endued with great energy, began from that time to worship kine every day. Do thou also, O son, conduct thyself in the same way."'"

---

forms of the cow. Viswarupa implies the same thing. Matara implies mothers, kine being regarded as the mothers of all.

[380] Ghee is regarded so sacred because of its use in sacrifices. It is with the aid of ghee that the deities have become what they are. Itself sacred, it is also cleansing at the same time.

SECTION LXXXII.

"'Yudhishthira said, "I have heard that the dung of the cow is endued with Sree. I desire to hear how this has been brought about. I have doubts, O grandsire, which thou shouldst dispel."[381]

"'Bhishma said, "In this connection is cited the old story, O monarch, of the conversation between kine and Sree, O best of the Bharatas! Once on a time the goddess Sree, assuming a very beautiful form, entered a herd of kine. The kine, beholding her wealth of beauty, became filled with wonder.

""'The kine said, 'Who art thou, O goddess? Whence hast thou become unrivalled on earth for beauty? O highly blessed goddess, we have been filled with wonder at thy wealth of beauty. We desire to know who thou art. Who, indeed, art thou? Whither wilt thou proceed? O thou of very superior splendour of complexion, do tell us in detail all we wish to know.'

""'Sri said, 'Blessed be ye, I am dear unto all creatures. Indeed, I am known by the name of Sri. Forsaken by me, the Daityas have been lost for ever. The deities, viz., Indra, Vivaswat, Soma, Vishnu, Varuna, and Agni, having obtained me, are sporting in joy and will do so for ever. Verily, the Rishis and the deities, only when they are endued with me, have success. Ye kine, those beings meet with destruction into whom I do not enter. Religion, wealth, and pleasure, only when endued with me, become sources of happiness. Ye kine who are givers of happiness, know that I am possessed of even such energy! I wish to always reside in every one of you. Repairing to your presence, I solicit you. Be all of you endued with Sri.'

""'The kine said, 'Thou art fickle and restless. Thou sufferest thyself to be enjoyed by many persons. We do not desire to have thee. Blessed be thou, go wheresoever thou pleasest. As regards ourselves, all of us are possessed of good forms. What need have we with thee? Go wheresoever thou likest. Thou hast already (by answering our questions) gratified us exceedingly.'

""'Sri said, 'Is it proper with you, ye kine that you do not welcome me? I am difficult of being attained. Why then do you not accept me? It seems, ye creatures of excellent vows, that the popular proverb is true, viz., that it is certain that when one come to another of one's own accord and without being sought, one meets with disregard. The Gods, the Danavas, the Gandharvas, the Pisachas, the Uragas, the Rakshasas and human beings succeed in obtaining me only after undergoing the severest austerities. You who have such energy, do ye take me. Ye amiable ones, I am never disregarded by any one in the three worlds of mobile and immobile creatures.'

""'The kine said, 'We do not disregard thee, O goddess. We do not show thee a slight! Thou art fickle and of a very restless heart. It is for this only that we take leave of thee. What need of much talk? Do thou go wheresoever thou choosest. All of us are endued with excellent forms. What need have we with thee, O sinless one?'

""'Sri said, 'Ye givers of honours, cast off by you in this way, I shall certainly be an object of disregard with all the world. Do ye show me grace. Ye are all highly blessed. Ye are ever ready to grant protection unto those that seek your protection. I have come to you soliciting your protection. I have no fault. Do you rescue me (from this situation). Know that I shall always be devoted to you. I am desirous of residing in any parts,

---

[381] Sri is the goddess of Prosperity. The answer of Bhishma will explain the question fully.

however repulsive, of your bodies. Indeed, I wish to reside in even your rectum. Ye sinless ones, I do not see that ye have any part in your bodies that may be regarded as repulsive, for ye are sacred, and sanctifying, and highly blessed. Do ye, however, grant my prayer. Do ye tell me in which part, of your bodies I shall take up my residence.'"

"'Bhishma continued, "Thus addressed by Sri, the kine, always auspicious and inclined to kindness unto all who are devoted to them, took counsel with one another, and then addressing Sri, and unto her, O king, these words.

""The kine said, 'O thou of great fame, it is certainly desirable that we should honour thee. Do thou live in our urine and dung. Both these are sacred, O auspicious goddess!'

""Sri said, 'By good luck, ye have shown me much grace implying your desire to favour me. Let it be even as ye say! Blessed be ye all, I have really been honoured by you, ye givers of happiness!'"

"'Bhishma continued, "Having, O Bharata, made this compact with the kine, Sri, there and then, in the very sight of those kine, rendered herself invisible. I have thus told thee, O son, the glory of the dung of kine. I shall once again discourse to thee on the glory of kine. Do thou listen to me."'"

SECTION LXXXIII.

"'Bhishma said, "They who make gifts of kine, and who subsist upon the remnants of things offered as libations on the sacred fire, are regarded, O Yudhishthira, as always performing sacrifices of every kind. No sacrifice can be performed without the aid of curds and ghee. The very character as sacrifice which sacrifices have, depends upon ghee. Hence ghee (or, the cow from which it is produced) is regarded as the very root of sacrifice. Of all kinds of gifts, the gift of kine is applauded as the highest. Kine are the foremost of all things. Themselves sacred, they are the best of cleansers and sanctifiers. People should cherish kine for obtaining prosperity and even peace. The milk, curds, and ghee that kine yield are capable of cleansing one from every kind of sin. Kine are said to represent the highest energy both in this world and the world that is above. There is nothing that is more sacred or sanctifying than kine, O chief of Bharata's race. In this connection is recited the ancient narrative, O Yudhishthira, of the discourse between the Grandsire and the chief of celestials. After the Daityas had been defeated and Sakra had become the lord of the three worlds all creatures grew in prosperity and became devoted to the true religion. Then, on one occasion, the Rishis, the Gandharvas, the Kinnaras, the Uragas, the Rakshasas, the Deities, the Asuras, the winged creatures and the Prajapatis, O thou of Kuru's race, all assembled together and adored the Grandsire. There were Narada and Parvata and Viswavasu and Haha-Huhu, who sang in celestial strains for adoring that puissant lord of all creatures. The deity of wind bore thither the fragrance of celestial flowers. The Seasons also, in their embodied forms, bore the perfumes of flowers peculiar to each, unto that conclave of celestials, that gathering of all creatures of the universe, where celestial maidens danced and sang in accompaniment with celestial music. In the midst of that assembly, Indra, saluting the Lord of all the deities and bowing his head unto him with reverence, asked him, saying, 'I desire, O Grandsire, to know why the region of kine is higher, O holy one, than the region of the deities themselves who are the lords of all the worlds. What austerities, what Brahmacharya, O lord, did kine perform in consequence of which they are able to reside happily in a region that is even above that of the deities?' Thus addressed by Indra, Brahman said unto the slayer of Vala, 'Thou hast always, O slayer of Vala, disregarded kine. Hence, thou art not acquainted with the glorious pre-eminence of kine. Listen now to me, O puissant one, as I explain to thee the high energy and glorious pre-eminence of kine, O chief of the celestials! Kine have been said to be the limbs of sacrifice. They represent sacrifice itself, O Vasava! Without them, there can be no sacrifice. With their milk and the Havi produced therefrom, they uphold all creatures. Their male calves are engaged in assisting at tillage and thereby produce diverse kinds of paddy and other seeds. From them flow sacrifices and Havya and Kavya, and milk and curds and ghee. Hence, O chief of the deities, kine are sacred. Afflicted by hunger and thirst, they bear diverse burdens. Kine support the Munis. They uphold all creatures by diverse acts. O Vasava, kine are guileless in their behaviour. In consequence of such behaviour and of many well-performed acts, they are enabled to live always in regions that are even above ours. I have thus explained to thee today, O thou of a hundred sacrifices, the reason, O Sakra of kine residing in a place that is high above that of the deities. Kine obtained many excellent forms, O Vasava, and are themselves givers of boons (to others). They are called Surabhis. Of sacred deeds and endued with many auspicious indications, they are highly sanctifying. Listen to me also, O slayer of Vala, as I tell thee in detail the reason why kine,—the offspring of Surabhi,—have descended on the earth, O best of the deities. In day of yore, O son, when in the Devayuga the high souled Danavas became lords of the three worlds, Aditi underwent the severest austerities and got Vishnu within her womb (as the reward thereof). Verily, O chief of the celestials, she had stood upon one leg for many long years, desirous of having a son.[382] Beholding the great goddess Aditi thus undergoing the severest austerities, the daughter of Daksha, viz., the illustrious Surabhi, herself devoted to righteousness, similarly underwent very severe austerities upon the breast of the delightful mountains of Kailasa that are resorted to by both the deities and the Gandharvas. Established on the highest Yoga she also stood upon one leg for eleven thousand years. The deities with the Rishis and the great Nagas all became scorched with the severity of her penances. Repairing thither with me, all of them began to adore that auspicious goddess. I then addressed that goddess endued with penances and said, "O goddess, O thou of faultless conduct, for what purpose, dost thou undergo such severe austerities. O highly blessed one, I am gratified with thy penances, O beautiful one! Do thou, O goddess, solicit what boon thou desirest. I shall grant thee whatever thou mayst ask." Even these were my words unto her, O Purandara. Thus addressed by me, Surabhi answered me, saying, "I have no need, O Grandsire, of boons. Even this, O sinless one, is a great boon to me that thou hast been gratified with me." Unto the illustrious Surabhi, O chief of the celestials who said so unto me, O lord of Sachi, I answered even in these words, O foremost of the deities, viz., "O goddess, at this exhibition of thy freedom from cupidity and desire and at these penances of thine, O thou of beautiful face, I have been exceedingly gratified. I, therefore, grant thee the boon of immortality. Thou shalt dwell in a region that is higher than the three worlds, through my grace. That region shall be known to all by the name of Goloka. Thy offspring, ever engaged in doing good acts, will reside in the world of men. In fact, O highly blessed one, thy daughters will reside there. All kinds of enjoyment, celestial and human, that thou mayst think of, will immediately be thine. Whatever happiness exists in Heaven, will also be thine, O blessed one." The regions, O thou of a hundred eyes, that are Surabhi's are endued with means for the gratification of every wish. Neither Death, nor Decrepitude, nor fire, can overcome its denizens. No ill luck, O Vasava, exists there. Many delightful woods, and delightful

---

[382] Devendreshu is evidently a misreading for Daitendreshu.

ornaments and objects of beauty may be seen there. There many beautiful cars, all excellently equipped, which move at the will of the rider, may be seen, O Vasava. O thou of eyes like lotus-petals, it is only by Brahmacharya, by penances, by Truth, by self-restraint, by gifts, by diverse kinds of righteous deeds, by sojourns to sacred waters, in fact, by severe austerities and righteous acts well-performed, that one can attain to Goloka. Thou hast asked me, O Sakra, and I have answered thee in full. O slayer of Asuras, thou shouldst never disregard kine.'"

"'Bhishma continued, "Having heard these words of the self-born Brahman, O Yudhishthira, Sakra of a thousand eyes began from that time to worship kine every day and to show them the greatest respect. I have thus told thee everything about the sanctifying character of kine, O thou of great splendour. The sacred and high pre-eminence and glory of kine, that is capable of cleansing one from every sin, has, O chief of men, been thus explained to thee. That man who with senses withdrawn from every other object will recite this account unto Brahmanas, on occasions when Havya and Kavya are offered, or at sacrifices, or on occasions of adoring the Pitris, succeeds in conferring upon his ancestors an inexhaustible felicity fraught with the fruition of every wish. That man who is devoted to kine succeeds in obtaining the fruition of every wish of his. Indeed, even those women that are devoted to kine succeed in obtaining the accomplishment of every wish of theirs. He that desireth sons obtaineth them. He that desireth daughters obtaineth them. He that desireth wealth succeedeth in acquiring it and he that desireth religious merit succeedeth in winning it. He that desireth knowledge acquireth it and he that desireth felicity succeedeth in acquiring it. Indeed, O Bharata, there is nothing that is unattainable to one that is devoted to kine."'"

SECTION LXXXIV.

"'Yudhishthira said, "Thou hast, O grandsire, discoursed to me on the gift of kine that is fraught with great merit. In the case of kings observant of their duties, that gift is most meritorious. Sovereignty is always painful. It is incapable of being borne by persons of uncleansed souls. In the generality of cases, kings fail to attain to auspicious ends. By always making, however, gifts of earth, they succeed in cleansing themselves (of all their sins). Thou hast, O prince of Kuru's race, discoursed to me on many duties. Thou hast discoursed to me on the gifts of kine made by king Nriga in days of old. The Rishi Nachiketa, in ancient times, had discoursed on the merits of this act. The Vedas and the Upanishads also have laid down that in all sacrifices,—in fact, in all kinds of religious acts,—the Dakshina should be earth or kine or gold. The Srutis, however, declare that in all Dakshinas, gold is superior and is, indeed, the best. I desire, O grandsire, to hear thee discourse truly on this topic. What is gold? How did it spring up? When did it come into existence? What is its essence? Who is its presiding deity? What are its fruits? Why is it regarded as the foremost of all things? For what reason do men of wisdom applaud the gift of gold? For what reason is gold regarded as the best Dakshinas in all sacrifices? Why also is gold regarded as a cleanser superior to earth itself and kine? Why, indeed, is it regarded so superior as a Dakshina? Do thou, O grandsire, discourse to me on all this!"

"'Bhishma said, "Listen, O king, with concentrated attention to me as I recite to thee in detail the circumstances connected with the origin of gold as understood by me. When my father Santanu of great energy departed from this world, I proceeded to Gangadwara for performing his Sraddha. Arrived there, I commenced the Sraddha of my father. My mother Jahnavi, coming there, rendered me great help. Inviting many ascetics crowned with success and causing them to take their seats before me, I commenced the preliminary rites consisting of gifts of water and of other things. Having with a concentrated mind performed all preliminary rites as laid down in the scriptures, I set myself to duly offer the obsequial cake. I then saw, O king, that a handsome arm, adorned with Angadas and other ornaments, rose up, piercing the ground, through the blades of Kusa grass which I had spread. Beholding that arm rise from the ground, I became filled with wonder. Indeed, O chief of Bharata's race, I thought that my father had come himself for accepting the cake I was about to offer. Reflecting then, by the light of the scriptures, the conviction soon came upon me that the ordinance does occur in the Vedas that the cake should not be presented into the hand of him whose Sraddha is performed. Even this was the conviction that took possession of my mind, viz., that the obsequial cake should never be presented in this world by a man into the visible hand of the man whose obsequial rites are performed. The Pitris do not come in their visible forms for taking the cake. On the other hand, the ordinance provides that it should be presented on the blades of Kusa grass spread on the earth for the purpose. I then, disregarding that hand which constituted an indication of my father's presence, and recollecting the true ordinance depending upon the authority of the scriptures respecting the mode of presenting the cake, offered the entire cake, O chief of the Bharatas, upon those blades of Kusa grass that were spread before me. Know, O prince of men, that what I did was perfectly consistent with the scriptural ordinance. After this, the arm of my sire, O monarch, vanished in our very sight. On that night as I slept, the Pitris appeared to me in a dream. Gratified with me they said, O chief of Bharata's race, even these words, 'We have been pleased with thee, for the indication thou hast afforded today of thy adherence to the ordinance. It has pleased us to see that thou hast not swerved from the injunctions of the scriptures. The scriptural ordinance, having been followed by thee, has become more authoritative, O king. By such conduct thou hast honoured and maintained the authority of thyself, the scriptures, the auditions of the Vedas, the Pitris and the Rishis, the Grandsire Brahman himself, and those seniors, viz., the Prajapatis. Adherence to the scriptures has been maintained. Thou hast today, O chief of the Bharatas, acted very properly. Thou hast made gifts of earth and kine. Do thou make gifts of gold. The gifts of gold is very cleansing. O thou that art well-conversant with duties, know that by such acts of thine, both ourselves and our forefathers will all be cleansed of all our sins. Such gifts rescue both ancestors and descendants to the tenth degree of the person who makes them.' Even these were the words that my ancestors, appearing unto me in a dream, said unto me. I then awoke, O king, and became filled with wonder. Indeed, O chief of Bharata's race, I set my heart then upon making gifts of gold. Listen now, monarch, to this old history. It is highly praiseworthy and it extends the period of his life who listens to it. It was first recited to Rama, the son of Jamadagni. In former days Jamadagni's son Rama, filled with great wrath, exterminated the Kshatriyas from off the face of the earth for thrice seven times. Having subjugated the entire earth the heroic Rama of eyes like lotus-petals began to make preparations for performing a Horse-sacrifice, O king, that is praised by all Brahmanas and Kshatriyas and that is capable of granting the fruition of every wish. That sacrifice cleanses all creatures and enhances the energy and splendour of those who succeed in performing it. Endued with great energy, Rama, by the performance of that sacrifice became purified. Having, however, performed that foremost of sacrifices, the high-souled Rama failed yet to attain to perfect lightness of heart. Repairing unto Rishis conversant with every branch of learning as also the deities, Rama of Bhrigu's race questioned them. Filled with repentance and compassion, he addressed them, saying, 'Ye highly blessed ones, do ye declare that which is more cleansing still for men engaged in fierce deeds.' Thus addressed by him, those great Rishis, fully acquainted with the Vedas and the scriptures, answered him, saying, 'O Rama, guided by the authority of the Vedas, do thou honour all learned Brahmanas. Following this conduct for some time do thou once more ask the regenerate Rishis as to what should be done by thee for cleansing thyself. Follow the advice which those persons of great wisdom give.' Repairing then to Vasishtha and Agastya and Kasyapa, that delighter of the Bhrigus, endued with great energy, asked them that question, 'Ye foremost of Brahmanas, even this is the wish that has arisen in my heart. How, indeed, may I succeed in cleansing myself? By what acts and rites may this be brought about? Or, if by gifts, what is that article by giving away which this wish of mine may be accomplished? Ye foremost of righteous persons, if your minds be inclined to do me a favour, then do tell me, ye that are endued with wealth of asceticism, what is that by which I may succeed in cleansing myself.'

""The Rishis said, 'O delighter of the Bhrigus, the mortal that has sinned becomes cleansed by making gifts of kine, of earth, and of wealth. Even this is what we have heard. There is another gift that is regarded as a great cleanser. Listen to us, O regenerate Rishi, as we discourse on it. That article is excellent and is endued with wonderful aspect and is, besides, the offspring of Fire. In days of yore, the god Agni burnt all the world. It has been heard by us that from his seed sprung gold of bright complexion. It came to be celebrated under the name of good complexioned. By making gifts of gold thou art sure to have thy wish crowned with fruition.' Then the illustrious Vasishtha in especial, of rigid vows, addressing him, said, 'Hear, O Rama, how gold, which has the splendour of fire sprang into existence. That gold will confer merit on thee. In matters of gifts, gold is highly applauded. I shall also tell thee what is gold, whence it has come, and how it has come to be invested with superior attributes. Listen to me, O thou of mighty arms, as I discourse upon these topics. Know this as certain that gold is of the essence of Fire and Soma. The goat is Fire (for if given, it leads to the region of the deity of fire); the sheep is Varuna (for it leads to the region of Varuna the lord of waters); the horse is Surya (for it leads to the region of Surya); elephants are Nagas (for they lead to the world of Nagas); buffaloes are Asuras (for they lead to the region of Asuras); cocks and boars are Rakshasas (for they lead to the regions of the Rakshasas), O delighter of the Bhrigus; earth is sacrifice, kine, water, and Soma (for it leads to the merits of sacrifice, and to the region of kine, of the lord of waters and of Soma). Even these are the declarations of the Smritis. Churning the entire universe, a mass of energy was found. That energy is gold. Hence, O regenerate Rishi, compared to all these objects (which I have named above) gold is certainly superior. It is a precious thing, high and excellent.[383] It is for this reason that the deities and Gandharvas and Uragas and Rakshasas and human beings and Pisachas hold it with care. All these beings, O son of Bhrigu's race, shine in splendour, with the aid of gold, after converting it into crowns and armlets and diverse kinds of ornaments. It is also for this reason that gold is regarded as the most cleansing of all cleansing things such as earth and kine and all other kinds of wealth, O prince of men. The gift of gold, O puissant king, is the highest gift. It is distinguished above the gifts of earth, of kine, and of all other things. O thou that art endued with the effulgence of an immortal, gold is an eternal cleanser. Do thou make gifts of it unto the foremost of

---

[383] The commentator explains that hence, by making gifts of gold, one comes to be regarded as making gifts of the entire universe.

Brahmanas as it is the foremost of cleansing things. Of all kinds of Dakshina, gold is the best. They who make gifts of gold are said to be givers of all things. Indeed, they who make gifts of gold come to be regarded as givers of deities. Agni is all the deities in one, and gold has Agni for its essence. Hence it is that the person who makes gifts of gold gives away all the deities. Hence, O chief of men, there is no gift higher than the gift of gold.'

""""Vasishtha continued, 'Hear once more, O regenerate Rishi, as I discourse upon it, the pre-eminence of gold, O foremost of all wielders of weapons. I heard this formerly in the Purana, O son of Bhrigu's race. I represent the speech of Prajapati himself. After the wedding was over of the illustrious and high-souled Rudra armed with the trident, O son of Bhrigu's race, with the goddess who became his spouse, on the breast of that foremost of mountains, viz., Himavat, the illustrious and high-souled deity wished to unite himself with the goddess. Thereupon all the deities, penetrated with anxiety, approached Rudra. Bending their heads with reverence and gratifying Mahadeva and his boon giving spouse Uma, both of whom were seated together, they addressed Rudra, O perpetuator of Bhrigu's race, saying, "This union, O illustrious and sinless one, of thine with the goddess, is a union of one endued with penances with another of penances as severe! Verily, it is the union, O lord, of one possessed of very great energy with another whose energy is scarcely less! Thou, O illustrious one, art of energy that is irresistible. The goddess Uma, also is possessed of energy that is equally irresistible. The offspring that will result from a union like this, will, without doubt, O illustrious deity, be endued with very great might. Verily, O puissant lord, that offspring will consume all things in the three worlds without leaving a remnant. Do thou then, O lord of all the universe, O thou of large eyes, grant unto these deities prostrated before thee, a boon from desire of benefiting the three worlds! Do thou, O puissant one, restrain this high energy of thine which may become the seed of offspring. Verily, that energy is the essence of all forces in the three worlds. Ye two, by an act of congress, are sure to scorch the universe! The offspring that will be born of you two will certainly be able to afflict the deities! Neither the goddess Earth, nor the Firmament, nor Heaven, O puissant one, nor all of them together, will be able to bear thy energy, we firmly believe. The entire universe is certain to be burnt through the force of thy energy. It behoveth thee, O puissant one, to show us favour, O illustrious deity. That favour consists in thy not begetting a son, O foremost of the deities, upon the goddess Uma. Do thou, with patience, restrain thy fiery and puissant energy!" Unto the deities that said so the holy Mahadeva having the bull for his sign, O regenerate Rishi, answered, saying, "So be it!" Having said so, the deity that has the bull for his vehicle, drew up his vital seed. From that time he came to be called by the name of Urdhvaretas (one that has drawn up the vital seed). The spouse of Rudra, however, at this endeavour of the deities to stop procreation, became highly incensed. In consequence of her being of the opposite sex (and, therefore, endued with little control upon her temper) she used harsh words, thus, "Since ye have opposed my lord in the matter of procreating a child when he was desirous of procreating one upon me, as the consequence of this act, ye deities, ye all shall become sonless. Verily, since ye have opposed the birth of issue from me, therefore, ye shall have no offspring of your own." At the time this curse was denounced, O perpetuator of Bhrigu's race, the deity of fire was not there. It is in consequence of this curse of the goddess that the deities have become childless. Rudra, solicited by them, held in himself his energy of incomparable puissance. A small quantity, however, that came out of his body fell down on the earth. That seed, falling on the earth, leaped into a blazing fire and there began to grow (in size and power) most wonderfully. The energy of Rudra, coming in contact with another energy of great puissance, became identified with it in respect of essence. Meanwhile, all the deities having Sakra at their head, were scorched a good deal by the Asura named Taraka. The Adityas, the Vasus, the Rudras, the Maruts, the Aswins, and the Sadhyas all became exceedingly afflicted in consequence of the prowess of that son of Diti. All the regions of the deities, their beautiful cars, and their palatial mansions, and the retreats of the Rishis, were snatched away by the Asuras. Then the deities and the Rishis, with cheerless hearts, sought the protection of the illustrious and puissant Brahman of unfading glory.'"""

SECTION LXXXV.

"""The Deities said, "The Asura named Taraka who has received boons from thee, O puissant one, is afflicting the deities and the Rishis. Let his death be ordained by thee. O Grandsire, great has been our fear from him. O illustrious one, do thou rescue us. We have no other refuge than thee."

"""Brahman said, "I am equal in my behaviour towards all creatures. I cannot, however, approve of unrighteousness. Let Taraka, that opponent of the deities and Rishis, be quickly destroyed. The Vedas and the eternal duties shall not be exterminated, ye foremost of celestials! I have ordained what is proper in this matter. Let the fever of your hearts be dispelled."

"""The Deities said, "In consequence of thy having granted him boons, that son of Diti has been proud of his might. He is incapable of being slain, by the deities. How then will his death be brought about? The boon which, O Grandsire, he has obtained from thee is that he should not be slayable by deities or Asuras or Rakshasas. The deities have also been cursed by the spouse of Rudra in consequence of their endeavour in former days to stop propagation. The curse denounced by her has been, O lord of the universe, even this, viz., that they are not to have any offspring."

"""Brahman said, "Ye foremost of deities, Agni was not there at the time the curse was denounced by the goddess. Even he will beget a son for the destruction of the enemies of the gods. Transcending all the deities and Danavas and Rakshasas and human beings and Gandharvas and Nagas and feathery creatures, the offspring of Agni with his dart, which in his hands will be a weapon incapable of being baffled if once hurled at the foe, will destroy Taraka from whom your fear hath arisen. Verily, all other enemies of yours will also be slain by him. Will is eternal. That Will is known by the name of Kama and is identical with Rudra's seed a portion of which fell into the blazing form of Agni. That energy, which is a mighty substance, and which resembles a second Agni, will be cast by Agni into Ganga for producing a child upon her in order to effect the destruction of the enemies of the gods. Agni did not come within the range of Uma's curse. The eater of sacrificial libations was not present there when the curse was denounced. Let the deity of fire, therefore, be searched out. Let him now be set to this task. Ye sinless ones, I have told you what the means are for the destruction of Taraka. The curses of those that are endued with energy fail to produce any effect upon those that are endued with energy. Forces, when they come into contact with something that is endued with stronger force, become weakened. They that are endued with penances are competent to destroy even the boon-giving deities who are indestructible. Will, or Like, or Desire (which is identifiable with Agni) sprang in former times and is the most eternal of all creatures. Agni is the Lord of the universe. He is incapable of being apprehended or described. Capable of going everywhere and existing in all things, he is the Creator of all beings. He lives in the hearts of all creatures. Endued with great puissance, He is older than Rudra himself. Let that eater of sacrificial libations, who is a mass of energy, be searched out. That illustrious deity will accomplish this desire of your hearts." Hearing these words of the Grandsire, the high-souled gods then proceeded to search out the god of fire with hearts cheerful in consequence of their purpose having been achieved. The gods and the Rishis then searched every part of the three worlds, their hearts filled with the thought of Agni and eagerly desiring to obtain a sight of him. Endued with penances, possessed of prosperity, celebrated over all the worlds, those high-souled ones, all crowned with ascetic success, sojourned over every part of the universe, O foremost one of Bhrigu's race. They failed, however, to find out the eater of sacrificial libations who had concealed himself by merging his self into self.[384] About this time, a frog, living in water, appeared on the surface thereof from the nethermost regions, with cheerless heart in consequence of having been scorched by the energy of Agni. The little creature addressed the deities who had become penetrated with fear and who were all very eager to obtain a sight of the deity of fire, saying, "Ye gods, Agni is now residing in the nethermost regions. Scorched by the energy of that deity, and unable to bear it longer, I have come hither. The illustrious bearer of sacrificial libations, ye gods, is now under the waters. He has created a mass of waters within which he is staying. All of us have been scorched by his energy. If, ye gods, ye desire to obtain a sight of him,—verily, if ye have any business with him,—do ye go to him thither. Do, indeed, repair thither. As regards ourselves, we shall fly from this place, ye deities, from fear of Agni." Having said this much, the frog dived into the water. The eater of sacrificial libations learnt of the treachery of the frog. Coming to that animal, he cursed the whole batrachian race, saying, "Ye shall henceforth be deprived of the organ of taste." Having denounced this curse on the frog, he left the spot speedily for taking up his abode elsewhere. Verily, the puissant deity did not show himself. Seeing the plight to which the frogs were reduced for having done them a service, the deities, O best of the Bhrigus, showed favour unto those creatures. I shall tell thee everything regarding it. Do thou listen to me, O mighty-armed hero.

""""The Deities said, "Though deprived of tongues through the curse of Agni and, therefore, reft of the sensation of taste, ye shall yet be able to utter diverse kinds of speech. Living within holes, deprived of food, reft of consciousness, wasted and dried up, and more dead than alive, all of you will be held by the Earth nevertheless. Ye shall also be able to wander about at night-time when everything is enveloped in thick darkness." Having said this unto the frogs, the deities once more went over every part of the earth for finding out the deity of blazing flames. In spite of all their efforts, however, they failed to get at him. Then, O perpetuator of Bhrigu's race, an elephant, as large and mighty as the elephant of Sakra, addressed the gods, saying, "Agni is now residing within this Aswattha tree!" Incensed with wrath, Agni cursed all the elephants, O descendant of Bhrigu saying, "Your tongues will be bent back." Having been pointed out by the elephants, the deity of fire cursed all elephants even thus and then went away and entered the heart of the Sami tree from the desire of residing within it for some time. Listen now, O puissant hero, what favour was shown unto the elephants, O foremost one of Bhrigu's race, by the deities of unbaffled prowess who were all gratified with the service a representative of their had done them.

""""The Deities said, "With the aid of even your tongues bent inwards ye shall be able to eat all things, and with even those tongues ye shall be able to utter cries that will only

---

[384] i.e., into water, for water is identical with Agni.

be indistinct." Having blessed the elephants in this way, the denizens of Heaven once more resumed their search after Agni. Indeed, having issued out of the Aswattha tree, the deity of fire had entered the heart of Sami. This new abode of Agni was divulged by a parrot. The gods thereupon proceeded to the spot. Enraged with the conduct of the parrot, the deity of blazing flames cursed the whole parrot race, saying, "Ye shall from this day be deprived of the power of speech." Indeed, the eater of sacrificial libations turned up the tongues of all the parrots. Beholding Agni at the place pointed out by the parrot, and witnessing the curse denounced upon him, the gods, feeling a compassion for the poor creature, blessed him, saying, "In consequence of thy being a parrot, thou shalt not be wholly deprived of the power of speech. Though thy tongue has been turned backwards, yet speech thou shalt have, confined to the letter K. Like that of a child or an old man, thy speech shall be sweet and indistinct and wonderful." Having said these words unto the parrot, and beholding the deity of fire within the heart of the Sami, the gods made Sami wood a sacred fuel fit for producing fire in all religious rites. It was from that time that fire is seen to reside in the heart of the Sami. Men came to regard the Sami as proper means for producing fire (in sacrifice).[385] The waters that occur in the nethermost regions had come into contact with the deity of blazing flames. Those heated waters, O thou of Bhrigu's race, are vomited forth by the mountain springs. In consequence, indeed, of Agni having resided in them for some time, they became hot through his energy. Meanwhile, Agni, beholding the gods, became grieved. Addressing the deities, he asked them, "What is the reason of your presence here?" Unto him the deities and the great Rishi said, "We wish to set thee to a particular task. It behoveth thee to accomplish it. When accomplished, it will redound greatly to thy credit."

""'Agni said, "Tell me what your business is. I shall, ye gods, accomplish it. I am always willing to be set by you to any task you wish. Do not scruple, therefore, to command me."

""'The Deities said, "There is an Asura of the name of Taraka who has been filled with pride in consequence of the boon he has obtained from Brahman. Through his energy he is able to oppose and discomfit us. Do thou ordain his destruction. O sire, do thou rescue these deities, these Prajapatis, and these Rishis, O highly blessed Pavaka! O puissant one, do thou beget a heroic son possessed of thy energy, who will dispel, O bearer of sacrificial libations, our fears from that Asura. We have been cursed by the great goddess Uma. There is nothing else than thy energy which can be our refuge now. Do thou, therefore, O puissant deity, rescue us all." Thus addressed, the illustrious and irresistible bearer of sacrificial libations answered, saying, "Be it so", and he than proceeded towards Ganga otherwise called Bhagirathi. He united himself in (spiritual) congress with her and caused her to conceive. Verily, in the womb of Ganga the seed of Agni began to grow even as Agni himself grows (when supplied with fuel and aided by the wind). With the energy of that god, Ganga became exceedingly agitated at heart. Indeed, she suffered great distress and became unable to bear it. When the deity of blazing flames cast his seed endued with great energy into the womb of Ganga, a certain Asura (bent on purposes of his own) uttered a frightful roar. In consequence of that frightful roar uttered by the Asura for purposes of his own (and not for terrifying her), Ganga became very much terrified and her eyes rolled in fear and betrayed her agitation. Deprived of consciousness, she became unable to bear her body and the seed within her

---

[385] This refers to the practice of making the sacrificial fire by rubbing two sticks of Sami. It is a very inflammable wood and is used hence in all sacred rites.

womb. The daughter of Jahnu, inseminated with the energy of the illustrious deity, began to tremble. Overwhelmed with the energy of the seed she held in her womb, O learned Brahmana, she then addressed the deity of blazing fire, saying, "I am no longer capable, O illustrious one, of bearing thy seed in my womb. Verily, I am overcome with weakness by this seed of thine. The health I had in days before is no longer mine. I have been exceedingly agitated, O illustrious one, and my heart is dead within me, O sinless one. O foremost of all persons endued with penances, I am incapable of bearing thy seed any longer. I shall cast it off, compelled by the distress that has overtaken me, and not by caprice. There has been no actual contact of my person with thy seed, O illustrious deity of blazing flames! Our union, having for its cause the distress that has overtaken the deities, has been suitable and not of the flesh, O thou of great splendour. Whatever merit or otherwise there may be in this act (intended to be done by me), O eater of sacrificial libations, must belong to thee. Verily, I think, the righteousness or unrighteousness of this deed must be thine." Unto her the deity of fire said, "Do thou bear the seed. Do, indeed, bear the foetus endued with my energy. It will lead to great results. Thou art, verily, capable of bearing the entire earth. Thou wilt gain nothing by not holding this energy." That foremost of streams, though thus passed by the deity of fire as also by all the other deities, cast off the seed on the breast of Meru, that foremost of all mountains. Capable (somehow) of bearing that seed, yet oppressed by the energy of Rudra (for Agni is identical with Rudra), she failed to hold that seed longer in consequence of its burning energy. After she had cast it off, through sheer distress, that blazing seed having the splendour of fire, O perpetuator of Bhrigu's race, Agni saw her, and asked that foremost of streams, "Is it all right with the foetus thou hast cast off? Of what complexion has it been, O goddess? Of what form does it look? With what energy does it seem to be endued? Do thou tell me all about it."

"'"'Ganga said, "The foetus is endued with the complexion of gold. In energy it is even like thee, O sinless one! Of an excellent complexion, perfectly stainless, and blazing with splendour, it has illuminated the entire mountain. O foremost of all persons endued with penances, the fragrance emitted by it resembles the cool perfume that is scattered by lakes adorned with lotuses and Nyphoea stellata, mixed with that of the Nauclea Cadamba. With the splendour of that foetus everything around it seemed to be transformed into gold even as all things on mountain and low land seem to be transformed into gold by the rays of the Sun. Indeed, the splendour of that foetus, spreading far, falls upon mountains and rivers and springs. Indeed, it seems that the three worlds, with all their mobile and immobile creatures, are being illuminated by it. Even of this kind is thy child, O illustrious bearer of sacrificial libations. Like unto Surya or thy blazing self, in beauty it is even like a second Soma." Having said these words, the goddess disappeared there and then. Pavaka also, of great energy, having accomplished the business of the deities proceeded to the place he liked, O delighter of the Bhrigus. It was in consequence of the result of this act that the Rishis and the deities bestowed the name of Hiranyaretas upon the deity of fire.[386] And because the Earth held that seed (after the goddess Ganga had cast it upon her), she also came to be called by the name of Vasumati. Meanwhile, that foetus, which had sprung from Pavaka and been held for a time by Ganga,[387] having fallen on a forest of reeds, began to grow and at last assumed a wonderful form. The presiding goddess of the constellation Krittika beheld that form

---

[386] Hiranyaretas implies having gold for his vital seed.

[387] Vasumati implies endued with wealth, so called because the seed of Agni, identified with gold, is wealth of the highest kind and fell on the Earth who from that time began to hold it.

resembling the rising sun. She thenceforth began to rear that child as her son with the sustenance of her breast. For this reason, that child of pre-eminent splendour came to be called Kartikeya after her name. And because he grew from seed that fell out of Rudra's body, he came to be called Skanda. The incident also of his birth having taken place in the solitude of a forest of reeds, concealed from everybody's view, led to his being called by the name of Guha. It was in this way that gold came into existence as the offspring of the deity of blazing flames.[388] Hence it is that gold came to be looked upon as the foremost of all things and the ornament of the very gods. It was from this circumstance that gold came to be called by the name of Jatarupam.[389] It is the foremost of all costly things, and among ornaments also it is the foremost. The cleanser among all cleansing things, it is the most auspicious of all auspicious objects. Gold is truly the illustrious Agni, the Lord of all things, and the foremost of all Prajapatis. The most sacred of all sacred things is gold, O foremost of re-generate ones. Verily, gold is said to have for its essence Agni and Soma.'

""'Vasishtha continued, 'This history also, O Rama, called Brahmadarsana, was heard by me in days of yore, respecting the achievement of the Grandsire Brahman who is identifiable with the Supreme Soul. To a sacrifice performed in days of yore by that foremost of gods, viz., Lord Rudra, O thou of great might, who on that occasion had assumed the form of Varuna, there came the Munis and all the deities with Agni at their head. To that sacrifice also came all the sacrificial limbs (in their embodied forms), and the Mantra called Vashat in his embodied form. All the Samans also and all the Yajushes, numbering by thousands and in their embodied forms, came there. The Rig-Veda also came there, adorned with the rules of orthoepy. The Lakshanas, the Suras, the Niruktas, the Notes arranged in rows, and the syllable Om, as also Nigraha and Pragraha, all came there and took their residence in the eye of Mahadeva. The Vedas with the Upanishads, Vidya and Savitri, as also, the Past, the Present, and the Future, all came there and were held by the illustrious Siva. The puissant Lord of all then poured libations himself into his own self. Indeed, the wielder of Pinaka caused that Sacrifice of multifarious form to look exceedingly beautiful. He is Heaven, Firmament, Earth, and the Welkin. He is called the Lord of the Earth. He is the Lord whose sway is owned by all obstacles. He is endued with Sri and He is identical with the deity of blazing flames. That illustrious deity is called by various names. Even He is Brahman and Siva and Rudra and Varuna and Agni and Prajapati. He is the auspicious Lord of all creatures. Sacrifice (in his embodied form), and Penance, and all the union rites, and the goddess Diksha blazing with rigid observances, the several points of the compass with the deities that respectively preside over them, the spouses of all the deities, their daughters, and the celestial mothers, all came together in a body to Pasupati, O perpetuator of Bhrigu's race. Verily, beholding that sacrifice of the high-souled Mahadeva who had assumed the form of Varuna, all of them became highly pleased. Seeing the celestial damsels of great beauty, the seed of Brahman came out and fell upon the earth. In consequence of the seed having fallen on the dust, Pushan (Surya) took up that dust mixed with the particles of seed from the earth with his hands and cast it into the sacrificial fire. Meanwhile, the sacrifice with the sacred fire of blazing flames was commenced and it went on. Brahman (as the Hotri) was pouring libations on the fire. While thus employed, the grandsire became excited with desire (and his seed came out). As soon as that seed came out, he took it up with the

---

[388] Skanda is derived from Skanna or fallen out. Guha implies secret. The secrecy of his birth in the wilderness led to the bestowal of this name. He has many other names.

[389] Jatarupa refers to the incident of its having assumed an excellent form after its birth from Agni.

sacrificial ladle and poured it as a libation of ghee, O delighter of the Bhrigus, with the necessary Mantras, on the blazing fire. From that seed, Brahman of great energy caused the four orders of creatures to spring into existence. That seed of the Grandsire was endued with the three attributes of Sattwa, Rajas, and Tamas. From that element in it which represented the principle of Rajas, sprang all mobile creatures endued with the principle of Pravritti or action.[390] From the element of Tamas in it, sprang all immobile creatures. The principle of Sattwa, however, which dwelt in that seed, entered both kinds of existences. That attribute of Sattwa is of the nature of Tejas or Light (being identical with Buddhi or the Understanding). It is eternal and of it is unending Space.[391] In all creatures the attribute of Sattwa is present and is identical with that light which shows what is right and what is wrong. When the seed of Brahman was thus poured as a libation on that sacrificial fire, there sprang from it, O mighty one, three beings into existence. They were three male persons, endued with bodies that partook of the characters of the circumstances from which they respectively sprang. One arose first from the flames of the fire (called Bhrig) and hence he came to be called by the name of Bhrigu. A second came from the burning charcoals (called Angara) and hence he came to be called by the name of Angiras. The third sprang from a heap of extinguished charcoals and he came to be called by the name of Kavi. It has been already said that the first came out with flames emanating from his body and hence he was called Bhrigu. From the rays of the sacrificial fire sprang another called Marichi. From Marichi (afterwards) sprang Kasyapa. It has been already said that from the (burning) charcoals sprang Angiras. The (diminutive) Rishis called Valakhilyas sprang from the blades of Kusa grass spread out in that sacrifice. From the same blades of Kula grass, O thou of great puissance, sprang Atri. From the ashes of the fire sprang all those that are numbered among the regenerate Rishis, viz., the Vaikhanasas, endued with penances and devoted to Vedic lore and all excellent accomplishments. From the eyes of Agni sprang the twin Aswins endued with great beauty of person. At last, from his ears, sprang all the Prajapatis. The Rishis sprang from the pores of Agni's body. From his sweat sprang Chhandas, and from his strength sprang Mind. For this reason, Agni has been said to be all the deities in his individual self, by Rishis endued with Vedic lore, guided by the authority of the Vedas. The pieces of wood that keep alive the flames of Agni are regarded as the Months. The Juices that the fuel yields constitute the Fortnights. The liver of Agni is called the Day and Night, and his fierce light is called the Muhurtas. The blood of Agni is regarded as the source of the Rudras. From his blood sprang also the gold-complexioned deities called the Maitradevatas. From his smoke sprang the Vasus. From his flames sprang the Rudras as also the (twelve) Adityas of great effulgence. The Planets and Constellations and other stars that have been set in their respective orbits in the firmament, are regarded as the (burning) charcoals of Agni. The first Creator of the universe declared Agni to be Supreme Brahma and Eternal, and the giver of all wishes. This is verily a mystery.

""'After all these births had taken place, Mahadeva who had assumed the form of Varuna (for his sacrifice) and who had Pavana for his soul, said, "This excellent Sacrifice is mine. I am the Grahapati in it. The very beings that first sprang from the sacrificial fire are mine. Without doubt, they should be regarded as my offspring. Know this, ye gods who range through the skies! They are the fruits of this Sacrifice."

---

[390] The commentator explains,—Pravrittipradhanam jangamamabhut.

[391] Sa guna refers to Sattwa. Tejas is identical with Buddhi, because Buddhi, like Light, discovers all things. Sattwa, again, being of the nature of space, or rather being space itself, is of universal form; that is, Sattwa is all-pervading.

"'"'Agni said, "These offspring have sprung from my limbs. They have all depended upon me as the cause of their starting into life. They should, therefore, be regarded as my children. Mahadeva in the form of Varuna is in error in respect of this matter."[392] After this, the master of all the worlds, the Grandsire of all creatures, viz., Brahman, then said, "These children are mine. The seed was mine which I poured upon the sacrificial fire. I am the accomplisher of this Sacrifice. It was I who poured on the sacrificial fire the seed that came out of myself. The fruit is always his who has planted the seed. The principal cause of these births is the seed owned by me." The deities then repaired to the presence of the Grandsire and having bowed their heads unto him joined their hands in reverence and they said unto him, "All of us, O illustrious one, and the entire universe of mobile and immobile creatures, are thy offspring. O sire, let Agni of blazing flames, and the illustrious and puissant Mahadeva who has, for this sacrifice, assumed the form of Varuna, have their wish (in the matter of the offspring)." At these words, although born of Brahman, the puissant Mahadeva in the form of Varuna, the ruler of all aquatic creatures received the firstborn one, viz., Bhrigu endued with the effulgence of the sun as his own child. The Grandsire then intended that Angiras should become the son of Agni. Conversant with the truth in respect of everything, the Grandsire then took Kavi as his own son. Engaged in procreating creatures for peopling the earth, Bhrigu who is regarded as a Prajapati thence came to be called as Varuna's offspring. Endued with every prosperity, Angiras came to be called the offspring of Agni, and the celebrated Kavi came to be known as the child of Brahman himself. Bhrigu and Angiras who had sprung from the flame and the charcoals of Agni respectively, became the procreators of extensive races and tribes in the world. Verily, these three, viz., Bhrigu and Angiras and Kavi, regarded as Prajapati, are the progenitors of many races and tribes. All are the children of these three. Know this, O puissant hero. Bhrigu begot seven sons all of whom became equal to him in merits and accomplishments. Their names are Chyavana, Vajrasirsha, Suchi, Urva, Sukra, that giver of boons, Vibhu, and Savana. These are the seven. They are children of Bhrigu and are hence Bhargavas. They are also called Varunas in consequence of their ancestor Bhrigu having been adopted by Mahadeva in the form of Varuna. Thou belongest to the race of Bhrigu. Angiras begot eight sons. They also are known as Varunas. Their names are Vrihaspati, Utathya, Payasya, Santi, Dhira, Virupa, Samvarta, and Sudhan was the eighth. These eight are regarded also as the offspring of Agni. Freed from every evil, they are devoted to knowledge only. The sons of Kavi who was appropriated by Brahman himself are also known as Varunas. Numbering eight, all of them became progenitors of races and tribes. Auspicious by nature, they are all conversant with Brahma. The names of the eight sons of Kavi are Kavi, Kavya, Dhrishnu, Usanas endued with great intelligence, Bhrigu, Viraja, Kasi, and Ugra conversant with every duty. These are the eight sons of Kavi. By them the whole world has been peopled. They are all Prajapatis, and by them have been procreated many offspring. Thus, O chief of Bhrigu's race, hath the whole world been peopled with the progeny of Angiras, and Kavi and Bhrigu. The puissant and supreme Lord Mahadeva in the form of Varuna which he had assumed for his sacrifice had first, O learned Brahmana, adopted both Kavi and Angiras. Hence, these two are regarded as of Varuna. After that the eater of sacrificial libations, viz., the deity of blazing flames, adopted Angiras. Hence, all the progeny of Angiras are known as belonging to the race of Agni. The Grandsire Brahman was, in olden days, gratified by all the deities who said unto him, "Let these lords of the universe

---

[392] Avasatmaka is explained by the commentator as bhranta.

(referring to Bhrigu and Angiras and Kavi and their descendants) rescue us all. Let all of them become progenitors of offspring (for peopling the earth). Let all of them become endued with penances. Through thy grace, let all these rescue the world (from becoming an uninhabited wilderness). Let them become procreators and extenders of races and tribes and let them increase thy energy. Let all of them become thorough masters of the Vedas and let them be achievers of great deeds. Let all of them be friends to the cause of the deities. Indeed, let all of them become endued with auspiciousness. Let them become founders of extensive races and tribes and let them be great Rishis. Let all of them be endued with high penances and let all of them be devoted to high Brahmacharya, All of us, as also all these are thy progeny, O thou of great puissance. Thou, O Grandsire, art the Creator of both, deities and the Brahmanas. Marichi is thy first son. All these also that are called Bhargavas are thy progeny. (Ourselves also are so). Looking at this fact, O Grandsire, we shall all aid and support one another. All these shall, in this way, multiply their progeny and establish thyself at the commencement of each creation after the universal destruction." Thus addressed by them, Brahman, the Grandsire of all the worlds, said unto them, "So be it! I am gratified with you all!" Having said so unto the deities he proceeded to the place he had come from. Even this is what happened in days of old in that sacrifice of the high-souled Mahadeva, that foremost one of all the deities, in the beginning of creation, when he for the purposes of his sacrifice had assumed the form of Varuna. Agni is Brahman. He is Pasupati. He is Sarva. He is Rudra. He is Prajapati.[393] It is well-known that gold is the offspring of Agni. When fire is not obtainable (for the purposes of a sacrifice), gold is used as substitute. Guided by the indications afforded by the auditions of the Veda, one that is conversant with authorities and that knows the identity of gold with fire, acts in this way. Placing a piece of gold on some blades of Kusa grass spread out on the ground, the sacrificer pours libations upon it. Upon also the pores of an ant-hill, upon the right ear of a goat, upon a piece of level earth, upon the waters of a Tirtha, or on the hand of a Brahmana, if libations are poured, the illustrious deity of fire becomes gratified and regards it as a source of his own aggrandisement as also that of the deities through his. Hence, it is that we have heard that all the deities regard Agni as their refuge and are devoted to him. Agni sprang from Brahman, and from Agni sprang gold.[394] Hence, it has been heard by us, that those persons observant of righteousness that make gifts of gold are regarded as giving away all the deities. The man who makes gifts of gold attains to a very high end. Regions of blazing effulgence are his. Verily, O Bhargava, he becomes installed as the king of kings in heaven. That person who, at sunrise, makes a gift of gold according to the ordinance and with proper Mantras, succeeds in warding off the evil consequences foreshadowed by ominous dreams. The man who, as soon as the sun has risen, makes a gift of gold becomes cleansed of all his sins. He who makes a gift of gold at midday destroys all his future sins. He who with restrained soul, makes a gift of gold at the second twilight succeeds in attaining to a residence with Brahman and the deity of wind and Agni and Soma in their respective regions. Such a man attains to auspicious fame in regions of great felicity that belong to Indra himself. Attaining to great fame in this world also, and cleansed of all his sins, he sports in joy and happiness. Verily, such a man attains to many other regions of happiness and becomes unequalled for glory and fame. His course perfectly unobstructed, he succeeds in going everywhere at will. He has never to fall

---

[393] These are different names of Brahman and Mahadeva.
[394] The 'hence' here does not refer to what preceded immediately, but has reference to what has been said of the identity of Agni with Brahman and Rudra.

down from the regions to which he attains and the glory he acquires becomes great. Indeed, by making gifts of gold one attains to innumerable regions of felicity all of which he enjoys for eternity. That man who, having ignited a fire at sunrise, makes gifts of gold in view of the observance of a particular vow, succeeds in attaining to the fruition of all his wishes. It has been said that gold is identical with Agni. The gift of gold, therefore, is productive of great felicity. The gift of gold leads to the possession of those merits and accomplishments that are desired, and cleanses the heart.[395] I have thus told thee, O sinless one, the origin of gold. O thou of puissance, hear how Kartikeya grew up, O delighter of Bhrigu's race. After a long time Kartikeya grew up. He was then, O perpetuator of Bhrigu's race, chosen by all the deities with Indra at their head, as the generalissimo of the celestial forces. He slew the Daitya Taraka as also many other Asuras, at the command of the chief of the celestials, O Brahmana, and actuated also by the desire of benefiting all the worlds. I have also, O thou of great might, discoursed to thee on the merits of making gifts of gold. Do thou, therefore, O foremost of all speakers make gifts of gold.'"

"'Bhishma continued, "Thus addressed by Vasishtha, Jamadagni's son of great prowess then made gifts of gold unto the Brahmanas and became cleansed of his sins. I have thus told thee, O king, everything about the merits of the gifts of gold and about its origin also, O Yudhishthira. Do thou also, therefore, make abundant gifts of gold unto the Brahmanas. Verily, O king, by making such gifts of gold, thou wilt surely be cleansed of all thy sins!"'"

SECTION LXXXVI.

"'Yudhishthira said, "Thou hast, O grandsire, discoursed to me, in detail on the merits that attach to the gift of gold agreeably with the ordinances laid down in the scriptures as indicated in the auditions of the Veda. Thou hast also narrated what the origin is of gold. Do thou tell me now how Taraka met with destruction. Thou hast said, O king, that Asura had become unslayable by the gods. Do thou tell me in detail how his destruction was brought about. O perpetuator of Kuru's race, I desire to hear this from thee. I mean the details of Taraka's slaughter. Great is my curiosity to hear the narrative."

"'Bhishma said, "The gods and the Rishis, O monarch, reduced to great distress (by Taraka's prowess and the conduct of Ganga in casting off Agni's seed), urged the six Krittikas to rear that child. Amongst the celestial ladies there were none, save these, that could, by their energy, bear the seed of Agni in their wombs. The god of fire became exceedingly gratified with those goddesses for their readiness to sustain the conception caused by the cast off seed of Agni which was endued with his own high energy. When the energy of Agni, O king, was divided into six portions and placed within the channels (leading to the womb), the six Krittikas began to nourish the portion that each held in her womb. As the high-souled Kumara, however, began to grow within their wombs, their bodies being afflicted by his energy, they failed to obtain peace anywhere (in heaven or on earth). Filled with energy as their bodies were, the time at last came for delivery. All of them, it so happened, O prince of men, delivered at the same time. Though held in six different wombs, yet all the portions, as they came out, united into one. The goddess Earth held the child, taking it up from a heap of gold. Verily, the child, endued with excellent form, blazed with splendour even like the god of Fire. Of beautiful features, he

---

[395] Pravartakam implies leading to Pravritti for righteous acts or Chittasuddhi.

began to grow in a delightful forest of reeds. The six Krittikas beheld that child of theirs looking like the morning sun in splendour. Filled with affection for him,—indeed, loving him very much,—they began to rear him with the sustenance of their breasts. In consequence of his having been born of the Krittikas and reared by them, he came to be known throughout the three worlds as Kartikeya. Having sprung from the seed which had fallen off from Rudra he was named Skanda, and because of his birth in the solitude of a forest of reeds he came to be called by the name of Guha (the secret-born). The gods numbering three and thirty, the points of the compass (in their embodied forms) together with the deities presiding over them, and Rudra and Dhatri and Vishnu and Yama and Pushan and Aryaman and Bhaga, and Angas and Mitra and the Sadhyas and Vasava and the Vasus and the Aswins and the Waters and the Wind and the Firmament and Chandramas and all the Constellations and the Planets and Surya, and all the Ricks and Samans and Yajuses in their embodied forms, came there to behold that wonderful child who was the son of the deity of blazing flames. The Rishis uttered hymns of praise and the Gandharvas sang in honour of that child called Kumara of six heads, twice six eyes, and exceedingly devoted to the Brahmanas. His shoulders were broad, and he had a dozen arms, and the splendour of his person resembled that of fire and Aditya. As he lay stretched on a clump of heath, the gods with the Rishis, beholding him, became filled with great delight and regarded the great Asura as already slain. The deities then began to bring him diverse kinds of toys and articles that could amuse him. As he played like a child, diverse kinds of toys and birds were given unto him. Garuda of excellent feathers gave unto him a child of his, viz., a peacock endued with plumes of variegated hue. The Rakshasas gave unto him a boar and a buffalo. Aruna himself gave him a cock of fiery splendour. Chandramas gave him a sheep, and Aditya gave him some dazzling rays of his. The mother of all kine, viz., Surabhi, gave him kine by hundreds and thousands. Agni gave him a goat possessed of many good qualities. Ila gave him an abundant quantity of flowers and fruit. Sudhanwan gave him a riding chariot and a car of Kuvara. Varuna gave him many auspicious and excellent, products of the Ocean, with some elephants. The chief of the celestials gave him lions and tigers and pards and diverse kinds of feathery denizens of the air, and many terrible beasts of prey and many umbrellas also of diverse kinds. Rakshasas and Asuras, in large bands, began to walk in the train of that puissant child. Beholding the son of Agni grow up, Taraka sought, by various means, to effect his destruction, but he failed to do anything unto that puissant deity. The god in time invested Agni's son born in the solitude (of a forest of reeds) with the command of their forces. And they also informed him of the oppressions committed upon them by the Asura Taraka. The generalissimo of the celestial forces grew up and became possessed of great energy and puissance. In time Guha slew Taraka, with his irresistible dart. Verily, Kumara slew the Asura as easily as if in sport. Having accomplished the destruction of Taraka he re-established the chief of the deities in his sovereignty of the three worlds. Endued with mighty prowess, the celestial generalissimo blazed with beauty and splendour. The puissant Skanda became the protector of the deities and did what was agreeable to Sankara. The illustrious son of Pavaka was endued with a golden form. Verily, Kumara is always the leader of the celestial forces. Gold is the puissant energy of the god of fire and was born with Kartikeya (from the same seed). Hence is Gold highly auspicious and, as a valuable, is excellent and endued with inexhaustible merit. Even thus, O son of Kuru's race, did Vasishtha recite this discourse unto Rama of Bhrigu's race in days of old. Do thou, therefore, O king of men, try to make gifts of Gold. By making gifts of Gold, Rama became cleansed of all his sins, and finally attained to a high place in heaven that is unattainable by other men."'"

SECTION LXXXVII.

"'Yudhishthira said, "Thou hast discoursed to me, O thou of righteous soul, on the duties of the four orders. Do thou, after the same manner, O king, discourse to me now on all the ordinances respecting the Sraddha (of deceased ancestors)."'

"Vaisampayana continued, 'Thus addressed by Yudhishthira, the son of Santanu set himself to declare unto him the following ritual, consistent with the ordinance of the Sraddha.'

"'Bhishma said, "Listen, O king, with close attention, to me as I discourse to you on the ritual of the Sraddha. That ritual is auspicious, worthy of praise, productive of fame and progeny, and is regarded as a sacrifice, O scorcher of foes, in honour of the Pitris. Gods or Asuras or human beings, Gandharvas or Uragas or Rakshasas, Pisachas or Kinnaras,—every one should always worship the Pitris. It is seen that people worship the Pitris first, and gratify the deities next by offering them their adorations. Hence, one should always worship the Pitris with every care.[396] It is said, O king, that the Sraddha performed in honour of the Pitris is performable afterwards. But this general rule is restrained by a special one (which directs that the Sraddha in honour of the Pitris should be performed on the afternoon of the day of the New moon).[397] The (deceased) grandsires become gratified with the Sraddha that may be performed on any day. I shall, however, tell thee now what the merits and demerits are of the respective lunar days (in view of their adaptability to the performance of the Sraddha). I shall discourse to thee, O sinless one, what fruits are attained on what days by performing the Sraddha. Do thou listen to me with close attention. By adoring the Pitris on the first day of the lighted fortnight, one obtains in one's abode beautiful spouses capable of producing many children all possessed of desirable accomplishments. By performing the Sraddha on the second day of the lighted fortnight one gets many daughters. By performing it on the third day, one acquires many steeds. By performing it on the fourth day, one gets a large herd of smaller animals (such as goats and sheep) in one's house. They, O king, who perform the Sraddha on the fifth day, get many sons. Those men who perform the Sraddha on the sixth day acquire great splendour. By performing it on the seventh day, O monarch, one acquires great fame. By performing it on the eighth day one makes great profits in trade. By performing it on the ninth day one acquires many animals of uncloven hoofs. By performing it on the tenth day one acquires much wealth in kine. By performing it on the eleventh day one becomes the possessor of much wealth in clothes and utensils (of brass and other metals). Such a man also obtains many sons all of whom become endued with Brahma splendour. By performing the Sraddha on the twelfth day one always beholds, if one desires, diverse kinds of beautiful articles made of silver and gold. By performing the Sraddha on the thirteenth day one attains to eminence over one's kinsmen. Without doubt, all the young men in the family of him who performs the Sraddha on the fourteenth day

---

[396] The commentator explains that the Pitris should be worshipped on the day of the New moon, the deities should then be worshipped on the first day of the lighted fortnight. Or, on any other day of the lighted fortnight, the Pitri-sacrifice or Sraddha should be performed first; the Deva-sacrifice or Ishti should then be performed.

[397] Anwaharyam, the commentator explains, is paschatkartavyam, i.e., subsequently performable (subsequent, i.e., to the worship of the gods). There is a special ordinance, however, which lays down that the Sraddha should be performed on the afternoon of the day of the new moon. The gods should be adored on the first day of the lighted fortnight. Hence, owing to this especial ordinance, the Sraddha must precede the worship of the gods, and not succeed it.

meet with death. Such a man becomes entangled in war. By performing the Sraddha on the day of the new moon, one obtains the fruition of every wish. In the dark fortnight, all the days commencing with the tenth (and ending with that of the new moon), leaving only the fourteenth day out, are laudable days for the performance of the Sraddha. Other days of that fortnight are not so. Then, again, as the dark fortnight is better than the lighted one, so the afternoon of the day is better than the forenoon in the matter of the Sraddha.""''

SECTION LXXXVIII.

"'Yudhishthira said, "O thou of great puissance, tell me what that object is which, if dedicated to the Pitris, becomes inexhaustible! What Havi, again, (if offered) lasts for all time? What, indeed, is that which (if presented) becomes eternal?"

"'Bhishma said, "Listen to me, O Yudhishthira, what those Havis are which persons conversant with the ritual of the Sraddha regard as suitable in view of the Sraddha and what the fruits are that attach to each. With sesame seeds and rice and barley and Masha and water and roots and fruits, if given at Sraddhas, the Pitris, O king, remain gratified for the period of a month.[398] Manu has said that if a Sraddha is performed with a copious measure of sesame, such Sraddha becomes inexhaustible. Of all kinds of food, sesame seeds are regarded as the best. With fishes offered at Sraddhas, the Pitris remain gratified for a period of two months. With mutton they remain gratified for three months and with the flesh of the hare for four. With the flesh of the goat, O king, they remain gratified for five months, with bacon for six months, and with the flesh of birds for seven. With venison obtained from those deer that are called Prishata, they remain gratified for eight months, and with that obtained from the Ruru for nine months, and with the meat of the Gavaya for ten months. With the meat of the buffalo their gratification lasts for eleven months. With beef presented at the Sraddha, their gratification, it is said, lasts for a full year. Payasa mixed with ghee is as much acceptable to the Pitris as beef. With the meat of the Vadhrinasa the gratification of the Pitris lasts for twelve years.[399] The flesh of the rhinoceros, offered to the Pitris on the anniversaries of the lunar days on which they died, becomes inexhaustible. The potherb called Kalasaka, the petals of the Kanchana flower, and meat of the goat also, thus offered, prove inexhaustible.[400] In this connection, O Yudhishthira, there are some verses, originally sung by the Pitris, that are sung (in the world). They were communicated to me in former days by Sanatkumara.—'He that has taken birth in our race should give us Payasa mixed with ghee on the thirteenth day (of the dark fortnight), under the constellation Magha, during the Sun's southward course. One born in our race should, under the constellation Magha, as if in the observance of a vow, offer the meat of goat or the petals of the Kanchana flower. One should also offer us, with due rites, Payasa mixed with ghee, dedicating it on a spot covered by the shadow of an elephant.'—Many sons should be coveted so that even one may go to Gaya (for performing the Sraddha of his ancestors), where stands the banian that is celebrated over

---

[398] Masha, is the Phascolus Roxburghii.

[399] It is difficult to understand what is meant by Vadhrinasa here. It means either a large bull, or a kind of bird, or a variety of the goat. Probably the bull is intended.

[400] Pitrikshaye is mrita-tithau. Kalasaka is explained by Nilakantha as identical with the common potherb called Shuka or the country sorrel (Rumex visicarius, Linn). Some hold that it is something like the sorrel. Lauham is the petals of the Kanchana flower (Bauhinia acuminata, Linn).

all the worlds and that makes all offerings made under its branches inexhaustible.[401] Even a little of water, roots, fruits, meat, and rice, mixed with honey, if offered on the anniversary of the day of death becomes inexhaustible.""

SECTION LXXXIX.

"'Bhishma continued, "Listen to me, O Yudhishthira, as I tell thee what those optional Sraddhas are that should be performed under the different constellations and that were first spoken of by Yama unto king Sasavindu.[402] That man who always performs the Sraddha under the constellation Krittika is regarded as performing a sacrifice after establishing the sacred fire. Such a person, freed from fear, ascends to heaven with his children. He that is desirous of children should perform the Sraddha under the constellation Rohini, while he that is desirous of energy should do it under the constellation Mrigasiras. By performing the Sraddha under the constellation Ardra, a man becomes the doer of fierce deeds. A mortal, by performing the Sraddha under Punarvasu, makes such again by agriculture. The man that is desirous of growth and advancement should perform the Sraddha under Pushya. By doing it under the constellation Aslesha one begets heroic children. By doing it under the Maghas one attains to pre-eminence among kinsmen. By doing it under the prior Phalgunis, the doer of it becomes endued with good fortune. By doing the Sraddha under the later Phalgunis one attains to many children; while by performing it under Hasta, one attains to the fruition of one's wishes. By performing it under the constellation Chitra one obtains children endued with great beauty. By doing it under the constellation Swati, one makes much profit by trade. The man that desires children acquires the fruition of his wish by performing the Sraddha under the constellation Visakha. By doing it under Anuradha one becomes a king of kings.[403] By making offerings in honour of the Pitris under the constellation Jyeshtha with devotion and humility, one attains to sovereignty, O foremost one of Kuru's race. By doing the Sraddha under Mula one attains to health, and by doing it under the prior Ashadha, one acquires excellent fame. By performing it under the later Ashadha one succeeds in roving over the whole world, freed from every sorrow. By doing it under the constellation Abhijit one attains to high knowledge. By doing it under Sravana one, departing from this world, attains to a very high end. The man that performs the Sraddha under the constellation Dhanishtha becomes the ruler of a kingdom. By doing it under the constellation presided over by Varuna (viz., Satabhisha), one attains to success as a physician. By performing the Sraddha under the constellation of the prior Bhadrapada one acquires large property in goats and sheep; while by doing it under the later Bhadrapada one acquires thousands of kine. By performing the Sraddha under the constellation Revati one acquires much wealth in utensils of white brass and copper. By doing it under Aswini one acquires many steeds, while under Bharani one attains to longevity. Listening to these ordinances about the Sraddha, king Sasavindu acted accordingly, and succeeded in easily subjugating and ruling the whole earth.""

---

[401] To this day the sanctity of Gaya is universally recognised by all Hindus. Sraddhas are performed there under the banian called the Akshaya or inexhaustible banian.

[402] All religious acts are either nitya or kamya. The former imply acts that are obligatory and by doing which no particular merit is acquired but by not doing which sin is incurred. The latter imply those optional acts which, if done, produce merit but which, if omitted, leads to no sin.

[403] Literally, 'set in motion a body of kings,' i.e., become an Overlord.

SECTION XC.

"'Yudhishthira said, "It behoves thee, O foremost one of Kuru's race, to tell me unto what kind of Brahmanas, O grandsire, should the offers made at Sraddhas be given away."

"'Bhishma said, "The Kshatriya who is conversant with the ordinances about gift should never examine Brahmanas (when making gifts unto them). In all acts, however, that relate to the worship of the deities and the Pitris, an examination has been said to be proper. The deities are worshipped on earth by men only when they are filled with devotion that comes from the deities themselves. Hence, one should, approaching them, make gifts unto all Brahmanas (without any examination of their merits), regarding such gifts as are made to the deities themselves. In Sraddhas, however, O monarch, the man of intelligence should examine the Brahmanas (to be employed for assisting the doers of the Sraddha in getting through the ritual and making gifts unto them of the offerings made to the Pitris). Such examination should concern itself with their birth and conduct and age and appearance and learning and nobility (or otherwise) of parentage. Amongst the Brahmanas there are some that pollute the line and some that sanctify it. Listen to me, O king, as I tell thee who those Brahmanas are that should be excluded from the line.[404] He that is full of guile, or he that is guilty of foeticide, or he that is ill of consumption, or he that keeps animals, or is destitute of Vedic study, or is a common servant of a village, or lives upon the interest of loans, or he that is a singer, or he that sells all articles, or he that is guilty of arson, or he that is a poisoner or he that is a pimp by profession, or he that sells Soma, or he that is a professor of palmistry, or he that is in the employ of the king, or he that is seller of oil, or he that is a cheat and false swearer, or he that has a quarrel with his father, or he that tolerates a paramour of his wife in his house, or he that has been cursed, or he that is a thief, or he that lives by some mechanical art, or he that puts on disguises, or he that is deceitful in his behaviour, or he that is hostile to those he calls his friends, or he that is an adulterer, or he that is a preceptor of Sudras, or he that has betaken himself to the profession of arms, or he that wanders with dogs (for hunting), or he that has been bit by a dog, or he that has wedded before his elder brothers, or he that seems to have undergone circumcision,[405] he that violates the bed of his preceptor, he that is an actor or mime, he that lives by setting up a deity and he that lives by calculating the conjunctions of stars and planets and asterisms,[406] are regarded as fit to be excluded from the line. Persons conversant with the Vedas say that the offerings made at Sraddhas, if eaten by such Brahmanas, go to fill the stomachs of Rakshasas (instead of filling those of the Pitris), O Yudhishthira. That person who having eaten at a Sraddha does not abstain that day from study of the Vedas or who has sexual congress that day with a Sudra woman, must know that his Pitris, in consequence of such acts of his, have to lie for a month on his dung. The offerings made at Sraddhas if presented to a Brahmana who sells Soma, become converted into human ordure; if presented to a Brahmana who is engaged in the practice of Medicine, they become converted into pus and blood; if presented to one who lives by setting up a deity, they fail to produce any fruit; if presented to one who lives upon the interest of loans they lead to infamy; if presented to one who is engaged in

---

[404] When Brahmanas are fed, they are made to sit in long lines. They that are stained with vices are excluded from the line. Such exclusion from the line is regarded as equal to complete outlawry.

[405] i.e., who have undergone a natural circumcision.

[406] Implying soothsayers.

trade, they become productive of no fruits either here or hereafter. If presented to a Brahmana who is born of a widowed mother (by a second husband), they become as fruitless as libations poured on ashes.[407] They who present the Havya and Kavya (offered at Sraddhas) unto such Brahmanas as are divested of the duties ordained for them and of those rules of good conduct that persons of their order should observe, find such presents productive of no merits hereafter. That man of little intelligence who makes gifts of such articles unto such men knowing their dispositions, obliges, by such conduct, his Pitris to eat human ordure in the next world. Thou shouldst know that these wretches among Brahmanas deserve to be excluded from the line. Those Brahmanas also of little energy who are engaged in instructing Sudras are of the same class. A Brahmana that is blind stains sixty individual of the line; one that is destitute of virile power a hundred; while one that is afflicted with white leprosy stains as many as he looks upon, O king. Whatever offerings made at Sraddhas are eaten by one with his head wrapped round with a cloth, whatever is eaten by one with face southwards, and whatever is eaten with shoes or sandals on all goes to gratify the Asuras. Whatever, again, is given with malice, and whatever is given without reverence, have been ordained by Brahmana himself as the portion of the prince of Asuras (viz., Vali). Dogs, and such Brahmanas as are polluters of lines, should not be allowed to cast their eyes upon the offerings made at Sraddhas. For this reason, Sraddhas should be performed in a spot that is properly hedged around or concealed from the view. That spot should also be strewn with sesame seeds. That Sraddha which is performed without sesame seeds, or that which is done by a person in anger, has its Havi robbed by Rakshasas and Pisachas. Commensurate with the number of Brahmanas seen by one that deserves to be excluded from the line, is the loss of merit he causes of the foolish performer of the Sraddha who invites him to the feast.

""I shall now, O chief of Bharata's race, tell thee who are sanctifiers of the line. Do thou find them out by examination. All those Brahmanas that are cleansed by knowledge, Vedic study, and vows and observances, and they that are of good and righteous behaviour, should be known as sanctifiers of everything. I shall now tell thee who deserve to sit in the line. Thou shouldst know them to be such whom I shall indicate presently. He that is conversant with the three Nachiketas, he that has set up the five sacrificial fires, he that knows the five Suparnas, he that is conversant with the six branches (called Angas) of the Veda, he that is a descendant of sires who were engaged in teaching the Vedas and is himself engaged in teaching, he that is well-conversant with the Chhandas, he that is acquainted with the Jeshtha Saman, he that is obedient to the sway of his parents, he that is conversant with the Vedas and whose ancestors have been so for ten generations, he that has congress with only his wedded wives and this at their seasons, and he who has been cleansed by knowledge, by the Veda, and by vows and observances,—even such a Brahmana,—sanctifies the line. He who reads the Atharva-siras, who is devoted to the observance of Brahmacharya practices, and who is steady in observance of righteous vows, who is truthful and of righteous conduct, and who is duly observant of the duties laid down for his order, they also that have undergone fatigue and labour for bathing in the waters of tirthas, that have undergone the final bath after performing sacrifices with proper Mantras that are freed from the sway of wrath, that are not restless, that are endued with forgiving dispositions, that are self-restrained masters of their senses, and they are devoted to the good of all creatures,—these should be invited to

---

[407] This is a common form of expression to imply the fruitlessness of an act. Libations should be poured on the blazing fire. If poured on the ashes, they lead to no merit, for only Agni in his blazing form can bear them to the intended places.

Sraddhas. Anything given to these becomes inexhaustible. These indeed, are sanctifiers of lines. There are others also, highly blessed, that should be regarded as sanctifiers of the line. They are Yatis and those that are conversant with the religion of Moksha, and they that are devoted to Yoga, and they that properly observe excellent vows and they that, with collected mind recite (sacred) histories unto foremost of Brahmanas. They that are conversant with Bhashyas, they also that are devoted to grammatical studies, they that study the Puranas and they that study the Dharmasastras and having studied them (i.e., the Puranas and Dharmasastras) act up to the standard laid down in them, he that has lived (for the stated period) in the abode of his preceptor, he that is truthful in speech, he that is a giver of thousands, they that are foremost in (their knowledge of) all the Vedas and the scriptural and philosophical aphorisms,—these sanctify the line as far they look at it. And because they sanctify all who sit in the line, therefore are they called sanctifiers of lines. Utterers of Brahma say that even a single person that happens to be the descendant of sires who were teachers of the Veda and that is himself a Vedic teacher, sanctifies full seven miles around him. If he that is not a Ritwik and that is not a Vedic teacher takes the foremost seat in a Sraddha, with even the permission of the other Ritwiks there present, he is said to take (by that act of his) the sins of all who may be sitting in the line. If, on the other hand, he happens to be conversant with the Vedas and freed from all those faults that are regarded as capable of polluting the line, he shall not, O king, be regarded as fallen (by taking the foremost seat in a Sraddha). Such a man would then be really a sanctifier of the line. For these reasons, O king, thou shouldst properly examine the Brahmanas before inviting them to Sraddhas. Thou shouldst invite only such among them as are devoted to the duties laid down for their order, and as are born in good families, and as are possessed of great learning. He who performs Sraddhas for feeding only his friends and whose Havi does not gratify the deities and the Pitris, fails to ascend to Heaven. He who collects his friends and relatives only on the occasion of the Sraddha he performs (without keeping an eye on properly honouring deserving persons by inviting and feeding them), fails to proceed (after death) by the path of the deities (which is a lighted one and free from all afflictions and impediments). The man who makes the Sraddha he performs an occasion for only gathering his friends, never succeeds in ascending to heaven. Verily, the man who converts the Sraddha into an occasion for treating his friends, becomes dissociated from heaven even like a bird dissociated from the perch when the chain tying it breaks.[408] Therefore, he that performs a Sraddha should not honour (on such occasions) his friends. He may make gifts of wealth unto them on other occasions by collecting them together. The Havi and the Kavi offered at Sraddhas should be served unto them that are neither friends nor foes but are only indifferent or neutral. As seed sown on a sterile soil does not sprout forth, or as one that has not sown does not get a share of the produce, even so that Sraddha the offerings in which are eaten by an unworthy person, yields no fruit either here or hereafter.[409] That Brahmana who is

---

[408] The idea is that heaven is the result of one's deeds. It is attached to the fruits of one's acts. The man falling off from heaven is identical with heaven being dissociated from the fruits of his acts. Hence such a falling off at the man or the dissociation of heaven is likened to a bird's dissociation from its perch when the chain tying it to the perch is broken. The simile seems to be far-fetched.

[409] It is painful to see how very careless the Vernacular versions of the Anusasana have been. From want of space the numerous errors that have been committed have not been pointed out. At times, however, the errors appear to be so grave that one cannot pass them by in silence. In the second half of the first line, whether the reading be avapta as in the Bengal texts or chavapta as in the Bombay texts, the meaning is that the Avapta or one that has not sown na vijabhagam prapnuyat, i.e., would not get a share of the produce. The Burdwan translators make a mess of it, while K. P. Singha skips over it.

destitute of Vedic study is like a fire made by burning grass or straw; and becomes soon extinguished even like such a fire. The offerings made at Sraddhas should not be given to him even as libations should not be poured on the ashes of the sacrificial fire. When the offerings made at Sraddhas are exchanged by the performers with one another (instead of being given away unto worthy persons), they come to be regarded as Pisacha presents. Such offerings gratify neither the gods nor the Pitris. Instead of reaching the other world, they wander about even here like a cow that has lost her calf wandering about within the fold. As those libations of ghee that are poured upon the extinguished ashes of a sacrificial fire never reach either the gods or the Pitris, after the same manner a gift that is made to a dancer or a singer or a Dakshina presented to a lying or deceitful person, produces no merit. The Dakshina that is presented to a lying or deceitful person destroys both the giver and the receiver without benefiting them in any respect. Such a Dakshina is destructive and highly censurable. The Pitris of the person making it have to fall down from the path of the deities. The gods know them to be Brahmanas who always tread, O Yudhishthira, within the bounds set up by the Rishis who are conversant with all duties, and who have a firm faith in their efficacy. Those Brahmanas that are devoted to Vedic study, to knowledge, to penances, and to acts, O Bharata, should be known as Rishis. The offerings made at Sraddhas should be given unto those that are devoted to knowledge. Verily, they are to be regarded as men who never speak ill of the Brahmanas. Those men should never be fed on occasions of Sraddhas who speak ill of Brahmanas in course of conversation in the midst of assemblies. If Brahmanas, O king, be calumniated, they would destroy three generations of the calumniator.[410] This is the declaration, O king, of the Vaikhanasa Rishis. Brahmanas conversant with the Vedas should be examined from a distance. Whether one likes them or feels a dislike for them, one should give unto such Brahmanas the offerings made at Sraddhas. That man who feeds thousands upon thousands of false Brahmanas acquires merit that is attainable by feeding even one Brahmana if the latter happens to be possessed of a knowledge of the Vedas, O Bharata!"'"

SECTION XCI.

"'Yudhishthira said, "By whom was the Sraddha first conceived and at what time? What also is its essence? During the time when the world was peopled by only the descendants of Bhrigu and Angiras, who was the muni that established the Sraddha? What acts should not be done at Sraddha? What are those Sraddhas in which fruits and roots are to be offered? What species also of paddy should be avoided in Sraddhas? Do thou tell me all this, O grandsire!"

"'Bhishma said, "Listen to me, O ruler of men, as I tell thee how the Sraddha was introduced, the time of such introduction, the essences of the rite, and the Muni who conceived it. From the Self-born Brahman sprang Atri, O thou of Kuru's race. In Atri's race was born a Muni of the name of Dattatreya. Dattatreya got a son of the name of Nimi possessed of wealth of asceticism. Nimi got a son named Srimat who was endued with great beauty of person. Upon the expiration of a full thousand years, Srimat, having undergone the severest austerities, succumbed to the influence of Time and departed from this world. His sire Nimi, having performed the Purificatory rites according to the ritual laid down in the ordinance, became filled with great grief, thinking continually of the loss

---

[410] The sense is that the calumniator, his sire, and son meet with destruction in consequence of such an act.

of his son.[411] Thinking of that cause of sorrow the high-souled Nimi collected together various agreeable objects (of food and drink) on the fourteenth day of the moon. The next morning he rose from bed. Pained his heart was with grief, as he rose from sleep that day—he succeeded in withdrawing it from the one object upon which it had been working. His understanding succeeded in busying itself with other matters. With concentrated attention he then conceived the idea of a Sraddha. All those articles of his own food, consisting of fruits and roots, and all those kinds of staple grains that were agreeable to him, were carefully thought of by that sage possessed of wealth of penances. On the day of the New moon he invited a number of adorable Brahmanas (to his asylum). Possessed of great wisdom, Nimi caused them to be seated on seats (of Kusa grass) and honoured them by going around their persons. Approaching seven such Brahmanas whom he had brought to his abode together, the puissant Nimi gave unto them food consisting of Syamaka rice, unmixed with salt. Towards the feet of those Brahmanas engaged in eating the food that was served unto them a number of Kusa blades was spread out on the seats they occupied, with the top ends of the blades directed towards the south. With a pure body and mind and with concentrated attention, Nimi, having placed those blades of sacred grass in the way indicated, offered cakes of rice unto his dead son, uttering his name and family. Having done this, that foremost of Munis became filled with regret at the idea of having achieved an act that had not (to his knowledge) been laid down in any of the scriptures. Indeed, filled with regret he began to think of what he had done.[412] 'Never done before by the Munis, alas, what have I done! How shall I (for having done an act that has not been ordained) avoid being cursed by the Brahmanas (as an introducer of strange rites)?' He then thought of the original progenitor of his race. As soon as he was thought of, Atri endued with wealth of penances came there. Beholding him exceedingly afflicted with grief on account of the death of his son, the immortal Atri comforted him with agreeable counsels. He said unto him, 'O Muni, this rite that thou hast conceived, is a sacrifice in honour of the Pitris. Let no fear be thine, O thou that art possessed of the wealth of asceticism! The Grandsire Brahman himself, in days of old, laid it down! This rite that thou hast conceived has been ordained by the Self-born himself. Who else than the Self-born could ordain this ritual in Sraddhas? I shall presently tell thee, O son, the excellent ordinance laid down in respect of Sraddhas. Ordained by the Self-born himself, O son, do thou follow it. Listen to me first! Having first performed the Karana on the sacred fire with the aid of Mantras, O thou that art possessed of wealth of penances, one should always pour libations next unto the deity of fire, and Soma, and Varuna. Unto the Viswedevas also, who are always the companions of the Pitris, the Self-born then ordained a portion of the offerings. The Earth also, as the goddess that sustains the offerings made at Sraddhas, should then be praised under the names of Vaishnavi, Kasyapi, and the inexhaustible.[413] When water is being fetched for the Sraddha, the deity Varuna of great puissance should be praised. After this, both Agni and Soma should be invoked with reverence and gratified (with libations), O sinless one. Those deities that are called by the name of Pitris were created by the Self-born. Others also, highly blessed, viz., the Ushnapsa, were created by him. For all these shares have been ordained of the offerings made at Sraddhas. By adoring all these deities at Sraddhas,

---

[411] These purificatory rites, after the usual period of mourning, consists in shaving and bathing and wearing new clothes.
[412] The act, as explained by the commentator, consisted in the father's doing that with reference to the son which, as the ordinance went, was done by sons with reference to sires.
[413] In one of the vernacular versions, the wrong reading Kshama is adopted for Akshaya.

the ancestors of the persons performing them become freed from all sins. The Pitris referred to above as those created by the Self-born number seven. The Viswedevas having Agni for their mouth (for it is through Agni that they feed), have been mentioned before. I shall now mention the names of those high-souled deities who deserve shares of the offerings made at Sraddhas. Those names are Vala, Dhriti, Vipapa, Punyakrit, Pavana, Parshni, Kshemak, Divysanu, Vivaswat, Viryavat, Hrimat, Kirtimat, Krita, Jitatman, Munivirya, Diptaroman, Bhayankara, Anukarman, Pratia, Pradatri, Ansumat, Sailabha, Parama Krodhi, Dhiroshni, Bhupati, Sraja, Vajrin, and Vari,—these are the eternal Viswedevas. There are others also whose names are Vidyutvarchas, Somavarchas, and Suryasri. Others also are numbered amongst them, viz., Somapa, Suryasavitra, Dattatman, Pundariyaka, Ushninabha, Nabhoda, Viswayu, Dipti, Chamuhara, Suresa, Vyomari, Sankara Bhava, Isa, Kartri, Kriti, Daksha, Bhuvana, Divya, Karmakrit, Ganita Panchavirya, Aditya, Rasmimat, Saptakrit, Somavachas, Viswakrit, Kavi, Anugoptri, Sugoptri, Naptri, and Iswara:—these highly blessed ones are numbered as the Viswedevas. They are eternal and conversant with all that occurs in Time. The species of paddy which should not be offered at Sraddhas are those called Kodrava, and Pulka. Assafoetida also, among articles used in cooking, should not be offered, as also onions and garlic, the produce of the Moringa pterygosperma, Bauhinia Variegata, the meat of animals slain with envenomed shafts, all varieties of Sucuribita Pepo, Sucuribita lagenaria, and black salt. The other articles that should not be offered at Sraddhas are the flesh of the domesticated hog, the meat of all animals not slaughtered at sacrifices, Nigella sativa, salt of the variety called Vid, the potherb that is called Sitapaki, all sprouts (like those of the bamboo), and also the Trapa bispinosa. All kinds of salt should be excluded from the offerings made at Sraddhas, and also the fruits of the Eugenia Jamblana. All articles, again, upon which any one has spat or upon which tears have fallen should not be offered at Sraddhas. Among offerings made to the Pitris or with the Havya and Kavya offered to the deities, the potherb called Sudarsana (Menispermum tomentosum, Rox) should not be included. Havi mixed with this is not acceptable to Pitris. From the place where the Sraddha is being performed, the Chandala and the Swapacha should be excluded, as also all who wear clothes steeped in yellow, and persons affected with leprosy, or one who has been excasted (for transgressions), or one who is guilty of Brahmanicide, or a Brahmana of mixed descent or one who is the relative of an excasted man. These all should be excluded by persons possessed of wisdom from the place where a Sraddha is being performed,' Having said these words in days of old unto the Rishi Nimi of his own race, the illustrious Atri possessed of wealth of penances then went back to the Grandsire's assembly in Heaven."'"

SECTION XCII.

"'Bhishma said, "After Nimi had acted in the way described above, all the great Rishis began to perform the sacrifice in honour of the Pitris (called the Sraddha) according to rites laid down in the ordinance. Firmly devoted to the discharge of all duties, the Rishis, having performed Sraddhas, began to also offer oblations (unto the Pitris) of sacred waters, with attention. In consequence, however, of the offerings made by persons of all classes (unto the Pitris), the Pitris began to digest that food. Soon they, and the deities also with them, became afflicted with indigestion. Indeed, afflicted with the heaps of food that all persons began to give them, they repaired to the presence of Soma. Approaching Soma they said, 'Alas, great is our affliction in consequence of the food that is offered to us at Sraddhas. Do thou ordain what is necessary for our ease.' Unto them Soma answered, saying, 'If, ye gods, ye are desirous of obtaining ease, do ye repair then unto the abode of the Self-born. Even he will do what is for your good.' At these words of Soma, the deities and the Pitris then proceeded, O Bharata, to the Grandsire where he was seated on the summit of the mountains of Meru.

""""The Deities said, 'O illustrious one, with the food that is offered us in sacrifices and Sraddhas, we are being exceedingly afflicted. O lord, show us grace and do what would be for our good.' Hearing these words of theirs, the Self-born said unto them in reply, 'Here, the god of fire is sitting beside me, Even he will do what is for your benefit.'

""""Agni said, 'Ye sires, when a Sraddha comes, we shall together eat the offerings made to us. If ye eat those offerings with me, ye shall then, without doubt, succeed in digesting them easily.' Hearing these words of the deity of fire, the Pitris became easy of heart. It is for this reason also that in making offerings at Sraddhas a share is first offered to the deity of fire, O king. If a portion of the offerings be first made to the deity of fire at a Sraddha, O prince of men, Rakshasas of regenerate origin cannot then do any injury to such a Sraddha.[414] Beholding the deity of fire at a Sraddha Rakshasas fly away from it. The ritual of the Sraddha is that the cake should first be offered to the (deceased) sire. Next, one should be offered to the grandsire. Next should one be offered to the great-grandsire. Even this is the ordinance in respect of the Sraddha. Over every cake that is offered, the offerer should, with concentrated attention, utter the Savitri Mantras. This other Mantra also should be uttered, viz., unto Soma who is fond of the Pitris. A woman that has become impure in consequence of the advent of her season, or one whose ears have been cut off, should not be allowed to remain where a Sraddha is being performed. Nor should a woman (for cooking the rice to be offered in the Sraddha) be brought from a Gotra other than that of the person who is performing the Sraddha.[415] While crossing river, one should offer oblations of water unto one's Pitris, naming them all. Indeed, when one comes upon a river one should gratify one's Pitris with oblations of water. Having offered oblations of water first unto the ancestors of one's own race, one should next offer such oblations to one's (deceased) friends and relatives. When one crosses a stream on a car unto which is yoked a couple of oxen of variegated hue, or from them that cross a stream on boats, the Pitris expect oblations of water. Those that know this always offer oblations of water with concentrated attention unto the Pitris. Every fortnight on the day of the New moon, one should make offerings unto one's deceased ancestors. Growth, longevity, energy, and prosperity become all attainable through devotion to the Pitris. The Grandsire Brahman, Pulastya, Vasishtha, Pulaha, Angiras, Kratu and the great Rishi Kasyapa—these, O prince of Kuru's race, are regarded as great masters of Yoga. They are numbered among the Pitris. Even this is the high ritual in respect of the Sraddha, O monarch! Through Sraddhas performed on earth the deceased members of one race become freed from a position of misery. I have thus, O prince of Kuru's race, expounded to thee agreeably with the scriptures, the ordinances in respect of Sraddhas. I shall once more discourse to thee on gifts.""""

---

[414] Ravana and other Rakshasas who spring from Pulastya's line are known as Brahma-Rakshasas or Rakshasas of regenerate origin.

[415] Ravana and other Rakshasas who spring from Pulastya's line are known as Brahma-Rakshasas or Rakshasas of regenerate origin.

SECTION XCIII.

"'Yudhishthira said, "If Brahmanas that are in the observance of a vow (viz., fast) eat, at the invitation of a Brahmana, the Havi (offered at a Sraddha), can they be charged with the transgression or a violation of their vow, or should they refuse the invitation of a Brahmana when such invitation is received by them? Tell me this, O grandsire!"

"'Bhishma said, "Let those Brahmanas eat, impelled by desire, who are observant of such vows as are not indicated in the Vedas. As regards those Brahmanas, however, that are observant of such vows are indicated in the Vedas, they are regarded as guilty of a breach of their vow, O Yudhishthira, by eating the Havi of a Sraddha at the request of him who performs the Sraddha."

"'Yudhishthira said, "Some people say that fast is a penance. Is penance really identifiable with fast or is it not so? Tell me this, O grandsire!"

"'Bhishma said, "People do regard a regular fast for a month or a half month as a penance. The truth, however, is that one who mortifies one's own body is not to be regarded either as an ascetic or as one conversant with duty.[416] Renunciation, however, is regarded as the best of penances. A Brahmana should always be an abstainer from food, and observe the vow called Brahmacharya.[417] A Brahmana should always practise self-denial restraining even speech, and recite the Vedas. The Brahmana should marry and surround himself with children and relatives, from desire of achieving righteousness. He should never sleep. He should abstain from meat. He should always read the Vedas and the scriptures. He should always speak the truth, and practise self-denial. He should eat Vighasa (viz., what remains after serving the deities and guests). Indeed, he should be hospitable towards all that come to his abode. He should always eat Amrita (viz., the food that remains in the house after all the family, including guests and servants have eaten) He should duly observe all rites and perform sacrifices."

"'Yudhishthira said, "How may one come to be regarded as always observant of fasts? How may one become observant of vows? How, O king, may one come to be an eater of Vighasa? By doing what may one be said to be found of guest?"

"'Bhishma said, "He who takes food only morning and evening at the prescribed hours and abstains from all food during the interval between, is said to be an abstainer from food. He who has congress with only his wedded wife and that only at her season, is said to be observant of the vow of Brahmacharya. By always making gifts, one comes to be regarded as truthful in speech. By abstaining from all meat obtained from animals slaughtered for nothing, one becomes an abstainer from meat.[418] By making gifts one becomes cleansed of all sins, and by abstaining from sleep during daytime one comes to be regarded as always awake. He who always eats what remains after serving the needs of guests and servants is said to always eat Amrita. He who abstains from eating till Brahmanas have eaten (of that food), is regarded as conquering heaven by such

---

[416] i.e., that fast which mortifies the body is not to be regarded as equivalent to penance. True penance is something else. An observer of such a fast is not to be regarded as an ascetic. Such fasts, again, are sinful instead of being meritorious.

[417] By Upavasa in the second line is meant abstention from food between the two prescribed hours for eating, and not that fast which mortifies the body. One may, again, eat the most luxurious food without being attached to it. One also, by repining at one's abstinence, may come to be regarded as actually enjoying the most luxurious food.

[418] Meat of animals slaughtered in sacrifices is allowable. By taking such meat, one does not become an eater of meat. In fact, one may etc.

abstention. He who eats what remains after serving the deities, the Pitris, and relatives and dependants, is said to eat Vighasa. Such men acquire many regions of felicity in the abode of Brahman himself. There, O king, they dwell in the company of Apsaras and Gandharvas. Indeed, they sport and enjoy all sports of delight in those regions, with the deities and guests and the Pitris in their company, and surrounded by their own children and grandchildren. Even such becomes their high end."

"'Yudhishthira said, "People are seen to make diverse kinds of gifts unto the Brahmanas. What, however, is the difference, O grandsire, between the giver and the receiver?"

"'Bhishma said, "The Brahmana accepts gifts from him that is righteous, and from him that is unrighteous. If the giver happens to be righteous, the receiver incurs little fault. If on the other hand, the giver happens to be unrighteous the receiver sinks in hell. In this connection is cited an old history of the conversation between Vrishadarbhi and the seven Rishis, O Bharata. Kasyapa and Atri and Vasishtha and Bharadwaja and Gautama and Viswamitra and Jamadagni, and the chaste Arundhati (the wife of Vasishtha), all had a common maidservant whose name was Ganda. A Sudra of the name of Pasusakha married Ganda and became her husband. Kasyapa and others, in days of old, observed the austerest penances and roved over the world, desirous of attaining to the eternal region of Brahman by the aid of Yoga-meditation. About that time, O delighter of the Kurus, there occurred a severe drought. Afflicted by hunger, the whole world of living creatures became exceedingly weak. At a sacrifice which had been performed in former times by Sivi's son he had given away unto the Ritwiks a son of his as the sacrificial present. About this time, unendued with longevity as the prince was, he died of starvation. The Rishis named, afflicted with hunger, approached the dead prince and sat surrounding him. Indeed, those foremost of Rishis, beholding the son of him at whose sacrifice they had officiated, O Bharata, thus dead of starvation, began to cook the body in a vessel, impelled by the pangs of hunger. All food having disappeared from the world of men, those ascetics, desirous of saving their lives, had recourse, for purposes of sustenance, to such a miserable shift. While they were thus employed. Vrishadarbha's son, viz., king Saivya, in course of his roving, came upon those Rishis. Indeed, he met them on his way, engaged in cooking the dead body, impelled by the pangs of hunger.

"""The son of Vrishadarbha said, 'The acceptance of a gift (from me) will immediately relieve you all. Do you, therefore, accept a gift for the support of your bodies! Ye ascetics endued with wealth of penances, listen to me as I declare what wealth I have! That Brahmana who solicits me (for gifts) is ever dear to me. Verily, I shall give unto you a thousand mules. Unto each of you I shall give a thousand kine of white hair, foremost in speed, each accompanied by a bull, and each having a well-born calf, and, therefore, yielding milk. I shall also give unto you a thousand bulls of white complexion and of the best breed and capable of bearing heavy burdens. I shall also give you a large number of kine, of good disposition, the foremost of their kind, all fat, and each of which, having brought forth her first calf, is quick with her second.[419] Tell me what else I shall give of foremost villages, of grain, of barley, and of even the rarer and costly jewels. Do not seek to eat this food that is inedible. Tell me what I should give unto you for the support of your bodies!'

"""The Rishis said, 'O king, an acceptance of gifts from a monarch is very sweet at

---

[419] Prashthauhi means a cow pregnant with her second calf. Grishti means a cow that has brought forth only her first calf.

first but it is poison in the end. Knowing this well, why do you, O king, tempt us then with these offers? The body of the Brahmana is the field of the deities. By penance, it is purified. Then again, by gratifying the Brahmana, one gratifies the deities. If a Brahmana accepts the gifts made to him by the king, he loses, by such acceptance, the merit that he would otherwise acquire by his penances that day. Indeed, such acceptance consumes that merit even as a blazing conflagration consumes a forest. Let happiness be thine, O king, as the result of the gifts thou makest to those that solicit thee!' Saying these words unto them, they left the spot, proceeding by another way. The flesh those high-souled ones had intended to cook remained uncooked. Indeed, abandoning that flesh, they went away, and entered the woods in search of food. After this, the ministers of the king, urged by their master, entered those woods and plucking certain figs endeavoured to give them away unto those Rishis. The officers of the king filled some of those figs with gold and mixing them with others sought to induce those ascetics to accept them. Atri took up some of those figs, and finding them heavy refused to take them. He said, 'We are not destitute of knowledge. We are not fools! We know that there is gold within these figs. We have our senses about us. Indeed, we are awake instead of being asleep. If accepted in this world, those will produce bitter consequence hereafter. He who seeks happiness both here and hereafter should never accept these.'

""Vasishtha said, 'If we accept even one gold coin, it will be counted as a hundred or even a thousand (in assigning the demerit that attaches to acceptance). If, therefore, we accept many coins, we shall surely attain to an unhappy end hereafter!'

""Kasyapa said, 'All the paddy and barley on earth, all the gold and animals and women that occur in the world, are incapable of gratifying the desire of a single person. Hence, one possessed of wisdom should dispelling cupidity, adopt tranquillity!'

""Bharadwaja said, 'The horns of a Ruru, after their first appearance, begin to grow with the growth of the animal. The cupidity of man is even like this. It has no measure!'

""Gautama said, 'All the objects that exist in the world are incapable of gratifying even a single person. Man is even like the ocean, for he can never be filled (even as the ocean can never be filled by all the waters that are discharged into it by the rivers).'

""Viswamitra said, 'When one desire cherished by a person becomes gratified, there springs up immediately another whose gratification is sought and which pierces him like a shaft.'

""Jamadagni said, 'Abstention from accepting gifts supports penances as their foundation. Acceptance, however, destroys that wealth (viz., the merit of penances).'

""Arundhati said, 'Some people are of opinion that things of the world may be stored with a view to spend them upon the acquisition of righteousness (by gifts and sacrifices). I think, however, that the acquisition of righteousness is better than that of worldly wealth.'

""Ganda said, 'When these my lords, who are endued with great energy, are so very much afraid of this which seems to be a great terror a weak man as I am fear it the more.'

""Pasusakha said, 'The wealth there is in righteousness is very superior. There is nothing superior to it. That wealth is known to the Brahmans. I wait upon them as their servant, only for learning to value that wealth.'

""The Rishis (all together) said, 'Let happiness be his, as the result of the gifts he makes, who is the king of the people of this land. Let his gift be successful who has sent these fruits to us, enclosing gold within them.'"

"Bhishma continued, "Having said these words, those Rishis of steadfast vows, abandoning the figs having gold within them, left that spot and proceeded to whatever destination they liked.

""The ministers said, 'O king, coming to know of the existence of gold within the figs, the Rishis have gone away! Let this be known to thee!'"

"'Bhishma continued, "Thus addressed by his ministers, king Vrishadarbhi became filled with wrath against all those Rishis. Indeed, to take vengeance upon them, the monarch entered his own chamber. Observing the austerest of penances, he poured on his sacred fire libations of ghee, accompanying each with Mantras uttered by him. From that fire there then arose as the result of the incantation, a form capable of striking every one with fear. Vrishadarbhi named her as Yatudhani. That form which had been from the incantations of the king, looking as terrible as the Last Night, appeared with joined hands before the monarch. Addressing king Vrishadarbhi, she said, 'What shall I accomplish?'

""Vrishadarbhi said, 'Go and follow the seven Rishis, as also Arundhati, and the husband of their maid-servant, and the maid-servant herself, and comprehend what the meanings are of their names. Having ascertained their names, do thou slay all of them. After slaying them thou mayst go whatever destination thou likest.'"[420]

"'Bhishma continued, "Saying, 'So be it!' the Rakshasi who had been named Yatudhani, in her proper form, proceeded to that forest in which the great Rishis wandered in search of food. Indeed, O king, those great Rishis, with Atri among them, roved within the forest, subsisting upon fruits and roots. In course of their wanderings they saw a mendicant of broad shoulders, and plump arms and legs and well-nourished face and abdomen. Of limbs that were all adipose, he was wandering with a dog in his company. Beholding that mendicant whose limbs were all well-developed and handsome, Arundhati exclaimed, addressing the Rishis, 'None of you will ever be able to show such well-developed features!'

""Vasishtha said, 'The sacred fire of this person is not like ours for while he is able to pour libations on it, morning and evening, none of us are able to do the same. It is for this reason that we see both him and his dog so well-developed.'

""Atri said, 'This man does not, like us, feel the pangs of hunger. His energy has not sustained, like ours, any diminution. Acquired with the greatest difficulty, his Vedas have not, like ours, disappeared. Hence, it is that we see both him and his dog so well-developed.'[421]

""Viswamitra said, 'This man is not, like us, unable to observe the eternal duties inculcated in the scriptures. I have become idle. I feel the pangs of hunger. I have lost the knowledge I had acquired. This man is not like us in this respect. Hence I see both him and his dog so well-developed.'

""Jamadagni said, 'This man has not to think of storing his annual grain and fuel as we are compelled to do. Hence I see both him and his dog so well-developed!'

""Kasyapa said, 'This man has not, like us, four brothers of the whole blood who are begging from house to house, uttering the words, "Give—Give!" Hence it is that I see him and his dog so well-developed.'

""Bharadwaja said, 'This man hath no regret like ours for having condemned and cursed his spouse. He hath not acted so wickedly and senselessly. Hence I see both him and his dog so well-developed!'

---

[420] The commentator explains that the direction about ascertaining the names of the Rishis and the meanings of those names proceed from the kings' desire of cautioning the Rakshasi lest in going to destroy them she might herself meet with destruction.

[421] In other words, Vasishtha attributes the leanness or emaciation of himself and his companions to the failure to discharge their daily rites of religious practice.

""Gautama said, 'This man hath not like us only three pieces of covering made of Kusa grass, and a single Ranku-skin, each of which again, is three years old. Hence it is that I see both him and his dog so well-developed!'"

"'Bhishma continued, "The wandering mendicant, beholding those great Rishis, approached them, and accosted them all by touching their hand according to the custom. Conversing then with each other about the difficulty of obtaining sustenance in that forest and the consequent necessity of bearing the pangs of hunger, all of them left that spot. Indeed, they wandered through that wilderness, all bent upon a common purpose, viz., the plucking of fruits and the extraction of roots for sustenance. One day, as they were wandering they beheld a beautiful lake overgrown with lotuses. Its banks were covered with trees that stood thickly near one another. The waters of the lake were pure and transparent. Indeed, the lotuses that adorned the lake were all of the hue of the morning sun. The leaves that floated on the water were of the colour of lapis lazuli. Diverse kinds of aquatic fowls were sporting on its bosom. There was but one path leading to it. The banks were not miry and the access to the water was easy. Urged by Vrishadarbhi, the Rakshasi of frightful mien who had sprung from his incantations and who had been named Yatudhani, guarded the lake. Those foremost of Rishis, with Pasusakha in their company, proceeded towards the lake, which was thus guarded by Yatudhani for the object of gathering some lotus stalks.[422] Beholding Yatudhani of frightful aspect standing on the banks of the lake, those great Rishis addressed her, saying, 'Who art thou that thus standest alone in these solitary woods? For whom dost thou wait here? What, indeed, is thy purpose? What dost thou do here on the banks of this lake adorned with lotuses?'

""Yatudhani said, 'It matters not who I am. I deserve not to be questioned (respecting my name and race and purposes). Ye that are possessed of ascetic wealth, know that I am the guard set to watch this lake.'

""The Rishis said, 'All of us are hungry. We have nothing else to eat. With thy permission we would gather some lotus-stalks!'

""Yatudhani said, 'Agreeably with a compact, do ye take the lotus-stalks as ye please. Ye must, one by one, give me your names. Ye may then, without delay, take the stalks!'"

"Bhishma continued, "Ascertaining that her name was Yatudhani and that she stood there for slaying them (after knowing, from the meanings their names, what the extent was of their power), Atri, who was famishing with hunger, addressed her, and said these words.'

""Atri said, 'I am called Atri because I cleanse the world from sin. For, again, thrice studying the Vedas every day, I have made days of my nights. That, again, is no night in which I have not studied the Vedas. For these reasons also I am called Atri, O beautiful lady!'

""Yatudhani said, 'O thou of great effulgence, the explanation thou hast given me of thy name is incapable of being comprehended by me. Do thou, therefore, go and plunge into this tank filled with lotuses!'

""Vasishtha said, 'I am endued with the wealth (that consists of the Yoga attributes of puissance, etc.) I lead, again, a domestic mode of life, and am regarded as the foremost of all persons that lead such a mode of life. In consequence of being endued with (such) wealth, of my living as a householder, and of my being regarded as the foremost of all householders, I am called Vasishtha.'

---

[422] Lotus-stalks are eaten in India and are mentioned by Charaka as heavy food.

""'Yatudhani said, 'The etymological explanation of thy name is perfectly incomprehensible to me, in as much as the inflections which the original roots have undergone are unintelligible. Go and plunge into this lake of lotuses!'

""'Kasyapa said, 'I always protect my body, and in consequence of my penances I have become endued with effulgence. For thus protecting the body and for this effulgence that is due to my penances, I have come to be called by the name of Kasyapa!'

""'Yatudhani said, 'O thou of great effulgence, the etymological explanation thou hast given of thy name is incapable of being comprehended by me. Go and plunge into this lake filled with lotuses!'

""'Bharadwaja said, 'I always support my sons, my disciples, the deities, the Brahmanas, and my wife. In consequence of thus supporting all with ease, I am called Bharadwaja!'

""'Yatudhani said, 'The etymological explanation thou hast given me of thy name is perfectly incomprehensible to me, in consequence of the many inflections the root has undergone. Go and plunge into this lake filled with lotuses!'

""'Gotama said, 'I have conquered heaven and earth by the aid of self-restraint. In consequence of my looking upon all creatures and objects with an equal eye, I am like a smokeless fire. Hence I am incapable of being subjugated by thee. When, again, I was born, the effulgence of my body dispelled the surrounding darkness. For these reasons I am called Gotama!'

""'Yatudhani said, 'The explanation thou hast given me of thy name, O great ascetic, is incapable of being understood by me. Go and plunge into this lake of lotuses!'

""'Viswamitra said, 'The deities of the universe are my friends. I am also the friend of the universe. Hence, O Yatudhani, know that I am called Viswamitra!'

""'Yatudhani said, 'The explanation thou hast given of thy name is incomprehensible to me in consequence of the inflections the root has undergone. Go and plunge into this lake of lotuses!'

""'Jamadagni said, 'I have sprung from the sacrificial fire of the deities. Hence am I called Jamadagni, O thou of beautiful features!'

""'Yatudhani said, 'The etymological explanation thou hast given me, O great ascetic, of thy name, is incomprehensible to me (in consequence of the diverse inflections the root has undergone). Do thou go and plunge into this lake of lotuses!'

""'Arundhati said, 'I always stay by the side of my husband, and hold the earth jointly with him. I always incline my husband's heart towards me. I am, for these reasons called Arundhati!'

""'Yatudhani said, 'The explanation thou hast given me of thy name is perfectly incomprehensible to me in consequence of the inflections the roots have undergone. Go and plunge into this lake of lotuses!'

""'Ganda said, 'The Ganda means a portion of the cheek. As I have that portion a little elevated above the others, I am, O thou that hast sprung from the sacrificial fire of Saivya, called by the name of Ganda!'

""'Yatudhani said, 'The explanation which thou hast given me of thy name is perfectly incomprehensible to me in consequence of the inflections which the root has undergone. Go and plunge into this lake of lotuses!'

""'Pasusakha said, 'I protect and tend all animals that I see, and I am always a friend to all animals. Hence am I called Pasusakha, O thou that hast sprung from the (sacrificial) fire (of king Vrishadarbhi).'

""'Yatudhani said, 'The explanation thou hast given me of thy name is perfectly incomprehensible to me in consequence of the inflections which the roots have undergone. Go and plunge into this lake of lotuses!'

""'Sunahsakha said,[423] 'I am incapable of explaining the etymology of my name after the manner of these ascetics. But know, O Yatudhani, that I am called by the name of Sunahsakha!'

""'Yatudhani said, 'Thou hast mentioned thy name only once. The explanation thou hast offered I have not able to catch. Do thou, therefore, mention it again, O regenerate one!'

""'Sunahsakha said, 'Since thou hast been unable to catch my name in consequence of my having mentioned it only once, I shall strike thee with my triple stick! Struck with it, be thou consumed into ashes without delay!'"

"'Bhishma continued, "Struck then, on the head, by the Sannyasin, with his triple stick which resembled the chastisement inflicted by a Brahmana, the Rakshasi who had sprung from the incantations of king Vrishadarbhi fell down on the earth and became reduced to ashes.[424] Having thus destroyed the mighty Rakshasi, Sunahsakha thrust his stick into the earth and sat himself down on a grassy plot of land. The Rishis then, having, as they liked, plucked a number of lotuses and taken up a number of lotus-stalks, came up from the lake, filled with joy. Throwing on the ground the heap of lotuses which they had gathered with much toil, they plunged once more into it for offering oblations of water to the Pitris. Coming up, they proceeded to that part of the bank where they had deposited the lotus-stalks. Reaching that spot, those foremost of men found that the stalks were nowhere to be seen.

""'The Rishis said, 'What sinful and hard-hearted man has stolen away the lotus-stalks gathered by our hungry selves from desire of eating?'"

"'Bhishma continued, "Those foremost of regenerate persons, suspecting one another, O crusher of foes, said, 'We shall each have to swear to our innocence!' All those ascetics then, famishing with hunger and worn out with exertion, agreeing to the proposal, took these oaths.

""'Atri said, 'Let him who has stolen the lotus-stalk touch kine with his foot, make water facing the sun, and study the Vedas on excluded days!'

""'Vasishtha said, 'Let him who has stolen the lotus-stalks abstain from studying the Vedas, or leash hounds, or be a wandering mendicant unrestrained by the ordinances laid down for that mode of life, or be a slayer of persons that seek his protection, or live upon the proceeds of the sale of his daughter, or solicit wealth from those that are low and vile!'

""'Kasyapa said, 'Let him who has stolen the lotus-stalks utter all kinds of words in all places, give false evidence in a court of law, eat the flesh of animals not slain in sacrifices, make gifts to undeserving persons or to deserving persons at unseasonable times, and have sexual congress with women during daytime!'

""'Bharadwaja said, 'Let him who has stolen the lotus-stalks be cruel and unrighteous in his conduct towards women and kinsmen and kine. Let him humiliate Brahmanas, in disputations, by displaying his superior knowledge and skill. Let him study the Riks and

---

[423] Sunahsakha implies a friend of dogs. The newcomer who had joined the roving Rishis had a dog with him. Hence, he is called by the name of Sunahsakha.

[424] Brahma-danda literally means the stick in the hand of a Brahmana. Figuratively, it implies the chastisement inflicted by a Brahmana in the form of a curse. As such it is more effective than the thunderbolt in the hands of Indra himself, for the thunderbolt blasts only those objects that lie within its immediate range. The Brahmana's curse, however, blasts even those that are unborn.

the Yajuses, disregarding his preceptor! Let him pour libations upon fires made with dry grass or straw!'[425]

""Jamadagni said, 'Let him who has stolen the lotus-stalks be guilty of throwing filth and dirt on water. Let him be inspired with animosity towards kine. Let him be guilty of having sexual congress with women at times other than their season. Let him incur the aversion of all persons. Let him derive his maintenance from the earnings of his wife! Let him have no friends and let him have many foes! Let him be another's guest for receiving in return those acts of hospitality which he has done to that other!'[426]

""Gotama said, 'Let him who has stolen the lotus-stalks be guilty of throwing away the Vedas after having studied them! Let him cast off the three sacred fires! Let him be a seller of the Soma (plant or juice)! Let him live with that Brahmana who resides in a village which has only one well from which water is drawn by all classes and who has married a Sudra woman!'

""Viswamitra said, 'Let him who has stolen the lotus-stalks be fated to see his preceptors and seniors and his servants maintained by others during his own life-time. Let him not have a good end. Let him be the father of many children! Let him be always impure and a wretch among Brahmanas! Let him be proud of his possessions! Let him be a tiller of the soil and let him be filled with malice! Let him wander in the season of rains. Let him be a paid servant! Let him be the priest of the king! Let him assist at the sacrifices of such impure persons as do not deserve to be assisted at their sacrifices!'

""Arundhati said, 'Let her who has stolen the lotus-stalks always humiliate her mother-in-law! Let her be always vexed with her husband! Let her eat whatever good things come to her house without sharing them with others! Disregarding the kinsmen of her lord, let her live in her husband's house and eat, at the day's close, the flour of fried barely! Let her come to be regarded as unenjoyable (in consequence of the stains that would tarnish her)! Let her be the mother of a heroic son!'[427]

""Ganda said, 'Let her who has stolen the lotus-stalks be always a speaker of falsehoods! Let her always quarrel with her kinsmen! Let her bestow her daughter in marriage for a pecuniary consideration! Let her eat the food which she has cooked, alone and without sharing it with anybody! Let her pass her whole life in slavery! Indeed, let her who has stolen the lotus-stalks be quick with child in consequence of sexual congress under circumstances of guilt.'

""Pasusakha said, 'Let him who has stolen the lotus-stalks be born of a slave-mother. Let him have many children all of whom are worthless! And let him never bow to the deities.'

""Sunahsakha said, 'Let him who has removed the lotus-stalks obtain the merit of bestowing his daughter in marriage upon a Brahmana, who has studied all the Samans and the Yajuses and who has carefully observed the vow of Brahmacharya. Let him perform the final ablutions after having studied all the Atharvans!'

""All the Rishis said, 'The oath thou hast taken is no oath at all, for all the acts which

[425] Libations should always be poured upon a blazing fire. Fire made with dry grass or straw blaze up quickly and become soon extinguished. By pouring libations, therefore, upon such fires, one practically pours them upon ashes and gains no merit.

[426] To derive the means of sustenance from a wife was always viewed with feelings of aversion in this country. It seems, therefore, that the custom of domesticating sons-in-law was not unknown in ancient times. To receive acts of hospitality in return for those rendered was regarded as not only meanness but also destructive of merit.

[427] Jnatinam is an instance of the genitive in what is called Anadara. The meaning, therefore, is disregarded them. For a Brahmana woman to bring forth a son devoted to heroic deeds is a reproach.

deposited on the bank) had been taken away by somebody. The foremost of Rishis, Agastya, addressing them all, said, 'Who has taken away the good stalks which I had extracted and deposited here? I suspect some one amongst you must have done the act. Let him who has taken them away give them back to me. It behoves you not thus to misappropriate my stalks! It is heard that Time assails the energy of Righteousness. That Time has come upon us. Hence, Righteousness is afflicted. It is meet that I should go to heaven for good, before unrighteousness assails the world and establishes itself here![428] Before the time comes when Brahmanas, loudly uttering the holy Vedas, within the precincts of villages and inhabited places, cause the Sudras to hear them, before the time comes when kings often against the rules of Righteousness from motives of policy, I shall go to heaven for good! Before men cease to regard the distinctions between the lower, the middle, and the higher classes, I shall go to heaven for good. Before Ignorance assails the world and envelops all things in darkness, I shall go to heaven for good.[429] Before the time comes when the strong begin to lord it over the weak and treat them as slaves, I shall go to heaven for good. Indeed, I dare not remain on earth for witnessing these things.' The Rishis, much concerned at what he said, addressed that great ascetic and said, 'We have not stolen thy stalks! Thou shouldst not harbour these suspicions against us. O great Rishi, we shall take the most frightful oaths!' Having said these words, conscious of their own innocence, and desirous of upholding the cause of righteousness, those Rishis and sages of royal descent then began to swear, one after another, the following oaths.

""Bhrigu said, 'Let him who has stolen thy stalks censure when censured, assail when assailed, and eat the flesh that is attached to the back-bone of animals (slaughtered in sacrifice)!'[430]

""Vasishtha said, 'Let him who has stolen thy stalks neglect his Vedic studies, leash hounds, and having taken himself to the mendicant order live in a city or town!'[431]

""Kasyapa said, 'Let him who has stolen thy stalks sell all things in all places, misappropriate deposits, and give false evidence!'

""Gautama said, 'Let him who has stolen thy stalks live, displaying pride in all things, with an understanding that does not see all creatures with an equal eye, and always yielding himself to the influence of desire and wrath! Let him be a cultivator of the soil, and let him be inspired by malice!'[432]

""Angiras said, 'Let him who has stolen thy stalks be always impure! Let him be a censurable Brahmana (for his misdeeds)! Let him leash hounds. Let him be guilty of Brahmanicide. Let him be averse to expiations after having committed transgressions!'

""Dhundhumara said, 'Let him who has stolen thy stalks be ungrateful to his friends! Let him take birth in a Sudra woman! Let him eat alone any good food (coming to the

---

[428] The scriptures declare that Righteousness loses its strength as Time advances. In the Krita age, it exists in entirety. In the Treta, it loses a quarter. In the Dwapara, another quarter is lost. In the Kali age, full three quarters are lost and only a quarter is all that remains.

[429] The Rishis think that the distinctions between the lower, the middling, and the higher classes of society are eternal, and nothing can be a greater calamity than the effacement of those distinctions. Equality of men, in their eyes, is an unmitigated evil.

[430] Forgiveness is the duty of the Brahmana. To fall off from forgiveness is to fall off from duty. To censure when censured and assail the assailer, are grave transgressions in the case of a Brahmana. The idea of retaliation should never enter the Brahmana's heart; for the Brahmana is the friend of the universe. His behaviour to friend and foe should be equal. To eat the flesh that attaches itself to the back-bone of a slaughtered animal is also a grave transgression.

[431] A religious mendicant should always wander over the Earth, sleeping where night overtakes him. For such a man to reside in a city or town is sinful.

[432] To till the soil is a transgression for a Brahmana.

house), without sharing it with others!'[433]

""'Dilipa said, 'Let him who has stolen thy stalks descend to those regions of misery and infamy which are reserved for that Brahmana who resides in a village having but one well and who has sexual congress with a Sudra woman!'[434]

""'Puru said, 'Let him who has stolen thy stalks adopt the occupation of a physician! Let him be supported by the earnings of his wife! Let him draw his sustenance from his father-in-law!'

""'Sukra said, 'Let him who has stolen thy stalks eat the flesh of animals not slain in sacrifices! Let him have sexual congress at day-time! Let him be a servant of the king!'

""'Jamadagni said, 'Let him who has stolen thy stalks study the Vedas on forbidden days or occasions! Let him feed friends at Sraddhas performed by him! Let him eat at the Sraddha of a Sudra!'

""'Sivi said, 'Let him who has stolen thy stalks die without having established a fire (for daily worship)! Let him be guilty of obstructing the performance of sacrifices by others! Let him quarrel with those that are observant of penances!'

""'Yayati said, 'Let him who has stolen thy stalks be guilty of having sexual congress with his wife when she is not in her season and when he is himself in the observance of a vow and bears matted locks on his head! Let him also disregard the Vedas!'

""'Nahusha said, 'Let him who has stolen thy stalks live in domesticity after having betaken himself to the vow of mendicancy! Let him act in whatever way he pleases (and without restraint of any kind), after having undergone the initiatory rites in view of a sacrifice or some solemn observance! Let him take pecuniary gratification for prelections to disciples (on any branch of knowledge that the latter come to learn)!'

""'Amvarisha said, 'Let him who has stolen thy stalks be cruel and unrighteous in his behaviour towards women and kinsmen and kine! Let him be guilty also of Brahmanicide!'

""'Narada said, 'Let him who has stolen thy stalks be one that identifies the body with the soul! Let him study the scriptures with a preceptor that is censurable! Let him chant the Vedas, offending at each step against the rules of orthoepy! Let him disregard all his seniors!'

""'Nabhaga said, 'Let him who has stolen thy stalks always speak false-hoods and quarrel with those that are righteous! Let him bestow his daughter in marriage after accepting a pecuniary gratification offered by his son-in-law!'

""'Kavi said, 'Let him who has stolen thy stalks he guilty of striking a cow with his foot! Let him make water, facing the sun! Let him cast off the person that seeks shelter at his hands!'

""'Viswamitra said, 'Let him who has stolen thy stalks become a servant that behaves with deceit towards his master! Let him be the priest of a king! Let him be the Ritwik of one that should not be assisted at his sacrifices!'

""'Parvata said, 'Let him who has stolen thy stalks be the chief of a village! Let him make journeys on asses! Let him leash hounds for a living!'

""'Bharadwaja said, 'Let him who has stolen thy stalks be guilty of all the demerits that become his who is cruel in his behaviour and untruthful in speech!'

""'Ashtaka said, 'Let him who has stolen thy stalks be a king destitute of wisdom capricious and sinful in his behaviour, and disposed to rule the Earth unrighteously!'

---

[433] Good food should never be taken alone. It should always be shared with children and servants.

[434] A village having only one well should be abandoned by a Brahmana, for he should not draw water from such a well which is used by all classes of the population.

"""Galava said, 'Let him who has stolen thy stalks be more infamous than a sinful man! Let him be sinful in his acts towards his kinsmen and relatives! Let him proclaim the gifts he makes to others!'

"""Arundhati said, 'Let her who has stolen thy stalks speak ill of her mother-in-law! Let her feel disgust for her lord. Let her eat alone any good food that comes to her house!'

"""The Valakhilyas said, 'Let him who has stolen thy stalks stand on one foot at the entrance of a village (for earning his subsistence)! Let him. while knowing all duties, be guilty of every breach!'[435]

"""Sunahsakha said, 'Let him who has stolen thy stalks be a Brahmana that sleeps in happiness, having disregarded his daily Homa! Let him, after becoming a religious mendicant, behave in whatever way he pleases, without observing any restraint!'

"""Surabhi said, 'Let her who has stolen thy stalks be milked, with her (hind) legs bound with a rope of human hair, and with the aid of a calf not her own, and, while milked, let her milk be held in a vessel of white brass!'"[436]

"'Bhishma continued, "After the Rishis and the royal sages had sworn these diverse oaths, O Kuru king, the thousand-eyed chief of the deities, filled with joy, cast his looks on the angered Rishi Agastya. Addressing the Rishi who was very angry at the disappearance of his lotus-stalks, Maghavat thus declared what was passing in his mind. Hear, O king, what the words were that Indra spoke in the midst of those regenerate and celestial Rishis and royal sages.

"""Sakra said, 'Let him who has stolen thy stalks be possessed of the merit of him who bestows his daughter in marriage upon a Brahmana that has duly observed the vow of Brahmacharya or that has duly studied the Samans and the Yajuses! Let him also have the merit of one that undergoes the final bath after completing one's study of the Atharva Veda! Let him who has stolen thy stalks have the merit of having studied all the Vedas. Let him be observant of all duties and righteous in his behaviour! Indeed, let him go to the region of Brahman!'

"""Agastya said, 'Thou hast, O slayer of Vala, uttered a benediction instead of a curse! (It is evident), thou hast taken my stalks! Give them to me, for that is the eternal duty!'

"""Indra said, 'O holy one, I did not remove thy stalks, led by cupidity! Indeed, I removed them from desire of hearing this conclave recite what the duties are that we should observe. It behoveth thee not to give way to anger! Duties are the foremost of Srutis. Duties constitute the eternal path (for crossing the sea of the world)! I have listened to this discourse of the Rishis (on duties) that is eternal and immutable, and that transcends all change![437] Do thou then, O foremost of learned Brahmanas, take back these stalks of thine! O holy one, it behoves thee to forgive my transgression, O thou that art free from every fault!'"

"'Bhishma continued, "Thus addressed by the chief of the deities, the ascetic, viz., Agastya, who had been very angry, took back his stalks. Endued with great intelligence, the Rishi became cheerful. After this, those denizens of the woods proceeded to diverse

---

[435] The penance that is involved in standing on one foot should be practised, like all other penances, in the woods. To practise a penance on the way leading to a village so that people may be induced to make gifts, is a transgression of a grave kind.

[436] Some kine that are vicious have their hind legs tied with a rope while they are milked. If the rope be made of human hair, the pain felt is supposed to be very great. To obtain the aid of a calf belonging to another cow is regarded as sinful. To the cow also, the process of sucking cannot be agreeable. If the milk is held in a vessel of white brass, it becomes unfit for gods and guests.

[437] The discourse is called eternal and immutable because of its subject being so. Duties are eternal truths.

other sacred waters. Indeed, repairing to those sacred waters they performed their ablutions everywhere. The man who reads this narrative with close attention on every Parva day, will not have to become the progenitor of an ignorant and wicked son. He will never be destitute of learning. No calamity will ever touch him. He will, besides, be free from every kind of sorrow. Decrepitude and decay will never be his. Freed from stains and evil of every kind, and endued with merit, he is sure to attain to Heaven. He who studies this Sastra observed by the Rishis, is sure, O prince of men, to attain to the eternal region of Brahman that is full of felicity!""[438]

SECTION XCV.

"'Yudhishthira said, "O chief of Bharata's race, by whom was the custom of giving umbrellas and sandals at obsequial ceremonies introduced? Why was it introduced and for what purpose are those gifts made? They are given not only at obsequial ceremonies but also at other religious rites. They are given on many occasions with a view to acquiring religious merit. I wish to know, in detail, O regenerate one, the true meaning of this custom!"

"'Bhishma said, "Do thou, O prince, attentively listen to the details I shall recite in respect of the custom of giving away umbrellas and shoes at religious rites, and as to how and by whom it was introduced. I shall also tell thee in full, O prince, how it acquired the force of a permanent observance and how it came to be viewed as a meritorious act. I shall, in this connection, recite the narrative of the discourse between Jamadagni and the high-souled Surya. In ancient times, the illustrious Jamadagni, O puissant king, of Bhrigu's race, was engaged in practising with his bow. Taking his aim, he shot arrow after arrow. His wife Renuka used to pick up the shafts when shot and repeatedly bring them back to that descendant, endued with blazing energy, of Bhrigu's race. Pleased with the whizzing noise of his arrows and the twang of his bow, he amused himself thus by repeatedly discharging his arrows which Renuka brought back into him. One day, at noontide, O monarch, in that month when the sun was in Jyesthamula, the Brahmana, having discharged all his arrows, said to Renuka, 'O large-eyed lady, go and fetch me the shafts I have shot from my bow, O thou of beautiful eye-brows! I shall again shoot them with my bow.' The lady proceeded on her errand but was compelled to sit under the shade of a tree, in consequence of her head and feet being scorched by the heat of the sun. The black-eyed and graceful Renuka, having rested for only a moment, feared the curse of her husband and, therefore, addressed herself again to the task of collecting and bringing back the arrows. Taking them with her, the celebrated lady of graceful features came back, distressed in mind and her feet smarting with pain. Trembling with fear, she approached her husband. The Rishi, filled with wrath, repeatedly addressed his fair-faced spouse, saying, 'O Renuka, why hast thou been so late in returning?'

""Renuka said, 'O thou that art endued with wealth of penances, my head and feet were scorched by the rays of the sun! Oppressed by the heat, I had betaken myself to the shade of a tree! Just this has been the cause of the delay! Informed of the cause, do thou, O lord, cease to be angry with me!'

""Jamadagni said, 'O Renuka, this very day shall I destroy, with the fiery energy of my weapons, the star of day with his blazing rays, that has afflicted thee in this way!'"

---

[438] This discourse on duties delivered by the Rishis is called a Sastra. Literally, anything that governs men, i.e., regulates their behaviour, is called a Sastra. As such, the enumeration of duties occurring in this Lesson, although it has been made by a reference to their breaches, is therefore, a Sastra.

"'Bhishma continued, "Drawing his celestial bow, and taking up many arrows, Jamadagni stood, turning his face towards the sun and watching him as he moved (in his diurnal course). Then, O son of Kunti, beholding him addressed for fight, Surya approached him in the guise of a Brahmana, and said unto him. 'What has Surya done to displease thee? Coursing through the firmament, he draws up the moisture from the earth, and in the form of rains he pours it down once more on her. It is through this, O regenerate one, that the food of human beings springs up,—food that is so agreeable to them! The Vedas say that it is food that constitutes the life-breaths. O Brahmana, hidden in the clouds and encompassed by his rays, the sun drenches the seven islands with showers of rain. O puissant one, the moisture, thus poured, diffusing itself into the leaves and fruits of vegetables and herbs, is transformed into food. O son of Bhrigu, the rites of nativity, religious observances of every kind, investiture with the sacred thread, gifts of kine, weddings, all articles in view of sacrifices, the rules for the governance of men, gifts, all sorts of union (between man and man), and the acquisition of wealth, have their origin in food! Thou knowest this well! All the good and agreeable things in the universe, and all the efforts made by living creatures, flow from food. I duly recite what is well-known to thee! Indeed, thou fully knowest all that I have said! Do thou, therefore, O regenerate Rishi, appease thy anger! What wilt thou gain by annihilating the sun?"'"

SECTION XCVI.

"'Yudhishthira said, "What did that foremost of ascetics, viz., Jamadagni endued with great energy, do when thus besought by the maker of day?"

"'Bhishma said, "O descendant of Kuru, despite all the supplications of Surya, the sage Jamadagni, endued with the effulgence of fire, continued to cherish his anger. Then, O king, Surya, in the guise of a Brahmana, bowed his head unto him and addressed him, with folded hands, in these soft words, 'O regenerate Rishi, the sun is always in motion! How shalt thou pierce the Lord of day who is continually moving forward?'

"'"Jamadagni said, 'With the eye of knowledge I know thee to be both moving and motionless! I shall surely read thee a lesson this day. At midday thou seemest to stay in the heavens for a moment. It is then, O Surya, that I shall pierce thee with my arrows! There is no swerving from this my resolution!'

"'"Surya said, 'O regenerate Rishi, without doubt, thou knowest me, O best of archers! But, O holy one, though I have offended, behold, I am a suppliant for thy protection!'"

"'Bhishma continued, "At this, the adorable Jamadagni smilingly addressed the maker of day, saying, 'O Surya, when thou hast sought my protection, thou hast nothing to fear! He would transcend the simplicity that exists in Brahmanas, the stability that exists in the Earth, the mildness existing in the Moon, the gravity existing in Varuna, the effulgence existing in Agni, the brightness of Meru, and the heat of the sun, who would slay a suppliant for protection! The man that can slay a suppliant is capable of violating the bed of his preceptor, of slaying a Brahmana, and of drinking alcohol. Do thou, therefore, think of some remedy for this evil, by which people may be relieved when heated by thy rays!'"

"'Bhishma continued, "So saying, that excellent descendant of Bhrigu remained silent for a while, and Surya forthwith made over to him an umbrella and a pair of sandals.

"'"Surya said, 'Do thou, O great Rishi, take this umbrella wherewith the head may be protected and my rays warded off. This pair of sandals is made of leather for the protection of the feet. From this day forth the gift of these articles in all religious rites shall be established as an inflexible usage!'"

"'Bhishma continued, "This custom of giving umbrellas and shoes was introduced by Surya! O descendant of Bharata, these gifts are considered meritorious in the three worlds. Do thou, therefore, give away umbrellas and shoes to Brahmanas. I have no doubt that thou shalt then acquire great religious merit by the act. O foremost one of Bharata's race, he who gives away a white umbrella with a hundred ribs to a Brahmana, attains to eternal felicity after death and resides in the region of Indra, respected by Brahmanas, Apsaras, and Devas. O puissant one, he who gives shoes to Snataka Brahmanas as also to Brahmanas practising the rites of religion whose feet have become sore with the heat of the sun, attains to regions coveted by the very deities. Such a man, O Bharata, dwells in happiness in the highest Heaven after his death. O foremost one of Bharata's race, I have thus recited to thee in full, the merits of giving away shoes and umbrellas at religious ceremonies!"'"

SECTION XCVII.

"'Yudhishthira said, "O foremost one of Bharata's race, do thou relate to me all the duties of the household mode and tell me all that a man should do in order to attain to prosperity in this world."

"'Bhishma said, "O Bharata, I shall, in this connection, recite to thee the old story of Vasudeva and the goddess Earth. The puissant Vasudeva, O excellent prince of Bharata's race, after hymning the praises of the goddess Earth, questioned her about this very topic that thou hast enquired about.

"""Vasudeva said, 'Having adopted the state of a householder, what acts should I, or one like me, perform and how are such acts to fructify in good?'

"""The goddess Earth said, 'O Madhava, the Rishis, the deities, the Pitris, and men should be worshipped, and sacrifices should be performed, by a householder. Do thou also learn this from me that the deities are always pleased with sacrifices, and men are gratified with hospitality. Therefore, the householder should gratify them with such objects as they desire. By such acts, O slayer of Madhu, the Rishis also are gratified. The householder, abstaining from food, should daily attend to his sacred fire and to his sacrificial offerings. The deities, O slayer of Madhu, are gratified with such acts. The householder should daily offer oblations of food and water, or of fruits, roots and water, for the gratification of the Pitris, and the Vaiswadeva offering should be performed with rice boiled, and oblations of clarified butter unto Agni, Soma, and Dhanwantari. He should offer separate and distinct oblations unto Prajapati. He should make sacrificial offerings in due order; to Yama in the Southern region, to Varuna in Western region, to Soma in the Northern region, to Prajapati within the homestead, to Dhanwantari in the North-eastern region, and to Indra in the Eastern region. He should offer food to men at the entrance of his house. These, O Madhava, are known as the Vali offerings. The Vali should be offered to the Maruts and the deities in the interior of one's house. To the Viswedevas it should be offered in open air, and to the Rakshasas and spirits the offerings should be made at night. After making these offerings, the householder should make offerings unto Brahmanas, and if no Brahmana be present, the first portion of the food should be thrown into the fire. When a man desires to offer Sraddha to his ancestors, he should, when the Sraddha ceremony is concluded, gratify his ancestors and then make the

Vali offerings in due order. He should then make offerings unto the Viswedevas. He should next invite Brahmanas and then properly regale guests arrived at his house, with food. By this act, O prince, are guests gratified. He who does not stay in the house long, or, having come, goes away after a short time, is called a guest. To his preceptor, to his father, to his friend and to a guest, a householder should say, "I have got this in my house to offer thee today!" And he should offer it accordingly every day. The householder should do whatever they would ask him to do. This is the established usage. The householder, O Krishna, should take his food last of all after having offered food to all of them. The householder should worship, with offerings of Madhuparka his king, his priest, his preceptor, and his father-in-law as also Snataka Brahmanas even if they were to stay in his house for a whole year. In the morning as well as in the evening, food should be offered on the ground to dogs, Swapachas,[439] and birds. This is called the Vaiswadeva offering. The householder, who performs these ceremonies with a mind unclouded by passion, obtains the blessings of the Rishis in this world, and after death attains to the heavenly regions."'

"'Bhishma continued, "The puissant Vasudeva, having listened to all this from the goddess Earth, acted accordingly. Do thou also act in the same way. By performing these duties of a householder, O king, thou shalt acquire fame in this world and attain to heaven after death!"'"

SECTION XCVIII.

"'Yudhishthira said, "Of what kind is the gift of light, O chief of Bharata's race? How did this gift originate? What are the merits that attach to it? Do thou tell me all this."

"'Bhishma said, "In this connection, O Bharata, is recited the old narrative of the discourse between Manu, that lord of creatures, and Suvarna. There was in days of yore an ascetic, O Bharata, of the name of Suvarna. His complexion was like that of gold and hence he was called Suvarna (the gold-complexioned). Endued with a pure lineage, good behaviour, and excellent accomplishments, he had mastered all the Vedas. Indeed, by the accomplishments he possessed, he succeeded in surpassing many persons of high lineage. One day that learned Brahmana saw Manu, the lord of all creatures, and approached him. Meeting with each other, they made the usual enquiries of politeness. Both of them were firm in the observance of truth. They sat down on the delightful breast of Meru, that mountain of gold. Seated there they began to converse with each other on diverse subjects connected with the high-souled deities and regenerate Rishis and Daityas of ancient times. Then Suvarna, addressing the Self-born Manu, said these words, 'It behoveth thee to answer one question of mine for the benefit of all creatures. O lord of all creatures, the deities are seen to be worshipped with presents of flowers and other good scents. What is this? How has this practice been originated? What also are the merits that attach to it? Do thou discourse to me on this topic.'

"'"Manu said, 'In this connection is recited the old history of the discourse between Sukra and the high-souled (Daitya) Vali. Once on a time, Sukra of Bhrigu's race approached the presence of Vali, the son of Virochana, while he was ruling the three worlds. The chief of the Asuras, that giver of sacrificial presents in abundance, having worshipped the descendant of Bhrigu with the Arghya (and offering him a seat), sat down

[439] Literally, they who cook for dogs, i.e., keep dogs as companions; meaning members of the lowest caste.

after his guest had seated himself. This very topic that thou hast stated relating to the merits attaching to the gift of flowers and incense and lamps, came up on the occasion. Indeed, the chief of the Daityas put this high question to Sukra, that most learned of all ascetics.

"""Vali said, "O foremost of all persons conversant with Brahma, what, indeed, is the merit of giving flowers and incense and lamps? It behoveth thee, O foremost of Brahmanas, to discourse to me on this."

"""Sukra said, "Penance first sprang into life. Afterwards came Dharma (or compassion and other virtues). In the interval between started into life many creepers and herbs.[440] Innumerable were the species of those. All of them have (the deity) Soma for their lord. Some of these creepers and herbs came to be regarded as Amrita and some came to be regarded as Poison. Others that were neither this nor that formed one class. That is Amrita which gives immediate gratification and joy to the mind. That is Poison which tortures the mind exceedingly by its odour. Know again that Amrita is highly auspicious and that Poison is highly inauspicious. All the (deciduous) herbs are Amrita. Poison is born of the energy of fire. Flowers gladden the mind and confer prosperity. Hence, men of righteous deeds bestowed the name Sumanas on them. That man who in a state of purity offers flowers into the deities finds that the deities become gratified with him, and as the consequence of such gratification bestow prosperity upon him. O ruler of the Daityas, those deities unto whom worshippers offer flowers, O lord, uttering their names the while, become gratified with the offers in consequence of their devotion. The (deciduous) herbs are of diverse kinds and possess diverse kinds of energy. They should be classed as fierce, mild, and powerful. Listen to me as I tell thee which trees are useful for purposes of sacrifice and which are not so. Hear also what garlands are acceptable to Asuras, and what are beneficial when offered to the deities. I shall also set forth in their due order what garlands are agreeable to the Rakshasas, what to the Uragas, what to the Yakshas, what to human beings, and what to the Pitris, in proper order. Flowers are of diverse kinds. Some are wild; some are from trees that grew in the midst of human habitations; some belong to trees that never grow unless planted on well-tilled soil; some are from trees growing on mountains; some are from trees that are not prickly; and some from trees that are prickly. Fragrance, beauty of form, and taste also may offer grounds of classification. The scent that flowers yield is of two kinds, agreeable and disagreeable. Those flowers that emit agreeable scent should be offered to the deities. The flowers of trees that are destitute of thorns are generally white in hue. Such flowers are always acceptable to the deities, O lord! One possessed of wisdom should offer garlands of aquatic flowers, such as the lotus and the like, unto the Gandharvas and Nagas and Yakshas. Such plants and herbs as produce red flowers, as are possessed of keen scent, and as are prickly, have been laid down in the Atharvana as fit for all acts of incantation for injuring foes. Such flowers as are possessed of keen energy, as are painful to the touch, as grow on trees and plants having thorns, and as are either bloody-red or black, should be offered to (evil) spirits and unearthly beings. Such flowers as gladden the mind and heart, as are very agreeable when pressed, and as are of beautiful form, have been said, O lord, to be worthy of being offered to human beings. Such flowers as grow on cemeteries and crematoria, or in places dedicated to the deities, should not be brought and used for marriage and other rites having growth and prosperity for their object, or for acts

---

[440] The commentator takes Tapah or Penance as indicative of the duties of the four orders of life, and Dharma as indicative of compassion and other virtues.

of dalliance and pleasure in secrecy. Such flowers as are born on mountains and in vales, and as are agreeable in scent and aspect, should be offered unto the deities. Sprinkling them with sandal-paste, such agreeable flowers should be duly offered according to the ordinances of the scriptures. The deities become gratified with the scent of flowers; the Yakshas and Rakshasas with their sight, the Nagas with their touch; and human beings with all three, viz., scent, sight, and touch. Flowers, when offered to the deities gratify them immediately. They are capable of accomplishing every object by merely wishing its accomplishment. As such, when gratified with devotees offering them flowers, they cause all the objects cherished by their worshippers to be immediately accomplished. Gratified, they gratify their worshippers. Honoured, they cause their worshippers to enjoy all honours. Disregarded and insulted, they cause those vilest of men to be ruined and consumed. I shall, after this, speak to thee of the merits that attach to the ordinances about the gift of incense. Know, O prince of Asuras, that incenses are of diverse kinds. Some of them are auspicious and some inauspicious. Some incenses consist of exudations. Some are made of fragrant wood set on fire. And some are artificial, being made by the hand, of diverse articles mixed together. Their scent is of two kinds, viz., agreeable and disagreeable. Listen to me as I discourse on the subject in detail.[441] All exudations except that of the Boswellia serrata are agreeable to the deities. It is, however, certain that the best of all exudations is that of the Balsamodendron Mukul. Of all Dhupas of the Sari class, the Aquilaria Agallocha is the best. It is very agreeable to the Yakshas, the Rakshasas, and Nagas. The exudation of the Boswellia serrata, and others of the same class, are much desired by the Daityas. Dhupas made of the exudation of the Shorea robusta and the Pinus deodara, mixed with various spirits of strong scent, are, O king, ordained for human beings. Such Dhupas are said to immediately gratify the deities, the Danavas, and spirits. Besides these, there are many other kinds of Dhupas used by men of purposes of pleasure or enjoyment. All the merits that have been spoken of as attaching to the offer of flowers should be known equally to attach to the gift of such Dhupas as are productive of gratification. I shall now speak of the merits that attach to the gift of lights, and who may give them at what time and in what manner, and what should be the kind of lights that should be offered. Light is said to be energy and fame and has an upward motion. Hence the gift of light, which is energy, enhances the energy of men.[442] There is a hell of the name of Andhatamas. The period also of the sun's southward course is regarded as dark. For escaping that hell and the darkness of this period, one should give lights during the period when the sun is in his northward course. Such an act is applauded by the good.[443] Since, again, light has an upward course and is regarded as a remedy for darkness, therefore, one should be a giver of light. Even this is the conclusion of the scriptures. It is owing to the lights offered that the deities have become endued with beauty, energy, and resplendence. By abstention from such an act, the Rakshasas have become endued with the opposite attributes. Hence, one should always give lights. By giving lights a man becomes endued with keen vision and resplendence. One that gives lights should not be an object of jealousy with others. Lights, again, should not be stolen, nor extinguished when given by others. One that steals a light becomes blind. Such a man

---

[441] Dhupas are incenses offered to the deities. Being of inflammable substances, they are so made that they may burn slowly or smoulder silently. They are the inseparable accompaniments of a worship of the deities.

[442] Tejas is explained by the commentator, as used here for Kanti or beauty, and prakasam for kirti; there is no necessity, however, for rejecting the ordinary meaning of Tejas which is energy.

[443] The sense seems to be that if a man dies during that period when the sun is in his southward course, he is dragged through a thick darkness. For escaping that darkness, one should give lights at the period mentioned.

has to grope through darkness (in the next world) and becomes destitute of resplendence. One that gives lights shines in beauty in the celestial regions like a row of lights. Among lights, the best are those in which ghee is burnt. Next in order are those in which the juice of (the fruits yielded by) deciduous herbs is burnt. One desirous of advancement and growth should never burn (for light) fat or marrow or the juice that flows from the bones of creatures.[444] The man who desires his own advancement and prosperity should always give lights at descents from mountains, in roads through forests and inaccessible regions, under sacred trees standing in the midst of human habitations, and in crossings of streets. The man who gives lights always illumines his race, attains to purity of soul and effulgence of form. Verily, such a man, after death, attains to the companionship of the luminous bodies in the firmament. I shall now discourse to thee upon the merits, with the fruits they bring about, that attach to Vali offerings made to the deities, the Yakshas, the Uragas, human beings, spirits, and Rakshasas. Those unscrupulous and wicked men that eat without first serving Brahmanas and deities and guests and children, should be known as Rakshasas. Hence, one should first offer the food one has got ready unto the deities after having worshipped them duly with restrained senses and concentrated attention. One should offer the Vali unto the deities, bending one's head in reverence. The deities are always supported by food that householders offer. Verily, they bless such houses in which offerings are made to them. The Yakshas and Rakshasas and Pannagas, as also guests and all homeless persons, are supported by the food that are offered by persons leading the domestic mode of life. Indeed, the deities and the Pitris derive their sustenance from such offerings. Gratified with such offerings they gratify the offerer in return with longevity and fame and wealth. Clean food, of agreeable scent and appearance, mixed with milk and curds, should, along with flowers, be offered to the deities. The Valis that should be offered to Yakshas and Rakshasas should be rich with blood and meat, with wines and spirits accompanying, and adorned with coatings of fried paddy.[445] Valis mixed with lotuses and Utpalas are very agreeable to the Nagas. Sesame seeds, boiled in raw sugar, should be offered to the spirits and other unearthly Beings. He who never takes any food without first serving therefrom the Brahmanas and deities and guests, becomes entitled to first portions of food. Such a man becomes endued with strength and energy. Hence, one should never take any food without first offering a portion thereof to the deities after worshipping them with reverence. One's house always blazes forth with beauty in consequence of the household deities that live in it. Hence, he that desires his own advancement and prosperity should worship the household deities by offering them the first portion of every food.'" Even thus did the learned Kavi of Bhrigu's race discourse to Vali, the chief of the Asuras. That discourse was next recited by Manu unto the Rishi Suvarna. Suvarna, in his turn, recited it to Narada. The celestial Rishi Narada recited unto me the merits that attach to the several acts mentioned. Informed of those merits, do thou, O son, perform the several acts mentioned!'"'"

---

[444] What is meant by the juice of deciduous herbs is oil of mustard seeds and castor seeds, etc.
[445] Well-fried paddy, reduced to powder, is sometimes used for giving a coating to dishes of meat.

SECTION XCIX.

"'Yudhishthira said, "I have, O chief of the Bharatas, heard what the merits are that are won by presenters of flowers and incense and lights. I have heard thee speak also of the merits that attach to a due observance of the ordinances in respect of the presentation of the Vali. It behoveth thee, O grandsire, to discourse unto me once more on this subject. Indeed, tell me, O sire, once more of the merits of presenting incense and lights. Why are Valis offered on the ground by persons leading the domestic mode of life?"

"'Bhishma said, "In this connection is recited the old narrative of the discourse between Nahusha and Agastya and Bhrigu. The royal sage Nahusha, O monarch, possessed of wealth of penances, acquired the sovereignty of Heaven by his own good deeds. With restrained senses, O king, he dwelt in Heaven, engaged in doing diverse acts of both human and celestial nature. From that high-souled monarch flowed diverse kinds of human acts and diverse kinds of celestial acts also, O chief of men. The diverse rites with respect to the sacrificial fire, the collection of sacred fuel and of Kusa grass, as also of flowers, and the presentation of Vali consisting of food adorned with fried paddy (reduced to powder), and the offer of incense and of light,—all these, O monarch, occurred daily in the abode of that high-souled king while he dwelt in heaven. Indeed, though dwelling in heaven, he performed the sacrifice of Japa (or silent recitation) and the sacrifice of meditation. And, O chastiser of foes, Nahusha, although he had become the chief of the deities, yet worshipped all the deities, as he used to do in days of yore, with due rites and ceremonies. Some time after, Nahusha realised his position as the chief of all the deities. This filled him with pride. From that time all his acts (of the kind spoken of) were suspended. Filled with arrogance in consequence of the boon he had received from all the deities, Nahusha caused the very Rishis to bear him on their shoulders. In consequence, however, of his abstention from all religious acts, his energy began to sustain a diminution. The time was very long for which Nahusha filled with pride, continued to employ the foremost of Rishis, possessed of wealth of penances, as the bearers of his vehicles. He caused the Rishis to discharge by turns his humiliating work. The day came when it was Agastya's turn to bear the vehicles, O Bharata. At that time, Bhrigu, that foremost of all persons conversant with Brahma, repaired to the presence of Agastya while the latter was seated in his asylum, and addressing him, said, 'O great ascetic, why should we patiently put up with such indignity inflicted on us by this wicked-souled Nahusha who has become the chief of the deities?'

""'Agastya said, 'How can I succeed in cursing Nahusha, O great Rishi? It is known to thee how the boon-giving (Brahman) himself has given Nahusha the best of boons! Coming to heaven, the boon that Nahusha solicited was that whoever would come within the range of his vision would, deprived of all energy, come within his sway. The self-born Brahman granted him even this boon, and it is for that reason that neither thyself nor I have been able to consume him. Without doubt, it is for this reason that none else amongst the foremost of Rishis has been able to consume or hurl him down from his high position. Formerly, O Lord, nectar was given by Brahman to Nahusha for quaffing. For that reason also we have become powerless against him. The supreme deity, it seems, gave that boon to Nahusha for plunging all creatures into grief. That wretch among men behaves most unrighteously towards the Brahmanas. O foremost of all speakers, do thou tell us what should be done in view of the situation. Without doubt, I shall do what thou wilt advise.'

""Bhrigu said, 'It is at the command of the Grandsire that I have come to thee with the view of counteracting the puissance of Nahusha who is possessed of great energy but who has been stupefied by fate. That exceedingly wicked-souled wight who has become the chief of the deities will today yoke thee to his car. With the aid of my energy I shall today hurl him down from his position as Indra in consequence of his having transcended all restraints! I shall today, in thy very sight, re-establish the true Indra in his position—him, viz., who has performed a hundred horse-sacrifices,—having hurled the wicked-souled and sinful Nahusha from that seat! That unrighteous chief of the deities will today insult thee by a kick, in consequence of his understanding being afflicted by fate and for bringing about his own downfall. Incensed at such an insult I shall today curse that sinful wretch, that enemy of the Brahmanas, that has transcended all restraints, saying, "Be thou transformed into a snake!" In thy very sight, O great ascetic, I shall today hurl down on the earth the wicked-souled Nahusha who shall be deprived of all energy in consequence of the cries of "Fie" that will be uttered from all sides.[446] Verily, I shall hurl down Nahusha today, that wight of unrighteous deeds, who has, besides, been stupefied by lordship and power. I shall do this, if it be acceptable to thee, O ascetic!' Thus addressed by Bhrigu, Mitravaruna's son Agastya of unfading puissance and glory, became highly gratified and freed from every anxiety.""""

SECTION C.

"'Yudhishthira said, "How was Nahusha plunged into distress? How was he hurled down on the earth? How, indeed, was he deprived of the sovereignty of the gods? It behoveth thee to recite everything to me."

"'Bhishma said, "Even thus did those two Rishis, viz., Bhrigu and Agastya, converse with each other. I have already told thee how Nahusha, when he first became the chief of the gods, acted in a becoming way. Verily, all acts of human and celestial nature flowed from that high souled royal sage! The offering of light, and all other rites of a similar kind, the due presentation of Valis, and all rites as are performed on especially sacred days,—all these were properly observed by the high-souled Nahusha who had become the sovereign of the deities.[447] Pious acts are always observed by those that are possessed of wisdom, in both the world of men and that of the deities. Verily, O foremost of kings, if such acts are observed, householders always succeed in acquiring prosperity and advancement. Even such is the effect of the gift of lamps and of incense, as also of bows and prostrations, to the deities. When food is cooked, the first portion thereof should be offered to a Brahmana. The particular offerings called Vali should also be presented to the household deities. The deities become gratified with such gifts.[448] It is also well-known that the measure of gratification which the deities derive from such offerings is a hundred times as great as that which the householder himself derives from making them. Persons endued with piety and wisdom make offerings of incense and lights, accompanying them with bows and prostrations. Such acts are always fraught with advancement and prosperity to those that do them. Those rites which the learned go

---

[446] It will be remembered that the only chastisement that was in vogue in the Krita age was the crying of 'Fie' on an offender.

[447] The Bombay text has vatsakah for utsavah. If the former reading be adopted, it would mean those rites that are performed for the prosperity and longevity of children. Of course, in such rites also the deities are worshipped and propitiated.

[448] For Dwijaya some text read Grahaya meaning guests.

through in course of their ablutions, and with the aid of waters, accompanied with bows unto the gods, always contribute to the gratification of the gods. When worshipped with proper rites, the highly blessed Pitris, Rishis possessed of wealth of asceticism, and the household deities, all become gratified. Filled with such ideas, Nahusha, that great king, when he obtained the sovereignty of the deities, observed all these rites and duties fraught with great glory. Some time after the good fortune of Nahusha waned, and as the consequence thereof, he disregarded all these observances and began to act in defiance of all restraints in the manner I have already adverted to. The chief of the deities, in consequence of his abstention from observing the ordinances about the offers of incense and light, began to decline in energy. His sacrificial rites and presents were obstructed by Rakshasas. It was at this time that Nahusha yoked that foremost of Rishis, viz., Agastya, to his car. Endued with great strength, Nahusha, smiling the while, set that great Rishi quickly to the task, commanding him to bear the vehicle from the banks of the Saraswati (to the place he would indicate). At this time, Bhrigu, endued with great energy, addressed the son of Mitravaruna, saying, 'Do thou close thy eyes till I enter into the matted locks on thy head.' Having said this, Bhrigu of unfading glory and mighty energy entered into the matted locks of Agastya who stood still like a wooden post for hurling king Nahusha from the throne of Heaven. Soon after Nahusha saw Agastya approach him for bearing his vehicle. Beholding the lord of the deities Agastya addressed him, saying, 'Do thou yoke me to thy vehicle without delay. To what region shall I bear thee? O lord of the deities, I shall bear thee to the spot which thou mayst be pleased to direct.' Thus addressed by him, Nahusha caused the ascetic to be yoked to his vehicle. Bhrigu, who was staying within the matted locks of Agastya, became highly pleased at this act of Nahusha. He took care not to cast his eyes upon Nahusha. Fully acquainted with the energy which the illustrious Nahusha had acquired in consequence of the boon which Brahman had granted him, Bhrigu conducted himself in this way. Agastya also, though treated by Nahusha in this way, did not give way to wrath. Then, O Bharata, king Nahusha urged Agastya on with his goad. The righteous-souled Rishi did not still give way to anger. The lord of the deities, himself giving way to anger, then struck Agastya on the head with his left foot. When the Rishi was thus struck on the head, Bhrigu, who was staying within Agastya's matted locks, became incensed and cursed Nahusha of sinful soul, saying, 'Since thou hast struck with thy foot on the head of this great Rishi, do thou, therefore, fall down on the earth, transformed into a snake, O wretch of wicked understanding!' Thus cursed by Bhrigu who had not been seen, Nahusha immediately became transformed into a snake and fell down on the earth, O chief of Bharata's race! If O monarch, Nahusha had seen Bhrigu, the latter would not then have succeeded, by his energy, in hurling the former down on the earth. In consequence of the various gifts that Nahusha had made, as also his penances and religious observances though hurled down on the earth, O king, he succeeded in retaining his memory. He then began to propitiate Bhrigu with a view to the working out of the curse. Agastya also, filled with compassion, joined Nahusha in pacifying Bhrigu for bringing about an end of the curse. At last Bhrigu felt compassion for Nahusha and provided for the working out of the curse.

""Bhrigu said, 'There will appear a king (on earth) of the name of Yudhishthira, the foremost of his race. He will rescue thee from this curse.' Having said this, the Rishi vanished in the very sight of Nahusha. Agastya also, of mighty energy, having thus accomplished the business of the true Indra, that performer of a hundred sacrifices, returned to his own asylum, worshipped by all members of the regenerate order. Thou hast, O king, rescued Nahusha from Bhrigu's curse. Verily, rescued by thee, he ascended to the region of Brahman in thy sight. As regards Bhrigu, having hurled Nahusha on the earth, he went to the region of Brahman and informed the Grandsire of it. The Grandsire, having called Indra back, addressed the deities, saying. 'Ye deities, through the boon I had granted him, Nahusha had obtained the sovereignty of heaven. Deprived, however, of that sovereignty by the enraged Agastya, he has been hurled on the earth. Ye deities, ye will not succeed in living without a chief. Do ye, therefore, once more install Indra in the sovereignty of Heaven.' Unto the Grandsire, O son of Pritha, who said so unto them, the deities filled with joy, replied, saying, 'So be it!' The divine Brahman then, O best of monarchs, installed Indra in the sovereignty of heaven. Made once more the chief of the deities, Vasava began to shine in beauty and resplendence. Even this is what occurred in days of yore through the transgression of Nahusha. In consequence, however, of the merits he had acquired through acts of the kind I have mentioned Nahusha succeeded in once more regaining his lost position. Hence, when evening comes, persons leading the domestic mode of life should give lights. The giver of lights is sure to acquire celestial sight after death. Verily, givers of light become as resplendent as the full moon. The giver of lights becomes endued with beauty of form and strength for as many years as correspond with the number of twinkles for which the lights given by him burn or blaze.""'[449]

SECTION CI.

"'Yudhishthira said, "Where do those foolish, wretched, and sinful men go, O chief of men, that steal or misappropriate such articles as belong to Brahmanas?"

"'Bhishma said, "I shall, in this connection, O Bharata, recite to thee the old narrative of a conversation between a Chandala and a low Kshatriya.[450]

"""The person of the royal order said, 'Thou seemest, O Chandala, to be old in years, but thy conduct seems to be like that of a boy! Thy body is besmeared with the dust raised by dogs and asses, but without minding that dust thou art anxious about the little drops of vine milk that have fallen upon thy body! It is plain that such acts as are censured by the pious are ordained for the Chandala. Why, indeed, dost thou seek to wash off the spots of milk from thy body?'[451]

"""The Chandala said, 'Formerly, O king, certain kine belonging to Brahmana were stolen. While they were being carried away, some milk from their udders fell upon a number of Soma plants that grew by the roadside. Those Brahmanas that drank the juice of the plants thus bedewed with milk, as also the king who performed the sacrifice in which that Soma was drunk, had to sink in hell. Indeed, for having thus appropriated some thing that had belonged to a Brahmana, the king with all the Brahmanas that had assisted him had to go to hell. All those men also, Brahmanas and Kshatriyas, that drank milk or ghee or curds, in the palace of the king who had stolen the Brahmana's kine, had to fall into hell. The stolen kine also, shaking their bodies, slew with their milk the sons and grandsons of those that had stolen them, as also the king and the queen although the latter treated the animals with great care and attention. As regards myself, O king, I used to live in the observance of the vow of Brahmacharya in that place where these kine were

---

[449] 'Jwalante' has 'dwipah' for its nominative understood. A twinkle occupies an instant of time. What is said here is that the giver of lights becomes endued with beauty and strength for as many years as the number of instants for which the lights given by him are seen to burn.

[450] 'Kshatrabandhu' implies a low or vile Kshatriya.

[451] Literally, 'Why dost thou dip such parts of thy body into a pond of water?'

placed after they had been stolen away. The food I had obtained by begging became sprinkled over with the milk of those kine. Having taken that food, O thou of the royal order, I have, in this life, become a Chandala. The king who had stolen the kine belonging to a Brahmana obtained an infamous end. Hence, one should never steal or appropriate anything that belongs to a Brahmana. Behold to what state I am reduced in consequence of my having eaten food that had been sprinkled over with milk belonging to a Brahmana! It is for this reason that Soma plants become unsaleable by a person possessed of wisdom. They who sell the Soma plant are censured by the wise. Indeed, O son, they who purchase Soma and they who sell it, both sink in the hell called Raurava when, departing from this world, they repair to the region of Yama. That man who, possessing a knowledge of the Vedas, duly sells Soma, becomes in his next life a usurer and quickly meets with destruction. For three hundred times he has to sink into hell and become transformed into an animal that subsists upon human ordure. Serving a person that is vile and low, pride, and rape upon a friend's wife, if weighed against one another in a balance, would show that pride, which transcends all restraints, is the heaviest. Behold this dog, so sinful and disagreeably pale and lean! (He was a human being in his former life). It is through pride that living creatures attain to such a miserable end. As regards myself, I was born in a large family, in a former birth of mine, O lord, and I was a thorough master of all branches of knowledge and all the sciences. I knew the gravity of all these faults, but influenced by pride, I became blinded and ate the meat attached to the vertebral columns of animals. In consequence of such conduct and such food, I have come to this state. Behold the reverses brought about by Time! Like a person whose cloth has taken fire at one end, or who is pursued by bees, behold, I am running, penetrated with fear, and smeared with dust! They that lead the domestic mode of life are rescued from all sins by a study of the Vedas, as also by gifts of other kinds, as declared by the wise.[452] O thou of the royal order, a Brahmana that is sinful in conduct, becomes rescued from all his sins by the study of the Vedas if he betakes himself to the forest mode of life and abstains from attachment of every kind. O chief of Kshatriyas, I am in this life, born in a sinful order! I fail to see clearly how I may succeed in cleansing myself from all sins. In consequence of some meritorious act of a former life, I have not lost the memory of my previous lives. O king, I throw myself on the mercy! I ask thee! Do thou resolve my doubt. By what auspicious course of conduct should I wish to achieve my emancipation? O foremost of men, by what means shall I succeed in getting rid of my status as a Chandala?'

""The person of the royal order said, 'Know, O Chandala, the means by which thou mayst be able to attain to emancipation. By casting off thy life-breaths for the sake of a Brahmana thou mayst attain a desirable end! By throwing thy body on the fire of battle as a libation to the beasts and birds of prey for the sake of a Brahmana, indeed, by casting off thy life-breaths thus, thou mayst achieve emancipation! By no other means wilt thou succeed in achieving it!'"

"Bhishma continued, "Thus addressed, that Chandala, O scorcher of foes, poured his life-breaths as a libation on the fire of battle for the sake of protecting a Brahmana's wealth and as the consequence of that act attained to a very desirable end. Hence, O son, thou shouldst always protect the property of the Brahmanas, if, O chief of Bharata's race, thou desirest, O thou of mighty arms, an end that is eternal felicity!"""

---

[452] The study of the Vedas is regarded as equivalent in merit of gifts. Hence actual gifts of articles are spoken of as 'gifts of other kinds.'

SECTION CII.

"'Yudhishthira said, "O grandsire, it has been said that all pious men attain to the same region after death. Is it true, O Bharata, that there is difference of position or status among them?"

"'Bhishma said, "By different deeds, O son of Pritha, men attain to different regions. They who are righteous in conduct attain to regions of felicity, while they who are sinful attain to regions that are fraught with misery. In this connection is cited the old narrative of the discourse, O son, between the ascetic Gautama and Vasava. A certain Brahmana of the name of Gautama, mild and self-restrained and with all his senses under complete control, beheld an infant elephant that had lost its mother and that was exceedingly cheerless on that account. Full of compassion and steady in the observance of his vows, the ascetic nursed that infant animal. After a long time the little beast grew up into a large and mighty elephant. One day, Indra, assuming the form of king Dhritarashtra, seized that mighty elephant which was as huge as a hill and from whose rent temples the juice was trickling down. Beholding the elephant dragged away, the great ascetic Gautama of rigid vows addressed king Dhritarashtra and said, 'O ungrateful Dhritarashtra, do not rob me of this elephant. It is looked upon by me as a son and I have reared it with much pain. It is said that between the righteous, friendship springs up if only they exchange seven words.[453] Thou shouldst see, O king, that the sin of injuring a friend does not touch thee! It behoveth thee not, O king, to take away by force this elephant that brings me my fuel and water, that protects my asylum when I am away, that is exceedingly docile and obedient to his instructor, that is mindful of doing all the offices that his preceptor commands, that is mild and well-broken, and that is grateful and very dear to me! Indeed, thou shouldst not bear it away, disregarding my protestations and cries!'

"''Dhritarashtra said, 'I shall give thee a thousand kine, a hundred maid-servants, and five hundred pieces of gold. I shall also, O great Rishi, give thee diverse other kinds of wealth. What use can Brahmanas have with elephants?'

"''Gautama said, 'Keep, O king, thy kine and maid-servants and coins of gold and various gems and diverse other kinds of wealth! What, O monarch, have Brahmanas to do with wealth?'

"''Dhritarashtra said, 'Brahmana, have no use for elephants. Verily, O learned Brahmana, elephants are meant for persons of the royal order. In taking away an animal, viz., this foremost of elephants, for my use as vehicle, I cannot be regarded as committing any sin. Do thou cease obstructing me in this way, O Gautama!'

"''Gautama said, 'O illustrious king, repairing even to that region of Yama where the righteous live in joy and the sinful in grief, I shall take from thee this my elephant!'

"''Dhritarashtra said, 'They that are destitute of (religious) acts, they that have no faith and are atheists, they that are of sinful souls and are always engaged in gratifying their senses, only they have to go to the region of Yama and endure the misery he inflicts. Dhritarashtra shall go to a higher region, and not thither!'

"''Gautama said, 'The region of Yama is such that men are there controlled. No untruth can be told there. Only truth prevails in that place. There the weak persecute the strong. Repairing thither I shall force thee to yield up this elephant to me!'

---

[453] Literally 'friendship is seven-word.' Sometimes the same expression is understood as meaning 'seven-paced.' The sense, of course, is that if the righteous meet and exchange seven words (or, walk with each other for only seven steps), they become friends.

""""Dhritarashtra said, 'Only those persons, that intoxicated with pride, conduct themselves towards their eldest sister and father and mother as towards foes, have to repair, O great ascetic, to such a region. I shall repair to a higher region. Indeed, Dhritarashtra shall not have to go thither!'

""""Gautama said, 'The region, called Mandakini, of king Vaisravana is attained by those highly blessed persons for whom are every joy and comfort. There Gandharvas and Yakshas and Apsaras live (gladdening all the denizens with enchanting dances and music). Repairing even thither, O king, I shall force thee to yield up this elephant to me!'

""""Dhritarashtra said, 'Those persons who regard hospitality to guests as a vow, who are observant of good vows (having other objects), who give shelter to Brahmanas, and who eat what remains after distribution among all those that are dependent upon them, adorn the region called Mandakini of Kuvera. (I shall not go thither, for a higher region is reserved for me)!'

""""Gautama said, 'If thou repairest to those delightful woods decked with flowers, that stand on the summit of Meru, that echo with melodious voice of Kinnaris, and that are graced with beautiful Jamvus of wide-spreading branches, I shall proceed even thither and force thee to yield up this elephant to me!'

""""Dhritarashtra said, 'Those Brahmanas that are endued with mild dispositions, that are devoted to truth, that are possessed of great learning in the scriptures, that are compassionate unto all creatures, that study the Puranas with all the histories, that pour libations on the sacred fire and make gifts of honey unto the Brahmanas, repair to such regions, O great Rishi! I shall repair to a region that is higher. Indeed Dhritarashtra shall not go thither. If thou art acquainted with any other well-known region of felicity, speak unto me, for I shall repair even thither!'

""""Gautama said, 'If thou proceedest to the woods owned by Narada and held dear by him, that are adorned with flowers and that echo with the melodious songs of the prince of Kinnaras, and that are the eternal abode of Gandharvas and Apsaras, I shall follow thee thither and force thee to yield up this elephant to me!'

""""Dhritarashtra said, 'They who never solicit alms, they who cultivate music and dancing, and always rove about in joy, proceed to such regions. O great Rishi, I shall repair to a region that is higher. Indeed, Dhritarashtra shall not have to go thither!'

""""Gautama said, 'If thou goest to that region where the Uttara-Kurus blaze in beauty and pass their days in gladness, O king, in the company of the very deities, where those beings that have their origin in fire, those that have their origin in water, and those having their origin in mountains, reside in happiness, and where Sakra raineth down the fruition of every wish, and where women live in perfect freedom, unrestrained by rules of any kind regulating their conduct or motions, and where there is no feeling of jealousy between the sexes,—if thou repairest thither, even thither shall I proceed and force thee to yield up this elephant to me!'

""""Dhritarashtra said, 'Those men that are freed from desire with respect to all articles of enjoyment, that abstain from meat, that never take up the rod of chastisement, and never inflict the least harm on mobile and immobile creatures, that have constituted themselves the soul of all creatures, that are entirely freed from the idea of meum, that have cast off attachments of every kind, that regard gain and loss as also praise and blame as equal,—only those men, O great Rishi, repair to such regions. I shall repair to a higher region. Verily, Dhritarashtra shall not go thither!'

""""Gautama said, 'Next to these blaze in beauty those eternal regions, redolent with excellent perfumes, that are free from passions of every kind and that are destitute of sorrow. These constitute the abode of the high-souled king Soma. If thou repairest thither, even thither shall I proceed and force thee to yield up this elephant to me!'

""Dhritarashtra said, 'Those men that always make gifts without receiving any gift, who never accept any service from others, who own nothing which they cannot give to a deserving person, who are hospitable to all creatures, who are inclined to show grace to every one, who are endued with forgiving dispositions, who never speak ill of others, who protect all creatures by throwing over them the shroud of compassion, and who are always righteous in their behaviour,—only those men, O great Rishi, proceed to such regions. I shall proceed to a higher region. Verily, Dhritarashtra shall not go there!'

""Gautama said, 'Next to these blaze in beauty other regions that are eternal, free from passion and darkness and sorrow, and that lie at the foot of the high-souled deity of the Sun. If thou repairest thither, even thither shall I go and force thee to yield up this elephant to me!'

""Dhritarashtra said, 'Those men that are attentive to the study of the Vedas, that are devoted to the service of their preceptors, that are observant of penances and excellent vows, that are firm in truth, that never utter anything that smacks of disobedience or enmity to their preceptors, that are always alert, and ever ready in service of seniors and preceptors,—they repair, O great Rishi, to such regions, they that are pure (of mind and body), that are endued with cleansed souls, that are of restrained speech, that are firm in truth, and that are well-versed in the Vedas. I shall proceed to a higher region! Verily, Dhritarashtra shall not go thither!'

""Gautama said, 'Next to those are the eternal regions that blaze in beauty, that are redolent with excellent perfumes, that are free from passion, and that are free from every sorrow. They constitute the abode of the high-souled king Varuna. If thou proceedest thither, even thither shall I go and force thee to yield up this elephant to me!'

""Dhritarashtra said, 'Those men who worship the deities by observing the vow called Chaturmasya, that perform a hundred and ten sacrifices, that pour libations every day on their sacred fire with devotion and faith for three years agreeably with the ordinances declared in the Vedas, that bear without flinching the burden of all duties, that walk steadily along the way trod by the righteous, that steadily sustain the course of conduct followed by the righteous-souled,—only they repair to such regions. I shall repair to a higher region. Verily, Dhritarashtra shall not go thither!'

""Gautama said, 'Above them are the regions of Indra, free from passion and sorrow, that are difficult of access and coveted by all men. Proceeding even to the abode of Indra himself of mighty energy, I shall, O king, force thee to yield up this elephant to me!'

""Dhritarashtra said, 'He who lives for a hundred years, who is endued with heroism, who studies the Vedas, and who performs sacrifices with devotion, verily, such men proceed to the region of Sakra. I shall repair to a higher region. Verily, Dhritarashtra shall not go there!'

""Gautama said, 'Above the Heavens are the regions of the Prajapatis of superior felicity abounding in every happiness, and divested of sorrow. Belonging to those puissant ones from whom the creation has sprung, they are coveted by all persons. If thou repairest thither, even thither shall I go and force thee to yield up this elephant to me!'

""Dhritarashtra said, 'Those kings that have bathed upon the completion of the Rajasuya sacrifice, that are endued with righteous souls, that have protected their subjects properly, and that have washed their limbs with sanctified water upon the completion of the horse-sacrifice, repair to such regions. Verily, Dhritarashtra shall not go there!'

""Gautama said, 'Next to those, blaze in beauty those eternal regions, redolent with delicious perfumes, free from passion, and transcending all sorrow. Those are the regions of kine difficult of attainment where oppression can never be. If thou repairest thither, I shall proceed even thither and force thee to yield up this elephant to me!'

"'Dhritarashtra said, 'He who, owning thousand kine, gives away a hundred kine every year, or owning a hundred kine gives away ten every year to the best of his might, or owning only ten or even five kine gives away therefrom one cow, and they who attain to a mature old age practising the vows of Brahmacharya all their days, who obey the declarations of the Vedas, and who, endued with energy of mind, betake themselves to pilgrimages to sacred waters and shrines, dwell in felicity in the region of kine. They who repair to Prabhasa and Manasa, the lakes of Pushkara, the large lake called Mahatsara, the sacred woods of Naimisha, Vahuda, Karatoya, Ganga, Gayasiras, Vipasa, Sthulavaluka, Krishna, the five rivers (of the Punjab), the extensive lake called Mahahrada, Gomati, Kausiki, Champa, Saraswati, Drisadwati, and Yamuna,—indeed, those illustrious Brahmanas, steady in the observance of vows, who go to these sacred waters,—repair to the regions of which thou speakest. Endued with celestial bodies and adorned with celestial garlands those blessed individuals, always emitting the most delightful perfumes, repair to those regions of joy and gladness. Verily, Dhritarashtra shall not go there!'

"'Gautama said, 'Next to these are regions where there is no fear of the least cold or heat, no hunger, no thirst, no pain, no sorrow, no joy, no one that is agreeable or disagreeable, no friend, and no enemy: where decrepitude and death are not, and where there is neither righteousness nor sin. Proceeding even to that region which is freed from passion, which abounds with equable happiness, and where there is wisdom and the attribute of Sattwa,—verily, proceeding to even that sacred abode of the self-born Brahman,—I shall force thee to yield up this elephant to me!'

"'Dhritarashtra said, 'They who are freed from all attachments, who are possessed of cleansed souls, who are steady in the observance of the foremost vows, who are devoted to the Yoga that depends on tranquillising the mind, and who have (in this life) attained to the happiness of heaven,—those persons wedded to the attribute of Sattwa—attain to the sacred region of Brahman. O great ascetic, thou shalt not be able to discover Dhritarashtra there!'

"'Gautama said, 'There where the foremost of Rathantaras is sung, where altars are strewn with the sacred Kusa blades, for the performance of Pundarika sacrifices, there where Soma-drinking Brahmanas go on vehicles drawn by excellent steeds,[454] proceeding even thither I shall force thee to yield up this elephant. I think, thou art the slayer of Vritra, viz., the deity that has performed a hundred sacrifices, engaged in roving through all the regions of the universe! I hope, I have not, through mental weakness (not recognising thee before) committed any fault by the words I have addressed thee!'

"'The deity of a hundred sacrifices said, 'Yes, I am Maghavat. I came to the world of human beings, for seizing this elephant. I bow to thee. Do thou command me! I shall readily accomplish all that thou mayst be pleased to say!'

"'Gautama said, 'Do thou give me, O chief of the deities, this elephant that is of white complexion and that is so young, for it is only ten years of age. I have brought it up as a child of my own. Dwelling in these woods, it has grown under my eye and has been to me a dear companion. Do thou set free this my child that thou hast seized and wishest

---

[454] The Bombay text has Somapithi and upavati instead of upayanti. The Bengal text reads Somavithi which seems to be inaccurate. The sense seems to be that of Somapithi or drinker of (sacrificial) soma.

to drag away!'

""The deity of a hundred sacrifices said, 'This elephant that has been a son to thee, O foremost of Brahmanas, cometh to thee looking wishfully at thee! Behold, it sniffs thy feet with its nostrils! My salutations to thee! Do thou pray for my welfare!'

""Gautama said, 'O chief of the deities, I do always think of thy good! I always offer thee worship! Do thou also, O Sakra, bestow thy blessings on me! Given by thee, I accept this elephant!'

""The deity of a hundred sacrifices said, 'Amongst all those high-souled and foremost of Rishis that firmly adhere to truth and that have the Vedas planted in their heart, thou alone hast been able to recognise me. For this reason I am exceedingly pleased with thee! Do thou, therefore, O Brahmana, come with me quickly, accompanied by this thy son! Thou deservest to attain to diverse regions of great felicity without the delay of even a single day!'"

"'Bhishma continued, "Having said these words, the wielder of the thunderbolt, taking Gautama with him and placing him before, along with his son, viz., that elephant, proceeded to heaven, that is difficult of attainment by even the righteous. He who would listen to this history every day or would recite it, restraining his senses the while, proceedeth (after death) to the region of Brahman even as Gautama himself."'"

SECTION CIII.

"'Yudhishthira said, "Thou hast discoursed to us on diverse kinds of gift, on tranquillity of soul, on Truth, on compassion, on contentment with one's wedded wife, and the merits of gift. It is known to thee, O grandsire, that there is nothing whose puissance is superior to that of penances. It behoveth thee to expound to us what constitutes the highest penances."

"'Bhishma said, "I tell thee, O Yudhishthira, that one attains to a region of felicity that corresponds with the kind of penances that one observes. This is what I hold, O son of Kunti, that there is no penance that is superior to abstention from food! In this connection is recited the ancient narrative of the discourse between Bhagiratha and the illustrious Brahman (the Grandsire of the Creation). It has been heard by us, O Bharata, that Bhagiratha attained to that region which transcends that of the deities, of kine, and of the Rishis. Beholding this, O monarch, the Grandsire Brahman, addressing Bhagiratha, said, 'How, O Bhagiratha, hast thou attained to this region that is so difficult of attainment? Neither the deities, nor Gandharvas, nor human beings, O Bhagiratha succeed in coming here without having practised the severest austerities. How, indeed, hast thou attained to this region?'

""Bhagiratha said, 'I used to make gifts of hundreds of thousands of gold coin unto the Brahmanas, observing the Brahmacharya vow all the while, it is not through the merit on those gifts, O learned one, that I have attained to this region. I performed the Ekaratra sacrifice for ten times, and the Pancharatra sacrifice for as many times. The Ekadasaratra sacrifice was performed by me eleven times. The great sacrifice of Jyotishtoma was performed by me a hundred times. It is not, however, through the merits of those sacrifices that I have attained to this region of felicity.[455] For a hundred years I lived continuously by the side of the holy Jahnavi, all the while practising the severest

---

[455] The Ekaratra, Pancharatra, and Ekadasaratra, sacrifices consist of fasts and gifts for the periods indicated by the names, viz., one night, five nights, and eleven nights.

austerities. There I made gifts unto the Brahmanas of thousands of male and female slaves. By the side of the Pushkara lakes I made gifts unto the Brahmanas, for a hundred thousand times, a hundred thousand steeds, and two hundred thousand kine. I also gave away a thousand damsels of great beauty, each adorned with golden moons, and sixty thousand more decked with ornaments of pure gold. It is not, however, through the merits of those acts that I have succeeded in attaining to these regions.[456] O lord of the universe, performing those sacrifices known by the name of Gosava, I gave away ten Arvudas of kine, presenting each Brahmana with ten kine, each of whom was accompanied with her calf, each of whom yielded milk at the time, and with each of whom were given a vessel of gold and one of white brass for milking her. Performing many Soma sacrifices, I gave away unto each Brahmana ten kine each of whom yielded milk, and each of whom had brought forth only her first calf, besides making presents unto them of hundreds of kine belonging to that species which is known by the name of Rohini. I also gave away unto the Brahmanas twice ten Prayutas of other kine, all yielding milk. It is not through the merit of those gifts, O Brahman, that I have succeeded in attaining to this region of felicity. I also gave away a hundred thousand horses of the Valhika breed, all white of complexion, and adorned with garlands of gold. It is not, however, through the merits of those acts that I have attained to this region. I gave away eight crores of golden coins unto the Brahmanas, O Brahman, and then another ten crores also, in each sacrifice that I performed. It is not, however, through the merits of those acts that I have attained to this region of felicity. I also gave away ten and then seven crores of steeds, O Grandsire, each of green complexion, each having ears that were dark, and each adorned with garlands of gold. I also gave away ten and seven thousand elephants of huge size, of teeth as large as plough-shares, each having those whorls on its body which are called Padmas, and each adorned with garlands of gold. I gave away ten thousand cars, O Grandsire, whose limbs were made of gold, and which were adorned with diverse ornaments of gold. I also gave away seven thousand other cars with steeds yoked unto each. All the steeds that were yoked unto them were adorned with ornaments of gold. Those cars represented the Dakshinas of a sacrifice and were of exactly that kind which is indicated in the Vedas. In the ten great Vajapeya sacrifices that I performed, I gave away a thousand horses each endued with the puissance of Indra himself, judged by their prowess and the sacrifices they had performed. Spending a vast sum of money, O Grandsire, and performing eight Rajasuya sacrifices, I gave away (unto the Brahmanas that officiated in them) a thousand kings whose necks were adorned with garlands of gold, after having vanquished them in battle. It is not, however, through the merits of those acts that I have attained to this region. In those sacrifices, O Lord of the universe, the presents that flowed from me were as copious as the stream of Ganga herself. Unto each Brahmana I gave two thousand elephants decked with gold, as many steeds adorned with golden ornaments, and a hundred villages of the best kind. Verily, I gave these unto each Brahmana for three times in succession. Observant of penances, subsisting on regulated diet, adopting tranquillity of soul, and restraining speech, I dwelt for a long time on the breast of Himavat by the side of that Ganga whose irresistible current (as it fell from heaven) was borne by

---

[456] 'Golden moons' imply those well-carved and beautifully fringed discs of gold that are worn by Hindu ladies on the forehead and that hang by thin chains of gold attached to the hair. In Bengal, ladies of respectable houses wear a kind of ornament called 'Chandrahara' or the moon-wreath. This ornament is worn round the waist, on the hip. Several chains of gold, from half a dozen to a dozen, having a large disc of well-carved gold to which they are attached, constitute this really very beautiful ornament. The disc is divided into two halves, attached to each other by hinges, so that in sitting down, the ornament produces no inconvenience.

Mahadeva on his head. It is not through the merit of these acts, O Grandsire, that I have attained to this region. Throwing the Sami, I adored the gods in myriads of such sacrifices as are completed in course of a single day, and such others as take twelve days for completing, and others still as can be completed in three and ten days, besides many Pundarikas. I have not attained to this region through the merits of any of those sacrifices.[457] I gave unto the Brahmanas eight thousand white-complexioned bulls, each graced with a beautiful hump, and each having one of its horns covered with gold. Unto them I also gave beautiful wives whose necks were adorned with chains of gold. I also gave away large heaps of gold and wealth of other kinds. Verily, I gave away hills of gems and precious stones. Villages, numbering by thousands and teeming with wealth and corn, were also given away by me. With all my senses about me, I gave away unto the Brahmanas a hundred thousand kine each of whom had brought forth only her first calf, at many great sacrifices which I performed. It is not, however, through the merits of those acts that I have attained to this region. I adored the deities in a sacrifice that is completed in eleven days. Twice I adored them in sacrifices that are completed in twelve days. I adored them also many a time in the horse-sacrifices. Six and ten times I performed the Arkayana sacrifice. It is not through the merits of those acts that I have attained to this region. I also gave unto each Brahmana a forest of Kanchana trees extending for a Yojana on every side, and with each tree adorned with jewels and gems. It is not through the merits of that act that I have attained to this region. For thirty years, with heart perfectly freed from wrath, I observed the Turayana vow that is possessed of very superior merit, and gave away unto the Brahmanas every day nine hundred kine. Indeed, O Lord of the universe, every one of those kine belonged to the Rohini species, and yielded milk at the time I gave them away. It is not through the merits of those acts, O chief of the deities, that I have attained to this region. I worshipped thirty fires, O Brahmana, every day. I adored the deities in eight sacrifices in which the fat of all animals was poured on the fire. I adored them in seven sacrifices in which the fat of human beings was poured on the fire. I adored them in a thousand and twenty-eight Viswajit sacrifices. It is not through the merits of those sacrifices O Lord of all the deities, that I have attained to this region. On the banks of Sarayu and Vahuda and Ganga as also in the woods of Naimisha, I gave away millions of kine unto the Brahmanas. It is not through the merits of those acts that I have attained to this region. The vow of fast had been known to Indra. He had, however, kept it a secret. Sukra, the descendant of Bhrigu, obtained a knowledge of it by means of spiritual sight acquired through penances. Blazing with energy as he does, it is Usanas who first made it known to the universe. I observed that vow, O boon giving Deity! When I accomplished that very superior vow, the Brahmanas became all gratified with me. A thousand Rishis came thither. All those Brahmanas and Rishis, O puissant lord, gratified with me, said, "Do thou repair to the region of Brahman!" It is in consequence of the merits of that vow that I have succeeded in attaining to this region of very superior felicity. There is no doubt in this. Asked by the Supreme Ordainer of all things, I have duly expounded the merits of the vow of fast. In my opinion, there is no penance higher than fast. I vow to thee, O foremost of all the deities! Be thou propitious unto me!'"

"Bhishma continued, "King Bhagiratha, who had said so and who deserved every

---

[457] In the Santi Parva it has been explained that in ancient times kings sometimes performed sacrifices causing altars to be raised at small distances from one another. These distances were measured by hurling a heavy piece of wood called Sami, so that throwing the Sami from one altar, the next altar would be created upon the spot where it fell.

honour was on the conclusion of his speech, honoured by Brahman according to the rites ordained for that purpose. Do thou, therefore, O Yudhishthira, observe the vow of fast and worship the Brahmanas every day. The words uttered by Brahmanas can accomplish everything both here and hereafter. Indeed, the Brahmanas should ever be gratified with gifts of robes, food and white complexioned kine and good dwelling houses and mansions. The very deities should gratify the Brahmanas. Freeing thyself from cupidity, do thou practise this vow of very superior merit that is not known to all!"'"

SECTION CIV.

"'Yudhishthira said, "Man, it is said, is endued with a period of life extending for a hundred years, and with energy and might that are considerable. Why then, O grandsire, do human beings die even when they are very young? By what does a man become endued with longevity, and by what is his life shortened? Through what does a man acquire the fame that rests upon great achievements? Through what does one attain to wealth and prosperity? Is it by penances, or Brahmacharya, or silent recitation of sacred Mantras, or drugs? Is it by his acts, or speech? Do thou explain to me this, O grandsire!"

"'Bhishma said, "I shall tell thee what thou askest me. In fact, I shall tell thee what the reason is for which one becomes shortlived, and what the reason is for which one becomes endued with longevity. I shall also explain to thee the reason for which one succeeds in acquiring the fame that rests on great achievements, and the reason for which one succeeds in acquiring wealth and prosperity. Indeed, I shall enlighten thee as to the manner in which one must live in order to be endued with all that is beneficial for him. It is by conduct that one acquires longevity, and it is by conduct that one acquires wealth and prosperity. Indeed, it is by conduct that one acquires the fame that rests upon great achievements both here and hereafter. The man whose conduct is improper or wicked never acquires a long life. All creatures become afraid of such a man and are oppressed by him. If, therefore, one wishes one's own advancement and prosperity, one should, in this world, betake to conduct that is proper and good. Good conduct succeeds in dispelling the inauspiciousness and misery of even one that is sinful.[458] Righteousness has conduct for its indication. They that are good and righteous are so in consequence of the conduct they follow. The indications, again, of good conduct are afforded by the acts of those that are good or righteous. People esteem that man who acts righteously and who does good acts even if they only hear of him without actually seeing him. They that are atheists, they that are destitute of all acts, they that are disobedient to preceptors and transgress the injunctions of the scriptures, they that are unacquainted with and, therefore, unobservant of duties, and they that are wicked of conduct, become shortlived. They that are of improper behaviour, they that transgress all restraints, they that are unscrupulous in respect of sexual congress, become shortlived here and have to go to Hell hereafter. Even those men live for a hundred years who, though destitute of all accomplishments, betake themselves to propriety and righteousness of conduct and become endued with faith and freed from malice. He that is free from wrath, that is truthful in speech, that never does any injury to any creature in the universe, that is divested of malice and crookedness and insincerity, succeeds in living for a hundred years. He who always breaks little clods of earth, or tears up the grass that grows under his feet, or cuts off his nails with his teeth, or

---

[458] i.e. if a sinful man mends his conduct, he succeeds in warding off the misery and evils to which he would otherwise be subject in consequence of his sins.

288

is always impure, or very restless, never succeeds in acquiring a long life.[459] One should wake up from sleep at the hour known as the Brahma Muhurta and then think of both religion and profit. Getting up from bed, one should then wash one's face and mouth, and joining one's hands in an attitude of reverence, say the morning prayers.[460] In this way, one should when evening comes, say one's evening prayers also, restraining speech (with other people) the while. One should never look at the rising sun, nor at the setting sun.[461] Nor should one look at the sun when he is in eclipse; nor at his image in the water; nor at midday when he is at the meridian. The Rishis, in consequence of their adoring the two twilights with great regularity succeeded in attaining to longevity. Hence, one should, restraining speech, say one's prayers regularly at the two twilights. As regards those Brahmanas that do not say their prayers at the two twilights, a righteous king should set them to accomplish such acts as are ordained for the Sudras. Persons of every order should never have sexual congress with other people's wives. There is nothing that shortens life so effectually as sexual congress with other people's wives. For as many thousand years shall the adulterer have to live in Hell as the number of pores on the bodies of the women with whom he may commit the offence. One should dress one's hair, apply collyrium to one's eyes, and wash one's teeth, as also worship the deities, in the forenoon. One should not gaze at urine or faeces, or tread on it or touch it with one's feet. One should not set out on a journey at early dawn, or at midday, or in the evening twilight, or with a companion that is unknown, or with a Sudra, or alone. While going along a road, one should, standing aside, always make way to a Brahmana, to kine, to kings, to an old man, to one that is weighted with a burden, to a woman quick with child, or to one that is weak. When one meets a large tree that is known, one should walk round it. One should also, when coming upon a spot where four roads meet, walk round it before pursuing one's journey. At midday, or at midnight, or at night in general, or at the two twilights, one should not proceed to spots where four roads meet. One should never wear sandals or clothes that have been worn by another. One should always observe the vow of Brahmacharya, and should never cross one's legs. One should observe the vow of Brahmacharya on the day of the new moon, as also on that of the full moon, as also on the eighth lunar day of both fortnights. One should never eat the flesh of animals not slain in sacrifice. One should never eat the flesh of the back of an animal. One should avoid censuring and calumniating others, as also all kinds of deceitful behaviour.[462] One should never pierce others with wordy shafts. Indeed, one should never utter any cruel speech. One should never accept a gift from a person that is low and vulgar. One should never utter such words as trouble other people or as are inauspicious or are as sinful. Wordy shafts fall from the mouth. Pierced therewith, the victim grieves day and night. The man of wisdom should never shoot them for piercing the vitals of other people. A forest, pierced with shafts or cut down with the axe, grows again. The man, however, that is pierced with words unwisely spoken, becomes the victim of wounds that fester and lead

[459] What is said here is this: certain persons have the ugly habit of picking up little clods of earth and pound them into dust, while sitting on the ground and engaged in talking. The habit also of tearing the grass while sitting on the ground may be marked. It should be remembered that the people of India in ancient times used often to sit on the bare ground. As to cutting off the nails with the teeth, it is an ugly habit with many young men.

[460] The Brahma Muhurta is that when the sun is just below the horizon.

[461] The prayers said in the morning and the evening are also spoken of as adoring the two twilights.

[462] 'One should always observe the vow of Brahmacharya' means that one should abstain from sexual congress except with one's wedded wives and in the proper season.

to death.[463] Barbed arrows and Nalikas and broadheaded shafts are capable of being extracted from the body. Wordy shafts, however, are incapable of being extracted, for they lie embedded in the very heart. One should not taunt a person that is defective of a limb or that has a limb in excess, or one that is destitute of learning, or one that is miserable, or one that is ugly or poor, or one that is destitute of strength. One should avoid atheism, calumniating the Vedas, censuring the deities, malice, pride, arrogance, and harshness. One should not, in wrath, take up the rod of chastisement for laying it upon another. Only the son or the pupil, it has been said, can be mildly chastised for purposes of instruction. One should not speak ill of Brahmanas; nor should he point at the stars with one's fingers. If asked, one should not say what the lunation is on a particular day. By telling it, one's life becomes shortened. Having answered calls of nature or having walked over a road, one should wash one's feet. One should also wash one's feet before sitting to recite the Vedas or to eat any food. These are the three things which are regarded as pure and sacred by the deities and as such fit for the Brahmana's use, viz., that whose impurity is unknown, that which has been washed in water, and that which has been well-spoken of. Samyava, Krisara, meat, Sashakuli and Payasa should never be cooked for one's own self. Whenever cooked, these should be offered to the deities.[464] One should attend every day to one's fire. One should every day give alms. One should, restraining speech the while, clean one's teeth with the tooth-stick. One should never be in bed when the sun is up. If one fails any day to be up with the sun, one should then perform an expiation. Rising from bed, one should first salute one's parents, and preceptors, or other seniors deserving of respect. By so doing one attains to long life. The tooth-stick should be cast off when done with, and a new one should be used every day. One should eat only such food as is not forbidden in the scriptures, abstaining from food of every kind on days of the new moon and the full moon. One should, with senses restrained, answer calls of nature, facing the north. One should not worship the deities without having first washed one's teeth. Without also worshipping the deities first, one should never repair to any person save one's preceptor or one that is old in years or one that is righteous or one that is possessed of wisdom. They that are wise should never see themselves in an unpolished or dirty mirror. One should never have sexual congress with a woman that is unknown or with one that is quick with child. One should never sleep with head turned towards the north or the west. One should not lie down upon a bed-stead that is broken or rickety. One should not sleep on a bed without having examined it first with the aid of a light. Nor should one sleep on a bed with another (such as wife) by one's side. One should never sleep in a transverse direction. One should never make a compact with atheists or do anything in conjunction with them.[465] One should never drag a seat with the foot and sit on it. One should never bathe in a state of nudity, nor at night. One possessed of intelligence should never suffer one's limbs to be rubbed or pressed after bathing. One should never smear unguents upon one's body without having first taken bath. Having bathed, one should never wave one's cloth in the air (for drying it). One should not always wear wet clothes. One should never take off one's body the garlands of

---

[463] The Bombay text reads the second line differently. What is meant, is that the wounds inflicted by wordy shafts rankle and fester and lead to death.

[464] Samyava is a thin cake of unleavened bread, fried with ghee, pounded and again made up into an oblong form with fresh bread, sugar and spices, and again fried with ghee. Krisara is a kind of liquid food made of milk, sesame, rice, sugar, and spices. Sashkuli is a kind of pie. Payasa is rice boiled in sugar and milk.

[465] Antarddhane implies 'in darkness'; hence one should always examine the bed with a light before one lies down on it.

flowers one may wear. Nor should one wear such garlands over one's outer garments. One should never even talk with a woman during the period of her functional change. One should not answer a call of nature on a field (where crops are grown) or at a place too near an inhabited village. One should never answer a call of nature on a water. One should first wash one's mouth thrice with water before eating any food. Having finished one's meals, one should wash one's mouth thrice with water and twice again. One should eat, with face turned eastwards, one's food, restraining speech the while and without censuring the food that is eaten. One should always leave a remnant of the food that is placed before one for eating. Having finished one's meals, one should mentally touch fire. If one eats with face turned eastwards, one becomes endued with longevity. By eating with face turned southwards, one acquires great fame. By eating with face turned westwards, one acquires great wealth. By eating with face turned northwards, one becomes truthful in speech. Having finished one's meals one should wash all the upper holes of one's body with water.[466] Similarly, all the limbs, the navel, and the palms of the hands should be washed with water. One should never seat oneself upon husk of corn, or upon hair, or upon ashes, or upon bones. One should, on no account, use the water that has been used by another for bathing. One should always perform the Homa for propitiating the deities, and recite the Savitri Mantra. One should always eat in a seated posture. One should never eat while walking. One should never answer a call of nature in a standing posture. One should never answer a call of nature on ashes or in a cow-pen. One should wash one's feet before sitting to one's meals. One should never sit or lie down for sleep with wet feet. One who sits to one's meals after having washed one's feet, lives for a hundred years. One should never touch these three things of great energy, while one is in an impure state, viz., fire, a cow, and a Brahmana. By observing this rule, one acquires longevity. One should not, while one is in an impure state, cast one's eyes on these three things of great energy, viz., the sun, the moon, and the stars. The life-breaths of a young man go upwards when an old and venerable person comes to his abode. He gets them back by standing up and properly saluting the guest. Old men should always be saluted. One should, upon seeing them, offer seats with one's own hand. After the old man has taken his seat, one should seat oneself and remain with hands joined in reverence. When an old man goes along the road, one should always follow him instead of walking ahead. One should never sit on a torn or broken seat. One should, without using it any longer, cast away a broken vessel of white brass. One should never eat without a piece of upper garment wrapping one's body. One should never bathe in a state of nudity. One should never sleep in a state of nudity. One should never even touch the remnants of other people's dishes and plates. One should never, while one is in an impure state, touch another's head, for it is said in the scriptures that the life-breaths are all concentrated in the head. One should never strike another on the head or seize another by the hair. One should not join one's hands together for scratching one's head. One should not, while bathing, repeatedly dip one's head in water. By so doing one shortens one's life. One who has bathed by dipping the head in water should not, afterwards, apply oil to any part of one's body. One should never take a meal without eating some sesame. One should never teach (the Vedas or any scriptures) at a time when one is impure. Nor should one study while one is impure. When a storm rises or a bad odour permeates in the atmosphere, one should never think of the Vedas. Persons conversant with ancient history

---

[466] Pranan, the commentator explains, implies the upper holes of the body, such as the nostrils, the ear-holes and the eyes.

recite a Gatha sung by Yama in days of old. He that runs while impure or studies the Vedas under similar circumstances, indeed, that regenerate Brahman who studies the Vedas at forbidden times, loses his Vedas and shortens his life. Hence, one should never study the Vedas with concentrated attention at forbidden times. They who answer a call of nature, with face towards the sun, or towards a blazing fire, or towards a cow, or towards a regenerate person, or on the road, become shortlived. At daytime both calls of nature should be answered with face turned towards the north. At night, those calls should be answered facing the south. By so doing one does not shorten one's life. One that wishes to live long should never disregard or insult any of these three, however weak or emaciated they may appear to be, viz., the Brahmana, the Kshatriya, and the snake. All three are endued with virulent poison. The snake, if angry, burns the victim with only a glance of its eyes. The Kshatriya also, if angry, burns the objects of his wrath, as soon as he sees him, with his energy. The Brahmana, stronger than any of these two, destroys not only the objects of his wrath but his whole race as well, not by vision alone but by thought also.[467] The man of wisdom should, therefore, tend these three with care. One should never engage in any disputation with one's preceptor. O Yudhishthira, if the preceptor becomes angry, he should always be pacified by due honours being paid to him. Even if the preceptor happens to be entirely wrong, one should still follow and honour him. Without doubt, calumnious sayings against the preceptor always consume the lives of those that utter them. One should always answer a call of nature at a spot far removed from one's habitation. One should wash one's feet at a distance from one's habitation. One should always throw the remnants of one's dishes and plates at a spot far removed from one's habitation. Verily, he who desires his own good should do all these. One should not wear garlands of red flowers. Indeed, they who are possessed of wisdom should wear garlands of flowers that are white in hue. Rejecting the lotus and the lily, O thou of great might, one may bear on one's head, however, a flower that is red, even if it be an aquatic one.[468] A garland of gold can under no circumstances become impure. After one has bathed, O king, one should use perfumes mixed with water.[469] One should never wear one's upper garment for covering the lower limbs or the lower garments for covering the upper ones. Nor should one wear clothes worn by another. One should not, again, wear a piece of cloth that has not its lateral fringes.[470] When one goes to bed, O king, one should wear a different piece of cloth. When making a journey also on a road, one should wear a different piece of cloth. So also, when worshipping the deities, one should wear a different piece of cloth.[471] The man of intelligence should smear his limbs with unguents made of Priyangu, sandalwood, Vilwa, Tagara, and Kesara.[472] In observing a fast, one should purify oneself by a bath, and adorn one's person with ornaments and

---

[467] The Brahmana is more powerful than the other two, for while the other two cannot injure except when they have their foe within sight, the Brahmana can do so even by not seeing his enemy.

[468] The custom in India, with especially all orthodox Brahmanas, is to wear a single flower on the head, inserted into the coronal lock. This flower may be a red one, it is said, after the prohibition in the previous verse about the wearing of garlands made of red flowers.

[469] What is stated here is that dry perfumes should not be used, but those which are pounded with water and made into a paste.

[470] The cloth worn by a Hindu has two lateral fringes which contain a lesser number of threads than the body of the cloth.

[471] It has been said that Hinduism is a vast system of personal hygiene. These directions about change of attire are scrupulously observed by every rigid Hindu to this day. No change seems to have taken place in the daily habits of the people.

[472] Priyangu is the Aglaia Roxburghiana. Vilwa is the Egle marmelos. Tagara is the Taberuaemontana coronaria, Linn. Kesara is probably the Eclipta alba, Hassk.

unguents. One should always abstain from sexual congress on days of the full moon and the new moon. One should never, O monarch, eat off the same plate with another even if that other happens to be of one's own or equal rank. Nor should one ever eat any food that has been prepared by a woman in her functional period. One should never eat any food or drink, any liquid whose essence has been taken off. Nor should one eat anything without giving a portion thereof to persons that wishfully gaze at the food that one happens to take. The man of intelligence should never sit close to one that is impure. Nor should one sit close to persons that are foremost in piety.[473] All food that is forbidden in ritual acts should never be taken even on other occasions. The fruits of the Ficus religiosa and the Ficus Bengalensis as also the leaves of the Crotolaria Juncea, and the fruits of the Ficus glomerata, should never be eaten by one who is desirous of his own good. The flesh of goats, of kine, and the peacock, should never be eaten. One should also abstain from dried flesh and all flesh that is stale. The man of intelligence should never eat any salt, taking it up with his hand. Nor should he eat curds and flour of fried barley at night. One should abstain also from flesh of animals not slain in sacrifices. One should, with concentrated attention, eat once in the morning and once in the evening, abstaining entirely from all food, during the interval. One should never eat any food in which one may detect a hair. Nor should one eat at the Sraddha of an enemy. One should eat silently; one should never eat without covering one's person with an upper garment, and without sitting down.[474] One should never eat any food placing it on the bare ground. One should never eat except in a sitting posture. One should never make any noise while eating.[475] The man of intelligence should first offer water and then food to one that has become his guest, and after having served the guest thus, should then sit to his meals himself. He who sits down to dinner in a line with friends and himself eats any food without giving thereof to his friends, is said to eat virulent poison. As regards water and Payasa and flour of fried barley and curds and ghee and honey, one should never, after drinking or eating these, offer the remnants thereof to others. One should never, O chief of men, eat any food doubtingly.[476] One desirous of food should never drink curds at the conclusion of a meal. After the meal is finished, one should wash one's mouth and face with the (right) hand only, and taking a little water should then dip the toe of the right foot in it. After washing, one should touch the crown of one's head with the (right) hand. With concentrated attention, one should next touch fire. The man who knows how to observe all these ordinances with care, succeeds in attaining to the foremost place among his kinsmen. One should, after finishing one's meals, with one's nose and eyes and ears and navel and both hands wash with water. One should not, however, keep one's hands wet. Between the tip and the root of the thumb is situate the sacred Tirtha known by the name of Brahma. On the back of the little finger, it is said, is situate the Deva-tirtha. The intervening space between the thumb and the forefinger, O Bharata, should be used for discharging the Pitri rites, after touching water according to the ordinance.[477] One should never indulge in other people's calumny. Nor should one ever utter anything that is disagreeable. The man that desires his own good should never seek to provoke against

---

[473] Na is the nom. sing. of Nri, implying man.

[474] One of the Vernacular translations takes valena as signifying child and para-sraddha as meaning the first or adya sraddha.

[475] This noise refers to that of chewing or sucking or licking, etc. It is an ugly habit with some people.

[476] Doubting, for example, as to whether he would be able to digest it or not, or whether what he is taking is clean or not, or whether it would be too much for him.

[477] In offering certain articles at the Sraddha, the articles are first placed on this part of the right hand and then offered with due Mantras to the Pitris.

himself the wrath of others. One should never seek to converse with a person that has fallen away from his order. The very sight of such a person should be avoided. One should never come in contact with a fallen person. By avoiding such contact one succeeds in attaining to a long life. One should never indulge in sexual congress at day-time. Nor should one have congress with a maiden, nor with a harlot nor with a barren woman. One should never have congress with a woman that has not bathed after the expiry of her functional period. By avoiding such acts one succeeds in attaining to a long life. After washing the several limbs directed, in view of religious acts, one should wash one's lips thrice, and once more twice. By doing this, one becomes purified and fit for religious acts. The several organs of sense should each be washed once, and water should also be sprinkled over the whole body. Having done this, one should go through the worship of the Pitris and the deities, agreeably with the ordinances of the Vedas. Listen to me, O thou of Kuru's race, as I tell thee what purification is cleansing and beneficial for a Brahmana. Before beginning to eat and after finishing the meal, and in all acts requiring purification, the Brahmana should perform the achamana with water placed on the limb called the Brahmatirtha.[478] After ejecting any matter from the throat or spitting, one should wash one's mouth before one can become pure. A kinsman who happens to be old, or a friend who happens to be poor, should be established in one's house and his comforts looked after as if he were a member of the family. By doing this, one succeeds in acquiring both fame and long life. The establishment of pigeons in one's house is fraught with blessedness, as also of parrots both male and female. If female these taken to one's abode, they succeed in dispelling calamity. The same is the case with cockroaches, If fireflies and vultures and wood-pigeons and bees enter a house or seek residence in it, acts of propitiating the deities should be performed. These are creatures of evil omen, as also ospreys. One should never divulge the secrets of high-souled men; one should never have sexual congress with a forbidden woman. Nor should one ever have such congress with the spouse of a king or with women that are the friends of queens. One should never cultivate intimacy with physicians, or with children, or with persons that are old, or with one's servants, O Yudhishthira. One should always provide for friends, for Brahmanas, and for such as seek one's protection. By doing this, O king, one acquires a long life. The man of wisdom should reside in such a house as has been constructed with the aid of a Brahmana and an engineer skilled in his profession, if indeed, O king, he desires his own good.[479] One should not, O king, sleep at the evening twilight. Nor should one study at such an hour for acquiring any branch of knowledge. The man of intelligence should never eat also at such an hour. By acting in this way one acquires a long life. One should never perform any act in honour of the Pitris at night time. One should not deck one's person after finishing one's meals. One should bathe at night, if one desires one's own advancement. One should also, O Bharata, always abstain from the flour of fried barley at night. The remnants of food and drink, as also the flowers with which one has worshipped the deities, should never be used. Inviting a guest at night, one should never, with excessive courtesy, force him to eat to the point of gratification. Nor should one eat oneself to the point of gratification, at night. One should not slay a bird (for eating it),

---

[478] The achamana is not exactly washing, when one is directed to perform the achamana after having eaten, there it, of course, implies an act of washing. At the commencement, however, of religious acts, the rite of achamana consists in merely touching the lips and some other parts with water.

[479] The Brahmana's aid is necessary in selecting the ground, and settling the longitudinal and other directions of the house, as also in fixing the day of commencing the work of building.

especially after having fed it.[480] One possessed of wisdom should wed a maiden born in a high family, endued with auspicious indications, and of full age. Begetting children upon her and thus perpetuating one's race by that means, one should make over one's sons to a good preceptor for acquiring general knowledge, O Bharata, as also a knowledge of the especial customs of the family, O monarch. The daughters that one may beget should be bestowed upon youths of respectable families, that are again possessed of intelligence. Sons should also be established and a portion of the family inheritance, given to them, O Bharata, as their provision. One should bathe by dipping one's head in water before one sits down to perform any act in honour of the Pitris of the deities. One should never perform a Sraddha under the constellation of one's nativity. No Sraddha should be performed under any of the Bhadrapadas (prior or later), nor under the constellation Krittika, O Bharata. The Sraddha should never be performed under any of those constellations that are regarded as fierce (such as Aslesha, etc.) and any of those that, upon calculation, seem to be hostile. Indeed, in this respect, all these constellations should be avoided which are forbidden in treatises on astrology. One should sit facing either the east or the north while undergoing a shave at the hands of the barber. By so doing, O great king, one succeeds in acquiring a long life. One should never indulge in other people's calumny or self-reproach, for, O chief of the Bharatas, it is said that calumny is sinful, whether of others or of oneself. In wedding, one should avoid a woman that is deficient of any limb. A maiden too, if such, should also be avoided. A woman of the same Pravaras should also be avoided; as also one that has any malformation; as also one that has been born in the race to which one's mother belongs.[481] One possessed of wisdom should never have sexual congress with a woman that is old, or one that has abandoned the domestic mode of life for entering the forest mode, or one that is true to her lord, or one whose organs of generation are not healthy or well-formed.[482] It behoveth thee not to wed a woman that is of a yellow complexion, or one that is afflicted with leprosy, or one born in a family in which there has been epilepsy, or one that is low in birth and habits, or one that is born in a family in which the disease called Switra (leprosy) has appeared, or one belonging by birth to a race in which there are early deaths. Only that maiden who is endued with auspicious indications, and who is accomplished for qualifications of diverse kinds, who is agreeable and handsome, should be wedded. One should wed, O Yudhishthira, in a family that is higher or at least equal to one's own. One who is desirous of one's own prosperity, should never wed a woman that is of an inferior order or that has fallen away from the order of her birth. Carefully igniting the fire, one should accomplish all those acts which have been ordained and declared in the Vedas or by the Brahmanas.[483] One should never seek to injure women. Spouses should always be protected. Malice always shortens life. Hence, one should always abstain from cherishing malice. Sleep at day-time shortens life. To sleep after the sun has risen shortens life. They who sleep at any of the twilights, or at nightfall or who go to sleep in a state of impurity, have their lives shortened. Adultery always shortens

---

[480] I adopt the meaning which Nilakantha points out. According to him, this verse forbids the killing of birds at night time and their killing after having fed and adopted them. Indeed, one may buy such birds killed by others for food. The word Dwija, however, may mean both hair and nails. The first part of the line, therefore, may be taken as a prohibition against the cutting of hair and nails after eating. The words na samarcha reta, in that case, would be difficult to interpret. Probably, it is this that has led the commentator to take Dwija here for a bird. Some texts read panam for na cha.

[481] Pravaras indicate the race in which one is born. They are named from the names of the Vedic Rishis.

[482] The commentator explains that ayonim implies of unknown birth and viyonim of mean birth.

[483] Brahmanih here refers to the rituals in the Vedas and not persons of the first order.

life. One should not remain in a state of impurity after shaving.[484] One should, O Bharata, carefully abstain from studying or reciting the Vedas, and eating, and bathing, at eventide. When the evening twilight comes, one should collect one's senses for meditation, without doing any act. One should, O king, bathe and then worship the Brahmanas. Indeed, one should bathe before worshipping the deities and reverentially saluting the preceptor. One should never go to a sacrifice unless invited. Indeed, one may go there without an invitation if one wishes only to see how the sacrifice is conducted. If one goes to a sacrifice (for any other purpose) without an invitation and if one does not, on that account, receive proper worship from the sacrificer, one's life becomes shortened. One should never go alone on a journey to foreign parts. Nor should one ever proceed alone to any place at night. Before evening comes, one should come back to one's house and remain within it. One should always obey the commands of one's mother and father and preceptor, without at all judging whether those commands are beneficial or otherwise. One should, O king, attend with great care to the Vedas and the science of arms. Do then, O king, carefully attend to the practice of riding an elephant, a steed, and a war-chariot. The man who attends to these with care succeeds in attaining to happiness. Such a king succeeds in becoming unconquerable by foes, and sway his servants and kinsmen without any of them being able to get the better of him. The king that attains to such a position and that carefully attends to the duty of protecting his subjects, has never to incur any loss. Thou shouldst acquire, O king, the science of reasoning, as also the science of words, the science of the Gandharvas, and the four and sixty branches of knowledge known by the name of Kala. One should every day hear the Puranas and the Itihasas and all the other narratives that exist, as also the life-stories of all high-souled personages. When one's spouse passes through functional period, one should never have congress with her, nor even summon her for conversation. The man endued with wisdom may accept her companionship on the fourth day after the bath of purification. If one indulges in congress on the fifth day from the first appearance of the functional operation, one gets a daughter. By indulging in congress on the sixth day, one happens to have a son. The man of wisdom should in the matter of congress, attend to this rule (about odd and even days). Kinsmen and relatives by marriage and friends should all be treated with respect. One should, according to the best of one's power, adore the deities in sacrifices, giving away diverse kinds of articles as sacrificial Dakshina. After the period ordained for the domestic mode of life has been passed, one should, O king, enter the life of a forest recluse. I have thus told thee all the indications, in brief, of persons who succeed in living long.[485] What remains untold by me should be heard by thee from the mouths of persons well-versed in the three Vedas, O Yudhishthira. Thou shouldst know that conduct is the root of prosperity. Conduct is the enhancer of fame. It is conduct that prolongs life. It is conduct that destroys all calamities and evils. Conduct has been said to be superior to all the branches of knowledge. It is conduct that begets righteousness, and it is righteousness that prolongs life. Conduct is productive of fame, of long life, and of heaven. Conduct is the most efficacious rite of propitiating the deities (for bringing about auspiciousness of every kind). The Self-born Brahman himself has said that one should

---

[484] The fact is, one is directed to bathe after a shave. One is considered impure after a shave until one bathes.

[485] Uddesa means, as the commentator explains, in brief.

show compassion unto all orders of men."""[486]

SECTION CV.

"'Yudhishthira said, "Tell me, O chief of Bharata's race, how the eldest brother should behave towards his younger brothers and how the younger brothers should behave towards their eldest brother."

"'Bhishma said, "Do thou, O son, always behave towards thy younger brothers as their eldest brother should. Thou art always the eldest of all these thy brothers. That high conduct which the preceptor should always adopt towards his disciples should be adopted by thee towards thy younger brothers. If the preceptor happens to be unendued with wisdom, the disciple cannot possibly behave towards him in a respectful or proper way. If the preceptor happens to be possessed of purity and highness of conduct, the disciple also succeeds in attaining to conduct of the same kind, O Bharata. The eldest brother should at times be blind to the acts of his younger brothers, and though possessed of wisdom should at times act as if he does not understand their acts. If the younger brothers be guilty of any transgression, the eldest brother should correct them by indirect ways and means. If there be good understanding among brothers and if the eldest brother seek to correct his younger brothers by direct or ostensible means, persons that are enemies, O son of Kunti, that are afflicted with sorrow at the sight of such good understanding and who, therefore, always seek to bring about a disunion, set themselves to disunite the brothers and cause dissension among them. It is the eldest brother that enhances the prosperity of the family or destroys it entirely. If the eldest brother happens to be unendued with sense and wicked in behaviour, he brings about the destruction of the whole family. The eldest brother who injures his younger brothers ceases to be regarded as the eldest and forfeits his share in the family property and deserves to be checked by the king. That man who acts deceitfully, has, without doubt, to go to regions of grief and every kind of evil. The birth of such a person serves no useful purpose even as the flowers of the cane.[487] That family in which a sinful person takes birth becomes subject to every evil. Such a person brings about infamy, and all the good acts of the family disappear. Such among the brothers as are wedded to evil acts forfeit their shares of the family property. In such a case, the eldest brother may appropriate the whole Yautuka property without giving any portion thereof to his younger brothers. If the eldest brother makes any acquisition, without using the paternal property and by going to a distant place he may appropriate for his own use, such acquisitions, without giving any share thereof to his younger brothers. If unseparated brothers desire (during the lifetime of their father) to portion the family property, the father should give equal shares unto all his sons. If the eldest brother happens to be of sinful acts and undistinguished by accomplishments of any kind he may be disregarded by his younger brothers. If the wife or the younger brother happens to be sinful, her or his good must still be looked after. Persons conversant with the efficacy of righteousness say that righteousness is the highest good. The Upadhyaya is superior to even ten Acharyas. The sire is equal to ten Upadhyayas. The mother is equal to ten sires or even the whole earth. There is no senior equal to the

---

[486] The word rendered conduct in the concluding verse of this lesson is acharah. It implies not only one's behaviour to one's own self and others, i.e., to beings inferior, equal, and superior. The word acharah, therefore, includes the entire body of acts that one does in this life, including the very sentiments that one cherishes.

[487] The flower of the cane cannot be plucked for being offered to the deities.

mother. Verily, she transcends all in respect of the reverence due to her.[488] It is for this reason that people regard the mother to deserve so much reverence. After the father has ceased to breathe, O Bharata, the eldest brother should be regarded as the father. It is the eldest brother who should assign unto them their means of support and protect and cherish them. All the younger brothers should bow to him and obey his authority. Indeed, they should live in dependence upon him even as they did upon their father while he was alive. So far as the body is concerned, O Bharata, it is the father and the mother that create it. That birth, however, which the Acharya ordains, is regarded as the true birth, that is, besides, really unfading and immortal. The eldest sister, O chief of Bharata's race, is like unto the mother. The wife of the eldest brother also is like unto the mother, for the younger brother, in infancy, receives suck from her.""[489]

SECTION CVI.

"'Yudhishthira said, "The disposition is seen, O grandsire, in all the orders of men, including the very Mlechchhas, of observing fasts. The reason, however, of this is not known to us. It has been heard by us that only Brahmanas and Kshatriyas should observe the vow of fasts. How, O grandsire, are the other orders to be taken as earning any merit by the observance of fasts? How have vows and fasts come to be observed by persons of all orders, O king? What is that end to which one devoted to the observance of fasts attains? It has been said that fasts are highly meritorious and that fasts are a great refuge. O prince of men, what is the fruit that is earned in this world by the man that observe fasts? By what means is one cleansed of one's sins? By what means doth one acquire righteousness? By what means, O best of the Bharatas, doth one succeed in acquiring heaven and merit? After having observed a fast, what should one give away, O king? O, tell me, what those duties are by which one may succeed in obtaining such objects as lead to happiness?"'

"Vaisampayana continued, 'Unto Kunti's son by the deity of Dharma, who was conversant with every duty and who said so unto him, Santanu's son, Bhishma, who was acquainted with every duty, answered in the following words.'

"Bhishma said, "In former days, O king, I heard of these high merits, O chief of Bharata's race, as attaching to the observance of fasts according to the ordinance. I had, O Bharata, asked the Rishi Angiras of high ascetic merit, the very same questions which thou hast asked me today. Questioned by me thus, the illustrious Rishi, who sprang from the sacrificial fire, answered me even thus in respect of the observance of fasts according to the ordinance.

""Angiras said, 'As regards Brahmanas and Kshatriyas, fasts for three nights at a

---

[488] An Acharya is an ordinary instructor. He is called an Upadhyaya who teaches the Vedas. The Upadhyaya is greater than even ten Acharyas or ordinary teachers. The father, again, deserves ten times as much respect as is paid to the Upadhyaya. As regards the mother, again, the reverence due to her is greater than what is due to the father. The mother is equal to the whole earth.

[489] Many of the verses of this Lesson are from Manu. The relative positions of the Acharya, the Upadhyaya, the father, and the mother, as given in verse 15, is not consistent with Manu. Verse 15 would show that the Upadhyaya was regarded as very much superior of the Acharya. In Manu, II—140-41, he is called an Acharya who taught all the Vedas, without any remuneration. He, on the other hand, who taught a particular Veda for a living, was called an Upadhyaya. The first line of verse 19 corresponds with Manu, II—148. The sense is that that birth which one derives from one's parents is subject to death; while the birth derived from the preceptor is true regeneration, unfading and immortal. It is a question whether any other nation paid such respect to persons employed in teaching.

stretch are ordained for them, O delighter of the Kurus. Indeed, O chief of men, a fast for one night, for two nights, and for three nights, may be observed by them. (They should never go beyond three nights). As regards Vaisyas and Sudras, the duration of fasts prescribed for them is a single night. If, from folly, they observe fasts for two or three nights, such fasts never lead to their advancement. Indeed, for Vaisyas and Sudras, fasts for two nights have been ordained (on certain special occasions). Fasts for three nights, however, have not been laid down for them by persons conversant with and observant of duties. That man of wisdom who, with his senses and soul under control, O Bharata, fasts, by abstaining from one of the two meals, on the fifth and the sixth days of the moon as also on the day of the full moon, becomes endured with forgiveness and beauty of person and conversance with the scriptures. Such a person never becomes childless and poor. He who performs sacrifices for adoring the deities on the fifth and sixth days of the moon, transcends all the members of his family and succeeds in feeding a large number of Brahmanas. He who observes fasts on the eighth and the fourteenth days of the dark fortnight, becomes freed from maladies of every kind and possessed of great energy. The man who abstains from one meal every day throughout the month called Margasirsha, should, with reverence and devotion, feed a number of Brahmanas. By so doing he becomes freed from all his sins. Such a man becomes endued with prosperity, and all kinds of grain become his. He becomes endued with energy. In fact, such a person reaps an abundance of harvest from his fields, acquires great wealth and much corn. That man, O son of Kunti, who passes the whole month of Pausha, abstaining every day from one of two meals, becomes endued with good fortune and agreeable features and great fame. He who passes the whole month of Magha, abstaining every day from one of the two meals, takes birth in a high family and attains to a position of eminence among his kinsmen. He who passes the whole month of Bhagadaivata, confining himself every day to only one meal becomes a favourite with women who, indeed, readily own his sway. He who passes the whole of the month of Chaitra, confining himself every day to one meal, takes birth in a high family and becomes rich in gold, gems, and pearls. The person, whether male or female, who passes the month of Vaisakha, confining himself or herself every day to one meal, and keeping his or her senses under control, succeeds in attaining to a position of eminence among kinsmen. The person who passes the month of Jyaishtha confining himself every day to one meal a day, succeeds in attaining to a position of eminence and great wealth. If a woman, she reaps the same reward. He who passes the month of Ashadha confining himself to one meal a day and with senses steadily concentrated upon his duties, becomes possessed of much corn, great wealth, and a large progeny. He who passes the month of Sravana, confining himself to one meal a day, receives the honours of Abhisheka wherever he may happen to reside, and attains to a position of eminence among kinsmen whom he supports. That man who confines himself to only one meal a day for the whole month of Proshthapada, becomes endued with great wealth and attains to swelling and durable affluence. The man who passes the month of Aswin, confining himself to one meal a day, becomes pure in soul and body, possessed of animals and vehicles in abundance, and a large progeny. He who passes the month of Kartika, confining himself to one meal every day, becomes possessed of heroism, many spouses, and great fame. I have now told thee, O chief of men what the fruits are that are obtained by men by observing fasts for the two and ten months in detail. Listen now, O king, to me as I tell thee what the rules are in respect of each of the lunar days. The man who, abstaining from it every day, takes rice at the expiration of every fortnight, becomes possessed of a great many kine, a large progeny, and a long life. He who observes a fast for three nights every month and conducts himself thus for two and ten years, attains to a position of supremacy among his kinsmen and associates, without a rival to contest his claim and without any anxiety caused by any one endeavouring to rise to the same height. These rules that I speak of, O chief of Bharata's race, should be observed for two and ten years. Let the inclination be manifested towards it. That man who eats once in the forenoon and once after evening and abstains from drinking (or eating anything) in the interval, and who observes compassion, towards all creatures and pours libations of clarified butter on his sacred fire every day, attains to success, O king, in six years. There is no doubt in this. Such a man earns the merit that attaches to the performance of the Agnishtoma sacrifice. Endued with merit and freed from every kind of stain, he attains to the region of the Apsaras that echo with the sound of songs and dance, and passes his days in the company of a thousand damsels of great beauty. He rides on a car of the complexion of melted gold and receives high honours in the region of Brahma. After the exhaustion of that merit such a person comes back to earth and attains to pre-eminence of position. That man who passes one whole year, confining himself every day to only one meal, attains to the merit of the Atiratra sacrifice. He ascends to heaven after death and receives great honours there. Upon the exhaustion of that merit he returns to earth and attains to a position of eminence. He who passes one whole year observing fasts for three days in succession and taking food on every fourth day, and abstaining from injury from every kind, adheres to truthfulness of speech and keeps his senses under control, attains to the merit of the Vajapeya sacrifice. Such a person ascends to heaven after death and receives high honours there. That man, O son of Kunti, who passes a whole year observing fasts for five days and taking food on only the sixth day, acquires the merit of the Horse-sacrifice. The chariot he rides is drawn by Chakravakas. Such a man enjoys every kind of happiness in heaven for full forty thousand years. He who passes a whole year observing fasts for seven days and taking food on only every eighth day, acquires the merit of the Gavamaya sacrifice. The chariot he rides is drawn by swans and cranes. Such a person enjoys all kinds of happiness in Heaven for fifty thousand years. He who passes a whole year, O king, eating only at intervals of a fortnight, acquires the merit of a continuous fast for six months. This has been said by the illustrious Angiras himself. Such a man dwells in heaven for sixty thousand years. He is roused every morning from his bed by the sweet notes of Vinas and Vallakis and flutes, O king. He who passes a whole year, drinking only a little water at the expiration of every month, acquires, O monarch, the merit of the Viswajit sacrifice. Such a man rides a chariot drawn by lions and tigers. He dwells in heaven for seventy thousand years in the enjoyment of every kind of happiness. No fast for more than a month, O chief of men, has been ordained. Even this, O son of Pritha, is the ordinance in respect of fasts that has been declared by sages conversant with duties. That man who, unafflicted by disease and free from every malady, observes a fast, verily acquires, at every step the merits that attach to Sacrifices. Such a man ascends to Heaven on a car drawn by swans. Endued with puissance, he enjoys every kind of happiness in heaven for a hundred years. A hundred Apsaras of the most beautiful features wait upon and sport with him. He is roused from his bed every morning by the sound of the Kanchis and the Nupuras of those damsels.[490] Such a person rides on a car drawn by a thousand swans. Dwelling, again, in a region teeming with hundreds of the most beautiful damsels, he passes his time in great joy. The person who

---

[490] Kanchi is an ornament worn by ladies round the waist or hips. There is a shining disc of gold or silver, which dangles on the hip. It is commonly called Chandra-hara. The Nupura is an anklet of silver, with moving bullets placed within, so that when the wearer moves, these make an agreeable sound.

is desirous of heaven does not like the accession of strength when he becomes weak, or the cure of wounds when he is wounded, or the administration of healing drugs when he is ill, or soothing by others when he is angry, or the mitigation, by the expenditure of wealth, of sorrows caused by poverty. Leaving this world where he suffers only privations of every kind, he proceeds to heaven and rides on cars adorned with gold, his person embellished with ornaments of every kind. There, in the midst of hundreds of beautiful damsels, he enjoys all kinds of pleasure and happiness, cleansed of every sin. Indeed, abstaining from food and enjoyments in this world, he takes leave of this body and ascends to heaven as the fruit of his penances. There, freed from all his sins, health and happiness become his and whatever wishes arise in his mind become crowned with fruition. Such a person rides on a celestial car of golden complexion, of the effulgence of the morning sun, set with pearls and lapis lazuli, resounding with the music of Vinas and Murajas, adorned with banners and lamps, and echoing with the tinkle of celestial bells, such a person enjoys all kinds of happiness in heaven for as many years as there are pores in his body. There is no Sastra superior to the Veda. There is no person more worthy of reverence than the mother. There is no acquisition superior to that of Righteousness, and no penance superior to fast. There is nothing, more sacred, in heaven or earth, than Brahmanas. After the same manner there is no penance that is superior to the observance of fasts. It was by fasts that the deities have succeeded in becoming denizens of heaven. It is by fasts that the Rishis have attained to high success. Viswamitra passed a thousand celestial years, confining himself every day to only one meal, and as the consequence thereof attained to the status of a Brahmana. Chyavana and Jamadagni and Vasishtha and Gautama and Bhrigu—all these great Rishis endued with the virtue of forgiveness, have attained to heaven through observance of fasts. In former days Angiras declared so unto the great Rishis. The man who teaches another the merit of fasts have never to suffer any kind of misery. The ordinances about fasts, in their due order, O son of Kunti, have flowed from the great Rishi Angiras. The man who daily reads these ordinances or hears them read, becomes freed from sins of every kind. Not only is such a person freed from every calamity, but his mind becomes incapable of being touched by any kind of fault. Such a person succeeds in understanding the sounds of all creatures other than human, and acquiring eternal fame, become foremost of his species."'"

SECTION CVII.

"'Yudhishthira said, "O high-souled grandsire, thou hast duly discoursed to us on the subject of Sacrifices, including the merits in detail that attach to them both here and hereafter. It should be remembered, however, O grandsire, that Sacrifices are incapable of being performed, by people that are poor, for these require a large store of diverse kinds of articles. Indeed, O grandsire, the merit attaching to Sacrifices can be acquired by only kings and princes. That merit is incapable of being acquired by those that are destitute of wealth and divested of ability and that live alone and are helpless. Do thou tell us, O grandsire, what the ordinances are in respect of those acts that are fraught with merit equal to what attaches to sacrifices and which, therefore, are capable of being performed by persons destitute of means."[491]

"'Bhishma said, "Listen, O Yudhishthira! Those ordinances that I have told thee

---

[491] In verse 3, Avaguna means Nirguna; Ekatma means alone and asamhta implies without associates i.e., helpless.

of,—those, viz., that were first promulgated by the great Rishi Angiras, and that have reference to meritorious fasts for their soul,—are regarded as equal to Sacrifices (in respect of the fruits they bring about both here and hereafter). That man who takes one meal in the forenoon and one at night, without taking any food or drink during the interval, and who observes this regulation for a period of six years in succession, abstaining all the while from injuring any creature and regularly pouring libations on his sacred fire every day, attains, without doubt, to success. Such a man acquires hereafter a car of the complexion of heated gold, and attains to a residence, for millions of years, in the region of Prajapati, in the company of celestial damsels, that ever echoes with the sound of music and dance, and blazes with the effulgence of fire. He who passes three years, confining himself every day to one meal and abstaining all the while from congress with any other woman save his own wedded wife, attains to the merit of the Agnishtoma sacrifice. Such a man is regarded as having performed a Sacrifice, with plenty of gifts in gold, that is dear to Vasava himself. By practising truthfulness of speech, making gifts, reverencing the Brahmanas, avoiding malice, becoming forgiving and self-restrained, and conquering wrath, a man attains to the highest end. Riding on a car of the complexion of white clouds that is drawn by swans, he lives, for millions and million of years, in the company of Apsaras. Fasting for a whole day and eating only one meal on the second day, he who pours libations upon his sacred fire for the period of a whole year,—verily, he who observes such a fast and attends every day to his fire and rises every day from bed before sunrise, attains to the merit of the Agnishtoma sacrifice. Such a man acquires a car drawn by swans and cranes. Surrounded by the most beautiful damsels, he resides in the region of Indra. That man who eats only one meal every third day, and pours libations every day on his sacred fire for a period of a whole year,—indeed, he who thus attends to his fire every day and wakes up from sleep every morning before the sun is up, attains to the high merit of the Atiratra sacrifice. He acquires a car drawn by peacocks and swans and cranes. Proceeding to the region of the seven (celestial) Rishis, he takes up his residence there, surrounded by Apsaras of great beauty. It is well-known that such residence lasts for full three Padmas of years.[492] Fasting for three days in succession, he who takes only one meal every fourth day, and pours libations every day on his sacred fire, acquires the high merit of the Vajapeya sacrifice. The car he acquires is graced by celestial damsels of great beauty that have Indra for their father. He resides in the region of Indra for millions and millions of years and experiences great happiness by witnessing the sports of the chief of the deities. Fasting for four days in succession, he who eats only one meal every fifth day, and pours libations on the sacred fire every day for the period of a whole year, and who lives without cupidity, telling the truth, reverencing the Brahmanas, abstaining from every kind of injury, and avoiding malice and sin, acquires the merit of the Vajapeya sacrifice. The car he rides is made of gold and drawn by swans and endued with the effulgence of many suns rising together. He acquires a palatial mansion of pure white. He lives there in great happiness for full one and fifty Padmas of years.[493] Fasting for five days, he who takes food on only the sixth day, and pours libations on his sacred fire every day for a whole year, and who performs three ablutions in course of the day for purifying himself and saying his prayers and doing his worship,

---

[492] A Padma is a very large number. Instead of rendering such words exactly, I have, in some of the preceding verses, following the sense, put down 'millions upon millions of years.'

[493] Avartanani means years. Four and twelve make sixteen, Sara is arrow. The arrows are five in number as possessed by Kama, the deity of love. The number of fires also is seven. The compound saragniparimana, therefore, implies five and thirty. Adding this to sixteen, the total comes up to one and fifty.

and who leads a life of Brahmacharya, divested of malice in his conduct, acquires the merit of the Gomedha sacrifice. He acquires an excellent car adorned with pure gold, possessed of the effulgence of a blazing fire and drawn by swans and peacocks. He sleeps on the lap of Apsaras and is awakened every morning by the melodious tinkle of Nupuras and Kanchis. He leads such a life of happiness for ten thousand million years and three thousand million besides and eight and ten Padmas and two Patakas.[494] Such a man resides also, honoured by all, in the region of Brahma for as many years as there are hairs on the bodies of hundreds of bears. Fasting for six days, he who eats only one meal every seventh day and pours libations on the sacred fire every day, for a full year, restraining speech all the while and observing the vow of Brahmacharya, and abstaining from the use of flowers and unguents and honey and meat, attains to the region of the Maruts and of Indra. Crowned with the fruition of every desire as it springs up in the mind, he is waited upon and adored by celestial damsels. He acquires the merits of a sacrifice in which abundance of gold is given away. Proceeding to the regions named, he lives there for countless years in the greatest happiness.[495] He who shows forgiveness to all and fasting for seven days eats on every eighth day for a whole year, and, pouring libations every day on the sacred fire, adores the deities regularly, acquires the high merits of the Paundarika sacrifice. The car he rides is of a colour like that of the lotus. Without doubt, such a man acquires also a large number of damsels, possessed of youth and beauty, some having complexions that are dark, some with complexions like that of gold, and some that are Syamas, whose looks and attitudes are of the most agreeable kind. He who fasts for eight days and takes only one meal on every ninth day for a whole year, and pours libations on the sacred fire every day, acquires the high merits of a thousand Horse-sacrifices. The car he rides in Heaven is as beautiful as a lotus. He always makes his journeys on that car, accompanied by the daughters of Rudra adorned with celestial garlands and endued with the effulgence of the midday sun or the fires of blazing flames. Attaining to the regions of Rudra, he lives there in great happiness for countless years. He who fasts for nine days and takes only one meal every tenth day for a whole year, and pours libations on his sacred fire every day, acquires the high merit of a thousand Horse-sacrifices, and attains to the companionship of Brahmanas' daughters endued with beauty capable of charming the hearts of all creatures. These damsels, possessed of such beauty, and some of them possessed of complexion like that of the lotus and some like that of the same flower of the blue variety, always keep him in joy.[496] He acquires a beautiful vehicle, that moves in beautiful circles and that looks like the dense cloud called Avarta, verily, it may be said to resemble also an ocean-wave. That vehicle resounds with the constant tinkle of rows of pearls and gems, and the melodious blare of conchs, and is adorned with columns made of crystals and diamonds, as also with an altar constructed of the same minerals. He makes his journeys on such a car, drawn by swans and cranes and lives for millions and millions of years in great happiness in heaven. He who fasts for ten days and eats only ghee on every eleventh day for a whole year and pours libations on his sacred fire every day, who never, in word or thought, covets the companionship of other people's wives and who never utters an untruth even for the sake of his mother and father, succeeds in

---

[494] A countless number almost.

[495] Here the exact number of years is not stated.

[496] Some of the most beautiful ladies in Indian mythology and history have been of dark complexion. Draupadi, the queen of the Pandavas, was dark in colour and was called Krishna. As to women called Syamas, the description given is that their bodies are warm in winter and cold in summer, and their complexion is like that of heated gold.

beholding Mahadeva of great puissance seated on his car. Such a person acquires the high merit of a thousand Horse-sacrifices. He beholds the car of the Self-born Brahman himself approach for taking him on it. He rides in it, accompanied by celestial damsels possessed of great beauty, and complexion as effulgent as that of pure gold. Endued with the blazing splendour of the Yoga-fire, he lives for countless years in a celestial mansion in heaven, full of every happiness. For those countless years he experiences the joy of bending his head in reverence unto Rudra adored by deities and Danavas. Such a person obtains every day the sight of the great deity. That man who having fasted for eleven days eats only a little ghee on the twelfth, and observes this conduct for a whole year, succeeds in obtaining the merits attaching to all the sacrifices. The car he rides in is possessed of the effulgence of a dozen suns. Adorned with gems and pearls and corals of great value, embellished with rows of swans and snakes and of peacocks and Chakravakas uttering their melodious notes, and beautified with large domes, is the residence to which he attains in the region of Brahman. That abode, O king, is always filled with men and women (who wait upon him for service). Even this is what the highly blessed Rishi Angiras, conversant with every duty, said (regarding the fruits of such a fast). That man who having fasted for twelve days eats a little ghee on the thirteenth, and bears himself in this way for a whole year, succeeds in attaining to the merits of the divine sacrifice. Such a man obtains a car of the complexion of the newly-blown lotus, adorned with pure gold and heaps of jewels and gems. He proceeds to the region of the Maruts that teem with celestial damsels, that are adorned with every kind of celestial ornament, that are redolent with celestial perfumes, and that contain every element of felicity. The number of years he resides in those happy regions is countless.[497] Soothed with the sound of music and the melodious voice of Gandharvas and the sounds and blare of drums and Panavas, he is constantly gladdened by celestial damsels of great beauty. That man who having fasted for thirteen days eats a little ghee on the fourteenth day, and bears himself in this way for a full year, obtains the merits of the Mahamedha sacrifice.[498] Celestial damsels of indescribable beauty, and whose age cannot be guessed for they are for ever young in appearance, adorned with every ornament and with armlets of blazing effulgence, wait upon him with many cars and follow him in his journeys. He is waked every morning from his bed by the melodious voice of swans, the tinkle of Nupuras, and the highly agreeable jingle of Kanchis. Verily, he resides in a superior abode, waited upon by such celestial damsels, for years as countless as the sands on the shores of Ganga. That man who, keeping his senses under control, fasts for a fortnight and takes only one meal on the sixteenth day, and bears himself in this way for a whole year, pouring libations every day on his sacred fire, acquires the high merits that attach to a thousand Rajasuya sacrifices. The car he rides in is possessed of great beauty and is drawn by swans and peacocks. Riding in such a vehicle, that is, besides, adorned with garlands of pearls and the purest gold and graced with bevies of celestial damsels decked with ornaments of every kind, having one column and four arches and seven altars exceedingly auspicious, endued with thousands of banners and echoing with the sound of music, celestial and of celestial attributes, embellished with gems and pearls and corals, and possessed of the effulgence of lightning, such a man lives in heaven for a thousand Yugas, having elephants and rhinoceroses for dragging that vehicle of his. That man who having fasted for fifteen days takes one meal on the sixteenth day and bears himself in

[497] A very large figure is given.
[498] This sacrifice consisted of the slaughter of a human being.

this way for one whole year, acquires the merits attaching to the Soma sacrifice. Proceeding to Heaven he lives in the company of Soma's daughters. His body fragrant with unguents whose perfumes are as sweet as those of Soma himself, he acquires the power of transporting himself immediately to any place he likes. Seated on his car he is waited upon by damsels of the most beautiful features and agreeable manners, and commands all articles of enjoyment. The period for which he enjoys such happiness consists of countless years.[499] That man who having fasted for sixteen days eats a little ghee on the seventeenth day and bears himself in this way for a whole year, pouring libations every day on his sacred fire, proceeds to the regions of Varuna and Indra, and Rudra and the Maruts and Usanas and Brahman himself. There he is waited upon by celestial damsels and obtains a sight of the celestial Rishi called Bhurbhuva and grasps the whole universe in his ken. The daughters of the deity of the deities gladden him there. Those damsels, of agreeable manners and adorned with every ornament, are capable of assuming two and thirty forms. As long as the Sun and the Moon move in firmament, so long does that man of wisdom reside in those regions of felicity, subsisting upon the succulence of ambrosia and nectar. That man who having fasted for seventeen days eats only one meal on the eighteenth day, and bears himself in this way for a whole year, succeeds in grasping the seven regions, of which the universe consist, in his ken. While performing his journeys on his car he is always followed by a large train of cars producing the most agreeable rattle and ridden by celestial damsels blazing with ornament and beauty. Enjoying the greatest happiness, the vehicle he rides in is celestial and endued with the greatest beauty. It is drawn by lions and tigers, and produces a rattle as deep as the sound of the clouds. He lives in such felicity for a thousand Kalpas subsisting upon the succulence of ambrosia that is as sweet as nectar itself. That man who having fasted for eighteen days eats only one meal on the nineteenth day and bears himself in this way for a full year, succeeds in grasping within his ken all the seven regions of which the universe consists. The region to which he attains is inhabited by diverse tribes of Apsaras and resounds with the melodious voice of Gandharvas. The car he rides in is possessed of the effulgence of the sun. His heart being freed from every anxiety, he is waited upon by the foremost of celestial damsels. Decked with celestial garlands, and possessed of beauty of form, he lives in such happiness for millions and millions of years. That man who having fasted for nineteen days eats only one meal on every twentieth day and bears himself in this way for a full year, adhering all the while to truthfulness of speech and to the observance of other (excellent) rituals, abstaining also from meat, leading the life of a Brahmacharin, and devoted to the good of all creatures, attains to the extensive regions of great happiness, belonging to the Adityas. While performing his journeys on his own car, he is followed by a large train of cars ridden by Gandharvas and Apsaras decked with celestial garlands and unguents. That man who having fasted for twenty days takes a single meal on the twenty-first day and bears himself in this way for a full year, pouring libations every day on his sacred fire, attains to the regions of Usanas and Sakra, of the Aswins and the Maruts, and resides there in uninterrupted happiness of great measure. Unacquainted with sorrow of every kind, he rides in the foremost of cars for making his journeys, and waited upon by the foremost of celestials, damsels, and possessed of puissance, he sports in joy like a celestial himself. That man who having fasted for one and twenty days takes a single meal on the twenty-second day and bears himself in this way for a full year, pouring libations on his sacred

---

[499] The exact number of years is given, consisting of a fabulous figure.

fire every day, abstaining from injuring any creature, adhering to truthfulness of speech, and freed from malice attains to the regions of the Vasus and becomes endued with effulgence of the sun. Possessed of the power of going everywhere at will, subsisting upon nectar, and riding in the foremost of cars, his person decked with celestial ornaments, he sports in joy in the company of celestial damsels. That man who having fasted for two and twenty days takes a single meal on the twenty-third day and bears himself in this way for a full year, thus regulating his diet and keeping his senses under control, attains to the regions of the deity of Wind, of Usanas, and of Rudra. Capable of going everywhere at will and always roving at will, he is worshipped by diverse tribes of Apsaras. Riding in the foremost of cars and his person decked with celestial ornaments, he sports for countless years in great felicity in the company of celestial damsels. That man who having fasted for three and twenty days eats a little ghee on the twenty-fourth day, and bears himself in this way for a full year, pouring libations on his sacred fire, resides for countless years in great happiness in the regions of the Adityas, his person decked with celestial robes and garlands and celestial perfumes and unguents. Riding in an excellent car made of gold and possessed of great beauty and drawn by swans, he sports in joy in the company of thousands and thousands of celestial damsels. That man who having fasted for four and twenty days eats a single meal on the twenty-fifth day and bears himself thus for a full year, succeeds in obtaining a car of the foremost kind, full of every article of enjoyment. He is followed in his journeys by a large train of cars drawn by lions and tigers, and producing a rattle as deep as the roar of the clouds ridden by celestial damsels, and all made of pure gold and possessed of great beauty. Himself riding on an excellent celestial car possessed of great beauty, he resides in those regions for a thousand Kalpas, in the company of hundreds of celestial damsels, and subsisting upon the succulence of ambrosia that is sweet as nectar itself. That man who having fasted for five and twenty days eats only one meal on the twenty-sixth day, and bears himself thus for a full year in the observance of such a regulation in respect of diet, keeping his senses under control, freed from attachment (to worldly objects), and pouring libations every day on his sacred fire,—that blessed man,—worshipped by the Apsaras, attains to the regions of the seven Maruts and of the Vasus. When performing his journeys he is followed by a large train of cars made of excellent crystal and adorned with all kinds of gems, and ridden by Gandharvas and Apsaras who show him every honour. He resides in those regions, in enjoyment of such felicity, and endued with celestial energy, for two thousand Yugas. That man who having fasted for six and twenty days eats a single meal on the twenty-seventh day and bears himself in this way for a full year, pouring libations every day on his sacred fire, acquires great merit and proceeding to Heaven receives honours from the deities. Residing there, he subsists on nectar, freed from thirst of every kind, and enjoying every felicity. His soul purified of every dross and performing his journeys on a celestial car of great beauty, he lives there, O king, bearing himself after the manner of the celestial Rishis and the royal sages. Possessed of great energy, he dwells there in great happiness in the company of celestial damsels of highly agreeable manners, for three thousand Yugas and Kalpas. That man who having fasted for seven and twenty days eats a single meal on the twenty-eighth day and bears himself in this way for a full year, with soul and senses under perfect control, acquires very great merit, which, in fact, is equal to what is acquired by the celestial Rishis. Possessed of every article of enjoyment, and endued with great energy, he blazes with the effulgence of the midday sun. Sportive damsels of the most delicate features and endued with splendour of complexion, having deep bosoms, tapering thighs and full and round hips, decked with celestial ornaments, gladden him with their company while he rides on a delightful and excellent car possessed of the effulgence of the sun and equipped with every article of enjoyment, for thousands and thousands of Kalpas. That man who having fasted for eight and twenty days eats a single meal on the twenty-ninth day, and bears himself in this way for a full year, adhering all the while to truthfulness of speech, attains to auspicious regions of great happiness that are worshipped by celestial Rishis and royal sages. The car he obtains is endued with the effulgence of the sun and the moon, made of pure gold and adorned with every kind of gem, ridden by Apsaras and Gandharvas singing melodiously. Thereon he is attended by auspicious damsels adorned with celestial ornaments of every kind. Possessed of sweet dispositions and agreeable features, and endued with great energy, these gladden him with their company. Endued with every article of enjoyment and with great energy, and possessed of the splendour of a blazing fire, he shines like a celestial, with a celestial form having every excellence. The regions he attains are those of the Vasus and the Maruts, of the Sadhyas and the Aswins, of the Rudras and of Brahman himself. That man who having fasted for a full month takes a single meal on the first day of the following month and bears himself in this way for a full year, looking on all things with an equal eye attains to the regions of Brahman himself. There he subsists upon the succulence of ambrosia. Endued with a form of great beauty and highly agreeable to all, he shines with energy and prosperity like the sun himself of a thousand rays. Devoted to Yoga and adorned with celestial robes and garlands and smeared with celestial perfumes and unguents, he passes his time in great happiness, unacquainted with the least sorrow. He shines on his car attended by damsels that blaze forth with effulgence emitted by themselves. Those damsels, the daughters of the celestial Rishis and the Rudras, adore him with veneration. Capable of assuming diverse forms that are highly delightful and highly agreeable, their speech is characterised by diverse kinds of sweetness, and they are able to gladden the person they wait upon in diverse kinds of ways. While performing his journeys, he rides on a car that looks like the firmament itself in colour (for subtlety of the material that compose it). In his rear are cars that look like the moon; before him are those that resemble the clouds; on his right are vehicles that are red; below him are those that are blue; and above him are those that are of variegated hue. He is always adored by those that wait upon him. Endued with great wisdom, he lives in the region of Brahman for as many years as are measured by the drops of rain that fall in course of a thousand years on that division of the earth which is called Jamvudwipa. Verily, possessed of the effulgence of a deity, he lives in that region of unalloyed felicity for as many years as the drops of rain that fall upon the earth in the season of showers. The man who, having fasted for a whole month, eats on the first day of the following month, and bears himself in this way for ten years, attains to the status of a great Rishi. He was not to undergo any change of form while proceeding to heaven for enjoying the rewards of his acts in his life. Verily, even this is the status to which one attains by restraining speech, practising self-denial, subjugating wrath, sexual appetite, and the desire to eat, pouring libations on the sacred fire, and regularly adoring the two twilights. That man who purifies himself by the observance of these and similar vows and practices, and who eats in this way, becomes as stainless as ether and endued with effulgence like that of the sun himself.[500] Such a man, O king, proceeding to heaven in even his own carnal form, enjoys all the felicity that is there like a deity at his will.

---

[500] Abhravakasasila is explained by Nilakantha as having the attribute of the Avakasa or place of Abhra or the clouds. Hence, as stainless as the ether, which, of course, is the purest of all the elements.

"I have thus told thee, O chief of the Bharatas, what the excellent ordinances are in respect of sacrifices, one after another, as dependent upon the fruits of fasts.[501] Poor men, O son of Pritha (who are unable to perform sacrifices) may, nevertheless, acquire the fruits thereof (by the observance of fasts). Verily, by observing these fasts, even a poor man may attain to the highest end, O foremost one of Bharata's race, attending all the while, besides, to the worship of the deities and the Brahmanas. I have thus recited to thee in detail the ordinances in respect of fasts. Do not harbour any doubt in respect of those men that are so observant of vows, that are so heedful and pure and high-souled, that are so freed from pride and contentions of every kind, that are endued with such devoted understandings, and that pursue their end with such steadiness and fixity of purpose without ever deviating from their path."'"

SECTION CVIII.

"'Yudhishthira said, "Do thou tell me, O grandsire, of that which is regarded as the foremost of all Tirthas. Indeed, it behoveth thee to expound to me what that Tirtha is which conduces to the greatest purity."[502]

"'Bhishma said, "Without doubt, all Tirthas are possessed of merit. Listen, however, with attention to me as I tell thee what the Tirtha, the cleanser, is of men endued with wisdom. Adhering to eternal Truth, one should bathe in the Tirtha called Manasa, which is unfathomable (for its depth), stainless, and pure, and which has Truth for its waters and the understanding for its lake.[503] The fruits in the form of cleansing, that one acquires by bathing in that Tirtha, are freedom from cupidity, sincerity, truthfulness, mildness (of behaviour), compassion, abstention from injuring any creature, self-restraint, and tranquillity. Those men that are freed from attachments, that are divested of pride, that transcend all pairs of opposites (such as pleasure and pain, praise and blame, heat and cold, etc.), that have no spouses and children and houses and gardens, etc., that are endued with purity, and that subsist upon the alms given to them by others, are regarded as Tirthas. He who is acquainted with the truths of all things and who is freed from the idea of meum, is said to be the highest Tirtha.[504] In searching the indications of purity, the gaze should ever be directed towards these attributes (so that where these are present, thou mayst take purity to be present, and where these are not, purity also should be concluded to be not). Those persons from whose souls the attributes of Sattwa and Rajas and Tamas have been washed off, they who, regardless of (external) purity and impurity pursue the ends they have proposed to themselves, they who have renounced everything, they who are possessed of omniscience and endued with universal sight, and they who are of pure conduct, are regarded as Tirthas possessing the power of cleansing. That man

---

[501] Sacrifices have for their soul either the actual rites laid down in the scriptures or fasts of several kinds. The observance of fasts is equal to the performance of sacrifices, for the merits of both are equal.

[502] The word Tirtha as already explained (in the Santi Parva) means a sacred water. There can be no Tirtha without water, be it a river, a lake, or even a well. Bhishma, however, chooses to take the word in a different sense.

[503] The language is figurative. By Manasa is not meant the trans-Himalayan lake of that name, which to this day is regarded as highly sacred and draws numerous pilgrims from all parts of India. The word is used to signify the Soul. It is fathomless in consequence of nobody being able to discover its origin. It is pure and stainless by nature. It is represented here as having Truth for its waters and the Understanding for its lake. Probably, what is meant by this is that the Understanding, containing the waters of Truth, forms a part of this Tirtha as the lakes of Pushkara form a part of the Tirtha called by that name.

[504] Once freed from the idea of meum implies him who identifies himself with all creatures; him, that is, in whom the idea of self has been extinguished.

whose limbs only are wet with water is not regarded as one that is washed. He, on the other hand, is regarded as washed who has washed himself by self-denial. Even such a person is said to be pure both inwardly and outwardly. They who never concern themselves with what is past, they who feel no attachment to acquisitions that are present, indeed, they who are free from desire, are said to be possessed of the highest purity. Knowledge is said to constitute the especial purity of the body. So also freedom from desire, and cheerfulness of mind. Purity of conduct constitutes the purity of the mind. The purity that one attains by ablutions in sacred waters is regarded as inferior. Verily, that purity which arises from knowledge, is regarded as the best. Those ablutions which one performs with a blazing mind in the waters of the knowledge of Brahma in the Tirtha called Manasa, are the true ablutions of those that are conversant with Truth. That man who is possessed of true purity of conduct and who is always devoted to the preservation of a proper attitude towards all, indeed, he who is possessed of (pure) attributes and merit, is regarded as truly pure. These that I have mentioned have been said to be the Tirthas that inhere to the body. Do thou listen to me as I tell thee what those sacred Tirthas are that are situate on the earth also. Even as especial attributes that inhere to the body have been said to be sacred, there are particular spots on earth as well, and particular waters, that are regarded as sacred. By reciting the names of the Tirthas, by performing ablutions there, and by offering oblations to the Pitris in those places, one's sins are washed off. Verily, those men whose sins are thus washed off succeed in attaining to heaven when they leave this world. In consequence of their association with persons that are righteous, through the especial efficacy of the earth itself of those spots and of particular waters, there are certain portions of the earth that have come to be regarded as sacred. The Tirthas of the mind are separate and distinct from those of the earth. That person who bathes in both attains to success without any delay. As strength without exertion, or exertion without strength can never accomplish anything singly, and as these, when combined, can accomplish all things, even so one that becomes endued with the purity that is contributed by the Tirthas in the body as also by that which is contributed by the Tirthas on the earth, becomes truly pure and attains to success. That purity which is derived from both sources is the best."'"

SECTION CIX.

"'Yudhishthira said, "It behoveth thee, O grandsire, to tell me what are the highest, the most beneficial, and the most certain fruit of all kinds of fasts in this world."

"'Bhishma said, "Listen, O king, to what was sung by the Self-born himself and by accomplishing which a person, without doubt, attains to the highest happiness. That man who fasts on the twelfth day of the moon in the month called Margasirsha and worships Krishna as Kesava for the whole day and night, attains to the merit of the Horse-sacrifice and becomes cleansed of all his sins. He who, after the same manner, fasts on the twelfth day of the moon in the month of Pausha and worships Krishna as Narayana, for the whole day and night, attains to the merits of the Vajapeya sacrifice and the highest success. He who fasts on the twelfth day of the moon in the month of Magha and worships Krishna as Madhava, for the whole day and night, attains to the merits of the Rajasuya sacrifice, and rescues his own race (from misery).[505] He who fasts on the twelfth day of the moon in the

[505] Such a man, through the merit he acquires, causes his deceased ancestors and descendants to be freed from every kind of misery in the next world.

month of Phalguna and worships Krishna as Govinda, for the whole day and night, attains to the merit of the Atiratra sacrifice and goes to the region of Soma. He who fasts on the twelfth day of the moon in the month of Chaitra and worships Krishna as Vishnu, for the whole day and night, attains to the merit of the Pundarika sacrifice and proceeds to the region of the deities. By observing a similar fast on the twelfth day of the month of Vaisakha and worshipping Krishna as the slayer of Madhu for the whole day and night, one attains to the merits of the Agnishtoma sacrifice and proceeds to the region of Soma. By observing a fast on the twelfth lunar day in the month of Jyaishtha and worshipping Krishna as him who had (in Vali's sacrifice) covered the universe with three steps of his, one attains to the merits of the Gomedha sacrifice and sports with the Apsaras in great happiness. By observing a fast on the twelfth day of the moon in the month of Ashadha and worshipping Krishna as the dwarf (who beguiled the Asura king Vali), one attains to the merits of the Naramedha[506] sacrifice and sports in happiness with the Apsaras. By observing a fast for the twelfth lunar day of the month Sravana and worshipping Krishna for day and night as Sridhara, one attains to the merits of the sacrifice called Panchayajna and acquires a beautiful car in Heaven whereon he sports in joy. By observing a fast on the twelfth day of the moon in the month of Bhadrapada and worshipping Krishna as Hrishikesa for the whole day and night, one attains to the merits of the Sautramani sacrifice and becomes cleansed of all sins. By observing a fast for the twelfth day of the moon in the month of Aswin and worshipping Krishna as Padmanabha, one attains without doubt, to the merits of the sacrifice in which a thousand kine are given away. By observing a fast for the twelfth day of the moon in the month of Kartika and worshipping Krishna as Damodara, one attains, without doubt, to the combined merits of all the sacrifices. He who, in this way, adores Krishna for a whole year as Pundarikaksha, acquires the power of recollecting the incidents of his past births and wins much wealth in gold. Similarly, he who worships Krishna every day as Upendra attains to identity with him. After Krishna has been worshipped in this way, one should, at the conclusion of one's vow, feed a number of Brahmanas or make gifts unto them of ghee. The illustrious Vishnu, that ancient Being, has himself said that there is no fast that possesses merits superior to what attach to fast of this kind."'"

SECTION CX.

"Vaisampayana said, 'Approaching the Kuru grandsire, venerable in years, viz., Bhishma, who was then lying on his bed of arrows, Yudhishthira possessed of great wisdom put the following question.'

"'Yudhishthira said, "How, O grandsire, does one acquire beauty of form and prosperity and agreeableness of disposition? How, indeed, does one become possessed of religious merit and wealth and pleasure? How does one become endued with happiness?"

"'Bhishma said, "In the month of Margasirsha, when the moon comes in conjunction with the asterism called Mula, when his two feet are united with that very asterism, O king, when Rohini is in his calf, when his knee-joints are in Aswini, and his shins are in the two Ashadhas, when Phalguni makes his anus, and Krittika his waist, when his navel is in Bhadrapada, his ocular region in Revati, and his back on the Dhanishthas, when Anuradha makes his belly, when with his two arms he reaches the Visakhas, when his two hands are indicated by Hasta, when Punarvasu, O king, makes his fingers, Aslesha

---

[506] In the Naramedha, a human being was offered up as the sacrifice.

his nails, when Jyeshtha is known for his neck, when by Sravana is pointed out his ears, and his mouth by Pushya, when Swati is said to constitute his teeth and lips, when Satabhisha is his smile and Magha his nose, when Mrigasiras is known to be in his eye, and Chitra in his forehead, when his head is in Bharani, when Ardra constitutes his hair, O king, the vow called Chandravrata should be commenced. Upon the completion of that vow, gift of ghee should be made unto Brahmanas conversant with the Vedas. As the fruit of that vow, one becomes possessed about knowledge. Indeed, one becomes, in consequence of such a vow, as full (of every blessed attribute) as the moon himself when he is at full."'"

SECTION CXI.

"'Yudhishthira said, "O grandsire, O thou that art possessed of great wisdom and conversant with all the scriptures, I desire to know those excellent ordinances in consequence of which mortal creatures have to travel through their rounds of rebirth. What is that conduct by following which, O king, men succeed in attaining to high heaven, and what is that conduct by which one sinks in Hell? When, abandoning the dead body that is as inert as a piece of wood or clod of earth, people proceed to the other world, what are those that follow them thither?"

"'Bhishma said, "Yonder comes the illustrious Vrihaspati of great intelligence! Do thou ask his blessed self. The subject is an eternal mystery. None else is capable of explaining the matter. There is no speaker like Vrihaspati."

"Vaisampayana said, 'While the son of Pritha and the son of Ganga were thus speaking with each other, there came to that spot from the firmament the illustrious Vrihaspati of cleansed soul. King Yudhishthira, and all others, with Dhritarashtra at their head, stood up and received Vrihaspati with proper honours. Verily, the worship they offered to the preceptor of the celestials was excellent. Then Dharma's royal son, Yudhishthira, approaching the illustrious Vrihaspati, asked him the question in proper form, desirous of knowing the truth.'

"'Yudhishthira said, "O illustrious one, thou art conversant with all duties and all the scriptures. Do thou tell me, what is truly the friend of mortal creatures? Is the father, or mother, or son, or preceptor, or kinsmen, or relatives, or those called friends, that may be said to truly constitute the friend of a mortal creature? One goes to the next world, leaving one's dead body that is like a piece of wood or a clod of earth. Who is it that follows him thither?"

"'Vrihaspati said, "One is born alone, O king, and one dies alone; one crosses alone the difficulties one meets with, and one alone encounters whatever misery falls to one's lot. One has really no companion in these acts. The father, the mother, the brother, the son, the preceptor, kinsmen, relatives, and friends, leaving the dead body as if it were a piece of wood or a clod of earth, after having mourned for only a moment, all turn away from it and proceed to their own concerns. Only Righteousness follows the body that is thus abandoned by them all. Hence, it is plain, that Righteousness is the only friend and that Righteousness only should be sought by all. One endued with righteousness would attain to that high end which is constituted by heaven. If endued with unrighteousness, he goes to Hell. Hence, the man of intelligence should always seek to acquire religious merit through wealth won by lawful means. Piety is the one only friend which creatures have in the world hereafter. Let by cupidity, or stupefaction, or compassion, or fear, one destitute of much knowledge is seen to do improper acts, for the sake of even another, his judgment thus stupefied by cupidity.[507] Piety, wealth and pleasure,—these three constitute the fruit of life. One should acquire these three by means of being free from impropriety and sin."

"'Yudhishthira said, "I have carefully heard the words spoken by thy illustrious self,—these words that are fraught with righteousness, and that are highly beneficial. I wish now to know of the existence of the body (after death).[508] The dead body of man becomes subtil and unmanifest. It becomes invisible. How is it possible for piety to follow it?"

"'Vrihaspati said, "Earth, Wind, Ether, Water, Light, Mind, Yama (the king of the dead), Understanding, the Soul, as also Day and Night, all together behold as witnesses the merits (and demerits) of all living creatures. With these, Righteousness follows the creature (when dead).[509] When the body becomes bereft of life, skin, bones, flesh, the vital seed, and blood, O thou of great intelligence, leave it at the same time. Endued with merit (and demerit) Jiva (after the destruction of this body) attains to another. After the attainment by Jiva of that body, the presiding deities of the five elements once more behold as witnesses all his acts good and bad. What else dost thou wish to hear? If endued with righteousness, Jiva enjoys happiness. What other topic, belonging to this or the other world, shall I discourse upon?"

"'Yudhishthira said, "Thy illustrious self has explained how Righteousness follows Jiva. I desire to know how the vital seed is originated."

"'Vrihaspati said, "The food that these deities, O king, who dwell in the body, viz., Earth, Wind, Ether, Water, Light, and Mind eat, gratifies them. When those five elements become gratified, O monarch, with Mind numbering as their sixth, their vital seed then becomes generated, O thou of cleansed soul! When an act of union takes place between male and female, the vital seed flows out and causes conception. I have thus explained to thee what thou hast asked. What else dost thou wish to hear?"

"'Yudhishthira said, "Thou hast, O illustrious one, said how conception takes place. Do thou explain how the Jiva that takes birth grows (by becoming possessed of body)."

"'Vrihaspati said, "As soon as Jiva enters the vital seed, he becomes overwhelmed by the elements already mentioned. When Jiva becomes disunited therewith, he is said to attain to the other end (viz., death). Endued as Jiva becomes with all those elements, he attains, in consequence thereof, a body. The deities, that preside over those elements behold as witnesses all his acts, good and bad. What else dost thou wish to hear?"

"'Yudhishthira said, "Leaving off skin and bone and flesh, and becoming destitute of all those elements, in what does Jiva reside, O illustrious one, for enjoying and enduring happiness and misery?"

"'Vrihaspati said, "Endued with all his acts, the Jiva quickly enters the vital seed, and utilizing the functional flow of women, takes birth in time, O Bharata. After birth, the Jiva receives woe and death from the messengers of Yama. Indeed, misery and a painful round of rebirth are his inheritance. Endued with life, O king, the Jiva in this world, from the moment of his birth, enjoys and endures his own (previous) acts, depending upon righteousness (and its reverse). If the Jiva, according to the best of his power, follows righteousness from the day of his birth, he then succeeds in enjoying, when reborn,

---

[507] The sense seems to be this: One that is not possessed of much learning is liable to do improper acts. These acts are all done for another, viz., one's body and the senses and not oneself. The para here is, the Not-self.

[508] Nichayam is, as explained by the commentator Avasthitim.

[509] The sense is that when these leave the body, they are accompanied by Righteousness.

happiness without interruption. If, on the other hand, without following righteousness without interruption, he acts sinfully, he reaps happiness at first as the reward of his righteousness and endures misery after that. Endued with unrighteousness, the Jiva has to go to the dominions of Yama and suffering great misery there, he has to take birth in an intermediate order of being.[510] Listen to me as I tell thee what the different acts are by doing which the Jiva, stupefied by folly, has to take birth in different orders of being, as declared in the Vedas, the scriptures, and the (sacred) histories. Mortals have to go to the frightful regions of Yama. In those regions, O king, there are places that are fraught with every merit and that are worthy on that account of being the abodes of the very deities. There are, again, places in those regions that are worse than those which are inhabited by animals and birds. Indeed, there are spots of these kinds in the abode of Yama which (so far as its happier regions are concerned) is equal to the region of Brahman himself in merits. Creatures, bound by their acts, endure diverse kinds of misery. I shall, after this, tell thee what those acts and dispositions are in consequence of which a person obtains to an end that is fraught with great misery and terror. If a regenerate person, having studied the four Vedas, becomes stupefied by folly and accepts a gift from a fallen man, he has then to take birth in the asinine order. He has to live as an ass for five and ten years. Casting off his asinine form, he has next to take birth as an ox, in which state he has to live for seven years. Casting off his bovine form, he has next to take birth as a Rakshasa of regenerate order. Living as Rakshasa of the regenerate order for three months, he then regains his status (in his next birth) of a Brahmana.[511] A Brahmana, by officiating at the sacrifice of a fallen person, has to take birth as a vile worm. In this form he has to live for five and ten years, O Bharata. Freed from the status of a worm, he next takes birth as an ass. As an ass he has to live for five years, and then a hog, in which state also he has to remain for as many years. After that, he takes birth as a cock, and living for five years in that form, he takes birth as a jackal and lives for as many years in that state. He has next to take birth as a dog, and living thus for a year he regains his status of humanity. That foolish disciple who offends his preceptor by doing any injury to him, has certainly to undergo three transformations in this world. Such a person, O monarch, has in the first instance to become a dog. He has then to become a beast of prey, and then an ass. Living his asinine form, he has to wander for some time in great affliction as a spirit. After the expiration of that period, he has to take birth as a Brahmana. That sinful disciple who even in thought commits adultery with the wife of his preceptor, has in consequence of such a sinful heart, to undergo many fierce shapes in this world. First taking birth in the canine order he has to live for three years. Casting off the canine form when death comes, he takes birth as a worm or vile vermin. In this form he has to live for a year. Leaving that form he succeeds in regaining his status as a human being of the regenerate order. If the preceptor kills, without reason, his disciple who is even as a son to him, he has, in consequence of such a wilful act of sin on his part, to take birth as a beast of prey. That son who disregards his father and mother, O king, has to take birth, after leaving off his human form as an animal of the asinine order. Assuming the asinine form he has to live for ten years. After that he has to take birth as a crocodile, in which form he has to live for a year. After that he regains the human form. That son with whom his parents become angry, has, in consequence of his evil thoughts towards them, to take birth as an ass. As an ass he has to live for ten months. He has then to take birth as a dog and to remain as

---

[510] Intermediate, i.e., between deities and human beings; hence, animals and birds.
[511] Brahma-Rakshasa is a Rakshasa that belongs, like Ravana and others, by birth to the regenerate order.

such for four and ten months. After that he has to take birth as a cat and living in that form for seven months he regains his status of humanity. Having spoken ill of parents, one has to take birth as a Sarika. Striking them, one has to take birth, O king, as tortoise. Living as a tortoise for ten years, he has next to take birth as a porcupine. After that he has to take birth as a snake, and living for six months in that form he regains the status of humanity. That man who, while subsisting upon the food that his royal master supplies, commits acts that are injurious to the interests of his master,—that man, thus stupefied by folly, has after death to take birth as an ape. For ten years he has to live as an ape, and after that for five years as a mouse. After that he has to become a dog, and living in that form for a period of six months he succeeds in regaining his status of humanity. That man who misappropriates what is deposited with him in trustfulness has to undergo a hundred transformations. He at last takes birth as a vile worm. In that order he has to live for a period of ten and five years, O Bharata. Upon the exhaustion of his great demerit in this way, he succeeds in regaining his status of humanity. That man who harbours malice towards others has, after death, to take birth as a Sarngaka. That man of wicked understanding who becomes guilty of breach of trust has to take birth as a fish. Living as a fish for eight years, he takes birth, O Bharata, as a deer. Living as a deer for four months, he has next to take birth as a goat. After the expiration of a full year he casts off his goatish body, he takes birth then as a worm. After that he succeeds in regaining his status of humanity. That shameless insensate man who, through stupefaction, steals paddy, barley, sesame, Masha, Kulattha, oil-seeds, oats, Kalaya, Mudga, wheat, Atasi, and other kinds of corn, has to take birth as a mouse.[512] After leading the life for some time he has to take birth as a hog. As soon as he takes birth as a hog he has to die of disease. In consequence of his sin, that foolish man has next to take birth as a dog, O king. Living as a dog for five years, he then regains his status of humanity. Having committed an act of adultery with the spouse of another man, one has to take birth as a wolf. After that he has to assume the forms of a dog and jackal and vulture. He has next to take birth as a snake and then as a Kanka and then as a crane.[513] That man of sinful soul who, stupefied by folly, commits an act of sexual congress with the spouse of a brother, has to take birth as a male Kokila and to live in that form for a whole year, O king. He who, through lust, commits an act of sexual congress with the wife of a friend, or the wife of preceptor, or the wife of his king, has, after death, to take the form of a hog. He has to live in his porcine form for five years and then to assume that of a wolf for ten years. For the next five years he has to assume that of a wolf for ten years. For the next five years he has to live as a cat and then for the next ten years as a cock. He has next to live for three months as an ant, and then as a worm for a month. Having undergone these transformations he has next to live as a vile worm for four and ten years. When his sin becomes exhausted by such chastisement, he at last regains the status of humanity. When a wedding is about to take place, or a sacrifice, or an act of gifts is about to be made, O thou of great puissance, the man who offers any obstruction, has to take birth in his next life as a vile worm. Assuming such a form he has to live, O Bharata, for five and ten years. When his demerit is exhausted by such suffering, he regains the status of humanity. Having once bestowed his daughter in marriage upon a person, he who seeks to bestow her again upon a second husband, has, O king, to take birth among vile worms. Assuming such a form, O Yudhisthira, he has to live for a period of three and ten

---

[512] Masha is Phaseolus Roxburghii, Kulatta is Dolichos biflosus, Roxb. Kalaya is Pisum Sativum, Linn. Mudga is Phaseolus Mango, Linn. Atasi is Linum usitattisimam, Linn.

[513] A Kanka is a bird of prey.

years. Upon the exhaustion of his demerit by such sufferance, he regains the status of humanity. He who eats without having performed the rites in honour of the deities or those in honour of the Pitris or without having offered (even) oblations of water to both the Rishis and the Pitris, has to take birth as a crow. Living as a crow for a hundred years he next assumes the form of a cock. His next transformation is that of a snake for a month. After this, he regains the status of humanity. He who disregards his eldest brother who is even like a sire, has, after death, to take birth in the order of cranes. Having assumed that form he has to live in it for two years. Casting off that form at the conclusion of that period, he regains the status of humanity. That Sudra who has sexual intercourse with a Brahmana woman, has, after death, to take birth as a hog. As soon as he takes birth in the porcine order he dies of disease, O king. The wretch has next to take birth as a dog, O king, in consequence of his dire act of sin. Casting off his canine form he regains upon the exhaustion of his demerit, the status of humanity. The Sudra who begets offspring upon a Brahmana woman, leaving off his human form, becomes reborn as a mouse. The man who becomes guilty of ingratitude O king, has to go to the regions of Yama and there to undergo very painful and severe treatment at the hands of the messengers, provoked to fury, of the grim king of the dead. Clubs with heavy hammers and mallets, sharp-pointed lances, heated jars, all fraught with severe pain, frightful forests of sword-blades, heated sands, thorny Salmalis—these and many other instruments of the most painful torture such a man has to endure in the regions of Yama, O Bharata! The ungrateful person, O chief of Bharata's race, having endured such terrible treatment in the regions of the grim king of the dead, has to come back to this world and take birth among vile vermin.[514] He has to live as a vile vermin for a period of five and ten years, O Bharata. He has then to enter the womb and die prematurely before birth. After this, that person has to enter the womb a hundred times in succession. Indeed, having, undergone a hundred rebirths, he at last becomes born as a creature in some intermediate order between man and inanimate nature. Having endured misery for a great many years, he has to take birth as a hairless tortoise. A person that steals curds has to take birth as a crane. One becomes a monkey by stealing raw fish. That man of intelligence who steals honey has to take birth as a gadfly. By stealing fruits or roots or cakes one becomes an ant. By stealing Nishpava one becomes a Halagolaka.[515] By stealing Payasa one becomes in one's next birth a Tittiri bird. By stealing cakes one becomes a screech-owl. That man of little intelligence who steals iron has to take birth as a cow. That man of little understanding who steals white brass has to take birth as a bird of the Harita species. By stealing a vessel of silver one becomes a pigeon. By stealing a vessel of gold one has to take birth as a vile vermin. By stealing a piece of silken cloth, one becomes a Krikara. By stealing a piece of cloth made of red silk, one becomes a Vartaka.[516] By stealing a piece of muslin one becomes a parrot. By stealing a piece of cloth that is of fine texture, one becomes a duck after casting off one's human body. By stealing a piece of cloth made of cotton, one becomes a crane. By stealing a piece of cloth made of jute, one becomes a sheep in one's next life. By stealing a piece of linen, one has to take birth as a hare. By stealing different kinds of colouring matter one has to take

---

[514] He is repeatedly struck with the clubs and hammers and mallets. He is frequently impaled. He is confined with fiery vessels. He is dragged with forests of sword-blades. He is made to walk over heated sand. He is rubbed against thorny Salmalis. The Salmali is the Bombox Malabaricum.

[515] The commentator explains that Nishpava means Rajamasha which is a kind of bears. It is the Dolichas catjung. Halagolaka is a long-tailed worm.

[516] A Krikara is a kind of partridge. It is spelt also as Krikala or Krikana. A Vartaka is a sort of quail.

birth as a peacock. By stealing a piece of red cloth one has to take birth as a bird of the Jivajivaka species. By stealing unguents (such as sandal-paste) and perfumes in this world, the man possessed of cupidity, O king, has to take birth as a mole. Assuming the form of a mole one has to live in it for a period of five and ten years. After the exhaustion of his demerit by such sufferings he regains the status of humanity. By stealing milk, one becomes a crane. That man, O king, who through stupefaction of the understanding, steals oil, has to take birth, after casting off this body, as an animal that subsists upon oil as his form.[517] That wretch who himself well armed, slays another while that other is unarmed, from motives of obtaining his victim's wealth or from feelings of hostility, has, after casting off his human body, to take birth as an ass. Assuming that asinine form he has to live for a period of two years and then he meets with death at the edge of a weapon. Casting off in this way his asinine body he has to take birth in his next life as a deer always filled with anxiety (at the thought of foes that may kill him). Upon the expiration of a year from the time of his birth as a deer, he has to yield up his life at the point of a weapon. Thus casting off his form of a deer, he next takes birth as a fish and dies in consequence of being dragged up in net, on the expiration of the fourth month. He has next to take birth as a beast of prey. For ten years he has to live in that form, and then he takes birth as a pard in which form he has to live for a period of five years. Impelled by the change that is brought about by time, he then casts off that form, and his demerit having been exhausted he regains the status of humanity. That man of little understanding who kills a woman has to go to the regions of Yama and to endure diverse kinds of pain and misery. He then has to pass through full one and twenty transformations. After that, O monarch, he has to take birth as a vile vermin. Living as a vermin for twenty years, he regains the status of humanity. By stealing food, one has to take birth as a bee. Living for many months in the company of other bees, his demerit becomes exhausted and he regains the status of humanity. By stealing paddy, one becomes a cat. That man who steals food mixed with sesame cakes has in his next birth to assume the form of a mouse large or small according to the largeness or smallness of the quantity stolen. He bites human beings every day and as the consequence thereof becomes sinful and travels through a varied round of rebirths. That man of foolish understanding who steals ghee has to take birth as a gallinule. That wicked person who steals fish has to take birth as a crow. By stealing salt one has to take birth as a mimicking bird. That man who misappropriates what is deposited with him through confidence, has to sustain a diminution in the period of his life, and after death has to take birth among fishes. Having lived for some time as a fish he dies and regains the human form. Regaining, however, the status of humanity, he becomes short-lived. Indeed, having committed sins, O Bharata, one has to take birth in an order intermediate between that of humanity and vegetables. Those people are entirely unacquainted with righteousness which has their own hearts for its authority. Those men that commit diverse acts of sin and then seek to expiate them by continuous vows and observances of piety, become endued with both happiness and misery and live in great anxiety of heart.[518] Those men that are of sinful conduct and that yield to the influence of cupidity and stupefaction, without doubt, take birth as Mlechchhas that do not deserve to be associated with. Those men on the other hand, who abstain from sin all their lives, become free from disease of every kind, endued with beauty of form and possessed of wealth. Women also, when they act in the

---

[517] Tailapayin is, literally, one that drinks oil. That name is applied to a cockroach.
[518] Vyathitah and vyadhitah are the correct readings.

way indicated, attain to births of the same kind. Indeed, they have to take births as the spouses of the animals I have indicated. I have told thee all the faults that relate to the appropriation of what belongs to others. I have discoursed to thee very briefly on the subject, O sinless one. In connection with some other subject, O Bharata, thou shalt again hear of those faults. I heard all this, O king, in days of old, from Brahman himself, and I asked all about it in a becoming way, when he discoursed on it in the midst of the celestial Rishis. I have told thee truly and in detail all that thou hadst asked me. Having listened to all this, O monarch, do thou always set thy heart on righteousness."'"

SECTION CXII.

"'Yudhishthira said, "Thou hast told me, O regenerate one, what the end is of unrighteousness or sin. I desire now to hear, O foremost of speakers, of what the end is of Righteousness. Having committed diverse acts of sin, by what acts of people succeed in attaining to an auspicious end in this world? By what acts also do people attain to an auspicious end in heaven?"

"'Vrihaspati said, "By committing sinful acts with perverted mind, one yields to the sway of unrighteousness and as a consequence goeth to hell. That man who, having perpetrated sinful acts through stupefaction of mind, feels the pangs of repentance and sets his heart on contemplation (of the deity), has not to endure the consequences of his sins. One becomes freed from one's sins in proportion as one repents for them. If one having committed a sin, O king, proclaims it in the presence of Brahmanas conversant with duties, one becomes quickly cleansed from the obloquy arising from one's sin. Accordingly as one becomes cleansed therefrom fully or otherwise, like a snake freed from his diseased slough. By making, with a concentrated mind, gifts of diverse kinds unto a Brahmana, and concentrating the mind (on the deity), one attains to an auspicious end. I shall now tell thee what those gifts are, O Yudhisthira, by making which a person, even if guilty of having committed sinful acts, may become endued with merit. Of all kinds of gifts, that of food is regarded as the best. One desirous of attaining to merit should, with a sincere heart, make gifts of food. Food is the life-breath of men. From it all creatures are born. All the worlds of living creatures are established upon food. Hence food is applauded. The deities, Rishis, Pitris, and men, all praise food. King Rantideva, in days of old, proceeded to Heaven by making gifts of food. Food that is good and that has been acquired lawfully, should be given, with a cheerful heart, unto such Brahmanas as are possessed of Vedic lore. That man has never to take birth in an intermediate order, whose food, given with a cheerful heart is taken by a thousand Brahmanas. A person, O chief of men, by feeding ten thousand Brahmanas, becomes cleansed of the piety and devoted to Yoga practices. A Brahmana conversant with the Vedas, by giving away food acquired by him as alms, unto a Brahmana devoted to the study of the Vedas, succeeds in attaining to happiness here. That Kshatriya who, without taking anything that belongs to a Brahmana, protects his subjects lawfully, and makes gifts of food, obtained by the exercise of his strength, unto Brahmanas foremost in Vedic knowledge, with concentrated heart, succeeds by such conduct, O thou of righteous soul, in cleansing himself, O son of Pandu, of all his sinful acts. That Vaisya who divides the produce of his fields into six equal shares and makes a gift of one of those shares unto Brahmanas, succeeds by such conduct in cleansing himself from every sin. That Sudra who, earning food by hard labour and at the risk of life itself, makes a gift of it to Brahmanas, becomes cleansed from every sin. That man who, by putting forth his physical strength, earns food without doing any act of injury to any creature, and makes gift of it unto Brahmanas succeeds in avoiding all calamities. A person by cheerfully making gifts of food acquired by lawful means unto Brahmanas pre-eminent for Vedic lore, becomes cleansed of all his sins. By treading in the path of the righteous one becomes freed from all sins. A person by making gifts of such food as is productive of great energy, becomes himself possessed of great energy. The path made by charitable persons is always trod by those that are endued with wisdom. They that make gifts of food are regarded as givers of life. The merit they acquire by such gifts is eternal. Hence, a person should, under all circumstances, seek to earn food by lawful means, and having earned to make always gifts of it unto deserving men. Food is the great refuge of the world of living creatures. By making gifts of food, one has never to go to hell. Hence, one should always make gifts of food, having earned it by lawful means. The householder should always seek to eat after having made a gift of food unto a Brahmana. Every man should make the day fruitful by making gifts of food.[519] A person by feeding, O king, a thousand Brahmanas all of whom are conversant with duties and the scriptures and the sacred histories, has not to go to Hell and to return to this world for undergoing rebirths. Endued with the fruition of every wish, he enjoys great felicity hereafter. Possessed of such merit, he sports in happiness, freed from every anxiety, possessed of beauty of form and great fame and endued with wealth. I have thus told thee all about the high merit of gifts of food. Even this is the root of all righteousness and merit, as also of all gifts, O Bharata!"'"

SECTION CXIII.

"'Yudhishthira said, "Abstention from injury, the observance of the Vedic ritual, meditation, subjugation of the senses, penances, and obedient services rendered to the preceptors,—which amongst these is fraught with the greatest merit with respect to a person?"

"'Vrihaspati said, "All these six are fraught with merit. They are different doors of piety. I shall discourse upon them presently. Do thou listen to them, O chief of the Bharatas! I shall tell thee what constitutes the highest good of a human being. That man who practises the religion of universal compassion achieves his highest good. That man who keeps under control the three faults, viz., lust, wrath, and cupidity, by throwing them upon all creatures (and practises the virtue of compassion), attains to success.[520] He who, from motives of his own happiness, slays other harmless creatures with the rod of chastisement, never attains to happiness, in the next world. That man who regards all creatures as his own self, and behaves towards them as towards his own self, laying aside the rod of chastisement and completely subjugating his wrath, succeeds in attaining to happiness. The very deities, who are desirous of a fixed abode, become stupefied in ascertaining the track of that person who constitutes himself the soul of all creatures and looks upon them all as his own self, for such a person leaves no track behind.[521] One

---

[519] That day is sterile or lost in which no gift is made of food.

[520] Kama and krodha are mentioned: but the use of cha gives by implication cupidity. What is meant by nidhaya sarvabhuteshu is, dividing them into infinite small parts, to cast them off from oneself to others. It is painful to see how the Burdwan translators misunderstand verses 2 and 3. They read Hanti for Hanta and write ridiculous nonsense.

[521] In the first line, after Sarvabhutani, atmatwena is understood. The sense of this verse seems to be this: such a man leaves no trace behind him, for he becomes identified with Brahma. He is, therefore, said to be apada. The deities on the other hand, are padaishinah, for they desire a fixed abode such as heaven or a spot fraught with felicity.

should never do that to another which one regards as injurious to one's own self. This, in brief, is the rule of Righteousness. One by acting in a different way by yielding to desire, becomes guilty of unrighteousness. In refusals and gifts, in happiness and misery, in the agreeable, and the disagreeable, one should judge of their effects by a reference to one's own self.[522] When one injures another, the injured turns round and injures the injurer. Similarly, when one cherishes another, that other cherishes the cherisher. One should frame one's rule of conduct according to this. I have told thee what Righteousness is even by this subtile way."'

"Vaisampayana continued, 'The preceptor of the deities, possessed of great intelligence, having said this unto king Yudhishthira the just, ascended upwards for proceeding to Heaven, before our eyes.'"

SECTION CXIV.

"Vaisampayana said, 'After this, king Yudhishthira, endued with great energy, and the foremost of eloquent men, addressed his grandsire lying on his bed of arrows, in the following words.'

"'Yudhishthira said, "O thou of great intelligence, the Rishis and Brahmanas and the deities, led by the authority of the Vedas, all applaud that religion which has compassion for its indication. But, O king, what I ask thee is this: how does a man, who has perpetrated acts of injury to others in word, thought and deed, succeed in cleansing himself from misery?"

"'Bhishma said, "Utterers of Brahma have said that there are four kinds of compassion or abstention from injury. If even one of those four kinds be not observed, the religion of compassion, it is said, is not observed. As all four-footed animals are incapable of standing on three legs, even so the religion of compassion cannot stand if any of those four divisions or parts be wanting. As the footprints of all other animals are engulfed in those of the elephant, even so all other religions are said to be comprehended in that of compassion. A person becomes guilty of injury through acts, words and thoughts.[523] Discarding it mentally at the outset, one should next discard in word and thought. He who, according to this rule, abstains from eating meat is said to be cleansed in a threefold way. It is heard that utterers of Brahma ascribe to three causes (the sin of eating meat). That sin may attach to the mind, to words, and to acts. It is for this reason that men of wisdom who are endued with penances refrain from eating meat. Listen to me, O king, as I tell thee what the faults are that attach to the eating of meat. The meat of other animals is like the flesh of one's son. That foolish person, stupefied by folly, who eats meat is regarded as the vilest of human beings. The union of father and mother produces an offspring. After the same manner, the cruelty that a helpless and sinful wretch commits, produces its progeny of repeated rebirths fraught with great misery. As the tongue is the cause of the knowledge or sensation of taste, so the scriptures declare, attachment proceeds from taste.[524] Well-dressed, cooked with salt or without salt, meat, in whatever form one may take it, gradually attracts the mind and enslaves it. How will

---

[522] The sense is that when one refuses a solicitation one should think how one would feel if another were to refuse the solicitations one addressed to that other. So with regard to the rest.

[523] By committing a slaughter, one becomes guilty of it. By inciting others to it one becomes guilty. By mentally committing an act of slaughter, one becomes guilty of it.

[524] i.e. by eating meat, one feels the desire for meat increasing. A taste or predilection for meat is thus created. Hence, the best course is total abstinence.

those foolish men that subsist upon meat succeed in listening to the sweet music of (celestial) drums and cymbals and lyres and harps? They who eat meat applaud it highly, suffering themselves to be stupefied by its taste which they pronounce to be something inconceivable, undescribable, and unimaginable. Such praise even of meat is fraught with demerit. In former days, many righteous men, by giving the flesh of their own bodies, protected the flesh of other creatures and as a consequence of such acts of merit, have proceeded to heaven. In this way, O monarch the religion of compassion is surrounded by four considerations. I have thus declared to thee that religion which comprises all other religions within it."'"

SECTION CXV.

"'Yudhishthira said, "Thou hast told it many times that abstention from injury is the highest religion. In Sraddhas, however, that are performed in honour of the Pitris, persons for their own good should make offerings of diverse kinds of meat. Thou hast said so while discoursing formerly upon the ordinances in respect of Sraddhas. How can meat, however, be procured without slaying a living creature? Thy declarations, therefore, seem to me to be contradictory. A doubt has, therefore, arisen in our mind respecting the duty of abstaining from meat. What are the faults that one incurs by eating meat, and what are the merits that one wins? What are the demerits of him who eats meat by himself killing a living creature? What are the merits of him who eats the meat of animals killed by others? What the merits and demerits of him who kills a living creature for another? Or of him who eats meat buying it of others? I desire, O sinless one, that thou shouldst discourse to me on this topic in detail. I desire to ascertain this eternal religion with certainty. How does one attain to longevity? How does one acquire strength? How does one attain to faultlessness of limbs? Indeed, how does one become endued with excellent indications?"

"'Bhishma said, "Listen to me, O scion of Kuru's race, what the merit is that attaches to abstention from meat. Listen to me as I declare to thee what the excellent ordinances, in truth, are on this head. Those high-souled persons who desire beauty, faultlessness of limbs, long life, understanding, mental and physical strength, and memory, should abstain from acts of injury. On this topic, O scion of Kuru's race, innumerable discourses took place between the Rishis. Listen, O Yudhishthira, what their opinion was. The merit acquired by that person, O Yudhishthira, who, with the steadiness of a vow, adores the deities every month in horse-sacrifices, is equal to his who discards honey and meat. The seven celestial Rishis, the Valakhilyas, and those Rishis who drink the rays of the sun, endued with great wisdom, applaud abstention from meat. The Self-born Manu has said that that man who does not eat meat, or who does not slay living creatures, or who does not cause them to be slain, is a friend of all creatures. Such a man is incapable of being oppressed by any creature. He enjoys the confidence of all living beings. He always enjoys, besides, the approbation and commendation of the righteous. The righteous-souled Narada has said that that man who wishes to increase his own flesh by eating the flesh of other creatures, meets with calamity. Vrihaspati has said that that man who abstains from honey and meat acquires the merit of gifts and sacrifices and penances. In my estimation, these two persons are equal, viz., he who adores the deities every month in a horse-sacrifice for a space of hundred years and he who abstains from honey and meat. In consequence of abstention from meat one comes to be regarded as one who always adores the deities in sacrifices, or as one who always makes gifts to others, or as one who always undergoes the severest austerities. That man who having eaten meat gives it up afterwards, acquires merit by such an act that is so great that a study of all the Vedas or a performance, O Bharata, of all the sacrifices, cannot bestow its like. It is exceedingly difficult to give up meat after one has become acquainted with its taste. Indeed, it is exceedingly difficult for such a person to observe the high vow of abstention from meat, a vow that assures every creature by dispelling all fear. That learned person who giveth to all living creatures the Dakshina of complete assurance comes to be regarded, without doubt, as the giver of life-breaths in this world.[525] Even this is the high religion which men of wisdom applaud. The life-breaths of other creatures are as dear to them as those of one's to one's own self. Men endued with intelligence and cleansed souls should always behave towards other creatures after the manner of that behaviour which they like others to observe towards themselves. It is seen that even those men who are possessed of learning and who seek to achieve the highest good in the form of Emancipation, are not free from the fear of death. What need there be said of those innocent and healthy creatures endued with love of life, when they are sought to be slain by sinful wretches subsisting by slaughter? For this reason, O monarch, know that the discarding of meat is the highest refuge of religion, of heaven, and of happiness. Abstention from injury is the highest religion. It is, again, the highest penance. It is also the highest truths from which all duty proceeds. Flesh cannot be had from grass or wood or stone. Unless a living creature is slain, it cannot be had. Hence is the fault in eating flesh. The deities who subsist upon Swaha, Swadha, and nectar, are devoted to truth and sincerity. Those persons, however, who are for gratifying the sensation of taste, should be known as Rakshasas wedded to the attribute of Passion. That man who abstains from meat, is never put in fear, O king, by any creature, wherever he may be, viz., in terrible wildernesses or inaccessible fastnesses, by day or by night, or at the two twilights, in the open squares of towns or in assemblies of men, from upraised weapons or in places where there is great fright from wild animals or snakes. All creatures seek his protection. He is an object of confidence with all creatures. He never causes any anxiety in others, and himself has never to become anxious. If there were nobody who ate flesh there would then be nobody to kill living creatures. The man who kills living creatures kills them for the sake of the person who eats flesh. If flesh were regarded as inedible, there would then be no slaughter of living creatures. It is for the sake of the eater that the slaughter of living creatures goes on in the world. Since, O thou of great splendour, the period of life is shortened of persons who slaughter living creatures or cause them to be slaughtered, it is clear that the person who wishes his own good should give up meat entirely. Those fierce persons who are engaged in slaughter of living creatures, never find protectors when they are in need. Such persons should always be molested and persecuted even as beasts of prey. Through cupidity or stupefaction of the understanding, for the sake of strength and energy, or through association with the sinful, the disposition manifests itself in men for sinning. That man who seeks to increase his own flesh by (eating) the flesh of others, has to live in this world in great anxiety and after death has to take birth in indifferent races and families. High Rishis devoted to the observance of vows and self-restraint have said that abstention from meat is worthy of every praise, productive of fame and Heaven, and a great propitiation by itself. This I heard in days of old, O son of

---

[525] The sense is this: he who observes the vow of abstention from injury comes to be regarded as the giver of life-breaths in this world. The assurance given to all creatures of never injuring them on any occasion is the Dakshina or Sacrificial present of the great sacrifice that is constituted by universal compassion or abstention from injury.

Kunti, from Markandeya when that Rishi discoursed on the demerits of eating flesh. He who eats the flesh of animals that are desirous of living but that have been killed by either himself or others, incurs the sin that attaches to the slaughter for his act of cruelty. He who purchases flesh slays living creatures through his wealth. He who eats flesh slays living creatures through such act of eating. He who binds or seizes and actually kills living creatures is the slaughterer. Those are the three kinds of slaughter, each of these three acts being so. He who does not himself eat flesh but approves of an act of slaughter becomes stained with the sin of slaughter. By abstaining from meat and showing compassion to all creatures one becomes incapable of being molested by any creature, and acquires a long life, perfect health, and happiness. The merit that is acquired by a person by abstaining from meat, we have heard, is superior to that of one who makes presents of gold, of kine, and of land. One should never eat meat of animals not dedicated in sacrifices and that are, therefore, slain for nothing, and that has not been offered to the gods and Pitris with the aid of the ordinances. There is not the slightest doubt that a person by eating such meat goes to Hell. If one eats the meat that has been sanctified in consequence of its having been procured from animals dedicated in sacrifices and that have been slain for the purpose of feeding Brahmanas, one incurs a little fault. By behaving otherwise, one becomes stained with sin. That wretch among men who slays living creatures for the sake of those who would eat them, incurs great demerit. The eater's demerit is not so great. That wretch among men who, following the path of religious rites and sacrifices laid down in the Vedas, would kill a living creature from desire of eating its flesh, would certainly become a resident of hell. That man who having eaten flesh abstains from it afterwards, attains to great merit in consequence of such abstention from sin. He who arranges for obtaining flesh, he who approves of those arrangements, he who slays, he who buys or sells, he who cooks, and he who eats, are all regarded as eaters of flesh. I shall now cite another authority, depending upon that was declared by the ordainer himself, and established in the Vedas. It has been said that that religion which has acts for its indications has been ordained for householders, O chief of kings, and not for those men who are desirous of emancipation. Manu himself has said that meat which is sanctified with mantras and properly dedicated, according to the ordinances of the Vedas, in rites performed in honour of the Pitris, is pure. All other meat falls under the class of what is obtained by useless slaughter, and is, therefore, uneatable, and leads to Hell and infamy. One should never eat, O chief of Bharata's race, like a Rakshasa, any meat that has been obtained by means not sanctioned by the ordinance. Indeed, one should never eat flesh obtained from useless slaughter and that has not been sanctified by the ordinance. That man who wishes to avoid calamity of every kind should abstain from the meat of every living creature. It is heard that in the ancient Kalpa, persons, desirous of attaining to regions of merit hereafter, performed sacrifices with seeds, regarding such animals as dedicated by them. Filled with doubts respecting the propriety of eating flesh, the Rishis asked Vasu the ruler of the Chedis for solving them. King Vasu, knowing that flesh is inedible, answered that is was edible, O monarch. From that moment Vasu fell down from the firmament on the earth. After this he once more repeated his opinion, with the result that he had to sink below the earth for it. Desirous of benefiting all men, the high-souled Agastya, by the aid of his penances, dedicated, once for all, all wild animals of the deer species to the deities. Hence, there is no longer any necessity of sanctifying those animals for offering them to the deities and the Pitris. Served with flesh according to the ordinance, the Pitris become gratified. Listen to me, O king of kings, as I tell thee this, O sinless one. There is complete happiness in abstaining from meat, O monarch. He that undergoes severe austerities for a hundred years and he that abstains from meat, are both equal in point of merit. Even this is my opinion, In the lighted fortnight of the month of Karttika in especial, one should abstain from honey and meat. In this, it has been ordained, there is great merit. He who abstains from meat for the four months of the rains acquires the four valued blessings of achievements, longevity, fame and might. He who abstains for the whole month of Karttika from meat of every kind, transcends all kinds of woe and lives in complete happiness. They who abstain from flesh by either months or fortnights at a stretch have the region of Brahma ordained for them in consequence of their abstention from cruelty. Many kings in ancient days, O son of Pritha, who had constituted themselves the souls of all creatures and who were conversant with the truths of all things, viz., Soul and Not-soul, had abstained from flesh either for the whole of the month of Karttika or for the whole of the lighted fortnight in that month. They were Nabhaga and Amvarisha and the high-souled Gaya and Ayu and Anaranya and Dilipa and Raghu and Puru and Kartavirya and Aniruddha and Nahusha and Yayati and Nrigas and Vishwaksena and Sasavindu and Yuvanaswa and Sivi, the son of Usinara, and Muchukunda and Mandhatri, and Harischandra. Do thou always speak the truth. Never speak an untruth. Truth is an eternal duty. It is by truth that Harischandra roves through heaven like a second Chandramas. These other kings also, viz., Syenachitra, O monarch, and Somaka and Vrika and Raivata and Rantideva and Vasu and Srinjaya, and Dushmanta and Karushma and Rama and Alarka and Nala, and Virupaswa and Nimi and Janaka of great intelligence, and Aila and Prithu and Virasena, and Ikshvaku, and Sambhu, and Sweta, and Sagara, and Aja and Dhundhu and Suvahu, and Haryaswa and Kshupa and Bharata, O monarch, did not eat flesh for the month of Karttika and as the consequence thereof attained to heaven, and endued with prosperity, blazed forth with effulgence in the region of Brahman, adored by Gandharvas and surrounded by thousand damsels of great beauty. Those high-souled men who practise this excellent religion which is characterised by abstention from injury succeed in attaining to a residence in heaven. These righteous men who, from the time of birth, abstain from honey and meat and wine, are regarded as Munis. That man who practises this religion consisting of abstention from meat or who recites it for causing others to hear it, will never have to go to hell even if he be exceedingly wicked in conduct in other respects. He, O king, who (often-times) reads these ordinances about abstention from meat, that are sacred and adored by the Rishis, or hears it read, becomes cleansed of every sin and attains to great felicity in consequence of the fruition of every wish. Without doubt, he attains also to a position of eminence among kinsmen. When afflicted with calamity, he readily transcends it. When obstructed with impediments, he succeeds in freeing himself from them with the utmost ease. When ill with disease, he becomes cured speedily, and afflicted with sorrow he becomes liberated from it with greatest ease. Such a man has never to take birth in the intermediate order of animals or birds. Born in the order of humanity, he attains to great beauty of person. Endued with great prosperity, O chief of Kuru's race, he acquires great fame as well. I have thus told thee, O king, all that should be said on the subject of abstention from meat, together with the ordinances respecting both the religion of Pravritti and Nivritti as framed by the Rishis.""

SECTION CXVI.

"'Yudhishthira said, "Alas, those cruel men, who, discarding diverse kinds of food, covet only flesh, are really like great Rakshasas! Alas, they do not relish diverse kinds of cakes and diverse sorts of potherbs and various species of Khanda with juicy flavour so much as they do flesh! My understanding, for this reason, becomes stupefied in this matter. I think, when such is the case, that, there is nothing which can compare with flesh in the matter of taste. I desire, therefore, O puissant one, to hear what the merits are of abstention from flesh, and the demerits that attach to the eating of flesh, O chief of Bharata's race. Thou art conversant with every duty. Do thou discourse to me in full agreeably to the ordinances on duty, on this subject. Do tell me what, indeed, is edible and what inedible. Tell me, O grandsire, what is flesh, of what substances it is, the merits that attach to abstention from it, and what the demerits are that attach to the eating of flesh."

"'Bhishma said, "It is even so, O mighty-armed one, as thou sayest. There is nothing on earth that is superior to flesh in point of taste. There is nothing that is more beneficial then flesh to persons that are lean, or weak, or afflicted with disease, or addicted to sexual congress or exhausted with travel. Flesh speedily increases strength. It produces great development. There is no food, O scorcher of foes, that is superior to flesh. But, O delighter of the Kurus, the merits are great that attach to men that abstain from it. Listen to me as I discourse to thee on it. That man who wished to increase his own flesh by the flesh of another living creature is such that there is none meaner and more cruel than he. In this world there is nothing that is dearer to a creature than his life. Hence (instead of taking that valuable possession), one should show compassion to the lives of others as one does to one's own life. Without doubt, O son, flesh has its origin in the vital seed. There is great demerit attaching to its eating, as, indeed, there is merit in abstaining from it. One does not, however, incur any fault by eating flesh sanctified according to the ordinances of the Vedas. The audition is heard that animals were created for sacrifice. They who eat flesh in any other way are said to follow the Rakshasa practice. Listen to me as I tell thee what the ordinance is that has been laid down for the Kshatriyas. They do not incur any fault by eating flesh that has been acquired by expenditure of prowess. All deer of the wilderness were dedicated to the deities and the Pitris in days of old, O king, by Agastya. Hence, the hunting of deer is not censured. There can be no hunting without risk of one's own life. There is equality of risk between the slayer and the slain. Either the animal is killed or it kills the hunter. Hence, O Bharata, even royal sages betake themselves to the practice of hunting. By such conduct they do not become stained with sin. Indeed, the practice is not regarded as sinful. There is nothing, O delighter of the Kurus, that is equal in point of merit, either here or hereafter, to the practice of compassion to all living creatures. The man of compassion has no fear. Those harmless men that are endued with compassion have both this world and the next. Persons conversant with duty say that that Religion is worthy of being called Religion which has abstention from cruelty for its indication. The man of cleansed soul should do only such acts as have compassion for their soul. That flesh which is dedicated in sacrifices performed in honour of the deities and the Pitris is called Havi (and, as such, is worthy of being eaten). That man who is devoted to compassion and who behaves with compassion towards others, has no fear to entertain from any creature. It is heard that all creatures abstain from causing any fear unto such a creature. Whether he is wounded or fallen down or prostrated or weakened or bruised, in whatever state he may be, all creatures protect him. Indeed, they do so, under all circumstances, whether he is on even or uneven ground. Neither snakes nor wild animals, neither Pisachas nor Rakshasas, ever slay him. When circumstances of fear arise, he becomes freed from fear who frees others from situations of fear. There has never been, nor will there ever be, a gift that is superior to the gift of life. It is certain that there is nothing dearer to oneself than one's life. Death, O Bharata, is a calamity or evil unto all creatures. When the time comes for Death, a trembling of the whole frame is seen in all creatures. Enduring birth in the uterus, decrepitude and afflictions of diverse kinds, in this ocean of the world, living creatures may be seen to be continually going forward and coming back. Every creature is afflicted by death. While dwelling in the uterus, all creatures are cooked in the fluid juices, that are alkaline and sour and bitter, of urine and phlegm and faeces,—juices that produce painful sensations and are difficult to bear. There in the uterus, they have to dwell in a state of helplessness and are even repeatedly torn and pierced. They that are covetous of meat are seen to be repeatedly cooked in the uterus in such a state of helplessness. Attaining to diverse kinds of birth, they are cooked in the hell called Kumbhipaka. They are assailed and slain, and in this way have to travel repeatedly. There is nothing so dear to one as one's life when one comes to this world. Hence, a person of cleansed soul should be compassionate to all living creatures. That man, O king, who abstains from every kind of meat from his birth, without doubt, acquires a large space in Heaven. They who eat the flesh of animals who are desirous of life, are themselves eaten by the animals they eat, without doubt. Even this is my opinion. 'Since he hath eaten me, I shall eat him in return,'—even this, O Bharata, constitutes the character as Mansa of Mansa.[526] The slayer is always slain. After him the eater meets with the same fate. He who acts with hostility towards another (in this life) becomes the victim of similar acts done by that other. Whatever acts one does in whatever bodies, one has to suffer the consequences thereof in those bodies.[527] Abstention from cruelty is the highest Religion. Abstention from cruelty is the highest self-control. Abstention from cruelty is the highest gift. Abstention from cruelty is the highest penance. Abstention from cruelty is the highest sacrifice. Abstention from cruelty is the highest puissance. Abstention from cruelty is the highest friend. Abstention from cruelty is the highest happiness. Abstention from cruelty is the highest truth. Abstention from cruelty is the highest Sruti. Gifts made in all sacrifices, ablutions performed in all sacred waters, and the merit that one acquires from making all kinds of gifts mentioned in the scriptures,—all these do not come up to abstention from cruelty (in point of the merit that attaches to it). The penances of a man that abstains from cruelty are inexhaustible. The man that abstains from cruelty is regarded as always performing sacrifices. The man that abstains from cruelty is the father and mother of all creatures. Even these, O chief of Kuru's race, are some of the merits of abstention from cruelty. Altogether, the merits that attach to it are so many that they are incapable of being exhausted even if one were to speak for a hundred years.'"

---

[526] Mansa is flesh. This verse explains the etymology of the word, Mam (me) sa; Me he eateth, therefore, I shall eat him. The words following Me he should be supplied in order to get at the meaning.

[527] The sense is this: one, while endued with a human body injures another, the consequences of that injury the doer will suffer in his human body. One becomes a tiger and slays a deer. The consequences of that act one will have to endure while one becomes reborn as a tiger.

SECTION CXVII.

"'Yudhishthira said, "Desiring to die or desiring to live, many persons give up their lives in the great sacrifice (of battle). Tell me, O grandsire, what is the end that these attain to. To throw away life in battle is fraught with sorrow for men. O thou of great wisdom, thou knowest that to give up life is difficult for men whether they are in prosperity, or adversity, in felicity or calamity. In my opinion, thou art possessed of omniscience. Do thou tell me the reason of this."

"'Bhishma said, "In prosperity or adversity, in happiness or woe, living creatures, O lord of the earth, coming into this world, live according to a particular tenor. Listen to me as I explain the reason to thee. The question thou hast asked me is excellent, O Yudhishthira! In this connection, O king, I shall explain to thee the old narrative of the discourse that took place in former times between the Island-born Rishi and a crawling worm. In days of old, when that learned Brahmana, viz., the Island-born Krishna, having identified himself with Brahma, roamed over the world, he beheld, on a road over which cars used to pass, a worm moving speedily. The Rishi was conversant with the course of every creature and the language of every animal. Possessed of omniscience, he addressed the worm he saw in these words.

"'"Vyasa said, 'O worm, thou seemest to be exceedingly alarmed, and to be in great haste. Tell me, whither dost thou run, and whence hast thou been afraid.'

"'"The worm said, 'Hearing the rattle of yonder large car I am filled with fear. O thou of great intelligence, fierce is the roar it makes. It is almost come! The sound is heard. Will it not kill me? It is for this that I am flying away. The sound, as it is heard from a near point, I catch, of the bulls I hear. They are breathing hard under the whip of the driver, as they are drawing the heavy burden. I hear also the diverse sounds made by the men who are driving the bulls. Such sounds are incapable of being heard by a creature that like us has taken his birth in the order of worms. It is for this reason that I am flying from this situation of great fright. Death is felt by all creatures to be fraught with pain. Life is an acquisition difficult to make. Hence, I fly away in fear, I do not wish to pass from a state of happiness to one of woe.'"

"'Bhishma continued, "Thus addressed, the Island-born Vyasa said, 'O worm, whence can be thy happiness? Thou belongest to the intermediate order of being. I think, death would be fraught with happiness to thee! Sound, touch, taste, scent, and diverse kinds of excellent enjoyments are unknown to thee, O worm! I think, death will prove a benefit to thee!'

"'"The worm said, 'A living creature, in whatever situation he may be placed, becomes attached to it. In even this order of being I am happy, I think, O thou of great wisdom! It is for this that I wish to live. In even this condition, every object of enjoyment exists for me according to the needs of my body. Human beings and those creatures that spring from immobile objects have different enjoyments. In my former life I was a human being. O puissant one, I was a Sudra possessed of great wealth. I was not devoted to the Brahmanas. I was cruel, vile in conduct, and a usurer. I was harsh in speech. I regarded cunning as wisdom. I hated all creatures. Taking advantage of pretexts in compacts made between myself and others, I was always given to taking away what belonged to others. Without feeding servants and guests arrived at my house, I used to fill, when hungry, my own stomach, under the impulse of pride, covetous of good food. Greedy I was of wealth, I never dedicated, with faith and reverence, any food to the deities and the Pitris although duty required me to dedicate food unto them. Those men that came to me, moved by fear, for seeking my protection, I sent adrift without giving them any protection. I did not extend my protection to those that came to me with prayers for dispelling their fear. I used to feel unreasonable envy at seeing other people's wealth, and corn, and spouses held dear by them, and articles of drink, and good mansions. Beholding the happiness of others, I was filled with envy and I always wished them poverty. Following that course of conduct which promised to crown my own wishes with fruition, I sought to destroy the virtue, wealth, and pleasures of other people. In that past life of mine, I committed diverse deeds largely fraught with cruelty and such other passions. Recollecting those acts I am filled with repentance and grief even as one is filled with grief at the loss of one's dear son. In consequence of these acts of mine I do not know what the fruits are of good deeds. I, however, worshipped my old mother and on one occasion worshipped a Brahmana. Endued with birth and accomplishments, that Brahmana, in course of his wanderings, came to my house once as a guest. I received him with reverent hospitality. In consequence of the merit attaching to that act, my memory has not forsaken me. I think that in consequence of that act I shall once more succeed in regaining happiness. O thou of ascetic wealth, thou knowest everything. Do thou in kindness tell me what is for my good."'"

SECTION CXVIII.

"'"Vyasa said, 'It is in consequence of a meritorious act, O worm, that thou, though born in the intermediate order of being, art not stupefied. That act is mine, O worm, in consequence of which thou art not stupefied.[528] In consequence of the puissance of my penances, I am able to rescue a being of demerit by granting him a sight only of my person. There is no stronger might than the might that attaches to penances. I know, O worm, that thou hast taken birth in the order of worms through the evil acts of thy past life. If, however, thou thinkest of attaining to righteousness and merit, thou mayst again attain to it. Deities as well as beings crowned with ascetic success, enjoy or endure the consequence of acts done by them in this field of action. Amongst men also, when acts of merit are performed, they are performed from desire of fruit (and not with disregard for fruit). The very accomplishment that one seeks to acquire are sought from desire of the happiness they will bring.[529] Learned or ignorant (in a former life) the creature that is, in this life, destitute of speech and understanding and hands and feet, is really destitute of everything.[530] He that becomes a superior Brahmana adores, while alive, the deities of the sun and the moon, uttering diverse sacred Mantras. O worm, thou shalt attain to that state of existence. Attaining to that status, thou wilt enjoy all the elements converted into articles of enjoyment. When thou hast attained to that state, I shall impart to thee Brahma. Or, if thou wishest, I may place thee in any other status!' The worm, agreeing to the words of Vyasa, did not leave the road, but remained on it. Meanwhile, the large vehicle

---

[528] What the sage says is that the fact of the worm's being able to recollect the incidents of his past life is due to some meritorious act. That meritorious act is the very sight of the sage which the worm has been fortunate to obtain.

[529] The sense is that among human beings also, acts are done with the intention of securing happiness. In other words, human beings also enjoy the fruits of their good acts and endure those of their evil ones.

[530] Literally, the verse runs,—'what is that which would forsake a creature that is destitute of etc.,' meaning that such a creature has been already forsaken by everything. Hence, 'the worm that is destitute of speech, etc.' is destitute of everything. Its condition is really fraught with great misery.

which was coming in that direction came to that spot.[531] Torn to pieces by the assault of the wheels, the worm gave up his life-breath. Born at last in the Kshatriya order through the grace of Vyasa of immeasurable puissance, he proceeded to see the great Rishi. He had, before becoming a Kshatriya, to pass through diverse orders of being, such as hedgehog and Iguana and boar and deer and bird, and Chandala and Sudra and Vaisya. Having given an account of his various transformations unto the truth-telling Rishi, and remembering the Rishi's kindness for him, the worm (now transformed into a Kshatriya) with joined palms fell at the Rishi's feet and touched them with his head.

""""The worm said, 'My present status is that high one which is coveted by all and which is attainable by the possession of the ten well-known attributes. Indeed, I who was formerly a worm have thus attained to the status of a prince. Elephants of great strength, decked with golden chains, bear me on their backs. Unto my cars are yoked Kamvoja steeds of high mettle. Numerous vehicles, unto which are attached camels and mules, bear me. With all my relatives and friends I now eat food rich with meat. Worshipped by all, I sleep, O highly blessed one, on costly beds in delightful rooms into which disagreeable winds cannot blow. Towards the small hours of every night, Sutas and Magadhas and encomiasts utter my praises even as the deities utter the agreeable praises of Indra, their chief. Through the grace of thyself that art firm in truth and endued with immeasurable energy, I who was before a worm have now become a person of the royal order. I bow my head to thee, O thou of great wisdom. Do thou command me as to what I should do now. Ordained by the puissance of thy penances, even this happy status hath now become mine!'

""""Vyasa said, 'I have today been worshipped by thee, O king, with diverse words expressive of reverence. Transformed into a worm, thy memory had become clouded. That memory has again appeared. The sin thou committed in a former life has not yet been destroyed,—that sin, viz., which was earned by thee while thou wert a Sudra covetous of wealth and cruel in behaviour and hostile to the Brahmanas. Thou wert able to obtain a sight of my person. That was an act of merit to thee while thou wert a worm. In consequence of thy having saluted and worshipped me thou shalt rise higher, for, from the Kshatriya order thou shalt rise to the status of a Brahmana, if only thou castest off thy life-breaths on the field of battle for the sake of kine or Brahmanas. O prince, enjoying much felicity and performing many sacrifices with copious presents, thou shalt attain to heaven and transformed into eternal Brahma, thou wilt have perfect beatitude. Those that take birth in the intermediate order (of animals) become (when they rise) Sudras. The Sudra rises to the status of the Vaisya; and the Vaisya to that of the Kshatriya. The Kshatriya who takes pride in the discharge of the duties of his order, succeeds in attaining to the status of a Brahmana. The Brahmana, by following a righteous conduct, attains to heaven that is fraught with great felicity."""""

SECTION CXIX.

"'Bhishma said, "Having cast off the status of a worm and taken birth as a Kshatriya of great energy, the person (of whom I am speaking), remembering his previous transformations, O monarch, began to undergo severe austerities. Beholding those severe austerities of the Kshatriya who was well-conversant with religion and wealth, the Island-born Krishna, that foremost of Brahmanas, went to him.

---

[531] Jugupsita smritih jata is the paraphrase.

""Vyasa said, 'The penances that appertain, O worm, to the Kshatriya order consist of the protection of all creatures. Do thou regard these duties of the Kshatriya order to be the penances laid down for thee. Thou shalt then attain to the status of a Brahmana. Ascertaining what is right and what is wrong, and cleansing thy soul, do thou duly cherish and protect all creatures, judiciously gratifying all good desires and correcting all that is unholy. Be thou of cleansed soul, be thou contented and be thou devoted to the practice of righteousness. Conducting thyself in this way, thou wilt then, when thou castest off thy life-breaths, become a Brahmana!'"

"'Bhishma continued, "Although he had retired into the woods, yet, O Yudhishthira, having heard the words of the great Rishi he began to cherish and protect his subjects righteously. Soon, O best of kings, that worm, in consequence of the due discharge of the duty of protecting his subjects, became a Brahmana after casting off his Kshatriya body. Beholding him transformed into a Brahmana, the celebrated Rishi, viz., the Island-born Krishna of great wisdom, came to him.

""Vyasa said, 'O chief of Brahmanas, O blessed one, be not troubled (through fear of death)! He who acts righteously attains to respectable birth. He, on the other hand, who acts unrighteously attains to a low and vile birth, O thou that art conversant with righteousness, one attains to misery agreeably the measure of one's sin. Therefore, O worm, do not be troubled through fear of death. The only fear thou shouldst entertain is about the loss of righteousness. Do thou, therefore, go on practising righteousness.'

""The worm said, 'Through thy grace, O holy one, I have attained from happy to happier positions! Having obtained such prosperity as has its roots in righteousness, I think, my demerits have been lost.'"

"'Bhishma said, "The worm having, at the command of the holy Rishi, attained to the status of a Brahmana that is so difficult to attain, caused the earth to be marked with a thousand sacrificial stakes. That foremost of all persons conversant with Brahma then obtained a residence in the region of Brahman himself. Indeed, O son of Pritha, the worm attained to the highest status, viz., that of eternal Brahma, as the result of his own acts done in obedience to the counsels of Vyasa. Those bulls among Kshatriyas, also, who have cast off their life-breaths (on the field of Kurukshetra) exerting their energy the while, have all attained to a meritorious end. Therefore O king, do not mourn on their account."""

SECTION CXX.

"'Yudhishthira said, "Which amongst these three is superior, viz., knowledge, penances, and gifts? I ask thee, O foremost of righteous persons! Do tell me this, O grandsire!"

"'Bhishma said, "In this connection is cited the old narrative of the conversation between Maitreya and the Island-born Krishna. Once on a time, the Island-born Krishna, O king, while wandering over the world in disguise, proceeded to Baranasi and waited upon Maitreya who belonged by birth to a race of Munis.[532] Seeing Vyasa arrive, that foremost of Rishis, viz., Maitreya, gave him a seat and after worshipping him with due rites, fed him with excellent food. Having eaten that good food which was very wholesome and which produced every kind of gratification, the high-souled Krishna

---

[532] Swairini-kule implies, as the commentator explains, the race of Munis. Swam (Dharamaya) irayati is the etymology. Ajnata-charitam-dharan applied to Krishna-Dwaipayana. If it be read charam it would refer to Maitreya.

became exceedingly delighted and as he sat there, he even laughed aloud. Seeing Krishna laugh, Maitreya addressed him, saying, 'Tell me, O righteous-souled one, what the reason is of thy laughter! Thou art an ascetic, endued with capacity to control thy emotions. Great joy, it seems, has come over thee! Saluting thee, and worshipping thee with bent head, I ask thee this, viz., what the puissance is of my penances and what the high blessedness is that is thine! The acts I do are different from those which thou doest. Thou art already emancipated though still owning life-breaths. I, however, am not yet freed. For all that I think that there is not much difference between thee and me. I am again, distinguished by birth.'[533]

""Vyasa said, 'This wonder that has filled me hath arisen from an ordinance that looks like a hyperbole, and from its paradoxical statement for the comprehension of the people. The declaration of the Vedas seems to be untrue. But why should the Vedas say an untruth? It has been said that there are three tracks which constitute the best vows of a man. One should never injure; one should always tell the truth; and one should make gifts. The Rishis of old announced this, following the declarations of the Vedas. These injunctions were heard in days of old,—they should certainly be followed by us even in our times. Even a small gift, made under the circumstances laid down, produces great fruits.[534] Unto a thirsty man thou hast given a little water with a sincere heart. Thyself thirsty and hungry, thou hast, by giving me such food, conquered many high regions of felicity, O puissant one, as, one does by many sacrifices. I am exceedingly delighted with thy very sacred gift, as also with thy penances. Thy puissance is that of Righteousness: Thy appearance is that of Righteousness. The fragrance of Righteousness is about thee. I think that all thy acts are performed agreeably to the ordinance. O son, superior to ablutions in sacred waters, superior to the accomplishment of all Vedic vows, is gift. Indeed, O Brahmana, gift is more auspicious than all sacred acts. If it be not more meritorious than all sacred acts, there can be no question about its superiority. All those rites laid down in the Vedas which thou applaudest do not come up to gift, for gift without doubt, is as I hold, fraught with very superior merit. The track that has been made by those men who make gifts is the track that is trodden by the wise. They who make gifts are regarded as givers of even the life-breaths. The duties that constitute Righteousness are established in them. As the Vedas when well-studied, as the restraining of the senses, as a life of universal Renunciation, even so is gift which is fraught with very superior merit. Thou, O son, wilt rise from joy to greater joy in consequence of thy having betaken thyself to the duty of making gifts. The man of intelligence (who practises this duty) certainly rises from joy to greater joy. We have without doubt, met with many direct instances of this. Men endued with prosperity succeed in acquiring wealth, making gifts, performing sacrifices, and earning happiness as the result thereof. It is always observed, O thou of great wisdom, to happen naturally that happiness is followed by misery and misery is followed by happiness.[535] Men of wisdom have said

[533] Prithagatman implies one whose soul is still invested with upadhis; Sukhatman is one whose soul has transcended all upadhis.

[534] This literal version of the verse yields no sense. The meaning, however, is this: Atichccheda or Atichchanda implies a hyperbolic statement, Ativaua means a paradox. It is said that by gift of even a palmful of water one may attain to a place which is attainable by a hundred sacrifices. This ordinance, which looks like a hyperbole, and its statement by Vedic teachers that looks like a paradox, fill me with wonder. The Vedas say that no one attains to such a place without a hundred sacrifices. This seems to be untrue, for people do reach it by making even slight gifts to deserving persons at proper times.

[535] The sense is that those who pursue carnal pleasures meet with misery as the end, and those who practise austerities meet with felicity as their reward.

that human beings in this world have three kinds of conduct. Some are righteous, some are sinful, and some are neither righteous nor sinful. The conduct of the person who is devoted to Brahma is not regarded either way. His sins are never regarded as sins. So also the man who is devoted to the duties laid down for him is regarded as neither righteous nor sinful (for the observance of those duties). Those men that are devoted to sacrifices, gifts, and penances, are regarded as righteous. These, however, that injure other creatures and are unfriendly to them, are regarded as sinful. There are some men who appropriate what belongs to others. These certainly fall into Hell and meet with misery. All other acts that men do are indifferent, being regarded as neither righteous nor sinful. Do thou sport and grow and rejoice and make gifts and perform sacrifices. Neither men of knowledge nor those endued with penances will then be able to get the better of thee!'"'"

SECTION CXXI.

"'Bhishma said, "Thus addressed by Vyasa, Maitreya, who was a worshipper of acts, who had been born in a race endued with great prosperity, who was wise and possessed of great learning said unto him these words.

"'"Maitreya said, 'O thou of great wisdom, without doubt it is as thou hast said. O puissant one, with thy permission I desire to say something.'

"'"Vyasa said, 'Whatever thou wishest to say, O Maitreya, do thou say, O man of great wisdom, for I wish to hear thee.'

"'"Maitreya said. 'Thy words on the subject of Gift are faultless and pure. Without doubt, thy soul has been cleansed by knowledge and penances. In consequence of thy soul being cleansed, even this is the great advantage I reap from it. With the aid of my understanding I see that thou art endued with high penances. As regards ourselves we succeed in acquiring prosperity through only a sight of personages like thee I think, that is due to thy grace and flows from the nature of my own acts.[536] Penances, knowledge of the Vedas, and birth in a pure race,—these are the causes of the status which one acquires of a Brahmana. When one has these three attributes, then does he come to be called a regenerate person. If the Brahmana be gratified, the Pitris and the deities are also gratified. There is nothing superior to a Brahmana possessed of Vedic lore. Without the Brahmana, all would be darkness. Nothing would be known. The four orders would not exist. The distinction between Righteousness and Unrighteousness, Truth and Falsehood, would cease. On a well-tilled field, an abundant harvest can be reaped. Even so, one may reap great merit by making gifts unto a Brahmana possessed of great learning. If there were no Brahmanas endued with Vedic lore and good conduct for accepting gifts, the wealth possessed by wealthy people would be useless. The ignorant Brahmana, by eating the food that is offered to him, destroys what he eats (for it produces no merit to him who gives it). The food that is eaten also destroys the eater (for the eater incurs sin by eating what is offered to him). That ought to be properly termed an eatable which is given away to a deserving man, in all other cases, he that takes it makes the donor's gift thrown away and the receiver is likewise ruined for his improperly accepting it. The Brahmana possessed of learning becomes the subjugator of the food that he eats. Having eaten it, he begets other food. The ignorant who eats the food offered to him loses his right to the children he begets, for the latter become his whose food has enabled the progenitor to

---

[536] To obtain a sight of thee is the reward or result of my own acts. A sight of thy person leads to prosperity, through the kindness thou cherishest for us.

beget them. Even this is the subtle fault that attaches to persons eating other people's food when they have not the puissance to win that food. The merit which the giver acquires by making the gift, is equal to what the taker acquires by accepting the food. Both the giver and the acceptor depend equally upon each other. Even this is what the Rishis have said. There where Brahmanas exist, possessed of Vedic lore and conduct, people are enabled to earn the sacred fruits of gifts and to enjoy them both here and hereafter. Those men who are of pure lineage, who are exceedingly devoted to penances, and who make gifts, and study the Vedas, are regarded as worthy of the most reverent worship. It is those good men that have chalked out the path by treading on which one does not become stupefied. It is those men that are the leaders of others to heaven. They are the men who bear on their shoulders the burden of sacrifices and live for eternity."'"

SECTION CXXII.

"'Bhishma said, "Thus addressed, the holy one replied unto Maitreya, saying 'by good luck, thou art endued with knowledge. By good luck, thy understanding is of this kind! They that are good highly applaud all righteous attributes. That personal beauty and youth and prosperity do not succeed in overwhelming thee is due to good luck. This favour done to thee is due to the kindness of the deities. Listen to me as I discourse to thee upon what is even superior (in efficacy) to gift. Whatever scriptures and religious treatises there are, whatever (righteous) inclinations are observable in the world, they have flowed in their due order, agreeably with the lead of the Vedas, according to their due order. Following them I applaud gift. Thou praisest penances and Vedic lore. Penances are sacred. Penances are the means by which one may acquire the Vedas and heaven also. With the aid of penances and of knowledge, one attains to the highest fruits, we have heard. It is by penances that one destroys one's sins and all else that is evil. It has been heard by us that with whatever purpose in view one undergoes penances, one attains the fruition thereof in consequence of those penances. The same may be said of knowledge. Whatever is difficult to accomplish, whatever is difficult to conquer, what is difficult to attain, and whatever is difficult to cross, can all be achieved with the aid of penances. Of all things, penances are possessed of very superior might. The man who drinks alcohol, or he that takes by force what belongs to others, or he that is guilty of foeticide, or he that violates the bed of his preceptor, succeeds in crossing with the aid of penances. Indeed, one becomes cleansed of all these sins through penances. One possessed of all knowledge and, therefore, having true vision, and an ascetic of whatever kind, are equal. One should always bow unto these two.[537] All men who have the Vedas for their wealth should be worshipped. Similarly, all men endued with penances deserve to be worshipped. Those who make gifts obtain happiness hereafter and much prosperity here. Righteous men of this world, by making gifts of food obtain both this world and that of Brahman himself with many other regions of superior felicity. Those men who are adored by all, themselves adore him who makes gifts. Those men that are honoured everywhere themselves honour him who make gifts. Wherever the giver goes, he hears himself praised. He who does acts and he who omits to do them gets each what is proportionate to his acts and omissions. Whether one dwells in the upper regions or in the nether, one always attains to those places to which one becomes entitled by one's acts. As

---

[537] The sense is that an ascetic observant of penances, in whatever stage, and a man possessed of omniscience, are regarded as equal.

regards thyself, thou wilt certainly obtain whatever food and drink thou mayst covet, for thou art endued with intelligence, good birth, Vedic lore, and compassion! Thou art possessed of youth, O Maitreya! Thou art observant of vows. Be thou devoted to Righteousness. Do thou take instructions from me regarding those duties which thou shouldst first follow,—the duties, viz., of householders. In that house in which the husband is gratified with his wedded wife, and the wife gratified with her husband, all auspicious results ensue. As filth is washed away from the body with water, as darkness is dispelled by the splendour of fire even so is sin washed off by gifts and penances. Bless thee, O Maitreya, let mansions be thine! I depart hence in peace. Do thou keep in mind what I have said. Thou shalt then be able to reap many advantages!' Maitreya then walked round his illustrious guest and bowed his head unto him, and joining his hands in reverence said, 'Let blessing be to thee also, O holy one!'"'"

SECTION CXXIII.

"'Yudhishthira said, "O thou that art conversant with all duties, I desire to hear, in detail, what the excellent behaviour is of good and chaste women. Do thou, O grandsire, discourse to me on this."

"'Bhishma said, "Once on a time, in the celestial regions, a lady named Sumana of Kekaya's race addressing Sandili possessed of great energy and conversant with the truth relating to everything and endued with omniscience, said, 'By what conduct, O auspicious lady, by what course of acts, hast thou succeeded in attaining to heaven, purged of every sin? Thou blazest forth with thy own energy like a flame of fire. Thou seemest to be a daughter of the Lord of stars, come to heaven in thy own effulgence. Thou wearest vestments of pure white, and art quite cheerful and at thy ease. Seated on that celestial chariot, thou shinest, O auspicious dame, with energy multiplied a thousandfold. Thou hast not, I ween, attained to this region of happiness by inconsiderable penances and gifts and vows. Do thou tell me the truth'. Thus questioned sweetly by Sumana, Sandili of sweet smiles, addressing her fair interrogatrix, thus answered her out of the hearing of others, 'I did not wear yellow robes; nor barks of trees. I did not shave my head; nor did I keep matted locks on my head. It is not in consequence of these acts that I have attained to the status of a celestial. I never, in heedlessness, addressed any disagreeable or evil speech to my husband. I was always devoted to the worship of the deities, the Pitris, and the Brahmanas. Always heedful I waited upon and served my mother-in-law and father-in-law. Even this was my resolution that I should never behave with deceit. I never used to stay at the door of our house nor did I speak long with anybody. I never did any evil act; I never laughed aloud; I never did any injury. I never disclosed any secret. Even thus did I bear myself always. When my husband, having left home upon any business, used to come back, I always served him by giving him a seat, and worshipped him with reverence. I never ate food of any kind which was unknown to my husband and at which my husband was not pleased. Rising at early dawn I did and caused to be done whatever was brought about and required to be accomplished for the sake of relatives and kinsmen. When my husband leaves home for going to a distant place on any business, I remain at home engaged in diverse kinds of auspicious acts for blessing his enterprise. Verily, during the absence of my husband I never use collyrium, or ornaments; I never wash myself properly or use garlands and unguents, or deck my feet with lac-dye, or person with ornaments. When my husband sleeps in peace I never awake him even if important business required his attention. I was happy to sit by him lying asleep. I never urged my husband to exert more energetically for earning wealth to support his family and relatives. I always kept secrets without disclosing them to others. I used to keep always our premises clean. That woman who with concentrated attention, adheres to this path of duty, becomes the recipient of considerable honours in heaven like a second Arundhati.'"

"'Bhishma continued, "The illustrious and highly blessed Sandili, of righteous conduct, having said these words unto Sumana on the subject of woman's duties towards her husband, disappeared there and then. That man, O son of Pandu, who reads this narrative at every full moon and new moon, succeeds in attaining to heaven and enjoying great felicity in the woods of Nandana."'"

SECTION CXXIV.

"'Yudhishthira said, "Which is of superior efficacy, Conciliation or Gifts? Tell me, O chief of Bharata's race, which of these two is superior in point of efficacy."

"'Bhishma said, "Some become gratified by conciliation, while others are gratified by gifts. Every man, according to his own nature, affects the one or the other. Listen to me, O king, as I explain to thee the merits of conciliation, O chief of Bharata's race, so that the most furious creatures may be appeased by it. In this connection is cited the ancient narrative of how a Brahmana, who had been seized in the forest by a Rakshasa, was freed (with the aid of conciliation). A certain Brahmana, endued with eloquence and intelligence, fell into distress, for he was seized in a lone forest by a Rakshasa who wished to feed on him. The Brahmana, possessed of understanding and learning, was not at all agitated. Without suffering himself to be stupefied at the sight of that terrible cannibal, he resolved to apply conciliation and see its effect on the Rakshasa. The Rakshasa, respectfully saluting the Brahmana so far as words went, asked him this question, 'Thou shalt escape, but tell me for what reason I am pale of hue and so lean!' Reflecting for a brief space of time, the Brahmana accepted the question of the Rakshasa and replied in the following well-spoken words.

"'"The Brahmana said, 'Dwelling in a place that is distant from thy abode, moving in a sphere that is not thy own, and deprived of the companionship of thy friends and kinsmen, thou art enjoying vast affluence. It is for this that thou art so pale and lean. Verily, O Rakshasa, thy friends, though well-treated by thee, are still not well-disposed towards thee in consequence of their own vicious nature. It is for this that thou art pale and lean. Thou art endued with merit and wisdom and a well-regulated soul. Yet it is thy lot to see others that are destitute of merit and wisdom honoured in preference to thyself. It is for this that thou art pale and lean. Persons possessed of wealth and affluence much greater than thine but inferior to thee in point of accomplishments are, verily, disregarding thee. It is for this that thou art pale and lean. Though distressed through want of the means of support, thou art led by the highness of thy soul to disregard such means as are open to thee for drawing thy sustenance. It is for this that thou art pale and lean. In consequence of thy righteousness thou hadst stinted thyself for doing good to another. This other, O righteous Rakshasa, thinks thee deceived and subjugated (by his superior intelligence). It is for this that thou art pale and lean. I think, thou art grieving for those persons who with souls overwhelmed by the lust and wrath are suffering misery in this world. It is for this that thou art pale and lean. Though graced with the possession of wisdom, thou art ridiculed by others who are entirely destitute of it. Verily, persons of wicked conduct are condemning thee. It is for this that thou art pale and lean. Verily, some enemy of thine, with a friendly tongue, coming to thee behaved at first like a righteous person and then has left thee, beguiling thee like a knave. It is for this that thou art pale and lean. Thou art well-conversant with the course of world's affairs. Thou art well-skilled in all mysteries. Thou art endued with capacity. Those who know thee to be such do not yet respect and praise thee. It is for this that thou art pale and lean. Staying in the midst of bad men engaged together in some enterprise, thou hadst discoursed to them, dispelling their doubts. For all that they did not admit thy superior merits. It is for this that thou art pale and lean. Verily, though destitute of wealth and intelligence and Vedic lore, thou desirest yet, with the aid of thy energy alone, to accomplish something great. It is for this that thou art pale and lean. It seems that although thou art resolved to undergo severe austerities by retiring into the forest, yet thy kinsmen art not favourably inclined towards this project of thine. It is for this that thou art pale and lean. Some neighbour of thine, possessed of great wealth and endued with youth and handsome features, verily, covets thy dear spouse. It is for this that thou art pale and lean. The words spoken by thee, even when excellent, in the midst of wealthy men, are not regarded by them as wise or well-timed. It is for this that thou art pale and lean. Some dear kinsman of thine, destitute of intelligence though repeatedly instructed in the scriptures, has become angry. Thou hast not succeeded in pacifying him. It is for this that thou art pale and lean. Verily, somebody, having first set thee to the accomplishment of some object desirable to thee is now seeking to snatch the fruit thereof from thy grasp. It is for this that thou art pale and lean. Verily, though possessed of excellent accomplishments and worshipped by all on that account, thou art yet regarded by thy kinsmen as worshipped for their sake and not for thy own. It is for this that thou art pale and lean. Verily, through shame thou art unable to give out some purpose in thy heart, moved also by the inevitable delay that will occur in its accomplishment. It is for this that thou art pale and lean. Verily, thou desirest, with the aid of thy intelligence, to bring under thy influence, diverse persons with diverse kinds of understandings and inclinations. It is for this that thou art pale and lean.[538] Destitute of learning, without courage, and without much wealth, thou seekest such fame as is won by knowledge and prowess and gifts. Verily, it is for this that thou hast been pale and lean. Thou hast not been able to acquire something upon which thou hast set thy heart for a long time. Or, that which thou seekest to do is sought to be undone by somebody else. It is for this that thou art pale and lean. Verily, without being able to see any fault on thy part, thou hast been cursed by somebody. It is for this that thou art pale and lean.[539] Destitute of both wealth and accomplishments thou seekest in vain to dispel the grief of thy friends and the sorrows of sorrowing men. It is for this that thou art pale and lean. Beholding righteous persons the domestic mode of life, unrighteous persons living according to the forest mode, and emancipated persons attached to domesticity and fixed abodes, thou hast become pale and lean. Verily, thy acts connected with Righteousness, with Wealth, and with Pleasure, as also the well-timed words spoken by thee, do not bear fruit. It is for this that thou art pale and lean. Though endued with wisdom, yet desirous of living, thou livest with wealth obtained by thee in gift from somebody of evil conduct. It is for this that thou art pale and lean. Beholding unrighteousness increasing on every side and righteousness languishing, thou art filled with grief. It is for this that thou art pale and lean. Urged by time thou seekest to please all thy friends even when they are disputing and ranged on sides opposite to one another. It is for this that thou art pale and lean. Beholding persons possessed of Vedic lore

---

[538] Such an object can never be accomplished. Hence thy paleness and leanness.

[539] Though completely innocent, thou hast yet been cursed. The anxiety due to this has made thee so.

engaged in improper acts, and persons of learning unable to keep their senses under control, thou art filled with grief. It is for this that thou art pale and lean.' Thus praised, the Rakshasa worshipped that learned Brahmana in return, and making him his friend and bestowing sufficient wealth upon him in gift, let him off (without devouring him).""''

SECTION CXXV.

"'Yudhishthira said, "Tell me, O grandsire, how a poor man, desirous of achieving his own good, should bear himself after having acquired the status of humanity and come into this region of acts that is so difficult to attain. Tell me also what is the best of all gifts, and what should be given under what circumstances. Tell me, O son of Ganga, who art truly deserving of honour and worship. It behoveth thee to discourse to us on these mysteries."'

"Vaisampayana continued, 'Thus questioned by that famous monarch, viz., the son of Pandu, Bhishma explained (in these words) unto that king these high mysteries appertaining to duty.'

"'Bhishma said, "Listen to me with concentrated attention, O king, as I explain to thee, O Bharata, these mysteries appertaining to duties, after the same manner in which the holy Vyasa had explained them to me in days of yore. This subject is a mystery to the very deities, O monarch. Yama of stainless deeds, with the aid of vows well-observed and Yoga meditation, had acquired the knowledge of these mysteries as the high fruits of his penances.[540] What pleases what deity, what pleases the Pitris, the Rishis, the Pramathas (associates of Mahadeva), the goddess Sri, Chitragupta (the recording assistant of Yama), and the mighty Elephants at the cardinal points of the compass, what constitutes the religion of the Rishis—the religion, which has many mysteries and which is productive of high fruits,—the merits of what are called great gifts, and the merits that attach to all the sacrifices, he who knows these, O sinless one, and knowing acts according to his knowledge, becomes freed from stains if he has stains and acquires the merits indicated. Equal to ten butchers is one oilman. Equal to ten oilmen is one drinker of alcohol. Equal to ten drinkers of alcohol is one courtezan. Equal to ten courtezans is a single (territorial) chief.[541] A great king is said to be equal to half of these all. Hence, one should not accept, gifts from these. On the other hand, one should attend to the science, that is sacred and that has righteousness for its indications, of the aggregate of three (viz., Religion, Wealth, and Pleasure). Amongst these, Wealth and Pleasure are naturally attractive. Hence, one should, with concentrated attention, listen to the sacred expositions of Religion (in particular), for the fruits are very great of listening to the mysteries of Religion. One should certainly hear every topic connected with Religion as ordained by the deities themselves. In it is contained the ritual in respect of the Sraddha in which have been declared the mysteries connected with the Pitris. The mysteries connected with all the deities have also been explained there. It comprehends the duties and practices, productive of great merit, of the Rishis also, together with the mysteries attaching to

---

[540] Yamena praptam is the sense, as explained by the commentator.

[541] The sense is this: one should not accept gifts made by a butcher or slayer of animals. Ten butchers are equal to a single oilman. By accepting a gift from an oilman, therefore, one incurs ten times as much sin as by accepting a gift from a butcher. In this way, the measure of sin goes on increasing according to the ratio given. A Nripa, as explained by the commentator, means here a small chief. A small king is equal to ten thousand butchers. A great king, however, is equal to half of that, i.e., five thousand butchers. In other words, by accepting a gift from a great king, a man incurs as much sin as is a full five thousand times of the sin which is incurred by accepting a gift from a butcher.

them. It contains an exposition of the merits of great sacrifices and those that attach to all kinds of gifts. Those men who always read the scriptures bearing on these topics, those who bear them properly in their mind, and he who, having listened to them, follows them in practice, are all regarded to be as holy and sinless as the puissant Narayana himself. The merits that attach to the gift of kine, those that belong to the performance of ablutions in sacred waters, those that are won by the performance of sacrifices,—all these are acquired by that man who treats guests with reverence. They who listen to these scriptures, they who are endued with faith, and they who have a pure heart, it is well-known, conquer many regions of happiness. Those righteous men who are endued with faith, become cleansed of all stains and no sin can touch them. Such men always increase in righteousness and succeed in attaining to heaven. Once on a time, a celestial messenger, coming to the court of Indra of his own accord, but remaining invisible, addressed the chief of the deities in these words, 'At the command of those two deities who are the foremost of all physicians, and who are endued with every desirable attribute, I have come to this place where I behold human beings and Pitris and the deities assembled together. Why, indeed, is sexual congress interdicted for the man who performs a Sraddha and for him also who eats at a Sraddha (for the particular day)? Why are three rice-balls offered separately at a Sraddha? Unto whom should the first of those balls be offered? Unto whom should the second one be offered? And whose has it been said is the third or remaining one? I desire to know all this.' After the celestial messenger had said these words connected with righteousness and duty, the deities who were seated towards the east, the Pitris also, applauding that ranger of the sky, began as follows.

""The Pitris said, 'Welcome art thou, and blessings upon thee! Do thou listen, O best of all rangers of the sky! The question thou hast asked is a high one and fraught with deep meaning. The Pitris of that man who indulges in sexual congress on the day he performs a Sraddha, or eats at a Sraddha, have to lie for the period of a whole month on his vital seed. As regards the classification of the rice-balls offered at a Sraddha, we shall explain what should be done with them one after another. The first rice-ball should be conceived as thrown into the waters. The second ball should be given to one of the wives to eat. The third ball should be cast into the blazing fire. Even this is the ordinance that has been declared in respect of the Sraddha. Even this is the ordinance that is followed in practice according to the rites of religion. The Pitris of that man who act according to this ordinance become gratified with him and remain always cheerful. The progeny of such a man increases and inexhaustible wealth always remains at his command.'

""The celestial messenger said, 'Thou hast explained the division of the rice-balls and their consignment one after another to the three (viz., water, the spouse, and the blazing fire), together with the reasons thereof.[542] Whom does that rice-ball which is consigned to the waters reach? How does it, by being so consigned, gratify the deities and how does it rescue the Pitris? The second ball is eaten by the spouse. That has been laid down in ordinance. How do the Pitris of that man (whose spouse eats the ball) become the eaters thereof? The last ball goes into the blazing fire. How does that ball succeed in finding its way to thee, or who is he unto whom it goes? I desire to hear this,—that is, what are the ends attained by the rice-balls offered at Sraddhas when thus disposed of by being cast into the water, given to the spouse, and thrown into the blazing fire!'

""The Pitris said, 'Great is this question which thou hast asked. It involves a mystery and is fraught with wonder. We have been exceedingly gratified with thee, O ranger of

---

[542] The reason is the declarations in the scriptures to that effect.

the sky! The very deities and the Munis applaud acts done in honour of the Pitris. Even they do not know what the certain conclusions are of the ordinances in respect of the acts done in honour of the Pitris. Excepting the high souled, immortal, and excellent Markandeya, that learned Brahmana of great fame, who is ever devoted to the Pitris, none amongst them is conversant with the mysteries of the ordinances in respect of the Pitris. Having heard from the holy Vyasa what the end is of the three rice-balls offered at the Sraddha, as explained by the Pitris themselves in reply to the question of the celestial messenger, I shall explain the same to thee. Do thou hear, O monarch, what the conclusions are with respect to the ordinances about the Sraddha. Listen with rapt attention, O Bharata, to me as I explain what the end is of the three rice-balls. That rice-ball which goes into water is regarded as gratifying the deity of the moon. That deity, thus gratified, O thou of great intelligence, gratifies in return the other deities and the Pitris also with them. It has been laid down that the second rice-ball should be eaten by the spouse (of the man that performs the Sraddha). The Pitris, who are ever desirous of progeny, confer children on the woman of the house. Listen now to me as I tell thee what becomes of the rice-ball that is cast into the blazing fire. With that ball the Pitris are gratified and as the result thereof they grant the fruition of all wishes unto the person offering it. I have thus told thee everything about the end of the three rice-balls offered at the Sraddha and consigned to the three (viz., water, the spouse, and the fire). That Brahmana who becomes the Ritwik at a Sraddha constitutes himself, by that act, the Pitri of the person performing the Sraddha. Hence, he should abstain that day from sexual intercourse with even his own spouse.[543] O best of all rangers of the sky, the man who eats at Sraddha should bear himself with purity for that day. By acting otherwise, one surely incurs the faults I have indicated. It cannot be otherwise. Hence, the Brahmana who is invited to a Sraddha for eating the offerings should eat them after purifying himself by a bath and bear himself piously for that day by abstaining from every kind of injury or evil. The progeny of such a person multiply and he also who feeds him reaps the same reward."'

"'Bhishma continued, "After the Pitris said so, a Rishi of austere penances, named Vidyutprabha, whose form shone with splendour like that of the sun, spoke. Having heard those mysteries of religion as propounded by the Pitris, he addressed Sakra, saying, 'Stupefied by folly, men slay numerous creatures born in the intermediate orders, such as worms and ants and snakes and sheep and deer and birds. Heavy is the measure of sin they incur by these acts. What, however, is the remedy?' When this question was asked, all the gods and Rishis endued with wealth of penances and the highly blessed Pitris, applauded that ascetic.

"'"Sakra said, 'Thinking in one's mind of Kurukshetra and Gaya and Ganga and Prabhasa and the lakes of Pushkara, one should dip one's head in water. By so doing one becomes cleansed of all one's sins like Chandramas freed from Rahu. One should bathe in this way for three days in succession and then fast for every day. Besides this, one should touch (after bathing) the back of a cow and bow one's head to her tail.' Vidyutprabha, after this, once more addressing Vasava, said, 'I shall declare a rite that is more subtle. Listen to me, O thou of a hundred sacrifices. Rubbed with the astringent powder of the hanging roots of the banian and anointed with the oil of Priyangu, one should eat the

---

[543] The sense, as explained by the commentator, is this: the Brahmana who becomes the Ritwik and eats at a Sraddha becomes a Pitri of the person performing the Sraddha. Hence, when his identity has been changed, he should, on that day, abstain from sexual congress with even his own spouse. By indulging in such congress, he incurs the sin of adultery.

Shashtika paddy mixed with milk. By so doing one becomes cleansed of all one's sins.[544] Listen now to another mystery unknown to many but which was discovered by the Rishis with the aid of meditation. I heard it from Vrihaspati while he recited it in the presence of Mahadeva. O chief of the deities, do thou hear it with Rudra in thy company, O lord of Sachi! If a person, ascending a mountain, stands there on one foot, with arms upraised and joined together, and abstaining from food looks at a blazing fire, he acquires the merits of severe penances and obtains the rewards that attach to fasts. Heated by the rays of the sun, he becomes cleansed of all his sins. One who acts in this way in both the summer and the winter seasons, becomes freed from every sin. Cleansed of every sin, one acquires a splendour of complexion for all time. Such a man blazes with energy like the Sun or shines in beauty like the Moon!' After this, the chief of the deities, viz., he of a hundred sacrifices, seated in the midst of the gods, then sweetly addressed Vrihaspati, saying these excellent words, 'O holy one, do thou duly discourse on what those mysteries of religion are that are fraught with happiness to human beings, and what the faults are which they commit, together with the mysteries that attach to them!'

""Vrihaspati said, 'They who pass urine, facing the sun, they who do not show reverence for the wind, they who do not pour libations on the blazing fire, they who milk a cow whose calf is very young, moved by the desire of obtaining from her as much milk as possible, commit sins. I shall declare what those faults are, O lord of Sachi! Do thou listen to me. The Sun, Wind, the bearer of sacrificial oblations, O Vasava, and kine who are the mothers of all creatures, were created by the Self-born himself, for rescuing all the worlds, O Sakra! These are the deities of human beings. Listen all of ye to the conclusions of religion. Those wicked men and wicked women who pass urine facing the sun, live in great infamy for six and eighty years. That man, O Sakra, who cherishes no reverence for the wind, gets children that fall away prematurely from the womb of his spouse. Those men who do not pour libations on the blazing fire find that the fire, when they do ignite it for such rites as they wish to perform, refuses to eat their libations.[545] Those men who drink the milk of kine whose calves are very young, never get children for perpetuating their races.[546] Such men see their children die and their races shrink. Even these are the consequences of the acts referred to, as observed by regenerate persons venerable for age in their respective races. Hence, one should always avoid that which has been interdicted, and do only that which has been directed to be done, if one is desirous of achieving prosperity. This that I say unto thee is very true.' After the celestial preceptor had said this, the highly blessed deities, with the Maruts, and the highly blessed Rishis questioned the Pitris, saying, 'Ye Pitris, at what acts of human beings, who are generally endued with little understanding, do ye become gratified? What gifts, made in course of such rites as are gone through for improving the position of deceased persons in the other world, become inexhaustible in respect of their efficacy?[547] By performing what acts can men become freed from the debt they owe to the Pitris? We desire to hear this. Great is the curiosity we feel.'

---

[544] Batakashaya is explained by the commentator as substance that is named by pounding the hanging roots of the banian. The Priyangu here mentioned is not the Aglaia Roxburghiana but the seed called Rajasarshapa, i.e., Brassica juncea; Sinapis ramasa, Roxb. The Shashtika paddy is that which ripens in sixty days.

[545] The sense seems to be that the libations, few and far between, of men who do not daily worship their fire are not borne by the fire to the destined places.

[546] Kshirapah means those that depend on the lacteal sustenance, hence, little children.

[547] Aurddhsadehikam danam means gifts made in course of Sraddhas and other rites that are observed for improving the position of a deceased person.

""""The Pitris said, 'Ye highly blessed ones, the doubt existing in your minds has been properly propounded. Listen as we declare what those acts are of righteous men that gratify us. Bulls endued with blue complexion should be set free. Gifts should be made to us, on the day of the new moon, of sesame seeds and water. In the season of rains, lamps should be lighted. By these acts of men, they can free themselves from the debt they owe to the Pitris.[548] Such gifts never become vain. On the other hand, they become inexhaustible and productive of high fruits. The gratification we derive from them is regarded to be inexhaustible. Those men who, endued with faith, beget offspring, rescue their deceased ancestors from miserable Hell'. Hearing these words of the Pitris, Vriddha-Gargya, possessed of wealth of penances and high energy, became filled with wonder so that the hair on his body stood erect. Addressing them he said, 'Ye that are all possessed of wealth of penances, tell us what the merits are that attach to the setting free of bulls endued with blue complexion. What merits, again, attach to the gift of lamps in the season of rains and the gift of water with sesame seeds?'

""""The Pitris said, 'If a bull of blue complexion, upon being set free, raises a (small) quantity of water with its tail, the Pitris (of the person that has set that bull free) become gratified with that water for full sixty thousand years. The mud such a bull raises with its horns from the banks (of a river or lake), succeeds, without doubt, in sending the Pitris (of the person that sets the animal free) to the region of Soma. By giving lamps in the season of rains, one shines with effulgence like Soma himself. The man who gives lamps is never subject to the attribute of Darkness. Those men who make gifts, on the day of the new moon, of sesame seeds and water, mixed with honey and using a vessel of copper, O thou that art possessed of wealth of penances, are regarded as duly performing a Sraddha with all its mysteries. These men get children of sound health and cheerful minds. The merit acquired by the giver of the Pinda (to the Pitris) takes the form of the growth of his race. Verily, he who performs these acts with faith, becomes freed from the debt he owes to the Pitris. Even thus has been laid down the proper time for the performance of the Sraddha, the ordinance in respect of the rites to be observed, the proper person that should be fed at the Sraddha, and the merits that attach to it.' I have declared everything to thee in due order.""""

SECTION CXXVI.

"'Bhishma said, "The chief of the deities, Indra, after the Pitri has ceased to speak, addressed the puissant Hari, saying, 'O Lord, what are those acts by which thou becomest gratified? How, indeed, do men succeed in gratifying thee?'

""""Vishnu said, 'That which I greatly hate is the detraction of Brahmanas; without doubt, if the Brahmanas are worshipped, I regard myself worshipped. All superior Brahmanas should always be saluted with reverence, after feeding them with hospitality. One should reverence one's own feet also (in the evening). I am gratified with men who act in this way, as also with those who worship and make offerings to the whirl that is noticeable on cowdung (when it first drops from the cow).[549] They who behold a Brahmana that is a dwarf in stature, or a boar that has just risen from water and that bears

---

[548] What is meant by the gift of lamps is the lighting of lamps in the sky. These are placed on long poles which are fastened to the tallest trees.

[549] The commentator explains that when evening comes, one should respectfully salute one's own feet. This custom has certainly died out in Bengal. A whirl is certainly observable on cowdung when it first drops from the cow; but the practice of making offering to it has also died out.

on his head a quantity of mud taken up from the bank, have never to meet with any evil. They become freed from every sin. That man who worships every day the Aswattha (Ficus religiosa) and the substance called Gorochana and the cow, is regarded as worshipping the whole universe with the deities and Asuras and human beings. Verily, staying within these, I accept, in my own form, the worship that is offered to them. The worship that is offered to these is the worship offered to me. This has been so as long as the worlds have been created. Those men of little understanding that worship me in a different way worship me in vain, for the worship of that kind I never accept. Verily, the worship of other kinds is not at all gratifying to me.'

""Indra said, 'Why dost thou applaud the circular marks on cowdung, the feet, the boar, the Brahmana that is a dwarf in stature, and mud raised up from the soil? It is thou who createst and it is thou who destroyest them. Thou art the eternal nature of all mortal or transitory things.'"

"'Bhishma continued, "Hearing these words of Indra, Vishnu smiled a little and then said, 'It was with my circular disc that the Daityas were slain. It was with my two feet that the world was covered. Assuming the form of a boar I slew Hiranyaksha. Assuming the form of a dwarf I conquered (the Asura) king Vali. Those high-souled men who worship these gratify me. Verily, they who worship me in these forms never meet with discomfiture. If one beholding a Brahmana leading the Brahmacharya mode of life arrived at one's house, offers unto him the first portion of one's food that belongs as of right to a Brahmana, and eats what remains thereafter, one is regarded as eating Amrita. If one, after adoring the morning twilight, stands with face directed towards the sun, one reaps the merit that attaches to the performance of ablutions in all tirthas and becomes cleansed of all sins. Ye Rishis possessed of wealth of penances, I have told you in details what constitutes a great mystery. On what else shall I discourse unto you? Tell me your doubts.'

""Baladeva said, 'Listen now to another great mystery that is fraught with happiness to men. Ignorant persons, unacquainted with it, meet with much distress at the hands of other creatures. That man who, rising at early dawn, touches a cow, ghee, and curds, as also mustard seeds and the larger variety thereof called Priyangu, becomes cleansed of all sins. As regards Rishis possessed of wealth of penances, they always avoid all creatures both before and behind, as also all that is impure while performing Sraddhas.'[550]

""The deities said, 'If a person, taking a vessel of copper, filling it with water, and facing the east, resolves upon a fast or the observance of a particular vow, the deities become gratified with him and all his wishes become crowned with success. By observing fasts, or vows in any other way, men of little understandings gain nothing.[551] In uttering the resolution about the observance of fasts and in making offerings to the deities, the use of a vessel of copper is preferable. In presenting the offerings to the deities, in (giving and accepting) alms, in presenting the ingredients of the Arghya and in offering oblations of water mixed with sesame seeds to the Pitris, a vessel of copper should be used. By doing these acts in any other way, one acquires little merit. Even these mysteries have been laid down relating to how the deities are gratified.'

""Dharma said, 'The offerings made in all rites in honour of the deities and in those

---

[550] The second line seems to be unintelligible. The reading I take is Sraddheshu and not Schidreshu.

[551] Vows and fasts, &c., should be observed after the Sankalpa or Resolution to that effect has been formally enunciated. Even a plunge in a piece of sacred water cannot be productive of merit unless the Sankalpa has been formally enunciated. The Sankalpa is the enunciation of the purpose for which the act is performed as also of the act that is intended to be performed.

in honour of the Pitris should never be given away to a Brahmana that has accepted service under the king, or that rings the bell or attends to subsidiary duties in acts of worship or at Sraddhas, or that keeps kine, or that is engaged in trade, or that follows some art as a profession, or that is an actor, or that quarrels with friends or that is destitute of Vedic studies, or that marries a Sudra woman.[552] The performer of the Sraddha who gives away such offerings unto such a Brahmana falls away from prosperity and multiplies not his race. He fails, again, to gratify his Pitris by doing such an act. From the house of that person whence a guest returns unsatisfied, the Pitris, the deities, and the sacred fires, all return disappointed in consequence of such treatment of the guest. That man who does not discharge the duties of hospitality towards the guest arrived at his abode, comes to be regarded as equally sinful with those that are slayers of women or of kine, that are ungrateful towards benefactors, that are slayers of Brahmanas, or that are violators of the beds of their preceptors.'

""Agni said, 'Listen ye with concentrated attention. I shall recite the demerits of that man of wicked understanding who lifts up his feet for striking therewith a cow or a highly blessed Brahmana or a blazing fire. The infamy of such a man spreads throughout the world and touches the confines of heaven itself. His Pitris become filled with fear. The deities also become highly dissatisfied on his account. Endued with great energy, Fire refuses to accept the libations poured by him. For a hundred lives he has to rot in hell. He is never rescued at any time. One should, therefore, never touch a cow with one's feet, or a Brahmana of high energy, or a blazing fire, if one is endued with faith and desires one's own good. These are the demerits declared by me of one who lifts up one's feet towards these three.'

""Viswamitra said, 'Listen to a high mystery that is unknown to the generality of men and that is connected with religion. He who offers the Pitris rice boiled in sugared milk, sitting with face directed to the south at noontide in the shade caused by an elephant's body, in the month of Bhadrapada, under the constellation Magha, acquires great merits. Listen to what those merits are. The man who makes such an offering to the Pitris under such circumstances, is regarded as performing a great Sraddha each year for thirteen years in succession.'[553]

""The kine said, 'That man becomes cleansed of all his sins who adores a cow with these Mantras, viz., 'O Vahula, O Samanga, O thou that art fearless everywhere, O thou that art forgiving and full of auspiciousness, O friend, O source of all plenty, in the region of Brahman, in days of yore, thou wert present with thy calf in the sacrifice of Indra, the wielder of the thunderbolt. Thou tookest thy station in the firmament and in the path of Agni. The deities with Narada among them adored thee on that occasion by calling thee Sarvamsaha. Such man attains to the region of Purandara. He acquires, besides, the merits that attach to kine, and the splendour of Chandramas also. Such a man becomes freed from every sin, every fear, every grief. At the end, he obtains residence in the happy region of the Thousand-eyed Indra!'"

"'Bhishma continued, "After this, the highly blessed and celebrated seven Rishis, with Vasishtha at their head, rose and circumambulating the Lotus-born Brahman, stood

---

[552] Vrishalipati literally means the husband of a Sudra woman. By actually marrying a woman of the lowest order, by marrying before the elder brother, by marrying a girl that has attained to puberty, and by certain other acts, a Brahmana comes to be regarded as a Vrishalipati.

[553] Kutapa is the hour about noontide. The shade of the elephant's body implies a particular instant of time that is regarded as very favourable for the Sraddha. The man that performs such a Sraddha is regarded as acquiring the merits attaching to Sraddhas regularly performed for thirteen years.

around him with hands joined in reverence. Vasishtha, that foremost of all persons conversant with Brahma, became their spokesman and asked this question that is beneficial to every creature, but especially so to Brahmanas and Kshatriyas, 'By doing what acts may men of righteous conduct who are, however, destitute of the good of this world, succeed in acquiring merits attaching to sacrifices?' Hearing this question of theirs, the Grandsire Brahman began to say what follows.

""Brahman said, 'Excellent is this question, ye highly blessed ones! It is at once auspicious and high and fraught with a mystery. This question that ye have put is subtil and is fraught with high benefit to mankind. Ye Rishis possessed of wealth of penances, I shall recite everything to you in detail. Do ye listen with attention to what I say as to how men acquire the merits attaching to sacrifices (even when they are unable to perform them through poverty.) In the lighted fortnight of the month of Pausha, when the constellation Rohini is in conjunction, if one, purifying oneself by a bath, lies under the cope of heaven, clad in a single piece of raiment, with faith and concentrated attention, and drinks the rays of the moon, one acquires the merits that attach to the performance of great sacrifices. Ye foremost of regenerate persons, this is a high mystery that I declare unto you in reply to your questions, ye that are possessed of insight into the subtil truths of all topics of enquiry.''''

SECTION CXXVII.

""Vibhavasu (otherwise called Surya) said, 'There are two offerings. One of those consists of a palmful of water and the other called Akshata consists of rice-grains with ghee. One should, on the day of the full moon, stand facing that bright orb and make unto him the two offerings mentioned, viz., a palmful of water and the rice-grains with ghee called Akshata. The man who presents these offerings is said to adore his sacred fire. Verily, he is regarded as one that has poured libations on the three (principal) fires. That man of little understanding who cutteth down a large tree on the day of the new moon, becomes stained with the sin of Brahmanicide. By killing even a single leaf one incurs that sin. That foolish man who chews a tooth-brush on the day of the new moon is regarded as injuring the deity of the moon by such an act. The Pitris of such a person become annoyed with him.[554] The deities do not accept the libations poured by such a man on days of the full moon and the new moon. His Pitris become enraged with him, and his race and the family become extinct.'

""Sree said, 'That sinful house, in which eating and drinking vessels and seats and beds lie scattered, and in which women are beaten, the deities and Pitris leave in disgust. Verily, without accepting the offerings made unto them by the owners of such houses, the deities and the Pitris fly away from such a sinful habitation.'

""Angiras said, 'The offspring of that man increase who stands every night for a full year under a Karanjaka tree with a lamp for lighting it, and holds besides in his hand the roots of the Suvarchala plant.'[555]

""Gargya said, 'One should always do the duties of hospitality to one's guests. One should give lamps in the hall or shed where sacrifices are performed. One should avoid sleep during the day, and abstain from all kinds of flesh or food. One should never injure

---

[554] In India the tooth-brush consists of a twig or a little branch. One end of it is chewed and softened. The softened fibres serve the purpose of a brush. Such a brush is used only once. It is thrown away after the brushing of the teeth is over.

[555] It is difficult to identify what plants are meant by Karanjaka and Suvarachala.

kine and Brahmanas. One should always recite names of the Pushkara lakes and the other sacred waters. Such a course of duty, is the foremost. Even this constitutes a high religion with its mysteries. If observed in practice, it is sure to produce great consequences. If a person performs even a hundred sacrifices, he is doomed to see the exhaustion of the merits attaching to the libations poured therein. The duties, however, which I have mentioned are such that when observed by a person endued with faith, their merit becomes inexhaustible. Listen now to another high mystery concealed from the view of many. The deities do not accept the libations (poured upon the fire) on the occasion of Sraddhas and rites in their honour or on the occasion of those rites that are performable on ordinary lunar days or on the especially sacred days of the full moon and the new moon, if they behold a woman in her season of impurity or one that is the daughter of a mother afflicted with leprosy. The Pitris of the man who allows such a woman to come near the place where the Sraddha is being performed by him, do not become gratified with him for thirteen years. Robed in raiment of white, and becoming pure in body and mind, one should invite Brahmanas and cause them to utter their benedictions (when one performs the Sraddha). On such occasions one should also recite the Bharata. It is by observing all these that the offerings made at Sraddhas become inexhaustible.'

""'Dhaumya said, 'Broken utensils, broken bedsteads, cocks and dogs, as also such trees as have grown within the dwelling houses, are all inauspicious objects. In a broken utensil is Kali himself, while in a broken bedstead is loss of wealth. When a cock or a dog is in sight, the deities do not eat the offerings made to them. Under the roots of a tree scorpions and snakes undoubtedly find shelter. Hence, one should never plant a tree within one's abode.'[556]

""'Jamadagni said, 'That man whose heart is not pure is sure to go to Hell even if he adores the deities in a Horse-sacrifice or in a hundred Vajapeya sacrifices, or if he undergoes the severest austerities with head downmost. Purity of heart is regarded as equal to sacrifices and Truth. A very poor Brahmana, by giving only a Prastha of powdered barley with a pure heart unto a Brahmana, attained to the region of Brahman himself. This is a sufficient proof (of the importance of purity of heart)."'"

SECTION CXXVIII.

""'Vayu said, 'I shall recite some duties the observance of which is fraught with happiness to mankind. Do ye listen also with concentrated attention to certain transgressions with the secret causes upon which they depend. That man who offers for the four months of the rainy season sesame and water (unto the Pitris), and food, according to the best of his power, unto a Brahmana well-conversant with the duties, who duly pours libations on the sacred fire, and makes offerings of rice boiled in sugared milk, who gives lamps in honour of the Pitris, with sesame and water,—verily he who does all this with faith and concentrated attention acquires all the merits that attach to a hundred sacrifices in which animals are offered to the deities. Listen to this other high mystery that is unknown to all. That man who thinks it all right when a Sudra ignites the

---

[556] Bhanda includes utensils of copper and brass such as plates and cups and jars and jugs. Broken utensils, to this day, are regarded inauspicious. They are rejected, as a rule, by every family. Kali (Evil?) has his abode in them, meaning that such utensils cause quarrels and disputes. Broken bed-steads also are regarded as capable of causing loss of wealth. Cocks and dogs should never be kept or reared in a house. The roots of trees afford shelter to scorpions and snakes and venomous insects and worms. One should not, therefore, plant trees or allow them to grow up within one's abode.

fire upon which he is to pour libations or who does not see any fault when women who are incompetent to assist at Sraddhas and other rites are allowed to assist at them, really becomes stained with sin.[557] The three sacrificial fires become enraged with such a person. In his next life he has to take birth as a Sudra. His Pitris, together with the deities are never gratified with him. I shall now recite what the expiations are which one must go through for cleansing oneself from such sins. Listen to me with attention. By performing those expiatory acts, one becomes happy and free from fever. Fasting all the while, one should, for three days, with concentrated attention, pour libation, on the sacred fire, of the urine of the cow mixed with cowdung and milk and ghee. The deities accept the offerings of such a man on the expiration of a full year. His Pitris also, when the time comes for him for performing the Sraddha, become gratified with him. I have thus recited what is righteous and what is unrighteous, with all their unknown details, in respect of human beings desirous of attaining to heaven. Verily, men who abstain from these transgressions or who having committed them undergo the expiatory rites indicated, succeed in attaining to heaven when they leave this world.'"""

SECTION CXXIX.

"""Lomasa said, 'The Pitris of those men who, without having wedded wives of their own, betake themselves to the wives of other people, become filled with disappointment when the time for the Sraddhas comes. He who betakes himself to the wives of other people, he who indulges in sexual union with a woman that is barren, and he who appropriates what belongs to a Brahmana, are equally sinful. Without doubt, the Pitris of such people cut them off without desiring to have any intercourse with them. The offerings they make fail to gratify the deities and the Pitris. Hence, one should always abstain from sexual congress with women that are the wedded wives of others, as also with women that are barren. The man who desires his own good should not appropriate what belongs to a Brahmana. Listen now to another mystery, unknown to all with regard to religion. One should, endued with faith, always do the bidding of one's preceptor and other seniors. On the twelfth lunar day, as also on the day of the full moon, every month, one should make gifts unto Brahmanas of ghee and the offerings that constitute Akshata. Listen to me as I say what the measure is of the merit that such a person acquires. By such an act one is said to increase Soma and the Ocean. Vasava, the chief of the celestials, confers upon him a fourth part of the merits that attach to a Horse-sacrifice. By making such gifts, a person becomes endued with great energy and prowess. The divine Soma, well-pleased with him, grants him the fruition of his wishes. Listen now to another duty, together with the foundation on which it rests, that is productive of great merit. In this age of Kali, that duty, if performed, brings about much happiness to men. That man who, rising at early dawn and purifying himself by a bath, attires himself in white robes and with the concentrated attention makes gifts unto Brahmanas of vessels full of sesame seeds, who makes offerings unto the Pitris of water with sesame seeds and honey, and who gives lamps as also the food called Krisara acquires substantial merits. Listen to me as I say what those merits are. The divine chastiser of Paka has ascribed these merits to the gift of vessels of copper and brass filled with sesame seeds. He who makes gifts of kine, he who makes gifts of land that are productive of eternal merit, he who performs the

---

[557] A Brahmana's fire should never be ignited by a Sudra. Women also should never be allowed to assist at Sraddhas for arranging the offerings.

Agnishtoma sacrifice with copious presents in the form of Dakshina to the Brahmanas, are all regarded by the deities as acquiring merits equal to those which one acquires by making gifts of vessels filled with sesame seeds. Gifts of water with sesame seeds are regarded by the Pitris as productive of eternal gratification to them. The grandsires all become highly pleased with gifts of lamps and Krisara. I have thus recited the ancient ordinance, laid down by the Rishis, that is highly applauded by both the Pitris and the deities in their respective regions.'"""

SECTION CXXX.

"'Bhishma said, "The Rishis there assembled, together with the Pitris and the deities, then, with concentrated attention, questioned Arundhati (the spouse of Vasishtha) who was endued with great ascetic merit. Possessed of abundant wealth of penances, Arundhati was equal to her husband, the high-souled Vasishtha in energy for in both vows and conduct she was her husband's equal. Addressing her they said, 'We desire to hear from thee the mysteries of duty and religion. It behoveth thee, O amiable lady, to tell us what thou regardest as a high mystery.'

"""Arundhati said, 'The great progress I have been able to achieve in penances is due to your consideration for me in thus remembering my poor self. With your gracious permission I shall now discourse on duties that are eternal, on duties that are high mysteries. I shall discourse thereon with the causes on which they depend. Listen to me as I discourse to you elaborately. A knowledge of these should be imparted unto him only that is possessed of faith or that has a pure heart. These four, viz., he that is bereft of faith, he that is full of pride, he that is guilty of Brahmanicide, and he that violates the bed of his preceptor, should never be talked to. Religion and duty should never be communicated unto them. The merits acquired by a person who gives away a Kapila cow every day for a period of two and ten years, or by a person who adores the deities every month in a sacrifice, or by him who gives away hundreds of thousands of kine in the great Pushkara, do not come up to those that are his with whom a guest is gratified. Listen now to another duty whose observance is fraught with happiness to mankind. It should be observed with its secret ritual by a person endued with faith. Its merits are certainly high. Listen to what they are. If a person, rising at early dawn and taking with him a quantity of water and a few blades of Kusa grass, proceeds into a cow-pen and arriving there washes a cow's horns by sprinkling thereon that water with those blades of Kusa grass and then causes the water to drip down on his own head, he is regarded, in consequence of such a bath, as one that has performed his ablutions in all the sacred waters that the wise have heard to exist in the three worlds and that are honoured and resorted to by Siddhas and Charanas.' After Arundhati had said these words, all the deities and Pitris applauded her, saying, 'Excellent, Excellent,' Indeed, all the beings there were highly gratified and all of them worshipped Arundhati.

"""Brahman said, 'O highly blessed one, excellent is the duty that thou hast enunciated, together with its secret ritual. Praise be to thee! I grant thee this boon, viz., that thy penances will continually increase!'

"""Yama said, 'I have heard from thee an excellent and agreeable discourse. Listen now to what Chitragupta has said and what is agreeable to me. Those words relate to duty with its secret ritual, and are worthy of being heard by the great Rishis, as also by men endued with faith and desirous of achieving their own good. Nothing is lost of either piety or sin that is committed by creatures. On days of the full moon and the new moon, those acts are conveyed to the sun where they rest. When a mortal goes into the region of the dead, the deity of the sun bears witness to all his acts. He that is righteous acquires the fruits of his righteousness there. I shall now tell you of some auspicious duties that are approved by Chitragupta. Water for drink, and lamps for lighting darkness, should always be given, as also sandals and umbrellas and Kapila kine with due rites. In Pushkara especially should one make the gift of a Kapila cow unto a Brahmana conversant with the Vedas. One should also always maintain one's Agnihotra with great care. Here is another duty which was proclaimed by Chitragupta. It behoveth them that are the best of creatures to listen to what the merits are of that duty separately. In course of time, every creature is destined to undergo dissolution. They that are of little understanding meet with great distress in the regions of the dead, for they become afflicted by hunger and thirst. Indeed, they have to rot there, burning in pain. There is no escape for them from such calamity. They have to enter into a thick darkness. I shall now tell you of those duties by performing which one may succeed in crossing such calamity. The performance of those duties costs very little but is fraught with great merit. Indeed, such performance is productive of great happiness in the other world. The merits that attach to the gift of water for drink are excellent. In the next world in especial, those merits are very high. For them that make gifts of water for drink there is ordained in the other world a large river full of excellent water. Indeed, the water contained in that river is inexhaustible and cool and sweet as nectar. He who makes gifts of water in this world drinks from that stream in the world hereafter when he goes thither. Listen now to the abundant merits that attach to the giving of lamps. The man who gives lamps in this world has never to even behold the thick darkness (of Hell). Soma and Surya and the deity of fire always give him their light when he repairs to the other world. The deities ordain that on every side of such a person there should be blazing light. Verily, when the giver of lights repairs to the world of the dead, he himself blazes forth in pure effulgence like a second Surya. Hence, one should give lights while here and water for drink in especial. Listen now to what the merits are of the person who makes the gift of a Kapila cow to a Brahmana conversant with the Vedas, especially if the gift be made in Pushkara. Such a man is regarded as having made a gift of a hundred kine with a bull, a gift that is productive of eternal merit. The gift of a single Kapila cow is capable of cleansing whatever sins the giver may be guilty of even if those sins be as grave. Brahmanicide, for the gift of a single Kapila cow is regarded as equal in point of merit to that of a hundred kine. Hence, one should give away a Kapila cow at that Pushkara which is regarded as the senior (of the two Tirthas known by that name) on the day of the full moon in the month of Karttika. Men that succeed in making such a gift have never to encounter distress of any kind, or sorrow, or thorns giving pain. That man who gives away a pair of sandals unto a superior Brahmana that is deserving of the gift, attains to similar merits. By giving away an umbrella a person obtains comfortable shade in the next world. (He will not have to be exposed to the sun). A gift made to a deserving person is never lost. It is certain to produce agreeable consequences to the giver.' Hearing these opinions of Chitragupta, Surya's hairs stood on their ends. Endued with great splendour, he addressed all the deities and the Pitris, saying 'Ye have heard the mysteries relating to duty, as propounded by the high-souled Chitragupta. Those human beings who, endued with faith, make these gifts unto high-souled Brahmanas, become freed from fear of every kind. These five kinds of men, stained with vicious deeds, have no escape. Verily, of sinful behaviour and regarded as the worst of men, they should never be talked to. Indeed they should always be avoided. Those five are he who is the slayer of a Brahmana, he who is the slayer of a cow, he who is addicted to sexual congress with other people's wives, he who is bereft of faith (in the Vedas), and he who derives his sustenance by selling the virtue of his wife. These men of sinful conduct, when they repair to the region of the dead, rot in hell like worms that live upon pus and blood. These five are avoided by the Pitris, the deities, the Snataka Brahmanas, and other regenerate persons that are devoted to the practice of penances.""'"

SECTION CXXXI.

"'Bhishma said, "Then all the highly blessed deities and the Pitris, and the highly blessed Rishis also, addressing the Pramathas, said,[558] 'Ye are all highly blessed beings. Ye are invisible wanderers of the night. Why do you afflict those men that are vile and impure and that are unclean? What acts are regarded as impediments to your power? What, indeed, are those acts in consequence of which ye become incompetent to afflict men? What are those acts that are destructive of Rakshasas and that prevent you from asserting your power over the habitations of men? Ye wanderers of the night, we desire to hear all this from you.'

""'The Pramathas said, 'Men are rendered unclean by acts of sexual congress. They who do not purify themselves after such acts, they who insult their superiors, they who from stupefaction eat different kinds of meat, the man also who sleeps at the foot of a tree, he who keeps any animal matter under his pillow while lying down for sleep, and he who lies down or sleeps placing the head where his feet should be placed or his feet where the head should be placed,—these men are regarded by us as unclean. Verily, these men have many holes. Those also are numbered in the same class who throw their phlegm and other unclean secretions into the water. Without doubt these men deserve to be slain and eaten up by us. Verily, we afflict those human beings who are given to such conduct. Listen now to what those acts are which are regarded as antidotes and in consequence of which we fail to do any injury to men. Those men upon whose persons occur streaks of Gorochana, or who hold Vachas in their hands, or who make gifts of ghee with those ingredients that go by the name of Akshata, or who place ghee and Akshata on their heads, or those who abstain from meat are incapable of being afflicted by us. That man in whose house the sacred fire burns day and night without being ever put out, or who keeps the skin or teeth of a wolf in his abode or a hill-tortoise, or from whose habitation the sacrificial smoke is seen to curl upwards, or who keeps a cat or a goat that is either tawny or black in hue, is free from our power. Verily, those householders who keep these things in their houses always find them free from the inroads of even the fiercest spirits that live on carrion. Those beings also, that like us range through different worlds in pursuit of pleasure, are unable to do any injury to such houses. Hence, ye deities, should men keep such articles in their houses,—articles that are destructive of Rakshasas (and other beings of the kind). We have thus told you everything about that respecting which ye had great doubts.""'"

---

[558] Pramathas are the ghostly companions of Mahadeva. Literally, the name implies smiters.

SECTION CXXXII.

"'Bhishma said, "After this, the Grandsire Brahman, sprung from the primeval lotus and resembling the lotus (in agreeableness and fragrance), addressed the deities with Vasava, the lord of Sachi, at their head,—'Yonder sits the mighty Naga who is a resident of the nether regions. Endued with great strength and energy, and with great prowess also, his name is Renuka. He is certainly a great being. Those mighty elephants endued with great energy and power, who hold the entire earth with her hills, waters, and lakes should be interviewed by this Renuka at your request. Let Renuka go to them and ask them about the mysteries of religion or duty.'—Hearing these words of the Grandsire, the deities, with well-pleased minds commissioned (the elephant) Renuka to where those upholders of the world are.

""Renuka, proceeding to where those elephants are, addressed them, saying, 'Ye mighty creatures, I have been commanded by the deities and the Pitris to question you about the mysteries of religion and duty. I desire to hear you discourse on that subject in detail. Ye highly blessed ones, do ye discourse on the subject as your wisdom may dictate.'

"""The (eight) elephants standing in the eight quarters said, 'On the auspicious eighth day of the dark fortnight in the month of Karttika when the constellation Aslesha is in the ascendant, one should make gifts of treacle and rice. Casting aside wrath, and living on regulated diet, one should make these offerings at a Sraddha, uttering these mantras the while—"Let Valadeva and other Nagas possessed of great strength, let other mighty snakes of huge bodies that are indestructible and eternal, and let all the other great snakes that have taken their birth in their race, make Vali offerings to me for the enhancement of my strength and energy. Verily, let my strength be as great as that of the blessed Narayana when he raised the submerged Earth!"—Uttering these mantras, one should make Vali offerings upon an ant-hill. When the maker of day retires to his chambers in the west, upon the ant-hill selected should offerings be made of raw sugar and rice. The ant-hill should previously be scattered with Gajendra flowers. Offerings should also be made of blue cloths and fragrant unguents. If offerings are made in this way, those beings that live in the nether regions, bearing the weight of the upper regions upon their heads or shoulders, become well-pleased and gratified. As regards ourselves, we also do not feel the labour of upholding the Earth, in consequence of such offerings being made to us. Afflicted with the burden we bear, even this is what we think (beneficial for men), without the slightest regard for selfish concerns. Brahmanas and Kshatriyas and Vaisyas and Sudras, by observing this rule for a full year, fasting on each occasion, acquire great merits from such gifts. We think that the making of such Vali offerings on the ant-hill is really fraught with very superior merits. By making such offerings, one is regarded as doing the duties of hospitality for a hundred years to all the mighty elephants that exist in the three worlds.' Hearing these words of the mighty elephants, the deities and the Pitris and the highly blessed Rishis, all applauded Renuka."""

SECTION CXXXIII.

""""Maheswara said, 'Searching your memories, excellent are the duties ye all have recited. Listen all of you now to me as I declare some mysteries relating to religion and duty. Only those persons whose understanding has been set on religion and who are possessed of faith, should be instructed in respect of those mysteries of duty and religion that are fraught with high merits. Hear what the merits are that become his who, with heart free from anxiety, gives food everyday, for a month, to kine and contents himself with one meal a day throughout such period. The kine are highly blessed. They are regarded as the most sacred of all sacred things. Verily, it is they that are upholding the three worlds with the deities, the Asuras, and human beings. Respectful services rendered to them are fraught with high merit and grave consequences. That man who every day gives food to kine advances every day in religious merit. Formerly, in the Krita age I had expressed my approval of these creatures. Afterwards Brahman, born of the primeval lotus, solicited me (to show kindness towards kine).[559] It is for this reason that a bull to this day stands as the device on my standard overhead. I always sport with kine. Hence should kine be worshipped by all. Kine are possessed of great power. They are givers of boons. If worshipped, they would grant boons. That person who gives food to kine even for a single day receives from those beneficent creatures for that act a fourth part of the merits he may win by all his good acts in life.'"""

SECTION CXXXIV.

""""Skanda said, 'I shall now declare a duty that is approved of by me. Do ye listen to it with concentrated attention. That person who takes a little earth from the horns of a bull of blue complexion, smears his body therewith for three days, and then performs his ablutions, acquires great merits. Hear what those merits are. By such an act he would wash away every stain and evil, and attain to sovereign sway hereafter. As many times he takes his birth in this world, so many times does he become celebrated for his heroism. Listen now to another mystery unknown to all. Taking a vessel of copper and placing therein some cooked food after having mixed it with honey, one should offer it as Vali unto the rising moon on the evening of the day when that luminary is at full. Do ye learn, with faith, what the merits are of the person that acts in this way. The Sadhyas, the Rudras, the Adityas, the Viswedevas, the twin Aswins, the Maruts, and the Vasus, all accept that offering. By such an offering Soma increases as also the ocean, that vast receptacle of waters. This duty that is declared by me and that is unknown to all, if performed, is certainly fraught with great happiness.'

""""Vishnu said, 'That person who, endued with faith and freed from malice, listens every day with concentrated attention to the mysteries in respect of religion and duty that are preserved by the high-souled deities and those mysteries also of the same kind that are preserved by the Rishis, has never to succumb to any evil. Such a person becomes also freed from every fear. That man who, with his senses under thorough control, reads these sections which treat of these auspicious and meritorious duties, together with their mysteries,—duties that have been declared (by the previous speakers), acquires all the

---

[559] Anujnatah literally implies permitted. These creatures, i.e., the kine, were permitted by me, means, perhaps, that they became my favourites. Brahman, it is said, solicited Maheswara to accept some kine in gift. The latter did accept some, and adopt from that time the device of the bull on his flag.

merits that attach to their actual performance. Sin can never overmaster him. Verily, such a man can never be stained with faults of any kind. Indeed, one wins abundant merits by reading these mysteries (as declared), or by reciting them to others, or by hearing them recited. The deities and the Pitris eat forever the Havya and the Kavya offered by such a creature. Both these, in consequence of the virtues of the offerer become inexhaustible. Even such is the merit that attaches to the person who, with concentrated attention, recites these mysteries to foremost of Brahmanas on days of the full moon or the new moon. Such a person, in consequence of such an act, becomes steady in the observance of all duties. Beauty of form and prosperity also become his. He succeeds, besides this, in becoming the favourite, for all time, of the Rishis and the deities and the Pitris. If a person becomes guilty of all sins save those which are classed as grave or heinous, he becomes cleansed of them all by only listening to the recitation of these mysteries about religion and duty.'"

"'Bhishma continued, "Even these, O king of men, are the mysteries in respect of religion and duty dwelling in the breasts of the deities. Held in high respect by all the gods and promulgated by Vyasa, they have now been declared by me for thy benefit. One who is conversant with religion and duty thinks that this excellent knowledge is superior (in value) to even the whole earth full of riches and wealth. This knowledge should not be imparted to one that is bereft of faith, or to one that is an atheist, or to one that has fallen away from the duties of his order, or to one that is destitute of compassion, or to one that is devoted to the science of empty disputations, or to one that is hostile to one's preceptors, or to one that thinks all creatures to be different from oneself."'"

SECTION CXXXV.

"'Yudhishthira said, "Who are those persons, O Bharata, from whom a Brahmana in this world may accept his food? From whom may a Kshatriya, a Vaisya, and a Sudra take their food respectively?"

"'Bhishma said, "A Brahmana may take his food from another Brahmana or from a Kshatriya or a Vaisya, but he must never accept food from a Sudra. A Kshatriya may take his food from a Brahmana, a Kshatriya or a Vaisya. He must, however, eschew food given by Sudras who are addicted to evil ways and who partake of all manner of food without any scruple. Brahmanas and Kshatriyas can partake of food given by such Vaisyas as tend the sacred fire every day, as are faultless in character, and as perform the vow of Chaturmasya. But the man who takes food from a Sudra, swallows the very abomination of the earth, and drinks the excretions of the human body, and partakes of the filth of all the world. He partakes of the very filth of the earth who takes his food thus from a Sudra. Verily, those Brahmanas that take their food from Sudras, take the dirt of the earth. If one engages in the service of a Sudra, one is doomed to perdition though one may duly perform all the rites of one's order. A Brahmana, a Kshatriya, or a Vaisya, so engaging, is doomed, although devoted to the due performance of religious rites. It is said that a Brahmana's duty consists in studying the Vedas and seeking the welfare of the human race; that a Kshatriya's duty consists in protecting men, and that a Vaisya's in promoting their material prosperity. A Vaisya lives by distributing the fruits of his own acts and agriculture. The breeding of kine and trade are the legitimate work in which a Vaisya may engage without fear of censure. The man who abandons his own proper occupation and betakes himself to that of a Sudra, should be considered as a Sudra and on no account should any food be accepted from him. Professors of the healing art, mercenary soldiers, the priest who acts as warder of the house, and persons who devote a whole year to study without any profit, are all to be considered as Sudras. And those who impudently partake of food offered at ceremonials in a Sudra's house are afflicted with a terrible calamity. In consequence of partaking such forbidden food they lose their family, strength, and energy, and attain to the status of animals, descending to the position of dogs, fallen in virtue and devoid of all religious observances. He who takes food from a physician takes that which is no better than excrement; the food of a harlot is like urine; that of a skilled mechanic is like blood. If a Brahmana approved by the good, takes the food of one who lives by his learning, he is regarded as taking the food of a Sudra. All good men should forego such food. The food of a person who is censured by all is said to be like a draught from a pool of blood. The acceptance of food from a wicked person is considered as reprehensible as the slaying of a Brahmana. One should not accept food if one is slighted and not received with due honours by the giver. A Brahmana, who does so, is soon overtaken by disease, and his race soon becomes extinct. By accepting food from the warder of a city, one descends to the status of the lowest outcaste. If a Brahmana accepts food from one who is guilty of killing either a cow or a Brahmana or from one who has committed adultery with his preceptor's wife or from a drunkard, he helps to promote the race of Rakshasas. By accepting food from a eunuch, or from an ungrateful person, or from one who has misappropriated wealth entrusted to his charge, one is born in the country of the Savaras situated beyond the precincts of the middle country. I have thus duly recited to thee the persons from whom food may be accepted and from whom it may not. Now tell me, O son of Kunti, what else thou wishest to hear from me today."'"

SECTION CXXXVI.

"'Yudhishthira said, "Thou hast told me in full of those from whom food may be accepted and of those from whom it should not be taken. But I have grave doubts on one point. Do thou, O sire, enlighten me, do thou tell me what expiation a Brahmana should make (for the sin he incurs) upon accepting the different kinds of food, those especially offered in honour of the gods and the oblations made to the manes."

"'Bhishma said, "I shall tell thee, O prince, how high-souled Brahmanas may be absolved from all sin incurred by accepting food from others. In accepting clarified butter, the expiation is made by pouring oblations on the fire, reciting the Savitri hymn. In accepting sesamum, O Yudhishthira, the same expiation has to be made. In accepting meat, or honey, or salt, a Brahmana becomes purified by standing till the rising of the sun. If a Brahmana accepts gold from any one, he becomes cleansed of all sins by silently reciting the great Vedic prayer (Gayatri) and by holding a piece of iron in his hand in the presence of the public. In accepting money or clothes or women or gold, the purification is the same as before. In accepting food, or rice boiled in milk and sugar, or sugarcane juice, or sugar-cane, or oil, or any sacred thing, one becomes purified by bathing thrice in the course of the day, viz., at morn, noon and eve. If one accepts paddy, flowers, fruits, water, half-ripe barley, milk, or curdled milk, or anything made of meal or flour, the expiation is made by reciting the Gayatri prayer a hundred times. In accepting shoes or clothes at obsequial ceremonies, the sin is destroyed by reciting devoutly the same hymn a hundred times. The acceptance of the gift of land at the time of an eclipse or during the period of impurity, is expiated by observing a fast during three successive nights. The Brahmana who partakes of oblations offered to deceased ancestors, in course of the dark fortnight, is purified by fasting for a whole day and night. Without performing his ablutions a Brahmana should not say his evening prayers, nor betake himself to religious meditation, nor take his food a second time. By so doing he is purified. For this reason, the Sraddha of deceased ancestors has been ordained to be performed in the afternoon and then the Brahmana who has been invited beforehand should be feasted. The Brahmana who partakes of food at the house of a dead person on the third day after the death, is purified by bathing three times daily for twelve days. After the expiration of twelve days, and going through the purification ceremonies duly, the sin is destroyed by giving clarified butter to Brahmanas. If a man takes any food in the house of a dead person, within ten days after the death, he should go through all the expiations before mentioned, and should recite the Savitri hymn and do the sin-destroying Ishti and Kushmanda penances. The Brahmana who takes his food in the house of a dead person for three nights, becomes purified by performing his ablutions thrice daily for seven days, and thus attains all the objects of his desire, and is never troubled by misfortunes. The Brahmana who takes his food in the company of Sudras is purged from all impurity by duly observing the ceremonies of purification. The Brahmana who takes his food in the company of Vaisyas is absolved from sin by living on alms for three successive nights. If a Brahmana takes his food with Kshatriyas, he should make expiation by bathing with his clothes on. By eating with a Sudra from off the same plate the Sudra loses his family respectability; the Vaisya by eating from off the same plate with a Vaisya, loses his cattle and friends. The Kshatriya loses his prosperity, and the Brahmana his splendour and energy. In such cases, expiations should be made, and propitiatory rites should be observed, and oblations offered to the gods. The Savitri hymn should be recited and the Revati rites and Kushmanda penances should be observed with the view of destroying the sin. If any of the above four classes partake of food partly eaten by a person of any other class, the expiation is undoubtedly made by smearing the body with auspicious substances like Rochana, Durva grass, and turmeric."''

SECTION CXXXVII.

"'Yudhishthira said, "O Bharata, of the two things charity and devotion, do thou condescend to tell me, O sire, which is the better in this world? Do thou, by this, remove a great doubt from my mind."

"'Bhishma said, "Do thou, listen to me as I recite the names of the princes who having been devoted to virtue, and having cleansed their hearts by penances and practised gifts and other acts of piety, undoubtedly attained to the different celestial regions. The Rishi Atreya revered by all, attained, O monarch, to the excellent celestial regions, by imparting the knowledge of the unconditional Supreme Being to his pupils. King Sivi, the son of Usinara, by offering the life of his dear son, for the benefit of a Brahmana, was translated from this world to heaven. And Pratardana, the king of Kasi, by giving his son to a Brahmana, secured to himself unique and undying fame in this as well as in the other world. Rantideva, the son of Sankriti, attained to the highest heaven by duly making gifts to the high-souled Vasishtha. Devavriddha too went to heaven by giving a hundred-ribbed and excellent golden umbrella to a Brahmana for a sacrifice. The worshipful Amvarisha too has attained to the region of the gods, by making a gift of all his kingdom to a Brahmana of great power. King Janamejaya of the solar race, went to the highest heaven by making a gift of ear-rings, fine vehicles, and cows to Brahmanas. The Royal sage Vrishadarbhi went to heaven by making gifts of various jewels and beautiful houses to Brahmanas. King Nimi of Vidarva, attained to heaven with his sons, friends and cattle, by giving his daughter and kingdom to the high-souled Agastya. The far-famed Rama, the son of Jamadagni, attained to the eternal regions, far beyond his expectation, by giving lands to Brahmanas. Vasishtha, the prince of Brahmanas, preserved all the creatures at a time of great drought when the god Parjjanya did not bestow his grateful showers upon the earth, and for this act he has secured eternal bliss for himself. Rama, the son of Dasaratha, whose fame is very high in this world, attained to the eternal regions by making gifts of wealth at sacrifices. The far-famed royal sage Kakshasena, went to heaven by duly making over to the high-souled Vasishtha the wealth which he had deposited with him. Marutta, the son of Parikshita and the grandson of Karandhama, by giving his daughter in marriage to Angiras, immediately went to heaven. The highly devout king of Panchalal Brahmadatta, attained the blessed way by giving away a precious conch-shell. King Mitrasaha, by giving his favourite wife Madayanti to the high-souled Vasishtha, ascended to heaven. Sudyumna, the son of Manu, by causing the proper punishment to be inflicted upon the high-souled Likhita, attained to the most blessed regions. The celebrated royal sage Saharachitta went to the blessed regions, by sacrificing his dear life for the sake of a Brahmana. The king Satadyumna went to heaven by giving to Maudgaya a golden mansion replete with all the objects of desire. In ancient times, king Sumanyu by giving to Sandilya heaps of food looking like a hill, proceeded to heaven. The Salwa prince Dyutimat of great splendour attained to the highest regions by giving his kingdom to Richika. The Royal sage Madiraswa by giving his slender-waisted daughter to Hiranyahasta went to the region of the gods. The lordly Lomapada attained all the vast objects of his desire by giving his daughter Santa in marriage to Rishyasringa. The royal sage Bhagiratha, by giving his famous daughter Hansi in marriage to Kautsa, went to the eternal regions. King Bhagiratha by giving hundreds and thousands of kine with their young ones to Kohala attained to the most blessed regions. These and many other men, O Yudhishthira, have attained to heaven, by the merit of their charities and penances and they have also returned from thence again and again. Their fame will endure as long as the world will last. I have related to thee, O Yudhishthira, this story of those good householders who have attained to eternal regions by dint of their charities and penances. By their charities and by performing sacrifices and by procreating offspring, these people have attained to the heavenly regions. O foremost scion of Kuru's race, by always performing acts of charity, these men applied their virtuous intellects to the performance of sacrifices and charities. O mighty prince, as night has approached I shall explain to thee in the morning whatever doubts may arise in thy mind.""

SECTION CXXXVIII.

"'Yudhishthira said, "I have heard from thee, O sire, the names of those kings that have ascended to heaven. O thou whose power is great in the observance of the vow of truth by following the religion of gift, how many kinds of gift are there that should be given? What are the fruits of the several kinds of gifts respectively? For what reasons, what kinds of gifts, made to what persons are productive of merits? Indeed, unto what persons should what gifts be made? For what reasons are how many kinds of gifts to be made? I desire to hear all this in detail."

"'Bhishma said, "Listen, O son of Kunti, in detail to me, O sinless one as I discourse on the subject of gifts. Indeed, I shall tell you, O Bharata, how gifts should be made unto all the orders of men. From desire of merit, from desire of profit, from fear, from free choice, and from pity, gifts are made, O Bharata! Gifts, therefore, should be known to be of five kinds. Listen now to the reasons for which gifts are thus distributed in five classes. With mind freed from malice one should make gifts unto Brahmanas, for by making gifts unto the one acquires fame here and great felicity hereafter. (Such gifts are regarded as made from desire of merit.) 'He is in the habit of making gifts; or he has already made gifts to me.' Hearing such words from solicitors one gives away all kinds of wealth unto a particular solicitor. (Such gifts are regarded as made from desire of profit.) 'I am not his, nor is he mine. If disregarded, he may injure me.' From such motives of fear even a man of learning and wisdom may make gifts unto an ignorant wretch. (Such gifts are regarded as made from fear.) 'This one is dear to me, I am also dear to him.' Influenced by considerations like these, a person of intelligence, freely and with alacrity, make gifts unto a friend. (Such gifts are regarded as made from free choice.) 'The person that solicits me is poor. He is, again, gratified with a little. 'From considerations such as these, one should always make gifts unto the poor, moved by pity. (Gifts made from such considerations are regarded as made from pity.) These are the five kinds of gift. They enhance the giver's merits and fame. The Lord of all creatures (Brahman himself) has said that one should always make gifts according to one's power.'"

SECTION CXXXIX.

"'Yudhishthira said, "O grandsire, thou art possessed of great wisdom. Indeed, thou art fully conversant with every branch of learning. In our great race thou art the only individual that swellest with all the sciences. I desire to hear from thee discourses that are interwoven with Religion and Profit, that lead to felicity hereafter, and that are fraught with wonder unto all creatures. The time that has come is fraught with great distress. The like of it does not generally come to kinsmen and friends. Indeed, save thee, O foremost of men, we have now none else that can take the place of an instructor. If, O sinless one, I with my brothers deserve the favour, it behoveth thee to answer the question I desire to ask thee. This one is Narayana who is endued with every prosperity and is honoured by all the kings. Even he waits upon thee, showing thee every indulgence and honouring thee greatly. It behoveth thee to discourse unto me, through affection, for my benefit as also for that of my brothers, in the presence of Vasudeva himself and of all these kings.'"

"Vaisampayana continued, 'Hearing these words of king Yudhishthira, Bhishma, the son of the river called after Bhagiratha, filled with joy in consequence of his affection for the monarch and his brothers, said what follows.'[560]

"'Bhishma said, "I shall certainly recite to thee discourses that are delightful, on the subject, O king, of the puissance of this Vishnu as displayed in days of yore and as I have heard (from my preceptors). Listen to me also as I describe the puissance of that great god who has a bull for his device. Listen to me as I narrate also the doubt that filled the mind of the spouse of Rudra and that of Rudra himself. Once on a time the righteous souled Krishna observed a vow extending for ten and two years. For beholding him who had gone through the rite of initiation for the observance of his great vow, there came to that place Narada and Parvata, and the Island-born Krishna, and Dhaumya, that foremost of silent reciters, and Devala, and Kasyapa, and Hastikasyapa. Other Rishis also, endued with Diksha and self-restraint, followed by their disciples and accompanied by many Siddhas and many ascetics of great merit, came there. The son of Devaki offered them

---

[560] Sambhrama here means, probably, joy, or that gratification which shows itself in horripilation. It may also mean alacrity.

such honours of hospitality as are deserving of the highest praise and as are offered unto the gods alone. Those great Rishis sat themselves down upon seats some of which were green and some endued with the colour of gold and some that were fraught with the plumes of the peacock and some that were perfectly new and fresh. Thus seated, they began to converse sweetly with one another on subjects connected with Religion and duty as also with many royal sages and deities. At that time the energy, in the form of fire, Narayana, rising from the fuel that consisted of the rigid observance of his vow, issued out of the mouth of Krishna of wonderful feats. That fire began to consume those mountains with their trees and creepers and little plants, as also with their birds and deer and beasts of prey and reptiles. Soon the summit of that mountain presented a distressing and pitiful appearance, Inhabited by animals of diverse kinds which began to utter cries of woe and pain, the summit soon became bereft of every living creature. That fire of mighty flames, having consumed everything without leaving a remnant at last came back to Vishnu and touched his feet like a docile disciple. That crusher of foes, viz., Krishna, beholding that mountain burnt, cast a benignant look upon it and thereby brought it back to its former condition. That mountain thereupon once more became adorned with flowering trees and creepers, and once more echoed with the notes and cries of birds and deer and animals of prey and reptiles. Seeing that wonderful and inconceivable sight, all the ascetics became amazed. Their hairs stood on end and their vision was blurred with tears. That foremost of speakers, Narayana, beholding those Rishis thus filled with wonder, addressed them in these sweet and refreshing words, 'Why, indeed, has wonder filled the hearts of this assemblage of Rishis, these ascetics that are always free from attachment of every kind, that are divested of the idea of meum, and that are fully conversant with every sacred science? It behoveth these Rishis possessed of wealth of penances and freed from every stain to explain to me truly this doubt that has arisen in my mind.'

""The Rishis said, 'It is thou that createst all the worlds, and it is thou that destroyest them again. It is thou that art Winter, it is thou that art Summer, and it is thou that art the season of rains. Of all the creatures, mobile and immobile, that are found on the earth, thou art the father, thou art the mother, thou art the master, and thou art the origin! Even this, O slayer of Madhu, is a matter of wonder and doubt with us. O source of all auspiciousness, it behoveth Thee to resolve to us that doubt, viz., the issue of fire from Thy mouth. Our fears being dispelled we shall then, O Hari, recite to thee what we have heard and seen.'

""Vasudeva said, 'The fire that issued from my mouth and that resembles the all-consuming Yuga-fire in splendour, and by which this mountain has been crushed and scorched, is nothing else than the energy of Vishnu. Ye Rishis, ye are persons that have subjugated wrath, that have brought your senses under complete control, that are endued with wealth of penances, and that are very gods in puissance. Yet ye have suffered yourselves to be agitated and distressed! I am now engaged wholly with the observances relating to rigid vow. Verily, in consequence of my observing the vows of an ascetic, a fire issued from my mouth. It behoves you not to suffer yourselves to be agitated. It is for observing a rigid vow that I came to this delightful and auspicious mountain. The object that has brought me here is to acquire by the aid of penances a son that would be my equal in energy. In consequence of my penances, the Soul existing in my body became transformed into fire and issued out of my mouth. That fire had repaired to behold the boon-giving Grandsire of all the universe. The Grandsire, ye foremost of ascetics, told my soul that half the energy of the great god having the bull for his device would take birth as my son. That fire returning from its mission, has come back to me and approached my feet like a disciple desirous of serving me dutifully. Indeed, casting off its fury it has come back to me to its own proper nature. I have thus told you, in brief, a mystery appertaining to Him who has the lotus for his origin and who is endued with great intelligence. Ye Rishis possessed of wealth of penances, ye should not give way to fear! Ye are endued with far-reaching vision. Ye can proceed to every place without any impediment. Blazing with vows observed by ascetics, ye are adorned with knowledge and science. I now ask you to tell me something that is highly wonderful which you have heard of or seen on earth or in heaven. I feel an eager desire to taste the honey of that speech which will drop from your lips, the honey that will, I am sure, be as sweet as a jet of nectar itself. If I behold anything on earth or in heaven, which is highly delightful and of wonderful aspect but which is unknown to all of you, ye Rishis that look like so many gods, I say that that is in consequence of my own Supreme Nature which is incapable of being obstructed by anything. Anything wonderful whose knowledge dwelleth in me or is acquired by my own inspiration ceases to appear wonderful to me. Anything, however, that is recited by pious persons and that is heard from those that are good, deserves to be accepted with respect and faith. Such discourses exist on earth for a long time and are as durable as characters engraved on rocks. I desire, therefore, to hear, at this meeting something dropping from the lips of persons that are good and that cannot fail to be productive of good to men.' Hearing these words of Krishna all those ascetics became filled with surprise. They began to gaze at Janardana with those eyes of theirs that were as beautiful and large as the petals of the lotus. Some of them began to glorify him and some began to worship him with reverence. Indeed, all of them then hymned the praises of the slayer of Madhu with words whose meanings were adorned with the eternal Riks. All those ascetics then appointed Narada, that foremost of all persons conversant with speech, to gratify the request of Vasudeva.

""The ascetics said, 'It behoveth thee, O Narada, to describe, in full, from the beginning, unto Hrishikesa, that wonderful and inconceivable incident which occurred, O puissant one, on the mountains of Himavat and which, O ascetic, was witnessed by those of us that had proceeded thither in course of our pilgrimage to the sacred waters. Verily, for the benefit of all the Rishis here assembled, it behoveth thee to recite that incident.' Thus addressed by those ascetics, the celestial Rishi, viz., the divine Narada, then recited the following story whose incidents had occurred some time before.""

SECTION CXL.

"'Bhishma said, "Then Narada, that holy Rishi, that friend of Narayana, recited the following narrative of the discourse between Sankara and his spouse Uma.

""Narada said, 'Once on a time the righteous-souled lord of all the deities, viz., Mahadeva with the bull for his device, practised severe penances on the sacred mountains of Himavat that are the resort of Siddhas and Charanas. Those delightful mountains are overgrown with diverse kinds of herbs and adorned with various species of flowers. At that time they were peopled by the different tribes of Apsaras and crowds of ghostly beings. There the great god sat, filled with joy, and surrounded by hundreds of ghostly beings who presented diverse aspects to the eye of the beholder. Some of them were ugly and awkward, some were of very handsome features, and some presented the most wonderful appearances. Some had faces like the lion's, some like the tiger's and some like the elephant's. In fact, the faces of those ghostly creatures presented every variety of animal faces. Some had faces resembling that of the jackal, some whose faces resembled the pard's, some like the ape's, some like the bull's. Some of them had faces like the owl's; some like the hawk's; some had faces like those of deer of diverse varieties. The great god was also surrounded by Kinnaras and Yakshas and Gandharvas and Rakshasas and diverse other created beings. The retreat to which Mahadeva had betaken himself also abounded with celestial flowers and blazed with celestial rays of light. It was perfumed with celestial sandal, and celestial incense was burnt on every side. And it echoed with the sounds of celestial instruments. Indeed, it resounded with the beat of Mridangas and Panavas, the blare of conchs, and the sound of drums. It teemed with ghostly beings of diverse tribes that danced in joy and with peacocks also that danced with plumes outspread. Forming as it did the resort of the celestial Rishis, the Apsaras danced there in joy. The place was exceedingly agreeable to the sight. It was exceedingly beautiful, resembling Heaven itself. Its entire aspect was wonderful and, indeed, it is indescribable in respect of its beauty and sweetness. Verily, with the penances of that great deity who sleeps on mountain breasts, that prince of mountains shone with great beauty. It resounded with the chant of the Vedas uttered by learned Brahmanas devoted to Vedic recitation. Echoing with the hum of bees, O Madhava, the mountain became incomparable in beauty. The ascetics, beholding the great deity who is endued with a fierce form and who looks like a great festival, became filled, O Janardana, with great joy. All the highly blessed ascetics, the Siddhas who have drawn in their vital seed, the Maruts, the Vasus, the Sadhyas, the Viswedevas, Vasava himself, the Yakshas, the Nagas, the Pisachas, the Regents of the world, the several sacred Fires, the Winds, and all the great creatures dwelt on that mountain with minds concentrated in Yoga. All the Seasons were present there and scattered those regions with all kinds of wonderful flowers. Diverse kinds of blazing herbs illuminated the woods and forests on that mountain. Various species of birds, filled with joy, hopped about and sang merrily on the delightful breast of that mountain. Those birds were exceedingly lovable in consequence of the notes they uttered. The high-souled Mahadeva sat, displayed in beauty, on one of the peaks that was adorned with excellent minerals, as if it served the purposes of a fine bedstead. Round his loins was a tiger-skin, and a lion-skin formed his upper garments. His sacred thread consisted of a snake. His arms were decked with a pair of red Angadas. His beard was green. He had matted locks on his head. Of terrible features, he it is that inspires with fear the hearts of all the enemies of the gods. It is he, again, that assures all creatures by dispelling their fears. He is adored by his worshippers as the deity having the bovine bull for his device. The great Rishis, beholding Mahadeva, bowed to him by touching the ground with their heads. Endued with forgiving souls, they all became (in consequence of the sight they had obtained of the great deity) freed from every sin and thoroughly cleansed. The retreat of that lord of all creatures with many terrible forms, shone with a peculiar beauty. Abounding with many large snakes, it became unapproachable and unbearable (by ordinary beings). Within the twinkling of the eye, O slayer of Madhu, everything there became exceedingly wonderful. Indeed, the abode of that great deity having the bovine bull for his device began to blaze with a terrible beauty. Unto Mahadeva seated there, came his spouse, the daughter of Himavat, surrounded by the wives of the ghostly beings who are the companions of the great deity. Her attire was like that of her lord and the vows she observed were like those of his. She held a jar on her loins that was filled with the waters of every Tirtha, and was accompanied by the presiding deities (of her own sex) of all the mountain streams. Those auspicious ladies walked in her train. The goddess approached raining flowers on every side and diverse kinds of sweet perfumes. She who loved to reside on the breast of Himavat advanced in this guise towards her great lord. The beautiful Uma, with smiling lips and desirous of playing a jest, covered from behind, with her two beautiful hands, the eyes of Mahadeva. As soon as Mahadeva's eyes were thus covered, all the regions became dark and life seemed to be extinct everywhere in the universe. The Homa rites ceased. The universe became suddenly deprived of the sacred Vashat also. All living creatures became cheerless and filled with fear. Indeed, when the eyes of the lord of all creatures were thus closed, the universe seemed to become sunless. Soon, however, that overspreading darkness disappeared. A mighty and blazing flame of fire emanated from Mahadeva's forehead. A third eye, resembling another sun, appeared (on it). That eye began to blaze forth like the Yuga-fire and began to consume that mountain. The large-eyed daughter of Himavat, beholding what occurred, bowed her head unto Mahadeva endued with that third eye which resembled a blazing fire. She stood there with gaze fixed on her lord. When the mountain forests burned on every side, with their Was and other trees of straight trunks, and their delightful sandals and diverse excellent medicinal herbs, herds of deer and other animals, filled with fright, came with great speed to the place where Hara sat and sought his protection. With those creatures almost filling it, the retreat of the great deity blazed forth with a kind of peculiar beauty. Meanwhile, that fire, swelling wildly, soared up to the very heavens and endued with the splendour and unsteadiness of lightning and looking like a dozen suns in might and effulgence, covered every side like the all-destroying Yuga-fire. In a moment, the Himavat mountains were consumed, with their minerals and summits and blazing herbs. Beholding Himavat crushed and consumed, the daughter of that prince of mountains sought the protection of the great deity and stood before him her hands joined in reverence. Then Sarva, seeing Uma overcome by an accession of womanly mildness and finding that she was unwilling to behold her father Himavat reduced to that pitiable plight, cast benignant looks upon the mountain. In a moment the whole of Himavat was restored to his former condition and became as beautiful to look at as ever. Indeed, the mountain put forth a cheerful aspect. All its trees became adorned with flowers. Beholding Himavat to his natural condition, the goddess Uma, divested of every fault, addressed her lord, that master of all creatures, the divine Maheswara, in these words.

"'"Uma said, "O holy one, O lord of all creatures, O deity that art armed with the trident, O thou of high vows, a great doubt has filled my mind. It behoveth thee to resolve that doubt for me. For what reason has this third eye appeared in thy forehead? Why also was the mountain consumed with the woods and all that belonged to it? Why also, O illustrious deity, hast thou restored the mountain to its former condition? Indeed, having burnt it once, why hast thou again caused it to be covered with trees?"

"'"Maheswara said, "O goddess without any fault, in consequence of thy having covered my eyes through an act of indiscretion the universe became in a moment devoid of light. When the universe became sunless and, therefore, all became dark, O daughter of the prince of mountains, I created the third eye desirous of protecting all creatures. The high energy of that eye crushed and consumed this mountain. For pleasing thee, however, O goddess, I once more made Himavat what he was by repairing the injury."

"'"Uma said, "O holy one, why are those faces of thine which are on the east, the north, and the west, so handsome and so agreeable to look at like the very moon? And why is that face of thine which is on the south so terrible? Why are thy matted locks tawny in hue and so erect? Why is thy throat blue after the manner of the peacock's plumes? Why, O illustrious deity, is the Pinaka always in thy hand? Why art thou always a Brahmacharin with matted locks? O lord, it behoves thee to explain all these to me. I am thy spouse who seeks to follow the same duties with thee. Further, I am thy devoted worshipper, O deity, having the bull for thy mark!'"

""'Narada continued, 'Thus addressed by the daughter of the prince of mountains, the illustrious wielder of Pinaka, the puissant Mahadeva, became highly gratified with her. The great god then addressed her saying, "O blessed lady, listen to me as I explain, with the reasons thereof, why my forms are so."'"""

SECTION CXLI.

""'The blessed and holy one said, "In days of yore, a blessed woman was created by Brahman, called Tilottama, by culling grains of beauty from every beautiful object in the universe. One day, that lady of beautiful face, unrivalled in the universe for beauty of form, came to me, O goddess, for circumambulating me but really impelled by the desire of tempting me. In whatever direction that lady of beautiful teeth turned, a new face of mine instantly appeared (so eager did I become to see her). All those faces of mine became agreeable to look at. Thus, in consequence of the desire of beholding her, I became four-faced, through Yoga-puissance. Thus, I showed my high Yoga-power in becoming four-faced. With that face of mine which is turned towards the east, I exercise the sovereignty of the universe. With that face of mine which is turned towards the north, I sport with thee, O thou of faultless features! That face of mine which is turned towards the west is agreeable and auspicious. With it I ordain the happiness of all creatures. That face of mine which is turned towards the south is terrible. With it I destroy all creatures. I live as a Brahmacharin with matted locks on my head, impelled by the desire of doing good to all creatures. The bow Pinaka is always in my hand for accomplishing the purposes of the deities. In days of yore, Indra, desirous of acquiring my prosperity, had hurled his thunderbolt at me. With that weapon my throat was scorched. For this reason I have become blue-throated."

""'Uma said, "When, O foremost of all creatures, there are so many excellent vehicles endued with great beauty, why is it that thou hast selected a bovine bull for thy vehicle?"

""'Maheswara said, "In the days of yore, the Grandsire Brahma created the celestial cow Surabhi yielding abundant milk. After her creation there sprang from her a large number of kine all of which yielded copious quantities of milk sweet as nectar. Once on a time a quantity of froth fell from the mouth of one of her calves on my body. I was enraged at this and my wrath scorched all the kine which thereupon became diversified in hue. I was then pacified by the Master of all the worlds, viz., Brahma, conversant with all topics. It was he who gave me this bull both as a vehicle for bearing me and as a device on my banner."

""'Uma said, "Thou hast many abodes in heaven, of diverse forms and possessed of every comfort and luxury. Why, O holy one, dost thou reside in the crematorium, abandoning all those delightful mansions? The crematorium is full of the hair and bones (of the dead), abounds with vulture and jackals, and is strewn with hundreds of funeral pyres. Full of carrion and muddy with fat and blood, with entrails and bones strewn all over it, and always echoing with the howls of jackals, it is certainly an unclean place."

""'Maheswara said, "I always wander over the whole earth in search of a sacred spot. I do not, however, see any spot that is more sacred than the crematorium. Hence, of all abodes, the crematorium pleases my heart most, shaded that it generally is by branches of the banian and adorned with torn garlands of flowers. O thou of sweet smiles, the multitudes of ghostly beings that are my companions love to reside in such spots. I do not like, O goddess, to reside anywhere without those ghostly creatures being by my side. Hence, the crematorium is a sacred abode to me. Indeed, O auspicious lady, it seems to me to be the very heaven. Highly sacred and possessed of great merit, the crematorium is much applauded by persons desirous of having holy abodes."

"'"Uma said, "O holy one, O lord of all creatures, O foremost of all observers of duties and religious rites, I have a great doubt, O wielder of Pinaka, O giver of boons. These ascetics, O puissant lord, have undergone diverse kinds of austerities. In the world are seen ascetics wandering everywhere under diverse forms and clad in diverse kinds of attire. For benefiting this large assemblage of Rishis, as also myself, do thou kindly resolve, O chastiser of all foes, this doubt of mine. What indications has Religion or Duty been said to possess? How, indeed, do men become unacquainted with the details of Religion or Duty to succeed in observing them? O puissant lord, O thou that art conversant with Religion, do thou tell me this."

"'"Narada continued, 'When the daughter of Himavat put this question, conclave of Rishis there present worshipped the goddess and adored her with words adorned with Riks and with hymns fraught with deep import.

"'"Maheswara said, "Abstention from injury, truthfulness of speech, compassion towards all beings, tranquillity of soul, and the making of gifts to the best of one's power, are the foremost duties of the householder. Abstention from sexual congress with the spouses of other men, protection of the wealth and the woman committed to one's charge, unwillingness to appropriate what is not given to one, and avoidance of honey and meat,—these are the five chief duties. Indeed, Religion or Duty has many branches all of which are fraught with happiness. Even these are the duties which these embodied creatures who regard duty as superior should observe and practise. Even these are the sources of merit."

"'"Uma said, "O holy one, I wish to ask thee another question about which I have great doubts. It behoveth thee to answer it and dispel my doubts. What are the meritorious duties of the four several orders? What duties appertain to the Brahmana? What to the Kshatriya? What are the indications of those duties that appertain to the Vaisya? And what kind of duties appertain to the Sudra?"

"'"The holy one said, "O highly blessed lady, the question thou hast asked is a very proper one. Those persons that belong to the regenerate order are regarded as highly blessed, and are, indeed, gods on earth. Without doubt, the observance of fasts (i.e., subjugation of the senses) is always the duty of the Brahmana. When the Brahmana succeeds in properly observing all his duties, he attains to identity with Brahma.[561] The proper observance of the duties of Brahmacharya, O goddess, are his ritual. The observance of vows and the investiture with the sacred thread are his other duties. It is by these that he becomes truly regenerate. He becomes a Brahmana for worshipping his preceptors and other seniors as also the deities. Verily, that religion which has for its soul the study of the Vedas is the source of all piety. Even that is the religion which those embodied creatures who are devoted to piety and duty should observe and practise."

"'"Uma said, "O holy one, my doubts have not been dispelled. It behoveth thee to explain in detail what the duties are of the four respective orders of men."

"'"Maheswara said, "Listening to the mysteries of religion and duty, observance of

---

[561] Upavasa here, as explained by the commentator, is used for Indriyajaya or subjugation of the senses.

the vows indicated in the Vedas, attention to the sacred fire, and accomplishment of the business of the preceptor, leading a mendicant life, always bearing the sacred thread, constant recitation of the Vedas, and rigid observance of the duties of Brahmacharya, are the duties of the Brahmana. After the period of study is over, the Brahmana, receiving the command of his preceptor, should leave his preceptor's abode for returning to his father's house. Upon his return he should duly wed a wife that is fit for him. Another duty of the Brahmana consists in avoiding the food prepared by the Sudra. Walking along the path of righteousness, always observing fasts and the practices of Brahmacharya, are his other duties.[562] The householder should keep up his domestic fire for daily worship. He should study the Vedas. He should pour libations in honour of the Pitris and the deities. He should keep his senses under proper control. He should eat what remains after serving gods and guests and all his dependants. He should be abstemious in food, truthful in speech, and pure both externally and internally. Attending to guests is another duty of the householder, as also the keeping up of the three sacrificial fires. The householder should also attend to the ordinary sacrifices that go by the name of Ishti and should also dedicate animals to the deities according to the ordinances. Indeed, the performance of sacrifices is his highest duty as also a complete abstention from injury to all creatures. Never to eat before serving the deities and guests and dependants is another duty of the householder. The food that remains after serving gods and guests and dependants is called Vighasa. The householder should eat Vighasa. Indeed, to eat after the members of one's family including servants and other dependants, is regarded as one of the special duties of the regenerate householder, who should be conversant with the Vedas. The conduct of husband and wife, in the case of householder, should be equal. He should every day make offerings of flowers and other articles unto those deities that preside over domesticity. The householder should take care that his house is every day properly rubbed (with cowdung and water). He should also observe fasts every day. Well-cleaned and well-rubbed, his house should also be every day fumigated with the smoke of clarified butter poured on his sacred fire in honour of the deities and the Pitris. Even these are the duties appertaining to the householder's mode of life as observable by a regenerate person. Those duties really uphold the world. Verily, those duties always and eternally flow from those righteous persons among the Brahmanas that lead a life of domesticity. Do thou listen to me with concentrated attention, O goddess, for I shall now tell thee what the duties are which appertain to the Kshatriya and about which thou hast asked me. From the beginning it has been said that the duty of the Kshatriya is to protect all creatures. The king is the acquirer of a fixed share of the merits earned by his subjects. By that means the king becomes endued with righteousness. That ruler of men who rules and protects his subjects righteously, acquires, by virtue of the protection he offers to others, many regions of felicity in the world to come. The other duties of a person of the kingly order consist of self-restraint and Vedic study, the pouring of libations on the sacred fire, the making of gifts, study, the bearing of the sacred thread, sacrifices, the performance of religious rites, the support of servants and dependants, and perseverance in acts that have been begun. Another duty of his is to award punishments according to the offences committed. It is also his duty to perform sacrifices and other religious rites according to the ordinances laid down in the Vedas. Adherence to the practice of properly judging the disputes of litigants before him, and a devotion to truthfulness of speech, and interference

---

[562] He who takes his meals at the proper hours is said to observe fasts. He who avoids sexual congress with other women and associates with only his wedded spouse and that at her season, is said to observe Brahmacharya.

for aiding the distressed, are the other duties by discharging which the king acquires great glory both here and hereafter. He should also lay down his life on the field of battle, having displayed great prowess on behalf of kine and Brahmanas. Such a king acquires in Heaven such regions of felicity as are capable of being won by the performance of Horse-sacrifices. The duties of the Vaisya always consist of the keeping of cattle and agriculture, the pouring of libations on the sacred fire, the making of gifts, and study. Trade, walking in the path of righteousness, hospitality, peacefulness, self-restraint, welcoming of Brahmanas, and renouncing things (in favour of Brahmanas), are the other eternal duties of the Vaisya. The Vaisya, engaged in trade and walking in the path of righteousness, should never sell sesame and perfumery and juices or liquid substances. He should discharge the duties of hospitality towards all. He is at liberty to pursue religion and wealth and pleasure according to his means and as much as is judicious for him. The service of the three regenerate classes constitutes the high duty of the Sudra. That Sudra who is truthful in speech and who has subdued his senses is regarded as having acquired meritorious penances. Verily, the Sudra, who having got a guest, discharges the duties of hospitality towards him, is regarded as acquiring the merit of high penances. That intelligent Sudra whose conduct is righteous and who worships the deities and Brahmanas, becomes endued with the desirable rewards of righteousness. O beautiful lady, I have thus recited to thee what the duties are of the four orders. Indeed, O blessed lady, I have told thee what their respective duties are. What else dost thou wish to hear?"

"""Uma said, "Thou has recited to me what the respective duties are of the four orders, auspicious and beneficial for them. Do thou now tell me, O holy one, what the common duties are of all the orders."

"""Maheswara said, "The foremost of all beings in the universe viz., the Creator Brahma, ever desirous of righteous accomplishments, created the Brahmanas for rescuing all the worlds. Among all created beings, they are, verily, gods on earth. I shall at the outset tell thee what the religious acts are which they should do and what the rewards are which they win through them. That religion which has been ordained for the Brahmanas is the foremost of all religions. For the sake of the righteousness of the world, three religions were created by the Self-born One. Whenever the world is created (or re-created), those religions are created by the Grandsire. Do thou listen. These are the three eternal religions. The religion that is propounded in the Vedas is the highest; that which is propounded in the Smritis is the next in the order of importance; the third in importance is that which is based upon the practices of those who are regarded as righteous. The Brahmans possessed of learning should have the three Vedas. He should never make the study of the Vedas (or recitation of the scriptures) the means of his living.[563] He should devote himself to the three well-known acts (of making gifts, studying the Vedas, and performing sacrifices). He should transcend the three (viz., lust, wrath, and covetousness). He should be the friend of all creatures. A person that possesses these attributes is called a Brahmana. The lord of the universe declared these six acts for the observance of Brahmanas. Listen to those eternal duties. The performance of sacrifices, officiating at the sacrifices of others, the making of gifts, the acceptance of gifts, teaching, and study, are the six acts by accomplishing which a Brahmans wins religious merit. Verily, the daily study of the Vedas is a duty. Sacrifice is (another) eternal duty. The making of gifts according to the measure of his power and agreeable to the

---

[563] To sell the Vedas or any kind of knowledge is a great sin.

ordinance, is, in his case, much applauded. Tranquillity of mind is a high duty that has always been current among them that are righteous. Householders of pure mind are capable of earning very great merit. Indeed, he who cleanses his soul by the performance of the five sacrifices, who is truthful in speech, who is free from malice, who makes gifts, who treats with hospitality and honour all regenerate guests, who lives in well-cleaned abodes, who is free from pride, who is always sincere in his dealings, who uses sweet and assuring words towards others, who takes pleasure in serving guests and others arrived at his abode, and who eats the food that remains after the requirements have been gratified of all the members of his family and dependants, wins great merit. That man who offers water to his guests for washing their feet and hands, who presents the Arghya for honouring the recipient, who duly gives seats, and beds, and lamps for lighting the darkness, and shelter to those that come to his abode, is regarded as highly righteous. That householder who rises at dawn and washes his mouth and face and serves food to his guests, and having honoured them duly dismisses them from his abode and follows them (as a mark of honour) for a little distance, acquires eternal merit. Hospitality towards all, and the pursuit of the aggregate of three, are the duties of the householder. The duties of the Sudra consist in the pursuit of the aggregate of three. The Religion ordained for the householder is said to have Pravritti for its chief indication. Auspicious, and beneficial to all creatures, I shall expound it to thee. The householder should always make gifts according to the measure of his power. He should also perform sacrifices frequently after the same manner. Indeed, he who wishes to achieve his own good should always achieve meritorious acts. The householder, should acquire wealth by righteous means. The wealth thus acquired should be carefully divided into three portions, keeping the requirements of righteousness in view. With one of those portions he should accomplish all acts of righteousness. With another he should seek to gratify his cravings for pleasure. The third portion he should lay out for increasing. The Religion of Nivritti is different. It exists for emancipation (from re-birth by absorption into Brahman). I shall tell thee the conduct that constitutes it. Listen to me in detail, O goddess. One of the duties inculcated by that religion is compassion towards all creatures. The man that follows it should not reside in one place for more than one day. Desirous of achieving emancipation, the followers of this Religion free themselves from the bonds of hope (or desire). They have no attachment to habitation, to the Kamandalu they bear for keeping water, to the robes that cover their loins, or the seat whereupon they rest, or the triple stick they bear in their hands, or the bed they sleep on, or the fire they want, or the chamber that houses them. A follower of this Religion sets his heart upon the workings of his soul. His mind is devoted to Supreme Brahman. He is filled with the idea of attaining to Brahman. He is always devoted to Yoga and the Sankhya Philosophy. He desires no other shelter than the foot of a tree. He houses himself in empty abodes of men. He sleeps on the banks of rivers. He takes pleasure in staying by such banks. He is freed from every attachment, and from every tie of affection. He merges the existence of his own soul into the Supreme Soul. Standing like a stake of wood, and abstaining from all food he does only such acts as point to Emancipation. Or, he may wander about, devoted to Yoga. Even these are the eternal duties of a follower of the Religion of Nivritti. He lives aloof from his species. He is freed from all attachments. He never resides in the same place for more than a day. Freed from all bonds he roves over the world. Emancipated from all ties, he never sleeps on even the same river-bank for more than a day. Even this is the religion of persons conversant with Emancipation as declared in the Vedas. Even this is the righteous path that is trodden by the righteous. He who follows in this track leaves no vestige behind. Bhikshus (or followers of the religion of Emancipation) are of four kinds. They are Kutichakas, Vahudakas, Hansas, and Paramahansas. The second is superior to the first, the third to the second, and the fourth to the third. There is nothing superior to the Paramahansa; nor is there anything inferior to it or beside it or before it. It is a condition that is divested of sorrow and happiness; that is auspicious and freed from decrepitude and death and that knows no change."[564]

""""Uma said, "Thou hast recited the religion of the householders, that of Emancipation, and that which is based upon the observances of the righteous. These paths are high and exceedingly beneficial to the world of living creatures. O thou that art conversant with every religion, I desire now to hear what is the high religion of the Rishis. I always have a liking for those that dwell in ascetic retreats. The perfume that emanates from the smoke of the libations of clarified butter poured on the sacred fire seems to pervade the entire retreats and make them delightful. Marking this, O great god, my heart becomes always filled with delight. O puissant deity, I have doubts regarding the religion of the ascetics. Thou art conversant with the details of all religions. Do thou enlighten me, O god of gods, in detail, respecting this topic truly about which I have asked thee, O great deity!"

""""The blessed and holy one said, "Yes, I shall recite to thee the high and excellent religion of the ascetics. By following the dictates of that religion, O auspicious lady, the ascetics attain to success through the severe penances they practise. O highly blessed one, do thou hear, from the beginning, what the duties are of those righteous Rishis that are conversant with every duty and that are known by the name of Phenapas. The Grandsire Brahma (during the days he devoted to the observance of penances) drank some nectar (in the form of water). That water had flowed in heaven from a great sacrifice. The froth of that water is highly auspicious and (in consequence of Brahma's having drunk it) it partook of His own nature. Those Rishis that subsist upon the measure of froth that thus issued (from the water indicated) are called Phenapas (Froth-eaters). Even this is the conduct of those pure-souled Rishis, O lady, possessed of wealth of penances! Listen now to me as I explain to thee who the Valkhilyas are. The Valkhilyas are ascetics that have won success by their penances. They reside in the solar disc. Adopting the means of subsistence that is followed by the birds, those Rishis, conversant with every duty of righteousness, live according to the Unchha mode. Their attire consists of deer-skins or barks of trees. Freed from every pair of opposites, the Valkhilyas, possessed of wealth of penances, walk in this track of righteousness. They are as big as a digit of the thumb. Distributed into classes, each class lives in the practice of the duties assigned to it. They desire only to practise penance. The merits they win by their righteous conduct are very high. They are regarded as having attained to an equality with the gods and exist for the accomplishment of the purposes of the gods. Having burnt off all their sins by severe penances, they blaze forth in effulgence, illuminating all the points of the compass. Others, called Chakracharas, are endued with cleansed souls and devoted to the practice of compassion. Righteous in their conduct and possessed of great sanctity, they live in the region of Soma. Thus residing near enough to the region of the Pitris, they duly subsist by drinking the rays of Soma. There are others called Samprakshalas and Asmkuttas and

---

[564] The correct reading of the latter half of the first line is nabaram natirogratah. The commentator explains, this means that 'there is nothing inferior to it or beside it or before it.' In the first part of the first line it has been said that there is nothing superior to it. The sense is that it includes all, being as comprehensive as Brahman.

Dantolukhalas.[565] These live near the Soma-drinking deities and others that drink flames of fire. With their wedded spouses, and with passions under complete control, they too subsist upon the rays of Soma. They pour libations of clarified butter on the sacred fire, and adore the Pitris under proper forms. They also perform the well-known sacrifices. Even this is said to constitute their religion. The religion of the Rishis, O goddess, is always observed by those who are houseless and who are free to rove through every region including that of the gods. There are, again, other classes about whom I shall speak presently. Do thou listen. It is necessary that they who observe the different religions of the Rishis, should subjugate their passions and know the Soul. Indeed, in my opinion, lust and wrath should be completely conquered. With corn (wealth) acquired by the Unchha mode, they should discharge the following duties, viz., the pouring of libations on the sacred fire, occupying a fixed seat employing oneself the while in the sacrifice called Dharmaratri, performance of she Soma-sacrifice, acquisition of especial knowledge, the giving of sacrificial presents which forms the fifth, the daily performance of sacrifices, devotion to the worship of the Pitris and the deities, hospitality towards all. Abstention from all luxurious viands prepared from cow's milk, taking a pleasure in tranquillity of heart, lying on bare rocks or the earth, devotion to Yoga, eating potherbs and leaves of trees, and subsisting upon fruits and roots and wind and water and moss, are some of the practices of the Rishis by which they attain to the end that belongs to persons unsubjugated (by the world). When the smoke has ceased to curl upwards from a house, when the husking machine has ceased to ply, when the hearth-fire has been extinguished, when all the inmates have taken their food, when dishes are no longer carried from room to room, when mendicants have ceased to walk the streets, it is then that the man who is devoted to the religion of truth and tranquillity of soul, desiring to have a guest (but finding his desire ungratified), should eat what remnant of food may still occur in the house. By acting in this way, one becomes a practiser of the religion of the Munis. One should not be arrogant, nor proud, nor cheerless and discontented; nor should one wonder at anything. Indeed, one should behave equally towards friends and foes. Verily, one who is the foremost of all persons conversant with duties should also be friendly towards all creatures."'"'''

SECTION CXLII.

'"''Uma said, "Forest recluses reside in delightful regions, among the springs and fountains of rivers, in bowers by the sides of streams and rills, on hills and mountains, in woods and forests, and in sacred spots full of fruits and roots. With concentrated attention and observant of vows and rules, they dwell in such places. I desire, O Sankara, to hear the sacred ordinances which they follow. These recluses, O god of all gods, are persons that depend, for the protection of their bodies, upon themselves alone."[566]

'"''Maheswara said, "Do thou hear with concentrated attention what the duties are of forest recluses. Having listened to them with one mind, O goddess, do thou set thy heart upon righteousness. Listen then to what the acts are that should be practised by righteous recluses crowned with success, observant of rigid vows and rules, and residing in woods

---

[565] Samprakshalas are those Rishis who wash all their utensils daily so that nothing is stored for them for the next day. Asmakuttas are those that use only two pieces of stone for husking their grain. Dantolukhalas are those that use their teeth for purposes of husking the grain they eat.

[566] Swasarirapa-jivishu implies persons that do not stand in need of the services of others for the support of their bodies.

and forests. Performing ablutions thrice a day, worshipping the Pitris and the deities, pouring libations on the sacred fire, performing those sacrifices and rites that go by the name of Ishti-homa, picking up the grains of Nivara-paddy, eating fruit and roots, and using oil that is pressed out from Inguda and castor-seeds are their duties. Having gone through the practices of Yoga and become crowned with (ascetic) success and freed from lust and wrath, they should seat themselves in the attitude called Virasana. Indeed, they should reside in those places which are inaccessible to cowards.[567] Observant of the excellent ordinances relating to Yoga, sitting in summer in the midst of four fires on four sides with the sun overhead, duly practising what is called Manduka Yoga, and always seated in the attitude called Virasana, and lying on bare rocks or the earth, these men, with hearts set upon righteousness, must expose themselves to cold and water and fire. They subsist upon water or air or moss. They use two pieces of stones only for husking their corn. Some of them use their teeth only for such a purpose. They do not keep utensils of any kind (for storing anything for the day to come). Some of them clothe themselves with rags and barks of trees or deer-skins. Even thus do they pass their lives for the measure of time allotted to them, according to the ordinances (set forth in the scriptures). Remaining in woods and forests, they wander within woods and forests, live within them, and are always to be found within them. Indeed, these forest recluses entering into woods and forests live within them as disciples, obtaining a preceptor, live with him. The performance of the rites of Homa is their duty, as also the observance of the five sacrifices. A due observance of the rules about distribution (in respect of time) of the fivefold sacrifices as laid down in the Vedas, devotion to (other) sacrifices, forming the eighth, observance of the Chaturmasya, performance of the Paurnamasya, and other sacrifices, and performance of the daily sacrifices, are the duties of these men dissociated from wives, freed from every attachment, and cleansed from every sin. Indeed, they should live even thus in the forest. The sacrificial ladle and the water-vessel are their chief wealth. They are always devoted to the three fires. Righteous in their conduct and adhering to the path of virtue, they attain to the highest end. These Munis, crowned with (ascetic) success and ever devoted to the religion of Truth, attain to the highly sacred region of Brahman or the eternal region of Soma. O auspicious goddess, I have thus recited to thee, in brief, the outlines of the religion that is followed by forest recluses and that has many practices in detail."

"""Uma said, "O holy one, O lord of all creatures, O thou that art worshipped by all beings, I desire to hear what the religion is of those Munis that are followers of the scriptures treating of ascetic success. Do thou recite it to me. Residing in woods and forests and well-accomplished in the scriptures of success, some amongst them live and act as they like, without being restrained by particular practices; others have wives. How, indeed, have their practices been laid down?"

"""Mahadeva said, "O goddess, the shaving of the head and the wearing of the brown robes are the indications of those recluses that rove about in freedom; while the indications of those that sport with wedded wives consist in passing their nights at home. Performing ablutions three times a day is the duty of the classes, while the Homa, with water and fruits from the wilderness, belongs to the wedded recluses as performed by the Rishis in general. Absorption, Yoga-meditation, and adherence to those duties that constitute piety and that have been laid down as such (in the scriptures and the Vedas) are some of the other duties prescribed for them. All those duties also of which I have spoken

---

[567] The great forests are called Virasthana for cowards cannot enter or reside in them.

to thee before as appertaining to recluses residing in forests, are the duties of these also. Indeed, if those duties are observed, they that observe them, attain to the rewards that attach to severe penances. Those forest recluses that lead wedded lives should confine the gratification of their senses to these wedded wives of theirs. By indulging in sexual congress with their wives at only those times when their seasons come, they conform to the duties that have been laid down for them. The religion which these virtuous men are to follow is the religion that has been laid down and followed by the Rishis. With their eyes set upon the acquisition of righteousness, they should never pursue any other object of desire from a sense of unrestrained caprice. That man who makes the gift unto all creatures of an assurance of perfect harmlessness or innocence, freed as his soul becomes from the stain of malice or harmfulness, becomes endued with righteousness. Verily, that person who shows compassion to all creatures, who adopts as a vow a behaviour of perfect sincerity towards all creatures, and who constitutes himself the soul of all creatures, becomes endued with righteousness. A bath in all the Vedas, and a behaviour of sincerity towards all creatures, are looked upon as equal in point of merit; or, perhaps, the latter is a little distinguished above the other in point of merit. Sincerity, it has been said, is Righteousness; while insincerity or crookedness is the reverse. That man who conducts himself with sincerity becomes endued with Righteousness. The man who is always devoted to sincerity of behaviour, succeeds in attaining to a residence among the deities. Hence, he who wishes to achieve the merit of righteousness should become endued with sincerity. Possessed of a forgiving disposition and of self-restraint, and with wrath under complete subjection, one should transform oneself into an embodiment of Righteousness and become freed from malice. Such a man, who becomes devoted, besides, to the discharge of all the duties of Religion, becomes endued with the merit of Righteousness. Freed from drowsiness and procrastination, the pious person, who adheres to the path of Righteousness to the best of his power, and becomes possessed of pure conduct, and who is venerable in years, comes to be regarded as equal to Brahma himself."

"""Uma said, "By what course of duties, O god, do those ascetics who are attached to their respective retreats and possessed of wealth of penances, succeed in becoming endued with great splendour? By what acts again, do kings and princes who are possessed of great wealth, and others who are destitute of wealth, succeed in obtaining high rewards? By what acts, O god, do denizens of the forest succeed in attaining to that place which is eternal and in adorning their persons with celestial sandal-paste? O illustrious god of three eyes, O destroyer of the triple city, do thou dispel this doubt of mine connected with the auspicious subject of the observance of penances by telling everything in detail."

"""The illustrious deity said, "Those who observe the vows relating to fasts and restrain their senses, who abstain from injury of any kind to any creature, and who practise truthfulness of speech, attain to success and ascending to Heaven sport in felicity with the Gandharvas as their companions, freed from every kind of evil. The righteous-souled man who lies down in the attitude which appertains to Manduka-Yoga, and who properly and according to the ordinance performs meritorious acts after having taken the Diksha, sports in felicity in the next world in the company of the Nagas. That man who lives in the company of deer and subsists upon such grass and vegetables as fall off from their mouths, and who has undergone the Diksha and attends to the duties attached to it, succeeds in attaining to Amaravati (the mansions of Indra). That man who subsists upon the moss he gathers and the fallen leaves of trees that he picks up, and endures all the severities of cold, attains to very high place. That man who subsists upon either air or water, or fruits and roots, attains in after life to the affluence that belongs to the Yakshas and sports in felicity in the company of diverse tribes of Apsaras. Having practised for two and ten years, according to the rites laid down in the ordinances, the vow relating to the endurance of the five fires in the summer season, one becomes in one's next life a king. That man who, having observed vows with respect to food, practises penances for two and twelve years, carefully abstaining from all interdicted food, taken at forbidden hours, during the periods becomes in his next life a ruler of earth.[568] That man who sits and lies on the bare ground with the cope of the firmament alone for his shelter, observes the course of duties that attach to Diksha, and then casts off his body by abstaining from all food, attains to great felicity in Heaven. The rewards of one who sits and lies down upon the bare ground (with the welkin alone for his shelter) are said to be excellent vehicles and beds, and costly mansions possessed of the resplendence of the moon, O lady! That man who, having subsisted upon abstemious diet and observed diverse excellent vows, lives depending upon his own self and then casts off his body by abstaining from all food, succeeds in ascending to heaven and enjoying all its felicity. That man who, having lived in entire dependence upon his own self, observes for two and ten years the duties that appertain to Diksha, and at last casts off his body on the great ocean, succeeds in attaining to the regions of Varuna after death. That man who, living in entire dependence upon his own self observes the duties that attach to Diksha for two and ten years, and pierces his own feet with a sharp stone, attains to the felicity of the region that belongs to the Guhyakas. He who cultivates self with the aid of self, who frees himself from the influence of all pairs of opposites (such as heat and cold, joy and sorrow, etc), who is freed from every kind of attachment, and who mentally observes for two and ten years such a course of conduct after Diksha, attains to Heaven and enjoys every happiness with the deities as his companions. He who lives in entire dependence upon his own self and observes for two and ten years the duties that attach to Diksha and finally casts off his body on the fire as an oblation to the deities, attains to the regions of Brahman and is held in high respect there. That regenerate man, O goddess, who having properly gone through the Diksha keeps his senses under subjugation, and placing his Self on Self frees himself from the sense of meum, desirous of achieving righteousness, and sets out, without a covering for his body, after the due observance of the duties of Diksha for two and ten years and after having placed his sacred fire on a tree, and walks along the path that belongs to heroes and lies down (when need for lying down comes) in the attitude of heroes, and conducts himself always after the manner of heroes, certainly attains to the end that is reserved for heroes.[569] Such a man repairs to the eternal region of Sakra where he becomes crowned with the fruition of all his wishes and where he sports in joy, his person decked with garlands of celestial flowers and celestial perfumes. Indeed, that righteous souled person lives happily in Heaven, with the deities as his companions. The hero, observant of the practices of heroes and devoted to that Yoga which belongs to heroes, living in the practice of Goodness, having renounced everything, having undergone the Diksha and subjugated his senses, and observing purity of both body and mind, is sure to attain to that path which is reserved for heroes. Eternal regions of happiness are his. Riding on a car that moves at the will of the rider, he roves

[568] Marum samsadhya implies abstention from even air and water as food or means of subsistence.
[569] It should be noted that the word Vira in the various compounds in which it occurs here, does not mean heroes of war. On the other hand, it signifies heroes of righteousness and penances. The path of heroes is the forest, for cowards cannot go there. The attitude of heroes (Virasana) is a kind of attitude for Yogins to sit in.

through all those happy regions as he likes. Indeed, dwelling in the region of Sakra, that blessed person always sports in joy, freed from every calamity."''''''

SECTION CXLIII.

'''''Uma said, "O holy one, O thou that didst tear off the eyes of Bhaga and the teeth of Pushan, O destroyer of the sacrifice of Daksha, O three-eyed deity, I have a great doubt. In days of yore, the Self-born One created the four orders. Through the evil consequence of what acts doth a Vaisya become a Sudra? Through what acts doth a Kshatriya become a Vaisya and a regenerate person (Brahmana) becomes a Kshatriya? By what means may such degradation of castes be prevented? Through what acts does a Brahmana take birth in his next life, in the Sudra order? Through what acts, O puissant deity, does a Kshatriya also descend to the status of Sudra? O sinless one, O lord of all created beings, do thou, O illustrious one, dispel this doubt of mine. How, again, can the three other orders naturally succeed in attaining to the status of Brahmanhood?"

'''''The illustrious one said, "The status of a Brahmana, O goddess, is exceedingly difficult to attain. O auspicious lady, one becomes a Brahmana through original creation or birth. After the same manner the Kshatriya, the Vaisya, and the Sudra, all become so through original creation. Even this is my opinion.[570] He, however, that is born a Brahmana falls away from his status through his own evil acts. Hence, the Brahmana, after having attained to the status of the first order, should always protect it (by his acts). If one, who is a Kshatriya or Vaisya, lives in the practice of those duties that are assigned to the Brahmana, after the manner of a Brahmana he becomes (in his next life) a Brahmana. That Brahmana who casts off the duties of his order for following those assigned for the Kshatriya, is regarded as one that has fallen away from the status of a Brahmana and that has become a Kshatriya. That Brahmana of little understanding, who, impelled by cupidity and folly, follows the practices assigned to Vaisyas forgetful of his status as a Brahmana that is exceedingly difficult to attain, comes to be regarded as one that has become a Vaisya. Similarly, one that is a Vaisya by birth may, by following the practices of a Sudra, become a Sudra. Indeed, a Brahmana, falling away from the duties of his own order, may descend to the status of even a Sudra. Such a Brahmana, falling away from the order of his birth and turned out of it, without attaining to the region of Brahmana (which is his goal if he duly observes his own duties), sinks into Hell and in his next birth becomes born as a Sudra. A highly blessed Kshatriya or a Vaisya, that abandons those practices of his that are consistent with the duties laid down for his order, and follows the practices laid down for the Sudra, falls away from his own order and becomes a person of mixed caste. It is in this way that a Brahmana, or a Kshatriya, or a Vaisya, sinks into the status of a Sudra. That man who has attained to clearness of vision through practice of the duties of his own order, who is endued with knowledge and science, who is pure (in body and mind), who is conversant with every duty and devoted to the practice of all his duties, is sure to enjoy the rewards of righteousness. I shall now recite to thee, O goddess, a saying uttered by Brahma (the Self-born) on this subject. Those that are righteous and desirous of acquiring merit always pursue with firmness the culture of the soul. The food that comes from cruel and fierce persons is censurable. So also is the food that has been cooked for serving a large number of persons. The same is

---

[570] Nisargat is literally through creation or original nature, or birth. Of course, what is implied is that one becomes a Brahmana, or Kshatriya, or Vaisya or Sudra, through original creation as such, by the Self-born, that is, birth.

said of the food that is cooked in view of the first Sraddha of a deceased person. So also is the food that is stained in consequence of the usual faults and the food that is supplied by a Sudra. These should never be taken by a Brahmana at any time.[571] The food of a Sudra, O goddess, is always disapproved of by the high-souled deities. Even this, I think, is the authority enunciated by the Grandsire with his own mouth. If a Brahmana, who has set up the sacred fire and who performs sacrifices, were to die with any portion of a Sudra's food remaining undigested in his stomach, he is sure to take birth in his next life as a Sudra. In consequence of those remains of a Sudra's food in his stomach, he falls away from the status of a Brahmana. Such a Brahmana becomes invested with the status of a Sudra. There is no doubt in this. This Brahmana in his next life becomes invested with the status of that order upon whose food he subsists through life or with the undigested portion of whose food in his stomach he breathes his last.[572] That man who, having attained to the auspicious status of a Brahmana which is so difficult to acquire, disregards it and eats interdicted food, falls away from his high status. That Brahmana who drinks alcohol, who becomes guilty of Brahmanicide or mean in his behaviour, or a thief, or who breaks his vows, or becomes impure, or unmindful of his Vedic studies, or sinful, or characterised by cupidity, or guilty of cunning or cheating, or who does not observe vows, or who weds a Sudra woman, or who derives his subsistence by pandering to the lusts of other people or who sells the Soma plant, or who serves a person of an order below his, falls away from his status of Brahmanahood.[573] That Brahmana who violates the bed of his preceptor, or who cherishes malice towards him, or who takes pleasure in speaking ill of him, falls away from the status of Brahmanahood even if he be conversant with Brahman. By these good acts, again, O goddess, when performed, a Sudra becomes a Brahmana, and a Vaisya becomes a Kshatriya. The Sudra should perform all the duties laid down for him, properly and according to the ordinance. He should always wait, with obedience and humility, upon person of the three other orders and serve them with care. Always adhering to the path of righteousness, the Sudra should cheerfully do all this. He should honour the deities and persons of the regenerate orders. He should observe the vow of hospitality to all persons. With senses kept under subjection and becoming abstemious in food, he should never approach his wife except in her season. He should ever search after persons that are holy and pure. As regards food, he should eat that which remains after the needs of all persons have been satisfied. If, indeed, the Sudra desires to be a Vaisya (in his next life), he should also abstain from meat of animals not slain in sacrifices. If a Vaisya wishes to be a Brahmana (in his next life), he should observe even these duties. He should be truthful in speech, and free from pride or arrogance. He should rise superior to all pairs of opposites (such as heat and cold, joy and sorrow, etc.) He should be observant of the duties of peace and tranquillity. He should adore the deities in sacrifices, attend with devotion to the study and recitation of the Vedas, and become pure in body and mind. He should keep his senses under

---

[571] Ugra means a fierce or cruel person. It is also applied to signify a person of a mixed caste whose occupation is the slaughter of animals in the chase. The commentator is silent. I think, the food supplied by a fierce or cruel person is meant here. What is said in this verse is that the several kinds of food spoken of here should be renounced by a good Brahmana.

[572] The sense is this: if a Brahmana dies with any portion of the food of a Sudra, a Vaisya, or a Kshatriya in his stomach, in his next life he has to take birth as a Sudra, a Vaisya, or a Kshatriya. If, again, during life he subsists upon food supplied to him by a Sudra, a Vaisya, or a Kshatriya, he has to take birth in his next life as a Sudra, a Vaisya, or a Kshatriya.

[573] Kundasin means a pander. It may also imply one who eats from off the vessel in which the food eaten has been cooked without, that is, using plates or leaves.

subjection, honour the Brahmanas, and seek the welfare of all the orders. Leading the domestic mode of life and eating only twice a day at the prescribed hours he should gratify his hunger with only such food as remains after the needs have been satisfied of all the members of his family with dependants and guests. He should be abstemious in food, and act without being impelled by the desire of reward. He should be free from egotism. He should adore the deities in the Agnihotra and pour libations according to the ordinance. Observing the duties of hospitality towards all persons, he should, as already said, eat the food that remains after serving all others for whom it has been cooked. He should, according to the ordinance laid down, worship the three fires. Such a Vaisya of pure conduct takes birth in his next life in a high Kshatriya family.[574] If a Vaisya, after having taken birth as a Kshatriya, goes through the usual purificatory rites, becomes invested with the sacred thread, and betakes himself to the observance of vows, he becomes, in his next life, an honoured Brahmana. Indeed, after his birth as a Kshatriya, he should make presents, adore the deities in great sacrifices with plentiful Dakshinas, study the Vedas, and desirous of attaining to Heaven should worship the three fires. He should interfere for dispelling the sorrows of the distressed, and should always righteously cherish and protect those subjects that own his sway. He should be truthful, and do all acts that have truth in them, and seek happiness in conduct like this. He should award punishments that are righteous, without laying aside the rod of chastisement for good. He should induce men to do righteous deeds. Guided by considerations of policy (in the matter of swaying his people), he should take a sixth of the produce of the fields.[575] He should never indulge in sexual pleasure, but live cheerfully and in independence, well-conversant with the science of Wealth or Profit. Of righteous soul, he should seek his wedded spouse only in her season. He should always observe fasts, keep his soul under control, devote himself to the study of the Vedas, and be pure in body and mind. He should sleep on blades of Kusa grass spread out in his fire chamber. He should pursue the aggregate of Three (viz., Righteousness, Wealth, and Pleasure), and be always cheerful. Unto Sudras desirous of food, he should always answer that it is ready. He should never desire any thing from motives of gain or pleasure. He should worship the Pitris and gods and guests. In his own house he should live the life of a mendicant. He should duly adore the deities in his Agnihotra, morning, noon, and evening every day, by pouring libations agreeably to the ordinance. With his face turned towards the foe, he should cast off his life-breath in battle fought for the benefit of kine and Brahmanas. Or he may enter the triple fires sanctified with Mantras and cast off his body. By pursuing this line of conduct he takes birth in his next life as a Brahmana. Endued with knowledge and science, purified from all dross, and fully conversant with the Vedas, a pious Kshatriya, by his own acts, becomes a Brahmana. It is with the aid of these acts, O goddess, that a person who has sprung from a degraded order, viz., a Sudra, may become a Brahmana refined of all stains and possessed of Vedic lore, One that is a Brahmana, when he becomes wicked in conduct and observes no distinction in respect of food, falls away from the status of Brahmanahood and becomes a Sudra. Even a Sudra, O goddess, that has purified his soul by pure deeds and that has subjugated all his senses, deserves to be waited upon and served with reverence as a Brahmana. This has been said by the Self-

---

[574] The sense seems to be this: a Vaisya ultimately becomes a Brahmana by observing the duties indicated in verses 30 to 33. As the immediate reward, however, of his observance of these duties, he becomes a great Kshatriya. What he should next do in order to become a Brahmana is said in the verses that follow.

[575] This may, besides, imply the taking of a sixth portion of the merits acquired by his subjects through the righteous deeds they perform.

born Brahmana himself. When a pious nature and pious deeds are noticeable in even a Sudra, he should, according to my opinion, be held superior to a person of the three regenerate classes. Neither birth, nor the purificatory rites, nor learning, nor offspring, can be regarded as grounds for conferring upon one the regenerate status. Verily, conduct is the only ground. All Brahmanas in this world are Brahmanas in consequence of conduct. A Sudra, if he is established on good conduct, is regarded as possessed of the status of a Brahmana. The status of Brahma, O auspicious lady, is equal wherever it exists. Even this is my opinion. He, indeed, is a Brahmana in whom the status of Brahma exists,—that condition which is bereft of attributes and which has no stain attached to it. The boon-giving Brahma, while he created all creatures, himself said that the distribution of human beings into the four orders dependent on birth is only for purposes of classification. The Brahmana is a great field in this world,—a field equipped with feet for it moves from place to place. He who plants seeds in that field, O beautiful lady, reaps the crop in the next world. That Brahmana who wishes to achieve his own good should always live upon the remains of the food that may be there in his house after gratifying the needs of all others. He should always adhere to the path of righteousness. Indeed, he should tread along the path that belongs to Brahma. He should live engaged in the study of the Samhitas and remaining at home he should discharge all the duties of a householder. He should always be devoted to the study of the Vedas, but he should never derive the means of subsistence from such study. That Brahmana who always conducts himself thus, adhering to the path of righteousness, worshipping his sacred fire, and engaged in the study of the Vedas, comes to be regarded as Brahma. The status of a Brahmana once gained, it should always be protected with care, O thou of sweet smiles, by avoiding the stain of contact with persons born in inferior orders, and by abstaining from the acceptance of gifts. I have thus told thee a mystery, viz., the manner in which a Sudra may become a Brahmana, or that by which a Brahmana falls away from his own pure status and becomes a Sudra."'''''

SECTION CXLIV.

"'''''Uma said, "O holy one, O Lord of all beings, O thou that art worshipped by the deities and Asuras equally, tell me what are the duties and derelictions of men. Indeed, O puissant one, resolve my doubts. It is by these three, viz., thought, word, and deed, that men become bound with bonds. It is by these same three that they become freed from those bonds. By pursuing what conduct, O god,—indeed, by what kind of acts,—by what behaviour and attributes and words, do men succeed in ascending to heaven?"

"'''''The god of gods said, "O goddess, thou art well-conversant with the true import of duties. Thou art ever devoted to righteousness and self-restraint. The question thou hast asked me is fraught with the benefit of all creatures. It enhances the intelligence of all persons. Do thou, therefore, listen to the answer. Those persons that are devoted to the religion of Truth, that are righteous and destitute of the indications of the several modes of life, and that enjoy the wealth earned by righteous means, succeed in ascending to heaven. Those men that are freed from all doubts, that are possessed of omniscience, and that have eyes to behold all things, are never enchained by either virtue or sin. Those men that are freed from all attachments can never be bound by the chains of action. They who never injure others in thought, word, or deed, and who never attach themselves to anything, can never be bound by acts. They who abstain from taking the lives of any creature, who are pious in conduct, who have compassion, who regard friends and foes in an equal light and who are self-restrained, can never be bound by acts. Those men that are endued with compassion towards all beings, that succeed in inspiring the confidence of all living creatures, and that have cast off malice in their behaviour, succeed in ascending to heaven. Those men that have no desire to appropriate what belongs to others, that keep themselves aloof from the wedded wives of others, and that enjoy only such wealth as has been earned by righteous means, succeed in ascending to heaven. Those men who behave towards the wives of other people as towards their own mothers and sisters and daughters, succeed in attaining to heaven. Those men that abstain from appropriating what belongs to others, that are perfectly contented with what they possess, and that live depending upon their own destiny, succeed in ascending to heaven. Those men that, in their conduct, always shut their eyes against association with other people's spouses, that are masters of their senses, and that are devoted to righteous conduct, succeed in ascending to heaven. Even this is the path, created by the gods, that the righteous should follow. This is the path, freed from passion and aversion, laid down for the righteous to follow. Those men who are devoted to their own spouses and who seek them only in their seasons, and who turn themselves away from indulgence in sexual pleasure, succeed in ascending to Heaven. Conduct marked by charity and penances, and characterised by righteousness of deeds and purity of both body and heart, should be followed by those that are wise for the sake of adding to their merit or for earning their means of subsistence. Those who wish to ascend to Heaven should follow in this track and not in any other."

"""Uma said, "Tell me, O illustrious deity, O sinless lord of all creatures, what are those words by which one becomes enchained and what are those words by uttering which one may be freed from one's bonds."

"""Maheswara said, "Those men who never tell lies for either themselves or for others, or in jest or for exciting laughter, succeed in ascending to Heaven. They who never tell lies for earning their subsistence or for earning merit or through mere caprice, succeed in ascending to Heaven. They who utter words that are smooth and sweet and faultless, and who welcome all whom they meet with sincerity, succeed in ascending to Heaven. They who never utter words that are harsh and bitter and cruel, and who are free from deceitfulness and evil of every kind, succeed in ascending to Heaven. Those men who never utter words that are fraught with deceit or that cause breach of understanding between friends, and who always speak what is true and what promotes good feelings, succeed in ascending to Heaven. Those men who avoid harsh speeches and abstain from quarrels with others, who are impartial in their behaviour to all creatures, and who have subjugated their souls, succeed in ascending to Heaven. They who abstain from evil speech or sinful conversation, who avoid such speeches as are disagreeable, and who utter only such words as are auspicious and agreeable, succeed in ascending to Heaven. They who never utter, under anger, such words as tear the hearts of other people, and who, even when under the influence of wrath, speak words that are peaceful and agreeable, succeed in ascending to Heaven. The religion, O goddess, appertaining to speech, should always be followed by men. It is auspicious and characterised by truth. They that are possessed of wisdom should always avoid untruth."

"""Uma said, "Do thou tell me, O god of gods, O wielder of Pinaka, O thou that art highly blessed, what those mental acts or thoughts are by which a person may be enchained."

"""Maheswara said, "Endued with merit that arises from mental acts, O goddess, one ascends to Heaven. Listen to me, O auspicious one, as I recite to thee what those acts are.

Listen to me, O thou of sweet face, how also a mind of ill-regulated features becomes enchained by ill-regulated or evil thoughts. Those men who do not seek even mentally, to take what belongs to others even when they see it lying in a lone forest, succeed in ascending to Heaven. Those men who care not to appropriate what belongs to others even when they see it lying in a house or a village that has been deserted, ascend to Heaven. Those men that do not seek, even mentally, to associate with the wedded spouses of others even when they behold them in deserted places and under the influence of desire, succeed in ascending to Heaven. Those men who, meeting with friends or foes, behave in the same friendly way towards all, succeed in ascending to Heaven. Those men that are possessed of learning and compassion, that are pure in body and mind, that are firm in their adherence to truth, and that are contented with what belongs to them, succeed in ascending to Heaven. Those men that do not bear ill-will to any creature, that do not stand in need of labour for their subsistence, that bear friendly hearts towards all beings, and that entertain compassion towards all, succeed in ascending to Heaven. Those men that are endued with faith, that have compassion, that are holy, that seek the company of holy men, and that are conversant with the distinctions between right and wrong, succeed in ascending to Heaven. Those men, O goddess, that are conversant with what the consequences are of good and bad deeds, succeed in ascending to Heaven. Those men that are just in all their dealings, that are endued with all desirable accomplishments, that are devoted to the deities and the Brahmanas, and that are endued with perseverance in the doing of good acts, succeed in ascending to Heaven. All these men, O goddess, succeed in ascending to Heaven through the meritorious consequences of their deeds. What else dost thou wish to hear?"

"'"Uma said, "I have a great doubt, O Maheswara, on a subject connected with human beings. It behoveth thee to explain it to me carefully. By what acts does a man succeed, O puissant deity, in acquiring a long life? By what penances also does one acquire a long life? By what acts does one become shortlived on earth? O thou that art perfectly stainless, it behoveth thee to tell me what the consequences are of acts (in the matter of bestowing a long or a short life on the doer). Some are seen to be possessed of great good fortune and some weighted with misfortune. Some are of noble birth while others of ignoble birth. Some are of such repulsive features as if they are made of wood, while others are of very agreeable features at even the first sight. Some appear to be destitute of wisdom while others are possessed of it. Some, again, are seen endued with high intelligence and wisdom, enlightened by knowledge and science. Some have to endure little pain, while others there are that are weighted with heavy calamities. Even such diverse sights are seen with respect to men. It behoveth thee, O illustrious one, to tell me the reason of all this."

"'"The god of gods said, "Verily, O goddess, I shall discourse to thee on the manifestation of the fruits of acts. It is by the rules of that manifestation that all human beings in this world enjoy or endure the consequences of their acts. That man who assumes a fierce aspect for the purpose of taking the lives of other creatures, who arms himself with stout sticks for injuring other creatures, who is seen with uplifted weapons, who slays living creatures, who is destitute of compassion, who always causes agitation to living beings, who refuses to grant protection to even worms and ants, who is endued with cruelty,—one who is such, O goddess, sinks in Hell. One who is endued with an opposite disposition and who is righteous in acts, is born as a handsome man. The man who is endued with cruelty, goes to Hell, while he that is endued with compassion ascends to Heaven. The man who goes to Hell has to endure excruciating misery. One who, having sunk in Hell, rises therefrom, takes birth as a man endued with short life. That man who is addicted to slaughter and injury, O goddess, becomes, through his sinful deeds, liable to destruction. Such a person becomes disagreeable to all creatures and endued with a short life. That man who belongs to what is called the White class, who abstains from the slaughter of living creatures, who has thrown away all weapons, who never inflicts any chastisement on anybody, who never injures any creatures, who never causes anybody to slay creatures for him, who never slays or strikes even when struck or attempted to be slain, who never sanctions or approves an act of slaughter, who is endued with compassion towards all creatures, who behaves towards others as towards his own self,—such a superior man, O goddess, succeeds in attaining to the status of a deity. Filled with joy, such a man enjoys diverse kinds of luxurious articles. If such a person ever takes birth in the world of men, he becomes endued with longevity and enjoys great happiness. Even this is the way of those that are of righteous conduct and righteous deeds and that are blessed with longevity, the way that was indicated by the Self-born Brahman himself and that is characterised by abstention from the slaughter of living creatures."'"'"

SECTION CXLV.

"'"'Uma said, "By what disposition, what conduct, what acts, and what gifts, does a man succeed in attaining to Heaven?"

"'"'Maheswara said, "He who is endued with a liberal disposition, who honours Brahmanas and treats them with hospitality, who makes gifts of food and drink and robes and other articles of enjoyment unto the destitute, the blind, and the distressed, who makes gifts of houses, erects halls (for use of the public), digs wells, constructs shelters whence pure and cool water is distributed (during the hot months unto thirsty travellers), excavates tanks, makes arrangements for the free distribution of gifts every day, gives to all seekers what each solicits, who makes gifts of seats and beds and conveyances, wealth, jewels and gems, houses, all kinds of corn, kine, fields, and women,—verily, he who always makes these gifts with a cheerful heart, becomes a denizen, O goddess, of Heaven. He resides there for a long period, enjoying diverse kinds of superior articles. Passing his time happily in the company of the Apsaras, he sports in the woods of Nandana and other delightful regions. After the exhaustion of his merits he falls down from Heaven and takes birth in the order of humanity, in a family, O goddess, that is possessed of wealth in abundance and that has a large command of every article of enjoyments. In that life he becomes endued with all articles for gratifying his wishes and appetites. Indeed, blessed with the possession of such articles, he becomes endued with affluence and a well-filled treasury. The self-born Brahman himself declared it in days of old that it is even such persons, O goddess, that become highly blessed and possessed of liberal dispositions and agreeable features. There are others, O goddess, that are incapable of making gifts. Endued with small understandings, they cannot make gifts even when solicited by Brahmanas and possessed of abundant wealth. Beholding the destitute, the blind, the distressed, and mendicants, and even guests arrived at their abodes, those persons, always filled with the desire of gratifying the organ of taste, turn away, even when expressly solicited by them. They never make gifts of wealth or robes, or viands, or gold, or kine, or any kind of food. Those men who are disinclined to relieve the distress of others, who are full of cupidity, who have no faith in the scriptures, and who never make gifts,—verily, these men of little understanding, O goddess, have to sink in Hell. In course of time, when their sufferings in Hell come to an end, they take birth in the order of humanity, in families that are entirely destitute of wealth. Always suffering from hunger and thirst, excluded from all decent society, hopeless of ever enjoying good things, they lead lives of great wretchedness. Born in families that are destitute of all articles of enjoyment, these men never succeed in enjoying the good things of the world. Indeed, O goddess, it is through their acts that persons become wretched and poor. There are others who are full of arrogance and pride caused by the possession of riches. Those senseless wretches never offer seats to those that deserve such an offer. Endued with little understandings they do not give way to them that deserve such an honour.[576] Nor do they give water for washing the feet to persons unto whom it should be given. Indeed, they do not honour, agreeably to the ordinance, with gifts of the Arghya, such persons as deserve to be honoured therewith. They do not offer water for washing the mouth unto such as deserve to have that honour. They do not treat their very preceptors, when the latter arrive at their houses, in the manner in which preceptors should be treated. Living in cupidity and arrogance, they refuse to treat their seniors and aged men with love and affection, even insulting those that deserve to be honoured and asserting their superiority over them without showing reverence and humility. Such men, O goddess, sink in Hell. When their sufferings come to an end after a long course of years, they rise from Hell, and take birth in the order of humanity, in low and wretched families. Indeed, they who humiliate their preceptors and seniors, have to take their birth in such castes as those of Swapakas and Pukkasas who are exceedingly vile and bereft of intelligence. He who is not arrogant or filled with pride, who is a worshipper of the deities and Brahmanas, who enjoys the respect of the world, who bows to every one that deserves his reverence, who utters smooth and sweet words, who benefits persons of all orders, who is always devoted to the good of all beings, who does not feel aversion for anybody, who is sweet-tongued, who is an utterer of agreeable and cooling words, who gives way to one that deserves to have way, who adores his preceptors in the manner in which preceptors deserve to be adored, who welcomes all creatures with proper courtesy, who does not hear ill will towards any creature, who lives, worshipping seniors and guests with such honours as they deserve, who is ever bent upon securing as many guests as possible, and who worships all who honour his house with their presence, succeeds, O goddess, in ascending to Heaven. Upon the exhaustion of his merit, he takes birth in the order of humanity in a high and respectable family. In that life he becomes possessed of all articles of enjoyment in abundance and jewels and gems and every kind of wealth in profusion. He gives unto deserving persons what they deserve. He becomes devoted to the observance of every duty and every act of righteousness. Honoured by all creatures and receiving their reverence, he obtains the fruits of his own acts. Even such a person acquires a high lineage and birth in this world. This that I have recited to thee was said by the Ordainer (Brahman) himself in days of old. That man who is fierce in conduct, who inspires terror in all creatures, who injures other beings with hands or feet or cords or sticks, or brick-bats or clods of hard clay, or other means of wounding and paining, O beautiful lady, who practises diverse kinds of deceit for slaying living creatures or vexing them, who pursues animals in the chase and causes them to tremble in fear,—verily, that man, who conducts himself in this way, is certain to sink in Hell. If in course of time he takes birth in the order of humanity, he is obliged to be born in a low and wretched race or family that is afflicted with impediments of every kind on every side. He becomes an object of

---

[576] In India an inferior should always stand aside for letting his superior pass. The Kshatriya should give way to the Brahmana, the Vaisya to the Kshatriya, and the Sudra to the Vaisya.

aversion to all the world. Wretched among men, he becomes so through the consequence of his own acts. Another, who is possessed of compassion, casts his eye on all creatures. Endued with a friendly vision, behaving towards all creatures as if he were their father, divested of every hostile feeling, with all his passions under complete control, he never vexes any creature and never inspires them with fear by means of his hands or feet which are always under his control. He inspires the confidence of all beings. He never afflicts any creature with either cords or clubs or brick-bats or clods of hard earth or weapons of any kind. His deeds are never fierce or cruel, and he is full of kindness. One who is endued with such practices and conduct certainly ascend to Heaven. There he lives like a god in a celestial mansion abounding with every comfort. If, upon the exhaustion of his merit, he has to take birth in the order of humanity, he becomes born as a man that has not to fight with difficulties of any kind or to encounter any fear. Indeed, he enjoys great happiness. Possessed of felicity, without the obligation of undergoing distressing labour for his subsistence, he lives freed from every kind of anxiety. Even this, O goddess, is the path of the righteous. In it there are no impediments or afflictions."

"""Uma said, "In the world some men are seen well-versed in inferences and the premises leading to them. Indeed, they are possessed of science and knowledge, have large progeny, and are endued with learning and wisdom. Others, O god, are destitute of wisdom, science, and knowledge, and are characterised by folly. By what particular acts does a person become possessed of wisdom? By what acts, again, does one become possessed of little wisdom and distorted vision? Do thou dispel this doubt of mine, O thou that art the foremost of all beings conversant with duties. Others there are, O god, that are blind from the moment of their birth. Others there are that are diseased and afflicted and impotent. Do thou, O god, tell me the reason of this."

"""Maheswara said, "Those men that always enquire, about what is for their benefit and what is to their detriment, Brahmanas learned in the Vedas, crowned with success, and conversant with all duties, that avoid all kinds of evil deeds and achieve only such deeds as are good, succeed in ascending to Heaven after departing from this world and enjoy great happiness as long as they live here. Indeed, upon the exhaustion of their merit when they take birth in the order of humanity, they become born as men possessed of great intelligence. Every kind of felicity and auspiciousness becomes theirs in consequence of that intelligence with which they are born. Those men of foolish understandings who cast wicked eyes upon the wedded spouses of other men, become cursed with congenital blindness in consequence of that sinfulness of theirs. Those men who, impelled by desire in their hearts, cast their eyes on naked women, those men of wicked deeds take birth in this world to pass their whole lives in one continuous disease. Those men of foolish and wicked deeds who indulge in sexual congress with women of orders different from their own,—those men of little wisdom,—have to take birth in their next lives as persons destitute of virility. Those men who cause animals to be slain, and those who violate the beds of their preceptors, and those who indulge promiscuously in sexual congress, have to take birth in their next lives as persons destitute of the virile power."

"""Uma said, "What acts, O foremost of the deities, are faulty, and what acts are faultless? What, indeed, are those acts by doing which a man succeeds in attaining to what is for your highest good?"

"""Maheswara said, "That man who is desirous of ascertaining what is righteousness, and who wishes to acquire prominent virtues and accomplishments, and who always puts questions to the Brahmanas with a view to find out the path that leads to his highest good, succeed in ascending to Heaven. If (after exhaustion of his merit) he takes birth in the order of humanity, he becomes endued with intelligence and memory and great wisdom. This, O goddess, is the line of conduct that the righteous are to follow and that is fraught with great benefit. I have told thee of it for the good of human beings."

""'Uma said, "There are men who hate righteousness and who are possessed of little understanding. They never wish to approach Brahmanas conversant with the Vedas. There are others who are observant of vows and who are devoted to the duty of performing Sraddhas. Others, again, are destitute of all vows. They are unmindful of observance and are like Rakshasas in conduct. Some there are who are devoted to the performance of sacrifices and some who are unmindful of the Homa. Through the consequences of what acts do men become possessed of These different natures?"

""'Maheswara said, "Through the Vedas, the limits have been assigned of all the acts of human beings. Those men that conduct themselves according to the authority of the Vedas, are seen (in their next lives) to become devoted to the observance of vows. Those men, however, who having become subject to the sway of folly accept unrighteousness for its reverse, become destitute of vows, transgress all restraints, and come to be regarded as Brahmarakshasas. Indeed, it is these men that become unmindful of the Homa, that never utter the Vashat and other sacred Mantras, and that come to be regarded as the lowest and vilest of men. Thus, O goddess, have I explained to thee the entire ocean of duties in respect of human beings for the sake of removing thy doubts, not omitting the sins of which they become guilty."'"""

SECTION CXLVI.

""'Narada said, 'Having said these words, the puissant Mahadeva himself became desirous of hearing (instead of talking), and with that view he questioned his dear spouse who was seated by his side and she was fully inclined to act up to his desire.'

""'Mahadeva said, "Thou, O goddess, art conversant with what is Supreme and what is not.[577] Thou art acquainted with all duties, O thou that lovest to reside in the retreats of ascetics. Thou art endued with every virtue, possessed of beautiful eyebrows and hair ending in the fairest curls, O daughter of Himavat, the king of mountains! Thou art skilled in every work. Thou art endued with self-restraint and thou lookest impartially upon all creatures. Divested of the sense of meum, thou art devoted to the practice of all the duties. O thou of beautiful features, I desire to ask thee about something. I wish that, asked by me, thou wilt discourse to me on that topic. Savitri is the chaste wife of Brahma. The chaste Sachi is the wife of Indra. Dhumrorna is the spouse of Markandeya, and Riddhi of (king) Vaisravana. Varuna has Gauri for his spouse, and Surya has Suvarchala. Rohini is the chaste wife of Sasin, and Swaha of Vibhavasu. Kasyapa has Aditi. All these regard their husbands as their gods. Thou hast, O goddess, conversed and associated with all of them every day. It is for this reason, O thou that art conversant with every duty, that I desire to question thee about the duties of women, O thou whose words are always consistent with righteousness. I desire to hear thee discourse on that subject from the beginning. Thou practisest all the duties of righteousness with me. Thy conduct is exactly like mine, and the vows thou observest are the same that are observed by me. Thy puissance and energy are equal to mine, and thou hast undergone the austerest penances. The subject, when discoursed upon by thee, will become endued with great merit. Indeed,

---

[577] i.e. Soul (including the Supreme Soul) and Not-soul.

that discourse will then become authoritative in the world. Women, in especial, are the highest refuge of women. O thou of beautiful hips, among human beings that course of conduct which thou wilt lay down will be followed from generation to generation.[578] Half of my body is made up of half thy body. Thou art always engaged in doing the work of the deities, and it is thou that art the cause of the peopling of the earth. O auspicious lady, all the eternal duties of women are well-known to thee. Do thou, therefore, tell me in detail what are the duties of thy sex."

"'"Uma said, "O holy one, O lord of all created things, O source of all that is past, present, and future, it is through thy grace that the words I am uttering are taking their rise in my mind. All these Rivers (that are of my sex), O god of gods, endued with the waters of all the Tirthas, are approaching thy presence for enabling thee to perform thy ablutions in them.[579] After consulting them I shall discourse on the topic named, in due order. That person who, though competent, is still free from egotism, is rightly called a Purusha.[580] As regards woman, O lord of all beings, she follows persons of her sex. By consulting these foremost of Rivers, they will be honoured by me. The sacred Saraswati is the foremost river of all rivers. She courses towards the ocean and is truly the first of all streams. Vipasa also here, and Vitasta, and Chandrabhaga, and Iravati, and Satadru, and the river Devika, and Kausiki, and Gomati.[581] and this celestial River who has in her all the sacred Tirthas, viz., the goddess Ganga, who having her rise in Heaven hath descended on the Earth and is regarded as the foremost of all streams." Having said this, the spouse of that god of gods, that foremost of all righteous persons, smilingly addressed all those Rivers of her sex. Indeed, the spouse of the great god, devoted to the performance of all duties, questioned those individuals of her sex about the duties of women. Verily, those foremost of rivers having Ganga for their first are all conversant with the duties of women.

"'"Uma said, "The illustrious god has asked a question relating to the duties of women. I desire to answer Sankara after having consulted with you. I do not see any branch of knowledge on Earth or Heaven that is capable of being mastered by any unaided individual. Ye rivers that run towards the ocean, it is for this that I seek your opinions!" It was in this way that those foremost of Rivers, all of whom were auspicious and highly sacred, were questioned by Siva's spouse. Then the celestial River Ganga, who worshipped the daughter of the prince of mountains in return, was selected for answering the question. Verily, she of sweet smiles is held as swelling with diverse kinds of understanding and well-conversant with the duties of women. The sacred goddess, capable of dispelling all fear of sin, possessed of humility in consequence of her intelligence, well acquainted with all duties, and enriched with an intelligence exceedingly comprehensive, sweetly smiling, uttered these, words, "O goddess, thou art always devoted to the due performance of all duties. Thou hast favoured me highly by thus questioning me! O sinless one, thou art honoured by the entire universe, yet thou askest me that am but a river. That person who, though himself competent (to discourse

---

[578] Gauri is another name for Earth.

[579] The Nadies or Rivers are feminine. Of course, among Rivers there are some that are masculine, notably, the Sindhu or Indus. Tirthas are places with sacred waters.

[580] One who is free from vanity or arrogance deserves to be called Purusha. The absence of vanity is implied by soliciting the help of others even when one is competent oneself. Females follow females, such being their nature. It is a compliment that Parvati pays to Siva for Siva's questioning her when he himself is well-acquainted with the topic upon which she is asked to discourse.

[581] The word Sindhu in this verse does not imply the river Indus, but stands for a river in general. Grammatically, it qualifies Devika before it. Devika is another name of Sarayu.

on a topic) yet asks another, or who pays a graceful tribute to another, certainly deserves, I think, to be regarded as righteous-souled. Verily, such a person deserves to be called learned and wise. That person never falls into disgrace who asks such speakers as are endued with knowledge and science and as are well-conversant with premises and inferences. A proud man, even when enriched with intelligence, by speaking in the midst of an assembly otherwise (that is, by relying upon his own powers alone and without reference to or consultation with others), finds himself uttering only words of weak import. Thou art possessed of spiritual insight, Thou art the foremost of all denizens in Heaven. Thou hast taken thy rise accompanied by diverse kinds of excellent merit. Thou, O goddess, art fully competent to discourse on the duties of women!" In this way, the goddess Uma was worshipped by Ganga and honoured with the ascription of many high merits. The beautiful goddess, thus praised, then began to discourse upon all the duties of women in full.

""""Uma said, "I shall, according to the ordinance, discourse on the subject of women's duties as far as they are known to me. Do ye all listen with concentrated attention! The duties of women arise as created at the outset by kinsmen in the rites of wedding. Indeed, a woman becomes, in the presence of the nuptial fire, the associate of her lord in the performance of all righteous deeds.[582] Possessed of a good disposition, endued with sweet speech, sweet conduct, and sweet features, and always looking at the face of her husband and deriving as much joy from it as she does from looking at the face of her child, that chaste woman who regulates her acts by observing the prescribed restraints, comes to be regarded as truly righteous in her conduct. Listening (with reverence) to the duties of wedded life (as expounded in the scriptures), and accomplishing all those auspicious duties, that woman who regards righteousness as the foremost of all objects of pursuit, who observes the same vows as those that are observed by her husband, who adorned with chastity, looks upon her spouse as a god, who waits upon and serves him as if he is a god, who surrenders her own will completely to that of her lord, who is cheerful, who observes excellent vows, who is endued with good features, and whose heart is completely devoted to her husband so much that she never thinks even of any other man, is regarded as truly righteous in conduct. That wife who, even when addressed harshly and looked upon with angry eyes by her lord, presents a cheerful aspect to him, is said to be truly devoted to her husband. She who does not cast her eyes upon the Moon or the Sun or a tree that has a masculine name, who is adored by her husband and who is possessed of beautiful features, is regarded as truly righteous. That woman who treats her husband with the affection which she shows towards her child, even when he (the husband) happens to be poor or diseased or weak or worn out with the toil of travelling, is regarded as truly righteous in her conduct. That woman who is endued with self-control, who has given birth to children, who serves her husband with devotion, and whose whole heart is devoted to him, is regarded as truly righteous in her conduct. That woman who waits upon and serves her lord with a cheerful heart, who is always cheerful of heart, and who is possessed of humility, is regarded as truly righteous in her conduct. That woman who always supports her kinsmen and relatives by giving them food, and whose relish in gratifying her desires or for articles of enjoyment, or for the affluence of which she is possessed, or for the happiness with which she is surrounded, falls short of her relish for her husband, is regarded as truly righteous in her

---

[582] According to the Hindu scriptures, marriage is not a contract. It is the union of two individuals of opposite sexes into one person for better performance of all deeds of piety.

conduct. That woman who always takes a pleasure in rising at early dawn, who is devoted to the discharge of all household duties, who always keeps her house clean, who rubs her house daily with cowdung, who always attends to the domestic fire (for pouring libations upon it), who never neglects to make offerings of flowers and other articles to the deities, who with her husband gratifies the deities and guests and all servants and dependants of the family with that share of food which is theirs by the ordinances, and who always takes, according to the ordinance, for herself, what food remains in the house after the needs have been met of gods and guests and servants, and who gratifies all people who come in contact with her family and feed them to their fill, succeeds in acquiring great merit. That woman who is endued with accomplishments, who gratifies the feet of her father-in-law and mother-in-law, and who is always devoted to her father and mother, is regarded as possessed of ascetic wealth. That woman who supports with food Brahmanas that are weak and helpless, that are distressed or blind or destitute, comes to be regarded as entitled to share the merit of her husband. That woman who always observes, with a light heart, vows that are difficult of observance, whose heart is devoted to her lord, and who always seeks good of her lord, is regarded as entitled to share the merits of her husband. Devotion to her lord is woman's merit; it is her penance; it is her eternal Heaven. Merit, penances, and Heaven become hers who looks upon her husband as her all in all, and who, endued with chastity, seeks to devote herself to her lord in all things. The husband is the god which women have. The husband is their friend. The husband is their high refuge. Women have no refuge that can compare with their husbands, and no god that can compare with him. The husband's grace and Heaven, are equal in the estimation of a woman; or, if unequal, the inequality is very trivial. O Maheswara, I do not desire Heaven itself if thou are not satisfied with me. If the husband that is poor, or diseased or distressed or fallen among foes, or afflicted by a Brahmana's curse, were to command the wife to accomplish anything that is improper or unrighteous or that may lead to destruction of life itself, the wife should, without any hesitation, accomplish it, guided by the code whose propriety is sanctioned by the law of Distress. I have thus, O god, expounded, at thy command, what the duties of women are. Verily, that woman who conducts herself in this way becomes entitled to a share of the merits won by her husband."'

"'"'Narada continued, 'Thus addressed, the great god applauded the daughter of the prince of mountains and then dismissed all persons that had assembled there, together with all his own attendants. The diverse tribes of ghostly beings, as also all the embodied Rivers, and the Gandharvas and Apsaras, all bowed their heads unto Mahadeva and departed for returning to the places whence they had come.'"'"'

SECTION CXLVII.

"'"'The Rishis said, "O wielder of Pinaka, O tearer of the eyes of Bhaga, O thou that art worshipped by all the universe, we desire to hear the glory of Vasudeva."

"'"'Maheswara said, "Hari is superior to the Grandsire himself. He is the Eternal Purusha. Otherwise called Krishna, he is endued with the splendour of gold, and shines with effulgence like a second sun. Possessed of ten arms, he is endued with great energy, and is the slayer of the foes of the gods. Having a whorl on his breast, he has curly locks of hair on his head. He is worshipped by all the deities. Brahman has risen from his abdomen. I have sprung from his head, All the luminaries in the firmament have sprung from his hair. From the bristles on his body have sprung all the gods and Asuras. From his body have sprung the Rishis as also all the eternal worlds. He is the veritable abode of the Grandsire and the abode of all the gods besides. He is the Creator of this whole Earth, and He is the Lord of the three worlds. He is also the Destroyer of all creatures mobile and immobile. He is verily the foremost of all the deities. He is their master. He is the chastiser of all foes. He is possessed of omniscience. He exists in everything. He is capable of going everywhere. He is of universal extent (pervading as he does everything). He is the Supreme Soul. He is the urger of all the senses. He covers the universe. He is the Supreme Lord. There is nothing in the three worlds that is superior to him. He is Eternal. He is the slayer of Madhu, and is otherwise called Govinda. The giver of honours, He will cause all the kings of Earth to be slain in battle, for achieving the purposes of the deities, taking birth in a human form. The deities, abandoned by Him, are unable to accomplish their purposes on earth. Without obtaining him as their leader they cannot do anything. He is the leader of all creatures and is adored by all the gods.[583] Within the abdomen of this Master of the gods who is ever devoted to the accomplishment of their purposes, of this one who is identical with Brahma and who is always the refuge of the regenerate Rishis, resides Brahma (the Grandsire). Indeed, the latter dwells happily in Hari's body which is the abode. I myself, that am called Sarva, also reside happily in that happy abode of mine. All the deities too reside in happiness in His body. Endued with great effulgence, he has eyes that resemble the petals of the lotus. Sri dwells within Him and He dwells always associated with her. The bow called Saranga and the discus (called Sudarsana) are his weapons, together with a sword. He has the enemy of the snakes (viz., Garuda) sitting on his standard. He is distinguished by excellent conduct, by purity (of both body and mind), by self-restraint, by prowess, by energy, by the handsomest form, by tallness and well-proportioned limbs, by patience, by sincerity, by affluence, by compassion, by excellence of form, and by might. He shines, endued with all celestial weapons of wonderful form and make. He has Yoga for his illusion. He is possessed of a thousand eyes. He is free from every stain or fault. He is high-minded. He is endued with heroism. He is an object of pride with all his friends. He is dear to all his kinsmen and relatives and they are dear to him. He is endued with forgiveness. He is free from pride or egotism. He is devoted to the Brahmanas and is their leader. He dispels the fears of all persons afflicted with fear. He enhances the joys of all his friends. He is the refuge of all creatures. He is ever engaged in protecting and cherishing the distressed. Possessed of a thorough acquaintance with all the scriptures, and every kind of affluence, He is worshipped by all beings. Conversant with all duties, He is a great benefactor of even enemies when they seek His protection. Conversant with policy and endued with policy, He is an utterer of Brahma and has all His senses under perfect control. For doing good to the deities, Govinda will take birth in the race of the high-souled Manu. Verily, endued with high intelligence, He will take birth in the auspicious and righteous race of that Prajapati. Manu will have a son of the name of Anga. After Anga will come Antardhaman. From Antardhaman will spring Havirdhaman, that lord of all creatures, free from every stain. Havirdhaman will have an illustrious son of the name of Rachinavarhi. He will have ten sons having Prachetas for their first. Prachetas will have a son named Daksha who will be regarded as a Prajapati. Daksha will beget a daughter who will be named Dakshayani. From Dakshayani will spring Aditya, and from Aditya will spring Manu. From Manu will spring a daughter named Ila and a

---

[583] Trivikrama is one who covered the three worlds with three steps of his. It implies Vishnu who assumed the form of a dwarf for beguiling the Asura king Vali.

son to be named Sudyumna. Ila will have Vudha for her husband, and from Vudha will spring Pururavas. From Pururavas will spring Ayu. From Ayu will spring Nahusha, and Nahusha will beget a son named Yayati. From Yayati will spring a mighty son of the name of Yadu, Yadu will beget Kroshtri. Kroshtri will beget a mighty son to be named Vrijinivat. From Vrijinivat will spring Ushadgu the unvanquished. Ushadgu will beget a son of the name of Chitraratha. Chitraratha will have a younger son of the name of Sura. Indeed, in the race of these mighty men, of energy celebrated over all the world, possessed of excellent conduct and diverse accomplishments, devoted to the performance of sacrifices and pure in behaviour,—in the pure race honoured by the Brahmanas, Sura will take his birth. He will be a foremost Kshatriya, endued with great energy, and possessed of great fame. Sura, that giver of honours, will beget a son, the spreader of his race, of the name of Vasudeva, otherwise called Anakadundhuvi. Vasudeva will have a son of the name of Vasudeva. He will have four hands. He will be exceedingly liberal, and will honour the Brahmanas greatly. Identical with Brahma, he will like and love the Brahmanas, and the Brahmanas will like and love him, that scion of Yadu's race will liberate many kings immured in the prison of the ruler of the Magadhas, after vanquishing that ruler named Jarasandha in his capital buried among mountains. Endued with great energy, he will be rich with the jewels and gems of all the rulers of the earth. Indeed, in energy he will be unrivalled on earth, possessed of great prowess, he will be the king of all kings of the earth. Foremost among all the Surasenas, the puissant one, residing at Dwaraka, will rule and protect the whole earth after vanquishing all her lords, conversant as he will be with the science of polity. Assembling together, do ye all adore Him, as ye adore the Eternal Brahman, with speech, floral wreaths, and excellent incense and perfumes. He who wishes to see me or the Grandsire Brahma should first see the illustrious Vasudeva of great puissance. If He is seen I am seen, as also the Grandsire Brahman, that foremost of all the gods. In this I do not deem there is any difference. Know this, ye Rishis of ascetic wealth! That person with whom the lotus-eyed Vasudeva becomes gratified, all the deities with Brahma amongst them will also become gratified with. That man who will seek the protection of Kesava will succeed in earning great achievements and victory and Heaven. He will be an instructor in religion and duties, and will earn great religious merit. All persons conversant with religion and duties should, with great alacrity, bow down unto that Lord of all the gods. By adoring that puissant one, one will acquire great merit. Endued with great energy, that god, with the desire of benefiting all creatures, created millions of Rishis for the sake of righteousness. Those millions of Rishis, thus created by that great Ordainer are now residing on the mountains of Gandhamadana, headed by Sanatkumara and engaged in the observance of penances. Hence, ye foremost of regenerate ones, that foremost of all eloquent persons, the righteous Vasudeva should be adored by all. The illustrious Hari, the puissant Narayana, is verily, the foremost of all beings in Heaven. Adored, he adores, and honoured he honours; unto them that make offerings to him, he makes offerings in return. Worshipped, he worships in return, if seen always, he sees the seers always. If one seeks His refuge and protection, He seeks the seeker as his refuge in return. Ye foremost of all righteous ones, if adored and worshipped, He adores and worships in return. Even this is the high practice of the faultless Vishnu. Even this is the vow that is practised by all righteous people, of that first of all deities, that puissant Lord of all creatures. He is always worshipped in the world. Verily, that Eternal Being is worshipped by even the deities. Those persons that are devoted to Him with the steadiness of a vow become liberated from calamity and fear in proportion to his devotion. The regenerate ones should always worship Him in thought, word, and deed. The son of Devaki should be seen by them with reverence and in order to see Him with reverence they should address themselves to the performance of penances. Ye foremost of ascetics, even this is the path that I show unto you. By beholding Him, ye will have behold all the foremost of deities. I too bow my head in reverence unto that Lord of the universe, that Grandsire of all the worlds, that mighty and vast boar. By beholding Him one beholds the Trinity. Ourselves, i.e., all the deities, reside in Him. He will have an elder brother who will become known over all the world as Vala. Having a plough for his weapon, in form he will look like a white hill. In fact, he will be endued with might capable of uplifting the whole earth. Upon the car of that divine person a tall palmyra, three-headed and made of gold, will form his proud standard. The head of that mighty-armed hero, that Lord of all the worlds, will be shaded by many high-souled snakes of vast bodies. All weapons of attack and defence will also come to him as soon as he will think of them. He is called Ananta (Infinite). Verily, that illustrious one is identical with the immutable Hari. Once on a time the mighty Garuda, the son of Kasyapa, was addressed by the deities in these words, 'Do thou, O puissant one, see if this one has any end!' Though possessed of great energy and might, Garuda, however, failed to find out the end of this illustrious one who is identical with the Supreme Soul. Supporting the whole earth on his head, he resides in the nether regions. He roves through the universe as Sesha, filled with great joy. He is Vishnu. He is the illustrious Ananta. He is the supporter of the earth. He that is Rama is Hrishikesa. He that is Achyuta is Ananta, the bearer of the earth. Both of those foremost of all creatures are celestial and endued with celestial prowess. One of them is armed with the discus and the other with the plough. They deserve every honour and should be seen. I have, through my kindness for you, have thus declared to you the nature of Vasudeva. Even this, ye ascetics possessed of wealth of penances, is Righteousness. I have declared all this to you so that ye may, with reverence and care, worship Krishna, that foremost one of Yadu's race."'"''

SECTION CXLVIII.

""'Narada said, 'At the conclusion of Mahadeva's speech, loud roars were heard in the firmament. Thunders bellowed, with flashes of lightening. The welkin was enveloped with blue and thick clouds. The deity of the clouds then poured pure water like to what he does in the season of rains. A thick darkness set in. The points of the compass could no longer be distinguished. Then on that delightful, sacred, and eternal breast of that celestial mountain, the assembled Rishis no longer saw the multitude of ghostly beings that associate with Mahadeva. Soon, however, the welkin cleared. Some of the Rishis set out for the sacred waters. Others returned whence they came. Verily, beholding that wonderful and inconceivable sight, they became filled with amazement. The discourse too between Sankara and Uma had been heard by them with the feelings, "That foremost of all Beings, of whom the high-souled Sankara spoke to us on that mountain, art Thou. Verily, thou art identical with Eternal Brahma. Some time also Mahadeva burnt Himavat with his energy. Thou too hast shown us a similar sight of wonder. Indeed, we have been put in remembrance of that fact by what we have witnessed today." O mighty-armed Janardana, I have thus, O puissant one, recited to thee the glory of that god of gods, viz., him that is called Kapardin or Girisa!'"

"Bhishma continued, "Thus addressed by those denizens of ascetic retreats, Krishna, the delighter of Devaki paid due honours unto all those Rishis. Filled with delight, those

Rishis once more addressed Krishna, saying, 'O slayer of Madhu, do Thou repeatedly show Thyself to us at all times! O puissant one, Heaven itself cannot rejoice us so much as a right of Thyself. Everything that was said by the illustrious Bhava (regarding Thyself) is true. O crusher of foes, we have told Thee all about that mystery. Thou art Thyself conversant with the truth of every topic. Since, however, asked by us, it pleased Thee to ask us in return, we have, for that reason, recited everything (about the discourse of Bhava with Uma) to Thee for only pleasing Thee. There is nothing in the three worlds that is unknown to Thee. Thou art fully conversant with the birth and origin of all things, indeed, with everything that operates as a cause (for the production of other objects). In consequence of the lightness of our character, we are unable to bear (within ourselves the knowledge of) any mystery (without disclosing it).[584] Indeed, in Thy presence, O puissant one, we indulge in incoherences from the lightness of our hearts. There is no wonderful thing that is unknown to Thee! Whatever is on earth, and whatever is in heaven, all is known to Thee! We take our leave of Thee, O Krishna, for returning to our respective abodes. Mayst Thou increase in intelligence and prosperity! O sire, Thou wilt soon get a son like unto Thee or even more distinguished than Thyself. He will be endued with great energy and splendour. He will achieve great feats, and become possessed of puissance as great as Thine!'"[585]

"'Bhishma continued, "After this, the great Rishis bowed unto that god of gods, that scion of Yadu's race, that foremost of all Beings. They then circumambulated Him and taking His leave, departed. As regards Narayana, who is endued with prosperity and blazing effulgence, He returned to Dwaraka after having duly observed that vow of His. His spouse Rukmini conceived, and on the expiration of the tenth month a son was born of her, possessed of heroism and honoured by all for his highly wonderful accomplishments. He is identical with that Kama (Desire) which exists in every creature and which pervades every existent condition. Indeed, he moves within the hearts of both gods and Asuras. This Krishna is that foremost of all persons. Even he, endued with the hue of the clouds is that four-handed Vasudeva. Through affection He has attached himself to the Pandavas, and you also, ye sons of Pandu, have attached yourselves to Him. Achievements, Prosperity, Intelligence, and the path that leads to heaven, are all there where this one, viz., the illustrious Vishnu of three steps, is. He is the three and thirty gods with Indra at their head. There is no doubt in this. He is the one Ancient God. He is the foremost of all gods. He is the refuge of all creatures. He is without beginning and without destruction. He is unmanifest. He is the high-souled slayer of Madhu. Endued with mighty energy, He has taken birth (among men) for accomplishing the purpose of the gods. Verily, this Madhava is the expounder of the most difficult truths relating to Profit or Wealth, and he is also their achiever. O son of Pritha, the victory thou hast obtained over thy enemies, thy unrivalled achievements, the dominion thou hast acquired over the whole earth, are all due to thy side having been taken up by Narayana. The fact of thy having got the inconceivable Narayana for thy protector and refuge, enabled thee to become an Adharyu (chief sacrificer) for pouring multitudes of kings as

---

[584] The sense seems to be this: Thou knowest all things, all mysteries, yet Thou canst bear all this knowledge within Thyself. We, however, are so light-minded, i.e., destitute of gravity, that we are unable to bear within ourselves the knowledge of a mystery. As soon as we got that knowledge from Mahadeva, we felt the desire of letting it out; and, indeed, we have let it out at thy request, and let out unto whom?—unto one that must be secretly laughing at us for our seeming pride.

[585] It is said that no person wishes to be vanquished by another in respect of anything. The only one whose victory or superiority, however, is bearable or, rather, prayed for, is the son. Hence, the Rishis wish unto Krishna a son even superior to him.

libations on the blazing fire of battle. This Krishna was thy great sacrificial ladle resembling the all-destroying fire that appears at the end of the Yuga. Duryodhana, with his sons, brothers and kinsmen, was much to be pitied inasmuch as, moved by wrath, he made war with Hari and the wielder of Gandiva. Many sons of Diti, many foremost of Danavas, of huge bodies and vast strength, have perished in the fire of Krishna's discus like insects in a forest conflagration. How incapable then must human beings be of battling against that Krishna,—human beings who, O tiger among men, are destitute of strength and might! As regards Jaya, he is a mighty Yogin resembling the all-destroying Yuga-fire in energy. Capable of drawing the bow equally with both hands, he is always in the van of fight. With his energy, O king, he has slain all the troops of Suyodhana. Listen to me as I tell thee what Mahadeva having the bovine bull for the device on his standard had recited unto the ascetics on the breast of the Himavat. His utterances constitute a Purana. The advancement of greatness, energy, strength, prowess, puissance, humility, and lineage that are in Arjuna can come up to only a third part of the measure in which those attributes reside in Krishna. Who is there that can transcend Krishna in these attributes? Whether that is possible or not, listen (and judge). There where the illustrious Krishna is, there is unrivalled Excellence.[586] As regards ourselves, we are persons of little understanding. Dependent upon the will of others, we are exceedingly unfortunate. Knowingly we betook ourselves to the eternal path of death. Thou, however, art devoted to sincerity of conduct. Having formerly pledged thyself against taking thy kingdom, thou didst not take it, desirous of maintaining thy pledge.[587] O king, thou makest too much of the slaughter of thy kinsmen and friends in battle (brought about, as thou believest, by thyself). Thou shouldst remember, however, O chastiser of foes, that it is not right to violate a pledge.[588] All those who have fallen on the field of battle have really been slain by Time. Verily, all of us have been slain by Time. Time is, indeed, all-powerful. Thou art fully conversant with the puissance of Time. Afflicted by Time, it does not behove thee to grieve. Know that Krishna Himself, otherwise called Hari, is that Time with blood-red eyes and with club in hand. For these reasons, O son of Kunti, it does not behove thee to grieve for thy (slain) kinsfolk. Be thou always free, O delighter of the Kurus, from grief. Thou hast heard of the glory and greatness of Madhava as recited by me. That is sufficient for enabling a good man to understand Him. Having heard the words of Vyasa as also of Narada endued with great intelligence, I have discoursed to thee on the adorableness of Krishna. I have myself added, from my own knowledge, something to that discourse. Verily, I have discoursed also on the surpassing puissance of Krishna as recited by Mahadeva, unto that conclave of Rishis (on the breast of the Himavat). The discourse too between Maheswara and the daughter of Himavat, O Bharata, has been recited by me to thee. He who will bear in mind that discourse when emanating from a foremost person, he who will listen to it, and he who will recite it (for other people's hearing), is sure to win what is highly beneficial. That man will find all his wishes fulfilled. Departing from this world he will ascend to Heaven. There is no doubt in this. That man who, desirous of obtaining what is beneficial for himself, should devote himself to Janardana. O king of the Kurus, it behoves thee also to always bear in mind those incidents of duty and righteousness which were declared by Maheswara. If thou

---

[586] The ward Pushti literally signifies growth or advancement. Hence, it stands generally for excellence of greatness.

[587] The correct reading is not pratisrayam but pratisravam which means promise or pledge.

[588] The pledge, probably, refers to the oaths taken by Bhima and others about the slaughter of the Kauravas.

conduct thyself according to those precepts, if thou bear the rod of chastisement rightly, if thou protect thy subjects properly, thou mayst be sure of attaining to heaven. It behoves thee, O king, to protect thy subjects always according to the dictates of righteousness. The stout rod of chastisement which the king bears has been said to be the embodiment of his righteousness or merit.[589] Hearing this discourse, fraught with righteousness, between Sankara and Uma, that I have recited in the presence of this righteous conclave, one should worship with reverence that god having the bovine bull for the device on his banner. One that becomes even desirous of listening to that discourse should worship Mahadeva with reverence. Verily, the person that wishes to obtain what is beneficial for him, should adore Mahadeva with a pure heart. Even this is the command of the faultless and high-souled Narada. Even he has commanded such worship of the great god, O son of Pandu, do thou obey that command of Narada. O puissant king, even these are the wonderful incidents that occurred on the sacred breast of the Himavat respecting Vasudeva and Sthanu, O son of Kunti. Those occurrences flowed from the very nature of those high-souled deities. Vasudeva, accompanied by the wielder of Gandiva, practised eternal penances in the retreat of Vadari for ten thousand years.[590] Verily, Vasudeva and Dhananjaya, both of eyes like lotus-petals, underwent severe austerities for the duration of three whole Yugas. I have learnt this from Narada and Vyasa, O king. The lotus-eyed and mighty-armed Vasudeva, while yet a child (in human form) achieved the great feat of slaying Kansa for the relief of his kinsmen. I do not venture, O son of Kunti, to enumerate the feats of this Ancient and Eternal Being, O Yudhishthira. Without doubt, O son, high and great benefits will be reaped by thee who ownest that foremost of all persons, viz., Vasudeva, for thy friend. I grieve for the wicked Duryodhana in respect of even the next world to which he has gone. It was for him that the whole earth has been depopulated with her steeds and elephants. Indeed, through the fault of Duryodhana, of Karna, of Sakuni, and of Duhsasana numbering the fourth, that the Kurus have perished."

"Vaisampayana continued, 'While that foremost of men, viz., the son of Ganga, addressed him in this strain, the Kuru king (Yudhishthira) remained entirely silent in the midst of those high-souled persons (who had assembled together for listening to the discourses of Bhishma). All the kings with Dhritarashtra amongst them became filled with wonder upon hearing the words of the Kuru grandsire. In their minds they worshipped Krishna and then turned towards him with hands joined in reverence. The Rishis also with Narada at their head, accepted and applauded the words of Bhishma and approved of them joyfully. These were the wonderful discourses recited by Bhishma which Pandu's son (Yudhishthira) with all his brothers heard with joy. Some time after, when king (Yudhishthira) saw that Ganga's son who had given away abundant wealth as presents unto the Brahmanas in the sacrifices performed by him, had rested and become refreshed, the intelligent king once more asked him as follows.'"

---

[589] The sense is this: the king acquires great merit by wielding the rod of chastisement properly, i.e., by punishing those that deserve punishment. The infliction of punishment is what keeps the subjects within the restraints of duty. The rod of chastisement, therefore, is the very embodiment of the righteousness or merit of the king.

[590] Vasudeva is Narayana, and Arjuna is Nara. Nara and Narayana had practised severe penances at Vadari on the breast of the Himavat for many thousand years. Vyasa afterwards adopted Vadari as his retreat.

388

SECTION CXLIX.

"Vaisampayana said, 'Having heard all the duties in their entirety and all those sacred acts and objects that cleanse human beings of their sins, Yudhishthira once more addressed the son of Santanu in the following words.'

"'Yudhishthira said, "Who may be said to be the one god in the world? Who may be said to be the one object which is our sole refuge? Who is he by worshipping whom or hymning whose praises human being would get what is beneficial? What religion is that which, according to thy judgment, is the foremost of all religions? What are those Mantras by reciting which a living creature becomes freed from the bonds of birth and life?"

"'Bhishma said, "One should always, with alacrity and throwing away all languor, hymn the praises of that Lord of the universe, that god of gods (viz., Vasudeva), who is Infinite and the foremost of all Beings, by uttering His thousand names. By always worshipping with reverence and devotion that immutable Being, by meditating on him, by hymning His praises and bowing the head unto Him, and by performing sacrifices unto Him, indeed by always praising Vishnu, who is without beginning and without end or destruction, who is the Supreme Lord of all the worlds, and who is the Master and Controller of the universe, one can succeed in transcending all sorrow. Verily, He is devoted to the Brahmanas, conversant with all duties and practices, the enhancer of the fame and achievement of all persons, the master of all the worlds, exceedingly wonderful, and the prime cause of the origin of all creatures. Even this, in my judgment, is the foremost religion of all religions, viz., one should always worship and hymn the praises of the lotus-eyed Vasudeva with devotion. He is the highest Energy. He is the highest Penance. He is the highest Brahma. He is the highest refuge. He is the most holy of all holies, the most auspicious of all auspicious objects. He is the god of all the gods and He is the immutable father of all creatures. On the advent of the primal Yuga, all creatures spring from Him. On the expiration, again of a Yuga, all things disappear in Him.[591] Hear, O king, the thousand names, possessed of great efficacy in destroying sins, of that foremost one in all the worlds that Master of the universe, viz., Vishnu. All those names derived from His attributes, secret and well-known, of the high-souled Vasudeva which were sung by Rishis, I shall recite to thee for the good of all. They are, Om! He that enters all things, besides Himself, He that covers all things, He unto whom sacrificial libations are poured, the Lord of the Past, the Present, and the Future, the Creator (or Destroyer) of all existent things, the upholder of all existent things, the Existent, the Soul of all, the Originator of all things (I—IX); of cleansed Soul, the Supreme Soul, the highest Refuge of all emancipated persons, the Immutable, He that lies enclosed in a case, the Witness, He that knows the material case in which He resides, the Indestructible (X—XVII);[592] He upon whom the mind rests during Yoga-abstraction, the Guide or

---

[591] The Hindu sages never attempt to speculate on the original creation of the universe. Their speculations, however, are concerned with what is called Avantara srishti or that creation which springs forth with the awakening of Brahman. Creation and Destruction have occurred ceaselessly and will occur ceaselessly. The original creation is impossible to conceive as Eternity cannot have a beginning.

[592] Putatman means, of cleansed Soul. This implies that though He is the Lord or ruler of all existent objects, yet He is dissociated from them. The Refuge of the Emancipated—Comp. Gita, 'Mamupetya tu Kaunteya punarjanma na vidyate,' etc., Purusha is He that lies in a pura or the nine-doored mansion, i.e., the body. Sakshi or Witness implies that He sees all things directly, without any medium obstructing His vision.

leader of all persons conversant with Yoga, the Lord of both Pradhana (or Prakriti) and Purusha. He that assumed a human form with a leonine head, He of handsome features and equipments, He of beautiful hair, the foremost of Purushas (XVIII—XXIV);[593] the embodiment of all things, the Destroyer of all things, He that transcends the three attributes of Sattwa, Rajas and Tamas, the Motionless, the Beginning of all things, the Receptacle into which all things sink at the universal Dissolution, the Immutable, He who takes birth at his own will, He who causes the acts of all living creatures to fructify (in the form of weal or woe), the Upholder of all things, the Source from which the primal elements have sprung, the Puissant One, He in whom is the unbounded Lordship over all things (XXV—XXXVII);[594] the Self-born, He that gives happiness to His worshippers, the presiding Genius (of golden form) in the midst of the Solar disc, the Lotus-eyed, Loud-voiced, He that is without beginning and without end. He that upholds the universe (in the form of Ananta and others), He that ordains all acts and their fruits, He that is superior to the Grandsire Brahma (XXXVIII—XLVI);[595] the Immeasurable, the Lord of the senses (or He that has curled locks), He from whose navel the primeval lotus sprang, the Lord of all the deities, the Artificer of the universe, the Mantra, He that weakens or emaciates all things, He that is vast, the Ancient one, He that is enduring (XLVII—LVI).[596] He that is incapable of being seized (by either the senses or the mind), the Eternal One, Krishna, the Red-eyed, He that kills all creatures at the time of the universal dissolution, He that is vast for knowledge and puissance and other attributes of the kind, He that resides in three parts (above, middle, and below) of every creature. That which cleanses, is auspicious, and high (LVII—LXIV).[597] He that urges all creatures in respect

Kshetrajna implies the Chit lying within the body and who knows the body; however, being inert, is not cognisant of the Chit it holds.

[593] He is called Yoga because of the mind resting upon Him while it is in Yoga abstraction. Pradhana, in Sankhya philosophy, is another name of Prakriti or original Nature. All things have sprung from the union of Prakriti and Purusha. Vasudeva, however, transcends Prakriti and Purusha and is their Lord. Narasinghavapu—He assumed the human form with a lion's head for slaying the Asura Hiranyakasipu, the father of Prahlada.

[594] Sarva implies the source of all existent and non-existent things and that in which all existent and non-existent things become merged at the universal dissolution. Sambhava signifies Him who takes birth at His own will. Acts cannot touch him. The birth of all other beings is determined by their acts in previous lives. Com. Gita, Paritranaya sadhunam etc. sambhavami yuge yuge. Bhuvana means one who attaches to acts their respective fruits i.e., he in consequence of whom the weal and woe of all creatures flow as due to acts.

[595] Sambhu implies one whose birth has not been determined by extraneous circumstances, or other influences than his own wish, the birth of all other creatures being determined by forces extraneous to themselves. Aditya may also mean the foremost one among the deities especially called the Adityas. They are twelve in number. Dhatri may also imply one who upholds everything in the universe by multiplying Himself infinitely. Dhaturuttama may, besides, signify one who as Chit is superior to all elements like Earth, Water, etc., which constitute all that is not-Chit.

[596] Aprameya is, literally, immeasurable. Sankara thus explains it: He has no such attributes as sound, etc; in consequence of this He is not an object of direct perception by the sense; nor can He be an object of inference, in consequence of there being nothing to which belong the same attributes as His, etc. His inconceivability is the foundation of His immeasurableness. Hrishikesa is regarded by European scholars as a doubtful word. The Hindu commentators do not regard it so. It implies the lord of the senses i.e., One who has his sense under complete control. Or, it may mean One who sways the sense of others, i.e., causes them to exercise their functions. Sankara proposes another meaning, viz. He that is the form of the Sun or the Moon and as such, the rays of light emanating from those luminaries and gladdening all creatures, are the hairs on His head. Manu is another name for Mantra or sacred words having great efficacy.

[597] Krishna is one of the foremost names of the supreme God-head. It means One who is always in transports of joy. It is derived from krish which implies to be, and na meaning final Emancipation or cessation of existence; the compound probably means One in whom every attribute has been extinguished; hence, absence of change, of sorrow, of gift, etc., or, eternal and highest joy. Lohitaksha is Red-eyed, from His eyes being of the hue of polished copper. Pratardana, according to Sankara, means the killer of all creatures. Others take it as

of all their acts. He that causes the life-breaths to act. He that causes all living creatures to live, the Eldest, the Foremost of all those that are regarded as the Lords of all creatures, He that has gold in his abdomen, He that has the Earth for his abdomen, the Lord of Sri or Lakshmi, the Slayer of Madhu (LXV—LXXII):[598] the Omnipotent, He that is endued with great prowess, He that is armed with the bow, He that is Possessed of a mind capable of bearing the contents of all treatises, He that roves through the universe, riding on Garuda. He that is well suited to the offerings made unto Him and that has the power to enjoy them properly, the Unrivalled, He that is incapable of being discomfited, He that knows all acts that are done, He that is identical with all acts, He that rests on His own true self (LXXIV—LXXXIV),[599] the Lord of all the deities, He that is the Refuge of all, the embodiment of the highest felicity, He whose seed is the universe, He that is the source of all things, the day (in consequence of His awakening Jiva who is steeped in the sleep of Nescience), the Year, the Snake (owing to His being incapable of being seized), the embodiment of Conviction, He that sees all things (LXXXV—XCIV):[600] the Unborn, the Lord of all creatures, He that has achieved success, He that is Success itself, He that is the beginning of all things (in consequence of His being the cause of all things), He that is above deterioration, He that is Righteousness in the form of the bovine bull and the great boar that raised the submerged Earth, He that is of immeasurable soul, He that stands aloof from all kinds of union (XCV—CIII);[601] He that is Pauaka among the deities called Vasus (or, He that dwells in His worshippers). He that is liberal soul, being freed from wrath and hatred and pride and other evil passions. Truth whose soul is equable in consequence of His thorough impartiality, He that has been measured by His worshippers, He that is always equal, being above all change or modification, He that never refuses to grant the wishes of His worshippers, He whose eyes are like the petals of the lotus, He whose acts are always characterised by Righteousness (or He who is always engaged in granting the wishes of those that are devoted to Him), He that is of the form of Righteousness (CIV—CXIII); He that destroys all creatures (or their pains), the Many headed, He that upholds the universe, He that is the source of the universe, He who is of pure or spotless fame, the Immortal One, He that is Eternal and Fixed, He that is possessed of beautiful limbs, (or, He the ascension unto whom is the best of all acts), He who has such knowledge having penance for its indication (CXIV—CXXII); He that goes everywhere (in the sense of pervading all things as their cause), the Omniscient One,

---

implying one who destroys the cheerlessness of his worshippers. Prabhuta is One who is Great or Vast in consequence of Knowledge, Puissance, Energy, and Renunciation, etc.; Pavitram, Mangalam, Param should be taken as one name, although each of them has a separate meaning.

[598] Pranada is interpreted variously. It may mean He that causes the life-breaths to operate; He that, as Time suspends the life-breaths (i.e., kills all creatures); He that connects the life-breaths (i.e., set them a-going when threatened with extinction; hence, healer of diseases). Prana implies He who is the cause of the life of every living creature being Himself, as it were, the life-breath that inspires them. Hiranyagarbha signifies He that is identical with the Grandsire. Bhugarbha is one who has the Earth for his abdomen, implying that all things on Earth are in His abdomen.

[599] Atmavan, other Beings are said to be Sariravan, Indriyavan, etc., in consequence of the possession of such attributes as Sarira, Indriya, etc. But the Supreme God-head is nothing but soul. He rests on his own true nature or essence without requiring anything extraneous like the deities or human beings whereon to live or exist.

[600] Aha is the day; He is so called because of Jiva being, as it were, awakened when he goes to Him. As long as Jiva is at a distance from Him, he is steeped in the sleep of Avidya or Nescience (a happy word which Professor Max Muller has coined) Samvatsara or the year. He is so called because Time is His essence. Vyala—He is a huge and fierce snake that inspires dread.

[601] Vrishakapi is otherwise explained by Valadeva Vidyabhushan, as He that showers blessings upon His worshippers and causes all His foes to tremble with fear.

He that blazes forth in unmodified effulgence, He whose troops are everywhere (in the form of devoted associates), (or He at whose very sight the Danava troops are scattered in all directions). He that is coveted (or sought) by all (or, He that grinds all His foes), He that is the Veda, He that is conversant with the Veda, He that is conversant with all the limbs (or branches) of the Veda, He that represents the limbs (or branches) of the Veda (i.e., all the subsidiary sciences), He that settles the interpretations of the Vedas, He that has no superior in wisdom (CXXIII—CXXXIII); He that is the master of all the worlds, He that is the master of the deities, He that is the Supervisor of both Righteousness and Unrighteousness (for giving the fruits thereof to those that seek the one or the other), He that is both Effect and Cause, (or, He whose life has not been determined by acts achieved on any previous occasion in consequence of His transcending Prakriti). He that is four-souled (in consequence of His four forms of Aniruddha, Pradyumna, Sankarshana and Vasudeva). He that is known by four forms (as above), He that has four horns (which appeared on Him when He had assumed a human form with a lion's head for slaying the Asura chief Hiranya-Kasipu), He that has four arms (for holding the conch, discus, mace, and lotus) (CXXXIV—CXLI); He that blazes forth in effulgence, He that is the giver of food and cherishes those that are good; He that does not bear or put up with those that are wicked, (or, He that puts up with the occasional transgressions of his devotees); He that existed before the universe started into life; He that is stainless; He that is ever victorious; He that vanquishes the very deities; He that is the material cause of the universe; He that repeatedly resides in material causes (CXLII—CL); He that is the younger brother of Indra, (or He that transcends Indra in accomplishments and attributes). He that took birth as a dwarf (from Aditi by her husband Kasyapa in order to beguile the Asura king Vali of the sovereignty of the three worlds, and bestow the same upon Indra who had been dispossessed of it), He that is tall (in allusion to the vast universal form of His which He assumed at the sacrifice of Vali for covering Heaven, Earth, and the Nether regions with three steps of His). He whose acts are never futile, He that cleanses (those that worship Him, those that hear of Him and those that think of Him), He that is endued with pre-eminent energy and strength, He that transcends Indra in all attributes, He that accepts all His worshippers, He that is the Creation itself in consequence of His being the Causes thereof, He that upholds His self in the same form without being ever subject to birth, growth, or death, He that sustains all creatures in their respective functions in the universe, He that controls the hearts of all creatures (CLI—CLXII); He that deserves to be known by those who wish to achieve what is for their highest good; He who is the celestial physician in the form of Dhanwantari, (or He who cures that foremost of all diseases, viz., the bonds that bind one to the world); He that is always engaged in Yoga; He that slays great Asuras for establishing Righteousness; He that is the Lord of that Lakshmi who sprang from the ocean when it was churned by the deities and the Asuras, (or, He that cherishes both the goddesses of prosperity and learning); He that is honey (in consequence of the pleasure He gives to those that succeed in having a taste of him); He that transcends the senses (or is invisible to those that turn away from Him); He that is possessed of great powers of illusion (manifested in His beguiling Mahadeva and the deities on many occasions); He that puts forth great energy (in achieving mighty feats); He that transcends all in might (CLXIII—CLXXII); He that transcends all in intelligence; He that transcends all in puissance; He that transcends all in ability; He that discovers the universe by the effulgence emanating from his body; He whose body is incapable of being ascertained by the eye (or any other sense organ of knowledge); He that is possessed of every beauty; He whose soul is incapable of being comprehended by either deities or men; He that held on his back, in the form of the vast tortoise, the huge mountain, Mandara, which was made the churning staff by the deities and the Asuras when they set themselves to churn the great ocean for obtaining therefrom all the valuables hid in its bosom; (or, He who held up the mountains of Govardhana in the woods of Brinda for protecting the denizens of that delightful place, who were especial objects of His kindness, from the wrath of Indra who poured incessant showers for days together with a view to drowning every thing) (CLXXIII—CLXXX); He that can shoot His shafts to a great distance, piercing through obstruction of every kind; He that raised the submerged Earth, having assumed the form of the mighty Boar; He on whose bosom dwells the goddess of Prosperity; (or He that is identical with Kama, the lord of Rati); He that is the Refuge of those that are righteous; He that is incapable of being won without thorough devotion; (or, He that is incapable of being immured or restrained by any one putting forth his powers); He that is the delight of the deities, or, He that is the embodiment of fullness of joy; He that rescued the submerged Earth; (or He that understands the hymns addressed to him by His devotees); He that is the Master of all eloquent persons (or He that dispels the calamities of all those who know him) (CLXXXI—CLXXXVIII); He that is full of blazing effulgence; He that suppressed the afflictions of His adorers; (or, He that assumes the form of Yama, the universal Destroyer, for chastising all persons that fall away from their duties); He that assumed the form of a Swan for communicating the Vedas to the Grandsire Brahman; (or, He that enters into the bodies of all persons); He that has Garuda, the prince of the feathery denizens of the welkin, for His vehicle; He that is the foremost of snakes in consequence of His identity with Sesha or Ananta who upholds on his head the vast Earth, (or, He that has the hood of the prince of snakes for His bed while He lies down to sleep on the vast expansion of water after the dissolution of the universe); He whose navel is as beautiful as gold; He that underwent the severest austerities in the form of Narayana at Vadari on the breast of Himavat; He whose navel resembles a lotus; (or, He from whose navel sprang the primeval lotus in which the Grandsire Brahma was born); He that is the Lord of all creatures (CLXXXIX—CXCVII); He that transcends death; (or, He that wards off Death from those that are devoted to him); He that always casts a kind eye on His worshippers; (or, He that sees all things in the universe); He that destroys all things; (or, He that drenches with nectar all those that worship Him with single-minded devotion); He that is the Ordainer of all ordainers; (or, He that unites all persons with the consequences of their acts); He that himself enjoys and endures the fruits of all acts, (or, He that assumed the form of Rama, the son of Dasaratha, and going into exile at the command of His sire made a treaty with Sugriva the chief of the Apes for aiding him in the recovery of his kingdom from the grasp of his elder brother Vali in return for the assistance which Sugriva promised Him for recovering from Ravana His wife Sita who had been ravished by that Rakshasa and borne away to his island home in Lanka), He that is always of the same form; (or, He that is exceedingly affectionate unto His worshippers); He that is always moving; (or, He that is of the form of Kama who springs up in the heart of every creature); He that is incapable of being endured by Danavas and Asuras (or, He that rescued His wife Sita after slaying Ravana, or, He that shows compassion towards even Chandalas and members of other low castes when they approach Him with devotion, in allusion to His friendship, in the form of Rama, for Guhaka the chief of the Chandalas, inhabiting the country known by the name of Sringaverapura); He that chastises the wicked; (or, He that regulates the conduct of all persons by the dictates of the Srutis and the Smritis); He whose soul has true knowledge for its indication; (or, He that destroyed Ravana, the foe of the gods, having assumed the form of Rama that was full of compassion and other amiable virtues); He that destroys the foes of the deities (or, He that slays those who obstruct or forbid the giving of presents unto deserving persons) (CXCVIII—CCVIII); He that is the instructor in all sciences and the father of all; He that is the instructor of even the Grandsire Brahma; He that is the abode or resting place of all creatures; He that is the benefactor of those that are good and is free from the stain of falsehood; He whose prowess is incapable of being baffled; He that never casts his eye on such acts as are not sanctioned or approved by the scriptures; He that casts his eye on such acts as are sanctioned or approved by the scriptures; (or, He whose eye never winks or sleeps); He that wears the unfading garland of victory called by the name of Vaijayanti; He that is the Lord of speech and that is possessed of great liberality insomuch that He rescued the lowest of the low and the vilest of the vile by granting them His grace (CCIX—CCXVIII); He that leads persons desirous of Emancipation to the foremost of all conditions, viz., Emancipation itself; (or, He that assumes the form of a mighty Fish and scudding through the vast expanse of waters that cover the Earth when the universal dissolution comes, and dragging the boat tied to His horns, leads Manu and others to safety); He that is the leader of all creatures; (or, He that sports in the vast expanse of waters which overwhelm all things at the universal dissolution); He whose words are the Veda and who rescued the Vedas when they were submerged in the waters at the universal dissolution; He that is the accomplisher of all functions in the universe; He that assumes the form of the wind for making all living creatures act or exert themselves; (or, He whose motions are always beautiful, or, who wishes His creatures to glorify Him); He that is endued with a thousand heads; He that is the Soul of the universe and as such pervades all things; He that has a thousand eyes and a thousand legs; (CCXIX—CCXXVI); He that causes the wheel of the universe to revolve at His will; He whose soul is freed from desire and who transcends those conditions that invest Jiva and to which Jiva is liable; He that is concealed from the view of all persons that are attached to the world; (or, He that has covered the eyes of all persons with the bandage of nescience); He that grinds those that turn away from him; He that sets the days a-going in consequence of His being identical with the Sun; He that is the destroyer of all-destroying Time itself; He that conveys the libations poured on the sacred fire unto those for whom they are intended; (or, He that bears the universe, placing it on only a minute fraction of His body); He that has no beginning; (or, He that has no fixed habitation); He that upholds the Earth in space (in the form of Sesha, or, rescues her in the form of the mighty boar or supports her as a subtil pervader) (CCXXVII—CCXXXV); He that is exceedingly inclined to grace, insomuch that He grants happiness to even foes like Sisupala; He that has been freed from the attributes of Rajas (passion) and Tamas (darkness) so that He is pure or stainless Sattwa by itself; (or, He that has obtained the fruition of all His wishes); He that supports the universe; He that feeds (or enjoys the universe); He that is displayed in infinite puissance; He that honours the deities, the Pitris, and His own worshippers; He that is honoured or adored by those that are themselves honoured or adored by others; (or, He whose acts are all beautiful and enduring); He that accomplishes the purposes of others; (or, He that is the benefactor of others); He that withdraws all things unto Himself at the universal dissolution; (or, He that destroys the foes of the deities or of His worshippers); He that has the waters for his home; (or, He that is the sole Refuge of all creatures or He that destroys the ignorance of all creatures) (CCXXXVI—CCXLVI); He that is distinguished above all, He that cherishes the righteous, He that cleanses all the worlds, He that crowns with fruition the desires of all creatures, He whose wishes are always crowned with fruition, He that gives success to all, He that bestows success upon those that solicit Him for it (CCXLVII—CCLVI); He that presides over all sacred days; (or, He that overwhelms Indra himself with His own excellent attributes), He that showers all objects of desire upon His worshippers, He that walks over all the universe, He that offers the excellent flight of steps constituted by Righteousness (unto those that desire to ascend to the highest place); He that has Righteousness in His abdomen; (or, He that protects Indra even as a mother protects the child in her womb); He that aggrandises (His worshippers), He that spreads Himself out for becoming the vast universe, He that is aloof from all things (though pervading them); He that is the receptacle of the ocean of Srutis (CCLVII—CCLXIV); He that is possessed of excellent arms (i.e., arms capable of upholding the universe); He that is incapable of being borne by any creature, He from whom flowed the sounds called Brahman (or Veda), He that is the Lord of all Lords of the universe, He that is the giver of wealth, He that dwells in His own puissance, He that is multiform, He that is of vast form, He that resides in the form of Sacrifice in all animals, He that causes all things to be displayed (CCLXV—CCLXXIV), He that is endued with great might, energy, and splendour; He that displays Himself in visible forms to His worshippers, He that scorches the unrighteous with His burning energy, He that is enriched with the sixfold attributes (of affluence, etc.), He that imparted the Veda to the Grandsire Brahma, He that is of the form of the Samans, Riks, and Yajuses (of the Veda); He that soothes His worshippers burning with the afflictions of the world like the rays of the moon cooling all living creatures of the world, He that is endued with blazing effulgence like the sun (CCLXXV—CCLXXXII); He from whose mind has sprung the moon, He that blazes forth in His own effulgence, He that nourishes all creatures even like the luminary marked by the hare, He that is the Master of the deities, He that is the great medicine for the disease of worldly attachment, He that is the great causeway of the universe, He that is endued with knowledge and other attributes that are never futile and with prowess that is incapable of being baffled (CCLXXXIII—CCLXXXIX); He that is solicited by all creatures at all times, viz., the Past, the Present, and the Future; He that rescues his worshippers by casting kind glances upon them, He that sanctifies even them that are sacred; He that merges the life-breath in the Soul; (or, He that assumes diverse forms for protecting both the Emancipated and the Unemancipated); He that kills the desires of those that are Emancipated; (or, He that prevents evil desires from arising in the minds of His worshippers); He that is the sire of Kama (the principle of desire or lust); He that is most agreeable, He that is desired by all creatures, He that grants the fruition of all desires, He that has the ability to accomplishing all acts (CCXC—CCXCIX); He that sets the four Yugas to begin their course; He that causes the Yugas to continually revolve as on a wheel, He that is endued with the diverse kinds of illusion (and, therefore, the cause from which spring the different kinds of acts that distinguish the different Yugas); He that is the greatest of eaters (in consequence of His swallowing all things at the end of every Kalpa); He that is incapable of being seized (by those that are not His worshippers); He that is manifest (being exceedingly vast); He that subjugates thousands of foes (of the deities); He that subjugates innumerable foes (CCC—CCCVIII); He that is desired (by even the Grandsire and Rudra, or He that is adored in sacrifices); He that is distinguished above all; He that is desired by those that are endued with wisdom and righteousness; He that has an ornament of (peacock's) feathers on His headgear; He that stupefies all creatures with His illusion; He that showers His grace on all His worshippers; He that kills the wrath of the righteous; He that fills the unrighteous with wrath; He that is the accomplisher of all acts; He who holds the universe on his arms; He that upholds the Earth (CCCIX—CCCXVIII); He that transcends the six well-known modifications (of inception, birth or appearance, growth, maturity, decline, and dissolution); He that is endued with great celebrity (in consequence of His feats); He that causes all living creatures to live (in consequence of His being the all-pervading soul); He that gives life; the younger brother of Vasava (in the form of Upendra or the dwarf); He that is the receptacle of all the waters in the universe; He that covers all creatures (in consequence of His being the material cause of everything); He that is never heedless (being always above error); He that is established on His own glory (CCCXIX—CCCXXVII); He that flows in the form of nectar; (or, He that dries up all things); He upholds the path of righteousness; He that bears the burden of the universe; He that gives desirable boons unto those that solicit them: He that causes the winds to blow; He that is the son of Vasudeva; (or, He that covers the universe with His illusions and sports in the midst of it); He that is endued with extraordinary lustre; He that is the originating cause of the deities; He that pierces all hostile towns (CCCXXVIII—CCCXXXVI); He that transcends all sorrow and grief; He that leads us safely across the ocean of life or the world; He that dispels from the hearts of all His worshippers the fear of rebirth; He that is possessed of infinite courage and prowess; He that is an offspring of Sura's race; He that is the master of all living creatures; He that is inclined to show His grace unto all; He that has come on earth for a hundred times (for rescuing the good, destroying the wicked, and establishing righteousness); He that holds a lotus in one of his hands; He whose eyes resemble the petals of the lotus (CCCXXXVII—CCCXLVI); He from whose navel sprang the primeval lotus; (or, He that is seated upon a lotus); He that is endued with eyes resembling the petals of the lotus; He that is adored by even worshippers as one seated within the lotus of His hearts; He that assumed the form of embodied Jiva (through His own illusion); He that is endued with puissance of every kind; He that grows in the form of the five primal elements; the Ancient Soul; He that is endued with vast eyes; He that has Garuda sitting on the standard of His car (CCCXLVII—CCCLV); He that is incomparable; the Sarabha (the lion-killing animal); He that strikes the wicked with terror; He that knows everything that has occurred in Time; He that accepts, in the forms of the deities, the butter poured on the sacrificial fire; He that is known by all kinds of evidence or proof; He upon whose breast sits Prosperity always; He that is victorious in every battle (CCCLVI—CCCLXIV); He that is above destruction; He that assumes a red form; (or, becomes wrathful unto the enemies of His worshippers); He that is an object of search with the righteous; He that is at the root of all things; He that has the mark of the string around his abdomen (for Yasoda had bound Him with a cord while He was Krishna); He that bears or forgives all injuries; He that upholds the Earth in the form of her mountains; He that is the foremost of all objects of worship; He that is endued with great speed; He that swallows vast quantities of food (CCCLXV—CCCLXXIV); He that caused the creation to start into life; He that always agitates both Prakriti and Purusha; He that shines with resplendence; (or, sports in joy); He that has puissance in his stomach; He that is the Supreme Master of all; He that is the material out of which the universe has been made; He that is the cause or Agent who has made the universe: He that is independent of all things; He that ordains variety in the universe; He that is incapable of being comprehended; He that renders Himself invisible by the screen of illusion (CCCLXXV—CCCLXXXV); He that is Chit divested of all attributes; He on whom all things rest; He in whom all things reside when the universal dissolution comes; He that assigns the foremost place to those that worship Him; He that is durable; He that is

endued with the highest puissance; He that has been glorified in the Vedanta; He that is
contented; He that is always full; He whose glance is auspicious (CCCLXXXVI—
CCCXCV); He that fills all Yogins with delight; He that is the end of all creatures (for it
is in Him that all things merge at the universal dissolution); He that is the faultless Path;
He that in the form of Jiva, leads to Emancipation; He that leads (Jiva to Emancipation);
He that has none to lead Him; He that is endued with great might; He that is the foremost
of all beings possessed of might; He that is the foremost of all Beings conversant with
duty and religion (CCCXCVI—CDIV); He that joins, at the time of creation, the
disunited elements for forming all objects; He that resides in all bodies; He that causes all
creatures to act in the form of Kshetrajna; He that creates all creatures after destroying
them at the universal dissolution; He unto whom every one bows with reverence; He that
is extended over the entire universe; He that owns the primeval golden egg as his
abdomen (whence, as from the female uterus), everything proceeds; He that destroys the
foes of the deities; He that overspreads all things (being the material cause whence they
spring); He that spreads sweet perfumes; He that disregards the pleasures of the senses
(CDV—CDXV); He that is identifiable with the seasons; He at whose sight alone all
worshippers succeed in obtaining the great object of their wish; He that weakens all
creatures; He that dwells in the firmament of the heart, depending upon His own glory
and puissance; He that is capable of being known everywhere (in consequence of His
omnipresence); He that inspires everyone with dread; He in whom all creatures dwell; He
that is clever in accomplishing all acts; He that constitutes the rest of all creatures (being,
as He is, the embodiment of Emancipation); He that is endued with competence greater
than that of other Beings (CDXVI—CDXXV); He in whom the whole Universe is spread
out; He that is Himself immobile and in whom all things rest for ever; He that is an object
of proof; He that is the Indestructible and unchanging seed; He that is sought by all (in
consequence of His being happiness); He that has no desire (in consequence of all His
desires having been gratified); He that is the great cause (which covers the universe): He
that has all sorts of things to enjoy; He that has great wealth wherewith to secure all
objects of desire (CDXXVI—CDXXXIV); He that is above despair; He that exists in the
form of Renunciation; He that is without birth; He that is the stake unto which
Righteousness is tethered; He that is the great embodiment of sacrifice; He who is the
nave of the starry wheel that revolves in the firmament;[602] He that is the Moon among the
constellations; He that is competent to achieve every feat; He that stays in His own soul
when all things disappear; He that cherishes the desire for Creation (CDXXXV—
CDXLIV); He that is the embodiment of all sacrifices; He that is adored in all sacrifices
and religious rites; He that is the most adorable of the deities present in the sacrifices that
men perform; He that is the embodiment of all such sacrifices in which animals are
offered up according to the ordinance; He that is adored by persons before they take any
food;[603] He that is the Refuge of those that seek emancipation; He that beholds the acts
and omissions of all creatures; He whose soul transcends all attributes; He that is
possessed of omniscience; He that is identical with knowledge that is unacquired,
unlimited, and capable of accomplishing everything (CDXLV—CDLIV); He that is
observant of excellent vows (chief amongst which is the granting of favour unto one that
solicits it with a pure heart); He that has a face always full of delight; He that is

[602] Vishnu is supposed to be within the constellation called Sisumara or the Northern Bear. The stars,
without changing their places per se, seem to revolve round this point within the constellation named.
[603] In India, no man should worship the deities, with a full stomach. Indeed, one must abstain from every
kind of food and drink if one has to worship the deities formally.

exceedingly subtle; He that utters the most agreeable sounds (in the form of the Veda or as Krishna playing on the lute); He that gives happiness (to all His worshippers); He that does good to others without expecting any return; He that fills all creatures with delight; He that has subdued wrath; He that has mighty arms (so mighty that He has slain as if in sport the mightiest of Asuras); He that tears those that are unrighteous (CDLV—CDLXIV); He that causes those persons who are destitute of knowledge of the soul to be steeped in the deep sleep of His illusion; He that relies on Himself (being entirely independent of all persons and things); He that overspreads the entire universe; He that exists in infinite forms; He that is engaged in vocations infinite in number; He that lives in everything; He that is full of affection towards all His worshippers; He that is the universal father (all living creatures of the universe being as calves sprung from Him); He that holds, in the form of the vast Ocean, all jewels and gems in His abdomen, He that is the Lord of all treasures (CDLXV—CDLXXIV); He that is the protector of righteousness; He that accomplishes all the duties of righteousness; He that is the substratum of righteousness; He that is existent for all time; He that is non-existent (in the form of the universe, for the manifested universe is the result of illusion); He that is destructible (in the form of the universe); He that is indestructible as Chit; He that is, in the form of Jiva, destitute of true knowledge; He that is, in the form of the Sun, endued with a thousand rays; He that ordains (even all such great and mighty creatures as Sesha and Garuda, etc.); He that has created all the Sastras (CDLXXV—CDLXXXV); He that exists, in the form of the Sun, as the centre of innumerable rays of light; He that dwells in all creatures; He that is possessed of great prowess; He that is the Master of even Yama and others of similar puissance; He that is the oldest of the deities (existing as He does from the beginning); He that exists in His own glory, casting off all conditions; He that is the Lord of even all the deities; He that is the ruler of even him that upholds the deities (viz., Indra) (CDLXXXVI—CDXCIII); He that transcends birth and destruction; He that tended and protected kine (in the form of Krishna); He that nourishes all creatures; He that is approachable by knowledge alone; He that is Ancient; He that upholds the elements which constitute the body; He that enjoys and endures (weal and woe, in the form of Jiva); He that assumed the form of a vast Boar; (or, He that, in the form of Rama, was the Lord of a large monkey host); He that gave plentiful presents unto all in a grand sacrifice performed by Him (CDXCIV—DII); He that drinks Soma in every sacrifice; He that drinks nectar; He that, in the form of Soma (Chandramas), nourishes all the herbs and plants; He that conquers foes in a trice when even they are infinite in number; He that is of universal form and is the foremost of all existent entities; He that is the chastiser; He that is victorious over all; He whose purposes are incapable of being baffled; He that deserves gifts; He that gives what His creatures have not and who protects what they have (DIII—DXII); He that holds the life-breaths; He that beholds all His creatures as objects of direct vision; He that never beholds anything beside His own Self; He that gives emancipation; He whose footsteps (three in number) covered Heaven, Earth, and the Nether regions; He who is the receptacle of all the water; He that overwhelms all Space, all Time, and all things; He that lies on the vast expanse of waters after the universal dissolution; He that causes the destruction of all things (DXIII—DXXI); He that is without birth; He that is exceedingly adorable; He that appears in His own nature; He that has conquered all foes (in the form of wrath and other evil passions); He that delights those that meditate on Him; He that is joy; He that fills others with delight; He that swells with all causes of delight; He that has truth and other virtues for His indications; He whose foot steps are in the three worlds (DXXII—DXXX); He that is the first of the Rishis (being conversant with the entire Vedas); He that is identical with the preceptor Kapila; He that is the knower of the Universe; He that is Master of the Earth; He that has their feet; He that is the guardian of the deities; He that has large horns (in allusion to the piscatory form in which He saved Manu on the occasion of the universal deluge by scudding through the waters with Manu's boat tied to His horns); He that exhausts all acts by causing their doers to enjoy or endure their fruits; (or, He that grinds the Destroyer himself) (DXXXI—DXXXVIII); the great Boar: He that is understood or apprehended by the aid of the Vedanta; He that has beautiful troops (in the form of His worshippers); He that is adorned with golden armlets; He that is concealed (being knowledge with the aid of the Upanishads only); He that is deep (in knowledge and puissance); He that is difficult of access; He that transcends both word and thought, that is armed with the discus and the mace (DXXXIX—DXLVII); the Ordainer; He that is the cause (in the form of helper of the universe); He that has never been vanquished; He that is the Island-born Krishna; He that is enduring (in consequence of His transcending decay): He that mows all things and is Himself above deterioration; the Varuna (the deity of the waters); the son of Varuna (in the form of Vasishtha or Agastya); He that is immovable as a tree; He that is displayed in His own true form in the lotus of the heart; He that creates, preserves, and destroys by only a fiat of the mind (DXLVIII—DLVIII); He that is possessed of the sixfold attributes (of sovereignty etc.); He that destroys the sixfold attributes (at the universal dissolution); He that is felicity (in consequence of His swelling with all kinds of prosperity); He that is adorned with the triumphal garland (called Vaijayanta); He that is armed with the plough (in allusion to His incarnation as Valadeva); He that took birth from the womb of Aditi (in the form of the dwarf that beguiled Vali); He that is endued with effulgence like unto the Sun's; He that endures all pairs of opposites (such as heat and cold, pleasure and pain, etc.); He that is the foremost Refuge of all things (DLIX—DLXVII); He that is armed with the best of bows (called Saranga); He that was divested of His battle-axe (by Rama of Bhrigu's race);[604] He that is fierce; He that is the giver of all objects of desire; He that is so tall as to touch the very heavens with his head (in allusion to the form He assumed at Vali's sacrifice); He whose vision extends over the entire universe; He that is Vyasa (who distributed the Vedas); He that is the Master of speech or all learning; He that has started into existence without the intervention of genital organs (DLXVIII—DLXXVI); He that is hymned with the three (foremost) Samans; He that is the singer of the Samans; He that is the Extinction of all worldly attachments (in consequence of His being the embodiment of Renunciation); He that is the Medicine; He that is the Physician (who applies the medicine); He that has ordained the fourth or last mode of life called renunciation (for enabling His creatures to attain to emancipation); He that causes the passions of His worshippers to be quieted (with a view to give them tranquillity of soul); He that is contented (in consequence of His utter dissociation with all worldly objects); He that is the Refuge of devotion and tranquillity of Soul (DLXXVII—DLXXXV); He that is possessed of beautiful limbs; He that is the giver of tranquillity of soul; He that is Creator; He that sports in joy on the bosom of the earth; He that sleeps (in Yoga) lying on the body of the prince of snakes, Sesha, after the universal dissolution; the Benefactor of kine; (or, He that took a human form for relieving the earth of the weight of her population); the Master of the universe;

---

[604] Rama of Bhrigu's race went to Mahadeva for acquiring the science of arms. While dwelling in Siva's retreat, he had a quarrel with Karttikeya or Kumara, the son of Siva's loins. Rama worsted his preceptor's son in battle, at which his preceptor, gratified with him, made him a present of his own battle-axe, wherewith the regenerate hero exterminated the Kshatriyas for full one and twenty times.

the Protector of the universe; He that is endued with eyes like those of the bull; He that cherishes Righteousness with love (DLXXXVI—DXCV): He that is the unreturning hero; He whose soul has been withdrawn from all attachments; He that reduces to a subtle form the universe at the time of the universal dissolution; He that does good to His afflicted worshippers; He whose name, as soon as heard, cleanses the hearer of all his sins; He who has the auspicious whorl on His breast; He in whom dwells the goddess of Prosperity for ever; He who was chosen by Lakshmi (the goddess of Prosperity) as her Lord; He that is the foremost one of all Beings endued with prosperity (DXCVI—DCIV); He that give prosperity unto His worshippers; the Master of prosperity; He that always lives with those that are endued with prosperity; He that is the receptacle of all kinds of prosperity; He that gives prosperity unto all persons of righteous acts according to the measure of their righteousness; He that holds the goddess of Prosperity on his bosom; He that bestows prosperity upon those that hear of, praise, and mediate on Him; He that is the embodiment of that condition which represents the attainment of unattainable happiness; He that is possessed of every kind of beauty; He that is the Refuge of the three worlds (DCV—DCXIV); He that is possessed of beautiful eye; He that is possessed of beautiful limbs; He that is possessed of a hundred sources of delight; He that represents the highest delight; He that is the Master of all the luminaries in the firmament (for it is He that maintains them in their places and orbits); He that has subjugated His soul; He whose soul is not swayed by any superior Being; He that is always of beautiful acts; He whose doubts have all been dispelled (for He is said to behold the whole universe as an Amlaka in His palm) (DCXV—DCXXIII); He that transcends all creatures; He whose vision extends in all directions: He that has no Master; He that at all times transcends all changes; He that (in the form of Rama) had to lie down on that bare ground; He that adorns the earth (by His incarnations); He that is puissance's self; He that transcends all grief; He that dispels the griefs of all His worshippers as soon as they remember Him (DCXXIV—DCXXXII); He that is possessed of effulgence, He that is worshipped by all; He that is the water-pot (as all things reside within Him); He that is of pure soul; He that cleanses all as soon as they hear of him; He that is free and unrestrained; He whose car never turns away from battles; He that is possessed of great wealth; He whose prowess is incapable of being measured (DCXXXIII—DCXLI); He that is the slayer of the Asura named Kalanemi; He that is the Hero; He that has taken birth in the race of Sura; He that is the Lord of all the deities; the soul of the three worlds; the Master of the three worlds; He that has the solar and lunar rays for his hair; the slayer of Kesi; He that destroys all things (at the universal dissolution) (DCXLII—DCL); the Deity from whom the fruition of all desires is sought; He that grants the wishes of all; He that has desires; He that has a handsome form; He that is endued with thorough knowledge of Srutis and Smritis; He that is possessed of a form that is indescribable by attributes; He whose brightest rays overwhelm heaven; He that has no end; He that (in the form of Arjuna or Nara) acquired vast wealth on the occasion of his campaign of conquest (DCLI—DCLX); He who is the foremost object of silent recitation, of sacrifice, of the Vedas, and of all religious acts; He that is the creator of penances and the like; He that is the form of (the grandsire) Brahman, He that is the augmentor of penances; He that is conversant with Brahma; He that is of the form of Brahmana; He that has for His limbs Him that is called Brahma; He that knows all the Vedas and everything in the universe; He that is always fond of Brahmanas and of whom the Brahmanas also are fond (DCLXI—DCLXX); He whose footsteps cover vast areas; He whose feats are mighty; He who is possessed of vast energy; He that is identical with Vasuki, the king of the snakes; He that is the foremost of all sacrifices; He that is Japa, that first of sacrifices; He that is the foremost of all offerings made in sacrifices (DCLXXI—DCLXXVIII);[605] He that is hymned by all; He that loves to be hymned (by his worshippers); He that is himself the hymns uttered by His worshippers; He that is the very act of hymning; He that is the person that hymns; He that is fond of battling (with everything that is evil); He that is full in every respect; He that fills others with every kind of affluence; He that destroys all sins as soon as He is remembered; He whose acts are all righteous; He that transcends all kinds of disease (DCLXXIX—DCLXXXIX); He that is endued with the speed of the mind; He that is the creator and promulgator of all kinds of learning; He whose vital seed is gold; He that is giver of wealth (being identical with Kuvera the Lord of treasures); He that takes away all the wealth of the Asuras; the son of Vasudeva; He in whom all creatures dwell; He whose mind dwells in all things in thorough identity with them; He that takes away the sins of all who seek refuge in him (DCXC—DCXCVIII); He that is attainable by the righteous; He whose acts are always good; He that is the one entity in the universe; He that displays Himself in diverse forms; He that is the refuge of all those that are conversant with truth; He who has the greatest of heroes for his troops;[606] He that is the foremost of the Yadavas; He that is the abode of the righteous; He that sports in joy (in the woods of Brinda) on the banks of Yamuna (DCXCIX—DCCVII); He in whom all created things dwell; the deity that overwhelms the universe with His Maya (illusion); He in whom all foremost of Beings become merged (when they achieve their emancipation); He whose hunger is never gratified; He that humbles the pride of all; He that fills the righteous with just pride; He that swells with joy; He that is incapable of being seized; He that has never been vanquished (DCCVIII—DCCXVI); He that is of universal form; He that is of vast form; He whose form blazes forth with energy and effulgence; He that is without form (as determined by acts); He that is of diverse forms; (He that is unmanifest); He that is of a hundred forms; He that is of a hundred faces (DCCXVII—DCCXXIV); He that is one; He that is many (through illusion); He that is full of felicity; He that forms the one grand topic of investigation; He from whom is this all; He that is called THAT; He that is the highest Refuge; He that confines Jiva within material causes; He that is coveted by all; He that took birth in the race of Madhu; He that is exceedingly affectionate towards His worshippers (DCCXXV—DCCXXXV); He that is of golden complexion; He whose limbs are like gold (in hue); He that is possessed of beautiful limbs; He whose person is decked with Angadas made with sandal-paste; He that is the slayer of heroes; He that has no equal; He that is like cipher (in consequence of no attributes being affirmable of Him); He that stands in need of no blessings (in consequence of His fulness); He that never swerves from His own nature and puissance and knowledge; He that is mobile in the form of wind (DCCXXXVI—DCCXLV); He that never identifies Himself with anything that is not-soul;[607] He that confers honours on His worshippers; He that is honoured by all; He that is the Lord of the three worlds; He that upholds the three worlds; He that is possessed of intelligence and memory capable of holding in His mind the contents of all treatises; He that took birth in a sacrifice; He that is worthy of the highest praise; He whose intelligence and memory are never futile; He that upholds the earth (DCCXLVI—DCCLV); He that pours forth heat in the form of the

---

[605] Many of these words beginning with Mahat represent Krishna's own words as spoken to Arjuna in the Gita. 'I am the foremost of sacrifices; I am the foremost of sacrificers,' etc.

[606] Referring to Hanumat and others among the apes that Rama led against Ravana.

[607] The universe consists of Soul and Not-soul. Jiva, when cased in matter or Not-soul takes Not-soul for himself, in his ignorance. In fact until true knowledge is attained, the body is taken for self.

Sun; He that is the bearer of great beauty of limbs; He that is the foremost of all bearers of weapons; He that accepts the flowery and leafy offerings made to Him by His worshippers; He that has subdued all his passions and grinds all His foes; He that has none to walk before Him; He that has four horns; He that is the elder brother of Gada (DCCLVI—DCCLXIV); He that has four arms; He from whom the four Purushas have sprung; He that is the refuge of the four modes of life and the four orders of men; He that is of four souls (Mind, Understanding, Consciousness, and Memory); He from whom spring the four objects of life, viz., Righteousness, Wealth, Pleasure, and Emancipation; He that is conversant with the four Vedas; He that has displayed only a fraction of His puissance (DCCLXV—DCCLXXII); He that sets the wheel of the world to revolve round and round; He whose soul is dissociated from all worldly attachments; He that is incapable of being vanquished; He that cannot be transcended; He that is exceedingly difficult of being attained; He that is difficult of being approached; He that is difficult of access; He that is difficult of being brought within the heart (by even Yogins); He that slays even the most powerful foes (among the Danavas) (DCCLXXIII—DCCLXXXI); He that has beautiful limbs; He that takes the essence of all things in the universe; He that owns the most beautiful warp and woof (for weaving this texture of fabric of the universe); He that weaves with ever-extending warp and woof; He whose acts are done by Indra; He whose acts are great; He who has no acts undone; He who has composed all the Vedas and scriptures (DCCLXXXII—DCCLXXXIX); He whose birth is high; He that is exceedingly handsome; He whose heart is full of commiseration; He that has precious gems in His navel; He that has excellent knowledge for His eye; He that is worthy of worship by Brahman himself and other foremost ones in the universe; He that is giver of food; He that assumed horns at the time of the universal dissolution; He that has always subjugated His foes most wonderfully; He that knows all things; He that is ever victorious over those that are of irresistible prowess (DCCXC—DCCXCIX); He whose limbs are like gold; He that is incapable of being agitated (by wrath or aversion or other passion); He that is Master of all those who are masters of all speech; He that is the deepest lake; He that is the deepest pit; He that transcends the influence of Time; He in whom the primal elements are established (DCCC—DCCCVI); He that gladdens the earth; He that grants fruits which are as agreeable as the Kunda flowers (Jasmim pubescens, Linn); He that gave away the earth unto Kasyapa (in His incarnation as Rama); He that extinguishes the three kinds of misery (mentioned in the Sankhya philosophy) like a rain-charged cloud cooling the heat of the earth by its downpour; He that cleanses all creatures; He that has none to urge Him; He that drank nectar; He that has an undying body; He that is possessed of omniscience; He that has face and eyes turned towards every direction (DCCCVII—DCCCXVI); He that is easily won (with, that is, such gifts as consist of flowers and leaves); He that has performed excellent vows; He that is crowned with success by Himself; He that is victorious over all foes; He that scorches all foes; He that is the ever-growing and tall Banian that overtops all other trees; He that is the sacred fig tree (Ficus glomerata, Willd); He that is the Ficus religiosa; (or, He that is not durable, in consequence of His being all perishable forms in the universe even as he is all the imperishable forms that exist); He that is the slayer of Chanura of the Andhra country (DCCCXVII—DCCCXXV); He that is endued with a thousand rays; He that has seven tongues (in the forms of Kali, Karali, etc.); He that has seven flames (in consequence of His being identical with the deity of fire); He that has seven horses for bearing His vehicle; (or, He that owns the steed called Sapta); He that is formless; He that is sinless: He that is inconceivable; He that dispels all fears; He that destroys all fears

(DCCCXXVI—DCCCXXXIV); He that is minute; He that is gross; He that is emaciated; He that is adipose; He that is endued with attributes; He that transcends all attributes; He that is unseizable; He that suffers Himself to be easily seized (by His worshippers); He that has an excellent face; He that has for His descendants the people of the accidental regions; He that extends the creation consisting of the fivefold primal elements (DCCCXXXV—DCCCXLVI); He that bears heavy weights (in the form of Ananta); He that has been declared by the Vedas; He that is devoted to Yoga; He that is the lord of all Yogins; He that is the giver of all wishes; He that affords an asylum to those that seek it; He that sets Yogins to practise Yoga anew after their return to life upon the conclusion of their life of felicity in heaven; He that invests Yogins with puissance even after the exhaustion of their merits; He that has goodly leaves (in the form of the Schhandas of the Vedas, Himself being the tree of the world); He that causes the winds to blow (DCCCXLVII—DCCCLVI); He that is armed with the bow (in the form of Rama); He that is conversant with the science of arms; He that is the rod of chastisement; He that is chastiser; He that executes all sentences of chastisement; He that has never been vanquished; He that is competent in all acts; He that sets all persons to their respective duties; He that has none to set Him to any work; He that has no Yama to slay Him (DCCCLVII—DCCCLXVI); He that is endued with heroism and prowess; He that has the attribute of Sattwa (Goodness); He that is identical with Truth; He that is devoted to Truth and Righteousness; He that is sought by those who are resolved to achieve emancipation; (or, He towards whom the universe proceeds when the dissolution comes); He that deserves to have all objects which His worshippers present unto Him; He that is worthy of being adored (with hymns and flowers and other offering of reverence); He that does good to all; He that enhances the delights of all (DCCCLXVII—DCCCLXXV); He whose track is through the firmament; He that blazes forth in His own effulgence; He that is endued with great beauty; He that eats the offerings made on the sacrificial fire; He that dwells everywhere and is endued with supreme puissance; He that sucks the moisture of the earth in the form of the Sun; He that has diverse desires; He that brings forth all things; He that is the parent of the universe; He that has the Sun for His eye (DCCCLXXVI—DCCCLXXXV); He that is Infinite; He that accepts all sacrificial offerings; He that enjoys Prakriti in the form of Mind; He that is giver of felicity; He that has taken repeated births (for the protection of righteousness and the righteous); He that is First-born of all existent things; He that transcends despair (in consequence of the fruition of all His wishes); He that forgives the righteous when they trip; He that is the foundation upon which the universe rests; He that is most wonderful (DCCCLXXXVI—DCCCXCV); He that is existent from the beginning of Time; He that has been existing from before the birth of the Grandsire and others; He that is of a tawny hue; (or, He that discovers or illumines all existent things by His rays); He that assumed the form of the great Boar; He that exists even when all things are dissolved; He that is the giver of all blessings; He that creates blessings; He that is identifiable with all blessings; He that enjoys blessings; He that is able to scatter blessings (DCCCXCVI—CMV); He that is without wrath; He that lies ensconced in folds (in the form of the snake Sesha); (or, He that is adorned with ear-rings); He that is armed with the discus; He that is endued with great prowess; He whose sway is regulated by the high precepts of the Srutis and the Smritis; He that is incapable of being described by the aid of speech; He whom the Vedantas have striven to express with the aid of speech; He that is the dew which cools those who are afflicted with the three kinds of grief; He that lives in all bodies, endued with the capacity of dispelling darkness (CMVI—CMXIV); He that is divested of wrath;

He that is well-skilled in accomplishing all acts by thought, word, and deed; He that can accomplish all acts within the shortest period of time; He that destroys the wicked; He that is the foremost of all forgiving persons; He that is foremost of all persons endued with knowledge; He that transcends all fear; He whose names and feats, heard and recited, lead to Righteousness (CMXV—CMXXII), He that rescues the Righteous from the tempestuous ocean of the world; He that destroys the wicked; He that is Righteousness; He that dispels all evil dreams; He that destroys all bad paths for leading His worshippers to the good path of emancipation; He that protects the universe by staying in the attribute of Sattwa; He that walks along the good path; He that is Life; He that exists overspreading the universe (CMXXIII—CMXXXI); He that is of infinite forms; He that is endued with infinite prosperity; He that has subdued wrath; He that destroys the fears of the righteous; He that gives just fruits, on every side, to sentient beings according to their thoughts and acts; He that is immeasurable Soul; He that bestows diverse kinds of fruits on deserving persons for their diverse acts; He that sets diverse commands (on gods and men); He that attaches to every act its proper fruit (CMXXXII—CMXL); He that has no beginning; He that is the receptacle of all causes as well as of the earth; He that has the goddess of Prosperity ever by his side; He that is the foremost of all heroes; He that is adorned with beautiful armlets; He that produces all creatures; He that is the original cause of the birth of all creatures; He that is the terror of all the wicked Asuras; He that is endued with terrible prowess (CMXLI—CMXLIX); He that is the receptacle and abode of the five primal elements; He that gulps down His throat all creatures at the time of the universal dissolution; He whose smile is as agreeable as the sight of flowers; (or, He who laughs in the form of flowers); He that is always wakeful; He that stays at the head of all creatures; He whose conduct consists of those acts which the Righteous do; He that revives the dead (as in the case of Parikshit and others); He that is the initial syllable Om; He that has ordained all righteous acts (CML—CMLVIII); He that displays the truth about the Supreme Soul; He that is the abode of the five life-breaths and the senses; He that is the food which supports the life of living creatures; He that causes all living creatures to live with the aid of the life-breath called Prana; He that is the great topic of every system of philosophy; He that is the One Soul in the universe; He that transcends birth, decrepitude, and death (CMLIX—CMLXV); He that rescues the universe in consequence of the sacred syllable Bhuh, Bhuvah, Swah, and the others with which Homa offerings are made; He that is the great rescuer; He that is the sire of all; He that is the sire of even the Grandsire (Brahman); He that is of the form of Sacrifice; He that is the Lord of all sacrifices (being the great deity that is adored in them); He that is the sacrificer; He that has sacrifices for his limbs; He that upholds all sacrifices (CMLXVI—CMLXXV); He that protects sacrifices; He that has created sacrifices; He that is the foremost of all performers of sacrifices; He that enjoys the rewards of all sacrifices; He that causes the accomplishment of all sacrifices; He that completes all sacrifices by accepting the full libation at the end; He that is identical with such sacrifices as are performed without desire of fruit; He that is the food which sustains all living creatures; He that is also the eater of that food (CMLXXVI—CMLXXXIV); He that is Himself the cause of His existence; He that is self-born; He that penetrated through the solid earth (and repairing to the nether regions slew Hiranyaksha and others); He that sings the Samans; He that is the delighter of Devaki; He that is the creator of all; He that is the Lord of the earth; He that is the destroyer of the sins of his worshippers (CMLXXXV—CMXCII); He that bears the conch (Panchajanya) in His hands; He that bears the sword of knowledge and illusion; He that sets the cycle of the

Yugas to revolve ceaselessly; He that invests Himself with consciousness and senses; He that is endued with the mace of the most solid understanding. He that is armed with a car-wheel; He that is incapable of being agitated; He that is armed with all kinds of weapons (CMXCIII—M). Om, salutations to Him!

"Even thus have I recited to thee, without any exception, the thousand excellent names of the high-souled Kesava whose glory should always be sung. That man who hears the names every day or who recites them every day, never meets with any evil either here or hereafter. If a Brahmana does this he succeeds in mastering the Vedanta; if a Kshatriya does it, he becomes always successful in battle. A Vaisya, by doing it, becomes possessed of affluence, while a Sudra earns great happiness. If one becomes desirous of earning the merit of righteousness, one succeeds in earning it (by hearing or reciting these names). If it is wealth that one desires, one succeeds in earning wealth (by acting in this way). So also the man who wishes for enjoyments of the senses succeeds in enjoying all kinds of pleasures, and the man desirous of offspring acquires offspring (by pursuing this course of conduct). That man who with devotion and perseverance and heart wholly turned towards him, recites these thousand names of Vasudeva every day, after having purified himself, succeeds in acquiring great fame, a position of eminence among his kinsmen, enduring prosperity, and lastly, that which is of the highest benefit to him (viz., emancipation itself). Such a man never meets with fear at any time, and acquires great prowess and energy. Disease never afflicts him; splendour of complexion, strength, beauty, and accomplishments become his. The sick become hale, the afflicted become freed from their afflictions; the affrighted become freed from fear, and he that is plunged in calamity becomes freed from calamity. The man who hymns the praises of that foremost of Beings by reciting His thousand names with devotion succeeds in quickly crossing all difficulties. That mortal who takes refuge in Vasudeva and who becomes devoted to Him, becomes freed of all sins and attains to eternal Brahma. They who are devoted to Vasudeva have never to encounter any evil. They become freed from the fear of birth, death, decrepitude, and disease. That man who with devotion and faith recites this hymn (consisting of the thousand names of Vasudeva) succeeds in acquiring felicity of soul, forgiveness of disposition, Prosperity, intelligence, memory, and fame. Neither wrath, nor jealousy, nor cupidity, nor evil understanding ever appears in those men of righteousness who are devoted to that foremost of beings. The firmament with the sun, moon and stars, the welkin, the points of the compass, the earth and the ocean, are all held and supported by the prowess of the high-souled Vasudeva. The whole mobile and immobile universe with the deities, Asuras, and Gandharvas, Yakshas, Uragas and Rakshasas, is under the sway of Krishna. The senses, mind, understanding, life, energy, strength and memory, it has been said, have Vasudeva for their soul. Indeed, this body that is called Kshetra, and the intelligent soul within, that is called the knower of Kshetra, also have Vasudeva for their soul. Conduct (consisting of practices) is said to be the foremost of all topics treated of in the scriptures. Righteousness has conduct for its basis. The unfading Vasudeva is said to be the lord of righteousness. The Rishis, the Pitris, the deities, the great (primal) elements, the metals, indeed, the entire mobile and immobile universe, has sprung from Narayana. Yoga, the Sankhya Philosophy, knowledge, all mechanical arts, the Vedas, the diverse scriptures, and all learning, have sprung from Janardana. Vishnu is the one great element or substance which has spread itself out into multifarious forms. Covering the three worlds, He the soul of all things, enjoys them all. His glory knows no diminution, and He it is that is the Enjoyer of the universe (as its Supreme Lord). This hymn in praise of the illustrious Vishnu composed by Vyasa, should be recited by that person who wishes to acquire happiness and that which is the highest benefit (viz., emancipation). Those persons that worship and adore the Lord of the universe, that deity who is inborn and possessed of blazing effulgence, who is the origin or cause of the universe, who knows on deterioration, and who is endued with eyes that are as large and beautiful as the petals of the lotus, have never to meet with any discomfiture."'"

SECTION CL.

"'Yudhishthira said, "O grandsire, O thou of great wisdom, O thou that art conversant with all branches of knowledge, what is that subject of silent recitation by reciting which every day one may acquire the merit of righteousness in a large measure? What is that Mantra for recitation which bestows success if recited on the occasion of setting out on a journey or in entering a new building, or at the commencement of any undertaking, or on the occasion of sacrifices in honour of the deities or of the Pitris? It behoveth thee to tell me what indeed, what Mantra it is, which propitiates all malevolent influences, or leads to prosperity or growth, or protection from evil, or the destruction of foes, or the dispelling of fears, and which, at the same time, is consistent with the Vedas."

"'Bhishma said, "Hear, O king, with concentrated attention, what that Mantra is which was declared by Vyasa. It was ordained by Savitri and is possessed of great excellence. It is capable of cleansing a person immediately of all his sins. Hear, O sinless one, as I recite to thee the ordinances in respect of that Mantra. Indeed, O chief of the sons of Pandu, by listening to those ordinances, one becomes cleansed of all one's sins. One who recites this Mantra day and night becomes never stained by sin. I shall now declare it to thee what that Mantra is. Do thou listen with concentrated attention. Indeed, the man that hears it becomes endued with long life, O prince, and attaining to the fruition of all his wishes, sports in felicity both here and hereafter. This Mantra, O king, was daily recited by the foremost of royal sages devoted to the practice to Kshatriya duties and steadily observant of the vow of truth. Indeed, O tiger among kings, those monarchs who, with restrained senses and tranquil soul, recite this Mantra every day, succeed in acquiring unrivalled prosperity—Salutations to Vasishtha of high vows after having bowed with reverence unto Parasara, that Ocean of the Vedas! Salutations to the great snake Ananta, and salutations to all those who are crowned with success, and who are of unfading glory! Salutations to the Rishis, and unto Him that is the Highest of the High, the god of gods, and the giver of boons unto all those that are foremost. Salutations unto Him of a thousand heads, Him that is most auspicious, Him that has a thousand names, viz., Janardana! Aja, Ekapada, Ahivradhna, the unvanquished Pinakin, Rita Pitrirupa, the three-eyed Maheswara, Vrishakapi, Sambhu, Havana, and Iswara—these are the celebrated Rudras, eleven in number, who are the lords of all the worlds. Even these eleven high-souled ones have been mentioned as a hundred in the Satarudra (of the Vedas). Ansa, Bhaga, Mitra, Varuna the lord of waters, Dhatri, Aryaman, Jayanta, Bhaskara, Tvashtri, Pushan, Indra and Vishnu, are said to comprise a tale of twelve. These twelve are called Adityas and they are the sons of Kasyapa as the Sruti declares. Dhara, Dhruva, Some, Savitra. Anila, Anala, Pratyusha, and Prabhava, are the eight Vasus named in the scriptures, Nasataya and Dasra are said to be the two Aswins. They are the sons of Martanda born of his spouse Samjna, from whose nostrils they came out. After this I shall recite the names of those who are the witnesses of all acts in the worlds. They take note of all sacrifices, of all gifts, of all good acts. Those lords among the deities behold everything although they are invisible. Indeed, they behold all the good and bad acts of all beings. They are Mrityu, Kala, the Viswedevas, the Pitris endued with forms, the great Rishis possessed of wealth of penances, the Munis, and others crowned with success and devoted to penances and emancipation. These of sweet smiles, bestow diverse benefits upon those men that recite their names. Verily, endued with celestial energy, they bestow diverse regions of felicity created by the Grandsire upon such men. They reside in all the worlds and attentively note all acts. By reciting the names of those lords of all living creatures, one always becomes endued with righteousness and wealth and enjoyments in copious measure. One acquires hereafter diverse regions of auspiciousness and felicity created by the Lord of the universe. These three and thirty deities, who are the lords of all beings as also Nandiswara of huge body, and that pre-eminent one who has the bull for the device on his banner, and those masters of all the worlds, viz., the followers and associates of him called Ganeswara, and those called Saumyas, and called the Rudras, and those called the Yogas, and those that are known as the Bhutas, and the luminaries in the firmament, the Rivers, the sky, the prince of birds (viz., Garuda), all those persons on earth who have become crowned with success in consequence of their penances and who are existing in an immobile or mobile form, the Himavat, all the mountains, the four Oceans, the followers and associates of Bhava who are possessed of prowess equal to that of Bhava himself, the illustrious and ever-victorious Vishnu, and Skanda, and Ambika,—these are the great souls by reciting whose name with restrained senses, one becomes cleansed of all sins. After this I shall recite the names of those foremost Rishis who are known as Manavas. They are Yavakrita, and Raibhya, and Arvavasu, and Paravasu, and Aushija, and Kakshivat, and Vala the son of Angiras. Then comes Kanwa the son of the Rishi Medhatithi, and Varishada. All these are endued with the energy of Brahma and have been spoken of (in the scriptures) as creators of the universe. They have sprung from Rudra and Anala and the Vasus. By reciting their names people obtain great benefits. Indeed, by doing good deeds on earth, people sport in joy in heaven, with the deities. These Rishis are the priests of Indra. They live in the east. That man who, with rapt attention, recites the names of these Rishis, succeeds in ascending to the regions of Indra and obtaining great honours there. Unmachu, Pramchu, Swastyatreya of great energy, Dridhavya, Urdhvavahu, Trinasoma, Angiras, and Agastya of great energy, the son of Mitravaruna,—these seven are the Ritwiks of Yama the king of the dead, and dwell in the southern quarter. Dridheyu and Riteyu, and Pariyadha of great fame, and Ekata, and Dwita, and Trita—the last three endued with splendour like that of the sun,—and Atri's son of righteous soul, viz., the Rishi Saraswata,—these seven who had acted as Ritwiks in the great sacrifice of Varuna—have taken up their abodes in the western quarter. Atri, the illustrious Vasishtha, the great Rishi Kasyapa, Gotama, Bharadwaja, Viswamitra, the son of Kusika, and Richika's fierce son Jamadagni of great energy,—these seven are the Ritwiks of the Lord of treasures and dwell in the northern quarter. There are seven other Rishis that live in all directions without being confined to any particular one. They, it is, who are the inducers of fame and of all this beneficial to men, and they have been sung as the creators of the worlds. Dharma, Kama, Kala, Vasu, Vasuki, Ananta, and Kapila,—these seven are the upholders of the world. Rama, Vyasa, Drona's son Aswatthaman, are the other Rishis (that are regarded as the foremost). These are the great Rishis as distributed into seven groups, each group consisting of seven. They are the creators of that peace and good that men enjoy. They are said to be the Regents of the several points of the compass. One should turn one's face to that direction in which one of these Rishis live if one wishes to worship him. Those Rishis are the creators of all creatures and have been regarded as the cleansers of all. Samvarta, Merusavarna, the righteous Markandeya, and Sankhya and Yoga, and Narada and the great Rishi Durvasa,—these are endued with severe penance and great self-restraint, and are celebrated over the three worlds. There are others who are equal to Rudra himself. They live in the region of Brahman. By naming them with reverence a sonless man obtains a son, and a poor man obtains wealth. Indeed, by naming them, one acquires success in religion, and wealth and pleasure. One should also take the name of that celebrated king who was Emperor of all the earth and equal to a Prajapati, viz., that foremost of monarchs, Prithu, the son of Vena. The earth became his daughter (from love and affection). One should also name Pururavas of the Solar race and equal unto Mahendra himself in prowess. He was the son of Ila and celebrated over the three worlds. One should, indeed, take the name of that dear son of Vudha. One should also take the name of Bharata, that hero celebrated over the three worlds. He also who in the Krita age adored the gods in a grand Gomedha sacrifice, viz., Rantideva of great splendour, who was equal unto Mahadeva himself, should be named. Endued with penances, possessed of every auspicious mark, the source of every kind of benefit to the world, he was the conqueror of the universes. One should also take the name of the royal sage Sweta of illustrious fame. He had gratified the great Mahadeva and it was for his sake that Andhaka was slain. One should also take the name of the royal sage Bhagiratha of great fame, who, through the grace of Mahadeva, succeeded in bringing down the sacred river from heaven (for flowing over the earth and cleansing all human beings of their sins). It was Bhagiratha who caused the ashes of the sixty thousand sons of Sagara to be overflowed with the sacred waters of Ganga and thereby rescued them from their sin. Indeed, one should take the names of all these that were endued with the blazing effulgence of fire, great beauty of person, and high energy. Some of them were of awe-inspiring forms and great might. Verily, one should take the names of these deities and Rishis and kings, those lords of the universe,—who are enhancers of fame. Sankhya, and Yoga which is highest of the high, and Havya and Kavya and that refuge of all the Srutis, viz., Supreme Brahma, have been declared to be the sources of great benefit to all creatures. These are sacred and sin-cleansing and have been spoken of very highly. These are the foremost of medicines for allaying all diseases, and are the inducers of the success in respect of all deeds. Restraining one's senses, one should, O Bharata, take the names of these, morning and evening. It is these that protect. It is these that shower rain. It is these that shine and give light and heat. It is these that blow. It is these that create all things. These are regarded as the foremost of all, as the leaders of the universe, as highly clever in the accomplishment of all things, as endued with forgiveness, as complete masters of the senses. Indeed, it has been said that they dispel all the evils to which human beings are subject. These high-souled ones are the witnesses of all good and bad deeds. Rising up in the morning one should take their names, for by this, one is sure to acquire all that is good. He who takes the names of them becomes freed from the fear of fires and of thieves. Such a man never finds his way obstructed by any impediment. By taking the names of these high-souled ones, one becomes free from bad dreams of every kind. Cleared from every sin, such men take birth in auspicious families. That regenerate person who, with restrained senses, recites these names on the occasions of performing the initiatory rites of sacrifices and other religious observances, becomes, as the consequence thereof, endued with righteousness, devoted to the study of the soul, possessed of forgiveness and self-restraint, and free from malice. If a man that is afflicted with disease recites them, he becomes freed from his sin in the form of disease. By reciting them within a house, all evils are dispelled from the inmates. By reciting them within a field, the growth is helped of all kinds of crops. Reciting them at the time of setting out on a journey, or while one is away from one's home, one meets with good fortune. These names lead to the protection of one's own self, of one's children and spouses, of one's wealth, and of one's seeds, and plants. The Kshatriya who recites these names at the time of joining a battle sees destruction overtake his foes and good fortune crown him and his party. The man who recites these names on the occasions of performing the rites in honour of the deities or the Pitris, helps the Pitris and deities eat the sacrificial Havya and Kavya. The man that recites them becomes freed from fear of diseases and beasts of prey, of elephants and thieves. His load of anxiety becomes lightened, and he becomes freed from every sin. By reciting these excellent Savitri Mantras on board a vessel, or in a vehicle, or in the courts of kings, one attains to high success. There where these Mantras are recited, fire does not burn wood. There children do not die, nor snakes dwell. Indeed, at such places, there can be no fear of the king, nor of Pisachas and Rakshasas.[608] Verily, the man who recites these Mantras ceases to have any fear of fire or water or wind or beasts of prey. These Savitri Mantras, recited duly, contribute to the peace and well-being of all the four orders. Those men who recite them with reverence become freed from every sorrow and at last attain to a high end. Even these are the results achieved by them that recite these Savitri Mantras which are of the form of Brahma. That man who recites these Mantras in the midst of kine sees his kine become fruitful. Whether when setting out on a journey, or entering a house on coming back, one should recite these Mantras on every occasion. These Mantras constitute a great mystery of the Rishis and are the very highest of those which they silently recite. Even such are these Mantras unto them who practise the duty of recitation and pour libations on the sacrificial fire. This that I have said unto thee is the excellent opinion of Parasara. It was recited in former days unto Sakra himself. Representing as it does Truth or Eternal Brahman, I have declared it in full to thee. It constitutes that heart of all creatures, and is the highest Sruti. All the princes of the race of Soma and of Surya, viz., the Raghavas and the Kauravas, recite these Mantras every day after having purified themselves, These constitute the highest end of human creatures. There is rescue from every trouble and calamity in the daily recitation of the names of the deities of the seven Rishis, and of Dhruva. Indeed, such recitation speedily frees one from distress. The sages of olden times, viz., Kasyapa, Gotama, and others, and Bhrigu Angiras and Atri and others, and Sukra, Agastya, and Vrihaspati, and others, all of whom are regenerate Rishis, have adored these Mantras. Approved of by the son of Bharadwaja, these Mantras were attained by the sons of Richika. Verily, having acquired them again from Vasishtha, Sakra and the Vasus went forth to battle and succeeded in subjugating the Danavas. That man who makes a present of a hundred kine with their horns covered with plates of gold unto a Brahmana possessed of much learning and well-conversant with the Vedas, and he who causes the excellent Bharata story to be recited in his house every day, are said to acquire equal merits. By reciting the name of Bhrigu one's righteousness becomes enhanced. By bowing to Vasishtha one's energy become enhanced. By bowing unto Raghu, one becomes victorious in battle. By reciting the praises of the Aswins, one becomes freed from diseases. I have thus, O king, told thee of the Savitri Mantras which are identical with eternal Brahman. If thou wishest to question me on any other topic thou

---

[608] The sense is that untimely deaths do not occur in such places; nor fear of oppression or unlawful chastisement by the king; etc.

mayst do so. I shall, O Bharata, answer thee.""'

SECTION CLI.

"'Yudhishthira said, "Who deserve to be worshipped? Who are they unto whom we should bow? How, indeed, should we behave towards whom? What course of conduct, O grandsire, towards what classes of persons is regarded faultless?"

"'Bhishma said, "The humiliation of Brahmanas would humiliate the very deities. By bowing unto Brahmanas one does not, O Yudhishthira, incur any fault. They deserve to be worshipped. They deserve to have our salutations. Thou shouldst behave towards them as if they are thy sons. Indeed, it is those men endued with great wisdom that uphold all the worlds. The Brahmanas are the great causeways of Righteousness in respect of all the worlds. Their happiness consists in renouncing all kinds of wealth. They are devoted to the vow of restraining speech. They are agreeable to all creatures, and observant of diverse excellent vows. They are the refuge of all creatures in the universe. They are the authors of all the regulations which govern the worlds. They are possessed of great fame. Penances are always their great wealth. Their power consists in speech. Their energy flows from the duties they observe. Conversant with all duties, they are possessed of minute vision, so that they are cognizant of the subtlest considerations. They are of righteous desires. They live the observance of well-performed duties. They are the causeways of Righteousness. The four kinds of living creatures exist, depending upon them as their refuge. They are the path or road along which all should go. They are the guides of all. They are the eternal upholders of all the sacrifices. They always uphold the heavy burdens of sires and grandsires. They never droop under heavy weights even when passing along difficult roads like strong cattle. They are attentive to the requirements of Pitris and deities and guests. They are entitled to eat the first portions of Havya and Kavya. By the very food they eat, they rescue the three worlds from great fear. They are as it were, the Island (for refuge) for all worlds. They are the eyes of all persons endued with sight. The wealth they possess consists of all the branches of knowledge known by the name of Siksha and all the Srutis. Endued with great skill, they are conversant with the most subtle relations of things. They are well-acquainted with the end of all things, and their thoughts are always employed upon the science of the soul. They are endued with the knowledge of the beginning, the middle, and the end of all things, and they are persons in whom doubts no longer exist in consequence of feeling certain of their knowledge. They are fully aware of the distinctions between what is superior and what is inferior. They it is who attain to the highest end. Freed from all attachments, cleansed of all sins, transcending all pairs of opposites (such as heat and cold, happiness and misery, etc.), they are unconnected with all worldly things. Deserving of every honour, they are always held in great esteem by persons endued with knowledge and high souls. They cast equal eyes on sandal-paste and filth or dirt, on what is food and what is not food. They see with an equal eye their brown vestments of coarse cloth and fabrics of silk and animal skins. They would live for many days together without eating any food, and dry up their limbs by such abstention from all sustenance. They devote themselves earnestly to the study of the Vedas, restraining their senses. They would make gods of those that are not gods, and not gods of those that are gods. Enraged, they can create other worlds and other Regents of the worlds than those that exist. Through the course of those high-souled ones, the ocean became so saline as to be undrinkable. The fire of their wrath yet burns in the forest of Dandaka, unquenched by time. They are the gods of the gods, and the cause of all cause. They are the authority of all authorities. What man of intelligence and wisdom is there that would seek to humiliate them? Amongst them the young and the old all deserve honours. They honour one another (not in consequence of distinctions of age but) in consequence of distinctions in respect of penances and knowledge. Even the Brahmana that is destitute of knowledge is a god and is a high instrument for cleansing others. He amongst them, then, that is possessed of knowledge is a much higher god and like unto the ocean when full (to the brim). Learned or unlearned, Brahmana is always a high deity. Sanctified or unsanctified (with the aid of Mantras), Fire is ever a great deity. A blazing fire even when it burns on a crematorium, is not regarded as tainted in consequence of the character of the spot whereon it burns. Clarified butter looks beautiful whether kept on the sacrificial altar or in a chamber. So, if a Brahmana be always engaged in evil acts, he is still to be regarded as deserving of honour. Indeed, know that the Brahmana is always a high deity."'"

SECTION CLII.

"'Yudhishthira said, "Tell us, O king, what is that reward attached to the worship of Brahmanas, seeing which thou worshippest them, O thou of superior intelligence! Indeed, what is that success, flowing from their worship, guided by which thou worshippest them?"

"'Bhishma said, "In this connection is cited this old narrative of a conversation between Pavana and Arjuna, O Bharata! Endued with a thousand arms and great beauty the mighty Kartavirya, in days of yore, became the lord of all the world. He had his capital in the city of Mahishmati. Of unbaffled prowess, that chief of the Haihaya race of Kshatriyas swayed the whole earth with her belt of seas, together with all her islands and all her precious mines of gold and gems. Keeping before him the duties of the Kshatriya order, as also humility and Vedic knowledge, the king made large gifts of wealth unto the Rishi Dattatreya. Indeed, the son of Kritavirya thus adored the great ascetic who, becoming pleased with him, asked him to solicit three boons. Thus requested by the Rishi in respect of boons, the king addressed him, saying, 'Let me become endued with a thousand arms when I am in the midst of my troops. While, however, I remain at home let me have, as usual only two arms! Indeed, let combatants, when engaged in battle, behold me possessed of a thousand arms, observant also of high vows, let me succeed in subjugating the whole earth by dint of my prowess. Having acquired the earth righteously, let me sway her with vigilance. There is a fourth boon which, O foremost of regenerate persons, I solicit thee to grant. O faultless one, in consequence of the disposition to favour me, it behoveth thee to grant it to me. Dependent that I am on thee, whenever I may happen to go wrong, let the righteous come forth to instruct and set me right!' Thus addressed, the Brahmana replied unto the king, saying, 'So let it be!' Even thus were those boons acquired by that king of blazing effulgence. Riding then on his car whose splendour resembled that of fire or the Sun, the monarch, blinded by his great prowess, said, 'Who, indeed, is there that can be regarded as my equal in patience and energy, in fame and heroism, in prowess and strength?' After he had uttered these words, an invisible voice in the welkin said, 'O ignorant wretch, dost thou not know that the Brahmana is superior to the Kshatriya? The Kshatriya, assisted by the Brahmana rules all creatures!'

"'"Arjuna said, 'When gratified, I am able to create many creatures. When angry, I am able to destroy all. In thought, word, and deed, I am the foremost. The Brahmana is certainly not above me! The first proposition here is that the Brahmana is superior to the Kshatriya. The counter-proposition is that the Kshatriya is superior. Thou hast said, O invisible being that the two are united together (in the act upon which the Kshatriya's superiority is sought to be based). A distinction, however, is observable in this. It is seen that Brahmanas take refuge with Kshatriyas. The Kshatriyas never seek the refuge of Brahmanas. Indeed, throughout the earth, the Brahmanas, accepting such refuge under the pretence of teaching the Vedas, draw their sustenance from the Kshatriyas. The duty of protecting all creatures is vested in Kshatriyas. It is from the Kshatriyas that the Brahmanas derive their sustenance. How then can the Brahmana be superior to the Kshatriyas? Well, I shall from today, bring under my subjection, your Brahmanas who are superior to all creatures but who have mendicancy for their occupation and who are so self-conceited! What the virgin Gayatri has said from the welkin is not true. Robed in skins, the Brahmanas move about in independence. I shall bring those independent wights under my subjection. Deity or man, there is none in the three worlds who can hurl me from the sovereignty I enjoy. Hence, I am certainly superior to the Brahmanas. This world that is now regarded as having Brahmanas for its foremost denizens shall soon be made such as to have Kshatriyas for its foremost denizens. There is none that is capable of bearing my might in battle!' Hearing these words of Arjuna, the welkin-ranging goddess became agitated. Then the god of wind, addressing the king from the sky, said, 'Cast off this sinful attitude. Bow unto the Brahmanas. By injuring them thou wilt bring about troubles on thy kingdom. The Brahmanas will either slay thee, king though thou art, or, endued with great might that they are, they will drive thee away from thy kingdom, despoiling thee of thy energy!' The king, hearing this speech, addressed the speaker, saying, 'Who, indeed, art thou?' The god of wind answered, 'I am the god of wind and the messenger of the deities! I say unto thee what is for thy benefit.'

""Arjuna said, 'Oh, I see that thou hast today shown thy devotion and attachment to the Brahmanas. Tell me now what kind of earthly creature is the Brahmana! Tell me, does a superior Brahmana resemble the Wind in any respect? Or, is he like Water, or Fire, or the Sun, or the Firmament?""

SECTION CLIII.

""The god of wind said, 'Hear, O deluded man, what the attributes are that belong to Brahmanas all of whom are endued with high souls. The Brahmana is superior to all those which, O king, thou hast named! In days of yore, the earth, indulging in a spirit of rivalry with the king of the Angas, forsook her character as Earth. The regenerate Kasyapa caused destruction to overtake her by actually paralysing her. The Brahmanas are always unconquerable, O king, in heaven as also on earth. In days of yore, the great Rishi Angiras, through his energy, drank off all the waters. The high-souled Rishi, having drank off all the waters as if they were milk, did not feel yet his thirst to be slaked. He, therefore, once more caused the earth to be filled with water by raising a mighty wave. On another occasion, when Angiras became enraged with me, I fled away, leaving the world, and dwelt for a long time concealed in the Agnihotra of the Brahmanas through fear of that Rishi. The illustrious Purandara, in consequence of his having coveted the body of Ahalya, was cursed by Gautama, yet, for the sake of Righteousness and wealth, the Rishi did not destroy outright the chief of the deities. The Ocean, O king, that was full in former days of crystal water, cursed by the Brahmanas, became saline in taste.[609] Even Agni who is of the complexion of gold, and who blazes with effulgence when destitute of smoke, and whose flames uniting together burn upwards, when cursed by the angry Angiras, became divested of all these attributes.[610] Behold, the sixty thousand sons of Sagara, who came here to adore the Ocean, have all been pulverised by the Brahmana, Kapila of golden complexion. Thou art not equal to the Brahmanas. Do thou, O king, seek thy own good. The Kshatriya of even great puissance bows to Brahmana children that are still in their mothers' wombs. The large kingdom of the Dandakas was destroyed by a Brahmana. The mighty Kshatriya Talajangala was destroyed by a single Brahmana, viz., Aurva. Thou too hast acquired a large kingdom, great might, religious merit, and learning, which are all difficult of attainment, through the grace of Dattatreya. Why dost thou, O Arjuna, worship Agni everyday who is a Brahmana? He is the bearer of sacrificial libations from every part of the universe. Art thou ignorant of this fact? Why, indeed, dost thou suffer thyself to be stupefied by folly when thou art not ignorant of the fact that a superior Brahmana is the protector of all creatures in the world and is, indeed, the creator of the living world? The Lord of all creatures, Brahman, unmanifest, endued with puissance, and of unfading glory, who created this boundless universe with its mobile and immobile creatures (is a Brahman). Some persons there are, destitute of wisdom, who say that Brahman was born of an Egg. From the original Egg, when it burst forth, mountains and the points of the compass and the waters and the earth and the heavens all sprang forth into existence. This birth of the creation was not seen by any one. How then can Brahman be said to have taken his birth from the original Egg, when especially he is declared as Unborn? It is said that vast uncreate Space is the original Egg. It was from this uncreate Space (or Supreme Brahman) that the Grandsire was born. If thou askest, "Whereon would the Grandsire, after his birth from uncreate Space, rest, for there was then nothing else?" The answer may be given in the following words, "There is an existent Being of the name of Consciousness. That mighty Being is endued with great energy. There is no Egg. Brahman, however, is existent. He is the creator of the universe and is its king!" Thus addressed by the god of wind, king Arjuna remained silent.'"[611]

SECTION CLIV.

"'The god of wind said, 'Once on a time, O king, a ruler of the name of Anga desired to give away the whole earth as sacrificial present unto the Brahmanas. At this, the earth became filled with anxiety. "I am the daughter of Brahman. I hold all creatures. Having obtained me, alas, why does this foremost of kings wish to give me away unto the Brahmanas? Abandoning my character as the soil, I shall now repair to the presence of my sire. Let this king with all his kingdom meet with destruction." Arrived at this conclusion, she departed for the region of Brahman. The Rishi Kasyapa, beholding goddess Earth on the point of departing, himself immediately entered the visible embodiment of the goddess, casting off his own body, by the aid of Yoga. The earth thus penetrated by the spirit of Kasyapa, grew in prosperity and became full of all kinds of

[609] The Bengal reading mrishtascha varina is incorrect. The Bombay reading mrishtasya varinsha is correct.
[610] The word kavi used in this verse, means Agni or fire, as explained by the commentator. One of the vernacular translators wrongly takes it as implying the preceptor Sukara.
[611] The last verse, as read in the Bengal texts, is vicious. Nastyandam astitu Brahma, etc., is the correct reading.

vegetable produce. Indeed, O king for the time that Kasyapa pervaded the earth, Righteousness became foremost everywhere and all fears ceased. In this way, O king, the earth remained penetrated by the spirit of Kasyapa for thirty thousand celestial years, fully alive to all those functions which it used to discharge while it was penetrated by the spirit of Brahman's daughter. Upon the expiry of this period, the goddess returned from the region of Brahman and arrived here bowed unto Kasyapa and from that time became the daughter of that Rishi. Kasyapa is a Brahmana. Even this was the feat, O king, that a Brahmana did. Tell me the name of the Kshatriya who can be held to be superior to Kasyapa!' Hearing these words, king Arjuna remained silent. Unto him the god of wind once more said, 'Hear now, O king, the story of Utathya who was born in the race of Angiras. The daughter of Soma, named Bhadra, came to be regarded as unrivalled in beauty. Her sire Soma regarded Utathya to be the fittest of husbands for her. The famous and highly blessed maiden of faultless limbs, observing diverse vows, underwent the severest austerities from the desire of obtaining Utathya for her lord. After a while, Soma's father Atri, inviting Utathya to his house, bestowed upon him the famous maiden. Utathya, who used to give away sacrificial presents in copious measure, duly received the girl for his wife. It so happened, however, that the handsome Varuna had, from a long time before, coveted the girl. Coming to the woods where Utathya dwelt, Varuna stole away the girl when she had plunged into the Yamuna for a bath. Abducting her thus, the Lord of the waters took her to his own abode. That mansion was of a wonderful aspect. It was adorned with six hundred thousand lakes. There is no mansion that can be regarded more beautiful than that palace of Varuna. It was adorned with many palaces and by the presence of diverse tribes of Apsaras and of diverse excellent articles of enjoyment. There, within that palace, the Lord of waters, O king, sported with the damsel. A little while after, the fact of the ravishment of his wife was reported to Utathya. Indeed, having heard all the facts from Narada, Utathya addressed the celestial Rishi, saying, "Go, O Narada, unto Varuna and speak with due severity unto him. Ask him as to why he has abducted my wife, and, indeed, tell him in my name that he should yield her up. Thou mayst say to him further, 'Thou are a protector of the worlds, O Varuna, and not a destroyer! Why then hast thou abducted Utathya's wife bestowed upon him by Soma?'" Thus requested by Utathya, the celestial Rishi Narada repaired to where Varuna was and addressing him, said, "Do thou set free the wife of Utathya. Indeed, why hast thou abducted her?" Hearing these words of Narada, Varuna replied unto him, saying, "This timid girl is exceedingly dear to me. I dare not let her go!" Receiving this reply, Narada repaired to Utathya and cheerlessly said, "O great ascetic, Varuna has driven me out from his house, seizing me by the throat. He is unwilling to restore to thee thy spouse. Do thou act as thou pleasest." Hearing these words of Narada, Angiras became inflamed with wrath. Endued with wealth of penances, he solidified the waters and drank them off, aided by his energy. When all the waters were thus drunk off, the Lord of that element became very cheerless with all his friends and kinsfolk. For all that, he did not still give up Utathya's wife. Then Utathya, that foremost of regenerate persons, filled with wrath, commanded Earth, saying, "O amiable one, do thou show land where there are at present the six hundred thousand lakes." At these words of the Rishi, the Ocean receded from the spot indicated, and land appeared which was exceedingly sterile. Unto the rivers that flowed through that region, Utathya said, "O Saraswati, do thou become invisible here. Indeed, O timid lady, leaving this region, go thou to the desert! O auspicious goddess, let this region, destitute of thee, cease to become sacred." When that region (in which the lord of waters dwelt) became dry, he repaired to Angiras, taking with him Utathya's spouse, and made her over to him. Getting back his wife, Utathya became cheerful. Then, O chief of the Haihaya race, that great Brahmana rescued both the universe and the Lord of waters from the situation of distress into which he had brought them. Conversant with every duty, the Rishi Utathya of great energy, after getting back his spouse, O king, said so unto Varuna, "I have recovered my wife, O Lord of waters, with the aid of my penances and after inflicting such distress on thee as made thee cry aloud in anguish!" Having said this, he went home, with that wife of his. Even such, O king, was Utathya, that foremost of Brahmanas. Shall I go on? Or, will you yet persist in thy opinion? What, is there a Kshatriya that is superior to Utathya?"'"

SECTION CLV.

"'Bhishma said, "Thus addressed, king Arjuna remained silent. The god of wind once more spoke to him, 'Listen now, O king, to the story of the greatness of the Brahmana Agastya. Once on a time, the gods were subjugated by the Asuras upon which they became very cheerless. The sacrifices of the deities were all seized, and the Swadha of the Pitris was also misappropriated. Indeed, O Chief of the Haihayas, all the religious acts and observances of human beings also were suspended by the Danavas. Divested of their prosperity, the deities wandered over the earth as we have heard. One day, in course of their wandering they met Agastya of high vows, that Brahmana, O king, who was endued with great energy and splendour which was as blazing as that of the sun. Saluting him duly, the deities made the usual enquiries of politeness. They then, O King, said these words unto that high-souled one, "We have been defeated by the Danavas in battle and have, therefore, fallen off from affluence and prosperity. Do thou, therefore, O foremost of ascetics, rescue us from this situation of great fear." Thus informed of the plight to which the deities had been reduced, Agastya became highly incensed (with the Danavas). Possessed of great energy, he at once blazed forth like the all-consuming fire at the time of the universal dissolution. With the blazing rays that then emanated from the Rishi, the Danavas began to be burnt. Indeed, O king, thousands of them began to drop down from the sky. Burning with the energy of Agastya, the Danavas, abandoning both heaven and earth, fled towards the southern direction. At that time the Danava king Vali was performing a Horse-sacrifice in the nether regions. Those great Asuras who were with him in those regions or who were dwelling in the bowels of the earth, were not burnt. The deities, upon the destruction of their foes, then regained their own regions, their fears entirely dispelled. Encouraged by what he accomplished for them, they then solicited the Rishi to destroy those Asuras who had taken refuge within the bowels of the earth or in the nether regions. Thus solicited by the gods, Agastya replied unto them, saying, "Yes, I am fully competent to consume those Asuras that are dwelling underneath the earth; but if I achieve such a feat, my penances will suffer a diminution. Hence, I shall not exert my power." Even thus, O king, were the Danavas consumed by the illustrious Rishi with his own energy. Even thus did Agastya of cleansed soul, O monarch, accomplish that feat with the aid of his penances. O sinless one, even so was Agastya as described by me! Shall I continue? Or, will you say anything in reply? Is there any Kshatriya who is greater than Agastya?"'

"'Bhishma continued, "Thus addressed, king Arjuna remained silent. The god of wind once more said, 'Hear, O king, one of the great feats of the illustrious Vasishtha. Once on a time the deities were engaged in performing a sacrifice on the shores of the lake Vaikhanasa. Knowing of his puissance, the sacrificing gods thought of Vasishtha and made him their priest in imagination. Meanwhile, seeing the gods reduced and emaciated in consequence of the Diksha they were undergoing, a race of Danavas, of the name of Khalins, of statures as gigantic as mountains, desired to slay them. Those amongst the Danavas that were either disabled or slain in the fight were plunged into the waters of the Manasa lake and in consequence of the boon of the Grandsire they instantly came back to vigour and life. Taking up huge and terrible mountain summits and maces and trees, they agitated the waters of the lake, causing them to swell up to the height of a hundred yojanas. They then ran against the deities numbering ten thousand. Afflicted by the Danavas, the gods then sought the protection of their chief, Vasava. Sakra, however, was soon afflicted by them. In his distress he sought the protection of Vasishtha. At this, the holy Rishi Vasishtha assured the deities, dispelling their fears. Understanding that the gods had become exceedingly cheerless, the ascetic did this through compassion. He put forth his energy and burnt, without any exertion, those Danavas called Khalins. Possessed of wealth of penances, the Rishi brought the River Ganga, who had gone to Kailasa, to that spot. Indeed, Ganga appeared, piercing through the waters of the lake. The lake was penetrated by that river. And as that celestial stream, piercing through the waters of the lake, appeared, it flowed on, under the name of Sarayu. The place whereon those Danavas fell came to be called after them. Even thus were the denizens of Heaven, with Indra at their head, rescued from great distress by Vasishtha, It was thus that those Danavas, who had received boons from Brahman, were slain by that high-souled Rishi. O sinless one, I have narrated to thee the feat which Vasishtha accomplished. Shall I go on? Or, will you say anything! Was there a Kshatriya who could be said to surpass the Brahmana Vasishtha?"'"

SECTION CLVI.

"'Bhishma said, "Thus addressed, Arjuna remained silent. The god of wind once more addressed him, saying, 'Hear me, O foremost one of the Haihayas, as I narrate to thee the achievement of the high-souled Atri. Once on a time as the gods and Danavas were fighting each other in the dark, Rahu pierced both Surya and Soma with his arrows. The gods, overwhelmed by darkness, began to fall before the mighty Danavas, O foremost of kings! Repeatedly struck by the Asuras, the denizens of heaven began to lose their strength. They then beheld the learned Brahmana Atri, endued with wealth of penances, engaged in the observance of austerities. Addressing that Rishi who had conquered all his senses and in whom wrath had been extinguished, they said "Behold, O Rishi, these two, viz., Soma and Surya, who have both been pierced by the Asuras with their arrows! In consequence of this, darkness has overtaken us, and we are being struck down by the foe. We do not see the end of our troubles! Do thou, O lord of great puissance, rescue us from this great fear."

"'"The Rishi said, "How, indeed, shall I protect you?" They answered, saying, "Do thou thyself become Chandramas. Do thou also become the sun, and do thou begin to slay these robbers!" Thus solicited by them, Atri assumed the form of the darkness-destroying Soma. Indeed, in consequence of his agreeable disposition, he began to look as handsome and delightful as Soma himself. Beholding that the real Soma and the real Surya had become darkened by the shafts of the foe, Atri, assuming the forms of those luminaries, began to shine forth in splendour over the field of battle, aided by the puissance of his penances. Verily Atri made the universe blaze forth in light, dispelling all its darkness. By putting forth his puissance, he also subjugated the vast multitudes of those enemies of the deities. Beholding those great Asuras burnt by Atri, the gods also, protected by Atri's energy, began to despatch them quickly. Putting forth his prowess and mastering all his energy, it was even in this way that Atri illumined the god of day, rescued the deities, and slew the Asuras! Even this was the feat that regenerate one, aided by his sacred fire,—that silent reciter of Mantras, that one clad in deer-skins,— accomplished! Behold, O royal sage, that act achieved by that Rishi who subsisted upon fruits only! I have thus narrated to thee, in detail, the feat of the high-souled Atri. Shall I go on? Or, will you say anything? Is there a Kshatriya that is superior to this regenerate Rishi?'

"""Thus addressed, Arjuna remained silent. The god of wind once more spake unto him, 'Hear, O king, the feat achieved by the high-souled Chyavana (in days of old). Having passed his promise to the twin Aswins, Chyavana addressed the chastiser of Paka, saying, "Do thou make the Aswins drinkers of Soma with all other deities!"

"""Indra said, "The Aswins have been cast away by us. How then, can they be admitted into the sacrificial circle for drinking Soma with the others? They are not numbered with the deities. Do not, therefore, tell us so! O thou of great vows, we do not wish to drink Soma in the company of the Aswins. Whatever other behest thou mayst be pleased to utter, O learned Brahmana, we are ready to accomplish."

"""Chyavana said, "The twin Aswins shall drink Soma with all of you! Both of them are gods, O chief of the deities, for they are the sons of Surya. Let the gods do what I have said. By acting according to those words, the gods will reap great advantage. By acting otherwise, evil will overtake them."

"""Indra said, "I shall not, O foremost of regenerate persons, drink Soma with the Aswins! Let others drink with them as they please! As regards myself, I dare not do it."

"""Chyavana said, "If, O slayer of Vala, thou wilt not obey my words, thou shalt, this very day, drink Soma with them in sacrifice, compelled by me!"

"""The god of wind said, 'Then Chyavana, taking the Aswins with him, commenced a great religious rite for their benefit. The gods all became stupefied by Chyavana with his Mantras. Beholding that feat commenced by Chyavana, Indra became incensed with wrath. Taking up a huge mountain he ran against that Rishi. The chief of the deities was also armed with the thunderbolt. Then the illustrious Chyavana, endued with penances, cast an angry glance upon Indra as he advanced. Throwing a little water at him, he paralysed the chief of the deities with his thunderbolt and mountain. As the result of the religious rite he had commenced, he created a terrible Asura hostile to Indra. Made of the libations he had poured on the sacred fire, that Asura was called Mada, of mouth gaping wide. Even such was the Asura that the great ascetic created with the aid of Mantras. There were a thousand teeth in his mouth, extending for a hundred yojanas. Of terrible mien, his fangs were two hundred yojanas in length. One of his cheeks rested on the earth and the other touched the heavens. Indeed, all the gods with Vasava seemed to stand at the root of that great Asura's tongue, even as fishes when they enter into the wide open mouth of a leviathan. While standing within the mouth of Mada, the gods held a quick consultation and then addressing Indra, said, "Do thou soon bend thy head in reverence unto this regenerate personage! Freed from every scruple, we shall drink Soma with the Aswins in our company!" Then Sakra, bowing down his head unto Chyavana, obeyed his behest. Even thus did Chyavana make the Aswins drinkers of Soma with the other gods. Calling back Mada, the Rishi then assigned him the acts he was to do. That Mada was commanded to take up his residence in dice, in hunting, in drinking, and in women. Hence, O king, those men that betake themselves to these, meet with destruction, without doubt. Hence, one should always cast off these faults to a great distance. Thus, O king, I have narrated to thee the feat achieved by Chyavana. Shall I go on? Or, will you say anything in reply? Is there a Kshatriya that is higher than the Brahmana Chyavana?"'''

SECTION CLVII.

"'Bhishma said, "Hearing these words of the god of wind, Arjuna remained silent. At this, the god of wind once more addressed him, saying, 'When the denizens of heaven, with Indra at their head, found themselves within the mouth of the Asura Mada, at that time Chyavana took away from them the earth. Deprived previously of heaven and now shorn of the earth also, the gods became very cheerless. Indeed, those high-souled ones, afflicted with grief, then threw themselves unreservedly upon the Grandsire's protection.'

"'"The gods said, "O thou that art adored by all creatures of the universe, the earth has been taken away from us by Chyavana, while we have been deprived of heaven by the Kapas, O puissant one!"

"'"Brahman said, "Ye denizens of heaven, do you, with Indra at your head, repair quickly and seek the protection of the Brahmanas. By gratifying them you will succeed in regaining both the regions as before." Thus instructed by the Grandsire, the deities repaired to the Brahmanas and became suppliants for their protection. The Brahmanas replied, enquiring, "Whom shall we subjugate?" Thus asked, the deities said unto them, "Do ye subjugate the Kapas." The Brahmanas then said, "Bringing them down on the earth first, we shall speedily subjugate them." After this, the Brahmanas commenced a rite having for its object the destruction of the Kapas. As soon as this was heard of by the Kapas, they immediately despatched a messenger of theirs, named Dhanin, unto those Brahmanas. Dhanin, coming to them as they sat on the earth, thus delivered to them the message of the Kapas. "The Kapas are even like you all! (They are not inferior to any of you). Hence, what will be the effect of these rites which you seem to be bent upon achieving? All of them are well-conversant with the Vedas and possessed of wisdom. All of them are mindful of sacrifices. All of them have Truth for their vow, and for these reasons all of them are regarded as equal to great Rishis. The goddess of Prosperity sports among them, and they, in their turn, support her with reverence. They never indulge in acts of fruitless congress with their wives, and they never eat the flesh of such animals as have not been killed in sacrifices. They pour libations on the blazing sacrificial fire (every day) and are obedient to the behests of their preceptors and seniors. All of them are of souls under perfect control, and never take any food without dividing it duly among their children. They always proceed on cars and other vehicles together (without any of them riding his own vehicle while others journey on foot). They never indulge in acts of congress with their spouses when the latter are in midst of their functional period. They all act in such a way as to attain to regions of felicity hereafter. Indeed, they are always righteous in their deeds. When women quick with child or old men have not eaten, they never eat anything themselves. They never indulge in play or sports of any kind in the forenoon. They never sleep during the day. When the Kapas have these and many other virtues and accomplishments, why, indeed, would you seek to subjugate them? You should abstain from the endeavour! Verily, by such abstention ye would achieve what is for your good."

"'"The Brahmanas said, "Oh, we shall subjugate the Kapas! In this matter, we art one with the deities. Hence, the Kapas deserve slaughter at your hands. As regards Dhanin, he should return whence he came!" After this, Dhanin, returning to the Kapas, said unto them, "The Brahmanas are not disposed to do you any good!" Hearing this, all the Kapas took up their weapons and proceeded towards the Brahmanas. The Brahmanas, beholding the Kapas advancing against them with the standards of their cars upraised, forthwith created certain blazing fires for the destruction of the Kapas. Those eternal fires, created with the aid of Vedic Mantras, having effected the destruction of the Kapas, began to shine in the firmament like so many (golden) clouds. The gods, having assembled together in battle, slew many of the Danavas. They did not know at that time that it was the Brahmanas who had effected their destruction. Then Narada of great energy, coming there, O king, informed the deities how their foes, the Kapas, had been really slain by the Brahmanas of mighty energy (and not by deities themselves). Hearing these words of Narada, the denizens of heaven became highly gratified. They also applauded those regenerate allies of theirs that were possessed of great fame. The energy and prowess of the deities then began to increase, and worshipped in all the worlds, they acquired also the boon of immortality!' After the god of wind had said these words, king Arjuna worshipped him duly and addressing him answered in these words. Hear, O mighty armed monarch, what Arjuna said.

""Arjuna said, 'O puissant god, always and by all means do I live for the Brahmanas! Devoted to them, I worship them always! Through the grace of Dattatreya I have obtained this might of mine! Through his grace have I been able to accomplish great feats in the world and achieve high merit! Oh, I have, with attention, heard of the achievements, O god of the wind, of the Brahmanas with all their interesting details as recited by thee truly.'

""The god of wind said, 'Do thou protect and cherish the Brahmanas, in the exercise of those Kshatriya duties which are thine by birth. Do thou protect them even as thou protectest thy own senses! There is danger to thee from the race of Bhrigu! All that, however, will take place on a distant day.""""

SECTION CLVIII.

"'Yudhishthira said, "Thou always worshippest, O king, Brahmanas of praiseworthy vows. Whatever, however is that fruit seeing which thou worshippest them, O king? O thou of high vows, beholding what prosperity attaching to the worship of the Brahmanas dost thou worship them? Tell me all this, O thou of mighty arms!"

"'Bhishma said, "Here is Kesava endued with great intelligence. He will tell thee everything. Of high vows and endued with prosperity, even he will tell you what the prosperity is that attaches to the worship of Brahmanas. My strength, ears, speech, mind, eyes, and that clear understanding of mine (are all clouded today). I think, the time is not distant when I shall have to cast off my body. The sun seems to me to go very slowly.[612] Those high duties, O king, that are mentioned in the Puranas as observed by Brahmanas and Kshatriyas and Vaisyas and Sudras, have all been recited by me. Do thou, O son of Pritha, learn from Krishna what little remains to be learnt on that head. I know Krishna truly. I know who he is and what his ancient might is. O chief of the Kauravas, Kesava is of immeasurable soul. Whenever doubts arise, it is he who upholds Righteousness then.[613] It is Krishna who created the earth, and sky, and the heavens. Indeed, the earth

---

[612] To an afflicted person the day seems long.

[613] The sense is that it is this Kesava who upholds the cause of Righteousness when dangers overtake it, cf. 'Yada yada hi dharmasya, etc.' in the Gita. It does not mean that when doubts are entertained by persons on questions of morality, it is Kesava who dispels them.

has sprung from Krishna's body. Of terrible prowess and existing from the beginning of time, it is Krishna who became the mighty Boar and raised the submerged Earth. It is He who created all the points of the compass, together with all the mountains. Below Him are the welkin, heaven, the four cardinal points, and the four subsidiary points. It is from him that the entire creation has flowed. It is He who has created this ancient universe. In His navel appeared a Lotus. Within that Lotus sprang Brahma himself of immeasurable energy. It was Brahma, O son of Pritha, who rent that darkness which existed surpassing the very ocean (in depth and extent). In the Treta age, O Partha, Krishna existed (on the earth), in the form of Righteousness. In the Treta age, he existed in the form of Knowledge. In the Dwapara age, he existed in the form of might. In the Kali age he came to the earth in the form of unrighteousness. It is He who in days of yore slew the Daityas. It is He who is the Ancient God. It is He who ruled the Asuras in the form of their Emperor (Valin). It is He who is the Creator of all beings. It is He who is also the future of all created Beings. It is He who is also the protector of this universe fraught with the seed of destruction. When the cause of Righteousness languishes, this Krishna takes birth in the race of either the gods or among men. Staying on Righteousness, this Krishna of cleansed soul (on such occasion) protects both the higher and the lower worlds. Sparing those that deserve to be spared, Krishna sets himself to the slaughter of the Asura, O Partha! It is he who is all acts proper and improper and it is he who is the cause. It is Krishna who is the act done, the act to be done, and the act that is being done. Know that that illustrious one is Rahu and Soma and Sakra. It is he that is Viswakarma. It is he that is of universal form. He is the destroyer and he is the Creator of the universe. He is the wielder of the Sula (lance); He is of human form; and He is of terrible form. All creatures sing his praises, for he is known by his acts. Hundreds of Gandharvas and Apsaras and deities always accompany him. The very Rakshasas hymn his praise. He is the Enhancer of Wealth; He is the one victorious Being in the universe. In Sacrifices, eloquent men hymn His praises. The singers of Samans praise Him by reciting the Rathantaras. The Brahmanas praise Him with Vedic Mantras. It is unto Him that the sacrificial priests pour their libations. The deities with Indra at their head hymned His praise when He lifted up the Gobardhana mountains for protecting the cow-herds of Brindavana against the incessant showers that Indra poured in rage. He is, O Bharata, the one Blessing unto all creatures. He, O Bharata, having entered the old Brahma cave, beheld from that place the original cover of the world in the beginning of Time.[614] Agitating all the Danavas and the Asuras, this Krishna of foremost feats rescued the earth. It is unto Him that people dedicate diverse kinds of food. It is unto Him that the warriors dedicate all kinds of their vehicles at the time of war. He is eternal, and it is under that illustrious one that the welkin, earth, heaven, all things exist and stay. He it is who has caused the vital seed of the gods Mitra and Varuna to fall within a jar, whence sprang the Rishi known by the name of Vasishtha. It is Krishna who is the god of wind; it is He who is the puissant Aswins; it is He who is that first of gods, viz., the sun possessed of a thousand rays. It is He by whom the Asuras have been subjugated. It is He who covered the three worlds with three steps of His. He is the soul of the deities and human beings, and Pitris. It is He who is the Sacrifice performed by those persons that are conversant with the rituals of sacrifices. It is He who rises every day in the firmament (in the form of the sun) and divides Time into day and night, and courses for half the year northwards and for half the year southwards. Innumerable rays of light emanate from Him upwards and downwards

---

[614] Refers to the existence of Brahma when all else is nought.

and transversely and illumine the earth. Brahmanas conversant with the Vedas adore Him. Taking a portion of His rays the sun shines in the firmament. Month after month, the sacrificer ordains Him as a sacrifice. Regenerate persons conversant with the Vedas sing His praises in sacrifices of all kinds. He it is that constitutes the wheel of the year, having three naves and seven horses to drag it. It is in this way that He supports the triple mansion (of the seasons). Endued with great energy, pervading all things, the foremost of all creatures, it is Krishna who alone upholds all the worlds. He is the sun, the dispeller of all darkness. He is the Creator of all. Do thou, O hero, approach that Krishna! Once on a time, the high-souled and puissant Krishna dwelt, for a while, in the form of Agni in the forest of Khandava among some straw or dry grass. Soon was He gratified (for he consumed all the medicinal herbs in that forest). Capable of going everywhere at will, it was Krishna who, having subjugated the Rakshasas and Uragas, poured them as libations upon the blazing fire. It is Krishna who gave unto Arjuna a number of white steeds. It is He who is the creator of all steeds. This world (or, human life) represents his car. He it is that yokes that car for setting it in motion. That car has three wheels (viz., the three attributes of Sattwa, Rajas, and Tamas). It has three kinds of motion (for it goes upwards or downwards or transversely, implying superior, inferior, and intermediate birth as brought about by acts). It has four horses yoked to it (viz., Time, Predestiny, the will of the deities, and one's own will). It has three naves (white, black, and mixed, implying good acts, evil acts and acts that are of a mixed character). It is this Krishna who is the refuge of the five original elements with the sky among them. It is He who created the earth and heaven and the space between. Indeed, it is this Krishna of immeasurable and blazing energy who has created the forests and the mountains. It is this Krishna who, desirous of chastising Sakra who was about to hurl his thunder at him, crossed the rivers and once paralysed him. He is the one great Indra that is adored by the Brahmanas in great sacrifices with the aid of a thousand old Riks. It was this Krishna, O king, who alone was able to keep the Rishi Durvasa of great energy as a guest for some time in his house. He is said to be the one ancient Rishi. He is the Creator of the universe. Indeed, He creates everything from His own nature. Superior to all the deities it is He who teaches all the deities. He scrupulously observes all ancient ordinances. Know, O king, that this Krishna, who is called Vishwaksena, is the fruit of all acts that relate to pleasure, of all acts that are founded on the Vedas, and of all acts that appertain to the world. He is the white rays of light that are seen in all the worlds. He is the three worlds. He is the three Regents of all the worlds. He is the three sacrificial fires. He is the three Vyahritis; indeed, this son of Devaki is all the gods together. He is the year; He is the Seasons; He is the Fortnights; He is the Day and the Night; He is those divisions of time which are called Kalas, and Kashthas, and Matras, and Muhurtas, and Lavas, and Kshanas. Know that this Vishwaksena is all these. The Moon and the Sun, the Planets, the Constellations, and the Stars, all the Parva days, including the day of the full moon, the conjunctions of the constellations and the seasons, have, O son of Pritha, flowed from this Krishna who is Vishwaksena. The Rudras, the Adityas, the Vasus, the Aswins, the Sadhyas, the Viswedevas, the diverse Maruts, Prajapati himself, the mother of the deities, viz., Aditi, and the seven Rishis, have all sprung from Krishna. Transforming Himself into the Wind, He scatters the universe. Of Universal form, He becomes Fire that burns all things. Changing Himself into Water, He drenches and submerges all, and assuming the form of Brahman, He creates all the diverse tribes of animate and inanimate creatures. He is Himself the Veda, yet he learns all the Vedas. He is Himself all the ordinances, yet He observes all the ordinances that have been laid down in matters connected with

Righteousness and the Vedas and that force or might which rules the world. Indeed, know, O Yudhishthira, that this Kesava is all the mobile and immobile universe. He is of the form of the most resplendent light. Of universal form, this Krishna is displayed in that blazing effulgence. The original cause of the soul of all existent creatures. He at first created the waters. Afterwards He created this universe. Know that this Krishna is Vishnu. Know that He is the soul of the universe. Know that He is all the seasons; He is these diverse wonderful vegetations of Nature which we see; He is the clouds that pour rain and the lightening that flashes in the sky. He is the elephant Airavata. In fact, He is all the immobile and mobile universe. The abode of the universe and transcending all attributes, this Krishna is Vasudeva. When He becomes Jiva He comes to be called Sankarshana. Next, He transforms Himself into Pradyumna and then into Aniruddha. In this way, the high-souled Krishna, who has Himself for His origin divides (or displays) Himself in fourfold form. Desirous of creating this universe which consists of the fivefold primal elements, He sets himself to his task, and causes it to go on in the fivefold form of animate existence consisting of deities and Asuras and human beings and beasts and birds. He it is that then creates the Earth and the Wind, the Sky, Light, and also Water, O son of Pritha! Having created this universe of immobile and mobile objects distributed into four orders of being (viz., viviparous, oviparous, vegetable and filth-born), he then created the earth with her fivefold seed. He then created the firmament for pouring copious showers of water on the earth.[615] Without doubt, O king, it is this Krishna who has created this universe. His origin is in his own self; it is He who causes all things to exist through his own puissance. He it is that has created the deities, the Asuras, the human beings, the world, the Rishis, the Pitris, and all creatures. Desirous of creating, that Lord of all creatures duly created the whole universe of life. Know that good and evil, mobile and immobile, have all flowed from this One who is Vishwaksena. Whatever exists, and whatever will spring into existence, all is Kesava. This Krishna is also the death that overtakes all creatures when their end comes. He is eternal and it is He who upholds the cause of Righteousness. Whatever existed in the past, and whatever we do not know, verily, all that also is this Vishwaksena. Whatever is noble and meritorious in the universe, indeed, whatever of good and of evil exists, all that is Kesava who is inconceivable. Hence, it is absurd to think of anything that is superior to Kesava. Kesava is even such. More than this, He is Narayana, the highest of the high, immutable and unfading. He is the eternal and immutable cause of the entire mobile and immobile universe with its beginning, middle, and end, as also of all creatures whose birth follows their wish.""'

SECTION CLIX.

"'Yudhishthira said, "Do thou tell us, O slayer of Madhu, what the prosperity is that attaches to the worship of the Brahmanas. Thou art well-conversant with this topic. Verily, our grandsire knows thee."

"'Vasudeva said, "Hear, O king, with rapt attention to me, O chief of Bharata's race, as I recite to thee what the merits of the Brahmanas are, in accordance with truth, O foremost one of Kuru's race! Once on a time while I was seated at Dwaravati, O delighter of the Kurus, my son Pradyumna, enraged by certain Brahmanas, came to me and said, 'O

---

[615] The fivefold seed consists of the four orders of creatures and acts which determine the conditions of all beings.

slayer of Madhu, what merit attaches to the worship of the Brahmanas? Whence is their lordship derived both here and hereafter? O giver of honours, what rewards are won by constantly worshipping the Brahmanas? Do thou kindly explain this clearly to me, for my mind is disturbed by doubts in respect of this.' When these words were addressed to me by Pradyumna, I answered him as follows. Do thou hear, O king, with close attention, what those words were, 'O child of Rukmin, listen to me as I tell thee what the prosperity is that one may win by worshipping the Brahmanas. When one sets oneself to the acquisition of the well-known aggregate of three (viz., Righteousness, Wealth, and Pleasure), or to the achievement of Emancipation, or to that of fame and prosperity, or to the treatment and cure of disease, or to the worship of the deities and the Pitris, one should take care to gratify the regenerate ones. They are each a king Soma (that sheds such agreeable light in the firmament.) They are dispensers of happiness and misery. O child of Rukmini, whether in this or in the next world, O son, everything agreeable has its origin in the Brahmanas. I have no doubt in this! From the worship of the Brahmanas flow mighty achievements and fame and strength. The denizens of all the worlds, and the Regents of the universe, are all worshippers of Brahmanas. How then, O son, can we disregard them, filled with the idea that we are lords of the earth? O mighty-armed one, do not suffer thy wrath to embrace the Brahmanas as its object. In this as also in the next world, Brahmanas are regarded as beings. They have direct knowledge of everything in the universe. Verily, they are capable of reducing everything into ashes, if angry. They are capable of creating other worlds and other Regents of worlds (than those that exist). Why then should not persons who are possessed of energy and correct knowledge behave with obedience and respect towards them? Formerly, in my house, O son, dwelt the Brahmana Durvasa whose complexion was green and tawny. Clad in rags, he had a stick made of the Vilwa tree.[616] His beard was long and he was exceedingly emaciated. He was taller in stature than the tallest man on earth. Wandering over all the worlds, viz., that which belongs to human beings and those that are for the deities and other superior beings, even this was the verse which he sang constantly among assemblies and in public squares. "Who is there that would cause the Brahmana Durvasa to dwell in his house, doing the duties of hospitality towards him? He becomes enraged with every one if he finds even the slightest transgression. Hearing this regarding my disposition, who is there that will give me refuge? Indeed, he that would give me shelter as a guest should not do anything to anger me!" When I saw that no one ventured to give him shelter in his house, I invited him and caused him to take up his residence in my abode. On certain days he would eat the food sufficient for the needs of thousands of persons. On certain other days he would eat very little. On some days he would go out of my house and would not return. He would sometimes laugh without any ostensible reason and sometimes cry as causelessly. At that time there was nobody on earth that was equal to him in years. One day, entering the quarters assigned to him he burnt all the beds and coverlets and all the well-adorned damsels that were there for serving him. Doing this, he went out. Of highly praiseworthy vows, he met me shortly after this and addressing me, said, "O Krishna, I wish to eat frumenty without delay!" Having understood his mind previously, I had set my servants to prepare every kind of food and drink. Indeed, many excellent viands had been kept ready. As soon as I was asked, I caused hot frumenty to be brought and offered to the ascetic. Having eaten some, he quickly said unto me, "Do thou, O Krishna, take some of this frumenty and smear all thy limbs with it!" Without any scruple I did as

---

[616] Eagle marmelos, Linn.

directed. Indeed, with the remnant of that frumenty I smeared my body and head. The ascetic at that time saw thy mother of sweet face standing near. Laughing the while, he smeared her body also with that frumenty. The ascetic then caused thy mother, whose body was smeared over with frumenty, to be yoked unto a car without any delay. Ascending that car he set out of my house. Endued with great intelligence, that Brahmana blazed with effulgence like fire, and struck, in my presence, my Rukmini endued with youth, as if she were an animal destined to drag the cars of human beings. Beholding this, I did not feel the slightest grief born of malice or the desire to injure the Rishi. Indeed, having yoked Rukmini to the car, he went out, desirous of proceeding along the high road of the city. Seeing that extraordinary sight, some Dasarhas, filled with wrath, addressed one another and began to converse in this way, "Who else is there on earth that would draw breath after having yoked Rukmini to a car! Verily, let the world be filled with Brahmanas only! Let no other orders take birth here. The poison of a virulent snake is exceedingly keen. Keener than poison is a Brahmana. There is no physician for a person that has been bitten or burnt by the virulent snake of a Brahmana." As the irresistible Durvasa proceeded on the car, Rukmini tottered on the road and frequently fell down. At this the regenerate Rishi became angry and began to urge Rukmini on by striking her with the whip. At last, filled with a towering passion, the Brahmana leapt down from the car, and fled towards the south, running on foot, over a pathless ground. Beholding that foremost of Brahmanas flying along the pathless ground, we followed him, although we were smeared with frumenty, exclaiming behind him, "Be gratified with us, O holy one!" Endued with great energy, the Brahmana, seeing me, said, "O mighty-armed Krishna, thou hast subdued wrath by the strength of thy nature. O thou of excellent vows, I have not found the slightest fault in thee! O Govinda, I have been highly gratified with thee. Do thou solicit the fruition of such wishes as thou pleasest! Behold duly, O son, what the puissance is of myself when I become gratified with any one. As long as deities and human beings will continue to entertain a liking for food, so long will every one among them cherish the same liking for thee that they cherish for their food! As long, again, as there will be Righteousness in the several world, so long will the fame of thy achievements last! Indeed, thy distinction will last so long in the three worlds! O Janardana, agreeable thou shalt be to all persons! Whatever articles of thine have been broken or burnt or otherwise destroyed (by me), thou shalt see restored, O Janardana, to their former state or they will reappear even in a better form! As long, again, O thou of unfading glory, as thou wilt wish to live, so long wilt thou have no fear of death assailing thee through such parts of thy body as have been smeared with the frumenty I gave thee! O son, why didst thou not smear that frumenty on the soles of thy feet as well? By not doing it, thou have acted in a way that is not approved by me!" Even these were the words that he said, well-pleased with me on that occasion. After he had ceased speaking, I saw that my body became endued with great beauty and splendour. Unto Rukmini also, the Rishi, well-pleased with her, said, "O beautiful lady, thou shalt be the foremost one of thy sex in fame, and great glory and achievements will be thine. Decrepitude or disease or loss of complexion will never be thine! Every one will see thee engaged in waiting upon Krishna, possessed as thou already art with a fragrant odour which is always present in thee. Thou shalt become the foremost of all spouses, numbering sixteen thousand, O Kesava. At last, when the time comes for thy departure from the world, thou shalt attain to the inseparable companionship of Krishna hereafter!" Having said these words unto thy mother, the Rishi once more addressed me and uttering following words, left the spot. Indeed, the Rishi Durvasa, blazing like a fire, said, "O Kesava, let thy understanding be always disposed even thus towards the Brahmana!" Verily after uttering these words, that Brahmana disappeared there and then before my eyes. After his disappearance I took to the observance of the vow of uttering certain Mantras silently without being heard by anybody. Verily, from that day I resolved to accomplish whatever behests I should receive from the Brahmanas. Having adopted this vow, O son, along with thy mother, both of us, with hearts filled with joy re-entered our palace. Entering our house I saw that everything which the Rishi had broken or burnt had reappeared and become new. Beholding those new articles, which had besides become more durable, I became filled with wonder. Verily, O son of Rukmini, from that day forth I have always worshipped the Brahmanas in my mind!' Even this, O chief of Bharata's race, is what I said on that occasion regarding the greatness of those Brahmanas who are the foremost of their order. Do thou also, O son of Kunti, worship the highly blessed Brahmanas every day with gifts of wealth and kine, O puissant one! It was in this way that I acquired the prosperity I enjoy, the prosperity that is born of the grace of Brahmanas. Whatever, again, Bhishma has said of me, O chief of the Bharatas, is all true!"'"

SECTION CLX.

"'Yudhishthira said, "It behoveth thee, O slayer of Madhu, to expound to me that knowledge which thou hast acquired through the grace of Durvasa! O foremost of all persons endued with intelligence, I desire to know everything about the high blessedness and all the names of that high-souled one truly and in detail!"[617]

"'Vasudeva said, "I shall recite to thee the good that I have acquired and the fame that I have won through the grace of that high-souled one. Verily, I shall discourse to thee on the topic, after having bowed unto Kapardin. O king, listen to me as I recite to thee that Sata-rudriya which I repeat with restrained senses, every morning after rising from bed. The great lord of all creatures, viz., the Grandsire Brahman himself, endued with wealth of penances, composed those Mantras, after having observed especial penances for some time. O sire it is Sankara who created all the creatures in the universe, mobile and immobile. There is no being that is higher, O monarch, than Mahadeva. Verily, he is the highest of all beings in the three worlds. There is no one who is capable of standing before that high-souled Being. Indeed, there is no Being in the three worlds that can be regarded as his equal. When he stands, filled with rage, on the field of battle, the very odour of his body deprives all foes of consciousness and they that are not slain tremble and fall down. His roars are terrible, resembling those of the clouds. Hearing those roars in battle, the very hearts of the deities break in twain. When the wielder of Pinaka becomes angry and assuming a terrible form merely casts his eye upon deity, Asura, Gandharva, or snake, that individual fails to obtain peace of mind by taking shelter in the recesses of even a mountain-cave. When that lord of all creatures, viz., Daksha, desirous of performing a sacrifice, spread his sacrifice out, the dauntless Bhava, giving way to wrath (at Daksha's slight of him), pierced (the embodied) sacrifice, shooting his shaft from his terrible bow, he roared aloud. Indeed, when Maheswara became angry and suddenly pierced with his shaft the embodied form of sacrifice, the deities become filled with grief, losing happiness and tranquillity of heart. In consequence of the twang of his bow-string the whole universe became agitated. The deities and the Asuras, O son of

---

[617] Durvasa is regarded as a portion of Mahadeva. The question of Yudhishthira, therefore, really relates to Mahadeva although the name that occurs is of Durvasa.

Pritha, all became cheerless and stupefied. The ocean rolled in agitation and the earth trembled to her centre. The hills and mountains began to move from their bases and ran on every side. The vault of the welkin became cracked. All the worlds became enveloped in gloom. Nothing could be seen. The light of all the luminaries became darkened, along with that of the sun himself, O Bharata! The great Rishis, penetrated with fear and desirous of doing good to themselves and the universe, performed the usual rites of propitiation and peace. Meanwhile, Rudra of terrible prowess rushed against the deities. Filled with rage, he tore out the eyes of Bhaga. Incensed with wrath, he assailed Pushan with his foot. He tore out the teeth of that god as he sat employed in eating the large sacrificial ball (called Purodasa). Trembling with fear, the deities bent their heads to Sankara. Without being appeased, Rudra once more placed on his bow-string a sharp and blazing arrow. Beholding his prowess, the deities and the Rishis became all alarmed. Those foremost of gods began to pacify him! Joining their hands in reverence, they began to recite the Sata-rudriya Mantras. At last Maheswara, thus praised by the deities, became gratified. The deities than assigned a large share (of the sacrificial offerings) to him. Trembling with fear, O king, they sought his protection. When Rudra became gratified, the embodiment of sacrifice, which had been pierced in twain, became once more united. Whatever limbs of his had been destroyed by the shafts of Mahadeva, became once more whole and sound. The Asuras possessed of great energy had in days of yore three cities in the firmament. One of these had been made of iron, one of silver, and the third of gold. With all his weapons, Maghavat, the chief of the deities, was unable to pierce those cities. Afflicted by the Asuras, all the deities then sought the protection of the great Rudra. Assembled together the high-souled deities addressed him, saying, 'O Rudra, the Asuras threaten to exert their destructive influence in all acts! Do thou slay the Daityas and destroy their city for the protection of the three worlds, O giver of honours!' Thus addressed by them, he replied, saying, 'So be it!' and then made Vishnu his excellent shaft-head. He made the deity of fire his shaft-reed, and Surya's son Yama the wings of that shaft. He made the Vedas his bow and the goddess Savitri his excellent bow-string. And he made the Grandsire Brahma his charioteer. Applying all these, he pierced the triple city of the Asuras with that shaft of his, consisting of three Parvans and three Salyas.[618] Indeed, O Bharata, the Asuras with their cities, were all burnt by Rudra with that shaft of his whose complexion was like that of the sun and whose energy resembled that of the fire which appears at the end of the Yuga for consuming all things. Beholding that Mahadeva changed into a child with five locks of hair lying on the lap of Parvati, the latter asked the deities as to who he was. Seeing the child, Sakra became suddenly filled with jealousy and wrath and resolved to kill him with his thunder. The child, however, paralysed the arm, looking like a mace of iron, of Indra with the thunderbolt in it. The deities all became stupefied, and they could not understand that the child was the Lord of universe. Verily, all of them along with the very Regents of the world, found their intellects stupefied in the matter of that child who was none else than the Supreme Being. Then the illustrious Grandsire Brahma, reflecting with the aid of his penances, found out that that child was the foremost of all Beings, the lord of Uma, Mahadeva of immeasurable prowess. He then praised the Lord. The deities also began to hymn the praises of both Uma and Rudra. The arm (which had been paralysed) of the slayer of Vala then became restored to its former state. The Mahadeva, taking birth as the

---

[618] A Parvam is a knot. Reeds and bamboos consist of a series of knots. The space between two knots is called a Salya.

Brahmana Durvasa of great energy, resided for a long time at Dwaravati in my house. While residing in my abode he did diverse acts of mischief. Though difficult of being borne, I bore them yet from magnanimity of heart. He is Rudra; he is Shiva; he is Agni; he is Sarva; he is the vanquisher of all; he is Indra, and Vayu, and the Aswins and the god of lightning. He is Chandramas; he is Isana; he is Surya; he is Varuna; he is Time; he is the Destroyer; he is Death; he is the Day and the Night; he is the fortnight; he is the seasons; he is the two twilights; he is the year. He is Dhatri and he is Vidhatri; and he is Viswakarma; and he is conversant with all things. He is the cardinal points of the compass and the subsidiary points also. Of universal form, he is of immeasurable soul. The holy and illustrious Durvasa is of the complexion of the celestials. He sometimes manifests himself singly; sometimes divides himself into two portions; and sometimes exhibits himself in many, a hundred thousand forms. Even such is Mahadeva. He is, again, that god who is unborn. In even a hundred years one cannot exhaust his merits by reciting them.""''

SECTION CLXI.

"'Vasudeva said, "O mighty-armed Yudhishthira, listen to me as I recite to thee the many names of Rudra as also the high blessedness of that high-souled one. The Rishis describe Mahadeva as Agni, and Sthanu, and Maheswara; as one-eyed, and three-eyed, of universal form, and Siva or highly auspicious. Brahmanas conversant with the Vedas say that that god has two forms. One of these is terrible, and the other mild and auspicious. Those two forms, again, are subdivided into many forms. That form which is fierce and terrible is regarded as identical with Agni and Lightning and Surya. The other form which is mild and auspicious is identical with Righteousness and water and Chandramas. Then, again, it is said that half his body is fire and half is Soma (or the moon). That form of his which is mild and auspicious is said to be engaged in the practice of the Brahmacharya vow. The other form of his which is supremely terrible is engaged in all operations of destruction in the universe. Because he is great (Mahat) and the Supreme Lord of all (Iswara), therefore he is called Maheswara. And since he burns and oppresses, is keen and fierce, and endued with great energy, and is engaged in eating flesh and blood and marrow, he is said to be Rudra. Since he is the foremost of all the deities, and since his dominion and acquisitions are very extensive, and since he protects the extensive universe, therefore he is called Mahadeva. Since he is of the form or colour of smoke, therefore he is called Dhurjati. Since by all his acts he performs sacrifices for all and seeks the good of every creature, therefore he is called Siva or the auspicious one. Staying above (in the sky) he burns the lives of all creatures and is, besides, fixed in a particular route from which he does not deviate. His emblem, again, is fixed and immovable for all time. He is, for these reasons, called Sthanu. He is also of multiform aspect. He is present, past, and future. He is mobile and immobile. For this he is called Vahurupa (of multiform aspect). The deities called Viswedevas reside in his body. He is, for this, called Viswarupa (of universal form). He is thousand-eyed; or, he is myriad-eyed; or, he has eyes on all sides and on every part of his body. His energy issues through his eyes. There is no end of his eyes. Since he always nourishes all creatures and sports also with them, and since he is their lord or master, therefore he is called Pasupati (the lord of all creatures). Since his emblem is always observant of the vow of Brahmacharya, all the worlds worship it accordingly. This act of worship is said to gratify him highly. If there is one who worship him by creating his image, another who worships his emblem, the latter it is that attains to great prosperity for ever. The Rishis, the deities, the Gandharvas, and the Apsaras, worship that emblem of his which is ever erect and upraised. If his emblem is worshipped, Maheswara becomes highly gratified with the worshipper. Affectionate towards his devotees, he bestows happiness upon them with a cheerful soul. This great god loves to reside in crematoria and there he burns and consumes all corpses. Those persons that perform sacrifices on such grounds attain at the end to those regions which have been set apart for heroes. Employed in his legitimate function, he it is that is regarded as the Death that resides in the bodies of all creatures. He is, again, those breaths called Prana and Apana in the bodies of all embodied beings. He has many blazing and terrible forms. All those forms are worshipped in the world and are known to Brahmanas possessed of knowledge. Amongst the gods he has many names all of which are fraught with grave import. Verily, the meanings of those names are derived from either his greatness or vastness, or his feats, or his conduct. The Brahmanas always recite the excellent Sata-rudriya in his honour, that occurs in the Vedas as also that which has been composed by Vyasa. Verily, the Brahmanas and Rishis call him the eldest of all beings. He is the first of all the deities, and it was from his mouth that he created Agni. That righteous-souled deity, ever willing to grant protection to all, never gives up his suppliants. He would much rather abandon his own life-breaths and incur all possible afflictions himself. Long life, health and freedom from disease, affluence, wealth, diverse kinds of pleasures and enjoyments, are conferred by him, and it is he also who snatches them away. The lordship and affluence that one sees in Sakra and the other deities are verily his. It is he who is always engaged in all that is good and evil in the three worlds. In consequence of his fullest control over all objects of enjoyment he is called Iswara (the Supreme Lord or Master). Since, again, he is the master of the vast universe, he is called Maheswara. The whole universe is pervaded by him in diverse forms. It is that deity whose mouth roars and burns the waters of the sea in the form of the huge mare's head!"""[619]

SECTION CLXII.

"Vaisampayana said, 'After Krishna, the son of Devaki, had said these words, Yudhishthira once more asked Bhishma the son of Santanu, saying, "O thou of great intelligence, O foremost of all persons conversant with duties, which, indeed, of the two, direct perception and the scriptures, is to be regarded as authority for arriving at a conclusion?"

"'Bhishma said, "I think, there is no doubt in this. Listen to me, O thou of great wisdom! I shall answer thee. The question thou hast asked is certainly proper. It is easy to cherish doubt. But the solution of that doubt is difficult. Innumerable are the instances, in respect of both direct perception and audition (or the scriptures), in which doubts may arise. Certain persons, who delight in the name of logicians, verily imagining themselves to be possessed of superior wisdom, affirm that direct perception is the only authority. They assert that nothing, however true, is existent which is not directly perceivable; or, at least they doubt the existence of those objects. Indeed, such assertions involve an absurdity and they who make them are of foolish understanding, whatever may be their pride of learning. If, on the other hand, thou doubtest as to how the one (indivisible Brahman) could be the cause, I answer that one would understand it only after a long

---

[619] The allusion is to the fiery mare's head which is supposed to wander through the ocean.

course of years and with the assistance of Yoga practised without idleness. Indeed, O Bharata, one that lives according to such means as present themselves (without, i.e., one's being wedded to this or that settled mode of life), and one that is devoted (to the solution of the question), would be capable of understanding it. None else, truly, is competent for comprehending it. When one attains to the very end of reasons (or reasoning processes), one then attains to that excellent and all comprehending knowledge—that vast mass of effulgence which illumines all the universe (called Brahma). That knowledge, O king, which is derived from reason (or inferences) can scarcely be said to be knowledge. Such knowledge should be rejected. It should be noted that it is not defined or comprehended by the word. It should, therefore, be rejected!"[620]

"'Yudhisthira said, "Tell me, O grandsire, which among these (four) is most authoritative, viz., direct perception, inference from observation, the science of Agama or scriptures, and diverse kinds of practices that distinguish the good."

"'Bhishma said, "While Righteousness is sought to be destroyed by wicked persons possessed of great might, it is capable of being protected for the time being by those that are good exerting themselves with care and earnestness. Such protection, however, avails not in the long run, for destruction does overtake Righteousness at the end. Then, again, Righteousness often proves a mask for covering Unrighteousness, like grass and straw covering the mouth of a deep pit and concealing it from the view. Hear, again, O Yudhisthira! In consequence of this, the practices of the good are interfered with and destroyed by the wicked. Those persons who are of evil conduct, who discard the Srutis—indeed, those wicked wights who are haters of Righteousness,—destroy that good course of conduct (which could otherwise be set up as a standard). Hence, doubts attach to direct perception, inference, and good conduct.[621] Those, therefore, among the good that are possessed of understanding born of (or cleansed by) the scriptures and that are ever contented, are to be regarded as the foremost. Let those that are anxious and deprived of tranquillity of soul, approach these. Indeed, O Yudhishthira, do thou pay court to them and seek of them the solutions of thy doubt![622] Disregarding both pleasure and wealth which always follow cupidity and awakened into the belief that only Righteousness should be sought, do thou, O Yudhishthira, wait upon and ask those persons (for enlightening thyself). The conduct of those persons never goes wrong or meets with destruction, as also their sacrifices and Vedic study and rites. Indeed, these

---

[620] Verses 4 to 9 are extremely difficult. They represent so many surceases. Nilakantha, however, has shown great ingenuity in expounding them. In the first line of 4, drishtam refers to pratyaksham, and srutam to sruti or agama. Hence, what is meant by the first line is,—Innumerable are the cases of both direct perception and scriptural assertion in which the scriptures are regarded as more authoritative, and those is which direct perception is regarded as more authoritative. In 5, the speaker refers to the atomic and other theories of the creation derived from Reason. Bhishma declares it as his opinion that all such theories are untenable or groundless. In the first line of 6, the word Ekam implies Brahma. The sense is, if thou thinkest that Brahma alone is the cause of the universe and in thinking so becomest landed on doubt. The reply to this is that Yoga for a long course of years will enable thee to comprehend the sufficiency of unassisted Brahma to evolve the universe. In 7, anekam pranayatram kalpamanena refers to one who without leading any particular or settled mode of life lives just as it suits him to live, that is, who leads the life of a religious mendicant never thinking of the morrow. In 9, anihaddham vacha implies what is not defined or indicated by the words of the Vedas or scriptures. The Burdwan Pundits have made a mess of the whole passage, or, rather, of nearly the whole of this section.

[621] Teshu is equivalent to praryakshanumanachareshu. The sense, therefore, is that the three, viz., direct perception, inference, and good conduct being, for these reasons, fallible, the only infallible standard that remain, is audition of the scriptures, or, as verse 14 puts it, men with understandings born of the scriptures.

[622] Atripyantah are men who like Yudhishthira are filled with anxiety as to what they should do. Seekers after the right are so called.

three, viz., conduct as consisting of overt acts, behaviour in respect of (mental) purity, and the Vedas together constitute Righteousness."

"'Yudhishthira said, "O grandsire, my understanding is once more stupefied by doubt. I am on this side the ocean, employed in searching after the means of crossing it. I do not, however, behold the other shore of the ocean! If these three, viz., the Vedas, direct perception (or acts that are seen), and behaviour (or, mental purity) together constitute what is to be regarded as authority, it can be alleged that there is difference between them. Righteousness then becomes really of three kinds, although it is one and indivisible."

"'Bhishma said, "Righteousness is sometimes seen to be destroyed by wicked wights of great power. If thou thinkest, O king, that Righteousness should really be of three kinds, my reply is that thy conclusion is warranted by reason. The truth is that Righteousness is one and indivisible, although it is capable of being viewed from three different points. The paths (indications) of those three that constitute the foundation of Righteousness have each been laid down. Do thou act according to the instructions laid down. Thou shouldst never wrangle about Righteousness and then seek to have those doubts solved into which thou mayst arrive. O chief of the Bharatas, let no doubts like these ever take possession of thy mind! Do thou obey what I say without scruple of any kind. Follow me like a blind man or like one who, without being possessed of sense himself, has to depend upon that of another. Abstention from injury, truth, absence of wrath (or forgiveness), and liberality of gifts,—these four, O king, that hast no foe, do thou practise, for these four constitute eternal Righteousness! Do thou also, O mighty-armed prince, pursue that conduct towards the Brahmanas which is consistent with what has been observed towards them by thy sires and grandsires. These are the principal indications of Righteousness. That man of little intelligence who would destroy the weight of authority by denying that to be a standard which has always been accepted as such would himself fail to become an authority among men. Such a man becomes the cause of much grief in the world. Do thou reverence the Brahmanas and treat them with hospitality. Do thou always serve them in this way. The universe rests on them. Do thou understand them to be such!"

"'Yudhishthira said, "Tell me, O grandsire, what the respective ends are of those that hate Righteousness and of those that adore and observe it!"

"'Bhishma said, "Those men that hate Righteousness are said to have their hearts overwhelmed by the attributes of passion and darkness. Such men have always to go to Hell. Those men, on the other hand, O monarch, who always adore and observe Righteousness, those men who are devoted to truth and sincerity, are called good. They always enjoy the pleasures or felicity of heaven. In consequence of their waiting upon their preceptors with reverence their hearts always turn towards Righteousness. Verily, they who adore Righteousness attain to the regions of the deities. Those individuals, whether human beings or deities who divest themselves of cupidity and malice and who emaciate or afflict their bodies by the observance of austerities, succeed, in consequence of the Righteousness which then becomes theirs to attain to great felicity. Those that are gifted with wisdom have said that the Brahmanas, who are the eldest sons of Brahmana, represent Righteousness. They that are righteous always worship them, their hearts regarding them with as much love and affection as a hungry man's stomach entertains for ripe and delicious fruits."

"'Yudhishthira said, "What is the appearance presented by those that are wicked, and what are those acts which they that are called good are to do? Explain to me this, O holy one! Indeed, tell me what the indications are of the good and the wicked."

"'Bhishma said, "They that are wicked are evil in their practices, ungovernable or incapable of being kept within the restraints of rules, and foul mouthed. They, on the other hand, that are good, are always good in their acts. Verily, the acts these men do are regarded as the indications of that course of conduct which is called good. They that are good or righteous, O monarch, never answer the two calls of nature on the public road, or in the midst of a cow-pen, or on a field of paddy. After feeding the five they take their own food.[623] They never talk while eating, and never go to sleep with wet hands (i.e., without rubbing them dry with towels or napkins). Whenever they see any of the following, they circumambulate them for showing them reverence, viz., a blazing fire, a bull, the image of a deity, a cow-pen, a place where four roads meet, and an old and virtuous Brahmana. They give the way, themselves standing aside, unto those that are old, those that are afflicted with burdens, ladies, those that hold high appointments in the village or town administration, Brahmanas, kine, and kings. The righteous or good man is he that protects his guests, servants and other dependents, his own relatives, and all those that seek his protection. Such a man always welcomes these with the usual enquiries of politeness. Two times have been appointed by the deities for human beings to take their food, viz., morning and evening. During the interval one should not eat anything. By following this rule about eating, one is said to observe a fast. As the sacred fire waits for libations to be poured upon it when the hour for Homa arrives, even so a woman, when her functional period is over, expects an act of congress with her husband. One that never approaches one's spouses at any other time save after the functional period, is said to observe the vow of Brahmacharya. Amrita (nectar), Brahmanas, and kine,—these three are regarded as equal. Hence, one should always worship, with due rites, Brahmanas and kine. One does not incur any fault or stain by eating the meat of animals slain in sacrifices with the aid of Tantras from the Yajur Veda. The flesh of the back-bone, or that of animals not slain in sacrifice, should be avoided even as one avoids the flesh of one's own son. One should never cause one's guest to go without food whether when one resides in one's own country or in a foreign land. After completing one's study one should present the Dakshina unto one's preceptor. When one sees one's preceptor, one should congratulate him with reverence and worshipping him present him a seat. By worshipping one's preceptor, one increases the period of one's life as also one's fame and prosperity. One should never censure the old, nor send them on any business.[624] One should never be seated when any one that is old is standing. By acting in this way one protects the duration of one's life. One should never cast one's eyes on a naked woman, nor a naked man. One should never indulge in sexual congress except in privacy. One should eat also without being seen by others. Preceptors are the foremost of Tirthas; the heart is the foremost of all sacred objects; knowledge is the foremost of all objects of search; and contentment is the foremost of all happiness. Morning and evening one should listen to the grave counsels of those that are aged. One attains to wisdom by constant waiting upon those that are venerable for years. While reading the Vedas or employed in eating, one should use one's right hand. One should always keep one's speech and mind under thorough control, as also one's senses. With well-cooked frumenty, Yavaka, Krisara, and Havi (clarified butter), one should worship the Pitris and

---

[623] The five who must be first fed are the deities, the Pitris, the guests, diverse creatures included under the word Bhutus, and lastly relatives.

[624] Some texts read nabhibhavet, meaning one should never vanquish an old man (i.e., assert one's superiority over him).

the deities in the Sraddha called Ashtaka. The same should be used in worshipping the Planets. One should not undergo a shave without calling down a blessing upon oneself. If one sneezes, one should be blessed by those present. All that are ill or afflicted with disease, should be blessed. The extension of their lives should be prayed for.[625] One should never address an eminent person familiarly (by using the word Twam). Under even the great difficulties one should never do this. To address such a person as Twam and to slay him are equal, persons of learning are degraded by such a style of address. Unto those that are inferior, or equal, or unto disciples, such a word can be used. The heart of the sinful man always proclaims the sins he has committed. Those men who have deliberately committed sins meet with destruction by seeking to conceal them from the good. Indeed, they that are confirmed sinners seek to conceal their sinful acts from others.[626] Such persons think that their sins are witnessed by neither men nor the deities. The sinful man, overwhelmed by his sins, takes birth in a miserable order of being. The sins of such a man continually grow, even as the interest the usurer charge (on the loans he grants) increase from day to day. If, having committed a sin, one seeks to have it covered by righteousness, that sin becomes destroyed and leads to righteousness instead of other sins.[627] If a quantity of water be poured upon salt, the latter immediately dissolves away. Even so when expiation is performed, sin dissolves away. For these reasons one should never conceal a sin. Concealed, it is certain to increase. Having committed a sin, one should confess it in the presence of those that are good. They would destroy it immediately. If one does not enjoy in good time what one has stored with hope, the consequence is that the stored wealth finds another owner after the death of him who has stored it. The wise have said that the mind of every creature is the true test of Righteousness. Hence, all creatures in the world have an innate tendency to achieve Righteousness. One should achieve Righteousness alone or single-handed. Verily, one should not proclaim oneself Righteous and walk with the standard of Righteousness borne aloft for purpose of exhibition. They are said to be traders in Righteousness who practise it for enjoying the fruits it brings about. One should adore the deities without giving way to sentiments of pride. Similarly, one should serve one's preceptor without deceit. One should make arrangements for securing to oneself invaluable wealth in the hereafter which consists in gifts made here to deserving persons."'"

SECTION CLXIII.

"'Yudhishthira said, "It is seen that if a person happens to be unfortunate, he fails to acquire wealth, how great so ever his strength. On the other hand, if one happens to be fortunate, he comes to the possession of wealth, even if he be a weakling or a fool. When, again, the time does not come for acquisition, one cannot make an acquisition with even one's best exertion. When, however, the time comes for acquisition, one wins great wealth without any exertion. Hundreds of men may be seen who achieve no result even when they exert their best. Many persons, again, are seen to make acquisitions without

---

[625] In his excellent work on the Curiosities of Literature Mr. D'Israeli attempts to trace the origin of the custom of uttering a blessing on people who sneeze. The custom seems, however, to be very ancient and widespread. It exists to this day in India, among the Hindus at any rate, as it existed in the days of the Mahabharata.

[626] It seems that the author is of opinion that one lightens one's sins by admissions before the wise. To conceal a sin after having committed it proves the confirmed sinner.

[627] 'Covered by righteousness' implies 'if, having once tripped, the sinner restrains himself and engages to do acts of righteousness.'

any exertion. If wealth were the result of exertion, then one could, with exertion, acquire it immediately. Verily, if the case were so, no man of learning could then be seen to take the protection for the sake of his livelihood, of one destitute of learning. Among men, that which is not (destined) to be attained, O chief of the Bharatas, is never attained. Men are seen to fail in achieving results even with the aid of their best exertions. One may be seen to seek wealth by hundreds of means (and yet failing to acquire it); while another, without at all seeking it, becomes happy in its possession. Men may be seen doing evil acts continually (for wealth) and yet failing to acquire it. Others are in the enjoyment of wealth without doing any evil act whatever. Others, again, who are observant of the duties assigned to them by the scriptures, are without wealth. One may be seen to be without any knowledge of the science of morals and policy even after one has studied all the treatises on that science. One, again, may be seen appointed as the prime minister of a king without having at all studied the science of morals and policy. A learned man may be seen that is possessed of wealth. One destitute of learning may be seen owning wealth. Both kinds of men, again, may be seen to be entirely destitute of wealth. If, by the acquisition of learning one could acquire the happiness of wealth, then no man of learning could be found living, for the very means of his subsistence, under the protection of one destitute of learning. Indeed, if one could obtain by the acquisition of learning, all desirable objects like a thirsty individual having his thirst slaked upon obtaining water, then none in this world would have shown idleness in acquiring learning. If one's time has not come, one does not die even if one be pierced with hundreds of shafts. On the other hand, one lays down one's life, if one's hour has come, even if it be a blade of grass with which one is struck."

"'Bhishma said, "If one, setting oneself to undertaking involving even great exertions, fails to earn wealth, one should then practise severe austerities. Unless seeds be sown, no crops appear. It is by making gifts (to deserving persons in this life) that one acquires (in one's next life) numerous objects of enjoyment, even as one becomes possessed of intelligence and wisdom by waiting upon those that are venerable for years. The wise have said that one becomes possessed of longevity by practising the duty of abstention from cruelty to all creatures. Hence, one should make gifts and not solicit (or accept them when made by others). One should worship those individuals that are righteous. Verily, one should be sweet-speeched towards all, and always do what is agreeable to others. One should seek to attain to purity (both mental and external). Indeed, one should always abstain from doing injury to any creature. When in the matter of the happiness and woe of even insects and ants, their acts (of this and past lives) and Nature constitute the cause, it is meet, O Yudhishthira, that thou shouldst be tranquil!"'"[628]

---

[628] What is stated here is this: the condition of all living creatures is determined by their acts of this and past lives. Nature, again, is the cause of acts. What of felicity and misery, therefore, one sees in this world, must be ascribed to these two causes. As regards the self also, O Yudhishthira, thou art not freed from that universal law. Do thou, therefore, cease to cherish doubts of any kind. If thou seest a learned man that is poor, or an ignorant man that is wealthy, if thou seest exertion failing and the absence of exertion leading to success, thou must always ascribe the result to acts and Nature.

SECTION CLXIV.

"'Bhishma said, "If one does acts oneself that are good or causes others to accomplish them, one should then expect to attain to the merits of righteousness. Similarly, if one does acts oneself that are evil, and causes others to accomplish them, one should never expect to attain to the merits of righteousness.[629] At all times, it is Time that, entering the understandings of all creatures, sets them to acts of righteousness or unrighteousness, and then confer felicity or misery upon them. When a person, beholding the fruits of Righteousness, understands Righteousness to be superior, it is then that he inclines towards Righteousness and puts faith in it. One, however, whose understanding is not firm, fails to put faith in it. As regards faith in Righteousness, it is this (and nothing else). To put faith in Righteousness is the indication of the wisdom of all persons. One that is acquainted with both (i.e., what should be done and what should not be done), with a view to opportuneness, should, with care and devotion, achieve what is right. Those Righteous men who have in this life been blessed with affluence, acting of their own motion, take particular care of their souls so that they may not, in their next lives, have to take birth as persons with the attribute of Passion predominating in them. Time (which is the supreme disposer of all things) can never make Righteousness the cause of misery. One should, therefore, know that the soul which is righteous is certainly pure (i.e., freed from the element of evil and misery). As regards Unrighteousness, it may be said that, even when of large proportions, it is incapable of even touching Righteousness which is always protected by Time and which shines like a blazing fire. These are the two results achieved by Righteousness, viz., the stainlessness of the soul and unsusceptibility of being touched by Unrighteousness. Verily, Righteousness is fraught with victory. Its effulgence is so great that it illumines the three worlds. A man of wisdom cannot catch hold of a sinful person and forcibly cause him to become righteous. When seriously urged to act righteously, the sinful only act with hypocrisy, impelled by fear. They that are righteous among the Sudras never betake themselves to such hypocrisy under the plea that persons of the Sudra order are not permitted to live according to any of the four prescribed modes. I shall tell thee particularly what the duties truly are of the four orders. So far as their bodies are concerned, the individuals belonging to all the four orders have the five primal elements for the constituent ingredients. Indeed, in this respect, they are all of the same substance. For all that, distinctions exist between them in respect of both practices relating to life or the world and the duties of righteousness. Notwithstanding these distinctions, sufficient liberty of action is left to them in consequence of which all individuals may attain to an equality of condition. The regions of felicity which represent the consequences or rewards of Righteousness are not eternal, for they are destined to come to an end. Righteousness, however, is eternal. When the cause is eternal, why is the effect not so?[630] The answer to this is as follows. Only that Righteousness is eternal which is not promoted by the desire of fruit or reward. (That Righteous, however, which is prompted by the desire of reward, is not eternal. Hence, the reward though undesired

---

[629] What is stated here is this: one may become righteous by accomplishing oneself righteous deeds or inducing or helping others to do them. Similarly, one becomes unrighteous by doing oneself acts that are evil or by inducing or helping others to do them.

[630] Righteousness leads to regions of felicity. The former is said to be eternal, while the latter are not so. The question asked (or doubt raised) is why is the effect not eternal when the cause is eternal? It is explained below.

that attaches to the first kind of Righteousness, viz., attainment of identity with Brahman, is eternal. The reward, however, that attaches to that Righteousness prompted by desire of fruit. Heaven is not eternal).[631] All men are equal in respect of their physical organism. All of them, again, are possessed of souls that are equal in respect of their nature. When dissolution comes, all else dissolve away. What remains is the inceptive will to achieve Righteousness. That, indeed, reappears (in next life) of itself.[632] When such is the result (that is, when the enjoyments and endurance of this life are due to the acts of a past life), the inequality of lot discernible among human beings cannot be regarded in any way anomalous. So also, it is seen that those creatures that belong to the intermediate orders of existence are equally subject, in the matter of their acts, to the influence of example."'''

SECTION CLXV.

"Vaisampayana said, 'That perpetuator of Kuru's race, viz., Yudhishthira the son of Pandu, desirous of obtaining such good as is destructive of sins, questioned Bhishma who was lying on a bed of arrows, (in the following words).'

"'Yudhishthira said, "What, indeed, is beneficial for a person in this world? What is that by doing which one may earn happiness? By what may one be cleansed of all one's sins? Indeed, what is that which is destructive of sins?"'

"Vaisampayana continued, 'In this connection, the royal son of Santanu, O foremost of men, duly recited the names of the deities unto Yudhishthira who was desirous of hearing.'

"'Bhishma said, "O son, the following names of the deities with those of the Rishis, if duly recited morning, noon, and evening, become efficacious cleansers of all sins. Acting with the aid of one's senses (or knowledge and action), whatever sins one may commit by day or by night or by the two twilights, consciously, or unconsciously one is sure to be cleansed therefrom and become thoroughly pure by reciting these names. One that takes those names has never to become blind or deaf; indeed, by taking those names, one always succeeds in attaining to what is beneficial. Such a man never takes birth in the intermediate order of beings, never goes to hell, and never becomes a human being of any of the mixed castes. He has never to fear the accession of any calamity. When death comes, he never becomes stupefied. The master of all the deities and Asuras, resplendent with effulgence, worshipped by all creatures, inconceivable, indescribable, the life of all living beings, and unborn, is the Grandsire Brahma, the Lord of the universe. His chaste spouse is Savitri. Then comes that origin of the Vedas, the creator Vishnu, otherwise called Narayana of immeasurable puissance. Then comes the three-eyed Lord of Uma; then Skanda the generalissimo of the celestial forces; then Visakha; then Agni the eater of sacrificial libations; then Vayu the god of wind; then Chandramas; then Aditya the god of the sun, endued with effulgence; then the illustrious Sakra the lord of Sachi; and Yama with his spouse Dhumorna; and Varuna with Gauri; Kuvera the lord of treasures, with his spouse Riddhi; the amiable and illustrious cow Surabhi; the great Rishi Visravas; Sankalpa, Ocean, Ganga; the other sacred Rivers; the diverse Maruts; the Valkhilyas crowned with success of penances; the island-born Krishna; Narada; Parvata; Viswavasu;

---

[631] There are two kinds of Righteousness, viz., nishkama and sakama. The former leads to attainment of Brahma, the latter to heaven and felicity. Brahma is eternal; the latter not so. Nishkama Righteousness being eternal, leads to an eternal reward. Sakama Righteousness not being so, does not lead to an eternal reward. The word Kala here means Sankalpa, hence Dhruvahkalah means nishkama Dharma.
[632] Here, Calah means 'Sankalpa'.

the Hahas; the Huhus; Tumvuru; Chitrasena; the celestial messenger of wide celebrity; the highly blessed celestial maidens, the celestial Apsaras, Urvasi, Menaka, Rambha; Misrakesi, Alamvusha, Viswachi, Ghritachi, Panchachuda, Tilottama; the Adityas, the Vasus, the Aswins, the Pitris; Dharma (Righteousness); Vedic lore, Penances, Diksha, Perseverance (in religious acts), the Grandsire, Day and Night, Kasyapa the son of Marichi, Sukra, Vrihaspati, Mangala the son of Earth, Vudha, Rahu, Sanischara, the Constellations, the Seasons, the Months, the Fortnights, the Year, Garuda, the son of Vinata, the several Oceans, the sons of Kadru, viz., the Snakes, Satadru, Vipasa, Chandrabhaga, Saraswati, Sindhu, Devika, Prabhasa, the lakes of Pushkara, Ganga, Mahanadi, Vena, Kaveri, Narmada, Kulampuna Visalya, Karatoya, Amvuvahini, Sarayu, Gandaki, the great river Lohita, Tamra, Aruna, Vetravati, Parnasa, Gautami, the Godavari, Vena, Krishnavena, Dwija, Drishadvati, Kaveri, Vankhu, Mandakini Prayaga, Prabhasa, the sacred Naimisha, the spot sacred to Visweswara or Mahadeva, viz., Kasi, that lake of crystal water, Kurukshetra full of many sacred waters, the foremost of oceans (viz., the ocean of milk), Penances, Gifts, Jamvumarga, Hiranwati, Vitasta, the river Plakshavati, Vedasmriti, Vedavati, Malava, Aswavati, all sacred spots on Earth, Gangadwara, the sacred Rishikulya, the river Chitravaha, the Charmanwati, the sacred river Kausiki, the Yamuna, the river Bhimarathi, the great river Vahuda, Mahendravani, Tridiva Nilika, Saraswati, Nanda, the other Nanda, the large sacred lake, Gaya, Phalgutirtha Dharmarayana (the sacred forest) that is peopled with the deities, the sacred celestial river, the lake created by the Grandsire Brahma which is sacred and celebrated over the three worlds, and auspicious and capable of cleansing all sins, the Himavat mountain endued with excellent herbs, the Vindhya mountain variegated with diverse kinds of metals, containing many Tirthas and overgrown with medicinal herbs, Meru, Mahendra, Malaya, Sweta endued with silver, Sringavat, Mandara, Nila, Nishada, Dardurna, Chitrakuta, Anjanabha, the Gandhamadana mountains; the sacred Somagiri, the various other mountains, the cardinal points of the compass, the subsidiary points, the Earth, all the trees, the Viswedevas, the Firmament, the Constellations, the Planets, and the deities,—let these all, named and unnamed, rescue and cleanse us! The man who takes the names of these becomes cleansed of all his sins. By hymning their praises and gratifying them, one becomes freed from every fear. Verily, the man who delights in uttering the hymns in praise of the deities becomes cleansed of all such sins as lead to birth in impure orders. After this recital of the deities, I shall name those learned Brahmanas crowned with ascetic merit and success and capable of cleaning one of every sin. They are Yavakrita and Raibhya and Kakshivat and Aushija, and Bhrigu and Angiras and Kanwa, and the puissant Medhatithi, and Varhi possessed of every accomplishment. These all belong to the eastern region. Others, viz., Unmuchu, Pramuchu, all highly blessed, Swastyatreya of great energy, Agastya of great prowess, the son of Mitra and Varuna; Dridhayu and Urdhavahu, those two foremost and celebrated of Rishis,—these live in the southern region. Listen now to me as I name those Rishis that dwell in the western region. They are Ushango with his uterine brothers, Parivyadha of great energy, Dirghatamas, Gautama, Kasyapa, Ekata, Dwita, Trita, the righteous-souled son of Atri (viz., Durvasa), and puissant Saraswat. Listen now to me as I name those Rishis that worship the deities in sacrifices, dwelling in the northern region. They are Atri, Vasishtha, Saktri, Parasara's son Vyasa of great energy; Viswamitra, Bharadwaja, Jamadagni, the son of Richika, Rama, Auddalaka, Swetaketu, Kohala, Vipula, Devala, Devasarman, Dhaumya, Hastikasyapa, Lomasa, Nachiketa, Lomaharsana, Ugrasravas, and Bhrigu's son Chyavana. This is the tale of Rishis possessed of Vedic lore. They are primeval Rishis, O king, whose names, if taken, are capable of cleansing one of every sin. After this I shall recite the names of the principal kings. They are Nriga, Yayati, Nahusha, Yadu, Puru of great energy, Sagara, Dhundhumara, Dilipa of great prowess, Krisaswa, Yauvanaswa, Chitraswa, Satyavat, Dushmanta, Bharata who became an illustrious Emperor over many kings, Yavana, Janaka, Dhrishtaratha, Raghu, that foremost of kings, Dasaratha, the heroic Rama, that slayer of Rakshasas, Sasavindu. Bhagiratha, Harischandra, Marutta, Dridharatha, the highly fortunate Alarka, Aila, Karandhama, that foremost of men, Kasmira, Daksha, Amvarisha, Kukura, Raivata of great fame, Kuru, Samvarana, Mandhatri of unbaffled prowess, the royal sage Muchukunda, Jahnu who was much favoured by Janhavi (Ganga), the first (in point of time) of all kings, viz., Prithu the son of Vena, Mitrabhanu, Priyankara, Trasadasyu, Sweta that foremost of royal sages, the celebrated Mahabhisha, Nimi Ashtaka, Ayu, the royal sage Kshupa, Kaksheyu, Pratardana, Devodasa, Sudasa, Kosaleswara, Aila, Nala, the royal sage Manu, that lord of all creatures, Havidhara, Prishadhara, Pratipa, Santanu, Aja, the senior Varhi, Ikshwaku of great fame, Anaranya, Janujangha, the royal sage Kakshasena, and many others not named (in history). That man who rising at early dawn takes the names of these kings at the two twilights, viz., at sunset and sunrise, with a pure body and mind and without distracted attention, acquires great religious merit. One should hymn the praises of the deities, the celestial Rishis, and the royal sages and say, 'These lords of the creation will ordain my growth and long life and fame! Let no calamity be mine, let no sin defile me, and let there be no opponents or enemies of mine! Without doubt, victory will always be mine and an auspicious end hereafter!'"'"

SECTION CLXVI.

"Janamejaya said, 'When that foremost person among the Kauravas, viz., Bhishma, was lying on a bed of arrows,—a bed that is always coveted by heroes,—and when the Pandavas, were sitting around him, my great grandsire Yudhishthira of much wisdom, heard these expositions of mysteries with respect to the subject of duty and had all his doubts solved. He heard also what the ordinance are that apply to the subjects of gifts, and thus had all his doubts removed with respect to the topics of righteousness and wealth. It behoveth thee, O learned Brahmana, to tell me now what else did the great Pandava king do.'

"Vaisampayana said, 'When Bhishma became silent, the entire circle of king (who were seated around him) became perfectly silent. Indeed, they all sat motionless there, like figures painted on canvass. Then Vyasa the son of Satyavati, having reflected for a moment, addressed the royal son of Ganga, saying, "O king, the Kuru chief Yudhishthira has been restored to his own nature, along with all brothers and followers. With Krishna of great intelligence by his side, he bends his head in reverence unto thee. It behoveth thee to give him leave for returning to the city." Thus addressed by the holy Vyasa, the royal son of Santanu and Ganga dismissed Yudhishthira and his counsellors. The royal son of Santanu, addressing his grandson in a sweet voice, also said, "Do thou return to the city, O king! Let fever of thy heart be dispelled. Do thou adore the deities in diverse sacrifices distinguished by large gifts of food and wealth, like Yayati himself, O foremost of kings, endued with devotion and self-restraint. Devoted to the practice of the Kshatriya order, do thou, O son of Pritha, gratify the Pitris and the deities. Thou shalt then earn great benefits. Indeed, let the fever of thy heart be dispelled. Do thou gladden all thy subjects. Do thou assure them and establish peace among all. Do thou also honour all thy well-wishers with such rewards as they deserve! Let all thy friends and well-wishers live, depending on thee for their means, even as birds live, depending for their means upon a full-grown tree charged with fruit and standing on a sacred spot. When the hour comes for my departure from this world, do thou come here, O king. The time when I shall take leave of my body is that period when the sun, stopping in his south-ward course, will begin to return northwards!" The son of Kunti answered, "So be it!" And saluted his grandsire with reverence and then set out, with all his relatives and followers, for the city called after the elephant. Placing Dhritarashtra at the head and also Gandhari who was exceedingly devoted to her lord, and accompanied by the Rishis and Kesava, as also by the citizens and the inhabitants of the country and by his counsellors, O monarch, that foremost one of Kuru's race entered the city named after the elephant.'"

SECTION CLXVII.

"Vaisampayana said, 'Then the royal son of Kunti, having duly honoured the citizens and the inhabitants of the province, dismissed them to their respective homes. The Pandava king then consoled these women, who had lost their heroic husbands and sons in the battle, with abundant gift of wealth. Having recovered his kingdom, Yudhishthira of great wisdom caused himself to be duly installed on the throne. That foremost of men then assured all his subjects by diverse acts of good will. That foremost of righteous men then set himself to earn the substantial blessing of the Brahmanas, of the foremost military officers, and the leading citizens. The blessed monarch having passed fifty nights in the capital recollected the time indicated by his grandsire as the hour of his departure from this world. Accompanied by a number of priests he then set out of the city named after the elephant, having seen that the sun ceasing to go southwards had begun to proceed in his northward course. Yudhishthira the son of Kunti took with him a large quantity of clarified butter and floral garlands and scents and silken cloths and excellent sandalwood and Aquilaria Agallocha and dark sloe wood, for cremating the body of Bhishma. Diverse kinds of costly garlands and gems also were among those stores. Placing Dhritarashtra ahead and queen Gandhari celebrated for her virtues, and his own mother Kunti and all his brothers also, Yudhishthira of great intelligence, accompanied by Krishna and Vidura of great wisdom, as also by Yuyutsu and Yuyudhana, and by his other relatives and followers forming a large train, proceeded, his praises hymned the while by eulogists and bards. The sacrificial fires of Bhishma were also borne in the procession. Thus accompanied, the king set out from his city like a second chief of the deities. Soon he came upon the spot where the son of Santanu was still lying on his bed of arrows. He beheld his grandsire waited upon with reverence by Parasara's son Vyasa of great intelligence, by Narada, O royal sage, by Devala and Asita, and also by the remnant of unslain kings assembled from various parts of the country. Indeed, the king saw that his high-souled grandsire, as he lay on his heroic bed, was guarded on all sides by the warriors appointed for that duty. Alighting from his car, King Yudhishthira with his brothers saluted his grandsire, the chastiser of all foes. They also saluted the Rishis with the island-born Vyasa at their head. They were saluted in return by them. Accompanied by his priests each of whom resembled the grandsire Brahman himself, as also by his brothers, Yudhishthira of unfading glory then approached that spot whereon Bhishma lay on his bed of arrows surrounded by these reverend Rishis. Then king Yudhishthira the just, at the head of his brothers, addressed that foremost one of Kuru's race, viz., the son of the River Ganga, as he lay on that bed of his, saying, "I am

Yudhishthira, O king! Salutations to thee, O son of the River Janhavi! If thou hearest me still, tell me what I am to do for thee! Bearing with me thy sacrificial fires, I have come here, O king, and wait upon thee at the hour indicated! Preceptors of all branches of learning, Brahmanas, Ritwiks, all my brothers, thy son, viz., king Dhritarashtra of great energy, are all here with my counsellors as also Vasudeva of great prowess. The remnant of unslain warriors, and all the denizens of Kurujangala, are also here. Opening thy eyes, O chief of Kuru's race, do thou behold them! Whatever should be done on this occasion has all been arranged and provided for by me. Indeed, at this hour which thou hadst indicated, all things have been kept ready!"

"Vaisampayana continued, 'Thus addressed by Kunti's son of great intelligence, the son of Ganga opened his eyes and saw all the Bharatas assembled there and standing around him. The mighty Bhishma then, taking the strong hand of Yudhishthira, addressed him in a voice deep as that of the clouds. That thorough master of words said, "By good luck, O son of Kunti, thou hast come here with all thy counsellors, O Yudhishthira! The thousand-rayed maker of day, the holy Surya has begun his northward course. I have been lying on my bed here for eight and fifty nights. Stretched on these sharp-pointed arrows I have felt this period to be as long as if it was a century. O Yudhishthira, the lunar month of Magha has come. This is, again, the lighted fortnight and a fourth part of it ought by this (according to my calculations) be over." Having said so unto Yudhishthira the son of Dharma, Ganga's son Bhishma then saluted Dhritarashtra and said unto him as follows.'

"'Bhishma said, "O king, thou art well-conversant with duties. All thy doubts, again, relating to the science of wealth have been well-solved. Thou hast waited upon many Brahmanas of great learning. The subtle sciences connected with the Vedas, all the duties of religion, O king, and the whole of the four Vedas, are well-known to thee! Thou shouldst not grieve, therefore, O son of Kuru! That which was pre-ordained has happened. It could not be otherwise. Thou hast heard the mysteries relating to the deities from the lips of the island-born Rishi himself. Yudhishthira and his brothers are morally as much thy sons as they are the sons of Pandu. Observant of the duties of religion, do thou cherish and protect them. In their turn, they are always devoted to the service of their seniors. King Yudhishthira the just is pure-souled. He will always prove obedient to thee! I know that he is devoted to the virtue of compassion or abstention from injury. He is devoted to his seniors and preceptors. Thy sons were all wicked-souled. They were wedded to wrath and cupidity. Overwhelmed by envy, they were all of wicked behavior. It behoveth thee not to grieve for them!"'

"Vaisampayana continued, 'Having said this much unto Dhritarashtra of great wisdom, the Kuru hero then addressed Vasudeva of mighty arms.'

"'Bhishma said, "O holy one, O god of all gods, O thou that art worshipped by all the deities and Asuras, O thou that didst cover the three worlds with three steps of thine, salutations to thee, O wielder of the conch, the discus, and the mace! Thou art Vasudeva, thou art of golden body, thou art the one Purusha (or active agent), thou art the creator (of the universe), thou art of vast proportions. Thou art Jiva. Thou art subtle. Thou art the Supreme and eternal Soul. Do thou, O lotus-eyed one, rescue me, O foremost of all beings! Do thou, give me permission, O Krishna, to depart from this world, O thou that art Supreme felicity, O foremost of all beings! The sons of Pandu should ever be protected by thee. Thou art, indeed, already their sole refuge. Formerly, I spoke to the foolish Duryodhana of wicked understanding that thither is Righteousness where Krishna is, and that there is victory where Righteousness is. I further counselled him that relying on Vasudeva as his refuge, he should make peace with the Pandavas. Indeed, I repeatedly told him, 'This is the fittest time for thee to make peace!' The foolish Duryodhana of wicked understanding, however, did not do my bidding. Having caused a great havoc on earth, at last, he himself laid down his life. Thee, O illustrious one, I know to be that ancient and best of Rishis who dwelt for many years in the company of Nara, in the retreat of Vadari. The celestial Rishi Narada told me this, as also Vyasa of austere penances. Even they have said unto me that. Thyself and Arjuna are the old Rishis Narayana and Nara born among men. Do thou, O Krishna, grant me leave, I shall cast off my body. Permitted by thee, I shall attain to the highest end!"

"'Vasudeva said, "I give thee leave, O Bhishma! Do thou, O king, attain to the status of the Vasus, O thou of great splendour, thou hast not been guilty of a single transgression in this world. O royal sage, thou art devoted to thy sire. Thou art, therefore, like a second Markandeya! It is for that reason that death depends upon thy pleasure even as thy slave expectant of reading thy pleasure!"'

"Vaisampayana continued, 'Having said these words, the son of Ganga once more addressed the Pandavas headed by Dhritarashtra, and other friends and well-wishers of his, "I desire to cast off my lifebreaths. It behoveth you to give me leave. Ye should strive for attaining to truth. Truth constitutes the highest power. Ye should always live with Brahmanas of righteous conduct, devoted to penances, ever abstaining from cruel behaviour, and who have their souls under control!" Having said these words unto his friends and embraced them all, the intelligent Bhishma once more addressed Yudhishthira, saying, "O king, let all Brahmanas, especially those that are endued with wisdom, let them who are preceptors, let those who are priests capable of assisting as sacrifices, be adorable in thy estimation."'"

SECTION CLXVIII.

"Vaisampayana said, 'Having said so unto all the Kurus, Bhishma, the son of Santanu, remained silent for some time, O chastiser of foes. He then held forth his life-breaths successively in those parts of his body which are indicated in Yoga. The life-breaths of that high-souled one, restrained duly, then rose up. Those parts of the body of Santanu's son, in consequence of the adoption, of Yoga, from which the life-breaths went up, became soreless one after another. In the midst of those high-souled persons, including those great Rishis with Vyasa at their head, the sight seemed to be a strange one, O king. Within a short time, the entire body of Bhishma became shaftless and soreless. Beholding it, all those distinguished personages with Vasudeva at their head, and all the ascetics with Vyasa, became filled with wonder. The life-breaths, restrained and unable to escape through any of the outlets, at last pierced through the crown of the head and proceeded upwards to heaven. The celestial kettle-drums began to play and floral showers were rained down. The Siddhas and regenerate Rishis, filled with delight, exclaimed, "Excellent, Excellent!" The life-breaths of Bhishma, piercing through the crown of his head, shot up through the welkin like a large meteor and soon became invisible. Even thus, O great king, did Santanu's son, that pillar of Bharata's race, united himself with eternity. Then the high-souled Pandavas and Vidura, taking a large quantity of wood and diverse kinds of fragrant scents, made a funeral pyre. Yuyutsu and others stood as spectators of the preparations. Then Yudhishthira and the high-souled Vidura wrapped Bhishma's body with silken cloth and floral garlands. Yuyutsu held an excellent umbrella, over it Bhimasena and Arjuna both held in their hands a couple of yak-tails of

440

pure white. The two sons of Madri held two head-gears in their hands. Yudhishthira and Dhritarashtra stood at the feet of the lord of the Kurus, taking up palmyra fans, stood around the body and began to fan it softly. The Pitri sacrifice of the high-souled Bhishma was then duly performed. Many libations were poured upon the sacred fire. The singers of Samans sang many Samans. Then covering the body of Ganga's son with sandal wood and black aloe and the bark wood, other fragrant fuel, and setting fire to the same, the Kurus with Dhritarashtra and others, stood on the right sight of the funeral pyre. Those foremost ones of Kuru's race, having thus cremated the body of the son of Ganga, proceeded to the sacred Bhagirathi, accompanied by the Rishis. They were followed by Vyasa, by Narada, by Asita, by Krishna, by the ladies of the Bharata race, as also by such of the citizens of Hastinapore as had come to the place. All of them, arrived at the sacred river, duly offered oblation of water unto the high-souled son of Ganga. The goddess Bhagirathi, after those oblations of water had been offered by them unto her son, rose up from the stream, weeping and distracted by sorrow. In the midst of her lamentations, she addressed the Kurus, "Ye sinless ones, listen to me as I say unto you all that occurred (with respect to my son). Possessed of royal conduct and disposition, and endued with wisdom and high birth, my son was the benefactor of all the seniors of his race. He was devoted to his sire and was of high vows. He could not be vanquished by even Rama of Jamadagni's race with his celestial weapons of great energy. Alas, that hero has been slain by Sikhandin. Ye kings, without doubt, my heart is made of adamant, for it does not break even at the disappearance of that son from my sight! At the Self choice at Kasi, he vanquished on a single car the assembled Kshatriyas and ravished the three princesses (for his step-brother Vichitravirya)! There was no one on earth that equalled him in might. Alas, my heart does not break upon hearing the slaughter of that son of mine by Sikhandin!" The puissant Krishna, hearing the goddess of the great river indulging in these lamentations consoled her with many soothing words. Krishna said, "O amiable one, be comforted. Do not yield to grief, O thou of beautiful features! Without doubt, thy son has gone to the highest region of felicity! He was one of the Vasus of great energy. Through a curse, O thou of beautiful features, he had to take birth among men. It behoveth thee not to grieve for him. Agreeably to Kshatriya duties, he was slain by Dhananjaya on the field of battle while engaged in battle. He has not been slain, O goddess, by Sikhandin. The very chief of the celestials himself could not slay Bhishma in battle when he stood with stretched bow in hand. O thou of beautiful face, thy son has, in felicity, gone to heaven. All the gods assembled together could not slay him in battle. Do not, therefore, O goddess Ganga, grieve for that son of Kuru's race. He was one of the Vasus, O goddess! Thy son has gone to heaven. Let the fever of thy heart be dispelled."'

"Vaisampayana continued, 'That foremost of all rivers, thus addressed by Krishna and Vyasa, cast off her grief, O great king, and became restored to equanimity. All the kings there present, headed by Krishna, O monarch, having honoured that goddess duly, received her permission to depart from her banks.'"

THE END OF ANUSASANA PARVA

BOOK 14. ASWAMEDHA PARVA

SECTION I. (*Aswamedhika Parva*)

OM! HAVING BOWED down unto Narayana, and Nara the foremost of male beings, and unto the goddess Saraswati, must the word Jaya be uttered.

"Vaisampayana said, 'After the king Dhritarashtra had offered libations of water (unto the manes of Bhisma), the mighty-armed[633] Yudhishthira, with his senses bewildered, placing the former in his front, ascended the banks (of the river), his eyes suffused with tears, and dropt down on the bank of the Ganga like an elephant pierced by the hunter. Then incited by Krishna, Bhima took him up sinking. "This must not be so," said Krishna, the grinder of hostile hosts. The Pandavas, O king, saw Yudhishthira, the son of Dharma, troubled and lying on the ground, and also sighing again and again. And seeing the king despondent and feeble, the Pandavas, overwhelmed with grief, sat down, surrounding him. And endowed with high intelligence and having the sight of wisdom, king Dhritarashtra, exceedingly afflicted with grief for his sons, addressed the monarch, saying,—"Rise up, O thou tiger among the Kurus. Do thou now attend to thy duties. O Kunti's son, thou hast conquered this Earth according to the usage of the Kshatriyas. Do thou now, O lord of men, enjoy her with thy brothers and friends. O foremost of the righteous, I do not see why thou shouldst grieve. O lord of the Earth, having lost a hundred sons like unto riches obtained in a dream, it is Gandhari and I, who should mourn. Not having listened to the pregnant words of the high-souled Vidura, who sought our welfare, I, of perverse senses, (now) repent. The virtuous Vidura, endowed with divine insight, had told me,—'Thy race will meet with annihilation owing to the transgressions of Duryodhana. O king, if thou wish for the weal of thy line, act up to my advice. Cast off this wicked-minded monarch, Suyodhana, and let not either Karna or Sakuni by any means see him. Their gambling too do thou, without making any fuss suppress, and anoint the righteous king Yudhishthira. That one of subdued senses will righteously govern the Earth. If thou wouldst not have king Yudhishthira, son of Kunti, then, O monarch, do thou, performing a sacrifice, thyself take charge of the kingdom, and regarding all creatures with an even eye, O lord of men, do thou let thy kinsmen, O thou advancer of thy kindred, subsist on thy bounty.' When, O Kunti's son, the far-sighted Vidura said this, fool that I was I followed the wicked Duryodhana. Having turned a deaf ear to the sweet speech of that sedate one, I have obtained this mighty sorrow as a consequence, and have been plunged in an ocean of woe. Behold thy old father and mother, O king, plunged in misery. But, O master of men, I find no occasion for thy grief."'"

SECTION II.

"Vaisampayana said, 'Thus addressed by the intelligent king Dhritarashtra Yudhishthira, possessed of understanding, became calm. And then Kesava (Krishna) accosted him,—"If a person indulges excessively in sorrow for his departed forefathers, he grieves them. (Therefore, banishing grief), do thou (now) celebrate many a sacrifice with suitable presents to the priests; and do thou gratify the gods with Soma liquor, and

---

[633] Mahavahu occurs twice in this passage. One of the epithets is left out on the score of redundancy.

the manes of thy forefathers with their due food and drink. Do thou also gratify thy guests with meat and drink and the destitute with gifts commensurate with their desires. A person of thy high intelligence should not bear himself thus. What ought to be known hath been known by thee; what ought to be done, hath also been performed. And thou hast heard the duties of the Kshatriyas, recited by Bhishma, the son of Bhagirathi, by Krishna Dwaipayana, Narada and Vidura. Therefore thou shouldst not walk the way of the stupid; but pursuing the course of thy forefathers, sustain the burthen (of the empire). It is meet that a Kshatriya should attain heaven for certain by his (own) renown. Of heroes, those that came to be slain never shall have to turn away (from the celestial regions). Renounce thy grief, O mighty sovereign. Verily, what hath happened was destined to happen so. Thou canst in no wise see those that have been slain in this war."—Having said this unto Yudhishthira, prince of the pious, the high-spirited Govinda paused; and Yudhishthira answered him thus, "O Govinda, full well do I know thy fondness for me. Thou hast ever favoured me with thy love and thy friendship. And, O holder of the mace and the discus, O scion of Yadu's race, O glorious one, if (now) with a pleased mind thou dost permit me to go to the ascetic's retreat in the woods, then thou wouldst compass what is highly desired by me. Peace find I none after having slain my grand-father, and that foremost of men, Karna, who never fled from the field of battle. Do thou, O Janarddana, so order that I may be freed from this heinous sin and that my mind may be purified." As Pritha's son was speaking thus, the highly-energetic Vyasa, cognisant of the duties of life, soothing him, spoke these excellent words, "My child, thy mind is not yet calmed; and therefore thou art again stupefied by a childish sentiment. And wherefore, O child, do we over and over again scatter our speech to the winds? Thou knowest duties of the Kshatriyas, who live by warfare. A king that hath performed his proper part should not suffer himself to be overwhelmed by sorrow. Thou hast faithfully listened to the entire doctrine of salvation; and I have repeatedly removed thy misgivings arising out of desire. But not paying due heed to what I have unfolded, thou of perverse understanding hast doubtless forgotten it clean. Be it not so. Such ignorance is not worthy of thee. O sinless one, thou knowest all kinds of expiation; and thou hast also heard of the virtues of kings as well as the merits of gifts. Wherefore then, O Bharata, acquainted with every morality and versed in all the Agamas, art thou overwhelmed (with grief) as if from ignorance?"""

SECTION III.

"'Vyasa said, "O Yudhishthira, thy wisdom, I conceive, is not adequate. None doth any act by virtue of his own power. It is God, who engageth him in acts good or bad, O bestower of honour. Where then is the room for repentance? Thou deemest thyself as having perpetrated impious acts. Do thou, therefore, O Bharata, harken as to the way in which sin may be removed. O Yudhishthira, those that commit sins, can always free themselves from them through penance, sacrifice and gifts. O king, O foremost of men, sinful people are purified by sacrifice, austerities and charity. The high-souled celestials and Asuras perform sacrifices for securing religious merit; and therefore sacrifice are of supreme importance. It is through sacrifices that the high-souled celestials had waxed so wondrously powerful; and having celebrated rites did they vanquish the Danavas. Do thou, O Yudhishthira, prepare for the Rajasuya, and the horse-sacrifice, as well as, O

Bharata, for the Sarvamedha and the Naramedha.[634] And then as Dasaratha's son, Rama, or as Dushmanta's and Sakuntala's son, thy ancestor, the lord of the Earth, the exceedingly puissant king Bharata, had done, do thou agreeably to the ordinance celebrate the Horse-sacrifice with Dakshinas." Yudhishthira replied, "Beyond a doubt, the Horse-sacrifice purifieth princes. But I have a purpose of which it behoveth thee to hear. Having caused this huge carnage of kindred, I cannot, O best of the regenerate ones, dispense gifts even on a small scale; I have no wealth to give. Nor can I for wealth solicit these juvenile sons of kings, staying in sorry plight, with their wounds yet green, and undergoing suffering. How, O foremost of twice-born ones, having myself destroyed the Earth can I, overcome by sorrow, levy dues for celebrating a sacrifice? Through Duryodhana's fault, O best of ascetics, the kings of the Earth have met with destruction, and we have reaped ignominy. For wealth Duryodhana hath wasted the Earth; and the treasury of that wicked-minded son of Dhritarashtra is empty. (In this sacrifice), the Earth is the Dakshina; this is the rule that is prescribed in the first instance. The usual reversal of this rule, though sanctioned, is observed, by the learned as such. Nor, O ascetic, do I like to have a substitute (for this process). In this matter, O reverend sir, it behoveth thee to favour me with thy counsel." Thus addressed by Pritha's son, Krishna Dwaipayana, reflecting for a while, spoke unto the righteous king,—"This treasury, (now) exhausted, shall be full. O son of Pritha, in the mountain Himavat (The Himalayas) there is gold which had been left behind by Brahmanas at the sacrifice of the high-souled Marutta."[635] Yudhishthira asked, "How in that sacrifice celebrated by Marutta was so much gold amassed? And, O foremost of speakers, when did he reign?" Vyasa said "If, O Pritha's son, thou art anxious to hear concerning that king sprung from the Karandhama race, then listen to me as I tell thee when that highly powerful monarch possessed of immense wealth reigned."'"

SECTION IV.

"'Yudhishthira said, "O righteous one, I am desirous of hearing the history of that royal sage Marutta. Do thou, O Dwaipayana, relate this unto me, O sinless one."

"'Vyasa said, "O child, in the Krita age Manu was lord (of the Earth) wielding the sceptre. His son was known under the name of Prasandhi. Prasandhi had a son named Kshupa, Kshupa's son was that lord (of men), king Ikshwaku. He, O king, had a hundred sons endowed with pre-eminent piety. And all of them were made monarchs by king Ikshwaku. The eldest of them, Vinsa by name became the model of bowmen. Vinsa's son, O Bharata, was the auspicious Vivinsa. Vivinsa, O king, had five and ten sons; all of them were powerful archers, reverencial to the Brahmanas and truthful, gentle and ever speaking fair. The eldest brother, Khaninetra, oppressed all his brothers. And having conquered the entire kingdom rid of all troubles, Khaninetra could not retain his supremacy; nor were the people pleased with him. And dethroning him, they, O foremost of monarchs, invested his son Suvarcha with the rights of sovereignty and (having effected this) experienced joy (in their hearts). Seeing the reverses sustained by his sire as well as his expulsion from the empire, he was ever intent on bringing about the welfare of the people, being devoted to the Brahmanas, speaking the truth, practising purity and

---

[634] i.e., human sacrifice. From this it appears that the sacrifice of human beings was in vogue at the time.

[635] King Marutta celebrated a sacrifice in the Himalayas, bestowing gold on Brahmanas. Not being able to carry the entire quantity, they had carried as much as they could, throwing away the remainder.

restraining his senses and thoughts. And the subjects were well pleased with that high-minded one constant in virtue. But he being constantly engaged in virtuous deeds, his treasures and vehicles became greatly reduced. And on his treasury having become depleted, the feudatory princes swarming round him began to give him trouble. Being thus oppressed by many foes while his treasury, horses and vehicles were impoverished, the king underwent great tribulation along with his retainers and the denizens of his capital. Although his power waned greatly, yet the foes could not slay the king, for his power, O Yudhishthira, was established in righteousness. And when he had reached the extreme of misery along with the citizens, he blew his hand (with his mouth), and from that there appeared a supply of forces. And then he vanquished all the kings living along the borders of his dominions. And from this circumstance O king, he hath been celebrated as Karandhama. His son, (the first) Karandhama who was born at the beginning of the Treta age, equalled Indra himself and was endowed with grace, and invincible even by the immortals. At that time all the kings were under his control; and alike by virtue of his wealth and for his prowess, he became their emperor. In short, the righteous king Avikshit by name, became like unto Indra himself in heroism; and he was given to sacrifices, delight took in virtue and held his senses under restraint. And in energy he resembled the sun and in forbearance Earth herself; in intelligence, he was like Vrihaspati, and in calmness the mountain Himavat himself. And that king delighted the hearts of his subjects by act, thought, speech, self-restraint, and forbearance. He performed hundreds of horse-sacrifices, and the potent and learned Angira himself served him as priest. His son surpassed his sire in the possession of good qualities. Named Marutta, that lord of kings was righteous and of great renown, and possessed the might of ten thousand elephants. He was like unto Vishnu's second self. Desirous of celebrating a sacrifice, that virtuous monarch, coming to Mount Meru on the northern side of Himavat, caused thousands of shining golden vessels to be forged. There on a huge golden hill he performed the rites. And goldsmiths made basins and vessels and pans and seats without number. And the sacrificial ground was near this place. And that righteous lord of Earth, king Marutta, along with other princes, performed a sacrifice there.""'

SECTION V.

"'Yudhishthira said, "O best of speakers, how did that king become so powerful? And how, O twice-born one, did he obtain so much gold? And where now, O reverend sire, is all his wealth? And, O ascetic, how can we secure the same?"

"'Vyasa thereupon said,—"As the numerous offspring of the Prajapati Daksha, the Asuras and the Celestials challenged each other (to encounter), so in the same way Angira's sons, the exceedingly energetic Vrihaspati and the ascetic, Samvarta, of equal vows, challenged each other, O king. Vrihaspati began to worry Samvarta again and again. And constantly troubled by his elder brother, he, O Bharata, renouncing his riches, went to the woods, with nothing to cover his body save the open sky.[636] (At that time), Vasava having vanquished and destroyed the Asuras, and obtained the sovereignty of the celestial regions had appointed as his priest Angira's eldest son, that best of Brahmanas, Vrihaspati. Formerly Angira was the family-priest of king Karandhama. Matchless among men in might, prowess and character; powerful like unto Satakratu, righteous souled and of rigid vows, O king, he had vehicles, and warriors, and many adherents, and

---

[636] Digambara, i.e., in naked state.

superb and costly bedsteads, produced through dint of meditation by the breath of his mouth. And by his native virtues, the monarch had brought all the princes under his sway. And having lived as long as he desired, he ascended to the heaven in his corporal embodiment. And his son named Avikshit—conqueror of foes,—righteous like unto Yayati, brought all the Earth under his dominion. And both in merit and might the king resembled his sire. He had a son named Marutta, endowed with energy, and resembling Vasava himself. This earth clad in oceans, felt herself drawn towards him. He always[637] used to defy the lord of the celestials; and O son of Pandu, Vasava also defied Marutta. And Marutta,—master of Earth—was pure and possessed of perfections. And in spite of his striving, Sakra could not prevail over him. And incapable of controlling him, he riding on the horse, along with the celestials summoning Vrihaspati, spoke to him thus, 'O Vrihaspati, if thou wishest to do what is agreeable to me, do not perform priestly offices for Marutta on behalf of the deities or the ancestral Manes. I have, O Vrihaspati, obtained the sovereignty of the three worlds, while Marutta is merely the lord of the Earth. How, O Brahmana, having acted as priest unto the immortal king of the celestials, wilt thou unhesitatingly perform priestly function unto Marutta subject to death? Good betide thee! Either espouse my side or that of the monarch, Marutta or forsaking Marutta, gladly come over to me.'—Thus accosted by the sovereign of the celestials, Vrihaspati, reflecting for a moment, replied unto the king of the immortals. 'Thou art the Lord of creatures, and in thee are the worlds established, And thou hast destroyed Namuchi, Viswarupa and Vala. Thou, O hero, alone encompassest the highest prosperity of the celestials, and, O slayer of Vala, thou sustainest the earth as well as the heaven. How, O foremost of the celestials, having officiated as thy priest, shall I, O chastiser of Paka, serve a mortal prince? Do thou listen to what I say. Even if the god of fire cease to cause heat and warmth, or the earth change its nature, or the sun ceases to give light, I shall never deviate from the truth (that I have spoken).'"

"Vaisampayana continued,—'On hearing this speech from Vrihaspati Indra became cured of his envious feelings, and then praising him he repaired to his own mansion.'"

SECTION VI.

"'Vyasa said, "The ancient legend of Vrihaspati and the wise Marutta is cited in this connection. On hearing of the compact made by Angira's son Vrihaspati with the lord of the gods (Indra), king Marutta made the necessary preparations for a great sacrifice. The eloquent grandson of Karandhama, (Marutta) having conceived the idea of a sacrifice in his mind, went to Vrihaspati and addressed him thus, 'O worshipful ascetic, I have intended to perform the sacrifice which thou didst propose to me once on a previous occasion and in accordance with thy instructions, and I now desire to appoint thee as officiating priest in this sacrifice, the materials whereof have also been collected by me.—O excellent one, thou art our family priest, therefore do thou take those sacrificial things and perform the sacrifice thyself.'

"""Vrihaspati said, 'O lord of the earth, I do not desire to perform thy sacrifice. I have been appointed as priest by the Lord of the gods (Indra) and I have promised to him to act as such.'

"""Marutta said, 'Thou art our hereditary family priest, and for this reason I entertain great regard for thee, and I have acquired the right of being assisted at sacrifices by thee,

---

[637] Nityada always, left out on the ground of redundancy.

and therefore it is meet that thou shouldst officiate as priest at my sacrifice.'

"'"Vrihaspati said, 'Having, O Marutta, acted as priest to the Immortals, how can I act as such to mortal men, and whether thou dost depart hence or stay, I tell thee, I have ceased to act as priest to any but the Immortals. O thou of mighty arms, I am unable to act as thy priest now. And according to thy own desire, thou canst appoint any one as thy priest who will perform thy sacrifice.'"

"'Vyasa said, "Thus told, king Marutta became confused with shame, and while returning home with his mind oppressed by anxiety, he met Narada on his way. And that monarch on seeing the divine Rishi Narada stood before him with due salutation, with his hands clasped together. Then Narada addressing him thus said,—'O royal sage, thou seemest to be not well-pleased in thy mind; is all well with thee? Where hast thou been, O sinless one, and whence the cause of this thy mental disquietude? And, O king, if there be no objection to thy telling it to me, do thou, O best of kings, disclose (the cause of thy anxiety) to me, so that, O prince, I may allay the disquietude of thy mind with all my efforts.'"'

"Vaisampayana continued, 'Thus addressed by the great Rishi Narada, king Marutta informed him of the rebuff he had received from his religious preceptor.'

"'"Marutta said, 'Seeking for a priest to officiate at my sacrifice, I went to that priest of the Immortals, Vrihaspati, the son of Angira, but he did not choose to accept my offer. Having met with this rebuff from him, I have no desire to live any longer now, for by his abandoning me thus, I have, O Narada, become contaminated with sin.'"

"'Vyasa said, "Thus told by that king, Narada, O mighty prince, made this reply to him with words which seemed to revive that son of Avikshit.'

"'"Narada said, 'The virtuous son of Angira, Samvarta by name is wandering over all the quarters of the earth in a naked state to the wonder of all creatures; do thou, O prince, go to him. If Vrihaspati does not desire to officiate at thy sacrifice, the powerful Samvarta, if pleased with thee, will perform thy sacrifice.'

"'"Marutta said, 'I feel as if instilled with new life, by these thy words, O Narada, but O the best of speakers, do thou tell me where I can find Samvarta, and how I can remain by his side, and how I am to act so that he may not abandon me, for I do not desire to live if I meet with a rebuff from him also.'

"'"Narada said, 'Desirous of seeing Maheswara, O prince, he wanders about at his pleasure in the city of Varanasi, in the garb of a mad man. And having reached the gate of that city, thou must place a dead body somewhere near it, and the man who shall turn away on seeing the corpse, do thou, O prince, know that man to be Samvarta, and knowing him, do thou follow his footsteps wheresoever that powerful man chooses to go and finding him (at length) in a lonely place thou must seek his protection with thy hands clasped together in supplication to him. And if he enquires of thee as to the person who has given thee the information about his own self, do thou tell him that Narada has informed thee about Samvarta. And if he should ask thee to follow me, thou must tell him without any hesitation, that I have entered into the fire.'"

"'Vyasa said, "Having signified his assent to the proposal of Narada, that royal sage after duly worshipping him, and taking his permission, repaired to the city of Varanasi, and having reached there, that famous prince did as he had been told, and remembering the words of Narada, he placed a corpse at the gate of the city. And by coincidence, that Brahmana also entered the gate of the city at the same time. Then on beholding the corpse, he suddenly turned away. And on seeing him turn back, that prince, the son of Avikshit followed his footsteps with his hands clasped together, and with the object of receiving instruction from him. And then finding him in a lonely place, Samvarta covered the king with mud and ashes and phlegm and spittle. And though thus worried and oppressed by Samvarta, the king followed that sage with his hands clasped together in supplication and trying to appease him. At length overcome with fatigue, and reaching the cool shade of a sacred fig tree with many branches, Samvarta desisted from his course and sat himself to rest.""'"

SECTION VII.

""'Samvarta said, 'How hast thou come to know me, and who has referred thee to me, do thou tell this to me truly, if thou wishest me to do what is good to thee. And if thou speak truly, thou shalt attain all the objects of thy desire, and shouldst thou tell a lie, thy head shall be riven in a hundred pieces.'

""'Marutta said, 'I have been told by Narada, wandering on his way, that thou art the son of our family-priest, and this (information) has inclined my mind (towards thee), with exquisite satisfaction.'

""'Samvarta said, 'Thou hast told this to me truly. He (Narada) knows me to be a performer of sacrifices. Now tell me where is Narada living at present.'

""'Marutta said, 'That prince of celestial saints (Narada) having given me this information about thee, and commended me to thy care, has entered into the fire.'"

"'Vyasa said, "Hearing these words from the king (Marutta) Samvarta was highly gratified, and he said (addressing Marutta), 'I too am quite able to do all that.' Then, O prince, that Brahmana, raving like a lunatic, and repeatedly scolding Marutta with rude words, again accosted him thus, 'I am afflicted with a cerebral disorder, and, I always act according to the random caprices of my own mind. Why art thou bent upon having this sacrifice performed by a priest of such a singular disposition? My brother is able to officiate at sacrifices, and he has gone over to Vasava (Indra), and is engaged in performing his sacrifices, do thou therefore have thy sacrifice performed by him. My elder brother has forcibly taken away from me all my household goods and mystical gods, and sacrificing clients, and has now left to me only this physical body of mine, and, O son of Avikshit, as he is worthy of all respect from me, I cannot by any means officiate at thy sacrifice, unless with his permission. Thou must therefore go to Vrihaspati first, and taking his permission thou canst come back to me, if thou hast any desire to perform a sacrifice, and then only shall I officiate at thy sacrifice.'

""'Marutta said, 'Do thou listen to me, O Samvarta, I did go to Vrihaspati first, but desiring the patronage of Vasava, he did not wish to have me as his sacrificer. He said, "Having secured the priesthood of the Immortals, I do not desire to act for mortals, and, I have been forbidden by Sakra (Indra) to officiate at Marutta's sacrifice, as he told me that Marutta having become lord of the earth, was always filled with a desire to rival him." And to this thy brother assented by saying to the Slayer of Vala (Indra),—"Be it so." Know thou, O best of ascetics, that as he had succeeded in securing the protection of the Lord of the Celestials, I repaired to him with gratified heart, but he did not agree to act as my priest. And thus repulsed, I now desire to spend all I possess, to have this sacrifice performed by thee, and to outstrip Vasava by the merit of thy good offices. As I have been repulsed by Vrihaspati for no fault of mine, I have now no desire, O Brahmana, to go to him to seek his aid in this sacrifice.'

""'Samvarta said, 'I can certainly, O king, accomplish all that thou desirest, if only thou agree to do all that I shall ask thee to do, but I apprehend that Vrihaspati and

Purandara (Indra) when they will learn that I am engaged in performing thy sacrifice, will be filled with wrath, and do all they can to injure thee. Therefore, do thou assure me of thy steadfastness, so as to ensure my coolness and constancy, as otherwise, if I am filled with wrath against thee, I shall reduce (destroy) thee and thy kindred to ashes.'

""Marutta said, 'If ever I forsake thee, may I never attain the blessed regions as long as the mountains shall exist, and the thousand-rayed sun continue to emit heat: if I forsake thee, may I never attain true wisdom, and remain for ever addicted to worldly (material) pursuits.'

""Samvarta said, 'Listen, O son of Avikshit, excellent as it is the bent of thy mind to perform this act, so too, O king, have I in my mind the ability to perform the sacrifice, I tell thee, O king, that thy good things will become imperishable, and that thou shalt lord it over Sakra and the Celestials with Gandharvas. For myself, I have no desire to amass wealth or sacrificial presents, I shall only do what is disagreeable to both Indra and my brother, I shall certainly make thee attain equality with Sakra, and I tell thee truly that I shall do what is agreeable to thee.'""""

SECTION VIII.

""Samvarta said, 'There is a peak named Munjaban on the summits of the Himalaya mountains, where the adorable Lord of Uma (Mahadeva) is constantly engaged in austere devotional exercises. There the mighty and worshipful god of great puissance, accompanied by his consort Uma, and armed with his trident, surrounded by wild goblins of many sorts, pursuing his random wish or fancy, constantly resides in the shade of giant forest trees, or in the caves, or on the rugged peaks of the great mountain. And there the Rudras, the Saddhyas, Viswedevas, the Vasus, Yama, Varuna, and Kuvera with all his attendants, and the spirits and goblins, and the two Aswins, the Gandharvas, the Apsaras, the Yakshas, as also the celestial sages, the Sun-gods, as well as the gods presiding over the winds, and evil spirits of all sorts, worship the high-souled lord of Uma, possessed of diverse characteristics. And there, O king, the adorable god sports with the wild and playful followers of Kuvera, possessed of weird and ghostly appearances. Glowing with its own splendour, that mountain looks resplendent as the morning sun. And no creature with his natural eyes made of flesh, can ever ascertain its shape or configuration, and neither heat nor cold prevails there, nor doth the sun shine nor do the winds blow. And, O king, neither doth senility nor hunger, nor thirst, nor death, nor fear afflict any one at that place. And, O foremost of conquerors, on all sides of that mountain, there exist mines of gold, resplendent as the rays of the sun. And O king, the attendants of Kuvera, desirous of doing good to him, protect these mines of gold from intruders, with uplifted arms. Hie thee thither, and appease that adorable god who is known by the names of Sarva, Bedha, Rudra, Sitikantha, Surapa, Suvarcha, Kapardi, Karala, Haryyaksha, Varada, Tryaksha, Pushnodantabhid, Vamana, Siva, Yamya, Avyaktarupa, Sadvritta, Sankara, Kshemya, Harikesa, Sthanu, Purusha, Harinetra, Munda, Krishna, Uttarana, Bhaskara, Sutirtha, Devadeva, Ranha, Ushnishi, Suvaktra, Sahasraksha, Midhvan, Girisa, Prasanta, Yata, Chiravasa, Vilwadanda, Siddha, Sarvadandadhara, Mriga, Vyadha, Mahan, Dhanesa, Bhava, Vara, Somavaktra, Siddhamantra, Chakshu, Hiranyavahu, Ugra, Dikpati, Lelihana, Goshtha, Shiddhamantra, Vrishnu, Pasupati, Bhutapati, Vrisha, Matribhakta, Senani, Madhyama, Sruvahasta, Yati, Dhanwi, Bhargava, Aja, Krishnanetra, Virupaksha, Tikshnadanshtra, Tikshna, Vaiswanaramukha, Mahadyuti, Ananga, Sarva, Dikpati, Bilohita, Dipta, Diptaksha, Mahauja, Vasuretas, Suvapu, Prithu, Kritivasa, Kapalmali,

Suvarnamukuta, Mahadeva, Krishna, Tryamvaka, Anagha, Krodhana, Nrisansa, Mridu, Vahusali, Dandi, Taptatapa, Akrurakarma, Sahasrasira, Sahasra-charana, Swadha-swarupa, Vahurupa, Danshtri, Pinaki, Mahadeva, Mahayogi, Avyaya, Trisulahasta, Varada, Tryamvaka, Bhuvaneswara, Tripuraghna, Trinayana, Trilokesa, Mahanja, Sarvabhuta-prabhava, Sarvabhuta-dharana, Dharanidhara, Isana, Sankara, Sarva, Siva, Visveswara, Bhava, Umapati, Pasupati, Viswarupa, Maheswara, Virupaksha, Dasabhuja, Vrishavadhwaja, Ugra, Sthanu, Siva, Rudra, Sarva, Girisa, Iswara, Sitakantha, Aja, Sukra, Prithu, Prithuhara, Vara, Viswarupa, Virupaksha, Vahurupa, Umapati, Anangangahara, Hara, Saranya, Mahadeva, Chaturmukha. There bowing unto that deity, must thou crave his protection. And thus, O prince, making thy submission to that high-souled Mahadeva of great energy, shalt thou acquire that gold. And the men who go there thus, succeed in obtaining the gold.' Thus instructed, Marutta, the son of Karandhama, did as he was advised, and made superhuman arrangements for the performance of his sacrifice. And artisans manufactured vessels of gold for that sacrifice. And Vrihaspati too, hearing of the prosperity of Marutta, eclipsing that of the gods, became greatly grieved at heart, and distressed at the thought that his rival Samvarta should become prosperous, became sick at heart, and the glow of his complexion left him, and his frame became emaciated. And when the lord of the gods came to know that Vrihaspati was much aggrieved, he went to him attended by the Immortals and addressed him thus."'

SECTION IX.

"'Indra said, 'Dost thou, O Vrihaspati, sleep in peace, and are thy servants agreeable to thee, dost thou seek the welfare of the gods, and do the gods, O Brahmana, protect thee?'

"'Vrihaspati said, 'I do sleep in peace in my bed, O Lord of the gods, and my servants are to my liking and I always seek the welfare of the gods, and they cherish me well.'

"'Indra said, 'Whence then is this pain, mental or physical, and why art thou pale and altered in appearance (complexion) at present? Tell me, O Brahmana, who those people are, who have caused thee pain, so that I may kill them all.'

"'Vrihaspati said, 'O Indra, I have heard that Marutta will perform a great sacrifice at which exquisite presents will be given by him (to Brahmanas) and that at his sacrifice Samvarta will act as the officiating priest, and therefore do I desire that he may not officiate as priest at that sacrifice.'

"'Indra said, 'Thou, O Brahmana, hast attained all the object of thy desire when thou hast become the excellent priest of the gods, versed in all the sacred hymns, and hast overreached the influence of death and dotage, what can Samvarta do to thee now?'

"'Vrihaspati said, 'Prosperity of a rival is always painful to one's feelings, and for this reason too, thou dost with thy attendant gods persecute the Asuras with their kith and kin, and kill the most prosperous among them; hence, O Lord of the gods, am I changed in appearance at the thought that my rival is prospering, therefore, O Indra, do thou, by all means, restrain Samvarta and king Marutta.'

"'Indra turning to Agni said, 'Do thou, O Jataveda, following my direction, go to king Marutta to present Vrihaspati to him, and say unto him that this Vrihaspati will officiate at his sacrifice and make him immortal.'

"'Agni said, 'I shall presently, O adorable one, repair thither as thy messenger, to present Vrihaspati to king Marutta, and to make Indra's words true, and to show respect to Vrihaspati, Agni departed.'"

"'Vyasa said, "Then the high-souled fire-god went on his errand, devastating all the forests and trees, like unto the mighty wind, roaring and revolving at random at the end of the winter season."

"'"Marutta said, 'Behold! I find the fire-god come in his own embodiment, this day, therefore do thou, O Muni, offer him a seat and water, and a cow, and water for washing the feet.'

"'"Agni said, 'I accept thy offerings of water, seat, and water for washing the feet, O sinless one, do thou know me as the messenger of Indra, come to thee, in accordance with his directions.'

"'"Marutta said, 'O Fire-god, is the glorious Lord of the Celestials happy, and is he pleased with us, and are the other gods loyal to him? Do thou enlighten me duly on all these points.'

"'"Agni said, 'O lord of the earth, Sakra is perfectly happy, he is pleased with thee, and wishes to make thee free from senility, and all the other gods are loyal to him. Do thou, O king, listen to the message of the Lord of the Celestials. And the object for which he has sent me to thee is to present Vrihaspati to Marutta. O prince, let this priest (of the Celestials) perform thy sacrifice, and make thee, who art only a mortal, attain immortality.'

"'"Marutta said, 'This twice-born Brahmana Samvarta will perform my sacrifice, and I pray to Vrihaspati, that he having acted as priest to Mahendra (Indra), it does not look well for him now to act as priest to mortal men.'

"'"Agni said, 'If this Vrihaspati officiate as thy priest, then shalt thou by the blessings of Devaraja (Indra) attain the highest region in the celestial mansion and attaining fame shalt thou certainly conquer the heavenly region. And, O lord of men, if Vrihaspati act as thy priest, thou shalt be able to conquer all the regions inhabited by men, and the heavenly regions, and all the highest regions created by Prajapati and even the entire kingdom of the gods.'

"'"Samvarta said, 'Thou must never come again thus to present Vrihaspati to Marutta: for know, O Pavaka, (Agni) if thou dost, I losing my temper, will burn thee with my fierce evil eyes.'"

"'Vyasa said, "Then Agni apprehending destruction by fire, and trembling like the leaves of the Aswattha tree (Ficus religiosa), returned to the gods, and the high-souled Sakra seeing that carrier of oblations (Agni) in the company of Vrihaspati said as follows:

"'"Indra said, 'O Jataveda (Agni), didst thou go to present Vrihaspati to Marutta according to my direction? What did that sacrificing king say unto thee and did he accept my message?'

"'"Agni said, 'Thy message was not acceptable by Marutta and when urged by me, he clasping the hands of Vrihaspati, repeatedly said, that Samvarta would act as his priest. And he also observed that he did not desire to attain the worldly and the heavenly regions and all the highest regions of Prajapati, and that if he were so minded, he would accept the terms of Indra.'

"'"Indra said, 'Do thou go back to that king and meeting him, tell him these words of mine, full of significance, and if he obey them not, I shall strike him with my thunderbolt.'

"'"Agni said, 'Let this king of the Gandharvas repair thither as thy messenger, O Vasava, for, I am afraid to go thither myself. Know, O Sakra, that highly incensed Samvarta, used to ascetic practices, told me these words in a rage. 'I shall burn thee with my fierce evil eyes if thou on any account come again here to present Vrihaspati to king Marutta.'

""""Sakra said, 'O Jataveda, it is thou who dost burn all other things and there is none else who can reduce thee to ashes. All the world is afraid to come in contact with thee. O carrier of oblations, these words of thine are worthy of no credence.'

""""Agni said, 'Thou, O Sakra, hast encompassed the dominion of the heaven and the earth and the firmament by the might of thy own arms, but even thus how could Vritra (of old) wrest from thee the sovereignty of the celestial regions?'

""""Indra said, 'I can reduce my foes to submission and can even reduce the size of a mountain to an atom, if I will it. But, O Vahnni, as I do not accept the libation of Soma if offered by a foe, and as I do not strike the weak with my thunderbolt, Vritra seemed to triumph over me for a time. But who among mortals can live in peace by creating feud with me. I have banished the Kalakeyas to the earth, and removed the Danavas from heaven, and have terminated the existence of Prahlada in heaven. Can there be any man who can live in peace by provoking my enmity?'

""""Agni said, 'Dost thou, O Mahendra, remember that in olden times when the sage Chyavana officiated at the sacrifice of Saryati with the twin gods Aswins and himself appropriated the Soma offering alone, thou wert filled with wrath, and when bent upon preventing Saryati's sacrifice, thou didst violently strike Chyavana with thy thunderbolt? But that Brahmana, O Purandara, giving way to passion, was able by the power of his devotions to seize and hold fast by hand with thy thunder-bolt in it. And in a rage, he again created a terrible looking enemy of thine, the Asura named Mada assuming all shapes, on beholding whom thou didst shut thine eyes with fear, whose one huge jaw was placed on earth, and the other extended to the celestial regions, and who looked terrible with his thousand sharp teeth extending over a hundred Yojanas, and had four prominent ones thick-set, and shining like a pillar of silver, and extending over two hundred Yojanas. And when grinding his teeth he pursued thee with his terrible and uplifted pike with the object of killing thee. Thou on beholding that terrible monster, presented a (pitiful) spectacle to all the by-standers. Then, O slayer of Danavas, overcome with fear of the monster, with thy hands clasped in supplication, thou didst seek the protection of the great sage. The might of Brahmanas, O Sakra, is greater than that of the Kshatriyas. None are more powerful than Brahmanas and knowing duly, as I do, the power of Brahmanas, I do not, O Sakra, desire to come in conflict with Samvarta.""""

SECTION X.

""""Indra said, 'Even so it is; the might of Brahmanas is great and there are none more powerful than Brahmanas, but I can never bear with equanimity the insolent pride of Avikshita's son, and so shall I smite him with my thunderbolt. Therefore, O Dhritarashtra, do thou according to my direction repair to king Marutta attended by Samvarta, and deliver this message to him—"Do thou, O prince, accept Vrihaspati as thy spiritual preceptor, as otherwise, I shall strike thee with my terrific thunderbolt.""""

"'Vyasa said, "Then Dhritarashtra betook himself to that monarch's court and delivered this message to him from Vasava.

""""Dhritarashtra said, 'O lord of men, know that I am Dhritarashtra the Gandharva, come here with the object [of] delivering to thee the message of Indra. Do thou, O lion among kings, listen to the words which the high-souled lord of all the worlds meant for thee,—That one of incomprehensible achievements (Indra) only said this much, "Do thou accept Vrihaspati as thy officiating priest for the sacrifice, or if thou do not comply with my request, I shall strike thee with my terrific thunderbolt.'"

""'Marutta said, 'Thou, O Purandara, the Viswadevas, the Vasus and the Aswins ye all know, that in this world there is no escape from the consequences of playing false to a friend; it is a great sin like unto that of murdering a Brahman. Let Vrihaspati (therefore) officiate as priest to that Mahendra the supreme Deva (god), the highest one wielding the thunderbolt, and O prince, Samvarta will act as my priest, as neither his (Indra's) words, nor thine commend themselves to me.'

""'The Gandharva said, 'Do thou, O lion among princes, listen to the terrible war-cry of Vasava roaring, in the heavens. Assuredly, and openly will Mahendra hurl his thunderbolt at thee. Do thou therefore be-think thyself of thy good, for this is the time to do it.'"

"'Vyasa said, "Thus accosted by Dhritarashtra, and hearing the roar of howling Vasava, the king communicated this intelligence to Samvarta steadfast in devotion and the highest of all virtuous men.

""'Marutta said, 'Verily this rain-cloud floating in the air indicates that Indra must be near at present, therefore, O prince of Brahmanas, I seek shelter from thee. Do thou, O best of Brahmanas, remove this fear of Indra from my mind. The Wielder of the thunderbolt is coming encompassing the ten directions of space with his terrible and superhuman refulgence and my assistants at this sacrificial assembly have been overcome with fright.'

""'Samvarta said, 'O lion among kings, thy fear of Sakra will soon be dispelled, and I shall soon remove this terrible pain by means of my magic lore (incantation); be calm and have no fear of being overpowered by Indra. Thou hast nothing to fear from the god of a hundred sacrifices. I shall use my staying charms, O king, and the weapons of all the gods will avail them not. Let the lightening flash in all the directions of space, and the winds entering into the clouds pour down the showers amid the forests and the waters deluge the heavens and the flashes of lightning that are seen will avail not. Thou hast nothing to fear, let Vasava pour down the rains and blast his terrific thunderbolt where he will, floating among the watery masses (clouds) for thy destruction, for the god Vahnni (Agni) will protect thee in every way, and make thee attain all the objects of thy desire.'

""'Marutta said, 'This appalling crash of the thunderbolt together with the howling of the winds, seem terrible to my ears and my heart is afflicted again and again, O Brahmana, and my peace of mind is gone at present.'

""'Samvarta said, 'O king, the fear in thy mind from this terrible thunderbolt will leave thee presently. I shall dispel the thunder by the aid of the winds, and setting aside all fear from thy mind, do thou accept a boon from me according to thy heart's desire, and I shall accomplish it for thee.'

""'Marutta said, 'I desire, O Brahmana, that Indra all on a sudden should come in person at this sacrifice, and accept the oblation offered to him, and that all the other gods also come and take their own shares of the offerings and accept the libations of Soma offered to them.'

""'Samvarta said, 'I have by the power of my incantations attracted Indra in person to this sacrifice. Behold, O monarch, Indra coming with his horses, and worshipped by the other gods hastening to this sacrifice.'

""'Then the lord of the Devas attended by the other gods and riding in his chariot drawn by the most excellent steeds, approached the sacrificial altar of that son of Avikshit and drank the Soma libations of that unrivalled monarch. And king Marutta with his priest rose to receive Indra coming with the host of gods and well-pleased in mind, he welcomed the lord of the Devas with due and foremost honours according to the Sastras.

""""Samvarta said, 'Welcome to thee, O Indra, by thy presence here, O learned one, this sacrifice has been made grand. O slayer of Vala and Vritra, do thou again quaff this Soma juice produced by me today.'

""""Marutta said, 'Do thou look with kindness upon me, I bow unto thee, O Indra, by thy presence, my sacrifice has been perfected, and my life too blessed with good results. O Surendra, this excellent Brahmana, the younger brother of Vrihaspati is engaged in performing my sacrifices.'

""""Indra said, 'I know thy priest, this highly energetic ascetic, the younger brother of Vrihaspati, at whose invitation I have come to this sacrifice. I am, O monarch, well-pleased with thee and my resentment against thee hath been destroyed.'

""""Samvarta said, 'If, O prince of the Devas, thou art pleased with us, do thou thyself give all the directions for this sacrifice, and O Surendra, thyself ordain the sacrificial portions (for the gods), so that, O god, all the world may know that it hath been done by thee.'"

""'Vyasa said, "Thus accosted by the son of Angira, Sakra himself gave directions to all the gods to erect the hall of assembly, and a thousand well-furnished excellent rooms looking grand as in a picture, and speedily to complete the staircase massive and durable, for the ascent of the Gandharvas and Apsaras and to furnish that portion of the sacrificial ground reserved for the dance of the Apsaras, like unto the palace of Indra in the heaven. O king, thus directed, the renowned dwellers of heaven speedily fulfilled the directions of Sakra. And then, O king, Indra well-pleased and adored, thus said to king Marutta,—'O prince, by associating with thee at this sacrifice, thine ancestors who have gone before thee, as well as the other gods have been highly gratified and have accepted the oblations offered by thee. And now, O king, let the foremost of regenerate beings offer on the sacrificial altar a red bull appertaining to the Fire-god and a sacred and duly consecrated blue bull with a variegated skin, appertaining to the Viswedevas.' Then, O king, the sacrificial ceremony grew in splendour, wherein the gods themselves collected the food, and Sakra, the lord of the gods, possessed of horses, and worshipped by the Brahmanas, became an assistant at the sacrifice. And then the high-souled Samvarta ascending the altar, and looking radiant as the second embodiment of the blazing fire, loudly addressing the gods with complaisance, offered oblations of clarified butter to the fire with incantation of the sacred hymns. And then the slayer of Vala first drank the Soma juice, and then the assembly of other gods drank Soma. And then in happiness and with the king's permission they returned home and well-pleased and delighted. Then that monarch, the slayer of his enemies, with a delighted heart, placed heaps of gold on diverse spots, and distributing the immense wealth to the Brahmanas, he looked glorious like Kuvera, the god of wealth. And with a buoyant heart, the king filled his treasury with different kinds of wealth, and with the permission of his spiritual preceptor, he returned (to his kingdom) and continued to rule the entire realm extending to the borders of the sea. So virtuous in this world was that king, at whose sacrifice such an enormous quantity of gold was collected, and now, O prince, thou must collect that gold and worshipping the gods with due rites, do thou perform this sacrifice."

"Vaisampayana continued, 'Then the Pandava prince Yudhishthira was delighted on hearing this speech of the son of Satyavati (Vyasa), and desirous of performing his sacrifice with those riches, he held repeated consultations with his ministers.'"

SECTION XI.

"Vaisampayana said, 'When Vyasa of wonderful achievements had concluded his speech to the king, the highly-puissant son of Vasudeva (Krishna) also addressed him. Knowing the king, the son of Pritha, afflicted in mind, and bereft of his relatives and kinsmen slain in battle, and appearing crest-fallen like the sun darkened eclipse, or fire smothered by smoke, that prop of the Vrishni race (Krishna), comforting the son of Dharma, essayed to address him thus.

"'Vasudeva said, "All crookedness of heart leads to destruction (perdition?) and all rectitude leads to Brahman (spiritual excellence). If this and this only is the aim and object of all true wisdom, then what can mental distraction do (to one who understands this)? Thy Karma has not yet been annihilated, nor have thy enemies been subjugated, for thou dost not yet know the enemies that are still lurking within thine own flesh. I shall (therefore) relate to thee truly as I have heard it, the story of the war of Indra with Vritra as it took place. In ancient times the Prithivi (earth), O king, was encompassed by Vritra, and by this abstraction of earthly matter, the seat of all odour, there arose bad odours on all sides, and the Performer of a hundred sacrifices (Indra), being much enraged by this act, hurled his thunderbolt at Vritra. And being deeply wounded by the thunderbolt of mighty Indra, Vritra entered into the (waters), and by doing so he destroyed their property. The waters being seized by Vritra, their liquid property left them. At this Indra became highly enraged and again smote him with his thunderbolt. And he (Vritra) smitten by the thunderbolt by the most powerful Indra betook himself to the Jyoti (luminous matter) and abstracted its inherent property. The luminous matter being overwhelmed by Vritra and its property, colour and form being thereby lost, the wrathful Indra again hurled his thunderbolt at him. And thus wounded again by Indra of immeasurable power, Vritra entered all on a sudden into the Vayu (gaseous matter). and thereafter made away with its inherent property. And this matter being overpowered by Vritra and its property, viz., touch being lost, Indra became again filled with wrath and flung his thunderbolt at him. And wounded therein by the mighty (Indra), he overwhelmed the Akasa (ether), and took away its inherent property, and the Akasa being overwhelmed by Vritra, and its property, sound being destroyed, the god of a hundred sacrifices highly incensed, again smote him with his thunderbolt. And thus smitten by the mighty Indra, he suddenly entered into his (Sakra's) body, and took away its essential attributes. And overtaken by Vritra, he was filled with great illusion. And, O venerable sir, the mightiest of Bharata's race, we have heard that Vasishtha comforted Indra (when he was thus afflicted) and that the god of a hundred sacrifices slew Vritra in his body by means of his invisible thunderbolt, and know, O prince, that this religious mystery was recited by Sakra to the great sages, and they in turn told it to me."'"

SECTION XII.

"'Vasudeva said, "There are two kinds of ailments, physical and mental. They are produced by the mutual action of the body and mind on each other, and they never arise without the interaction of the two. The ailment that is produced in the body, is called the physical ailment, and that which has its seat in the mind, is known as the mental ailment. The cold, the warm (phlegm and bile) as well as the windy humours, O king, are the essential transformations generated in the physical body, and when these humours are evenly distributed, and are present in due proportions, they are said to be symptomatic of good health. The warm humour is acted upon (allayed) by the cold, and the cold by the warm. And Sattwa, Rajas and Tamas are the attributes of the soul, and it is said by the learned that their presence in due proportions indicates health (of the mind). But if any of the three preponderates, some remedy is enjoined (to restore the equilibrium). Happiness is overcome by sorrow, and sorrow by pleasure. Some people while afflicted by sorrow, desire to recall (past) happiness, while others, while in the enjoyment of happiness, desire to recall past sorrow. But thou, O son of Kunti, dost neither desire to recall thy sorrows nor thy happiness; what else dost thou desire to recall barring this delusion of sorrow? Or, perchance, O son of Pritha, it is thy innate nature, by which thou art at present overpowered. Thou dost not desire to recall to thy mind the painful sight of Krishna standing in the hall of assembly with only one piece of cloth to cover her body, and while she was in her menses and in the presence of all the Pandavas. And it is not meet that thou shouldst brood over thy departure from the city, and thy exile with the hide of the antelope for thy robe, and thy wanderings in the great forest, nor shouldst thou recall to thy mind the affliction from Jatasura, the fight with Chitrasena, and thy troubles from the Saindhavas. Nor is it proper, O son of Pritha, and conqueror of thy foes, that thou shouldst recall the incident of Kichaka's kicking Draupadi, during the period of thy exile passed in absolute concealment, nor the incidents of the fight which took place between thyself and Drona and Bhishma. The time has now arrived, when thou must fight the battle which each must fight single-handed with his mind. Therefore, O chief of Bharata's race, thou must now prepare to carry the struggle against thy mind, and by dint of abstraction and the merit of thine own Karma, thou must reach the other side of (overcome) the mysterious and unintelligible (mind). In this war there will be no need for any missiles, nor for friends, nor attendants. The battle which is to be fought alone and single-handed has now arrived for thee. And if vanquished in this struggle, thou shalt find thyself in the most wretched plight, and O son of Kunti, knowing this, and acting accordingly, shalt thou attain success. And knowing this wisdom and the destiny of all creatures, and following the conduct of thy ancestors, do thou duly administer thy kingdom."'"

SECTION XIII.

"'Vasudeva said, "O scion of Bharata's race, salvation is not attained by foregoing the external things (like kingdom, etc), it is only attained by giving up things which pander to the flesh (body). The virtue and happiness which are attainable by the person who has renounced only the external objects, but who is at the same time engrossed by passions and weakness of the flesh, let these be the portion of our enemies. The word with two letters is Mrit-yu (death of the soul or perdition), and the word with three letters is Sas-wa-ta (Brahman) or the eternal spirit. The consciousness that this or that thing is mine, or the state of being addicted to worldly objects is Mrityu and the absence of that feeling is Saswatam. And these two, Brahman and Mrityu, O king, have their seats in the souls of all creatures, and remaining unseen, they, without doubt, wage war with each other. And if, O Bharata, it be true that no creature is ever destroyed, then one doth not make oneself guilty of the death of a creature by piercing (destroying) its body. What matters the world to a man, if having acquired the sovereignty of the whole earth with its mobile and immobile creation, he does not become attached to it, or engrossed in its enjoyment. But the man who having renounced the world, has taken to the life of the recluse in the forest, living on wild roots and edibles, if such a man, O son of Pritha, has a craving for the good things of the world, and is addicted to them, he may be said to bear Mrityu (death) in his mouth. Do thou, O Bharata, watch and observe the character of thy external and internal enemies, (by means of thy spiritual vision). And the man who is able to perceive the nature of the eternal reality is able to overreach the influence of the great fear (perdition). Men do not look with approbation upon the conduct of those who are engrossed in worldly desires and there is no act without having a desire (at its root) and all (Kama) desires are, as it were, the limbs (offshoots) of the mind. Therefore, wise men knowing this subjugate their desires. The Yogi who holds communion with the Supreme Spirit, knows Yoga to be the perfect way (to salvation) by reason of the practices of his many former births. And remembering that, what the soul desires, is not conducive to piety and virtue, but that the suppression of the desires is at the root of all true virtue, such men do not engage in the practice of charity, Vedic learning, asceticism and Vedic rites whose object is attainment of worldly prosperity, ceremonies, sacrifices, religious rules and meditation, with the motive of securing any advantage thereby. By way of illustration of this truth, the sages versed in ancient lore, recite these Gathas called by the name of Kamagita, do thou O Yudhishthira, listen to the recital of them in detail. (Kama says) No creature is able to destroy me without resorting to the proper methods (viz., subjugating of all desires and practice of Yoga etc.) If a man knowing my power, strive to destroy me by muttering prayers etc., I prevail over him by deluding him with the belief that I am the subjective ego within him. If he wish to destroy me by means of sacrifices with many presents, I deceive him by appearing in his mind as a most virtuous creature amongst the mobile creation, and if he wish to annihilate me by mastering the Vedas and Vedantas, I over reach him by seeming to his mind to be the soul of virtue amongst the immobile creation. And if the man whose strength lies in truth, desire to overcome me by patience, I appear to him as his mind, and thus he does not perceive my existence, and if the man of austere religious practices, desire to destroy me by means of asceticism, I appear in the guise of asceticism in his mind, and thus he is prevented from knowing me, and the man of learning, who with the object of attaining salvation desires to destroy me, I frolic and laugh in the face of such a man intent on salvation. I am the everlasting one without a compeer, whom no creature can kill or destroy. For this reason thou too, O prince, divert thy desires (Kama) to Virtue, so that, by this means, thou mayst attain what is well for thee. Do thou therefore make preparations for the due performance of the horse sacrifice with presents, and various other sacrifices of great splendour, and accompanied with presents. Let not therefore grief overpower thee again, on beholding thy friends lying slain on the battlefield. Thou canst not see the men slain in this battle alive again. Therefore shouldst thou perform magnificent sacrifices with presents, so that thou mayst attain fame in this world, and reach the perfect way (hereafter)."'"

SECTION XIV.

"Vaisampayana said, 'With such speeches as these, was the royal saint Yudhishthira, bereft of his friends, consoled by those sages of great ascetic merits. And O monarch, that lord of men exhorted by the worshipful Viswarasraba himself, and by Dwaipayana (Vyasa), Krishna Devasthana, Narada, Bhima, Nakula, Krishna (Draupadi), Sahadeva, and the sharpwitted Vijaya, as well as by other great men, and Brahmanas versed in the Sastras, became relieved of all mental affliction and sorrow arising from the death of his dear relations. And that monarch Yudhishthira after performing the obsequial ceremonies of his departed friends, and honouring the Brahmanas and Devas (gods), brought the kingdom of the earth with its girdle of oceans, under his sway. And that prince of Kuru's race having regained his kingdom, with a tranquil mind, thus addressed Vyasa, Narada and the other sages who were present. "I have been comforted by the words of so great, ancient and aged saints as yourselves, and I have now no cause left for the least affliction. And likewise, I have attained great wealth, with which I may worship the gods. Therefore, with your assistance, I shall now perform the sacrifice, O the best of regenerate beings. We have heard that those (Himalayan) regions are full of wonders. Therefore, O Brahmana, saint and grandsire do thou so ordain that under thy protection we may safety reach the Himalaya mountains, the performance of my sacrifice being entirely within thy control, and then the adorable celestial saint Narada and Devasthana have also addressed exquisite and well-meaning words for our well being. No unlucky man in times of great tribulation and distress, has ever the good fortune to secure the services of such preceptors and friends approved by all virtuous men." Thus addressed by the king, those great saints, bidding the king and Krishna and Arjuna to repair to the Himalayan regions, then and there vanished in the presence of the assembled multitude, and the king, the lordly son of Dharma, then seated himself there for a while. And the Pandavas then in consequence of the death of Bhishma, were engaged in performing his funeral ceremonies. And their time, while thus engaged, seemed too long in passing and performing the last rites to the mortal remains of Bhishma, Karna and other foremost Kauravas, they gave away large presents to Brahmanas. And then the foremost descendant of Kuru again performed with Dhritarashtra the funeral rites (of the heroes slain in battle), and having given away immense wealth to the Brahmanas, the Pandava chief with Dhritarashtra in advance, made this entry into the city of Hastina Nagar, and consoling his lordly uncle, possessed of eyes of wisdom, that virtuous prince continued to administer the earth with his brothers.'"

SECTION XV.

"Janamejaya said, 'O the best of regenerate beings, when the Pandavas had reconquered and pacified their kingdom, what did the two warriors, Vasudeva and Dhananjaya do?'

"Vaisampayana said, 'O lord of the earth, Vasudeva and Dhananjaya were highly pleased when the Pandavas had succeeded in regaining and pacifying their dominions, and they deported themselves with great satisfaction, like unto Indra and his consort in the celestial regions, and amidst picturesque woodland sceneries, and tablelands of mountains, and sacred places of pilgrimage, and lakes and rivers, they travelled with great pleasure like the two Aswins in the Nandana garden of Indra. And, O Bharata, the high-souled Krishna and the son of Pandu (Dhananjaya) entering the beautiful hall of assembly at Indraprastha, whiled away their time in great merriment. And there, O prince, they passed their time in recounting the stirring incidents of the war, and the sufferings of their past lives. And those two high-souled ancient sages, glad at heart, recited the genealogy of the races of saints and gods. Then Kesava, knowing the full import of all matters, addressed Partha in a sweet and beautiful speech of excellent style and import. And then Janarddana comforted the son of Pritha afflicted by the death of his sons, and thousands of other relatives. And he of great ascetic merit and knowing the science of all things having duly consoled him, Arjuna rested for a while, as if a great burden had been removed from his own person. Then Govinda (Krishna) consoling

Arjuna with sweet speech addressed these well-reasoned words to him.

"'Vasudeva said, "O Arjuna, the terror of thine enemies, this whole earth has been conquered by the king, the son of Dharma, relying on the power of thy arms. And O the best of men, the virtuous king Yudhishthira now enjoys the sovereignty of the earth without a rival, by the might of Bhimasena and the twin brothers. O thou who knowest what virtue is, it was by righteousness alone that the king has been able to regain his kingdom free from all enemies (thorns), and it was by the action of righteousness that king Suyodhana has been killed in battle, and, O son of Pritha and pillar of the Kuru race, the wicked sons of Dhritarashtra, avaricious, always rude in speech, and bent upon an unrighteous course of conduct, having been exterminated with their followers, the king, the son of Dharma and lord of the earth, now peaceably enjoys the entire kingdom of the earth with thy aid, and I too, O son of Pandu, have been pleasantly whiling away my time in thy company, amidst woodland scenes. O terror of thine enemies, what more need I tell thee, but that where thou and Pritha, and the king, the son of Dharma, and the mighty Bhimasena and the two sons of Madri are, there am I attracted with exquisite delight. O descendant of Kuru, in these delightful and sacred and heaven-like halls of assembly a long time hath fleeted away in thy company without my seeing Vasudeva, Valadeva and other leaders of the Vrishni race. And now I am desirous of repairing to the city of Dwaravati. Do thou therefore, O most valorous of men, assent to my departure. When king Yudhishthira was smitten heavily with affliction, I with Bhishma, have recited to him many appropriate legends suited to the occasion with a view of assuaging his grief, and the pliant and high-minded Yudhishthira, though our sovereign and versed in all lore paid due heed to our words. That son of Dharma honours truth, and is grateful and righteous, therefore will his virtue and good sense and the stability of his power always endure. And now, O Arjuna, if it pleases thee, do thou go to that high-minded prince and tell him of my intention to depart from this place. For, O thou of mighty arms, even if death cometh to me, I am unwilling to do anything that may displease him, leaving alone my going to the city of Dwaravati. O son of Pritha and descendant of Kuru, I now tell thee truly, desiring to do only what is good and agreeable to thee, and there can be nothing equivocal in it in any way, that the necessity for my staying here no longer exists, because, O Arjuna, that monarch the son of Dhritarashtra hath been slain with his armies and attendants, and the earth, my friend, with its girdle of seas and its mountains and woods and forests, and the kingdom of the Kuru king filled with various gems, have passed under the sway of that wise son of Dharma. And O foremost prince of Bharata's race, may that virtuous prince administer the entire kingdom of the earth in righteousness, and with the respect and approbation of numerous high-souled Siddhas, and having his praises always extolled by the court heralds. Do thou, O chieftain of Kuru's race, accompany me to-day to the presence of the king, the great aggrandiser of the Kuru race, and sound him of my intended return to Dwaraka. As Yudhishthira the high-souled king of the Kurus always commands my love and respect, I have, O son of Pritha, placed this my body and all the wealth that I have in my house, at his disposal. And O prince Partha (son of Pritha), when this earth has come under thy sway and that of the worshipful Yudhishthira of excellent character, there no longer remains any necessity for my staying here except for my affection for thee." And O monarch, when the redoubtable Arjuna had been thus accosted by the noble-hearted Janarddana, he, showing all the honours due to him, sorrowfully replied by merely saying "be it so.""'

SECTION XVI. (*Anugita Parva*)

"Janamejaya said, 'When the high-souled Kesava and Arjuna after slaying their enemies repaired to the assembly rooms, what conversation, O regenerate one, took place between them?'

"Vaisampayana said, 'The son of Pritha (Arjuna), having recovered his own kingdom, joyously spent his time, without doing anything else, in the company of Krishna, his heart filled with delight, in that palace of celestial beauty. One day, those two listlessly proceeded to a particular part of the palace that looked, O king, like a veritable portion of Heaven. Themselves filled with delight, they were then surrounded by their relatives and attendants. Pandu's son, Arjuna, filled with joy in the company of Krishna, surveyed that delightful mansion, and then addressed his companion, saying, "O mighty-armed one, thy greatness became known to me upon the approach of the battle. O son of Devaki, thy form also, as the Lord of the universe, then became known to me! What thy holy self said unto me at that time, O Kesava, through affection, has all been forgotten by me, O chief of men, in consequence of the fickleness of my mind. Repeatedly, however, have I been curious on the subject of those truths. Thou again, O Madhava, wilt repair to Dwaraka soon."'

"Vaisampayana continued, 'Thus addressed by him, Krishna of mighty energy, that foremost of speakers, embraced Phalguna and replied unto him as follows.

"'Vasudeva said, "I made thee listen to truths that are regarded as mysteries. I imparted to thee truths that are eternal. Verily, I discoursed to thee on Religion in its true form and on all the eternal regions. It is exceedingly disagreeable to me to learn that thou didst not, from folly, receive what I imparted. The recollection of all that I told thee on that occasion will not come to me now. Without doubt, O son of Pandu, thou art destitute of faith and thy understanding is not good. It is impossible for me, O Dhananjaya, to repeat, in detail, all that I said on that occasion. That religion (about which I discoursed to thee then) is more than sufficient for understanding Brahma. I cannot discourse on it again in detail. I discoursed to thee on Supreme Brahma, having concentrated myself in Yoga. I shalt now, however, recite to thee an old history upon the same topic. O foremost of all persons, observant of duty, listen to everything I now say, so that, with an understanding adapted to my teaching, thou mayst succeed in attaining to the highest end. O chastiser of foes, on one occasion, a Brahmana came to us from the regions of Heaven. Of irresistible energy, he came from the regions of the Grandsire. He was duly reverenced by us. Listen, O son of Pritha, without yielding to scruples of any kind, to what he, O chief of Bharata's race, said, in answer to our enquiries, agreeably to heavenly forms.

""The Brahmana said, 'That which thou askest me, O Krishna, connected with the religion of Moksha (Emancipation), led by thy compassion for all creatures (and not for thy own good),—that, indeed, which destroys all delusion, O thou that art possessed of supreme puissance[638] I shall now tell thee duly, O slayer of Madhu. Do thou listen with concentrated attention as I discourse to thee, O Madhava. A Brahmana of the name of Kasyapa, possessed of penances and the foremost of all persons conversant with duties, came to a certain other Brahmana who had become conversant with all the mysteries of

---

[638] Bhutanam etc. is explained by Nilakantha as no swasya, and the vocative vibho is taken as Paramatman.

religion.[639] Indeed, the latter had mastered all the knowledge which the scriptures teach respecting the departure and reappearance of beings and possessed that direct knowledge of all things which Yoga gives. He was well skilled in the truths of all topics relating to the world. He had mastered the truth about pleasure and pain. He knew the truth about birth and death, and understood the distinctions between merit and demerit. He was a beholder of the ends attained to by embodied creatures high and low in consequence of their acts. He lived like one emancipated from the world. Crowned with ascetic success and possessed of perfect tranquillity of soul, he had all his senses under complete control. He seemed to blaze with the resplendence of Brahma and was capable of going everywhere at will. He knew the science of disappearing at will from before the eyes of all. He used to rove in the company of invisible Siddhas and celestial musicians. He used to sit and converse with them on some spot retired from the bustle of humanity. He was as unattached to all things as the wind. Kasyapa having heard of him truly, desired to see him. Possessed of intelligence, that foremost of all Brahmanas, approached the sage. Himself possessed of penances, Kasyapa, moved by the desire of acquiring merit, fell, with a rapt heart, at the feet of the sage when he had seen all those wonderful attributes. Filled with wonder at the sight of those extraordinary accomplishments, Kasyapa began to wait upon that foremost of all Brahmanas, with the dutiful reverence of a disciple waiting upon his preceptor and succeeded in propitiating him. By his devotion, O scorcher of foes, rendering to him the obedience due from a disciple to a preceptor, Kasyapa gratified that Brahmana who possessed all these accomplishments and was endued, besides, with scriptural learning and excellent conduct. Gratified with Kasyapa, that Brahmana one day addressed him cheerfully and spoke as follows, with an eye to the highest success. Listen to those words, O Janarddana, as I repeat them.'

""'The ascetic crowned with success said, 'By diverse acts, O son, as also by the aid of merit, mortal creatures attain to diverse ends here and residence in Heaven. Nowhere is the highest happiness; nowhere can residence be eternal. There are repeated falls from the highest regions acquired with such sorrow. In consequence of my indulgence in sin, I had to attain to diverse miserable and inauspicious ends, filled as I was with lust and wrath, and deluded by cupidity. I have repeatedly undergone death and rebirth. I have eaten diverse kinds of food, I have sucked at diverse breasts. I have seen diverse kinds of mothers, and diverse fathers dissimilar to one another. Diverse kinds of happiness have been mine and diverse kinds of misery, O sinless one. On diverse occasions have I been separated from what was agreeable and united with what was disagreeable. Having earned wealth with great toil I have had to put up with its loss. Insults and excessive misery I have received from king and relatives. Mental and physical pain, of great severity, have been mine. Humiliations I have undergone, and death and immurement under circumstances of great severity. Falls into Hell have been mine, and great tortures in the domains of Yama. Decrepitude and diseases have repeatedly assailed me, and calamities, as frequent, in copious measure. In this world I have repeatedly undergone all those afflictions that flow from a perception of all pairs of opposites. After all this, one day, overwhelmed with sorrow, blank despair came upon me. I took refuge in the Formless. Afflicted as I was with great distress, I gave up the world with all its joys and sorrows.[640] Understanding then this path, I exercised myself in it in this world.

[639] Agatagamam implies, as explained by the commentator, praptasastrarahasyam.

[640] Nirakarasritena is explained by Nilakantha as Asamprajnatas-samadhi-samadhigamya Brhamabhavasritena, implying reliance on Brahman by having recourse to Samadhi or a suspension of all

Afterwards, through tranquillity of soul, I attained to this success that thou seest. I shall not have to come to this world again (after my departure hence). Verily, till I attain to absorption into eternal Brahman, till, in fact, the final dissolution of the universe, I shall look on those happy ends that will be mine, and on those beings that constitute this universe.[641] Having acquired this excellent success, I shall, after departing from this world, proceed, to what is above it (i.e., Satyaloka) and thence to what is higher (i.e., absorption into Brahman). Verily, I shall attain to the condition, which is unmanifest aspect of Brahman. Let no doubt be thine as regards this. O scorcher of foes, I shall not return to this world of mortal creatures. O thou of great wisdom, I have become gratified with thee. Tell me what I shall do for thee. The time has come for the accomplishment of that purpose for which thou hast come hither. Verily, I know that object for which thou hast sought me. I shall soon depart from this world. Hence it is that I have given thee this hint. O thou of great wisdom and experience, I have been highly gratified with thee for thy behaviour. Do thou question me. I shall discourse on what is beneficial to thee, agreeably to thy desire. I think thy intelligence is great. Indeed, I applaud it much, for it was with the aid of that intelligence that thou wert able to recognise me. Surely, O Kasyapa, thou art possessed of great intelligence.""""

SECTION XVII.

"'Vasudeva said, "touching the feet of that sage, the Brahmana asked him some questions that were exceedingly difficult to answer. That foremost of all righteous persons then discoursed on those duties that were referred to.

""""Kasyapa said, 'How does the body dissolve away, and how is another acquired? How does one become emancipated after passing through a repeated round of painful rebirths? Enjoying Prakriti for some time, how does Jiva cast off the particular body (which Prakriti gives)? How does Jiva, freed from the body, attain to what is different from it (viz., Brahman)? How does a human being enjoy (and endure the fruits of) the good and bad acts done by him? Where do the acts exist of one that is devoid of body?'[642]

""""The Brahmana said,—'Thus urged by Kasyapa, the emancipated sage answered those questions one after another. Do thou listen to me, O scion of the Vrishi race, as I recite to thee the answers he made.'

""""The Emancipated sage said, 'Upon the exhaustion of those acts capable of prolonging life and bringing on fame which are done in a particular body that Jiva assumes, the embodied Jiva, with the span of his life shortened, begins to do acts hostile to life and health. On the approach of destruction, his understanding turns away from the proper course. The man of uncleansed soul, after even a correct apprehension of his constitution and strength and of the season of both his own life and of the year, begins to

---

functions of both body and mind (through Yoga) and arrival at that state which is one of perfect unconsciousness.

[641] The dissolution here spoken of is the Mahapralaya and not the Khanda or Avantara Pralayas. Till then, the sage will look upon all beings, i.e., their repeated migrations.

[642] The commentator explains that altogether seven questions are asked. The first is about the dissolution of the body. The second relates to the manner of re-acquiring a body. The third has reference to the manner in which rebirth may be avoided. The fourth relates to the causes that operate for giving a body to Jiva. By Prakriti is meant Nature or that Nescience which is the cause of body. The fifth relates to the Anyat or Param, viz., how final Emancipation or absorption into Brahman takes place. The sixth pertains to the manner in which the fruits of acts are enjoyed or endured. The seventh enquires after the way in which acts attach to Jiva even when devoid of a body.

eat at irregular intervals and to eat such food as is hostile to him.[643] At such a time he indulges in practices that are exceedingly harmful. He sometimes eats excessively and sometimes abstains altogether from food. He eats bad food or bad meat or takes bad drinks, or food that has been made up of ingredients incompatible with one another. He eats food that is heavy in excess of the measure that is beneficial, or before the food previously taken has been digested. He indulges in physical exercise and sexual pleasure in excess of the due measure, or through avidity for work, suppresses the urgings of his corporeal organism even when they become pronounced. Or, he takes food that is very juicy, or indulges in sleep during daytime. Food that is not properly digested, of itself excites the faults, when the time comes.[644] From such excitement of the faults in his body, he gets disease ending in death itself. Sometimes the person engages in perverse or unnatural acts like hanging (for bringing about his death). Through these causes the living body of the creature dissolves away. Understand correctly the manner as I declare it to thee.[645] Urged on by the Wind which becomes violent, the heat in the body, becoming excited and reaching every part of the body one after another, restrains all the (movements of the) vital breaths. Know truly that excited all over the body, the heat becomes very strong, and pierces every vital part where life may be said to reside. In consequence of this, Jiva, feeling great pain, quickly takes leave of its mortal casement. Know, O foremost of regenerate persons, that when the vital parts of the physical organism become thus afflicted, Jiva slips away from the body, overwhelmed with great pain. All living creatures are repeatedly afflicted with birth and death. It is seen, O chief of Brahmanas, that the pain which is felt by a person when casting off his bodies is like what is felt by him when first entering the womb or when issuing out of it. His joints become almost dislocated and he derives much distress from the waters (of the womb).[646] Urged on by (another) violent wind, the wind that is in the body becomes excited through cold, and dissolves away the union of matter (called the body) into its respective elements numbering five.[647] That wind which resides in the vital breaths called Prana and Apana occurring within this compound of the five primal elements, rushes upwards, from a situation of distress, leaving the embodied creature. It is even thus that the wind leaves the body. Then is seen breathlessness. The man then becomes destitute of heat, of breath, of beauty, and of consciousness. Deserted by Brahman (for Jiva is Brahman), the person is said to be dead. By those ducts through which he perceives all sensuous objects, the

---

[643] Kala here means both the season of the year and the age of the person. Food that is beneficial in summer is not so in winter, or that which is beneficial in youth is otherwise at old age. All the texts that I have seen have viditwa and not aviditiwa which Telang takes in his version for the Sacred Books of the East. Kala is always interpreted by the commentators of Charaka as referring to either period of life or period of the year. This, as well as the following verses, relates to the laws of health as expounded by Charaka.

[644] The faults are three, viz., Wind, Bile, and Phlegm. When existing in a state of harmony, they produce health. When one is excited or two, or all, indisposition sets in. They are called dosha or faults, because of their liability to be excited and produce disease. Telang, not suspecting that the whole passage is a reproduction of a passage in the ancient work edited by Charaka, misunderstands some expressions and wrongly renders doshan into 'disorders.'

[645] Jivitam in the second line seems to be an objective of sariram in the first.

[646] Garbha-sankramane is explained by Nilakantha as entering the foetus in the womb after casting off the body appertaining to the other world. I think Telang is not correct in his version of 19 and 20. Atisarpana can never imply 'exhaustion'; hence, karmanam can never be the reading he adopts. Besides tadrisam seems to settle the question. The tortures felt at death are similar to those at birth.

[647] Sambutatwam is sanhatatwam. Niyachachati is nasyyati. Vayu is understood in the second line, or that in the first line of the next verse may be taken as the nom. of niyachachati.

bearer of the body no longer perceives them. It is the eternal Jiva who creates in the body in those very ducts the life-breaths that are generated by food. The elements gathered together become in certain parts firmly united. Know that those parts are called the vitals of the body. It is said so in the Sastras. When those vital parts are pierced, Jiva, rising up, enters the heart of the living creature and restrains the principle of animation without any delay. The creature then, though still endued with the principle of consciousness, fails to know anything. The vital parts being all overwhelmed, the knowledge of the living creature becomes overwhelmed by darkness. Jiva then, who has been deprived of everything upon which to stay, is then agitated by the wind. He then, deeply breathing a long and painful breath, goes out quickly, causing the inanimate body to tremble. Dissociated from the body, Jiva, however, is surrounded by his acts. He becomes equipped on every side with all his auspicious acts of merit and with all his sins. Brahmanas endued with knowledge and equipped with the certain conclusions of the scriptures, know him, from indications, as to whether he is possessed of merit or with its reverse. Even as men possessed of eyes behold the fire-fly appearing and disappearing amid darkness, men possessed of the eye of knowledge and crowned with success of penances, behold, with spiritual vision, Jiva as he leaves the body, as he is reborn, and as he enters the womb. It is seen that Jiva has three regions assigned to him eternally. This world where creatures dwell is called the field of action. Accomplishing acts good or bad, all embodied creatures attain to the fruits thereof. In consequence of their own acts, creatures acquire even here superior or inferior enjoyments. Doers of evil deeds here, in consequence of those acts of theirs, attain to Hell. This condition of sinking with head downwards, in which creatures are cooked, is one of great misery. It is such that a rescue therefrom is exceedingly difficult. Indeed, one should strive hard for saving oneself from this misery. Those regions where creatures dwell when they ascend from this world I shall now declare truly. Do thou listen to me with attention. By listening to what I say, thou shalt attain to firmness of understanding and a clear apprehension of (good and bad) acts. Know that even those are the regions of all creatures of righteous deeds, viz., the stellar worlds that shine in the firmament, the lunar disc, and the solar disc as well that shines in the universe in its own light. Upon the exhaustion, again, of their merits, they fall away from those regions repeatedly. There, in Heaven itself, is distinction of inferior, superior, and middling felicity. There, in Heaven itself, is discontent at sight of prosperity more blazing than one's own. Even these are the goals which I have mentioned in detail. I shall, after this, discourse to you on the attainment by Jiva of the condition of residence in the womb. Do thou hear me, with concentrated attention, O regenerate one, as I speak to thee!'"""

SECTION XVIII.

"""The Brahmana said, 'The acts, good and bad, that a Jiva does are not subject to destruction. Upon attainment of body after body, those acts produce fruits corresponding with them.[648] As a fruit-bearing tree, when the season comes of productivity, yields a large quantity of fruit, similarly merit, achieved with a pure heart, yields a large crop (of felicity). After the same fashion, sin, done with a sinful heart, produces a large crop of misery. The Soul (or Jiva), placing the mind ahead, addresses himself to action. Hear then how Jiva, equipt with all his acts and overwhelmed with lust and wrath, enters the womb.

---

[648] Pachante is phalam prayachhanti.

464

The vital seed, mixed with blood, enters the womb of females and becomes the field (of Jiva), good or bad, born of (his) acts. In consequence of his subtlety and the condition of being unmanifest, Jiva does not become attached to anything even after attaining to a body. Therefore, he is called Eternal Brahman.[649] That (viz., Jiva or Brahman) is the seed of all creatures. It is in consequence of Him that living creatures live. That Jiva, entering all the limbs of the foetus part by part, accepting the attribute of mind, and residing within all the regions that belong to Prana, supports (life). In consequence of this, the foetus becoming endued with mind begins to move its limbs.[650] As liquified iron, poured (into a mould), takes the form of the mould, know that the entrance of Jiva into the foetus is even such. As fire, entering a mass of iron, heats it greatly, do thou know that the manifestation of Jiva in the foetus is such. As a lamp, burning in a room, discovers (all things within it), after the same manner mind discovers the different limbs of the body.[651] Whatever acts, good or bad, Jiva does in a former body, have certainly to be enjoyed or endured by him. By such enjoyment and endurance former acts are exhausted, and other acts, again, accumulate, till Jiva succeed in acquiring a knowledge of the duties included in that contemplation which leads to Emancipation. Regarding this, I shall tell thee those acts by which Jiva, O best of men, while coursing through a repeated round of re-births, becomes happy. Gifts, observances of austerity, Brahmacharyya, bearing Brahman according to the ordinances laid down, self-restraint, tranquillity, compassion for all creatures, restraint of passions, abstentions from cruelty as also from appropriating what belongs to others, refraining from doing even mentally all acts that are false and injurious to living creatures on the Earth, reverently serving mother and father, honouring deities and guests, worship of preceptors, pity, purity, constant restraint of all organs, and causing of all good acts, are said to constitute the conduct of the good. From observance of such conduct, arises Righteousness which protects all creatures eternally. Such conduct one would always behold among persons that are good. Verily, such conduct resides there eternally. That course of practices to which persons of tranquil souls adhere indicates Righteousness. Among them is thrown that course of practices which constitutes eternal Righteousness. He who would betake himself to that Righteousness would never have to attain to a miserable end. It is by the conduct of the good that the world is restrained in the paths of Righteousness when it falls away. He that is a Yogin is Emancipated, and is, therefore, distinguished above these (viz., the good).[652] Deliverance from the world takes place, after a long time, of one who acts righteously and well on every occasion as he should. A living creature thus always meets with the acts done by him in a former life. All these acts constitute the cause in consequence of which he comes into this world in a state different from his true form.[653] There is a doubt in the world as

[649] Nilakantha explains this verse in a different way. According to him it means,—'in consequence of his subtlety and imperceptibility, Jiva does not become attached to anything. For this reason, one possessed of a knowledge of Brahman, having become cognisant of Brahman and attained the great object of his desire, succeeds in becoming so (i.e., dissociated from all things).' This interpretation seems to be a little far-fetched.

[650] Chetasa indicates upadhibhutena, for previously, Jiva was without upadhi. Pranasthaneshu implies Indriyagolokeshu or those vital parts which constitute the seats of the senses. Chetana does not, I think, mean 'consciousness.' It implies mind.

[651] Causes them to grow. I do not follow Nilakantha here.

[652] Nilakantha points out that one of the cha's indicates the reason or cause. Hence, the use of 'therefore' in the text.

[653] Vikrita does not necessarily mean degraded. It implies 'changed or altered.' Jiva, who is pure and immaculate, takes birth in this world, falling away from his true status of Brahman owing to his acts. Acts, again, are eternal, no beginning being conceivable.

regards the question. By what was the acceptance (by Jiva) of a body first determined. The Grandsire of all the worlds, viz., Brahma having first formed a body of his own, then created the three worlds, in their entirety, of mobile and immobile creatures. Having first himself assumed a body, he then created Pradhana. That Pradhana is the material cause of all embodied creatures, by whom is all this covered and whom all came to know as the highest. This that is seen is said to be destructible; while the other is immortal and indestructible. This that (is seen) is said to be Kshara (the destructible); that, however, which is Para (the other) is the Immortal, (as also) Akshara (the Indestructible). Of each Purusha taken distributively, the whole is duality among these three.[654] Seen first (to appear in an embodied form) Prajapati (then) created all the primal elements and all immobile creatures. Even this is the ancient audition. Of that (acceptance of body), the Grandsire ordained a limit in respect of time, and migrations among diverse creatures and return or rebirth. All that I say is proper and correct, like to what a person who is endued with intelligence and who has seen his soul, would say on this topic of previous births.[655] That person who looks upon pleasure and pain as inconstant, which, indeed, is the correct view, who regards the body as an unholy conglomeration, and destruction as ordained in action, and who remembers that what little of pleasure there is, is really all pain, will succeed in crossing this terrible ocean of worldly migration that is so difficult to cross. Though assailed by decrepitude and death and disease, he that understands Pradhana beholds with an equal eye that Consciousness which dwells in all beings endued with consciousness. Seeking the supreme seat, he then becomes utterly indifferent to all (other) things. O best of men, I shall now impart instruction to thee, agreeably to truth, concerning this. Do thou, O learned Brahmana, understand in completeness that which constitutes the excellent knowledge, as I declare it, of that indestructible seat.'"'"

SECTION XIX.

"'"The Brahmana said, 'He who becomes absorbed in the one receptacle (of all things), freeing himself from even the thought of his own identity with all things,—indeed, ceasing to think of even his own existence,—gradually casting off one after another, will succeed in crossing his bonds.[656] That man who is the friend of all, who endures all, who is attached to tranquillity, who has conquered all his senses, who is divested of fear and wrath, and who is of restrained soul, succeeds in emancipating himself. He who behaves towards all creatures as towards himself, who is restrained,

---

[654] Parantwa-maritam-aksharam indicates two things, viz., Amritam and Aksharam. The first line speaks of Kshara, or the material case, or body; then of that which is para or other. This other is of two kinds, viz., Amritam or suddha-chaitanyam, implying Brahman in its condition of purity; and Aksharamt or Jiva as existing in the material case. In the second line, trayanam refers to Kshara, Amrita, and Akshara. Mithunam is duality, referring to that which is composed of Kshara and Akshara. What is stated in this verse is that every Purusha is a duality, made up of Kshara and Akshara. Telang gives a different version of the verse. He ignores the word trayanam totally, and takes Mithunam as implying a couple (male and female). All the texts I have seen contain trayanam.

[655] Atra purvajamnani (vishaye) yatha kaschit Medhavi etc., (vadet), seems to be the correct order of the words. Telang translates the first line differently.

[656] Ekayana is the one receptacle of all things, viz., Brahman. Tushni implies ahamevedam sarvamasmityabhimanamapyakurvan i.e., 'without even retaining the consciousness of his own identity with everything.' Kinchikachintayan—i.e., not even thinking that he is existing. Purvam purvam parityajya implies the gradual merging of the grosser in the subtler, i.e., the successive stages of Yoga before absorption into Brahman. I follow Nilakantha.

pure, free from vanity and divested of egoism is regarded as emancipated from everything. He also is emancipated who looks with an equal eye upon life and death, pleasure and pain, gain and loss, agreeable and disagreeable. He is in every way emancipated who does not covet what belongs to others, who never disregards any body, who transcends all pairs of opposites, and whose soul is free from attachment. He is emancipated who has no enemy, no kinsman, and no child, who has cast off religion, wealth, and pleasure, and who is freed from desire or cupidity. He becomes emancipated who acquires neither merit nor demerit, who casts off the merits and demerits accumulated in previous births, who wastes the elements of his body for attaining to a tranquillised soul, and who transcends all pairs of opposites. He who abstains from all acts, who is free from desire or cupidity, who looks upon the universe as unenduring or as like an Aswattha tree, ever endued with birth, death and decrepitude, whose understanding is fixed on renunciation, and whose eyes are always directed towards his own faults, soon succeeds in emancipating himself from the bonds that bind him.[657] He that sees his soul void of smell, of taste and touch, of sound, of belongings, of vision, and unknowable, becomes emancipated.[658] He who sees his soul devoid of the attributes of the five elements to be without form and cause, to be really destitute of attributes though enjoying them, becomes emancipated.[659] Abandoning, with the aid of the understanding, all purposes relating to body and mind, one gradually attains to cessation of separate existence, like a fire unfed with fuel.[660] One who is freed from all impressions, who transcends all pairs of opposites, who is destitute of all belongings, and who uses all his senses under the guidance of penances, becomes emancipated.[661] Having become freed from all impressions, one then attains to Brahma which is Eternal and supreme, and tranquil, and stable, and enduring, and indestructible. After this I shall declare the science of Yoga to which there is nothing superior, and how Yogins, by concentration, behold the perfect soul.[662] I shall declare the instructions regarding it duly. Do thou learn from me those doors by which directing the soul within the body one beholds that which is without beginning and end.[663] Withdrawing the senses from their objects, one should fix the mind upon the soul; having previously undergone the severest austerities, one should practise that concentration of mind which leads to Emancipation.[664] Observant of penances and always practising concentration of mind, the learned Brahmana, endued with intelligence, should observe the precepts of the science of Yoga, beholding the soul in the body. If the good man succeeds in concentrating the mind on the soul, he then, habituated to

---

[657] The first half of the second line of 8 is read differently in the Bengal texts. Aswasthamavasam mudham implies 'without ease or happiness, endued with slavery and ignorance.'

[658] The Soul being destitute of these becomes Chinmatra, i.e., a pure Chit without the attributes superinduced upon it by Nescience or ignorance.

[659] Formlessness implies subtlety. 'Without cause' implies increate or as identical with eternal Brahman. Dissociation from attributes while enjoying them implies an emancipate condition.

[660] Nirvana, according to orthodox commentators, implies the annihilation or cessation of separate or individual existence by absorption into universal and eternal Brahman.

[661] The impressions caused by objects outside self are destroyed by those belonging to contemplation. The latter, again, should be destroyed before absorption into Brahman can occur.

[662] Siddham is explained as 'destitute of the errors due to Nescience.'

[663] Attnanam is Chittam; atmani is dehe; charayan is antarmukham kritwa; nityam is adyantasunyam. So Nilakantha.

[664] 'Fixing the mind upon the soul' is that concentration which leads to Emancipation. This becomes possible in consequence of severe austerities undergone previously.

exclusive meditation, beholds the Supreme soul in his own soul. Self-restrained, and always concentrated, and with all his senses completely conquered, the man of cleansed soul, in consequence of such complete concentration of mind, succeeds in beholding the soul by the soul. As a person beholding some unseen individual in a dream recognises him, saying,—This is he,—when he sees him after waking, after the same manner the good man having seen the Supreme Soul in the deep contemplation of Samadhi recognises it upon waking from Samadhi.[665] As one beholds the fibrous pith after extracting it from a blade of the Saccharum Munja, even so the Yogin beholds the soul, extracting it from the body. The body has been called the Saccharum Munja, and the fibrous pith is said to stand for the soul. This is the excellent illustration propounded by persons conversant with Yoga. When the bearer of a body adequately beholds the soul in Yoga, he then has no one that is master over him, for he then becomes the lord of the three worlds.[666] He succeeds in assuming diverse bodies according as he wishes. Turning away decrepitude and death, he neither grieves nor exults. The self-restrained man, concentrated in Yoga, can create (for himself) the godship of the very gods. Casting off his transient body he attains to immutable Brahma.[667] No fear springs up in him at even the sight of all creatures falling victims to destruction (before his eyes). When all creatures are afflicted,—he can never be afflicted by any one. Devoid of desire and possessed of a tranquil mind, the person in Yoga is never shaken by pain and sorrow and fear, the terrible effects that flow from attachment and affection. Weapons never pierce him; death does not exist for him. Nowhere in the world can be seen any one that is happier than he. Having adequately concentrated his soul, he lives steadily on himself. Turning off decrepitude and pain and pleasure, he sleeps in comfort. Casting off this human body he attains to (other) forms according to his pleasure. While one is enjoying the sovereignty that Yoga bestows, one should never fall away from devotion to Yoga.[668] When one, after adequate devotion to Yoga, beholds the Soul in oneself, one then ceases to have any regard for even him of a hundred sacrifices (Indra).[669] Hear now how one, habituating oneself to exclusive meditation, succeeds in attaining to Yoga. Thinking of that point of the compass which has the Sun behind it, the mind should be fixed, not outside, but in the interior of that mansion in which one may happen to live. Residing within that mansion, the mind should then, with all its outward and inward (operations), behold in that particular room in which one may stay. At that time when, having deeply meditated, one beholds the All (viz., Brahman, the Soul of the universe), there is then nothing external to Brahman where the mind may dwell. Restraining all the senses in a forest that is free from noise and that is uninhabited, with mind fixed thereon, one should meditate on the All (or universal Brahman) both outside and inside one's body. One

---

[665] I expand the verse a little to make it intelligible. The sense is this: having seen the supreme Soul in Samadhi, upon awaking from it, he recognises it in the universe, i.e., regards the universe to be nothing else than the Supreme Soul.

[666] This may also mean 'he has none superior to him; not even he that is the Lord of the universe.'

[667] The first line seems to be doubtful. The sense, as I understand it, is,—such a person becomes the god of the very gods. The causal verb karayate may be taken as equivalent to karoti.

[668] I follow Nilakantha in rendering the second line. The sense is clear, viz., that one should not fall away from the practice of Yoga, tempted by the puissance that Yoga brings. Telang renders the line 'one practising concentration should never become despondent.' I think, Nilakantha is right.

[669] Nilakantha notes that this indicates that only that Yogin who has not advanced much may be tempted by the desire of enjoyment. He, however, who has adequately devoted himself to Yoga feels no regard for Indra himself but can turn him away like Diogenes dismissing Alexander the Great.

should meditate on the teeth, the palate, the tongue, the throat, the neck likewise; one should also meditate on the heart and the ligatures of the heart!'[670]

""The Brahmana continued, 'Thus addressed by me, that intelligent disciple, O slayer of Madhu, once more asked me about this religion of Emancipation that is so difficult to explain. How does this food that is eaten from time to time become digested in the stomach? How does it become transformed into juice? How, again, into blood? How does it nourish the flesh, the marrow, the sinews, the bones? How do all these limbs of embodied creatures grow? How does the strength grow of the growing man? How occurs the escape of all such elements as are not nutritive, and of all impurities separately? How does this one inhale and again, exhale? Staying upon what particular part does the Soul dwell in the body? How does Jiva, exerting himself, bear the body? Of what colour and of what kind is the body in which he dwells again (leaving a particular body)? O holy one, it behoveth thee to tell me all this accurately, O sinless one,'—even thus was I interrogated by that learned Brahmana, O Madhava. I replied unto him, O thou of mighty arms, after the manner I myself had heard, O chastiser of all foes. 'As one placing some precious object in one's store-room should keep one's mind on it, so, placing the mind within one's own body, one should then, restraining all the senses, seek after the Soul, avoiding all heedlessness. One would, becoming always assiduous in this way and gratified with one's own self, within a very short time attain to that Brahma by beholding which one would become conversant with Pradhana.[671] He is not capable of being seized by the eye; nor even by all the senses.[672] It is only with the lamp of the mind that great Soul can be seen. He has hands and feet on all sides; he has ears on all sides; he dwells, pervading all things in the world.[673] Jiva beholds the Soul as extracted from the body (like the stalk from a blade of Saccharum Munja, when knowledge comes). Then casting off Brahma as invested with form, by holding the mind in the body, he beholds Brahma as freed from all attributes.[674] He sees the Soul with his mind, smiling as it were at the time. Depending upon that Brahma, he then attains to Emancipation in me.[675] O

---

[670] I have endeavoured to render verses 33 to 37 as literally as possible, under the guide of Nilakantha, omitting his inferences. The passage relates to the mysteries of Yoga. In the second line of 33, drishtapurvam disam, which has been rendered 'that point of the compass which has the Sun behind it,' means the instructions laid down in the Vedanta as based upon Srutis. Drishtam implies 'Sruti', for it is as authoritative as anything seen. 'Pura' implies a city, a citadel, or a mansion. Here it refers to the body. The avasatha within the pura refers to the chakra or nervous centres beginning with what is called the muladhara. At the time when Brahman is realised, the whole universe appears as Brahman and so nothing exists, besides Brahman, upon which the mind can then dwell. Telang, I think, is not correct in rendering manaschasya ... vahyatah as 'his mind should not any way wander outside'. The correct version would 'the mind is then nowhere,' implying that at that time the mind has nothing else to dwell upon. Kayamabhyantaram is kayamabhi and antaram, i.e., both within and without the body. The several parts of the body named, beginning with teeth, etc, refer to eating and other operations, all of which influence the mind and dispose it for purity and otherwise.

[671] i.e., that from which the entire universe has been created.

[672] Probably, 'by any of the senses'. The plural form occurs in the original.

[673] This answers the questions respecting the form of the Soul, says Nilakantha.

[674] I render this verse, following Nilakantha's gloss. The second line of 50, according to that commentator, refers to the ascension of the Yogin from Brahma vested with attributes to Brahma divested of all attributes. The tam does not refer to body, as Telang takes it, but to Brahma as endued with hands and feet on all sides, etc. Deheswam dharayan means 'restraining the mind within the body'. Kevalam Brahma is Brahma without attributes.

[675] The speaker here is the regenerate visitor of Krishna. The latter is repeating the words of that visitor. In this verse, Krishna, forgetting that he is merely reciting the words of another, refers to himself as the Supreme Brahman in whom one must merge for attaining to Emancipation.

foremost of regenerate ones, all this mystery has now been declared by me. I ask thy permission, for I shall leave this spot. Do thou (also) go withersoever thou pleasest.' Thus addressed by me, O Krishna, on that occasion, that disciple of mine, endued with austere penances, that Brahmana of rigid vows, went away according to his pleasure."

"'Vasudeva continued, "That best of Brahmanas, O son of Pritha, having said these words unto me, on that occasion, properly relating to the religion of Emancipation, disappeared then and there. Has this discourse been heard by thee, O son of Pritha, with mind directed solely towards it? Even this was what thou didst hear on that occasion while thou wert on thy car. It is my opinion, O son of Pritha, that this is difficult of being comprehended by one whose understanding is confused, or who has acquired no wisdom by study, or who eats food incompatible with his body, or whose Soul is not purified.[676] O chief of Bharata's race, this is a great mystery among the deities that has been declared (to thee). At no time or place, O son of Pritha, has this been heard by man in this world. O sinless one, no other man than thyself is deserving of hearing it. It is not, at this time, capable of being easily understood by one whose inner soul is confused. The world of the deities is filled, O son of Kunti, with those who follow the religion of actions. The cessation of the mortal form (by practising the religion of inaction) is not agreeable to the deities.[677] That goal, O son of Pritha, is the highest which is constituted by eternal Brahman where one, casting off the body, attains to immortality and becomes always happy. By adhering to this religion, even they who are of sinful birth, such as women and Vaisyas and Sudras, attain to the highest goal. What need be said then, O son of Pritha, of Brahmanas and Kshatriyas possessed of great learning, always devoted to the duties of their own orders and who are intent on (the acquisition of) the region of Brahma? This has been laid down with the reasons (on which it rests); and also the means for its acquisition; and its complete attainment and fruit, viz., Emancipation and the ascertainment of the truth regarding pain. O chief of Bharata's race, there is nothing else that is fraught with happiness greater than this. That mortal, O son of Pandu, who, endued with intelligence, and faith, and prowess, renounces as unsubstantial what is regarded as substantial by the world, succeeds within a short time in obtaining the Supreme by these means. This is all that is to be said,—there is nothing else that is higher than this. Yoga takes place in his case, O son of Pritha, who devotes himself to its constant practice for a period of six months."'"

SECTION XX.

"'Vasudeva said, "In this connection is cited the ancient narrative, O son of Pritha, of the discourse that took place between a married couple. A certain Brahmana's spouse, beholding the Brahmana, her husband who was a complete master of every kind of knowledge and wisdom, seated in seclusion, said unto him,—'Into what region shall I go, depending on thee as my husband,—thee that art seated, having cast off all (religious) acts, that art harsh in thy conduct towards me, and that art so undiscerning?[678] It has been

676 The second line of 56 is read variously.
677 Heaven is the reward of those who follow the religion of Pravritti or acts, such as sacrifices, religious observances, etc. The followers, however, of the religion of Nivritti or inaction, i.e., they who betake themselves to the path of knowledge, become emancipated. The deities derive their sustenance from the former and become even jealous of the latter, for the emancipate state is higher than that of the deities themselves.
678 Avichakshanam is undiscerning, in the sense of the husband's not knowing that the interrogatrix as wife, has no other refuge than her lord with all his defects.

heard by us that a wife attains to those regions which are acquired by her husband. What, indeed, is the goal that I shall attain, having obtained thee for my husband?'—Thus questioned, that Brahmana of tranquil soul then said unto her, smilingly,—'O blessed dame, I am not offended with these words of thine, O sinless one. Whatever acts exist that are adopted with the aid of others, that are seen (in consequence of their grossness), and that are true, are done as acts by men devoted to acts.[679] Those persons that are destitute of knowledge, only store delusion by acts. Freedom from acts, again, is incapable of being attained in this world for even a moment. From birth to the attainment of a different form, action good or bad, and accomplished by acts, mind, or speech, exists in all beings. Those paths (of action) which are characterised by visible objects (such as Soma-juice and ghee for libations) being destroyed by Rakshasas, turning away from them I have perceived the seat (of the soul) that is in the body, without the aid of the soul.[680] There dwells Brahma transcending all pairs of opposites; there Soma with Agni, and there the urger of the understanding (viz., Vayu) always moves, upholding all creatures.[681] It is for that seat that the Grandsire Brahman and others, concentrated in Yoga, worship the Indestructible. It is for that seat that men of learning and excellent vows, of tranquil souls, and of senses completely vanquished, strive.[682] That is not capable of being smelt by the sense of smell; nor tasted by the tongue; or touched by the organs of touch. It is by the mind that that is attained. It is incapable of being conquered by the eye. It transcends the sense of hearing. It is destitute of scent, taste, touch, and form as attributes. It is that from which proceeds the well-ordained universe, and it is that upon which it rests. The life-breaths called Prana and Apana and Samana and Vyana and Udana flow from it, and it is that into which they again enter. The breaths Prana and Apana move between Samana and Vyana. When the soul sleeps, both Samana and Vyana are absorbed.[683] Between Apana and Prana, Udana dwells, pervading all. Hence, Prana and Apana do not desert a sleeping person. In consequence of its controlling all the life-winds, the controlling breath is called Udana. Hence, utterers of Brahman undergo penances which have myself for their goal.[684] In the midst of all those life-breaths that swallow up one another and move within the body, blazes forth the fire called Vaiswanara made up of seven flames. The nose, the tongue, the eye, the skin, the ear which numbers the fifth, the mind, and the understanding,—these are the seven tongues of that Vaiswanara's flame. That which is smelt, that which is seen, that which is drunk, that which is touched, as also that which is heard, that which is thought of, and that which is understood,—these are the seven sorts of fuel for me. That which smells, that which eats, that which sees, that which touches, that which hears numbering the fifth; that which

---

[679] I follow Nilakantha. Telang adopts the views of Arjuna Misra and renders the first line as 'whatever acts are seized (by the touch, or seen, or heard, etc.') Grahyam, according to Nilakantha, implies those acts, like Diksha, etc, which are adopted with the aid of others.

[680] This seat, says Nilakantha, is called Avimukta and lies between the eyebrows and the nose.

[681] Nilakantha interprets this mystically. By Soma he understands the artery or duct called Ida, and by Agni the duct called Pingala. Dhira is Buddhipreraka; vyavayam is sancharam. Dhirobhutani dharayan nityam vyavayam kurute is the order of the words. The sense is this: in this spot is seated Brahman; there Ida and Pingala meet; and there also is Vayu which urges the understanding and upholds all living creatures.

[682] Yatra is not to be taken as a locative here. It is equivalent to yatah or for which.

[683] Tasmin is taken, by Nilakantha as Apana sahite Prane.

[684] Utkarshena anayati, hence Udana, says Nilakantha. The sense of the whole passage seems to be this. Worldly life is regulated by the life-breaths. These are attached to the Soul and lead to its individual manifestations. Udana controls all the breaths. Udana is controlled by penance. It is penance then that destroys the round of rebirths and leads to absorption into Brahman.

thinks, and that which understands,—these are the seven great officiating priests. Behold, O blessed one, learned sacrificers duly casting seven libations in seven ways in the seven fires, viz., that which is smelt, that which is drunk, that which is seen, that which is touched, as also that which is heard, that which is thought of, and that which is understood, create them in their own wombs.[685] Earth, Wind, Ether, Water, and Light numbering as the fifth, Mind, and Understanding—these seven are called wombs (of all things). All the attributes which constitute the sacrificial offerings, enter into the attribute that is born of the fire, and having dwelt within that dwelling became reborn in their respective wombs. Thither also, viz., in that which generates all beings, they remain absorbed during the period for which dissolution lasts. From that is produced smell, from that is produced taste, from that is produced colour, and from that is produced touch; from that is produced sound; from that arises doubt; and from that is produced resolution. This is what is known as the sevenfold creation. It is in this very way that all this was comprehended by the ancients. By the three full and final libations, the full become full with light.'"""

SECTION XXI.

"""The Brahmana said, 'In this connection is cited the following ancient story. Do thou understand, of what kind the institution is of the ten Hotris (sacrificing priests). The ear, the skin, the two eyes, the tongue, the nose, the two feet, the two hands, the genital organ, the lower duct, and speech,—these, O beautiful one, are the ten sacrificing priests. Sound and touch, colour and taste, scent, speech, action, motion, and the discharge of vital seed, of urine and of excreta, are the ten libations. The points of the compass, Quarters, Wind, Sun, Moon, Earth, Fire, Vishnu, Indra, Prajapati, and Mitra,—these, O beautiful one, are the ten (sacrificial) fires. The ten organs (of knowledge and action) are the sacrificing priests. The libations, O beautiful one, are ten. The objects of the senses are the fuel that are cast into these ten fires,[686] as also the mind, which is the ladle, and the wealth (viz., the good and bad acts of the sacrificer). What remains is the pure, highest knowledge. We have heard that all this universe was well differentiated (from Knowledge). All objects of knowledge are Mind. Knowledge only perceives (i.e., discovers the Mind without being attached to it). The knower (or Jiva), encased in subtle form, lives within the gross body that is produced by the vital seed. The bearer of the body is the Garhapatya fire. From that is produced another. Mind is the Ahavaniya fire. Into it is poured the oblation. From that was produced the Veda (or Word); (then was born Mind); Mind (desirous of creation) sets itself on the Veda (or the Word). Their arises form (or colour) undistinguished by particular colours. It runs towards the Mind.'[687]

---

[685] The meaning seems to be this: they who renounce sensuous objects can create them when they like. One casting off smell that has earth for its object can create earth when he likes.

[686] What is stated in this passage is, shortly, this: the ear, etc, are the Hotris or sacrificing priests who are to pour libations on the sacrificial fire. The perceptions and functions of those organs constitute the Havi or libations that are to be poured. The points, wind, etc, are the Agni or sacred fires on which they are to be poured. These statements are recapitulated in verse 5. The objects of the senses, of the same as those in verse 3, are the fuel, previously described as Havi or libations, which are to be burnt off by being cast into the fires.

[687] The Hridaya or heart is the Garhapatya fire. From it is produced another fire, the Ahavaniya, viz., the mind. 'The heart was pierced. From the heart arose mind, for the mind arose Chandramas,' is the declaration of the Sruti cited by Nilakantha. The Ahavaniya fire or mind is the mouth. Asyam ahavaniya is the Sruti. Annamayam hi Somya manas, apomayah pranah, tejomayi vak is the Sruti that bears upon this. Food or fire, poured into the mouth develops into speech or word. Vachaspati implies the Veda or word. First arises the

""The Brahmana's wife said, 'Why did Word first arise and why did Mind arise afterwards, seeing that Word starts into existence after having been thought upon by Mind? Upon that authority can it be said that Mati (Prana) takes refuge in Mind? Why, again, in dreamless slumber, though separated from Mind, does not Prana apprehend (all objects)? What is that which restrains it then?'[688]

""The Brahmana said, 'The Apana breath, becoming the lord (i.e., bringing the Prana under its control), in consequence of such lordship over it, makes it identical with itself. That restrained motion of the Prana breath (which for the time becomes identical with that of the Apana) has been said to be the motion of the mind. Hence the mind is dependent upon Prana, not Prana upon the mind. Therefore, in dreamless slumber, upon the disappearance of mind, Prana does not disappear. But since thou askest me a question about word and mind, I shall, therefore, relate to thee a discourse between them. Both Word and Mind, repairing to the Soul of matter,[689] asked him,—"Do thou say who amongst us is superior. Do thou, O puissant one, dispel our doubt."—On that occasion, the holy one made this answer.—"The mind undoubtedly (is superior)." Unto him Word said,—"I yield to thee the fruition of all thy desires!"'[690]

""The Brahmana said, 'Know that I have two minds, immovable and movable. That which is immovable is, verily, with me; the movable is in your dominion.[691] That mind is verily called movable which, in the form of Mantra, letter, or voice, is referable to your dominion. Hence, thou art superior (to the other mind which concerns itself with only the external world). But since, coming of thy own accord, O beautiful one, thou enterest into the engagement (about the fruition of all wishes), therefore, filling myself with breath, I utter thee.[692] The goddess Word used always to dwell between Prana and Apana. But, O blessed one, sinking into Apana, though urged upwards, in consequence of becoming dissociated from Prana, she ran to Prajapati and said,—Be gratified with me, O holy one.—The Prana appeared, once more fostering Word. Hence, Word, encountering deep exhalation, never utters anything. Word always flows as endued with utterance or unendued with it.[693] Amongst those two, Word without utterance is superior to Word with utterance. Like a cow endued with excellent milk, she (Word without utterance) yields diverse kinds of meaning. This one always yields the Eternal (viz., Emancipation), speaking of Brahman. O thou of beautiful smiles, Word is a cow, in consequence of her

---

word, the mind sets itself upon it, desirous of creation. This corresponds with the Mosaic Genesis.—'God said, let there be light, and there was light.' The word was first.

[688] The last question seems to be this: in dreamless slumber, the mind disappears totally. If it is the mind upon which Prana rests, why does not Prana also disappear? It is seen to separate itself from mind, for it continues to exist while mind does not exist. If so, i.e., if existing, as it must be admitted to do, why does it not apprehend objects? What is it that restrains its powers of apprehension?

[689] Bhutatmanam is ordinary Prajapati. Nilakantha takes it to mean here individual Jiva or self.

[690] It is through words that desirable fruits, visible and invisible, are acquired. Of course, word means both ordinary speech and Vedic Mantras.

[691] The speaker is the Brahmana, which Nilakantha explains to mean 'the Brahmana named Manas or Mind'. Instead of such a learned interpretation, we may take it as implying that the Brahmana is repeating the answer which Bhutatman, i.e., Prajapati or Jiva, made to Word. The Brahmana is the real speaker. He recites the words of Jiva. Immovable, according to Nilakantha, means 'that which is seizable by the external senses'; and 'movable', that which is beyond the ken of the senses, such as heaven, etc. The external world being only a manifestation of the mind, it is spoken of here as identical with it. So, the ideas in the mind which are not due to the senses, are only the mind. This is the movable mind. That mind depends on word or the scriptures.

[692] Telang gives a different version of this verse. I offer a verbal rendering, without attempting to explain it.

[693] i.e., as noisy or noiseless.

puissance which is both divine and not divine. Behold the distinction of these two subtle forms of Word that flow.'[694]

""The Brahmana's wife said, 'What did the goddess of Word then say, in days of old, when, though impelled by the Wish to speak, Speech could not come out?'

""The Brahmana said, 'The Word that is generated in the body by Prana, then attains to Apana from Prana. Then transformed into Udana and issuing out of the body, envelops all the quarters, with Vyana. After that, she dwells in Samana. Even in this way did Word formerly speak. Hence Mind, in consequence of being immovable, is distinguished, and the goddess Word, in consequence of being movable, is also distinguished.""""

SECTION XXII.

""The Brahmana said, 'In this connection is cited the ancient story, O blessed one, of what the institution is of the seven sacrificing priests. The nose, the eye, the tongue, the skin, and the ear numbering the fifth, the mind, and the understanding,—these are the seven sacrificing priests standing distinctly from one another. Dwelling in subtle space, they do not perceive one another. Do thou, O beautiful one, know these sacrificing priests that are seven by their nature.'

""The Brahmana's wife said, 'How is it that dwelling in subtle space, these do not perceive one another? What are their (respective) natures, O holy one? Do thou tell me this, O lord.'

""The Brahmana said, 'Not knowing the qualities (of any object) is ignorance (of that object); while knowledge of the qualities is (called) knowledge (of the object which possesses those qualities). These seven never succeed in apprehending or knowing the qualities of one another. The tongue, the eye, the ear too, the skin, the mind, and the understanding, do not succeed in apprehending smells. It is the nose alone that apprehends them. The nose, the tongue, the ear also, the skin, the mind, and the understanding, never succeed in apprehending colours. It is the eye alone that apprehends them. The nose, the tongue, the eye too, the ear, the understanding, and the mind, never succeed in apprehending sensations of touch. It is the skin alone that apprehends them. The nose, the tongue, the eye, the skin, the mind, and the understanding, never succeed in apprehending sounds. It is the ear alone that apprehends them. The nose, the tongue, the eye, the skin, the ear, and the understanding never succeed in apprehending doubt. It is the mind that apprehends it. The nose, the tongue, the eye, the skin, the ear, and the mind, never succeed in apprehending determination (certainty in respect of knowledge). It is the understanding alone that apprehends it. In this connection, is cited, O beautiful lady, this ancient narrative of a discourse between the senses and the mind.'

""The mind said, "The nose does not smell without me. (Without me) the tongue does not apprehend taste. The eye does not seize colour, the skin does not feel touch, the ear does not apprehend sound, when deprived of me. I am the eternal and foremost one among all the elements. It always happens that destitute of myself, the senses never shine, like habitations empty of inmates or fires whose flames have been quenched. Without me, all creatures fail to apprehend qualities and objects, with even the senses exerting themselves, even as fuel that is wet and dry (failing to ignite a fire)."

---

[694] I have given as close a verbal rendering of the passage as possible. The sense, however, is not very intelligible to me. The gloss of Nilakantha is as unintelligible as the text. Telang also has given a verbal rendering which differs from the above slightly. His foot-notes do not, I think, bring out the meaning at all. As regards the two vernacular versions, both are useless.

""""Hearing these words, the Senses said, "Even this would be true as thou thinkest in this matter, if, indeed, thou couldst enjoy pleasures without either ourselves or our objects.[695] What thou thinkest, would be true, if, when we are extinct, there be gratification and support of life, and a continuation of thy enjoyments, or, if, when we are absorbed and objects are existing, thou canst have thy enjoyments by thy desire alone, as truly as thou hast them with our aid. If, again, thou deemest thy power over our objects to be always complete, do thou then seize colour by the nose, and taste by the eye. Do thou also take smell by the ear, and sensations of touch by the tongue. Do thou also take sounds by the skin, and likewise touch by the understanding. They that are powerful do not own the dominion of any rules. Rules exist for those only that are weak. Do thou seize enjoyments unenjoyed before; it behoves thee not to enjoy what has been tasted before (by others). As a disciple repairs to a preceptor for the sake of (acquiring) the Srutis, and then, having acquired the Srutis, dwells on their import (by obeying their injunctions), even so dost thou regard as thine those objects which are shown by us, past or future, in sleep or in wakefulness. Of creatures, again, that are of little intelligence, when their mind becomes distracted and cheerless, life is seen to be upheld upon our objects discharging their functions.[696] It is seen also that a creature, after having formed even innumerable purposes and indulged in dreams, when afflicted by the desire to enjoy, runs to objects of sense at once.[697] One entering upon enjoyments depending on mental purposes alone and unconnected with actual objects of sense, always meets with death upon the exhaustion of the life-breaths, like an enkindled fire upon the exhaustion of fuel. True it is that we have connections with our respective attributes; true it is, we have no knowledge of one another's attributes. But without us thou canst have no perception. Without us no happiness can come to thee."""""

SECTION XXIII.

""""The Brahmana said, 'In this connection, O blessed lady, is cited the ancient story of what kind the institution is of the five sacrificing priests. The learned know this to be a great principle that Prana and Apana and Udana and Samana and Vyana are the five sacrificing priests.'

""""The Brahmana's wife said, 'That naturally there are seven sacrificing priests is what was my former conviction. Let the great principle be declared to me as to how, verily, the number is five of the sacrificing priests.'

""""The Brahmana said, 'The wind nursed by Prana afterwards takes birth in Apana. The wind nursed in Apana then becomes developed into Vyana. Nursed by Vyana, the wind is then developed into Udana. Nursed in Udana, the wind is then generated as Samana. Those good beings in days of yore asked the first-born Grandsire, saying—"Do thou say who amongst us is the foremost. He (whom thou wilt indicate) will be our chief."

""""Brahmana said, '"He upon whose extinction all the life-breaths become extinct in the bodies of living creatures, he upon whose moving they move, is verily the foremost (among you). Do ye go where ye like."

---

[695] The correct reading is cha after arthan and not twam after it. Hence, the Senses say that, 'without ourselves and without those which are our objects, thou canst not have thy enjoyments.'

[696] Thus creatures may exist through us, even though mind may be out of order.

[697] Both mental purposes and dreams having failed to gratify him.

"""Prana said, "Upon my extinction all the life-breaths become extinct in the bodies of living creatures. Upon my moving they once more move. I am (therefore) the foremost. Behold, I go into extinction!'"

"""The Brahmana continued, 'Prana then became extinct and once more moved about. Then Samana and Udana also, O blessed one, said these words—"Thou dost not dwell here, pervading all this, as we do. Thou art not the foremost amongst us, O Prana. (Only) Apana is under thy dominion." Prana then moved about, and unto him Apana spoke.

"""Apana said, "When I become extinct, all the life-winds become extinct in the bodies of living creatures. When I move about, they again move about. I am, therefore, the foremost. Behold, I go into extinction!"

"""The Brahmana continued, 'Unto Apana who said so, both Vyana and Udana said— "O Apana, thou art not the foremost. (Only) Prana is under thy dominion." Then Apana began to move about. Vyana once more addressed him saying, "I am the foremost of all (the life-winds). Listen, for what reason. When I become extinct, all the life-winds become extinct in the bodies of living creatures. When I move about, they once more move about. I am (therefore) the foremost. Behold, I go into extinction!"

"""The Brahmana continued, 'Then Vyana went into extinction and once more began to move about. At this, Prana and Apana and Udana and Samana addressed him, saying, "Thou art not the foremost among us, O Vyana! (Only) Samana is under thy dominion."—Vyana then began to move about and Samana said unto him,—"I am the foremost of you all. Listen, for what reason. When I become extinct, all the life-winds become extinct in the bodies of living creatures. When I begin to move about, they once more move about. Hence, I am the foremost. Behold, I go into extinction!" Then Samana began to move about. Unto him Udana said, "I am the foremost of all the life-winds. Listen, for what reason. When I become extinct, all the life-winds become extinct in the bodies of living creatures. When I move about they once more move about. Hence, I am the foremost. Behold, I go into extinction!"—Then Udana, after having gone into extinction, began once more to move about, Prana and Apana and Samana and Vyana said, unto him, O Udana, "thou art not the foremost one among us, only Vyana is under thy dominion."

"""The Brahmana continued, 'Unto them assembled together, the Lord of creatures, Brahma, said, "No one of you is superior to others. Ye are all endued with particular attributes. All are foremost in their own spheres, and all possess special attributes." Thus said unto them, that were assembled together, the Lord of all creatures. There is one that is unmoving, and one that is moving. In consequence of special attributes, there are five life-winds. My own self is one. That one accumulates into many forms. Becoming friendly unto one another, and gratifying one another, depart in peace. Blessings to ye, do ye uphold one another!"'"

SECTION XXIV.

"""The Brahmana said, 'In this connection is cited the ancient story of the discourse between Narada and the Rishi Devamata.'

"""Devamata said, "What verily, comes first into existence, of a creature that takes birth? Is it Prana, or Apana, or Samana, or Vyana, or Udana?"

"""Narada said, "By whatever the creature is created, that first comes unto him which is other (or separate from him). The life winds are to be known as existing in pairs, viz., those that move transversely, upwards, and downwards."

""""Devamata said, "By whom (among the life-winds) is a creature produced? Who (amongst) them comes first? Do thou tell me what the pairs are of the life-winds, that move transversely, upwards, and downwards."

""""Narada said, "From Sankalpa (wish) arises Pleasure. It also arises from sound. It arises also from taste; it arises too from colour. From the semen, united with blood, first flows Prana. Upon the semen being modified by Prana, flows Apana. Pleasure arises from the semen as well. It arises from taste also. This is the form (effect) of Udana. Pleasure is produced from union. Semen is generated by desire. From desire is produced the menstrual flow. In the union of semen and blood, generated by Samana and Vyana, the pair that consists of Prana and Apana, enters, moving transversely and upwards, Vyana and Samana both form a pair that moves transversely. Agni (fire) is all the deities. Even this is the teaching of the Veda. The knowledge of Agni arises in a Brahmana with intelligence. The smoke of that fire is of the form of (the attribute called) Darkness. The attribute that is known by the name of Passion is in its ashes. The quality of goodness arises from that portion of the fire into which the oblation is poured.[698] They that are conversant with sacrifices know that Samana and Vyana are from the attribute of Goodness. Prana and Apana are portions of the oblation (of clarified butter). Between them is the Fire. That is the excellent form (or seat) of Udana, as the Brahmanas know. Listen as I say which is distinct from the pairs. Day and Night constitute a pair. Between them is the Fire. That is the excellent seat of Udana as the Brahmanas know. The existent and the non-existent form a pair. Between them is the Fire. That is the excellent seat of Udana as the Brahmanas know. First is Samana; then Vyana. The latter's function is managed through it (viz., Samana). Then, secondly, Samana once more comes into operation. Only Vyana exists for tranquillity. Tranquillity is eternal Brahman. This is the excellent seat of Udana as the Brahmanas know.""""""[699]

SECTION XXV.

""""The Brahmana said, 'In this connection is recited the ancient story of what the institution is of the Chaturhotra (sacrifice). The ordinances are now being duly declared of that in its entirety. Listen to me, O amiable lady, as I declare this wonderful mystery. The agent, the instrument, the action and Emancipation,—these, O beautiful lady, are the four sacrificing priests by whom the universe is enveloped. Hear in its entirety the assignment of causes (relating to this topic). The nose, the tongue, the eye, the skin, the ear numbering the fifth, the mind, and the understanding,—these seven should be understood as being caused by (the knowledge of) qualities. Smell, taste, colour, sound, touch, numbering the fifth, the objects of the mind, and the objects of the understanding, these seven are caused by action. He who smells, he who eats, he who sees, he who speaks, he who hears, numbering the fifth, he who thinks, and he who understands— these seven should be known as caused by the agent. Possessed of qualities, these enjoy

---

[698] The reading sarvam in the second line is incorrect, though Nilakantha adopts it. The different portions of the fire are indicated as the different attributes. The smoke is of the form of Darkness (Tamas); the ashes are the attributes of Passion; while the blazing flame, that into which the oblation is thrown, is the attribute of Goodness.

[699] I give a close rendering of these verses, without endeavouring to bring out the sense as explained by the commentators. The printed texts are not correct. The text adopted by Nilakantha differs from that of Arjuna Misra. The very order of the verses is not uniform in all the texts.

their own qualities, agreeable or disagreeable.[700] As regards the Soul, that is destitute of qualities. These seven are the causes of Emancipation. With them that are learned and possessed of sufficient understanding, the qualities, which are in the position of deities, eat the oblations, each in its proper place, and agreeably to what has been ordained. The person who is destitute of learning, eating diverse kind of food, becomes seized with the sense of mineness.[701] Digesting food for himself, he becomes ruined through the sense of mineness. The eating of food that should not be eaten, and the drinking of wine, ruin him. He destroys the food (he takes), and having destroyed that food, he becomes destroyed himself. The man of learning, however, being possessed of puissance, destroys his food for reproducing it. The minutest transgression does not arise in him from the food he takes. Whatever is thought of by the mind, whatever is uttered by speech, whatever is heard by the ear, whatever is seen by the eye, whatever is touched by the (sense of) touch, whatever is smelt by the nose, constitute oblations of clarified butter which should all, after restraining the senses with the mind numbering the sixth, be poured into that fire of high merits which burns within the body, viz., the Soul.[702] The sacrifice constituted by Yoga is going on as regards myself. The spring whence that sacrifice proceeds is that which yields the fire of knowledge. The upward life-wind Prana is the Stotra of that sacrifice. The downward life-wind Apana is its Sastra. The renunciation of everything is the excellent Dakshina of that sacrifice. Consciousness, Mind, and Understanding—these becoming Brahma, are its Hotri, Adhwaryyu, and Udgatri. The Prasastri, his Sastra, is truth.[703] Cessation of separate existence (or Emancipation) is the Dakshina. In this connection, people conversant with Narayana recite some Richs. Unto the divine Narayana were animals offered in days of yore.[704] Then are sung some Samanas. On that topic occurs an authority. O timid one, know that the divine Narayana is the soul of all.'"""

SECTION XXVI.

"""The Brahmana said, 'There is one Ruler. There is no second beside him. He that is Ruler resides in the heart. I shall speak now of him. Impelled by Him, I move as directed, like water along an inclined plane. There is one Preceptor. There is no second beside him. He resides in the heart, and of him I shall now speak. Be instructed by that preceptor; they who are always endued with feelings of animosity are like snakes. There is one kinsman. There is no second beside him. He resides in the heart of him I shall now speak. Instructed by him, kinsmen become possessed of kinsmen, and the seven Rishis, O son of Pritha, shine in the firmament. There is one dispeller. There is no second beside him. He resides in the heart. Of him I shall now speak. Having lived with that instructor under the

---

[700] 'These' refers to action, agent and instrument. The qualities of which they are possessed are goodness, passion, and darkness.

[701] What is stated in these two verses is this: it is the Senses that enjoy and not the Soul. This is well known to those that are learned. On the other hand, those that are not learned, regard this or that to be theirs, when in reality they are different from them. They are their selves, and not their senses, although they take themselves for the latter, ignorantly identifying themselves with things which they are not.

[702] What is stated here is this: Restraining the senses and the mind, the objects of those senses and the mind should be poured as libations on the sacred fire of the Soul that is within the body.

[703] i.e., truth is the Sastra of the Prasastri.

[704] Narayana is taken by Nilakantha to stand here for either the Veda or the Soul. The animals offered up to Narayana in days of old were the senses offered up as sacrifices.

proper mode of living, Sakra attained to the sovereignty of all the worlds.[705] There is one enemy. There is no second beside him. He resides in the heart. Of him I shall now speak. Instructed by that preceptor all snakes in the world are always endued with feelings of animosity. In this connection is cited the ancient story of the instruction of the snakes, the deities, and the Rishis by the Lord of all creatures. The deities and the Rishis, the snakes, and the Asuras, seated around the Lord of all creatures, asked him, saying,—"Let that which is highly beneficial for us be declared." Unto them that enquired about what is highly beneficial, the holy one uttered only the word Om, which is Brahman in one syllable. Hearing this, they ran away in various directions. Amongst them that thus ran in all directions from desire of self-instruction, the disposition first arose in snakes of biting. Of the Asuras, the disposition, born of their nature for ostentations, pride arose. The deities betook themselves to gifts, and the great Rishis to self-restraint. Having repaired to one teacher, and having been instructed (refined) by one word, the snakes, the deities, the Rishis, and the Danavas, all betook themselves to diverse different dispositions. It is that one who hears himself when speaking, and apprehends it duly. Once, again, is that heard from him when he speaks. There is no second preceptor.[706] It is in obedience to his counsels that action afterwards flows. The instructor, the apprehender, the hearer, and the enemy, are pleased within the heart. By acting sinfully in the world it is he that becomes a person of sinful deeds. By acting auspiciously in the world, it is he who becomes a person of auspicious deeds. It is he who becomes a person of unrestrained conduct by becoming addicted to the pleasures of sense, impelled by desire. It is he who becomes a Brahmacharin by always devoting himself to the subjugation of his senses. It is he, again, that casts off vows and actions and takes refuge on Brahman alone. By moving in the world, identifying himself the while with Brahman, he becomes a Brahmacharin. Brahman is his fuel; Brahman is his fire; Brahman is his origin; Brahman is his water; Brahman is his preceptor: he is rapt in Brahman. Brahmacharyya is even so subtle, as understood by the wise. Having understood it, they betook themselves to it, instructed by the Kshetrajna!"""[707]

SECTION XXVII.

""""The Brahmana said, 'Having crossed that impassable fastness (the world) which has purposes for its gadflies and mosquitoes, grief and joy for its cold and heat, heedlessness for its blinding darkness, cupidity and diseases for its reptiles, wealth for its one danger on the road, and lust and wrath its robbers, I have entered the extensive forest of (Brahman)'.

""""The wife of the Brahmana said, 'Where is that foremost, O thou of great wisdom? What are its trees? What its rivers? What its mountains and hills? How far is that forest?'

""""The Brahmana said, 'There exists nothing that is separate from it. There is nothing more delightful than it. There is nothing that is unseparated from it. There is nothing more afflicting than it. There is nothing smaller than that. There is nothing vaster than that. There is nothing minuter than that. There is no happiness that can resemble it.

---

[705] Srota here means preceptor or dispeller of doubts. Amaratwam is the status of the immortal head of all.

[706] I think Telang is not correct in his rendering of this verse. What is stated here is plain, viz., that it is He who is the preceptor and the disciple. Ayam srinoti,—'prochyamanam grihnati,—tat prichchatah ato bhuyas anye srinanti' is the grammar of the construction. The conclusion then comes—'gururanyo na vidyate'.

[707] One who understands the truth.

Regenerate persons, entering into it, at once transcend both joy and sorrow. They (then) never stand in fear of any creature, nor does any creature stand in fear of them. In that forest are seven large trees, seven fruits, and seven guests. There are seven hermitages, seven (forms of) Yoga concentration, and seven (forms) of initiation. Even this a description of that forest.[708] The trees which stand filling that forest, produce excellent flowers and fruits of five colours. The trees which stand there filling that forest, produce flowers and fruits that are of excellent colours and that are, besides, of two kinds. The trees which stand there filling that forest, produce flowers and fruits that are endued with fragrance and that are, besides, of two colours. The trees which stand there filling that forest, produce flowers and fruits that are possessed of fragrance and that are, besides, of one colour. The two trees which stand filling that forest, produce many flowers and fruits that are of unmanifest colours. There is one fire here, possessed of a good mind. That is connected with Brahmana. The five senses are the fuel here. The seven forms of Emancipation flowing from them are the seven forms of Initiation. The qualities are the fruits, and the guests eat those fruits. There, in diverse places, the great Rishis accept hospitality. When they, having been worshipped, become annihilated, then another forest shines forth. In that forest, Intelligence is the tree; Emancipation is the fruit; Tranquillity is the shade of which it is possessed. It has knowledge for its resting house, contentment for its water, and the Kshetrajna for its sun. Its end cannot be ascertained upwards, downwards, or horizontally. Seven females always dwell there, with faces downwards, possessed of effulgence, and endued with the cause of generations. They take up all the different tastes from all creatures, even as inconstancy sucks up truth. In that itself dwell, and from that emerge, the seven Rishis who are crowned with ascetic success, with those seven having Vasishtha for their foremost. Glory, effulgence, greatness, enlightenment, victory, perfection, and energy, these seven always follow this same like rays following the sun. Hills and mountains also exist there, collected together; and rivers and streams bearing waters in their course, waters that are born of Brahma. And there happens a confluence also of streams in the secluded spot for sacrifice. Thence those that are contented with their own souls proceed to the Grandsire. Those whose wishes have been reduced, whose wishes have been directed to excellent vows, and whose sins have been burnt off by penances, merging themselves in their souls, succeed in attaining to Brahman. Tranquillity is praised by those who are conversant with the forest of knowledge. Keeping that forest in view, they take birth so as not to lose courage. Even such is that sacred forest that is understood by Brahmanas, and understanding it, they live (in accordance with the ordinance), directed by the Kshetrajna.'"""

SECTION XXVIII.

"""The Brahmana said, 'I do not smell scents. I do not perceive tastes. I do not see colours. I do not touch. I do not likewise hear the diverse sounds (that arise). Nor do I entertain purposes of any kind. It is Nature that desires such objects as are liked; it is Nature that hates such objects as are disliked. Desire and aversion spring from Nature, after the manner of the upward and the downward life-winds when souls have entered

[708] The seven large trees are the five senses, the mind, and the understanding. The fruits are the pleasures and pains derived from or through them. The guests are the powers of each sense, for it is they that receive those pleasures and pains. The hermitages are those very trees under which the guests take shelter. The seven forms of Yoga are the extinctions of the seven senses. The seven forms of initiation are the repudiation, one after another, of the actions of the seven senses.

animate bodies. Separated from them are others; in them are eternal dispositions; (these as also) the soul of all creatures. Yogins would behold in the body. Dwelling in that, I am never attached to anything through desire and wrath, and decrepitude and death. Not having any desire for any object of desire, and not having any aversion for any evil, there is no taint on my natures, as there is no taint of a drop of water on (the leaves of) the lotus. Of this constant (principle) which looks upon diverse natures, they are inconstant possessions.[709] Though actions are performed, yet the assemblage of enjoyments does not attach itself to them, even as the assemblage of rays of the sun does not attach to the sky. In this connection is recited an ancient story of a discourse between an Adhwaryu and a Yati. Do thou hear it, O glorious lady. Beholding an animal sprinkled with water at a sacrificial ceremony, a Yati said unto the Adhwaryu seated there these words in censure,—"This is destruction of life!" unto him the Adhwaryu said in reply,—"This goat will not be destroyed. The animal (sacrificed) meets with great good, if the Vedic declaration on this subject be true. That part of this animal which is of earth will go to earth. That part of this one which is born of water, will enter into water. His eye will enter the sun; his ear will enter the different points of the horizon; his life-winds will enter the sky. I who adhere to the scriptures incur no fault (by assisting at the killing of this animal)."

""The Yati said, "If thou beholdest such good to the goat in this dissociation with (his) life-winds, then this sacrifice is for the goat. What need hast thou for it? Let the brother, father, mother, and friend (of this goat) give thee their approval in this. Taking him (to them) do thou consult them. This goat is especially dependent. It behoveth thee to see them who can give their consent in this. After hearing their consent, the matter will become fit for consideration. The life-winds of this goat have been made to return to their respective sources. Only the inanimate body remains behind. This is what I think. Of those who wish to enjoy felicity by means of the inanimate body (of an animal) which is comparable with fuel, the fuel (of sacrifice) is after all the animal himself. Abstention from cruelty is the foremost of all duties. Even this is the teaching of the elders. We know this is the proposition, viz.,—No slaughter (of living creatures).—If I say anything further, (it will then appear that) diverse kinds of faulty actions are capable of being done by thee. Always abstaining from cruelty to all creatures is what meets with our approbation. We establish this from what is directly perceptible. We do not rely on what is beyond direct perception."

""The Adhwaryu said, "Thou enjoyest the properties of smell which belong to the earth. Thou drinkest the tastes which appertain to water. Thou seest colours which belong to lighted bodies. Thou touchest the properties which have their origin in wind. Thou hearest the sounds which have their origin in space (or ether). Thou thinkest thoughts with the mind. All these entities, thou art of opinion, have life. Thou dost not then abstain from taking life. Really, thou art engaged in slaughter. There can be no movement without slaughter. Or, what dost thou think, O regenerate one."

""The Yati said, "The Indestructible and the Destructible constitute the double manifestation of the soul. Of these the Indestructible is existent. The Destructible is said to be exceedingly non-existent.[710] The life-wind, the tongue, the mind, the quality of goodness, along with the quality of passion, are all existent. The Atman is above these forms and hence is without duality and hope. As regards one that is freed from these

---

[709] The correct reading is bhavantyanityah and vahuswabhavan.

[710] Swabhava is explained by Nilakantha as sutaram abhava.

existent objects, that transcends all pairs of opposites, that does not cherish any expectation, that is alike to all creatures, that is liberated from the idea of meum, that has subjugated his self, and that is released from all his surroundings,—for him no fear exists from any source!"[711]

""""The Adhwaryu said, "O foremost of intelligent men, one should reside with those that are good. Hearing thy opinion my understanding shines with light. O illustrious one, I come to thee, believing thee to be a god; and I say I have no fault, O regenerate one, by performing these rites with the aid of Mantras!"'[712]

""""The Brahmana continued, 'With this conclusion, the Yati remained silent after this. The Adhwaryu also proceeded with the great sacrifice, freed from delusion. The Brahmanas understand Emancipation, which is exceedingly subtle, to be of this kind and having understood it, they live accordingly directed by the Kshetrajna, that beholder of all topics.'"""

SECTION XXIX.

""""The Brahmana said, 'In this connection is cited the ancient story, O lady, of the discourse between Kartaviryya and the Ocean. There was a king of the name of Kartaviryya-Arjuna who was endued with a thousand arms. He conquered, with his bow, the Earth, extending to the shores of the ocean. It has been heard by us that, once on a time, as he was walking on the shores of the sea, proud of his might, he showered hundreds of shafts on that vast receptacle of waters. The Ocean, bowing down unto him, said, with joined hands,—"Do not, O hero, shoot thy shafts (at me)! Say, what shall I do to thee. With these mighty arrows shot by thee, those creatures which have taken shelter in me are being killed, O tiger among kings. Do thou, O lord, grant them security."

""""Arjuna said, "If any wielder of the bow exists that is equal to me in battle, and that would stand against me in the field, do thou name him to me!"

""""The Ocean said, "If thou hast heard, O king, of the great Rishi Jamadagni, his son is competent to duly receive thee as a guest."—Then that king proceeded, filled with great wrath. Arrived at that retreat, he found Rama himself. With his kinsmen he began to do many acts that were hostile to Rama, and caused much trouble to that high-souled hero. Then the energy, which was immeasurable of Rama blazed forth, burning the troops of the foe, O lotus-eyed one. Taking up his battle-axe, Rama suddenly put forth his power, and hacked that thousand-armed hero, like a tree of many branches. Beholding him slain and prostrated on the earth, all his kinsmen, uniting together, and taking up their darts, rushed at Rama, who was then seated, from all sides. Rama also, taking up his bow and quickly ascending on his car, shot showers of arrows and chastised the army of the king. Then, some of the Kshatriyas, afflicted with the terror of Jamadagni's son, entered mountain-fastnesses, like deer afflicted by the lion. Of them that were unable, through fear of Rama, to discharge the duties ordained for their order, the progeny

---

[711] The sense seems to be this: the life-winds indicate the operations of the several organs of action; the tongue, which stands here for all the organs of perception, of the sensual perceptions; the mind, of all the internal operations; the quality of goodness, of all pleasure; and the quality of passion, of all kinds of pain. These, therefore include the whole external and the internal worlds. He that is free from these, transcends sin, for sin is destroyed by freedom from these, knowledge being the means of attaining to that freedom.

[712] 'I have no fault etc.'—The sense seems to be that by doing these rites with the aid of Mantras I have done that which has been approved from ages past by those who have always been regarded wise. My eyes, however, have now been opened by thee. I should not be held responsible for what I did while I was ignorant.

became Vrishalas owing to their inability to find Brahmanas.[713] In this way Dravidas and Abhiras and Pundras, together with the Savaras, became Vrishalas through those men who had Kshatriya duties assigned to them (in consequence of their birth), falling away (from those duties). Then the Kshatriyas that were begotten by the Brahmanas upon Kshatriya women that had lost their heroic children, were repeatedly destroyed by Jamadagni's son. The slaughter proceeded one and twenty times. At its conclusion a bodiless voice, sweet and proceeding from heaven, and which was heard by all people, spoke to Rama, "O Rama, O Rama, desist! What merit it dost thou see, O son, in thus destroying repeatedly these inferior Kshatriyas?"[714] In this way, O blessed dame, his grandsires, headed by Richika, addressed that high-souled one, saying. "Do thou desist." Rama, however, unable to forgive the slaughter of his sire, replied unto those Rishis saying, "It behoves you not to forbid me." The Pitris then said, "O foremost of all victorious men, it behoves thee not to slay these inferior Kshatriyas. It is not proper that thyself, being a Brahmana, should slay these kings."'"'"

SECTION XXX.

'"'"'The Pitris said, "In this connection is cited this old history. Having heard it, thou shouldst act according to it, O foremost of all regenerate persons. There was a royal sage of the name Alarka endued with the austerest of penances. He was conversant with all duties, truthful in speech, of high soul, and exceedingly firm in his vows. Having, with his bow, conquered the whole Earth extending to the seas, and thereby achieved an exceedingly difficult feat, he set his mind on that which is subtle. While sitting at the root of a tree, his thoughts, O thou of great intelligence, abandoning all those great feats, turned towards that which is subtle.

'"'"'Alarka said, 'My mind has become strong. Having conquered the mind, one's conquest becomes permanent. Though surrounded by foes, I shall (henceforth) shoot my arrows at other objects. Since in consequence of its unsteadiness, it sets all mortals to accomplish acts, I shall shoot very sharp-pointed shafts at the mind.'

'"'"'The mind said, 'These arrows, O Alarka, will never pierce me through. They will pierce only thy own vital parts. Thy vital parts being pierced, thou shalt die. Do thou look out for other arrows with which to destroy me.' Hearing these words and reflecting upon them, he said as follows.

'"'"'Alarka said, 'Smelling very many perfumes, the nose hankers after them only. Hence I shall shoot whetted arrows at the nose.'

'"'"'The nose said, 'These arrows will never cross through me, O Alarka. They will pierce only thy own vital parts, and thy vital parts being pierced, thou shalt die. Do thou look for other arrows with which to destroy me.' Hearing these words and reflecting upon them, he said as follows.

'"'"'Alarka said, 'This one (viz., the tongue), enjoying savoury tastes, hankers after them only. Hence I shall shoot whetted shafts at the tongue.'

---

[713] Kshatriyas always require Brahmanas for assisting them in their acts. These particular Kshatriyas, through fear of Rama, fled to the forests and mountains. They could not, accordingly, find Brahmanas for assisting them. Their children, therefore, fell away from the status of Kshatriyas and became Vrishalas or Sudras.

[714] Kshatriya-bandhu always implies low or inferior Kshatriyas, as Brahma-bandhu implies low or inferior Brahmanas. The expression, very probably, is similar to Brahman-sangat in current Bengali. It does not surely mean 'kinsmen of Kshatriyas'.

""""The tongue said, 'These arrows, O Alarka, will not cross through me. They will only pierce thy own vital parts and thy vital parts being pierced, thou shalt die. Do thou look for other arrows with which to destroy me.' Hearing these words and reflecting upon them, he said as follows.

""""Alarka said, 'The skin, touching diverse objects of touch, hankers after them only. Hence, I shall tear off the skin with diverse arrows equipt with the feathers of the Kanka.'

""""The skin said, 'These arrows will not, O Alarka, cross through me. They will pierce thy own vital parts only, and thy vital parts being pierced, thou shalt die. Do thou look for other arrows with which to destroy me.' Hearing these words and reflecting on them, he said as follows.

""""Alarka said, 'Hearing diverse sounds, (the ear) hankers after them only. Hence, I shall shoot whetted shafts at the ear.'

""""The ear said, 'These arrows will not, O Alarka, cross through me. They will pierce thy own vital parts only, and thy vital parts being pierced, thou shalt die. Do thou then look for other arrows with which to destroy me.' Hearing these words and reflecting upon them, he said as follows.

""""Alarka said, 'Seeing many colours, the eye hankers after them only. Hence, I shall destroy the eye with sharp-pointed arrows.'

""""The eye said. 'These arrows will not, O Alarka, cross through me at all. They will pierce thy own vital parts only, and thy vital parts being pierced, thou shalt die. Do thou then look for other arrows with which to destroy me!' Hearing these words and reflecting upon them, he said as follows.

""""Alarka said, 'This (viz., the understanding) forms many determinations with the aid of ratiocination. Hence, I shall shoot whetted arrows at the understanding.'

""""The understanding said, 'These arrows will not, O Alarka, cross through me at all. They will pierce thy vital parts only, and thy vital parts being pierced, thou shalt die. Do thou then look for other arrows with which to destroy me!'"

"""The Brahmana continued, "'Then Alarka, employing himself, even there, on penances difficult to perform and exceedingly austere, failed to obtain, by the high power (of his penances) arrows for casting at these seven. Endued with puissance, he then, with mind well concentrated, began to reflect. Then O best of regenerate ones, Alarka, that foremost of intelligent men, having reflected for a long time, failed to obtain anything better than Yoga. Setting his mind on one object, he remained perfectly still, engaged in Yoga.[715] Endued with energy, he quickly slew all the senses with one arrow, having entered by Yoga into his soul and thereby attained to the highest success. Filled with wonder, that royal sage then sang this verse: 'Alas, it is a pity that we should have accomplished all acts that are external! Alas, that we should have, endued with the thirst for enjoyment, courted (the pleasures of) sovereignty before now! I have learnt this afterwards. There is no happiness that is higher than Yoga.'—Do thou know this, O Rama. Cease to slay the Kshatriyas. Do thou practise the austerest of penances. Thou wilt then attain to what is good.'"—Thus addressed by his grandsires, Jamadagni's son practised the austerest penances,—and having practised them, that highly blessed one

---

[715] The vocative, 'O foremost of regenerate ones' applies to Jamadagni's son. The narration is that of the Pitris. All the copies, however, represent this as the Brahmana's speech to his wife. Indeed, the Brahmana is only reciting to his wife the speech of the Pitris to Rama. The Yoga here spoken of is, as Nilakantha explains the Raja-Yoga. Previously, Alarka had been bent upon Hatha-Yoga which frequently ends in the destruction of the person practising it.

attained to that success which is difficult to reach.'"""

SECTION XXXI.

"""The Brahmana said, 'There are three foes in the world. They are said to be ninefold, agreeably to their qualities. Exultation, satisfaction, and joy,—these three qualities appertain to Goodness.[716] Cupidity, wrath, and hatred, these three qualities are said to appertain to Passion. Lassitude, procrastination, and delusion, these three qualities appertain to darkness. Cutting these with showers of arrows, the man of intelligence, free from procrastination, possessed of a tranquil soul, and with his senses under subjection, ventures to vanquish others.[717] In this connection, persons conversant with (the occurrence of) ancient cycles recite some verses which were sung in days of old by king Amvarisha who had acquired a tranquil soul. When diverse kinds of faults were in the ascendant and when the righteous were afflicted, Amvarisha of great fame put forth his strength for assuming sovereignty.[718] Subduing his own faults and worshipping the righteous, he attained to great success and sang these verses.—"I have subdued many faults. I have killed all foes. But there is one, the greatest, vice which deserves to be destroyed but which has not been destroyed by me! Urged by that fault, this Jiva fails to attain to freedom from desire. Afflicted by desire, one runs into ditches without knowing it. Urged by that fault, one indulges in acts that are forbidden. Do thou cut off, cut off, that cupidity with sharp-edged swords. From cupidity arise desires. From desire flows anxiety. The man who yields to desire acquires many qualities that appertain to passion. When these have been acquired, he gets many qualities that appertain to Darkness. In consequence of those qualities, he repeatedly takes birth, with the bonds of body united, and is impelled to action. Upon the expiration of life, with body becoming dismembered and scattered, he once meets with death which is due to birth itself.[719] Hence, duly understanding this, and subduing cupidity by intelligence, one should desire for sovereignty in one's soul. This is (true) sovereignty. There is no other sovereignty here. The soul, properly understood, is the king." Even these were the verses sung by king Amvarisha of great celebrity, on the subject of sovereignty which he kept before him,— that king who had cut off the one foremost fault viz., cupidity.'"""

SECTION XXXII.

"""The Brahmana said, 'In this connection is cited the old narrative, O lady, of the discourse between a Brahmana and (king) Janaka. King Janaka (on a certain occasion), desirous of punishing him, said unto a Brahmana who had become guilty of some

---

[716] Praharsha, rendered 'exultation', is explained by Nilakantha as the joy that is felt at the certainty of attaining what is desired. Priti is that satisfaction which is felt when the object desired is attained. Ananda is what arises while enjoying the attained object.

[717] The sense seems to be this. Having first conquered the internal foes mentioned, the man of intelligence, bent on effecting his deliverance, should then seek to vanquish all external foes standing in his way.

[718] Nilakantha explains that dosha here refers to attachment, cupidity and the rest; while Sadhu implies not men but the virtues of tranquillity and the rest.

[719] I think Telang renders this verse wrongly. Samhatadehabandhanah does not mean 'with bodily frame destroyed' but 'with bodily frame united.' If samhata be taken as destroyed, the compound bhinna-vikirna-dehah in the second line would be a useless repetition. The meaning is that with bodily frame or the bonds of body united, he takes birth. When he dies, that frame becomes dismembered and scattered.

offence, "Thou shalt not dwell within my dominions." Thus addressed, the Brahmana replied unto that best of kings, saying, "Tell me, O king, what the limits are of the territories subject to thee. I desire, O lord, to dwell within the dominions of another king. Verily, I wish to obey thy behest, O lord of Earth, agreeably to the scriptures."—Thus addressed by that celebrated Brahmana, the king, hearing repeated and hot sighs, said not a word in reply. Like the planet Rahu overwhelming the Sun, a cloudedness of understanding suddenly overwhelmed that king of immeasurable energy as he sat plunged in thought. When that cloudedness of understanding passed away and the king became comforted, he spoke after a short while these words unto that Brahmana.

"""Janaka said, "Although a (large) inhabited tract is subject to me within this ancestral kingdom of mine, yet I fail to find my dominion, searching through the whole Earth. When I failed to find it on the Earth, I then searched Mithila (for it). When I failed to find it in Mithila, I then searched for it among my own children. When I failed to find it even there, a cloudedness of understanding came over me. After that cloudedness of understanding passed away, intelligence came back to me. Then I thought that I have no dominion, or that everything is my dominion. Even this body is not mine, or the whole Earth is mine. At the same time, O best of regenerate persons, I think that that is as much mine as it is of others. Do thou, therefore, dwell (here) as long as thy choice leads thee, and do thou enjoy as long as thou pleasest.'"

"""The Brahmana said, "'When there is a large inhabited tract in thy ancestral kingdom, tell me, depending upon what understanding, has the idea of meum been got rid of by thee. What also is that understanding depending upon which thou hast come to the conclusion that everything constitutes thy dominion? What, indeed, is the notion through which thou hast no dominion, or everything is thy dominion?'"

"""Janaka said, "All conditions here, in all affairs, have been understood by me to be terminable. Hence, I could not find that which should be called mine.[720] (Considering) whose is this, I thought of the Vedic text about anybody's property. I could not, therefore, find, by my understanding, what should be (called) mine.[721] Depending upon this notion, I got rid of idea of mineness. Hear now what that notion is depending upon which I came to the conclusion that I have dominion everywhere. I do not desire for my own self those smells that are even in my nose. Therefore, the earth, subjugated by me, is always subject to me.[722] I do not desire for my own self those tastes that exist in contact with even my tongue. Therefore, water, subjugated by me, is always subject to me. I do not desire for my own self the colour or light that appertains to my eye. Therefore, light subjugated by me, is always subject to me. I do not desire for my own self those sensations of touch which are in contact with even my skin. Therefore, the wind, subjugated by me, is always subject to me. I do not desire for my own self those sounds which are in contact with even my ear. Therefore sounds, subjugated by me, are always subject to me. I do not desire for my own self the mind that is always in my mind. Therefore the mind,

---

[720] The conditions referred to are affluence and indigence, as explained by Nilakantha.

[721] This is, rather, obscure. Nilakantha observes that the Vedic text referred to is: 'Do not covet anybody's property.' What Janaka says seems to be this: Thinking of this prohibition about coveting other people's property, I thought how could it be ascertained what belongs to others.

[722] The sense seems to be this: the property of smell attaches to earth. I do not desire smell for my own enjoyment. If it is perceived, it is perceived by the organ of smell. The earth, therefore, is subject to me, not I to the earth. I have transcended my sensations, and, therefore, the objects to which they inhere. The whole world represents only the objects of the sensations. The latter being mastered, the whole world has been mastered by me.

subjugated by me, is subject to me. All these acts of mine are for the sake of the deities, the Pitris, the Bhutas, together with guests."[723]—The Brahmana then, smiling, once more said unto Janaka,—"Know that I am Dharma, who have come here today for examining thee. Thou art verily the one person for setting this wheel in motion, this wheel that has the quality of Goodness for its circumference, Brahmin for its nave, and the understanding for its spokes, and which never turns back!'"""[724]

SECTION XXXIII.

"""The Brahmana said, 'I do not, O timid one, move in this world in that manner which thou, according to thy own understanding, censurest. I am a Brahmana possessed of Vedic knowledge. I am emancipated. I am a forest recluse. I am an observer of the duties of a house-holder. I observe vows. I am not what thou seest me in good and bad acts. By me is pervaded everything that exists in this universe. Whatever creatures exist in the world, mobile or immobile, know that I am the destroyer of them all, even as fire is (the destroyer) of all kinds of wood. Of sovereignty over the whole Earth or over Heaven (on the one hand), or this knowledge (of my identity with the universe), this knowledge is my wealth.[725] This is the one path for Brahmanas, by which they who understand it proceed to house-holds, or abodes in the forest, or residence with preceptors, or among mendicants.[726] With numerous unconfused symbols, only one knowledge is worshipped. Those who, whatever the symbols and modes of life to which they adhere, have acquired an understanding having tranquillity for its essence, attain to that one entity even as numerous rivers all meeting the Ocean.[727] The path is traversable with the aid of the understanding and not of this body. Actions have both beginning and end, and the body has actions for its bonds.[728] Hence, O blessed lady, thou needst have no apprehension in respect of the world hereafter. With thy heart intent upon the real entity, it is my soul into which thou wilt come.'"""

SECTION XXXIV.

"""The Brahmana's wife said, 'This is incapable of being understood by a person of little intelligence as also by one whose soul has not been cleansed. My intelligence is very little, and contracted, and confused. Do thou tell me the means by which the knowledge (of which thou speakest) may be acquired. I wish to learn from thee the source from which this knowledge flows.'

---

[723] i.e., I live and act for these and not my own self.

[724] Nilakantha's reading is erroneous, Brahma-labhasya should be Brahmana-bhasya. So also durvarasya is incorrect. Nemi may also mean the line or track that is made by a wheel as it moves. If taken in this sense, it would mean 'that is confined to, or that cannot deviate from the track constituted by goodness'. The nave, Brahman, is, of course, the Vedas.

[725] The sense seems to be this. The sovereignty of the whole Earth or of Heaven, and this knowledge of my identity with the universe—of these two alternatives, I would freely choose the latter. Hence, he says—'This knowledge is my wealth.'

[726] These are different modes of life.

[727] The sense is this: the knowledge to be acquired is that all is one. Diverse ways there are for acquiring it. Those, again, that have attained to tranquillity have acquired it.

[728] Actions are perishable and can lead to no lasting result. It is by the understanding that that knowledge, leading to what is permanent, is to be attained.

""The Brahmana said, 'Know that intelligence devoted to Brahman, is the lower Arani; the preceptor is the upper Arani; penances and conversance with the scriptures are to cause the attrition. From this is produced the fire of knowledge.'

""The Brahmana's wife said, 'As regards this symbol of Brahman, which is designated Kshetrajna, where, indeed, occurs a description of it by which it is capable of being seized?'

""The Brahmana said, 'He is without symbols, and without qualities. Nothing exists that may be regarded as his cause. I shall, however, tell thee the means by which he can be seized or not. A good means may be found; viz., perception of hearing, etc. as flowers are perceived by bees. That means consists of an understanding cleansed by action. Those whose understandings have not been so cleansed, regard that entity, through their own ignorance, as invested with the properties of knowledge and others.[729] It is not laid down that this should be done, of that this should not be done, in the rules for achieving Emancipation,—those, that is, in which a knowledge of the soul arises only in him who sees and hears.[730] One should comprehend as many parts, unmanifest and manifest by hundreds and thousands, as one is capable of comprehending here. Indeed, one should comprehend diverse objects of diverse import, and all objects of direct perception. Then will come, from practice (of contemplation and self-restraint, etc.), that above which nothing exists.'"[731]

"'The holy one continued, "Then the mind of that Brahmana's wife, upon the destruction of the Kshetrajna, became that which is beyond Kshetrajna, in consequence of the knowledge of Kshetra."[732]

"'Arjuna said, "Where, indeed, is that Brahmana's wife, O Krishna, and where is that foremost of Brahmanas, by both of whom was such success attained. Do thou, tell me about them, O thou of unfading glory."

"'The blessed and holy one said, "Know that my mind is the Brahmana, and that my understanding is the Brahmana's wife. He who has been spoken of as Kshetrajna is I myself, O Dhananjaya!"'"

SECTION XXXV.

"'Arjuna said, "It behoveth thee to expound Brahma to me,—that which is the highest object of knowledge. Through thy favour, my mind is delighted with these subtle

---

[729] I expand this verse a little for making it intelligible. A literal version would run as follows: Good means may be seen, perceived as by bees. Action is (cleansed) understanding; through folly it is invested with the symbols of knowledge. Karmabudhhi never means 'action and knowledge' as rendered by Telang. Abudhitwatt means 'through ignorance.' This ignorance is of those persons whose understandings have not been cleansed by action.

[730] What is stated here is this. In the matter of achieving Emancipation, no ordinances have been laid down, positive or negative, like those in respect of other things. If one wishes to attain to Heaven, he should do this and abstain from the other. For achieving Emancipation, however, only seeing and hearing are prescribed. Seeing implies contemplation, and hearing, the receiving of instructions from the preceptor. Nilakantha explains hearing as Vedantadisravanam (vide his comment on the word 'srutam' in verse 3 above).

[731] The speaker wishes to inculcate that one should first contemplate an object of direct perception, such as earth, etc. Then on such 'unperceived' objects as operations of the mind. Such contemplation will gradually lead to that which is Supreme. The abhyasa or practice referred to in the second line is the practice of sama, dama, etc. I do not think that Telang's version of 8 and 9 brings out the meaning clearly.

[732] The sense is that when her individual soul became merged into the Supreme soul, she became identified with Brahman. This, was, of course, due to the knowledge of Kshetra as something separate from Kshetrajna.

disquisitions."

"'Vasudeva said,—"In this connection is recited the old history of the discourse between a preceptor and his disciple on the subject of Brahman. Once on a time, O scorcher of foes, an intelligent disciple questioned a certain Brahmana of rigid vows who was his preceptor, as he was seated (at his ease), saying,—'What, indeed, is the highest good? Desirous of attaining to that which constitutes the highest good, I throw myself at thy feet, O holy one. O learned Brahmana, I solicit thee, bending my head, to explain to me what I ask.'—Unto that disciple, O son of Pritha, who said so, the preceptor said,—'O regenerate one, I shall explain to thee everything about which thou mayst have any doubts.'—Thus addressed, O foremost one of Kuru's race, by his preceptor, that disciple who was exceedingly devoted to his preceptor, spoke as follows, with joined hands. Do thou hear what he said, O thou of great intelligence.

"""The Disciple said, 'Where am I? Whence art thou? Explain that which is the highest truth. From what source have sprung all creatures mobile and immobile? By what do creatures live? What is the limit of their life? What is truth? What is penance, O learned Brahmana? What are called attributes by the good? What paths are to be called auspicious? What is happiness? What is sin? O holy one, O thou of excellent vows, it behoves thee to answer these questions of mine, O learned Rishi, correctly, truly, and accurately. Who else is there in this world than thee that is capable of answering these questions? Do thou answer them, O foremost of all persons conversant with duties. My curiosity is great. Thou art celebrated in all the worlds as one well skilled in the duties relating to Emancipation. There is none else than thou that is competent to remove all kinds of doubts. Afraid of worldly life, we have become desirous of achieving Emancipation.'"

"'Vasudeva said, "Unto that disciple who had humbly sought his instruction and put the questions duly, who was devoted to his preceptor and possessed of tranquillity, and who always behaved in a manner that was agreeable (to his instructor), who lived so constantly by the side of his instructor as to have almost become his shadow, who was self-restrained, and who had the life of a Yati and Brahmacharin, O son of Pritha, that preceptor possessed of intelligence and observant of vows, duly explained all the questions, O foremost one of Kuru's race, O chastiser of all foes.

"""The preceptor said, 'All this was declared (in days of old) by Brahma himself (the Grandsire of all the worlds). Applauded and practised by the foremost of Rishis, and depending on a knowledge of the Vedas, it involves a consideration of what constitutes the real entity. We regard knowledge to be the highest object, and renunciation as the best penance. He who, with certainty, knows the true object of knowledge which is incapable of being modified by circumstances, viz., the soul abiding in all creatures, succeeds in going whithersoever he wishes and comes to be regarded as the highest. That learned man who beholds the residence of all things in one place and their severance as well, and who sees unity in diversity, succeeds in freeing himself from misery. He who does not covet anything and does not cherish the idea of mineness with regard to anything, comes to be regarded, although residing in this world, as identifiable with Brahman. He who is conversant with the truth about the qualities of Pradhana (or Nature), acquainted with the creation of all existent objects, divested of the idea of mineness, and without pride, succeeds, without doubt, in emancipating himself. Understanding properly that great tree which has the unmanifest for its seed sprout, and the understanding for its trunk, and high consciousness of self for its branches, and the senses for the cells whence its twigs issue, and the (five) great elements for its flower-buds, and the gross elements for its smaller boughs, which is always endued with leaves, which always puts forth flowers, and upon which all existent objects depend, whose seed is Brahman, and which is eternal,—and cutting all topics with the sharp sword of knowledge, one attains to immortality and casts off birth and death. The conclusions with regard to the past, present, and future, etc, and religion, pleasure and wealth, which are all well known to conclaves of Siddhas, which appertain to remote cycles, and which are, indeed, eternal, I shall declare to thee, O thou of great wisdom. These constitute what is called Good. Men of wisdom, understanding them in this world, attain to success. In days of old, the Rishis Vrihaspati and Bharadwaja, and Gautama and Bhargava, and Vasishtha and Kasyapa, and Viswamitra, and Atri, assembled together for the purpose of asking one another. They thus assembled together after having travelled over all paths and after they had got tired with the acts each of them had done. Those regenerate persons, placing the sage son of Angiras at their head, proceeded to the region of the Grandsire. There they beheld Brahma perfectly cleansed of all sin. Bowing their heads unto that high-souled one who was seated at his ease, the great Rishis, endued with humility, asked him this grave question regarding the highest good. "How should a good man act? How would one be released from sin? What paths are auspicious for us? What is truth, and what is sin? By what action are the two paths, northern and southern, obtained? What is destruction? What is Emancipation? What is birth and what is death of all existent objects?" I shall tell thee, O disciple, what the Grandsire, thus addressed, said unto them, conformably to the scriptures. Do thou listen.

""'Brahma said, "It is from Truth that all creatures, mobile and immobile, have been born. They live by penance (of action). Understand this, O ye of excellent vows. In consequence of their own actions they live, transcending their own origin.[733] For Truth, when united with qualities, becomes always possessed of five indications. Brahman is Truth. Penance is truth. Prajapati is truth. It is from Truth that all creatures have sprung. Truth is the universe of being. It is for this that Brahmanas who are always devoted to Yoga, who have transcended wrath and sorrow, and who always regard Religion as the causeway (along which every one must pass for avoiding the morass below), take refuge in Truth. I shall now speak of those Brahmanas who are restrained by one another and possessed of knowledge, of the orders, and of those who belong to the four modes of life. The wise say that Religion or duty is one, (though) having four quarters. Ye regenerate ones, I shall speak to ye now of that path which is auspicious and productive of good. That path has constantly been trod over by men possessed of wisdom in order to achieve an identity with Brahman. I shall speak now of that path which is the highest and which is exceedingly difficult of being understood. Do you understand, in all its details, ye highly blessed ones, what is the highest seat. The first step has been said to be the mode of life that appertains to Brahmacharins. The second step is domesticity. After this is the residence in the woods. After that it should be known is the highest step, viz., that relating to Adhyatma.[734] Light, ether (or space), sun, wind, Indra, and Prajapati,—one sees these as long as one does not attain to Adhyatma. I shall declare the means (by which that Adhyatma may be attained). Do ye first understand them. The forest mode of life that is followed by ascetics residing in the woods and subsisting upon fruits and roots

---

[733] Their origin is Brahman or Truth. They live, dissociated from their origin, in consequence of their acts. When their acts cease, they return to and become merged in Brahman.

[734] i.e., that course of life which has for its object the acquisition of knowledge relating to the soul. This, of course, includes the knowledge that is needed for achieving identification with the Supreme Soul or Brahman.

and air is laid down for the three regenerate classes. The domestic mode of life is ordained for all the orders. They that are possessed of wisdom say that Religion or duty has Faith for its (chief) indication. Thus have I declared to you the paths leading to the deities. They are adopted by those that are good and wise by their acts. Those paths are the causeways of piety. That person of rigid vows who adopts any one of these modes separately, always succeeds in time to understand the production and destruction of all creatures. I shall now declare, accurately and with reasons, the elements which reside in parts in all objects. The great soul, the unmanifest, egoism (consciousness of identity), the ten and one organs (of knowledge and action), the five great elements, the specific characteristics of the five elements,—these constitute the eternal creation. The number of elements has been said to be four and twenty, and one (more). That person of wisdom who understands the production and destruction of all these elements, that man among all creatures, never meets with delusion. He who understands the elements accurately, all the qualities, all the deities, succeeds in cleansing himself of all sin. Freed from all bonds, such a man succeeds in enjoying all regions of spotless purity."""""[735]

SECTION XXXVI.

"""""Brahma said, "That which is unmanifest, which is indistinct, all-pervading, everlasting, immutable, should be known to become the city (or mansion) of nine portals, possessed of three qualities, and consisting of five ingredients. Encompassed by eleven including Mind which distinguishes (objects), and having Understanding for the ruler, this is an aggregate of eleven.[736] The three ducts that are in it support it constantly. These are the three Nadis. They run continually, and have the three qualities for their essence: Darkness, Passion, and Goodness. These are called the (three) qualities. These are coupled with one another. They exist, depending on one another. They take refuge in one another, and follow one another. They are also joined with one another. The five (principal) elements are characterised by (these) three qualities. Goodness is the match of Darkness. Of Goodness the match is Passion. Goodness is also the match of Passion, and of Goodness the match is Darkness. There where Darkness is restrained, Passion is seen to flow. There where Passion is restrained, Goodness is seen to flow. Darkness should be known to have the night (or obscurity) for its essence. It has three characteristics, and is (otherwise) called Delusion. It has unrighteousness (or sin) also for its indication, and it is always present in all sinful acts. This is the nature of Darkness and it appears also as confined with others. Passion is said to have activity for its essence. It is the cause of successive acts. When it prevails, its indication, among all beings, is production. Splendour, lightness, and faith,—these are the form, that is light, of Goodness among all creatures, as regarded by all good men. The true nature of their characteristics will now be declared by me, with reasons. These shall be stated in aggregation and separation. Do ye understand them. Complete delusion, ignorance, illiberality, indecision in respect of action, sleep, haughtiness, fear, cupidity, grief, censure of good acts, loss of memory, unripeness of judgment, absence of faith, violation of all rules of conduct, want of discrimination, blindness, vileness of behaviour, boastful assertions of performance when

---

[735] The specific characteristics of the five elements are, as frequently referred before, smell attaching to earth, sound to ether, taste, to water, etc. The deities referred to in the last verse are probably the senses.

[736] The total eleven is made up of the three qualities, the five elements, the group of organs and senses as one, egoism and understanding.

there has been no performance, presumption of knowledge in ignorance, unfriendliness (or hostility), evilness of disposition, absence of faith, stupid reasoning, crookedness, incapacity for association, sinful action, senselessness, stolidity, lassitude, absence of self-control, degradation,—all these qualities are known as belonging to Darkness. Whatever other states of mind, connected with delusion, exist in the world, all appertain to Darkness. Frequent ill-speaking of other people, censuring the deities and the Brahmanas, illiberality, vanity, delusion, wrath, unforgiveness, hostility towards all creatures, are regarded as the characteristics of Darkness. Whatever undertakings exist that are unmeritorious (in consequence of their being vain or useless), what gifts there are that are unmeritorious (in consequence of the unworthiness of the donees, the unreasonableness of the time, the impropriety of the object, etc.), vain eating,—these also appertain to Darkness. Indulgence in calumny, unforgiveness, animosity, vanity, and absence of faith are also said to be characteristics of Darkness. Whatever men there are in this world who are characterised by these and other faults of a similar kind, and who break through the restraints (provided by the scriptures), are all regarded as belonging to the quality of Darkness. I shall now declare the wombs where these men, who are always of sinful deeds, have to take their birth. Ordained to go to hell, they sink in the order of being. Indeed, they sink into the hell of (birth in) the brute creation. They become immobile entities, or animals, or beasts of burden; or carnivorous creatures, or snakes, or worms, insects, and birds; or creatures of the oviparous order, or quadrupeds of diverse species; or lunatics, or deaf or dumb human beings, or men that are afflicted by dreadful maladies and regarded as unclean. These men of evil conduct, always exhibiting the indications of their acts, sink in Darkness. Their course (of migrations) is always downwards. Appertaining to the quality of Darkness, they sink in Darkness. I shall, after this, declare what the means are of their improvement and ascent; indeed, by what means they succeed in attaining to the regions that exist for men of pious deeds. Those men who take birth in orders other than humanity, by growing up in view of the religious ceremonies of Brahmanas devoted to the duties of their own order and desirous of doing good to all creatures, succeed, through the aid of such purificatory rites, in ascending upwards. Indeed, struggling (to improve themselves), they at last attain to the same regions with these pious Brahmanas. Verily, they go to Heaven. Even this is the Vedic audition.[737] Born in orders other than humanity and growing old in their respective acts, even thus they become human beings that are, of course, ordained to return. Coming to sinful births and becoming Chandalas or human beings that are deaf or that lisp indistinctly, they attain to higher and higher castes, one after another in proper turn, transcending the Sudra order, and other (consequences of) qualities that appertain to Darkness and that abide in it in course of migrations in this world.[738] Attachment to objects of desire is regarded as great delusion. Here Rishis and Munis and deities become deluded, desirous of pleasure. Darkness, delusion, the great delusion, the great obscurity called wrath, and death, that blinding obscurity, (these are the five great afflictions). As regards wrath, that is the great obscurity (and not aversion or hatred as is sometimes included in the list). With respect then to its colour (nature), its characteristics, and its source, I have, ye learned Brahmanas, declared to you, accurately and in due order,

---

[737] Anyatha pratipannah is explained by Nilakantha as 'born in other orders'. Telang takes it as 'Behaving in a contrary way.' 'How can goats and sheep behave otherwise?' The sense seems to be that those born as goats, succeed in ascending upwards through the efficacy of the religious acts of the Brahmanas. By becoming sacrificial victims they regain their true position.

[738] Qualities abiding in Darkness etc, imply those qualities that are permanently attached to Darkness.

everything about (the quality of) Darkness. Who is there that truly understands it? Who is there that truly sees it? That, indeed, is the characteristic of Darkness, viz., the beholding of reality in what is not real. The qualities of Darkness have been declared to you in various ways. Duly has Darkness, in its higher and lower forms, been described to you. That man who always bears in mind the qualities mentioned here, will surely succeed in becoming freed from all characteristics that appertain to Darkness."'''

SECTION XXXVII.

'''"Brahma said, "Ye best of beings, I shall now declare to you accurately what (the quality of) Passion is. Ye highly blessed ones, do you understand what those qualities are that appertain to Passion. Injuring (others), beauty, toil, pleasure and pain, cold and heat, lordship (or power), war, peace, arguments, dissatisfaction, endurance,[739] might, valour, pride, wrath, exertion, quarrel (or collision), jealousy, desire, malice, battle, the sense of meum or mineness, protection (of others), slaughter, bonds, and affliction, buying and selling, lopping off, cutting, piercing and cutting off the coat of mail that another has worn,[740] fierceness, cruelty, vilifying, pointing out the faults of others, thoughts entirely devoted to worldly affairs, anxiety, animosity, reviling of others, false speech, false or vain gifts, hesitancy and doubt, boastfulness of speech, dispraise and praise, laudation, prowess, defiance, attendance (as on the sick and the weak), obedience (to the commands of preceptors and parents), service or ministrations, harbouring of thirst or desire, cleverness or dexterity of conduct, policy heedlessness, contumely, possessions, and diverse decorations that prevail in the world among men, women, animals, inanimate things, houses, grief, incredulousness, vows and regulations, actions with expectation (of good result), diverse acts of public charity, the rites in respect of Swaha salutations, rites of Swadha and Vashat, officiating at the sacrifices of others, imparting of instruction, performance of sacrifices, study, making of gifts, acceptance of gifts, rites of expiation, auspicious acts, the wish to have this and that, affection generated by the merits of the object for which or whom it is felt, treachery, deception, disrespect and respect, theft, killing, desire of concealment, vexation, wakefulness, ostentation, haughtiness, attachment, devotion, contentment, exultation, gambling, indulgence in scandal, all relations arising out of women, attachment to dancing, instrumental music and songs—all these qualities, ye learned Brahmanas, have been said to belong to Passion. Those men on Earth who meditate on the past, present, and the future, who are devoted to the aggregate of three, viz., Religion, Wealth, and Pleasure, who acting from impulse of desire, exult on attaining to affluence in respect of every desire, are said to be enveloped by Passion. These men have downward courses. Repeatedly reborn in this world, they give themselves up to pleasure. They covet what belongs to this world as also all those fruit, that belong to the world hereafter. They make gifts, accept gifts, offer oblations to the Pitris, and pour libations on the sacrificial fire. The qualities of Passion have (thus) been declared to you in their variety. The course of conduct also to which it leads has been properly described to you. The man who always understands these qualities, succeeds in always freeing himself from all of them which appertain to Passion."'''''

---

[739] Some texts read Santapah and not Sanghatah. The meaning then will be grief or sorrow.

[740] This may refer to the exposure of other people's weaknesses by tearing open their veils or covers.

SECTION XXXVIII.

"""'Brahma said, "I shall, after this discourse to you on that excellent quality which is the third (in the order of our enumeration). It is beneficial to all creatures in the world, and unblamable, and constitutes the conduct of those that are good. Joy, satisfaction, nobility, enlightenment, and happiness, absence of stinginess (or liberality), absence of fear, contentment, disposition for faith, forgiveness, courage, abstention from injuring any creature, equability, truth, straightforwardness, absence of wrath, absence of malice, purity, cleverness, prowess, (these appertain to the quality of Goodness). He who is devoted to the duty of Yoga, regarding knowledge to be vain, conduct to be vain, service to be vain, and mode of life to be vain, attains to what is highest in the world hereafter. Freedom from the idea of meum, freedom from egoism, freedom from expectations, looking on all with an equal eye, and freedom from desire,—these constitute the eternal religion of the good. Confidence, modesty, forgiveness, renunciation, purity, absence of laziness, absence of cruelty, absence of delusion, compassion to all creatures, absence of the disposition to calumniate, exultation, satisfaction, rapture, humility, good behaviour, purity in all acts having for their object the attainment of tranquillity, righteous understanding, emancipation (from attachments), indifference, Brahmacharyya, complete renunciation, freedom from the idea of meum, freedom from expectations, unbroken observance of righteousness, belief that gifts are vain, sacrifices are vain, study is vain, vows are vain, acceptance of gifts is vain, observance of duties is vain, and penances are vain—those Brahmanas in this world, whose conduct is marked by these virtues, who adhere to righteousness, who abide in the Vedas, are said to be wise and possessed of correctness of vision. Casting off all sins and freed from grief, those men possessed of wisdom attain to Heaven and create diverse bodies (for themselves). Attaining the power of governing everything, self-restraint, minuteness, these high-souled ones make by operations of their own mind, like the gods themselves dwelling in Heaven. Such men are said to have their courses directed upwards. They are veritable gods capable of modifying all things. Attaining to Heaven, they modify all things by their very nature. They get whatever objects they desire and enjoy them.[741] Thus have I, ye foremost of regenerate ones, described to you what that conduct is which appertains to the quality of goodness. Understanding these duly, one acquires whatever objects one desires. The qualities that appertain to goodness have been declared particularly. The conduct which those qualities constitute has also been properly set forth. That man who always understands these qualities, succeeds in enjoying the qualities without being attached to them."""""

SECTION XXXIX.

"""'Brahma said, "The qualities are incapable of being declared as completely separate from one another. Passion and Goodness and Darkness are seen existing in a state of union. They are attached to one another. They depend on one another. They have one another for their refuge. They likewise follow one another. As long as goodness exists, so long does Passion exist. There is no doubt in this. As long as Darkness and Goodness exist, so long does Passion exist. They make their journey together, in union, and moving collectively. They, verily, move in body, when they act with cause or without

---

[741] Vibhajanti implies enjoyments in this connection. Telang starts a needless objection to this word.

cause. Of all these which act with one another, however, much they may differ in their development, the manner in which their increase and diminution take place will now be declared. There where Darkness exists in an increased measure, in the lower creatures (for example), Passion exists in a smaller measure and Goodness in a measure that is still less. There where Passion exists in a copious measure, in creatures of middle course, Darkness exists in a smaller measure and Goodness in a measure that is still less. There where Goodness exists in a copious measure, in creatures of upward courses, Darkness should be known to exist in a small measure and Passion in a measure that is still less. Goodness is the spring that causes the modifications of the senses. It is the great enlightener. No duty has been laid down that is higher than Goodness. They who abide in Goodness proceed upwards. They who abide in Passion remain in the middle. They who abide in Darkness, being characterised by qualities that are low, sink downwards. Darkness occurs in the Sudra; Passion in the Kshatriya; and Goodness, which is the highest, in the Brahmana. The three qualities exist even thus in the three orders. Even from a distance, the three qualities of darkness and Goodness and Passion, are seen to exist in a state of union and more collectively. They are never seen in a state of separation.[742] Beholding the sun rising, men of evil deeds become inspired with fear. Travellers on their way become afflicted with heat, and suffer distress. The Sun is Goodness developed, men of evil deeds represent Darkness; the heat which travellers on their way feel is said to be a quality of Passion. The sun representing light is Goodness; the heat is the quality of Passion; the shading (or eclipse) of the sun on Parvana days should be known to represent Darkness. Even thus, the three qualities exist in all luminous bodies. They act by turns in diverse places in diverse ways. Among immobile objects, the quality of Darkness exists in a very large measure. The qualities appertaining to Passion are those properties of theirs which undergo constant changes. Their oleaginous attributes appertain to Goodness.[743] The Day should be understood as threefold. The Night has been ordained to be threefold. So also are fortnight, months, years, seasons, and conjunctions.[744] The gifts that are wide are threefold. Threefold is sacrifice that flows. Threefold are the worlds; threefold the deities; threefold is knowledge; and threefold the path or end. The past, the Present, and the Future; Religion, Wealth, and Pleasure. Prana, Apana, and Udana; these also are fraught with the three qualities. Whatever object exists in this world, everything in it is fraught with the three qualities. The three qualities act by turns in all things and in all circumstances. Verily, the three qualities always act in an unmanifest form. The creation of those three, viz., Goodness, Passion, and Darkness is eternal. The unmanifest, consisting of the three qualities, is said to be darkness, unperceived, holy, Constant, unborn, womb, eternal, Nature, change or modification, destruction, Pradhana, production, and absorption, undeveloped, not small (i.e., vast), unshaking, immovable, fixed, existent, and non-

---

[742] 'From even a distance' implies that upon even a cursory view; without even being examined minutely.

[743] What is said here is this: the three qualities exist in even the immobile objects of the universe. As regards Darkness, it predominates in them. As regards Passion, it dwells in such properties of theirs as pungency, sourness, sweetness, etc, which change with time or in consequence of cooking or through admixture. Their only properties are said to appertain to Goodness. Tiryagbhavagatam is explained by Nilakantha as adhikyam gatam. Telang thinks this is unwarrantable. His own version, however, of the first line is untenable. What can be the tiryagbhava or 'form of lower species' of immobile objects? Telang frequently forgets that Nilakantha represents a school of interpretation not founded by him but which existed from a time long anterior to him.

[744] 'Conjunctions' are evidently the periods joining the seasons, i.e., the close of one season and the beginning of another.

existent. All these names should be known by those who meditate on matters connected with the soul. That person who accurately knows all the names of the unmanifest, and the qualities, as also the pure operations (of the qualities), is well conversant with the truth about all distinctions and freed from the body, becomes liberated from all the qualities and enjoys absolute happiness.""""

SECTION XL.

""""Brahma said, "From the unmanifest first sprang Mahat (the Great Soul) endued with great intelligence, the source of all the qualities. That is said to be the first creation. The Great Soul is signified by these synonymous words—the Great Soul, Intelligence, Vishnu, Jishnu, Sambhu of great valour, the Understanding, the means of acquiring knowledge, the means of perception, as also fame, courage, and memory. Knowing this, a learned Brahmana has never to encounter delusion. It has hands and feet on every side, it has ears on every side. It stands, pervading everything in the universe. Of great power, that Being is stationed in the heart of all. Minuteness, Lightness and Affluence, are his. He is the lord of all, and identical with effulgence, and knows not decay. In Him are all those who comprehend the nature of the understanding, all those who are devoted to goodness of disposition, all those who practise meditation, who are always devoted to Yoga, who are firm in truth, who have subdued their senses, who are possessed of knowledge, who are freed from cupidity, who have conquered wrath, who are of cheerful hearts, who are endued with wisdom, who are liberated from ideas of meum (and teum), and who are devoid of egoism. All these, freed from every kind of attachment, attain to the status of Greatness. That person who understands that holy and high goal, viz., the Great Soul, becomes freed from delusion. The self-born Vishnu becomes the Lord in the primary creations. He who thus knows the Lord lying in the cave, the Supreme, Ancient Being, of universal form, the golden one, the highest goal of all persons endued with understanding,—that intelligent man lives, transcending the understanding.""""

SECTION XLI.

""""Brahma said, "That Mahat who was first produced is called Egoism. When it sprang up as I, it came to be called as the second creation. That Egoism is said to be the source of all creatures, for these have sprung from its modifications. It is pure effulgence and is the supporter of consciousness. It is Prajapati. It is a deity, the creator of deities, and of mind. It is that which creates the three worlds. It is said to be that which feels—I am all this.—That is the eternal world existing for those sages who are contented with knowledge relating to the soul, who have meditated on the soul, and who have won success by Vedic study and sacrifices. By consciousness of soul one enjoys the qualities. That source of all creatures, that creator of all creatures, creates (all creatures) even in this way. It is that which causes all changes. It is that which causes all beings to move. By its own light it illuminates the universe likewise.""""

SECTION XLII.

""Brahma said, "From Egoism were verily born the five great elements. They are earth, air, ether, water, and light numbering the fifth. In these five great elements, in the matter of the sound, touch, colour, taste, and smell, all creatures become deluded. When at the close of the destruction of the great elements, the dissolution of the universe approaches, ye that are possessed of wisdom, a great fear comes upon all living creatures. Every existent object is dissolved into that from which it is produced. The dissolution takes place in an order that is the reverse of that in which creation takes place. Indeed, as regards birth, they are born from one another. Then, when all existent objects, mobile and immobile, become dissolved, wise men endued with powerful memory never dissolve. Sound, touch, colour, taste, and smell numbering the fifth, are effects. They are, however, inconstant, and called by the name of delusion. Caused by the production of cupidity, not different from one another, without reality, connected with flesh and blood, and depending upon one another, existing outside the soul, these are all helpless and powerless. Prana and Apana, and Udana and Samana and Vyana,—these five winds are always closely attached to the soul. Together with speech, mind, and understanding, they constitute the universe of eight ingredients. He whose skin, nose, ear, eyes, tongue, and speech are restrained, whose mind is pure, and whose understanding deviates not (from the right path), and whose mind is never burnt by those eight fires, succeeds in attaining to that auspicious Brahman to which nothing superior exists. Those which have been called the eleven organs and which have sprung from Egoism, I shall now, ye regenerate ones, mention particularly. They are the ear, the skin, the two eyes, the tongue, the nose numbering the fifth, the two feet, the lower duct, the organ of generation, the two hands, and speech forming the tenth. These constitute the group of organs, with mind numbering as the eleventh. One should first subdue this group. Then will Brahman shine forth (in him). Five amongst these are called organs of knowledge, and five, organs of action. The five beginning with the ear are truly said to be connected with knowledge. The rest, however, that are connected with action, are without distinction. The mind should be regarded as belonging to both. The understanding is the twelfth in the top. Thus have been enumerated the eleven organs in due order. Learned men, having understood these, think they have accomplished everything. I shall, after this, enumerate all the various organs. Space (or Ether) is the first entity. As connected with the soul, it is called the ear. As connected with objects, that is sound. The presiding deity (of this) is the quarters. The Wind is the second entity. As connected with the soul, it is known as the skin. As connected with objects, it is known as objects of touch; and the presiding deity there is touch. The third is said to be Light. As connected with the soul, it is known as the eye. As connected with objects, it is colour; and the sun is its deity. The fourth (entity) should be known as Water. As connected with the soul, it is said to be the tongue. As connected with objects, it is taste, and the presiding deity there is Soma. The fifth entity is Earth. As connected with the soul, it is said to be the nose. As connected with objects, it is scent; and the presiding deity there is the wind. Thus has the manner been declared of how the five entities are divided into sets of three. After this I shall declare everything about the diverse (other) organs. Brahmanas conversant with the truth say that the two feet are mentioned as connected with the soul. As connected with objects, it is motion; and Vishnu is there the presiding deity. The Apana wind, whose motion is downward, as connected with the soul, is called the lower duct. As connected with objects, it is the excreta that is ejected; and the presiding deity there is Mitra. As connected with the soul, the organ of generation is mentioned, the producer of all beings. As connected with objects, it is the vital seed; and the presiding deity is Prajapati. The two hands are mentioned as connected with the soul by persons conversant with the relations of the soul. As connected with objects, it is actions; and the presiding deity there is Indra. Next, connected with the soul is speech which relates to all the gods. As connected with objects, it is what is spoken. The presiding deity there is Agni. As connected with the soul, the mind is mentioned, which moves within the soul of the five elements.[745] As connected with objects, it is the mental operation; and the presiding deity is Chandramas (moon). As connected with the soul is Egoism, which is the cause of the whole course of worldly life. As connected with objects, it is consciousness of self; and the presiding deity there is Rudra. As connected with the soul is the understanding, which impels the six senses. As connected with objects, it is that which is to be understood, and the presiding deity there is Brahma. Three are the seats of all existent objects. A fourth is not possible. These are land, water, and ether. The mode of birth is fourfold. Some are born of eggs; some are born of germs which spring upwards, penetrating through the earth; some are born of filth; and some are born of fleshy balls in wombs. Thus is the mode of birth seen to be of four kinds, of all living creatures. Now, there are other inferior beings and likewise those that range the sky. These should be known to be born of eggs as also those which crawl on their breasts. Insects are said to be born of filth, as also other creatures of a like description. This is said to be the second mode of birth and is inferior. Those living creatures that take birth after the lapse of some time, bursting through the earth, are said to be germ-born beings, ye foremost of regenerate persons. Creatures of two feet or of many feet and those which move crookedly, are the beings born of wombs. Among them are some that are deformed, ye best of men. The eternal womb of Brahma should be known to be of two kinds, viz., penance and meritorious acts. Such is the doctrine of the learned.[746] Action should be understood to be of various kinds, such as sacrifice, gifts made at sacrifices, and the meritorious duty of study for every one that is born; such is the teaching of the ancients. He who duly understands this, comes to be regarded as possessed of Yoga, ye chief of regenerate persons. Know also that such a man becomes freed too from all his sins. I have thus declared to you duly the doctrine of Adhyatma.[747] Ye Rishis conversant with all duties, a knowledge of this is acquired by those who are regarded as persons of knowledge. Uniting all these together, viz., the senses, the objects of the senses, and the five great entities, one should hold them in the mind.[748] When everything is attenuated (by absorption) in the mind, one no longer esteems the pleasures of life. Learned men, whose understandings are furnished with knowledge, regard that as true happiness.[749] I shall after this, tell thee of renunciation with respect to all entities by means, gentle and hard, which produces attachment to subtle topics and which is fraught with auspiciousness. That conduct which consists in

---

[745] This probably implies that the mind, through the aid of the senses, enters into all things or succeeds in knowing them.

[746] The sense seems to be that through these one succeeds in taking birth as a Brahmana.

[747] A repetition occurs here of about 5 verses. The passage is evidently an interpolation originally caused by carelessness.

[748] Nilakantha explains that this implies that one should regard these as really undistinguished from the mind. Indeed, created by the mind itself, these should always be taken as having no real existence beyond the mind.

[749] 'That' here refers to the attenuation of all things by absorption into the mind.

498

treating the qualities is not qualities, which is free from attachment, which is living alone, which does not recognise distinctions, and which is full of Brahman, is the source of all happiness.[750] The learned man who absorbs all desires into himself from all sides like the tortoise withdrawing all its limbs, who is devoid of passion, and who is released from everything, becomes always happy. Restraining all desires within the soul, destroying his thirst, concentrated in meditation, and becoming the friend of good heart towards all creatures, he succeeds in becoming fit for assimilation with Brahman. Through repression of all the senses which always hanker after their objects, and abandonment of inhabited places, the Adhyatma fire blazes forth in the man of contemplation. As a fire, fed with fuel, becomes bright in consequence of the blazing flames it puts forth, even so, in consequence of the repression of the senses, the great soul puts forth its effulgence. When one with a tranquil soul beholds all entities in one's own heart, then, lighted by one's own effulgence, one attains to that which is subtler than the subtle and which is unrivalled in excellence. It is settled that the body has fire for colour, water for blood and other liquids, wind for sense of touch, earth for the hideous holder of mind (viz., flesh and bones, etc.), space (or ether) for sound; that it is pervaded by disease and sorrow; that it is overwhelmed by five currents; that it is made up of the five elements; that it has nine doors and two deities;[751] that it is full of passion; that it is unfit to be seen (owing to its unholy character); that it is made up of three qualities; that it has three constituent elements, (viz., wind, bile and phlegm); that it is delighted with attachments of every kind, that it is full of delusions.[752] It is difficult of being moved in this mortal world, and it rests on the understanding as its support. That body is, in this world, the wheel of Time that is continually revolving.[753] That (body), indeed, is a terrible and unfathomable ocean and is called delusion. It is this body which stretches forth, contracts, and awakens the (whole) universe with the (very) immortals.[754] By restraining the senses, one casts off lust, wrath, fear, cupidity, enmity, and falsehood, which are eternal and, therefore, exceedingly difficult to cast off.[755] He who has subjugated these in this world, viz., the three qualities and the five constituent elements of the body, has the Highest for his seat in Heaven. By him is Infinity attained. Crossing the river, that has the five senses for its steep banks, the mental inclinations for its mighty waters, and delusion for its lake, one should subjugate both lust and wrath. Such a man freed from all faults, then beholds the Highest, concentrating the mind within the mind and seeing self in self. Understanding all things, he sees his self, with self, in all creatures, sometimes as one and sometimes as

---

[750] Gunagunam is treating the qualities as not qualities; i.e., regarding bravery, magnanimity, etc, as really not merits, for these lead to pride. Ekacharyyam is ekantavasam, i.e., life in seclusion, or living without depending upon others. Anantaram is nirastasamastabheda or non-recognition of all distinctions. Some texts read Brahmamatah meaning 'existing among Brahmanas'. Ekapadam sukham is samastasukhagarbham, i.e., the source or fountain of all happiness.

[751] The two deities are Jiva and Iswara.

[752] The correct reading, in 53 seems to be samsargabhiratam and not samsayabhiratam.

[753] In the second line, the correct words are martya and sarva. The sense of the second line seems to be that this body is ceaselessly revolving, for Emancipation is difficult to achieve. Hence this body is, as it were, the wheel of Time. Nilakantha's explanation does not seem to be satisfactory.

[754] I do not think that Telang is correct in his version of this verse. What is said here seems to be this. The body is, as it were the wheel of Time; the body is the ocean of delusion; the body is the creator, destroyer and reawakener of the universe. Through the body creatures act, and hence creation, destruction, and re-creation are due to the body. This accords with what is said elsewhere regarding the body.

[755] It would be wrong to take satah as implying 'the good,' the finite verses in every text being singular.

diverse, changing form from time to time.[756] Without doubt he can perceive numerous bodies like a hundred lights from one light. Verily he is Vishnu, and Mitra, and Varuna, and Agni, and Prajapati. He is the Creator and the ordainer: he is the Lord possessed of puissance, with faces turned in all directions. In him, the heart of all creatures, the great soul, becomes resplendent. Him all conclaves of learned Brahmanas, deities and Asuras, and Yakshas, and Pisachas, the Pitris, and birds, and bands of Rakshasas, and bands of ghostly beings, and all the great Rishis, praise.""""

SECTION XLIII.

""""Brahma said, "Among men, the royal Kshatriya is (endued with) the middle quality. Among vehicles, the elephant (is so); and among denizens of the forest the lion; among all (sacrificial) animals, the sheep; among all those that live in holes, is the snake; among cattle, the bovine bull; among females, the mule.[757] There is no doubt in this that in this world, the Nyagrodha, the Jamvu, the Pippala, the Salmali, and Sinsapa, the Meshasringa, and the Kichaka, are the foremost ones among trees.[758] Himavat, Patipatra, Sahya, Vindhya, Trikutavat, Sweta, Nila, Bhasa, Koshthavat, Guruskandha, Mahendra and Malayavat,—these are the foremost of mountains. Likewise the Maruts are the foremost of the Ganas. Surya is the lord of all the planets, and Chandramas of all the constellations. Yama is the lord of the Pitris; Ocean is the lord of all rivers. Varuna is the king of the waters. Indra is said to be the king of the Maruts. Arka is the king of all hot bodies, and Indra of all luminous bodies. Agni is the eternal lord of the elements, and Vrihaspati of the Brahmanas. Soma is the lord of (deciduous) herbs, and Vishnu is the foremost of all that are endued with might. Tashtri is the king of Rudras, and Siva of all creatures. Sacrifice is the foremost of all initiatory rites, and Maghavat of the deities. The North is the lord of all the points of the compass; Soma of great energy is the lord of all learned Brahmanas. Kuvera is the lord of all precious gems, and Purandara of all the deities. Such is the highest creation among all entities. Prajapati is the lord of all creatures. Of all entities whatever, I, who am full of Brahman, am the foremost. There is no entity that is higher than myself or Vishnu. The great Vishnu, who is full of Brahman, is the king of kings over all. Know him to be the ruler, the creator, the uncreated Hari. He is the ruler of men and Kinnaras and Yakshas and Gandharvas, and Snakes and Rakshasas, and deities and Danavas and Nagas. Among those that are followed by persons full of desire is the great goddess Maheswari of beautiful eyes. She is otherwise called by the name of Parvati. Know that the goddess Uma is the foremost and the most auspicious of women. Among women that are a source of pleasure, the foremost are the Apsaras who are possessed of great splendour.[759] Kings are desirous of acquiring piety, and Brahmanas are causeways of piety. Therefore, the king should always strive to protect the twice-born ones. Those kings in whose dominions good men languish are regarded as bereft of the virtues of their order. Hereafter they have to go into wrong

---

[756] The correct reading seems to be atmana as the last word of the first line, and not atman.

[757] What is said here is that the quality of passion predominates in these.

[758] Nyagrodha is the Ficus Bengalensis, Linn. Jamvu is Eugenia Jambolana, Lamk. Pippala is Ficus religiosa, Linn. Salmali is Bombax Malabaricum. Sinsapa is Dalbergia Sissoo, Roxb. Meshasringa is Asclepia geminata, Roxb. Kichaka is a variety of mountain bamboo. Here however it evidently implies the Nimba or Melia Azadirachta, Linn.

[759] Nilakantha is for taking the second line as consisting of two propositions. It would be better to take satinam as referring to strinam, and vasumatyah, as an adjective of Apsarasah.

500

paths. Those kings in whose dominions good men are protected, rejoice in this world and enjoy happiness hereafter. Verily, those high-souled ones attain to the highest seat. Understand this, ye foremost of regenerate ones. I shall after this state the everlasting indications of duties. Abstention from injury is the highest duty. Injury is an indication of unrighteousness. Splendour is the indication of the deities. Men have acts for their indications. Ether (or space) has sound for its characteristic. Wind has touch for its characteristic. The characteristic of lighted bodies is colour, and water has taste for its characteristic. Earth, which holds all entities, has smell for its characteristic. Speech has words for its characteristic, refined into vowels and consonants. Mind has thought for its characteristic. Thought has, again, been said to be the characteristic of the understanding. The things thought of by the mind are ascertained with accuracy by the understanding. There is no doubt in this, viz., that the understanding, by perseverance, perceives all things. The characteristic of mind is meditation. The characteristic of the good man is to live unperceived.[760] Devotion has acts for its characteristic. Knowledge is the characteristic of renunciation. Therefore keeping knowledge before his view, the man of understanding should practise renunciation. The man who has betaken himself to renunciation and who is possessed of knowledge, who transcends all pairs of opposites, as also darkness, death, and decrepitude, attains to the highest goal. I have thus declared to you duly what the indications are of duty. I shall, after this, tell you of the seizure (comprehension) of qualities. Smell, which appertains to earth, is seized by the nose. The wind, that dwells in the nose is likewise appointed (as an agent) in the perception of smell. Taste is the essence of water. That is seized by the tongue. Soma, who resides in the tongue, is appointed likewise in the perception of taste. The quality of a lighted body is colour. That is seized by the eye. Aditya who always resides in the eye has been appointed in the perception of colour. Touch always appertains to the wind (as its quality). That is perceived by the skin. The wind that always resides in the skin has been appointed in apprehending touch. The quality of ether is sound. That is seized by the ear. All the quarters, which reside in the ear, have been appointed in apprehending sound. The quality of the mind is thought. That is seized by the understanding. The upholder of consciousness, residing in the heart, has been appointed in apprehending the mind. The understanding is apprehended in the form of determination or certitude, and Mahat in the form of knowledge. The unperceived (Prakriti) has been, it is evident, appointed for the seizure of all things after certitude. There is no doubt in this.[761] The Kshetrajna which is eternal and is destitute of qualities as regards its essence, is incapable of being seized by symbols. Hence, the characteristic of the Kshetrajna, which is without symbols, is purely knowledge. The unmanifest resides in the symbol called Kshetra, and is that in which the qualities are produced and absorbed. I always see, know, and hear it (though) it is hidden. Purusha knows it: therefore is he called Kshetrajna. The Kshetrajna perceives also the operations of the qualities and absence of their operations. The qualities, which are created repeatedly, do not know themselves, being unintelligent, as entities to be created and endued with a beginning, middle, and end. No one else attains, only the Kshetrajna attains, to that which is the highest and great and which transcend the qualities and those entities which are born of the qualities. Hence one who understands duties, casting off

[760] The sense seems to be that good men never allow others to know what their acts are. They are strangers to ostentation.

[761] The sense seems to be that the knowledge of one's own identity and of things as discriminated from one another is presided over by Prakriti. If the question is asked whence is the knowledge—'I am so,' and that 'this is so,' the answer is that it comes from Prakriti or Nature.

qualities and the understanding, and having his sins destroyed, and transcending the qualities, enters the Kshetrajna. One that is free from all pairs of opposites, that never bends his head to any one, that is divested of Swaha, that is immovable, and homeless, is the Kshetrajna. He is the Supreme Lord.""""

SECTION XLIV.

""""Brahma said, "I shall now tell you truly about all that which has a beginning, middle, and end, and which is endued with name and characteristics, together with the means of apprehension. It has been said that the Day was first. Then arose Night. The Months are said to have the lighted fortnights first. The constellations have Sravana for their first; the Seasons have that of dews (viz., Winter) for their first. Earth is the source of all smells; and Water of all tastes. The solar light is the source of all colours; the Wind of all sensations of touch. Likewise, of sound the source is space (or Ether). These are the qualities of elements. I shall, after this, declare that which is the first and the highest of all entities. The sun is the first of all lighted bodies. Fire is said to be the first of all the elements. Savitri is the first of all branches of learning. Prajapati is the first of all the deities. The syllable Om is the first of all the Vedas, and the life-wind Prana is the first of all winds. All that is called Savitri which is prescribed in this world.[762] The Gayatri is the first of all metres; of all (sacrificial) animals the first is the goat. Kine are the first of all quadrupeds. The twiceborn ones are the first of all human beings. The hawk is the first of all birds. Of sacrifices the first is the pouring of clarified butter on the fire. Of all reptiles the first, O foremost of regenerate ones, is the snake. The Krita is the first of all the Yugas; there is no doubt in this. Gold is the first of all precious things. Barley is the first of all plants. Food is the first of all things to be eaten or swallowed. Of all liquid substances to be drunk, water is the foremost. Of all immobile entities without distinction, Plaksha is said to be the first, that ever holy field of Brahman. Of all the Prajapatis I am the first. There is no doubt in this. Of inconceivable soul, the self-existent Vishnu is said to be my superior.[763] Of all the mountains the great Meru is said to be the first-born. Of all the cardinal and subsidiary points of the horizon, the eastern is said to be the foremost and first-born. Ganga of three courses is said to be the firstborn of all rivers. Likewise, of all wells and reservoirs of waters, the ocean is said to be the first-born. Iswara is the supreme Lord of all the deities and Danavas and ghostly beings and Pisachas, and snakes and Makshasas and human beings and Kinnaras and Yakshas. The great Vishnu, who is full of Brahma, than whom there is no higher being in the three worlds, is the first of all the universe. Of all the modes of life, that of the householder is the first. Of this there is no doubt. The Unmanifest is the source of all the worlds as, indeed, that is the end of every thing. Days end with the sun's setting and Nights with the sun's rising. The end of pleasure is always sorrow, and the end of sorrow is always pleasure. All accumulations have exhaustion for their end, and all ascent have falls for their end. All associations have dissociations for their end, and life has death for its end. All action ends in destruction, and all that is born is certain to meet with death. Every mobile and immobile thing in this world is transient. Sacrifice, gift, penances, study,

[762] As explained by Nilakantha, the word Savitri is used here to imply all forms of worship observed by Brahmanas, etc, and the Mlecchas as well. This turning back to explain a word used before is said to be an instance of "looking back like the lion."

[763] Telang, I think, renders this verse wrongly. In the first line it is said that Brahman is superior to the Prajapatis. In the second it is pointed out that Vishnu is superior to Brahman.

vows, observances,—all these have destruction for their end. Of Knowledge, there is no end. Hence, one that is possessed of a tranquil soul, that has subjugated his senses, that is freed from the sense of meum, that is devoid of egoism, is released from all sins by pure knowledge."'"""

SECTION XLV.

"""'Brahma said, "The wheel of life moves on. It has the understanding for its strength; the mind for the pole (on which it rests); the group of senses for its bonds, the (five) great elements for its nave, and home for its circumference.[764] It is overwhelmed by decrepitude and grief, and it has diseases and calamities for its progeny. That wheel relates in time and place. It has toil and exercise for its noise. Day and Night are the rotations of that wheel. It is encircled by heat and cold. Pleasure and pain fire its joints, and hunger and thirst are the nails fixed into it. Sun-shine and shade are the ruts (it causes). It is capable of being agitated during even such a short space of time as is taken up by the opening and the closing of the eyelid. It is enveloped in the terrible waters of delusion. It is ever revolving and void of consciousness. It is measured by months and half-months. It is not uniform (being ever-changing), and moves through all the worlds. Penances and vows are its mud. Passion's force is its mover. It is illuminated by the great egoism, and is sustained by the qualities. Vexations (caused by the non-acquisition of what is desired) are the fastenings that bind it around. It revolves in the midst of grief and destruction. It is endued with actions and the instruments of action. It is large and is extended by attachments. It is rendered unsteady by cupidity and desire. It is produced by variegated Ignorance. It is attended upon by fear and delusion, and is the cause of the delusion of all beings. It moves towards joy and pleasure, and has desire and wrath for its possession. It is made up of entities beginning with Mahat and ending with the gross elements. It is characterised by production and destruction going on ceaselessly. Its speed is like that of the mind, and it has the mind for its boundary.[765] This wheel of life that is associated with pairs of opposites and devoid of consciousness, the universe with the very immortals should cast away, abridge, and check. That man who always understands accurately the motion and stoppage of this wheel of life, is never seen to be deluded, among all creatures. Freed from all impressions, divested of all pairs of opposites, released from all sins, he attains to the highest goal. The householder, the Brahmacharin, the forest recluse and the mendicant,—these four modes of life have all been said to have the householder's mode for their foundation. Whatever system of rules is prescribed in this world, their observance is beneficial. Such observance has always been highly spoken of. He who has been first cleansed by ceremonies, who has duly observed vows, who belongs in respect of birth to a race possessed of high qualifications, and who understands the Vedas, should return (from his preceptor's house).[766] Always devoted to

---

[764] It is difficult to understand which part of the wheel is intended to be expressedly 'bandhanam' or the bond; I take it for the spokes. Pariskandha is Samuha or the materials that together compose an object. Here it may be taken for the nave or centre. Home is called the circumference, because, as the circumference limits the wheel, even so home (wife and children) limits the affections and acts of life.

[765] The words Kalachakram pravartate have been rendered in the first verse of this lesson. In verse 9, the words asaktaprabhavapavyam are explained by Nilakantha differently. Manas-krantam, I take, is equivalent to 'be bounded by the mind.' I do not know whence Telang gets 'never fatigued' as the substitute of this word.

[766] Implying that he should go to the house of his preceptor, study and serve there, and after completing his course, return for leading a life of domesticity.

his wedded spouse, conducting himself after the manner of the good, with his senses under subjugation, and full of faith, one should in this world perform the five sacrifices. He who eats what remains after feeding deities and guests, who is devoted to the observance of Vedic rites, who duly performs according to his means sacrifices and gifts, who is not unduly active with his hands and feet, who is not unduly active with his eye, who is devoted to penances, who is not unduly active with his speech and limits, comes under the category of Sishta or the good. One should always bear the sacred thread, wear white (clean) clothes, observe pure vows, and should always associate with good men, making gifts and practising self-restraint. One should subjugate one's lust and stomach, practise universal compassion, and be characterised by behaviour that befits the good. One should bear a bamboo-stick, and a water-pot filled with water. Having studied, one should teach; likewise should also make sacrifices himself and officiate at the sacrifices of others. One should also make gifts made to oneself. Verily, one's conduct, should be characterised by these six acts. Know that three of these acts should constitute the livelihood of the Brahmanas, viz., teaching (pupils), officiating at the sacrifices of others, and the acceptance of gifts from a person that is pure. As to the other duties that remain, numbering three, viz., making of gifts, study, and sacrifice, these are accompanied by merit.[767] Observant of penances, self-restrained, practising universal compassion and forgiveness, and looking upon all creatures with an equal eye, the man that is conversant with duties should never be heedless with regard to those three acts. The learned Brahmana of pure heart, who observes the domestic mode of life and practises rigid vows, thus devoted and thus discharging all duties to the best of his power, succeeds in conquering Heaven."''''''

SECTION XLVI.

"''''Brahma said, "Duly studying thus to the best of his power, in the way described above, and likewise living as a Brahmacharin, one that is devoted to the duties of one's own order, possessed of learning, observant of penances, and with all the senses under restraint, devoted to what is agreeable and beneficial to the preceptor, steady in practising the duty of truth, and always pure, should, with the permission of the preceptor, eat one's food without decrying it. He should eat Havishya made from what is obtained in alms, and should stand, sit, and take exercise (as directed).[768] He should pour libations on the fire twice a day, having purified himself and with concentrated mind. He should always bear a staff made of Vilwa or Palasa.[769] The robes of the regenerate man should be linen, or of cotton, or deer-skin, or a cloth that is entirely brown-red. There should also be a girdle made of Munja-grass. He should bear matted locks on head, and should perform his ablutions every day. He should bear the sacred thread, study the scriptures, divest himself of cupidity, and be steady in the observance of vows. He should also gratify the deities with oblations of pure water, his mind being restrained the while. Such a Brahmacharin is worthy of applause. With vital seed drawn up and mind concentrated, one that is thus devoted succeeds in conquering Heaven. Having attained to the highest

---

[767] The sense seems to be that these last three duties are productive of merit and should, therefore, be performed. The first three however, are sources of living.

[768] Havishya is food cooked in a particular way and offered to the deities. It must be free from meat. There may be milk or ghee in it, but the cooking must be done in a single pot or vessel continuously; no change of vessels is allowed.

[769] Vilwa is the Aegle marmelos, and Palasa is the Butea frondosa of Roxburgh.

seat, he has not to return to birth. Cleansed by all purificatory rites and having lived as a Brahmacharin, one should next go out of one's village and next live as an ascetic in the woods, having renounced (all attachments). Clad in animal skins or barks of trees he should perform his ablutions morning and evening. Always living within the forest, he should never return to an inhabited place. Honouring guests when they come, he should give them shelter, and himself subsist upon fruits and leaves and common roots, and Syamaka. He should, without being slothful subsist on such water as he gets, and air, and all forest products. He should live upon these, in due order, according to the regulations of his initiation.[770] He should honour the guest that comes to him with alms of fruits and roots. He should then, without sloth, always give whatever other food he may have. Restraining speech the while, he should eat after gratifying deities and guests. His mind should be free from envy. He should eat little, and depend always on the deities. Self-restrained, practising universal compassion, and possessed of forgiveness, he should wear both beard and hair (without submitting to the operations of the barber). Performing sacrifices and devoting himself to the study of the scriptures, he should be steady in the observance of the duty of truth. With body always in a state of purity, endued with cleverness, ever dwelling in the forest, with concentrated mind, and senses in subjection, a forest-recluse, thus devoting himself, would conquer Heaven. A householder, or Brahmacharin, or forest-recluse, who would wish to achieve Emancipation, should have recourse to that which has been called the best course of conduct. Having granted unto all creatures the pledge of utter abstention from harm, he should thoroughly renounce all action. He should contribute to the happiness of all creatures, practise universal friendliness, subjugate all his senses, and be an ascetic. Subsisting upon food obtained without asking and without trouble, and that has come to him spontaneously, he should make a fire. He should make his round of mendicancy in a place whence smoke has ceased to curl up and where all the inhabitants have already eaten.[771] The person who is conversant with the conduct that leads to Emancipation should seek for alms after the vessels (used in cooking) have been washed. He should never rejoice when he obtains anything, and never be depressed if he obtains nothing. Seeking just what is needed for supporting life, he should, with concentrated mind, go about his round of mendicancy, waiting for the proper time. He should not wish for earnings in common with others, nor eat when honoured. The man who leads the life of mendicancy should conceal himself for avoiding gifts with honour. While eating, he should not eat such food as forms the remains of another's dish, nor such as is bitter, or astringent, or pungent. He should not also eat such kinds of food as have a sweet taste. He should eat only so much as is needed to keep him alive. The person conversant with Emancipation should obtain his subsistence without obstructing any creature. In his rounds of mendicancy he should never follow another (bent on the same purpose). He should never parade his piety; he should move about in a secluded place, freed from passion. Either an empty house, or a forest, or the foot of some tree, or a river, or a mountain-cave, he should have recourse to for shelter. In summer he should pass only one night in an inhabited place; in the season of rains he may live in one place. He should move about the world like a worm, his path

---

[770] At first he should live on fruits and roots and leaves, etc. Next on water, and then on air. There are different sects of forests recluses. The course of life is settled at the time of the initiatory rites.

[771] What is stated here is this. The Sannyasin should not ask for alms: or, if he ever seeks for alms, he should seek them in a village or house where the cooking has been already done and where every one has already eaten. This limitation is provided as otherwise the Sannyasin may be fed to his fill by the householder who sees him.

pointed out by the Sun. From compassion for creatures, he should walk on the Earth with his eyes directed towards it. He should never make any accumulations and should avoid residence with friends. The man conversant with Emancipation should every day do all his acts with pure water. Such a man should always perform his ablutions with water that has been fetched up (from the river or the tank).[772] Abstention from harm, Brahmacharyya, truth, simplicity, freedom from wrath, freedom from decrying others, self-restraint, and habitual freedom from backbiting: these eight vows, with senses restrained, he should steadily pursue. He should always practise a sinless mode of conduct, that is not deceptive and not crooked. Freed from attachment, he should always make one who comes as a guest eat (at least) a morsel of food. He should eat just enough for livelihood, for the support of life. He should eat only such food as has been obtained by righteous means, and should not pursue the dictates of desire. He should never accept any other thing than food and clothing only. He should, again, accept only as much as he can eat and nothing more. He should not be induced to accept gifts from others, nor should he make gifts to others. Owing to the helplessness of creatures, the man of wisdom should always share with others. He should not appropriate what belongs to others, nor should he take anything without being asked. He should not, having enjoyed anything become so attached to it as to desire to have it once more. One should take only earth and water and pebbles and leaves and flowers and fruits, that are not owned by any body, as they come, when one desires to do any act. One should not live by the occupation of an artisan, nor should one covet gold. One should not hate, nor teach (one that does not seek to be taught); nor should one have any belongings. One should eat only what is consecrated by faith. One should abstain from controversies. One should follow that course of conduct which has been said to be nectarine. One should never be attached to anything, and should never enter into relations of intimacy with any creature. One should not perform, nor cause to perform, any such action as involves expectation of fruit or destruction of life or the hoarding of wealth or articles. Rejecting all objects, content with a very little, one should wander about (homeless) pursuing an equal behaviour towards all creatures mobile and immobile. One should never annoy another being; not should one be annoyed with another. He who is trusted by all creatures is regarded as the foremost of those persons that understand Emancipation. One should not think of the past, nor feel anxious about the future. One should disregard the present, biding time, with concentrated mind.[773] One should never defile anything by eye, mind, or speech. Nor should one do anything that is wrong, openly or in secret. Withdrawing one's senses like the tortoise withdrawing its limbs, one should attenuate one's senses and mind, cultivate a thoroughly peaceful understanding, and seek to master every topic. Freed from all pairs of opposites, never bending one's head in reverence, abstaining from the rites requiring the utterance of Swaha, one should be free from mineness, and egoism. With cleansed soul, one should never seek to acquire what one has not and protect what one has. Free from expectations, divested of qualities, wedded to tranquillity, one should be free from all attachments and should depend on none. Attached to one's own self and comprehending all topics, one becomes emancipated without doubt. Those who perceive the self, which is without hands and feet and back, which is without head and without stomach, which is free from the operation of all qualities, which is absolute, untainted, and stable, which is without smell, without taste, and touch, without colour, and without

---

[772] He should never plunge into a stream or lake or tank for bathing.

[773] Kalakankhi implies, probably 'simply biding time', i.e., allowing time to pass indifferently over him.

sound, which is to be comprehended (by close study), which is unattached, which is without flesh, which is free from anxiety, unfading, and divine, and, lastly, which though dwelling in a house resides in all creatures, succeed in escaping death. There the understanding reaches not, nor the senses, nor the deities, nor the Vedas, nor sacrifices, nor the regions (of superior bliss), nor penance, nor vows. The attainment to it by those who are possessed of knowledge is said to be without comprehension of symbols. Hence, the man who knows the properties of that which is destitute of symbols, should practise the truths of piety.[774] The learned man, betaking himself to a life of domesticity, should adopt that conduct which is conformable to true knowledge. Though undeluded, he should practise piety after the manner of one that is deluded, without finding fault with it. Without finding fault with the practices of the good, he should himself adopt such a conduct for practising piety as may induce others to always disrespect him. That man who is endued with such a conduct is said to be the foremost of ascetics. The senses, the objects of the senses, the (five) great elements, mind, understanding, egoism, the unmanifest, Purusha also, after comprehending these duly with the aid of correct inferences, one attains to Heaven, released from all bonds. One conversant with the truth, understanding these at the time of the termination of his life, should meditate, exclusively resting on one point. Then, depending on none, one attains to Emancipation. Freed from all attachments, like the wind in space, with his accumulations exhausted, without distress of any kind, he attains to his highest goal.'"""'

SECTION XLVII.

'"""Brahma said, "The ancients who were utterers of certain truth, say that Renunciation is penance. Brahmanas, dwelling in that which has Brahman for its origin, understand Knowledge to be high Brahman.[775] Brahman is very far off, and its attainments depends upon a knowledge of the Vedas. It is free from all pairs of opposites, it is divested of all qualities; it is eternal; it is endued with unthinkable qualities: it is supreme. It is by knowledge and penance that those endued with wisdom behold that which is the highest. Verily, they that are of untainted minds, that are cleansed of every sin, and that have transcended all passion and darkness (succeed in beholding it). They who are always devoted to renunciation, and who are conversant with the Vedas, succeed in attaining to the supreme Lord who is identical with the path of happiness and peace, by the aid of penance. Penance, it has been said, is light. Conduct leads to piety. Knowledge is said to be the highest. Renunciation is the best penance. He who understands self through accurate determination of all topics, which is unperturbed, which is identical with Knowledge, and which resides in all entities, succeeds in going everywhere. The learned man who beholds association, and dissociation, and unity in diversity, is released from misery. He who never desires for anything, who despises nothing, becomes eligible, even when dwelling in this world, for assimilation with Brahman. He who is conversant with the truths about qualities of Pradhana, and understands the Pradhana as existing in all entities who is free from mineness and egoism, without doubt becomes emancipated. He who is freed from all pairs of opposites, who does not bend his head to any body, who

---

[774] The sense seems to be this: the self or soul is without qualities. He who knows the self, or rather he who pursues the self with the desire of knowing it, should practise the truths of Piety laid down above. They constitute the path that leads to the self.

[775] 'That which has Brahman for its origin' implies the Vedas.

has transcended the rites of Swadha, succeeds by the aid of tranquillity alone in attaining to that which is free from pairs of opposites, which is eternal, and which is divested of qualities. Abandoning all action, good or bad, developed from qualities, and casting off both truth and falsehood, a creature, without doubt, becomes emancipated. Having the unmanifest for the seed of its origin, with the understanding for its trunk, with the great principle of egoism for its assemblage of boughs, with the senses for the cavities of its little sprouts, with the (five) great elements for its large branches, the objects of the senses for its smaller branches, with leaves that are ever present, with flowers that always adorn it and with fruits both agreeable and disagreeable always produced, is the eternal tree of Brahman which forms the support of all creatures. Cutting and piercing that tree with knowledge of truth as the sword, the man of wisdom, abandoning the bonds which are made of attachment and which cause birth, decrepitude and death, and freeing himself from mineness and egoism, without doubt, becomes emancipated. These are the two birds, which are immutable, which are friends, and which should be known as unintelligent. That other who is different from these two is called the Intelligent. When the inner self, which is destitute of knowledge of nature, which is (as it were) unintelligent, becomes conversant with that which is above nature, then, understanding the Kshetra, and endued with an intelligence that transcends all qualities and apprehends everything, one becomes released from all sins.""'"

SECTION XLVIII.

"'"Brahma said, "Some regard Brahman as a tree. Some regard Brahman as a great forest. Some regard Brahman as unmanifest. Some regard it as transcendant and freed from every distress. They think that all this is produced from and absorbed into the unmanifest. He who, even for the short space of time that is taken by a single breath, when his end comes, becomes equable, attaining to the self, fits himself for immortality. Restraining the self in the self, even for the space of a wink, one goes, through the tranquillity of the self, to that which constitutes the inexhaustible acquisition of those that are endued with knowledge. Restraining the life-breaths again and again by controlling them according to the method called Pranayama, by the ten or the twelve, he attains to that which is beyond the four and twenty. Thus having first acquired a tranquil soul, one attains to the fruition of all one's wishes.[776] When the quality of Goodness predominates in that which arises from the Unmanifest, it becomes fit for immortality. They who are conversant with Goodness applaud it highly, saying that there is nothing higher than Goodness. By inference we know that Purusha is dependent on Goodness. Ye best of regenerate ones, it is impossible to attain to Purusha by any other means. Forgiveness, courage, abstention from harm, equability, truth, sincerity, knowledge, gift, and renunciation, are said to be the characteristics of that course of conduct which arises out of Goodness. It is by this inference that the wise believe in the identity of Purusha and Goodness, There is no doubt in this. Some learned men that are devoted to knowledge assert the unity of Kshetrajna and Nature. This, however, is not correct. It is said that

---

[776] Commentators differ about what is implied by the ten or the twelve. Nilakantha thinks that the ten mean the eight characteristics of Yoga, viz., Yama, Niyama, Asana, Pranayama, Pratyahara, Dharana, Dhyana, Samadhi, and Tarka and Vairagya. The twelve would imply the first eight, and these four, viz., Maitri, Karuna, Mudita, and Upeksha. If ten plus twelve or two and twenty be taken, then that number would be made up by the five modes of Yama, the five of Niyama, the remaining six of Yoga (beginning with Asana and ending with Samadhi), the four beginning with Maitri, and the two, viz., Tarka and Vairagya.

Nature is different from Purusha: that also will imply a want to consideration. Truly, distinction and association should be known (as applying to Purusha and Nature). Unity and diversity are likewise laid down. That is the doctrine of the learned. In the Gnat and Udumbara both unity and diversity are seen. As a fish in water is different from it, such is the relation of the two (viz., Purusha and Nature). Verily, their relation is like that of water drops on the leaf of the lotus."'

""'The preceptor continued, 'Thus addressed, those learned Brahmanas, who were the foremost of men, felt some doubts and (therefore) they once more questioned the Grandsire (of all creatures).'""'[777]

SECTION XLIX.

""'The Rishis said,—"Which among the duties is deemed to be the most worthy of being performed? The diverse modes of duty, we see, are contradictory. Some say that (it remains) after the body (is destroyed). Others say that it does not exist. Some say that everything is doubtful. Others have no doubts.[778] Some say that the eternal (principle) is not eternal. Some say that it exists, and some that it exists not. Some say it is of one form, or two-fold, and others that it is mixed. Some Brahmanas who are conversant with Brahman and utterers of truth regard it to be one. Others, that it is distinct; and others again that it is manifold. Some say that both time and space exist; others, that it is not so. Some bear matted locks on their heads and are clad in deer-skins. Others have shaven crowns and go entirely naked. Some are for entire abstention from bathing, and some for bathing. Such differences of views may be seen among deities and Brahmanas conversant with Brahman and endued with perceptions of truth. Some are for taking food; while some are devoted to fasts. Some applaud action; others applaud perfect tranquillity. Some applaud Emancipation; some, various kinds of enjoyments. Some desire diverse kinds of wealth; some, poverty. Some say that means should be resorted to; others, that this is not so. Some are devoted to a life of abstention from harm; others are addicted to destruction. Some are for merit and glory, others say that this is not so. Some are devoted to goodness; others are established on doubt. Some are for pleasure; some are for pain. Other people say that it is meditation. Other learned Brahmanas say that it is Sacrifice. Others, again, say that it is gift. Others applaud penances; others, the study of the scriptures. Some say that knowledge and renunciation (should be followed). Others who ponder on the elements say that it is Nature. Some extol everything; others, nothing. O foremost one of the deities, duty being thus confused and full of contradictions of various kinds, we are deluded and unable to come to any conclusion. People stand up for acting, saying,—This is good,—This is good—He that is attached to a certain duty applauds that duty as the best. For this reason our understanding breaks down and our mind is distracted. We therefore, wish, O best of all beings, to know what is good. It behoves thee

---

[777] What is said in this Lesson seems to be this: the Unmanifest or Prakriti is that condition in which all the three qualities of Goodness, Passion, and Darkness exist in a state of combination. The unmanifest is the condition existing before creation. When one particular quality, viz., Goodness prevails over the others, there arises Purusha, viz., that from whom everything flows. The relation of Purusha and Nature is both unity and diversity. The three illustrations of the Gnat and the Udumbara, the fish and water, and water drops and the lotus leaf, explain the relation between Purusha and Nature. He is in Nature, yet different from it. There is both association and dissociation.

[778] The doubts appertain to duties, that is whether they should be done or not, and whether they have any effects here and hereafter.

to declare to us, after this, what is (so) mysterious, and what is the cause of the connection between the Kshetrajna and Nature." Thus addressed by those learned Brahmanas, the illustrious creator of the worlds, endued with great intelligence and possessed of a righteous soul, declared to them accurately what they asked.'"""

SECTION L.

"""Brahma said, "Well then, I shall declare to you what you ask. Learn what was told by a preceptor to a disciple that came unto him. Hearing it all, do you settle properly (what it should be). Abstention from harming any creature is regarded as the foremost of all duties. That is the highest feat, free from anxiety and constituting an indication of holiness. The ancients who were beholders of the certain truth, have said that knowledge is the highest happiness. Hence, one becomes released of all sins by pure knowledge. They that are engaged in destruction and harm, they that are infidels in conduct, have to go to Hell in consequence of their being endued with cupidity and delusion. Those who, without procrastination, perform acts, impelled thereto by expectation become repeatedly born in this world and sport in joy. Those men who, endued with learning and wisdom, perform acts with faith, free from expectations, and possessed of concentration of mind, are said to perceive clearly. I shall, after this, declare how the association and the dissociation takes place of Kshetrajna and Nature. Ye best of men, listen. The relation here is said to be that between the object and the subject.[779] Purusha is always the subject; and Nature has been said to be the object. It has been explained, by what has been said in a previous portion of the discourse where it has been pointed out, that they exist after the manner of the Gnat and the Udumbara. An object of enjoyment as it is, Nature is unintelligent and knows nothing. He, however, who enjoys it, is said to know it. Kshetrajna being enjoyer, Nature is enjoyed. The wise have said that Nature is always made up of pairs of opposites (and consists of qualities). Kshetrajna is, on the other hand, destitute of pairs of opposites, devoid of parts, eternal, and free, as regards its essence, from qualities. He resides in everything alike, and walks with knowledge. He always enjoys Nature, as a lotus leaf (enjoys) water. Possessed of knowledge, he is never tainted even if brought into contact with all the qualities. Without doubt, Purusha is unattached like the unsteady drop of water on the lotus-leaf. This is the certain conclusion (of the scriptures) that Nature is the property of Purusha. The relation between these two (viz., Purusha and Nature) is like that existing between matter and its maker. As one goes into a dark place taking a light with him, even so those who wish for the Supreme proceed with the light of Nature.[780] As long as matter and quality (which are like oil and wick) exist, so long the light shines. The flame, however, becomes extinguished when matter and quality (or oil and wick) are exhausted. Thus Nature is manifest; while Purusha is said to be unmanifest. Understand this, ye learned Brahmanas. Well, I shall now tell you something more. With even a thousand (explanations), one that has a bad understanding succeeds not in acquiring knowledge. One, however, that is endued with intelligence succeeds in attaining happiness, through only a fourth share (of explanations). Thus should the accomplishment of duty be understood as dependent on means. For the man of

---

[779] The thinking or enjoying agent is subject, and that which is thought or enjoyed is object. Subject and object an two well known words in Sir W. Hamilton's philosophy. I follow Telang in adopting them.

[780] Sattawa pradipa, rendered 'light of Nature,' implies, as Nilakantha explains, knowledge, which is a manifestation of Nature. Arjuna Misra's interpretation seems to be better. He says that knowledge,—that is, knowledge of truth,—is acquired by the self through Nature.

intelligence, having knowledge of means, succeeds in attaining to supreme felicity. As some man travelling along a road without provisions for his journey, proceeds with great discomfort and may even meet with destruction before he reaches the end of his journey, even so should it be known that ill acts there may not be fruits.[781] The examination of what is agreeable and what is disagreeable in one's own self is productive of benefit.[782] The progress in life of a man that is devoid of the perception of truth is like that of a man who rashly journeys on a long road unseen before. The progress, however, of those that are endued with intelligence is like that of men who journey along the same road, riding on a car unto which are yoked (fleet) steeds and which moves with swiftness. Having ascended to the top of a mountain, one should not cast one's eyes on the surface of the earth.[783] Seeing a man, even though travelling on a car, afflicted and rendered insensible by pain, the man of intelligence journeys on a car as long as there is a car path.[784] The man of learning, when he sees the car path end, abandons his car for going on. Even thus proceeds the man of intelligence who is conversant with the ordinances respecting truth and Yoga (or Knowledge and Devotion). Conversant with the qualities, such a man proceeds, comprehending what is next and next.[785] As one that plunges, without a boat, into the terrible ocean, with only one's two arms, through delusion, undoubtedly wishes for destruction; while the man of wisdom, conversant with distinctions, goes into the water, with a boat equipt with oars, and soon crosses the lake without fatigue, and having crossed it attains to the other shore and casts off the boat, freed from the thought of meum. This has been already explained by the illustration of the car and the pedestrian. One who has been overwhelmed by delusion in consequence of attachment, adheres to it like a fisherman to his boat. Overcome by the idea of meum, one wanders within its narrow range. After embarking on a boat it is not possible in moving about on land. Similarly, it is not possible in moving about on water after one has mounted on a car. There are thus various actions with regard to various objects. And as action is performed in this world, so does it result to those that perform them. That which is void of smell, void of taste, and void of touch and sound, that which is meditated upon by the sages with the aid of their understanding, is said to be Pradhana. Now, Pradhana is unmanifest. A development of the unmanifest is Mahat. A development of Pradhana when it has become Mahat is Egoism. From egoism is produced the development called the great elements. And of the great elements respectively, the objects of sense are said to be the developments. The unmanifest is of the nature of seed. It is productive in its essence. It has been heard by us that the great soul has the virtues of a seed, and that is a product. Egoism is of the nature of seed and is a product again and again. And the five great elements are of the nature of seed and products. The objects of the five great elements are

---

[781] The sense seems to be this: one who proceeds, on a journey must provide oneself with the necessary means, otherwise one is sure to feel discomfort or meet with even destruction. So, in the journey of life, one must provide oneself with knowledge as the means. One may then avoid all discomfort and danger. Action does not constitute the proper means. It may or may not produce fruits.

[782] i.e., one should not care for the external.

[783] i.e., one need not do acts enjoined by the scriptures after one has attained to knowledge which is the highest seat.

[784] The sense is this: riding on a car may not always be comfortable. As long as there is a car path, one should travel on one's car. If, however, the road be such as not to be fit for a car to proceed along it, one should avoid a car in going over it, for the car instead of conducing to comfort, would, on such a path, be productive of only discomfort.

[785] i.e., first action with desire; then action without desire; then knowledge, according to Arjuna Misra. Nilakantha explains that action is first, then Yoga, then the state of Hansa or Paramahansa.

endued with the nature of seed, and yield products. These have Chitta for their property. Among them, space has one quality; wind is said to have two. Light, it is said, is endued with three qualities; and water as possessed of four qualities. Earth, teeming with mobiles and immobiles, should be known as possessed of five qualities. She is a goddess that is the source of all entities and abounds with examples of the agreeable and the disagreeable. Sound, likewise touch, colour, taste, and smell numbering the fifth,—these are the five qualities of earth, ye foremost of regenerate persons. Smell always belongs to earth, and smell is said to be of various kinds. I shall state at length the numerous qualities of smell. Smell is agreeable or disagreeable, sweet, sour, pungent, diffusive and compact, oily and dry, and clear. Thus smell, which belongs to the earth, should be known as of ten kinds.[786] Sound, touch, likewise colour, and taste have been said to be the qualities of water. I shall now speak of the qualities of taste. Taste has been said to be of various kinds. Sweet, sour, pungent, bitter, astringent, and saline likewise. Taste, which has been said to appertain to water, is thus of six varieties. Sound, touch, and likewise colour,—these are the three qualities which light is said to be possessed of. Colour is the quality of light, and colour is said to be of various kinds. White, dark, likewise red, blue, yellow, and grey also, and short, long, minute, gross, square and circular, of these twelve varieties in colour which belongs to light. These should be understood by Brahmanas venerable for years, conversant with duties, and truthful in speech. Sound and touch should be known as the two qualities of wind. Touch has been said to be of various kinds. Rough, cold and likewise hot, tender and clear, hard, oily, smooth, slippery, painful and soft, of twelve kinds is touch, which is the quality of wind, as said by Brahmanas crowned with success, conversant with duties, and possessed of a sight of truth. Now space has only one quality, and that is said to be sound. I shall speak at length of the numerous qualities of sound. Shadaja, Rishabha, together with Gandhara, Madhyama, and likewise Panchama; after this should be known Nishada, and then Dhaivata.[787] Besides these, there are agreeable sounds and disagreeable sounds, compact, and of many ingredients. Sound which is born of space should thus be known to be of ten kinds. Space is the highest of the (five) elements. Egoism is above it. Above egoism is understanding. Above understanding is the soul. Above the soul is the Unmanifest. Above the Unmanifest is Purusha. One who knows which is superior and inferior among existent creatures, who is conversant with the ordinances in respect of all acts, and who constitutes himself the soul of all creatures, attains to the Unfading Soul.""""

SECTION LI.

""""Brahma said, "Since the mind is the ruler of these five elements, in the matter of controlling and bringing them forth, the mind, therefore, is the soul of the elements. The mind always presides over the great elements. The understanding proclaims power, and is called the Kshetrajna.[788] The mind yokes the senses as a charioteer yokes good steeds. The senses, the mind, and the understanding are always joined to the Kshetrajna. The individual soul, mounting the chariot to which big steeds are yoked and which has the understanding for the reins, drives about on all sides. With all the senses attached to it

---

[786] Katu is not bitter but pungent or sharp, as that which is attached to chillies.

[787] These are the notes of the Hindu Gamut.

[788] The understanding operates on what is placed before it by the mind. The understanding, therefore, is, as it were, the lord exercising power or sovereignty, being served by the mind.

(for steeds), with the mind for the charioteer, and the understanding for the eternal reins, exists the great Brahman-car. Verily, that man endued with learning and wisdom who always understands the Brahman-car in this way, is never overwhelmed by delusion in the midst of all entities. This forest of Brahman begins with the Unmanifest and ends with gross objects. It includes mobile and immobile entities, and receives light from the radiance of the sun and the moon, and is adorned with planets and constellations. It is decked, again, on all sides with nets of rivers and mountains. It is always embellished likewise by diverse kinds of waters. It is the means of subsistence for all creatures. It is, again, the goal of all living creatures. In that forest the Kshetrajna always moves about. Whatever entities exist in this world, mobile and immobile, are the very first to be dissolved away. After this (are dissolved) those qualities which compose all entities. After the qualities (are dissolved) the five elements. Such is the gradation of entities. Gods, men, Gandharvas, Pisachas, Asuras, and Rakshasas, have all sprung from Nature, and not from actions, not from a cause. The Brahmanas, who are creators of the universe, are born here again and again. All that springs from them dissolves, when the time comes, in those very five great elements like billows in the ocean. All the great elements are beyond those elements that compose the universe. He that is released from those five elements goes to the highest goal. The puissant Prajapati created all this by the mind only. After the same manner Rishis attained to the status of deities by the aid of penance. After the same manner, those who have achieved perfection, who were capable of the concentration of Yoga, and who subsist on fruits and roots, likewise perceive the triple world by penance. Medicines and herbs and all the diverse sciences are acquired by means of penance alone, for all acquisition has penance for its root. Whatever is difficult of acquisition, difficult to learn, difficult to vanquish, difficult to pass through, are all achievable by penance, for penance is irresistible. One that drinks alcoholic liquors, one that slays a Brahmana, one that steals, one that destroys a foetus, one that violates one's preceptor's bed, becomes cleansed of such sin by penance well performed. Human beings, Pitris, deities, (sacrificial) animals, beasts and birds, and all other creatures mobile and immobile, by always devoting themselves to penances, become crowned with success by penance alone. In like manner, the deities, endued with great powers of illusion, have attained to Heaven. Those who without idleness perform acts with expectations, being full of egoism, approach the presence of Prajapati. Those high-souled ones, however, who are devoid of mineness and freed from egoism through the pure contemplation of Yoga, attain to the great and highest regions. Those who best understand the self, having attained to Yoga contemplation and having their minds always cheerful, enter into the unmanifest accumulation of happiness. Those persons who are freed from the idea of mineness as also from egoism and who are reborn after having attained to the fullness of Yoga contemplation, enter (when they depart from such life) into the highest region reserved for the great, viz., the Unmanifest. Born from that same unmanifest (principle) and attaining to the same once more, freed from the qualities of Darkness and Passion, and adhering to only the quality of Goodness, one becomes released from every sin and creates all things.[789] Such a one should be known to be Kshetrajna in perfection. He that knows him, knows the Veda.[790] Attaining to pure

[789] Sarvan srijati i.e., creates all things by attaining to the condition of the universal cause, for the unmanifest is the universal cause. Between such a one and the Supreme Soul there is no difference. Even this is said in the last sentence.

[790] The man who reads the book called Veda is not truly conversant with the Veda. He, however, who knows Kshetrajna, is regarded as truly knowing the Veda.

knowledge from (restraining) the mind, the ascetic should sit self-restrained. One necessarily becomes that on which one's mind is set. This is an eternal mystery. That which has the unmanifest for its beginning and gross qualities for its end, has been said to have Nescience for its indication. But do you understand that whose nature is destitute of qualities? Of two syllables is Mrityu (death); of three syllable is the eternal Brahman. Mineness is death, and the reverse of mineness is the eternal.[791] Some men who are led by bad understanding applaud action. Those, however, that are numbered among the high-souled ancients never applaud action. By action is a creature born with body which is made up of the sixteen.[792] (True) Knowledge swallows up Purusha (Self with consciousness of body). Even this is what is highly acceptable to eaters of Amrita.[793] Therefore, those whose vision extends to the other end (of the ocean of life) have no attachment for actions. This Purusha, however, is full of knowledge and not full of action.[794] He dies not who understands Him that is immortal, immutable, incomprehensible, eternal and indestructible—Him that is the restrained Soul and that transcends all attachments. He who thus understands the Soul to which there is nothing prior which is uncreated, immutable, unconquered, and incomprehensible even to those that are eaters of nectar, certainly becomes himself incomprehensible and immortal through these means. Expelling all impressions and restraining the Soul in the Soul, he understands that auspicious Brahman than which nothing greater exists. Upon the understanding becoming clear, he succeeds in attaining to tranquillity. The indication of tranquillity is like what takes place in a dream.[795] This is the goal of those emancipated ones who are intent on knowledge. They behold all those movements which are born of successive developments.[796] This is the goal of those who are unattached to the world. This is the eternal usage. This is the acquisition of men of knowledge. This is the uncensured mode of conduct. This goal is capable of being attained by one that is alike to all creatures, that is without attachment, that is without expectations, and that looks equally on all things. I have now declared everything to you, ye foremost of regenerate Rishis. Do you act in this way forthwith; you will then acquire success."

""The preceptor continued, 'Thus addressed by the preceptor Brahma, those high-souled sages acted accordingly and then attained to many regions (of great felicity). Do thou also, O blessed one, duly act according to the words of Brahma as declared by me, O thou of pure soul. Thou wilt then attain to success.'"

---

[791] The argument is that Mrityu or death being of two syllables, the correspondence is justifiable between it and Mama or mineness which also is of two syllables. So in the case of Brahman and na-mama. Of course, what is meant by mineness being death and not-mineness being Brahman or emancipation, cannot be unintelligible to one who has carefully read the preceding sections.

[792] i.e., the five great elements, four organs of knowledge with mind, and the four organs of action.

[793] The word Purusha here is used in the sense of dehabhimani Jiva or individual self with consciousness of body. True knowledge destroys this condition of Jiva, for the man of knowledge identifies himself with the universe and thereby assimilates himself to Brahman. By eaters of Amrita are meant they who never take any food without offering portions thereof to the deities, Pitris, and guests. Of course, Yogins of piety are implied by it.

[794] Purusha here implies Jiva divested of consciousness of body.

[795] The meaning is this: in a dream what is seen is all unreal. So, when tranquillity has been attained, all the surroundings become unreal. Nilakantha gives a slightly different interpretation; it is this: when tranquillity has been attained, the Soul lives without attachment to the body and all external objects. Indeed, the Soul then lives completely in itself even as it works in course of a dream.

[796] The sense is that they behold all worldly objects, present, past and future, which are, of course, due to development of previous causes.

"'Vasudeva said,—"Thus instructed in the principles of high religion by the preceptor, the pupil, O son of Kunti, did everything accordingly, and then attained to Emancipation. Having done all that he should have done, the pupil, O perpetuator of Kuru's race, attained to that seat repairing whither one has not to grieve."

"'Arjuna said, "Who, indeed, was that Brahmana, O Krishna, and who the pupil, O Janarddana. Truly, if it is fit to be heard by me, do thou then tell me, O lord!"

"'Vasudeva said, "I am the preceptor, O mighty-armed one, and know that the mind is my pupil. Through my affection for thee, O Dhananjaya, I have related this mystery to thee. If thou hast any love for me, O perpetuator of Kuru's race, do thou then, after having heard these instructions relating to the Soul, always act duly (according to them), O thou of excellent vows. Then when this religion has been duly practised, O mower of foes, thou wilt become freed from all thy sins and attain to absolute emancipation. Formerly, when the hour of battle came, this very religion, O thou of mighty arms, was declared by me (to thee)! Do thou, therefore, set thy mind on it. And now, O chief of Bharata's race, it is long since that I saw the lord my sire. I wish to see him again, with thy leave, O Phalguna!'"

"Vaisampayana continued, 'Unto Krishna who had said so, Dhananjaya said in reply,—"We shall go to-day from this town to the city called after the elephant. Meeting king Yudhishthira of virtuous soul there, and informing him (of thy intention) thou shalt then repair to thy own city!'""

SECTION LII.

"Vaisampayana said, 'After this, Krishna ordered Daruka, saying—"Let my car be yoked."—Within a very short space of time Daruka informed (his master), saying,—"It has been yoked."—The son of Pandu then commanded all his attendants, saying,—"Prepare yourselves and be ready. We shall repair to-day to the city named after the elephant." Thus addressed, O king, those troops accoutred themselves, and informed Pritha's son of immeasurable energy, saying,—"Everything is equipt." Then those two, viz., Krishna and the son of Pandu, ascended their car and proceeded on the journey, the loving friends engaged the while in delightful conversation. Unto Vasudeva seated on the car, Dhananjaya of great energy once more said these words, O chief of Bharata's race!—"O perpetuator of the Vrishni race, the king has obtained victory through thy grace. All his foes have been slain, and he has recovered his kingdom without a thorn in it (to make it disagreeable). O slayer of Madhu, through thee the Pandavas are endued with a powerful protector. Having obtained thee for our raft we have crossed the Kuru ocean. O thou that hast this universe for thy handiwork, salutations to thee, O Soul of the universe, O best of all beings in the universe. I know thee in that measure in which I am approved by thee.[797] O slayer of Madhu, the soul of every creature is always born of thy energy. Playful sport (in the form of creation, preservation, and destruction) is thine. Earth and sky, O lord, are thy illusion. This whole universe, consisting of mobile and immobile objects, is established on thee. Thou createst, by modification, the four orders of Being (viz., viviparous, oviparous, filth-born, and vegetables). Thou createst the Earth, the Welkin, and Heaven, O slayer of Madhu. The stainless lunar light is thy smile. The

---

[797] This line is rather obscure. The sense seems to be this: no one can know the Supreme Deity if it is not the latter's pleasure to be known. One, therefore, understands Him in exactly that measure in which it is His pleasure to be known.

seasons are thy senses. The ever-moving wind is thy breath, and death, existing eternally, is thy wrath. In thy grace is the goddess of prosperity. Verily, Sree is always established in thee, O thou of the highest intelligence. Thou art the sport (in which creatures engage); thou art their contentment; thou their intelligence, thou their forgiveness, thou their inclinations, thou their beauty. Thou art the universe with its mobile and immobile objects. At the end of the cycle, it is thou, O sinless one, that art called destruction. I am incapable of reciting all thy qualities in course of even a long period. Thou art the Soul and the Supreme Soul. I bow to thee, O thou of eyes like the petals of the lotus. O thou that art irresistible, I have learnt it from Narada and Devala and the Island-born (Vyasa), and the Kuru grandsire also, that all this (universe) rests on thee. Thou art the one Lord of all creatures. This, O sinless one, that thou hast declared unto me in consequence of thy favour for myself, I shall duly accomplish in its entirety, O Janarddana. Exceedingly wonderful is this which thou hast done from desire of doing what is agreeable to us, viz., the destruction in battle of the Kaurava (prince), the son of Dhritarashtra. That host had been burnt by thee which I (subsequently) vanquished in battle. That feat was achieved by thee in consequence of which victory became mine. By the power of thy intelligence was shown the means by which was duly affected the destruction of Duryodhana in battle, as also of Karna, as of the sinful king of the Sindhus; and Bhurisravas. I shall accomplish all that which, O son of Devaki, pleased with me thou hast declared to myself. I do not entertain any scruple in this. Repairing to king Yudhishthira of righteous soul, I shall, O sinless one, urge him to dismiss thee, O thou that art conversant with every duty. O lord, thy departure for Dwaraka meets with my approbation. Thou shalt soon see my maternal uncle, O Janarddana. Thou shalt also see the irresistible Valadeva and other chiefs of the Vrishni race."—Thus conversing with each other, the two reached the city named after the elephant. They then, with cheerful hearts, and without any anxiety, entered the palace of Dhritarashtra which resembled the mansion of Sakra. They then saw, O monarch, king Dhritarashtra, and Vidura of great intelligence, and king Yudhishthira and the irresistible Bhimasena, and the two sons of Madri by Pandu; and the unvanquished Yuyatsu, seated before Dhritarashtra and Gandhari of great wisdom, and Pritha, and the beautiful Krishna, and the other ladies of Bharata's race with Subhadra counting first. They also saw all those ladies that used to wait upon Gandhari. Then approaching king Dhritarashtra, those two chastisers of foes announced their names and touched his feet. Indeed, those high-souled ones also touched the feet of Gandhari and Pritha and king Yudhishthira the Just, and Bhima. Embracing Vidura also, they enquired after his welfare. In the company of all those persons, Arjuna and Krishna then approached king Dhritarashtra (again). Night came and then king Dhritarashtra of great intelligence dismissed all those perpetuators of Kuru's race as also Janarddana for retiring to their respective chambers. Permitted by the king all of them entered their respective apartments. Krishna of great energy proceeded to the apartments of Dhananjaya. Worshipped duly and furnished with every object of comfort and enjoyment, Krishna of great intelligence passed the night in happy sleep with Dhananjaya as his companion. When the night passed away and morning came, the two heroes, finishing their morning rites and dealing their persons properly, proceeded to the mansion of king Yudhishthira the just. There Yudhishthira the just, of great might, sat with his ministers. The two high-souled ones, entering that well-adorned chamber, beheld king Yudhishthira the just like the two Aswins beholding the chief of the celestials. Meeting the king, he of Vrishni's race as also that foremost hero of Kuru's race, obtaining the permission of Yudhishthira who was highly pleased with them, sat themselves down. Then the king, gifted with great intelligence, seeing those two friends, became desirous of addressing them. Soon that best of monarchs, that foremost of speakers addressed them in the following words.'

"'Yudhishthira said, "Ye heroes, ye foremost ones of Yadu's and Kuru's race, it seems that ye two are desirous of saying something to me. Do ye say what is in your mind. I shall soon accomplish it. Do not hesitate."

"'Thus addressed, Phalguna, well conversant with speech, humbly approached king Yudhishthira the just and then said these words.—"Vasudeva here, of great prowess, O king, is long absent from home. He desires, with thy permission, to see his sire. Let him go, if thou thinkest it meet, to the city of the Anarttas. It behoveth thee, O hero, to grant him permission!"

"'Yudhishthira said, "O lotus-eyed one, blessed be thou. O slayer of Madhu, do thou go this very day to the city of Dwaravati for seeing, O puissant one, that foremost one of Sura's race. O mighty-armed Kesava, thy departure is approved by me. Thou hast not seen my maternal uncle as also the goddess Devaki, for a long time. Meeting my maternal uncle and repairing to Valadeva also, O giver of honours, thou wilt, O thou of great wisdom, worship both of them at my word as they deserve.[798] Do thou also think of me daily as also of Bhima, that foremost of mighty men, and of Phalguna and Nakula and Sahadeva, O giver of honours. Having seen the Anarttas, and thy sire, O mighty-armed one, and the Vrishnis, thou wilt come back to my horse-sacrifice, O sinless one. Do thou then depart, taking with thee diverse kinds of gems and various sorts of wealth. Do thou, O hero of the Satwata race, also take with thee whatever else thou likest. It is through thy grace, O Kesava, that the whole Earth, O hero, has come under our dominion and all our foes have been slain."

"'When king Yudhishthira the just of Kuru's race said so, Vasudeva, that foremost of men, said these words (in reply).

"'Vasudeva said, "O mighty-armed one, all jewels and gems, all wealth, and the entire Earth, are thine and thine alone. Whatever wealth exists in my abode, thou, O lord, art always the owner thereof." Unto him Yudhishthira, the son of Dharma, said,—"Be it so"—and then duly worshipped (Krishna) the eldest brother, endued with great energy, of Gada. Vasudeva then proceeded to his paternal aunt (Kunti). Duly honouring her, he circumambulated her person. He was properly accosted by her in return, and then by all the others having Vidura for their first. The four-armed eldest brother of Gada then set out from Nagapura on his excellent car.[799] Placing his sister, the lady Subhadra, on the car, the mighty-armed Janarddana then, with the permission of both Yudhishthira and (Kunti) his paternal aunt, set out, accompanied by a large train of citizens. The hero who had the foremost of apes on his banner, as also Satyaki, and the two sons of Madravati, and Vidura of immeasurable intelligence, and Bhima himself whose tread resembled that of a prince of elephants, all followed Madhava. Janarddana of mighty energy causing all those extenders of the Kuru kingdom and Vidura also to return, addressed Daraka, and Satyaki, saying,—"Urge the steeds to speed." Then that grinder of hostile masses, viz., Janarddana of great prowess, accompanied by Satyaki, the foremost one of Sini's race, proceeded to the city of the Anarttas, after having slain all his foes, like He of a hundred sacrifices proceeding to Heaven (after slaughtering all his foes)."'

---

[798] Krishna's father Vasudeva is maternal uncle. Yudhishthira asks Krishna to worship Vasudeva and Valadeva on his behalf, i.e., he charges Krishna to bear to them a message of respect and love from him.

[799] The city of Hastinapura is sometimes called Nagapura, both Hasti and Naga being words expressive of the elephant. 'The city called after the elephant' is the usual description of the Kuru capital.

SECTION LIII.

"Vaisampayana said, 'As he of Vrishni's race was proceeding to Dwaraka, those foremost princes of Bharata's race, those chastisers of foes embraced him and fell back with their attendants. Phalguna repeatedly embraced the Vrishni hero, and as long as he was within the range of vision, he repeatedly turned his eyes towards him. With great difficulty, the son of Pritha withdrew his gaze that had fallen on Govinda. The unvanquished Krishna also (did the same). The indications that were manifested on the occasion of that high-souled one's departure, I shall now detail. Do thou listen to me. The wind blew with great speed before the car, clearing the path of sand-grains and dust and thorns. Vasava rained pure and fragrant showers and celestial flowers before the wielder of Saranga. As the mighty-armed hero proceeded, he came upon the desert ill supplied with water. There he beheld that foremost of ascetics, named Utanka, of immeasurable energy. The hero of large eyes and great energy worshipped that ascetic. He was then worshipped by the ascetic in return. Vasudeva then enquired after his welfare. That foremost of Brahmanas, viz., Utanka, politely accosted by Madhava, honoured him duly and then addressed him in these words.—"O Saurin, having repaired to the mansions of the Kurus and the Pandavas, hast thou succeeded in establishing a durable understanding between them such as should exist between brothers? It behoves thee to tell me everything. Dost thou come, O Kesava, after having united them in peace,—them that are thy relatives and that are ever dear to thee, O foremost one of Vrishni's race? Will the five sons of Pandu, and the children of Dhritarashtra, O scorcher of foes, sport in the world in joy with thee? Will all the kings enjoy happiness in their respective kingdoms, in consequence of the pacification of the Kauravas brought about by thee? Has that trust, O son, which I had always reposed on thee, borne fruit with regard to the Kauravas?"

"'The blessed and holy one said, "I strove my best at first, for bringing about a good understanding, in regard to the Kauravas. When I could not by any means succeed in establishing them on peace, it happened that all of them, with their relatives and kinsmen, met with death. It is impossible to transgress destiny by either intelligence or might. O great Rishi, O sinless one, this also cannot be unknown to thee. They (the Kauravas) transgressed the counsels which Bhishma and Vidura gave them referring to me.[800] Encountering one another they then became guests of Yama's abode. Only the five Pandavas constitute the remnant of the unslain, all their friends and all their children having been slaughtered. All the sons of Dhritarashtra also with their children and kinsmen, have been slain." When Krishna had said these words, Utanka, filled with wrath, and with eyes expanded in rage, addressed him in these words.

"'Utanka said,—"Since, though able, O Krishna, thou didst not rescue those foremost ones of Kuru's race, who were thy relatives and, therefore, dear to thee, I shall, without doubt, curse thee. Since thou didst not forcibly compel them to forbear, therefore, O slayer of Madhu, I shall, filled with wrath, denounce a curse on thee. It seems, O Madhava, that though fully able (to save them), thou wert indifferent to these foremost of Kurus who, overwhelmed by insincerity and hypocrisy have all met with destruction."

"'Vasudeva said, "O scion of Bhrigu's race, listen to what I say in detail. Do thou accept my apologies also. O thou of Bhrigu's race, thou art an ascetic. After having heard my words relating to the soul, thou mayst then utter thy curse. No man is able, by a little

---

[800] Mahyam is equal to 'mam uddisya' i.e., referring to my divine nature.

ascetic merit, to put me down. O foremost of ascetics, I do not wish to see the destruction of all thy penances. Thou hast a large measure of blazing penances. Thou hast gratified thy preceptors and seniors.[801] O foremost of regenerate ones, I know that thou hast observed the rules of Brahmacharyya from the days of thy infancy. I do not, therefore, desire the loss or diminution of thy penances achieved with so much pain."'"

SECTION LIV.

"'Utanka said, "Do thou, O Kesava, tell me that faultless Adhyatma. Having heard thy discourse I shall ordain what is for thy good or denounce a curse to thee, O Janarddana."

"'Vasudeva said, "Know that the three qualities of Darkness and Passion and Goodness exist, depending on me as their refuge. So also, O regenerate one, know that the Rudras and the Vasus have sprung from me. In me are all creatures, and in all creatures do I exist; know this. Let no doubt arise in thy mind respecting this. So also, O regenerate one, know that all the tribes of the Daityas, all the Yakshas, Gandharvas, Rakshasas, Nagas, Apsaras, have sprung from me. Whatever has been called existent and non-existent, whatever is manifest and not-manifest, whatever is destructible and indestructible, all have me for their soul. Those fourfold courses of duty which, O ascetic, are known to attach to the (four) modes of life, and all the Vedic duties, have me for their soul. Whatever is non-existent, whatever is existent and non-existent, and whatever transcends that which is existent and non-existent,—all these which constitute the universe—are from me. There is nothing higher (or beyond) me who am the eternal god of gods.[802] O perpetuator of Bhrigu's race, know that all the Vedas beginning with (the original syllable) Om are identical with me. Know, O son of Bhrigu's race, that I am the sacrificial stake; I am the Soma (drunk in sacrifices); I am the Charu (cooked in sacrifices for being offered to the deities); I am the Homa (that is performed); I am those acts which sacrificers perform for gratifying the deities; I am even the pourer of the sacrificial libation: and I am the Havi or libation that is poured. I am the Adharyu. I am the Kalpaka; and I am the highly sanctified sacrificial Havi. It is me whom the Udgatri, in the great sacrifice, hymns by the sound of his songs. In all rites of expiation, O Brahmana, the utterers of auspicious Mantras and benedictions fraught with peace hymn my praises who am the artificer, O foremost of regenerate ones, of the universe. Know, O best of regenerate person, that Dharma is my eldest-born offspring, sprung from my mind, O learned Brahmana, whose essence is compassion for all creatures. Constantly transforming myself, I take birth in diverse wombs, O best of men, for upholding that son of mine, with the aid of men now existing in or departed from the world. Indeed, I do this for protecting Righteousness and for establishing it. In those forms that I assume for the purpose, I am known, O son of Bhrigu's race, in the three worlds as Vishnu and Brahman and Sakra. I am the origin and I am the destruction of all things. I am the creator of all existent objects and I am their destroyer. Knowing no change myself, I am the destroyer

---

[801] An ascetic loses his penances by cursing another rightly or wrongly. Hence, forgiveness was always practised by the Brahmanas who were ascetics. A Brahmana's strength consisted in forgiveness. The more forgiving he was, the more powerful he became.

[802] The first asat or non-existent refers to such objects as the horns of the hare. The second, viz., sadasat, or existent and non-existent refers to such objects as exist and meet with destruction. Sadasat param or that which transcends the existent and non-existent, refers to the unmanifest. The universe consists of these three. All this is from Vasudeva.

of all those creatures that live in sinfulness. In every Yuga I have to repair the causeway of Righteousness, entering into diverse kinds of wombs from desire of doing good to my creatures. When, O son of Bhrigu's race, I live in the order of the deities, I then verily act in every respect as a deity. When I live in the order of the Gandharvas, I then, O son of Bhrigu's race, act in every respect as a Gandharva. When I live in the order of the Nagas, I then act as a Naga, and when I live in the order of Yakshas or that of Rakshasas, I act after the manner of that order. Born now in the order of humanity, I must act as a human being. I appealed to them (the Kauravas) most piteously. But stupefied as they were and deprived of their senses, they refused to accept my words. I frightened them, filled with wrath, referring to some great fear (as the consequence of their slighting my message). But once more I showed themselves my usual (human) form. Possessed as they were of unrighteousness, and assailed by the virtue of Time, all of them have been righteously slain in battle, and have, without doubt, gone to Heaven. The Pandavas also, O best of Brahmanas, have acquired great fame. I have thus told thee all that thou hadst asked me.""

SECTION LV.

"'Utanka said, "I know thee, O Janarddana, to be the creator of the universe. Without doubt, this knowledge that I have is the result of thy grace towards me. O thou of unfading glory, my heart is possessed of cheerful tranquillity in consequence of its being devoted to thee. Know, O chastiser of foes, that my heart is no longer inclined to curse thee. If, O Janarddana, I deserve the least grace from thee, do thou then show me once thy sovereign form."'

"Vaisampayana continued, 'Gratified with him, the holy one then showed Utanka that eternal Vaishnava form which Dhananjaya of great intelligence had seen. Utanka beheld the high-souled Vasudeva's universal form, endued with mighty arms. The effulgence of that form was like that of a blazing fire of a thousand suns. It stood before him filling all space. It had faces on every side. Beholding that high and wonderful Vaishnava form of Vishnu, in act, seeing the Supreme Lord (in that guise), the Brahmana Utanka became filled with wonder.'

"'Utanka, said, "O thou whose handiwork is the universe, I bow to thee, O Soul of the universe, O parent of all things. With thy feet thou hast covered the whole Earth, and with thy head thou fillest the firmament. That which lies between the Earth and the firmament has been filled by thy stomach. All the points of the compass are covered by thy arms. O thou of unfading glory, thou art all this. Do thou withdraw this excellent and indestructible form of thine. I wish to behold thee now in thy own (human) form which too is eternal!"'

"Vaisampayana continued, 'Unto him, O Janamejaya, Govinda of gratified soul said these words,—"Do thou ask for some boon." Unto him Utanka, however, said—"Even this is a sufficient boon from thee for the present, O thou of great splendour, in that, O Krishna, I have beheld this form of thine, O foremost of all beings." Krishna, however, once more said unto him—"Do not scruple in this matter. This must be done. A sight of my form cannot be fruitless."

"'Utanka said, "I must accomplish that, O lord, which thou thinkest should be done. I desire to have water wherever my wish for it may arise. Water is scarce in such deserts." Withdrawing that energy, the Supreme Lord then said unto Utanka—"Whenever thou wilt require water, think of me!" Having said so, he proceeded towards Dwaraka.

Subsequently, one day, the illustrious Utanka, solicitous of water and exceedingly thirsty, wandered over the desert. In course of his wanderings he thought of Krishna of unfading glory. The intelligent Rishi then beheld in that desert a naked hunter (of the Chandala class), all besmeared with dirt, surrounded by a pack of dogs. Extremely fierce-looking, he carried a sword and was armed with bow and arrows. That foremost of regenerate ones beheld copious streams of water issuing from the urinary organs of that hunter. As soon as Utanka had thought of Krishna, that hunter smilingly addressed him, saying,—"O Utanka, O thou of Bhrigu's race, do thou accept this water from me. Beholding thee afflicted by thirst I have felt great compassion for thee." Thus addressed by the hunter, the ascetic showed no inclination to accept that water. The intelligent Utanka even began to censure Krishna of unfading glory. The hunter, however, repeatedly addressed the Rishi, saying,—"Drink!" The ascetic refused to drink the water thus offered. On the other hand, with heart afflicted by hunger and thirst, he even gave way to wrath. Disregarded by the high-souled Rishi through that conviction, the hunter, O king, with his pack of dogs, disappeared there and then. Beholding that (wonderful) disappearance, Utanka became filled with shame. He even thought that Krishna, that slayer of foes, had beguiled him (in the matter of the boon he had granted). Soon after, the holder of the conch and discus and mace, endued with great intelligence, came to Utanka by the way (along which the hunter had come). Addressing Krishna, the Brahmana said,—"O foremost of beings, it was scarcely proper for thee to offer water unto foremost of Brahmanas in the form of a hunter's urine, O lord." Unto Utanka who said these words, Janarddana of great intelligence replied, comforting him with many soft words—"That form which it was proper to assume for offering thee water, in that form was water offered to thee. But, also, thou couldst not understand it. The wielder of the thunder bolt, Purandara, was requested by me for thy sake. My words to that puissant deity were—'Do thou give nectar in the form of water unto Utanka.' The chief of the celestials replied to me saying—'It is not proper that a mortal should become immortal. Let some other boon be granted to Utanka.'—O son of Bhrigu's race, these words were repeatedly addressed to me. The lord of Sachi, however, was once more requested by me in these words, viz., 'even nectar should be given to Utanka.'—The chief of the celestials then, comforting me, said,—'If, O thou of great intelligence, nectar is to be given to him, I shall then assume the form of a hunter and give it to that high-souled descendant of Bhrigu's race. If that son of Bhrigu accepts it thus, I then go to him, O lord, for giving it unto him. If, however, he sends me away from disregard,—I shall not then give it to him on any account.'—Having made this compact with me, Vasava appeared before thee, in that disguise, for giving thee nectar. Thou, however, didst disregard him and send him away, seeing that the illustrious one had put on the guise of a Chandala. Thy fault has been great. Once more, with regard to thy desire, I am prepared to do what is in my power. Indeed, this painful thirst of thine, I shall arrange, shall be slaked. On those days, O regenerate one, in which thou wilt feel a desire for water, clouds well-charged with water will rise over this desert. Those clouds, O son of Bhrigu's race, will give thee savoury water to drink. Verily, those clouds will become known in the world as Utanka-clouds." Thus addressed by Krishna, Utanka became filled with gladness, and to this day, O Bharata, Utanka-clouds (appear and) shower rain on any deserts.'"

SECTION LVI.

"Janamejaya said, 'With what penances was the high-souled Utanka endued so that he entertained the wish to denounce a curse on Vishnu himself, who is the source of all puissance?'

"Vaisampayana said, 'O Janamejaya, Utanka was endued with austere penances. He was devoted to his preceptor. Endued with great energy, he abstained from worshipping anybody else. All the children of the Rishis, O Bharata, entertained even this wish, viz., that their devotion to preceptors should be as great as that of Utanka. Gautama's gratification with and affection for Utanka, among his numerous disciples, were very great, O Janamejaya. Indeed, Gautama was highly pleased with the self-restraint and purity of behaviour that characterised Utanka, and with his acts of prowess and the services he rendered to him. One after another, thousands of disciples received the preceptor's permission to return home (after the completion of their pupilage). In consequence, however, of his great affection for Utanka, Gautama could not permit him to leave his retreat. Gradually, in course of time, O son, decrepitude overtook Utanka, that great ascetic. The ascetic, however, in consequence of his devotion to his preceptor, was not conscious of it. One day, he set out, O monarch, for fetching fuel for his preceptor. Soon after Utanka brought a heavy load of fuel. Toil-worn and hungry and afflicted by the load he bore on his head, O chastiser of foes, he threw the load down on the Earth, O king. One of his matted locks, white as silver, had become entangled with the load. Accordingly, when the load was thrown down, with it fell on the earth that matted lock of hair. Oppressed as he had been by that load and overcome by hunger, O Bharata, Utanka, beholding that sign of old age, began to indulge in loud lamentations from excess of sorrow. Conversant with every duty, the daughter of his preceptor, who was possessed of eyes that resembled the petals of the lotus, and of hips that were full and round, at the command of her sire, sought, with downcast face, to hold Utanka's tears in her hands. Her hands seemed to burn with those tear-drops that she held. Unable, accordingly, to hold them longer, she was obliged to throw them down on the Earth. The Earth herself was unable to hold those tear-drops of Utanka. With a gratified heart, Gautama then said unto the regenerate Utanka,—"Why, O son, is thy mind so afflicted with grief today? Tell me calmly and quietly, O learned Rishi, for I wish to hear it in detail."

"'Utanka said, "With mind entirely devoted to thee, and wholly bent upon doing what is agreeable to thee, with my heart's devotion turned to thee, and with thoughts entirely dwelling on thee, (I have resided here till) decrepitude has come upon me without my knowing it at all. I have not, again, known any happiness. Though I have dwelt with thee for a hundred years, yet thou hast not granted me permission to depart. Many disciples of thine, that were my juniors, have, however, been permitted by thee to return. Indeed, hundreds and thousands of foremost Brahmanas have, equipt with knowledge, been permitted by thee (to depart from thy retreat and set themselves up as teachers)!"

"'Gautama said, "Through my love and affection for thee, and in consequence of thy dutiful services to me, a long time has elapsed without my knowing it, O foremost of Brahmanas. If, however, O thou of Bhrigu's race, the desire is entertained by thee of leaving this place, do thou go without delay, receiving my permission."

"'Utanka said, "What shall I present to my preceptor? Tell me this, O best of regenerate persons. Having brought it, I shall go hence, O lord, with thy permission."

"'Gautama said, "The good that the gratification of the preceptor is the final fee.[803] Without doubt, O regenerate one. I have been highly gratified with thy conduct. Know, O perpetuator of Bhrigu's race, that I have been exceedingly gratified with thee for this. If thou becomest a young man today of sixteen years, I shall bestow on thee, O regenerate one, this my own daughter for becoming thy wife. No other woman save this one is capable of waiting upon thy energy." At these words of Gautama, Utanka once again became a youth and accepted that famous maiden for his wife. Receiving the permission of his preceptor, he then addressed his preceptor's wife, saying,—"What shall I give thee as final fee for my preceptor? Do thou command me. I desire to accomplish, with wealth or even my life, what is agreeable and beneficial to thee. Whatever gem, exceedingly wonderful and of great value, exists in this world, I shall bring for thee with the aid of my penances. I have no doubt in this."

"'Ahalya said, "I am highly gratified with thee, O learned Brahmana, with thy unintermitting devotion, O sinless one. This is enough. Blessed be thou, go whithersoever thou likest."'

"Vaisampayana continued, 'Utanka, however, O monarch, once more, said these words,—"Do thou command me, O mother. It is meet that I should do something that is agreeable to thee."

"'Ahalya said, "Blessed be thou, bring for me those celestial ear-rings that are worn by the wife of Saudasa. That which is due to thy preceptor will then be well-discharged." Replying unto her "So be it,"—Utanka departed, O Janamejaya, resolved to bring those ear-rings for doing what was agreeable to his preceptor's wife. That foremost of Brahmanas, Utanka, proceeded without any loss of time to Saudasa who had (through the curse of Vasishtha) become a cannibal, in order to solicit the ear-rings from him. Gautama meanwhile said unto his wife,—"Utanka is not to be seen today." Thus addressed, she informed him how he had departed for fetching the jewelled ear-rings (of Saudasa's queen). At this, Gautama said,—"Thou hast not acted wisely. Cursed (by Vasishtha), that king (who has been transformed into a man-eater) will verily slay Utanka."

"'Ahalya said, "Without knowing this, O holy one, I have set Utanka to this task. He shall not, however, incur any danger through thy grace." Thus addressed by her, Gautama said,—"Let it be so!" Meanwhile, Utanka met king Saudasa in a deserted forest."'

SECTION LVII.

"Vaisampayana said, 'Beholding the king, who had become so, of frightful mien, wearing a long beard smeared with the blood of human beings, the Brahmana Utanka, O king, did not become agitated. That monarch of great energy, inspiring terror in every breast and looking like a second Yama, rising up, addressed Utanka, saying,—"By good luck, O best of Brahmanas, thou hast come to me at the sixth hour of the day when I am in search of food."

"'Utanka said, "O king, know that I have come hither in course of my wanderings for

---

[803] To this day preceptors in India have to feed and teach their disciples without any pecuniary compensation. In fact, the sale of knowledge has been strictly forbidden. Pupils, however, after completing their studies, had to give the final Dakshina which varied according to their means. The kings and princes of India thought themselves honoured if solicited by pupils in search of the final Dakshina. What Gautama says here is that the object of the final present is to gratify the preceptor. He (Gautama), however, had already been gratified with the dutiful conduct of Utanka. There was no need, therefore, of any present.

the sake of my preceptor. The wise have said that while one is employed for the sake of one's preceptor, one should not be injured."

"'The king said, "O best of Brahmanas, food has been ordained for me at the sixth hour of the day. I am hungry. I cannot, therefore, allow thee to escape today."

"'Utanka said, "Let it be so, O king. Let this compact be made with me. After I have ceased to wander for my preceptor, I shall once more come and place myself within thy power. It has been heard by me, O best of kings, that the object I seek for my preceptor is under thy control, O monarch. Therefore, O ruler of men, I solicit thee for it. Thou daily givest many foremost of gems unto superior Brahmanas. Thou art a giver, O chief of men, from whom gifts may be accepted, know that I too am a worthy object of charity present before thee, O best of kings. Having accepted from thee in gift that object for my preceptor which is under thy control, I shall, O king, in consequence of my compact, once more come back to thee and place myself under thy power. I assure thee truly of this. There is no falsehood in this. Never before have I spoken anything untrue, no, not even in jest. What shall I say then of other occasions?"

"'Saudasa said, "If the object thou seekest for thy preceptor is capable of being placed in thy hands by me, if I be regarded as one from whom a gift may be accepted, do thou then say what that object is."

"'Utanka said, "O foremost of men, O Saudasa, in my estimation thou art a worthy person from whom gifts may be accepted. I have, therefore, come to thee for begging of thee the jewelled ear-rings (worn by thy queen)."

"'Saudasa said, "Those jewelled ear-rings, O learned and regenerate Rishi, belong to my wife. They should be asked from her. Do thou, therefore, solicit some other thing from me. I shall give it to thee, O thou of excellent vows."

"'Utanka said, "If we be regarded as any authority, do thou cease then to urge this pretext. Do thou give those jewelled ear-rings to me. Be thou truthful in speech, O king.'"

"Vaisampayana continued, 'Thus addressed, the king once more addressed Utanka and said unto him, "Do thou, at my word, go to my venerable queen, O best of men, and ask her, saying,—Give!—She of pure vows, thus solicited by thee, will certainly, at my command, give thee, O foremost of regenerate persons, those jewelled ear-rings of hers without doubt."

"'Utanka said, "Whither, O ruler of men, shall I be able to meet thy queen? Why dost thou not thyself go to her?"

"'Saudasa said, "Thou wilt find her today in the vicinity of a foremost fountain. I cannot see her today as the sixth hour of the day has come."'

"Vaisampayana continued, 'Thus addressed, Utanka, O chief of Bharata's race, then left that spot. Beholding Madayanti, he informed her of his object. Hearing the command of Saudasa, that lady of large eyes replied unto the highly intelligent Utanka, O Janamejaya, in these words: "It is even so, O regenerate one. Thou shouldst, however, O sinless one, assure me that thou dost not say what is untrue. It behoves thee to bring me some sign from my husband. These celestial ear-rings of mine, made of costly gems, are such that the deities and Yakshas and great Rishis always watch for opportunities for bearing them away. If placed at any time on the Earth, this costly article would then be stolen by the Nagas. If worn by one who is impure in consequence of eating, it would then be taken away by the Yakshas. If the wearer falls asleep (without taking care of these precious ear-rings) the deities would then take them away. O best of Brahmanas, these ear-rings are capable of being taken away, when such opportunities present themselves, by deities and Rakshasas and Nagas, if worn by a heedless person. O best of regenerate ones, these ear-rings, day and night, always produce gold. At night, they shine brightly, attracting the rays of stars and constellations. O holy one, if worn by any one, he would be freed from hunger and thirst and fear of every kind. The wearer of these ear-rings is freed also from the fear of poison and fire and every kind of danger. If worn by one of short stature, these become short. If worn by one of tall stature, these grow in size. Even of such virtues are these ear-rings of mine. They are praised and honoured everywhere. Indeed, they are known over the three worlds. Do thou, therefore, bring me some sign (from my husband).""'"

SECTION LVIII.

"Vaisampayana said, 'Utanka, coming back to king Saudasa who was always well-disposed towards all his friends, solicited him for some sign (to convince Madayanti of the fact of his being really commissioned by the king). That foremost one of Ikshwaku's race then gave him a sign.'

"'Saudasa said, "This my present condition is intolerable. I do not behold any refuge. Knowing this to be my wish, do thou give away the jewelled ear-rings."[804] Thus addressed by the king, Utanka went back to the queen and reported to her the words of her lord. Hearing those words, the queen gave unto Utanka her jewelled ear-rings. Having obtained the ear-rings, Utanka came back to the king and said unto him, "I desire to hear, O monarch, what the import is of those mysterious words which thou saidst as a sign to thy queen."

"'Saudasa said, "Kshatriyas are seen to honour the Brahmanas from the very beginning of the creation. Towards the Brahmanas, however, many offences arise (on the part of Kshatriyas). As regards myself, I am always bent in humility before them. I am overtaken by a calamity through a Brahmana. Possessed of Madayanti, I do not see any other refuge. Indeed, O foremost of all persons having of a high goal, I do not behold any other refuge for myself in the matter of approaching the gates of Heaven, or in continuing here, O best of regenerate ones. It is impossible for a king that is hostile to Brahmanas to continue living in this world or in attaining to happiness in the next. Hence have I given thee these my jewelled ear-rings which were coveted by thee.[805] Do thou now keep the compact which thou hast made with me today."

"'Utanka said, "O king, I shall certainly act according to my promise. I shall truly come back and place myself under thy power. There is, however, a question, O scorcher of foes, which I wish to ask thee."

"'Saudasa said, "Say, O learned Brahmana, what is in thy mind. I shall certainly reply unto thy words. I shall dispel whatever doubt may be in thy mind. I have no hesitation in this."

"'Utanka said, "Those who are skilled in the rules of duty say that Brahmanas are of restrained speech. One who behaves wrongly towards friends is regarded as vile as a

---

[804] These words of the king are intended to be reported to his queen who would understand the allusion. The sense is this: cursed by Vasishtha, I have become a cannibal. My condition is intolerable. By this gift of the ear-rings to a deserving Brahmana, much merit may arise. That merit may relieve me.

[805] This also is an allusion to the dreadful curse of Vasishtha. The king refers to Madayanti as his only refuge. She may save him by doing an act or special merit, viz., giving away her costly ear-rings to a truly deserving Brahmana.

thief.[806] Thou, again, O king, hast become my friend today. Do thou then, O foremost of men, give me such counsel as is approved by the wise. As regards myself, I have now obtained the fruition of my wishes. Thou, again, art a cannibal. Is it proper for me to come back to thee or not?"

"'Saudasa said, "If it is proper (for me), O foremost of superior Brahmanas, to say what thou askest, I should then, O best of regenerate ones, tell thee that thou shouldst never come back to me. O perpetuator of Bhrigu's race, by acting even thus, thou wilt attain to what is beneficial to thee. If thou comest back, O learned Brahmana, thou wilt surely meet with death."'

"Vaisampayana continued, 'Thus addressed by the intelligent king in respect of what was beneficial for him, Utanka took leave of the monarch and set out for the presence of Ahalya. Desirous of doing what was agreeable to the wife of his preceptor, he took the ear-rings with him and set out with great speed for reaching the retreat of Gautama. Protecting them even in the manner directed by Madayanti, that is, binding them within the folds of his black deer-skin, he proceeded on his way. After he had proceeded for some distance, he became afflicted by hunger. He there beheld a Vilwa tree bent down with the weight of (ripe) fruits.[807] He climbed that tree. Causing his deer-skin, O chastiser of foes, to hang on a branch, that foremost of regenerate persons then began to pluck some fruits. While he was employed in plucking those fruits with eyes directed towards them, some of them fell, O king, on that deerskin in which those ear-rings had been carefully tied by that foremost of Brahmanas. With the strokes of the fruits, the knot became untied. Suddenly that deer-skin, with the ear-rings in it, fell down. When the knot being unfastened, the deer-skin fell down on the ground, a snake who was there beheld those jewelled ear-rings. That snake belonged to the race of Airavata. With great promptness he took up the ear-rings in his mouth and then entered an anthill. Beholding the ear-rings taken away by that snake, Utanka, filled with wrath and in great anxiety of mind, came down from the tree. Taking his staff he began to pierce that anthill. That best of Brahmanas, burning with wrath and the desire for revenge, ceaselessly employed himself for five and thirty days in that task. The goddess Earth, unable to bear the force of Utanka's walking staff and with body torn therewith, became exceedingly anxious. Unto that regenerate Rishi then, who continued to dig the Earth from desire of making a path to the nether regions inhabited by the Nagas, the chief of the celestials, armed with the thunder, came there, on his car drawn by green horses. Endued with great energy, he beheld that foremost of Brahmanas, as he sat there engaged in his task.'

"Vaisampayana continued, 'Assuming the garb of a Brahmana afflicted with the sorrow of Utanka, the chief of the celestials addressed him, saying, "This (purpose of thine) is incapable of being achieved. The regions of the Nagas are thousands of Yojanas removed from this place. I think that thy purpose is not capable of being achieved with thy walking staff."

"'Utanka said, "If, O Brahmana, the ear-rings be not recovered by me from the regions of the Nagas, I shall cast off my life-breaths before thy eyes, O foremost of regenerate persons!"'

"Vaisampayana said, 'When the thunder-armed Indra failed to divert Utanka from his

[806] The sense is this: a Brahmana is never loose of tongue. He is truthful. Hence, having passed my word to thee about my return, thou mayst be sure that I would keep my word. One, again, that acts improperly towards a friend, comes to be regarded as a thief. By this, Utanka reminds the king that he should not inflict any wrong on him by carrying out his intention of eating him up.
[807] Vilwa is the Aegle marmalos.

purpose, he united the latter's walking staff with the force of thunder. Then, O Janamejaya, the Earth, opening with those strokes having the force of thunder, yielded a way to the (nether) regions inhabited by the Nagas. By that path Utanka entered the world of Nagas. He saw that that region lay extended thousands of Yojanas on all sides. Indeed, O blessed one, it was equipt with many walls made of pure gold and decked with jewels and gems. There were many fine tanks of water furnished with flights of stair-cases made of pure crystal, and many rivers of clear and transparent water. He saw also many trees with diverse species of birds perching on them. That perpetuator of Bhrigu's race behold the gate of that region which was full five Yojanas high and a hundred Yojanas in width. Beholding the region of the Nagas, Utanka became very cheerless. Indeed, he despaired of getting back the earrings. Then there appeared unto him a black steed with a white tail. His face and eyes were of a coppery hue, O thou of Kuru's race, and he seemed to blaze forth with energy. Addressing Utanka, he said, "Do thou blow into the Apana duct of my body. Thou wilt then, O learned Brahmana, get back thy ear-rings which have been taken away by a descendant of Airavata's race! Do not loathe to do my bidding, O son. Thou didst it often at the retreat of Gautama in former days."

"'Utanka said, "How did I know thee in the retreat of my preceptor? Indeed, I wish to hear how I did in those days what thou biddest me do now."

"'The steed said, "Know, O learned Brahmana, that I am the preceptor of thy preceptor, for I am the blazing Jatavedas (deity of fire). By thee I was often worshipped for the sake of thy preceptor, O child of Bhrigu's race, duly and with a pure heart and body. For that reason I shall accomplish what is for thy good. Do my bidding without delay." Thus addressed by the deity of fire, Utanka did as he was directed. The deity then, gratified with him, blazed up for consuming everything. From the pores of his body, O Bharata, in consequence of his very nature, a thick smoke issued threatening terrors to the world of Nagas. With that mighty and wide-spreading smoke, O Bharata, everything became enveloped in gloom, so that nothing, O king, could any longer be seen in the world of the Nagas. Cries of woe were heard throughout the mansions of the Airavatas, uttered by the Nagas headed by Vasuki, O Janamejaya. Enveloped by that smoke, the palaces could no longer be seen, O Bharata. These resembled woods and hill overwhelmed by a thick forest. With eyes that were red in consequence of that smoke, and afflicted by the energy of the deity of fire, the Nagas came out of their mansions to the high-souled son of Bhrigu's race for ascertaining what was the matter. Having heard what the matter was from that ascetic of immeasurable energy, all the Nagas, with fear depicted on their eyes, offered him their worship according to due forms. Indeed, all the Nagas placing the old and the young one's before them, bowed unto him with their heads and joining their hands addressed him, saying, "Be gratified with us, O holy one!" Having gratified that Brahmana and offered him water to wash his feet and the ingredients of the Arghya (for honouring him), the Nagas gave him those celestial and highly-adored ear-rings. Thus honoured by them, Utanka of great prowess, circumambulating the deity of fire, started for the retreat of his preceptor. Indeed, repairing quickly to Gautama's asylum, O king, he presented those ear-rings unto the wife of his preceptor, O sinless one. That best of Brahmanas also told his preceptor everything about Vasuki and the other Nagas that had occurred. It was even thus, O Janamejaya, that the high-souled Utanka, having wandered through the three worlds, fetched those jewelled ear-rings (for his preceptor's wife). Of such prowess, O chief of Bharata's race, was the ascetic Utanka. So austere were the penances with which he was endued. I have thus told thee what thou hadst asked me.'"

SECTION LIX.

"Janamejaya said, 'After having conferred that boon on Utanka, O foremost of regenerate persons, what did the mighty-armed Govinda of great celebrity next do?'

"Vaisampayana said, 'Having granted that boon to Utanka, Govinda, accompanied by Satyaki, proceeded to Dwaraka on his car drawn by his large steeds endued with great speed. Passing many lakes and rivers and forests and hills, he at last came upon the delightful city of Dwaravati. It was at the time, O king, when the festival of Raivataka had begun, that he of eyes like lotus-petals arrived with Satyaki as his companion. Adorned with many beautiful things and covered with diverse Koshas made of jewels and gems, the Raivataka hill shone, O king, with great splendour. That high mountain, decked with excellent garlands of gold and gay festoons of flowers, with many large trees that looked like the Kalpa trees of Indra's garden, and with many golden poles on which were lighted lamps, shone in beauty through day and night. By the caves and fountains the light was so great that it seemed to be broad day. On all sides beautiful flags waved on the air with little bells that jingled continuously. The entire hill resounded with the melodious songs of men and women. Raivataka presented a most charming prospect like Meru with all his jewels and gems. Men and women, excited and filled with delight, O Bharata, sang aloud. The swell of music that thus rose from that foremost of mountains seemed to touch the very heavens. Everywhere were heard shouts and loud whoops of men who were in all stages of excitement. The cackle of thousands of voices made that mountain delightful and charming. It was adorned with many shops and stalls filled with diverse viands and enjoyable articles. There were heaps of cloths and garlands, and the music of Vinas and flutes and Mridangas was heard everywhere. Food mixed with wines of diverse kinds was stored here and there. Gifts were being ceaselessly made to those that were distressed, or blind, or helpless. In consequence of all this, the festival of that mountain became highly auspicious. There were many sacred abodes built on the breast of that mountain, O hero, within which resided many men of righteous deeds. Even thus did the heroes of Vrishni's race sport in that festival of Raivataka. Equipt with those mansions, that mountain shone like a second Heaven. At the arrival of Krishna, O chief of Bharata's race, that prince of mountains resembled the blessed abode of Indra himself. Worshipped (by his relatives), Krishna then entered a beautiful mansion. Satyaki also went to his own quarters with a delighted soul. Govinda entered his residence after a long absence, having accomplished feats of great difficulty like Vasava amid the Danava host. The heroes of the Bhoja, Vrishni, and Andhaka races, all came forward to receive that high-souled one like the deities advancing to receive him of a hundred sacrifices. Endued with great intelligence, he honoured them in return and enquired after their welfare. With a gratified heart he then saluted his father and mother. The mighty-armed hero was embraced by both of them and comforted too (by numerous evidences of affection). He then took his seat with all the Vrishnis sitting around him. Having washed his feet and dispelled his fatigue, Krishna of mighty energy, as he sat there, then recounted the chief incidents of the great battle in answer to the questions put to him by his sire.'"

SECTION LX.

"'Vasudeva said, "O thou of Vrishni's race, I have repeatedly heard men speaking of the wonderful battle (between the Kurus and the Pandavas). Thou, however, O mighty-armed one, hast witnessed it with thy own eyes. Do thou, therefore, O sinless one, describe the battle in detail. Indeed, tell me how that battle took place between the high-souled Pandavas (on the one side) and Bhishma and Karna and Kripa and Drona and Salya and others (on the other side), between, in fact, numerous other Kshatriyas well-skilled in arms, differing from one another in mien and attire, and hailing from diverse realms."'

"Vaisampayana continued, 'Thus addressed by his sire, he of eyes like lotus-petals narrated, in the presence of his mother also, how the Kaurava heroes had been slain in battle.'

"'Vasudeva said, "The feats were highly wonderful that were achieved by those high-souled Kshatriyas. In consequence of their large number, they are incapable of being enumerated in even hundreds of years. I shall however, mention only the foremost of them. Do thou listen, therefore, to me as I mention in brief those feats achieved by the kings of Earth, O thou of godlike splendour. Bhishma of Kuru's race became the generalissimo, having eleven divisions of the Kaurava princes under his command, like Vasava of the celestial forces.[808] Sikhandin of great intelligence, protected by the blessed Arjuna, became the leader of the seven divisions of the sons of Pandu. The battle between the Kurus and the Pandavas (under these leaders) raged for ten days. It was so fierce as to make one's hair stand on its end. Then Sikhandin, in great battle, aided by the wielder of Gandiva, slew, with innumerable arrows, the son of Ganga fighting bravely. Lying on a bed of arrows, Bhishma waited like an ascetic till the sun leaving his southward path entered on his northerly course when that hero gave up his life-breaths. Then Drona, that foremost of all persons conversant with arms, that greatest of men under Duryodhana, like Kavya himself of the lord of the Daityas, became generalissimo.[809] That foremost of regenerate persons, ever boasting of his prowess in battle, was supported by the remnant of the Kaurava force consisting then of nine Akshauhinis, and protected by Kripa and Vrisha and others. Dhrishtadyumna conversant with many mighty weapons, and possessed of great intelligence, became the leader of the Pandavas. He was protected by Bhima like Varuna protected by Mitra. That high-souled hero, always desirous of measuring his strength with Drona, supported by the (remnant of the) Pandava army, and recollecting the wrongs inflicted (by Drona) on his sire (Drupada, the king of the Panchalas), achieved great feats in battle. In that encounter between Drona and the son of Prishata, the kings assembled from diverse realms were nearly exterminated. That furious battle lasted for five days. At the conclusion of that period, Drona, exhausted, succumbed to Dhrishtadyumna. After that, Karna became the generalissimo of Duryodhana's forces. He was supported in battle by the remnant of the Kaurava host which numbered five Akshauhinis. Of the sons of Pandu there were then three Akshauhinis. After the slaughter of innumerable heroes, protected by Arjuna, they came to battle. The Suta's son Karna, though a fierce warrior, encountering Partha, came to his end on the second day, like an insect encountering a blazing fire. After the fall of Karna, the Kauravas became dispirited

---

[808] Chamu here is used in a general sense, viz., a division. Of course it stands for an Akshauhini.

[809] Kavi or Kavya is another name of Sukra, the preceptor of the Daityas.

and lost all energy. Numbering three Akshauhinis, they gathered round the ruler of the Madras. Having lost many car-warriors and elephants and horsemen, the remnant of the Pandava army, numbering one Akshauhini and penetrated with cheerlessness, supported Yudhishthira (as their leader). The king Yudhishthira, in the battle that ensued, achieved the most difficult feats and slew, before half the day was over, the king of the Madras. After the fall of Salya, the high-souled Sahadeva of immeasurable prowess slew Sakuni, the man who had brought about the quarrel (between the Pandavas and the Kurus). After the fall of Sakuni, the royal son of Dhritarashtra, whose army had suffered an extensive carnage and who on that account had become exceedingly cheerless, fled from the field, armed with his mace. Then Bhimasena of great prowess, filled with wrath, pursued him and discovered him within the waters of the Dwaipayana lake. With the remnant of their army, the Pandavas surrounded the lake and, filled with joy, encountered Duryodhana concealed within the waters. Their wordy shafts, penetrating through the waters, pierced Duryodhana. Rising up from the lake, the latter approached the Pandavas, armed with his mace, desirous of battle. Then, in the great battle that ensued, the royal son of Dhritarashtra was slain by Bhimasena who put forth his great prowess, in the presence of many kings. After this the remnant of the Pandava army, as it slept in the camp, was slaughtered at night time by Drona's son who was unable to put up with the slaughter of his father (at the hands of Dhrishtadyumna). Their sons slain, their forces slain, only the five sons of Pandu are alive with myself and Yuyudhana. With Kripa and the Bhoja prince Kritavarman, the son of Drona represents the unslain remnant of the Kaurava army. Dhritarashtra's son Yuyutsu also escaped slaughter in consequence of his having adopted the side of the Pandavas. Upon the slaughter of the Kaurava king (Suyodhana) with all his followers and allies, Vidura and Sanjaya have come to the presence of king Yudhishthira the just. Even thus did that battle occur, O lord, for eight and ten days. Many kings of Earth, slain therein, have ascended to Heaven.'"

"Vaisampayana continued, 'The Vrishnis, as they heard, O king, that dreadful account became filled with grief and sorrow and pain.'"

SECTION LXI.

"Vaisampayana said, 'After the high-souled Vasudeva of great prowess had finished his narration of the great battle of the Bharatas before his sire, it was plain that that hero had passed over the slaughter of Abhimanyu. The motive of the high-souled one was that his sire might not hear what was highly unpleasant to him. Indeed, the intelligent Krishna did not wish that his sire Vasudeva should, on hearing the dreadful intelligence of the death of his daughter's son, be afflicted with sorrow and grief. (His sister) Subhadra, noticing that the slaughter of her son had not been mentioned, addressed her brother, saying,—"Do thou narrate the death of my son, O Krishna"—and fell down on the earth (in a swoon). Vasudeva beheld his daughter fallen on the ground. As soon as he saw this, he also fell down, deprived of his senses by grief. (Regaining his senses) Vasudeva, afflicted with grief at the death of his daughter's son, O king, addressed Krishna, saying, "O lotus-eyed one, thou art famed on Earth for being truthful in speech. Why, however, O slayer of foes, dost thou not tell me today of the death of my daughter's son? O puissant one, tell me in detail of the slaughter of thy sister's son. Possessed of eyes resembling thine, alas, how was he slain in battle by foes? Since my heart does not from grief break into a hundred pieces, it seems, O thou of the Vrishni's race, that it does not die with men when its hour does not come. Oh, at the time of his fall, what words did he utter, apostrophising his mother? O lotus-eyed one what did that darling of mine, possessed of restless eyes, say unto me? I hope he has not been slain by foes while retreating from battle with his back towards them? I hope, O Govinda, that, his face did not become cheerless while fighting? He was possessed, O Krishna, of mighty energy. From a spirit of boyishness, that puissant hero, boasting (of his prowess) in my presence, used to speak of his skill (in battle). I hope that boy does not lie on the field, slain deceitfully by Drona and Karna and Kripa and others? Do thou tell me this. That son of my daughter always used to challenge Bhishma and that foremost of all mighty warriors, viz., Karna, in battle." Unto his sire who, from excess of grief, indulged in such lamentations, Govinda, more afflicted than he answered in these words. "His face did not become cheerless as he fought in the van of battle. Fierce though that battle was, he did not turn his back upon it. Having slain hundreds and thousands of kings of Earth, he was brought to grief by Drona and Karna and at last succumbed to the son of Dussasana. If, O lord, he had been encountered, one to one, without intermission, he was incapable of being slain in battle by even the wielder of the thunderbolt. When his sire Arjuna was withdrawn from the main body by the Samsaptakas (who challenged to fight him separately), Abhimanyu was surrounded by the enraged Kaurava heroes headed by Drona in battle. Then, O sire, after he had slaughtered a very large number of foes in battle, thy daughter's son at last succumbed to the son of Dussasana. Without doubt, he has gone to Heaven. Kill this grief of thine, O thou of great intelligence. They that are of cleansed understandings never languish when they meet with any calamity. He by whom Drona and Karna and others were checked in battle,—heroes that were equal to Indra himself in might—why would not he ascend to Heaven? O irresistible one, do thou kill this grief of thine. Do not suffer thyself to be swayed by wrath. That conqueror of hostile cities has attained in that sanctified goal which depends upon death at the edge of weapons. After the fall of that hero, this my sister Subhadra stricken with grief, indulged in loud lamentations, when she saw Kunti, like a female osprey. When she met Draupadi, she asked her in grief,—'O reverend lady, where are all our sons? I desire to behold them.' Hearing her lamentations, all the Kaurava ladies embraced her and wept sitting around her. Beholding (her daughter-in-law) Uttara, she said,—'O blessed girl, where has thy husband gone? When he comes back, do thou, without losing a moment, apprise me of it. Alas, O daughter of Virata, as soon he heard my voice, he used to come out of his chamber without the loss of a moment. Why does not thy husband come out today? Alas, O Abhimanyu, thy maternal uncles—mighty car-warriors—are all hale. They used to bless thee when they saw thee come here prepared to go out for battle. Do thou tell me the incidents of battle today as before, O chastiser of foes. Oh. why dost thou not answer me today—me who am weeping so bitterly?'—Hearing these lamentations of this daughter of the Vrishni race, Pritha, deeply afflicted with grief, addressed her and slowly said,—'O Subhadra, though protected by Vasudeva and Satyaki and by his own sire, thy youthful son has yet been slain. That slaughter is due to the influence of Time! O daughter of Yadu's race, mortal thy son was. Do not grieve. Irresistible in battle, thy son has, without doubt, attained to the highest goal. Thou art born in a high race of high-souled Kshatriyas. Do not grieve, O thou of restless glances, O girl of eyes like lotus-petals. Do thou cast thy eyes on Uttara who is quick with child. O blessed lady, do not yield to sorrow. This auspicious girl will soon bring forth a son to that hero.' Having comforted her in this way, Kunti, conversant with every duty, O perpetuator of Yadu's race, casting off her grief, O irresistible one, made arrangements for Abhimanyu's obsequial rites, with the acquiescence of king Yudhishthira and Bhima, and the twins (viz., Nakula and Sahadeva) who in prowess resembled Yama himself. She also made many presents unto the Brahmanas, and bestowed upon them many kine, O perpetuator of Yadu's race. Then the Vrishni dame (Kunti), comforted a little, addressed the daughter of Virata, saying,—'O faultless daughter of Virata, thou shouldst not indulge in grief. For the sake of thy husband, O thou of rotund hips, protect the child in thy womb.'—Having said these words, O thou of great splendour, Kunti ceased. With her permission I have brought Subhadra here. It was even thus, O giver of honours, that thy daughter's son met with his death. Cast off thy burning grief, O irresistible one. Indeed, do not set thy heart on sorrow."'"

SECTION LXII.

"Vaisampayana said, 'Having heard these words of his son Vasudeva, that descendant of Sura, of righteous soul, casting off his grief, made excellent obsequial offerings (unto Abhimanyu). Vasudeva also performed those rites for the ascension (to Heaven) of his high-souled nephew, that hero who was ever the darling of his sire (Vasudeva). He duly fed six millions of Brahmanas, endued with great energy, with edibles possessed of every recommendation. Presenting many clothes unto them, Krishna gratified the thirst for wealth of those Brahmanas. Wonderful were the heaps of gold, the number of kine and of beds and clothes, that were then given away. The Brahmanas loudly declared—"Let (Krishna's wealth) increase." Then Vasudeva of Dasarha's race, and Valadeva, and Satyaki, and Satyaka, each performed the obsequial rites of Abhimanyu. Exceedingly afflicted with grief, they failed to attain comfort. The same was the case with the sons of Pandu in the city called after the elephant. Deprived of Abhimanyu, they failed to obtain peace of mind. The daughter of Virata, O monarch, for many days, totally abstained from all food, exceedingly afflicted by grief on account of the death of her husband. At this all her relatives became plunged into excess of grief. They all feared that the embryo in her womb might be destroyed. Then Vyasa, ascertaining the state of things by his spiritual vision, came there. The highly intelligent Rishi, endued with great energy, arrived (at the palace), addressed Pritha of large eyes, as also Uttara herself, saying,—"Let this grief be abandoned. O famous lady, a son endued with mighty energy will be born to thee, through the puissance of Vasudeva and at my word. That son will rule the Earth after the Pandavas (have departed from it)." Beholding Dhananjaya, he said unto him, in the hearing of king Yudhishthira the just, and gladdening him with his words, "O Bharata, thy grandson, O highly blessed one, will become a high-souled prince. He will righteously rule the whole Earth to the verge of the sea. Therefore, O foremost one of Kuru's race, cast off this grief, O mower of foes. Do not doubt this. This will truly happen. That which was uttered by the Vrishni hero on a former occasion, will, without doubt, happen. Do not think otherwise. As regards Abhimanyu, he has gone to the regions of the deities, conquered by him with his own acts. That hero should not be grieved for by thee or, indeed, by the other Kurus." Thus addressed by his grandsire, Dhananjaya of righteous soul, O king, cast off his grief and even became cheerful. Thy sire, O prince, that art conversant with all duties, began to grow in that womb, O thou of great intelligence, like the Moon in the lighted fortnight. Then Vyasa urged the royal son of Dharma for performing the horse-sacrifice. Having said so, he made himself invisible there and then. The intelligent king Yudhishthira the just, hearing the words of Vyasa, set his mind on the journey for bringing wealth (for the sacrifice).'"

532

SECTION LXIII.

"Janamejaya said, 'Having heard these words, O regenerate one, that were spoken by the high-souled Vyasa in respect of the horse-sacrifice, what steps were taken by Yudhishthira? Do thou tell me, O foremost of regenerate ones, how the king succeeded in obtaining the wealth which Marutta had buried in the Earth.'

"Vaisampayana said, 'Having heard the words of the Island-born ascetic, king Yudhishthira the just, summoned all his brothers, viz., Arjuna and Bhimasena and the twin sons of Madri, in proper time and then said unto them (the following words),—"Ye heroes, you have heard the words which the highly intelligent and high-souled Krishna has said from his friendship for and the desire of doing good to the Kurus![810] Verily, you have heard those words that have been uttered by that ascetic of abundant penances, that great sage desirous of bestowing prosperity on his friends, that preceptor of righteous behaviour, viz., Vyasa of wonderful feats. You have heard what Bhishma also said, and what Govinda too of great intelligence has uttered. Remembering those words, ye sons of Pandu, I desire to obey them duly. By obeying those words of theirs great blessedness will attach to all of you. Those words spoken by those utterers of Brahma are certain (if obeyed) to bring in their train considerable benefit. Ye perpetuators of Kuru's race, the Earth has become divested of her wealth. Ye kings, Vyasa, therefore, informed us of the wealth (that lies buried in the Earth) of Marutta. If you think that wealth abundant or sufficient, how shall we bring it (to our capital)? What, O Bhima, dost thou think as regards this?" When the king, O perpetuator of Kuru's race, said these words, Bhimasena, joining his hands, said these words in reply,—"The words thou hast said, O thou of mighty-arms, on the subject of bringing the wealth indicated by Vyasa, are approved by me. If, O puissant one, we succeed in getting the wealth kept there by the son of Avikshita, then this sacrifice, O king, purposed by us will be easily accomplished. Even this is what I think. We shall, therefore, bowing our heads unto the high-souled Girisa, and offering due worship unto that deity, bring that wealth. Blessed be thou. Gratifying that god of gods, as also his companions and followers, in words, thought, and deed, we shall, without doubt, obtain that wealth. Those Kinnaras of fierce mien who are protecting that treasure will certainly yield to us if the great deity having the bull for his sign become gratified with us!"—Hearing these words uttered by Bhima, O Bharata, king Yudhishthira the son of Dharma became highly pleased. The others, headed by Arjuna, at the same time, said, "So be it." The Pandavas then, having resolved to bring that wealth, ordered their forces to march under the constellation Dhruba and on the day called by the same name.[811] Causing the Brahmanas to utter benedictions on them, and having duly worshipped the great god Maheswara, the sons of Pandu set out (on their enterprise). Gratifying that high-souled deity with Modakas and frumenty and with cakes made of meat, the sons of Pandu set out with cheerful hearts. While they thus set out, the citizens, and many foremost of Brahmanas, with cheerful hearts, uttered auspicious blessings (on their heads). The Pandavas, circumambulating many Brahmanas that daily worshipped their fires, and bending their heads unto them, proceeded on their journey. Taking the permission of king Dhritarashtra who was afflicted with grief on account of the death of

---

[810] Krishna implies Vyasa here. The great Rishi was called 'the island-born Krishna'.

[811] The commentator explains that by the constellation Dhruba is implied Rohini and the Uttaras numbering three. Sunday, again is called the Dhruba-day.

his sons, his queen (Gandhari), and Pritha also of large eyes, and keeping the Kaurava prince Yuyutsu, the son of Dhritarashtra, in the capital, they set out, worshipped by the citizens and by many Brahmanas possessed of great wisdom.'"

SECTION LXIV.

"Vaisampayana said, 'They then set out, with cheerful hearts, and accompanied by men and animals all of whom and which were equally cheerful. They filled the whole Earth with the loud clatter of their wheels. Their praises hymned by eulogists and Sutas and Magadhas and bards, and supported by their own army, they looked like so many Adityas adorned with their own rays. With the white umbrella held over his head, king Yudhishthira shone with beauty like the lord of the stars on the night when he is at full. That foremost of men, the eldest son of Pandu, accepted, with due forms, the blessings and cheers of his gladdened subjects as he proceeded on his way. As regards the soldiers that followed the king, their confused murmurs seemed to fill the entire welkin. That host crossed many lakes and rivers and forests and pleasure gardens. They at last came upon the mountains. Arrived at that region where that wealth was buried, O king, the royal Yudhishthira fixed his camp with all his brothers and troops. The region selected for the purpose, O chief of Bharata's race, was perfectly level and auspicious. There the king pitched his camp, placing in his van such Brahmanas as were endued with penances and learning and self-restraint, as also his priest Agnivesya, O thou of Kuru's race, who was well-conversant with the Vedas and all their branches.[812] Then the royal sons of Pandu, and the other kings (who accompanied that expedition), and the Brahmanas and priests well-skilled in sacrificial rites, having duly performed some propitiatory ceremonies, spread themselves all over that spot. Having duly placed the king and his ministers in the middle, the Brahmanas caused the camp to be pitched by laying out six roads and nine divisions.[813] King Yudhishthira caused a separate encampment to be duly made for the infuriate elephants that accompanied his force. When everything was complete, he addressed the Brahmanas, saying, "Ye foremost of Brahmanas, let that be done which you think should be done in view of the matter at hand. Indeed, let an auspicious day and constellation be fixed for it. Let not a long time pass away over our heads as we wait in suspense here. Ye foremost of learned Brahmanas, having formed this resolution, let that be done which should be done after this." Hearing these words of the king, the Brahmanas with those amongst them that were well-skilled in the performance of religious rites, became filled with gladness and desirous of doing what was agreeable to king Yudhishthira the just, said these words in reply, "This very day is an auspicious one with an auspicious constellation. We shall, therefore, strive to accomplish those high rites we propose. We shall today, O king, live upon water alone. Do you all fast also today." Hearing those words of those foremost Brahmanas, the royal sons of Pandu passed that night, abstaining from all food, and lying confidently on beds of Kusa grass, like blazing fires in a sacrifice. And the night wore away as they listened to the discourses of the learned Brahmanas (on diverse subjects). When the cloudless morning came, those foremost of Brahmanas addressed the royal son of Dharma (saying as follows).'"

---

[812] Agnivesya was another name of Dhaumya.

[813] Three roads running north to south, and three running cast to west and intersecting the former, are the six roads that are directed to be laid out in pitching encampments. Those give nine squares with two boundary lines at right angles with each other.

SECTION LXV.

"'The Brahmanas said, "Let offerings be made unto the high-souled Mahadeva of three eyes. Having duly dedicated those offerings, O king, we shall then strive to gain our object." Hearing these words of those Brahmanas, Yudhishthira caused offerings to be duly made unto that deity who loved to lie down on mountain-breasts. Gratifying the (sacrificial) fire with (libations of) sanctified butter according to the ordinance, the priest (Dhaumya) cooked Charu with the aid of Mantras and performed the necessary rites. He took up many flowers and sanctified them with Mantras, O king. With Modakas and frumenty and meat, he made offerings to the deity. With diverse kinds of flowers and with fried paddy, of very superior kind, Dhaumya, well-versed in the Vedas, performed the remaining rites. He next presented offerings according to the ordinance unto those ghostly beings who formed Mahadeva's train. And offerings were next made to Kuvera, the chief of the Yakshas, and unto Manibhadra also. Unto the other Yakshas also and unto them that were the foremost ones among the ghostly companions of Mahadeva, the priest offered due worship, having filled many jugs with food, with Krisaras and meat and Nivapas mixed with sesame seeds. The king gave away unto the Brahmanas thousands of kine. He then directed the presentation, according to due rites, of offerings unto those night-wandering beings (who live with Mahadeva). Surcharged, as it were, with the scent of Dhupas, and filled with the fragrance of flowers, that region, sacred to the deity of deities, O king, became exceedingly delightful. Having performed the worship of Rudra and of all the Ganas, the king, placing Vyasa ahead, proceeded towards the place where the treasure was buried. Once more worshipping the Lord of treasures, and bowing unto him with reverence and saluting him properly, with diverse kinds of flowers and cakes and Krisara, having worshipped those foremost of gems, viz., Sankha and Nidhi, and those Yakshas who are the lords of gems, and having worshipped many foremost of Brahmanas and caused them to utter blessings, the king endued with great puissance, strengthened by the energy and the auspicious benedictions of those Brahmanas, caused that spot to be excavated. Then numerous vessels of diverse and delightful forms, and Bhringaras and Katahas and Kalasas and Bardhamanakas, and innumerable Bhajanas of beautiful forms, were dug out by king Yudhishthira the just. The wealth thus dug out was placed in large "Karaputas" for protection.[814] A portion of the wealth was caused to be borne upon the shoulders of men in stout balances of wood with baskets slung like scales at both ends. Indeed, O king, there were other methods of conveyance there for bearing away that wealth of the son of Pandu.[815] There were sixty thousands of camels and a hundred and twenty thousand horses, and of elephants, O monarch, there were one hundred thousand. Of cars there were as many, and of carts, too as many, and of she-elephants as many. Of mules and men the number was untold. That wealth which Yudhishthira caused to be dug out was even so much. Sixteen thousand coins were placed on the back of each camel; eight thousand on each car; four and twenty thousand on each elephant; (while proportionate loads were placed on horses and mules and on the backs, shoulder and heads of men). Having loaded these vehicles with that

---

[814] Karaputa is made up of two wooden chests united with each other by chains or cords and intended to be borne by camels and bullocks.

[815] The first line of 17 is exceedingly terse. Literally rendered, it runs,—'Each vessel was united with another, and became half the (total) weight slung on balance.'

wealth and once more worshipping the great deity Siva, the son of Pandu set out for the city called after the elephant, with the permission of the Island-born Rishi, and placing his priest Dhaumya in the van. That foremost of men, viz., the royal son of Pandu, made short marches every day, measured by a Goyuta (4 miles). That mighty host, O king, afflicted with the weight they bore, returned, bearing that wealth, towards the capital, gladdening the hearts of all those perpetuators of the Kuru race.'"

SECTION LXVI.

"Vaisampayana said, 'Meanwhile, Vasudeva of great energy accompanied by the Vrishnis, came to the city called after the elephant. While leaving that city for returning to his own Dwaraka, he had been requested by the son of Dharma to come back. Hence, knowing that the time fixed for the horse-sacrifice had come, that foremost of men came back (to the Kuru capital). Accompanied by the son of Rukmini, by Yuyudhana, by Charudeshna, by Samva, by Gada, by Kritavarman, by the heroic Sarana, by Nisatha, and by the Unmukha, Vasudeva came with Valadeva at the head of the train, with Subhadra also accompanying him. Indeed, that hero came for seeing Draupadi and Uttara and Pirtha and for comforting those Kshatriya ladies of distinction who had been bereft of many of their protectors. Beholding those heroes come, king Dhritarashtra, as also the high-souled Vidura, received them with due honours. That foremost of men, viz., Krishna of great energy, well adored by Vidura and Yuyutsu, continued to reside in the Kuru capital. It was while the Vrishni heroes, O Janamejaya, were residing in the Kuru city, O king, that thy sire, that slayer of hostile heroes, was born. The royal Parikshit, O monarch, afflicted by the Brahma weapon (of Aswatthaman), upon coming out of the womb, lay still and motionless, for life he had not. By his birth he had gladdened the citizens but soon plunged them into grief. The citizens, learning of the birth of the prince, uttered a leonine shout. That noise proceeded to the utmost verge of every point of the compass. Soon, however, (when it was known that the prince was bereft of life), that noise ceased. With great haste Krishna, his senses and mind considerably affected, with Yuyudhana in his company, entered the inner apartments of the palace. He beheld his own paternal aunt (Kunti) coming, loudly weeping and calling upon him repeatedly. Behind her were Draupadi and the famous Subhadra, and the wives of the relatives of the Pandavas, all weeping piteously. Meeting Krishna, Kunti, that daughter of the Bhoja race, said unto him, O foremost of monarchs, these words in a voice chocked with tears, "O Vasudeva, O mighty-armed hero, Devaki by having borne thee, has come to be regarded as an excellent genetrix. Thou art our refuge, and our glory. This race (of Pandu) depends upon thee for its protector. O Yadava hero, O puissant one, this child of thy sister's son, has come out of the womb, slain by Aswatthaman. O Kesava, do thou revive him. O delighter of the Yadavas, even this was vowed by thee, O puissant one, when Aswatthaman had inspired the blade of grass into a Brahma-weapon of mighty energy. Indeed, O Kesava, thy words were even these, 'I shall revive that child if he comes out of the womb dead.'—That child, O son, has been born dead. Behold him, O foremost of men. It behoveth thee, O Madhava, to rescue Uttara and Subhadra and Draupadi and myself, and Dharma's son (Yudhishthira), and Bhima and Phalguna, and Nakula, and the irresistible Sahadeva. In this child are bound the life-breaths of the Pandavas and myself. O thou of the Dasarha race, on him depends the obsequial cake of Pandu, as also of my father-in-law, and of Abhimanyu too, blessed be thou, that darling nephew of thine who was so very like unto thee. Do thou accomplish today what will be beneficial to all these.

I urge thee earnestly, O Janarddana. Uttara, O slayer of foes, always repeats the words said unto her by Abhimanyu. Without doubt, O Krishna, those words were highly agreeable to her. O thou of the Dasarha race, Arjuna's son said unto this daughter of Virata,—'Thy son, O blessed girl, will go to my maternal uncles. Taking up his residence with the Vrishnis and Andhakas, he will obtain from them the science of arms, indeed, diverse wonderful weapons and the whole of the science of politics and morality.' Even these were the words, O son, that that slayer of hostile heroes, viz., the son of Subhadra, that irresistible hero, said unto Uttara, from his affection for her. O slayer of Madhu, bowing our heads unto thee, we pray thee for making those words of Abhimanyu true. In view also of the time that has come, do thou accomplish what is highly beneficial." Having said these words unto that hero of the Vrishni's race, Pritha of large eyes, raised her arms upwards and with the other ladies in her company, fell down on the Earth. All of them, with eyes rendered muddy by tears, repeatedly exclaimed, saying, "Alas, the son of Vasudeva's nephew has been born dead." After Kunti had said so, Janarddana took hold of her, O Bharata, and gently raising her from the Earth, comforted her as follows.'"

SECTION LXVII.

"Vaisampayana said, 'After Kunti had sat up, Subhadra, beholding her brother, began to weep aloud, and afflicted with excessive grief, said,—"O thou of eyes like lotus petals, behold the grandson of Arjuna of great intelligence. Alas, the Kuru race having been thinned, a child has been born that is feeble and dead. The blade of grass (inspired into a weapon of great efficacy), uplifted by Drona's son for compassing the destruction of Bhimasena, fell upon Uttara and Vijaya and myself.[816] Alas, that blade, O Kesava, is still existing unextracted in me, after having pierced my heart, since I do not, O irresistible hero, behold this child with (his sire who was) my son. What will the righteous-souled king Yudhishthira the just say? What will Bhimasena and Arjuna and the two sons of Madravati also say? Hearing that Abhimanyu's son was born and found dead, the Pandavas, O thou of Vrishni's race, will regard themselves as cheated by Aswatthaman. Abhimanyu, O Krishna, was the favourite of all the Pandava brothers, without doubt. Hearing this intelligence, what will those heroes, vanquished by the weapon of Drona's son say? What grief, O Janarddana, can be greater than this viz., that Abhimanyu's son should be born dead! Bowing unto thee with my head, O Krishna, I seek to gratify thee today. Behold, O foremost of men, these two standing here, viz., Pritha and Draupadi. When, O Madhava, the son of Drona sought to destroy the embryos even in the wombs of the ladies of the Pandavas, at that time, O grinder of foes, thou saidst in wrath unto Drona's son (ever these words), 'O wretch of a Brahmana, O vilest of men, I shall disappoint thy wish. I shall revive the son of Kiritin's son.' Hearing these words of thine and well knowing thy puissance, I seek to gratify thee, O irresistible hero. Let the son of Abhimanyu be revived. If having pledged thyself previously thou dost not accomplish thy auspicious vow, do thou then know for certain, O chief of the Vrishni race, that I shall cast off my life. If, O hero, this son of Abhimanyu doth not revive when thou, O irresistible one, art alive and near, of what other use wilt thou be to me? Do thou, therefore, O irresistible one, revive this son of Abhimanyu,—this child possessed of eyes similar to his,—even as a rain-charged cloud revives the lifeless crops (on a field). Thou, O Kesava, art righteous-souled, truthful, and of prowess incapable of being baffled. It

---

[816] Vilava is Arjuna.

behoveth thee, O chastiser of foes, to make thy words truthful. If only thou wishest it, thou canst revive the three worlds (of being) if dead. What need I say, therefore, of this darling child, born but dead, of thy sister's son? I know thy puissance, O Krishna. Therefore, do I solicit thee. Do thou show this great favour to the sons of Pandu. It behoveth thee, O mighty-armed one, to show compassion to this Uttara or to me, thinking that I am thy sister or even a mother that hath lost her son, and one that hath thrown herself upon thy protection."'"

SECTION LXVIII.

"Vaisampayana said, 'Thus addressed, O king, (by his sister and others), the slayer of Kesin, exceedingly afflicted by grief, answered,—"So be it!"—These words were uttered with sufficient loudness and they gladdened all the inmates of the inner apartments of the palace. The puissant Krishna, that foremost of men, by uttering these words, gladdened all the people assembled there, like one pouring cold water on a person afflicted with sweat. He then quickly entered the lying-in room in which thy sire was born. It was duly sanctified, O chief of men, with many garlands of white flowers, with many well-filled water pots arranged on every side; with charcoal, soaked in ghee, of Tinduka wood, and mustard seeds, O thou of mighty arms; with shining weapons properly arrayed, and several fires on every side. And it was peopled by many agreeable and aged dames summoned for waiting (upon thy grandmother). It was also surrounded by many well-skilled and clever physicians, O thou of great intelligence. Endued with great energy, he also saw there all articles that are destructive of Rakshasas, duly placed by persons conversant with the subject. Beholding the lying-in room in which thy sire was born thus equipt, Hrishikesa became very glad and said,—"Excellent, Excellent!" When he of Vrishni's race said so and presented such a cheerful countenance, Draupadi, repairing thither with great speed, addressed the daughter of Virata, saying,—"O blessed lady, here comes to thee thy father-in-law, the slayer of Madhu, that ancient Rishi of inconceivable soul, that unvanquished one."—Virata's daughter, checking her tears, said these words in a voice suffocated with grief. Covering herself properly, the princess waited for Krishna like the deities reverentially waiting for him. The helpless lady, with heart agitated by grief, beholding Govinda coming, indulged in these lamentations, "O lotus-eyed one, behold us two deprived of our child. O Janarddana, both Abhimanyu and myself have been equally slain. O thou of Vrishni's race, O slayer of Madhu, I seek to gratify thee by bending my head, O hero, unto thee. Do thou revive this child of mine that has been consumed by the weapon of Drona's son. If king Yudhishthira the just, or Bhimasena, or thyself, O lotus-eyed one, had, on that occasion, said, 'Let the blade of grass (inspired by Aswatthaman into a Brahma-weapon) destroy the unconscious mother'—O puissant one, then I would have been destroyed and this (sad occurrence) would not have happened. Alas, what benefit has been reaped by Drona's son by accomplishing this cruel deed, viz., the destruction of the child in the womb by his Brahma-weapon. The self-same mother now seeks to gratify thee, O slayer of foes, by bending her head. Surely, O Govinda, I shall cast off my life-breaths if this child does not revive. In him, O righteous one, were placed many expectations by me. Alas, when these have been frustrated by Drona's son, what need have I, O Kesava, to bear, the burden of life? The hope, O Krishna, was cherished by me that with my child on my lap, O Janarddana, I would salute thee with reverence. Alas, O Kesava, that hope has been destroyed. O foremost of all beings, at the death of this heir of Abhimanyu of restless eyes, all the hopes in my breast have been destroyed. Abhimanyu of restless eyes, O slayer of Madhu, was exceedingly dear to thee. Behold this child of his slain by the Brahma-weapon. This child is very ungrateful and very heartless, like his sire, for, behold, disregarding the prosperity and affluence of the Pandavas, he has gone to Yama's abode. I had, before this, vowed, O Kesava, that if Abhimanyu fell on the field of battle, O hero, I would follow him without any loss of time. I did not, however, keep my vow, cruel that I am and fond of life. If I repair to him now, what, indeed, will Phalguna's son say?"'"

SECTION LXIX.

"Vaisampayana said, 'The helpless Uttara, desirous of getting back her child, having indulged in these piteous lamentations, fell down in affliction on the earth like a demented creature. Beholding the princess fallen on the earth deprived of her son and with her body uncovered, Kunti as also all the (other) Bharata ladies deeply afflicted, began to weep aloud. Resounding with the voice of lamentation, the palace of the Pandavas, O king, was soon converted into a mansion of sorrow where nobody could remain. Exceedingly afflicted by grief on account of her son, Virata's daughter, O king, seemed to be struck down for some time by sorrow and cheerlessness. Regaining consciousness, O chief of Bharata's race, Uttara took up her child on her lap and said these words: "Thou art the child of one who was conversant with every duty. Art thou not conscious then of the sin thou committest, since thou dost not salute this foremost one of the Vrishni's race? O son, repairing to thy sire tell him these words of mine, viz.,—it is difficult for living creatures to die before their time comes, since though reft of thee, my husband, and now deprived of my child also, I am yet alive when I should die, unendued as I am with everything auspicious and everything possessed of value.—O mighty-armed one, with the permission of king Yudhishthira the just I shall swallow some virulent poison or cast myself on the blazing fire. O sire, difficult of destruction is my heart since, though I am deprived of husband and child, that heart of mine does not yet break into a thousand pieces. Rise, O son and behold this thy afflicted great-grandmother. She is deeply afflicted with grief, bathed in tears, exceedingly cheerless, and plunged in an ocean of sorrow. Behold the reverend princess of Panchala, and the helpless princess of the Satwata race. Behold myself, exceedingly afflicted with grief, and resembling a deer pierced by a hunter. Rise, O child, and behold the face of this lord of the worlds, that is endued with great wisdom, and possessed of eyes like lotus-petals and resembling thy sire of restless glance." Beholding Uttara, who indulged in these lamentations, fallen on the earth, all those ladies, raising her, caused her to sit up. Having sat up, the daughter of the king of the Matsyas, summoning her patience, joined her hands in reverence and touched the earth with her head for saluting Kesava of eyes like the petals of the lotus. That foremost of beings, hearing those heart-rending lamentations of hers, touched water and withdrew the (force of the) Brahma-weapon.[817] That hero of unfading glory, belonging to the race of the Dasarhas, promised to give the child his life. Then he of pure soul, said these words in the hearing of the whole universe,—"O Uttara, I never utter an untruth. My words will prove true. I shall revive this child in the presence of all creatures. Never before have I uttered an untruth even in jest. Never have I turned back from battle.

---

[817] Before performing any rite or act of a grave nature, Hindus are required to touch water or perform what is called the 'achamana'. A little quantity of water is taken on the palm of the right hand, and with it are touched the lips, the nostrils, the ears, and the eyes.

(By the merit of those acts) let this child revive! As righteousness is dear to me, as Brahmanas are specially dear to me, (by the merit of that disposition of mine) let Abhimanyu's son, who is born dead, revive! Never hath a misunderstanding arisen between me and my friend Vijaya. Let this dead child revive by that truth! As truth and righteousness are always established in me, let this dead child of Abhimanyu revive (by the merit of these)! As Kansa and Kesi have been righteously slain by me, let this child revive today by that truth!" After these words were uttered by Vasudeva, that child, O foremost one of Bharata's race, became animate and began gradually to move, O monarch."'

SECTION LXX.

"Vaisampayana said, 'When the Brahma-weapon was withdrawn by Krishna, at that time, the laying-in room was illumined by thy father with his energy. All the Rakshasas (that had come there) were forced to leave the room and many of them met with destruction. In the welkin a voice was heard, saying, "Excellent, O Kesava, Excellent!"— The blazing Brahma-weapon then returned to the Grandsire (of all the worlds). Thy sire got back his life-breaths, O king. The child began to move according to his energy and might. The Bharata ladies became filled with joy. At the command of Govinda, the Brahmanas were made to utter benedictions. All the ladies, filled with joy, praised Janarddana. Indeed, the wives of those Bharata lions, viz., Kunti and Drupada's daughter and Subhadra, and Uttara, and the wives of other lions among men, like (ship-wrecked) persons who have reached the shore after having obtained a boat, became exceedingly glad. Then wrestlers and actors and astrologers and those who enquire after the slumbers (of princes), and bands of bards and eulogists all uttered the praises of Janarddana, while uttering benedictions fraught with the praises of the Kuru race, O chief of the Bharatas. Uttara, rising up at the proper time, with a delighted heart and bearing her child in her arms, reverentially saluted the delighter of the Yadus. Rejoicing greatly, Krishna made gifts unto the child of many valuable gems. The other chiefs of the Vrishni race, did the same. Then the puissant Janarddana, firmly adhering to truth, bestowed a name on the infant who was thy sire, O monarch.—"Since this child of Abhimanyu has been born at a time when this race has become nearly extinct, let his name be Parikshit!" Even this is what he said. Then thy father, O king, began to grow, and gladden all the people, O Bharata. When thy father was a month old, O hero, the Pandavas came back to their capital, bringing with them a profusion of wealth. Hearing that the Pandavas were near, those foremost ones of the Vrishni race went out. The citizens decked the city called after the elephant with garlands of flowers in profusions, with beautiful pennons and standards of diverse kinds. The citizens also, O king, adorned their respective mansions. Desirous of doing what was beneficial to the sons of Pandu, Vidura ordered diverse kinds of worship to be offered to the deities established in their respective temples. The principal streets of the city were adorned with flowers. Indeed, the city was filled with the hum of thousands of voices which resembled the softened roar of distant ocean waves. With dancers all engaged in their vocation, and with the voice of singers, the (Kuru) city then resembled the mansion of Vaisravana himself.[818] Bards and eulogists, O king, accompanied by beautiful women were seen to adorn diverse retired spots in the city. The

[818] The abode of Vaisravana is called Alaka. Vaisravana is, of course, Kuvera, the lord of treasures, friend of Mahadeva, and chief of the Yakshas.

pennons were caused by the wind to float gaily on every part of the city, as if bent upon showing the Kurus the southern and the northern points of the compass. All the officers also of the government loudly proclaimed that that was to be a day of rejoicing for the entire kingdom as an indication of the success of the enterprise for bringing a profusion of gems and other valuables.'"[819]

SECTION LXXI.

"Vaisampayana said, 'Hearing that the Pandavas were near, that crusher of foes, viz., Vasudeva, accompanied by his ministers, went out for seeing them.

"'The Pandavas then, uniting with the Vrishnis according to the usual formalities, together entered, O king, the city named after the elephant. With the hum of voices and the clatter of cars of that mighty host, the Earth and the welkin, and the firmament itself, became as it were entirely filled. The Pandavas, with rejoicing hearts, accompanied by their officers and friends entered the capital, placing that treasure in their van. Repairing, agreeably to custom, to king Dhritarashtra first, they worshipped his feet, announcing their respective names. Those foremost ones of Bharata's race, O chief of kings, then paid their respectful salutations to Gandhari, the daughter of Suvala and to Kunti. They next worshipped (their uncle) Vidura and met Yuyutsu, the son of Dhritarashtra by his Vaisya wife. Those heroes were then worshipped by others and they blazed forth in beauty, O king. After this, O Bharata, those heroes heard the tidings of that highly wonderful and marvellous and glad-some birth of thy father. Hearing of that feat of Vasudeva of great intelligence, they all worshipped Krishna, the delighter of Devaki, who was every way worthy of worship. Then, after a few days, Vyasa, the son of Satyavati, endued with great energy, came to the city named after the elephant. The perpetuators of Kuru's race worshipped the great Rishi according to the usual custom. Indeed, those heroes, with those foremost princes of the Vrishni and the Andhaka races, paid the sage their adorations. After having conversed on various subjects, Dharma's son Yudhishthira addressed Vyasa and said, "This treasure, O holy one, which has been brought through thy grace I wish to devote to that great sacrifice known by the name of the horse-sacrifice. O best of ascetics, I desire to have thy permission. We are all, O Rishi, at thy disposal, and at that of the high-souled Krishna."

"'Vyasa said, "I give thee permission, O king. Do what should be done after this. Do thou worship the deities duly by performing the horse-sacrifice with profuse gifts. The horse-sacrifice, O king, is a cleanser of all sins. Without doubt, having worshipped the deities by that sacrifice thou wilt surely be cleansed of all sins."'

"Vaisampayana continued, 'Thus addressed, the Kuru king Yudhisthira of righteous soul then set his heart, O monarch, on making the necessary preparations for the horse-sacrifice. Having represented all this unto the Island-born Krishna, the king endued with great eloquence approached Vasudeva and said,—"O foremost of all beings, the goddess Devaki has, through thee, come to be regarded as the most fortunate of mothers! O thou of unfading glory, do thou accomplish that which I shall now tell thee, O mighty-armed one. O delighter of the Kurus, the diverse enjoyments we enjoy have all been acquired through thy puissance. The whole Earth has been subjugated by thee with the aid of thy prowess and intelligence. Do thou, therefore, cause thyself to undergo the rites of initiation. Thou art our highest preceptor and master. If thou performest the sacrifice, O

---

[819] The last line is slightly expanded.

thou of the Dasarha race, I shall be cleansed from every sin. Thou art Sacrifice. Thou art the Indestructible. Thou art this All. Thou art Righteousness. Thou art Prajapati. Thou art the goal of all creatures. Even this is my certain conclusion."

"'Vasudeva said, "O mighty-armed one, it becomes thee to say so, O chastiser of foes. Thou art the goal of all creatures. Even this is my certain conclusion. Amongst the heroes of the Kuru race, in consequence of thy righteousness, thou shinest today in great glory. They have all been cast into the shade, O king, by thee. Thou art our king, and thou art our senior. With my approval freely granted, do thou adore the deities in the sacrifice suggested. Do thou, O Bharata, appoint us to whatever tasks thou likest. Truly, do I pledge myself that I shall accomplish all, O sinless one, that thou mayst bid me accomplish. Bhimasena and Arjuna and the two sons of Madravati will be sacrificing when thou, O king, sacrificest."'"[820]

SECTION LXXII.

"Vaisampayana said, 'Thus addressed by Krishna, Yudhishthira, the son of Dharma, endued with great intelligence, saluted Vyasa and said these words: "Do thou cause me to be initiated when the proper hour, as thou truly knowest, comes for that rite. This my sacrifice is entirely dependent on thee."

"'Vyasa said, "Myself, O son of Kunti, and Paila and Yajnavalkya, shall without doubt, achieve every rite at the proper time. The rite of initiating thee will be performed on the day of full moon belonging to the month of Chaitra. Let all the necessaries of the sacrifice, O foremost of men, be got ready. Let Sutas well-versed in the science of horses, and let Brahmanas also possessed of the same lore, select, after examination, a worthy horse in order that thy sacrifice may be completed. Loosening the animal according to the injunctions of the scriptures, let him wander over the whole Earth with her belt of seas, displaying thy blazing glory, O king!"'

"Vaisampayana continued, 'Thus addressed (by the Rishi), Yudhishthira, the son of Pandu, that lord of Earth, answered,—"So be it!"—and then, O monarch, he accomplished all that that utterer of Brahma had directed. All the articles necessary for the sacrifice, O king, were duly procured. The royal son of Dharma, possessed of immeasurable soul, having procured all the necessaries, informed the Island-born Krishna of it. Then Vyasa of great energy said unto the royal son of Dharma,—"As regards ourselves, we are all prepared to initiate thee in view of the sacrifice. Let the Sphya and the Kurcha and all the other articles that, O thou of Kuru's race, may be needed for thy sacrifice, be made of gold.[821] Let the horse also be loosened today, for roaming on the Earth, agreeably to the ordinances of the scriptures. Let the animal, duly protected, wander over the Earth."

"'Yudhishthira said, "Let arrangements be made by thee, O regenerate one, about loosening this horse for enabling it to wander over the Earth at its will. It behoveth thee, O ascetic, to say who will protect this steed while roaming over the Earth freely according to its will."'

"Vaisampayana continued, 'Thus addressed (by king Yudhishthira), O monarch, the

---

[820] The sense is this: thou art the eldest brother of the Pandavas; if thou sacrificest, thy brothers also will come to be regarded as sacrificing with thee.

[821] Sphya was a wooden sword or scimitar, used for slaying the sacrificial animal. Kurcha is a handful of Kusa grass. All these things are directed by Vyasa to be made of pure gold.

Island-born Krishna said,—"He who is born after Bhimasena, who is the foremost of all bowmen, who is called Jishnu, who is endued with great patience and capable of overcoming all resistance,—he will protect the horse. That destroyer of the Nivatakavachas is competent to conquer the whole Earth. In him are all celestial weapons. His body is like that of a celestial in its powers of endurance. His bow and quivers are celestial. Even he will follow this horse.—He is well versed in both Religion and wealth. He is a master of all the sciences. O foremost of kings, he will agreeably to the scriptures, cause the steed to roam and graze at its will. This mighty-armed prince, of dark complexion, is endued with eyes resembling the petals of the lotus. That hero, the father of Abhimanyu, will protect the steed. Bhimasena also is endued with great energy. The son of Kunti is possessed of immeasurable might. He is competent to protect the kingdom, aided by Nakula, O monarch. Possessed of great intelligence and fame, Sahadeva will, O thou of Kuru's race, duly attend to all the relatives that have been invited to thy capital." Thus addressed by the Rishi, that perpetuator of Kuru's race, viz., Yudhishthira, accomplished every injunction duly and appointed Phalguna to attend to the horse.

"'Yudhishthira said, "Come, O Arjuna, let the horse, O hero, be protected by thee. Thou alone art competent to protect it, and none else. Those kings, O mighty-armed hero, who will come forward to encounter thee, try, O sinless one, to avoid battles with them to the best of thy power. Thou shouldst also invite them all to this sacrifice of mine. Indeed, O mighty-armed one go forth but try to establish friendly relations with them."'

"Vaisampayana continued, 'The righteous-souled king Yudhishthira, having said so unto his brother Savyasachin, commanded Bhima and Nakula to protect the city. With the permission of king Dhritarashtra, Yudhishthira then set Sahadeva, that foremost of warriors, to wait upon all the invited guests.'"

SECTION LXXIII.

"Vaisampayana said, 'When the hour for initiation came, all those great Ritwijas duly initiated the king in view of the horse-sacrifice. Having finished the rites of binding the sacrificial animals, the son of Pandu, viz., king Yudhishthira the just endued with great energy, the initiation being over, shone with great splendour along with those Ritwijas. The horse that was brought for the horse-sacrifice was let loose, agreeably to the injunctions of the scriptures, that utterer of Brahma, viz., Vyasa himself of immeasurable energy. The king Yudhishthira the just, O monarch, after his initiation, adorned with a garland of gold around his neck, shone in beauty like a blazing fire. Having a black deer skin for his upper garment, bearing a staff in hand, and wearing a cloth of red silk, the son of Dharma, possessed of great splendour, shone like a second Prajapati seated on the sacrificial altar. All his Ritwijas also, O king, were clad in similar robes. Arjuna also shone like a blazing fire. Dhananjaya, unto whose car were yoked white steeds, then duly prepared, O king, to follow that horse of the complexion of a black deer, at the command of Yudhishthira. Repeatedly drawing his bow, named Gandiva, O king, and casing his hand in a fence made of iguana skin, Arjuna, O monarch, prepared to follow that horse, O ruler of men, with a cheerful heart. All Hastinapore, O king, with very children, came out at that spot from desire of beholding Dhananjaya, that foremost of the Kurus on the eve of his journey. So thick was the crowd of spectators that came to behold the horse and the prince who was to follow it, that in consequence of the pressure of bodies, it seemed a fire was created. Loud was the noise that arose from that crowd of men who assembled together for beholding Dhananjaya the son of Kunti, and it seemed to fill all the points of the compass and the entire welkin. And they said,—"There goes the son of Kunti, and there that horse of blazing beauty. Indeed, the mighty-armed hero follows the horse, having armed himself with his excellent bow."—Even these were the words which Jishnu of noble intelligence heard. The citizens also blessed him, saying,—"Let blessings be thine! Go thou safely and come back, O Bharata." Others, O chief of men uttered these words—"So great is the press that we do not see Arjuna. His bow, however, is visible to us. Even that is celebrated bow Gandiva of terrible twang. Blessed be thou. Let all dangers fly from thy path. Let fear nowhere inspire thee. When he returns we shall behold him, for it is certain that he will come back." The high-souled Arjuna repeatedly heard these and similar other sweet words of men and women, O chief of the Bharatas. A disciple of Yajnavalkya, who was well-versed in all sacrificial rites and who was a complete master of the Vedas, proceeded with Partha for performing auspicious rites in favour of the hero. Many Brahmanas also, O king, all well-conversant with the Vedas, and many Kshatriyas too, followed the high-souled hero, at the command, O monarch, of Yudhishthira the just. The horse then roamed, O foremost of men, wherever he liked over the Earth already conquered by Pandavas with the energy of their weapons. In course of the horse's wanderings, O king, many great and wonderful battles were fought between Arjuna and many kings. These I shall describe to thee. The horse, O king, roamed over the whole Earth. Know, O monarch, that from the north it turned towards the East. Grinding the kingdoms of many monarchs that excellent horse wandered. And it was followed slowly by the great car-warrior Arjuna of white steeds. Countless, O monarch, was the fete of Kshatriyas,—of kings in myriads—who fought with Arjuna on that occasion, for having lost their kinsmen on the field of Kurukshetra. Innumerable Kiratas also, O king, and Yavanas, all excellent bowmen, and diverse tribes of Mlechcchas too, who had been discomfited before (by the Pandavas on the field of Kurukshetra), and many Aryan kings, possessed of soldiers and animals endued with great alacrity, and all irresistible in fight encountered the son of Pandu in battle. Thus occurred innumerable battles in diverse countries, O monarch, between Arjuna and the rulers of diverse realms who came to encounter him. I shall, O sinless king, narrate to thee those battles only which raged with great fury and which were the principal ones among all he fought.'"

SECTION LXXIV.

"Vaisampayana said. 'A battle took place between the diadem-decked (Arjuna) and the sons and grandsons of the Trigartas whose hostility the Pandavas has incurred before and all of whom were well-known as mighty car-warriors. Having learnt that that foremost of steeds, which was intended for the sacrifice, had come to their realm, these heroes, casing themselves in mail, surrounded Arjuna. Mounted on their cars, drawn by excellent and well-decked horses, and with quivers on their backs, they surrounded that horse, O king, and endeavoured to capture it. The diadem-decked Arjuna, reflecting on that endeavour of theirs, forbade those heroes, with conciliatory speeches, O chastiser of foes. Disregarding Arjuna's message, they assailed him with their shafts. The diadem-decked Arjuna resisted those warriors who were under the sway of darkness and passion. Jishnu addressed them smilingly and said, "Desist, ye unrighteous ones. Life is a benefit (that should not be thrown away)." At the time of his setting out, he had been earnestly ordered by king Yudhishthira the just, not to slay those Kshatriyas whose kinsmen had been slain before on the field of Kurukshetra. Recollecting these commands of king

Yudhishthira the just who was endued with great intelligence, Arjuna asked the Trigartas to forbear. But they disregarded Arjuna's injunction. Then Arjuna vanquished Suryavarman, the king of the Trigartas, in battle, by shooting countless shafts at him and laughed in scorn. The Trigarta warriors, however, filling the ten points with the clatter of their cars and car-wheels, rushed towards Dhananjaya. Then Suryavarman, displaying his great lightness of hand, pierced Dhananjaya with hundreds of straight arrows, O monarch. The other great bowmen who followed the king and who were all desirous of compassing the destruction of Dhananjaya, shot showers of arrows on him. With countless shafts shot from his own bow-string, the son of Pandu, O king, cut off those clouds of arrows; upon which they fell down. Endued with great energy, Ketuvarman, the younger brother of Suryavarman, and possessed of youthful vigour, fought, for the sake of his brother, against Pandu's son possessed of great fame. Beholding Ketuvarman approaching towards him for battle, Vibhatsu, that slayer of hostile heroes, slew him with many sharp-pointed arrows. Upon Ketuvarman's fall, the mighty car-warrior Dhritavarman, rushing on his car towards Arjuna, showered a perfect downpour of arrows on him. Beholding that lightness of hand displayed by the youth Dhritavarman, Gudakesa of mighty energy and great prowess became highly gratified with him. The son of Indra could not see when the young warrior took out his arrows and when he placed them on his bow-string aiming at him. He only saw showers of arrows in the air. For a brief space of time, Arjuna gladdened his enemy and mentally admired his heroism and skill. The Kuru hero, smiling the while, fought with that youth who resembled an angry snake. The mighty armed Dhananjaya, glad as he was in beholding the valour of Dhritavarman, did not take his life. While, however, Partha of immeasurable energy fought mildly with him without wishing to take his life, Dhritavarman shot a blazing arrow at him. Deeply pierced in the hand by that arrow, Vijaya became stupefied and his bow Gandiva fell down on the Earth from his relaxed grasp. The form of that bow, O king, when it fell from the grasp of Arjuna, resembled, O Bharata, that of the bow of Indra (that is seen in the welkin after a shower). When that great and celestial bow fell down, O monarch, Dhritavarman laughed loudly in battle. At this, Jishnu, excited with rage, wiped the blood from his hand and once more taking up his bow, showered a perfect downpour of arrows. Then a loud and confused noise arose, filling the welkin and touching the very heavens as it were, from diverse creatures who applauded that feat of Dhananjaya. Beholding Jishnu inflamed with rage and looking like Yama himself as he appears at the end of the Yuga, the Trigarta warriors hastily surrounded him, rushing from their posts and desirous of rescuing Dhritavarman. Seeing himself surrounded by his foes, Arjuna became more angry than before. He then quickly despatched eight and ten of their foremost warriors with many shafts of hard iron that resembled the arrows of the great Indra himself. The Trigarta warriors then began to fly. Seeing them retreat, Dhananjaya, with great speed, shot many shafts at them that resembled wrathful snakes of virulent poison, and laughed aloud. The mighty car-warriors of the Trigartas, with dispirited hearts, fled in all directions, exceedingly afflicted by Dhananjaya with his arrows. They then addressed that tiger among men, that slayer of the Samsaptaka host (on the field of Kurukshetra), saying, "We are your slaves. We yield to thee.[822] Do thou command us, O Partha. Lo, we wait here as the most docile of thy servants. O delighter

---

[822] It will be remembered that the Samsaptaka host which had engaged Arjuna for several days on the field of Kurukshetra, all consisted of Trigarta warriors led by their king Susarman, Samsaptaka means 'sworn'. Those soldiers who took the oath that they would either conquer or die, wore called by that name.

of the Kurus, we shall execute all thy commands." Hearing these words expressive of their submission, Dhananjaya, said unto them, "Do ye, O kings, save your lives, and accept my dominion.""'"

SECTION LXXV.

"Vaisampayana said, 'That foremost of steeds then proceeded to the realm of Pragjyotisha and began to wander there. At this, Bhagadatta's son, who was exceedingly valorous in battle, came out (for encountering Arjuna). King Vajradatta, O chief of the Bharatas, finding the (sacrificial) steed arrived within his realm, fought (for detaining it). The royal son of Bhagadatta, issuing out of his city, afflicted the steed that was coming (and seizing it), marched back towards his own place. Marking this, the mighty-armed chief of the Kuru race, speedily stretched his Gandiva, and suddenly rushed towards his foe. Stupefied by the shafts sped from Gandiva, the heroic son of Bhagadatta, letting off loose the steed, fled from Partha.[823] Once more entering his capital, that foremost of kings, irresistible in battle, cased himself in mail, and mounting on his prince of elephants, came out. That mighty car-warrior had a white umbrella held over his head, and was fanned with a milk-white yak-tail. Impelled by childishness and folly, he challenged Partha, the mighty car-warrior of the Pandavas, famed for terrible deeds in battle, to an encounter with him. The enraged prince then urged towards Arjuna that elephant of his, which resembled a veritable mountain, and from whose temples and mouth issued streams of juice indicative of excitement. Indeed, that elephant showered its secretions like a mighty mass of clouds pouring rain. Capable of resisting hostile feats of its own species, it had been equipped agreeably to the ordinances of the treatises (on war-elephants). Irresistible in battle, it had become so infuriate as to be beyond control. Urged on by the prince with the iron-hook, that mighty elephant then seemed (as it advanced) as if it would cut through the welkin (like a flying hill). Beholding it advance towards him, O king, Dhananjaya, filled with rage and standing on the earth, O Bharata, encountered the prince on its back. Filled with wrath, Vajradatta quickly sped at Arjuna a number of broad-headed shafts endued with the energy of fire and resembling (as they coursed through the air) a cloud of speedily-moving locusts. Arjuna, however, with shafts sped from Gandiva, cut off those arrows, some into two and some into three pieces. He cut them off in the welkin itself with those shafts of his coursing through the welkin. The son of Bhagadatta, beholding his broad-headed shafts thus cut off, quickly sped at Arjuna a number of other arrows in a continuous line. Filled with rage at this, Arjuna, more quickly than before, shot at Bhagadatta's son a number of straightly coursing arrows equipt with golden wings. Vajradatta of mighty energy, struck with great force and pierced with these arrows in that fierce encounter, fell down on the Earth. Consciousness, however, did not desert him. Mounting on his prince of elephants again in the midst of that battle the son of Bhagadatta, desirous of victory, very coolly sped a number of shafts at Arjuna. Filled with wrath, Jishnu then sped at the prince a number of arrows that looked like blazing flames of fire and that seemed to be so many snakes of virulent poison. Pierced therewith, the mighty elephant, emitting a large quantity of blood, looked like a mountain of many springs discharging rills of water coloured with red chalk.'"

---

[823] The reading in every edition seems to be vicious. For obvious reasons, I read Parthadupadravat instead of Parthamupadravat.

SECTION LXXVI.

"Vaisampayana said, 'Thus waged that battle, O chief of the Bharatas, for three days between Arjuna and that prince like the encounter between him of a hundred sacrifices and Vritra. On the fourth day, Vajradatta of great might laughed loudly and, addressing Arjuna, said these words: "Wait, wait, O Arjuna. Thou shalt not escape me with life. Slaying thee I shall duly discharge the water-rite of my sire. My aged sire, Bhagadatta, who was the friend of thy sire, was slain by thee in consequence of his weight of years. Do thou, however, fight me that am but a boy!"[824] Having said these words, O thou of Kuru's race, king Vajradatta, filled with rage, urged his elephant towards the son of Pandu. Urged on by Vajradatta of great intelligence, that prince of elephants, as if desirous of cutting through the welkin, rushed towards Dhananjaya. That prince of elephants drenched Arjuna with a shower of juice emitted from the end of his trunk, like a mass of blue clouds drenching a hill with its downpour. Indeed, urged on by the king, the elephant, repeatedly roaring like a cloud, rushed towards Phalguna, with that deep noise emitted from its mouth. Verily, urged on by Vajradatta, that prince of elephants quickly moved towards the mighty car-warrior of the Kurus, with the tread of one that seemed to dance in excitement. Beholding that beast of Vajradatta advance towards him, that slayer of foes, viz., the mighty Dhananjaya, relying on Gandiva, stood his ground without shaking with fear. Recollecting what an obstacle Vajradatta was proving to the accomplishment of his task, and remembering the old enmity of the house (of Pragjyotisha towards the Pandavas), the son of Pandu became exceedingly inflamed with wrath against the king. Filled with rage, Dhananjaya impeded the course of that beast with a shower of arrows like the shore resisting the surging sea. That prince of elephants possessed of beauty (of form), thus impeded by Arjuna, stopped in its course, with body pierced with many an arrow, like a porcupine with its quills erect. Seeing his elephant impeded in its course, the royal son of Bhagadatta, deprived of sense by rage, shot many whetted arrows at Arjuna. The mighty-armed Arjuna baffled all those arrows with many foe-slaying shafts of his. The feat seemed to be exceedingly wonderful. Once more the king of the Pragjyotishas, inflamed with ire, forcibly urged his elephant, which resembled a mountain, at Arjuna. Beholding the beast once more advancing towards him, Arjuna shot with great strength a shaft at it that resembled a veritable flame of fire. Struck deeply in the very vitals, O king, by the son of Pandu, the beast suddenly fell down on the Earth like a mountain summit loosened by a thunder-bolt. Struck with Dhananjaya's shaft, the elephant, as it lay on the Earth, looked like a huge mountain cliff lying on the ground, loosened by the bolt of Indra. When the elephant of Vajradatta was prostrated on the ground, the son of Pandu, addressing the king who had fallen down with his beast, said,—"Do not fear. Indeed, Yudhishthira of mighty energy said unto me while commissioning me for this task even these words,—'Thou shouldst not, O Dhananjaya, slay those kings (who may encounter thee in battle). O tiger among men, thou shouldst regard thy task as accomplished if only thou disablest those hostile kings. Thou shouldst not also, O Dhananjaya, slay the warriors of those kings who may come forth to fight thee, with all their kinsmen and friends. They should be requested to come to the horse-sacrifice of Yudhishthira.'—Having heard these commands of my brother, I shall not slay thee, O king. Rise up; let no fear be thine; return to thy city safe and sound, O lord of

---

[824] Bhagadatta was the friend of Indra, the father of Arjuna.

Earth. When the day of full moon in the month of Chaitra comes, thou shalt, O great king, repair to that sacrifice of king Yudhishthira the just, for it takes place on that day." Thus addressed by Arjuna, the royal son of Bhagadatta, defeated by the son of Pandu, said,—"So be it."'"

SECTION LXXVII.

"Vaisampayana said, 'There occurred a great battle between the diadem-decked Arjuna and the hundreds of Saindhavas who still lived after the slaughter of their clan (on the field of Kurukshetra). Hearing that he of white steeds had entered their territories, those Kshatriyas came out against him, unable to bear that foremost one of Pandu's race. Those warriors who were as terrible as virulent poison, finding the horse within their dominion, seized it without being inspired with any fear of Partha who was the younger brother of Bhimasena. Advancing against Vibhatsu who waited on foot, armed with his bow, upon the sacrificial steed, they assailed him from a near point. Defeated in battle before, those Kshatriyas of mighty energy, impelled by the desire of victory, surrounded that foremost of men. Proclaiming their names and families and their diverse feats, they showered their arrows on Partha. Pouring showers of arrows of such fierce energy as were capable of impeding the course of hostile elephants, those heroes surrounded the son of Kunti, desirous of vanquishing him in battle. Themselves seated on cars, they fought Arjuna of fierce feats who was on foot. From every side they began to strike that hero, that slayer of the Nivatakavachas, that destroyer of the Samasaptakas, that killer of the king of the Sindhus. Surrounding him on every side as within a cage by means of a thousand cars and ten thousand horses, those brave warriors expressed their exaltation. Recollecting the slaughter by Dhananjaya of Jayadratha in battle, O thou of Kuru's race, they poured heavy showers of arrows on that hero like a mass of clouds showering a heavy downpour. Overwhelmed with that arrowy shower, Arjuna looked like the sun covered by a cloud. That foremost son of Pandu, in the midst of that cloud of arrows, resembled a bird in the midst of an iron cage, O Bharata. Seeing the son of Kunti thus afflicted with shafts, cries of Oh and Alas were uttered by the three worlds and the Sun himself became shorn of his splendour. Then, O king, a terrible wind began to blow, and Rahu swallowed up both the Sun and the Moon at the same time. Many meteors struck the solar disc and then shot in different directions. The prince of mountains, viz., Kailasa, began to tremble. The seven (celestial) Rishis, as also the other Rishis of Heaven, penetrated with fear, and afflicted with grief and sorrow, breathed hot sighs. Piercing through the welkin, those meteors fell on the lunar disc as well. All the points of the compass became filled with smoke and assumed a strange aspect. Reddish clouds, with flashes of lightning playing in their midst and the bow of Indra measuring them from side to side, suddenly covered the welkin and poured flesh and bloods on the Earth. Even such was the aspect which all nature assumed when that hero was overwhelmed with showers of shafts. Indeed, when Phalguna, that foremost one among the Bharatas, was thus afflicted, those marvels were seen. Overwhelmed by that dense cloud of arrows, Arjuna became stupefied. His bow, Gandiva, fell down from his relaxed grip and his leathern fence also slipped down. When Dhananjaya became stupefied, the Saindhava warriors once more shot at that senseless warrior, without loss of time, innumerable other shafts. Understanding that the son of Pritha was deprived of consciousness, the deities, with hearts penetrated by fear, began to seek his welfare by uttering diverse benedictions. Then the celestial Rishis, the seven Rishis, and the regenerate Rishis, became engaged in silent recitations from desire of giving victory to Pritha's son of great intelligence. When at last the energy of Partha blazed forth through those acts of the denizens of Heaven, that hero, who was conversant with celestial weapons of high efficacy, stood immovable like a hill. The delighter of the Kurus then drew his celestial bow. And as he repeatedly stretched the bowstring, the twang that followed resembled the loud sound of some mighty machine. Like Purandara pouring rain, the puissant Arjuna then, with that bow of his, poured incessant showers of shafts on his foes. Pierced by those shafts the Saindhava warriors with their chiefs became invisible like trees when covered with locusts. They were frightened at the very sound of Gandiva, and afflicted by fear they fled away. In grief of heart they shed tears and uttered loud lamentations. The mighty warrior moved amidst that host of foes with the celerity of a fiery wheel, all the time piercing those warriors with his arrows. Like the great Indra, the wielder of the thunder-bolt, that slayer of foes, viz., Arjuna, shot from his bow in every direction that shower of arrows which resembled a sight produced by magic (instead of any human agency). The Kaurava hero, piercing the hostile host with showers of arrows, looked resplendent like the autumnal Sun when he disperses the clouds with his powerful rays.'"

SECTION LXXVIII.

"Vaisampayana said, 'The irresistible wielder of Gandiva, addresst for battle, stood immovable on the field like Himavat himself. The Saindhava warriors, once more rallying, showered in great wrath repeated down-pours of shafts on him. The mighty-armed hero, laughing at his foes, who had once more rallied but who were on the point of death, addressed them in these soft words,—"Do ye fight to the best of your power and do ye endeavour to vanquish me. Do ye however, accomplish all necessary acts, for a great danger awaits you all. See, I fight all of you, baffling your clouds of arrows. Bent as you are on battle, tarry a little. I shall soon quell your pride." The wielder of Gandiva, having said these words in wrath, recollected, however, the words, O Bharata, of his eldest brother. Those words were,—"Thou shouldst not, O child, slay those Kshatriyas who will come against thee for battle. They should, however, be vanquished by thee." That foremost of men, Phalguna, had been thus addressed by king Yudhishthira the just, of great soul. He, therefore, began to reflect in this strain. "Even thus was I commissioned by my brother. Warriors advancing against me should not be slain. I must act in such a way as not to falsify the words of king Yudhishthira the just." Having arrived at this conclusion, Phalguna, that foremost of men, then said unto those Saindhavas who were all fierce in battle, these words:—"I say what is for your benefit. Though staying before me. I do not wish to slay you. He amongst you who will say unto me that he has been vanquished by me and that he is mine, will be spared by me. Having heard these words of mine, act towards me in that way which may best conduce to your benefit. By acting in a different way you will place yourselves in a situation of great fear and danger." Having said these words unto those heroic warriors the chief of the Kurus began to fight them. Arjuna was inflamed with wrath. His foes, desirous of victory, were equally enraged. The Saindhavas then, O king, shot hundreds and thousands of straight arrows at the wielder of Gandiva. Dhananjaya, with his own whetted shafts, cut off those arrows of sharp and terrible points, resembling snakes of virulent poison, before they could come up to him. Having cut off those sharp arrows equipt with Kanka feathers, Arjuna pierced each of the warriors opposed to him with a whetted shaft. The Saindhava Kshatriyas, recollecting that it was Dhananjaya who had slain their king Jayadratha, then hurled at him darts and javelins with great force. The diadem-decked Dhananjaya of great might baffled their intent by cutting off all those weapons before any of them could reach him. At length the son of Pandu became highly angry. With many straight and broad-headed arrows, he felled the heads of many of those warriors who were rushing at him from desire of victory. Many fled, many rushed at Arjuna; many moved not, all of them, however, uttered such a loud noise (of wrath and grief) that it resembled the roar of the ocean. As they were slain by Partha of immeasurable might, they fought him, each according to his strength and prowess. Their animals being all exhausted, Partha succeeded in depriving a large number of those warriors of their senses by means of his sharpest shafts in that battle. Then Dussala, their queen, the daughter of Dhritarashtra, knowing that they were rendered cheerless by Arjuna, took her grandson in her arms and repaired to Arjuna. The child was the son of Suratha (the son of Jayadratha). The brave prince proceeded to his maternal uncle on his car for the safety of all the Saindhava warriors. The queen, arrived at the presence of Dhananjaya, began to weep in sorrow. The puissant Dhananjaya, seeing her, cast off his bow. Abandoning his bow, Partha duly received his sister and enquired of her as to what he could do for her. The queen replied unto him, saying,—"O chief of the Bharatas, this child is the son of thy sister's son. He salutes thee, O Partha. Look at him, O foremost of men." Thus addressed by her, Partha enquired after his son (Suratha), saying—"Where is he?" Dussala then answered him, saying,—"Burning with grief on account of the slaughter of his sire, the heroic father of this child died in great affliction of heart. Listen to me how he met with his death. O Dhananjaya, he had heard before that his sire Jayadratha had been slain by thee, O sinless one. Exceedingly afflicted with grief at this, and hearing of thy arrival here as the follower and protector of the sacrificial horse, he at once fell down and gave up his life-breaths. Verily, deeply afflicted with grief as he was, as soon as he heard of thy arrival he gave up his life. Seeing him prostrate on the Earth, O lord, I took his infant son with me and have come to thee, desirous of thy protection." Having said these words, the daughter of Dhritarashtra began to lament in deep affliction. Arjuna stood before her in great cheerlessness of heart. His face was turned towards the Earth. The cheerless sister then said unto her brother, who was equally cheerless, these words: "Behold thy sister. Behold the child of thy sister's son. O perpetuator of Kuru's race, O thou that art fully conversant with every duty, it behoveth thee to show mercy to this child, forgetting the Kuru prince (Duryodhana) and the wicked Jayadratha. Even as that slayer of hostile heroes, Parikshit, has been born of Abhimanyu, so has this mighty-armed child, my grandson, sprung from Suratha. Taking him with me, O chief of men, I have come to thee, desirous of the safety of all the warriors. Do thou listen to these words of mine. This child of that wicked foe of thine hath now come to thee, O mighty-armed hero. It behoveth thee, therefore to show mercy to this infant. O chastiser of foes, this infant seeks to gratify thee by bending his head. He solicits thee for peace. O mighty-armed hero, be inclined to make peace. O thou that art conversant with every duty, be thou gratified with the child whose friends and kinsmen have all been slain and who himself knows nothing of what has happened. Do not yield to wrath. Forgetting his disreputable and cruel grandfather, who offended against thee so highly, it behoveth thee to show thy grace towards this child." Recollecting queen Gandhari and king Dhritarashtra, Dhananjaya, afflicted with grief, addressed Dussala who had said so unto him, and answered her, censuring Kshatriya practices the while. "Fie on Duryodhana, that mean wight, covetous of kingdom and full of vanity! Alas, it was for him that all my kinsmen have been despatched by me to the abode of Yama." Having said so, Dhananjaya comforted his sister and became inclined to make peace. Cheerfully he embraced her and then dismissed her, telling her to return to her palace. Dussala bade all her warriors desist from that great battle, and worshipping Partha, she of beautiful face retraced her steps towards her abode. Having vanquished those heroes, viz., the Saindhavas, thus, Dhananjaya began to follow that steed which roved at its will. The heroic Arjuna duly followed that sacrificial horse even as the divine wielder of Pinaka had in days of yore followed the deer through the firmament.[825] The steed, at its will, wandered through various realms one after another, enhancing the feats of Arjuna. In course of time, O chief of men, the horse wandering at its pleasure, at last arrived within the dominions of the ruler of Manipura, followed by the son of Pandu.'"

SECTION LXXIX.

"Vaisampayana said, 'The ruler of Manipura, Vabhruvahana, hearing that his sire Arjuna had arrived within his dominions, went out with humility, with a number of Brahmanas and some treasure in his van.[826] Remembering, however, the duties of Kshatriyas, Dhananjaya of great intelligence, seeing the ruler of Manipura arrive in that guise, did not approve of it. The righteous-souled Phalguna angrily said, "This conduct of thine is not becoming. Thou hast certainly fallen away from Kshatriya duties. I have come here as the protector of Yudhishthira's sacrificial horse. Why, O son, wilt thou not fight me, seeing that I have come within thy dominions? Fie on thee, O thou of foolish understanding, fie on thee that hast fallen away from Kshatriya duties! Fie on thee that would receive me peacefully, even though I have come here for battling with thee. In thus receiving me peacefully thou actest like a woman. O thou of wretched understanding, if I had come to thee, leaving aside my arms, then would this behaviour of thine have been fit, O worst of men." Learning that these words were addressed by her husband, the daughter of the Snake-king, viz., Ulupi unable to tolerate it, pierced through the Earth and came up to that spot.[827] She beheld her son standing there perfectly cheerless and with face hanging down. Indeed, the prince was repeatedly rebuked by his sire who was desirous of battle with him, O monarch. The daughter of the snake, with every limb possessed of beauty, viz., Ulupi, said these words consistent with righteousness and duty unto the prince who was conversant with righteousness and duty,—"Know that I am thy mother Ulupi that am the daughter of a snake. Do thou accomplish my behest, O son, for thou wouldst then attain to great merit. Fight thy father, this foremost one of Kuru's race, this hero that is irresistible in battle. Without doubt, he will then be gratified with thee." In this way was king Vabhruvahana incited against his sire by his (step) mother. At last, endued as he was with great energy, he made up his mind, O chief of the Bharatas, to fight Dhananjaya. Putting on his armour of bright gold and his effulgent head-gear, he ascended an excellent car which had hundreds of quivers ready on it. That car was equipt with necessaries for battle and had steeds yoked to it that were endued with the speed of the mind. It had excellent wheels and a strong Upashkara, and was adorned with golden ornaments of every kind. Raising his standard which was decorated most beautifully and which bore the device of a lion in gold, the handsome prince Vabhruvahana proceeded against his sire for battle. Coming upon the sacrificial steed which was protected by

---

[825] The allusion is to Mahadeva's pursuing Sacrifice when the latter fled from him in the form of a deer.

[826] The Brahmanas were to receive Arjuna duly and the treasure was intended as a present or offering of respect.

[827] Ulupi was one of the wives of Arjuna. She was, therefore, the step-mother of Vabhruvahana.

Partha, the heroic prince caused it to be seized by persons well-versed in horse-lore. Beholding the steed seized, Dhananjaya became filled with joy. Standing on the Earth, that hero began to resist the advance of his son who was on his car. The king afflicted the hero with repeated showers of shafts endued with whetted points and resembling snakes of virulent poison. The battle that took place between sire and son was incomparable. It resembled the encounter between the deities and the Asuras of old. Each was gratified with obtaining the other for an antagonist. Then Vabhruvahana, laughing, pierced the diadem-decked Arjuna, that foremost of men, in the shoulder with a straight shaft. Equipt with feathers, that shaft penetrated Arjuna's body like a snake penetrating on an anthill. Piercing the son of Kunti through, the shaft went deep into the Earth. Feeling acute pain, the intelligent Dhananjaya rested awhile, supporting himself on his excellent bow. He stood, having recourse to his celestial energy and seemed to outward appearance like one deprived of life. That foremost of men, then regaining consciousness, praised his son highly. Possessed of great splendour, the son of Sakra said, "Excellent, Excellent, O mighty-armed one, O son of Chitrangada! O son, beholding this feat, so worthy of thee, I am highly gratified with thee. I shall now shoot these arrows at thee, O son. Stand for fight (without running away)." Having said these words, that slayer of foes shot a shower of arrows on the prince. King Vabhruvahana, however, with his own broad-headed shafts, cut all those arrows which were shot from Gandiva and which resembled the thunder-bolt of Indra in splendour, some in twain and some into three parts. Then the standard, decked with gold and resembling a golden palmyra, on the king's car was cut off by Partha with some excellent shafts of his. The son of Pandu, laughing, next slew the king's steeds endued with large size and great speed. Descending from his car, the king inflamed with rage, fought his sire on foot. Gratified with the prowess of his son, that foremost one of the sons of Pritha, viz., the son of the wielder of the thunder-bolt, began to afflict him greatly. The mighty Vabhruvahana, thinking that his father was no longer able to face him, again afflicted him with many shafts resembling snakes of virulent poison. From a spirit of boyishness he then vigorously pierced his father in the breast with a whetted shaft equipt with excellent wings. That shaft, O king, penetrated the body of Pandu's son and reaching his very vital caused him great pain. The delighter of the Kurus, Dhananjaya, deeply pierced therewith by his son, then fell down in a swoon on the Earth, O king. When that hero, that bearer of the burthens of the Kurus fell down, the son of Chitrangada also became deprived of his senses. The latter's swoon was due to his exertions in battle as also to his grief at seeing his sire slain. He had been pierced deeply by Arjuna with clouds of arrows. He, therefore, fell down at the van of battle embracing the Earth. Hearing that her husband had been slain and that her son had fallen down on the Earth, Chitrangada, in great agitation of mind, repaired to the field of battle. Her heart burning with sorrow, weeping piteously the while, and trembling all over, the mother of the ruler of Manipura saw her slain husband."'

SECTION LXXX.

"Vaisampayana said, 'That lady of eyes like lotus petals, having indulged in copious lamentations, and burning with grief, at last lost her senses and fell down on the Earth. Regaining consciousness and seeing Ulupi, the daughter of the snake chief, queen Chitrangada endued with celestial beauty, said unto her these words, "Behold, O Ulupi, our ever-victorious husband slain in battle, through thee, by my son of tender years. Art thou conversant with the practices of the respectable? Art thou a wife devoted to thy lord? It is through thy deed that thy husband is laid low, slain in battle. If Dhananjaya hath offended against thee in every respect, do thou forgive him. I solicit thee, do thou revive that hero. O righteous lady, thou art conversant with piety. Thou art, O blessed one, known (for thy virtues) over the three worlds. How is it that having caused thy husband to be slain by my son, thou dost not indulge in grief? O daughter of the snake chief, I do not grieve for my slain son. I grieve for only my husband who has received this hospitality from his son." Having said these words unto the queenly Ulupi, the daughter of the snake chief, the illustrious Chitrangada proceeded to where her husband lay on the Earth and addressing him, said, "Rise, O dear lord, thou occupiest the foremost place in the affections of the Kuru king (Yudhishthira). Here is that steed of thine. It has been set free by me. Verily, O puissant one, this sacrificial steed of king Yudhishthira the just, should be followed by thee. Why then dost thou lie still on the Earth? My life-breaths depend on thee, O delighter of the Kurus. How is it that he who is the giver of other people's life-breaths casts off his own life-breaths today? Behold, O Ulupi, this goodly sight of thy husband lying prostrate on the ground. How is it that thou dost not grieve, having caused him to be slain through my son when thou didst excite with thy words? It is fit that this boy should succumb to the power of death and lie thus on the ground beside his own sire. Oh, let Vijaya, let him that is called Gudakesa, let this hero with reddish eyes, come back to life. O blessed lady, polygamy is not fault with men. Women only incur fault by taking more than one husband. Do not, therefore, harbour such thoughts (of vengeance).[828] This relationship was ordained by the Supreme ordainer himself. It is, besides, an eternal and unchangeable one. Do thou attend to that relationship. Let thy union (with Dhananjaya) be made true. If, having slain thy husband through my son, thou dost not revive him today before my eyes, I shall then cast off my life-breaths. Without doubt, O reverend lady, afflicted as I am with grief and deprived as I am of both husband and son, I shall sit here today in Praya in thy very sight!" Having said so unto the daughter of the snake chief, who was a co-wife with her to Arjuna, the princess Chaitravahini sat in Praya, O king, restraining speech.[829]

"Vaisampayana continued, 'Ceasing to lament, the cheerless queen, taking upon her lap the feet of her husband, sat there, sighing heavily and wishing also the restoration of her son to life. King Vabhruvahana then, regaining consciousness, saw his mother seated in that guise on the field of battle. Addressing her he said, "What can be more painful than the sight of my mother, who has been brought up in luxury, lying on the bare ground beside her heroic husband stretched thereon? Alas, this slayer of all foes, this foremost of all wielders of weapons, hath been slain by me in battle. It is evident that men do not die till their hour comes.[830] Oh, the heart of this princess seems to be very hard since it does not break even at the sight of her mighty-armed and broad-chested husband lying dead on the ground. It is evident that one does not die till one's hour comes, since neither myself, nor my mother is deprived of life (at even such a sight). Alas, alas, the golden coat of mail of this foremost hero of Kuru's race, slain by me, his son, knowingly, is lying on the ground, cut off from his body. Alas, ye Brahmanas, behold my heroic sire lying prostrate on the Earth, on a hero's bed, slain by his son. What benefit is done to this hero, slain by

---

[828] Yahubharyyata, meaning polygamy in the first line, should, as the noun of reference for Eshah be taken as vahunam bharyyata, i.e., polyandry, in the second line.

[829] To sit in Praya is to remain seated in a particular spot, abstaining from food and drink with a view to cast off one's life-breaths.

[830] The sense is, that 'grief does not kill; one does not die till one's hour comes. If it were otherwise, I would have died, so heavy is the load of my affliction.'

me in battle, by those Brahmanas who were commissioned to attend upon this foremost one of Kuru's race engaged in following the steed? Let the Brahmanas direct what expiation should now be undergone by me, a cruel and sinful wretch, that has slain his own sire in battle. Having slain my own sire, I should, suffering every kind of misery, wander over the Earth, cruel that I am, covering myself with his skin. Give me the two halves of my sire's head today, (so that I may wander over the Earth with them for that period), for there is no other expiation for me that have slain my own sire. Behold, O daughter of the foremost of snakes, thy husband slain by me. Verily, by slaying Arjuna in battle I have accomplished what is agreeable to thee. I shall today follow in the track by which my sire has gone. O blessed one, I am unable to comfort myself. Be happy today, O mother, seeing myself and the wielder of Gandiva both embrace death today. I swear to thee by truth itself (that I shall cast off my life-breaths)." Having said these words, the king, deeply afflicted with grief, O monarch, touched water, and exclaimed in sorrow, "Let all creatures, mobile and immobile, listen to me. Do thou also listen to me, O mother. I say the truth, O best of all daughters of the snakes. If this best of men, Jaya, my sire, does not rise up, I shall emaciate my own body, sitting on the field of battle. Having slain my sire, there is no rescue for me (from that dire sin). Afflicted as I am with the sin of slaying my sire, I shall without doubt have to sink in Hell. By slaying a heroic Kshatriya one becomes cleansed by making a gift of a hundred kine. By slaying my sire, however, so dire has been my sin that any rescue is impossible. This Dhananjaya, the son of Pandu, was the one hero endued with mighty energy. Possessed of righteous soul, he was the author of my being. How can I be rescued after having slain him?" Having uttered these lamentations, the high-souled son of Dhananjaya, king Vabhruvahana, touched water and became silent, vowing to starve himself to death.'

"Vaisampayana continued, 'When the king of Manipura, that chastiser of foes, afflicted with grief, along with his mother, sat down to starve himself to death, Ulupi then thought of the gem that has the virtue of reviving a dead man. The gem, the great refuge of the snakes, thus thought of, came there. The daughter of the prince of snakes taking it up, uttered these words that highly gladdened the combatants standing on the field. "Rise up, O son. Do not grieve. Jishnu has not been vanquished by thee. This hero is incapable of being vanquished by men as also by the deities with Vasava himself at their head. I have exhibited this illusion, deceiving your senses, for the benefit of this foremost of men, viz., thy illustrious sire. O thou of Kuru's race, desirous of ascertaining the prowess of thyself, his son, this slayer of hostile heroes, O king, came here for battling with thee. It was for that reason, O son, that thou wert urged by me to do battle. O puissant king, O son, do not suspect that thou hast committed any, even the least, fault, by accepting his challenge. He is a Rishi, of a mighty soul, eternal and indestructible. O dear son, Sakra himself is incapable of vanquishing him in battle. This celestial gem has been brought by me, O king. It always revives the snakes as often as they die. O puissant king, do thou place this gem on the breast of thy sire. Thou shalt then see the son of Pandu revived." Thus addressed, the prince who had committed no sin, moved by affection for his sire, then placed that gem on the breast of Pritha's son of immeasurable energy. After the gem had been placed on his breast, the heroic and puissant Jishnu became revived. Opening his red eyes he rose up like one who had slept long. Beholding his sire, the high-souled hero of great energy, restored to consciousness and quite at his ease, Vabhruvahana worshipped him with reverence. When that tiger among men, O puissant one, awoke from the slumber of death with every auspicious sign of life, the chastiser of Paka rained down celestial flowers. Kettle-drums struck by nobody, produced their music deep as the

roar of the cloud. A loud uproar was heard in the welkin consisting of the words—
"Excellent, Excellent!" The mighty-armed Dhananjaya, rising up and well-comforted,
embraced Vabhruvahana and smelled his head. He saw sitting at a distance from his son,
this latter's mother afflicted with grief, in the company of Ulupi. Dhananjaya asked,—
"Why is it that every thing in the field of battle seems to bear the indications of grief,
wonder, and joy? If, O slayer of foes, the cause is known to thee, do thou then tell me.
Why has thy mother come to the field of battle? Why also has Ulupi, the daughter of the
prince of snakes, come here? I know that thou hadst fought this battle with me at my own
command. I desire to know what the cause is that has brought out the ladies." The
intelligent ruler of Manipura, thus questioned by Dhananjaya, gratified him by bending
his head in reverence, and then said,—"Let Ulupi be questioned."'"

SECTION LXXXI.

"'Arjuna said, "What business brought thee here, O daughter (-in-law) of Kuru's race,
and what also is the cause of the arrival on the field of battle of her who is the mother of
the ruler of Manipura? Dost thou entertain friendly motives towards this king, O daughter
of a snake? O thou of restless glances, dost thou wish good to me too? I hope, O thou of
ample hips, that neither I, nor this Vabhruvahana here, have, O beautiful lady, done any
injury to thee unconsciously? Has Chitrangada of faultless limbs, descended from the
race of Chitravahana, done thee any wrong?" Unto him, the daughter of the prince of
snakes answered smilingly, "Thou hast not offended me, nor has Vabhruvahana done me
any wrong; nor this prince's mother who is always obedient to me as a hand-maid. Listen,
how all this has been brought about by me. Thou shouldst not be angry with me. Indeed, I
seek to gratify thee by bending my head in reverence. O thou of Kuru's race, all this has
been done by me for thy good, O puissant one. O mighty-armed Dhananjaya, hear all that
I have done. In the great battle of the Bharata princes, thou hadst slain the royal son of
Santanu by unrighteous ways. What I have done has expiated thy sin. Thou didst not
overthrow Bhishma while battling with thee. He was engaged with Sikhandin. Relying on
him as thy help, thou didst compass the overthrow of Santanu's son. If thou hadst died
without having expiated thy sin, thou wouldst then have fallen without doubt into Hell in
consequence of that sinful act of thine. Even this which thou hast got from thy son is the
expiation of that sin. Formerly, O ruler of Earth, I heard this said by the Vasus while they
were in the company of Ganga, O thou of great intelligence. After the fall of Santanu's
son, those deities, viz., the Vasus, coming to the banks of Ganga, bathed in her waters,
and calling the goddess of that stream, they uttered these terrible words having the
sanction of Bhagirathi herself, viz.,—'Santanu's son Bhishma has been slain by
Dhananjaya. Verily, O goddess, Bhishma then was engaged with another, and had ceased
to fight. For this fault we shall today denounce a curse on Dhananjaya.'—To this, the
goddess Ganga readily assented, saying,—'Be it so!'—Hearing these words I became very
much afflicted and penetrating into the nether regions represented everything to my sire.
Informed of what had happened, my sire became plunged in grief. Repairing to the
Vasus, he solicited them for thy sake, repeatedly gratifying them by every means in his
power. They then said unto him, 'Dhananjaya has a highly blessed son who, endued with
youth, is the ruler of Manipura. He will, standing on the field of battle, cast Dhananjaya
down on the Earth. When this will happen, O prince of snakes, Arjuna will be freed from
our curse. Do thou go back.'—Thus addressed by the Vasus, he came back and informed
me of what had happened. Having learnt all this, O hero, I have freed thee from the curse

of the Vasus even in this way. The chief of the deities himself is incapable of vanquishing thee in battle. The son is one's own self. It is for this that thou hast been vanquished by him. I cannot be held, O puissant one, to have committed any fault. How, indeed, wouldst thou hold me censurable?"—Thus addressed (by Ulupi), Vijaya became cheerful of heart and said unto her, "All this that thou hast done, O goddess, is highly agreeable to me." After this, Jaya addressed his son, the ruler of Manipura, and said unto him in the hearing of Chitrangada, the daughter (-in-law) of Kuru's house, "the Horse-sacrifice of Yudhishthira will take place on the day of full moon in the coming month of Chaitra. Come there, O king, with thy mother and thy counsellors and officers." Thus addressed by Partha, king Vabhruvahana of great intelligence, with tearful eyes, said these words to his sire, "O thou that art conversant with every duty, I shall certainly repair, at thy command, to the great Horse-sacrifice, and take upon myself the task of distributing food among the regenerate ones. For, however, showing thy grace towards me, thou enter thy own city with thy two wives. Let no scruple be thine as regards this, O thou that art fully acquainted with every duty. O lord, having lived for one night in thy own mansion in happiness, thou mayst then follow the steed, O foremost of victorious warriors." The ape-bannered son of Kunti, thus addressed by his son, answered the child of Chitrangada, saying "Thou knowest, O mighty-armed one, what vow I am observing. O thou of large eyes, till the termination of this my vow, I cannot enter thy city. O foremost of men, this sacrificial horse wanders at will. (I have to follow it always.) Blessings on thee! I must go away. Place I have none wherein to rest for even a short while." The son of the chastiser of Paka then, duly worshipped by his son and obtaining the permission of his two wives, left the spot and proceeded on his way.'"

SECTION LXXXII.

"Vaisampayana said, 'The (sacrificial) steed, having wandered over the whole Earth bounded by the ocean, then ceased and turned his face towards the city called after the elephant. Following as he did that horse, the diadem-decked Arjuna also turned his face towards the Kuru capital. Wandering at his will, the steed then came to the city of Rajagriha. Beholding him arrived within his dominion, O monarch, the heroic son of Sahadeva, observant of Kshatriya duties, challenged him to battle. Coming out of his city, Meghasandhi, mounted on his car and equipt with bow and arrows and leathern fence, rushed towards Dhananjaya who was on foot. Possessed of great energy, Meghasandhi approaching Dhananjaya, O king, said these words from a spirit of childishness and without any skill. "This steed of thine, O Bharata, seems to move about, protected by women only. I shall take away the horse. Do thou strive to free him. Although my sires did not teach thee in battle, I, however, shall do the duties of hospitality to you. Do thou strike me, for I shall strike thee." Thus addressed, the son of Pandu, smiling the while, answered him, saying, "To resist him who obstructs me is the vow cast on me by my eldest brother. Without doubt, O king, this is known to thee. Do thou strike me to the best of thy power. I have no anger." Thus addressed, the ruler of Magadha first struck the son of Pandu, showering his arrows on him like the thousand-eyed Indra showering heavy downpour of rain. Then, O chief of Bharata's race, the heroic wielder of Gandiva, with shafts sped from his excellent bow, baffled all the arrows shot carefully at him by his antagonist. Having thus baffled that cloud of arrows, the ape-bannered hero sped a number of blazing arrows at his foe that resembled snakes with fiery mouths. These arrows he shot at his flag and flag-staff and car and poles and yoke and the horses, sparing the body of his foe and his car-driver. Though Partha who was capable of shooting the bow with the left hand (as well as with the right) spared the body of the prince of Magadha, yet the latter thinking that his body was protected by his own prowess, shot many arrows at Partha. The wielder of Gandiva, deeply struck by the prince of Magadha, shone like a flowering Palasa (Butea frondosa) in the season of spring. Arjuna had no desire of slaying the prince of Magadha. It was for this that, having struck the son of Pandu, he succeeded in remaining before that foremost of heroes. Then Dhananjaya, becoming angry, drew his bow with great force, and slew his antagonist's steeds and then struck off the head of his car-driver. With a razor-headed shaft he then cut off Meghasandhi's large and beautiful bow, and then his leathern fence. Then cutting off his flag and flag-staff, he caused it to fall down. The prince of Magadha, exceedingly afflicted, and deprived of his steeds and bow and driver, took up a mace and rushed with great speed at the son of Kunti. Arjuna then with many shafts of his equipt with vulturine feathers cut off into fragments, that mace of his advancing foe which was adorned with bright gold. Thus cut off into fragments, that mace with its begemmed bonds and knots all severed, fell on the Earth like a she-snake helplessly hurled down by somebody. When his foe became deprived of his car, his bow, and his mace, that foremost of warriors, viz., the intelligent Arjuna, did not wish to strike him. The ape-bannered hero then, comforting his cheerless foe who had been observant of Kshatriya duties, said unto him these words, "O son, thou hast sufficiently displayed thy adherence to Kshatriya duties. Go now. Great have been the feats, O king, which thou hast accomplished in battle although thou art very young in years. The command I received from Yudhishthira was that kings who oppose me should not be slain. It is for this thou livest yet, O monarch, although thou hast offended me in battle." Thus addressed, the ruler of Magadha considered himself vanquished and spared. Thinking then that it was his duty to do so, he approached Arjuna and joining his hands in reverence worshipped him. And he said, "Vanquished have I been by thee. Blessed be thou, I do not venture to continue the battle. Tell me what I am to do now for thee. Regard thy behest as already accomplished." Comforting him again, Arjuna once more said unto him, "Thou shouldst repair to the Horse-sacrifice of our king which takes place at the coming full moon of Chaitra." Thus addressed by him, the son of Sahadeva said, "So be it,"—and then duly worshipped that horse as also Phalguna, that foremost of warriors. The sacrificial horse then, equipt with beautiful manes, proceeded at his will along the sea-coast, repairing to the countries of the Bangas, the Pundras, and the Kosalas. In those realms Dhananjaya, with his bow Gandiva, O king, vanquished innumerable Mlechccha armies one after another.'"

SECTION LXXXIII.

"Vaisampayana said, 'Worshipped by the ruler of Magadha, Pandu's son having white steeds yoked unto his car, proceeded along the south, following the (sacrificial) steed. Turning round in course of his wanderings at will, the mighty steed came upon the beautiful city of the Chedis called after the oyster.[831] Sarabha, the son of Sisupala, endued with great strength, first encountered Arjuna in battle and then worshipped him with due honours. Worshipped by him, O king, that best of steeds then proceeded to the realms of the Kasis, the Angas, the Kosalas, the Kiratas, and the Tanganas. Receiving due honours in all those realms, Dhananjaya turned his course. Indeed, the son of Kunti then

---

[831] The name of the city was Suktimati.

proceeded to the country of the Dasarnas. The ruler of that people was Chitrangada who was endued with great strength and was a crusher of foes. Between him and Vijaya occurred a battle exceedingly terrible. Bringing him under his sway the diadem-decked Arjuna, that foremost of men, proceeded to the dominions of the Nishada king, viz., the son of Ekalavya. The son of Ekalavya received Arjuna in battle. The encounter that took place between the Kuru hero and the Nishadas was so furious as to make the hair stand on end. Unvanquished in battle, the valiant son of Kunti defeated the Nishada king who proved an obstacle to the sacrifice. Having subjugated the son of Ekalavya, O king, the son of Indra, duly worshipped by the Nishadas, then proceeded towards the southern ocean. In those regions battle took place between the diadem-decked hero and the Dravidas and Andhras and the fierce Mahishakas and the hillmen of Kolwa. Subjugating those tribes without having to accomplish any fierce feats, Arjuna proceeded to the country of the Surashtras, his footsteps guided by the horse. Arrived at Gokarna, he repaired thence to Prabhasa. Next he proceeded to the beautiful city of Dwaravati protected by the heroes of the Vrishni race. When the beautiful sacrificial horse of the Kuru king reached Dwaravati, the Yadava youths, used force against that foremost of steeds. King Ugrasena, however, soon went out and forbade those youths from doing what they meditated. Then the ruler of the Vrishnis and the Andhakas, issuing out of his palace, with Vasudeva, the maternal uncle of Arjuna, in his company, cheerfully met the Kuru hero and received him with due rites. The two elderly chiefs honoured Arjuna duly. Obtaining their permission, the Kuru prince then proceeded to where the horse he followed, led him. The sacrificial steed then proceeded along the coast of the western ocean and at last reached the country of the five waters which swelled with population and prosperity. Thence, O king, the steed proceeded to the country of Gandharas. Arrived there, it wandered at will, followed by the son of Kunti. Then occurred a fierce battle between the diadem-decked hero and the ruler of Gandharas, viz., the son of Sakuni, who had a bitter remembrance of the grudge his sire bore to the Pandavas.'"

SECTION LXXXIV.

"Vaisampayana said, 'The heroic son of Sakuni, who was a mighty car-warrior among the Gandharas, accompanied by a large force, proceeded against the Kuru hero of curly hair.[832] That force was properly equipt with elephants and horses and cars, and was adorned with many flags and banners. Unable to bear and, therefore, burning to avenge, the slaughter of their king Sakuni, those warriors, armed with bows, rushed together at Partha. The unvanquished Vibhatsu of righteous soul addressed them peacefully, but they were unwilling to accept the beneficial words of Yudhishthira (through Arjuna). Though forbidden by Partha with sweet words, they still gave themselves up to wrath and surrounded the sacrificial steed. At this, the son of Pandu became filled with wrath. Then Arjuna, carelessly shooting from Gandiva many shafts with razor-like heads that blazed with splendour, cut off the heads of many Gandhara warriors. While thus slaughtered by Partha, the Gandharas, O king, exceedingly afflicted, set free the horse, moved by fear and desisted from battle. Resisted, however, by those Gandhara combatants who still surrounded him on every side, the son of Pandu, possessed of great energy, felled the heads of many, previously naming those whom he thus despatched. When the Gandhara warriors were thus being slain all around him in battle, the royal son of Sakuni came

---

[832] The etymology of Gudakesa as the lord of Gudaka or sleep, is fanciful.

forward to resist the son of Pandu. Unto the Gandhara king who was fighting with him, impelled by Kshatriya duty, Arjuna said, "I do not intend to slay the kings who fight with me, in consequence of the commands of Yudhishthira. Cease, O hero, to fight with me. Do not court defeat." Thus addressed the son of Sakuni, stupefied by folly, disregarded that advice and covered with many swift arrows the Kuru hero who resembled Sakra himself in the feats he accomplished in battle. Then Partha, with a crescent-shaped arrow, cut off the head-gear of his foe. Of immeasurable soul, he also caused that head-gear to be borne along a great distance like the head of Jayadratha (after he had cut it off in the battle of Kurukshetra). Beholding this feat, all the Gandhara warriors became filled with wonder. That Arjuna voluntarily spared their king was well understood by them. The prince of the Gandharas then began to fly away from the field, accompanied by all his warriors who resembled a flock of frightened deer. The Gandharas, through fear, lost their senses and wandered over the field, unable to escape. Arjuna, with his broad-headed shafts, cut off the heads of many. Many there were who lost their arms in consequence of Arjuna's arrows, but so stupefied were they with fear that they were not aware of the loss of that limb. Verily, the Gandhara army was exceedingly afflicted with those large shafts which Partha sped from Gandiva. That army, which then consisted of frightened men and elephants and horses, which lost many warriors and animals, and which had been reduced to a rabble and put to rout, began to wander and wheel about the field repeatedly. Among those foes who were thus being slaughtered none could be seen standing in front of the Kuru hero famed for foremost of feats. No one could be seen who was able to bear the prowess of Dhananjaya. Then the mother of the ruler of the Gandharas, filled with fear, and with all the aged ministers of state, came out of her city, bearing an excellent Arghya for Arjuna. She forbade her brave son of steady heart from fighting any longer, and gratified Jishnu who was never fatigued with toil. The puissant Vibhatsu worshipped her and became inclined to show kindness towards the Gandharas. Comforting the son of Sakuni, he said, "Thou hast not, O mighty-armed hero, done what is agreeable to me by setting thy heart upon these measures of hostility. O slayer of heroes, thou art my brother, O sinless one.[833] Recollecting my mother Gandhari, and for the sake of Dhritarashtra also, I have not taken thy life. It is for this, O king, that thou livest still. Many of thy followers, however, have been slain by me. Let not such a thing happen again. Let hostilities cease. Let not thy understanding again go astray. Thou shouldst go to the Horse-sacrifice of our king which comes off on the day of full moon of the month of Chaitra.""

SECTION LXXXV.

"Vaisampayana said, 'Having said these words, Partha set out, following the horse which wandered at its will. The sacrificial steed then turned towards the road that led to the city called after the elephant. Yudhishthira heard from his intelligence-bearers that the steed had turned back. And hearing also that Arjuna was hale and hearty, he became filled with joy.[834] Hearing also the feats, accomplished by Vijaya in the country of the

---

[833] Sakuni was the maternal uncle of Duryodhana and, therefore, of Arjuna also. Sakuni's son and Arjuna, hence, were cousins.

[834] The word chara does not mean always a spy. The ancient kings of India had their spies it is true, but they had a regular intelligence department. It was the business of these men to send correct reports to the king of every important occurrence. The news letter-writers of the Mussalman time, or Harkaras, were the successors of the charas of Hindu times.

Gandharas as also in another realms, the king became exceedingly glad. Meanwhile, king Yudhishthira the just, seeing that the twelfth day of the lighted fortnight in the month of Magha had come, and noticing also that the constellation was favourable, summoned all his brothers, viz., Bhima and Nakula and Sahadeva. Endued with great energy, the king, O thou of Kuru's race, that foremost of all persons conversant with duties, said these words in proper time. Indeed, that foremost of all speakers, addressing Bhima, the first of all smiters, said;—"Thy younger brother (Arjuna), O Bhimasena, is coming back with the horse. I have learnt this from those men who had followed Arjuna. The time (for the sacrifice) is come. The sacrificial horse is near. The day of full moon of the month of Magha is at hand. The month is about to expire, O Vrikodara. Let, therefore, learned Brahmanas conversant with the Vedas look for a sacrificial spot for the successful accomplishment of the Horse-sacrifice." Thus addressed, Bhima obeyed the royal behest. He became very glad upon hearing that Arjuna of curly hair was about to come back. Then Bhima went out with a number of men well conversant with the rules of laying out sacrificial grounds and constructing buildings. And he took with him many Brahmanas well-versed in all the rites of sacrifices. Bhima selected a beautiful spot and caused it to be duly measured out for laying the sacrificial compound. Numerous houses and mansions were constructed on it and high and broad roads also were laid out. Soon enough the Kaurava hero caused that ground to teem with hundreds of excellent mansions. The surface was levelled and made smooth with jewels and gems, and adorned with diverse structures made of gold. Columns were raised, ornamented with bright gold, and high and wide triumphal arches also were constructed on that sacrificial compound. All these were made of pure gold. The righteous-souled prince also caused apartments to be duly constructed for the accommodation of ladies and of the numerous kings who, hailing from many realms, were expected to grace the sacrifice with their presence. The son of Kunti also caused many mansions to be duly erected for Brahmanas who were expected to come from diverse realms. Then the mighty-armed Bhimasena, at the command of the king, sent out messengers to the great kings of the Earth. Those best of kings, came to the Horse-sacrifice of the Kuru monarch for doing what was agreeable to him. And they brought many gems with them and many female slaves and horses and weapons. The sounds that arose from those high-souled kings who resided within those pavilions touched the very heavens and resembled the noise made by the roaring ocean. King Yudhishthira, the delighter of the Kurus, assigned unto the monarchs who thus came to his sacrifice diverse kinds of food and drink, and beds also of celestial beauty. The chief of the Bharatas, viz., king Yudhishthira the just, assigned several stables well filled with different kinds of corn and sugarcane and milk to the animals (that came with the guests). To that great sacrifice of king Yudhishthira the just who was possessed of high intelligence, there also came a large number of Munis all of whom were utterers of Brahman. Indeed, O lord of Earth, all the foremost ones among the regenerate class that were then alive, came to that sacrifice, accompanied by their disciples. The Kuru king received them all. King Yudhishthira of mighty energy, casting off all pride, himself followed all his guests to the pavilions that had been assigned for their residence. Then all the mechanics and engineers, having completed the arrangements of the sacrifice informed king Yudhishthira of it. Hearing that everything was ready, king Yudhishthira the just, full of alertness and attention, became highly glad along with his brothers all of whom honoured him duly.'

"Vaisampayana continued, 'When the great sacrifice of Yudhishthira commenced, many eloquent dialecticians started diverse propositions and disputed thereon, desirous of vanquishing one another.[835] The (invited) kings beheld the excellent preparations of that sacrifice, resembling those of the chief himself of the deities, made, O Bharata, by Bhimasena. They beheld many triumphal arches made of gold, and many beds and seats and other articles of enjoyment and luxury, and crowds of men collected at different spots. There were also many jars and vessels and cauldrons and jugs and lids and covers. The invited kings saw nothing there that was not made of gold. Many sacrificial stakes also were set up, made, according to the directions of the scriptures of wood, and adorned with gold. Endued with great effulgence, these were duly planted and dedicated (with scriptural Mantras). The king saw all animals, again, which belong to land and all those which belong to water, collected there on the occasion. And they also beheld many kine and many buffaloes and many old women, and many aquatic animals, many beasts of prey and many species of birds, and many specimens of viviparous and oviparous creatures, and many that are filth-born, and many belonging to the vegetable kingdom, and many animals and plants that live or grow on mountains. Beholding the sacrificial compound thus adorned with animals and kine and corn, the invited kings became filled with wonder. Large heaps of costly sweet-meats were kept ready for both the Brahmanas and the Vaisyas. And when the feeding was over of a hundred thousand Brahmanas, drums and cymbals were beat. And so large was the number fed that the sounds of drums and cymbals were repeatedly heard, indeed, from day to day those sounds continued. Thus was performed that sacrifice of king Yudhishthira of great intelligence. Many hills of food, O king, were dedicated on the occasion. Many large tanks were seen of curds and many lakes of ghee. In that great sacrifice, O monarch, was seen the entire population of Jamvudwipa, with all its realms and provinces, collected together. Thousands of nations and races were there. A large number of men, O chief of Bharata's race, adorned with garlands and wearing bright ear-rings made of gold, taking innumerable vessels in their hands, distributed the food unto the regenerate classes by hundreds and thousands. The attendants of the Pandavas gave away unto the Brahmanas diverse kinds of food and drink which were, besides, so costly as to be worthy of being eaten and drunk by kings themselves.'"

SECTION LXXXVI.

"Vaisampayana said, 'Beholding those kings—lords of Earth—all conversant with the Vedas, arrive, king Yudhishthira, addressing Bhimasena, said,—"O chief of men, let proper honours be paid to these kings who have come (to my sacrifice), for these foremost of men are all worthy of the highest honours." Thus addressed by king Yudhishthira of great fame Pandu's son Bhimasena of mighty energy did as he was enjoined, assisted by the twins. The foremost of all men, viz., Govinda, came there, accompanied by the Vrishnis, and with Valadeva in the van. He was accompanied by Yuyudhana and Pradyumna and Gada, and Nisatha and Samvo and Kritavarman. The mighty car-warrior Bhima offered them the most reverential worship. Those princes then entered the palaces, adorned with gems, that were assigned to them. At the end of a conversation he had with Yudhishthira, the slayer of Madhu referred to Arjuna who had been emaciated in consequence of many fights. The son of Kunti repeatedly asked Krishna, that chastiser of foes, about Arjuna. Unto Dharma's son, the lord of all the universe began to speak about Jishnu, the son of Sakra. "O king, a confidential agent of

---

[835] Hetuvadins are dialecticians or philosophers who dispute on the reasons of things.

mine residing in Dwaraka came to me. He had seen Arjuna, that foremost of Pandu's sons. Indeed, the latter has been very much emaciated with the fatigue of many battles. O puissant monarch, that agent of mine informed me that the mighty-armed hero is very near to us. Do thou set thyself to accomplish thy Horse-sacrifice." Thus addressed, king Yudhishthira the just, said unto him,—"By good luck, O Madhava, Arjuna comes back safely. I desire to ascertain from thee, O delighter of the Yadavas, what has been said in this matter by that mightiest of heroes among the sons of Pandu." Thus addressed by king Yudhishthira the just, the lord of the Vrishnis and the Andhakas, that foremost of eloquent men, said these words unto that monarch of righteous soul,—"My agent, recollecting the words of Partha, reported them thus to me, O great king,—'Yudhishthira, O Krishna, should be told these words of mine when the time comes. O chief of the Kauravas, many kings will come (to thy sacrifice). When they arrive, high honours should be paid unto them. This would, indeed, be worthy for us. O giver of honours, the king should further be informed at my request that he should do what is necessary for preventing a carnage similar to what took place at the time of presenting the Arghya (on the occasion of the Rajasuya-sacrifice). Let Krishna also approve of this. Let not, O king, through the ill-feeling of kings, the people be slaughtered.' My man further reported, O king, these words of Dhananjaya. Listen as I repeat them, 'O monarch, the ruler of Manipura, my dear son Vabhruvahana, will come at the sacrifice. Do thou honour him duly for my sake, O puissant one. He is always attached and deeply devoted to me.'"— Hearing these words, king Yudhishthira the just, approved of them and said as follows."'

SECTION LXXXVII.

"'Yudhishthira said, "I have heard, O Krishna, thy agreeable words. They are such as deserve to be spoken by thee. Gladsome and sweet as nectar are they, indeed, they fill my heart with great pleasure, O puissant one. O Hrishikesa, I have heard that innumerable have been the battles which Vijaya has fought with the kings of the Earth. For what reason is Partha always dissociated from ease and comfort? Vijaya is exceedingly intelligent. This, therefore, pains my heart very much. I always, O Janarddana, think, when I am withdrawn from business, of Kunti's son Jishnu. The lot of that delighter of the Pandus is exceedingly miserable. His body has every auspicious mark. What, however, O Krishna, is that sign in his excellent body in consequence of which he has always to endure misery and discomfort? That son of Kunti has to bear an exceedingly large share of unhappiness. I do not see any censurable indication in his body. It behoves thee to explain the cause to me if I deserve to hear it." Thus addressed, Hrishikesa, that enhancer of the glory of the Bhoja princes, having reflected for a long time, answered as follows—"I do not see any censurable feature in this prince, except that the cheek bones of this lion among men are a little too high. It is in consequence of this that that foremost of men has always to be on the road. I really do not see anything else in consequence of which he could be made so unhappy." Thus answered by Krishna of great intelligence, that foremost of men, viz., king Yudhishthira, said unto the chief of the Vrishnis that it was even so. The princess Draupadi, however, looked angrily and askance at Krishna, (for she could not bear the ascription of any fault to Arjuna). The slayer of Kesi, viz., Hrishikesa, approved of that indication of love (for his friend) which the princess of

Panchala, who also was his friend, displayed.[836] Bhimasena and the other Kurus, including the sacrificial priests, who heard of the agreeable triumphs of Arjuna in course of his following the horse, became highly gratified. While they were still engaged in discoursing on Arjuna, an envoy came from that high-souled hero bearing a message from him. Repairing to the presence of the Kuru king, the intelligent envoy bowed his head in reverence and informed him of the arrival of that foremost of men, viz., Phalguna. On receipt of this intelligence, tears of joy covered the king's eyes. Large gifts were made to the messenger for the very agreeable tidings he had brought. On the second day from that date, a loud din was heard when that foremost of men, that chief of the Kurus, came. The dust raised by the hoofs of that horse as it walked in close adjacence to Arjuna, looked as beautiful as that raised by the celestial steed Uchchaisravas. And as Arjuna advanced he heard many gladdening words uttered by the citizens. "By good luck, O Partha, thou art out of danger. Praise to you and king Yudhishthira! Who else than Arjuna could come back after having caused the horse to wander over the whole Earth and after having vanquished all the kings in battle? We have not heard of such a feat having been achieved by even Sagara and other high-souled kings of antiquity. Future kings also will never be able to accomplish so difficult a feat, O foremost one of Kuru's race, as this which thou hast achieved." Listening to such words, agreeable to the ear, of the citizens, the righteous-souled Phalguna entered the sacrificial compound. Then king Yudhishthira with all his ministers, and Krishna, the delighter of the Yadus, placing Dhritarashtra in their van, went out for receiving Dhananjaya. Saluting the feet of his sire (Dhritarashtra), and then of king Yudhishthira the just of great wisdom, and then worshipping Bhima and others, he embraced Kesava. Worshipped by them all and worshipping them in return according to due rites, the mighty-armed hero, accompanied by those princes, took rest like a ship-wrecked man tossed on the waves resting on reaching the shore. Meanwhile king Vabhruvahan of great wisdom, accompanied by his mothers (Chitrangada and Ulupi), came to the Kuru capital. The mighty-armed prince duly saluted all his seniors of Kuru's race and the other kings present there, and was honoured by them all in return. He then entered the excellent abode of his grand-mother Kunti.'"

SECTION LXXXVIII.

"Vaisampayana said, 'Entering the palace of the Pandavas the mighty-armed prince saluted his grand-mother in soothing and sweet accents. Then queen Chitrangada, and (Ulupi) the daughter of (the snake) Kauravya, together approached Partha and Krishna with humility. They then met Subhadra and the other ladies of the Kuru race with due formalities. Kunti gave them many gems and costly things. Draupadi and Subhadra and the other ladies of Kuru's race all made presents to them. The two ladies took up their residence there, using costly beds and seats, treated with affection and respect by Kunti herself from desire of doing what was agreeable to Partha. King Vabhruvahana of great energy, duly honoured (by Kunti), then met Dhritarashtra according to due rites. Repairing then to king Yudhishthira and Bhima and the other Pandavas, the mighty prince of Manipura saluted them all with humility. They all embraced him with great affection and honoured him duly. And those mighty car-warriors highly gratified with

---

[836] It is worthy of note that Draupadi was always styled by Krishna as his sakhi or 'friend'. Krishna was highly chivalrous to the other sex at an age when women were universally regarded as the inferiors of men.

him, made large gifts of wealth unto him. The king of Manipura then humbly approached Krishna, that hero armed with the discus and the mace, like a second Pradyumna approaching his sire. Krishna gave unto the king a very costly and excellent car adorned with gold and unto which were yoked excellent steeds. Then king Yudhishthira the just, and Bhima, and Phalguna, and the twins, each separately honoured him and made costly presents unto him. On the third day, the sage Vyasa, the son of Satyavati, that foremost of eloquent men, approaching Yudhishthira said,—"From this day, O son of Kunti, do thou begin thy sacrifice. The time for it has come. The moment for commencing the rite is at hand. The priests are urging thee. Let the sacrifice be performed in such a way that no limb may become defective. In consequence of the very large quantity of gold that is required for this sacrifice, it has come to be called the sacrifice of profuse gold. Do thou also, O great king, make the Dakshina of this sacrifice three times of what is enjoined. Let the merit of thy sacrifice increase threefold. The Brahmanas are competent for the purpose.[837] Attaining to the merits then of three Horse-sacrifices, each with profuse presents, thou shalt be freed, O king, from the sin of having slain thy kinsmen. The bath that one performs upon completion of the Horse-sacrifice, O monarch, is highly cleansing and productive of the highest merit. That merit will be thine, O king of Kuru's race." Thus addressed by Vyasa of immeasurable intelligence, the righteous-souled Yudhishthira of great energy underwent the Diksha for performance of the Horse-sacrifice.[838] The mighty-armed monarch then performed the great Horse-sacrifice characterised by gifts of food and presents in profusion and capable of fructifying every wish and producing every merit. The priests, well conversant with the Vedas, did every rite duly, moving about in all directions. They were all well-trained, and possessed of omniscience. In nothing was there a swerving from the ordinances and nothing was done improperly. Those foremost of regenerate persons followed the procedure as laid down (in the scriptures) and as it should be followed in those points about which no directions are given.[839] Those best of regenerate ones, having first performed the rite called Pravargya, otherwise called Dharma, then duly went through the rite of Abhishava, O king.[840] Those foremost of Soma-drinkers, O monarch, extracting the juice of the Soma, then performed the Savana rite following the injunctions of the scriptures. Among those that came to that sacrifice none could be seen who was cheerless, none who was poor, none who was hungry, none who was plunged into grief, and none that seemed to be vulgar. Bhimasena of mighty energy at the command of the king, caused food to be ceaselessly distributed among those that desired to eat. Following the injunctions of the scriptures, priests, well-versed in sacrificial rites of every kind, performed every day all the acts necessary to complete the great sacrifice. Amongst the Sadasayas of king Yudhishthira of great intelligence there was none who was not well conversant with the six branches of (Vedic) learning.

---

[837] The sense is this: for a horse-sacrifice, the Dakshina or sacrificial present, payable to the principal Ritwija or to be distributed among all the Ritwijas including the other Brahmanas, is enjoined to be of a certain measure. Vyasa advises Yudhishthira to make that Dakshina triple of what the enjoined measure is. By thus increasing the Dakshina, the merit of the sacrificer will increase correspondingly.

[838] The Diksha is the ceremony of initiation. Certain mantras are uttered in which the intention is declared of performing what is desired to be performed.

[839] The Karma of a sacrifice or religious rite is the procedure. It is, of course, laid down in the scriptures on the ritual. There are certain acts, however, which, though not laid down, should be done agreeably to reasonable inferences. What is said, therefore, in the second line of 20 is that the procedure was fully followed, both as laid down and as consistent with inferences.

[840] Pravargya is a special preliminary rite performed in a sacrifice. 'Abhishva' is the extraction of the juice of the Soma plant after its consecration with Mantras.

There was none among them that was not an observer of vows, none that was not an Upadhyaya, none that was not well versed in dialectical disputations. When the time came for erecting the sacrificial stake, O chief of Bharata's race, six stakes were set up that were made of Vilwa,[841] six that were made of Khadira, and six that were made of Saravarnin. Two stakes were set up by the priests that were made of Devadaru in that sacrifice of the Kuru king, and one that was made of Sleshmataka. At the command of the king, Bhima caused some other stakes to be set up, for the sake of beauty only, that were made of gold. Adorned with fine cloths supplied by the royal sage, those stakes shone there like Indra and the deities with the seven celestial Rishis standing around them in Heaven. A number of golden bricks were made for constructing therewith a Chayana. The Chayana made resembled in beauty that which had been made for Daksha, the lord of creatures (on the occasion of his great sacrifice). The Chayana measured eight and ten cubits and four stories or lairs. A golden bird, of the shape of Garuda, was then made, having three angles.[842] Following the injunctions of the scriptures, the priests possessed of great learning then duly tied to the stakes both animals and birds, assigning each to its particular deity.[843] Bulls, possessed of such qualifications as are mentioned in the scriptures, and aquatic animals were properly tied to the stakes after the rites relating to the sacrificial fire had been performed. In that sacrifice of the high-souled son of Kunti, three hundred animals were tied to the stakes set up, including that foremost of steeds. That sacrifice looked exceedingly beautiful as if adorned with the celestial Rishis, with the Gandharvas singing in chorus and the diverse tribes of Apsaras dancing in merriment. It teemed, besides, with Kimpurushas and was adorned with Kinnaras. All around it were abodes of Brahmanas crowned with ascetic success. There were daily seen the disciples of Vyasa, those foremost of regenerate ones, who are compilers of all branches of learning, and well conversant with sacrificial rites. There was Narada, and there was Tumvuru of great splendour. There were Viswavasu and Chitrasena and others, all of whom were proficient in music. At intervals of the sacrificial rites, those Gandharvas, skilled in music and well versed in dancing, used to gladden the Brahmanas who were engaged in the sacrifice.'"

SECTION LXXXIX.

"Vaisampayana said, 'Having cooked, according to due rites, the other excellent animals that were sacrificed, the priests then sacrificed, agreeably to the injunctions of the scriptures, that steed (which had wandered over the whole world). After cutting that horse into pieces, conformably to scriptural directions, they caused Draupadi of great intelligence, who was possessed of the three requisites of mantras, things, and devotion, to sit near the divided animal. The Brahmanas then with cool minds, taking up the marrow of that steed, cooked it duly, O chief of Bharata's race. King Yudhishthira the just, with all his younger brothers, then smelled, agreeably to the scriptures, the smoke,

---

[841] Vitwa is the Aegle marmelos, Linn. Khadira is Acacia catechu, Linn, or Mimosa catechu; Saravarnin is otherwise called, as explained by Nilakantha, Palasa. It is the Butea frondosa of Roxburgh. Devadaru is Pinus Deodara of Roxburgh, or Cedruz Deodara. Sleshmataka is a small tree identified with the Cordia latifolia. Here probably, some other tree is intended.

[842] It is difficult to understand what these constructions or figures were. They were probably figures drawn on the sacrificial altar, with gold-dust. At the present day, powdered rice, coloured red, yellow, blue, etc, is used.

[843] Each animal is supposed to be agreeable to a particular deity.

capable of cleansing one from every sin, of the marrow that was thus cooked. The remaining limbs, O king, of that horse, were poured into the fire by the sixteen sacrificial priests possessed of great wisdom. Having thus completed the sacrifice of that monarch, who was endued with the energy of Sakra himself, the illustrious Vyasa with his disciples eulogised the king greatly. Then Yudhishthira gave away unto the Brahmanas a thousand crores of golden nishkas, and unto Vyasa he gave away the whole Earth. Satyavati's son Vyasa, having accepted the Earth, addressed that foremost one of Bharata's race, viz., king Yudhishthira the just, and said, "O best of kings, the Earth which thou hast given me I return unto thee. Do thou give me the purchasing value, for Brahmanas are desirous of wealth (and have no use with the Earth)." The high-souled Yudhishthira of great intelligence staying with his brothers in the midst of the kings invited to his sacrifice, said unto those Brahmanas, "The Dakshina ordained in the scriptures for the great Horse-sacrifice is the Earth. Hence, I have given away unto the sacrificial priests the Earth conquered by Arjuna. Ye foremost of Brahmanas, I shall enter the woods. Do ye divide the Earth among yourselves. Indeed, do you divide the Earth into four parts according to what is done in the Chaturhotra sacrifice. Ye best of regenerate ones I do not desire to appropriate what now belongs to the Brahmanas. Even this, ye learned Brahmanas, has been the intention always cherished by myself and my brothers." When the king said these words, his brothers and Draupadi also said, "Yes, it is even so." Great was the sensation created by this announcement. Then, O Bharata, an invisible voice was heard in the welkin, saying,—"Excellent, Excellent!" The murmurs also of crowds of Brahmanas as they spoke arose. The Island-born Krishna, highly applauding him, once more addressed Yudhishthira, in the presence of the Brahmanas, saying, "The Earth has been given by thee to me. I, however, give her back to thee. Do thou give unto these Brahmanas gold. Let the Earth be thine." Then Vasudeva, addressing king Yudhishthira the just, said, "It behoveth thee to do as thou art bid by the illustrious Vyasa." Thus addressed, the foremost one of Kuru's race, along with all his brothers, became glad of soul, and gave away millions of golden coins, in fact, trebling the Dakshina ordained for the Horse-sacrifice. No other king will be able to accomplish what the Kuru king accomplished on that occasion after the manner of Marutta. Accepting that wealth, the Island-born sage, Krishna, of great learning, gave it unto the sacrificial priests, dividing it into four parts. Having paid that wealth as the price of the Earth, Yudhishthira, cleansed of his sins and assured of Heaven rejoiced with his brothers. The sacrificial priests, having got that unlimited quantity of wealth, distributed it among the Brahmanas gladly and according to the desire of each recipient. The Brahmanas also divided amongst themselves, agreeably to Yudhishthira's permission, the diverse ornaments of gold that were in the sacrificial compound, including the triumphal arches, the stakes, the jars, and diverse kinds of vessels. After the Brahmanas had taken as much as they desired, the wealth that remained was taken away by Kshatriyas and Vaisyas and Sudras and diverse tribes of Mlechcchas. Thus gratified with presents by king Yudhishthira of great intelligence, the Brahmanas, filled with joy, returned to their respective abodes. The holy and illustrious Vyasa respectfully presented his own share, which was very large, of that gold unto Kunti. Receiving that gift of affection from her father-in-law, Pritha became glad of heart and devoted it to the accomplishment of diverse acts of merit. King Yudhishthira, having bathed at the conclusion of his sacrifice and become cleansed of all his sins, shone in the midst of his brothers, honoured by all, like the chief of the celestials in the midst of the denizens of Heaven. The sons of Pandu, surrounded by the assembled kings, looked as beautiful, O king, as the planets in the midst of the stars. Unto those kings they made presents of various jewels and gems, and elephants and horses and ornaments of gold, and female slaves and cloths and large measures of gold. Indeed, Pritha's son by distributing that untold wealth among the invited monarchs, shone, O king, like Vaisravana, the lord of treasures. Summoning next the heroic king Vabhruvahana, Yudhishthira gave unto him diverse kinds of wealth in profusion and gave him permission to return home. The son of Pandu, for gratifying his sister Dussala, established her infant grandson in his paternal kingdom. The Kuru king Yudhishthira, having a full control over his senses, then dismissed the assembled kings all of whom had been properly classed and honoured by him.[844] The illustrious son of Pandu, that chastiser of foes, then duly worshipped the high-souled Govinda and Valadeva of great might, and the thousands of other Vrishni heroes having Pradyumna for their first. Assisted by his brothers, he then dismissed them for returning to Dwaraka. Even thus was celebrated that sacrifice of king Yudhishthira the just, which was distinguished by a profuse abundance of food and wealth and jewels and gems, and oceans of wines of different kinds. There were lakes whose mire consisted of ghee, and mountains of food. There were also, O chief of Bharata's race, miry rivers made of drinks having the six kinds of taste. Of men employed in making and eating the sweetmeats called Khandavaragas, and of animals slain for food, there was no end.[845] The vast space abounded with men inebriated with wine, and with young ladies filled with joy. The extensive grounds constantly echoed with the sounds of drums and the blare of conches. With all these, the sacrifice became exceedingly delightful. "Let agreeable things be given away,"—"Let agreeable food be eaten,"—these were the sounds that were repeatedly heard day and night in that sacrifice. It was like a great festival, full of rejoicing and contented men. People of diverse realms speak of that sacrifice to this day. Having showered wealth in torrents, and diverse objects of desire, and jewels and gems, and drinks of various kinds, the foremost one of Bharata's race, cleansed of all his sins, and his purpose fulfilled, entered his capital.'"

SECTION XC.

"Janamejaya said, 'It behoveth thee to tell me of any wonderful incident that occurred in the sacrifice of my grandsires.'

"Vaisampayana said, 'Hear, O chief of kings of a most wonderful incident that occurred, O puissant monarch, at the conclusion of that great horse-sacrifice. After all the foremost of Brahmanas and all the kinsmen and relatives and friends, and all the poor, the blind, and the helpless ones had been gratified, O chief of Bharata's race, when the gifts made in profusion were being spoken of on all sides, indeed, when flowers were rained down on the head of king Yudhishthira the just, a blue-eyed mongoose, O sinless one, with one side of his body changed into gold, came there and spoke in a voice that was as loud and deep as thunder. Repeatedly uttering such deep sounds and thereby frightening all animals and birds, that proud denizen of a hole, with large body, spoke in a human voice and said, "Ye kings, this great sacrifice is not equal to a prastha of powdered barley given away by a liberal Brahmana of Kurukshetra who was observing the Unccha vow." Hearing these words of the mongoose, O king, all those foremost of Brahmanas became

---

[844] Suvibhaktan implies that they were properly classed or grouped so that there was no dispute or dissatisfaction among them regarding questions of precedence.

[845] Nilakantha explains that Khandavaraga was made of piper longum and dried ginger (powdered), and the juice of Phaseolus Mungo, with sugar. Probably, it is identical with what is now called Mungka laddu in the bazars of Indian towns.

filled with wonder. Approaching the mongoose, they then asked him, saying, "Whence hast thou come to this sacrifice, this resort of the good and the pious? What is the extent of thy might? What thy learning? And what thy refuge? How should we know thee that thus censurest this our sacrifice? Without having disregarded any portion of the scriptures, everything that should be done has been accomplished here according to the scriptures and agreeably to reason, with the aid of diverse sacrificial rites. Those who are deserving of worship have been duly worshipped here according to the way pointed out by the scriptures. Libations have been poured on the sacred fire with the aid of proper mantras. That which should be given has been given away without pride. The regenerate class have been gratified with gifts of diverse kinds. The Kshatriyas have been gratified with battles fought according to just methods. The grandsires have been gratified with Sraddhas. The Vaisyas have been gratified by the protection offered to them, and many foremost of women have been gratified by accomplishing their desires. The Sudras have been gratified by kind speeches, and others with the remnants of the profuse wealth collected on the spot. Kinsmen and relatives have been gratified by the purity of behaviour displayed by our king. The deities have been gratified by libations of clarified butter and acts of merit, and dependants and followers by protection. That therefore, which is true, do thou truly declare unto these Brahmanas. Indeed, do thou declare what is agreeable to the scriptures and to actual experience, asked by the Brahmanas who are eager to know. Thy words seem to demand credit. Thou art wise. Thou bearest also a celestial form. Thou hast come into the midst of learned Brahmanas. It behoveth thee to explain thyself." Thus addressed by those regenerate persons, the mongoose, smiling, answered them as follows. "Ye regenerate ones, the words I have uttered are not false. Neither have I spoken them from pride. That which I have said may have been heard by you all. Ye foremost of regenerate persons, this sacrifice is not equal in merit to the gift of a prastha of powdered barley. Without doubt, I should say this, ye foremost of Brahmanas. Listen to me with undivided attention as I narrate what happened to thee truly. Wonderful and excellent was the occurrence that fell out. It was witnessed by me and its consequences were felt by me. The incident relates to a liberal Brahmana dwelling in Kurukshetra in the observance of the Unccha vow. In consequence of that incident he attained to Heaven, ye regenerate ones, along with his wife and son and daughter-in-law. And in consequence of what then happened half my body became transformed into gold."

"'The Mongoose continued, "Ye regenerate ones, I shall presently tell you what the excellent fruit was of the gift, made by a Brahmana, of a very little measure (of powdered barley) obtained by lawful means. On that righteous spot of ground known by the name of Kurukshetra, which is the abode of many righteous persons, there lived a Brahmana in the observance of what is called the Unccha vow. That mode of living is like unto that of the pigeon.[846] He lived there with his wife and son and daughter-in-law and practised penances. Of righteous soul, and with senses under complete control, he adopted the mode of living that is followed by a parrot. Of excellent vows, he used to eat everyday at the sixth division.[847] If there was nothing to eat at the sixth division of the day, that excellent Brahmana would fast for that day and eat the next day at the sixth division. On one occasion, ye Brahmanas, there occurred a dreadful famine in the land. During that time there was nothing stored in the abode of that righteous Brahmana. The herbs and

---

[846] The unccha vow consists of subsisting upon grains of corn picked up after the manner of the pigeon from the field after the crops have been cut and removed by the owners.

[847] The day of 12 hours is divided into 8 divisions.

plants were all dried up and the whole realm became void of foodstore. When the accustomed hours came for eating, the Brahmana had nothing to eat. This occurred day after day. All the members of his family were afflicted with hunger but were obliged to pass the days as best they could. One day, in the month of Jaishtha, while the Sun was in the meridian, the Brahmana was engaged in picking up grains of corn. Afflicted by heat and hunger, he was practising even this penance. Unable to obtain grains of corn, the Brahmana soon became worn out with hunger and toil. Indeed, with all the members of his family, he had no food to eat. That best of Brahmanas passed the days in great suffering. One day, after the sixth division came, he succeeded in obtaining a prastha of barley. That barley was then reduced by those ascetics to powder for making what is called Saktu of it. Having finished their silent recitations and other daily rites, and having duly poured libations on the sacred fire, those ascetics divided that little measure of powdered barley amongst themselves so that the share of each came up to the measure of a Kudava.[848] As they were about to sit down for eating, there came unto their abode a guest. Beholding the person who came as a guest, all of them became exceedingly glad. Indeed, seeing him, they saluted him and made the usual enquiries of welfare. They were of pure minds, self-restrained, and endued with faith and control over the passions. Freed from malice, they had conquered wrath. Possessed of piety, they were never pained at the sight of other people's happiness. They had cast off pride and haughtiness and anger. Indeed, they were conversant with every duty, ye foremost of regenerate ones. Informing their guest of their own penances and of the race or family to which they belonged, and ascertaining from him in return those particulars, they caused that hungry guest of theirs to enter their cottage. Addressing him they said, 'This is the Arghya for thee. This water is for washing thy feet. There are scattered some Kusa grass for thy seat, O sinless one. Here is some clean Saktu acquired by lawful means, O puissant one. Given by us, O foremost of regenerate persons, do thou accept it,' Thus addressed by them, that Brahmana accepted the Kudava of powdered barley that was offered to him and ate it all. But his hunger, O king, was not appeased by what he ate. The Brahmana in the observance of the Unccha vow, seeing that his guest's hunger was still unappeased, began to think of what other food he could place before him for gratifying him. Then his wife said unto him,—'Let my share be given unto him. Let this foremost of regenerate persons be gratified and let him then go whithersoever he will.' Knowing that his chaste wife who said so was herself afflicted by hunger, that best of Brahmanas could not approve of her share of the powdered barley being given to the guest. Indeed, that best of Brahmanas possessed of learning, knowing from his own state that his aged, toil-worn, cheerless, and helpless wife was herself afflicted by hunger and seeing that lady who had been emaciated into mere skin and bone was quivering with weakness, addressed her and said, 'O beautiful one, with even animals, with even worms and insects, wives are fed and protected. It behoveth thee not, therefore, to say so. The wife treats her lord with kindness and feeds and protects him. Everything appertaining to religion, pleasure, and wealth, careful nursing, offspring for perpetuating the race, are all dependent on the wife. Indeed, the merits of a person himself as also of his deceased ancestors depend also on her. The wife should know her lord by his acts. Verily, that man who fails to protect his wife earns great infamy here and goes into Hell hereafter. Such a man falls down from even a position of great fame and never succeeds in acquiring regions of happiness hereafter.' Thus addressed, she answered him, saying, 'O regenerate one, our religious acts and

---

[848] A prastha is made up of four Kudavas. A Kudava is equal to about twelve double handfuls.

wealth are united. Do thou take a fourth of this barley. Indeed, be gratified with me. Truth, pleasure, religious merit, and Heaven as acquirable, by good qualities, of women, as also all the objects of their desire, O foremost of regenerate ones, are dependent on the husband. In the production of offspring the mother contributes her blood. The father contributes his seed. The husband is the highest deity of the wife. Through the grace of the husband, women obtain both pleasure and offspring as the reward. Thou art my Pati (lord) for the protection thou givest me. Thou art my Bhartri for the means of sustenance thou givest me. Thou art, again, boon-giver to me in consequence of thy having presented me a son. Do thou, therefore, (in return for so many favours), take my share of the barley and give it unto the guest. Overcome by decrepitude, thou art of advanced years. Afflicted by hunger thou art exceedingly weakened. Worn out with fasts, thou art very much emaciated. (If thou couldst part with thy share, why should not I part with mine).' Thus addressed by her, he took her share of the powdered barley and addressing his guest said,—'O regenerate one, O best of men, do thou accept this measure of powdered barley as well.' The Brahmana, having accepted that quantity, immediately ate it up, but his hunger was not yet appeased. Beholding him ungratified, the Brahmana in the observance of the Unccha vow became thoughtful. His son then said unto him, 'O best of men, taking my share of the barley do thou give it to the guest. I regard this act of mine as one of great merit. Therefore, do it. Thou shouldst be always maintained by me with great care. Maintenance of the father is a duty which the good always covet. The maintenance of the father in his old age is the duty ordained for the son. Even this is the eternal sruti (audition) current in the three worlds, O learned Rishi. By barely living thou art capable of practising penances. The life-breath is the great deity that resides in the bodies of all embodied creatures.'[849]

""""The father, at this, said, 'If thou attainest to the age of even a thousand years, thou wilt still seem to me to be only a little child. Having begotten a son, the sire achieves success through him. O puissant one, I know that the hunger of children is very strong. I am old. I shall somehow succeed in holding my life-breaths. Do thou, O son, become strong (by eating the food that has fallen to thy share). Old and decrepit as I am, O son, hunger scarcely afflicts me. I have, again, for many years, practised penances. I have no fear of death.'

""""The son said, 'I am thy offspring. The Sruti declares that one's offspring is called putra because one is rescued by him. One's own self, again, takes birth as one's son. Do thou, therefore, rescue thyself by thy own self (in the form of thy son).'

""""The father said, 'In form thou art like me. In conduct and in self-restraint also thou art my like. Thou hast been examined on various occasions by me. I shall, therefore, accept thy share of the barley, O son.' Having said this, that foremost of regenerate persons cheerfully took his son's share of the barley and smilingly presented it to his regenerate guest. Having eaten that barley also, the guest's hunger was not appeased. The righteous-souled host in the observance of the unccha vow became ashamed (at the thought that he had nothing more to give). Desirous of doing what was agreeable to him, his chaste daughter-in-law then, bearing her share of the barley, approached him and said, 'Through thy son, O learned Brahmana, I shall obtain a son. Do thou, therefore, take my

---

[849] This verse is rather obscure. I am not sure that I have understood it correctly. The sense seems to be this: thou art capable of enduring much. Indeed, by barely living, thou art capable of earning religious merit, for life-breath is a great deity. He should not be cast off. Thy life is at stake, for if this guest be not gratified, the thought of it will kill thee. Do thou, therefore, protect thy life by gratifying this guest with my share of the barley.

share of the barley and give it unto this guest. Through thy grace, numerous regions of beatitude will be mine for eternity. Through the grandson one obtains those regions repairing whither one has not to endure any kind of misery. Like the triple aggregate beginning with Religion, or the triple aggregate of sacred fires, there is a triple aggregate of everlasting Heavens, depending upon the son, the grandson, and the great-grandson. The son is called Putra because he frees his sires from debt. Through sons and grandsons one always enjoys the happiness of those regions which are reserved for the pious and the good.'

""'The father-in-law said, 'O thou of excellent vows and conduct, beholding thee wasted by wind and sun, deprived of thy very complexion, emaciated and almost destitute of consciousness through hunger, how can I be such a transgressor against the rules of righteousness as to take thy share of the barley? O auspicious damsel, it behoves thee not to say so, for the sake of those auspicious results for which every family must strive.[850] O auspicious damsel, how can I behold thee at even this, the sixth division of the day, abstaining from food and observing vows? Thou art endued with purity and good conduct and penances. Alas, even thou hast to pass thy days in so much misery. Thou art a child, afflicted by hunger, and belongest to the softer sex. Thou shouldst be always protected by me. Alas, I have to see thee worn out with fasts, O thou that art the delighter of all thy kinsmen.'

""'The daughter-in-law said, 'Thou art the senior of my senior since thou art the deity of my deity. Thou art verily the god of my god. Do thou, therefore, O puissant one, take my share of the barley. My body, life-breaths, and religious rites have all one purpose viz., the service of my senior. Through thy grace, O learned Brahmana, I shall obtain many regions of happiness hereafter. I deserve to be looked after by thee. Know, O regenerate one, that I am wholly devoted to thee. Cherishing also this thought, viz., that my happiness is thy concern, it behoveth thee to take this my share of the barley.'

""'The father-in-law said, 'O chaste lady, in consequence of such conduct of thine thou wilt for ever shine in glory, for endued with vows and steadiness in religious rites, thy eyes are directed to that conduct which should be observed towards seniors. Therefore, O daughter-in-law, I shall take thy share of the barley. Thou deservest not to be deceived by me, reckoning all thy virtues. Thou art truly, O blessed damsel, the foremost of all persons observing the duties of righteousness.' Having said so unto her, the Brahmana took her share of the barley and gave it unto his guest. At this the guest became gratified with the high-souled Brahmana endued with great piety. With gratified soul, that first of regenerate person, possessed of great eloquence, who was none else than the deity of Righteousness in a human form, then addressed that foremost of Brahmanas and said, 'O best of regenerate ones, I am exceedingly gratified with this pure gift of thine, this gift of what was acquired by lawful means by thee, and which thou didst freely part with, agreeably to the rules of righteousness. Verily, this gift of thine is being bruited about in Heaven by the denizens of that happy region. Behold, flowers have been rained down from the firmament on the Earth. The celestial Rishis, the deities, the Gandharvas, those who walk before the deities, and the celestial messengers, are all praising thee, struck with wonder at thy gift. The regenerate Rishis who dwell in the regions of Brahma, seated on their cars, are solicitous of obtaining thy sight. O foremost of regenerate persons, go to Heaven. The Pitris residing in their own region have all been

---

[850] The sense is this: for the sake of those auspicious results after which every family should strive, the daughter-in-law should be well treated. How then can I deprive thee of food?

rescued by thee. Others also who have not attained to the position of Pitris have equally been rescued by thee for countless Yugas. For thy Brahmacharyya, thy gifts, thy sacrifices, thy penances, and thy acts of piety done with a pure heart, go thou to Heaven. O thou of excellent vows, thou practisest penances with great devotion. Thy gifts have, therefore, gratified the deities highly, O best of regenerate ones. Since thou hast made this gift, in a season of great difficulty, with a pure heart, thou hast, by this act of thine, conquered Heaven. Hunger destroys one's wisdom and drives off one's righteous understanding. One whose intelligence is overwhelmed by hunger casts off all fortitude. He, therefore, that conquers hunger conquers Heaven without doubt. One's righteousness is never destroyed as long as one cherishes the inclination of making gifts. Disregarding filial affection, disregarding the affection one feels for one's wife, and reckoning righteousness as the foremost, thou hast paid no heed to the cravings of nature. The acquisition of wealth is an act of slight merit. Its gift to a deserving person is fraught with greater merit. Of still greater merit is the (proper) time. Lastly, devotion (in the matter of gift) is fraught with the highest merit. The door of Heaven is very difficult to see. Through heedlessness men fail to obtain a sight of it. The bar of Heaven's door has cupidity for its seed. That bar is kept fastened by desire and affection. Verily, Heaven's door is unapproachable. Those men who subdued wrath and conquered their passions, those Brahmanas who are endued with penances and who make gifts according to the measure of their ability, succeed in beholding it. It has been said that he that gives away a hundred, having a thousand, he that gives away ten, having a hundred, and he that gives a handful of water, having no wealth, are all equal in respect of the merit they earn. King Rantideva, when divested of all his wealth, gave a small quantity of water with a pure heart. Through this gift, O learned Brahmana, he went to Heaven. The deity of righteousness is never gratified so much with large gifts of costly things as with gifts of even things of no value, if acquired lawfully and given away with devotion and faith. King Nriga had made gifts of thousands of kine unto the regenerate class. By giving away only one cow that did not belong to him, he fell into Hell. Usinara's son Sivi of excellent vows, by giving away the flesh of his own body, is rejoicing in Heaven, having attained to the regions of the righteous. Mere wealth is not merit. Good men acquire merit by exerting to the best of their power and with the aid of pious meals. One does not acquire such merit by means of even diverse sacrifices as with even a little wealth that has been earned lawfully. Through wrath, the fruits of gifts are destroyed. Through cupidity one fails to go to Heaven. One conversant with the merits of gift, and leading a just course of conduct succeeds, through penances, in enjoying Heaven. The fruit, O Brahmana, of this gift made by thee (of a prastha of powdered barley) is much greater than what one acquires by many Rajasuya sacrifices with profuse gifts or many Horse-sacrifices. With this prastha of powdered barley thou hast conquered the eternal region of Brahman. Go thou in happiness, O learned Brahmana, to the abode of Brahman that is without the stain of darkness. O foremost of regenerate persons, a celestial car is here for all of you. Do thou ascend it as pleasest thee. O Brahmana, I am the deity of Righteousness. Behold me! Thou hast rescued thy body. The fame of thy achievement will last in the world. With thy wife, thy son, and thy daughter-in-law, go now to Heaven.'—After the deity of Righteousness had said these words, that Brahmana, with his wife, son and daughter-in-law, proceeded to Heaven. After that learned Brahmana, conversant with all duties, had thus ascended to Heaven with his son, daughter-in-law, and wife numbering the fourth, I came out of my hole. There with the scent of that powdered barley, with the mire caused by the water (which the Brahmana had given to his guest), with the contact (of my body) with the celestial flowers that had been rained down, with the particles of the barley-powder which that good man had given away, and the penances of that Brahmana, my head became gold. Behold, in consequence of the gift of that Brahmana who was firm in truth, and his penances, half of this my ample body has become golden. Ye regenerate ones, for converting the rest of my body into gold I repeatedly repair, with a cheerful heart, to the retreats of ascetics and the sacrifices performed by kings. Hearing of this sacrifice of the Kuru king endued with great wisdom, I came hither with high hopes. I have not, however, been made gold. Ye foremost of Brahmanas, it was for this that I uttered those words, viz., that this sacrifice can by no means compare with (the gift of) that prastha of powdered barley. With the grains of that prastha of powdered barley, I was made gold on that occasion. This great sacrifice however, is not equal to those grains. Even this is my opinion." Having said those words unto all those foremost of Brahmanas, the mongoose disappeared from their sight. Those Brahmanas then returned to their respective homes.'

"Vaisampayana continued, 'O conquerer of hostile towns, I have now told thee all relating to that wonderful incident which occurred in that great Horse-sacrifice. Thou shouldst not, O king, think highly of sacrifice. Millions of Rishis have ascended to Heaven with the aid of only their penances. Abstention from injury as regards all creatures, contentment, conduct, sincerity, penances, self-restraint, truthfulness, and gifts are each equal in point of merit to sacrifice.'"

SECTION XCI.

"Janamejaya said, 'O puissant Rishi, kings are attached to sacrifices. The great Rishis are attached to penances. Learned Brahmanas are observant of tranquillity of mind, peacefulness of behaviour, and self-restraint. Hence it seems that nothing can be seen in this world which can compare with the fruits of sacrifices. Even this is my conviction. That conviction, again, seems to be undoubtedly correct. Innumerable kings, O best of regenerate persons, having worshipped the deities in sacrifices, earned high fame here and obtained Heaven hereafter. Endued with great energy, the puissant chief of the deities viz., Indra of a thousand eyes, obtained the sovereignty over the deities through the many sacrifices he performed with gifts in profusion and attained to the fruition of all his wishes. When king Yudhishthira, with Bhima and Arjuna by him, resembled the chief of the deities himself in prosperity and prowess, why then did that mongoose depreciate that great Horse-sacrifice of the high-souled monarch?'

"Vaisampayana said, 'Do thou listen to me, O king, as I discourse to thee duly, O Bharata, on the excellent ordinances relating to sacrifice and the fruits also, O ruler of men, that sacrifice yields. Formerly, on one occasion Sakra performed a particular sacrifice. While the limbs of the sacrifice were spread out, the Ritwijas became busy in accomplishing the diverse rites ordained in the scriptures. The pourer of libations, possessed of every qualification, became engaged in pouring libations of clarified butter. The great Rishis were seated around. The deities were summoned one by one by contented Brahmanas of great learning uttering scriptural Mantras in sweet voices. Those foremost of Adhwaryyus, not fatigued with what they did, recited the Mantras of the Yajurveda in soft accents. The time came for slaughtering the animals. When the animals selected for sacrifice were seized, the great Rishis, O king, felt compassion for them. Beholding that the animals had all become cheerless, those Rishis, endued with wealth of penances, approached Sakra and said unto him, "This method of sacrifice is not auspicious. Desirous of acquiring great merit as thou art, this is verily an indication of thy unacquaintance with sacrifice. O Purandara, animals have not been ordained to be slaughtered in sacrifices. O puissant one, these preparations of thine are destructive of merit. This sacrifice is not consistent with righteousness. The destruction of creatures can never be said to be an act of righteousness. If thou wishest it, let thy priests perform thy sacrifice according to the Agama. By performing a sacrifice according to the (true import of the) scriptural ordinances, great will be the merit achieved by thee. O thou of a hundred eyes, do thou perform the sacrifice with seeds of grain that have been kept for three years. Even this, O Sakra, would be fraught with great righteousness and productive of fruits of high efficacy." The deity of a hundred sacrifices, however, influenced by pride and overwhelmed by stupefaction, did not accept these words uttered by the Rishis. Then, O Bharata, a great dispute arose in that sacrifice of Sakra between the ascetics as to how sacrifices should be performed, that is, should they be performed with mobile creatures or with immobile objects. All of them were worn out with disputation. The Rishis then, those beholders of truth, having made an understanding with Sakra (about referring the matter to arbitration) asked king Vasu, "O highly blessed one, what is the Vedic declaration about sacrifices? Is it preferable to perform sacrifices with animals or with seeds and juices?" Hearing the question, king Vasu, without all judging of the strength or weakness of the arguments on the two sides, at once answered, saying, "Sacrifices may be performed with whichever of the two kinds of objects is ready." Having answered the question thus, he had to enter the nether regions. Indeed the puissant ruler of the Chedis had to undergo that misery for having answered falsely. Therefore, when a doubt arises, no person, however wise, should singly decide the matter, unless he be the puissant and self-born Lord himself of creatures. Gifts made by a sinner with an impure understanding, even when they are very large, become lost. Such gifts go for nothing. By the gifts made by a person of unrighteous conduct,—one, that is, who is of sinful soul and who is a destroyer, just fame is never acquired either here or hereafter. That person of little intelligence who, from desire of acquiring merit, performs sacrifices with wealth acquired by unrighteous means, never succeeds in earning merit. That low wretch of sinful soul, who hypocritically assuming a garb of righteousness makes gifts unto Brahmanas, only creates the conviction in men about his own righteousness (without earning true merit). That Brahmana of uncontrolled conduct, who acquires wealth by sinful acts, ever overwhelmed by passion and stupefaction, attains at last to the goal of the sinful. Someone, overwhelmed by cupidity and stupefaction, becomes bent on strong wealth. He is seen to persecute all creatures, urged by a sinful and impure understanding. He who, having acquired wealth by such means, makes gifts or performs sacrifices therewith, never enjoys the fruits of those gifts or sacrifices in the other world in consequence of the wealth having been earned by unrighteous means. Men endued with wealth of penances, by giving away, to the best of their power, grains of corn picked up from the fields or roots or fruits or pot-herbs or water or leaves, acquire great merit and proceed to Heaven. Even such gifts, as also compassion to all creatures, and Brahmacharyya, truthfulness of speech and kindness, and fortitude, and forgiveness, constitute the eternal foundations of Righteousness which itself is eternal. We hear of Viswamitra and other kings of ancient times. Indeed, Viswamitra, and Asita, and king Janaka, and Kakshasena and Arshtisena, and king Sindhudwipa,—these and many other kings, endued with wealth of penances, having made gifts of articles acquired lawfully, have attained to high success. Those amongst Brahmanas and Kshatriyas and Vaisyas and Sudras who betake themselves to penances, O Bharata, and who purify themselves by

574

gifts and other acts of righteousness, proceed to Heaven.'"

SECTION XCII.

"Janamejaya said, 'If, O illustrious one, Heaven is the fruit of wealth acquired by lawful means, do thou discourse to me fully on it. Thou art well-conversant with the subject and therefore, it behoveth thee to explain it. O regenerate one, thou hast said unto me what the high fruit was that accrued unto that Brahmana, who lived according to the Unccha mode, through his gift of powdered barley. Without doubt, all thou hast said is true. In what way, however, was the attainment held certain of the highest end in all sacrifices? O foremost of regenerate persons, it behoveth thee to expound this to me in all its details.'

"Vaisampayana said, 'In this connection is cited this old narrative, O chastiser of foes, of what occurred in former days in the great sacrifice of Agastya. In olden days, O king, Agastya of great energy, devoted to the good of all creatures, entered into a Diksha extending for twelve years.[851] In that sacrifice of the high-souled Rishi many Hotris were engaged that resembled blazing fires in the splendour of their bodies. Among them were men that subsisted upon roots or fruits, or that used two pieces of stone only for husking their corn, or that were supported by only the rays (of the moon). Among them were also men who never took any food unless it was placed before them by others solicitous of feeding them, and those who never ate anything without having first served the deities, the Pitris, and guests, and those who never washed the food which they took. There were also Yatis and Bikshus among them, O king. All of them were men who had obtained a sight of the deity of Righteousness in his embodied form. They had subjugated wrath and acquired a complete mastery over all their senses. Living in the observance of self-restraint, they were freed from pride and the desire of injuring others. They were always observant of a pure conduct and were never obstructed (in the prosecution of their purposes) by their senses. Those great Rishis attended that sacrifice and accomplished its various rites. The illustrious Rishi (Agastya) acquired the food that was collected in that sacrifice and that came up to the required measure, by lawful means according to the best of his power. Numerous other ascetics at that time performed large sacrifices. As Agastya, however, was engaged in that sacrifice of his, the thousand-eyed Indra, O best of the Bharatas, ceased to pour rain (on the Earth). At the intervals, O king, of the sacrificial rites, this talk occurred among those Rishis of cleansed souls about the high-souled Agastya, viz., "This Agastya, engaged in sacrifice, is making gifts of food with heart purged of pride and vanity. The deity of the clouds, however, has ceased to pour rain. How, indeed, will food grow? This sacrifice of the Rishi, ye Brahmanas, is great and extends for twelve years. The deity will not pour rain for these twelve years. Reflecting on this, it behoveth you to do some favour unto this Rishi of great intelligence, viz., Agastya of severe penances." When these words were said, Agastya of great prowess, gratifying those ascetics by bending his head, said, "If Vasava does not pour rain for those twelve years, I shall then perform the mental sacrifice. Even this is the eternal ordinance. If Vasava does not pour rain for these twelve years, I shall then perform the Touch-sacrifice. Even this is the eternal sacrifice. If Vasava does not pour rain for these

---

[851] The Diksha consists of the initiatory rites undergone by one desirous of performing a particular sacrifice or completing a particular vow. Some auspicious day is selected. Mantras are uttered and the purpose is expressed in words. There were many long-extending sacrifices which were partly of the nature of vows. Till their completion the performer or observer is said to undergo the period of Diksha.

twelve years, I shall then, putting forth all my exertion, make arrangements for other sacrifices characterised by the observance of the most difficult and severe vows. This present sacrifice of mine, with seeds, has been arranged for by me with labour extending for many years.[852] I shall, with seeds, accomplish much good. No impediment will arise. This my sacrifice is incapable of being baffled. It matters little whether the deity pours rains or no downpours happen. Indeed, if Indra does not, of his own will, show any regard for me, I shall, in that case, transform myself into Indra and keep all creatures alive. Every creature, on whatever food he has been nourished, will continue to be nourished on it as before. I can even repeatedly create a different order of things. Let gold and whatever else of wealth there is, come to this place today. Let all the wealth that occurs in the three worlds come here today of its own accord. Let all the tribes of celestial Apsaras, all the Gandharvas along with the Kinnaras, and Viswavasu, and others there are (of that order), approach this sacrifice of mine. Let all the wealth that exists among the Northern Kurus, come of their own accord to these sacrifices. Let Heaven, and all those who have Heaven for their home, and Dharma himself, come hither."—After the ascetic had uttered these words, everything happened as he wished, in consequence of his penances, for Agastya was endued with a mind that resembled a blazing fire and was possessed of extraordinary energy. The Rishis who were there beheld the power of penances with rejoicing hearts. Filled with wonder they then said these words of grave import.'

"'The Rishis said, "We have been highly gratified with the words thou hast uttered. We do not, however, wish that thy penances should suffer any diminution. Those sacrifices are approved by us which are performed by lawful means. Indeed, we desire duly those sacrifices which rest on lawful means.[853] Earning our food by lawful means and observant of our respective duties, we shall seek to go through sacrificial initiations and the pouring of libations on the sacred fire and the other religious rites. We should adore the deities, practising Brahmacharyya by lawful means. Completing the period of Brahmacharyya we have come out of our abode, observing lawful methods. That understanding, which is freed from the desire of inflicting any kind of injury on others, is approved by us. Thou shouldst always, O puissant one, command such abstention from injury in all sacrifices. We shall then be highly gratified, O foremost of regenerate ones. After the completion of thy sacrifice, when dismissed by thee, we shall then, leaving this place, go away." As they were saying these words, Purandara, the chief of the deities, endued with great energy, beholding the power of Agastya's penances, poured rain. Indeed, O Janamejaya, till the completion of the sacrifice of that Rishi of immeasurable prowess, the deity of rain poured rain that met the wishes of men in respect of both quantity and time. Placing Vrihaspati before him, the chief of the deities came there, O royal sage, and gratified the Rishi Agastya. On the completion of that sacrifice, Agastya, filled with joy, worshipped those great Rishis duly and then dismissed them all.'

"Janamejaya said, 'Who was that mongoose with a golden head, that said all those words in a human voice? Asked by me, do thou tell me this.'

"Vaisampayana said, 'Thou didst not ask me before and, therefore, I did not tell thee. Hear as I tell thee who that mongoose was and why he could assume a human voice. In

---

[852] The first line of 20 is differently read in the Bombay text. It runs,—'steadfastly observing my vow, I shall make arrangements for many sacrifices, creating the articles I want by thought alone (or fiats of my will).'

[853] Probably, the sense is this: If a Brahmana produced extraordinary results by his penances, a portion of his penances was supposed to be destroyed. The Rishis did not like that any portion of Agastya's penances should be spent for completing his sacrifice.

former times, the Rishi Jamadagni proposed to perform a Sraddha. His Homa cow came to him and the Rishi milked her himself. He then placed the milk in a vessel that was new, durable and pure. The deity Dharma, assuming the form of Anger, entered that vessel of milk. Indeed, Dharma was desirous of ascertaining what that foremost of Rishis would do when seeing some injury done to him. Having reflected thus, Dharma spoiled that milk. Knowing that the spoiler of his milk was Anger, the ascetic was not at all enraged with him. Anger, then, assuming the form of a Brahmana lady, showed himself to the Rishi. Indeed, Anger, finding that he had been conquered by that foremost one of Bhrigu's race, addressed him, saying, "O chief of Bhrigu's race, I have been conquered by thee. There is a saying among men that the Bhrigus are very wrathful. I now find that that saying is false, since I have been subdued by thee. Thou art possessed of a mighty soul. Thou art endued with forgiveness. I stand here today, owning thy sway. I fear thy penances, O righteous one. Do thou, O puissant Rishi, show me favour."

"'Jamadagni said, "I have seen thee, O Anger, in thy embodied form. Go thou whithersoever thou likest, without any anxiety. Thou hast not done me any injury today. I have no grudge against thee. Those for whom I had kept this milk are the highly blessed Pitris. Present thyself before them and ascertain their intentions." Thus addressed, penetrated with fear, Anger vanished from the sight of the Rishi. Through the curse of the Pitris he became a mongoose. He then began to gratify the Pitris in order to bring about an end of his curse. By them he was told these words, "By speaking disrespectfully of Dharma thou shalt attain to the end of thy curse." Thus addressed by them he wandered over places where sacrifices were performed and over other sacred places, employed in censuring great sacrifices. It was he that came to the great sacrifice of king Yudhishthira. Dispraising the son of Dharma by a reference to the prastha of powdered barley, Anger became freed from his curse, for Yudhishthira (as Dharma's son) was Dharma's self. Even this is what occurred in the sacrifice of that high-souled king. Mongoose disappeared there in our very sight.'"[854]

THE END OF ASWAMEDHA PARVA

BOOK 15. ASRAMAVASIKA PARVA

SECTION I. (*Asramavasa Parva*)

OM! AFTER HAVING bowed down to Narayana, and Nara, the foremost of men, and unto the goddess Saraswati also, must the word Jaya be uttered.

"Janamejaya said, 'After having acquired their kingdom, how did my grandsires, the high-souled Pandavas, conduct themselves towards the high-souled king Dhritarashtra? How, indeed, did that king who had all his counsellors and sons slain, who was without a refuge, and whose affluence had disappeared, behave? How also did Gandhari of great fame conduct herself? For how many years did my high-souled grandsires rule the kingdom? It behoveth thee to tell me all this.'

"Vaisampayana said, 'Having got back their kingdom, the high-souled Pandavas,

---

[854] It is difficult to resist the conviction that as much of this section as relates to the mongoose is an interpolation. The Brahmanas could not bear the idea of a sacrifice with such profusion of gifts, as that of Yudhishthira, being censurable. Hence the invention about the transformation of the mongoose. Truly speaking, the doctrine is noble of the gift of a small quantity of barley made under the circumstances being superior in point of merit to even a Horse-sacrifice performed by a king with gifts in profusion made to the Brahmanas.

their foes all slain, ruled the Earth, placing Dhritarashtra at their head. Vidura, and Sanjaya and Yuyutsu of great intelligence, who was Dhritarashtra's son by his Vaisya wife, used to wait upon Dhritarashtra. The Pandavas used to take the opinion of that king in all matters. Indeed, for ten and five years, they did all things under the advice of the old king. Those heroes used very often to go to that monarch and sit beside him, after having worshipped his feet, agreeably to the wishes of king Yudhishthira the just. They did all things under the command of Dhritarashtra who smelt their heads in affection. The daughter of king Kuntibhoja also obeyed Gandhari in everything. Draupadi and Subhadra and the other ladies of the Pandavas behaved towards the old king and the queen as if they were their own father-in-law and mother-in-law. Costly beds and robes and ornaments, and food and drink and other enjoyable articles, in profusion and of such superior kinds as were worthy of royal use, were presented by king Yudhishthira unto Dhritarashtra. Similarly Kunti behaved towards Gandhari as towards a senior. Vidura, and Sanjaya, and Yuyutsu, O thou of Kuru's race, used to always wait upon the old king whose sons had all been slain. The dear brother-in-law of Drona, viz., the very superior Brahmana, Kripa, that mighty bowman, also attended upon the king. The holy Vyasa also used to often meet with the old monarch and recite to him the histories of old Rishis and celestial ascetics and Pitris and Rakshasas. Vidura, under the orders of Dhritarashtra, superintended the discharge of all acts of religious merit and all that related to the administration of the law. Through the excellent policy of Vidura, by the expenditure of even a small wealth, the Pandavas obtained numerous agreeable services from their feudatories and followers. King Dhritarashtra liberated prisoners and pardoned those that were condemned to death. King Yudhishthira the just never said anything to this. On those occasions when the son of Amvika went on pleasure excursions, the Kuru king Yudhishthira of great energy used to give him every article of enjoyment. Aralikas, and juice-makers, and makers of Ragakhandavas waited on king Dhritarashtra as before.[855] Pandu's son, collected costly robes and garlands of diverse kinds and duly offered them to Dhritarashtra. Maireya wines, fish of various kinds, and sherbets and honey, and many delightful kinds of food prepared by modifications (of diverse articles), were caused to be made for the old king as in his days of prosperity. Those kings of Earth who came there one after another, all used to wait upon the old Kuru monarch as before. Kunti, and Draupadi, and she of the Sattwata race, possessed of great fame, and Ulupi, the daughter of the snake chief, and queen Chitrangada, and the sister of Dhrishtaketu, and the daughter of Jarasandha,—these and many other ladies, O chief of men, used to wait upon the daughter of Suvala like maids of all work. That Dhritarashtra, who was deprived of all his children, might not feel unhappy in any matter, was what Yudhishthira often said unto his brothers to see. They also, on their part, listening to these commands of grave import from king Yudhishthira, showed particular obedience to the old king. There was one exception, however. It embraced Bhimasena. All that had followed from that match at dice which had been brought about by the wicked understanding of Dhritarashtra, did not disappear from the heart of that hero. (He remembered those incidents still).'"

---

[855] The derivation of Aralikas is explained by Nilakantha thus; Potherbs cut off with a kind of weapon called Ara are called Aralu. They who were expert in cooking those potherbs were called Aralikas. Ragakhandava was manufactured from piper longum, dry ginger, sugar, and the juice of Phaseolus Mango.

SECTION II.

"Vaisampayana said, 'Thus worshipped by the Pandavas, the royal son of Amvika passed his time happily as before, waited upon and honoured by the Rishis. That perpetuator of Kuru's race used to make those foremost of offerings which should be given to the Brahmanas. The royal son of Kunti always placed those articles under Dhritarashtra's control. Destitute of malice as king Yudhishthira was, he was always affectionate towards his uncle. Addressing his brothers and councillors, the king said, "King Dhritarashtra should be honoured both by myself and you all. He indeed, is a well-wisher of mine who is obedient to the commands of Dhritarashtra. He, on the other hand, who behaves otherwise towards him, is my enemy. Such a man should certainly be punished by me." On days of performing the rites ordained for the Pitris, as also in the Sraddhas performed for his sons and all well-wishers, the high-souled Kuru king Dhritarashtra, gave away unto Brahmanas, as each deserved, as profuse measures of wealth as he liked. King Yudhishthira the just, and Bhima, and Arjuna, and the twins, desirous of doing what was agreeable to the old king, used to execute all his orders. They always took care that the old king who was afflicted with the slaughter of his sons and grandsons,—with, that is, grief caused by the Pandavas themselves,—might not die of his grief. Indeed, the Pandavas bore themselves towards him in such a way that that Kuru hero might not be deprived of that happiness and all those articles of enjoyment which had been his while his sons lived. The five brothers, viz., the sons of Pandu, behaved themselves even thus towards Dhritarashtra, living under his command. Dhritarashtra also, seeing them so humble and obedient to his commands and acting towards him as disciples towards preceptors, adopted the affectionate behaviour of a preceptor towards them in return. Gandhari, by performing the diverse rites of the Sraddha and making gifts unto Brahmanas of diverse objects of enjoyment, became freed from the debt she owed to her slain children. Thus did that foremost of righteous men, viz., king Yudhishthira the just, possessed of great intelligence, along with his brothers, worship king Dhritarashtra.'

"Vaisampayana continued, 'Possessed of great energy, that perpetuator of Kuru's race, viz., the old king Dhritarashtra, could not notice any ill-will in Yudhishthira. Seeing that the high-souled Pandavas were in the observance of a wise and righteous conduct, king Dhritarashtra, the son of Amvika, became gratified with them. Suvala's daughter, Gandhari, casting off all sorrow for her (slain) children, began to show great affection for the Pandavas as if they were her own children. Endued with great energy, the Kuru king Yudhishthira, never did anything that was disagreeable to the royal son of Vichitraviryya. On the other hand, he always behaved towards him in a highly agreeable way. Whatever acts, grave or light, were directed by king Dhritarashtra, or the helpless Gandhari to be done, were all accomplished with reverence, O monarch, by that slayer of hostile heroes, viz., the Pandava king. The old king became highly gratified with such conduct of Yudhishthira. Indeed, he was grieved at the remembrance of his own wicked son. Rising every day at early dawn, he purified himself and went through his recitations, and then blessed the Pandavas by wishing them victory in battle. Making the usual gifts unto the Brahmanas and causing them to utter benedictions, and pouring libations on the sacred fire, the old king prayed for long life to the Pandavas. Indeed, the king had never derived that great happiness from his own sons which he always derived from the sons of Pandu. King Yudhishthira at that time became as agreeable to the Brahmanas as to the Kshatriyas, and the diverse bands of Vaisyas and Sudras of his realm. Whatever wrongs were done to him by the sons of Dhritarashtra, king Yudhishthira, forgot them all, and reverenced his uncle. If any man did anything that was not agreeable to the son of Amvika, he became thereby an object of hatred to the intelligent son of Kunti. Indeed, through fear of Yudhishthira, nobody could talk of the evil deeds of either Duryodhana or Dhritarashtra. Both Gandhari and Vidura also were well pleased with the capacity the king Ajatasatru showed for bearing wrongs. They were, however, not so pleased, O slayer of foes, with Bhima. Dharma's son, Yudhishthira, was truly obedient to his uncle. Bhima, however, at the sight of Dhritarashtra, became very cheerless. That slayer of foes, seeing Dharma's son reverencing the old king, reverenced him outwardly with a very unwilling heart.'"

SECTION III.

"Vaisampayana said, 'The people who lived in the Kuru kingdom failed to notice any variance in the cordiality that subsisted between king Yudhishthira and the father of Duryodhana. When the Kuru king recollected his wicked son, he then could not but feel unfriendly, in his heart, towards Bhima. Bhimasena also, O king, impelled by a heart that seemed to be wicked, was unable to put up with king Dhritarashtra. Vrikodara secretly did many acts that were disagreeable to the old king. Through deceitful servitors he caused the commands of his uncle to be disobeyed. Recollecting the evil counsels of the old king and some acts of his, Bhima, one day, in the midst of his friends, slapped his armpits, in the hearing of Dhritarashtra and of Gandhari. The wrathful Vrikodara, recollecting his foes Duryodhana and Karna and Dussasana, gave way to a transport of passion, and said these harsh words: "The sons of the blind king, capable of fighting with diverse kinds of weapons, have all been despatched by me to the other world with these arms of mine that resemble a pair of iron clubs. Verily, these are those two arms of mine, looking like maces of iron, and invincible by foes, coming within whose clasp the sons of Dhritarashtra have all met with destruction. These are those two well-developed and round arms of mine, resembling a pair of elephantine trunks. Coming within their clasp, the foolish sons of Dhritarashtra have all met with destruction. Smeared with sandal-paste and deserving of that adornment are those two arms of mine by which Duryodhana has been despatched to the other world along with all his sons and kinsmen." Hearing these and many other words, O king, of Vrikodara, that were veritable darts, king Dhritarashtra gave way to cheerlessness and sorrow. Queen Gandhari, however, who was conversant with every duty and possessed of great intelligence, and who knew what Time brings on its course, regarded them as untrue. After five and ten years had passed away, O monarch, king Dhritarashtra afflicted (constantly) by the wordy darts of Bhima, became penetrated with despair and grief. King Yudhishthira the son of Kunti, however, knew it not; nor Arjuna of white steeds, nor Kunti; nor Draupadi possessed of great fame; nor the twin sons of Madri, conversant with every duty and who were always engaged in acting after the wishes of Dhritarashtra. Employed in doing the behests of the king, the twins never said anything that was disagreeable to the old king. Then Dhritarashtra one day honoured his friends by his confidence. Addressing them with tearful eyes, he said these words.'

"'Dhritarashtra said, "How the destruction of the Kurus has happened is well known to you. All that was brought about by my fault though the Kauravas approved of all my counsels. Fool that I was, I installed the wicked minded Duryodhana, that enhancer of the terrors of kinsmen, to rule over the Kurus. Vasudeva had said unto me, 'Let this sinful wretch of wicked understanding be killed along with all his friends and counsellors.' I did not listen to those words of grave import. All wise men gave me the same beneficial advice. Vidura, and Bhishma, and Drona, and Kripa, said the same thing. The holy and high-souled Vyasa repeatedly said the same, as also Sanjaya and Gandhari. Overwhelmed, however, by filial affection, I could not follow that advice. Bitter repentance is now my lot for my neglect. I also repent for not having bestowed that blazing prosperity, derived from sires and grand sires, on the high-souled Pandavas possessed of every accomplishment. The eldest brother of Gada foresaw the destruction of all the kings; Janarddana, however, regarded that destruction as highly beneficial.[856] So many Anikas of troops, belonging to me, have been destroyed. Alas, my heart is pierced with thousands of darts in consequence of all these results. Of wicked understanding as I am, now after the lapse of five and ten years, I am seeking to expiate my sins. Now at the fourth division of the day or sometimes at the eighth division, with the regularity of a vow, I eat a little food for simply conquering my thirst. Gandhari knows this. All my attendants are under the impression that I eat as usual. Through fear of Yudhishthira alone I concealed my acts, for if the eldest son of Pandu came to know of my vow, he would feel great pain. Clad in deer-skin, I lie down on the Earth, spreading a small quantity of Kusa grass, and pass the time in silent recitations. Gandhari of great fame passes her time in the observance of similar vows. Even thus do we both behave, we that have lost a century of sons none of whom ever retreated from battle. I do not, however, grieve for those children of mine. They have all died in the observance of Kshatriya duties." Having said these words, the old king then addressed Yudhishthira in particular and said, "Blessed be thou, O son of the princess of Yadu's race. Listen now to what I say. Cherished by thee, O son, I have lived these years very happily. I have (with thy help) made large gifts and performed Sraddhas repeatedly.[857] I have, O son, to the best of my power, achieved merit largely. This Gandhari, though destitute of sons, has lived with great fortitude, looking all the while at me. They whom inflicted great wrongs on Draupadi and robbed thee of thy affluence,—those cruel wights—have all left the world, slain in battle agreeably to the practice of their order.

""I have nothing to do for them, O delighter of the Kurus. Slain with their faces towards battle, they have attained to those regions which are for wielders of weapons.[858] I should now accomplish what is beneficial and meritorious for me as also for Gandhari. It behoveth thee, O great king, to grant me permission. Thou art the foremost of all righteous persons. Thou art always devoted to righteousness. The king is the preceptor of all creatures. It is for this that I say so. With thy permission, O hero, I shall retire into the woods, clad in rags and barks. O king, alone with this Gandhari, I shall live in the woods, always blessing thee. It is meet, O son, for the members of our race, to make over sovereignty, when old age comes, to children and lead the forest mode of life. Subsisting there on air alone, or abstaining from all food, I shall, with this wife of mine, O hero, practise severe austerities. Thou shalt be a sharer of these penances, O son, for thou art the king. Kings are sharers of both auspicious and inauspicious acts done in their

---

[856] It will be remembered, Earth, unable to bear her load of population, prayed to the Grandsire for lightening that load. The Grandsire urged Vishnu to do the needful. Hence Vishnu incarnated himself as Krishna and brought about a lightening of Earth's load.

[857] Mahadana implies such gifts as elephants, boats, cars, horses, etc. Everybody does not accept these gifts, for their acceptance causes a Brahmana to fall away from his status.

[858] Some of the Bengal texts read avimukham hatah for abhimukam hatah. The sense is the same.

kingdom."[859]

"'Yudhishthira said, "When thou, O king, art thus subject to grief, sovereignty does not please me at all. Fie on me that am of wicked understanding, devoted to the pleasures of rule, and utterly heedless of my true concerns. Alas, I, with all my brothers, was ignorant of thyself having so long been afflicted with grief, emaciated with fasts, abstaining from food, and lying on the bare ground. Alas, foolish that I am, I have been deceived by thee that hast deep intelligence, inasmuch as, having inspired me with confidence at first thou hast latterly undergone such grief. What need have I of kingdom or of articles of enjoyment, what need of sacrifices or of happiness, when thou, O king, hast undergone so much affliction? I regard my kingdom as a disease, and myself also as afflicted. Plunged though I am in sorrow, what, however, is the use of these words that I am addressing thee? Thou art our father, thou art our mother; thou art our foremost of superiors. Deprived of thy presence, how shall we live? O best of king, let Yuyutsu, the son of thy loins, be made king, or, indeed, anybody else whom thou mayst wish. I shall go into the woods. Do thou rule the kingdom. It behoveth thee not to burn me that am already burned by infamy. I am not the king. Thou art the king. I am dependent on thy will. How can I dare grant permission to thee that art my preceptor? O sinless one, I harbour no resentment in my heart on account of the wrongs done to us by Suyodhana. It was ordained that it should be so. Both ourselves and others were stupefied (by fate). We are thy children as Duryodhana and others were. My conviction is that Gandhari is as much my mother as Kunti. If thou, O king of kings, goest to the woods leaving me, I shall then follow thee. I swear by my soul. This Earth, with her belt of seas, so full of wealth, will not be a source of joy to me when I am deprived of thy presence. All this belongs to thee. I gratify thee, bending my head. We are all dependent on thee, O king of kings. Let the fever of thy heart be dispelled. I think, O lord of Earth, that all this that has come upon thee is due to destiny. By good luck, I had thought, that waiting upon thee and executing thy commands obediently, I would rescue thee from the fever of thy heart."

"'Dhritarashtra said, "O delighter of the Kurus, my mind is fixed, O son, on penances. O puissant one, it is meet for our race that I should retire into the woods. I have lived long under thy protection, O son, I have for many years been served by thee with reverence. I am now old. It behoveth thee, O king, to grant me permission (to take up my abode in the woods).'"

"Vaisampayana continued, 'Having said these words unto king Yudhishthira, the just, king Dhritarashtra, the son of Amvika, trembling the while and with hands joined together, further said unto the high-souled Sanjaya and the great car-warrior Kripa, these words, "I wish to solicit the king through you. My mind has become cheerless, my mouth has become dry, through the weakness of age and the exertion of speaking." Having said so, that perpetuator of Kuru's race, viz., the righteous-souled old king, blessed with prosperity, leaned on Gandhari and suddenly looked like one deprived of life. Beholding him thus seated like one deprived of consciousness, that slayer of hostile heroes, viz., the royal son of Kunti, became penetrated by a poignant grief.

"'Yudhishthira said, "Alas, he whose strength was equal to that of a hundred thousand elephants, alas, that king sitteth today, leaning on a woman. Alas! he by whom the iron image of Bhima on a former occasion was reduced to fragments, leaneth today

---

[859] The king gets a sixth share of the penances performed by the Rishis living under his protection. The demerit, again, of all evil deeds done within his realm is shared by the king, for such deeds become possible through absence of supervision by the king.

on a weak woman. Fie on me that am exceedingly unrighteous! Fie on my understanding! Fie on my knowledge of the scripture! Fie on me for whom this lord of Earth lieth today in a manner that is not becoming of him! I also shall fast even as my preceptor. Verily, I shall fast if this king and Gandhari of great fame abstain from food."'

"Vaisampayana continued, 'The Pandava king, conversant with every duty, using his own hand, then softly rubbed with cold water the breast and the face of the old monarch. At the touch of the king's hand which was auspicious and fragrant, and on which were jewels and medicinal herbs, Dhritarashtra regained his senses.[860]

"'Dhritarashtra said, "Do thou again touch me, O son of Pandu, with thy hand, and do thou embrace me. O thou of eyes like lotus petals, I am restored to my senses through the auspicious touch of thy hand. O ruler of men, I desire to smell thy head. The clasp of thy arms is highly gratifying to me. This is the eighth division of the day and, therefore, the hour of taking my food. For not having taken my food, O child of Kuru's race, I am so weak as to be unable to move. In addressing my solicitations to thee, great has been my exertion. Rendered cheerless by it, O son, I had fainted. O perpetuator of Kuru's race, I think that receiving the touch of thy hand, which resembles nectar in its vivifying effects I have been restored to my senses."'

"Vaisampayana said, 'Thus addressed, O Bharata, by the eldest brother of his father, the son of Kunti, from affection, gently touched every part of his body. Regaining his life-breaths, king Dhritarashtra embraced the son of Pandu with his arms and smelled his head. Vidura and others wept aloud in great grief. In consequence, however, of the poignancy of their sorrow, they said nothing to either the old king or the son of Pandu. Gandhari, conversant with every duty, bore her sorrow with fortitude, and loaded as her heart was, O king, said nothing. The other ladies, Kunti among them, became greatly afflicted. They wept, shedding copious tears, and sat surrounding the old king. Then Dhritarashtra, once more addressing Yudhishthira, said these words, "Do thou, O king, grant me permission to practise penances. By speaking repeatedly, O son, my mind becomes weakened. It behoveth thee not, O son, to afflict me after this." When that foremost one of Kuru's race was saying so unto Yudhishthira, a loud sound of wailing arose from all the warriors there present. Beholding his royal father of great splendour, emaciated and pale, reduced to a state unbecoming of him, worn out with fasts, and looking like a skeleton covered with skin, Dharma's son Yudhishthira shed tears of grief and once more said these words, "O foremost of men, I do not desire life and the Earth. O scorcher of foes, I shall employ myself in doing what is agreeable to thee. If I deserve thy favour, if I am dear to thee, do thou eat something. I shall then know what to do." Endued with great energy, Dhritarashtra then said to Yudhishthira,—"I wish, O son, to take some food, with thy permission." When Dhritarashtra said these words to Yudhishthira, Satyavati's son Vyasa came there and said as follows."'

---

[860] Formerly kings and noblemen wore jewels and medicinal herbs on their arms. The last were enclosed in drum-like capsules of gold, hermetically closed on both sides. It was believed that jewels and medicinal herbs are a great protection against many evils.

SECTION IV.

"'Vyasa said, "O mighty-armed Yudhishthira, do without any scruple what Dhritarashtra of Kuru's race has said. This king is old. He has, again, been made sonless. I think he will not be able to bear his grief long. The highly blessed Gandhari, possessed of great wisdom and endued with kindly speech, bears with fortitude her excessive grief owing to the loss of her sons. I also tell thee (what the old king says). Do thou obey my words. Let the old king have thy permission. Let him not die an inglorious death at home. Let this king follow the path of all royal sages of old. Verily, for all royal sages, retirement into the woods comes at last.'"

"Vaisampayana said, 'Thus addressed at that time by Vyasa of wonderful deeds, king Yudhishthira the just, possessed of mighty energy, said unto the great ascetic these words, "Thy holy self is held by us in great reverence. Thou alone art our preceptor. Thou alone art the refuge of this our kingdom as also of our race. I am thy son. Thou, O holy one, art my father. Thou art our king, and thou art our preceptor. The son should, agreeably to every duty, be obedient to the commands of his sire."'"

"Vaisampayana continued, 'Thus addressed by the king, Vyasa, that foremost of poets, foremost of all persons conversant with the Vedas, endued with great energy once more said unto Yudhishthira these words, "It is even so, O mighty-armed one. It is even as thou sayest, O Bharata. This king has reached old age. He is now in the last stage of life. Permitted both by me and thee, let this lord of Earth do what he proposes. Do not stand as an impediment in his way. Even this is the highest duty, O Yudhishthira, of royal sages. They should die either in battle or in the woods agreeably to the scriptures. Thy royal sire, Pandu, O king of kings, reverenced this old king as a disciple reverences his preceptor. (At that time) he adored the gods in many great sacrifices with profuse gifts consisting of hills of wealth and jewels, and ruled the Earth and protected his subjects wisely and well. Having obtained a large progeny and a swelling kingdom, he enjoyed great influence for thirteen years while you were in exile, and gave away much wealth. Thyself also, O chief of men, with thy servants, O sinless one, hast adored this king and the famous Gandhari with that ready obedience which a disciple pays to his preceptor. Do thou grant permission to thy father. The time has come for him to attend to the practice of penances. He does not harbour, O Yudhishthira, even the slightest anger against any of you."'"

"Vaisampayana continued, 'Having said these words, Vyasa soothed the old king. Yudhishthira then answered him, saying, "So be it." The great ascetic then left the palace for proceeding to the woods. After the holy Vyasa had gone away, the royal son of Pandu softly said these words unto his old father, bending himself in humility,—"What the holy Vyasa has said, what is thy own purpose, what the great bowman Kripa has said, what Vidura has expressed, and what has been asked for by Yuyutsu and Sanjaya, I shall accomplish with speed. All these are worthy of my respect, for all of them are well-wishers of our race. This, however, O king, I beg of thee by bending my head. Do thou first eat and afterwards go to thy forest retreat."'"

SECTION V.

"Vaisampayana said, 'Having received the king's permission, king Dhritarashtra of great energy then proceeded to his own palace, followed by Gandhari. With weakened strength and slow motion, that king of great intelligence walked with difficulty, like the leader, worn out with age, of an elephantine herd. He was followed by Vidura of great learning, and his charioteer Sanjaya, as also that mighty bowman Kripa, the son of Saradwata. Entering his mansion, O king, he went through the morning rites and after gratifying many foremost of Brahmanas he took some food. Gandhari conversant with every duty, as also Kunti of great intelligence, worshipped with offers of various articles by their daughters-in-law, then took some food, O Bharata. After Dhritarashtra had eaten, and Vidura also and others had done the same, the Pandavas, having finished their meals, approached and sat around the old king. Then the son of Amvika, O monarch, addressing Kunti's son who was seated near him and touching his back with his hand, said, "Thou shouldst always, O delighter of the Kurus, act without heedlessness as regards everything connected with thy kingdom consisting of eight limbs, O foremost of rulers, and in which the claims of righteousness should ever be kept foremost.[861] Thou art possessed, O son of Kunti, of intelligence and learning. Listen to me, O king, as I tell thee what the means are by which, O son of Pandu, the kingdom is capable of being righteously protected. Thou shouldst always, O Yudhishthira, honour those persons that are old in learning. Thou shouldst listen to what they would say, and act accordingly without any scruple. Rising at dawn, O king, worship them with due rites, and when the time comes for action, thou shouldst consult them about thy (intended) acts. When, led by the desire of knowing what would be beneficial to thee in respect of thy measures, thou honourest them, they will, O son, always declare what is for thy good, O Bharata. Thou shouldst always keep thy senses, as thou keepest thy horses. They will then prove beneficial to thee, like wealth that is not wasted. Thou shouldst employ only such ministers as have passed the tests of honesty, (i.e., as are possessed of loyalty, disinterestedness, continence, and courage), as are hereditary officers of state, possessed of pure conduct, self-restrained, clever in the discharge of business, and endued with righteous conduct. Thou shouldst always collect information through spies in diverse disguises, whose faithfulness have been tested, who are natives of thy kingdom, and who should not be known to thy foes. Thy citadel should be properly protected with strong walls and arched gates. On every side the walls, with watch-towers on them standing close to one another, should be such as to admit of six persons walking side by side on their top.[862] The gates should all be large and sufficiently strong. Kept in proper places those gates should be carefully guarded. Let thy purposes be accomplished through men whose families and conduct are well known. Thou shouldst always protect thy person also with care, in matters connected with thy food, O Bharata, as also in the hours of sport and eating and in matters connected with the garlands thou wearest and the beds thou liest upon. The ladies of thy household should be properly protected, looked over by aged and trusted servitors, of good behaviour, well-born, and possessed of learning, O Yudhishthira. Thou shouldst make ministers of Brahmanas possessed of learning, endued with humility, well-born, conversant with religion and

---

[861] The eight limbs of a kingdom are the law, the judge, the assessors, the scribe, the astrologer, gold, fire, and water.

[862] Atta is explained by Nilakantha as the space kept for the soldiers to tread upon.

wealth, and adorned with simplicity of behaviour. Thou shouldst hold consultations with them. Thou shouldst not, however, admit many persons into thy consultations. On particular occasions thou mayst consult with the whole of thy council or with a portion of it. Entering a chamber or spot that is well protected (from intruders) thou shouldst hold thy consultation. Thou mayst hold thy consultation in a forest that is divested of grass. Thou shouldst never consult at night time.[863] Apes and birds and other animals that can imitate human beings should all be excluded from the council chamber, as also idiots and lame and palsied individuals. I think that the evils that flow from the divulgence of the counsels of kings are such that they cannot be remedied. Thou shouldst repeatedly refer, in the midst of thy counsellors, to the evils that arise from the divulgence of counsels, O chastiser of foes, and to the merits that flow from counsels properly kept. Thou shouldst, O Yudhishthira, act in such a manner as to ascertain the merits and faults of the inhabitants of thy city and the provinces. Let thy laws, O king, be always administered by trusted judges placed in charge thereof, who should also be contented and of good behaviour. Their acts should also be ascertained by thee through spies. Let thy judicial officers, O Yudhishthira, inflict punishments, according to the law, on offenders after careful ascertainment of the gravity of the offences. They that are disposed to take bribes, they that are the violators of the chastity of other people's wives, they that inflict heavy punishments, they that are utterers of false speeches, they that are revilers, they that are stained by cupidity, they that are murderers, they that are doers of rash deeds, they that are disturbers of assemblies and the sports of others, and they that bring about a confusion of castes, should, agreeably to considerations of time and place, be punished with either fines or death.[864] In the morning thou shouldst see those that are employed in making thy disbursements. After that thou shouldst look to thy toilet and then to thy food. Thou shouldst next supervise thy forces, gladdening them on every occasion. Thy evenings should be set apart for envoys and spies. The latter end of the night should be devoted by thee to settle what acts should be done by thee in the day. Mid-nights and mid-days should be devoted to thy amusements and sports. At all times, however thou shouldst think of the means for accomplishing thy purposes. At the proper time, adorning thy person, thou shouldst sit prepared to make gifts in profusion. The turns for different acts, O son, ceaselessly revolve like wheels. Thou shouldst always exert thyself to fill thy treasuries of various kinds by lawful means. Thou shouldst avoid all unlawful means towards that end. Ascertaining through thy spies who thy foes are that are bent on finding out thy laches, thou shouldst, through trusted agents, cause them to be destroyed from a distance. Examining their conduct, thou shouldst O perpetuator of Kuru's race, appoint thy servants. Thou shouldst cause all thy acts to be accomplished through thy servitors: whether they are appointed for those acts or not. The commandant of thy forces should be of firm conduct, courageous, capable of bearing hardships, loyal, and devoted to thy good. Artisans and mechanics, O son of Pandu, dwelling in thy provinces, should always do thy acts like kine and asses.[865] Thou shouldst always, O Yudhishthira, be careful to ascertain thy own laches as also those of thy foes. The laches also of thy own men as also

---

[863] Grass may conceal the spies of foes. The darkness of night also may do the same.

[864] Adanaruchi is a very civil way of indicating corrupt officials and thieves. Inflictors of severe punishments were looked upon as tyrants deserving of being put down. Heavy fines were at one time interdicted in England. Sahasapriya is a doer of rash deeds, such as culpable homicide not amounting to murder, to adopt the terminology of the Indian Penal Code.

[865] i.e., content to work on receiving their food only. Their wages should not be higher that what is needed to feed them.

of the men of thy foes should equally be ascertained. Those men of thy kingdom, that are well skilled in their respective vocations, and are devoted to thy good, should be favoured by thee with adequate means of support. A wise king, O ruler of men, should always see that the accomplishments of his accomplished subjects might be kept up. They would then be firmly devoted to thee, seeing that they did not fall away from their skill.""

SECTION VI.

"'Dhritarashtra said, "Thou shouldst always ascertain the Mandalas that belong to thee, to thy foes, to neutrals, and to those that are disposed equally towards thee and thy foes, O Bharata.[866] The Mandalas also of the four kinds of foes, of these called Atatayins, and of allies, and the allies of foes, should be distinguished by thee, O crusher of foes.[867] The ministers of state, the people of the provinces, the garrisons of forts, and the forces, O foremost one of Kuru's race, may or may not be tampered with. (Thou shouldst, therefore, behave in such a manner that these may not be tampered with by thy foes). The twelve (enumerated above), O son of Kunti, constitute the principal concerns of kings. These twelve, as also sixty, having Ministers for their foremost, should be looked after by the king.[868] Professors conversant with the science of politics call these by the name of Mandala. Understand, O Yudhishthira, that the six incidents (of peace, war, march, halt, sowing dissensions, and conciliation) depend upon these. Growth and diminution should also be understood, as also the condition of being stationary. The attributes of the sixfold incidents, O thou of mighty arms, as resting on the two and seventy (already enumerated), should also be carefully understood. When one's own side has become strong and the side of the foe has become weak, it is then, O son of Kunti, that the king should war against the foe and strive to win victory. When the enemy is strong and one's own side is weak, then the weak king, if possessed of intelligence, should seek to make peace with the enemy. The king should collect a large store of articles (for his commissariat). When able to march out, he should on no account make a delay, O Bharata. Besides, he should on that occasion set his men to offices for which they are fit, without being moved by any other consideration. (When obliged to yield a portion of his territories) he should give his foe only such land as does not produce crops in abundance. (When obliged to give wealth), he should give gold containing much base metal. (When obliged to give a portion of his forces), he should give such men as are not noted for strength. One that is skilled in treaties should, when taking land or gold or men from the foe, take what is possessed of attributes the reverse of this.[869] In making treaties of peace, the son of the (defeated) king, should be demanded as a hostage, O chief of the Bharatas. A contrary course of conduct would not be beneficial, O son. If a calamity comes over

---

[866] The word Mandala has been explained below in verse 5. The distinction between Udasinas and Madhyasthas, as explained by Nilakantha, is that the former are neutrals, while the latter are those who cherish equal sentiments towards both the parties.

[867] The four kinds of foes, as explained by the commentator, are (1) foes proper, (2) allies of foes, (3) those that wish victory to both sides, and (4) those that wish defeat to both sides. As regards Atatayins, they are six, viz., (1) he that sets fire to one's house, (2) he that mixes poison with one's food, (3) he that advances, weapon in hand, with hostile intent, (4) he that robs one of one's wealth, (5) he that invades one's fields, and (6) he that steals one's wife.

[868] The sixty are thus made up. Eight consisting of agriculture and the rest; twenty-eight consisting of forces and the rest; fourteen consisting of atheists and the rest and eighteen consisting of counsels and the rest.

[869] i.e., land that is fertile, gold that is pure, and men that are strong.

the king, he should, with knowledge of means and counsels, strive to emancipate himself from it.[870] The king, O foremost of monarchs, should maintain the cheerless and the destitute (such as the blind, the deaf and dumb, and the diseased) among his people. Himself protecting his own kingdom, the king, possessed of great might, should direct all his efforts, either one after another or simultaneously, against his foes. He should afflict and obstruct them and seek to drain their treasury. The king that desires his own growth should never injure the subordinate chieftains that are under his sway. O son of Kunti, thou shouldst never seek to war with that king who desires to conquer the whole Earth. Thou shouldst seek to gain advantages by producing, with the aid of thy ministers, dissensions among his aristocracy and subordinate chieftains. A powerful king should never seek to exterminate weak kings, for these do good to the world by cherishing the good and punishing the wicked. O foremost of kings, thou shouldst live, adopting the behaviour of the cane.[871] If a strong king advances against a weak one, the latter should make him desist, by adopting conciliation and other modes. If unable to stop the invader in this way, then he, as also those that are disposed to do him good, should fall upon the foe for battling with him. Indeed, with his ministers and treasury and citizens, he should thus adopt force against the invader. If battling with the foe becomes hopeless, then he should fall, sacrificing his resources one after another. Casting off his life in this way, he will attain to liberation from all sorrow."'"

SECTION VII.

"'Dhritarashtra said, "O best of kings, thou shouldst also reflect properly on war and peace. Each is of two kinds. The means are various, and the circumstances also, under which war or peace may be made, are various, O Yudhishthira.[872] O thou of Kuru's race, thou shouldst, with coolness, reflect on the two (viz., thy strength and weakness) with regard to thyself. Thou shouldst not suddenly march against a foe that is possessed of contented and healthy soldiers, and that is endued with intelligence. On the other hand, thou shouldst think carefully of the means of vanquishing him.[873] Thou shouldst march against a foe that is not provided with contented and healthy combatants. When everything is favourable, the foe may be beaten. After that, however, the victor should retire (and stay in a strong position). He should next cause the foe to be plunged into various calamities, and sow dissensions among his allies. He should afflict the foe and inspire terror in his heart, and attacking him weaken his forces. The king, conversant with the scriptures that marches against a foe, should think of the three kinds of strength, and, indeed, reflect on his own strength and of his foe.[874] Only that king, O Bharata, who is endued with alacrity, discipline, and strength of counsels, should march against a foe.

---

[870] The wards Kasyanchidapadi should be construed with what follows.

[871] The cane yields when pressure is directed towards it. In the Santi Parva occurs the detailed conversation between the Ocean and the Rivers. The former enquired why, when the Rivers washed down the largest trees, they could not wash into the Ocean a single cane. The answer was that the cane was yielding; the trees were not so.

[872] War and peace are each of two kinds, i.e., war with a strong foe and that with a weak foe: peace with a strong foe and that with a weak foe. The Bengal texts wrongly read dividhopayam or vividhopayam.

[873] I expand this verse a little, following the commentator.

[874] Strength is of three kinds, as explained in the next verse.

When his position is otherwise, he should avoid defensive operations.[875] The king should provide himself with power of wealth, power of allies, power of foresters, power of paid soldiery, and power of the mechanical and trading classes, O puissant one.[876] Among all these, power of allies and power of wealth are superior to the rest. The power of classes and that of the standing army are equal. The power of spies is regarded by the king as equal in efficacy to either of the above, on many occasions, when the time comes for applying each. Calamity, O king, as it overtakes rulers should be regarded as of many forms. Listen, O thou of Kuru's race, as to what those diverge forms are. Verily of various kinds are calamities, O son of Pandu. Thou shouldst always count them, distinguishing their forms, O king, and strive to meet them by applying the well-known ways of conciliation and the rest (without concealing them through idleness). The king should, when equipt with a good force, march (out against a foe), O scorcher of enemies. He should attend also to the considerations of time and place, while preparing to march, as also to the forces he has collected and his own merits (in other respects). That king who is attentive to his own growth and advancement should not march unless equipt with cheerful and healthy warriors. When strong, O son of Pandu, he may march in even an unfavourable season. The king should make a river having quivers for its stones, steeds and cars for its current, and standards for the trees that cover its banks, and which is miry with foot-soldiers and elephants. Even such a river should the king apply for the destruction of his foe. Agreeably to the science known to Usanas, arrays called Sakata, Padma, and Vijra, should be formed, O Bharata, for fighting the enemy.[877] Knowing everything about the enemy's strength through spies, and examining his own strength himself the king should commence war either within his own territories or within those of his foe.[878] The king should always gratify his army, and hurl all his strongest warriors (against the enemy). First ascertaining the state of his kingdom, he should apply conciliation or the other well-known means. By all means, O king, should the body be protected. One should do that which is highly beneficial for one both here and hereafter. The king, O monarch, by behaving duly according to these ways, attains to Heaven hereafter, after ruling his subjects righteously in this world. O foremost one of Kuru's race, it is even thus that thou shouldst always seek the good of thy subjects for attaining to both the worlds.[879] Thou hast been instructed in all duties by Bhishma, by Krishna, and by Vidura, I should also, O best of kings, from the affection I bear thee, give thee these instructions. O giver of profuse presents in sacrifices, thou shouldst do all this duly. Thou shalt, by conducting thyself in this way, become dear to thy subjects and attain to felicity

---

[875] Utsaha is readiness or alacrity, of the forces to attack the foe: prabhusakti is the complete mastery of the king over his forces, i.e., through discipline. By strength of counsels, in this connection, is meant well-formed plans of attack and defence.

[876] Maulam is explained as the strength of money. In modern warfare also, money is called 'the sinews of war'. Atavivala or the force consisting of foresters, was, perhaps, the body of Irregulars that supported a regular army of combatants. Bhritavala implies the regular army, drawing pay from the state at all times. In India, standing armies have existed from remote times. Sreni-vala is, perhaps, the forces of artisans, mechanics, and engineers, who looked after the roads and the transport, as also of traders who supplied the army with provision.

[877] A sakata array was an array after the form of a car. It is described in Sukraniti fully, and occurs in the Drona Parva, ante. The Padma is a circular array with angular projections. It is the same with what is now called the starry array, many modern forts being constructed on this plan. The Vajra is a wedge-like array. It penetrates into the enemy's divisions like a wedge and goes out, routing the foe. It is otherwise called suchivyuha.

[878] i.e., meet the foe whether within his own kingdom or invade the foe's realm and thus oblige the foe to fall back for resisting him there.

[879] i.e., for obtaining fame here and felicity hereafter.

in Heaven. That king who adores the deities in a hundred horse-sacrifices, and he who rules his subjects righteously, acquire merit that is equal."'"

SECTION VIII.

"'Yudhishthira said, "O lord of Earth, I shall do as thou biddest me. O foremost of kings, I should be further instructed by thee. Bhishma has ascended to Heaven. The slayer of Madhu has departed (for Dwaraka). Vidura and Sanjaya also will accompany thee to the forest. Who else, therefore, than thee will teach me? Those instructions which thou imparted today, desirous of doing good to me, I shall certainly follow, O lord of Earth. Be thou assured of this, O king."'

"Vaisampayana continued, 'Thus addressed by king Yudhishthira the just, of great intelligence, the royal sage, Dhritarashtra, O chief of the Bharatas, wished to obtain the king's permission (about his retirement to the forest). And he said, "Cease, O son, great has been my toil." Having said these words, the old king entered the apartments of Gandhari. Unto that husband of hers who resembled a second Lord of all creatures, while resting on a seat, Gandhari of righteous conduct, conversant with the opportuneness of everything, said these words, the hour being suited to them,—"Thou hast obtained the permission of that great Rishi, viz., Vyasa himself. When, however, wilt thou go to the forest, with the permission of Yudhishthira?"

"'Dhritarashtra said, "O Gandhari, I have received the permission of my high-souled sire. With the permission of Yudhishthira (next obtained), I shall soon retire into the woods. I desire, however, to give away some wealth capable of following the status of Preta, in respect of all those sons of mine who were addicted to calamitous dice. Verily, I desire to make those gifts, inviting all the people to my mansion."'[880]

"Vaisampayana continued, 'Having said so (to Gandhari), Dhritarashtra sent for Yudhishthira. The latter, at his uncle's command, brought all the articles necessary. Many Brahmanas residing in Kuru-jangala, and many Kshatriyas, many Vaisyas, and many Sudras also, came to Dhritarashtra's mansion, with gratified hearts. The old king, coming out of the inner apartments, beheld them all, as also his subjects assembled together. Beholding all those assembled citizens and inhabitants of the provinces, and his well-wishers also thus gathered together, and the large number of Brahmanas arrived from diverge realms, king Dhritarashtra of great intelligence, O monarch, said these words,— "Ye all and the Kurus have lived together for many long years, well-wishers of each other, and each employed in doing good to the other. What I shall now say in view of the opportunity that has come, should be accomplished by you all even as disciples accomplish the biddings of their preceptors. I have set my heart upon retiring into the woods, along with Gandhari as my companion. Vyasa has approved of this, as also the son of Kunti. Let me have your permission too. Do not hesitate in this. That goodwill, which has always existed between you and us, is not to be seen, I believe, in other realms between the rulers and the ruled. I am worn out with this load of years on my head. I am destitute of children. Ye sinless ones, I am emaciated with fasts, along with Gandhari. The kingdom having passed to Yudhishthira, I have enjoyed great happiness. Ye foremost of men, I think that happiness has been greater than what I could expect from

[880] Those who die become at first what is called Preta. They remain so for one year, till the Sapindikarana Sraddha is performed. They then become united with the Pitris. The gifts made in the first Sraddha as also in the monthly ones, have the virtue of rescuing the Preta or bringing him an accession of merit. The gifts in annual Sraddhas also have the same efficacy.

Duryodhana's sovereignty. What other refuge can I have, old as I am and destitute of children, save the woods? Ye highly blessed ones, it behoves you to grant me the permission I seek." Hearing these words of his, all these residents of Kurujangala, uttered loud lamentations, O best of the Bharatas, with voices choked with tears. Desirous of telling those grief-stricken people something more, Dhritarashtra of great energy, once more addressed them and said as follows.'"

SECTION IX.

"'Dhritarashtra said, "Santanu duly ruled this Earth. Similarly, Vichitraviryya also, protected by Bhishma, ruled you. Without doubt, all this is known to you. It is also known to you how Pandu, my brother, was dear to me as also to you. He also ruled you duly. Ye sinless ones, I have also served you. Whether those services have come up to the mark or fallen short of it, it behoveth you to forgive me, for I have attended to my duties without heedlessness. Duryodhana also enjoyed this kingdom without a thorn in his side. Foolish as he was and endued with wicked understanding, he did not, however, do any wrong to you. Through the fault, however, of that prince of wicked understanding, and through his pride, as also through my own impolicy, a great carnage has taken place of persons of the royal order. Whether I have, in that matter, acted rightly or wrongly, I pray you with joined hands to dispel all remembrance of it from your hearts.—This one is old; this one has lost all his children; this one is afflicted with grief; this one was our king;— this one is a descendant of former kings;—considerations like these should induce you to forgive me. This Gandhari also is cheerless and old. She too has lost her children and is helpless. Afflicted with grief for the loss of her sons, she solicits you with me. Knowing that both of us are old and afflicted and destitute of children, grant us the permission we seek. Blessed be you, we seek your protection. This Kuru king, Yudhishthira, the son of Kunti, should be looked after by you all, in prosperity as well as in adversity. He will never fall into distress, he that has for his counsellors four such brothers of abundant prowess. All of them are conversant with both righteousness and wealth, and resemble the very guardians of the world. Like the illustrious Brahman himself, the Lord of the universe of creatures, this Yudhishthira of mighty energy will rule you. That which should certainly be said is now said by me. I make over to you it this Yudhishthira here as a deposit. I make you also a deposit in the hands of this hero. It behoves you all to forget and forgive whatever injury has been done to you by those sons of mine that are no longer alive, or, indeed, by any one else belonging to me. Ye never harboured any wrath against me on any previous occasion. I join my hands before you who are distinguished for loyalty. Here, I bow to you all. Ye sinless ones, I, with Gandhari by my side, solicit your pardon now for anything done to you by those sons of mine, of restless understandings, stained by cupidity, and ever acting as their desires prompted." Thus addressed by the old monarch, all those citizens and inhabitants of the provinces, filled with tears, said nothing but only looked at one another.'"

SECTION X.

"Vaisampayana said, 'Thus addressed, O thou of Kuru's race, by the old king, the citizens and the inhabitants of the provinces stood sometime like men deprived of consciousness. King Dhritarashtra, finding them silent, with their throats choked by grief, once more addressed them, saying, "Ye best of men, old as I am, sonless, and indulging, through cheerlessness of heart, in diverse lamentations along with this my wedded wife, I have obtained the permission, in the matter of my retirement into the forest, of my sire, the Island-born Krishna himself, as also of king Yudhishthira, who is conversant with every duty, ye righteous denizens of this kingdom. Ye sinless ones, I, with Gandhari, repeatedly solicit you with bent heads. It behoves you all to grant us permission."

"Vaisampayana continued, 'Hearing these pitiable words of the Kuru king, O monarch, the assembled denizens of Kurujangala all began to weep. Covering their faces with their hands and upper garments, all those men burning with grief, wept for a while as fathers and mothers would weep (at the prospect of a dear son about to leave them for ever). Bearing in their hearts, from which every other thought had been dispelled, the sorrow born of Dhritarashtra's desire to leave the world, they looked like men deprived of all consciousness. Checking that agitation of heart due to the announcement of Dhritarashtra's desire of going to the forest, they gradually were able to address one another, expressing their wishes. Settling their words in brief, O king, they charged a certain Brahmana with the task of replying unto the old monarch. That learned Brahmana, of good behaviour, chosen by unanimous consent, conversant with all topics, master of all the Richs, and named Samba, endeavoured to speak. Taking the permission of the whole assembly and with its full approbation, that learned Brahmana of great intelligence, conscious of his own abilities, said these words unto the king,—"O monarch, the answer of this assembly has been committed to my care. I shall voice it, O hero. Do thou receive it, O king. What thou sayest, O king of kings, is all true, O puissant one. There is nothing in it that is even slightly untrue. Thou art our well-wisher, as, indeed, we are thine. Verily, in this race of kings, there never was a king who coming to rule his subjects became unpopular with them. Ye have ruled us like fathers or brothers. King Duryodhana never did us any wrong. Do that, O king, which that righteous-souled ascetic, the son of Satyavati, has said. He is, verily, our foremost of instructors. Left by thee, O monarch, we shall have to pass our days in grief and sorrow, filled with remembrance of thy hundreds of virtues. We were well protected and ruled by king Duryodhana even as we had been ruled by king Santanu, or by Chitrangada, or by thy father, O monarch, who was protected by the prowess of Bhishma, or by Pandu, that ruler of Earth, who was overlooked by thee in all his acts. Thy son, O monarch, never did us the slightest wrong. We lived, relying on that king as trustfully as on our own father. It is known to thee how we lived (under that ruler). After the same manner, we have enjoyed great happiness, O monarch, for thousands of years, under the rule of Kunti's son of great intelligence and wisdom.[881] This righteous-souled king who performs sacrifices with gifts in profusion, follows the conduct of the royal sages of old, belonging to thy race, of meritorious deeds, having Kuru and Samvara and others and Bharata of great intelligence among them. There is nothing, O monarch, that is even slightly censurable in the matter of this Yudhishthira's rule. Protected and ruled by thee, we have all lived in great happiness. The slightest demerit is incapable of being alleged against thee and thy son. Regarding what thou hast said about Duryodhana in the matter of this carnage of kinsmen, I beg thee, O delighter of the Kurus (to listen to me)."

"'The Brahmana continued, "The destruction that has overtaken the Kurus was not brought about by Duryodhana. It was not brought about by thee. Nor was it brought about by Karna and Suvala's son. We know that it was brought about by destiny, and that it was

---

[881] The text in verse 2, where mention is made of thousands of years as embracing the rule of Yudhishthira, is evidently vitiated.

incapable of being counteracted. Verily, destiny is not capable of being resisted by human exertion. Eight and ten Akshauhinis of troops, O monarch, were brought together. In eight and ten days that host was destroyed by the foremost of Kuru warriors, viz., Bhishma and Drona and Kripa and others, and the high-souled Karna, and the heroic Yuyudhana, and Dhrishtadyumna, and by the four sons of Pandu, that is, Bhima and Arjuna and twins. This (tremendous) carnage, O king, could not happen without the influence of destiny. Without doubt, by Kshatriyas in particular, should foes be slain and death encountered in battle. By those foremost of men, endued with science and might of arms, the Earth has been exterminated with her steeds and cars and elephants. Thy son was not the cause of that carnage of high-souled kings. Thou wert not the cause, nor thy servants, nor Karna, nor Suvala's son. The destruction of those foremost ones of Kuru's race and of kings by thousands, know, was brought about by destiny. Who can say anything else in this? Thou art regarded as the Guru and the master of the whole world. We, therefore, in thy presence, absolve thy righteous-souled son. Let that king, with all his associates, obtain the regions reserved for heroes. Permitted by foremost of Brahmanas, let him sport blissfully in heaven. Thou also shalt attain to great merit, and unswerving steadiness in virtue. O thou of excellent vows, follow thou fully the duties indicated in the Vedas. It is not necessary for either thee or ourselves to look after the Pandavas. They are capable of ruling the very Heavens, what need then be said of the Earth? O thou of great intelligence, in prosperity as in adversity, the subjects of this kingdom, O foremost one of Kuru's race, will be obedient to the Pandavas who have conduct for their ornament. The son of Pandu makes those valuable gifts which are always to be made to foremost of regenerate persons in sacrifices and in obsequial rites, after the manner of all the great kings of antiquity. The high-minded son of Kunti is mild, and self-restrained, and is always disposed to spend as if he were a second Vaisravana. He has great ministers that attend on him. He is compassionate to even his foes. Indeed, that foremost one of Bharata's race is of pure conduct. Endued with great intelligence, he is perfectly straight-forward in his dealings and rules and protects us like a father protecting his children. From association with him who is the son of Dharma, O royal sage, Bhima and Arjuna and others will never do us the least wrong. They are mild, O thou of Kuru's race, unto them that are mild, and fierce like snakes of virulent poison unto them that are fierce. Possessed of great energy, those high-souled ones are always devoted to the good of the people. Neither Kunti, nor thy (daughter-in-law) Panchali, nor Ulupi, nor the princess of the Sattwata race, will do the least wrong to these people.[882] The affection which thou hast shown towards us and which in Yudhishthira is seen to exist in a still larger measure is incapable of being forgotten by the people of the city and the provinces. Those mighty car-warriors, viz., the sons of Kunti, themselves devoted to the duties of the righteousness, will protect and cherish the people even if these happen to be unrighteous. Do thou, therefore, O king, dispelling all anxiety of heart on account of Yudhishthira, set thyself to the accomplishment of all meritorious acts, O foremost of men.'"

"Vaisampayana continued, 'Hearing these words, fraught with righteousness and merit, of that Brahmana and approving of them, every person in that assembly said, "Excellent, Excellent" and accepted them as his own. Dhritarashtra also, repeatedly applauding those words, slowly dismissed that assembly of his subjects. Thus honoured by them and looked upon with auspicious glances, the old king, O chief of Bharata's race,

---

[882] The correct reading is jane and not kshane.

joined his hands and honoured them all in return. He then entered his own mansion with Gandhari. Listen now to what he did after that night had passed away.'"

SECTION XI.

"Vaisampayana said, 'After that night had passed away, Dhritarashtra, the son of Amvika, despatched Vidura to Yudhishthira's mansion. Endued with great energy and the foremost of all persons possessed of intelligence, Vidura, having arrived at Yudhishthira's mansion, addressed that foremost of men, that king of unfading glory, in these words, "King Dhritarashtra has undergone the preliminary rites for accomplishing his purpose of retiring into the woods. He will set out for the woods, O king, on the coming day of full moon of the month of Kartika. He now solicits from thee, O foremost one of Kuru's race, some wealth. He wishes to perform the Sraddha of the high-souled son of Ganga, as also of Drona and Somadatta and Valhika of great intelligence, and of all his sons as also of all well-wishers of his that have been slain, and, if thou permittest it, of that wicked-souled wight, viz., the ruler of the Sindhus."[883] Hearing these words of Vidura, both Yudhishthira, and Pandu's son Arjuna of curly hair, became very glad and applauded them highly. Bhima, however, of great energy and unappeasable wrath, did not accept those words of Vidura in good spirits, recollecting the acts of Duryodhana. The diadem-decked Phalguna, understanding the thoughts of Bhimasena, slightly bending his face downwards, addressed that foremost of men in these words, "O Bhima, our royal father who is advancing in years, has resolved to retire into the woods. He wishes to make gifts for advancing the happiness of his slain kinsmen and well-wishers now in the other world. O thou of Kuru's race, he wishes to give away wealth that belongs to thee by conquest. Indeed, O mighty-armed one, it is for Bhishma and others that the old king is desirous of making those gifts. It behoves thee to grant thy permission. By good luck it is, O thou of mighty arms that Dhritarashtra today begs wealth of us, he who was formerly begged by us. Behold the reverse brought about by Time. That king who was before the lord and protector of the whole Earth, now desires to go into the woods, his kinsmen and associates all slain by foes. O chief of men, let not thy views deviate from granting the permission asked for. O mighty-armed one, refusal, besides bringing infamy, will be productive of demerit. Do thou learn your duty in this matter from the king, thy eldest brother, who is lord of all. It becometh thee to give instead of refusing, O chief of Bharata's race." Vibhatsu who was saying so was applauded by king Yudhishthira the just. Yielding to wrath, Bhimasena said these words, "O Phalguna, it is we that shall make gifts in the matter of Bhishma's obsequies, as also of king Somadatta and of Bhurisravas, of the royal sage Valhika, and of the high-souled Drona, and of all others. Our mother Kunti shall make such obsequial offerings for Karna. O foremost of men, let not Dhritarashtra perform those Sraddhas. Even this is what I think. Let not our foes be gladdened. Let Duryodhana and others sink from a miserable to a more miserable position. Alas, it was those wretches of their race that caused the whole Earth to be exterminated. How hast thou been able to forget that anxiety of twelve long years, and our residence in deep incognito that was so painful to Draupadi? Where was

---

[883] It is difficult to imagine why the ruler of the Sindhus, Jayadratha, only should be regarded as a wrong-doer to the Pandavas. In the matter of the slaying of Abhimanyu he played a very minor part, by only guarding the entrance of the array against the Pandava warriors. It is true he had attempted to abduct Draupadi from the forest retreat of the Pandavas, but even in this, the wrong was not so great as that which Duryodhana and others inflicted on the Pandavas by dragging Draupadi to the court of the Kurus.

Dhritarashtra's affection for us then? Clad in a black deer-skin and divested of all thy ornaments, with the princess of Panchala in thy company, didst thou not follow this king? Where were Bhishma and Drona then, and where was Somadatta? Thou hadst to live for thirteen years in the woods, supporting thyself on the products of the wilderness. Thy eldest father did not then look at thee with eyes of parental affection. Hast thou forgotten, O Partha, that it was this wretch of our race, of wicked understanding, that enquired of Vidura, when the match at dice was going on,—'What has been won?'" Hearing thus far, king Yudhishthira, the son of Kunti, endued with great intelligence, rebuked him and told him to be silent.'"

<h2 style="text-align:center">SECTION XII.</h2>

'"Arjuna said, "O Bhima, thou art my elder brother and, therefore, my senior and preceptor. I dare not say anything more than what I have already said. The royal sage Dhritarashtra deserves to be honoured by us in every respect. They that are good, they that are distinguished above the common level, they that break not the distinctions which characterise the good, remember not the wrongs done to them but only the benefits they have received." Hearing these words of the high-souled Phalguna, the righteous-souled Yudhishthira, the son of Kunti, addressed Vidura and said these words, "Instructed by me, O Kshattri, do thou say unto the Kuru king that I shall give him as much wealth from my treasury as he wishes to give away for the obsequies of his sons, and of Bhishma and others among his well-wishers and benefactors. Let not Bhima be cheerless at this!"'

"Vaisampayana continued, 'Having said these words, king Yudhishthira the just, highly applauded Arjuna. Meanwhile Bhimasena began to cast angry glances at Dhananjaya. Then Yudhishthira, endued with great intelligence, once more addressed Vidura and said, "It behoves not king Dhritarashtra to be angry with Bhimasena. This Bhima of great intelligence was greatly afflicted by cold and rain and heat and by a thousand other griefs while residing in the woods. All this is not unknown to thee. Do thou, however, instructed by me, say unto the king, O foremost one of Bharata's race, that he may take from my house whatever articles he wishes and in whatever measure also he likes. Thou shalt also tell the king that he should not allow his heart to dwell on this exhibition of pride in which Bhima, deeply afflicted, has indulged. Whatever wealth I have and whatever Arjuna has in his house, the owner thereof is king Dhritarashtra. Even this thou shouldst tell him. Let the king make gifts unto the Brahmanas. Let him spend as largely as he likes. Let him free himself from the debt he owes to his sons and well-wishers. Let him be told besides,—O Monarch, this very body of mine is at thy disposal and all the wealth I have. Know this, and let there be no doubt in this."'"

<h2 style="text-align:center">SECTION XIII.</h2>

"Vaisampayana said, 'Thus addressed by king Yudhishthira, Vidura, that foremost of all intelligent persons, returned to Dhritarashtra and said unto him these words of grave import. "I at first reported thy message to king Yudhishthira. Reflecting on thy words, Yudhishthira of great splendour applauded them highly. Vibhatsu also, of great energy, places all his mansions, with all the wealth therein, as also his very life-breaths, at thy disposal. Thy son, king Yudhishthira, too, offers thee, O royal sage, his kingdom and life-breath and wealth and all else that belongs to him. Bhima, however, of mighty arms, recollecting all his innumerable sorrows, has with difficulty given his consent, breathing many heavy sighs. That mighty-armed hero, O monarch, was solicited by the righteous king as also by Vibhatsu, and induced to assume relations of cordiality towards thee. King Yudhishthira the just, has prayed thee not to give way to dissatisfaction for the improper conduct which Bhima has displayed at the recollection of former hostilities. This is generally the behaviour of Kshatriyas in battle, O king, and this Vrikodara is devoted to battle and the practices of Kshatriyas. 'Both myself and Arjuna, O king, repeatedly beg thee for pardoning Vrikodara. Be gracious unto us. Thou art our lord. Whatever wealth we have, thou mayst give away as thou likest, O ruler of Earth. Thou, O Bharata, art the Master of this kingdom and of all lives in it. Let the foremost one of Kuru's race give away, for the obsequial rites of his sons, all those foremost of gifts which should be given to the Brahmanas. Indeed, let him make those gifts unto persons of the regenerate order, taking away from our mansions jewels and gems, and kine, and slaves both male and female, and goats and sheep. Let gifts be made unto also those that are poor or sightless or in great distress, selecting the objects of his charity as he likes. Let, O Vidura, large pavilions be constructed, rich with food and drink of diverse tastes collected in profusion. Let reservoirs of water be constructed for enabling kine to drink, and let other works of merit be accomplished.'—Even these were the words said unto me by the king as also by Pritha's son Dhananjaya. It behoveth thee to say what should be done next." After Vidura had said these words, O Janamejaya, Dhritarashtra his satisfaction at them and set his heart upon making large presents on the day of full moon in the month of Kartika.'"

SECTION XIV.

"Vaisampayana said,—'Thus addressed by Vidura, king Dhritarashtra became highly pleased, O monarch, with the act of Yudhishthira and Jishnu. Inviting then, after proper examination, thousands of deserving Brahmanas and superior Rishis, for the sake of Bhishma, as also of his sons and friends, and causing a large quantity of food and drink to be prepared, and cars and other vehicles and clothes, and gold and jewels and gems, and slaves both male and female, and goats and sheep, and blankets and costly articles to be collected, and villages and fields, and other kinds of wealth to be kept ready, as also elephants and steeds decked with ornaments, and many beautiful maidens who were the best of their sex, that foremost of kings gave them away for the advancement of the dead, naming each of them in due order as the gifts were made. Naming Drona, and Bhishma, and Somadatta, and Valhika, and king Duryodhana, and each one of his other sons, and all his well-wishers with Jayadratha numbering first, those gifts were made in due order. With the approval of Yudhishthira, that Sraddha-sacrifice became characterised by large gifts of wealth and profuse presents of jewels and gems and other kinds of treasure. Tellers and scribes on that occasion, under the orders of Yudhishthira, ceaselessly asked the old king.—Do thou command, O monarch, what gifts should be made to these. All things are ready here.—As soon as the king spoke, they gave away what he directed.[884] Unto him that was to receive a hundred, a thousand was given, and unto him that was to

---

[884] The usual way in which gifts are made at the present day on occasions of Sraddhas and marriages or other auspicious rites very nearly resembles what is described here. Instead of dedicating each gift with mantras and water and making it over to the receiver, all the articles in a heap are dedicated with the aid of mantras. The guests are then assembled, and are called up individually. The Adhyaksha or superintendent, according to a list prepared, names the gifts to be made to the guest called up. The tellers actually make them over, the scribes noting them down.

receive a thousand was given ten thousand, at the command of the royal son of Kunti.[885] Like the clouds vivifying the crops with their downpours, that royal cloud gratified the Brahmanas by downpours of wealth. After all those gifts had been distributed, the king, O thou of great intelligence, then deluged the assembled guests of all the four orders with repeated surges of food and drink of diverse tastes. Verily, the Dhritarashtra-ocean, swelling high, with jewels and gems for its waters, rich with the villages and fields and other foremost of gifts constituting its verdant islands, heaps of diverse kinds of precious articles for its rich caves, elephants and steeds for its alligators and whirlpools, the sound of Mridangas for its deep roars, and clothes and wealth and precious stones for its waves, deluged the Earth. It was even in this way, O king, that that monarch made gifts for the advancement in the other world of his sons and grandsons and Pitris as also of himself and Gandhari. At last when he became tired with the task of making gifts in such profusion, that great Gift-sacrifice came to an end. Even thus did that king of Kuru's race perform his Gift-sacrifice. Actors and mimes continually danced and sang on the occasion and contributed to the merriment of all the guests. Food and drink of diverse tastes were given away in large quantities. Making gifts in this way for ten days, the royal son of Amvika, O chief of Bharata's race, became freed from the debts he owed to his sons and grandsons.'"

SECTION XV.

"Vaisampayana said,—'The royal son of Amvika, viz., Dhritarashtra, having settled the hour of his departure for the woods, summoned those heroes, the Pandavas. Possessed of great intelligence, the old monarch, with Gandhari, duly accosted those princes. Having caused the minor rites to be performed, by Brahmanas conversant with the Vedas, on that day which was the day of full moon in the month of Kartika, he caused the fire which he worshipped daily to be taken up. Leaving his usual robes he wore deer-skins and barks, and accompanied by his daughters-in-law, he set out of his mansion. When the royal son of Vichitraviryya thus set out, a loud wail was uttered by the Pandava and the Kaurava ladies as also by other women belonging to the Kaurava race. The king worshipped the mansion in which he had lived with fried paddy and excellent flowers of diverse kinds. He also honoured all his servants with gifts of wealth, and then leaving that abode set out on his journey. Then O son, king Yudhishthira, trembling all over, with utterance choked with tears, said these words in a loud voice, viz.,—"O righteous monarch, where dost thou go?"—and fell down in a swoon. Arjuna, burning with great grief, sighed repeatedly. That foremost of Bharata princes, telling Yudhishthira that he should not behave in that manner, stood cheerlessly and with heart plunged into distress. Vrikodara, the heroic Phalguna, the two sons of Madri, Vidura, Sanjaya, Dhritarashtra's son by his Vaisya wife, and Kripa, and Dhaumya, and other Brahmanas, all followed the old monarch, with voices choked in grief. Kunti walked ahead, bearing on her shoulders the hand of Gandhari who walked with her bandaged eyes. King Dhritarashtra walked confidently behind Gandhari, placing his hand on her shoulder.[886] Drupada's daughter Krishna, she of the Sattwata race, Uttara the daughter-in-law of the Kauravas, who had

---

[885] Each gift that was indicated by Dhritarashtra was multiplied ten times at the command of Yudhishthira.

[886] As Dhritarashtra was blind, his queen Gandhari, whose devotion to her lord was very great, had, from the days of her marriage, kept her eyes bandaged refusing to look on the world which her lord could not see.

recently become a mother, Chitrangada, and other ladies of the royal house-hold, all proceeded with the old monarch. The wail they uttered on that occasion, O king, from grief, resembled the loud lamentations of a swarm of she-ospreys. Then the wives of the citizens,—Brahmanas and Kshatriyas and Vaisyas and Sudras,—also came out into the streets from every side. At Dhritarashtra's departure, O king, all the citizens of Hastinapore became as distressed as they had been, O monarch, when they had witnessed the departure of the Pandavas in former days after their defeat at the match at dice. Ladies that had never seen the sun or the moon, came out into the streets on the occasion, in great grief, when king Dhritarashtra proceeded towards the great forest.'"

SECTION XVI.

"Vaisampayana said, 'Great was the uproar, at that time, O king, of both men and women standing on the terraces of mansions or on the Earth. Possessed of great intelligence, the old king, with joined hands, and trembling with weakness, proceeded with difficulty along the principal street which was crowded with persons of both sexes. He left the city called after the elephant by the principal gate and then repeatedly bade that crowd of people to return to their homes. Vidura had set his heart on going to the forest along with the king. The Suta Sanjaya also, the son of Gavalgani, the chief minister of Dhritarashtra, was of the same heart. King Dhritarashtra however, caused Kripa and the mighty car-warrior Yuyutsu to refrain from following him. He made them over into Yudhishthira's hands. After the citizens had ceased following the monarch, king Yudhishthira, with the ladies of his house-hold, prepared to stop, at the command of Dhritarashtra. Seeing that his mother Kunti was desirous of retiring into the woods, the king said unto her, "I shall follow the old monarch. Do thou desist. It behoveth thee, O queen, to return to the city, accompanied by these thy daughters-in-law. This monarch proceeds to the woods, firmly resolved to practise penances." Though king Yudhishthira said these words unto her, with his eyes bathed in tears, Kunti, however, without answering him, continued to proceed, catching hold of Gandhari.

"'Kunti said, "O king, never show any disregard for Sahadeva. He is very much attached to me, O monarch, and to thee also always. Thou shouldst always bear in mind Karna who never retreated from battle. Through my folly that hero has been slain in the field of battle. Surely, my son, this heart of mine is made of steel, since it does not break into a hundred pieces at not seeing that child born of Surya. When such has been the case, O chastiser of foes, what can I now do? I am very much to blame for not having proclaimed the truth about the birth of Surya's child. O crusher of foes, I hope thou wilt, with all thy brothers, make excellent gifts for the sake of that son of Surya. O mower of foes, thou shouldst always do what is agreeable to Draupadi. Thou shouldst look after Bhimasena and Arjuna and Nakula and Sahadeva. The burthens of the Kuru race have now fallen on thee, O king. I shall live in the woods with Gandhari, besmearing my body with filth, engaged in the performance of penances, and devoted to the service of my father-in-law and mother-in-law."'[887]

"Vaisampayana continued, 'Thus addressed by her, the righteous-souled Yudhishthira, with passions under complete control, became, with all his brothers,

---

[887] Nilakantha explains that as Dhritarashtra is Pandu's elder brother, therefore, Kunti regards him as Pandu's father. Queen Gandhari therefore is Kunti's mother-in-law. The eldest brother is looked upon as a father.

plunged into great distress. Endued with great intelligence, the king said not a word. Having reflected for a little while, king Yudhishthira the Just, cheerless and plunged in anxiety and sorrow, addressed his mother, saying,—"Strange, indeed, is this purpose of thine. It behoves thee not to accomplish it. I can never grant thee permission. It behoves thee to show us compassion. Formerly, when we were about to set out of Hastinapore for the woods, O thou of agreeable features, it was thou who, reciting to us the story of Vidula's instructions to her son, excited us to exertion. It behoves thee not to abandon us now. Having slain the kings of Earth, I have won sovereignty, guided by thy words of wisdom communicated through Vasudeva. Where now is that understanding of thine about which I had heard from Vasudeva? Dost thou wish now to fall away from those Kshatriya practices about which thou hadst instructed us? Abandoning ourselves, this kingdom, and this daughter-in-law of thine who is possessed of great fame, how wilt thou live in the inaccessible woods? Do thou relent!" Kunti, with tears in her eyes, heard these words of her son, but continued to proceed on her way. Then Bhima addressed her, saying,—"When, O Kunti, sovereignty has been won, and when the time has come for thee to enjoy that sovereignty thus acquired by thy children, when the duties of royalty await discharge by thee, whence has this desire got hold of thy mind? Why then didst thou cause us to exterminate the Earth? For what reason wouldst thou leave all and wish to take up thy abode in the woods? We were born in the woods. Why then didst thou bring us from the woods while we were children? Behold, the two sons of Madri are overwhelmed with sorrow and grief. Relent, O mother, O thou of great fame, do not go into the woods now. Do thou enjoy that prosperity which acquired by might, has become Yudhishthira's today." Firmly resolved to retire into the woods, Kunti disregarded these lamentations of her sons. Then Draupadi with a cheerless face, accompanied by Subhadra, followed her weeping mother-in-law who was journeying on from desire of going into the woods. Possessed of great wisdom and firmly resolved on retirement from the world, the blessed dame walked on, frequently looking at her weeping children. The Pandavas, with all their wives and servitors, continued to follow her. Restraining then her tears, she addressed her children in these words.'"

SECTION XVII.

"'Kunti said, "It is even so, O mighty-armed son of Pandu, as thou sayest. Ye kings, formerly when ye were cheerless, it was even in this way that I excited you all. Yes, seeing that your kingdom was wrested from you by a match at dice, seeing that you all fell from happiness, seeing that you were domineered over by kinsmen, I instilled courage and high thoughts into your minds. Ye foremost of men, I encouraged you in order that they that were the sons of Pandu might not be lost, in order that their fame might not be lost. You are all equal to Indra. Your prowess resembles that of the very gods. In order that you might not live, watching the faces of others, I acted in that way.[888] I instilled courage into thy heart in order that thou who art the foremost of all righteous persons, who art equal to Vasava, might not again go into the woods and live in misery. I instilled courage into your hearts in order that this Bhima who is possessed of the strength of ten thousand elephants and whose prowess and manliness are widely known, might not sink into insignificance and ruin. I instilled courage into your hearts in order that this Vijaya, who was born after Bhimasena, and who is equal unto Vasava himself

---

[888] To live watching the faces of others is to live in dependence on others.

might not be cheerless. I instilled courage into your hearts in order that Nakula and Sahadeva, who are always devoted to their seniors, might not be weakened and rendered cheerless by hunger. I acted in that way in order that this lady of well-developed proportions and of large expansive eyes might not endure the wrongs inflicted on her in the public hall without being avenged. In the very sight of you all, O Bhima, Dussasana, through folly, dragged her trembling all over like a plantain plant, during the period of her functional illness, and after she had been won at dice, as if she were a slave. All this was known to me. Indeed, the race of Pandu had been subjugated (by foes). The Kurus, viz., my father-in-law and others, were cheerless when she, desirous of a protector, uttered loud lamentations like a she-osprey. When she was dragged by her fair locks by the sinful Dussasana with little intelligence, I was deprived of my senses, O king. Know, that for enhancing your energy, I instilled that courage into your hearts by reciting the words of Vidula, O my sons. I instilled courage into your hearts, O my sons, in order that the race of Pandu, represented by my children, might not be lost. The sons and grandsons of that person who brings a race to infamy never succeed in attaining to the regions of the righteous. Verily, the ancestors of the Kaurava race were in danger of losing those regions of felicity which had become theirs. As regards myself, O my sons, I, before this, enjoyed the great fruits of that sovereignty which my husband had acquired. I made large gifts. I duly drank the Soma juice in sacrifice.[889] It was not for my own sake that I had urged Vasudeva with the stirring words of Vidula. It was for your sake that I had called upon you to follow that advice. O my sons, I do not desire the fruits of that sovereignty which has been won by my children. O thou of great puissance, I wish to attain, by my penances, to those regions of felicity which have been acquired by my husband. By rendering obedient service to my father-in-law and mother-in-law both of whom wish to take up their abode in the woods, and by penances, I desire, O Yudhishthira, to waste my body. Do thou cease to follow me, O foremost one of Kuru's race, along with Bhima and others. Let thy understanding be always devoted to righteousness. Let thy mind be always great."'"

SECTION XVIII.

"Vaisampayana said, 'Hearing these words of Kunti, the sinless Pandavas, O best of kings, became ashamed. They, therefore, desisted, along with the princess of Panchala, from following her.[890] Beholding Kunti resolved to go into the woods, the ladies of the Pandava household uttered loud lamentations. The Pandavas then circumambulated the king and saluted him duly. They ceased to follow further, having failed to persuade Pritha to return. Then Amvika's son of great energy, viz., Dhritarashtra, addressing Gandhari and Vidura and supporting himself on them, said, "Let the royal mother of Yudhishthira cease to go with us. What Yudhishthira has said is all very true. Abandoning this high prosperity of her sons, abandoning those high fruits that may be hers, why should she go into the inaccessible woods, leaving her children like a person of little intelligence? Living in the enjoyment of sovereignty, she is capable of practising penances and

---

[889] It has been pointed out before that mahadana means gifts of such things as elephants, horses, cars and other vehicles, boats, etc. The giver wins great merit by making them, but the receiver incurs demerit by acceptance, unless he happens to be a person of exceptional energy. To this day, acceptors of such gifts are looked upon as fallen men.

[890] The words that Kunti spoke were just. The opposition her sons offered was unreasonable. Hence, their shame.

observing the high vow of gifts. Let her, therefore, listen to my words. O Gandhari, I have been much gratified with the services rendered to me by this daughter-in-law of mine. Conversant as thou art with all duties, it behoveth thee to command her return." Thus addressed by her lord, the daughter of Suvala repeated unto Kunti all those words of the old king and added her own words of grave import. She, however, failed to cause Kunti to desist inasmuch as that chaste lady, devoted to righteousness, had firmly set her heart upon residing in the woods. The Kuru ladies, understanding how firm her resolution was regarding her retirement into the woods, and seeing that those foremost ones of Kuru's race (viz., their own lords), had ceased to follow her, set up a loud wail of lamentation. After all the sons of Pritha and all the ladies had retraced their steps, king Yudhishthira of great wisdom continued his journey to the woods. The Pandavas, exceedingly cheerless and afflicted with grief and sorrow accompanied by their wives, returned to the city, on their cars. At that time the city of Hastinapura, with its entire population of men, both old and young, and women, became cheerless and plunged into sorrow. No festivals of rejoicing were observed. Afflicted with grief, the Pandavas were without any energy. Deserted by Kunti, they were deeply afflicted with grief, like calves destitute of their dams. Dhritarashtra reached that day a place far removed from the city. The puissant monarch arrived at last on the banks of the Bhagirathi and took rest there for the night. Brahmanas conversant with the Vedas duly ignited their sacred fires in that retreat of ascetics. Surrounded by those foremost of Brahmanas, those sacred fires blazed forth in beauty. The sacred fire of the old king was also ignited. Sitting near his own fire, he poured libations on it according to due rites, and then worshipped the thousand-rayed sun as he was on the point of setting. Then Vidura and Sanjaya made a bed for the king by spreading some blades of Kusa grass. Near the bed of that Kuru hero they made another for Gandhari. In close proximity to Gandhari, Yudhishthira's mother Kunti, observant of excellent vows, happily laid herself down. Within hearing distance of those three, slept Vidura and others. The Yajaka Brahmanas and other followers of the king laid themselves down on their respective beds. The foremost of Brahmanas that were there chanted aloud many sacred hymns. The sacrificial fires blazed forth all around. That night, therefore, seemed as delightful to them as a Brahmi night.[891] When the night passed away, they all arose from their beds and went through their morning acts. Pouring libations then on the sacred fire, they continued their journey. Their first day's experience of the forest proved very painful to them on account of the grieving inhabitants of both the city and the provinces of the Kuru kingdom.'"

SECTION XIX.

"Vaisampayana said. 'Following the advice of Vidura, the king took up his abode on the banks of the Bhagirathi which were sacred and deserved to be peopled with the righteous. There many Brahmanas who had taken up their abode in the woods, as also many Kshatriyas and Vaisyas and Sudras, came to see the old monarch. Sitting in their midst, he gladdened them all by his words. Having duly worshipped the Brahmanas with their disciples, he dismissed them all. As evening came, the king, and Gandhari of great fame, both descended into the stream of the Bhagirathi and duly performed their ablutions for purifying themselves. The king and the queen, and Vidura and others, O Bharata, having bathed in the sacred stream, performed the usual rites of religion. After

---

[891] 'Brahmi night' implies a night in course of which sacred hymns are sung.

the king had purified himself by a bath, the daughter of Kuntibhoja gently led both him, who was to her as her father-in-law and Gandhari from the water into the dry bank. The Yajakas had made a sacrificial altar there for the king. Devoted to truth, the latter poured libations then on the fire. From the banks of the Bhagirathi the old king, with his followers, observant of vows and with senses restrained, then proceeded to Kurukshetra. Possessed of great intelligence, the king arrived at the retreat of the royal sage Satayupa of great wisdom and had an interview with him. Satayupa, O scorcher of foes, had been the great king of the Kekayas. Having made over the sovereignty of his kingdom to his son he had come into the woods. Satayupa, received king Dhritarashtra with due rites. Accompanied by him, the latter proceeded to the retreat of Vyasa. Arrived at Vyasa's retreat, the delighter of the Kurus received his initiation into the forest mode of life. Returning he took up his abode in the retreat of Satayupa. The high-souled Satayupa, instructed Dhritarashtra in all the rites of the forest mode, at the command of Vyasa. In this way the high-souled Dhritarashtra set himself to the practice of penances, and all his followers also to the same course of conduct. Queen Gandhari also, O monarch, along with Kunti, assumed barks of trees and deer-skins for her robe, and set herself to the observance of the same vows as her lord. Restraining their senses in thought, words, and deeds, as well as by eye, they began to practise severe austerities. Divested of all stupefaction of mind, king Dhritarashtra began to practise vows and penances like a great Rishi, reducing his body to skin and bones, for his flesh was all dried up, bearing matted locks on head, and his person clad in barks and skins. Vidura, conversant with the true interpretations of righteousness, and endued with great intelligence, as also Sanjaya, waited upon the old king with his wife. Both of them with souls under subjection, Vidura and Sanjaya also reduced themselves, and wore barks and rags.'"

SECTION XX.

"Vaisampayana said, 'Those foremost of ascetics, viz. Narada and Parvata and Devala of austere penances, came there to see king Dhritarashtra. The Island-born Vyasa with all his disciples, and other persons endued with great wisdom and crowned with ascetic success, and the royal sage Satayupa of advanced years and possessed of great merit, also came. Kunti worshipped them with due rites, O king. All those ascetics were highly gratified with the worship offered to them. Those great Rishis gladdened the high-souled king Dhritarashtra with discourses on religion and righteousness. At the conclusion of their converse, the celestial Rishi Narada, beholding all things as objects of direct perceptions, said the following words.'

"'Narada said, "There was a ruler of the Kekayas, possessed of great prosperity and perfectly fearless. His name was Sahasrachitya and he was the grandfather of this Satayupa. Resigning his kingdom to his eldest son endued with a large measure of righteousness, the virtuous king Sahasrachitya retired into the woods. Reaching the other end of blazing penances, that lord of Earth, endued with great splendour, attained to the region of Purandara where he continued to live in his company. On many occasions, while visiting the region of Indra, O king, I saw the monarch, whose sins had all been burnt off by penances, residing in Indra's abode. After the same manner, king Sailalaya, the grandfather of Bhagadatta, attained to the region of Indra by the power alone of his penances. There was another king, O monarch, of the name of Prishadhra who resembled the wielder of the thunder-bolt himself. That king also, by his penances proceeded from the Earth to Heaven. In this very forest, O king, that lord of Earth, Purukutsa, the son of

Mandhatri, attained to high success. That foremost of rivers, viz., Narmada, became the consort of that king. Having undergone penances in this very forest, that ruler of Earth proceeded to Heaven. There was another king, highly righteous, of the name of Sasaloman. He too underwent severe austerities in this forest and then ascended to Heaven. Thou also, O monarch, having arrived at this forest, shalt, through the grace of the Island-born, attain to a goal that is very high and that is difficult of attainment. Thou also, O foremost of kings, at the end of thy penances, become endued with great prosperity and, accompanied by Gandhari, attain to the goal reached by those high-souled ones. Dwelling in the presence of the slayer of Vala, Pandu thinks of thee always. He will, O monarch, certainly assist thee in the attainment of prosperity. Through serving thee and Gandhari, this daughter-in-law of thine, possessed of great fame, will attain to residence with her husband in the other world. She is the mother of Yudhishthira who is the eternal Dharma. We behold all this, O king, with our spiritual vision. Vidura will enter into the high-souled Yudhishthira. Sanjaya also, through meditation, will ascend from this world into Heaven.'"

"Vaisampayana continued, 'That high-souled chief of Kuru's race, possessed of learning, having, with his wife, heard these words of Narada, praised them and worshipped Narada with unprecedented honours. The conclave of Brahmanas there present became filled with great joy, and desirous of gladdening king Dhritarashtra, O monarch, themselves worshipped Narada with profound regards. Those foremost of regenerate persons also praised the words of Narada. Then the royal sage Satayupa, addressing Narada, said, "Thy holy self hath enhanced the devotion of the Kuru king, of all those people here, and of myself also, O thou of great splendour. I have, however, the wish to ask thee something. Listen to me as I say it. It has reference to the king Dhritarashtra, O celestial Rishi, that art worshipped by all the worlds. Thou art acquainted with the truth of every affair. Endued with celestial sight, thou beholdest, O regenerate Rishi, what the diverse goals are of human beings. Thou hast said what the goal has been of the kings mentioned by thee, viz., association with the chief of celestials. Thou hast not, however, O great Rishi, declared what those regions are that will be acquired by this king. O puissant one, I wish to hear from thee what region will be acquired by the royal Dhritarashtra. It behoveth thee to tell me truly the kind of region that will be his and the time when he will attain to it." Thus addressed by him, Narada of celestial sight and endued with austere penances, said in the midst of the assembly these words highly agreeable to the minds of all.'

"'Narada said, "Repairing at my will to the mansion of Sakra, I have seen Sakra the lord of Sachi; and there, O royal sage, I have beheld king Pandu. There a talk arose, O monarch, regarding this Dhritarashtra and those highly austere penances which he is performing. There I heard from the lips of Sakra himself that there are three years yet of the period of life allotted to this king. After that, king Dhritarashtra, accompanied by his wife Gandhari, will go to the regions of Kuvera and be highly honoured by that king of kings. He will go there on a car moving at his will, his person adorned with celestial ornaments. He is the son of a Rishi; he is highly blessed; he has burnt all his sins by his penances. Endued with a righteous soul, he will rove at will through the regions of the deities, the Gandharvas, and the Rakshasas. That about which thou hast enquired is a mystery of the gods. Through my affection for you, I have declared this high truth. Ye all are possessed of the wealth of Srutis and have consumed all your sins by your penances."'

"Vaisampayana continued, 'Hearing these sweet words of the celestial Rishi, all the persons there assembled, as also king Dhritarashtra, became greatly cheered and highly pleased. Having cheered Dhritarashtra of great wisdom with such talk, they left the spot, wending away by the path that belongs to those who are crowned with success.'"

SECTION XXI.

"Vaisampayana said, 'Upon the retirement of the chief of the Kurus into the forest, the Pandavas, O king, afflicted besides by grief on account of their mother, became very cheerless. The citizens also of Hastinapura were possessed by deep sorrow. The Brahmanas always talked of the old king. "How, indeed, will the king, who has become old, live in the solitary woods? How will the highly blessed Gandhari, and Pritha, the daughter of Kuntibhoja, live there? The royal sage has always lived in the enjoyment of every comfort. He will certainly be very miserable. Arrived in deep woods, what is now the condition of that personage of royal descent, who is, again, bereft of vision? Difficult is the feat that Kunti has achieved by separating herself from her sons. Alas casting off kingly prosperity, she chose a life in the woods. What, again, is the condition of Vidura who is always devoted to the service of his elder brother? How also is the intelligent son of Gavalgani who is so faithful to the food given him by his master?" Verily, the citizens, including those of even nonage meeting together, asked one another these questions. The Pandavas also, exceedingly afflicted with grief, sorrowed for their old mother, and could not live in their city long. Thinking also of their old sire, the king, who had lost all his children, and the highly blessed Gandhari, and Vidura of great intelligence, they failed to enjoy peace of mind. They had no pleasure in sovereignty, nor in women, nor in the study of the Vedas. Despair penetrated their souls as they thought of the old king and as they repeatedly reflected on that terrible slaughter of kinsmen. Indeed, thinking of the slaughter of the youthful Abhimanyu on the field of battle, of the mighty-armed Karna who never retreated from the fray, of the sons of Draupadi, and of other friends of theirs, those heroes became exceedingly cheerless. They failed to obtain peace of mind upon repeatedly reflecting that the Earth had become divested of both her heroes and her wealth. Draupadi had lost all her children, and the beautiful Subhadra also had become childless. They too were of cheerless hearts and grieved exceedingly. Beholding, however, the son of Virata's daughter, viz., thy sire Parikshit, thy grandsires somehow held their life-breaths.'"

SECTION XXII.

"Vaisampayana said, 'Those foremost of men, the heroic Pandavas,—those delighters of their mother—became exceedingly afflicted with grief. They who had formerly been always engaged in kingly offices, did not at that time attend to those acts at all in their capital. Afflicted with deep grief, they failed to derive pleasure from anything. If any body accosted them, they never honoured him with an answer. Although those irresistible heroes were in gravity like the ocean, yet they were now deprived of their knowledge and their very senses by the grief they felt. Thinking of their mother, the sons of Pandu were filled with anxiety as to how their emaciated mother was serving the old couple. "How, indeed, is that king, whose sons have all been slain and who is without refuge, living alone, with only his wife, in the woods that are the haunt of beasts of prey? Alas, how does that highly blessed queen, Gandhari, whose dear ones have all been slain, follow her blind lord in the solitary woods?"—Even such was the anxiety manifested by the Pandavas when they talked with one another. They then set their hearts upon seeing the king in his forest retreat. Then Sahadeva, bowing down to the king, said, "I see thy heart to be set upon seeing our sire. From my respect for thee, however, I could not speedily open my mouth on the subject of our journey to the woods. The time for that sojourn is now come. By good luck I shall see Kunti living in the observance of penances, with matted locks on her head, practising severe austerities, and emaciated with sleeping on blades of Kusa and Kasa. She was brought up in palaces and mansions, and nursed in every comfort and luxury. Alas, when shall I see my mother who is now toil-worn and plunged into exceeding misery? Without doubt, O chief of Bharata's race, the ends of mortals are exceedingly uncertain, since Kunti, who is a princess by birth, is now living in misery in the woods." Hearing these words of Sahadeva, queen Draupadi, that foremost of all women duly honouring the king said, with proper salutations,—"Alas, when shall I see queen Pritha, if, indeed, she be yet alive. I shall consider my life as not passed in vain if I succeed in beholding her once more, O king. Let this sort of understanding be ever stable in thee. Let thy mind always take a pleasure in such righteousness as is involved, O king of kings, in thy desire of bestowing such a high boon on us. Know, O king, that all these ladies of thy house are staying with their feet raised for the journey, from desire of beholding Kunti, and Gandhari, and my father-in-law." Thus addressed by queen Draupadi, the king, O chief of Bharata's race, summoned all the leaders of his forces to his presence and told them,—"Cause my army, teeming with cars and elephants, to march out. I shall behold king Dhritarashtra who is now living in the woods." Unto those that supervised the concerns of the ladies, the king gave the order, "Let diverse kinds of conveyances be properly equipt, and all my closed litters that count by thousands. Let carriages and granaries, and wardrobes, and treasuries, be equipt and ordered out, and let mechanics have the command to march out. Let men in charge of treasuries go out on the way leading to the ascetic retreats on Kurukshetra. Whoever amongst the citizens wishes to see the king is allowed to do so without any restriction. Let him proceed, properly protected. Let cooks and superintendents of kitchens, and the whole culinary establishment, and diverse kinds of edibles and viands, be ordered to be borne out on carts and conveyances. Let it be proclaimed that we march out tomorrow. Indeed, let no delay occur (in carrying out the arrangements). Let pavilions and resting houses of diverse kinds be erected on the way." Even these were the commands which the eldest son of Pandu gave, with his brothers. When morning came, O monarch, the king set out, with a large train of women and old men. Going out of his city, king Yudhishthira waited five days for such citizens as might accompany him, and then proceeded towards the forest.'"

SECTION XXIII.

"Vaisampayana said, 'That foremost one of Bharata's race, then ordered his troops, which were protected by heroes that were headed by Arjuna and that resembled the very guardians of the universe, to march out. Instantly, a loud clamour arose consisting of the words—Equip, Equip!—of horse-men, O Bharata, engaged in equipping and their steeds. Some proceeded on carriages and vehicles, some on horses of great speed, and some on cars made of gold endued with the splendour of blazing fires. Some proceeded on mighty elephants, and some on camels, O king. Some proceeded on foot, that belonged to that class of combatants which is armed with tiger-like claws.[892] The citizens and inhabitants of the provinces, desirous of seeing Dhritarashtra, followed the king on diverse kinds of conveyances. The preceptor Kripa also, of Gotama's race, that great leader of forces, taking all the forces with him, proceeded, at the command of the king, towards the old monarch's retreat. The Kuru king Yudhishthira, that perpetuator of Kuru's race, surrounded by a large number of Brahmanas, his praises sung by a large band of Sutas and Magadhas and bards, and with a white umbrella held over his head and encompassed around by a large number of cars, set out on his journey. Vrikodara, the son of the Wind-god, proceeded on an elephant as gigantic as a hill, equipt with strung bow and machines and weapons of attack and defence. The twin sons of Madri proceeded on two fleet steeds, well cased in mail, well protected, and equipt with banners. Arjuna of mighty energy, with senses under control, proceeded on an excellent car endued with solar effulgence and unto which were equipt excellent steeds of white hue. The ladies of the royal household, headed by Draupadi, proceeded in closed litters protected by the superintendents of women. They scattered copious showers of wealth as they proceeded. Teeming with cars and elephants and steeds, and echoing with the blare of trumpets and the music of Vinas, the Pandava host, O monarch, blazed with great beauty. Those chiefs of Kuru's race proceeded slowly, resting by delightful banks of rivers and lakes, O monarch. Yuyutsu of mighty energy, and Dhaumya, the priest at the command of Yudhishthira, were engaged in protecting the city. By slow marches, king Yudhishthira reached Kurukshetra, and then, crossing the Yamuna, that highly sacred river, he beheld from a distance the retreat, O thou of Kuru's race, of the royal sage of great wisdom and of Dhritarashtra. Then all the men became filled with joy and quickly entered the forest, filling it with loud sounds of glee, O chief of Bharata's race.'"

SECTION XXIV.

"Vaisampayana said, 'The Pandavas alighted, at a distance, from their cars and proceeded on foot to the retreat of the king, bending themselves in humility. All the combatants also, and all the denizens of the kingdom, and the spouses of the Kuru chiefs, followed them on foot. The Pandavas then reached the sacred retreat of Dhritarashtra which abounded with herds of deer and which was adorned with plantain plants. Many ascetics of rigid vows, filled with curiosity, came there for beholding the Pandavas who had arrived at the retreat. The king, with tears in his eyes, asked them, saying,—"Where has my eldest sire, the perpetuator of Kuru's race, gone?" They answered, O monarch, telling him that he had gone to the Yamuna for his ablutions, as also for fetching flowers and waters. Proceeding quickly on foot along the path pointed out by them, the Pandavas beheld all of them from a distance. Desirous of meeting with their sire they walked with a rapid pace. Then Sahadeva ran with speed towards the spot where Pritha was. Touching the feet of his mother, he began to weep aloud. With tears gushing down her cheeks, she saw her darling child. Raising her son up and embracing him with her arms, she informed Gandhari of Sahadeva's arrival. Then seeing the king and Bhimasena and Arjuna, and Nakula, Pritha endeavoured to advance quickly towards them. She was walking in advance of the childless old couple, and was dragging them forward. The Pandavas, beholding her, fell down on the earth. The puissant and high-souled monarch, endued

---

[892] Nakharaprasa-yodhina, Nilakantha explains, are those combatants who are armed with tiger-like claws made of iron and tied to their waists.

606

with great intelligence, recognising them by their voices and also by touch, comforted
them one after another. Shedding tears, those high-souled princes, with due formalities,
approached the old king and Gandhari, as also their own mother. Indeed, regaining their
senses, and once more comforted by their mother, the Pandavas took away from the king
and their aunt and mother the jars full of water which they had been carrying, forbearing
them themselves. The ladies of those lions among men, and all the women of the royal
household, as also all the inhabitants of the city and provinces, then beheld the old king.
King Yudhishthira presented all those individuals one after another to the old king,
repeating their names and races, and then himself worshipped his eldest sire with
reverence. Surrounded by them all, the old monarch, with eyes bathed in tears of joy,
regarded himself as once more staying in the midst of the city called after the elephant.
Saluted with reverence by all his daughters-in-law headed by Krishna, king Dhritarashtra,
endued with great intelligence, with Gandhari and Kunti, became filled with joy. He then
reached his forest-retreat that was applauded by Siddhas and Charanas, and that then
teemed with vast crowds of men all desirous of beholding him, like the firmament
teeming with innumerable stars.'"

SECTION XXV.

"Vaisampayana said, 'The king, O chief of Bharata's race, with those foremost of
men, viz., his brothers, who were all possessed of eyes that resembled lotus-petals, took
his seat in the retreat of his eldest sire. There sat around him many highly-blessed
ascetics, hailing from diverse regions, from desire of beholding the sons of that lord of
Kuru's race, viz., the Pandavas of wide chests. They said, "We wish to know who
amongst these is Yudhishthira, who are Bhima and Arjuna, who the twins, and who is
Draupadi of great fame." Then the Suta, Sanjaya, in answer to their queries, pointed out
to them the Pandavas, naming each, and Draupadi too as also the other ladies of the Kuru
household.'
"'Sanjaya said, "This one that is as fair of complexion as pure gold, that is endued
with a body which looks like that of a full-grown lion, that is possessed of a large
aquiline nose, and wide and expansive eyes that are, again, of a coppery hue, is the Kuru
king. This one, whose tread resembles that of an infuriate elephant, whose complexion is
as fair as that of heated gold, whose frame is of large and expansive proportions and
whose arms are long and stout, is Vrikodara. Behold him well! The mighty bowman who
sits besides him, of darkish complexion and youthful frame, who resembles the leader of
an elephantine herd, whose shoulders are as high as those of a lion, who walks like a
sporting elephant, and whose eyes are as expansive as the petals of a lotus, is the hero
called Arjuna. Those two foremost of men, that are sitting besides Kunti, are the twins,
resembling Vishnu and Mahendra. In this whole world of men, they have not their equals
in beauty and strength and excellence of conduct. This lady, of eyes as expansive as lotus
petals, who seems to have touched the middle age of life, whose complexion resembles
that of the blue lotus, and who looks like a goddess of Heaven, is Krishna, the embodied
form of the goddess of prosperity.[893] She who sits besides her, possessed of the
complexion of pure gold, who looks like the embodied rays of the moon, in the midst of
the other ladies, is, ye foremost of regenerate ones, the sister of that unrivalled hero who
wields the discus. This other, as fair as pure gold, is the daughter of the snake-chief and

[893] Suradevata is like karivringhati or govalivardda.

wife of Arjuna.[894] This other whose complexion is like that of pure gold or like that of Madhuka flowers, is the princess Chitrangada. This one, that is possessed of the complexion of an assemblage of blue lotuses, is the sister of that monarch, that lord of hosts, who used to always challenge Krishna. She is the foremost wife of Vrikodara. This is the daughter of the king of Magadha who was known by the name of Jarasandha. Possessed of the complexion of an assemblage of Champakas, she is the wife of the youngest son of Madravati. Possessed of a complexion as darkish as that of the blue lotus, she who sits there on the earth, and whose eyes are as expansive as lotus-petals, is the wife of the eldest son of Madravati. This lady whose complexion is as fair as that of heated gold and who sits with her child on her lap, is the daughter of king Virata. She is the wife of that Abhimanyu who, while divested of his car, was slain by Drona and others fighting from their cars.[895] These ladies, the hair on whose heads shows not the parted line, and who are clad in white, are the widows of the slain sons of Dhritarashtra. They are the daughters-in-law of this old king, the wives of his hundred sons, now deprived of both their husbands and children who have been slain by heroic foes. I have now pointed them out in the order of precedence. In consequence of their devotion to Brahmanas, their understandings and hearts are divested of every kind of crookedness. Possessed of pure souls, they have all been pointed out by me,—these princesses of the Kaurava household,—in answer to your queries.'"

"Vaisampayana continued, 'Thus that king of Kuru's race, of very advanced years, having met with those sons of him that was a deity among men, enquired about their welfare after all the ascetics had gone away. The warriors who had accompanied the Pandavas, leaving the retreat, sat themselves down at a little distance, alighting from their cars and the animals they rode. Indeed, after all the crowd, viz., the ladies, the old men, and the children, had been seated, the old king duly addressed them, making the usual enquiries of politeness.'"

SECTION XXVI.

"'Dhritarashtra said, "O Yudhishthira, art thou in peace and happiness, with all thy brothers and the inhabitants of the city and the provinces? Are they that live in dependance on thee also happy? Are thy ministers, and servitors, and all thy seniors and preceptors also, happy? Are those also that live in thy dominions free from fear? Dost thou follow the old and traditional conduct of rulers of men? Is thy treasury filled without disregarding the restraints imposed by justice and equity? Dost thou behave as thou shouldst towards foes, neutrals, and allies? Dost thou duly look after the Brahmanas, always making them the first gifts (ordained in sacrifices and religious rites)? What need I say of the citizens, and thy servants, and kinsmen,—are thy foes, O chief of Bharata's race, gratified with thy behaviour? Dost thou, O king of kings, adore with devotion the Pitris and the deities? Dost thou worship guests with food and drink, O Bharata? Do the Brahmanas in thy dominions, devoted to the duties of their order, walk along the path of righteousness? Do the Kshatriyas and Vaisyas and Sudras also within thy kingdom, and all thy relatives, observe their respective duties? I hope the women, the children, and the old, among thy subjects, do not grieve (under distress) and do not beg (the necessaries of

---

[894] Ulupi is implied.

[895] Implying the unfair character of the fight, for one on the earth should never be assailed by one on his car.

608

life). Are the ladies of thy household duly honoured in thy house, O best of men? I hope, O monarch, that this race of royal sages, having obtained thee for their king, have not fallen away from fame and glory.'"

"Vaisampayana continued, 'Unto the old king who said so, Yudhishthira, conversant with morality and justice, and well-skilled in acts and speech, spoke as follows, putting some questions about his welfare.'

"'Yudhishthira said, "Doth thy peace, O king, thy self-restraint, thy tranquillity of heart, grow? Is this my mother able to serve thee without fatigue and trouble? Will, O king, her residence in the woods be productive of fruits? I hope this queen, who is my eldest mother, who is emaciated with (exposure to) cold and wind and the toil of walking, and who is now devoted to the practice of severe austerities, no longer gives way, to grief for her children of mighty energy, all of whom, devoted to the duties of the Kshatriya order, have been slain on the field of battle. Does she accuse us, sinful wretches, that are responsible for their slaughter? Where is Vidura, O king? We do not see him here. I hope this Sanjaya, observant of penances, is in peace and happiness."'

"Vaisampayana continued, 'Thus addressed, Dhritarashtra answered king Yudhishthira, saying,—"O son, Vidura is well. He is performing austere penances, subsisting on air alone, for he abstains from all other food. He is emaciated and his arteries and nerves have become visible. Sometimes he is seen in this empty forest by Brahmanas." While Dhritarashtra was saying this Vidura was seen at a distance. He had matted locks on his head, and gravels in his mouth, and was exceedingly emaciated. He was perfectly naked. His body was besmeared all over with filth, and with the dust of various wild flowers. When Kshattri was beheld from a distance, the fact was reported to Yudhishthira. Vidura suddenly stopped, O king, casting his eyes towards the retreat (and seeing it peopled by so many individuals). King Yudhishthira pursued him alone, as he ran and entered the deep forest, sometimes not seen by the pursuer. He said aloud, "O Vidura, O Vidura, I am king Yudhishthira, thy favourite!"—Exclaiming thus, Yudhishthira, with great exertion, followed Vidura. That foremost of intelligent men, viz., Vidura, having reached a solitary spot in the forest, stood still, leaning against a tree. He was exceedingly emaciated. He retained only the shape of a human being (all his characteristic features having totally disappeared). Yudhishthira of great intelligence recognised him, however, (in spite of such change). Standing before him, Yudhishthira addressed him, saying, "I am Yudhishthira!" Indeed, worshipping Vidura properly, Yudhishthira said these words in the hearing of Vidura. Meanwhile Vidura eyed the king with a steadfast gaze. Casting his gaze thus on the king, he stood motionless in Yoga. Possessed of great intelligence, he then (by his Yoga-power) entered the body of Yudhishthira, limb by limb. He united his life-breaths with the king's life-breaths, and his senses with the king's senses. Verily, with the aid of Yoga-power, Vidura, blazing with energy, thus entered the body of king Yudhishthira the just. Meanwhile, the body of Vidura continued to lean against the tree, with eyes fixed in a steadfast gaze. The king soon saw that life had fled out of it. At the same time, he felt that he himself had become stronger than before and that he had acquired many additional virtues and accomplishments. Possessed of great learning and energy, O monarch, Pandu's son, king Yudhishthira the just, then recollected his own state before his birth among men.[896]

---

[896] Yudhishthira was Dharma's self, Vidura also was Dharma born as a Sudra through the curse of the Rishi Animandavya. Both, therefore, were of the same essence. When Vidura left his human body, he entered the body of Yudhishthira and thus the latter felt himself strengthened greatly by the accession.

Endued with mighty energy, he had heard of Yoga practice from Vyasa. King Yudhishthira the just, possessed of great learning, became desirous of doing the last rites to the body of Vidura, and wished to cremate it duly. An invisible voice was then heard,—saying,—"O king, this body that belonged to him called Vidura should not be cremated. In him is thy body also. He is the eternal deity of Righteousness. Those regions of felicity which are known by the name of Santanika will be his, O Bharata. He was an observer of the duties of Yatis. Thou shouldst not, O scorcher of foes, grieve for him at all." Thus addressed, king Yudhishthira the just, returned from that spot, and represented everything unto the royal son of Vichitraviryya. At this, that king of great splendour, all these men, and Bhimasena and others, became filled with wonder. Hearing what had happened, king Dhritarashtra became pleased and then, addressing the son of Dharma, said,—"Do thou accept from me these gifts of water and roots and fruits. It has been said, O king, that one's guest should take that which one takes oneself." Thus addressed, Dharma's son answered the king, saying,—"So be it." The mighty-armed king ate the fruits and roots which the monarch gave him. Then they all spread their beds under a tree and passed that night thus, having eaten fruits and roots and drunk the water that the old king had given them.'"

SECTION XXVII.

"Vaisampayana said, 'They passed that night which was characterised by auspicious constellations even thus, O king, in that retreat of righteous ascetics. The conversation that occurred was characterised by many reflections on morality and wealth. Consisting of delightful and sweet words, it was graced with diverse citations from the Srutis. The Pandavas, O king, leaving costly beds, laid themselves down, near their mother, on the bare ground. Indeed, those heroes passed that night, having eaten the food which was the food of the high-souled king Dhritarashtra. After the night had passed away, king Yudhishthira, having gone through his morning acts, proceeded to survey that retreat in the company of his brothers. With the ladies of his household, the servants, and his priest, the king roved about the retreat in all directions, as he pleased, at the command of Dhritarashtra. He beheld many sacrificial altars with sacred fires blazing on them and with many ascetics seated on them, that had performed their oblations and poured libations in honour of the deities. Those altars were overspread with fruits and roots of the forest, and with heaps of flowers. The smoke of clarified butter curled upwards from them. They were graced, besides, with many ascetics possessed of bodies that looked like the embodied Vedas and with many that belonged to the lay brotherhood. Herds of deer were grazing, or resting here and there, freed from every fear. Innumerable birds also were there, engaged in uttering their melodious notes, O king. The whole forest seemed to resound with the notes of peacocks and Datyuhas and Kokilas and the sweet songs of other warblers.[897] Some spots echoed with the chant of Vedic hymns recited by learned Brahmanas. Some were adorned with large heaps of fruits and roots gathered from the wilderness. King Yudhishthira then gave those ascetics jars made of gold or copper which he had brought for them, and many deer-skins and blankets and sacrificial ladles

---

[897] Nilakantha here implies the peacock and not the blue jay, for the word keka is applied to the notes of the peacock alone. Datyuhas are gallinules or a species of Chatakas whose cry resembles, Phatik jal—phatik jal—phatik jal! repeated very distinctly, the second syllable being lengthened greatly.

made of wood, and Kamandalus and wooden platters, and pots and pans, O Bharata.[898]
Diverse kinds of vessels, made of iron, and smaller vessels and cups of various sizes,
were also given away by the king, the ascetics taking them away, each as many as he
liked. King Yudhishthira of righteous soul, having thus roved through the woods and
beheld the diverse retreats of ascetics and made many gifts, returned to the place where
his uncle was. He saw king Dhritarashtra, that lord of Earth, at his ease, with Gandhari
beside him, after having finished his morning rites. The righteous-souled monarch saw
also his mother, Kunti, seated not much remote from that place, like a disciple with bent
head, endued with humility. He saluted the old king, proclaiming his name. "Sit down"
were the words the old king said. Receiving Dhritarashtra's permission, Yudhishthira sat
himself down on a mat of Kusa grass. Then the other sons of Pandu with Bhima among
them, O thou of Bharata's race, saluted the king and touched his feet and sat themselves
down, receiving his permission. The old Kuru king, surrounded by them, looked
exceedingly beautiful. Indeed, he blazed with a Vedic splendour like Vrihaspati in the
midst of the celestials. After they had sat themselves down, many great Rishis, viz.,
Satayupa and others, who were denizens of Kurukshetra, came there. The illustrious and
learned Vyasa, possessed of great energy, and reverenced by even the celestial Rishis,
showed himself, at the head of his numerous disciples, unto Yudhishthira. The Kuru king
Dhritarashtra, Kunti's son Yudhishthira of great energy, and Bhimasena and others, stood
up and advancing a few steps, saluted those guests. Approaching near, Vyasa, surrounded
by Satayupa and others, addressed king Dhritarashtra, saying,—"Be thou seated." The
illustrious Vyasa then took an excellent seat made of Kusa grass placed upon a black
deer-skin and covered with a piece of silken cloth. They had reserved that seat for him.
After Vyasa had been seated, all those foremost of regenerate persons, endued with
abundant energy, sat themselves down, having received the permission of the Island-born
sage.'"

SECTION XXVIII.

"Vaisampayana said, 'After the high-souled Pandavas had all been seated, Satyavati's
son Vyasa said,—"O Dhritarashtra of mighty arms, hast thou been able to achieve
penances? Is thy mind, O king, pleased with thy residence in the woods? Has the grief
that was thine, born of the slaughter of thy sons in battle, disappeared from thy heart? Are
all thy perceptions, O sinless one, now clear? Dost thou practise the ordinances of forest
life after having made thy heart firm? Does my daughter-in-law, Gandhari, allow herself
to be overwhelmed by grief? She is possessed of great wisdom. Endued with intelligence,
that queen understands both Religion and Wealth. She is well conversant with the truths
that relate to both prosperity and adversity. Does she still grieve? Does Kunti, O king,
who in consequence of her devotion to the service of her seniors, left her children, attend
to thy wants and serve thee with all humility? Have the high-minded and high-souled
king, Yudhishthira, the son of Dharma and Bhima and Arjuna and the twins been
sufficiently comforted? Dost thou feel delight at seeing them? Has thy mind become
freed from every stain? Has thy disposition, O king, become pure in consequence of the
increase of thy knowledge? This aggregate of three, O king, is the foremost of all

---

[898] Audumvaran is an adjective of kalasan. It means 'made of copper'. Praveni is a kutha or blanket. Sruk
is a ladle having the cup like cavity at one extremity only. Sruv is a ladle having cup-like cavities at both
extremities.

concerns, O Bharata, viz., abstension from injury to any creature, truth, and freedom from anger. Does thy forest life any longer prove painful to thee? Art thou able to earn with thy own exertions the products of the wilderness for thy food? Do fasts give thee any pain now? Hast thou learnt, O king, how the high-souled Vidura, who was Dharma's self, left this world? Through the curse of Mandavya, the deity of Righteousness became born as Vidura. He was possessed of great intelligence. Endued with high penances, he was high-souled and high-minded. Even Vrihaspati among the celestials, and Sukra among the Asuras, was not possessed of such intelligence as that foremost of persons. The eternal deity of Righteousness was stupefied by the Rishi Mandavya with an expenditure of his penances earned for a long time with great care.[899] At the command of the Grandsire, and through my own energy, Vidura of great intelligence was procreated by me upon a soil owned by Vichitraviryya. A deity of deities, and eternal, he was, O king, thy brother. The learned know him to be Dharma in consequence of his practices of Dharana and Dhyana.[900] He grows with (the growth of) truth, self-restraint, tranquillity of heart, compassion, and gifts. He is always engaged in penances, and is eternal. From that deity of Righteousness, through Yoga-puissance, the Kuru king Yudhishthira also took his birth. Yudhishthira, therefore, O king, is Dharma of great wisdom and immeasurable intelligence. Dharma exists both here and hereafter, and is like fire or wind or water or earth or space. He is, O king of kings, capable of going everywhere and exists, pervading the whole universe. He is capable of being beheld by only those that are the foremost of the deities and those that are cleansed of every sin and crowned with ascetic success. He that is Dharma is Vidura; and he that is Vidura is the (eldest) son of Pandu. That son of Pandu. O king, is capable of being perceived by thee. He stays before thee as thy servitor. Endued with great Yoga-puissance, thy high-souled brother, that foremost of intelligent men, seeing the high-souled Yudhishthira, the son of Kunti, has entered into his person. These also, O chief of Bharata's race, I shall unite with great benefit. Know, O son, that I am come here for dispelling thy doubts. Some feat that has never been accomplished before by any of the great Rishis, some wonderful effect of my penances,—I shall show thee. What object is that, O king, whose accomplishment thou desirest from me? Tell me what is that which thou wishest to see or ask or hear? O sinless one, I shall accomplish it.""'

SECTION XXIX. (*Putradarsana Parva*)

"Janamejaya said, 'Tell me. O learned Brahmana, what that wonderful feat was which the great Rishi Vyasa of high energy accomplished after his promise to the old king, made when Dhritarashtra, that lord of Earth, that foremost one of Kuru's race, had taken up his abode in the forest, with his wife and with his daughter-in-law Kunti; and after, indeed, Vidura had left his own body and entered into Yudhishthira, and at the time when all the sons of Pandu were staying in the ascetic retreat. For how many days did the Kuru king Yudhishthira of unfading glory stay, with his men, in the woods? On what food, O puissant one, did the high-souled Pandavas support themselves, with their men,

---

[899] Whenever a Brahmana cursed another, his penances underwent a diminution. Forgiveness was the highest virtue of the Brahmana. His power lay in forgiveness. Hence, when Mandavya cursed Dharma, he had to spend a portion of his hard-earned penances. Previously, the plea of minority or non-age could not be urged in the court of Dharma. Mandavya forced Dharma to admit that plea in the matter of punishment for offences.

[900] Both Dharana and Dhyana are processes or, rather, stages of Yoga. The former implies the fixing of the mind on one thing; the latter is the abstraction of the mind from surrounding objects.

and wives, while they lived in the woods? O sinless one, do thou tell me this.'

"Vaisampayana said, 'With the permission of the Kuru king, the Pandavas, O monarch, with their troops and the ladies of their household, supported themselves on diverse kinds of food and drink and passed about a month in great happiness in that forest. Towards the close of that period, O sinless one, Vyasa came there. While all those princes sat around Vyasa, engaged in conversation on diverse subjects, other Rishis came to that spot. They were Narada, and Parvata and Devala of austere penances, and Viswavasu and Tumvuru, and Chitrasena, O Bharata. Endued with severe penances, the Kuru king Yudhishthira, with the permission of Dhritarashtra, worshipped them according to due rites. Having obtained that worship from Yudhishthira, all of them sat down on sacred seats (made of Kusa grass), as also on excellent seats made of peacock feathers. After they had all taken their seats, the Kuru king of high intelligence took his seat there, surrounded by the sons of Pandu. Gandhari and Kunti and Draupadi, and she of the Sattwata race, and other ladies of the royal household also sat down. The conversation that then arose was excellent and had reference to topics connected with piety, and the Rishis of old, and the deities and the Asuras. At the close of that conversation Vyasa of great energy, that foremost of eloquent men, that first of all persons conversant with the Vedas, highly gratified, addressed the blind monarch and once more said,—"Burning as thou art with grief on account of thy children, I know, O king of kings, what object is cherished by thee in thy heart. The sorrow that always exists in the heart of Gandhari, that which exists in the heart of Kunti, and that also which is cherished by Draupadi in her heart, and that burning grief, on account of the death of her son, which Krishna's sister Subhadra also cherishes, are all known to me. Hearing of this meeting, O king, of thine with all these princes and princesses of thy house, I have come here, O delighter of the Kauravas, for dispelling thy doubts. Let the deities and Gandharvas, and all these great Rishis, behold today the energy of those penances which I have acquired for these long years. Therefore, O king, tell me what wish of thine I shall grant today. I am puissant enough to grant thee a boon. Behold the fruit of my penances." Thus addressed by Vyasa of immeasurable understanding, king Dhritarashtra reflected for a moment and then prepared to speak. He said,—"I am exceedingly fortunate. Lucky am I in obtaining thy favour. My life is crowned with success today,—since this meeting has happened between me and ye all of great piety. Today I shall attain to that highly happy goal which is reserved for me, since, ye ascetics endued with wealth of penances, ye who are equal to Brahma himself, I have succeeded in obtaining this meeting with you all. There is not the least doubt that this sight that I have obtained of you all has cleansed me of every sin. Ye sinless ones, I have no longer any fear in respect of my end in the next world. Full as I am of love for my children, I always cherish their remembrance. My mind, however, is always tortured by the recollection of the diverse acts of wrong which my wicked son of exceedingly evil understanding perpetrated. Possessed of a sinful understanding, he always persecuted the innocent Pandavas. Alas, the whole Earth has been devastated by him, with her steeds, elephants and men. Many high-souled kings, rulers of diverse realms, came for siding with my son and succumbed to death. Alas, leaving their beloved sires and wives and their very life-breaths, all those heroes have become guests of the king of the dead. What end, O regenerate one, has been attained by those men who have been slain, for the sake of their friend, in battle? What end also has been attained by my sons and grandsons who have fallen in the fray? My heart is always pained at the thought of my having brought about the slaughter of the mighty Bhishma, the son of Santanu, and of Drona, that foremost of Brahmanas, through my foolish and sinful son who was an injurer of his friends. Desirous of obtaining the sovereignty of the Earth, he caused the Kuru race, blazing with prosperity, to be annihilated. Reflecting on all this, I burn day and night with grief. Deeply afflicted with pain and grief, I am unable to obtain peace of mind. Indeed, O father, thinking of all this, I have no peace of mind."'

"Vaisampayana continued, 'Hearing these lamentations expressed in diverse ways, of that royal sage, the grief, O Janamejaya, of Gandhari, became fresh. The grief also of Kunti, of the daughter of Drupada, of Subhadra, and of the other members, male and female, and the daughters-in-law, of the Kuru race, became equally green. Queen Gandhari, with bandaged eyes, joining her hands, addressed her father-in-law. Deeply afflicted with grief on account of the slaughter of her sons, she said,—"O foremost of ascetics, sixteen years have passed over the head of this king grieving for the death of his sons and divested of peace of mind. Afflicted with grief on account of the slaughter of his children, this king Dhritarashtra, always breathes heavily, and never sleeps at night. O great Rishi, through the power of thy penances thou art competent to create new worlds. What need I say then about showing this king his children who are now in the other world? This Krishna, the daughter of Drupada, hath lost all her kinsmen and children. For this, she who is the dearest of my daughters-in-law grieves exceedingly. The sister of Krishna, viz., Subhadra of sweet speech, burning with the loss of her son, grieves as deeply. This lady that is respected by all, that is the wife of Bhurisravas, afflicted with grief on account of the fate that has overtaken her husband, always indulges in heart-rending lamentations. Her father-in-law was the intelligent Valhika of Kuru's race. Alas, Somadatta also was slain, along with his sire, in the great battle![901] Alas, a century of sons, heroes that never retreated from battle, belonging to this son of thine, this king of great intelligence and great prosperity, has been slain in battle. The hundred wives of those sons are all grieving and repeatedly enhancing the grief of both the king and myself. O great ascetic, stricken by that great slaughter, they have gathered round me. Alas, those high-souled heroes, those great car warriors, my fathers-in-law, Somadatta and others,—alas, what end has been theirs, O puissant one? Through thy grace, O holy one, that will happen in consequence of which this lord of Earth, myself, and this daughter-in-law of thine, viz., Kunti, shall all become freed from our grief." After Gandhari had said so, Kunti, whose face had become wasted through observance of many hard vows, began to think of her secret-born son endued with solar effulgence. The boon-giving Rishi Vyasa, capable of both beholding and hearing what happened at a remote distance, saw that the royal mother of Arjuna was afflicted with grief. Unto her Vyasa said,—"Tell me, O blessed one, what is in thy mind. Tell me what thou wishest to say." At this, Kunti, bending her head unto her father-in-law, and overcome with bashfulness, said these words unto him, relating to the occurrences of the past.'"

SECTION XXX.

"'Kunti said, "O holy one, thou art my father-in-law and therefore, my deity of deities. Verily, thou art my god of gods. Hear my words of truth. An ascetic named Durvasas, who is of the regenerate order and who is full of wrath, came to my father's house for eleemosynary charity. I succeeded in gratifying him by the purity of my external behaviour and of my mind, as also by refusing to notice the many wrongs he did.

---

[901] Valhika was the sire of Somadatta and the grandsire of Bhurisravas. Valhika, therefore, was the grand-father-in-law of the lady mentioned by Gandhari.

I did not give way to wrath although there was much in his behaviour quite capable of exciting that passion. Served with care, the great ascetic became highly pleased with me and disposed to grant me a boon. 'Thou must accept the boon I shall give,' were his words to me. Fearing his curse, I answered him, saying,—'So be it.' The regenerate Rishi once more said unto me,—'O blessed damsel, O thou of beautiful face, thou wilt become the mother of Dharma. Those deities whom thou wilt summon will be obedient to thee.' Having said those words, the regenerate one vanished away from my sight. I became filled with wonder. The mantra, however, which the Rishi gave has dwelt in my memory at all times. One day, sitting within my chamber I beheld the sun rising. Desiring to bring the maker of day before me, I recollected the words of the Rishi. Without any consciousness of the fault I committed, I summoned the deity from mere girlishness. The deity, however, of a thousand rays, (summoned by me) came to my presence. He divided himself in twain. With one portion he was in the firmament, and with the other he stood on the Earth before me. With one he heated the worlds and with another he came to me. He told me, while I was trembling at his sight, these words,—'Do thou ask a boon of me.' Bowing unto him with my head, I asked him to leave me. He replied unto me, saying,—'I cannot bear the idea of coming to thee fruitlessly. I shall consume thee as also that Brahmana who gave thee the Mantra as a boon.' The Brahmana who had done no evil—I wished to protect from Surya's curse. I therefore, said—'Let me have a son like thee, O god.' The deity of thousand rays then penetrated me with his energy and stupefied me completely. He then said unto me,—'Thou wilt have a son,' and then went back to the firmament. I continued to live in the inner apartments and desirous of saving the honour of my sire, I cast into the waters my infant son named Karna who thus came into the world secretly. Without doubt, through the grace of that god, I once more became a virgin, O regenerate one, even as the Rishi Durvasas had said unto me. Foolish that I am, although he knew me for his mother when he grew up, I yet made no effort to acknowledge him. This burns me, O regenerate Rishi, as is well-known to thee. Whether it is sinful or not so, I have told thee truth. It behoveth thee, O holy one, to gratify the craving I feel for beholding that son of mine. O foremost of ascetics, let this king also, O sinless one, obtain the fruition today of that wish of his which he cherishes in his bosom and which has become known to thee." Thus addressed by Kunti, Vyasa, that foremost of all persons, said unto her in reply,—"Blessed be thou; all that thou hast said unto me will happen. (As regards the birth of Karna) no fault is ascribable to thee. Thou wert restored to virginity. The deities are possessed of (Yoga) puissance. They are able to penetrate human bodies.[902] There are deities. They beget (offspring) by thought alone. By word, by sight, by touch, and by sexual union, also, they beget children. These are the five methods. Thou belongest to the order of humanity. Thou hast no fault (in what happened). Know this, O Kunti. Let the fever of thy heart be dispelled. For those that are mighty, everything is becoming. For those that are mighty, everything is pure. For those that are mighty, everything is meritorious. For those that are mighty, everything is their own."'"

---

[902] The puissance here referred to is that of Anima, Laghima, etc. i.e., the capacity of becoming minute and subtile, etc.

SECTION XXXI.

"'Vyasa said, "Blessed be thou, O Gandhari, thou shalt behold thy sons and brothers and friends and kinsmen along with thy sires this night like men risen from sleep. Kunti also shall behold Karna, and she of Yadu's race shall behold her son Abhimanyu. Draupadi shall behold her five sons, her sires, and her brothers also. Even before ye had asked me, this was the thought in my mind. I entertained this purpose when I was urged to that effect by the king, by thee, O Gandhari, and by Kunti. Thou shouldst not grieve for those foremost of men. They met with death in consequence of their devotion to the established practices of Kshatriyas. O faultless one, the work of the gods could not but be accomplished. It was for accomplishing that object that those heroes came down on Earth. They were all portions of the deities. Gandharvas and Apsaras, and Pisachas and Guhyakas and Rakshasas, many persons of great sanctity, many individuals crowned with success (of penances), celestial Rishis, deities and Danavas and heavenly Rishis of spotless character, met with death on the battle-field of Kurukshetra.[903] It is heard that he that was the intelligent king of the Gandharvas, and named Dhritarashtra, took birth in the world of men as thy lord Dhritarashtra. Know that Pandu of unfading glory and distinguished above all others, sprung from the Maruts. Kshattri and Yudhishthira are both portions of the deity of Righteousness. Know that Duryodhana was Kali, and Sakuni was Dwapara. O thou of good features, know that Dussasana and others were all Rakshasas. Bhimasena of great might, that chastiser of foes, is from the Maruts. Know that this Dhananjaya, the son of Pritha, is the ancient Rishi Nara. Hrishikesa is Narayana, and the twins are the Aswins. The foremost of heat-giving ones, viz., Surya, having divided his body in twain, continued with one portion to give heat to the worlds and with another to live (on Earth.) as Karna. He that took his birth as the son of Arjuna, that gladdener of all, that heir to the possessions of the Pandavas, who was slain by six great car-warriors (fighting together), was Soma. He was born of Subhadra. Through Yoga-puissance he had divided himself in twain. Dhrishtadyumna who sprung with Draupadi from the sacrificial fire, was an auspicious portion of the deity of fire. Sikhandin was a Rakshasa. Know that Drona was a portion of Vrihaspati, and that Drona's son is born of a portion of Rudra. Know that Ganga's son Bhishma was one of the Vasus that became born as a human being. Thus, O thou of great wisdom, the deities had taken birth as human beings, and after having accomplished their purposes have gone back to Heaven. That sorrow which is in the hearts of you all, relating to the return of these to the other world, I shall today dispel. Do you all go towards the Bhagirathi.—You will then behold all those that have been slain on the field of battle."'

"Vaisampayana continued, 'All the persons there present, having heard the words of Vyasa, raised a loud leonine shout and then proceeded towards the Bhagirathi. Dhritarashtra with all his ministers and the Pandavas, as also with all those foremost of Rishis and Gandharvas that had come there, set out as directed. Arrived at the banks of Ganga, that sea of men took up their abode as pleased them. The king possessed of great intelligence, with the Pandavas, took up his abode in a desirable spot, along with the ladies and the aged ones of his household. They passed that day as if it were a whole year, waiting for the advent of the night when they would behold the deceased princes.

---

[903] The sense is that those had been incarnated as human beings and fighting with one another met with death as regards their human existence.

The Sun then reached the sacred mountain in the west and all those persons, having bathed in the sacred stream, finished their evening rites.'"

SECTION XXXII.

"Vaisampayana said, 'When night came, all those persons, having finished their evening rites, approached Vyasa. Dhritarashtra of righteous soul, with purified body and with mind solely directed towards it, sat there with the Pandavas and the Rishis in his company. The ladies of the royal household sat with Gandhari in a secluded spot. All the citizens and the inhabitants of the provinces ranged themselves according to their years. Then the great ascetic, Vyasa, of mighty energy, bathing in the sacred waters of the Bhagirathi, summoned all the deceased warriors, viz., those that had fought on the side of the Pandavas, those that had fought for the Kauravas, including highly blessed kings belonging to diverse realms. At this, O Janamejaya, a deafening uproar was heard to arise from within the waters, resembling that which had formerly been heard of the forces of the Kurus and the Pandavas. Then those kings, headed by Bhishma and Drona, with all their troops, arose by thousands from the waters of the Bhagirathi. There were Virata and Drupada, with their sons and forces. There were the sons of Draupadi and the son of Subhadra, and the Rakshasa Ghatotkacha. There were Karna and Duryodhana, and the mighty car-warrior Sakuni, and the other children, endued with great strength, of Dhritarashtra, headed by Dussasana. There were the son of Jarasandha, and Bhagadatta, and Jalasandha of great energy, and Bhurisravas, and Sala, and Salya, and Vrishasena with his younger brother. There were prince Lakshmana (the son of Duryodhana), and the son of Dhrishtadyumna, and all the children of Sikhandin, and Dhrishtaketu, with his younger brother. There were Achala and Vrishaka, and the Rakshasa Alayudha, and Valhika, and Somadatta, and king Chekitana. These and many others, who for their number cannot be conveniently named, appeared on that occasion. All of them rose from the waters of the Bhagirathi, with resplendent bodies. Those kings appeared, each clad in that dress and equipt with that standard and that vehicle which he had while fighting on the field. All of them were now robed in celestial vestments and all had brilliant ear-rings. They were free from all animosity and pride, and divested of wrath and jealousy. Gandharvas sang their praises, and bards waited on them, chanting their deeds. Robed in celestial vestments and wearing celestial garlands, each of them was waited upon by bands of Apsaras. At that time, through the puissance of his penances, the great ascetic, the son of Satyavati, gratified with Dhritarashtra, gave him celestial vision. Endued with celestial knowledge and strength, Gandhari of great fame saw all her children as also all that had been slain in battle. All persons assembled there beheld with steadfast gaze and hearts filled with wonder that amazing and inconceivable phenomenon which made the hair on their bodies stand on its end. It looked like a high carnival of gladdened men and women. That wondrous scene looked like a picture painted on the canvas. Dhritarashtra, beholding all those heroes, with his celestial vision obtained through the grace of that sage, became full of joy, O chief of Bharata's race.'"

SECTION XXXIII.

"Vaisampayana said. 'Then those foremost of men divested of wrath and jealousy, and cleansed of every sin, met with one another, agreeably to those high and auspicious ordinances that have been laid down by regenerate Rishis. All of them were happy of hearts and looked like gods moving in Heaven. Son met with sire or mother, wives with husbands, brother with brother, and friend with friend, O king. The Pandavas, full of joy, met with the mighty bowman Karna as also with the son of Subhadra, and the children of Draupadi. With happy hearts the sons of Pandu approached Karna, O monarch, and became reconciled with him. All those warriors, O chief of Bharata's race, meeting with one another through the grace of the great ascetic, became reconciled with one another. Casting off all unfriendliness, they became established on amity and peace. It was even thus that all those foremost of men, viz., the Kauravas and other kings became united with the Kurus and other kinsmen of theirs as also with their children. The whole of that night they passed in great happiness. Indeed, the Kshatriya warriors, in consequence of the happiness they felt, regarded that place as Heaven itself. There was no grief, no fear, no suspicion, no discontent, no reproach in that region, as those warriors, O monarch, met with one another on that night. Meeting with their sires and brothers and husbands and sons, the ladies cast off all grief and felt great raptures of delight. Having sported with one another thus for one night, those heroes and those ladies, embracing one another and taking one another's leave returned to the places they had come from. Indeed, that foremost of ascetics dismissed that concourse of warriors. Within the twinkling of an eye that large crowd disappeared in the very sight of all those (living) persons. Those high-souled persons, plunging into the sacred river Bhagirathi proceeded, with their cars and standards, to their respective abodes. Some went to the regions of the gods, some to the region of Brahman, some to the region of Varuna, and some to the region of Kuvera. Some among those kings proceeded to the region of Surya. Amongst the Rakshasas and Pisachas some proceeded to the country of Uttara-Kurus. Others, moving in delightful attitudes, went in the company of the deities. Even thus did all those high-souled persons disappear with their vehicles and animals and with all their followers. After all of them had gone away, the great sage, who was standing in the waters of the sacred stream viz., Vyasa of great righteousness and energy, that benefactor of the Kurus, then addressed those Kshatriya ladies who had become widows, and said these words, "Let those amongst these foremost of women that are desirous of attaining to the regions acquired by their husbands cast away all sloth and quickly plunge into the sacred Bhagirathi."— Hearing these words of his, those foremost ladies, placing faith in them, took the permission of their father-in-law, and then plunged into the waters of the Bhagirathi. Freed from human bodies, those chaste ladies then proceeded, O king, with their husbands to the regions acquired by the latter. Even thus, those ladies of virtuous conduct, devoted to their husbands, entering the waters of the Bhagirathi, became freed from their mortal tenements and attained to the companionship of their husbands in the regions acquired by them. Endued with celestial forms, and adorned with celestial ornaments, and wearing celestial vestments and garlands, they proceeded to those regions where their husbands had found their abodes. Possessed of excellent behaviour and many virtues, their anxieties all dispelled, they were seen to ride on excellent cars, and endued with every accomplishment they found those regions of happiness which were theirs by right. Devoted to the duties of piety, Vyasa, at that time, becoming a giver of boons, granted unto all the men there assembled the fruition of the wishes they respectively cherished. People of diverse realms, hearing of this meeting between the hallowed dead and living human beings, became highly delighted. That man who duly listens to this narrative meets with everything that is dear to him. Indeed, he obtains all agreeable objects both here and hereafter. That man of learning and science, that foremost of righteous persons, who recites this narrative for the hearing of others acquires great fame here and an auspicious end hereafter, as also a union with kinsmen and all desirable objects. Such a man has not to undergo painful labour for his sustenance, and meets with all sorts of auspicious objects in life. Even these are the rewards reaped by a person who, endued with devotion to Vedic studies and with penances, recites this narrative in the hearing of others. Those persons who possessed of good conduct, devoted to self-restraint, cleansed of all sins by the gifts they make, endued with sincerity, having tranquil souls, freed from falsehood and the desire of injuring others, adorned with faith, belief in the scriptures, and intelligence, listen to this wonderful parvan, surely attain to the highest goal hereafter.'"

SECTION XXXIV.

Sauti said, "Hearing this story of the re-appearance and departure of his forefathers, king Janamejaya of great intelligence became highly pleased. Filled with joy, he once more questioned Vaisampayana on the subject of the reappearance of dead men, saying,—'How is it possible for persons whose bodies have been destroyed to re-appear in those very forms?' Thus asked, that foremost of regenerate persons, viz., the disciple of Vyasa, that first of speakers, possessed of great energy, thus answered Janamejaya.

"Vaisampayana said, 'This is certain, viz., that acts are never destroyed (without their consequences being enjoyed or endured). Bodies, O king, are born of acts; so also are features. The great primal elements are eternal (indestructible) in consequence of the union with them of the Lord of all beings. They exist with what is eternal. Accordingly, they have no destruction when the non-eternal are destroyed. Acts done without exertion are true and foremost, and bear real fruit. The soul, united however with such acts as require exertion for their accomplishment, enjoys pleasure and pain.[904] Though united so (that is, with pleasure and pain), yet it is a certain inference that the soul is never modified by them, like the reflection of creatures in a mirror. It is never destroyed.[905] As long as one's acts are not exhausted (by enjoyment or endurance of their fruits good and bad), so long does one regard the body to be oneself. The man, however, whose acts have been exhausted, without regarding the body to be self, takes the self to be something

[904] Nilakantha explains that anayasakritani karma implies the religion of Nivritti, for the religion of Pravritti consists of acts that require ayasa or exertion for their accomplishment. The religion of Nivritti or abstention from acts is said hereto be true and superior, and productive of real fruit, in the form, that is, of Emancipation. The soul, however, in the generality of cases, united with ebhih, by which is meant ayasa-kritam karma, that is, the acts done in pursuance of the religion of Pravritti, becomes embodied and, therefore, enjoys happiness or endures misery as the case may be.

[905] The sense seems to be this—when a creature stands before a mirror, its image is formed in the mirror; such reflection, however, never affects the mirror in the least, for when the object leaves the vicinity of the mirror, the image or reflection vanishes away. The soul is like the mirror. Pleasure and pain are like reflections in it. They come and go away without the soul being at all modified by them in anyway. Pleasure and pain are destructible, but not so the soul.

otherwise.[906] Diverse existent objects (such as the primal elements and the senses, etc.) attaining to a body, become united as one. To men of knowledge who understand the difference (between the body and self), those very objects become eternal.[907] In the Horse-sacrifice, this Sruti is heard in the matter of the slaying of the horse. Those which are the certain possessions of embodied creatures, viz., their life-breaths (and the senses, etc.), exist eternally even when they are borne to the other world. I shall tell thee what is beneficial, if it be agreeable to thee, O king. Thou hast, while employed in thy sacrifices, heard of the paths of the deities. When preparations were made for any sacrifice of thine, the deities became beneficially inclined to thee. When indeed, the deities were thus disposed and came to thy sacrifices, they were lords in the matter of the passage (from this to the next world) of the animals slain.[908] For this reason, the eternal ones (viz., Jivas), by adoring the deities in sacrifices, succeed in attaining to excellent goals. When the five primal elements are eternal, when the soul also is eternal, he called Purusha (viz., the soul invested with case) is equally so. When such is the case, he who beholds a creature as disposed to take diverse forms, is regarded as having an erroneous understanding. He who indulges in too much grief at separation is, I think, a foolish person. He who sees evil in separation should abandon union. By standing aloof, no unions are formed, and sorrow is cast off, for sorrow in the world is born of separation.[909] Only he who understands the distinction between body and self, and not another, becomes freed from the erroneous conviction. He that knows the other (viz., self) attains to the highest understanding and becomes freed from error.[910] As regards creatures. they appear from an invisible state, and once more disappear into invisibleness. I do not know him. He also does not know me. As regards myself, renunciation is not yet mine.[911] He that is not possessed of puissance enjoys or endures the fruits of all his acts in those too dies in which he does them. If the act be a mental one, its consequences are enjoyed or endured mentally; if it be done with the body, its consequences are to be enjoyed or endured in the body.'"[912]

---

[906] The ordinary man thinks this conglomeration of diverse objects to be his self. The man of wisdom who has exhausted his acts does not think so. He is freed from the obligation of taking a body.

[907] The sense probably is this. In the case of ordinary men, the component parts of the body dissolve away, while Yogins can keep such parts from dissolution as long as they like.

[908] The sense is, the deities bear away to the next world the animals slain in sacrifices. Though the bodies of such animals are apparently destroyed, yet their life-breaths and senses continue to exist.

[909] The sense is that as wives etc., when lost, are sources of sorrow, wise men should abstain from contracting such relations. They might then be free from sorrow.

[910] Paraparajnah is one that understands the distinction between body and self. Apara is, therefore, one that is not possessed of such knowledge; hence, as Nilakantha explains, it implies one who has not attained to Jnana nishtha. What is said in the second line is that he that adores saguna Brahma, succeeds afterwards, through such adoration, in reaching to nirguna Brahma.

[911] The sense seems to be this: we spring from the unmanifest and disappear once more in the unmanifest. The Bengal texts read the first line incorrectly. It is adarsanalapatitah. The second line is unintelligible. Naham tam vedini is taken by Nilakantha as implying 'I do not know him,' i.e., him that is Emancipate. Asau cha no vetti mam is explained as a due to karanabhat. But who is asau? 'I have no renunciation,' or 'renunciation is not yet mine,' implies that Emancipation, which directly flows from renunciation, is not mine.

[912] What is stated here is that if a man does an act that is bad, its consequences he will have to endure in a human body. The same with regard to rewards. By doing a meritorious act in one's human form, one will enjoy its good consequences in one's human body. So acts done mentally affect the mind and those done with the body affect the body.

It should be noted that the whole of the above translation is offered tentatively. A verbal rendering has been attempted. The chain of reasoning is not at all clear. The commentator has done much to elucidate the

620

SECTION XXXV.

"Vaisampayana said, 'King Dhritarashtra had never beheld his own sons. Obtaining eye-sight through the grace of the Rishi, he beheld, for the first time, O perpetuator of Kuru's race, those children of his that were very like his own self. That foremost of men, viz., the Kuru monarch, had learnt all the duties of kings, as also the Vedas and the Upanishads, and had acquired certitude of understanding (from the same source). Vidura of great wisdom attained to high success through the power of his penances. Dhritarashtra also attained to great success in consequence of having met the ascetic Vyasa.'

"Janamejaya said, 'If Vyasa, disposed to grant me a boon, kindly show me my sire in that form which he had, clad as he used to be clad, and as old as he was when he departed from this world, I may then believe all that thou hast told me. Such a sight will be most agreeable to me. Indeed, I shall regard myself crowned with success. I shall have gained a certainty of conclusion. O, let my wish be crowned with fruition through the grace of that foremost of Rishis.'"

Sauti said,—"After king Janamejaya had said these words, Vyasa of great energy and intelligence showed his grace and brought Parikshit (from the other world). King Janamejaya beheld his royal father, possessed of great beauty, brought down from Heaven, in the same form that he had and of the same age as he was (at the time of leaving this world). The high-souled Samika also, and his son Sringin, were similarly brought there. All the counsellors and ministers of the king beheld them. King Janamejaya. performing the final bath in his sacrifice, became highly glad. He poured the sacred water on his father, even as he caused it to be poured on himself. Having undergone the final bath, the king addressed the regenerate Astika who had sprung from the race of the Yayavaras and who was the son of Jaratkaru, and said these words,—'O Astika, this sacrifice of mine is fraught with many wonderful incidents, since this my sire has been seen by me—he who has dispelled all my sorrows.'

"Astika said, 'The performer of that sacrifice in which the ancient Rishi, the Island-born Vyasa, that vast receptacle of penances, is present, is sure, O foremost one of Kuru's race, to conquer both the worlds. O son of the Pandavas, thou hast heard a wonderful history. The snakes have been consumed into ashes and have followed the footsteps of thy sire. Through thy truthfulness, O monarch, Takshaka has with difficulty escaped a painful fate. The Rishis have all been worshipped. Thou hast seen also the end that has been attained by thy high-souled sire. Having heard this sin-cleansing history thou hast achieved abundant merit. The knots of thy heart have been untied through sight of this foremost of person. They that are the supporters of the wings of Righteousness, they that are of good conduct and excellent disposition, they at sight of whom sins become attenuated,—we should all bow to them.'"

Sauti continued, "Having heard this from that foremost of regenerate ones, King Janamejaya worshipped that Rishi, repeatedly honouring him in every way. Conversant with all duties he then asked the Rishi Vaisampayana of unfading glory about the sequel, O best of ascetics, of king Dhritarashtra's residence in the woods."

sense, but the original obscurities have scarcely been removed.

SECTION XXXVI.

"Janamejaya said, 'Having seen his sons and grandsons with all their friends and followers, what, indeed, did that ruler of men, viz., Dhritarashtra, and king Yudhishthira also, do?'

"Vaisampayana said, 'Beholding that exceedingly wonderful sight, viz., the reappearance of his children, the royal sage, Dhritarashtra, became divested of his grief and returned (from the banks of the Bhagirathi) to his retreat. The common people and all the great Rishis, dismissed by Dhritarashtra, returned to the places they respectively wished. The high-souled Pandavas, accompanied by their wives, and with a small retinue, went to the retreat of the high-souled monarch. Then Satyavati's son, who was honoured by regenerate Rishis and all other persons, arrived at the retreat, addressed Dhritarashtra, saying,—"O mighty-armed Dhritarashtra, O son of Kuru's race, listen to what I say. Thou hast heard diverse discourses from Rishis of great knowledge and sacred deeds, of wealth of penances and excellence of blood, of conversance with the Vedas and their branches, of piety and years, and of great eloquence. Do not set thy mind again on sorrow. He that is possessed of wisdom is never agitated at ill luck. Thou hast also heard the mysteries of the deities from Narada of celestial form. Thy children have all attained, through observance of Kshatriya practices, to that auspicious goal which is sanctified by weapons. Thou hast seen how they move about at will in great happiness. This Yudhishthira of great intelligence is awaiting thy permission, with all his brothers and wives and kinsmen. Do thou dismiss him. Let him go back to his kingdom and rule it. They have passed more than a month in thus residing in the woods. The station of sovereignty should always be well guarded. O king, O thou of Kuru's race, [thy] kingdom has many foes." Thus addressed by Vyasa of incomparable energy, the Kuru king, well-versed in words, summoned Yudhishthira and said unto him,—"O Ajatasatru, blessings on thee! Do thou listen to me, with all thy brothers. Through thy grace, O king, grief no longer stands in my way. I am living as happily, O son, with thee here as if I were in the city called after the elephant. With thee as my protector, O learned one, I am enjoying all agreeable objects. I have obtained from thee all those services which a son renders to his sire. I am highly gratified with thee. I have not the least dissatisfaction with thee, O mighty-armed one. Go now, O son, without tarrying here any longer. Meeting with thee, my penances are being slackened. This my body, endued with penances, I have been able to sustain only in consequence of my meeting with thee.[913] These two mothers of thine, subsisting now upon fallen leaves of trees, and observing vows similar to mine, will not live long. Duryodhana and others, who have become denizens of the other world, have been seen by us, through the puissance of Vyasa's penances and through (the merit of) this my meeting with thee. O sinless one, the purpose of my life has been attained. I now wish to set myself to the practice of the austerest of penances. It behoveth thee to grant me permission. On thee now the obsequial cake, the fame and achievements, and the race of our ancestors, rest. O mighty-armed one, do thou then depart either tomorrow or this very day. Do not tarry, O son. O chief of Bharata's race, thou hast repeatedly heard what the duties are of kings. I do not see what more I can say unto thee. I have no longer any need with thee, O thou of great puissance."'

"Vaisampayana continued, 'Unto the (old) monarch who said so, king Yudhishthira

---

[913] The Bengal reading manah is incorrect. It should be punah.

replied,—"O thou that art conversant with every rule of righteousness, it behoveth thee, not to cast me off in this way. I am guilty of no fault. Let all my brothers and followers depart as they like. With steadfast vows I shall wait upon thee and upon these two mothers of mine." Unto him Gandhari then said,—"O son, let it not be so. Listen, the race of Kuru is now dependant on thee. The obsequial cake also of my father-in-law depends on thee. Depart then, O son. We have been sufficiently honoured and served by thee. Thou shouldst do what the king says. Indeed, O son, thou shouldst obey the behests of thy sire.'"

"Vaisampayana continued,—'Thus addressed by Gandhari, King Yudhishthira, rubbing his eyes which were bathed in tears of affection, said these words of lament. "The king casts me off, as also Gandhari of great fame. My heart, however, is bound to thee. How shall I, filled as I am with grief, leave thee? I do not, however, at the same time, venture to obstruct thy penances, O righteous lady. There is nothing higher than penances. It is by penances that one attains to the Supreme. O queen, my heart no longer turns as of old towards kingdom. My mind is wholly set upon penances now. The whole Earth is empty now. O auspicious lady, she does not please me any longer. Our kinsmen have been reduced in number. Our strength is no longer what it was before. The Panchalas have been wholly exterminated. They exist in name only. O auspicious lady, I do not behold any one that may assist as their re-establishment and growth. All of them have been consumed to ashes by Drona on the field of battle. Those that remained were slain by Drona's son at night. The Chedis and the Matsyas, who were our friends, no longer exist. Only the tribes of the Vrishnis are all that remain, Vasudeva having upheld them. Beholding only the Vrishnis I wish to live. My desire of life, however, is due to my wish of acquiring merit and not wealth or enjoyment. Do thou cast auspicious looks upon us all. To obtain thy sight will be difficult for us. The king will commence to practise the most austere and unbearable of penances." Hearing these words, that lord of battle, the mighty-armed Sahadeva, with eyes bathed in tears, addressed Yudhishthira, saying,—"O chief of Bharata's race, I dare not leave my mother. Do thou return to the capital soon. I shall practise penances, O puissant one. Even here I shall emaciate my body by penances, engaged in serving the feet of the king and of these my mothers." Unto that mighty-armed hero, Kunti, after an embrace, said—"Depart, O son. Do not say so. Do my bidding. Do all of you go hence. Let peace be yours. Ye sons, let happiness be yours. By your stay here, our penances will be obstructed. Bound by the ties of my affection for thee, I shall fall off from my high penances. Therefore, O son, leave us. Short is the period that we have of life, O thou of great puissance." By these and diverse other speeches of Kunti, the minds of Sahadeva and king Yudhishthira were composed. Those foremost ones of Kuru's race, having received the permission of their mother as also of the (old) monarch, saluted the latter and began to take his leave.

"'Yudhishthira said, "Gladdened by auspicious blessings, we shall return to the capital. Indeed, O king, having received thy permission, we shall leave this retreat, freed from every sin." Thus addressed by the high-souled king Yudhishthira the just, that royal sage, viz., Dhritarashtra, blessed Yudhishthira and gave him permission. The king comforted Bhima, that foremost of all persons endued with great strength. Endued with great energy and great intelligence, Bhima showed his submissiveness to the king. Embracing Arjuna and clasping those foremost of men, viz., the twins also, and blessing them repeatedly, the Kuru king gave them permission to depart. They worshipped the feet of Gandhari and received her blessings also. Their mother Kunti then smelt their heads, and dismissed them. They then circumambulated the king like calves, when prevented from sucking their dams. Indeed, they repeatedly walked round him, looking steadfastly at him.[914] Then all the ladies of the Kaurava household, headed by Draupadi, worshipped their father-in-law according to the rites laid down in the scriptures, and took his leave. Gandhari and Kunti embraced each of them, and blessing them bade them go. Their mothers-in-law instructed them as to how they should conduct themselves. Obtaining leave, they then departed, with their husbands. Then loud sounds were heard, uttered by the charioteers that said,—"Yoke, yoke,"—as also of camels that grunted aloud and of steeds that neighed briskly. King Yudhishthira, with his wives and troops and all his kinsmen, set out for Hastinapura."'

SECTION XXXVII. (*Naradagamana Parva*)

"Vaisampayana said, 'After two years had elapsed from the date of the return of the Pandavas (from the retreat of their sire), the celestial Rishi, Narada, O king, came to Yudhishthira. The mighty-armed Kuru king, that foremost of speakers, viz., Yudhishthira, having duly worshipped him, caused him to take a seat. After the Rishi had rested awhile, the king asked him, saying,—"It is after a long time that I behold thy holy self arrived at my court. Art thou in peace and happiness, O learned Brahmana? What are those countries which thou hast passed through? What shall I do to thee? Do thou tell me. Thou art the foremost of regenerate ones, and thou art our highest refuge."

"'Narada said, "I have not seen thee for a long while. Hence it is that I have come to thee from my ascetic retreat. I have seen many sacred waters, and the sacred stream Ganga also, O king."

"'Yudhishthira said, "People dwelling on the banks of Ganga report that the high-souled Dhritarashtra is practising the austerest of penances. Hast thou seen him there? Is that perpetuator of Kuru's race in peace? Are Gandhari and Pritha, and the Suta's son Sanjaya also, in peace? How, indeed, is it faring with that royal sire of mine? I desire to hear this, O holy one, if thou hast seen the king (and knowest of his condition)."

"'Narada said, "Listen, O king, with calmness to me as I tell thee what I have heard and seen in that ascetic retreat. After thy return from Kurukshetra, O delighter of the Kurus, thy sire, O king, proceeded towards Gangadwara. That intelligent monarch took with him his (sacred) fire, Gandhari and his daughter-in-law Kunti, as also Sanjaya of the Suta caste, and all the Yajakas. Possessed of wealth of penances, thy sire set himself to the practice of severe austerities. He held pebbles of stone in his mouth and had air alone for his subsistence, and abstained altogether from speech. Engaged in severe penances, he was worshipped by all the ascetics in the woods. In six months the king was reduced only to a skeleton. Gandhari subsisted on water alone, while Kunti took a little every sixth day. The sacred fire, O monarch, (belonging to the Kuru king) was duly worshipped by the sacrificing assistants that were with him, with libations of clarified butter poured on it. They did this whether the king saw the rite or not. The king had no fixed habitation. He became a wanderer through those woods. The two queens, as also Sanjaya, followed him. Sanjaya acted as the guide on even and uneven land. The faultless Pritha, O king, became the eye of Gandhari. One day, that best of kings proceeded to a spot on the margin of Ganga. He then bathed in the sacred stream and finishing his ablutions turned his face towards his retreat. The wind rose high. A fierce forest-conflagration set in. It began to burn that forest all around. When the herds of animals were being burnt all around, as

---

[914] Nripam pradakshinam chakru is the construction. Nivarana has snanapanat understood after it.

also the snakes that inhabited that region, herds of wild boars began to take themselves to the nearest marshes and waters. When that forest was thus afflicted on all sides and such distress came upon all the living creatures residing there, the king, who had taken no food, was incapable of moving or exerting himself at all. Thy two mothers also, exceedingly emaciated, were unable to move. The king, seeing the conflagration approach him from all sides, addressed the Suta Sanjaya, that foremost of skilful charioteers, saying,—'Go, O Sanjaya, to such a place where the fire may not burn thee. As regards ourselves, we shall suffer our bodies to be destroyed by this fire and attain to the highest goal.' Unto him, Sanjaya, that foremost of speakers, said,—'O king, this death, brought on by a fire that is not sacred, will prove calamitous to thee. I do not, however, see any means by which thou canst escape from this conflagration. That which should next be done should be indicated by thee.' Thus addressed by Sanjaya the king once more said,—'This death cannot be calamitous to us, for we have left our home of our own accord. Water, fire, wind, and abstention from food,[915] (as means of death), are laudable for ascetics. Do thou, therefore, leave us, O Sanjaya, without any delay.' Having said these words to Sanjaya, the king concentrated his mind. Facing the east, he sat down, with Gandhari and Kunti. Beholding him in that attitude, Sanjaya walked round him. Endued with intelligence, Sanjaya said,—'Do thou concentrate thy soul, O puissant one.' The son of a Rishi, and himself possessed of great wisdom, the king acted as he was told. Restraining all the senses, he remained like a post of wood. The highly blessed Gandhari, and thy mother Pritha too, remained in the same attitude. Then thy royal sire was overtaken by the forest-conflagration. Sanjaya, his minister, succeeded in escaping from that conflagration. I saw him on the banks of Ganga in the midst of ascetics. Endued with great energy and great intelligence, he bade them farewell and then started for the mountains of Himavat. Even thus the high-souled Kuru king met with his death, and it was even thus that Gandhari and Kunti, thy two mothers, also met with death, O monarch. In course of my wanderings at will, I saw the bodies of that king and those two queens, O Bharata. Many ascetics came to that retreat, having heard of the end of king Dhritarashtra. They did not at all grieve for that end of theirs. There, O best of men, I heard all the details of how the king and the two queens, O son of Pandu, had been burnt. O king of kings, thou shouldst not grieve for him. The monarch, of his own will, as also Gandhari and thy mother, obtained that contact with fire.'"

"Vaisampayana continued,—'Hearing of the exit of Dhritarashtra from this world, the high-souled Pandavas all gave way to great grief. Loud sounds of wailing were heard within the inner apartments of the palace. The citizens also, hearing of the end of the old king, uttered loud lamentations. "O fie!" cried king Yudhishthira in great agony, raising his arms aloft. Thinking of his mother, he wept like a child. All his brothers too, headed by Bhimasena, did the same. Hearing that Pritha had met with such a fate, the ladies of the royal household tittered loud lamentations of grief. All the people grieved upon hearing that the old king, who had become childless, had been burnt to death and that the helpless Gandhari too had shared his fate. When those sounds of wailing ceased for a while, king Yudhishthira the just, stopping his tears by summoning all his patience, said these words.'"

---

[915] Vikarshanam is emaciation of the body by abstention from all food.

SECTION XXXVIII.

"'Yudhishthira said, "When such a fate overtook that high-souled monarch who was engaged in austere penances, notwithstanding the fact of his having such kinsmen as ourselves all alive, it seems to me, O regenerate one, that the end of human beings is difficult to guess. Alas, who would have thought that the son of Vichitraviryya would thus be burnt to death. He had a hundred sons each endued with mighty arms and possessed of great prosperity. The king himself had the strength of ten thousand elephants. Alas, even he has been burnt to death in a forest-conflagration! Alas, he who had formerly been fanned with palm leaves by the fair hands of beautiful women was fanned by vultures with their wings after he had been burnt to death in a forest-conflagration! He who was formerly roused from sleep every morning by bands of Sutas and Magadhas had to sleep on the bare ground through the acts of my sinful self. I do not grieve for the famous Gandhari who had been deprived of all her children. Observing the same vows as her husband, she has attained to those very regions which have become his. I grieve, however, for Pritha who, abandoning the blazing prosperity of her sons, became desirous of residing in the woods. Fie on this sovereignty of ours, fie on our prowess, fie on the practices of Kshatriyas! Though alive, we are really dead! O foremost of superior Brahmanas, the course of Time is very subtle and difficult to understand, inasmuch as Kunti, abandoning sovereignty, became desirous of taking up her abode in the forest. How is it that she who was the mother of Yudhishthira, of Bhima, of Vijaya, was burnt to death like a helpless creature. Thinking of this I become stupefied. In vain was the deity of fire gratified at Khandava by Arjuna. Ingrate that he is, forgetting that service he has burnt to death the mother of his benefactor! Alas, how could that deity burn the mother of Arjuna. Putting on the guise of a Brahmana, he had formerly come to Arjuna for soliciting a favour. Fie on the deity of fire! Fie on the celebrated success of Partha's shafts! This is another incident, O holy one, that appears to me to be productive of greater misery, for that lord of Earth met with death by union with a fire that was not sacred. How could such a death overtake that royal sage of Kuru's race who, after having ruled the whole Earth, was engaged in the practice of penances. In that great forest there were fires that had been sanctified with mantras. Alas, my father has made his exit from this world, coming in contact with an unsanctified fire! I suppose that Pritha, emaciated and reduced to a form in which all her nerves became visible, must have trembled in fear and cried aloud, saying,—'O son Yudhishthira,' and awaited the terrible approach of the conflagration. She must have also said,—'O Bhima, rescue me from this danger'—when she, my mother, was surrounded on all sides by that terrible conflagration. Among all her sons, Sahadeva, was her darling. Alas, that heroic son of Madravati did not rescue her." Hearing these lamentations of the king, those persons that were present there began to weep, embracing each other. In fact, the five sons of Pandu were so stricken with grief that they resembled living creatures at the time of the dissolution of the universe. The sound of lamentations uttered by those weeping heroes, filling the spacious chambers of the palace, escaped therefrom and penetrated the very welkin.'"

SECTION XXXIX.

"'Narada said, "The king has not been burnt to death by an unsanctified fire. I have heard this there. I tell thee, O Bharata, such has not been the fate of Vichitraviryya. It has been heard by us that when the old king endued with great intelligence and subsisting on air alone entered the woods (after his return from Gangadwara), he caused his sacrificial fires to be duly ignited. Having performed his sacred rites therewith, he abandoned them all. Then the Yajaka Brahmanas he had with him cast off those fires in a solitary part of the woods and went away as they liked on other errands, O foremost one of Bharata's race. The fire thus cast off grew in the woods. It then produced a general conflagration in the forest. Even this is what I have heard from the ascetics dwelling on the banks of Ganga. United with that (sacred) fire of his own, O chief of the Bharatas, the king, as I have already said unto thee, met with death on the banks of Ganga. O sinless one, this is what the ascetics have told me,—those, viz., whom I saw on the banks of the sacred Bhagirathi, O Yudhishthira. Thus O lord of Earth, king Dhritarashtra, coming into contact with his own sacred fire, departed from this world and attained to that high goal that has been his. Through service rendered by her to her seniors, thy mother, O lord of men, has attained to very great success. There is not the slightest doubt of this. It behoveth thee, O king of kings, to now discharge the rites of water to their honour, with all thy brothers. Let, therefore, the necessary steps be taken towards that end.'"

"Vaisampayana continued,—'Then that lord of Earth, that foremost of men, that upholder of the burthens of the Pandavas, went out, accompanied by all his brothers as well as the ladies of his household. The inhabitants of the city as also those of the provinces, impelled by their loyalty, also went out. They all proceeded towards the banks of Ganga, every one clad in only single peace of raiment. Then all those foremost of men, having plunged into the stream, placed Yuyutsu at their head, and began to offer oblations of water unto the high-souled king. And they also gave similar oblations unto Gandhari and Pritha, naming each separately and mentioning their families. Having finished those rites that cleanse the living, they came back but without entering their capital took up their residence outside of it. They also despatched a number of trusted people well conversant with the ordinances relating to the cremation of the dead, to Gangadwara where the old king had been burnt to death. The king, having rewarded those men beforehand, commanded them to accomplish those rites of cremation which the bodies of Dhritarashtra and Gandhari and Kunti still awaited.[916] On twelfth day, the king, properly purified, duly performed the Sraddhas of his deceased relations, which were characterised by gifts in abundance. Referring to Dhritarashtra, Yudhishthira made many gifts of gold and silver, of kine and costly beds. Uttering the names of Gandhari and Pritha, the king, endued with great energy, made many excellent gifts. Every man received what thing he wished and as much of it as he wished. Beds and food, and cars and conveyances, and jewels and gems, and other wealth were given away in profusion. Indeed, the king referring to his two mothers, gave away cars and conveyances, robes and coverlets, various kinds of food, and female slaves adorned with diverse ornaments. Having thus made many kinds of gifts in profusion, that lord of Earth then entered his capital called after the elephant. Those men who had gone to the banks of Ganga at the

---

[916] The verb anvacat from root sas can govern two objectives. Here the two objectives are purushan and krityani.

command of the king, having disposed of (by cremation) the remains of the king and two queens, returned to the city. Having duly honoured those remains with garlands and scents of diverse kinds and disposed of them, they informed Yudhishthira of the accomplishment of their task. The great Rishi Narada, having comforted king Yudhishthira of righteous soul, went away to where he liked. Even thus did king Dhritarashtra make his exit from this world after having passed three years in the forest and ten and five years in the city. Having lost all his children in battle, he had many gifts in honour of his kinsmen, relatives, and friends, his brethren and own people. King Yudhishthira after the death of his uncle, became very cheerless. Deprived of his kinsmen and relatives, he somehow bore the burthen of sovereignty.

"'One should listen with rapt attention to this Asramavasika Parvan, and having heard it recited, one should feed Brahmanas with Habishya, honouring them with scents and garlands.'"

THE END OF ASRAMAVASIKA PARVAN

BOOK 16. MAUSALA-PARVA

SECTION I.

Om! Having bowed down unto Narayana, and to Nara, the foremost of men, as also to the goddess Sarasvati, should the word "Jaya" be uttered.

"Vaishampayana said: 'When the thirty-sixth year (after the battle) was reached, the delighter of the Kurus, Yudhishthira, beheld many unusual portents. Winds, dry and strong, and showering gravels, blew from every side. Birds began to wheel, making circles from right to left. The great rivers ran in opposite directions. The horizon on every side seemed to be always covered with fog. Meteors, showering (blazing) coals, fell on the Earth from the sky. The Sun's disc, O king, seemed to be always covered with dust. At its rise, the great luminary of day was shorn of splendour and seemed to be crossed by headless trunks (of human beings). Fierce circles of light were seen every day around both the Sun and the Moon. These circles showed three hues. Their edges seemed to be black and rough and ashy-red in colour. These and many other omens, foreshadowing fear and danger, were seen, O king, and filled the hearts of men with anxiety. A little while after, the Kuru king Yudhishthira heard of the wholesale carnage of the Vrishnis in consequence of the iron bolt. The son of Pandu, hearing that only Vasudeva and Rama had escaped with life, summoned his brothers and took counsel with them as to what they should do. Meeting with one another, they became greatly distressed upon hearing that the Vrishnis had met with destruction through the Brahmana's rod of chastisement. The death of Vasudeva, like the drying up of the ocean, those heroes could not believe. In fact the destruction of the wielder of Saranga was incredible to them. Informed of the incident about the iron bolt, the Pandavas became filled with grief and sorrow. In fact, they sat down, utterly cheerless and penetrated with blank despair.'

"Janamejaya said: 'Indeed, O holy one, how was it that the Andhakas along with Vrishnis, and those great car-warriors, the Bhojas, met with destruction in the very sight of Vasudeva?'

"Vaishampayana continued: 'When the thirty-sixth year was reached (after the great battle) a great calamity overtook the Vrishnis. Impelled by Time, they all met with destruction in consequence of the iron bolt.'

"Janamejaya said: 'Cursed by whom did those heroes, the Vrishnis, the Andhakas, and the Bhojas, met with destruction? O foremost of regenerate persons, do thou tell me this in detail.'

"Vaishampayana continued: 'One day, the Vrishni heroes numbering Samva amongst them, saw Vishvamitra and Kanwa and Narada arrived at Dwaraka. Afflicted by the rod of chastisement wielded by the deities, those heroes, causing Samva to be disguised like a woman, approached those ascetics and said, "This one is the wife of Vabhru of immeasurable energy who is desirous of having a son. Ye Rishis, do you know for certain what this one will bring forth?"

"'Hear now, O king, what those ascetics, attempted to be thus deceived, said: "This heir of Vasudeva, by name Samva, will bring forth a fierce iron bolt for the destruction of the Vrishnis and the Andhakas. Ye wicked and cruel ones, intoxicated with pride, through that iron bolt ye will become the exterminators of your race with the exception of Rama and Janarddana. The blessed hero armed with the plough will enter the ocean, casting off his body, while a hunter of the name of Jara will pierce the high-souled Krishna while lying on the ground."

"'Endeavoured to be deceived by those wicked ones, those ascetics, with eyes red in wrath, looked at each other and uttered those words. Having said so they then proceeded to see Keshava. The slayer of Madhu, informed of what had taken place, summoned all the Vrishnis and told them of it. Possessed of great intelligence and fully acquainted with what the end of his race would be, he simply said that that which was destined would surely happen. Hrishikesa having said so, entered his mansion. The Lord of the universe did not wish to ordain otherwise. When the next day came, Samva actually brought forth an iron bolt through which all the individuals in the race of the Vrishnis and the Andhakas became consumed into ashes. Indeed, for the destruction of the Vrishnis and the Andhakas, Samva brought forth, through that curse, a fierce iron bolt that looked like a gigantic messenger of death. The fact was duly reported to the king. In great distress of mind, the king (Ugrasena) caused that iron bolt to be reduced into fine powder. Men were employed, O king, to cast that powder into the sea. At the command of Ahuka, of Janarddana, of Rama, and of the high-souled Vabhru, it was, again, proclaimed throughout the city that from that day, among all the Vrishnis and the Andhakas no one should manufacture wines and intoxicating spirits of any kind, and that whoever would secretly manufacture wines and spirits should be impaled alive with all his kinsmen. Through fear of the king, and knowing that it was the command of Rama also of unimpeachable deeds, all the citizens bound themselves by a rule and abstained from manufacturing wines and spirits.'"

SECTION II.

"Vaishampayana said: 'While the Vrishnis and the Andhakas were thus endeavouring (to avoid the impending calamity), the embodied form of Time (death) every day wandered about their houses. He looked like a man of terrible and fierce aspect. Of bald head, he was black and of tawny complexion. Sometimes he was seen by the Vrishnis as he peered into their houses. The mighty bowmen among the Vrishnis shot hundreds and thousands of shafts at him, but none of these succeeded in piercing him, for he was none else than the Destroyer of all creatures. Day by day strong winds blew, and many were the evil omens that arose, awful and foreboding the destruction of the Vrishnis and the Andhakas. The streets swarmed with rats and mice. Earthen pots showed cracks or broke from no apparent cause. At night, the rats and mice ate away the hair and nails of slumbering men. Sarikas chirped, sitting within the houses of the Vrishnis. The noise made by those birds ceased not for even a short while by day or by night. The Sarashas were heard to imitate the hooting of the owl, and goats imitated the cries, O Bharata, of jackals. Many birds appeared, impelled by Death, that were pale of complexion but that had legs red of hue. Pigeons were seen to always disport in the houses of the Vrishnis. Asses were born of kine, and elephants of mules. Cats were born of bitches, and mouse of the mongoose. The Vrishnis, committing sinful acts, were not seen to feel any shame. They showed disregard for Brahmanas and the Pitris and the deities. They insulted and humiliated their preceptors and seniors. Only Rama and Janardana acted differently. Wives deceived their husbands, and husbands deceived their wives. Fires, when ignited, cast their flames towards the left. Sometimes they threw out flames whose splendour was blue and red. The Sun, whether when rising or setting over the city, seemed to be surrounded by headless trunks of human form. In cook rooms, upon food that was clean and well-boiled, were seen, when it was served out for eating, innumerable worms of diverse kinds. When Brahmanas, receiving gifts, blessed the day or the hour (fixed for this or that undertaking) or when high-souled men were engaged in silent recitations, the heavy tread was heard of innumerable men running about, but no one could be seen to whom the sound of such tread could be ascribed. The constellations were repeatedly seen to be struck by the planets. None amongst the Yadavas could, however, obtain a sight of the constellation of his birth. When the Panchajanya was blown in their houses, asses of dissonant and awful voice brayed aloud from every direction. Beholding these signs that indicated the perverse course of Time, and seeing that the day of the new moon coincided with the thirteenth (and the fourteenth) lunation, Hrishikesa, summoning the Yadavas, said unto them these words: "The fourteenth lunation has been made the fifteenth by Rahu once more. Such a day had happened at the time of the great battle of the Bharatas. It has once more appeared, it seems, for our destruction." The slayer of Keshi, Janardana, thinking upon the omens that Time showed, understood that the thirty-sixth year had come, and that what Gandhari, burning with grief on account of the death of her sons, and deprived of all her kinsmen, had said was about to transpire. "The present is exactly similar to that time when Yudhishthira noted at such awful omens when the two armies had been arrayed in order of battle." Vasudeva, having said so, endeavoured to bring about those occurrences which would make Gandhari's words true. That chastiser of foes commanded the Vrishnis to make a pilgrimage to some sacred water. The messengers forthwith proclaimed at the command of Keshava that the Vrishnis should make a journey to the sea-coast for bathing in the sacred waters of the ocean.'"

SECTION III.

"Vaishampayana said: 'At that time the Vrishni ladies dreamed every night that a woman of black complexion and white teeth, entering their abodes, laughed aloud and ran through Dwaraka, snatching from them the auspicious threads in their wrists. The men dreamt that terrible vultures, entering their houses and fire-chambers, gorged themselves on their bodies. Their ornaments and umbrellas and standards and armour were seen to be taken away by terrible Rakshasas. In the very sight of the Vrishnis, the discus of Krishna, given by Agni, made of iron and having its nave composed of hardest adamant, ascended into the firmament. In the very sight of Daruka, the excellent car of Vasudeva, of solar effulgence, and properly equipped, was taken away by the horses yoked unto it. Those foremost of steeds, numbering four, (Saivya, Sugriva, Meghapushpa and Valahaka), and endued with the speed of thought, fled away, dragging the car after them along the surface of the ocean. The two great standards of Krishna's car and Valadeva's car, that with the device of Garuda and that bearing the device of the palmyra, which were reverently worshipped by those two heroes, were taken away by Apsaras who, day and night, called upon the Vrishnis and the Andhakas to set out on a pilgrimage to some sacred water. When these omens were seen and heard, those foremost of men, the mighty car-warriors of the Vrishnis and the Andhakas, became desirous of setting out, with their whole families, on a pilgrimage to some sacred water. They prepared diverse kinds of viands and edibles and diverse kinds of wines and meat. The troops of the Vrishnis and the Andhakas, blazing with beauty and endued with fierce energy, then set out from the city on cars and steeds and elephants. The Yadavas, then, with their wives, proceeded to Prabhasa and took up their residence there, each in the (temporary) habitation that was assigned to him, and all having an abundance of provisions consisting of edibles and drink.

"'Hearing that they had taken up their abode on the sea-coast, Uddhava, the wisest of men, who was, besides, well-versed in Yoga, proceeded there and took his leave (for departing). Krishna, with joined hands, saluted Uddhava, and seeing him bent on departing (from the world) and knowing that the destructions of the Vrishnis was at hand, did not feel any disposition to prevent him. The mighty car-warriors among the Vrishnis and the Andhakas, whose hour had come, then saw Uddhava proceed on his great journey, filling the whole welkin with his splendour. The Vrishnis, mixing with wine the food that had been cooked for high-souled Brahmanas, gave it away unto monkeys and apes. Those heroes of fierce energy then began their high revels, of which drinking formed the chief feature, at Prabhasa. The entire field echoed with the blare of hundreds of trumpets and abounded with actors and dancers plying their vocations. In the very sight of Krishna, Rama began to drink, with Kritavarma, Yuyudhana and Gada; and Vabhru also did the same. Then Yuyudhana, inebriated with wine, derisively laughing at and insulting Kritavarma in the midst of that assembly, said, "What Kshatriya is there who, armed with weapons, will slay men locked in the embraces of sleep and, therefore, already dead? Hence, O son of Hridika, the Yadavas will never tolerate what thou hast done." When Yuyudhana had said these words, Pradyumna, that foremost of car-warriors, applauded them, expressing his disregard for the son of Hridika.

"'Highly incensed at this, Kritavarma, emphasising his disregard for Satyaki, by pointing to him with his left hand, said these words: "Professing thyself to be a hero, how couldst thou so cruelly slay the armless Bhurishrava who, on the field of battle, (gave up all hostile intentions and) sat in praya?"

"'Hearing these words of his, Keshava, that slayer of hostile heroes, giving way to wrath, cast an angry glance at Kritavarma. Then Satyaki informed the slayer of Madhu as to how Kritavarma had behaved towards Satrajit for taking away from him the celebrated gem Syamantaka. Hearing the narrative, Satyabhama, giving way to wrath and tears, approached Keshava and sitting on his lap enhanced his anger (for Kritavarma). Then rising up in a rage, Satyaki said, "I swear to thee by Truth that I shall soon cause this one to follow in the wake of the five sons of Draupadi, and of Dhrishtadyumna and Shikhandi, they that were slain by this sinful wretch, while they were asleep, with the assistance of Drona's son. O thou of slender waist, Kritavarma's period of life and fame have come to their end."

"'Having said these words, Satyaki rushed at Kritavarma and severed his head with a sword in the very sight of Keshava. Yuyudhana, having achieved this feat, began to strike down others there present. Hrishikesa ran to prevent him from doing further mischief. At that time, however, O monarch, the Bhojas and Andhakas, impelled by the perverseness of the hour that had come upon them, all became as one man and surrounded the son of Sini. Janardana of mighty energy, knowing the character of the hour, stood unmoved without giving way to anger at the sight of those heroes rushing in wrath at Satyaki from every side. Urged by fate and inebriated with drink, they began to strike Yuyudhana with the pots from which they had been eating. When the son of Sini was being thus assaulted, Rukmini's son became highly enraged. He rushed forward for rescuing Satyaki who was engaged with the Bhojas and the Andhakas. Endued with might of arms and wealth of energy, those two heroes exerted themselves with great courage. But as the odds were overwhelming, both of them were slain in the very sight of Krishna. The delighter of the Yadus, beholding his own son, and the son of Sini too, slain, took up, in wrath, a handful of the Eraka grass that grew there. That handful of grass became a terrible bolt of iron endued with the energy of the thunderbolt. With it Krishna slew all those that came before him. Then the Andhakas and the Bhojas, the Saineyas and the Vrishnis, urged by Time, struck one another in that fearful melee. Indeed, O king, whoever amongst them took up in wrath a few blades of the Eraka grass, these, in his hands, became soon converted into a thunderbolt, O puissant one. Every blade of grass there was seen to be converted into a terrible iron bolt. All this, know, O king, was due to the curse denounced by Brahmanas. He who hurled a blade of grass saw that it pierced through even such things as were utterly impenetrable. In fact, every blade was seen to become a terrible bolt having the force of thunder. Son killed sire, and sire killed son, O Bharata. Inebriated with wine, they rushed and fell upon one another. The Kukuras and the Andhakas met with destruction like insects rushing at a blazing fire. As they were thus being slaughtered, no one among them thought of escaping by flight. Knowing that the hour of destruction had come, the mighty-armed Keshava stood there, eyeing everything. Indeed, the slayer of Madhu stood, raising a bolt of iron formed of a blade of grass. Beholding that Samva was slain, as also Charudeshna and Pradyumna and Aniruddha, Madhava became filled with rage. Beholding Gada lying dead on the ground, his wrath became enhanced. The wielder of Sarnga and the discus and the mace then exterminated the Vrishnis and the Andhakas. Hear, O king, what that conquerer of hostile towns, Vabhru of mighty energy and Daruka then said to Krishna, "O holy one, a very large number of men has been slain by thee. Turn now to where Rama has gone. We wish to go there where he has proceeded."'"

SECTION IV.

"Vaishampayana said: 'Then Daruka and Keshava and Vabhru left that spot, following in the wake of Rama (for discovering his retreat). They beheld that hero of infinite energy sitting thoughtfully, reclining his back against a tree, in a solitary spot of earth. Finding Rama of great soul, Krishna commanded Daruka, saying, "Going to the Kurus, inform Partha of this great slaughter of the Yadus. Let Arjuna come here quickly, hearing of the destruction of the Yadavas through the Brahmana's curse."

"'Thus addressed, Daruka, deprived of his senses by grief, proceeded on a car to the (capital of the) Kurus. After Daruka had gone away, Keshava, seeing Vabhru waiting on him, told him these words: "Do thou go quickly for protecting the ladies. Let not robbers do them any injury, tempted by the wealth (that is with them)." Thus commanded by

Keshava, Vabhru, still helpless with wine but cheerless at the slaughter of his kinsmen, departed. He had rested for a while by the side of Keshava, but as soon as he had proceeded to a distance, the iron-bolt, attaching itself to a mallet in the hands of a hunter, suddenly sprang of itself upon that solitary survivor of the Yadava race and slew him, who also had been included in the curse of the Brahmanas. Beholding Vabhru slain, Keshava of great energy addressed his elder brother and said, "Do thou, O Rama wait for me here till I place the ladies under the care of kinsmen."

"'Entering the city of Dwaravati, Janardana said these words unto his father, "Do thou protect all the ladies of our house, till Dhananjaya comes. At the skirts of the forest Rama is waiting for me. I shall meet him today. This great carnage of the Yadus has been beheld by me even as I beheld before the carnage of those Kshatriyas who were the foremost ones of Kuru's race. It is impossible for me to see this city of the Yadavas without the Yadus beside me. Know that proceeding to the woods I shall practise penances with Rama in my company." Having said these words, Krishna touched the feet of his father with his head, and quickly left his presence. Then a loud wail of sorrow arose from the ladies and children of his house. Hearing that loud sound of wailing uttered by the weeping ladies, Keshava retraced his foot-steps and said unto them, "Arjuna will come here. That foremost of men will relieve you of your grief."

"'Proceeding then to the forest, Keshava beheld Rama sitting in a solitary spot thereof. He also saw that Rama had set himself to Yoga and that from out his mouth was issuing a mighty snake. The colour of that snake was white. Leaving the human body (in which he had dwelt so long), that high-souled naga of a 1,000 heads and having a form as large as that of a mountain, endued besides with red eyes, proceeded along that way which led to the ocean. Ocean himself, and many celestial snakes, and many sacred Rivers were there, for receiving him with honour. There were Karkotaka and Vasuki and Takshaka and Prithusravas and Varuna and Kunjara, and Misri and Sankha and Kumuda and Pundarika, and the high-souled Dhritarashtra, and Hrada and Kratha and Sitikantha of fierce energy, and Chakramanda and Atishanda, and that foremost of Nagas called Durmukha, and Amvarisha, and king Varuna himself, O monarch. Advancing forward and offering him the Arghya and water to wash his feet, and with diverse other rites, they all worshipped the mighty Naga and saluted him by making the usual enquiries.

"'After his brother had thus departed from the (human) world, Vasudeva of celestial vision, who was fully acquainted with the end of all things, wandered for some time in that lonely forest thoughtfully. Endued with great energy he then sat down on the bare earth. He had thought before this of everything that had been fore-shadowed by the words uttered by Gandhari in former days. He also recollected the words that Durvasas had spoken at the time his body was smeared by that Rishi with the remnant of the Payasa he had eaten (while a guest at Krishna's house). The high-souled one, thinking of the destruction of the Vrishnis and the Andhakas, as also of the previous slaughter of the Kurus, concluded that the hour (for his own departure from the world) had come. He then restrained his senses (in Yoga). Conversant with the truth of every topic, Vasudeva, though he was the Supreme Deity, wished to die, for dispelling all doubts and establishing a certainty of results (in the matter of human existence), simply for upholding the three worlds and for making the words of Atri's son true. Having restrained all his senses, speech, and mind, Krishna laid himself down in high Yoga.

"'A fierce hunter of the name of Jara then came there, desirous of deer. The hunter, mistaking Keshava, who was stretched on the earth in high Yoga, for a deer, pierced him at the heel with a shaft and quickly came to that spot for capturing his prey. Coming up,

Jara beheld a man dressed in yellow robes, rapt in Yoga and endued with many arms. Regarding himself an offender, and filled with fear, he touched the feet of Keshava. The high-souled one comforted him and then ascended upwards, filling the entire welkin with splendour. When he reached Heaven, Vasava and the twin Ashvinis and Rudra and the Adityas and the Vasus and the Viswedevas, and Munis and Siddhas and many foremost ones among the Gandharvas, with the Apsaras, advanced to receive him. Then, O king, the illustrious Narayana of fierce energy, the Creator and Destroyer of all, that preceptor of Yoga, filling Heaven with his splendour, reached his own inconceivable region. Krishna then met the deities and (celestial) Rishis and Charanas, O king, and the foremost ones among the Gandharvas and many beautiful Apsaras and Siddhas and Saddhyas. All of them, bending in humility, worshipped him. The deities all saluted him, O monarch, and many foremost of Munis and Rishis worshipped him who was the Lord of all. The Gandharvas waited on him, hymning his praises, and Indra also joyfully praised him.'"

SECTION V.

"Vaishampayana said: 'Meanwhile Daruka, going to the Kurus and seeing those mighty car-warriors, the son of Pritha, informed them of how the Vrishnis had slain one another with iron bolts. Hearing that the Vrishnis along with the Bhojas and Andhakas and Kukuras had all been slain, the Pandavas, burning with grief, became highly agitated. Then Arjuna, the dear friend of Keshava, bidding them farewell, set out for seeing his maternal uncle. He said that destruction would soon overtake everything. Proceeding to the city of the Vrishnis with Daruka in his company, O puissant king, that hero beheld that the city of Dwaraka looked like a woman bereft of her husband. Those ladies who had, before this, the very Lord of the universe for their protector, were now lordless. Seeing that Partha had come for protecting them, they all set up a loud wail. 16,000 ladies had been wedded to Vasudeva. Indeed, as soon as they saw Arjuna arrive, they uttered a loud cry of sorrow. As soon as the Kuru prince met those beauteous ones deprived of the protection of Krishna and of their sons as well, he was unable to look at them, his vision being obstructed by tears. The Dwaraka river had the Vrishnis and the Andhakas for its water, steeds for its fishes, cars for its rafts, the sound of musical instruments and the rattle of cars for its waves, houses and mansions and public squares for its lakes. Gems and precious stones were its abundant moss. The walls of adamant were the garlands of flowers that floated on it. The streets and roads were the strong currents running in eddies along its surface. The great open squares were the still large lakes in its course. Rama and Krishna were its two mighty alligators. That agreeable river now seemed to Arjuna to be the fierce Vaitarani bound up with Time's net. Indeed, the son of Vasava, endued with great intelligence, beheld the city to look even thus, reft as it was of the Vrishni heroes. Shorn of beauty, and perfectly cheerless, it presented the aspect of a lotus flower in the season of winter. Beholding the sight that Dwaraka presented, and seeing the numerous wives of Krishna, Arjuna wailed aloud with eyes bathed in tears and fell down on the earth. Then Satya, the daughter of Satrajit, and Rukmini too, O king, fell down beside Dhananjaya and uttered loud wails of grief. Raising him then they caused him to be seated on a golden seat. The ladies sat around that high-souled one, giving expression to their feelings. Praising Govinda and talking with the ladies, the son of Pandu comforted them and then proceeded to see his maternal uncle.'"

SECTION VI.

"Vaishampayana said: 'The Kuru prince beheld the heroic and high-souled Anakadundubhi lying on the ground and burning with grief on account of his sons. The broad-chested and mighty-armed son of Pritha, more afflicted than his uncle, with eyes bathed in tears, touched his uncle's feet, O Bharata. The mighty-armed Anakadundubhi wished to smell the head of his sister's son but failed to do it, O slayer of foes. The old man of mighty arms, deeply afflicted, embraced Partha with his arms and wept aloud, remembering his sons, brothers, grandsons, daughters' sons, and friends.

"'Vasudeva said, "Without beholding those heroes, O Arjuna, who had subjugated all the kings of the Earth and the Daityas a hundred times, I am still alive! Methinks, I have no death! Through the fault of those two heroes who were thy dear disciples and who were much regarded by thee, also, O Partha, the Vrishnis have been destroyed. Those two who were regarded as Atirathas amongst the foremost of the Vrishnis, and referring to whom in course of conversation thou wert wont to indulge in pride, and who, O chief of Kuru's race, were ever dear to Krishna himself, alas, those two, O Dhananjaya, have been the chief causes of the destruction of the Vrishnis! I do not censure the son of Sini or the son of Hridika, O Arjuna. I do not censure Akrura or the son of Rukmini. No doubt, the curse (of the Rishis) is the sole cause. How is it that that lord of the universe, the slayer of Madhu, who had put forth his prowess for achieving the destruction of Kesin and Kansa, and Chaidya swelling with pride, and Ekalavya, the son of the ruler of the Nishadas, and the Kalingas and the Magadhas, and the Gandharas and the king of Kasi, and many rulers assembled together in the midst of the desert, many heroes belonging to the East and the South, and many kings of the mountainous regions, alas, how could he remain indifferent to such a calamity as the curse denounced by the Rishis? Thyself, Narada, and the Munis, knew him to be the eternal and sinless Govinda, the Deity of unfading glory. Alas, being puissant Vishnu himself, he witnessed, without interfering, the destruction of his kinsmen! My son must have himself allowed all this to happen. He was the Lord of the universe. He did not, however, wish to falsify the words of Gandhari and the Rishis, O scorcher of foes. In thy very sight, O hero, thy grandson, who had been slain by Ashvatthama, was revived through his energy. That friend, however, of yours did not wish to protect his kinsmen. Beholding his sons and grandsons and brothers and friends lying dead, he said unto me these words, O chief of Bharata's race, 'The destruction of this our race has at last come. Vibhatsu will come to this city, Dwaravati. Tell him what has occurred, this great carnage of the Vrishnis. I have no doubt that as soon as he will hear of the destruction of the Yadus, that hero of mighty energy will come here without any loss of time. Know, O father, that I am Arjuna and Arjuna is myself. That should be done by thee which he would say. The son of Pandu will do what is best for the women and the children. Even he will perform thy funeral rites. This city of Dwaravati, after Arjuna's departure, will, with its walls and edifices, be swallowed up by the ocean without any delay. As regards myself, retiring to some sacred place, I shall bide my hour, with the intelligent Rama in my company, observing strict vows all the while.' Having said these words unto me, Hrishikesa of inconceivable prowess, leaving me with the children, has gone away to some spot which I do not know. Thinking of those two high-souled brothers of thine, as also of the terrible carnage of my kinsmen, I have abstained from all food, and am emaciated with grief. I shall neither eat, nor live. By good luck thou meetest me, O son of Pandu. Do thou accomplish all, O Partha, that Krishna has said. This kingdom, with all these women, and all the wealth here, is thine now, O son of Pritha. As regards myself, O slayer of foes, I shall cast off my life-breaths dear though they be."'"

SECTION VII.

"Vaishampayana said: 'That scorcher of foes, Vibhatsu, thus addressed by his maternal uncle, replied, with great cheerlessness of heart, unto Vasudeva who was equally cheerless, saying, "O uncle, I am unable to look at this Earth when she is reft of that hero of Vrishni's race and those my other kinsmen. The king and Bhimasena and Sahadeva and Nakula and Yajnaseni, numbering the sixth, are of the same mind with myself in this matter. The time has come for the departure of the king also. Know this, that the hour of our departure too is at hand. Thou art the foremost of those that are well conversant with the course of time. I shall, however, O chastiser of foes, first remove to Indraprastha the women of the Vrishni race as also the children and the aged." Having said so unto his uncle, Arjuna next addressed Daruka, saying, "I wish to see without any delay the chief officers of the Vrishni heroes." Having uttered these words, the heroic Arjuna, grieving for those great car-warriors (who had been slain), entered the great hall of the Yadavas (where they used to hold their court), called Sudharma. When he had taken his seat there, all the citizens, including the Brahmanas, and all the ministers of state came and stood surrounding him. Then Partha, more grieved than they, addressed those grieving and cheerless citizens and officers who were more dead than alive, and said these words that were well suited to the occasion: "I shall take away with me the remnants of the Vrishnis and the Andhakas. The sea will soon engulf this city. Equip all your cars and place on them all your wealth. This Vajra (the grandson of Krishna) will be your king at Shakraprastha. On the seventh day from this, at sunrise, we shall set out. Make your preparations without delay."

"'Thus addressed by Pritha's son of pure deeds, all of them hastened their preparations with eagerness for achieving their safety. Arjuna passed that night in the mansion of Keshava. He was suddenly overwhelmed with great grief and stupefaction. When morning dawned, Vasudeva of great energy and prowess attained, through the aid of Yoga, to the highest goal. A loud and heart-rending sound of wailing was heard in Vasudeva's mansion, uttered by the weeping ladies. They were seen with dishevelled hair and divested of ornaments and floral wreaths. Beating their breasts with their hands, they indulged in heart-rending lamentations. Those foremost of women, Devaki and Bhadra and Rohini and Madira threw themselves on the bodies of their lord. Then Partha caused the body of his uncle to be carried out on a costly vehicle borne on the shoulders of men. It was followed by all the citizens of Dwaraka and the people of the provinces, all of whom, deeply afflicted by grief, had been well-affected towards the deceased hero. Before that vehicle were borne the umbrella which had been held over his head at the conclusion of the horse-sacrifice he had achieved while living, and also the blazing fires he had daily worshipped, with the priests that had used to attend to them. The body of the hero was followed by his wives decked in ornaments and surrounded by thousands of women and thousands of their daughters-in-law. The last rites were then performed at that spot which had been agreeable to him while he was alive. The four wives of that heroic son of Sura ascended the funeral pyre and were consumed with the body of their lord. All of them attained to those regions of felicity which were his. The son of Pandu burnt the body of his uncle together with those four wives of his, using diverse kinds of scents and perfumed wood. As the funeral pyre blazed up, a loud sound was heard of the burning wood and other combustible materials, along with the clear chant of Samans and the wailing of the citizens and others who witnessed the rite. After it was all over, the boys of the Vrishni and Andhaka races, headed by Vajra, as also the ladies, offered oblations of water to the high-souled hero.

"'Phalguna, who was careful in observing every duty, having caused this duty to be performed, proceeded, O chief of Bharata's race, next to the place where the Vrishnis were slaughtered. The Kuru prince, beholding them lying slaughtered all around, became exceedingly cheerless. He, however, did what was required to be done in view of that which had happened. The last rites were performed, according to the order of seniority, unto the bodies of those heroes slain by the iron bolts born, by virtue of the curse denounced by the Brahmanas, of the blades of Eraka grass. Searching out the bodies then of Rama and Vasudeva, Arjuna caused them to be burnt by persons skilled in that act. The son of Pandu, having next performed duly those sraddha rites that are done to the dead, quickly set out on the seventh day, mounting on his car. The widows of the Vrishni heroes, wailing aloud, followed the high-souled son of Pandu, Dhananjaya, on cars drawn by bullocks and mules and camels. All were in deep affliction. The servants of the Vrishnis, their horsemen, and their car-warriors too, followed the procession. The citizens and the inhabitants of the country, at the command of Pritha's son, set out at the same time and proceeded, surrounding that cavalcade destitute of heroes and numbering only women and the aged and the children. The warriors who fought from the backs of elephants proceeded on elephants as huge as hills. The foot-soldiers also set out, together with the reserves. The children of the Andhaka and the Vrishni races, all followed Arjuna. The Brahmanas and Kshatriyas, and Vaisyas, and wealthy Sudras, set out, keeping before them the 16,000 women that had formed Vasudeva's harem, and Vajra, the grandson of the intelligent Krishna. The widows of the other heroes of the Bhoja, the Vrishni, and the Andhaka races, lordless now, that set out with Arjuna, numbered many millions. That foremost of car-warriors, that conqueror of hostile towns, the son of Pritha, escorted this vast procession of Vrishnis, which still abounded with wealth, and which looked like a veritable ocean.

"'After all the people had set out, the ocean, that home of sharks and alligators, flooded Dwaraka, which still teemed with wealth of every kind, with its waters. Whatever portion of the ground was passed over, ocean immediately flooded over with his waters. Beholding this wonderful sight, the inhabitants of Dwaraka walked faster and faster, saying, "Wonderful is the course of fate!" Dhananjaya, after abandoning Dwaraka, proceeded by slow marches, causing the Vrishni women to rest in pleasant forests and mountains and by the sides of delightful streams. Arrived at the country of the five waters, the puissant Dhananjaya planted a rich encampment in the midst of a land that abounded with corn and kine and other animals. Beholding those lordless widows escorted by Pritha's son alone O Bharata, the robbers felt a great temptation (for plunder). Then those sinful wretches, with hearts overwhelmed by cupidity, those Abhiras of ill omen, assembled together and held a consultation. They said, "Here there is only one bowman, Arjuna. The cavalcade consists of children and the old. He escorts them, transgressing us. The warriors (of the Vrishnis) are without energy." Then those robbers, numbering by thousands, and armed with clubs, rushed towards the procession of the Vrishnis, desirous of plunder. Urged by the perverse course of time they fell upon that vast concourse, frightening it with loud leonine shouts and desirous of slaughter. The son of Kunti, suddenly ceasing to advance along the path, turned, with his followers, towards the place where the robbers had attacked the procession. Smiling the while, that mighty-armed warrior addressed the assailants, saying, "You sinful wretches, forbear, if ye love your lives. Ye will rue this when I pierce your bodies with my shafts and take your lives." Though thus addressed by that hero, they disregarded his words, and though repeatedly dissuaded, they fell upon Arjuna. Then Arjuna endeavoured to string his large, indestructible, celestial bow with some effort. He succeeded with great difficulty in stringing it, when the battle had become furious. He then began to think of his celestial weapons but they would not come to his mind. Beholding that furious battle, the loss of the might of his arm, and the non-appearance of his celestial weapons, Arjuna became greatly ashamed. The Vrishni warriors including the foot-soldiers, the elephant-warriors, and the car-men, failed to rescue those Vrishni women that were being snatched away by the robbers. The concourse was very large. The robbers assailed it at different points. Arjuna tried his best to protect it, but could not succeed. In the very sight of all the warriors, many foremost of ladies were dragged away, while others went away with the robbers of their own accord. The puissant Arjuna, supported by the servants of the Vrishnis, struck the robbers with shafts sped from Gandiva. Soon, however, O king, his shafts were exhausted. In former days his shafts had been inexhaustible. Now, however, they proved otherwise. Finding his shafts exhausted, he became deeply afflicted with grief. The son of Indra then began to strike the robbers with the horns of his bow. Those Mlecchas, however, O Janamejaya, in the very sight of Partha, retreated, taking away with them many foremost ladies of the Vrishnis and Andhakas. The puissant Dhananjaya regarded it all as the work of destiny. Filled with sorrow he breathed heavy sighs at the thought of the non-appearance of his (celestial) weapons, the loss of the might of his arms, the refusal of his bow to obey him, and the exhaustion of his shafts. Regarding it all as the work of destiny, he became exceedingly cheerless. He then ceased, O king, to make further efforts, saying, he had not the power which he had before. The high-souled one, taking with him the remnant of the Vrishni women, and the wealth that was still with them, reached Kurukshetra. Thus bringing with him the remnant of the Vrishnis, he established them at different places. He established the son of Kritavarma at the city called Marttikavat, with the remnant of the women of the Bhoja king. Escorting the remainder, with children and old men and women, the son of Pandu established them, who were reft of heroes, in the city of Indraprastha. The dear son of Yuyudhana, with a company of old men and children and women, the righteous-souled Arjuna established on the banks of the Sarasvati. The rule of Indraprastha was given to Vajra. The widows of Akrura then desired to retire into the woods. Vajra asked them repeatedly to desist, but they did not listen to him. Rukmini, the princess of Gandhara, Saivya, Haimavati, and queen Jamvabati ascended the funeral pyre. Satyabhama and other dear wives of Krishna entered the woods, O king, resolved to set themselves to the practice of penances. They began to live on fruits and roots and pass their time in the contemplation of Hari. Going beyond the Himavat, they took up their abode in a place called Kalpa. Those men who had followed Arjuna from Dwaravati, were distributed into groups, and bestowed upon Vajra. Having done all these acts suited to the occasion, Arjuna, with eyes bathed in tears, then entered the retreat of Vyasa. There he beheld the Island-born Rishi seated at his ease.'"

SECTION VIII.

"Vaishampayana said: 'As Arjuna entered the asylum of the truthful Rishi, he beheld the son of Satyavati seated in a secluded spot.

"'Approaching that Rishi of high vows and endued with a knowledge of all duties, he said, "I am Arjuna," and then awaited his pleasure. Satyavati's son, endued with high penances, answered, saying "Welcome!" Of tranquil soul, the great Muni further said, "Take thy seat." Seeing that the son of Pritha was exceedingly cheerless and breathing heavy sighs repeatedly and filled with despair, Vyasa addressed him, saying, "Hast thou been sprinkled with water from anybody's nails or hair, or the end of anybody's cloth, or from the mouth of a jar? Hast thou had sexual congress with any woman before the cessation of her functional flow? Hast thou slain a Brahmana? Hast thou been vanquished in battle? Thou lookest like one shorn of prosperity. I do not know that thou hast been defeated by anyone. Why then, O chief of Bharata's race, this exceedingly dejected aspect? It behoveth thee, O son of Pritha, to tell me all, if, indeed, there be no harm in telling it."

"'Arjuna said, "He whose complexion was like that of a (newly-risen) cloud, he whose eyes were like a pair of large lotus petals, Krishna, has, with Rama, cast off his body and ascended to Heaven. At Prabhasa, through iron bolts generated by the curse denounced by Brahmanas, the destruction has taken place of the Vrishni heroes. Awful hath that carnage been, and not even a single hero has escaped. The heroes of the Bhoja, the Andhaka, and the Vrishni races, O Brahmana, who were all endued with high souls, great might, and leonine pride, have slaughtered one another in battle. Possessed of arms that looked like maces of iron, and capable of bearing the strokes of heavy clubs and darts, alas, they have all been slain with blades of Eraka grass. Behold the perverse course of Time. 500,000 mighty-armed warriors have thus been laid low. Encountering one another, they have met with destruction. Thinking repeatedly of this carnage of the Yadava warriors of immeasurable energy and of the illustrious Krishna, I fail to derive peace of mind. The death of the wielder of Sarnga is as incredible as the drying up of the ocean, the displacement of a mountain, the falling down of the vault of heaven, or the cooling property of fire. Deprived of the company of the Vrishni heroes, I desire not to live in this world. Another incident has happened that is more painful than this, O thou that art possessed of wealth of penances. Repeatedly thinking of it, my heart is breaking. In my very sight, O Brahmana, thousands of Vrishni ladies were carried away by the Abhiras of the country of the five waters, who assailed us. Taking up my bow I found myself unequal to even string it. The might that had existed in my arms seemed to have disappeared on that occasion. O great ascetic, my weapons of diverse kinds failed to make their appearance. Soon, again, my shafts became exhausted. That person of immeasurable soul, of four arms, wielding the conch, the discus, and the mace, clad in yellow robes, dark of complexion, and possessing eyes resembling lotus-petals, is no longer seen by me. Alas, reft of Govinda, what have I to live for, dragging my life in sorrow? He who used to stalk in advance of my car, that divine form endued with great splendour and unfading puissance, consuming as he proceeded all hostile warriors, can no longer be seen by me. No longer beholding him who by his energy first burnt all hostile troops whom I afterwards despatched with shafts sped from Gandiva, I am filled with grief and my head swims, O best of men. Penetrated with cheerlessness and despair, I fail to obtain peace of mind. I dare not live, reft of the heroic Janardana. As soon as I heard that Vishnu had left the Earth, my eyes became dim and all things disappeared from my vision. O best of men, it behoveth thee to tell me what is good for me now, for I am now a wanderer with an empty heart, despoiled of my kinsmen and of my possession."

"'Vyasa said, "The mighty car-warriors of the Vrishni and the Andhaka races have all been consumed by the Brahmana's curse. O chief of Kuru's race, it behoveth thee not to grieve for their destruction. That which has happened had been ordained. It was the destiny of those high-souled warriors. Krishna suffered it to take place although he was fully competent to baffle it. Govinda was able to alter the very course of the universe with all its mobile and immobile creatures. What need then be said of the curse of even high-souled Brahmanas? He who used to proceed in front of thy car, armed with discus and mace, through affection for thee, was the four-armed Vasudeva, that ancient rishi. That high-souled one of expansive eyes, Krishna, having lightened the burthen of the Earth and cast off his (human) body, has attained to his own high seat. By thee also, O foremost of men, with Bhima for thy helpmate and the twins, O mighty-armed hero, has the great work of the gods been accomplished. O foremost one of Kuru's race, I regard thee and thy brothers as crowned with success, for ye have accomplished the great purpose of your lives. The time has come for your departure from the world. Even this, O puissant one, is what is beneficial for you now. Even thus, understanding and prowess and foresight, O Bharata, arise when days of prosperity have not outrun. These very acquisitions disappear when the hour of adversity comes. All this has Time for its root. Time is, indeed, the seed of the universe, O Dhananjaya. It is Time, again, that withdraws everything at its pleasure. One becomes mighty, and, again, losing that might, becomes weak. One becomes a master and rules others, and, again, losing that position, becomes a servant for obeying the behests of others. Thy weapons, having achieved success, have gone away to the place they came from. They will, again, come into thy hands when the Time for their coming approaches. The time has come, O Bharata, for you all to attain to the highest goal. Even this is what I regard to be highly beneficial for you all, O chief of Bharata's race."

"Vaishampayana continued: 'Having heard these words of Vyasa of immeasurable energy, the son of Pritha, receiving his permission, returned to the city named after the elephant. Entering it, the hero approached Yudhishthira and informed him of all that had taken place with reference to the Vrishnis.'"

THE END OF MAUSALA-PARVA

BOOK 17. MAHAPRASTHANIKA-PARVA

SECTION I.

Om! Having bowed down unto Narayana, and to Nara, the foremost of men, as also to the goddess Sarasvati, should the word "Jaya" be uttered.

"Janamejaya said: 'Having heard of that encounter with iron bolts between the heroes of the Vrishni and the Andhaka races, and having been informed also of Krishna's ascension to Heaven, what did the Pandavas do?'

"Vaishampayana said: 'Having heard the particulars of the great slaughter of the Vrishnis, the Kaurava king set his heart on leaving the world. He addressed Arjuna, saying, O thou of great intelligence, it is Time that cooks every creature (in his cauldron). I think that what has happened is due to the cords of Time (with which he binds us all). It behoveth thee also to see it.

"'Thus addressed by his brother, the son of Kunti only repeated the word "Time, Time!" and fully endorsed the view of his eldest brother gifted with great intelligence. Ascertaining the resolution of Arjuna, Bhimasena and the twins fully endorsed the words that Arjuna had said. Resolved to retire from the world for earning merit, they brought Yuyutsu before them. Yudhishthira made over the kingdom to the son of his uncle by his Vaisya wife. Installing Parikshit also on their throne, as king, the eldest brother of the Pandavas, filled with sorrow, addressed Subhadra, saying, This son of thy son will be the king of the Kurus. The survivor of the Yadus, Vajra, has been made a king. Parikshit will rule in Hastinapura, while the Yadava prince, Vajra, will rule in Shakraprastha. He should be protected by thee. Never set thy heart on unrighteousness.

"'Having said these words, king Yudhishthira the just, along with his brothers, promptly offered oblations of water unto Vasudeva of great intelligence, as also unto his old maternal uncle and Rama and others. He then duly performed the Sraddhas of all those deceased kinsmen of his. The king, in honour of Hari and naming him repeatedly, fed the Island-born Vyasa, and Narada, and Markandeya possessed of wealth of penances, and Yajnavalkya of Bharadwaja's race, with many delicious viands. In honour of Krishna, he also gave away many jewels and gems, and robes and clothes, and villages, and horses and cars, and female slaves by hundreds and thousands unto foremost of Brahmanas. Summoning the citizens, Kripa was installed as the preceptor and Parikshit was made over to him as his disciple, O chief of Bharata's race.

"'Then Yudhishthira once more summoned all his subjects. The royal sage informed them of his intentions. The citizens and the inhabitants of the provinces, hearing the king's words, became filled with anxiety and disapproved of them. "This should never be done," said they unto the king. The monarch, well versed with the changes brought about by time, did not listen to their counsels. Possessed of righteous soul, he persuaded the people to sanction his views. He then set his heart on leaving the world. His brothers also formed the same resolution. Then Dharma's son, Yudhishthira, the king of the Kurus, casting off his ornaments, wore barks of trees. Bhima and Arjuna and the twins, and Draupadi also of great fame, similarly clad themselves in bark of trees, O king. Having caused the preliminary rites of religion, O chief of Bharata's race, which were to bless them in the accomplishment of their design, those foremost of men cast off their sacred fires into the water. The ladies, beholding the princes in that guise, wept aloud. They seemed to look as they had looked in days before, when with Draupadi forming the sixth in number they set out from the capital after their defeat at dice. The brothers, however, were all very cheerful at the prospect of retirement. Ascertaining the intentions of Yudhishthira and seeing the destruction of the Vrishnis, no other course of action could please them then.

"'The five brothers, with Draupadi forming the sixth, and a dog forming the seventh, set out on their journey. Indeed, even thus did king Yudhishthira depart, himself the head of a party of seven, from the city named after the elephant. The citizens and the ladies of the royal household followed them for some distance. None of them, however, could venture to address the king for persuading him to give up his intention. The denizens of the city then returned; Kripa and others stood around Yuyutsu as their centre. Ulupi, the daughter of the Naga chief, O thou of Kunti's race, entered the waters of Ganga. The princess Chitrangada set out for the capital of Manipura. The other ladies who were the grandmothers of Parikshit centered around him. Meanwhile the high-souled Pandavas, O thou of Kuru's race, and Draupadi of great fame, having observed the preliminary fast, set out with their faces towards the east. Setting themselves on Yoga, those high-souled ones, resolved to observe the religion of Renunciation, traversed through various countries and reached diverse rivers and seas. Yudhishthira, proceeded first. Behind him was Bhima; next walked Arjuna; after him were the twins in the order of their birth; behind them all, O foremost one of Bharata's race, proceeded Draupadi, that first of women, possessed of great beauty, of dark complexion, and endued with eyes resembling lotus petals. While the Pandavas set out for the forest, a dog followed them.

"'Proceeding on, those heroes reached the sea of red waters. Dhananjaya had not cast off his celestial bow Gandiva, nor his couple of inexhaustible quivers, actuated, O king, by the cupidity that attaches one to things of great value. The Pandavas there beheld the deity of fire standing before them like a hill. Closing their way, the god stood there in his embodied form. The deity of seven flames then addressed the Pandavas, saying, "Ye heroic sons of Pandu, know me for the deity of fire. O mighty-armed Yudhishthira, O Bhimasena that art a scorcher of foes, O Arjuna, and ye twins of great courage, listen to what I say! Ye foremost ones of Kuru's race, I am the god of fire. The forest of Khandava was burnt by me, through the puissance of Arjuna and of Narayana himself. Let your brother Phalguna proceed to the woods after casting off Gandiva, that high weapon. He has no longer any need of it. That precious discus, which was with the high-souled Krishna, has disappeared (from the world). When the time again comes, it will come back into his hands. This foremost of bows, Gandiva, was procured by me from Varuna for the use of Partha. Let it be made over to Varuna himself."

"'At this, all the brothers urged Dhananjaya to do what the deity said. He then threw into the waters (of the sea) both the bow and the couple of inexhaustible quivers. After this, O chief of Bharata's race, the god of the fire disappeared then and there. The heroic sons of Pandu next proceeded with their faces turned towards the south. Then, by the northern coast of the salt sea, those princes of Bharata's race proceeded to the south-west. Turning next towards the west, they beheld the city of Dwaraka covered by the ocean. Turning next to the north, those foremost ones proceeded on. Observant of Yoga, they were desirous of making a round of the whole Earth.'"

SECTION II.

"Vaishampayana said: 'Those princes of restrained souls and devoted to Yoga, proceeding to the north, beheld Himavat, that very large mountain. Crossing the Himavat, they beheld a vast desert of sand. They then saw the mighty mountain Meru, the foremost of all high-peaked mountains. As those mighty ones were proceeding quickly, all rapt in Yoga, Yajnaseni, falling of from Yoga, dropped down on the Earth. Beholding her fallen down, Bhimasena of great strength addressed king Yudhishthira the just, saying, "O scorcher of foes, this princess never did any sinful act. Tell us what the cause is for which Krishna has fallen down on the Earth!"

"'Yudhishthira said: "O best of men, though we were all equal unto her she had great partiality for Dhananjaya. She obtains the fruit of that conduct today, O best of men."'

"Vaishampayana continued: 'Having said this, that foremost one of Bharata's race proceeded on. Of righteous soul, that foremost of men, endued with great intelligence, went on, with mind intent on itself. Then Sahadeva of great learning fell down on the Earth. Beholding him drop down, Bhima addressed the king, saying, "He who with great humility used to serve us all, alas, why is that son of Madravati fallen down on the Earth?"

"'Yudhishthira said, "He never thought anybody his equal in wisdom. It is for that fault that this prince has fallen down."

"Vaishampayana continued: 'Having said this, the king proceeded, leaving Sahadeva there. Indeed, Kunti's son Yudhishthira went on, with his brothers and with the dog. Beholding both Krishna and the Pandava Sahadeva fallen down, the brave Nakula, whose love for kinsmen was very great, fell down himself. Upon the falling down of the heroic Nakula of great personal beauty, Bhima once more addressed the king, saying, "This brother of ours who was endued with righteousness without incompleteness, and who always obeyed our behests, this Nakula who was unrivalled for beauty, has fallen down."

"'Thus addressed by Bhimasena, Yudhishthira said, with respect to Nakula, these words: "He was of righteous soul and the foremost of all persons endued with intelligence. He, however, thought that there was nobody that equalled him in beauty of person. Indeed, he regarded himself as superior to all in that respect. It is for this that Nakula has fallen down. Know this, O Vrikodara. What has been ordained for a person, O hero, must have to be endured by him."

"'Beholding Nakula and the others fall down, Pandu's son Arjuna of white steeds, that slayer of hostile heroes, fell down in great grief of heart. When that foremost of men, who was endued with the energy of Shakra, had fallen down, indeed, when that invincible hero was on the point of death, Bhima said unto the king, "I do not recollect any untruth uttered by this high-souled one. Indeed, not even in jest did he say anything false. What then is that for whose evil consequence this one has fallen down on the Earth?"

"'Yudhishthira said, "Arjuna had said that he would consume all our foes in a single day. Proud of his heroism, he did not, however, accomplish what he had said. Hence has he fallen down. This Phalguna disregarded all wielders of bows. One desirous of prosperity should never indulge in such sentiments."

"Vaishampayana continued: 'Having said so, the king proceeded on. Then Bhima fell down. Having fallen down, Bhima addressed king Yudhishthira the just, saying, "O king, behold, I who am thy darling have fallen down. For what reason have I dropped down? Tell me if thou knowest it."

"'Yudhishthira said, "Thou wert a great eater, and thou didst use to boast of thy strength. Thou never didst attend, O Bhima, to the wants of others while eating. It is for that, O Bhima, that thou hast fallen down."

"'Having said these words, the mighty-armed Yudhishthira proceeded on, without looking back. He had only one companion, the dog of which I have repeatedly spoken to thee, that followed him now.'"

SECTION III.

"Vaishampayana said: 'Then Shakra, causing the firmament and the Earth to be filled by a loud sound, came to the son of Pritha on a car and asked him to ascend it. Beholding his brothers fallen on the Earth, king Yudhishthira the just said unto that deity of a 1,000 eyes these words: "My brothers have all dropped down here. They must go with me. Without them by me I do not wish to go to Heaven, O lord of all the deities. The delicate princess (Draupadi) deserving of every comfort, O Purandara, should go with us. It behoveth thee to permit this."

"'Shakra said, "Thou shalt behold thy brothers in Heaven. They have reached it before thee. Indeed, thou shalt see all of them there, with Krishna. Do not yield to grief,

O chief of the Bharatas. Having cast off their human bodies they have gone there, O chief of Bharata's race. As regards thee, it is ordained that thou shalt go thither in this very body of thine."

"'Yudhishthira said, "This dog, O lord of the Past and the Present, is exceedingly devoted to me. He should go with me. My heart is full of compassion for him."

"'Shakra said, "Immortality and a condition equal to mine, O king, prosperity extending in all directions, and high success, and all the felicities of Heaven, thou hast won today. Do thou cast off this dog. In this there will be no cruelty."

"'Yudhishthira said, "O thou of a 1,000 eyes. O thou that art of righteous behaviour, it is exceedingly difficult for one that is of righteous behaviour to perpetrate an act that is unrighteous. I do not desire that union with prosperity for which I shall have to cast off one that is devoted to me."

"'Indra said, "There is no place in Heaven for persons with dogs. Besides, the (deities called) Krodhavasas take away all the merits of such persons. Reflecting on this, act, O king Yudhishthira the just. Do thou abandon this dog. There is no cruelty in this."

"'Yudhishthira said, "It has been said that the abandonment of one that is devoted is infinitely sinful. It is equal to the sin that one incurs by slaying a Brahmana. Hence, O great Indra, I shall not abandon this dog today from desire of my happiness. Even this is my vow steadily pursued, that I never give up a person that is terrified, nor one that is devoted to me, nor one that seeks my protection, saying that he is destitute, nor one that is afflicted, nor one that has come to me, nor one that is weak in protecting oneself, nor one that is solicitous of life. I shall never give up such a one till my own life is at an end."

"'Indra said, "Whatever gifts, or sacrifices spread out, or libations poured on the sacred fire, are seen by a dog, are taken away by the Krodhavasas. Do thou, therefore, abandon this dog. By abandoning this dog thou wilt attain to the region of the deities. Having abandoned thy brothers and Krishna, thou hast, O hero, acquired a region of felicity by thy own deeds. Why art thou so stupefied? Thou hast renounced everything. Why then dost thou not renounce this dog?" Yudhishthira said, "This is well known in all the worlds that there is neither friendship nor enmity with those that are dead. When my brothers and Krishna died, I was unable to revive them. Hence it was that I abandoned them. I did not, however, abandon them as long as they were alive. To frighten one that has sought protection, the slaying of a woman, the theft of what belongs to a Brahmana, and injuring a friend, each of these four, O Shakra, is I think equal to the abandonment of one that is devoted."'

"Vaishampayana continued: 'Hearing these words of king Yudhishthira the just, (the dog became transformed into) the deity of Righteousness, who, well pleased, said these words unto him in a sweet voice fraught with praise.

"'Dharma said: "Thou art well born, O king of kings, and possessed of the intelligence and the good conduct of Pandu. Thou hast compassion for all creatures, O Bharata, of which this is a bright example. Formerly, O son, thou wert once examined by me in the woods of Dwaita, where thy brothers of great prowess met with (an appearance of) death. Disregarding both thy brothers Bhima and Arjuna, thou didst wish for the revival of Nakula from thy desire of doing good to thy (step-) mother. On the present occasion, thinking the dog to be devoted to thee, thou hast renounced the very car of the celestials instead of renouncing him. Hence, O king, there is no one in Heaven that is equal to thee. Hence, O Bharata, regions of inexhaustible felicity are thine. Thou hast won them, O chief of the Bharatas, and thine is a celestial and high goal."'

"Vaishampayana continued: 'Then Dharma, and Shakra, and the Maruts, and the

Ashvinis, and other deities, and the celestial Rishis, causing Yudhishthira to ascend on a car, proceeded to Heaven. Those beings crowned with success and capable of going everywhere at will, rode their respective cars. King Yudhishthira, that perpetuator of Kuru's race, riding on that car, ascended quickly, causing the entire welkin to blaze with his effulgence. Then Narada, that foremost of all speakers, endued with penances, and conversant with all the worlds, from amidst that concourse of deities, said these words: "All those royal sages that are here have their achievements transcended by those of Yudhishthira. Covering all the worlds by his fame and splendour and by his wealth of conduct, he has attained to Heaven in his own (human) body. None else than the son of Pandu has been heard to achieve this."

'"Hearing these words of Narada, the righteous-souled king, saluting the deities and all the royal sages there present, said, "Happy or miserable, whatever the region be that is now my brothers', I desire to proceed to. I do not wish to go anywhere else."

'"Hearing this speech of the king, the chief of the deities, Purandara, said these words fraught with noble sense: "Do thou live in this place, O king of kings, which thou hast won by thy meritorious deeds. Why dost thou still cherish human affections? Thou hast attained to great success, the like of which no other man has ever been able to attain. Thy brothers, O delighter of the Kurus, have succeeded in winning regions of felicity. Human affections still touch thee. This is Heaven. Behold these celestial Rishis and Siddhas who have attained to the region of the gods."

'"Gifted with great intelligence, Yudhishthira answered the chief of the deities once more, saying, "O conqueror of Daityas, I venture not to dwell anywhere separated from them. I desire to go there, where my brothers have gone. I wish to go there where that foremost of women, Draupadi, of ample proportions and darkish complexion and endued with great intelligence and righteous of conduct, has gone."'"

THE END OF MAHAPRASTHANIKA-PARVA

BOOK 18. SVARGAROHANIKA-PARVA

SECTION I.

Om! Having bowed down into Narayana, and to Nara, the foremost of men, as also to the goddess Sarasvati, should the word "Jaya" be uttered.

"Janamejaya said, 'Having attained to Heaven, what regions were respectively attained by my grandsires of old, viz., the Pandavas and the sons of Dhritarashtra? I desire to hear this. I think that thou art conversant with everything, having been taught by the great Rishi Vyasa of wonderful feats.'

"Vaishampayana said, 'Listen now to what thy grandsires, Yudhishthira and others, did after having attained to Heaven, that place of the deities. Arrived at Heaven, king Yudhishthira the just, beheld Duryodhana endued with prosperity and seated on an excellent seat. He blazed with effulgence like the sun and wore all those signs of glory which belong to heroes. And he was in the company of many deities of blazing effulgence and of Sadhyas of righteous deeds. Yudhishthira, beholding Duryodhana and his prosperity, became suddenly filled with rage and turned back from the sight.

'"He loudly addressed his companions, saying, "I do not desire to share regions of felicity with Duryodhana who was stained by cupidity and possessed of little foresight. It was for him that friends, and kinsmen, over the whole Earth were slaughtered by us whom he had afflicted greatly in the deep forest. It was for him that the virtuous princess of Panchala, Draupadi of faultless features, our wife, was dragged into the midst of the assembly before all our seniors. Ye gods, I have no desire to even behold Suyodhana. I wish to go there where my brothers are."

"'Narada, smiling, told him, "It should not be so, O king of kings. While residing in Heaven, all enmities cease. O mighty-armed Yudhishthira, do not say so about king Duryodhana. Hear my words. Here is king Duryodhana. He is worshipped with the gods by those righteous men and those foremost of kings who are now denizens of Heaven. By causing his body to be poured as a libation on the fire of battle, he has obtained the end that consists in attainment of the region for heroes. You and your brothers, who were veritable gods on Earth, were always persecuted by this one. Yet through his observance of Kshatriya practices he has attained to this region. This lord of Earth was not terrified in a situation fraught with terror.

"'"O son, thou shouldst not bear in mind the woes inflicted on thee on account of the match at dice. It behoveth thee not to remember the afflictions of Draupadi. It behoveth thee not to remember the other woes which were yours in consequence of the acts of your kinsmen, the woes, viz., that were due to battle or to other situations. Do thou meet Duryodhana now according to the ordinances of polite intercourse. This is Heaven, O lord of men. There can be no enmities here."

"'Though thus addressed by Narada, the Kuru king Yudhishthira, endued with great intelligence, enquired about his brothers and said, "If these eternal regions reserved for heroes be Duryodhana's, that unrighteous and sinful wight, that man who was the destroyer of friends and of the whole world, that man for whose sake the entire Earth was devastated with all her horses and elephants and human beings, that wight for whose sake we were burnt with wrath in thinking of how best we might remedy our wrongs, I desire to see what regions have been attained by those high-souled heroes, my brothers of high vows, steady achievers of promises, truthful in speech, and distinguished for courage. The high-souled Karna, the son of Kunti, incapable of being baffled in battle, Dhrishtadyumna, Satyaki, the sons of Dhrishtadyumna and those other Kshatriyas who met with death in the observance of Kshatriya practices, where are those lords of Earth, O Brahmana? I do not see them here, O Narada. I desire to see, O Narada, Virata and Drupada and the other great Kshatriyas headed by Dhrishtaketu, as also Shikhandi, the Panchala prince, the sons of Draupadi, and Abhimanyu, irresistible in battle."'"

SECTION II.

"'Yudhishthira said, "Ye deities, I do not see here Radha's son of immeasurable prowess, as also my high-souled brothers, and Yudhamanyu and Uttamaujas, those great car-warriors that poured their bodies (as libations) on the fire of battle, those kings and princes that met with death for my sake in battle. Where are those great car-warriors that possessed the prowess of tigers? Have those foremost of men acquired this region? If those great car-warriors have obtained these regions, then only do you know, ye gods, that I shall reside here with those high-souled ones. If this auspicious and eternal region has not been acquired by those kings, then know, ye gods, that without those brothers and kinsmen of mine, I shall not live here. At the time of performing the water rites (after the battle), I heard my mother say, 'Do thou offer oblations of water unto Karna.' Since hearing those words of my mother, I am burning with grief. I grieve also incessantly at this, ye gods, that when I marked the resemblance between the feet of my mother and those of Karna of immeasurable soul, I did not immediately place myself under orders of that afflicter of hostile ranks. Ourselves joined with Karna, Shakra himself would have been unable to vanquish in battle. Wherever may that child of Surya be, I desire to see him. Alas, his relationship with us being unknown, I caused him to be slain by Arjuna. Bhima also of terrible prowess and dearer to me than my life-breaths, Arjuna too, resembling Indra himself, the twins also that resembled the Destroyer himself in prowess, I desire to behold. I wish to see the princess of Panchala, whose conduct was always righteous. I wish not to stay here. I tell you the truth. Ye foremost ones among the deities, what is Heaven to me if I am dissociated from my brothers? That is Heaven where those brothers of mine are. This, in my opinion, is not Heaven."

"'The gods said, "If thou longest to be there, go then, O son, without delay. At the command of the chief of the deities, we are ready to do what is agreeable to thee."'

"Vaishampayana continued: 'Having said so, the gods then ordered the celestial messenger, O scorcher of foes, saying, "Do thou show unto Yudhishthira his friends and kinsmen." Then the royal son of Kunti and the celestial messenger proceeded together, O foremost of kings, to that place where those chiefs of men (whom Yudhishthira had wished to see) were. The celestial messenger proceeded first, the king followed him behind. The path was inauspicious and difficult and trodden by men of sinful deeds. It was enveloped in thick darkness, and covered with hair and moss forming its grassy vesture. Polluted with the stench of sinners, and miry with flesh and blood, it abounded with gadflies and stinging bees and gnats and was endangered by the inroads of grisly bears. Rotting corpses lay here and there. Overspread with bones and hair, it was noisome with worms and insects. It was skirted all along with a blazing fire. It was infested by crows and other birds and vultures, all having beaks of iron, as also by evil spirits with long mouths pointed like needles. And it abounded with inaccessible fastnesses like the Vindhya mountains. Human corpses were scattered over it, smeared with fat and blood, with arms and thighs cut off, or with entrails torn out and legs severed.

"'Along that path so disagreeable with the stench of corpses and awful with other incidents, the righteous-souled king proceeded, filled with diverse thoughts. He beheld a river full of boiling water and, therefore, difficult to cross, as also a forest of trees whose leaves were sharp swords and razors. There were plains full of fine white sand exceedingly heated, and rocks and stones made of iron. There were many jars of iron all around, with boiling oil in them. Many a Kuta-salmalika was there, with sharp thorns and, therefore, exceedingly painful to the touch. The son of Kunti beheld also the tortures inflicted upon sinful men.

"'Beholding that inauspicious region abounding with every sort of foulness, Yudhishthira asked the celestial messenger, saying, "How far shall we proceed along a path like this? It behoveth thee to tell me where those brothers of mine are. I desire also to know what region is this of the gods?"

"'Hearing these words of king Yudhishthira the just, the celestial messenger stopped in his course and replied, saying, "Thus far is your way. The denizens of Heaven commanded me that having come thus far, I am to stop. If thou art tired, O king of kings, thou mayst return with me."

"'Yudhishthira, however, was exceedingly disconsolate and stupefied by the foul odour. Resolved to return, O Bharata, he retraced his steps. Afflicted by sorrow and grief, the righteous-souled monarch turned back. Just at that moment he heard piteous lamentations all around, "O son of Dharma, O royal sage, O thou of sacred origin, O son of Pandu, do thou stay a moment for favouring us. At thy approach, O invincible one, a delightful breeze hath begun to blow, bearing the sweet scent of thy person. Great hath been our relief at this. O foremost of kings, beholding thee, O first of men, great hath been our happiness. O son of Pritha, let that happiness last longer through thy stay here, for a few moments more. Do thou remain here, O Bharata, for even a short while. As long as thou art here, O thou of Kuru's race, torments cease to afflict us." These and many similar words, uttered in piteous voices by persons in pain, the king heard in that region, wafted to his ears from every side.

"'Hearing those words of beings in woe, Yudhishthira of compassionate heart exclaimed aloud, "Alas, how painful!" And the king stood still. The speeches of those woe-begone and afflicted persons seemed to the son of Pandu to be uttered in voices that he had heard before although he could not recognise them on that occasion.

"'Unable to recognise voices, Dharma's son, Yudhishthira, enquired, saying, "Who are you? Why also do you stay here?"

"'Thus addressed, they answered him from all sides, saying, "I am Karna!" "I am Bhimasena!" "I am Arjuna!" "I am Nakula!" "I am Sahadeva!" "I am Dhrishtadyumna!" "I am Draupadi!" "We are the sons of Draupadi!" Even thus, O king, did those voices speak.

"'Hearing those exclamations, O king, uttered in voices of pain suitable to that place, the royal Yudhishthira asked himself, "What perverse destiny is this? What are those sinful acts which were committed by those high-souled beings, Karna and the sons of Draupadi, and the slender-waisted princess of Panchala, so that their residence has been assigned in this region of foetid smell and great woe? I am not aware of any transgression that can be attributed to these persons of righteous deeds. What is that act by doing which Dhritarashtra's son, king Suyodhana, with all his sinful followers, has become invested with such prosperity? Endued with prosperity like that of the great Indra himself, he is highly adored. What is that act through the consequence of which these (high-souled ones) have fallen into Hell? All of them were conversant with every duty, were heroes, were devoted to truth and the Vedas; were observant of Kshatriya practices; were righteous in their acts; were performers of sacrifices; and givers of large presents unto brahmanas. Am I asleep or awake? Am I conscious or unconscious? Or, is all this a mental delusion due to disorders of the brain?"

"'Overwhelmed by sorrow and grief, and with his senses agitated by anxiety, king Yudhishthira indulged in such reflections for a long time. The royal son of Dharma then gave way to great wrath. Indeed, Yudhishthira then censured the gods, as also Dharma himself. Afflicted by the very foul odour, he addressed the celestial messenger, saying, "Return to the presence of those whose messenger thou art. Tell them that I shall not go back to where they are, but shall stay even here, since, in consequence of my companionship, these afflicted brothers of mine have become comforted." Thus addressed by the intelligent son of Pandu, the celestial messenger returned to the place where the chief of the deities was, viz., he of a hundred sacrifices. He represented unto him the acts of Yudhishthira. Indeed, O ruler of men, he informed Indra of all that Dharma's son had said.'"

SECTION III.

"Vaishampayana said, 'King Yudhishthira the just, the son of Pritha, had not stayed there for more than a moment when, O thou of Kuru's race, all the gods with Indra at their head came to that spot. The deity of Righteousness in his embodied form also came to that place where the Kuru king was, for seeing that monarch. Upon the advent of those deities of resplendent bodies and sanctified and noble deeds, the darkness that had overwhelmed that region immediately disappeared. The torments undergone by beings of sinful deeds were no longer seen. The river Vaitarani, the thorny Salmali, the iron jars, and the boulders of rock, so terrible to behold, also vanished from sight. The diverse repulsive corpses also, which the Kuru king had seen, disappeared at the same time. Then a breeze, delicious and fraught with pleasant perfumes, perfectly pure and delightfully cool, O Bharata, began to blow on that spot in consequence of the presence of the gods. The Maruts, with Indra, the Vasus with the twin Ashvinis, the Sadhyas, the Rudras, the Adityas, and the other denizens of Heaven, as also the Siddhas and the great Rishis, all came there where Dharma's royal son of great energy was.

"'Then Shakra, the lord of the deities, endued with blazing prosperity, addressed Yudhishthira and comforting him, said, "O Yudhishthira of mighty arms, come, come, O chief of men. These illusions have ended, O puissant one. Success has been attained by thee, O mighty-armed one, and eternal regions (of felicity) have become thine. Thou shouldst not yield to wrath. Listen to these words of mine. Hell, O son, should without doubt be beheld by every king. Of both good and bad there is abundance, O chief of men. He who enjoys first the fruits of his good acts must afterwards endure Hell. He, on the other hand, who first endures Hell, must afterwards enjoy Heaven. He whose sinful acts are many enjoys Heaven first. It is for this, O king, that desirous of doing thee good, I caused thee to be sent for having a view of Hell. Thou hadst, by a pretence, deceived Drona in the matter of his son. Thou hast, in consequence thereof, been shown Hell by an act of deception. After the manner of thyself, Bhima and Arjuna, and Draupadi, have all been shown the place of sinners by an act of deception. Come, O chief of men, all of them have been cleansed of their sins. All those kings who had aided thee and who have been slain in battle, have all attained to Heaven. Come and behold them, O foremost one of Bharata's race.

"'"Karna, the mighty bowman, that foremost of all wielders of weapons for whom thou art grieving, has also attained to high success. Behold, O puissant one, that foremost of men, viz., the son of Surya. He is in that place which is his own, O mighty-armed one. Kill this grief of thine, O chief of men. Behold thy brothers and others, those kings, that is, who had espoused thy side. They have all attained to their respective places (of felicity). Let the fever of thy heart be dispelled. Having endured a little misery first, from this time, O son of Kuru's race, do thou sport with me in happiness, divested of grief and all thy ailments dispelled. O mighty-armed one, do thou now enjoy, O king, the rewards of all thy deeds of righteousness of those regions which thou hast acquired thyself by thy penances and of all thy gifts. Let deities and Gandharvas, and celestial Apsaras, decked in pure robes and excellent ornaments, wait upon and serve thee for thy happiness. Do thou, O mighty-armed one, enjoy now those regions (of felicity) which have become thine through the Rajasuya sacrifice performed by thee and whose felicities have been enhanced by the sacrificial scimitar employed by thee. Let the high fruits of thy penances be enjoyed by thee. Thy regions, O Yudhishthira, are above those of kings. They are equal to those of Hariscandra, O son of Pritha. Come, and sport there in bliss. There where the royal sage Mandhatri is, there where king Bhagiratha is, there where Dushmanta's son Bharata is, there wilt thou sport in bliss. Here is the celestial river, sacred and sanctifying the three worlds. It is called Heavenly Ganga. Plunging into it, thou wilt go to thy own regions. Having bathed in this stream, thou wilt be divested of thy human nature. Indeed, thy grief dispelled, thy ailments conquered, thou wilt be freed from all enmities."

"'While, O Kuru king, the chief of the gods was saying so unto Yudhishthira, the deity of Righteousness, in his embodied form, then addressed his own son and said, "O king, I am greatly pleased, O thou of great wisdom, with thee, O son, by thy devotion to me, by thy truthfulness of speech, and forgiveness, and self-restraint. This, indeed, is the third test, O king, to which I put thee. Thou art incapable, O son of Pritha, of being swerved from thy nature or reason. Before this, I had examined thee in the Dwaita woods by my questions, when thou hadst come to that lake for recovering a couple of fire sticks. Thou stoodst it well. Assuming the shape of a dog, I examined thee once more, O son, when thy brothers with Draupadi had fallen down. This has been thy third test; thou hast expressed thy wish to stay at Hell for the sake of thy brothers. Thou hast become cleansed, O highly blessed one. Purified of sin, be thou happy.

"""O son of Pritha, thy brothers, O king, were not such as to deserve Hell. All this has been an illusion created by the chief of the gods. Without doubt, all kings, O son, must once behold Hell. Hence hast thou for a little while been subjected to this great affliction. O king, neither Arjuna, nor Bhima, nor any of those foremost of men, viz., the twins, nor Karna, ever truthful in speech and possessed of great courage, could be deserving of Hell for a long time. The princess Krishna too, O Yudhishthira, could not be deserving of that place of sinners. Come, come, O foremost one of the Bharatas, behold Ganga who spreads her current over the three worlds."

"'Thus addressed, that royal sage, viz., thy grandsire, proceeded with Dharma and all the other gods. Having bathed in the celestial river Ganga, sacred and sanctifying and ever adored by the Rishis, he cast off his human body. Assuming then a celestial form, king Yudhishthira the just, in consequence of that bath, became divested of all his enmities and grief. Surrounded by the deities, the Kuru king Yudhishthira then proceeded from that spot. He was accompanied by Dharma, and the great Rishis uttered his praises. Indeed, he reached that place where those foremost of men, those heroes, viz., the Pandavas and the Dhartarashtras, freed from (human) wrath, were enjoying each his respective status.'"

SECTION IV.

"Vaishampayana said, 'King Yudhishthira, thus praised by the gods, the Maruts and the Rishis, proceeded to that place where those foremost ones of Kuru's race were. He beheld Govinda endued with his Brahma-form. It resembled that form of his which had been seen before and which, therefore, helped the recognition. Blazing forth in that form of his, he was adorned with celestial weapons, such as the terrible discus and others in their respective embodied forms. He was being adored by the heroic Phalguna, who also was endued with a blazing effulgence. The son of Kunti beheld the slayer of Madhu also in his own form. Those two foremost of Beings, adored by all the gods, beholding Yudhishthira, received him with proper honours.

"'In another place, the delighter of the Kurus beheld Karna, that foremost one among all wielders of weapons, resembling a dozen Suryas in splendour. In another part he beheld Bhimasena of great puissance, sitting in the midst of the Maruts, and endued with a blazing form. He was sitting by the side of the God of Wind in his embodied form. Indeed, he was then in a celestial form endued with great beauty, and had attained to the highest success. In the place belonging to the Ashvinis, the delighter of the Kurus beheld Nakula and Sahadeva, each blazing with his own effulgence.

"'He also beheld the princess of Panchala, decked in garlands of lotuses. Having attained to Heaven, she was sitting there, endued with a form possessed of solar splendour. King Yudhishthira suddenly wished to question her. Then the illustrious Indra, the chief of the gods, spoke to him, "This one is Sree herself. It was for your sake that she took birth, as the daughter of Drupada, among human beings, issuing not from any mother's womb, O Yudhishthira, endued with agreeable perfume and capable of delighting the whole world. For your pleasure, she was created by the wielder of the trident. She was born in the race of Drupada and was enjoyed by you all. These five highly blessed Gandharvas endued with the effulgence of fire, and possessed of great energy, were, O king, the sons of Draupadi and yourself.

"''Behold Dhritarashtra, the king of the Gandharvas, possessed of great wisdom. Know that this one was the eldest brother of thy sire. This one is thy eldest brother, the son of Kunti, endued with effulgence of fire. The son of Surya, thy eldest brother, the foremost of men, even this one was known as the son of Radha. He moves in the company of Surya. Behold this foremost of Beings. Among the tribes of the Saddhyas, the gods, the Viswedevas, and the Maruts, behold, O king of kings, the mighty car-warriors of the Vrishnis and the Andhakas, viz., those heroes having Satyaki for their first, and those mighty ones among the Bhojas. Behold the son of Subhadra, invincible in battle, now staying with Soma. Even he is the mighty bowman Abhimanyu, now endued with the gentle effulgence of the great luminary of the night. Here is the mighty bowman Pandu, now united with Kunti and Madri. Thy sire frequently comes to me on his excellent car. Behold the royal Bhishma, the son of Santanu, now in the midst of the Vasus. Know that this one by the side of Brihaspati is thy preceptor Drona. These and other kings, O son of Pandu, who had warred on thy side now walk with the Gandharvas or Yakshas or other sacred beings. Some have attained to the status of Guhyakas, O king. Having cast off their bodies, they have conquered Heaven by the merit they had acquired through word, thought and deed."''

SECTION V.

"Janamejaya said, 'Bhishma and Drona, those two high-souled persons, king Dhritarashtra, and Virata and Drupada, and Sankha and Uttara, Dhrishtaketu and Jayatsena and king Satyajit, the sons of Duryodhana, and Shakuni the son of Subala, Karna's sons of great prowess, king Jayadratha, Ghatotkaca and others whom thou hast not mentioned, the other heroic kings of blazing forms, tell me for what period they remained in Heaven. O foremost of regenerate persons, was theirs an eternal place in Heaven? What was the end attained to by those foremost of men when their acts came to an end? I desire to hear this, O foremost of regenerate persons, and therefore have I asked thee. Through thy blazing penances thou seest all things.'"

Sauti said: "Thus questioned, that regenerate Rishi, receiving the permission of the high-souled Vyasa, set himself to answer the question of the king.

"Vaishampayana said, 'Every one, O king of men, is not capable of returning to his own nature at the end of his deeds. Whether this is so or not, is, indeed a good question asked by thee. Hear, O king, this which is a mystery of the gods, O chief of Bharata's race. It was explained (to us) by Vyasa of mighty energy, celestial vision and great prowess, that ancient ascetic, O Kauravya, who is the son of Parasara and who always observes high vows, who is of immeasurable understanding, who is omniscient, and who, therefore knows the end attached to all acts.

"'Bhishma of mighty energy and great effulgence attained to the status of the Vasus. Eight Vasus, O chief of Bharata's race, are now seen. Drona entered into Brihaspati, that foremost one of Angirasa's descendants. Hridika's son Kritavarma entered the Maruts. Pradyumna entered Sanatkumara whence he had issued. Dhritarashtra obtained the regions, so difficult of acquisition, that belong to the Lord of treasures. The famous Gandhari obtained the same regions with her husband Dhritarashtra. With his two wives, Pandu proceeded to the abode of the great Indra. Both Virata and Drupada, the king Dhrishtaketu, as also Nishatha, Akrura, Samva, Bhanukampa, and Viduratha, and Bhurishrava and Sala and king Bhuri, and Kansa, and Ugrasena, and Vasudeva, and Uttara, that foremost of men, with his brother Sankha, all these foremost of persons entered the deities. Soma's son of great prowess, named Varchas of mighty energy, became Abhimanyu, the son of Phalguna, that lion among men. Having fought, agreeably to Kshatriya practices, with bravery such as none else had ever been able to show, that mighty-armed and righteous-souled being entered Soma. Slain on the field of battle, O foremost of men, Karna entered Surya. Shakuni obtained absorption into Dwapara, and Dhrishtadyumna into the deity of fire. The sons of Dhritarashtra were all Rakshasas of fierce might. Sanctified by death caused by weapons, those high-souled beings of prosperity all succeeded in attaining to Heaven. Both Kshattri and king Yudhishthira entered into the god of Righteousness. The holy and illustrious Ananta (who had taken birth as Balarama) proceeded to the region below the Earth. Through the command of the Grandsire, he, aided by his Yoga power, supported the Earth. Vasudeva was a portion of that eternal god of gods called Narayana. Accordingly, he entered into Narayana. 16,000 women had been married to Vasudeva as his wives. When the time came, O Janamejaya, they plunged into the Sarasvati. Casting off their (human) bodies there, they re-ascended to Heaven. Transformed into Apsaras, they approached the presence of Vasudeva. Those heroic and mighty car-warriors, Ghatotkaca and others, who were slain in the great battle, attained to the status, some of gods and some of Yakshas. Those that had fought on the side of Duryodhana are said to have been Rakshasas. Gradually, O king, they have all attained to excellent regions of felicity. Those foremost of men have proceeded, some to the abode of Indra, some to that of Kuvera of great intelligence, and some to that of Varuna. I have now told thee, O thou of great splendour, everything about the acts, O Bharata, of both the Kurus and the Pandavas.'"

Sauti said: "Hearing this, ye foremost of regenerate ones, at the intervals of sacrificial rites, king Janamejaya became filled with wonder. The sacrificial priests then finished the rites that remained to be gone through. Astika, having rescued the snakes from fiery death), became filled with joy. King Janamejaya then gratified all the Brahmanas with copious presents. Thus worshipped by the king, they returned to their respective abodes. Having dismissed those learned Brahmanas, king Janamejaya came back from Takshasila to the city named after the elephant.

"I have now told everything that Vaishampayana narrated, at the command of Vyasa, unto the king at his snake sacrifice. Called a history, it is sacred, sanctifying and excellent. It has been composed by the ascetic Krishna, O Brahmana, of truthful speech.

He is omniscient, conversant with all ordinances, possessed of a knowledge of all duties, endued with piety, capable of perceiving what is beyond the ken of the senses, pure, having a soul cleansed by penances, possessed of the six high attributes, and devoted to Sankhya Yoga. He has composed this, beholding everything with a celestial eye that has been cleansed (strengthened) by varied lore. He has done this, desiring to spread the fame, throughout the world, of the high-souled Pandavas, as also of other Kshatriyas possessed of abundant wealth of energy.

"That learned man who recites this history of sacred days in the midst of a listening auditory becomes cleansed of every sin, conquers Heaven, and attains to the status of Brahma. Of that man who listens with rapt attention to the recitation of the whole of this Veda composed by (the Island-born) Krishna, a million sins, numbering such grave ones as Brahmanicide and the rest, are washed off. The Pitris of that man who recites even a small portion of this history at a Sraddha, obtain inexhaustible food and drink. The sins that one commits during the day by one's senses or the mind are all washed off before evening by reciting a portion of the Mahabharata. Whatever sins a Brahmana may commit at night in the midst of women are all washed off before dawn by reciting a portion of the Mahabharata.

"The high race of the Bharatas is its topic. Hence it is called Bharata. And because of its grave import, as also of the Bharatas being its topic, it is called Mahabharata. He who is versed in interpretations of this great treatise, becomes cleansed of every sin. Such a man lives in righteousness, wealth, and pleasure, and attains to Emancipation also, O chief of Bharata's race.

"That which occurs here occurs elsewhere. That which does not occur here occurs nowhere else. This history is known by the name of Jaya. It should be heard by every one desirous of Emancipation. It should be read by Brahmanas, by kings, and by women quick with children. He that desires Heaven attains to Heaven; and he that desires victory attains to victory. The woman quick with child gets either a son or a daughter highly blessed. The puissant Island-born Krishna, who will not have to come back, and who is Emancipation incarnate, made an abstract of the Bharata, moved by the desire of aiding the cause of righteousness. He made another compilation consisting of sixty lakhs of verses. Thirty lakhs of these were placed in the region of the deities. In the region of the Pitris fifteen lakhs, it should be known, are current; while in that of the Yakshas fourteen lakhs are in vogue. One lakh is current among human beings.

"Narada recited the Mahabharata to the gods; Asita-Devala to the Pitris; Suka to the Rakshasas and the Yakshas; and Vaishampayana to human beings. This history is sacred and of high import, and regarded as equal to the Vedas. That man, O Saunaka, who hears this history, placing a Brahmana before him, acquires both fame and the fruition of all his wishes. He who, with fervid devotion, listens to a recitation of the Mahabharata, attains (hereafter) to high success in consequence of the merit that becomes his through understanding even a very small portion thereof. All the sins of that man who recites or listens to this history with devotion are washed off.

"In former times, the great Rishi Vyasa, having composed this treatise, caused his son Suka to read it with him, along with these four Verses. Thousands of mothers and fathers, and hundreds of sons and wives arise in the world and depart from it. Others will (arise and) similarly depart. There are thousands of occasions for joy and hundreds of occasions for fear. These affect only him that is ignorant but never him that is wise. With uplifted arms I am crying aloud but nobody hears me. From Righteousness is Wealth as also Pleasure. Why should not Righteousness, therefore, be courted? For the sake neither of pleasure, nor of fear, nor of cupidity should any one cast off Righteousness. Indeed, for the sake of even life one should not cast off Righteousness. Righteousness is eternal. Pleasure and Pain are not eternal. Jiva is eternal. The cause, however, of Jiva's being invested with a body is not so.

"That man who, waking up at dawn, reads this Savittri of the Bharata, acquires all the rewards attached to a recitation of this history and ultimately attains to the highest Brahma. As the sacred Ocean, as the Himavat mountain, are both regarded as mines of precious gems, even so is this Bharata (regarded as a mine of precious gems). The man of learning, by reciting to others this Veda or Agama composed by (the Island-born) Krishna, earns wealth. There is no doubt in this that he who, with rapt attention, recites this history called Bharata, attains to high success. What need has that man of a sprinkling of the waters of Pushkara who attentively listens to this Bharata, while it is recited to him? It represents the nectar that fell from the lips of the Island-born. It is immeasurable, sacred, sanctifying, sin-cleansing, and auspicious."

SECTION VI.

"Janamejaya said, 'O holy one, according to what rites should the learned listen to the Bharata? What are the fruits (acquirable by hearing it)? What deities are to be worshipped during the several paranas? What should be the gifts that one should make, O holy one, at every parva or sacred day (during the continuance of the recitation)? What should be the qualification of the reciter to be engaged? Tell me all this!'

"Vaishampayana said, 'Hear, O king, what the procedure is, and what the fruits, O Bharata, are that will spring from ones listening (to a recitation of the Bharata). Even this, O king of kings, is what thou askest me. The deities of Heaven, O ruler of Earth, came to this world for sport. Having achieved their task, they ascended once more to Heaven. Listen to what I shall tell thee in brief. In the Mahabharata is to be found the births of Rishis and deities on the Earth. In this treatise, called Bharata, O foremost one of Bharata's race, are to be seen in one place the eternal Rudras, the Saddhyas, and the Viswedevas; the Adityas, the two deities named the Ashvinis, the regents of the World, the great Rishis, the Guhyakas, the Gandharvas, the Nagas, the Vidyadharas, the Siddhas, the diverse deities, the Self-born visible in a body, with many ascetics; the Hills and Mountains, Oceans and Seas and Rivers, the diverse tribes of Apsaras; the Planets, the Years, the Half-years, and the Seasons; and the whole universe of mobile and immobile entities, with all the gods and Asuras.

"'Hearing their celebrity, and in consequence of a recitation of their names and achievements, a man that has committed even terrible sins, will be cleansed. Having, with a concentrated soul and cleansed body, heard this history duly, from the beginning, and having reached its end, one should make Sraddha offerings, O Bharata, unto those (foremost of persons who have been mentioned in it). Unto the Brahmanas also, O chief of Bharata's race, should, with due devotion and according to ones power, be made large gifts and diverse kinds of gems, and kine, and vessels of white brass for milking kine, and maidens decked with every ornament, and possessed of every accomplishment suited to enjoyment, as also diverse kinds of conveyances, beautiful mansions, plots of land, and cloths. Animals also should be given, such as horses and elephants in rage, and beds, and covered conveyances borne on the shoulders of men, and well-decked cars. Whatever objects occur in the house, of the foremost kind, whatever wealth of great value occurs in it, should be given away unto Brahmanas. Indeed, one should give away one's own self, wives, and children.

"'One desirous of hearing the Bharata, should hear it without a doubting heart, with cheerfulness and joy; and as he proceeds listening to its recitation, he should according to the extent of his power, make gifts with great devotion.

"'Hear how a person that is devoted to truth and sincerity, that is self-restrained, pure (in mind), and observant of those acts which lead to purity of body, that is endued with faith, and that has subjugated wrath, attains to success (in the matter of a recitation of the Bharata). He should appoint as reciter one that is pure (of body), that is endued with good and pious conduct, that should be robed in white, that should have a complete mastery over his passions, that is cleansed of all offences, that is conversant with every branch of learning, that is endued with faith, that is free from malice, that is possessed of handsome features, that is blessed, self-restrained, truthful, and with passions under control, and that is beloved of all for the gifts he makes and the honours of which he is the possessor.

"'The reciter, seated at his ease, free from all bodily complaints, and with rapt attention, should recite the text without too much slowness, without a labouring voice, without being fast or quick, quietly, with sufficient energy, without confusing the letters and words together, in a sweet intonation and with such accent and emphasis as would indicate the sense giving full utterance to the three and sixty letters of the alphabet from the eight places of their formation. Bowing unto Narayana, and to Nara, that foremost of men, as also to the goddess Sarasvati, should the word Jaya be uttered.

"'Listening to the Bharata, O king, when recited, O thou of Bharata's race, by a reader of this kind, the listener, observant of vows all the while and cleansed by purificatory rites, acquires valuable fruits. When the first Parana is reached, the hearer should gratify Brahmanas with presents of all desirable objects. By doing this, one obtains the fruits of the Agnishtoma sacrifice. He acquires a large (celestial) car teeming with diverse orders of Apsaras (that wait upon him). With a glad heart, and with the deities in his company, he proceeds to Heaven, his heart rapt (in felicity).

"'When the second Parana is reached, the hearer acquires the fruits of the Atiratra vow. Indeed, he ascends a celestial car made entirely of precious gems. Wearing celestial garlands and robes, and decked with celestial unguents and always shedding a celestial fragrance around, he receives high honours in Heaven.

"'When the third Parana is reached, he acquires the fruits of the Dwadasaha vow. Indeed he resides in Heaven for myriads of years, like a god.

"'At the fourth Parana he acquires the fruits of the Vajapeya sacrifice.

"'At the fifth, twice those fruits are his. Ascending a celestial car that resembles the rising sun or a blazing fire, and with the deities for his companions, he goes to Heaven and sports in felicity for myriads of years in the abode of Indra.

"'At the sixth Parana, twice, and at the seventh, thrice those fruits become his. Ascending a celestial car that resembles the summit of the Kailasa mountains (in beauty), that is equipt with an altar made of stones of lapis lazuli and other precious gems, that is surrounded by beautiful objects of diverse kinds, that is decked with gems and corals, that moves at the will of the rider, and that teems with waiting Apsaras, he roves through all the regions of felicity, like a second deity of the Sun.

"'At the eight Parana, he acquires the fruits of the Rajasuya sacrifice. He ascends a car as beautiful as the rising moon, and unto which are yoked steeds white as the rays of the moon and endued with the speed of thought. He is served by women of the foremost beauty and whose faces are more charming than the moon. He hears the music of the garlands that encircle their waists and the Nupuras encircling their ankles. Sleeping with his head resting on the laps of women of transcendent beauty, he awakes greatly refreshed.

"'At the ninth Parana, he acquires, O Bharata, the fruits of that foremost of sacrifices, viz., the Horse-sacrifice. Ascending on a car equipt with a chamber consisting of a top supported by columns of gold, furnished with a seat made of stones of lapis lazuli, with windows on all sides made of pure gold, and teeming with waiting Apsaras and Gandharvas and other celestials, he blazes forth in splendour. Wearing celestial garlands and robes, and decked with celestial unguents, he sports in bliss, with deities for his companions, in Heaven, like a second deity himself.

"'Reaching the tenth Parana and gratifying Brahmanas, he acquires a car which tinkles with innumerable bells, which is decked with flags and banners, which is equipt with a seat made of precious gems, which has many arches made of lapis lazuli, which has a net-work of gold all round, which has turrets made of corals, which is adorned with Gandharvas and Apsaras well-skilled in singing, and which is fit for the residence of the Righteous. Crowned with a diadem of the complexion of fire, decked with ornaments of gold, his person smeared with celestial sandal paste, garnished with celestial wreaths, he roves through all celestial regions, enjoying all celestial objects of enjoyment, and endued with great splendour, through the grace of the deities.

"'Thus accoutred, he receives high honours in Heaven for many long years. With Gandharvas in his company, for full 21,000 years, he sports in bliss with Indra himself in abode of Indra. He roves at pleasure every day through the diverse regions of the gods, riding on celestial cars and conveyances, and surrounded by celestial damsels of transcendent beauty. He is able to go to the abode of the solar deity, of the lunar deity, and of Siva, O king. Indeed, he succeeds in living in the same region with Vishnu himself. It is even so, O monarch. There is no doubt in this. A person listening with faith, becomes even so. My preceptor has said this. Unto the reciter should be given all such objects as he may wish. Elephants and steeds and cars and conveyances, especially animals and the vehicles they draw, a bracelet of gold, a pair of ear-rings, sacred threads, beautiful robes, and perfumes in especial (should be given). By worshipping him as a deity one attains to the regions of Vishnu.

"'After this I shall declare what should be given away, as each parva is reached of the Bharata in course of its recitation, unto brahmanas, after ascertaining their birth, country, truthfulness, and greatness, O chief of Bharata's race, as also their inclination for piety, and unto Kshatriyas too, O king, after ascertainment of similar particulars. Causing the Brahmanas to utter benedictions, the business of recitation should be begun. When a parva is finished, the brahmanas should be worshipped to the best of one's power. At first, the reciter, clad in good robes and smeared with perfumed paste, should, O king, be duly fed with honey and frumenty of the best kind.

"'When the Astika-parva is being recited, brahmanas should be entertained with fruits and roots, and frumenty, and honey and clarified butter, and rice boiled with raw sugar.

"'When the Sabha-parva is being recited, brahmanas should be fed with habisya along with apupas and pupas and modakas, O king.

"'When the Aranyaka-parva is being recited, superior brahmanas should be fed with fruits and roots.

"'When the Arani-parva is reached, water-pots full of water should be given away. Many superior kinds of delicious food, also rice and fruits and roots, and food possessed of every agreeable attribute, should be presented unto the brahmanas.

"'During the recitation of the Virata-parva diverse kinds of robes should be given away; and during that of the Udyoga-parva, O chief of the Bharatas, the twice-born ones, after being decked with perfumes and garlands, should be entertained with food possessed of every agreeable quality.

"'During the recitation of the Bhishma-parva, O king of kings, after giving them excellent cars and conveyances, food should be given that is pure and well-cooked and possessed of every desirable attribute.

"'During the Drona-parva food of very superior kind should be given to learned brahmanas, as also beds, O monarch, and bows and good swords.

"'During the recitation of the Karna-parva, food of the foremost kind, besides being pure and well-cooked, should be presented unto the brahmanas by the house-holder with rapt mind.

"'During the recitation of the Shalya-parva, O king of kings, food with confectionery and rice boiled with raw sugar, as also cakes of wheat and soothing and nutritive viands and drinks should be presented.

"'During the recitation of the Gada-parva, brahmanas should be entertained with food mixed with mudga.

"'During the recitation of the Stri-parva, foremost of brahmanas should be entertained with gems and precious stones; and during the recitation of the Aishika-parva, rice boiled in ghee should first be given, and then food pure and well-cooked, and possessed of every desirable quality, should be presented.

"'During the recitation of the Shanti-parva, the brahmanas should be fed with havisya.

"'When the Asvamedhika-parva is reached, food possessed of every agreeable quality should be given; and when the Asramvasika is reached, brahmanas should be entertained with havisya.

"'When the Mausala is reached, scents and garlands possessed of agreeable qualities should be given away.

"'During the Mahaprasthanika, similar presents should be made, possessed of every quality of an agreeable kind.

"'When the Svarga-parva is reached, the brahmanas should be fed with havisya.

"'Upon the conclusion of the Harivansa, a 1,000 brahmanas should be fed. Unto each of them should be presented a cow accompanied with a piece of gold. Half of this should be presented to each poor man, O king.

"'Upon the conclusion of all the Parvas, the house-holder of wisdom should give unto the reciter a copy of the Mahabharata with a piece of gold. When the Harivansa Parva is being recited, Brahmanas should be fed with frumenty at each successive Parana, O king Having finished all the Parvas, one versed in the scriptures, robing himself in white, wearing garlands, decked with ornaments, and properly purified, should place a copy of the Mahabharata on an auspicious spot and cover it with a piece of silken cloth and worship it, according to due rites, with scents and garlands, offering each at a time Indeed, O king, the several volumes of this treatise should be worshipped by one with devotion and concentrated mind. Offerings should be made unto them of diverse kinds of food and garlands and drinks and diverse auspicious articles of enjoyment. Gold and other precious metals should be given as Dakshina. The names should then be taken of all the deities as also of Nara and Narayana. Then, adorning the persons of some foremost of Brahmanas with scents and garlands, they should be gratified with diverse kinds of gifts of enjoyable and very superior or costly articles. By doing this, one attains to the merits of the Atiratra sacrifice. Indeed, at each successive Parva, he acquires the merits that attach to the performance of a sacrifice. The reciter, O chief of the Bharatas, should be possessed of learning and endued with a good voice and a clear utterance respecting both letters and words. Even such a man should, O chief of the Bharatas, recite the Bharata. After entertaining a number of foremost Brahmanas, presents should be made unto them according to the ordinances. The reciter also, O chief of the Bharatas, should be decked with ornaments and fed sumptuously. The reciter being gratified, the house-holder attains to an excellent and auspicious contentment. If the Brahmanas are gratified, all the deities are gratified. After this, O chief of the Bharatas, Brahmanas should be duly entertained with diverse kinds of enjoyable articles and superior things.

"'I have thus indicated the ordinances, O foremost of men, (about the manner of reciting these scriptures) in answer to thy enquiries. Thou shouldst observe them with faith. In listening to a recitation of the Bharata and at each Parana, O best of kings, one that desires to attain to the highest good should listen with the greatest care and attention. One should listen to the Bharata every day. One should proclaim the merits of the Bharata every day. One in whose house the Bharata occurs, has in his hands all those scriptures which are known by the name of Jaya. The Bharata is cleansing and sacred. In the Bharata are diverse topics. The Bharata is worshipped by the very gods. The Bharata is the highest goal. The Bharata, O chief of the Bharatas, is the foremost of all scriptures. One attains to Emancipation through the Bharata. This that I tell thee is certain truth. One that proclaims the merits of this history called the Mahabharata, of the Earth, of the cow, of Sarasvati (the goddess of speech), of Brahmanas, and of Keshava, has never to languish.

"'In the Vedas, in the Ramayana, and in the sacred Bharata, O chief of Bharata's race, Hari is sung in the beginning, the middle, and at the end. That in which occur excellent statements relating to Vishnu, and the eternal Srutis, should be listened to by men desirous of attaining to the highest goal. This treatise is sanctifying. This is the highest indicator as regards duties; this is endued with every merit. One desirous of prosperity should listen to it. Sins committed by means of the body, by means of words, and by means of the mind, are all destroyed (through listening to the Bharata) as Darkness at sunrise. One devoted to Vishnu acquires (through this) that merit which is acquired by listening to the eighteen Puranas. There is no doubt in this. Men and women (by listening to this) would certainly attain to the status of Vishnu. Women desirous of having children should certainly listen to this which proclaims the fame of Vishnu. One desirous of attaining to the fruits that attach to a recitation of the Bharata should, according to one's power, give unto the reciter Dakshina, as also an honorarium in gold. One desirous of one's own good should give unto the reciter a Kapila cow with horns cased in gold and accompanied by her calf, covered with a cloth. Ornaments, O chief of Bharatas race, for the arms, as also those for the ears, should be given. Besides these, other kinds of wealth should be presented. Unto the reciter, O king of men, gift of land should be made. No gift like that of land could ever be or will be. The man that listens (to the Bharata) or that recites it to other people, becomes cleansed of all his sins and attains at last to the status of Vishnu. Such a man rescues his ancestors to the eleventh degree, as also himself with his wives and sons, O chief of Bharata's race. After concluding a recitation of the Bharata, one should, O king, perform a Homa with all its ten parts.

"'I have thus, O chief of men, told everything in thy presence. He that listens with devotion to this Bharata from the beginning becomes cleansed of every sin even if he be guilty of Brahmanicide or the violation of his preceptor's bed, or even if he be a drinker of alcohol or a robber of other people's wares, or even if he be born in the Chandala order. Destroying all his sins like the maker of day destroying darkness, such a man, without doubt, sports in felicity in the region of Vishnu like Vishnu himself.'"

THE END OF THE SVARGAROHANIKA-PARVA

THE EIGHTEEN PARVAS OF THE MAHABHARATA ARE THUS COMPLETE.